enthusiasm as he studied her, this woman who looked like an underling a man in his position would never have touched out of ethical considerations—but wasn't.

She wasn't his employee. He didn't pay her salary. And she wasn't bound to obey him in anything if she didn't feel like it.

But she had no idea that he knew that.

Achilles almost felt sorry for her. Almost.

Scandalous Royal Brides

Married for passion, made for scandal!

When personal assistant Natalie and Princess Valentina
meet they can't believe their eyes…they're the very
image of one another. They're so similar it's impossible
that they're anything but identical twins.

Dissatisfied with their lives, they impulsively agree to
swap places for six weeks only…

But will they want to return to their old lives
when the alpha heroes closest to them are intent on
making these scandalous women their brides?

Read Natalie and Prince Rodolfo's story in

The Prince's Nine-Month Scandal
Available now

And discover Princess Valentina
and Achilles Casilieris's story

The Billionaire's Secret Princess
Available now!

THE
BILLIONAIRE'S
SECRET PRINCESS

BY
CAITLIN CREWS

First Published in Great Britain 2017
By Mills & Boon, an imprint of HarperCollins*Publishers*
1 London Bridge Street, London, SE1 9GF

© 2017 Caitlin Crews

ISBN: 978-0-263-92444-2

Our policy is to use papers that are natural, renewable and recyclable
products and made from wood grown in sustainable forests. The logging
and manufacturing processes conform to the legal environmental
regulations of the country of origin.

Printed and bound in Spain
by CPI, Barcelona

USA TODAY bestselling and RITA® Award–nominated author **Caitlin Crews** loves writing romance. She teaches her favourite romance novels in creative writing classes at places like UCLA Extension's prestigious Writers' Program, where she finally gets to utilise the MA and PhD in English literature she received from the University of York in England. She currently lives in California, with her very own hero and too many pets. Visit her at caitlincrews.com.

To all the secret princesses
cruelly stuck working in horrible offices:
as long as you know the truth, that's what matters.

CHAPTER ONE

ACHILLES CASILIERIS REQUIRED PERFECTION.

In himself, certainly. He prided himself on it, knowing all too well how easy it was to fall far, far short. And in his employees, absolutely—or they would quickly find themselves on the other side of their noncompete agreements with indelible black marks against their names.

He did not play around. He had built everything he had from nothing, step by painstaking step, and he hadn't succeeded the way he had—building the recession-proof Casilieris Company and making his first million by the age of twenty-five, then expanding both his business and his personal fortune into the billions—by accepting anything less than 100 percent perfection in all things. Always.

Achilles was tough, tyrannical when necessary, and refused to accept what one short-lived personal assistant had foolishly called "human limitations" to his face.

He was a man who knew the monster in himself. He'd seen its face in his own mirror. He did not allow for "human limitations."

Natalie Monette was his current executive assistant and had held the position for a record five years because she had never once asserted that she was human as some kind of excuse. In point of fact, Achilles thought of her as a remarkably efficient robot—the highest praise he could think to bestow on anyone, as it removed the possibility of human error from the equation.

Achilles had no patience for human error.

Which was why his assistant's behavior on this flight today was so alarming.

The day had started out normally enough. When Achilles had risen at his usual early hour, it had been to find Natalie already hard at work in the study of his Belgravia town house. She'd set up a few calls to his associates in France, outlined his schedule for the day and his upcoming meetings in New York. They'd swung by his corporate offices in the City, where Achilles had handled a fire he thought she should have put out before he'd learned of it, but then she'd accompanied him in his car to the private airfield he preferred without appearing the least bit bothered that he'd dressed her down for her failure. And why should she be bothered? She knew he expected perfection and had failed to deliver it. Besides, Natalie was never bothered. She'd acquitted herself with her usual cool competence and attitude-free demeanor, the way she always did or she never would have lasted five minutes with him. Much less five years.

And then she'd gone into the bathroom at the airfield, stayed in there long enough that he'd had to go find her himself, and come out changed.

Achilles couldn't put his finger on *how* she'd changed, only that she had.

She still looked the part of the closest assistant to a man as feared and lauded as Achilles had been for years now. She looked like his public face the way she always did. He appreciated that and always had. It wasn't enough that she was capable of handling the complications of his personal and company business without breaking a sweat, that she never seemed to sleep, that she could protect him from the intrusive paparazzi and hold off his equally demanding board members in the same breath—it was necessary that she also look like the sort of woman who belonged in his exalted orbit for the rare occasions when he needed to escort someone to this or that function and couldn't trouble himself to expend the modicum of charm necessary to squire one of his mistresses. Today she wore one of her usual outfits, a pencil skirt and soft blouse and a feminine sort of sweater that wrapped around her torso and was no different from any other outfit she'd worn a million times before.

Natalie dressed to disappear in plain sight. But for some reason, she caught his eye this odd afternoon. He couldn't quite figure it out. It was as if he had never seen her before. It was as if she'd gone into the bathroom in the airport lounge and come out a completely different person.

Achilles sat back in his remarkably comfortable leather chair on the jet and watched her as she took her seat opposite him. Did he imagine that she hesitated? Was he making up the strange look he'd seen in her eyes before she sat down? Almost as if she was looking for clues instead of taking her seat as she always did?

"What took you so long in that bathroom?" he asked, not bothering to keep his tone particularly polite. "I should not have to chase down my own assistant, surely."

Natalie blinked. He didn't know why the green of her eyes behind the glasses he knew she didn't need for sight seemed...too bright, somehow. Or brighter, anyway, than they'd been before. In fact, now that he thought about it, everything about her was brighter. And he couldn't understand how anyone could walk into a regular lavatory and come out...gleaming.

"I apologize," she said quietly. Simply. And there was something about her voice then. It was almost…musical.

It occurred to Achilles that he had certainly never thought of Natalie's voice as anything approaching *musical* before. It had always been a voice, pure and simple. And she had certainly never *gleamed*.

And that, he thought with impatience, was one of the reasons that he had prized Natalie so much for all these years. Because he had never, ever noticed her as anything but his executive assistant, who was reasonably attractive because it was good business to give his Neanderthal cronies something worth gazing at while they were trying to ignore Achilles's dominance. But there was a difference between noting that a woman was attractive and *being attracted to* that woman. Achilles would not have hired Natalie if he'd been attracted to her. He never had been. Not ever.

But to his utter astonishment that was what seemed to be happening. Right here. Right now. His body was sending him unambiguous signals. He wasn't simply *attracted* to his assistant. What he felt roll in him as she crossed her legs at the ankle and smiled at him was far more than *attraction*.

It was need.

Blinding and impossible and incredibly, astonishingly inconvenient.

Achilles Casilieris did not do inconvenience, and he was violently opposed to *need*. It had been beaten into him as an unwanted child that it was the height of foolishness to want something he couldn't have. That meant he'd dedicated his adult life to never allowing himself to need anything at all when he could buy whatever took his fancy, and he hadn't.

And yet there was no denying that dark thread that wound in him, pulling tight and succeeding in surprising him—something else that happened very, very rarely.

Achilles knew the shadows that lived in him. He had no intention of revisiting them. Ever.

Whatever his assistant was doing, she needed to stop. Now.

"That is all you wish to say?" He sounded edgy. Dangerous. He didn't like that, either.

But Natalie hardly seemed to notice. "If you would like me to expand on my apology, Mr. Casilieris, you need only tell me how."

He thought there was a subtle rebuke in that, no matter how softly she'd said it, and that, too, was new. And unacceptable no matter how prettily she'd voiced it.

Her copper-colored hair gleamed. Her skin glowed as she moved her hands in her lap, which struck him as odd, because Natalie never sat there with her hands folded in her lap like some kind of diffident Catholic schoolgirl. She was always in motion, because she was always working. But tonight, Natalie appeared to be sitting there like some kind of regal Madonna, hands folded in her lap, long, silky legs crossed at the ankles, and an inappropriately serene smile on her face.

If it wasn't impossible, he would have thought that she really was someone else entirely. Because she looked exactly the same save for all that gold that seemed to wrap itself around her and him, too, making him unduly fascinated with the pulse he could see beating at her throat—except he'd never, ever noticed her that way before.

Achilles did not have time for this, whatever it was. There was entirely too much going on with his businesses at the moment, like the hotel deal he'd been trying to put together for the better part of the last year that was by no means assured. He hadn't become one of the most feared and fearsome billionaires in the world because he took time off from running his businesses to pretend to care about the personal lives of his employees.

But Natalie wasn't just any employee. She was the one he'd actually come to rely on. The only person he relied on in the world, to be specific.

"Is there anything you need to tell me?" he asked.

He watched her, perhaps too carefully. It was impossible not to notice the way she flushed slightly at that. That was strange, too. He couldn't remember a single instance Natalie had ever flushed in response to anything he'd done. And the truth was he'd done a lot. He didn't hide his flashes of irritation or spend too much time worrying about anyone else's feelings. Why should he? The Casilieris Company was about profit—and it was about Achilles. Who else's feelings should matter? One of the things he'd long prized about his assistant was that she never, ever reacted to anything that he did or said or shouted. She just did her job.

But today Natalie had spots of red, high on her elegant cheekbones, and she'd been sitting across from him for whole minutes now without doing a single thing that could be construed as her job.

Elegant? demanded an incredulous voice inside him. *Cheekbones?*

Since when had Achilles ever noticed anything of the kind? He didn't pay that much attention to the mistresses he took to his bed—which he deigned to do in the first place only after they passed through all the levels of his application process and signed strict confidentiality agreements. And the women who made it through were in no doubt as to why they were there. It was to please him, not render him disoriented enough to be focusing on their bloody *cheekbones*.

"Like what, for example?" She asked the question and then she smiled at him, that curve of her mouth that was suddenly wired to the hardest part of him, and echoed inside him like heat. Heat he didn't want. "I'll be happy to tell you anything you wish to hear, Mr. Casilieris. That is, after all, my job."

"Is that your job?" He smiled, and he doubted it echoed much of anywhere. Or was anything but edgy and a little but harsh. "I had started to doubt that you remembered you had one."

"Because I kept you waiting? That was unusual, it's true."

"You've never done so before. You've never dared." He tilted his head slightly as he gazed at her, not understanding why everything was different when nothing was. He could see that she was exactly the same as she always was, down to that single freckle centered on her left cheekbone that he wasn't even aware he'd noticed before now. "Again, has some tragedy befallen you? Were you hit over the head?" He did nothing to hide the warning or the menace in his voice. "You do not appear to be yourself."

But if he thought he'd managed to discomfit her, he saw in the next moment that was not to be. The flush faded from her porcelain cheeks, and all she did was smile at him again. With that maddeningly enigmatic curve of her lips.

Lips, he noticed with entirely too much of his body, that were remarkably lush.

This was insupportable.

"I am desolated to disappoint you," she murmured as the plane began to move, bumping gently along the tarmac. "But there was no tragedy." Something glinted in her green gaze, though her smile never dimmed. "Though I must confess in the spirit of full disclosure that I was thinking of quitting."

Achilles only watched her idly, as if she hadn't just said that. Because she couldn't possibly have just said that.

"I beg your pardon," he said after a moment passed and there was still that spike of something dark and furious in his chest. "I must have misheard you. You do not mean that you plan to quit this job. That you wish to leave *me*."

It was not lost on him that he'd phrased that in a way that should have horrified him. Maybe it would at some point. But today what slapped at him was that his assistant spoke of quitting without a single hint of anything like uncertainty on her face.

And he found he couldn't tolerate that.

"I'm considering it," she said. Still smiling. Unaware of her own danger or the dark thing rolling in him, reminding him of how easy it was to wake that monster that slept in him. How disastrously easy.

But Achilles laughed then, understanding finally catching up with him. "If this is an attempt to wrangle more money out of me, Miss Monette, I cannot say that I admire the strategy. You're perfectly well compensated as is. Overcompensated, one might say."

"Might one? Perhaps." She looked unmoved. "Then again, perhaps your rivals have noticed exactly how much you rely on me. Perhaps I've decided that I want more than being at the beck and call of a billionaire. Much less standing in as your favorite bit of target practice."

"It cannot possibly have bothered you that I lost my temper earlier."

Her smile was bland. "If you say it cannot, then I'm sure you must be right."

"I lose my temper all the time. It's never bothered you before. It's part of your job to not be bothered, in point of fact."

"I'm certain that's it." Her enigmatic smile seemed to deepen. "I must be the one who isn't any good at her job."

He had the most insane notion then. It was something about the cool challenge in her gaze, as if they were equals. As if she had every right to call him on whatever she pleased. He had no idea why he wanted to reach across the little space between their chairs and put his hands on her. Test her skin to see if it was as soft as it looked. Taste that lush mouth—

What the hell was happening to him?

Achilles shook his head, as much to clear it as anything else. "If this is your version of a negotiation, you should rethink your approach. You know perfectly well that there's entirely too much going on right now."

"Some might think that this is the perfect time, then, to talk about things like compensation and temper tantrums," Natalie replied, her voice as even and unbothered as ever. There was no reason that should make him grit his teeth. "After all, when one is expected to work twenty-two hours a day and is shouted at for her trouble, one's thoughts automatically turn to what one lacks. It's human nature."

"You lack nothing. You have no time to spend the money I pay you because you're too busy traveling the world—which I also pay for."

"If only I had more than two hours a day to enjoy these piles of money."

"People would kill for the opportunity to spend even five minutes in my presence," he reminded her. "Or have you forgotten who I am?"

"Come now." She shook her head at him, and he had the astonishing sense that she was trying to chastise him. *Him.* "It would not kill you to be more polite, would it?"

Polite.

His own assistant had just lectured him on his manners.

To say that he was reeling hardly began to scratch the surface of Achilles's reaction.

But then she smiled, and that reaction got more complicated. "I got on the plane anyway. I decided not to quit today." Achilles could not possibly have missed her emphasis on that final word. "You're welcome."

And something began to build inside him at that. Something huge, dark, almost overwhelming. He was very much afraid it was rage.

But that, he refused. No matter what. Achilles left his demons behind him a long time ago, and he wasn't going back. He refused.

"If you would like to leave, Miss Monette, I will not stop you," he assured her coldly. "I cannot begin to imagine what has led you to imagine I would try. I do not beg. I could fill your position with a snap of my fingers. I might yet, simply because this conversation is intolerable."

The assistant he'd thought he knew would have swallowed hard at that, then looked away. She would have smoothed her hands over her skirt and apologized as she did it. She had riled him only a few times over the years, and she'd talked her way out of it in exactly that way. He gazed at her expectantly.

But today, Natalie only sat there with distractingly perfect posture and gazed back at him with a certain serene confidence that made him want to...mess her up. Get his hands in that unremarkable ponytail and feel the texture of all that gleaming copper. Or beneath her snowy-white blouse. Or better yet, up beneath that skirt of hers.

He was so furious he wasn't nearly as appalled at himself as he should have been.

"I think we both know perfectly well that while you could snap your fingers and summon crowds of candidates for my position, you'd have a very hard time filling it to your satisfaction," she said with a certainty that...gnawed at him. "Perhaps we could dispense with the threats. You need me."

He would sooner have her leap forward and plunge a knife into his chest.

"I need no one," he rasped out. "And nothing."

His suddenly mysterious assistant only inclined her

head, which he realized was no response at all. As if she was merely patronizing him—a notion that made every muscle in his body clench tight.

"You should worry less about your replacement and more about your job," Achilles gritted out. "I have no idea what makes you think you can speak to me with such disrespect."

"It is not disrespectful to speak frankly, surely," she said. Her expression didn't change, but her green gaze was grave—very much, he thought with dawning incredulity, as if she'd expected better of him.

Achilles could only stare back at her in arrogant astonishment. Was he now to suffer the indignity of being judged by his own assistant? And why was it she seemed wholly uncowed by his amazement?

"Unless you plan to utilize a parachute, it would appear you are stuck right here in your distasteful position for the next few hours," Achilles growled at her when he thought he could speak without shouting. Shouting was too easy. And obscured his actual feelings. "I'd suggest you use the time to rethink your current attitude."

He didn't care for the brilliant smile she aimed at him then, as if she was attempting to encourage him with it. *Him.* He particularly didn't like the way it seemed too bright, as if it was lighting him up from the inside out.

"What a kind offer, Mr. Casilieris," she said in that self-possessed voice of hers that was driving him mad. "I will keep it in mind."

The plane took off then, somersaulting into the London sky. Achilles let gravity press him back against the seat and considered the evidence before him. He had worked with this woman for five years, and she had never spoken to him like that before. Ever. He hardly knew what to make of it.

But then, there was a great deal he didn't know what

to do with, suddenly. The way his heart pounded against his ribs as if he was in a real temper, when he was not the sort of man who lost control. Of his temper or anything else. He expected nothing less than perfection from himself, first and foremost. And temper made him think of those long-ago days of his youth, and his stepfather's hovel of a house, victim to every stray whim and temper and fist until he'd given himself over to all that rage and fury inside him and become little better than an animal himself—

Why was he allowing himself to think of such things? His youth was off-limits, even in his own head. What the hell was *happening*?

Achilles didn't like that Natalie affected him. But what made him suspicious was that she'd never affected him before. He'd approved when she started to wear those glasses and put her hair up, to make herself less of a target for the less scrupulous men he dealt with who thought they could get to him through expressing their interest in her. But he hadn't needed her to downplay her looks because *he* was entranced by her. He hadn't been.

So what had changed today?

What had emboldened her and, worse, allowed her to get under his skin?

He kept circling back to that bathroom in the airport and the fact she'd walked out of it a different person from the one who'd walked in.

Of course, she wasn't a *different person*. Did he imagine the real Natalie had suffered a body snatching? Did he imagine there was some elaborate hoax afoot?

The idea was absurd. But he couldn't seem to get past it. The plane hit its cruising altitude, and he moved from his chair to the leather couch that took pride of place in the center of the cabin that was set up like one of his high-end hotel rooms. He sat back with his laptop and pretended to be looking through his email when he was watching Natalie instead. Looking for clues.

She wasn't moving around the plane with her usual focus and energy. He thought she seemed tentative. Uncertain—and this despite the fact she seemed to walk taller than before. As if she'd changed her very posture in that bathroom. But who did something like that?

A different person would have different posture.

It was crazy. He knew that. And Achilles knew further that he always went a little too intense when he was closing a deal, so it shouldn't have surprised him that he was willing to consider the insane option today. Part of being the sort of unexpected, out-of-the-box thinker he'd always been was allowing his mad little flights of fancy. He never knew where they might lead.

He indulged himself as Natalie sat and started to look through her own bag as if she'd never seen it before. He pulled up the picture of her he kept in his files for security purposes and did an image search on it, because why not.

Achilles was prepared to discover a few photos of random celebrities she resembled, maybe. And then he'd have to face the fact that his favorite assistant might have gone off the deep end. She was right that replacing her would be hard—but it wouldn't be impossible. He hadn't overestimated his appeal—and that of his wildly successful company—to pretty much anyone and everyone. He was swamped with applicants daily, and he didn't even have an open position.

But then none of that mattered because his image search hit gold.

There were pages and pages of pictures. All of his assistant—except it wasn't her. He knew it from the exquisitely bespoke gowns she wore. He knew it from the jewels that flowed around her neck and covered her hands, drawing attention to things like the perfect manicure she had today—when the Natalie he knew almost never had time to care for her nails like that. And every picture he clicked on identified the woman in them not as Natalie Monette, assistant to Achilles Casilieris, but Her Royal Highness, Princess Valentina of Murin.

Achilles didn't have much use for royals, or really anyone with inherited wealth, when he'd had to go to so much trouble to amass his own. He'd never been to the tiny Mediterranean kingdom of Murin, mostly because he didn't have a yacht to dock there during a sparkling summer of endless lounging and, further, didn't need to take advantage of the country's famously friendly approach to taxes. But he recognized King Geoffrey of Murin on sight, and he certainly recognized the Murinese royal family's coat of arms.

It had been splashed all over the private jet he'd seen on the same tarmac as his back in London.

There was madness, Achilles thought then, and then there was a con job that no one would ever suspect—because who could imagine that the person standing in front of them, looking like someone they already knew, was actually someone else?

If he wasn't mistaken—and he knew he wasn't, because there were too many things about his assistant today that didn't make sense, and Achilles was no great believer in coincidence—Princess Valentina of Murin was trying to run a con.

On him.

Which meant a great many things. First, that his actual assistant was very likely pretending to be the princess somewhere, leaving him and her job in the hands of someone she had to know would fail to live up to Achilles's high standards. That suggested that second, she really wasn't all that happy in her position, as this princess had dared to throw in his face in a way he doubted Natalie ever would have. But it also suggested that third, Natalie had effectively given her notice.

Achilles didn't like any of that. At all. But the fourth thing that occurred to him was that clearly, neither this princess nor his missing assistant expected their little switch to be noticed. Natalie, who should have known better, must honestly have believed that he wouldn't notice an imposter in her place. Or she hadn't cared much if he did.

That was enraging, on some level. Insulting.

But Achilles smiled as Valentina settled herself across the coffee table from him, with a certain inbred grace that whispered of palaces and comportment classes and a lifetime of genteel manners.

Because she thought she was tricking him.

Which meant he could trick her instead. A prospect his body responded to with great enthusiasm as he studied her, this woman who looked like an underling whom a man in his position could never have touched out of ethical considerations—but wasn't.

She wasn't his employee. He didn't pay her salary, and she wasn't bound to obey him in anything if she didn't feel like it.

But she had no idea that he knew that.

Achilles almost felt sorry for her. Almost.

"Let's get started," he murmured, as if they'd exchanged no harsh words. He watched confusion move over her face in a blink, then disappear, because she was a royal princess and she was used to concealing her reactions. He planned to have fun with that. The possibilities were endless, and seemed to roll through him like heat. "We have so much work to do, Miss Monette. I hardly know where to begin."

CHAPTER TWO

BY THE TIME they landed in New York, Princess Valentina of Murin was second-guessing her spontaneous, impulsive decision to switch places with the perfect stranger she'd found wearing her face in the airport lounge.

Achilles Casilieris could make anyone second-guess anything, she suspected.

"You do not appear to be paying attention," he said silkily from beside her, as if he knew exactly what she was thinking. And who she was. And every dream she'd ever had since she was a girl—that was how disconcerting this man was, even lounging there beside her in the back of a luxury car doing nothing more alarming than *sitting*.

"I am hanging on your every word," she assured him as calmly as she could, and then she repeated his last three sentences back to him.

But she had no idea what he was talking about. Repeating conversations she wasn't really listening to was a skill she'd learned in the palace a long, long time ago. It came in handy at many a royal gathering. And in many longwinded lectures from her father and his staff.

You have thrown yourself into deep, deep water, she told herself now, as if that wasn't entirely too apparent already. As if it hadn't already occurred to her that she'd better learn how to swim, and fast.

Achilles Casilieris was a problem.

Valentina knew powerful men. Men who ruled countries. Men who came from centuries upon centuries of power and consequence and wielded it with the offhanded superiority of those who had never imagined *not* ruling all they surveyed.

But Achilles was in an entirely different league.

He took over the whole of the backseat of the car that had waited for them on the tarmac in the bright and sunny afternoon, looking roomy and spacious from the outside. He'd insisted she sit next to him on the plush backseat that should have been more than able to fit two people with room to spare. And yet Valentina felt crowded, as if he was pressing up against her when he wasn't. Achilles wasn't touching her, but still, she was entirely too *aware* of him.

He took up all the air. He'd done it on his plane, too.

She had the hectic notion, connected to that knot beneath her breastbone that was preventing her from taking anything like a deep breath, that it wasn't the enclosed space that was the issue. That he would have this same effect anywhere. All that brooding ruthlessness he didn't bother to contain—or maybe he couldn't contain even if he'd wanted to—seemed to hum around him like a kind of force field that both repelled and compelled at once.

If she was honest, the little glimpse she'd had of him in the airport had been the same—she'd just ignored it.

Valentina had been too busy racing into the lounge so she could have a few precious seconds alone. No staff. No guards. No cameras. Just her perched on the top of a closed toilet seat, shut away from the world, breathing. Letting her face do what it liked. Thinking of absolutely nothing. Not her duty. Not her father's expectations.

Certainly not her bloodless engagement to Prince Rodolfo of Tissely, a man she'd tuned out within moments of their first meeting. Or their impending wedding in two months' time, which she could feel bearing down on her like a thick hand around her throat every time she let herself think about it. It wasn't that she didn't *want* to do her duty and marry the Crown Prince of Tissely. She'd been promised in marriage to her father's allies since the day she was born. It was that she'd never given a great deal of thought to what it was she wanted, because *want* had never been an option available to her.

And it had suddenly occurred to her at her latest wedding dress fitting there in London that she was running out of time.

Soon she would be married to a man in what was really more of a corporate merger of two great European brands, the houses of Tissely and Murin. She'd be expected to produce the necessary heirs to continue the line. She would take her place in the great sweep of her family's storied history, unite two ancient kingdoms, and in so doing fulfill her purpose in life. The end.

The end, she'd thought in that bathroom stall, high-end and luxurious but still, a bathroom stall. *My life fulfilled at twenty-seven.*

Valentina was a woman who'd been given everything, including a healthy understanding of how lucky she was. She didn't often indulge herself with thoughts of what was and wasn't fair when there was no doubt she was among the most fortunate people alive.

But the thing was, it still didn't seem fair. No matter how hard she tried not to think about it that way.

She would do what she had to do, of course. She always had and always would, but for that single moment, locked away in a bathroom stall where no one could see her and no one would ever know, she basked in the sheer, dizzying unfairness of it all.

Then she'd pulled herself together, stepped out and had been prepared to march onto her plane and head back to the life that had been plotted out for her since the day she arrived on the planet.

Only to find her twin standing at the sinks.

Her identical twin—though that was, of course, impossible.

"What is this?" the other woman had asked when they'd faced each other, looking something close to scared. Or unnerved, anyway. "How...?"

Valentina had been fascinated. She'd been unable to keep herself from studying this woman who appeared to be wearing her body as well as her face. She was dressed in a sleek pencil skirt and low heels, which showed legs that Valentina recognized all too well, having last seen them in her own mirror. "I'm Valentina."

"Natalie."

She'd repeated that name in her head like it was a magic spell. She didn't know why she felt as if it was.

But then, running into her double in a London bathroom seemed something close enough to magic to count. Right then when she'd been indulging her self-pity about the unchangeable course of her own life, the universe had presented her with a glimpse of what else could be. If she was someone else.

An identical someone else.

They had the same face. The same legs, as she'd already noted. The same coppery hair that her double wore up in a serviceable ponytail and the same nose Valentina could trace directly to her maternal grandmother. What were the chances, she'd wondered then, that they *weren't* related?

And didn't that raise all kinds of interesting questions?

"You're that princess," Natalie had said, a bit haltingly.

But if Valentina was a princess, and if they were related as they surely had to be...

"I suspect you might be, too," she'd said gently.

"We can't possibly be related. I'm a glorified secretary who never really had a home. You're a royal princess. Presumably your lineage dates back to the Roman Conquest."

"Give or take a few centuries." Valentina tried to imagine having a job like that. Or any job. A secretary, glorified or otherwise, who reported to work for someone else and actually *did things* with her time that weren't directly related to being a symbol. She couldn't really wrap her head around it, or being effectively without a home, either, having been a part of Murin since her birth. As much Murin as its beaches and hills, its monuments and its palace. She might as well have been a park. "Depending which branch of the family you mean, of course."

"I was under the impression that people with lineages that could lead to thrones and crown jewels tended to keep better track of their members," Natalie had said, her tone just dry enough to make Valentina decide that given the right circumstances—meaning anywhere that wasn't a toilet—she'd rather like her doppelganger.

And she knew what the other woman had been asking.

"Conspiracy theorists claim my mother was killed and her death hushed up. Senior palace officials have assured me my whole life that no, she merely left to preserve her mental health, and is rumored to be in residence in a hospital devoted to such things somewhere. All I know is that I haven't seen her since shortly after I was born. According to my father, she preferred anonymity to the joys of motherhood."

And she waited for Natalie to give her an explanation in turn. To laugh, perhaps, and then tell her that she'd been raised by two perfectly normal parents in a happily normal somewhere else, filled with golden retrievers and school buses and pumpkin-spiced coffee drinks and whatever else normal people took for granted that Valentina only read about.

But instead, this woman wearing Valentina's face had looked stricken. "I've never met my father," she'd whispered. "My mother's always told me she has no idea who he was. And she bounces from one affair to the next pretty quickly, so I came to terms with the fact it was possible she really, truly didn't know."

And Valentina had laughed, because what else could she do? She'd spent her whole life wishing she'd had more of a family than her chilly father. Oh, she loved him, she did, but he was so excruciatingly proper. So worried about appearances. His version of a hug was a well-meaning critique on her latest public appearance. Love to her father was maintaining and bolstering the family's reputation across the ages. She'd always wanted a sister to share in the bolstering. A brother. A mother. *Someone.*

But she hadn't had anyone. And now she had a stranger who looked just like her.

"My father is many things," she'd told Natalie. It was too soon to say *our father.* And who knew? Maybe they were cousins. Or maybe this was a fluke. No matter that little jolt of recognition inside her, as if she'd been meant to know this woman. As if this was a reunion. "Including His Royal Majesty, King Geoffrey of Murin. What he is not now, nor has ever been, I imagine, is forgettable."

Natalie had shaken her head. "You underestimate my mother's commitment to amnesia. She's made it a life choice instead of a malady. On some level I admire it."

"My mother was the noblewoman Frederica de Burgh, from a very old Murinese family." Valentina watched Natalie closely as she spoke, looking for any hint of…anything, really, in her gaze. "Promised to my father at birth, raised by nuns and kept deliberately sheltered, and then widely held to be unequal to the task of becoming queen. Mentally. But that's the story they would tell, isn't it, to explain why she disappeared? What's your mother's name?"

Natalie sighed and swung her shoulder bag onto the counter. Valentina had the impression that she'd really, truly wanted not to answer. But she had. "She calls herself Erica."

And there it was. Valentina supposed it could be a coincidence that *Erica* was a shortened form of *Frederica*. But how many coincidences were likely when they resulted in two women who'd never met—who never should have met—who happened to be mirror images?

If there was something in her that turned over at the notion that her mother had, in fact, had a maternal impulse after all—just not for Valentina—well, this wasn't the time to think about that. It might never be the time to think about that. She'd spent twenty-seven years trying her best not to think about that.

She changed the subject before she lost her composure completely and started asking questions she knew she shouldn't.

"I saw Achilles Casilieris, out there in the lounge," she'd said instead. The notorious billionaire had been there on her way in, brooding in a corner of the lounge and scowling at the paper he'd been reading. "He looks even more fearsome in person. You can almost *see* all that brash command and dizzying wealth ooze from his pores, can't you?"

"He's my boss," Natalie had said, sounding amused—if rather darkly. "If he was really oozing anything, anywhere, it would be my job to provide first aid until actual medical personnel could come handle it. At which point he would bite my head off for wasting his precious time by not curing him instantly."

Valentina had been flooded with a rash of follow-up questions. Was the biting off of heads normal? Was it fun to work for a man who sounded half-feral? Most important, did Natalie like her life or merely suffer through it?

But then her mobile started buzzing in her clutch. She'd forgotten about ferocious billionaires and thought about things she knew too much about, like the daredevil prince she was bound to marry soon, instead, because their fathers had agreed regardless of whether either one of them liked it. She'd checked the mobile's display to be sure, but wasn't surprised to find she'd guessed correctly. Lucky her, she'd had another meeting with her husband-to-be in Murin that very afternoon. She'd expected it to go the way all their meetings so far had gone. Prince Rodolfo, beloved the world over for his good looks and devil-may-care attitude, would talk. She would listen without really listening. She'd long since concluded that foretold a very happy royal marriage.

"My fiancé," she'd explained, meeting Natalie's gaze again. "Or his chief of staff, to be more precise."

"Congratulations," Natalie murmured.

"Thank you, I'm very lucky." Valentina's mouth curved, though her tone was far more dry than Natalie's had been. "Everyone says so. Prince Rodolfo is objectively attractive. Not all princes can make that claim, but the tabloids have exulted over his abs since he was a teenager. Just as they have salivated over his impressive dating history, which has involved a selection of models and actresses from at least four continents and did not cease in any noticeable way upon our engagement last fall."

"Your Prince Charming sounds…charming," Natalie had said.

Valentina raised one shoulder, then dropped it. "His theory is that he remains free until our marriage, and then will be free once again following the necessary birth of his heir. More discreetly, I can only hope. Meanwhile, I am beside myself with joy that I must take my place at his side in two short months. Of course."

Natalie had laughed, and the sound had made Valentina's stomach flip. Because it sounded like her. It sounded exactly like her.

"It's going to be a terrific couple of months all around, then," her mirror image was saying. "Mr. Casilieris is in rare form. He's putting together a particularly dramatic deal and it's not going his way and he…isn't used to that. So that's me working twenty-two-hour days instead of my usual twenty for the foreseeable future, which is even more fun when he's cranky and snarling."

"It can't possibly be worse than having to smile politely while your future husband lectures you about the absurd expectation of fidelity in what is essentially an arranged marriage for hours on end. The absurdity is that *he* might be expected to curb his impulses for a year or so, in case you wondered. The expectations for *me* apparently involve quietly and chastely finding fulfillment in philanthropic works, like his sainted absentee mother, who everyone knows manufactured a supposed health crisis so she could live out her days in peaceful seclusion. It's easy to be philanthropically fulfilled while living in isolation in Bavaria."

Natalie had smiled. "Try biting your tongue while your famously short-tempered boss rages at you for no reason, for the hundredth time in an hour, because he pays you to stand there and take it without wilting or crying or selling whingeing stories about him to the press."

Valentina had returned that smile. "Or the hours and hours of grim palace-vetted prewedding press interviews in the company of a pack of advisers who will censor everything I say and inevitably make me sound like a bit of animated treacle, as out of touch with reality as the average overly sweet dessert."

"Speaking of treats, I also have to deal with the board of directors Mr. Casilieris treats like irritating schoolchildren, his packs of furious ex-lovers each with her own vendetta, all his terrified employees who need to be coached through meetings with him and treated for PTSD after, and every last member of his staff in every one of his households, who like me to be the one to ask him the questions they know will set him off on one of his scorch-the-earth rages." Natalie had moved closer then, and lowered her voice. "I was thinking of quitting, to be honest. Today."

"I can't quit, I'm afraid," Valentina had said. Regretfully.

But she'd wished she could. She'd wished she could just…walk away and not have to live up to anyone's expectations. And not have to marry a man whom she barely knew. And not have to resign herself to a version of the same life so many of her ancestors had lived. Maybe that was where the idea had come from. Blood was blood, after all. And this woman clearly shared her blood. What if…?

"I have a better idea," she'd said, and then she'd tossed it out there before she could think better of it. "Let's switch places. For a month, say. Six weeks at the most. Just for a little break."

"That's crazy," Natalie said at once, and she was right. Of course she was right.

"Insane," Valentina had agreed. "But you might find royal protocol exciting! And I've always wanted to do the things everyone else in the world does. Like go to a real job."

"People can't *switch places*." Natalie had frowned. "And certainly not with a princess."

"You could think about whether or not you really want to quit," Valentina pointed out, trying to sweeten the deal. "It would be a lovely holiday for you. Where will Achilles Casilieris be in six weeks' time?"

"He's never gone from London for too long," Natalie had said, as if she was considering it.

Valentina had smiled. "Then in six weeks we'll meet in London. We'll text in the meantime with all the necessary details about our lives, and on the appointed day we'll just meet up and switch back and no one will ever be the wiser. Doesn't that sound like *fun*?"

"It would never work," Natalie had replied. Which wasn't exactly a *no*. "No one will ever believe I'm you."

Valentina waved a hand, encompassing the pair of them. "How would anyone know the difference? I can barely tell myself."

"People will take one look at me and know I'm not you. *You* look like a *princess*."

"You, too, can look like a princess," Valentina assured her. Then smiled. "This princess, anyway. You already do."

"You're elegant. Poised. You've had years of training, presumably. How to be a diplomat. How to be polite in every possible situation. Which fork to use at dinner, for God's sake."

"Achilles Casilieris is one of the wealthiest men alive," Valentina had pointed out. "He dines with as many kings as I do. I suspect that as his personal assistant, Natalie, you have, too. And have likely learned how to navigate the cutlery."

"No one will believe it," Natalie had insisted. But she'd sounded a bit as if she was wavering.

Valentina tugged off the ring on her left hand and placed it down on the counter between them. It made an audible *clink* against the marble surface, as well it should, given it was one of the crown jewels of the kingdom of Tissely.

"Try it on. I dare you. It's an heirloom from Prince Rodolfo's extensive treasury of such items, dating back to the dawn of time, more or less." She smiled. "If it doesn't fit we'll never speak of switching places again."

But the ring had fit her double as if it had been made especially for her.

And after that, switching clothes was easy. Valentina found herself in front of the bathroom mirror, dressed like a billionaire's assistant, when Natalie walked out of the stall behind her in her own shift dress and the heels her favorite shoe designer had made just for her. It was like looking in a mirror, but one that walked and looked unsteady on her feet and was wearing her hair differently.

Valentina couldn't tell if she was disconcerted or excited. Both, maybe.

She'd eyed Natalie. "Will your glasses give me a headache, do you suppose?"

But Natalie had pulled them from her face and handed them over. "They're clear glass. I was getting a little too much attention from some of the men Mr. Casilieris works with, and it annoyed him. I didn't want to lose my job, so I started wearing my hair up and these glasses. It worked like a charm."

"I refuse to believe men are so idiotic."

Natalie had grinned as Valentina took the glasses and slid them onto her nose. "The men we're talking about weren't exactly paying me attention because they found me enthralling. It was a diversionary tactic during negotiations, and yes, you'd be surprised how many men fail to see a woman who looks smart."

She'd freed her hair from its utilitarian ponytail and shook it out, then handed the stretchy elastic to Valentina. It took Valentina a moment to re-create the ponytail on her own head, and then it was done.

And it really was like magic.

"This is crazy," Natalie had whispered.

"We have to switch places now," Valentina said softly, hearing the rough patch in her own voice. "I've always wanted to be...someone else. Someone normal. Just for a little while."

And she'd gotten exactly what she'd wanted, hadn't she?

"I am distressed, Miss Monette, that I cannot manage to secure your attention for more than a moment or two," Achilles said then, slamming Valentina back into this car he dominated so easily when all he was doing was sitting there.

Sitting there, filling up the world without even trying.

He was *devastating*. There was no other possible word that could describe him. His black hair was close-cropped to his head, which only served to highlight his strong, intensely masculine features. She'd had hours on the plane to study him as she'd repeatedly failed to do the things he'd expected of her, and she still couldn't really get her head around why it was that he was so...affecting. He shouldn't have been. Dark hair. Dark eyes that tended toward gold when his temper washed over him, which he'd so far made no attempt to hide. A strong nose that reminded her of ancient statues she'd seen in famous museums. That lean, hard body of his that wasn't made of marble or bronze but seemed to suggest both as he used it so effortlessly. A predator packed into a dark suit that seemed molded to him, whispering suggestions of a lethal warrior when all he was doing was taking phone calls with a five-hundred-thousand-dollar watch on one wrist that he didn't flash about, because he was Achilles Casilieris. He didn't need flash.

Achilles was something else.

It was the power that seemed to emanate from him, even when he was doing nothing but sitting quietly. It was the fierce hit of his intelligence, that brooding, unmistakable cleverness that seemed to wrap around him like a cloud. It was something in the way he looked at her, as if he saw too much and too deeply and no matter that Valentina's unreadable game face was the envy of Europe. Besides all that, there was something untamed about him. Fierce.

Something about him left her breathless. Entirely too close to reeling.

"Do you require a gold star every time you make a statement?" she asked, careful not to look at him. It was too hard to look away. She'd discovered that on the plane ride from London—and he was a lot closer now. So close she was sure she could feel the heat of his body from where she sat. "I'll be certain to make a note to celebrate you more often. Sir."

Valentina didn't know what she was doing. In Natalie's job, certainly, but also with this man in general. She'd learned one thing about powerful people—particularly men—and it was that they did not enjoy being challenged. Under any circumstances. What made her think Achilles would go against type and magically handle this well?

But she couldn't seem to stop herself.

And the fact that she had never been one to challenge much of anything before hardly signified. Or maybe that was why she felt so unfettered, she thought. Because this wasn't her life. This wasn't her remote father and his endless expectations for the behavior of his only child. This was a strange little bit of role-playing that allowed her to be someone other than Princess Valentina for a moment. A few weeks, that was all. Why not challenge Achilles while she was at it? *Especially* if no one else ever did?

She could feel his gaze on the side of her face, that brooding dark gold, and she braced herself. Then made sure her expression was nothing but serene as she turned to face him.

It didn't matter. There was no minimizing this man.

She could feel the hit of him—like a fist—deep in her belly. And then lower.

"Are you certain you were not hit in the head?" Achilles asked, his dark voice faintly rough with the hint of his native Greek. "Perhaps in the bathroom at the airport? I fear that such places can often suffer from slippery floors. Deadly traps for the unwary."

"It was only a bathroom," she replied airily. "It wasn't slippery or otherwise notable in any way."

"Are you sure?" And something in his voice and his hard gaze prickled into her then. Making her chest feel tighter.

Valentina did not want to talk about the bathroom, much less anything that had happened there. And there was something in his gaze that worried her—but that was insane. He couldn't have any idea that she'd run into her own twin. How could he? Valentina had been unaware that there was the faintest possibility she might have a twin until today.

Which made her think about her father and his many, many lectures about his only child in a new, unfortunate light. But Valentina thrust that aside. That was something to worry about when she was a princess again. That was a problem she could take up when she was back in Murin Castle.

Here, now, she was a secretary. An executive assistant, no more and no less.

"I beg your pardon, Mr. Casilieris." She let her smile deepen and ignored the little hum of...something deep inside her when his gaze seemed to catch fire. "Are you trying to tell me that you need a bathroom? Should I ask the driver to stop the car right here in the middle of the George Washington Bridge?"

She expected him to get angry again. Surely that was what had been going on before, back in London before the plane had taken off. She'd seen temper all over that fierce, hard face of his and gleaming hot in his gaze. More than that, she'd felt it inside her. As if the things he felt echoed within her, winding her into knots. She felt something a whole lot like a chill inch its way down her spine at that notion.

But Achilles only smiled. And that was far more dangerous than merely devastating.

"Miss Monette," he said and shook his head, as if she amused him, when she could see that the thing that moved over that ruthless face of his was far too intense to be simple *amusement*. "I had no idea that beneath your officious exterior you've been hiding a comedienne all this time. For five years you've worked at my side and never let so much as a hint of this whimsical side of your personality out into the open. Whatever could have changed?"

He knows. The little voice inside her was certain—and terrified.

But it was impossible. Valentina knew it was impossible, so she made herself smile and relax against the leather seat as if she'd never in her life been so at her ease. Very much as if she was not within scant inches of a very large, very powerful, very intense male who was eyeing her the way gigantic lions and tigers and jaguars eyed their food. When they were playing with it.

She'd watched enough documentaries and made enough state visits to African countries to know firsthand.

"Perhaps I've always been this amusing," she suggested, managing to tamp down her hysteria about oversize felines, none of which was particularly helpful at the moment. "Perhaps you've only recently allowed yourself to truly listen to me."

"I greatly enjoy listening to you," Achilles replied. There was a laziness in the way he sat there, sprawled out in the backseat of his car, that dark gold gaze on hers.

A certain laziness, yes—but Valentina didn't believe it for a second. "I particularly enjoy listening to you when you are doing your job perfectly. Because you know how much I admire perfection. I insist on it, in fact. Which is why I cannot understand why you failed to provide it today."

"I don't know what you mean."

But she knew what he meant. She'd been on the plane and she'd been the one to fail repeatedly to do what was clearly her job. She'd hung up on one conference call and failed entirely to connect another. She'd expected him to explode—if she was honest, there was a part of her that wanted him to explode, in the way that anyone might want to poke and poke and poke at some kind of blister to see if it would pop. But he hadn't popped. He hadn't lost his temper at all, despite the fact that it had been very clear to Valentina very quickly that she was a complete and utter disaster at doing whatever it was that Natalie did.

When Achilles had stared at her in amazement, however, she hadn't made any excuses. She'd only gazed right back, serenely, as if she'd meant to do whatever utterly incorrect thing it was. As if it was all some kind of strategy.

She could admit that she hadn't really thought the job part through. She been so busy fantasizing herself into some kind of normal life that it had never occurred to her that, normal or not, a life was still *a whole life*. She had no idea how to live any way but the way she'd been living for almost thirty years. How remarkably condescending, she'd thought up there on Achilles Casilieris's jet, that she'd imagined she could simply step into a job—especially one as demanding as this appeared to be—and do it merely because she'd decided it was her chance at something "normal."

Valentina had found the entire experience humbling, if she was honest, and it had been only a few hours since she'd switched places with Natalie in London. Who knew what else awaited her?

But Achilles was still sprawled there beside her, that unnerving look of his making her skin feel too small for her bones.

"Natalie, Natalie," he murmured, and Valentina told herself it was a good thing he'd used that name. It wasn't her name, and she needed the reminder. This wasn't about her. It wasn't her job to advocate for Natalie when the other woman might not wish for her to do anything like that. She was on a fast track to losing Natalie her job, and then what? Valentina didn't have to worry about her employment prospects, but she had no idea what the market was like for billionaire's assistants.

But maybe there was a part of her that already knew that there was no way Natalie Monette was a stranger to her. Certainly not on the genetic level. And that had implications she wasn't prepared to examine just yet, but she did know that the woman who was in all likelihood her long-lost identical twin did not have to work for Achilles Casilieris unless she wanted to.

How arrogant of you, a voice inside her said quietly. *Her Royal Highness, making unilateral decisions for others' lives without their input.*

The voice sounded a little too much like her father's.

"That is my name," Valentina said to Achilles, in case there had been any doubt. Perhaps with a little too much force.

But she had the strangest notion that he was...*tasting* the name as he said it. As if he'd never said it before. Did he call Natalie by her first name? Valentina rather thought not, given that he'd called her *Miss Monette* when she'd met him—but that was neither here nor there, she told herself. And no matter that she was a woman who happened to know the power of titles. She had many of her own. And her life was marked by those who used the different versions of her titles, not to mention the few who actually called her by her first name.

"I cannot tolerate this behavior," he said, but it wasn't in that same infuriated tone he'd used earlier. If anything, he sounded almost…indulgent. But surely that was impossible. "It borders on open rebellion, and I cannot have that. This is not a democracy, I'm afraid. This is a dictatorship. If I want your opinion, I'll tell you what it is."

There was no reason her heart should have been kicking at her like that, her pulse so loud in her ears she was sure he must be able to hear it himself.

"What an interesting way to foster employee loyalty," she murmured. "Really more of a scorch-the-earth approach. Do you find it gets you the results you want?"

"I do not need to breed employee loyalty," Achilles told her, sounding even lazier than before, those dark eyes of his on hers. "People are loyal to me or they are fired. You seem to have forgotten reality today, Natalie. Allow me to remind you that I pay you so much money that I own your loyalty, just as I own everything else."

"Perhaps," and her voice was a little too rough then. A little too shaky, when what could this possibly have to do with her? She was a visitor. Natalie's loyalty was no concern of hers. "I have no wish to be owned. Does anyone? I think you'll find that they do not."

Achilles shrugged. "Whether you wish it or do not, that is how it is."

"That is why I was considering quitting," she heard herself say. And she was no longer looking at him. That was still far too dangerous, too disconcerting. She found herself staring down at her hands, folded in her lap. She could feel that she was frowning, when she learned a long, long time ago never to show her feelings in public. "It's all very well and good for you, of course. I imagine it's quite pleasant to have minions. But for me, there's more to life than blind loyalty. There's more to life than work." She blinked back a strange heat. "I may not have experienced it myself, but I know there must be."

"And what do you think is out there?" He shifted in the seat beside her, but Valentina still refused to look back at him, no matter how she seemed almost physically compelled to do just that. "What do you think you're missing? Is it worth what you are throwing away here today, with this aggressive attitude and the childish pretense that you don't know your own job?"

"It's only those who are bored of the world, or jaded, who are so certain no one else could possibly wish to see it."

"No one is keeping you from roaming about the planet at will," he told her in a low voice. Too low. So low it danced along her skin and seemed to insinuate itself beneath her flesh. "But you seem to wish to burn down the world you know in order to see the one you don't. That is not what I would call wise. Would you?"

Valentina didn't understand why his words seemed to beat beneath her own skin. But she couldn't seem to catch her breath. And her eyes seemed entirely too full, almost scratchy, with an emotion she couldn't begin to name.

She was aware of too many things. Of the car as it slid through the Manhattan streets. Of Achilles himself, too big and too masculine in the seat beside her, and much too close besides. And most of all, that oddly weighted thing within her, rolling around and around until she couldn't tell the difference between sensation and reaction.

And him right there in the middle of it, confusing her all the more.

CHAPTER THREE

ACHILLES DIDN'T SAY another word, and that was worse. It left Valentina to sit there with her own thoughts in a whirl and nothing to temper them. It left no barrier between that compelling, intent look in his curiously dark eyes and her.

Valentina had no experience with men. Her father had insisted that she grow up as sheltered as possible from public life, so that she could enjoy what little privacy was afforded to a European princess before she turned eighteen. She'd attended carefully selected boarding schools run strictly and deliberately, but that hadn't prevented her classmates from involving themselves in all kinds of dramatic situations. Even then, Valentina had kept herself apart.

Your mother's defection was a stain on the throne, her father always told her. *It is upon us to render it clean and whole again.*

Valentina had been far too terrified of staining Murin any further to risk a scandal. She'd concentrated on her studies and her friends and left the teenage rebellions to others. And once out of school, she'd been thrust unceremoniously into the spotlight. She'd been an ambassador for her kingdom wherever she went, and more than that, she'd always known that she was promised to the Crown

Prince of Tissely. Any scandals she embroiled herself in would haunt two kingdoms.

She'd never seen the point.

And along the way she'd started to take a certain pride in the fact that she was saving herself for her predetermined marriage. It was the one thing that was hers to give on her wedding night that had nothing to do with her father or her kingdom.

Is it pride that's kept you chaste—or is it control? a little voice inside her asked then, and the way it kicked in her, Valentina suspected she wouldn't care for the answer. She ignored it.

But the point was, she had no idea how to handle men. Not on any kind of intimate level. These past few hours, in fact, were the longest she'd ever spent alone in the company of a man. It simply didn't happen when she was herself. There were always attendants and aides swarming around Princess Valentina. Always.

She told herself that was why she was having such trouble catching her breath. It was the novelty—that was all. It certainly wasn't *him*.

Still, it was almost a relief when the car pulled up in front of a quietly elegant building on the Upper West Side of Manhattan, perched there with a commanding view of Central Park, and came to a stop.

The late-afternoon breeze washed over her when she stepped from the car, smelling improbably of flowers in the urban sprawl of New York City. But Valentina decided to take it as a blessing.

Achilles remained silent as he escorted her into the building. He only raised his chin in the barest of responses to the greeting that came his way from the doormen in the shiny, obviously upscale lobby, and then he led her into a private elevator located toward the back and behind another set of security guards. It was a gleaming, shining thing that he operated with a key. And it was blessedly without any mirrors.

Valentina wasn't entirely sure whom she'd see if she looked at her own reflection just then.

There were too many things she didn't understand churning inside her, and she hadn't the slightest idea what she was doing here. What on earth she hoped to gain from this odd little lark across the planet, literally in another woman's shoes.

A break, she reminded herself sternly. A vacation. A little holiday away from all the duties and responsibilities of Princess Valentina, which was more important now than ever. She would give herself over to her single-greatest responsibility in a matter of weeks. She would marry Prince Rodolfo and make both of their fathers and all of their subjects very, very happy.

And a brief escape had sounded like bliss for that split second back there in London—and it still did, when she thought about what waited for her. The terribly appropriate royal marriage. The endlessly public yet circumspect life of a modern queen. The glare of all that attention that she and any children she bore could expect no matter where they went or what they did, yet she could never comment upon lest she seem ungrateful or entitled.

Hers was to wave and smile—that was all. She was marrying a man she hardly knew who would expect the marital version of the same. This was a little breather before the reality of all that. This was a tiny bit of space between her circumscribed life at her father's side and more of the same at her husband's.

She couldn't allow the brooding, unreadable man beside her to ruin it, no matter how unnerving his dark gold gaze was. No matter what fires it kicked up inside her that she hardly dared name.

The elevator doors slid open, delivering them straight

into the sumptuous front hall of an exquisitely decorated penthouse. Valentina followed Achilles as he strode deep inside, not bothering to spare her a glance as he moved. She was glad that he walked ahead of her, which allowed her to look around so she could get her bearings without seeming to do so. Because, of course, Natalie would already know her way around this place.

She took in the high ceilings and abundant windows all around. The sweeping stairs that led up toward at least two more floors. The mix of art deco and a deep coziness that suggested this penthouse was more than just a showcase; Achilles actually *lived* here.

Valentina told herself—sternly—that there was no earthly reason that notion should make her shiver.

She was absurdly grateful when a housekeeper appeared, clucking at Achilles in what it took Valentina longer than it should have to realize was Greek. A language she could converse in, though she would never consider herself anything like fluent. Still, it took her only a very few moments to understand that whatever the danger Achilles exuded and however ruthless the swath he cut through the entire world with a single glance, this woman thought he was wonderful.

She *beamed* at him.

It would not do to let that get to her, Valentina warned herself as something warm seemed to roll its way through her, pooling in the strangest places. She should not draw any conclusions about a man who was renowned for his fierceness in all things and yet let a housekeeper treat him like family.

The woman declared she would feed him no matter if he was hungry or not, lest he get skinny and weak, and bustled back in the direction of what Valentina assumed was the kitchen.

"You're looking around as if you are lost," Achilles

murmured, when Valentina didn't think she'd been looking around at all. "When you have spent more time in this penthouse over the last five years than I have."

Valentina hated the fact that she started a bit when she realized his attention was focused on her again. And that he was speaking in English, which seemed to make him sound that much more knowing.

Or possibly even mocking, unless she was very much mistaken.

"Mr. Casilieris," she said, lacing her voice with gentle reprove, "I work for you. I don't understand why you appear to be quite so interested in what you think is happening inside my head today. Especially when you are so mistaken."

"Am I?"

"Entirely." She raised her brows at him. "If I could suggest that we concentrate more on matters of business than fictional representations of what might or might not be going on inside my mind, I think we might be more productive."

"As productive as we were on the flight over?" His voice was a lazy sort of lash, as amused as it was on target.

Valentina only smiled, hoping she looked enigmatic and strategic rather than at a loss.

"Are *you* lost?" she asked him after a moment, because neither one of them had moved from the great entry that bled into the spacious living room, then soared up two stories, a quiet testament to his wealth and power.

"Careful, Miss Monette," Achilles said with a certain dark precision. "As delightful as I have found today's descent into insubordination, I have a limit. It would be in your best interests not to push me there too quickly."

Valentina had made a study out of humbly accepting all kinds of news she didn't wish to hear over the years. She bent her head, let her lips curve a bit—but not enough to be called a smile, only enough to show she was feeling... something. Then she simply stood there quietly. It was amazing how many unpleasant moments she'd managed to get through that way.

So she had no earthly idea why there was a part of her that wanted nothing more than to look Achilles straight in his dark eyes and ask him, *Or what?*

Somehow, thankfully, she refrained.

Servants came in behind them with luggage—some of which Valentina assumed must be Natalie's and thus hers—but Achilles did not appear to notice them. He kept his attention trained directly on her.

A lesser woman would have been disconcerted, Valentina thought. Someone unused to being the focus of attention, for example. Someone who hadn't spent a part of every day since she turned eighteen having cameras in her face to record every flutter of her eyelashes and rip apart every facet of whatever she happened to be wearing and how she'd done her hair. Every expression that crossed her face was a headline.

What was a cranky billionaire next to that?

"There's no need to repair to our chambers after the flight, I think," he said softly, and Valentina had that odd notion again. That he could see right through her. That he knew things he couldn't possibly know. "We can get right to it."

And there was no reason that that should feel almost... dirty. As if he was suggesting—

But, of course, that was absurd, Valentina told herself staunchly. He was Achilles Casilieris. He was renowned almost as much for his prowess in the sheets as he was for his dominance in the boardroom. In some circles, more.

He tended toward the sort of well-heeled women who

were mainstays on various charity circuits. Not for him the actresses or models whom so many other men of his stature preferred. That, apparently, was not good enough for Achilles Casilieris. Valentina had found herself with some time on the plane to research it herself, after Achilles had finished the final call she'd failed entirely to set up to his liking and had sat a while, a fulminating stare fixed on her. Then he'd taken himself off to one of the jet's finely appointed staterooms, and she'd breathed a bit easier.

A bit.

She'd looked around for a good book to read, preferably a paperback romance because who didn't like hope and happiness with a bit of sex thrown in to make it spicy, but there had been nothing of the sort. Achilles apparently preferred dreary economic magazines that trumpeted out recession and doom from all quarters. Valentina had kicked off her shoes, tucked her legs beneath her on the smooth leather chair she'd claimed for the flight, and indulged herself with a descent into the tabloid and gossip sites she normally avoided. Because she knew how many lies they told about her, so why would she believe anything she read about anyone else?

Still, they were a great way to get a sense of the kind of coverage a man like Achilles suffered, which would surely tell her...something. But the answer was...not much. He was featured in shots from charity events where other celebrities gathered like cows at a trough, but was otherwise not really a tabloid staple. Possibly because he was so sullen and scowling, she thought.

His taste in bedmates, however, was clear even without being splashed across screeching front pages all over the world. Achilles tended toward women who were less celebrated for their faces and more for their actions. Which wasn't to say they weren't all beautiful, of course. That seemed to be a requirement. But they couldn't only be beautiful.

This one was a civil rights attorney of some renown. That one was a journalist who spent most of her time in terrifying war zones. This one had started a charity to benefit a specific cancer that had taken her younger sister. That one was a former Olympic athlete who had dedicated her post-competition life to running a lauded program for at-risk teenagers.

He clearly had a type. Accomplished, beautiful women who did good in the world and who also happened to be wealthy enough all on their own. The uncharitable part of her suspected that last part was because he knew a woman of independent means would not be as interested in his fortune as a woman who had nothing. No gold diggers need apply, clearly.

But the point was, she knew she was mistaken about his potentially suggestive words. Because "assistant to billionaire" was not the kind of profession that would appeal to a man like Achilles. It saved no lives. It bettered nothing.

Valentina found herself glaring at his back as he led her into a lavish office suite on the first level of his expansive penthouse. When she stood in the center of the room, awaiting further instructions, he only crooked a brow. He leaned back against the large desk that stretched across one wall and regarded her with that hot sort of focus that made everything inside her seem to shift hard to the left.

She froze. And then she could have stood there for hours, for all she knew, as surely as if he'd caught her and held her fast in his fists.

"When you are ready, Miss Monette, feel free to take your seat." His voice was razor sharp, cut through with that same rough darkness that she found crept through her limbs. Lighting her up and making her feel something like sluggish. She didn't understand it. "Though I do love being kept waiting."

More chastened than she wanted to admit, Valentina moved to one of the seats set around a table to the right of the desk, at the foot of towering bookshelves stuffed full of serious-looking books, and settled herself in it. When he continued to stare at her as if she was deliberately keeping him waiting, she reached into the bag—Natalie's bag, which she'd liberated from the bathroom when she'd left the airport with Achilles—until she found a tablet.

A few texts with her double had given her the passwords she needed and some advice.

Just write down everything he says. He likes to forget he said certain things, and it's always good to have a record. One of my jobs is to function as his memory.

Valentina had wanted to text back her thoughts on that, but had refrained. Natalie might have wanted to quit this job, but that was up to her, not the woman taking her place for a few weeks.

"Anything else?" Achilles's voice had a dark edge. "Would you like to have a snack? Perhaps a brief nap? Tell me, is there any way that I can make you more comfortable, Miss Monette, such that you might actually take it upon yourself to do a little work today?"

And Valentina didn't know what came over her. Because she wanted to argue. She, who had made a virtue out of remaining quiet and cordial under any circumstances, wanted to fight. She didn't understand it. She knew it was Achilles. That there was something in him that made her want to do or say anything to get some kind of reaction. It didn't matter that it was madness. It was something about that look in his eyes. Something about that hard, amused mouth of his.

CAITLIN CREWS 51

It was something about *him*.

But Valentina reminded herself that this was not her life.

This was not her life and this was not her job, and none of this was hers to ruin. She was the steward of Natalie's life for a little while, nothing more. She imagined that Natalie would be doing the same for her. Maybe breathing a little bit of new life into the tired old royal nonsense she'd find waiting for her at Murin Castle, but that was all. Neither one of them was out to wreck what they found.

And she'd never had any trouble whatsoever keeping to the party line. Doing her father's bidding, behaving appropriately, being exactly the princess whom everyone imagined she was. She felt that responsibility—to her people, to her bloodline, to her family's history—deeply. She'd never acted out the way so many of her friends had. She'd never fought against her own responsibilities. It wasn't that she was afraid to do any of those things, but simply that it had never occurred to her to try. Valentina had always known exactly who she was and what her life would hold, from her earliest days.

So she didn't recognize this thing in her that wanted nothing more than to cause a commotion. To stand up and throw the tablet she held at Achilles's remarkably attractive head. To kick over the chair she was sitting in and, while she was at it, that desk of his, too, all brash steel and uncompromising masculinity, just like its owner.

She wanted to do *something*. Anything. She could feel it humming through her veins, bubbling in her blood. As if something about this normal life she'd tried on for size had infected her. Changed her. When it had only been a few hours.

He's a ruthless man, something reckless inside her whispered. *He can take it.*

But this wasn't her life. She had to protect it, not destroy it, no matter what was moving in her, poking at her, tempting her to act out for the first time in her life.

So Valentina smiled up at Achilles, forced herself to remain serene the way she always did, and got to work.

It was late into the New York night when Achilles finally stopped torturing his deceitful princess.

He made her go over byzantine contracts that rendered his attorneys babbling idiots. He questioned her on clauses he only vaguely understood himself, and certainly couldn't expect her to be conversant on. He demanded she prepare memos he had no intention of sending. He questioned her about events he knew she could not possibly know anything about, and the truth was that he enjoyed himself more than he could remember enjoying anything else for quite some time.

When Demetria had bustled in with food, Achilles had waved Valentina's away.

"My assistant does not like to eat while she works," he told his housekeeper, but he'd kept his gaze on Valentina while he'd said it.

"I don't," she'd agreed merrily enough. "I consider it a weakness." She'd smiled at him. "But you go right ahead."

Point to the princess, he'd thought.

The most amazing thing was that Princess Valentina never backed down. Her ability to brazen her way through the things she didn't know, in fact, was nothing short of astounding. Impressive in the extreme. Achilles might have admired it if he hadn't been the one she was trying to fool.

"It is late," he said finally, when he thought her eyes might glaze over at last. Though he would cast himself out his own window to the Manhattan streets below before he'd admit his might, too. "And while there is always more to do, I think it is perhaps wise if we take this as a natural stopping place."

Valentina smiled at him, tucked up in that chair of hers that she had long since claimed as her own in a way he couldn't remember the real Natalie had ever done, her green eyes sparkling.

"I understand if you need a rest," she said sweetly. Too sweetly. "Sir."

Achilles had been standing at the windows, his back to the mad gleam of Manhattan. But at that, he let himself lean back, his body shifting into something…looser. More dangerous.

And much, much hotter than contracts.

"I worry my hearing has failed me. Because it sounded very much as if you were impugning my manhood."

"Only if your manhood is so fragile that you can't imagine it requires a rest," she said, and aimed a sunny smile at him as if that would take away the sting of her words. "But you are Achilles Casilieris. You have made yourself a monument to manhood, clearly. No fragility allowed."

"It is almost as if you think debating me like this is some kind of strategy," he said softly, making no attempt to ratchet back the ruthlessness in his voice. Much less do something about the fire he could feel storming through him everywhere else. "Let me warn you, again, it is only a strategy if your goal is to find yourself without a job and without a recommendation. To say nothing of the black mark I will happily put beside your name."

Valentina waved a hand in the air, airily, dismissing him. And her possible firing, black marks—all of it. Something else he very likely would have found impressive if he'd been watching her do it to someone else.

"So many threats." She shook her head. "I understand that this is how you run your business and you're very successful, but really. It's exhausting. Imagine how many more bees you could get with honey."

He didn't want to think about honey. Not when there were only the two of them here, in this office cushioned by the night outside and the rest of the penthouse. No shared walls on these floors he owned. This late, none of the staff would be up. It was only Achilles and this princess pretending to be his assistant, and the buttery light of the few lamps they'd switched on, making the night feel thick and textured everywhere the light failed to reach.

Like inside him.

"Come here."

Valentina blinked, but her green gaze was unreadable then. She only looked at him for a moment, as if she'd forgotten that she was playing this game. And that in it, she was his subordinate.

"Come here," he said again. "Do not make me repeat myself, I beg you. You will not like my response."

She stood the way she did everything else, with an easy grace. With that offhanded elegance that did things to him he preferred not to examine. And he knew she had no desire to come any closer to him. He could feel it. Her wariness hung between them like some kind of smoke, and it ignited that need inside him. And for a moment he thought she might disobey him. That she might balk—and it was in that moment he thought she'd stay where she was, across the room, that he had understood how very much he wanted her.

In a thousand ways he shouldn't, because Achilles was a man who did not *want*. He took. Wanting was a weakness that led only to darkness—though it didn't feel like a weakness tonight. It felt like the opposite.

But he'd underestimated his princess. Her shoulders straightened almost imperceptibly. And then she glided toward him, head high like some kind of prima ballerina, her face set in the sort of pleasant expression he now knew she could summon and dispatch at will. He admired that, too.

And he'd thrown out that summons because he could. Because he wanted to. And he was experimenting with this new *wanting*, no matter how little he liked it.

Still, there was no denying the way his body responded as he watched her walk toward him. There was no denying the rich, layered tension that seemed to fill the room. And him, making his pulse a living thing as his blood seemed to heat in his veins.

Something gleamed in that green gaze of hers, but she kept coming. She didn't stop until she was directly beside him, so close that if she breathed too heavily he thought her shoulder might brush his. He shifted so that he stood slightly behind her, and jutted his chin toward the city laid out before them.

"What do you see when you look out the window?"

He felt more than saw the glance she darted at him. But then she kept her eyes on the window before them. On the ropes of light stretching out in all hectic directions possible below.

"Is that a trick question? I see Manhattan."

"I grew up in squalor." His voice was harsher than he'd intended, but Achilles did nothing to temper it. "It is common, I realize, for successful men to tell stories of their humble beginnings. Americans in particular find these stories inspiring. It allows them to fantasize that they, too, might better themselves against any odds. But the truth is more of a gray area, is it not? Beginnings are never quite so humble as they sound when rich men claim them. But me?" He felt her gaze on him then, instead of the mess of lights outside. "When I use the word *squalor*, that's an upgrade."

Her swallow was audible. Or perhaps he was paying her too close attention. Either way, he didn't back away.

"I don't know why you're telling me this."

"When you look through this window you see a city. A place filled with people going about their lives, traffic and isolation." He shifted so he could look down at her. "I see hope. I see vindication. I see all the despair and all the pain and all the loss that went into creating the man you see before you tonight. Creating this." And he moved his chin to indicate the penthouse. And the Casilieris Company while he was at it. "And there is nothing that I wouldn't do to protect it."

And he didn't know what had happened to him while he was speaking. He'd been playing a game, and then suddenly it seemed as if the game had started to play him— and it wasn't finished. Something clutched at him, as if he was caught in the grip of some massive fist.

It was almost as if he wanted this princess, this woman who believed she was tricking him—deceiving him—to understand him.

This, too, was unbearable.

But he couldn't seem to stop.

"Do you think people become driven by accident, Miss Monette?" he asked, and he couldn't have said why that thing gripping him seemed to clench harder. Making him sound far more intense than he thought he should have felt. Risking the truth about himself he carried inside and shared with no one. But he still didn't stop. "Ambition, desire, focus and drive—do you think these things grow on trees? But then, perhaps I'm asking the wrong person. Have you not told me a thousand times that you are not personally ambitious?"

It was one of the reasons he'd kept Natalie with him for so long, when other assistants to men like him used positions like hers as springboards into their own glorious careers. But this woman was not Natalie. If he hadn't known it before, he'd have known it now, when it was a full-scale struggle to keep his damned hands to himself.

"Ambition, it seems to me, is for those who have the freedom to pursue it. And for those who do not—" and Valentina's eyes seemed to gleam at that, making Achilles wonder exactly what her ambitions were "—it is nothing more than dissatisfaction. Which is far less worthy and infinitely more destructive, I think we can agree."

He didn't know when he'd turned to face her fully. He didn't know when he'd stopped looking at the city and was looking only at her instead. But he was, and he compounded that error by reaching out his hand and tugging on the very end of her silky, coppery ponytail where it kissed her shoulder every time she moved her head.

Her lips parted, as if on a soundless breath, and Achilles felt that as if she'd caressed him. As if her hands were on his body the way he wished they were, instead of at her sides.

"Are you dissatisfied?" It was amazing how difficult it was not to use her real name then. How challenging it was to stay in this game he suddenly didn't particularly want to play. "Is that what this is?"

Her green eyes, which had been so unreadable, suddenly looked slick. Dark and glassy with some or other emotion. He couldn't tell what it was, and still, he could feel it in him like smoke, stealing through his chest and making it harder than it should have been to breathe.

"There's nothing wrong with dissatisfaction in and of itself," she told him after a moment, then another, that seemed too large for him to contain. Too dark and much too edgy to survive intact, and yet here they both were. "You see it as disloyalty, but it's not."

"How can it be anything else?"

"It is possible to be both loyal and open to the possibility that there is a life outside the one you've committed yourself to." Her green eyes searched his. "Surely there must be."

"I think you will find that there is no such possibility." His voice was harsh. He could feel it inside him, like a stain. Like need. "We must all decide who we are, every moment of every day. You either keep a vow or you do not. There is no between."

She stiffened at that, then tried to force her shoulders back down to an easier, less telling angle. Achilles watched her do it. He watched something like distress cross her lovely face, but she hid that, too. It was only the darkness in her gaze that told him he'd scored a direct hit, and he was a man who took great pride in the strikes he leveled against anyone who tried to move against him. Yet what he felt when he looked at Valentina was not pride. Not pride at all.

"Some vows are not your own," she said fiercely, her gaze locked to his. "Some are inherited. It's easy to say that you'll keep them because that's what's expected of you, but it's a great deal harder to actually *do* it."

He knew the vows she'd made. That pointless prince. Her upcoming royal wedding. He assumed that was the least of the vows she'd inherited from her father. And he still thought it was so much smoke and mirrors to hide the fact that she, like so many of her peers, was a spoiled and pampered creature who didn't like to be told what to do. Wasn't that the reason *poor little rich girl* was a saying in the first place?

He had no sympathy for the travails of a rich, pampered princess. But he couldn't seem to unwind that little silken bit of copper from around his finger, either. Much less step back and put the space between them that he should have left there from the start.

Achilles shook his head. "There is no gray area. Surely

you know this. You are either who you say you are or you are not."

There was something like misery in those eyes of hers then. And this was what he'd wanted. This was why he'd been goading her. And yet now that he seemed to have succeeded, he felt the strangest thing deep in his gut. It was an unpleasant and unfamiliar sensation, and at first Achilles couldn't identify it. It was a low heat, trickling through him, making him restless. Making him as close to uncertain as he'd ever been.

In someone else, he imagined, it might be shame. But shame was not something Achilles allowed in himself. Ever.

This was a night full of things he did not allow, apparently. Because he wanted her. He wanted to punctuate this oddly emotional discussion with his mouth. His hands. The whole of his too-tight, too-interested body pressed deep into hers. He wanted to taste those sweetly lush lips of hers. He wanted to take her elegant face in his hands, tip her head back and sate himself at last. It seemed to him an age or two since he'd boarded his plane and realized his assistant was not who she was supposed to be. An agony of waiting and all that *want*, and he was not a man who agonized. Or waited. Or wanted anything, it seemed, but this princess who thought she could fool him.

What was the matter with him that some part of him wanted to let her?

He did none of the things he longed to do.

Achilles made himself do the hard thing, no matter how complicated it was. Or how complicated it felt, anyway. When really it was so simple. He let her go. He let her silky hair fall from between his fingers, and he stepped back, putting inches between them.

But that did nothing to ease the temptation.

"I think what you need is a good night's sleep," he told

her, like some kind of absurd nurturer. Something he had certainly never tried to be for anyone else in the whole of his life. He would have doubted it was possible—and he refused to analyze that. "Perhaps it will clear your head and remind you of who you are. Jet lag can make that so very confusing, I know."

He thought she might have scuttled from the room at that, filled with her own shame if there was any decency in the world, but he was learning that this princess was not at all who he expected her to be. She swallowed, hard. And he could still see that darkness in her eyes. But she didn't look away from him. And she certainly didn't scuttle anywhere.

"I know exactly who I am, Mr. Casilieris," she said, very directly, and the lenses in her glasses made her eyes seem that much greener. "As I'm certain you do, too. Jet lag makes a person tired. It doesn't make them someone else entirely."

And when she turned to walk from the room then, it was with her head held high, graceful and self-contained, with no apparent second thoughts. Or anything the least bit like shame. All he could read on her as she went was that same distracting elegance that was already too far under his skin.

Achilles couldn't seem to do a thing but watch her go.

And when the sound of her footsteps had faded away, deep into the far reaches of the penthouse, he turned back to the wild gleam of Manhattan on the other side of his windows. Frenetic and frenzied. Light in all directions, as if there was nothing more to the world tonight than this utterly mad tangle of life and traffic and people and energy and it hardly mattered what he felt so high above it. It hardly mattered at all that he'd betrayed himself. That this woman who should have been nothing to him made him act like someone he barely recognized.

And her words stayed with him. *I know exactly who I am.* They echoed around and around in his head until it sounded a whole lot more like an accusation.

As if she was the one playing this game, and winning it, after all.

CHAPTER FOUR

As THE DAYS PASSED, Valentina thought that she was getting the hang of this assistant thing—especially if she endeavored to keep a minimum distance between herself and Achilles when the night got a little too dark and close. And at all other times, for that matter.

She'd chalked up those odd, breathless moments in his office that first night to the strangeness of inhabiting someone else's life. Because it couldn't be anything else. Since then, she hadn't felt the need to say too much. She hadn't defended herself—or her version of Natalie. She'd simply tried to do the job that Natalie, apparently, did so well she was seen by other employees of the Casilieris Company as superhuman.

With every day she became more accustomed to the demands of the job. She felt less as if she really ought to have taken Achilles up on his offer of a parachute and more as if this was something she could handle. Maybe not well or like superhuman Natalie, but she could handle it all the same in her own somewhat rudimentary fashion.

What she didn't understand was why Achilles hadn't fired her already. Because it was perfectly clear to Valentina that her version of handling things in no way lived up to Achilles's standards.

And if she'd been any doubt about that, he was the first to tell her otherwise.

His corporate offices in Manhattan took up several floors at one of Midtown's most esteemed addresses. There was an office suite set aside for him, naturally enough, that sprawled across the top floor and looked out over Manhattan as if to underscore the notion that Achilles Casilieris was in every way on top of the world. Valentina was settled in the immediate outer office, guarded by two separate lines of receptionist and secretarial defense should anyone make it through security. It wasn't to protect Achilles, but to further illuminate his importance. And Natalie's, Valentina realized quickly.

Because Natalie controlled access to Achilles. She controlled his schedule. She answered his phone and his email, and was generally held to have that all-important insight into his moods.

"What kind of day is it?" the senior vice presidents would ask her as they came in for their meetings, and the fact they smiled as they said it didn't make them any less anxious to hear her answer.

Valentina quickly discovered that Natalie controlled a whole lot more than simple access. There was a steady line of people at her desk, coming to her to ask how best to approach Achilles with any number of issues, or plot how to avoid approaching him with the things they knew he'd hate. Over the course of her first week in New York City, Valentina found that almost everyone who worked for Achilles tried to run things past her first, or used her to gauge his reactions. Natalie was less the man's personal assistant, she realized, and more the hub around which his businesses revolved. More than that, she thought he knew it.

"Take that up with Natalie," he would say in the middle of a meeting, without even bothering to look over at her. Usually while cutting someone off, because even he appeared not to want to hear certain things until Natalie had assessed them first.

"Come up with those numbers and run them past Natalie," he would tell his managers, and sometimes he'd even sound irritated while he said such things.

"Why are you acting as if you have never worked a day in my company?" he'd demanded of one of his brand managers once. "I am not the audience for your uncertain first drafts, George. How can you not know this?"

Valentina had smiled at the man in the meeting, and then had been forced to sit through a brainstorming/therapy session with him afterward, all the while hoping that the noncommittal things she'd murmured were, at the very least, not the *opposite* of the sort of things Natalie might have said.

Not that she texted Natalie to find out. Because that might have led to a conversation Valentina didn't really want to have with her double about strange, tense moments in the darkness with her employer.

She didn't know what she was more afraid of. That Natalie had never had any kind of tension with Achilles and Valentina was messing up her entire life...or that she did. That *tension* was just what Achilles did.

Valentina concentrated on her first attempt at a normal life, complete with a normal job, instead. And whether Achilles was aware of it or not, Natalie had her fingers in everything.

Including his romantic life.

The first time Valentina had answered his phone to find an emotional woman on the other end, she'd been appalled.

"There's a crying woman on the phone," she'd told Achilles. It had taken her a day or so to realize that she wasn't only allowed to walk in and out of his office when necessary, but encouraged to do so. That particular afternoon Achilles had been sitting on the sofa in his office, his feet up on his coffee table as he'd scowled down at his laptop. He shifted that scowl to her instead, in a way that made Valentina imagine that whatever he was looking at had something to do with her—

But that was ridiculous. There was no *her* in this scenario. There was only Natalie, and Valentina very much doubted Achilles spent his time looking up his assistant on the internet.

"Why are you telling me this?" he'd asked her shortly. "If I wanted to know who called me, I would answer my phones myself."

"She's crying about you," Valentina had said. "I assume she's calling to share her emotions with you, the person who caused them."

"And I repeat—why are you telling me this." This time it wasn't a question, and his scowl deepened. "You are my assistant. You are responsible for fielding these calls. I'm shocked you're even mentioning another crying female. I thought you stopped bringing them to my attention years ago."

Valentina had blinked at that. "Aren't you at all interested in why this woman is upset?"

"No."

"Not at all. Not the slightest bit interested." She studied his fierce face as if he was an alien. In moments like this, she thought he must have been. "You don't even know which woman I'm referring to, do you?"

"Miss Monette." He bit out that name as if the taste of it irritated him, and Valentina couldn't have said why it put her back up when it wasn't even her name. "I have a number of mistresses, none of whom call that line to manufacture emotional upsets. You are already aware of this." And he'd set his laptop aside, as if he needed to concentrate fully on Valentina before him. It had made her spine prickle, from her neck to her bottom and back up again. "Please let me know exactly what agenda it is we are pursuing today, that you expect to interrupt me in order to have a discussion about nuisance calls. When I assure you, the subject does not interest me at all. Just as it did not interest me five years ago, when you vowed to stop bothering me about them."

There was a warning in that. Valentina had heard it, plain as day. But she hadn't been able to heed it. Much less stop herself.

"To be clear, what you're telling me is that tears do not interest you," she'd said instead of beating a retreat to her desk the way she should have. She'd kept her tone even and easy, but she doubted that had fooled either one of them.

"Tears interest me least of all." She'd been sure that there was a curve in that hard mouth of his then, however small.

And what was the matter with her that she'd clung to that as if it was some kind of lifeline? As if she needed such a thing?

As if what she really wanted was his approval, when she hadn't switched places with Natalie for him. He'd had nothing to do with it. Why couldn't she seem to remember that?

"If this is a common occurrence for you, perhaps you need to have a think about your behavior," she'd pointed out. "And your aversion to tears."

There had definitely been a curve in his mouth then, and yet somehow that hadn't made Valentina any easier.

"This conversation is over," he'd said quietly. Though not gently. "Something I suggest you tell the enterprising actress on the phone."

She'd thought him hideously cold, of course. Heartless, even. But the calls kept coming. And Valentina had quickly realized what she should perhaps have known from the start—that it would be impossible for Achilles to actually be out there causing harm to so many anonymous women when he never left the office. She knew this because she spent almost every hour of every day in his company. The man literally had no time to go out there smashing hearts left and right, the way she'd be tempted to believe he did if she paid attention only to the phone calls she received, laden with accusations.

"Tell him I'm falling apart," yet another woman on the phone said on this latest morning, her voice ragged.

"Sorry, but what's your name again?" Valentina asked, as brightly as possible. "It's only that he's been working rather hard, you see. As he tends to do. Which would, of course, make it extremely difficult for him to be tearing anyone apart in any real sense."

The woman had sputtered. But Valentina had dutifully taken her name into Achilles when he next asked for his messages.

"I somewhat doubted the veracity of her claim," Valentina murmured. "Given that you were working until well after two last night."

Something she knew very well since that had meant she'd been working even longer than that.

Achilles laughed. He was at his desk today, which meant he was framed by the vertical thrust of Manhattan behind him. And still, that look in his dark gold gaze made the city disappear. "As well you should. I have no idea who this woman is. Or any of them." He shrugged. "My attorneys are knee-deep in paternity suits, and I win every one of them."

Valentino was astonished by that. Perhaps that was naive. She'd certainly had her share of admirers in her day, strange men who claimed an acquaintance or who sent rather disturbing letters to the palace—some from distant prisons in foreign countries. But she certainly never had men call up and try to pretend they had relationships with her *to* her.

Then again, would anyone have told her if they had? That sat on her a bit uneasily, though she couldn't have said why. She only knew that his gaze was like a touch, and that, too, seemed to settle on her like a weight.

"It's amazing how many unhinged women seem to think that if they claim they're dating you, you might go along with it," she said before she could think better of it.

That dark gold gaze of his lit with a gleam she couldn't name then. And it sparked something deep inside her, making her fight to draw in a breath. Making her feel unsteady in the serviceable low heels that Natalie favored. Making her wish she'd worn something more substantial than a nice jacket over another pencil skirt. Like a suit of armor. Or her very own brick wall.

"There are always unhinged women hanging about," Achilles said in that quietly devastating way of his. "Trying to convince me that they have relationships with me that they adamantly do not. Why do you imagine that is, Miss Monette?"

She told herself he couldn't possibly know that she was one of those women, no matter how his gaze seemed to pin her where she stood. No matter the edge in his voice, or the sharp emphasis he'd put on *Miss Monette*.

Even if he suspected something was different with his assistant, he couldn't know. Because no one could know. Because Valentina herself hadn't known Natalie existed until she'd walked into that bathroom. And that meant all sorts of things, such as the fact that everything she'd been told about her childhood and her birth was a lie. Not to mention her mother.

But there was no way Achilles could know any of that.

"Perhaps it's you," she murmured in response. She smiled when his brows rose in that expression of sheer arrogance that never failed to make her feel the slightest bit dizzy. "I only mean that you're a public figure and people imagine you a certain way based on the kind of press coverage you allow. Unless you plan to actively get out there and reclaim your public narrative, I don't think there's any likelihood that it will change."

"I am not a public figure. I have never courted the public in any way."

Valentina checked a sigh. "You're a very wealthy man. Whether you like it or not, the public is fascinated by you."

Achilles studied her until she was forced to order herself not to fidget beneath the weight of that heavy, intense stare.

"I'm intrigued that you think the very existence of public fascination must create an obligation in me to cater to it," he said quietly. "It does not. In fact, it has the opposite effect. In me. But how interesting that you imagine you owe something to the faceless masses who admire you."

Valentina's lips felt numb. "No masses, faceless or otherwise, admire me, Mr. Casilieris. They have no idea I exist. I'm an assistant, nothing more."

His hard mouth didn't shift into one of those hard curves, but his dark gold eyes gleamed, and somehow that made the floor beneath her seem to tilt, then roll.

"Of course you are," he said, his voice a quiet menace that echoed in her like a warning. Like something far more dangerous than a simple warning. "My mistake."

Later that night, still feeling as off balance as if the floor really wasn't steady beneath her feet, Valentina found herself alone with Achilles long after everyone else in the office had gone home.

It had been an extraordinarily long couple of days,

something Valentina might have thought was business as usual for the Casilieris Company if so many of the other employees hadn't muttered about how grueling it was. Beneath their breath and when they thought she couldn't hear them, that was. The deal that Achilles was so determined to push through had turned out to have more tangles and turns than anyone had expected—especially, it seemed, Achilles. What that meant was long hour after long hour well into the tiny hours of the night, hunched over tables and conference rooms, arguing with fleets of attorneys and representatives from the other side over take-out food from fine New York restaurants and stale coffee.

Valentina was deep into one of the contracts Achilles had slid her way, demanding a fresh set of eyes on a clause that annoyed him, when she noticed that they were the only ones there. The Casilieris Company had a significant presence all over the planet, so there were usually people coming and going at all conceivable hours to be available to different workdays in distant places. Something Valentina had witnessed herself after spending so much time in these offices since she'd arrived in New York.

But when she looked up from the dense and confusing contract language for a moment to give her ever-impending headache a break, she could see from the long conference room table where she sat straight through the glass walls that allowed her to see all the way across the office floor. And there was no one there. No bustling secretaries, no ambitious VPs putting in ostentatiously late hours where the boss could see their vigilance and commitment. No overzealous interns making busy work for themselves in the cubicles. No late-night cleaning crews, who did their jobs in the dark so as not to bother the workers by day. There wasn't a soul. Anywhere.

Something caught in her chest as she realized that it was only the two of them. Just Valentina and the man across the table from her, whom she was trying very hard not to look at too closely.

It was an extraordinarily unimportant thing to notice, she chastised herself, frowning back down at the contract. They were always alone, really. In his car, on his plane, in his penthouse. Valentina had spent more time with this man, she thought, than with any other save her father.

Her gaze rose from the contract of its own accord. Achilles sat across from her in the quiet of the otherwise empty office, his laptop cracked open before him and a pile of contracts next to the sleek machine. He looked the way he always did at the end of these long days. *Entirely too good*, something in her whispered—though she shoved that aside as best she could. It did no good to concentrate on things like that, she'd decided during her tenure with him. The man's appearance was a fact, and it was something she needed to come to terms with, but she certainly didn't have to ogle him.

But she couldn't seem to look away. She remembered that moment in his penthouse a little too clearly, the first night they'd been in New York. She remembered how close they'd stood in that window, and the things he'd told her, that dark gold gaze of his boring into her. As if he had every intention of looking directly to her soul. More than that, she remembered him reaching out and taking hold of the end of the ponytail she'd worn, that he'd looked at as if he had no idea how it had come to be attached to her.

But she'd dreamed about it almost every time she'd slept, either way.

Tonight Achilles was lounging in a pushed-back chair, his hands on top of his head as if, had he had longer hair, he'd be raking his hands through it. His jaw was dotted with stubble after a long day in the office, and it lent him the look of some kind of pirate.

Valentina told herself—sternly—that there was no

need for such fanciful language when he already made her pulse heat inside her simply by being in the same room. She tried to sink down a bit farther behind the piles and piles of documents surrounding her, which she was viewing as the armor she wished she was wearing. The remains of the dinner she'd ordered them many hours before were scattered across the center of the table, and she took perhaps too much pride in the fact she'd completed so simple a task. Normal people, she was certain, ordered from take-out menus all the time, but Valentina never had before she'd taken over Natalie's life. Valentina was a princess. She'd discussed many a menu and sent requests to any number of kitchens, but she'd never ordered her own meal in her life, much less from stereotypical New Yorkers with accents and attitudes.

She felt as if she was in a movie.

Valentina decided she would take her victories where she found them. Even if they were as small and ultimately pointless as sending out for a takeaway meal.

"It's late," Achilles said, reminding her that they were all alone here. And there was something in his voice then. Or the way his gaze slammed into hers when she looked up again.

Or maybe it was in her—that catch. That little kick of something a little too much like excitement that wound around and around inside her. Making her feel…restless. Undone. Desperate for something she couldn't even name.

"And here I thought you planned to carry straight through until dawn," she said, as brightly as possible, hoping against hope he couldn't see anything on her face. Or hear it in her voice.

Achilles lowered his hand to the arms of his chair. But he didn't shift that gaze of his from hers. And she kept catching him looking at her like this. Exactly like this. Simmering. Dark and dangerous, and spun through with gold. In the cars they took together. Every morning when he walked out of his bedchamber and found her sitting in the office suite, already starting on the day's work as best she could. Across boardroom tables just like this one, no matter if they were filled with other people.

It was worse now. Here in the quiet of his empty office. So late at night it felt to Valentina as if the darkness was a part of her.

And Valentina didn't have any experience with men, but oh, the books she'd read. Love stories and romances and happy-ever-afters, and almost all of them started just like this. With a taut feeling in the belly and fire everywhere else.

Do not be absurd, she snapped at herself.

Because she was Princess Valentina of Murin. She was promised to another and had been since her birth. There wasn't space in her life for anything but that. Not even here, in this faraway place that had nothing at all to do with her real life. Not even with this man, whom she never should have met, and never would have had she not seized that moment in the London bathroom.

You can take a holiday from your life, apparently, she reminded herself. *But you still take you along with you wherever you go.*

She might have been playing Natalie Monette, but she was still *herself.* She was still the same person she'd always been. Dutiful. Mindful of what her seemingly inconsequential behavior might mean to her father, to the kingdom, to her future husband's kingdom, too. Whatever else she was—and she wasn't sure she knew anymore, not here in the presence of a man who made her head spin without seeming to try very hard—Valentina was a person who had always, always kept her vows.

Even when it was her father who had made them, not her.

"If you keep staring at me like that," Achilles said softly, a kind of ferociousness beneath his rough words that made her stomach knot, then seemed to kindle a different, deeper fire lower down, "I am not certain I'll be able to contain myself."

Valentina's mouth was dry. "I don't know what you mean."

"I think you do."

Achilles didn't move, she could see that he wasn't moving, and yet everything changed at that. He filled every room he entered—she was used to that by now—but this was something different. It was as if lightning flashed. It was if he was some kind of rolling thunder all his own. It was as if he'd called in a storm, then let it loose to fill all of the room. The office.

And Valentina, too.

"No," she whispered, her voice scratchy against all that light and rumble.

But she could feel the tumult inside her. It was fire and it was light and it threatened to burst free of the paltry cage of her skin. Surely she would burst. Surely no person could survive this. She felt it shake all through her, as if underlining her fear.

"I don't know what you mean, and I don't like what you're implying. I think perhaps we've been in this office too long. You seem to have mistaken me for one of your mistresses. Or worse, one of those desperate women who call in, hoping to convince you they ought to be one of them."

"On the contrary, Miss Monette."

And there was a starkness to Achilles's expression then. No curve on his stern mouth. No gleaming thing in the seductive gold of his dark eyes. But somehow, that only made it worse.

"You're the one who manages my mistresses. And

those who pretend to that title. How could I possibly confuse you for them?" He cocked his head slightly to one side, and something yawned open inside her, as if in response. "Or perhaps you're auditioning for the role?"

"No." Her voice was no less scratchy this time, but there was more power in it. *Or more fear*, something inside her whispered. "I am most certainly not auditioning for anything like that. Or anything at all. I already have a job."

"But you told me you meant to quit." She had the strangest notion then that he was enjoying himself. "Perhaps you meant you were looking to make a lateral move. From my boardroom to my bed?"

Valentina tried to summon her outrage. She tried to tell herself that she was deeply offended on Natalie's behalf, because of course this was about her, not Valentina herself... She tried to tell herself a whole lot of things.

But she couldn't quite get there. Instead, she was awash with unhelpful little visions, red hot and wild. Images of what a "lateral move" might look like. Of what his bed might feel like. Of him.

She imagined that lean, solidly muscled form stretched over hers, the way she'd read in so many books so many times. Something almost too hot to bear melted through her then, pulling deep in her belly, and making her breath go shallow before it shivered everywhere else.

As if it was already happening.

"I know that this might come as a tremendous shock," Valentina said, trying to make herself sound something like fierce—or unmoved, anyway. Anything other than thrown and yearning. "But I have no interest in your bed. Less than no interest."

"You are correct." And something gleamed bright and hot and unholy gold in that dark gaze of his. "I am in shock."

"The next time an aspiring mistress calls the office," Valentina continued coolly, and no matter that it cost her, "I'll be certain to put her through to you for a change. You can discuss lateral moves all day long."

"What if a random caller does not appeal to me?" he asked lazily, as if this was all a game to him. She told herself it was. She told herself the fact that it was a game made it safe, but she didn't believe it. Not when all the things that moved around inside her made it hard to breathe, and made her feel anything at all but *safe*. "What if it is I who wish to alter our working relationship after all these years?"

Valentina told herself that this was clearly a test. If, as this conversation seemed to suggest, Natalie's relationship with her boss had always been strictly professional, why would he want to change that now? She'd seen how distant he kept his romantic entanglements from his work. His work was his life. His women were afterthoughts. There was no way the driven, focused man she'd come to know a bit after the close proximity of these last days would want to muddy the water in his office, with the assistant who not only knew where all the bodies were buried, but oversaw the funeral rites herself.

This had to be a test.

"I don't wish to alter a thing," she told him, very distinctly, as if there was nothing in her head but thorny contract language. And certainly nothing involving that remarkably ridged torso of his. "If you do, I think we should revisit the compensation package on offer for my resignation."

Achilles smiled as if she delighted him. But in an entirely too wicked and too hot sort of way.

"There is no package, Miss Monette," he murmured. "And there will be no resignation. When will you understand? You are here to do as I wish. Nothing more and nothing less than that. And perhaps my wishes concerning your role here have changed."

He wants you to fall apart, Valentina snapped at herself. *He wants to see if this will break you. He's poking at* Natalie *about her change in performance, not at you. He doesn't know* you *exist.*

Because there could be no other explanation. And it didn't matter that the look in his eyes made her shudder, down deep inside.

"Your wishes concerning my role now involve me on my back?" It cost her to keep her voice that flat. She could feel it.

"You say that as if the very idea disgusts you." And that crook in the corner of his lethal mouth deepened, even as that look in his eyes went lethal. "Surely not."

Valentina forced herself to smile. Blandly. As if her heart wasn't trying to claw its way out of her chest.

"I'm very flattered by your offer, of course," she said.

A little too sweetly to be mistaken for sincerity.

Achilles laughed then. It was an unsettling sound, too rough and too bold. It told her too much. That he knew—everything. That he knew all the things that were moving inside her, white hot and molten and too much for her to handle or tamp down or control. There was a growing, impossible fire raging in places she hardly understood, rendering her a stranger to herself.

As if he was the one in control of her body, even sitting across the table, lounging in his seat as if none of this was a matter of any concern at all.

While she felt as if she was both losing pieces of herself—and seeing her true colors for the very first time.

"Are you letting me down easy?" Achilles asked.

There was still laughter in his voice, his gaze and, somehow, dancing in the air between them despite all that fire still licking at her. She felt it roll through her, as if those big hands of his were on her skin.

And then she was suddenly incapable of thinking about anything at all but that. His hands all over her body. Touching places only she had ever seen. She had to swallow hard. Then again. And still there was that ringing in her ears.

"Do think it will work?" he asked, laughter still making his words sound a little too much like the rough, male version of honey.

"I imagine it will work beautifully, yes." She held on to that smile of hers as if her life depended on it. She rather thought it did. It was that or tip over into all that fire, and she had no idea what would become of her if she let that happen. She had no idea what would be left. "Or, of course, I could involve Human Resources in this discussion."

Achilles laughed again, and this time it was rougher. Darker and somehow hotter at the same time. Valentina felt it slide all over her, making her breasts feel heavy and her hips restless. While deep between her legs, a slick ache bloomed.

"I admire the feigned naïveté," Achilles said, and he looked like a pirate again, all dark jaw and that gleam in his gaze. It lit her up. Everywhere. "I have obviously failed to appreciate your acting talent sufficiently. I think we both know what Human Resources will tell you. To suck it up or find another position."

"That does not sound at all like something Human Resources would say," Valentina replied crisply, rather than spending even a split second thinking about *sucking*. "It sounds as if you're laboring under the delusion that this is a cult of personality, not a business."

If she expected him to look at all abashed, his grin disabused her of it. "Do you doubt it?"

"I'm not sure that is something I would brag about, Mr. Casilieris."

His gaze was hot, and she didn't think he was talking about her job or his company any longer. Had he ever been?

"Is it bragging if it's true?" he asked.

Valentina stood then, because it was the last thing she wanted to do. She could have sat there all night. She could have rung in a new dawn, fencing words with this man and dancing closer and closer to that precipice she could feel looming between them, even if she couldn't quite see it.

She could have pretended she didn't feel every moment of this deep inside her, in places she shouldn't. And then pretend further she didn't know what it meant just because she'd never experienced any of it before outside the pages of a book.

But she did know. And this wasn't her life to ruin. And so she stood, smoothing her hands down her skirt and wishing she hadn't been quite so impetuous in that London bathroom.

If you hadn't been, you wouldn't be here, something in her replied. *Is that what you want?*

And she knew that she didn't. Valentina had a whole life left to live with a man she would call husband who would never know her, not really. She had duty to look forward to, and a lifetime of charity and good works, all of which would be vetted by committees and commented on by the press. She had public adulation and a marriage that would involve the mechanical creation of babies before petering off into a nice friendship, if she was lucky.

Maybe the making of the babies would be fun with her prince. What did she know? All she knew so far was that he didn't do...this. He didn't affect her the way Achilles did, lounging there like hard-packed danger across a conference table, his gaze too dark and the gold in it making her pulse kick at her.

She'd never felt anything like this before. She doubted she'd ever feel it again.

Valentina couldn't quite bring herself to regret it.

But she couldn't stay here tonight and blow up the rest of Natalie's life, either. That would be treating this little gift that she'd been given with nothing but contempt.

"Have I given you leave to go?" Achilles asked, with what she knew was entirely feigned astonishment. "I am clearly confused in some way. I keep thinking you work for me."

She didn't know how he could do that. How he could seem to loom over her when she was the one standing up and looking down at him.

"And because I'd like to continue working for you," Valentina forced herself to say in as measured a tone as she could manage, "I'm going to leave now. We can pick this up in the morning." She tapped the table with one finger. "Pick *this* up, I mean. These contracts and the deal. Not this descent into madness, which I think we can chalk up to exhaustion."

Achilles only watched her for a moment. Those hands that she could picture too easily against her own flesh curled over the armrests of his chair, and her curse was that she imagined she *was* that chair. His legs were thrust out before him, long and lean. His usual suit was slightly rumpled, his tie having been tugged off and tossed aside hours earlier, so she could see the olive skin at his neck and a hint of crisp, black hair. He looked simultaneously sleepy and breathlessly, impossibly lethal—with an intensity that made that hot ache between her legs seem to swallow her whole.

And the look in his eyes made everything inside her draw tight, then pulse harder.

"Do you have a problem with that?" she asked, and she meant to sound impatient. Challenging. But she thought both of them were entirely too aware that what came out instead was rather more plaintive than planned.

As if she was really asking him if he was okay with everything that had happened here tonight. She was clearly too dazed to function.

She needed to get away from him while she still had access to what little of her brain remained in all this smoke and flame.

"Do you require my permission?" Achilles lifted his chin, and his dark eyes glittered. Valentina held her breath. "So far tonight it seems you are laboring under the impression that you give the permission, not me. You make the rules, not me. It is as if I am here for no other purpose than to serve you."

And there was no reason at all that his words, spoken in that soft, if dangerous way, should make her skin prickle. But they did. As if a man like Achilles did not have to issue threats, he was the threat. Why pile a threat on top of the threat? When the look on his face would do.

"I will see you in the morning," Valentina said, resolutely. "When I'll be happy to accept your apology."

Achilles lounged farther down in his chair, and she had the strangest notion that he was holding himself back. Keeping himself in place. Goose bumps shivered to life over her shoulders and down her arms.

His gaze never left hers.

"Go," he said, and there was no pretending it wasn't an order. "But I would not lie awake tonight anticipating the contours of my apology. It will never come."

She wanted to reply to that, but her mouth was too dry and she couldn't seem to move. Not so much as a muscle.

And as if he knew it, Achilles kept going in that same intensely quiet way.

"Tonight when you can't sleep, when you toss and turn and stare up at yet another ceiling I own, I want you to think of all the other reasons you could be wide awake in the small hours of the night. All the things that I could do to you. Or have you do to me. All the thousands of ways I will be imagining us together, just like that, under the same roof."

"That is completely inappropriate, Mr. Casilieris, and I think you know it."

But she knew full well she didn't sound nearly as outraged as she should. And only partially because her voice was a mere whisper.

"Have you never wondered how we would fit? Have you not tortured herself with images of my possession?" Achilles's hard mouth curved then, a wicked crook in one corner that she knew, somehow, would haunt her. She could feel it deep inside her like its own bright fire. "Tonight, I think, you will."

And Valentina stopped pretending there was any way out of this conversation besides the precise images he'd just mentioned, acted out all over this office. She walked stiffly around the table and gave him a wide, wide berth as she passed.

When she made it to the door of the conference room, she didn't look behind her to see if he was watching. She knew he was. She could feel it.

Fire and lightning, thunder and need.

She ran.

And heard his laughter follow behind her like the leading edge of a storm she had no hope of outwitting, no matter how fast she moved.

CHAPTER FIVE

ACHILLES ORDINARILY ENJOYED his victory parties. Reveled in them, in fact. Not for him any nod toward false humility or any pretense that he didn't deeply enjoy these games of high finance with international stakes. But tonight he couldn't seem to get his head into it, and no matter that he'd been fighting to buy out this particular iconic Manhattan hotel—which he planned to make over in his own image, the blend of European elegance and Greek timelessness that was his calling card in the few hotels scattered across the globe that he'd deemed worthy of the Casilieris name—for nearly eighteen months.

He should have been jubilant. It irritated him—deeply—that he couldn't quite get there.

His group had taken over a New York steak house renowned for its high-end clientele and specialty drinks to match to celebrate the deal he'd finally put through today after all this irritating wrangling. Ordinarily he would allow himself a few drinks to blur out his edges for a change. He would even smile and pretend he was a normal man, like all the rest, made of flesh and blood instead of dollar signs and naked ambition—an improvement by far over the monster he kept locked up tight beneath. Nights like this were his opportunity to pretend to be like anyone else, and Achilles usually indulged that impulse.

He might not have been a normal man—he'd never been a normal man—but it amused him to pretend otherwise every now and again. He was renowned for his surliness as much as his high expectations, but if that was all there was to it—to him—he never would have gotten anywhere in business. It took a little charm to truly manipulate his enemies and his opponents and even his acolytes the way he liked to do. It required that he be as easy telling a joke as he was taking over a company or using his fiercest attorneys to hammer out a deal that served him, and only him, best.

But tonight he was charmless all the way through.

He stood at the bar, nursing a drink he would have much preferred to toss back and follow with a few more of the same, his attention entirely consumed by his princess as she worked the room. As ordered.

"Make yourself useful, please," he'd told her when they'd arrived. "Try to charm these men. If you can."

He'd been deliberately insulting. He'd wanted her to imagine he had some doubt that she could pull such a thing off. He'd wanted her to feel the way he did—grouchy and irritable and outside his own skin.

She made him feel like an adolescent.

But Valentina had not seemed the least bit cowed. Much less insulted—which had only made him feel that much more raw.

"As you wish," she'd murmured in that overly obsequious voice she used when, he thought, she most wanted to get her claws into him. She'd even flashed that bland smile of hers at him, which had its usual effect—making his blood seem too hot for his own veins. "Your slightest desire is my command, of course."

And the truth was, Achilles should have known better. The kind of men he liked to manipulate best, especially when it came to high-stakes deals like the one he'd closed tonight, were not the sort of men he wanted anywhere near his princess. If the real Natalie had been here, she would have disappeared. She would have dispensed her usual round of cool greetings and even cooler congratulations, none of which encouraged anyone to cozy up to her. Then she would have sat in this corner or that, her expression blank and her attention focused entirely on one of her devices. She would have done that remarkable thing she did, that he had never thought to admire as much as perhaps he should have, which was her ability to be both in the room and invisible at the same time.

Princess Valentina, by contrast, couldn't have stayed invisible if her life depended on it. She was the furthest thing from *invisible* that Achilles had ever seen. It was as if the world was cast into darkness and she was its only light, that bright and that impossibly silvery and smooth, like her own brand of moonlight.

She moved from one group to the next, all gracious smiles. And not that bland sort of smile she used entirely too pointedly and too well, which invariably worked his last nerve, but one he'd seen in too many photographs he'd looked at much too late at night. Hunched over his laptop like some kind of obsessed troll while she slept beneath the same roof, unaware, which only made him that much more infuriated.

With her, certainly. But with himself even more.

Tonight she was the consummate hostess, as if this was her victory celebration instead of his. He could hear her airy laugh from across the room, far more potent than another woman's touch. And worse, he could see her. Slender and graceful, inhabiting a pencil skirt and well-cut jacket as if they'd been crafted specifically for her. When he knew perfectly well that those were his assistant's clothes, and they certainly weren't bespoke.

But that was Valentina's power. She made everything in her orbit seem to be only hers. Crafted specifically and especially for her.

Including him, Achilles thought—and he hated it. He was not a man a woman could put on a leash. He'd never given a woman any kind of power over him in his life, and he didn't understand how this creature who was engaged in a full-scale deception—who was running a con on him *even now*—somehow seemed to have the upper hand in a battle he was terribly afraid only he knew they were fighting.

It was unconscionable. It made him want to tear down this building—hell, the whole city—with his bare hands.

Or better yet, put them on her.

All the men around her lapped it up, of course. They stood too close. They put their hands on her elbow, or her shoulder, to emphasize a point that Achilles did not have to hear to know did not require emphasis. And certainly did not require touch.

She was moonlight over this grim, focused life of his, and he had no idea how he was going to make it through a world cast in darkness without her.

If he was appalled by that sentiment—and he was, deeply and wholly—it didn't seem to matter. He couldn't seem to turn it off.

It was far easier to critique her behavior instead.

So Achilles watched. And seethed. He catalogued every single touch, every single laugh, every single time she tilted back her pretty face and let her sleek copper hair fall behind her, catching all the light in the room. He brooded over the men who surrounded her, knowing full well that each and every one of them was imagining her naked. Hell, so was he.

But he was the only person in this room who knew what he was looking at. They thought she was Natalie

Monette, his dependable assistant. He was the only one who knew who she really was.

By the time Valentina finished a full circuit of the room, Achilles was in a high, foul temper.

"Are you finished?" he asked when she came to stand by his side again, his tone a dark slap he did nothing at all to temper. "Or will you actually whore yourself out in lieu of dessert?"

He meant that to hurt. He didn't care if he was an ass. He wanted to knock her back a few steps.

But of course Valentina only shot him an arch, amused look, as if she was biting back laughter.

"That isn't very nice," she said simply.

That was all.

And yet Achilles felt that bloom of unfortunate heat inside him all over again, and this time he knew exactly what it was. He didn't like it any better than he had before, and yet there it sat, eating at him from the inside out.

It didn't matter if he told himself he didn't wish to feel shame. All Valentina had to do was look at him as if he was a misbehaving child, tell him he *wasn't being nice* when he'd built an entire life out of being the very opposite of nice and hailing that as the source of his vast power and influence—and there it was. Heavy in him, like a length of hard, cold chain.

How had he given this woman so much power over him? How had he failed to see that was what was happening while he'd imagined he was giving her the rope with which to hang herself?

This could not go on. He could not allow this to go on.

The truth was, Achilles couldn't seem to get a handle on this situation the way he'd planned to when he'd realized who she was on the plane. He'd imagined it would be an amusing sort of game to humble a high and mighty spoiled-rotten princess who had never worked a day in her life and imagined she could deceive *the* Achilles Casilieris so boldly. He'd imagined it would be entertaining—and over swiftly. He supposed he'd imagined he'd be shipping her back to her palace and her princessy life and her proper royal fiancé by the end of the first day.

But Valentina wasn't at all who he'd thought she'd be. If she was spoiled—and she had to be spoiled, by definition, he was certain of it—she hid it. No matter what he threw at her, no matter what he demanded, she simply did it. Not always well, but she did it. She didn't complain. She didn't try to weasel out of any tasks she didn't like. She didn't even make faces or let out those long-suffering sighs that so many of his support staff did when they thought he couldn't hear them.

In fact, Valentina was significantly more cheerful than any other assistant he'd ever had—including Natalie.

She was nothing like perfect, but that made it worse. If she was perfect, maybe he could have dismissed her or ignored her, despite the game she was playing. But he couldn't seem to get her out of his head.

It was that part he couldn't accept. Achilles lived a highly compartmentalized life by design, and he liked it that way. He kept his women in the smallest, most easily controlled and thus ignored space. It had been many, many years since he'd allowed sex to control his thoughts, much less his life. It was only sex, after all. And what was sex to a man who could buy the world if he so chose? It was a release, yes. Enjoyable, even.

But Achilles couldn't remember the last time he'd woken in the night, his heart pounding, the hardest part of him awake and aware. With nothing in his head but her. Yet it was a nightly occurrence since Valentina had walked onto his plane.

It was bordering on obsession.

And Achilles did not get obsessed. He did not *want*.

He did not *need*. He took what interested him and then he forgot about it when the next thing came along.

And he couldn't think of a single good reason why he shouldn't do the same with her.

"Do you have something you wish to say to me?" Valentina asked, her soft, smooth voice snapping him back to this party that bored him. This victory that should have excited him, but that he only found boring now.

"I believe I said it."

"You misunderstand me," she replied, smiling. From a distance it would look as if they were discussing something as light and airy as that curve to her mouth, he thought. Achilles would have been impressed had he not been close enough to see that cool gleam in her green gaze. "I meant your apology. Are you ready to give it?"

He felt his own mouth curve then, in nothing so airy. Or light.

"Do I strike you as a man who apologizes, Miss Monette?" he asked her, making no attempt to ease the steel in his voice. "Have I ever done so in all the time you've known me?"

"A man who cannot apologize is not quite a man, is he, Mr. Casilieris?" This time he thought her smile was meant to take away the sting of her words. To hide the insult a little. Yet it only seemed to make it worse. "I speak philosophically, of course. But surely the only people who can't bring themselves to apologize are those who fear that any admission of guilt or wrongdoing diminishes them. I think we can both agree that's the very opposite of strength."

"You must tell me if I appear diminished, then," he growled at her, and he had the satisfaction of watching that pulse in her neck go wild. "Or weak in some way."

He wasn't surprised when she excused herself and went back to working the crowd. But he was surprised he let her.

Not here, he cautioned that wild thing inside him that he'd never had to contend with before, not over a woman. And never so raw and bold. *Not now.*

Later that night, they sat in his car as it slid through the streets of Manhattan in the midst of a summer thunderstorm, and Achilles cautioned himself not to act rashly.

Again.

But Valentina sat there beside him, staring out the window with a faint smile on her face. She'd settled beside him on the wide, plush seat without a word, as if it hardly mattered to her if he spoke or not. If he berated her, if he ignored her. As if she was all alone in this car or, worse, as if her mind was far away on more interesting topics.

And he couldn't tolerate it.

Achilles could think of nothing but her, she was eating him alive like some kind of impossible acid, yet *her* mind was miles away. She didn't seem to notice or care what she did to him when he was the one who was allowing her grand deception to continue—instead of outing her the way he should have the moment he'd understood who she was.

His hands moved before he knew what he meant to do, as if they had a mind of their own.

He didn't ask. He didn't push or prod at her or fence more words, forcing some sort of temper or explosion that would lead them where he wanted her to go. He didn't stack that deck.

He simply reached across the backseat, wrapped his hand around the back of her neck and hauled her closer to him.

She came easily, as if she really was made of nothing but light. He pulled her until she was sprawled across his lap, one hand braced on his thigh and another at his side. Her body was as lithe and sweetly rounded as he'd imagined it would be, but better. Much, much better.

She smelled like a dream, something soft and something sweet, and all of it warm and female and *her*. Valentina.

But all he cared about was the fact that that maddening mouth of hers was close to his.

Finally.

"What are you doing?" she breathed.

"I should think that was obvious," he growled. "And overdue."

And then, at last, he kissed her.

He wasn't gentle. He wasn't anything like tentative. He was neither soft nor kind, because it was too late for that.

He claimed her. Took her. He reminded her who he was with every slick, intense slide of his tongue. Or maybe he was reminding himself.

And he couldn't stop himself once the taste of her exploded inside him, making him reel. He wanted more. He wanted everything.

But she was still fighting him, that stubbornness of hers that made his whole body tight and needy. Not with her body, which was wrapped around him, supple and sweet, in a way that made him feel drunk. Not with her arms, which she'd sneaked around his shoulders as if she needed to hold on to him to keep herself upright.

It was that mouth of hers that had been driving him wild since the start.

He pulled his lips from hers. Then he slid his hands up to take her elegant cheekbones between his palms. He tilted her face where he wanted it, making the angle that much slicker. That much sweeter.

"Kiss me back," he demanded, pulling back farther to scowl at her, all this unaccustomed need making him impatient. And testy.

She looked stunned. And entirely too beautiful. Her green eyes were wide and dazed behind those clear glasses she wore. Her lips were parted, distractingly soft and faintly swollen already.

Achilles was hard and he was greedy and he wanted nothing more than to bury himself inside her here and now, and finally get rid of this obsession that was eating him alive.

Or indulge in it awhile.

"In case you are confused," he told her, his voice still a growl, "that was an order."

She angled herself back, just slightly. As if she was trying to sit up straighter against him. He didn't allow it. He liked her like this. Off balance and under his control, and he didn't much care if that made him a savage. He'd only ever pretended to be anything else, and only occasionally, at that.

"I *am* kissing you back," she said, and there was a certain haughtiness in her voice that delighted him. It made him grin, imagining all the many ways he could make her pay for that high-born, inbred superiority that he wanted to lap up like cream.

"Not well enough," he told her.

Her cheeks looked crisp and red, but she didn't shrink away from him. She didn't so much as blink.

"Maybe we don't have any chemistry," she theorized in that same voice, making it sound as if that was a foregone conclusion. "Not every woman in the world finds you attractive, Mr. Casilieris. Did you ever think of that?"

Achilles pulled her even more off balance, holding her over his lap and in his arms, right where he wanted her.

"No," he said starkly, and he didn't care if his greed and longing was all over his face, revealing more to her than he had ever shared with anyone. Ever. "I don't think either of those things is a problem."

Then he set his mouth to hers, and proved it.

* * *

Valentina thought she'd died and gone to a heaven she'd never dreamed of before. Wicked and wild and *better*. So very much better than anything she could have come up with in her most brilliant and dark-edged fantasies.

She had never been truly kissed before—if that was even the word to describe something so dominant and so powerful and so deeply, erotically thrilling—but she had no intention of sharing her level of inexperience with Achilles. Not when he seemed so close to some kind of edge and so hell-bent on taking her with him, toppling over the side into all of this sensation and need.

So she simply mimicked him. When he tilted his head, she did the same. She balled up her hands in his exquisitely soft shirt, up there against the hard planes of his chest tucked beneath his dark suit coat. She was aware of his hard hands on her face. She exulted in his arms like steel, holding her and caging her against him. She lost herself in that desperately cruel mouth as it moved over hers, the touch of his rough jaw, the impossible heat.

God help her, the heat.

And she was aware of that hard ridge beneath her, suddenly. She couldn't seem to keep from wriggling against it. Once, daringly. Then again when she heard that deep, wild and somehow savagely beautiful male noise he made in response.

And Valentina forgot about her vows, old and forthcoming. She forgot about faraway kingdoms and palaces and the life she'd lived there. She forgot about the promises she'd made and the ones that had been made in her name, because all of that seemed insubstantial next to the sheer, overwhelming wonder of Achilles Casilieris kissing her like a man possessed in the back of his town car.

This was her holiday. Her little escape. This was nothing but a dream, and he was, too. A fantasy of the life she might have lived had she been anyone else. Had she ever been anything like normal.

She forgot where they were. She forgot the role she was supposed to be playing. There was nothing in all the world but Achilles and the wildness he summoned up with every drag of his mouth against hers.

The car moved beneath them, but all Valentina could focus on was him. That hot possession of his mouth. The fire inside her.

And the lightning that she knew was his, the thunder storming through her, teaching her that she knew less about her body than he did. Much, much less. When he shifted so he could rub his chest against hers, she understood that he knew her nipples had pebbled into hard little points. When he laughed slightly as he rearranged her arms around his shoulders, she understood that he knew all her limbs were weighted down with the force of that greedy longing coursing through her veins.

The more he kissed her, over and over again as if time had no meaning and he could do this forever, she understood that he knew everything.

When he pulled his mouth from hers again, Valentina heard a soft, whimpering sound of protest. It took her one shuddering beat of her heart, then another, to realize she'd made it.

She couldn't process that. It was so abandoned, so thoughtless and wild—how could that be her?

"If we do not get out of this car right now," Achilles told her, his gaze a dark and breathtaking gold that slammed into her and lit her insides on fire, "we will not get out of it for some time. Not until I've had my fill of you. Is that how you want our first time to go, *glikia mou*? In the backseat of a car?"

For a moment Valentina didn't know what he meant.

One hastily sucked-in breath later, she realized the car

had come to a stop outside Achilles's building. Her cheeks flushed with a bright heat, but worse, she knew that he could see it. He saw everything—hadn't she just realized the truth of that? He watched her as she flushed, and he liked it. That deeply male curve in the corner of his mouth made that plain.

Valentina struggled to free herself from his hold then, to climb off his lap and sit back on the seat herself, and she was all too aware that he let her.

She didn't focus on that. She couldn't. That offhanded show of his innate strength made her feel…slippery, inside and outside and high between her legs. She tossed herself off his lap, her gaze tangling with his in a way that made the whole world seem to spin a little, and then she threw herself out the door. She summoned a smile from somewhere and aimed it at the doormen.

Breathe, she ordered herself. *Just breathe.*

Because she couldn't do this. This wasn't who she was. She hadn't held on to her virginity all this time to toss it aside at the very first temptation…had she?

This couldn't be who she was. It couldn't.

She'd spent her whole life practicing how to appear unruffled and serene under any and all circumstances, though she couldn't recall ever putting it to this kind of test before. She made herself breathe. She made herself smile. She sank into the familiarity of her public persona, wielding it like that armor she'd wanted, because it occurred to her it was the toughest and most resilient armor she had.

Achilles followed her into that bright and shiny elevator in the back of the gleaming lobby, using his key to close the doors behind them. He did not appear to notice or care that she was newly armored, especially while he seemed perfectly content to look so…disreputable.

His suit jacket hung open, and she was sure it had to be

obvious to even the most casual observer that she'd had her hands all over his chest and his shirt. And she found it was difficult to think of that hard mouth of his as cruel now that she knew how it tasted. More, how it felt on hers, demanding and intense and—

Stop, she ordered herself. *Now.*

He leaned back against the wall as the elevator started to move, his dark gold eyes hooded and intent when they met hers. He didn't say a word. Maybe he didn't have to. Her heart was pounding so loud that Valentina was certain it would have drowned him out if he'd shouted.

But Achilles did not shout.

On the contrary, when the elevator doors shut behind them, securing them in his penthouse, he only continued to watch her in that same intense way. She moved into the great living room, aware that he followed her, silent and faintly lazy.

It made her nervous. That was what she told herself that fluttery feeling was, lodged there beneath her ribs. And lower, if she was honest. Much lower.

"I'm going to bed," she said. And then instantly wished she'd phrased that differently when she heard it echo there between them, seeming to fill up the cavernous space, beating as madly within her as her own frenzied heart. "Alone."

Achilles gave the impression of smiling without actually doing so. He thrust his hands into the pockets of his dark suit and regarded her solemnly, save for that glittering thing in his dark gaze.

"If that is what you wish, *glikia mou.*"

And that was the thing. It wasn't what she wished. It wasn't what she wanted, and especially not when he called her that Greek name that she thought meant *my sweet*. It made her want to taste that word on that mouth of his. It made her want to find out exactly how sweet he thought she was.

It made her want to really, truly be someone else so she could do all the things that trampled through her head, making her chest feel tight while the rest of her... yearned.

Her whole life had been an exercise in virtue and duty, and she'd thought that meant something. She'd thought that *said* something about who she was. Valentina had been convinced that she'd held on to her chastity all this time, long after everyone she'd known had rid themselves of theirs, as a gift to her future.

But the night all around her told her something different. It had stripped away all the lies she'd told herself—or Achilles had. All the places she'd run and hid across all these years. Because the truth was that she'd never been tested. Was it truly virtue if she'd never been the least bit tempted to give it away? Or was it only coincidence that she'd never encountered anything that had felt the least bit compelling in that regard? Was it really holding on to something if she'd never felt the least bit like getting rid of it?

Because everything tonight was different. Valentina was different—or, worse, she thought as she stared at Achilles across the little bit of space that separated them, she had never been who she'd imagined she was. She had never understood that it was possible that a body could drown out what the mind knew to be prudent.

Until now.

She had judged passion all her life and told herself it was a story that weak people told themselves and others to make their sins seem more interesting. More complicated and unavoidable. But the truth was, Valentina had never experienced passion in her life.

Not until Achilles.

"I am your assistant," she told him. Or perhaps she was telling herself. "This must never happen again. If it does, I can't work for you."

"I have already told you that I am more than happy to accommodate—"

"There will be no lateral moves," she threw at him, appalled to hear her voice shaking. "You might lie awake at night imagining what that means and what it would look like, but I don't. I won't."

"Liar."

If he had hauled off and hit her, Valentina didn't think she could have been any more surprised. Shocked. No one had ever called her a liar before, not in all her life.

Then again, chimed in a small voice deep inside, *you never used to lie, did you? Not to others and not to yourself.*

"I have no doubt that you enjoy doing as you please," she spat at him, horrified that any of this was happening and, worse, that she'd let it—when Valentina knew who she was and what she'd be going back to in a few short weeks. "No matter the consequences. But not everyone is as reckless as you."

Achilles didn't quite smirk. "And that is why one of us is a billionaire and the other is his assistant."

"And if we were having a discussion about how to make money," Valentina said from between her teeth, no sign of her trademark serenity, "I would take your advice— but this is my life."

Guilt swamped her as she said that. Because, of course, it wasn't her life. It was Natalie's. And she had the sick feeling that she had already complicated it beyond the point of return. It didn't matter that Natalie had texted her to say that she'd kissed Prince Rodolfo, far away in Murin and neck-deep in Valentina's real life, however little Valentina had thought about it since she'd left it behind.

Valentina was going to marry Rodolfo. That her double had kissed him, the way Valentina probably should have, wasn't completely out of line.

But this… This thing she was doing… It was unacceptable on every level. She knew that.

Maybe Natalie has this same kind of chemistry with Rodolfo, something in her suggested. *Maybe he was engaged to the wrong twin.*

Which meant, she knew—because she was that self-serving—that maybe the wrong twin had been working for Achilles all this time and all of this was inevitable.

She wasn't sure she believed that. But she couldn't seem to stop herself. Or worse, convince herself that she should.

Achilles was still watching her too closely. Once again, she had the strangest notion that he knew too much. That he could see too far inside her.

Don't be silly, she snapped at herself then. *Of course he can't. You're just looking for more ways to feel guilty.*

Because whatever else happened, there was no way Achilles Casilieris would allow the sort of deception Valentina was neck-deep in to take place under his nose if he knew about it. She was certain of that, if nothing else.

"This is what I know about life," Achilles said, his voice a silken thread in the quiet of the penthouse, and Valentina had to repress a little shiver that threatened to shake her spine apart. "You must live it. If all you do is wall yourself off, hide yourself away, what do you have at the end but wasted time?"

Her throat was dry and much too tight. "I would take your advice more seriously if I didn't know you had an ulterior motive."

"I don't believe in wasting time or in ulterior motives," he growled back at her. "And not because I want a taste of you, though I do. And I intend to have it, *glikia mou*, make no mistake. But because you have put yourself on hold. Do you think I can't see it?"

She thought she had to be reeling then. Nothing was solid. She couldn't help but put her hand out, steadying herself on the back of the nearest chair—though it didn't seem to help.

And Achilles was watching her much too closely, with far too much of that disconcerting awareness making his dark gaze shine. "Or is it that you don't know yourself?"

When she was Princess Valentina of Murin, known to the world before her birth. Her life plotted out in its every detail. Her name literally etched in stone into the foundations of the castle where her family had ruled for generations. She had never had the opportunity to lose herself. Not in a dramatic adolescence. Not in her early twenties. She had never been beside herself at some crossroads, desperate to figure out the right path—because there had only ever been one path and she had always known exactly how to walk it, every step of the way.

"You don't know me at all," she told him, trying to sound less thrown and more outraged at the very suggestion that she was any kind of mystery to herself. She'd never had that option. "You're my employer, not my confidant. You know what I choose to show you and nothing more."

"But what you choose to show, and how you choose to show it, tells me exactly who you are." Achilles shook his head, and it seemed to Valentina that he moved closer to her when she could see he didn't. That he was exactly where he'd always been—it was just that he seemed to take over the whole world. She wasn't sure he even tried; he just did. "Or did you imagine I achieved all that I've achieved without managing to read people? Surely you cannot be so foolish."

"I was about to do something deeply foolish," she said

tightly. And not exactly smartly. "But I've since come to my senses."

"No one is keeping you here." His hands were thrust deep into his pockets, and he stood where he'd stopped, a few steps into the living room from those elevator doors. His gaze was all over her, but nothing else was touching her. He wasn't even blocking her escape route back to the guest room on this floor.

And she understood then. He was giving her choice. He was putting it on her. He wasn't simply sweeping her off into all that wild sensation—when he must have known he could have. He easily could have. If he hadn't stopped in the car, what would they be doing now?

But Valentina already knew the answer to that. She could feel her surrender inside her like heat.

And she thought she hated him for it.

Or should.

"I'm going to sleep," she said. She wanted her voice to be fierce. Some kind of condemnation. But she thought she sounded more determined than resolved. "I will see you in the morning. Sir."

Achilles smiled. "I think we both know you will see me long before that. And in your dreams, *glikia mou*, I doubt I will be so chivalrous."

Valentina pressed her lips tight together and did not allow herself to respond to him. Especially because she wanted to so very, very badly—and she knew, somehow, that it would lead nowhere good. It couldn't.

Instead, she turned and headed for her room. It was an unremarkable guest room appropriate for staff, but the best thing about it was the lock on the door. Not that she thought he would try to get in.

She was far more concerned that she was the one who would try to get out.

"One of these days," he said from behind her, his voice

low and intense, "you will stop running. It is a foregone conclusion, I am afraid. And then what?"

Valentina didn't say a word. But she didn't have to.

When she finally made it to her room and threw the dead bolt behind her, the sound of it echoed through the whole of the penthouse like a gong, answering Achilles eloquently without her having to open her mouth.

Telling him exactly how much of a coward she was, in case he hadn't already guessed.

CHAPTER SIX

IN THE DAYS that followed that strange night and Achilles's world-altering kiss that had left her raw and aching and wondering if she'd ever feel like herself again, Valentina found she couldn't bear the notion that she was twenty-seven years old and somehow a stranger to herself.

Her future was set in stone. She'd always known that. And she'd never fought against all that inevitability because what was the point? She could fight as much as she wanted and she'd still be Princess Valentina of Murin, only with a stain next to her name. That had always seemed to her like the very definition of futility.

But in the days that followed that kiss, it occurred to her that perhaps it wasn't the future she needed to worry about, but her past. She hadn't really allowed herself to think too closely about what it meant that Natalie had been raised by the woman who was very likely Valentina's own mother. Because, of course, there was no other explanation for the fact she and Natalie looked so much alike. Identical twins couldn't just randomly occur, and certainly not when one of them was a royal. There were too many people watching royal births too closely. Valentina had accepted the story that her mother had abandoned her, because it had always been couched in terms of Frederica's mental illness. Valentina had imagined her mother living out her days in some or other institution somewhere, protected from harm.

But the existence of Natalie suggested that Frederica was instead a completely different person from the one Valentina had imagined all this time. The woman who now called herself Erica had clearly not wasted away in a mental institution, all soothing pastels and injections and no ability to contact her own child. On the contrary, this Erica had lived a complicated life after her time in the palace that had nothing to do with any hospital—and though she'd clearly had two daughters, she'd taken only one with her when she'd gone.

Valentina didn't entirely understand how she could be quite so hurt by a betrayal that had happened so long ago and that she hadn't known about until recently. She didn't understand why it mattered so much to her. But the more she tried to tell herself that it was silly to be so bothered, the more bothered she got.

It was only when she had gone round and round and round on that almost too many times to count that Valentina accepted the fact she was going to have to do something about it.

And all these years, she'd never known how to go about looking for her mother even if she'd wanted to. She would have had to ask her father directly, the very idea of which made her shudder—even now, across an ocean or two from his throne and his great reserve and his obvious reluctance to discuss Frederica at all. Barring that, she would have had to speak to one of the high-level palace aides whose role was to serve her father in every possible way and who therefore had access to most of the family secrets. She doubted somehow that they would have told her all the things that she wanted to know—or even a few of them. And they certainly would have run any questions she had past her father first, which would have defeated the purpose of asking them.

Valentina tried to tell herself that was why she'd never asked.

But now she was tucked up in a lethally dangerous billionaire's penthouse in New York City, away from all the palace intrigue and protocol, and far too aware of the things a man like Achilles could do with only a kiss. To say nothing of his businesses. What was an old family secret to a man like Achilles?

And even though in many ways she had fewer resources at her fingertips and fewer people to ask for ancient stories and explanations, in the end, it was very simple. Because Valentina had Natalie's mobile, which had to mean she had direct access to her own story. If she dared look for it.

The Valentina who had seen her own mirror image in a bathroom in London might not have dared. But the Valentina who had lost herself in the raw fire of Achilles's kiss, on the other hand, dared all manner of things.

It was that Valentina who opened up Natalie's list of contacts, sitting there in her locked bedroom in Achilles's penthouse. She scrolled down, looking for an entry that read *Mom*. Or *Mum*. Or any variation of *Mother* she could think of.

But there was nothing.

That stymied her, but she was aware enough to realize that the sensation deep in her belly was not regret. It was relief. As if, in the end, she preferred these mysteries to what was likely to be a vicious little slap of truth.

You are such a coward, she told herself.

Because it wasn't as if her father—or Valentina herself, for that matter—had ever been in hiding. The truth was that her mother could have located her at any point over these last twenty-seven years. That she hadn't done so told Valentina all she needed to know about Frederica's maternal feelings, surely.

Well. What she *needed* to know perhaps, but there was a great deal more she *wanted* to know, and that was the trouble.

She kept scrolling until she found an entry marked *Erica*. She thought that told her a great deal about Natalie's relationship with this woman who was likely mother to them both. It spoke of a kind of distance that Valentina had certainly never contemplated when she'd thought about her own mother from time to time over the past nearly thirty years. In her head, of course, any reunion with the woman she'd imagined had been locked away in a pleasantly secure institution would be filled with love. Regret. Soft, sweet arms wrapped around her, and a thousand apologies for somehow managing to abandon and then never find her way back to a baby who lived at one of the most famous addresses in the world.

She wasn't entirely sure why the simple fact of the woman's first name in a list of contacts made it so clear that all of that was a lie. Not just a harmless fantasy to make a motherless child feel better about her fate, but something infinitely more dangerous, somehow.

Valentina wanted to shut down the mobile phone. She wanted to throw it across the small room and pretend that she'd never started down this road in the first place.

But it occurred to her that possibly, she was trying to talk herself out of doing this thing she was certain she needed to do.

Because Achilles might have imagined that he could see these mysteries in her, but what scared Valentina was that she could, too. That he'd identified a terrible weakness in her, and that meant anyone could.

Perhaps she wasn't who she thought she was. Perhaps

she never had been. Perhaps, all this time, she'd imagined she'd been walking down a set path when she hadn't.

If she was honest, the very idea made her want to cry.

It had been important, she thought then, sitting crosslegged on the bed with the summer light streaming in from the windows—crucially important, even—to carry on the morning after that kiss as if nothing had changed. Because she had to pretend that nothing had. That she didn't know too much now. That she didn't think of that kiss every time she looked at Achilles. She'd gone to work, and she'd done her job, and she'd stayed as much in his presence as she ever did—and she thought that she deserved some kind of award for the acting she'd done. So cool, so composed.

So utterly unbothered by the fact she now knew how he tasted.

And she tried to convince herself that only she knew that she was absolutely full of it.

But one day bled into the next, and she'd found that her act became harder and harder to pull off, instead of easier. She couldn't understand it. It wasn't as if Achilles was doing anything, necessarily. He was Achilles, of course. There was always that look in his eyes, as if he was but waiting for her to give him a sign.

Any sign.

As if, were she to do so, he would drop everything he was doing—no matter where they were and what was happening around them—and sweep them right back into that storm of sensation that she found simmered inside her, waiting. Just waiting.

Just as he was.

It was the notion that she was the one who held the power—who could make all of that happen with a simple word or glance—that she found kept her up at night. It made her shake. It polluted her dreams and made her drift off entirely too many times while she was awake, only to be slapped back down to earth when Achilles's voice turned silken, as if he knew.

Somehow, this all made her determined to seek out the one part of her life that had never made sense, and had never fit in neatly into the tidy narrative she'd believed all her life and knew back and forth.

Today was a rare afternoon when Achilles had announced that he had no need of her assistance while he tended to his fitness in his personal gym because, he'd gritted at her, he needed to clear his head. Valentina had repaired to her bedroom to work out a few snarls in his schedule and return several calls from the usual people wanting advice on how to approach him with various bits of news he was expected to dislike intensely. She'd changed out of Natalie's usual work uniform and had gratefully pulled on a pair of jeans and a T-shirt, feeling wildly rebellious as she did so. And then a little bit embarrassed that her life was clearly so staid and old-fashioned that she found denim a personal revolution.

Many modern princesses dressed casually at times, she was well aware. Just as she was even more aware that none of them were related to her father, with his antiquated notions of propriety. And therefore none of them would have to suffer his disapproval should she find herself photographed looking "common" despite her ancient bloodline.

But she wasn't Princess Valentina here in New York, where no one cared what she wore. And maybe that was why Valentina pulled the trigger. She didn't cold-call the number that she'd found on her sister's phone—and there was something hard and painful in her chest even thinking that word, *sister*. She fed the number into a little piece of software that one of Achilles's companies had been working on, and she let it present her with information that she supposed she should have had some sort of scruple about using. But she didn't.

Valentina imagined that said something about her, too, but she couldn't quite bring herself to care about that the way she thought she ought to have.

In a push of a button, she had a billing address. Though the phone number itself was tied to the area code of a far-off city, the billing address was right here in Manhattan.

It was difficult not see that as some kind of sign.

Valentina slipped out of the penthouse then, without giving herself time to second-guess what she was about to do. She smiled her way through the lobby the way she always did, and then she set out into New York City by herself.

All by herself.

No guards. No security. Not even Achilles's brooding presence at her side. She simply walked. She made her way through the green, bright stretch of Central Park, headed toward the east side and the address Achilles's software had provided. No one spoke to her. No one called her name. No cameras snapped at her, recording her every move.

After a while, Valentina stopped paying attention to the expression on her face. She stopped worrying about her posture and whether or not her hair looked unkempt as the faint breeze teased at it. She simply...walked.

Her shoulders seemed to slip down an extra inch or two from her ears. She found herself breathing deeper, taking in the people she passed without analyzing them—without assuming they wanted something from her or were looking to photograph her supposedly "at large" in the world.

About halfway across the park it occurred to her that she'd never felt this way in her life. Alone. Free. Better yet, anonymous. She could have been anybody on the streets. There were locals all over the paths in the park, walking and talking and taking in the summer afternoon as if that was a perfectly normal pastime. To be out on their own, no one the wiser, doing exactly as they pleased.

Valentina realized that whatever happened next, this was the normal she'd spent her life looking for and dreaming about. This exact moment, walking across Central Park while summer made its cheerful noises all around her, completely and entirely on her own.

Freedom, it turned out, made her heart beat a little too fast and too hard inside her chest.

Once she made it to the east side, she headed a little bit uptown, then farther east until she found the address that had been on that billing statement. It looked like all the other buildings on the same block, not exactly dripping in luxury, but certainly no hovel. It was difficult for Valentina to determine the difference between kinds of dwellings in a place like this. Apartment buildings, huge blocks of too many people living on top of each other by choice, seemed strange to her on the face of it. But who was she to determine the difference between prosperous New Yorkers and regular ones? She had lived in a palace all her life. And she suspected that Achilles's sprawling penthouse wasn't a far cry from a palace itself, come to that.

But once she'd located the building she wanted and its dark green awning marked with white scrollwork, she didn't know what to do. Except wait there. As if she was some kind of daring sleuth, just like in the books she'd read as a little girl, when she was just...that same old motherless child, looking for a better story to tell herself.

She chided herself for that instantly. It felt defeating. Despairing. She was anonymous and free and unremarkable, standing on a city street. Nobody in the entire world knew where she was. Nobody would know where to look and nobody was likely to find her if they tried. Valentina couldn't decide if that notion made her feel small and fragile, or vast and powerful. Maybe both at the same time.

She didn't know how long she stood there. She ignored the first few calls that buzzed at her from Natalie's mobile tucked in her pocket, but then realized that standing about speaking on her phone gave her far more of a reason to be out there in the street. Instead of simply standing there doing nothing, looking like she was doing exactly what she was doing, which was looming around as she waited for somebody to turn up.

So she did her job, out there on the street. Or Natalie's job, anyway. She fielded the usual phone calls from the office and, if she was honest, liked the fact that she had somewhere to put all her nervous energy. She was half-afraid that Achilles would call and demand that she return to his side immediately, but she suspected that she was less afraid of that happening than she was hoping that it would, so she didn't have to follow this through.

Because even now, there was a part of her that simply wanted to retreat back into what she already knew. What she'd spent her life believing.

Afternoon was bleeding into evening, and Valentina was beginning to think that she'd completely outstayed her welcome. That Erica was in one of the other places she sometimes stayed, like the one in the Caribbean Natalie had mentioned in a text. That at any moment now it was likely that one of the doormen in the surrounding buildings would call the police to make her move along at last. That they hadn't so far she regarded as some kind of miracle. She finished up the last of the calls she'd been fielding, and told herself that it had been foolish to imagine that she could simply turn up one afternoon, stand around and solve the mysteries of her childhood so easily.

But that was when she saw her.

And Valentina didn't know exactly what it was that had

caught her eye. The hair was wrong, not long and coppery like her daughters' but short. Dark. And it wasn't as if Valentina had any memories of this woman, but still. There was something in the way she moved. The way she came down the block, walking quickly, a plastic bag hanging from one wrist and the other hand holding a phone to her ear.

But Valentina knew her. She knew that walk. She knew the gait and the way the woman cocked her head toward the hand holding her phone. She knew the way this woman carried herself.

She recognized her, in other words, when she shouldn't have. When, she realized, despite the fact she'd spent a whole summer afternoon waiting for this moment—she really didn't want to recognize her.

And she'd been nursing fantasies this whole time, little as she wanted to admit that, even to herself. She'd told herself all the things that she would do if this woman appeared. She'd worked out scenarios in her head.

Do you know who I am? she would ask, or demand, and this woman she had always thought of as Federica, but who went by a completely different name—the better to hide, Valentina assumed—would… Cry? Flail about? Offer excuses? She hadn't been able to decide which version she would prefer no matter how many times she'd played it out in her head.

And as this woman who was almost certainly her mother walked toward her, not looking closely enough to see that there was anyone standing down the block a ways in front of her, much less someone who she should have assumed was the daughter she knew as Natalie, Valentina realized what she should have known already. Or maybe, deep down, she had known it—she just hadn't really wanted to admit it.

There was nothing this woman could do to fix anything

or change anything or even make it better. She couldn't go back in time. She couldn't change the past. She couldn't choose Valentina instead of Natalie, if that had been the choice she'd made. Valentina wasn't even certain that was something she'd want, if she could go back in time herself, but the fact of the matter was that there was nothing to be done about it now.

And her heart beat at her and beat at her, until she thought it might beat its way straight out through her ribs, and even as it did, Valentina couldn't pretend that she didn't know that what she was feeling was grief.

Grief, thick and choking. Dark and muddy and deep.

For the childhood she'd never had, and hadn't known she'd missed until now. For the life she might have known had this woman been different. Had Valentina been different. Had her father, perhaps, not been King Geoffrey of Murin. It was all speculation, of course. It was that tearing thing in her belly and that weight on her chest, and that thick, deep mud she worried she might never find her way out of again.

And when Erica drew close to her building's green awning, coming closer to Valentina than she'd been in twenty-seven years, Valentina…said nothing. She let her hair fall forward to cover her face where she leaned against the brick wall. She pretended she was on a serious phone call while the woman who was definitely her mother—of course she was her mother; how had Valentina been tricking herself into pretending she could be anything but that?—turned into the building that Valentina had been staking out all afternoon, and was swallowed up into her own lobby.

For long moments, Valentina couldn't breathe. She wasn't sure she could think.

It was as if she didn't know who she was.

She found herself walking. She lost herself in the tumult of this sprawling mess of a bright and brash city, the noise of car horns in the street, and the blasts of conversation and laughter from the groups of strangers she passed. She made her way back to the park and wandered there as the summer afternoon took on that glassy blue that meant the hour was growing late.

She didn't cry. She hardly saw in front of her. She simply walked.

And dusk was beginning to steal in at last, making the long blocks cold in the long shadows, when she finally made it back to Achilles's building.

One of the doormen brought her up in the elevator, smiling at her as she stepped off. It made her think that perhaps she had smiled in return, though she couldn't tell. It was as if her body was not her own and her face was no longer under her control. She walked into Achilles's grand living room, and stood there. It was as if she still didn't know where she was. As if she still couldn't see. And the huge windows that let Manhattan in all around her only seemed to make her sense of dislocation worse.

"Where the hell have you been?"

That low growl came from above her. Valentina didn't have to turn and look to know that it was Achilles from on high, standing at the top of the stairs that led to his sprawling master suite.

She looked up anyway. Because somehow, the most dangerous man she'd ever met felt like an anchor.

He looked as if he'd just showered. He wore a T-shirt she could tell was soft from down two flights, stretched over his remarkable chest as if it was as enamored of him as she feared she was. Loose black trousers were slung low on his hips, and she had the giddy sense that if he did something like stretch, or breathe too heavily, she would be able to see a swathe of olive skin between the waistband and the hem of his T-shirt.

And suddenly, she wanted nothing more than to see exactly that. More than she could remember wanting anything else. Ever.

"Careful, *glikia mou*, or I will take you up on that invitation written all over your face," Achilles growled as if he was irritated...but she knew better.

Because he knew. He always knew. He could read her when no one else ever had. The masks she wore like they were second nature and the things she pretended for the whole of the rest of the world fooled everybody, but never him.

Never, ever him.

As if there was a real Valentina buried beneath the exterior she'd thought for years was the totality of who she was, and Achilles was the only one who had ever met her. Ever seen her. Ever suspected she existed and then found her, again and again, no matter how hard Valentina worked to keep her hidden away.

Her throat was dry. Her tongue felt as if it no longer fit in her own mouth.

But she couldn't bring herself to look away from him.

She thought about her mother and she thought about her childhood. She thought about the pride she'd taken in that virtue of hers that she'd clung to so fiercely all these years. Or perhaps not so fiercely, as it had been so untested. Was that virtue at all, she wondered?

Or was this virtue?

She had spent all of this time trying to differentiate herself from a woman she thought she knew, but who it turned out she didn't know at all. And for what? She was already trapped in the same life that her mother had abandoned.

Valentina was the one who hadn't left her father. She was the one who had prided herself on being perfect. She was the one who was decidedly not mentally ill, never too overwrought to do the job required of her by her blood and her father's expectations, nothing but a credit to her father in all ways. And she'd reveled in it.

More than reveled in it. It had become the cornerstone of her own self-definition.

And all of it was built on lies. The ones she told herself, and more than that, the lies that had been told to her for her entire life. By everyone.

All Valentina could think as she gazed up the stairs to the man she was only pretending was her employer was that she was done with lies. She wanted something honest. Even—especially—if it was raw.

And she didn't much care if there were consequences to that.

"You say that is if it is a threat," she said quietly. Distinctly. "Perhaps you should rethink your own version of an invitation before it gets you in trouble." She raised her brows in challenge, and knew it. Reveled in it, too. "Sir."

And when Achilles smiled then, it was with sheer masculine triumph, and everything changed.

He had thought she'd left him.

When Achilles had come out of the hard, brutal workout he'd subjected himself to that had done absolutely nothing to make his vicious need for her settle, Achilles had found her gone.

And he'd assumed that was it. The princess had finally had enough. She'd finished playing this down-market game of hers and gone back to her palaces and her ball gowns and her resplendent little prince who waited for her across the seas.

He'd told himself it was for the best.

He was a man who took things for a living and made an empire out of his conquests, and he had no business whatsoever putting his commoner's hands all over a woman of her pedigree. No business doing it, and worse, he shouldn't want to.

And maybe that was why he found himself on his treadmill again while he was still sucking air from his first workout, running as if every demon he'd vanquished in his time was chasing him all over again, and gaining. Maybe that was why he'd run until he'd thought his lungs might burst, his head might explode or his knees might give out beneath him.

Then he'd run more. And even when he'd exhausted himself all over again, even when he was standing in his own shower with his head bent toward the wall as if she'd bested him personally, it hadn't helped.

The fact of the matter was that he had a taste of Valentina, and nothing else would do.

And what enraged him the most, he'd found—aside from the fact he hadn't had her the way he'd wanted her— was that he'd let her think she'd tricked him all this time. That she would go back behind her fancy gates and her moats and whatever the hell else she had in that palace of hers that he'd looked up online and thought looked exactly like the sort of fairy tale he disdained, and she would believe that she'd played him for a fool.

Achilles thought that might actually eat him alive.

And now here she stood when he thought he'd lost her. At the bottom of his stairs, looking up at him, her eyes dark with some emotion he couldn't begin to define.

But he didn't want to define it. He didn't want to talk about her feelings, and he'd die before he admitted his own, and what did any of that matter anyway? She was here and he was here, and a summer night was creeping in outside.

And the only thing he wanted to think about was sating himself on her at last.

At last and for as long as he could.

Achilles was hardly aware of moving down the stairs even as he did it.

One moment he was at the top, staring down at Valentina's upturned face with her direct challenge ringing in him like a bell, and the next he was upon her. And she was so beautiful. So exquisitely, ruinously beautiful. He couldn't seem to get past that. It was as if it wound around him and through him, changing him, making him new each time he beheld her.

He told himself he hated it, but he didn't look away.

"There is no going back," he told her sternly. "There will be no pretending this didn't happen."

Her smile was entirely too graceful and the look in her green eyes too merry by far. "Do you get that often?"

Achilles felt like a savage. An animal. Too much like that monster he kept down deep inside. And yet he didn't have it in him to mind. He reached out and indulged himself at last while his blood hammered through his veins, running his fingers over that elegant cheekbone of hers, and that single freckle that marred the perfection of her face—and somehow made her all the more beautiful.

"So many jokes," he murmured, not sure how much of the gruffness in his voice was need and how much was that thing like temper that held him fast and fierce. "Everything is so hilarious, suddenly. How much longer do you think you will be laughing, *glikia mou*?"

"I think that is up to you," Valentina replied smoothly, and she was still smiling at him in that same way, graceful and knowing. "Is that why you require so much legal documentation before you take a woman to bed? Do you make them all laugh so much that you fear your reputation as a grumpy icon would take a hit if it got out?"

It was a mark of how far gone he was that he found that amusing. If anyone else had dreamed of saying such a thing to him, he would have lost his sense of humor completely.

He felt his mouth curve. "There is only one way to find out."

And Achilles had no idea what she might do next. He wondered if that was what it was about her, if that was why this thirst for her never seemed to ebb. She was so very different from all the women he'd known before. She was completely unpredictable. He hardly knew, from one moment to the next, what she might do next.

It should have irritated him, he thought. But instead it only made him want her more.

Everything, it seemed, made him want her more. He hadn't realized until now how pale and insubstantial his desires had been before. How little he'd wanted anything.

"There is something I must tell you." She pulled her bottom lip between her teeth after she said that, a little breathlessly, and everything in him stilled.

This was it, he thought. And Achilles didn't know if he was proud of her or sad, somehow, that this great charade was at an end. For surely that was what she planned to tell him. Surely she planned to come clean about who she really was.

And while there was a part of him that wanted to deny that what swirled between them was anything more than sex, simple and elemental, there was a far greater part of him that roared its approval that she should think it was right to identify herself before they went any further.

"You can tell me anything," he told her, perhaps more fiercely than he should. "But I don't know why you imagine I don't already know."

He was fascinated when her cheeks bloomed with that crisp, bright red that he liked a little too much. More each time he saw it, because he liked his princess a little flustered. A little off balance.

But something in him turned over, some foreboding perhaps. Because he couldn't quite imagine why it was that she should be *embarrassed* by the deception she'd practiced on him. He could think of many things he'd like her to feel for attempting to pull something like that over on him, and he had quite a few ideas about how she should pay for that, but embarrassment wasn't quite it.

"I thought you might know," she whispered. "I hope it doesn't matter."

"Everything matters or nothing does, *glikia mou*."

He shifted so he was closer to her. He wanted to care about whatever it was she was about to tell him, but he found the demands of his body were far too loud and too imperative to ignore. He put his hands on her, curling his fingers over her delicate shoulders and then losing himself in their suppleness. And in the delicate line of her arms. And in the sweet feel of her bare skin beneath his palms as he ran them down from her shoulders to her wrists, then back again.

And he found he didn't really care what she planned to confess to him. How could it matter when he was touching her like this?

"I do not require your confession," he told her roughly. "I am not your priest."

If anything, her cheeks flared brighter.

"I'm a virgin," she blurted out, as if she had to force herself to say it.

For a moment, it was as if she'd struck him. As if she'd picked up one of the sculptures his interior designer had littered about his living room and clobbered him with it.

"I beg your pardon?"

But she was steadier then. "You heard me. I'm a virgin. I thought you knew." She swallowed, visibly, but she didn't look away from him. "Especially when I didn't know how to kiss you."

Achilles didn't know what to do with that.

Or rather, he knew exactly what to do with it, but was

afraid that if he tossed his head back and let himself go
the way he wanted to—roaring out his primitive take on
her completely unexpected confession to the rafters—it
might terrify her.

And the last thing in the world he wanted to do was
terrify her.

He knew he should care that this wasn't quite the confession he'd expected. That as far as he could tell, Valentina had no intention of telling him who she was. Ever.
He knew that it should bother him, and perhaps on some
level it did, but the only thing he could seem to focus on
was the fact that she was untouched.

Untouched.

He was the only man in all the world who had ever
tasted her. Touched her. Made her shiver, and catch her
breath, and moan. That archaic word seemed to beat in
place of his heart.

Virgin. Virgin. Virgin.

Until it was as if he knew nothing but that. As if her innocence shimmered between them, beckoning and sweet,
and she was his for the taking.

And, oh, how Achilles liked to take the things he
wanted.

"Are you sure you wish to waste such a precious gift
on the likes of me?" he asked, and he heard the stark
greed beneath the laziness he forced into his tone. He
heard exactly how much he wanted her. He was surprised
it didn't seem to scare her the way he thought it should.
"After all, there is nothing particularly special about me.
I have money, that's all. And as you have reminded me,
I am your boss. The ethical considerations are legion."

He didn't know why he said that. Any of that. Was it to
encourage her to confess her real identity to him? Was it
to remind her of the role she'd chosen to play—although
not today, perhaps?

Or was it to remind him?

Either way, she only lifted her chin. "You don't have to take it," she said, as if it was of no import to her one way or the other. "Certainly not if you have some objection."

She lifted one shoulder, then dropped it, and the gesture was so quintessentially royal that it should have set Achilles's teeth on edge. But instead he found it so completely her, so entirely Princess Valentina, that it only made him harder. Hotter. More determined to find his way inside her.

And soon.

"I have no objection," he assured her, and there was no pretending his tone wasn't gritty. Harsh. "Are we finished talking?"

And the nerves he'd been unable to detect before were suddenly all over her face. He doubted she knew it. But she was braver than she ought to have been, his deceitful little princess, and all she did was gaze back at him. Clear and sure, as if he couldn't see the soft, vulnerable cast to her mouth.

Or maybe, he thought, she had no idea how transparent she was.

"Yes," Valentina said softly. "I'm ready to stop talking."

And this time, as he drew her to him, he knew it wouldn't end in a kiss. He knew they weren't going to stop until he'd had her at last.

He knew that she was not only going to be his tonight, but she was going to be only his. That no one had ever touched her before, and if he did it right, no one else ever would.

Because Achilles had every intention of ruining his princess for all other men.

CHAPTER SEVEN

VALENTINA COULDN'T BELIEVE this was happening.

At last.

Achilles took her mouth, and there was a lazy quality to his kiss that made her knees feel weak. He set his mouth to hers, and then he took his time. As if he knew that inside she was a jangle of nerves and longing, anticipation and greed. As if he knew she hardly recognized herself or all the needy things that washed around inside her, making her new.

Making her his.

He kissed her for a long while, it seemed to her. He slid his arms around her, he pulled her against his chest, and then he took her mouth with a thoroughness that made a dangerous languor steal all over her. All through her. Until she wasn't sure that she would be able to stand on her own, were he to let go of her.

But he didn't let go.

Valentina thought she might have fallen off the edge of the world anyway, because everything seemed to whirl and cartwheel around, but then she realized that what he'd done was stoop down to bend a little and then pick her up. As if she was as weightless as she felt. He held her in his arms, high against his chest, and she felt her shoes fall off her feet like some kind of punctuation. And when he gazed down into her face, she thought he looked like some kind of conquering warrior of old, though she chided herself for being so fanciful.

There was nothing fanciful about Achilles.

Quite the opposite. He was fierce and masculine and ruthless beyond measure, and still, Valentina couldn't think of anywhere she would rather be—or anyone she would rather be with like this. It all felt inevitable, as if she'd been waiting her whole life for this thing she hardly understood to sweep her away, just like this.

And it had come into focus only when she'd met Achilles.

Because he was her only temptation. She had never wanted anyone else. She couldn't imagine she ever would.

"I don't know what to do," she whispered, aware on some level that he was moving. That he was carrying her up those penthouse stairs as if she weighed nothing at all. But she couldn't bring herself to look away from his dark gold gaze. And the truth was, she didn't care. He could take her anywhere. "I don't want to disappoint you."

"And how would you do that?" His voice was so deep. So lazy and, unless she was mistaken, amused, even as that gaze of his made her quiver, deep inside.

"Well," she stammered out. "Well, I don't—"

"Exactly," he said, interrupting her with that easy male confidence that she found she liked a little too much. "You don't know, but I do. So perhaps, *glikia mou*, you will allow me to demonstrate the breadth and depth of my knowledge."

And when she shuddered, he only laughed.

Achilles carried her across the top floor, all of which was part of his great master bedroom. It took up the entire top level of his penthouse, bordered on all sides by the wide patio that was also accessible from a separate staircase below. The better to maintain and protect his privacy, she thought now, which she felt personally invested in at the moment. He strode across the hardwood floor with bold-colored rugs tossed here and there, and she took in the exposed brick walls and the bright, modern works of art that hung on them. This floor was all space and silence, and in between there were more of those breathtaking windows that brightened the room with the lights from the city outside.

Achilles didn't turn on any additional light. He simply took Valentina over to the huge bed that was propped up on a sleek modern platform crafted out of a bright, hard steel, and laid her out across it as if she was something precious to him. Which made her heart clutch at her, as if she wanted to be.

And then he stood there beside the bed, his hands on his lean hips, and did nothing but gaze down at her.

Valentina pushed herself up onto her elbows. She could feel her breath moving in and out of her, and it was as if it was wired somehow to all that sensation she could feel lighting her up inside. It made her breasts feel heavier. It made her arms and legs feel somehow restless and sleepy at once.

With every breath, she could feel that bright, hot ache between her legs intensify. And this time, she knew without a shred of doubt that he was aware of every last part of it.

"Do you have anything else to confess?" he asked her, and she wondered if she imagined the dark current in his voice then. But it didn't matter. She had never wanted anyone, but she wanted him. Desperately.

She would confess anything at all if it meant she could have him.

And it wasn't until his eyes blazed, and that remarkable mouth of his kicked up in one corner, that she realized she'd spoken out loud.

"I will keep that in mind," he told her, his voice a rasp into the quiet of the room. Then he inclined his head. "Take off your clothes."

It was as if he'd plugged her into an electrical outlet. She felt zapped. Blistered, perhaps, by the sudden jolt of power. It felt as if there were something bright and hot, wrapped tight around her ribs, pressing down. And down farther.

And she couldn't bring herself to mind.

"But—by myself?" she asked, feeling a little bit lightheaded at the very idea. She'd found putting on these jeans a little bit revolutionary. She couldn't imagine stripping them off in front of a man.

And not just any man. Achilles Casilieris.

Who didn't relent at all. "You heard me."

Valentina had to struggle then. She had to somehow shove her way out of all that wild electrical madness that was jangling through her body, at least enough so she could think through it. A little bit, anyway. She had to struggle to sit up all the way, and then to pull the T-shirt off her body. Her hands went to her jeans next, and she wrestled with the buttons, trying to pull the fly open. It was all made harder by the fact that her hands shook and her fingers felt entirely too thick.

And the more she struggled, the louder her breathing sounded. Until she was sure it was filling up the whole room, and more embarrassing by far, there was no possible way that Achilles couldn't hear it. Or see the flush that she could feel all over her, electric and wild. She wrestled the stiff, unyielding denim down over her hips, that bright heat that churned inside her seeming to bleed out everywhere as she did. She was sure it stained her, marking her bright hot and obvious.

She sneaked a look toward Achilles, and she didn't

know what she expected to see. But she froze when her eyes met his.

That dark gold gaze of his was as hot and demanding as ever. That curve in his mouth was even deeper. And there was something in the way that he was looking at her that soothed her. As if his hands were on her already, when they were not. It was as if he was helping her undress when she suspected that it was very deliberate on his part that he was not.

Because of course it was deliberate, she realized in the next breath. He was giving her another choice. He was putting it in her hands, again. And even while part of her found that inordinately frustrating, because she wanted to be swept away by him—or more swept away, anyway—there was still a part of her that relished this. That took pride in the fact that she was choosing to give in to this particular temptation.

That she was choosing to truly offer this particular man the virtue she had always considered such a gift.

It wasn't accidental. She wasn't drunk the way many of her friends had been, nor out of her mind in some other way, or even outside herself in the storm of an explosive temper or wild sensation that had boiled over.

He wanted her to be very clear that she was choosing him.

And Valentina wanted that, too. She wanted to choose Achilles. She wanted this.

She had never wanted anything else, she was sure of it. Not with this fervor that inhabited her body and made her light up from the inside out. Not with this deep certainty.

And so what could it possibly matter that she had never undressed for a man before? She was a princess. She had dressed and undressed in rooms full of attendants her whole life. Achilles was different from her collection of royal aides, clearly. But there was no need for her to be embarrassed, she told herself then. There was no need to go red in the face and start fumbling about, as if she didn't know how to remove a pair of jeans from her own body.

Remember who you are, she chided herself.

She was Princess Valentina of Murin. It didn't matter that seeing her mother might have shaken her. It didn't change a thing. That had nothing to do with who she was, it only meant that she'd become who she was in spite of the choices her mother had made. She could choose to do with that what she liked. And she was choosing to gift her innocence, the virginity she'd clung to as a badge of honor as if that differentiated her from the mother who'd left her, to Achilles Casilieris.

Here. Now.

And there was absolutely nothing to be ashamed about.

Valentina was sure that she saw something like approval in his dark gaze as she finished stripping her jeans from the length of her legs. And then she was sitting there in nothing but her bra and panties. She shifted up and onto her knees. Her hair fell down over her shoulders as she knelt on the bed, swirling across her bared skin and making her entirely too aware of how exposed she was.

But this time it felt sensuous. A sweet, warm sort of reminder of how much she wanted this. Him.

"Go on," he told her, a gruff command.

"That sounded a great deal like an order," Valentina murmured, even as she moved her hands around to her back to work the clasp of her bra. And it wasn't even a struggle to make her voice so airy.

"It was most definitely an order," Achilles agreed, his voice still gruff. "And I would suggest you obey me with significantly more alacrity."

"Or what?" she taunted him gently.

She eased open the silken clasp and then moved her hands around to the bra cups, holding them to her breasts when the bra would have fallen open. "Will you hold it against me in my next performance review? Oh, the horror."

"Are you defying me?"

But Achilles sounded amused, despite his gruffness. And there was something else in his voice then, she thought. A certain tension that she felt move inside her even before she understood what it was. Maybe she didn't have to understand. Her body already knew.

Between her legs, that aching thing grew fiercer. Brighter. And so did she.

"I think you can take it," she whispered.

And then she let the bra fall.

She felt the rush of cooler air over the flesh of her breasts. Her nipples puckered and stung a little as they pulled tight. But what she was concentrating on was that taut, arrested look on Achilles's face. That savage gleam in his dark gold eyes. And the way his fierce, ruthless mouth went flat.

He muttered something in guttural Greek, using words she had never heard before, in her blue-blooded academies and rarefied circles. But she knew, somehow, exactly what he meant.

She could feel it, part of that same ache.

He reached down to grip the hem of his T-shirt, then tugged it up and over his head in a single shrug of one muscled arm. She watched him do it, not certain she was breathing any longer and not able to make herself care about that at all, and then he was moving toward the bed.

Another second and he was upon her.

He swept her up in his arms again, moving her into the center of the bed, and then he bore her down to the mattress beneath them. And Valentina found that they fit together beautifully. That she knew instinctively what to do.

She widened her legs, he fit himself between them, and

she cushioned him there—that long, solid, hard-packed form of his—as if they'd been made to fit together just like this. His bare chest was a wonder. She couldn't seem to keep herself from exploring it, running her palms and her fingers over every ridge and every plane, losing herself in his hot, extraordinary male flesh. She could feel that remarkable ridge of his arousal again, pressed against her right where she ached the most, and it was almost too much.

Or maybe it really was too much, but she wanted it all the same.

She wanted him.

He set his mouth to hers again, and she could taste a kind of desperation on his wickedly clever mouth.

That wild sensation stormed through her, making her limp and wild and desperate for things she'd only ever read about before. He tangled his hands in her hair to hold her mouth to his, then he dropped his chest down against hers, bearing her down into the mattress beneath them. Making her feel glorious and alive and insane with that ache that started between her legs and bloomed out in all directions.

And then he taught her everything.

He tasted her. He moved his mouth from her lips, down the long line of her neck, learning the contours of her clavicle. Then he went lower, sending fire spinning all over her as he made his way down to one of her breasts, only to send lightning flashing all through her when he sucked her nipple deep into his mouth.

He tested the weight of her breasts in his faintly calloused palm, while he played with the nipple of the other, gently torturing her with his teeth, his tongue, his cruel lips. When she thought she couldn't take any more, he switched.

And then he went back and forth, over and over again,

until her head was thrashing against the mattress, and some desperate soul was crying out his name. Over and over again, as if she might break apart at any moment.

Valentina knew, distantly, that she was the one making those sounds. But she was too far gone to care.

Achilles moved his way down her body, taking his sweet time, and Valentina sighed with every inch he explored. She shifted. She rolled. She found herself lifting her hips toward him without his having to ask.

"Good girl," he murmured, and it was astonishing how much pleasure two little words could give her.

He peeled her panties down off her hips, tugged them down the length of her legs and then threw them aside. And when he was finished with that, he slid his hands beneath her bottom as he came back over her, lifted her hips up into the air and didn't so much as glance up at her before he set his mouth to the place where she needed him most.

Maybe she screamed. Maybe she fainted. Maybe both at once.

Everything seemed to flash bright, then smooth out into a long, lethal roll of sensation that turned Valentina red hot.

Everywhere.

He licked his way into her. He teased her and he learned her and he tasted her, making even that most private part of her his. She felt herself go molten and wild, and he made a low, rough sound of pleasure, deeply masculine and deliciously savage, and that was too much.

"Oh, no," she heard herself moan. "No—"

Valentina felt more than heard him laugh against the most tender part of her, and then everything went up in flames.

She exploded. She cried out and she shook, the pleasure so intense she didn't understand how anyone could live through it, but still she shook some more. She shook until she thought she'd been made new. She shook until she didn't care either way.

And when she knew her own name again, Achilles was crawling his way over her. He no longer wore those loose black trousers of his, and there was a look of unmistakably savage male triumph stamped deep on his face.

"Beautiful," he murmured. He was on his elbows over her, pressing himself against her. His wall of a chest. That fascinatingly hard part of him below. He studied her flushed face as if he'd never seen her before. "Am I the only man who has ever tasted you?"

Valentina couldn't speak. She could only nod, mute and still shaking.

She wondered if she might shake like this forever, and she couldn't seem to work herself up into minding if she did.

"Only mine," he said with a certain quiet ferocity that only made that shaking inside her worse. Or better. "You are only and ever mine."

And that was when she felt him. That broad smooth head of his hardest part, nudging against the place where she was nothing but soft, wet heat and longing.

She sucked in a breath, and Achilles took her face in his hands.

"Mine," he said again, in the same intense way.

It sounded a great deal like a vow.

Valentina's head was spinning.

"Yours," she whispered, and he grinned then, too fierce and too elemental.

He shifted his hips and moved a little farther against her, pressing himself against that entrance again, and Valentina found her hands in fists against his chest.

"Will it hurt?" she asked before she knew she meant

to speak. "Or is that just something they say in books, to make it seem more…"

But she couldn't quite finish that sentence. And Achilles's gaze was too dark and too bright at once, so intense she couldn't seem to stop shaking or spinning. And she couldn't bring herself to look away.

"It might hurt." He kept his attention on her, fierce and focused. "It might not. But either way, it will be over in a moment."

"Oh." Valentina blinked, and tried to wrap her head around that. "I suppose quick is good."

Achilles let out a bark of laughter, and she wasn't sure if she was startled or something like delighted to hear it. Both, perhaps.

And it made a knot she hadn't known was hardening inside her chest ease.

"I cannot tell if you are good for me or you will kill me," he told her then. He moved one hand, smoothing her hair back from her temple. "It will only hurt, or feel awkward, for a moment. I promise. As for the rest…"

And the smile he aimed at her then was, Valentina thought, the best thing she'd ever seen. It poured into her and through her, as bright and thick as honey, changing everything. Even the way she shook for him. Even the way she breathed.

"The rest will not be quick," Achilles told her, still braced there above her. "It will not be rushed, it will be thorough. Extremely thorough, as you know I am in all things."

She felt her breath stutter. But he was still going.

"And when I am done, *glikia mou*, we will do it again. And again. Until we get it right. Because I am nothing if not dedicated to my craft. Do you understand me?"

"I understand," Valentina said faintly, because it was

hard to keep her voice even when the world was lost somewhere in his commanding gaze. "I guess that's—"

But that was when he thrust his way inside her. It was a quick, hard thrust, slick and hot and overwhelming, until he was lodged deep inside her.

Inside her.

It was too much. It didn't hurt, necessarily, but it didn't feel good, either. It felt…like everything. Too much of everything.

Too hard. Too long. Too thick and too deep and too—

"Breathe," Achilles ordered her.

But Valentina didn't see how that was possible. How could she breathe when there was a person *inside* her? Even if that person was Achilles.

Especially when that person was Achilles.

Still, she did as he bade her, because he was *inside* her and she was beneath him and splayed open and there was nothing else to do. She breathed in.

She let it out, and then she breathed in again. And then again.

And with each breath, she felt less overwhelmed and more…

Something else.

Achilles didn't seem particularly worried. He held himself over her, one hand tangled in her hair as the other made its way down the front of her body. Lazily. Easily. He played with her breasts. He set his mouth against the crook of her neck where it met her shoulder, teasing her with his tongue and his teeth.

And still she breathed the way he'd told her to do. In. Out.

Over and over, until she couldn't remember that she'd balked at his smooth, intense entry. That she'd ever had a problem at all with *hard* and *thick* and *long* and *deep*.

Until all she could feel was fire.

Experimentally, she moved her hips, trying to get a better feel for how wide he was. How deep. How far inside her own body. Sensation soared through her every time she moved, so she did it again. And again.

She took a little more of him in, then rocked around a little bit, playing. Testing. Seeing how much of him she could take and if it would continue to send licks of fire coursing through her every time she shifted position, no matter how minutely.

It did.

And when she started to shift against him, restlessly, as if she couldn't help herself, Achilles lifted his head and grinned down her, something wild and dark and wholly untamed in his eyes.

It thrilled her.

"Please…" Valentina whispered.

And he knew. He always knew. Exactly what she needed, right when she needed it.

Because that was when he began to move.

He taught her about pace. He taught her depth and rhythm. She'd thought she was playing with fire, but Achilles taught her that she had no idea what real fire was.

And he kept his word.

He was very, very thorough.

When she began to thrash, he dropped down to get closer. He gathered her in his arms, holding her as he thrust inside her, again and again. He made her his with every deep, possessive stroke. He made her want. He made her need.

He made her cry out his name, again and again, until it sounded to Valentina like some kind of song.

This time, when the fire took her, she thought it might have torn her into far too many pieces for her to ever recover. He lost his rhythm then, hammering into her hard and wild, as if he was as wrecked as she was—

And she held him to her as he tumbled off that edge behind her, and straight on into bliss.

Achilles had made a terrible mistake, and he was not a man who made mistakes. He didn't believe in them. He believed in opportunities—it was how he'd built this life of his. Something that had always made him proud.

But this was a mistake. She was a mistake. He couldn't kid himself. He had never wanted somebody the way that he wanted Valentina. It had made him sloppy. He had concentrated entirely too much on her. Her pleasure. Her innocence, as he relieved her of it.

He hadn't thought to guard himself against her.

He never had to guard himself against anyone. Not since he'd been a child. He'd rather fallen out of the habit—and that notion galled him.

Achilles rolled to the side of the bed and sat there, running a hand over the top of his head. He could hear Valentina behind him, breathing. And he knew what he'd see if he looked. She slept hard, his princess. After he'd finished with her the last time, he'd thought she might have fallen asleep before he'd even pulled out of her. He'd held the weight of her, sprawled there on top of him, her breath heavy and her eyes shut tight so he had no choice but to marvel at the length of her eyelashes.

And it had taken him much longer than it should have to shift her off him, lay her beside him and cover her with the sheets. Carefully.

It was that unexpected urge to protect her—from himself, he supposed, or perhaps from the uncertain elements of his ruthlessly climate-controlled bedroom—that had made him go cold. Something a little too close to the sort of panic he did not permit himself to feel, ever, had pressed down on him then. And no amount of controlling his breath or ordering himself to stop the madness seemed to help.

He rubbed a palm over his chest now, because his heart was beating much too fast, the damned traitor.

He had wanted her too much, and this was the price. This treacherous place he found himself in now, that he hardly recognized. It hadn't occurred to him to guard himself against a virgin no matter her pedigree, and this was the result.

He felt things.

He felt things—and Achilles Casilieris did not *feel*. He refused to *feel*. The intensity of sex was physical, nothing more. Never more than that, no matter the woman and no matter the situation and no matter how she might beg or plead—

Not that Valentina had done anything of the sort.

He stood from the bed then, because he didn't want to. He wanted to roll back toward her, pull her close again. He bit off a filthy Greek curse, beneath his breath, then moved restlessly across the floor toward the windows.

Manhattan mocked him. It lay there before him, glittering and sparkling madly, and the reason he had a penthouse in this most brash and American of cities was because he liked to stand high above the sprawl of it as if he was some kind of king. Every time he came here he was reminded how far he'd come from his painful childhood. And every time he stayed in this very room, he looked out over all the wealth and opportunity and untethered American dreams that made this city what it was and knew that he had succeeded.

Beyond even the wildest dreams the younger version of Achilles could have conjured up for himself.

But tonight, all he could think about was a copperhaired innocent who had yet to tell him her real name, who had given him all of herself with that sweet enthusiasm that had nearly killed him, and left him…yearning.

And Achilles did not yearn.

He did not yearn and he did not let himself want things he could not have, and he absolutely, positively did not indulge in pointless nostalgia for things he did not miss. But as he stood at his huge windows overlooking Manhattan, the city that seemed to laugh at his predicament tonight instead of welcoming him the way it usually did, he found himself tossed back to the part of his past he only ever used as a weapon.

Against himself.

He hardly remembered his mother. Or perhaps he had beaten that sentimentality out of himself years ago. Either way, he knew that he had been seven or so when she had died, but it wasn't as if her presence earlier had done anything to save her children from the brute of a man whom she had married. Demetrius had been a thick, coarse sort of man, who had worked with his hands down on the docks and had thought that gave him the right to use those hands however he wished. Achilles didn't think there was anything the man had not beaten. His drinking buddies. His wife. The family dog. Achilles and his three young stepsiblings, over and over again. The fact that Achilles had not been Demetrius's own son, but the son of his mother's previous husband who had gone off to war and never returned, had perhaps made the beatings Demetrius doled out harsher—but it wasn't as if he spared his own flesh and blood from his fists.

After Achilles's mother had died under suspicious circumstances no one had ever bothered to investigate in a part of town where nothing good ever happened anyway, things went from bad to worse. Demetrius's temper worsened. He'd taken it out on the little ones, alternately kicking them around and then leaving them for seven-year-old Achilles to raise.

This had always been destined to end in failure, if not outright despair. Achilles understood that now, as an adult looking back. He understood it analytically and theoretically and, if asked, would have said exactly that. He'd been a child himself, etcetera. But where it counted, deep in those terrible feelings he'd turned off when he had still been a boy, Achilles would never understand. He carried the weight of those lives with him, wherever he went. No matter what he built, no matter what he owned, no matter how many times he won this or that corporate battle— none of that paid the ransom he owed on three lives he could never bring back.

They had been his responsibility, and he had failed. That beat in him like a tattoo. It marked him. It was the truth of him.

When it was all over—after Achilles had failed to notice a gas leak and had woken up only when Demetrius had returned from one of his drinking binges three days later to find the little ones dead and Achilles listless and nearly unresponsive himself—everything had changed. That was the cut-and-dried version of events, and it was accurate enough. What it didn't cover was the guilt, the shame that had eaten Achilles alive. Or what it had been like to watch his siblings' tiny bodies carried out by police, or how it had felt to stand at their graves and know that he could have prevented this if he'd been stronger. Bigger. *Better.*

Achilles had been sent to live with a distant aunt who had never bothered to pretend that she planned to give him anything but a roof over his head, and nothing more. In retrospect, that, too, had been a gift. He hadn't had to bother with any healing. He hadn't had to examine what had happened and try to come to terms with it. No one had cared about him or his grief at all.

And so Achilles had waited. He had plotted. He had taken everything that resembled a feeling, shoved it down as deep inside him as it would go, and made it over into hate. It had taken him ten years to get strong enough. To hunt Demetrius down in a sketchy bar in the same bad neighborhood where he'd brutalized Achilles's mother, beaten his own children and left Achilles responsible for what had happened to them.

And that whole long decade, Achilles had told himself that it was an extermination. That he could walk up to this man who had loomed so large over the whole of his childhood and simply rid the world of his unsavory presence. Demetrius did not deserve to live. There was no doubt about that, no shred of uncertainty anywhere in Achilles's soul. Not while Achilles's mother and his stepsiblings were dead.

He'd staked out his stepfather's favorite dive bar, and this one in the sense that it was repellant, not attractive to rich hipsters from affluent neighborhoods. He'd watched a ramshackle, much grayer and more frail version of the stepfather roaring in his head stumble out into the street. And he'd been ready.

He'd gone up to Demetrius out in the dark, cold night, there in a part of the city where no one would ever dream of interfering in a scuffle on the street lest they find themselves shanked. He'd let the rage wash over him, let the sweet taint of revenge ignite in his veins. He'd expected to feel triumph and satisfaction after all these years and all he'd done to make himself strong enough to take this man down—but what he hadn't reckoned with was that the drunken old man wouldn't recognize him.

Demetrius hadn't known who he was.

And that meant that Achilles had been out there in the

street, ready to beat down a defenseless old drunk who smelled of watered-down whiskey and a wasted life.

He hadn't done it. It wasn't worth it. He might have happily taken down the violent, abusive behemoth who'd terrorized him at seven, but he'd been too big himself at seventeen to find any honor in felling someone so vastly inferior to him in every way.

Especially since Demetrius hadn't the slightest idea who he'd been.

And Achilles had vowed to himself then and there that the night he stood in the street in his old neighborhood, afraid of nothing save the darkness inside him, would be the absolutely last time he let feelings rule him.

Because he had wasted years. Years that could have been spent far more wisely than planning out the extermination of an old, broken man who didn't deserve to have Achilles as an enemy. He'd walked away from Demetrius and his own squalid past and he'd never gone back.

His philosophy had served him well since. It had led him across the years, always cold and forever calculating his next, best move. Achilles was never swayed by emotion any longer, for good or ill. He never allowed it any power over him whatsoever. It had made him great, he'd often thought. It had made him who he was.

And yet Princess Valentina had somehow reached deep inside him, deep into a place that should have been black and cold and nothing but ice, and lit him on fire all over again.

"Are you brooding?" a soft voice asked from behind him, scratchy with sleep. Or with not enough sleep. "I knew I would do something wrong."

But she didn't sound insecure. Not in the least. She sounded warm, well sated. She sounded like his. She sounded like exactly who she was: the only daughter of one of Europe's last remaining powerhouse kings and the only woman Achilles had ever met who could turn him inside out.

And maybe that was what did it. The suddenly unbearable fact that she was still lying to him. He had this burning thing eating him alive from the inside out, he was cracking apart at the foundations, and she was still lying to him.

She was in his bed, teasing him in that way of hers that no one else would ever dare, and yet she lied to him. Every moment was a lie, even and especially this one. Every single moment she didn't tell him the truth about who she was and what she was doing here was more than a lie. More than a simple deception.

He was beginning to feel it as a betrayal.

"I do not brood," he said, and he could hear the gruffness in his own voice.

He heard her shift on the bed, and then he heard the sound of her feet against his floor. And he should have turned before she reached him, he knew that. He should have faced her and kept her away from him, especially when it was so dark outside and there was still so much left of the night—and he had clearly let it get to him.

But he didn't.

And in a moment she was at his back, and then she was sliding her arms around his waist with a familiarity that suggested she'd done it a thousand times before and knew how perfectly she would fit there. Then she pressed her face against the hollow of his spine.

And for a long moment she simply stood there like that, and Achilles felt his heart careen and clatter at his ribs. He was surprised that she couldn't hear it—hell, he was surprised that the whole of Manhattan wasn't alerted.

But all she did was stand there with her mouth pressed against his skin, as if she was holding him up, and through him the whole of the world.

Achilles knew that there was any number of ways to deal with this situation immediately. Effectively. No matter what name she called herself. He could call her out. He could ignore it altogether and simply send her away. He could let the darkness in him edge over into cruelty, so she would be the one to walk away.

But the simple truth was that he didn't want to do any of them.

"I have some land," he told her instead, and he couldn't tell if he was appalled at himself or simply surprised. "Out in the West, where there's nothing to see for acres and acres in all directions except the sky."

"That sounds beautiful," she murmured.

And every syllable was an exquisite pain, because he could feel her shape her words. He could feel her mouth as she spoke, right there against the flesh of his back. And he could have understood if it was a sexual thing. If that was what raged in him then. If it took him over and made him want to do nothing more than throw her down and claim her all over again. Sex, he understood. Sex, he could handle.

But it was much worse than that.

Because it didn't feel like fire, it felt…sweet. The kind of sweetness that wrapped around him, crawling into every nook and cranny inside him he'd long ago thought he'd turned to ice. And then stayed there, blooming into something like heat, as if she could melt him that easily.

He was more than a little worried that she could.

That she already had.

"Sometimes a man wants to be able to walk for miles in any direction and see no one," he heard himself say out loud, as if his mouth was no longer connected to the rest of him. "Not even himself."

"Or perhaps especially not himself," she said softly, her mouth against his skin having the same result as before.

Then he could feel her breathe, there behind him. There was a surprising amount of strength in the arms she still wrapped tight around his midsection. Her scent seemed to fill his head, a hint of lavender and something far softer that he knew was hers alone.

And the truth was that he wasn't done. He had never been a casual man in the modern sense, preferring mistresses who understood his needs and could cater to them over longer periods of time to one-night stands and such flashes in the pan that brought him nothing but momentary satisfaction.

He had never been casual, but this… This was nothing but trouble.

He needed to send her away. He had to fire Natalie, make sure that Valentina left, and leave no possible opening for either one of them to ever come back. This needed to be over before it really started. Before he forgot that he was who he was for a very good reason.

Demetrius had been a drunk. He'd cried and apologized when he was sober, however rarely that occurred. But Achilles was the monster. He'd gone to that bar to kill his stepfather, and he'd planned the whole thing out in every detail, coldly and dispassionately. He still didn't regret what he'd intended to do that night—but he knew perfectly well what that made him. And it was not a good man.

And that was all well and good as long as he kept the monster in him on ice, where it belonged. As long as he locked himself away, set apart.

It had never been an issue before.

He needed to get Valentina away from him, before he forgot himself completely.

"Pack your things," he told her shortly.

He shifted so he could look down at her again, drawing her around to his front and taking in the kick of those wide green eyes and that mouth he had sampled again and again and again.

And he couldn't do it.

He wanted her to know him, and even though that was the most treacherous thing of all, once it was in his head he couldn't seem to let it go. He wanted her to know him, and that meant he needed her to trust him enough to tell who she was. And that would never happen if he sent her away right now the way he should have.

And he was so used to thinking of himself as a monster. Some part of him—a large part of him—took a kind of pride in that, if he was honest. He'd worked so hard on making that monster into an impenetrable wall of wealth and judgment, taste and power.

But it turned out that all it took was a deceitful princess to make him into a man.

"I'm taking you to Montana," he told her gruffly, because he couldn't seem to stop himself.

And doomed them both.

CHAPTER EIGHT

ONE WEEK PASSED, and then another, and the six weeks Valentina had agreed to take stretched out into seven, out on Achilles's Montana ranch where the only thing on the horizon was the hint of the nearest mountain range.

His ranch was like a daydream, Valentina thought. Achilles was a rancher only in a distant sense, having hired qualified people to take care of the daily running of the place and turn its profit. Those things took place far away on some or other of his thousands of acres tucked up at the feet of the Rocky Mountains. They stayed in the sprawling ranch house, a sprawling nod toward log cabins and rustic ski lodges, the better to overlook the unspoiled land in all directions.

It was far away from everything and felt even farther than that. It was an hour drive to the nearest town, stout and quintessentially Western, as matter-of-fact as it was practical. They'd come at the height of Montana's short summer, hot during the day and cool at night, with endless blue skies stretching on up toward forever and nothing to do but soak in the quiet. The stunning silence, broken only by the wind. The sun. The exuberant moon and all those improbable, impossible stars, so many they cluttered up the sky and made it feel as if, were she to take a big enough step, Valentina could toss herself straight off the planet and into eternity.

And Valentina knew she was running out of time. Her wedding was the following week, she wasn't who she was pretending she was, and these stolen days in this faraway place of blue and gold were her last with this man. This stolen life had only ever been hers on loan.

But she would have to face that soon enough.

In Montana, as in New York, her days were filled with Achilles. He was too precise and demanding to abandon his businesses entirely, but there was something about the ranch that rendered him less overbearing. He and Valentina would put out what fires there might be in the mornings, but then, barring catastrophe, he let his employees earn their salaries the rest of the day.

While he and Valentina explored what this dreamy ranch life, so far removed from everything, had to offer. He had a huge library that she imagined would be particularly inviting in winter—not, she was forced to remind herself, that she would ever see it in a different season. A guest could sink into one of the deep leather chairs in front of the huge fireplace and read away a snowy evening or two up here in the mountains. He had an indoor pool that let the sky in through its glass ceiling, perfect for swimming in all kinds of weather. There was the hot tub, propped up on its own terrace with a sweeping view, which cried out for those cool evenings. It was a short drive or a long, pretty walk to the lake a little ways up into the mountains, so crisp and clear and cold it almost hurt.

But it was the kind of hurt that made her want more and more, no matter how it made her gasp and think she might lose herself forever in the cut of it.

Achilles was the same. Only worse.

Valentina had always thought of sex—or her virginity, anyway—as a single, solitary thing. Someday she would have sex, she'd always told herself. Someday she would get rid of her virginity. She had never really imagined that it wasn't a single, finite event.

She'd thought virginity, and therefore sex, was the actual breaching of what she still sometimes thought of as her maidenhead, as if she was an eighteenth-century heroine—and nothing more. She'd never really imagined much beyond that.

Achilles taught her otherwise.

Sex with him was threaded into life, a rich undercurrent that became as much a part of it as walking, breathing, eating. It wasn't a specific act. It was everything.

It was the touch of his hand across the dinner table, when he simply threaded their fingers together, the memory of what they'd already done together and the promise of more braided there between them. It was a sudden hot, dark look in the middle of a conversation about something innocuous or work-related, reminding her that she knew him now in so many different dimensions. It was the way his laughter seemed to rearrange her, pouring through her and making her new, every time she heard it.

It was when she stopped counting each new time he wrenched her to pieces as a separate, astonishing event. When she began to accept that he would always do that. Time passed and days rolled on, and all of these things that swirled between them only deepened. He became only more able to wreck her more easily the better he got to know her. And the better she got to know him.

As if their bodies were like the stars above them, infinite and adaptable, a great mess of joy and wonder that time only intensified.

But she knew it was running out.

And the more Achilles called her Natalie—which she thought he did more here, or perhaps she was far more sensitive to it now that she shared his bed—the more her terrible deception seemed to form into a heavy ball in the pit of her stomach, like some kind of cancerous thing that she very much thought might consume her whole.

Some part of her wished it would.

Meanwhile, the real Natalie kept calling her. Again and again, or leaving texts, but Valentina couldn't bring herself to respond to them. What would she say? How could she possibly explain what she'd done?

Much less the fact that she was still doing it and, worse, that she didn't want it to end no matter how quickly her royal wedding was approaching.

Even if she imagined that Natalie was off in Murin doing exactly the same thing with Rodolfo that Valentina was doing here, with all this wild and impossible hunger, what did that matter? They could still switch back, none the wiser. Nothing would change for Valentina. She would go on to marry the prince as she had always been meant to do, and it was highly likely that even Rodolfo himself wouldn't notice the change.

But Natalie had not been sleeping with Achilles before she'd switched places with Valentina. That meant there was no possible way that she could easily step back into the life that Valentina had gone ahead and ruined.

And was still ruining, day by day.

Still, no matter how self-righteously she railed at herself for that, she knew it wasn't what was really bothering her. It wasn't what would happen to Natalie that ate her up inside.

It was what would happen to her. And what could happen with Achilles. She found that she was markedly less sanguine about Achilles failing to notice the difference between Valentina and Natalie when they switched back again. In fact, the very notion made her feel sick.

But how could she tell him the truth? If she couldn't tell Natalie what she'd done, how could she possibly tell the man whom she'd been lying to directly all this time?

He thought he was having an affair with his assistant. A woman he had vetted and worked closely with for half a decade.

What was she supposed to say, *Oh, by the way, I'm actually a princess?*

The truth was that she was still a coward. Because she didn't know if what was really holding her back was that she couldn't imagine what she would say—or if she could imagine all too well what Achilles would do. And she knew that made her the worst sort of person. Because when she worried about what he would do, she was worried about herself. Not about how she might hurt him. Not about what it would do to him to learn that she had lied to him all this time. But the fact that it was entirely likely that she would tell him, and that would be the last she'd see of him. Ever.

And Valentina couldn't quite bear for this to be over.

This was her vacation. Her holiday. Her escape—and how had it never occurred to her that if that was true, it meant she had to go back? She'd known that in a general sense, of course, but she hadn't really thought it through. She certainly hadn't thought about what it would feel like to leave Achilles and then walk back to the stifling life she'd called her own for all these years.

It was one thing to be trapped. Particularly when it was all she'd ever known. But it was something else again to see exactly how trapped she was, to leave it behind for a while, and then knowingly walk straight back into that trap, closing the cage door behind her.

Forever.

Sometimes when she lay awake at night listening to Achilles breathe in the great bed next to her, his arms thrown over her as if they were slowly becoming one person, she couldn't imagine how she was ever going to make herself do it.

But time didn't care if she felt trapped. Or torn. It marched on whether she wanted it to or not.

"Are you brooding?" a low male voice asked from behind her, jolting her out of her unpleasant thoughts. "I thought that was my job, not yours."

Valentina turned from the rail of the balcony that ambled along the side of the master suite, where she was taking in the view and wondering how she could ever fold herself up tight and slot herself back into the life she'd left behind in Murin.

But the view behind her was even better. Achilles lounged against the open sliding glass door, naked save for a towel wrapped around his hips. He had taken her in a fury earlier, pounding into her from behind until she screamed out his name into the pillows, and he'd roared his own pleasure into the crook of her neck. Then he'd left her there on the bed, limp and still humming with all that passion, while he'd gone out for one of his long, brutal runs he always claimed cleared his head.

It had been weeks now, and he still took her breath. Now that she knew every inch of him, she found herself more in awe of him. All that sculpted perfection of his chest, the dark hair that narrowed at his lean hips, dipping down below the towel where she knew the boldest part of him waited.

She'd tasted him there, too. She'd knelt before the fireplace in that gorgeous library, her hands on his thighs as he'd sat back in one of those great leather chairs. He'd played with her hair, sifting strands of it through his fingers as she'd reached into the battered jeans he wore here on the ranch and had pulled him free.

He'd tasted of salt and man, and he'd let her play with him as she liked. He let her lick him everywhere until she learned his shape. He let her suck him in, then figure out how to make him as wild as he did when he tasted her in this same way. And she'd taken it as a personal triumph when he'd started to grip the chair. And when he'd lost himself inside her mouth, he'd groaned out that name he called her. *Glikia mou.*

Even thinking about it now made that same sweet, hot restlessness move through her all over again.

But time was her enemy. She knew that. And looking at him as he stood there in the doorway and watched her with that dark gold gaze that she could feel in every part of her, still convinced that he could see into parts of her she didn't know how to name, Valentina still didn't know what to do.

If she told him who she was, she would lose what few days with him she had left. This was Achilles Casilieris. He would never forgive her deception. Never. Her other option was never to tell him at all. She would go back to London with him in a few days as planned, slip away the way she'd always intended to do if a week or so later than agreed, and let the real Natalie pick up the pieces.

And that way, she could remember this the way she wanted to do. She could remember loving him, not losing him.

Because that was what she'd done. She understood that in the same way she finally comprehended intimacy. She'd gone and fallen in love with this man who didn't know her real name. This man she could never, ever keep.

Was it so wrong that if she couldn't keep him, she wanted to keep these sun-soaked memories intact?

"You certainly look like you're brooding." There was that lazy note to his voice that never failed to make her blood heat. It was no different now. It was that quick. It was that inevitable. "How can that be? There's nothing here but silence and sunshine. No call to brood about anything. Unless of course, it is your soul that is heavy." And she could have sworn there was something in his gaze then that dared her to come clean. Right then and there. As if, as ever, he knew what she was thinking. "Tell me, Natalie, what is it that haunts you?"

And it was moments like these that haunted her, but she couldn't tell him that. Moments like this, when she was certain that he knew. That he must know. That he was asking her to tell him the truth at last.

That he was calling her the wrong name deliberately, to see if that would goad her into coming clean.

But the mountains were too quiet and there was too much summer in the air. The Montana sky was a blue she'd never seen before, and that was what she felt in her soul. And if there was a heaviness, or a darkness, she had no doubt it would haunt her later.

Valentina wanted to live here. Now. With him. She wanted to *live*.

She had so little time left to truly *live*.

So once again, she didn't tell him. She smiled instead, wide enough to hide the fissures in her heart, and she went to him.

Because there was so little time left that she could do that. So few days left to reach out and touch him the way she did now, sliding her palms against the mouthwatering planes of his chest as if she was memorizing the heat of his skin.

As if she was memorizing everything.

"I don't know what you're talking about," she told him quietly, her attention on his skin beneath her hands. "I never do."

"I am not the mystery here," he replied, and though his voice was still so lazy, so very lazy, she didn't quite believe it. "There are enough mysteries to go around, I think."

"Solve this one, then," she dared him, going up on her toes to press her mouth to his.

Because she might not have truth and she might not have time, but she had this.

For a little while longer, she had this.

Montana was another mistake, because apparently, that was all he did now.

They spent weeks on his ranch, and Achilles made it all worse by the day. Every day he touched her, every day lost himself in her, every day he failed to get her to come clean with him. Every single day was another nail in his coffin.

And then, worse by far to his mind, it was time to leave.

Weeks in Montana, secluded from the rest of the world, and he'd gained nothing but a far deeper and more disastrous appreciation of Valentina's appeal. He hadn't exactly forced her to the light. He hadn't done anything but lose his own footing.

In all those weeks and all that sweet summer sunshine out in the American West, it had never occurred to him that she simply wouldn't tell him. He'd been so sure that he would get to her somehow. That if he had all these feelings churning around inside him, whatever was happening inside her must be far more extreme.

It had never occurred to him that he could lose that bet.

That Princess Valentina had him beat when it came to keeping herself locked up tight, no matter what.

They landed in London in a bleak drizzle that matched his mood precisely.

"You're expected at the bank in an hour," Valentina told him when they reached his Belgravia town house, standing there in his foyer looking as guileless and innocent as she ever had. Even now, when he had tasted every inch of her. Even now, when she was tearing him apart with that serene, untouchable look on her face. "And the board of directors is adamant—"

"I don't care about the bank," he muttered. "Or old men who think they can tell me what to do."

And just like that, he'd had enough.

He couldn't outright demand that Valentina tell him who she really was, because that wouldn't be her telling him of her own volition. It wouldn't be her trusting him.

It's almost as if she knows who you really are, that old familiar voice inside hissed at him. It had been years since he'd heard it, inside him or otherwise. But even though Demetrius had not been able to identify him on the streets when he'd had the chance, Achilles always knew the old man when he spoke. *Maybe she knows exactly what kind of monster you are.*

And a harsh truth slammed into him then, making him feel very nearly unsteady on his feet. He didn't know why it hadn't occurred to him before. Or maybe it had, but he'd shoved it aside out there in all that Montana sky and sunshine. Because he was Achilles Casilieris. He was one of the most sought-after bachelors in all the world. Legions of women chased after him daily, trying anything from trickery to bribery to outright lies about paternity claims to make him notice them. He was at the top of everyone's *most wanted* list.

But to Princess Valentina of Marin, he was nothing but a bit of rough.

She was slumming.

That was why she hadn't bothered to identify herself. She didn't see the point. He might as well have been the pool boy.

And he couldn't take it. He couldn't process it. There was nothing in him but fire and that raw, unquenchable need, and she was so cool. Too cool.

He needed to mess her up. He needed to do something to make all this…wildfire and feeling dissipate before it ate him alive and left nothing behind. Nothing at all.

"What are you doing?" she asked, and he took a little too much satisfaction in that appropriately uncertain note in her voice.

It was only when he saw her move that he realized he was stalking toward her, backing her up out of the gleaming foyer and into one of the town house's elegant sitting rooms. Not that the beauty of a room could do anything but fade next to Valentina.

The world did the same damned thing.

She didn't ask him a silly question like that again. And perhaps she didn't need to. He backed her up to the nearest settee, and took entirely too much pleasure in the pulse that beat out the truth of her need right there in her neck.

"Achilles..." she said hoarsely, but he wanted no more words. No more lies of omission.

No more *slumming*.

"Quiet," he ordered her.

He sank his hands into her gleaming copper hair, then dragged her mouth to his. Then he toppled her down to antique settee and followed her. She was slender and lithe and wild beneath him, rising to meet him with too much need, too much longing.

As if, in the end, this was the only place they were honest with each other.

And Achilles was furious. Furious, or something like it—something close enough that it burned in him as brightly. As lethally. He shoved her skirt up over her hips and she wrapped her legs around his waist, and she was panting already. She was gasping against his mouth. Or maybe he was breathing just as hard.

"Achilles," she said again, and there was something in her gaze then. Something darker than need.

But this was no time for sweetness. Or anything deeper. This was a claiming.

"Later," he told her, and then he took her mouth with

his, tasting the words he was certain, abruptly, he didn't want to hear.

He might be nothing to her but a walk on the wild side she would look back on while she rotted away in some palatial prison, but he would make sure that she remembered him.

He had every intention of leaving his mark.

Achilles tore off his trousers, freeing himself. Then he reached down and found the gusset of her panties, ripping them off and shoving the scraps aside to fit himself to her at last.

And then he stopped thinking about marks and memories, because she was molten hot and wet. She was his. He sank into her, groaning as she encased his length like a hot, tight glove.

It was so good. It was too good.

She always was.

He moved then, and she did, too, that slick, deep slide. And they knew each other so well now. Their bodies were too attuned to each other, too hot and too certain of where this was going, and it was never, ever enough.

He reached between them and pressed his fingers in the place where she needed him most, and felt her explode into a frenzy beneath him. She raised her hips to meet each thrust. She dug her fingers into his shoulders as if she was already shaking apart.

He felt it build in her, and in him, too. Wild and mad, the way it always was.

As if they could tear apart the world this way. As if they already had.

"No one will ever make you feel the way that I do," he told her then, a dark muttering near her ear as she panted and writhed. "No one."

And he didn't know if that was some kind of endearment, or a dire warning.

But it didn't matter, because she was clenching around him then. She gasped out his name, while her body gripped him, then shook.

And he pumped himself into her, wanting nothing more than to roar her damned name. To claim her in every possible way. To show her—

But he did none of that.

And when it was over, when the storm had passed, he pulled himself away from her and climbed to his feet again. And he felt something sharp and heavy move through him as he looked down at her, still lying there half on and half off the antique settee they'd moved a few feet across the floor, because he had done exactly as he set out to do.

He'd messed her up. She looked disheveled and shaky and absolutely, delightfully ravished.

But all he could think was that he still didn't have her. That she was still going to leave him when she was done here. That she'd never had any intention of staying in the first place. It ripped at him. It made him feel something like crazy.

The last time he'd ever felt anything like it, he'd been an angry seventeen-year-old in a foul-smelling street with an old drunk who didn't know who he was. It was a kind of anguish.

It was a grief, and he refused to indulge it. He refused to admit it was ravaging him, even as he pulled his clothes back where they belonged.

And then she made it even worse. She smiled.

She sat up slowly, pushing her skirt back into place and tucking the torn shreds of her panties into one pocket. Then she gazed up at him.

Achilles was caught by that look in her soft green eyes, as surely as if she'd reached out and wrapped her delicate hands around his throat. On some level, he felt as if she had.

"I love you," she said.

They were such small words, he thought through that thing that pounded in him like fear. Like a gong. Such small, silly words that could tear a man down without any warning at all.

And there were too many things he wanted to say then. For example, how could she tell him that she loved him when she wouldn't even tell him her name?

But he shoved that aside.

"That was sex, *glikia mou*," he grated at her. "Love is something different from a whole lot of thrashing around, half-clothed."

He expected her to flinch at that, but he should have known better. This was his princess. If she was cowed at all, she didn't show it.

Instead, she only smiled wider.

"You're the expert on love as in all things, of course," she murmured, because even here, even now, she was the only person alive who had ever dared to tease him. "My mistake."

She was still smiling when she stood up, then walked around him. As if she didn't notice that he was frozen there in some kind of astonishment. Or as if she was happy enough to leave him to it as she headed toward the foyer and, presumably, the work he'd always adored that seemed to loom over him these days, demanding more time than he wanted to give.

He'd never had a life that interested him more than his empire, until Valentina.

And he didn't have Valentina.

She'd left Achilles standing there with her declaration heavy in his ears. She'd left him half fire and a heart that long ago should have turned to ice. He'd been so certain it had when he was seven and had lost everything, including his sense of himself as anything like good.

He should have known then.

But it wasn't until much later that day—after he'd quizzed his security detail and household staff to discover she'd walked out with nothing but her shoulder bag and disappeared into the gray of the London afternoon—that he'd realized that had been the way his deceitful princess said goodbye.

CHAPTER NINE

VALENTINA COULDN'T KEEP her mind on her duties now that she was back in Murin. She couldn't keep her mind focused at all, come to that. Not on her duties, not on the goings-on of the palace, not on any of the many changes that had occurred since she'd come back home.

She should have been jubilant. Or some facsimile thereof, surely. She had walked back into her well-known, well-worn trap, expecting the same old cage, only to find that the trap wasn't at all what she had imagined it was— and the cage door had been tossed wide open.

When she'd left London that day, her body had still been shivering from Achilles's touch. She hadn't wanted to go. Not with her heart too full and a little bit broken at her own temerity in telling him how she felt when she'd known she had to leave. But it was time for her to go home, and there had been no getting around that. Her wedding to Prince Rodolfo was imminent. As in, the glittering heads of Europe's ancient houses were assembling to cheer on one of their own, and she needed to be there.

The phone calls and texts that she'd been ignoring that whole time, leaving Natalie to deal with it all on her own, had grown frantic. And she couldn't blame her sister, because the wedding was a mere day away. *Your twin sister*, she'd thought, those terms still feeling too unwieldy. She'd made her way to Heathrow Airport and bought herself a ticket on a commercial plane—the first time she'd ever done anything of the sort. One more normal thing to tuck away and remember later.

"Later" meaning after tomorrow, when she would be wed to a man she hardly knew.

It had taken Valentina a bit too long to do the right thing. To do the only possible thing and tear herself away from Achilles the way she should have done a long time ago. She should never have gone with him to Montana. She should certainly never have allowed them to stay there all that time, living out a daydream that could end only one way.

She'd known that going in, and she'd done it anyway. What did that make her, exactly?

Now I am awake, she thought as she boarded the plane. *Now I am awake and that will have to be as good as* alive, *because it's all I have left.*

She hadn't known what to expect from a regular flight into the commercial airport on the island of Murin. Some part of her imagined that she would be recognized. Her face was on the cover of the Murin Air magazines in every seat back, after all. She'd had a bit of a start when she'd sat down in the remarkably uncomfortable seat, pressed up against a snoring matron on one side and a very gray-faced businessman on the other.

But no one had noticed her shocking resemblance to the princess in the picture. No one had really looked at her at all. She flashed Natalie's passport, walked on the plane without any issues and walked off again in Murin without anyone looking at her twice—even though she was quite literally the spitting image of the princess so many were flocking to Murin to see marry her Prince Charming at last.

Once at the palace, she didn't bother trying to sneak

in because she knew she'd be discovered instantly—and that would hardly allow Natalie to switch back and escape, would it? So instead she'd walked up to the guard station around the back at the private family entrance, gazed politely at the guard who waited there and waited.

"But the...the princess is within," the guard had stammered. Maybe he was thrown by the fact Valentina was dressed like any other woman her age on the street. Maybe he was taken back because he'd never spoken to her directly before.

Or maybe it was because, if she was standing here in front of him, she wasn't where the royal guard thought she was. Which he'd likely assumed meant she'd sneaked out, undetected.

All things considered, she was happy to let that mystery stand.

Valentina had aimed a conspiratorial smile at the guard. "The princess can't possibly be within, given that I'm standing right here. But it can be our little secret that there was some confusion, if you like."

And then, feeling heavier than she ever had before and scarred somehow by what she'd gone through with Achilles, she'd walked back in the life she'd left so spontaneously and much too quickly in that London airport.

She'd expected to find Natalie as desperate to leave as she supposed, in retrospect, she had been. Or why else would she have suggested this switch in the first place?

But instead, she'd found a woman very much in love. With Crown Prince Rodolfo of Tissely. The man whom Valentina was supposed to marry the following day.

More than that, Natalie was pregnant.

"I don't know how it happened," Natalie had said, after Valentina had slipped into her bedroom and woken her up—by sitting on the end of the bed and pulling at Natalie's foot until she'd opened her eyes and found her double sitting there.

"Don't you?" Valentina had asked. "I was a virgin, but I had the distinct impression that you had not saved yourself for marriage all these years. Because why would you?"

Natalie had flushed a bit, but then her eyes had narrowed. "*Was* a virgin? Is that the past tense?" She'd blinked. "Not Mr. Casilieris."

But it wasn't the time then for sisterly confessions. Mostly because Valentina hadn't the slightest idea what she could say about Achilles that wasn't…too much. Too much and too unformed and unbearable, somehow, now that it was over. Now that none of it mattered, and never could.

"I don't think that you have a job with him anymore," Valentina had said instead, keeping her voice even. "Because I don't think you want a job with him anymore. You said you were late, didn't you? You're having a prince's baby."

And when Natalie had demurred, claiming that she didn't know one way or the other and it was likely just the stress of inhabiting someone else's life, Valentina had sprung into action.

She'd made it her business to find out, one way or another. She'd assured Natalie that it was simply to put her mind at ease. But the truth was a little more complicated, she admitted to herself as she made her way through the palace.

The fact was, she was relieved. That was what had washed through her when Natalie had confessed not only her love for Rodolfo, but her suspicions that she might be carrying his child. She'd pushed it off as she'd convinced one of her most loyal maids to run out into the city and buy her a few pregnancy tests, just to be certain. She'd shoved it to the side as she'd smuggled the tests back into her rooms, and then had handed them over to Natalie so she could find out for certain.

But there was no denying it. When Natalie had emerged from the bathroom with a dazed look on her face and a positive test in one hand, Valentina finally admitted the sheer relief that coursed through her veins. It was like champagne. Fizzy and a little bit sharp, washing through her and making her feel almost silly in response.

Because if Natalie was having Rodolfo's baby, there was no possible way that Valentina could marry him. The choice—though it had always been more of an expected duty than a choice—was taken out of her hands.

"You will marry him," Valentina had said quietly. "It is what must happen."

Natalie had looked pale. "But you... And I'm not... And you don't understand, he..."

"All of that will work out," Valentina had said with a deep certainty she very badly wanted to feel. Because it had to work out. "The important thing is that you will marry him in the morning. You will have his baby and you will be his queen when he ascends the throne. Everything else is spin and scandal, and none of that matters. Not really."

And so it was.

Once King Geoffrey had been brought into the loop and had been faced with the irrefutable evidence that his daughter had been stolen from him all those years ago—that Erica had taken Natalie and, not only that, had told Geoffrey that Valentina's twin had died at birth—he was more than on board with switching the brides at the wedding.

He'd announced to the gathered crowd that a most blessed miracle had occurred some months before. A daughter long thought dead had returned to him to take her rightful place in the kingdom, and they'd all kept it a secret to preserve everyone's privacy as they'd gotten to know each other.

Including Rodolfo, who had always been meant to be part of the family, the king had reminded the assembled crowd and the whole of the world, no matter how. And feelings had developed between Natalie and Rodolfo, where there had only ever been duty and honor between Valentina and her intended.

Valentina had seen this and stepped aside of her own volition, King Geoffrey had told the world. There had been no scandal, no sneaking around, no betrayals. Only one sister looking out for another.

The crowds ate it up. The world followed suit. It was just scandalous enough to be both believable and newsworthy. Valentina was branded as something of a Miss Lonely Hearts, it was true, but that was neither here nor there. The idea that she would sacrifice her fairy-tale wedding—and her very own Prince Charming—for her long-lost sister captured the public's imagination. She was more popular than ever, especially at home in Murin.

And this was a good thing, because now that her father had two heirs, he could marry one of his daughters off to fulfill his promises to the kingdom of Tissely, and he could prepare the other to take over Murin and keep its throne in the family.

And just like that, Valentina went from a lifetime preparing to be a princess who would marry well and support the king of a different country, to a new world in which she was meant to rule as queen in her own right.

If it was another trap, another cage, it was a far more spacious and comfortable one than any she had known before.

She knew that. There was no reason at all she should have been so unhappy.

"Your attention continues to drift, daughter," King Geoffrey said then.

Valentina snapped herself out of those thoughts in her head that did her no good and into the car where she sat with her father, en route to some or other glittering gala down at the water palace on the harbor. She couldn't even remember which charity it was this week. There was always another.

The motorcade wound down from the castle, winding its way along the hills of the beautiful capital city toward the gleaming Mediterranean Sea. Valentina normally enjoyed the view. It was pretty, first and foremost. It was home. It reminded her of so many things, of her honor and her duty and her love of her country. It renewed her commitment to her kingdom, and made her think about all the good she hoped she could do as its sovereign.

And yet these days, she wasn't thinking about Murin. All she could seem to think about was Achilles.

"I am preparing myself for the evening ahead," Valentina replied calmly enough. She aimed a perfectly composed smile at her father. "I live in fear of greeting a diplomat with the wrong name and causing an international incident."

Her father's gaze warmed, something that happened more often lately than it ever had before. Valentina chalked that up to the rediscovery of Natalie and, with it, some sense of family that had been missing before. Or too caught up in the past, perhaps.

"I have never seen you forget a name in all your life," Geoffrey said. "It's one among many reasons I expect you will make a far better queen than I have been a king. And I am aware I gave you no other choice, but I cannot regret that your education and talents will be Murin's gain, not Tissely's."

"I will confess," Valentina said then, "that stepping

aside so that Natalie could marry Rodolfo is not quite the sacrifice some have made it out to be."

Her father's gaze then was so canny that it reminded her that whatever else he was, King Geoffrey of Marin was a force to be reckoned with.

"I suspected not," he said quietly. "But there is no reason not to let them think so. It only makes you more sympathetic."

His attention was caught by something on his phone then. And as he frowned down at it, Valentina looked away. Back out the window to watch the sun drip down over the red-tipped rooftops that sloped all the way to the crystal blue waters below.

She let her hand move, slowly so that her father wouldn't notice, and held it over that faint roundness low in her belly she'd started to notice only a few weeks ago.

If her father thought she was a sympathetic figure now, she thought darkly, he would be delighted when she announced to him and the rest of the world that she was going to be a mother.

A single mother. A princess destined for his throne, with child.

Her thoughts went around and around, keeping her up at night and distracting her by day. And there were never any answers or, rather, there were never any good answers. There were never any answers she liked. Shame and scandal were sure to follow anything she did, or didn't do for that matter. There was no possible way out.

And even if she somehow summoned the courage to tell her father, then tell the kingdom, and then, far more intimidating, tell Achilles—what did she think might happen then? As a princess with no path to the throne, she had been expected to marry the Crown Prince of Tissely. As the queen of Murin, by contrast, she would be expected to marry someone of equally impeccable lineage. There were only so many such men alive, Valentina had met all of them, and none of them were Achilles.

No one was Achilles. And that shouldn't have mattered to her. There were so many other things she needed to worry about, like this baby she was going to be able to hide for only so long.

But he was the only thing she could seem to think about, even so.

The gala was as expected. These things never varied much, which was both their charm and their curse. There was an endless receiving line. There were music and speeches, and extremely well-dressed people milling about complimenting each other on the same old things. A self-congratulatory trill of laughter here, a fake smile there, and so it went. Dignitaries and socialites rubbing shoulders and making money for this or that cause the way they always did.

Valentina danced with her father, as tradition dictated. She was pleased to see Rodolfo and Natalie, freshly back from their honeymoon and exuding exactly the sort of happy charm that made everyone root for them, Valentina included.

Valentina especially, she thought.

She excused herself from the crush as soon as she could, making her way out onto one of the great balconies in this water palace that took its cues from far-off Venice and overlooked the sea. Valentina stood there for a long while, helplessly reliving all the things she'd been so sure she could lock away once she came back home. Over and over—

And she thought that her memory had gotten particularly sharp—and cruel. Because when she heard a foot against the stones behind her and turned, her smile already in place the way it always was, she saw him.

But it couldn't be him, of course. She assumed it was

her hormones mixing with her memory and making her conjure him up out of the night air.

"Princess Valentina," Achilles said, and his voice was low, a banked fury simmering there in every syllable. "I do not believe we have been introduced properly. You are apparently of royal blood you sought to conceal and I am the man you thought you could fool. How pleasant to finally make your acquaintance."

It occurred to her that she wasn't fantasizing at the same moment it really hit her that he was standing before her. Her heart punched at her. Her stomach sank.

And in the place she was molten for him, instantly, she ached. Oh, how she ached.

"Achilles…"

But her throat was so dry. It was in marked contrast to all that emotion that flooded her eyes at the sight of him that she couldn't seem to control.

"Are those tears, Princess?" And he laughed then. It was a dark, angry sort of sound. It was not the kind of laughter that made the world shimmer and change. And still, it was the best sound Valentina had heard in weeks. "Surely those are not tears. I cannot think of a single thing you have to cry about, Valentina. Not one. Whereas I have a number of complaints."

"Complaints?"

All she could seem to do was echo him. That and gaze at him as if she was hungry, and the truth was that she was. She couldn't believe he was here. She didn't care that he was scowling at her—her heart was kicking at her, and she thought she'd never seen anything more beautiful than Achilles Casilieris in a temper, right here in Murin.

"We can start with the fact that you lied to me about who you are," he told her. "There are numerous things to cover after that, culminating in your extremely bad decision to walk out. *Walk out*." He repeated it with three times the fury. "On *me*."

"Achilles." She swallowed, hard. "I don't think—"

"Let me be clear," he bit out, his dark gold gaze blazing as he interrupted her. "I am not here to beg or plead. I am Achilles Casilieris, a fact you seem to have forgotten. I do not beg. I do not plead. But I feel certain, princess, that you will do both."

He had waited weeks.

Weeks.

Having never been walked out on before—ever— Achilles had first assumed that she would return. Were not virgins forever making emotional connections with the men who divested them of their innocence? That was the reason men of great experience generally avoided virgins whenever possible. Or so he thought, at any rate. The truth was that he could hardly remember anything before Valentina.

Still, he waited. When the royal wedding happened the day after she'd left, and King Geoffrey made his announcement about his lost daughter—who, he'd realized, was his actual assistant and also, it turned out, a royal princess—Achilles had been certain it was only a matter of time before Valentina returned to London.

But she never came.

And he did not know when it had dawned on him that this was something he was going to have to do himself. The very idea enraged him, of course. That she had walked out on him at all was unthinkable. But what he couldn't seem to get his head around was the fact that she didn't seem to have seen the error of her ways, no matter how much time he gave her to open her damned eyes.

She was too beautiful and it was worse now, he thought

darkly, here in her kingdom, where she was no longer pretending anything.

Tonight she was dressed like the queen she would become one day, all of that copper hair piled high on the top of her head, jewels flashing here and there. Instead of the pencil skirts he'd grown accustomed to, she wore a deep blue gown that clung to her body in a way that was both decorous and alluring at once. And if he was not mistaken, made her curves seem more voluptuous than he recalled.

She was much too beautiful for Achilles's peace of mind, and worse, she did not break down and begin the begging or the pleading, as he would have preferred. He could see that her eyes were damp, though the tears that had threatened seemed to have receded. She smoothed her hand over her belly, as if the dress had wrinkles when it was very clear that it did not, and when she looked up from that wholly unnecessary task her green eyes were as guarded as her smile was serene.

As if he was a stranger. As if he had never been so deep inside her she'd told him she couldn't breathe.

"What are you doing here?" she asked.

"That is the wrong question."

She didn't so much as blink, and that smile only deepened. "I had no idea that obscure European charities were of such interest to men of your stature, and I am certain it was not on your schedule."

"Are you questioning how I managed to score an invite?" he asked, making no particular move to keep the arrogant astonishment from his voice. "Perhaps I must introduce myself again. There is no guest list that is not improved by my presence, princess. Even yours."

Her gaze became no less guarded. Her expression did not change. But still, Achilles thought something in her steeled. And her shoulders straightened almost imperceptibly.

"I must apologize to you," she said, very distinctly.

And this was what Achilles had wanted. It was why he'd come here. He had imagined it playing out almost exactly this way.

Except there was something in her tone that rubbed him the wrong way, now that it was happening. It was that guarded look in her eyes perhaps. It was the fact that she didn't close the distance between them, but stayed where she was, one hand on the balcony railing and the other at her side. As distant as if she was on some magazine cover somewhere instead of standing there in front of him.

He didn't like this at all.

"You will have to be more specific, I am afraid," he said coolly. "I can think of a great many apologies you owe me."

Her mouth curved, though he would not call it a smile, precisely.

"I walked into a bathroom in an airport in London and saw a woman I had never met before, who could only be my twin. I could not resist switching places with her." Valentina glanced toward the open doors and the gala inside, as if it called to her more than he did, and Achilles hated that, too. Then she looked back at him, and her gaze seemed darker. "Do not mistake me. This is a good life. It is just that it's a very specific, very planned sort of life and it involves a great many spotlights. I wanted a normal one, for a change. Just for a little while. It never occurred to me that that decision could affect anyone but me. I would never have done it if I ever thought that you—"

But Achilles couldn't hear this. Because it sounded entirely too much like a postmortem. When he had traveled across Europe to find her because he couldn't bear the thought that it had already ended, or that he hadn't picked up on the fact that she was leaving him until she'd already gone.

"Do you need me to tell you that I love you, Valentina?" he demanded, his voice low and furious. "Is that what this is? Tell me what you need to hear. Tell me what it will take."

She jolted as if he'd slapped her. And he hated that, so he took the single step that closed the distance between them, and then there was no holding himself back. Not when she was so close again—at last—after all these weeks. He reached over and wrapped his hands around her shoulders, holding her there at arm's length, like some kind of test of his self-control. He thought that showed great restraint, when all he wanted was to haul her toward him and get his mouth on her.

"I don't need anything," she threw at him in a harsh sort of whisper. "And I'm sorry you had to find out who I was after I left. I couldn't figure out how to tell you while I was still with you. I didn't want to ruin—"

She shook her head, as if distressed.

Achilles laughed. "I knew from almost the first moment you stepped on the plane in London. Did you imagine I would truly believe you were Natalie for long? When you could not perform the most basic of tasks she did daily? I knew who you were within moments after the plane reached its cruising altitude."

Her green eyes went wide with shock. Her lips parted. Even her face paled.

"You knew?"

"You have never fooled me," he told her, his voice getting a little too low. A little too hot. "Except perhaps when you claimed you loved me, then left."

Her eyes overflowed then, sending tears spilling down her perfect, elegant cheeks. And he was such a bastard that some part of him rejoiced.

Because if she cried for him, she wasn't indifferent to him. She was certainly not immune to him.

It meant that it was possible he hadn't ruined this, after all, the way he did everything else. It meant it was possible this was salvageable.

He didn't like to think about what it might mean if it wasn't.

"Achilles," she said again, more distinctly this time. "I never saw you coming—it never occurred to me that I could ever be anything but honorable, because I had never been tempted by anything in my life. Only you. The only thing I lied to you about was my name. Everything else was true. Is true." She shook her head. "But it's hopeless."

"Nothing is hopeless," he growled at her. "I have no intention of losing you. I don't lose."

"I'm not talking about a loss," she whispered fiercely, and he could feel a tremor go through her. "This isn't a game. You are a man who is used to doing everything in his own way. You are not made for protocol and diplomacy and the tedious necessities of excruciating propriety. That's not who you are." Her chin tilted up slightly. "But I'm afraid it is exactly who I am."

"I'm not a good man, *glikia mou*," he told her then, not certain what was gripping him. He only knew he couldn't let her go. "But you know this. I have always known who I am. A monster in fine clothes, rubbing shoulders with the elites who would spit on me if they could. If they did not need my money and my power."

Achilles expected a reaction. He expected her to see him at last as she had failed to see him before. The scales would fall from her eyes, perhaps. She would recoil, certainly. He had always known that it would take so very little for people to see the truth about him, lurking right there beneath his skin. Not hidden away at all.

But Valentina did not seem to realize what had happened. She continued to look at him the way she always did. There wasn't the faintest flicker of anything like revulsion, or bleak recognition, in her gaze.

If anything, her gaze seemed warmer than before, for all it was wet. And that made him all the more determined to show her what she seemed too blind to see.

"You are not hearing me, Valentina. I'm not speaking in metaphors. Do you have any idea what I have done? The lives that I have ruined?"

She smiled at that, through her tears. "I know exactly who you are," she said, with a bedrock certainty that shook him. "I worked for you. You did not wine me or dine me. You did not take me on a fancy date or try to impress me in any way. You treated me like an assistant, an underling, and believe me, there is nothing more revealing. Are you impatient? Are you demanding and often harsh? Of course." She shrugged, as if this was all so obvious it was hardly worth talking about. "You are a very powerful man. But you are not a monster."

If she'd reached over and wrenched his mangled little heart from between his ribs with her elegant hands and then held it there in front of him, it could not possibly have floored him more.

"And you will not convince me otherwise," she added, as if she could see that he was about to say something. "There's something I have to tell you. And it's entirely possible that you are not going to like it at all."

Achilles blinked. "How ominous."

She blew out a breath. "You must understand that there are no good solutions. I've had no idea how to tell you this, but our... What happened between us had consequences."

"Do you think that I don't know that?" he belted out at her, and he didn't care who heard him. He didn't care if the whole of her pretty little kingdom poured out of the party behind them to watch and listen. "Do you think that I would be here if I was unaware of the consequences?"

"I'm not talking about feelings—"

"I am," he snapped. "I have not felt anything in years. I have not wanted to feel. And thanks to you all I do now is feel. Too damned much, Valentina." She hadn't actually ripped his heart out, he reminded himself. It only felt as if she had. He forced himself to loosen his grip on her before he hurt her. "And it doesn't go anywhere. Weeks pass, and if anything grows worse."

"Achilles, please," she whispered, and the tears were falling freely again. "I never wanted to hurt you."

"I wish you had hurt me," he told her, something dark and bitter, and yet neither of those things threaded through him. "Hurt things heal. This is far worse."

She sucked in a breath as if he'd punched her. He forged on, throwing all the doom and tumult inside him down between them.

"I have never loved anything in my life, Princess. I have wanted things and I've taken them, but love has always been for other men. Men who are not monsters by any definition. Men who have never ruined anything— not lives, not companies and certainly not perfect, virginal princesses who had no idea what they were signing up for." He shook his head. "But there is nothing either one of us can do about it now. I'm afraid the worst has already happened."

"The worst?" she echoed. "Then you know…?"

"I love you, *glikia mou*," he told her. "There can be no other explanation, and I feel sorry for you, I really do. Because I don't think there's any going back."

"Achilles…" she whispered, and that was not a look of transported joy on her face. It wasn't close. "I'm so sorry. Everything is different now. I'm pregnant."

CHAPTER TEN

ACHILLES WENT SILENT. Stunned, if Valentina had to guess.

If that frozen astonishment in his dark gold gaze was any guide.

"And I am to be queen," she told him, pointedly. His hands were still clenched on her shoulders, and what was wrong with her that she should love that so much? That she should love any touch of his. That it should make her feel so warm and safe and wild with desire. All at once. "My father thought that he would not have an heir of his own blood, because he thought he had only one daughter. But now he has two, and Natalie has married Rodolfo. That leaves me to take the throne."

"I'm not following you," Achilles said, his voice stark. Something like frozen. "I can think of no reason that you have told me in one breath that I am to be a father and in the next you feel you must fill me in on archaic lines of succession."

"There is very strict protocol," she told him, and her voice cracked. She slid her hands over her belly. "My father will never accept—"

"You keep forgetting who I am," Achilles growled, and she didn't know if he'd heard a word she'd said. "If you are having my child, Valentina, this conversation is over. We will be married. That's an end to it."

"It's not that simple."

"On the contrary, there is nothing simpler."

She needed him to understand. This could never be. They could never happen. She was trapped just as surely as she'd ever been. Why couldn't he see that? "I am no longer just a princess. I'm the Crown Princess of Murin—"

"Princess, princess." Achilles shook his head. "Tell me something. Did you mean it when you told me that you loved me? Or did you only dare to tell me in the first place because you knew you were leaving?"

That walloped Valentina. She thought that if he hadn't been holding on to her, she would have staggered and her knees might well have given out from beneath her.

"Don't be ridiculous." But her voice was barely a whisper.

"Here's the difference between you and me, princess. I have no idea what love is. All I know is that you came into my life and you altered something in me." He let go of her shoulder and moved his hand to cover his heart, and broke hers that easily. "Here. It's changed now, and I can't change it back. And I didn't tell you these things and then leave. I accepted these things, and then came to find you."

She felt blinded. Panicked. As if all she could do was cower inside her cage—and worse, as if that was what she wanted.

"You have no idea what you're talking about," she told him instead. "You might be a successful businessman, but you know nothing about the realities of a kingdom like Murin."

"I know you better than you think. I know how desperate you are for a normal life. Isn't that why you switched places with Natalie?" His dark gaze was almost kind.

"But don't you understand? Normal is the one thing you can never be, *glikia mou*."

"You have no idea what you're talking about," she said again, and this time her voice was even softer. Fainter.

"You will never be normal, Valentina," Achilles said quietly. His fingers tightened on her shoulder. "I am not so normal myself. But together, you and I? We will be extraordinary."

"You don't know how much I wish that could happen." She didn't bother to wipe at her tears. She let them fall. "This is a cage, Achilles. I'm trapped in it, but you're not. And you shouldn't be."

He let out a breath that was too much like a sigh, and Valentina felt it shudder through her, too. Like foreboding.

"You can live in fear, or you can live the life you want, Valentina," he told her. "You cannot do both."

His dark gaze bored into her, and then he dropped his other hand, so he was no longer touching her.

And then he made it worse and stepped back.

She felt her hands move, when she hadn't meant to move at all. Reaching out for him, whether she wanted to or not.

"If you don't want to be trapped, don't be trapped," Achilles said, as if it was simple. And with that edge in his voice that made her feel something a little more pointed than simply restless. "I don't know how to love, but I will learn. I have no idea how to be a father, but I will dedicate myself to being a good one. I never thought that I'd be a husband to anyone, but I will be the husband you need. You can sit on your throne. You can rule your kingdom as you wish. I have no need to be a king. But I will be one for you." He held out his hand. "All you have to do is be brave, princess. That's all. Just be a little brave."

"It's a cage, Achilles," she told him again, her voice ragged. "It's a beautiful, beautiful cage, this life. And there's no changing it. It's been the same for untold centuries."

"Love me," he said then, like a bomb to her heart. What was left of it. "I dare you."

And the music poured out from the party within. Inside, her father ruled the way he always did, and her brand-new sister danced with the man Valentina had always imagined she would marry. Natalie had come out of nowhere and taken her rightful place in the kingdom, and the world hadn't ended when brides had been switched at a royal wedding. If anything, life had vastly improved for everyone involved. Why wasn't that the message Valentina was concentrating on?

She realized that all this time, she'd been focused on what she couldn't do. Or what she had to do. She'd been consumed with duty, honor—but none of it her choice. All of it thrust upon her by an accident of birth. If Erica had taken Valentina instead of Natalie, she would have met Achilles some time ago. They wouldn't be standing here, on this graceful balcony, overlooking the soothing Mediterranean and her father's kingdom.

Her whole life seemed to tumble around before her, year after year cracking open before her like so many fragile eggs against the stones beneath her feet. All the things she never questioned. All the certainties she simply accepted, because what was the alternative? She'd prided herself on her serenity in the face of anything that had come her way. On her ability to do what was asked of her, always. What was expected of her, no matter how unfair.

And she'd never really asked herself what she wanted to do with her life. Because it had never been a factor. Her life had been meticulously planned from the start.

But now Achilles stood before her, and she carried their baby inside her. And she knew that as much as she wanted to deny it, what he said was true. She was a coward. She'd used her duty to hide behind. She could have stayed in London, could have called off her wedding. But she hadn't.

And had she really imagined she could walk down that aisle to Rodolfo, having just left Achilles in London? Had she really intended to do that?

It was unimaginable. And yet she knew she'd meant to do exactly that.

She'd been saved from that vast mistake, and yet here she was, standing in front of the man she loved, coming up with new reasons why she couldn't have the one thing in her life she ever truly wanted.

All this time she'd been convinced that her life was the cage. That her royal blood trapped her.

But the truth was, she was the one who did that.

She was her own cage, and she always would be if she didn't do something to stop it right now. If she didn't throw open the door, step through the opening and allow herself to reach out for the man she already knew she loved.

Be brave, he'd told her, as if he knew she could do it. As if he had no doubt at all.

"I love you," she whispered helplessly. Lost somewhere in that gaze of his, and the simple fact that he was here. Right here in front of her, his hand stretched toward her, waiting for her with a patience she would have said Achilles Casilieris did not possess.

"Marry me, *glikia mou*. And you can love me forever." His mouth crept up in one corner, and all the scars Valentina had dug into her own heart when she'd left him seemed to glow a little bit. Then knit themselves into something more like art. "I'm told that's how it goes. But you know me. I always like to push the boundaries a little bit farther."

"Farther than forever?"

And she smiled at him then, not caring if she was still crying. Or laughing. Or whatever was happening inside her that was starting to take her over.

Maybe that was what it was to be brave. Doing whatever it was not because she felt it was right, but because it didn't matter what she felt. It was right, so she had to do it.

"Three forevers," Achilles said, as if he was promising them to her, here and now. "To start."

And he was still holding out his hand.

"Breathe," he murmured, as if he could see all the tumult inside her.

Valentina took a deep breath. She remembered lying in that bed of his with all of New York gleaming around them. He'd told her to breathe then, too.

In. Out.

Until she felt a little less full, or a little more able to handle what was happening. Until she had stopped feeling overwhelmed, and had started feeling desperate with need.

And this was no different.

Valentina breathed in, then out. Then she stepped forward and slid her hand into his, as easily as if they'd been made to fit together just like that, then let him pull her close.

He shifted to take her face in his hands, tilting her head back so he could fit his mouth to hers. Though he didn't. Not yet.

"Forever starts now," Valentina whispered. "The first one, anyway."

"Indeed." Achilles's mouth was so deliriously hard, and directly over hers. "Kiss me, Valentina. It's been too long."

And Valentina did more than kiss him. She poured herself into him, pushing herself up on her toes and winding her arms around his neck, and that was just the start.

Because there was forever after forever stacked up in front of them, just waiting for them to fill it. One after the next.

Together.

CHAPTER ELEVEN

ACHILLES MADE A terrible royal consort.

He didn't know who took more pride in that, he himself or the press corps, who finally had the kind of access to him they'd always wanted, and adored it.

But he didn't much care how bad he was at being the crown princess's billionaire, as long as he had Valentina. She allowed him to be as surly as he pleased, because she somehow found that charming. She'd even supported him when he'd refused to allow her father to give him a title, because he had no wish to become a Murinese citizen.

"I thank you," he had said to Geoffrey. "But I prefer not to swear my fealty to my wife by law, and title. I prefer to do it by choice."

Their wedding had been another pageant, with all the pomp and circumstance anyone could want for Europe's favorite princess. Achilles had long since accepted the fact that the world felt it had a piece of their story. Or of Valentina, certainly.

And he was a jealous bastard, but he tried not to mind as she waved and smiled and gave them what they wanted.

Meanwhile, as she grew bigger with his child she seemed to glow more by the day, and all those dark things in him seemed to grow lighter every time she smiled at him.

So he figured it was a draw.

She told him he wasn't a monster with that same deep certainty, as if she'd been there. As if she knew. And every time she did, he was more and more tempted to believe her.

She gave birth to their son the following spring, right about the time her sister was presenting the kingdom of Tissely with a brand-new princess of their own, because the ways in which the twins were identical became more and more fascinating all the time. The world loved that, too.

But not as much as Valentina and Natalie did.

And as Achilles held the tiny little miracle that he and Valentina had made, he felt another lock fall into place inside him. Maybe they could not be normal, Valentina and him. But that only meant that the love they would lavish on this child would be no less than remarkable.

And no less than he deserved.

This child would never live in the squalor his father had. He would never want for anything. No hand would be raised against him, and no fists would ever make contact with his perfect, sweet face. His parents would not abandon him, no stepfathers would abuse him, and it was entirely possible that he would be so loved that the world might drown in the force of it. Achilles would not be at all surprised.

Achilles met his beautiful wife's gaze over their child's head, lying with her in the bed in their private wing of the hospital. The public was locked outside, waiting to meet this latest member of the royal family. But that would happen later.

Here, now, it was only the three of them. His brand-new family and the world he would build for him. The world that Valentina would give their son.

Just as she'd given it to him.

"You are mine, *glikia mou*," he said softly as her gaze met his. Fiercely. "More now than ever."

And he knew that Valentina remembered. The first vows they'd taken, though neither of them had called it that, in his New York penthouse so long ago.

The smile she gave him then was brighter than the sun, and warmed him all the same. Their son wriggled in his arms, as if he felt it, too. His mother's brightness that had lit up a monster lost in his own darkness, and convinced him he was a man.

Not just a man, but a good one. For her.

Anything for her.

"Yours," she agreed softly.

And Achilles reckoned that three forevers would not be nearly enough with Valentina.

But he was Achilles Casilieris. Perfection was his passion.

If they needed more forever they'd have it, one way or another.

He had absolutely no doubt.

* * * * *

If you enjoyed
THE BILLIONAIRE'S SECRET PRINCESS
don't forget to read the first part of Caitlin Crews's
SCANDALOUS ROYAL BRIDES duet,

THE PRINCE'S NINE-MONTH SCANDAL

Available now!

MILLS & BOON®

MODERN™

POWER, PASSION AND IRRESISTIBLE TEMPTATION

0717/01

16

NEW ENGLAND

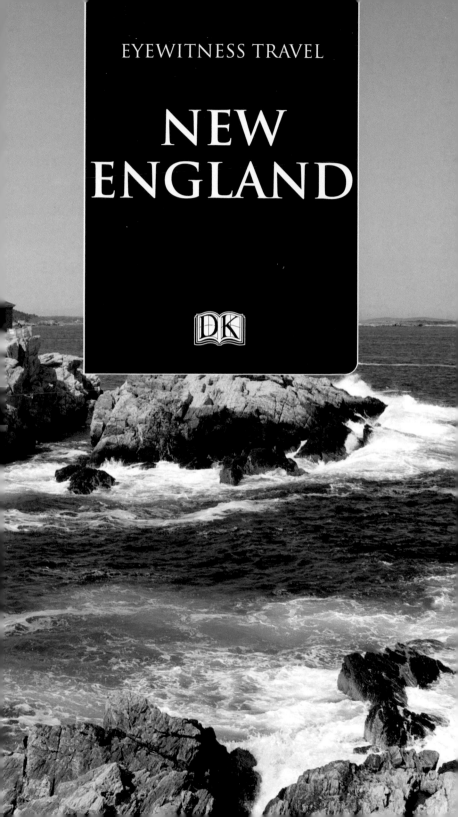

EYEWITNESS TRAVEL

NEW ENGLAND

DK

LONDON, NEW YORK,
MELBOURNE, MUNICH AND DELHI
www.dk.com

Produced By St. Remy Media Inc.,
Montréal, Canada

President Pierre Léveillé
Vice President, Finance Natalie Watanabe
Managing Editor Carolyn Jackson
Managing Art Director Diane Denoncourt
Production Manager Michelle Turbide
Director, Business Development Christopher Jackson
Editor Neale McDevitt
Art Directors Michel Giguère, Anne-Marie Lemay
Senior Research Editor Heather Mills
Researchers Tal Ashkenazi, Jessica Braun, Genevieve Ring
Picture Researcher Linda Castle
Map Coordinator Peter Alec Fedun
Senior Editor, Production Brian Parsons
Indexer Linda Cardella Cournoyer
Prepress Production Martin Francoeur, Jean Sirois
Main Contributors Eleanor Berman, Patricia Brooks, Tom Bross, Patricia Harris, Pierre Home-Douglas, Helga Loverseed, David Lyon
Photographers Alan Briere, Ed Homonylo, David Lyon
Illustrators Gilles Beauchemin, Martin Gagnon, Vincent Gagnon, Stéphane Jorisch, Patrick Jougla, Luc Normandin, Jean-François Vachon
Maps Dimension DPR

Printed and bound by
South China Printing Co. Ltd., China

First published in Great Britain in 2001
by Dorling Kindersley Limited
80 Strand, London WC2R 0RL

14 15 16 17 10 9 8 7 6 5 4 3 2 1

**Reprinted with revisions 2003, 2004, 2005, 2006, 2007,
2009, 2010, 2012, 2014**

A CIP catalogue record is available from the British Library
ISBN 978-1-40932-918-3

Floors are referred to throughout in accordance with American
usage; ie the "first floor" is the floor on street level

Front cover main image: Farmhouse in the beautiful Vermont countryside

◀ Portland Head Lighthouse, Cape Elizabeth, Maine

Contents

Vermont's dazzling fall foliage

West Quoddy Head Light, Maine

Boston

New England Region by Region

Travellers' Needs

Mansion in Waterbury, Vermont

Survival Guide

Costumed interpreter at Plimoth
Plantation, Plymouth,
Massachusetts

Mark Twain House in
Hartford, Connecticut

HOW TO USE THIS GUIDE

This guide helps you to get the most from your visit to New England. *Introducing New England* maps the region and sets it in its historical and cultural context. Each of the six states, along with the city of Boston, has its own chapter describing the important sights using maps, pictures,

and detailed illustrations. Suggestions on restaurants, accommodations, shopping, entertainment, and outdoor activities are covered in *Travelers' Needs*. The *Survival Guide* has tips on everything from changing currency in New England to getting around in Boston.

Boston

Boston has been divided into five sightseeing areas, each one opening with a list of the sights described. All the sights are numbered and plotted on an *Area Map*. The detailed information for each sight is presented in numerical order, making it easy to locate within the chapter.

Sights at a Glance lists the chapter's sights by category: Historic Streets and Squares; Historic Buildings, Churches, Museums, and Theaters; Waterfront Sights; Gardens and Zoos; and Parks and Cemeteries.

2 Street-by-Street map
This gives a bird's-eye view of the heart of each sightseeing area.

A suggested route for a walk covers the more interesting streets in the area.

All pages relating to Boston have yellow thumb tabs.

1 Area map
For easy reference, the sights are numbered and located on a map. The sights are also shown on the Boston Street Finder on pages 126–7.

A locator map shows where you are in relation to other areas of the city center.

Stars indicate the sights that no visitor should miss.

3 Detailed information on each sight
All the sights in Boston are described individually. Addresses, telephone numbers, opening hours, and information on admission charges and wheelchair access are also provided. The key to all the symbols used in the information block is shown on the back flap.

NEW HAMPSHIRE

New Hampshires are known for their fiercely independent nature, born of necessity in the early 1600s when European settlers established outposts in this mountainous and heavily forested region. This natural beauty is still in evidence, in the soaring peaks of the White Mountains, the pristine water of Lake Winnipesaukee, and the small, but scenic coastline.

Introduction

The landscape, history, and character of each state is described here, showing how the area has developed over the centuries and what it has to offer the visitors today.

New England Region by Region

In this book, New England has been divided into the six states, each of which has a separate chapter. The most interesting sights to visit have been numbered on the *Regional Map*.

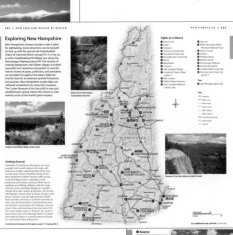

Exploring New Hampshire

Each state of New England can be quickly identified by its color coding, which is shown on the inside front cover.

2 Regional map

This shows the road network and gives an illustrated overview of the whole state. All the sights are numbered, and there are also useful tips on getting around the state.

Story boxes explore specific subjects further.

3 Detailed information

All the important towns and other places to visit are described individually. They are listed in order, following the numbering on the Regional Map. Within each town or city, there is detailed information on important buildings and other sights.

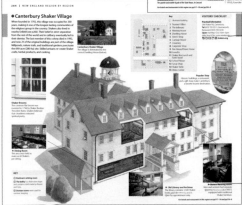

Canterbury Shaker Village

For all the top sights, a Visitors' Checklist provides the practical information you will need to plan your visit.

4 The top sights

These are given two or more pages. Historic buildings are dissected to reveal their interiors; museums and galleries have color-coded floor plans; national parks have maps showing facilities and trails.

Stars indicate the best features and works of art.

INTRODUCING NEW ENGLAND

DISCOVERING NEW ENGLAND

The following tours have been designed to take in as many of the region's highlights as possible, while keeping long-distance travel to a minimum. First comes a 2-day tour of Boston and suggested day trips, followed by the highlights of Eastern Massachusetts. These itineraries can be followed individually or combined to form a week-long tour. Next come two seven-day tours covering the

northern and southern parts of New England. A car is essential for these tours, but the region is quite simple to navigate. This is a lively destination and the area's cultural calendars are always buzzing, so be sure to consult with the states' visitor resources to learn about current happenings and special events. Pick, combine, and follow your favorite tours, or simply dip in and out and be inspired.

Waterplace Park, Rhode Island
A 4-acre (1.6-ha) walkway in downtown Providence, with cobblestone paths, Venetian-style footbridges, and free concerts in summers.

A Week in Southern New England

- Feel the energy of lively **Providence** while pausing for a glimpse of the city's past with a stroll down **Benefit Street's "Mile of History."**

- Relax on a cruise around picturesque **Newport**.

- Appreciate Connecticut's nautical past and present with visits to **Mystic Seaport** and the **Mystic Aquarium**.

- Enjoy a white clam pie at one of **New Haven's** famous pizzerias, and walk off the calories while touring **Yale University's** historic campus.

- Explore **Hartford's** many historical attractions.

- Visit the charming small towns that populate the **Berkshires**.

◀ Painting of the Boston Harbor circa 1750

A Week in Northern New England

- Explore **Mount Desert Island's** many charms, from the **Acadia National Park** to the town of **Bar Harbor**.

- Shop till you drop in Portland's **Old Port District**.

- Be one with nature in New Hampshire's **Lakes Region**.

- Take a hike, hit the slopes, or admire fall foliage in New Hampshire's scenic **White Mountains**.

- Fish, bike, or enjoy a canoe ride surrounded by Vermont's majestic **Green Mountains**.

- Enjoy a **Lake Champlain** pleasure cruise or stroll in bustling **Church Street**.

Portland Head Light, Maine
Erected in 1791 as part of Fort William, Portland Head Light is Maine's oldest lighthouse and is also one of the most photographed lighthouses in the world.

MAINE

Bar Harbor
Acadia
National Park
Mount
Desert
Island
Penobscot
Bay

*Atlantic
Ocean*

ebago
ake

Portland

rtsmouth

em

Peabody Essex Museum
Collections of China trade treasures, historic furniture, and Asian art in a soaring building by top architect Moshe Safdie.

Provincetown
Cape Cod
Cape Cod
Bay
uth
Hyannis
Chatham
ineyard
Haven
Edgartown
Nantucket
Martha's
Vineyard

Key

— A Week in Northern New England

— A Week in Southern New England

— A Week in Eastern Massachusetts

A Week in Eastern Massachusetts

- Explore **Salem's** many historic sights and the world-class **Peabody Essex Museum**.

- Soak in all the culture that **Boston** has to offer.

- Visit one of **Cape Cod's** inviting iconic towns such as **Hyannis** or **Provincetown**.

- Indulge in a relaxing visit to celeb-favorites **Martha's Vineyard** and **Nantucket**.

- Step back in time with a visit to **Plimoth Plantation**.

- Appreciate the area's role in the American Revolution at **Minute Man National Historical Park** in **Concord** and **Lexington**.

Boston Common and the Public Gardens

Two Days in Boston

Boston's importance in American history has left it with a unique architectural heritage. The city's wealth of sights, along with its many parks and gardens, make it a fascinating city to explore.

- **Arriving** Logan Airport, nestled on the water's edge in East Boston, is New England's primary air hub. From the airport, the MBTA provides a variety of transport options via bus, train, and boat. Boston's South Station and Back Bay Stations both provide direct rail and bus service throughout the area.

Day 1
Morning Compact and walkable, **Boston** can be easily explored on foot. Begin your day at **Boston Common and the Public Gardens** (pp68–9). The city's primary green spaces are great for people watching. If the Swan Boats are operating, indulge your inner child with a calming ride. Grab a coffee and stroll the **Back Bay's** (pp98–9) world-class shops before the crowds arrive.

Afternoon Score a bite at one of **Kenmore Square's** casual cafés, then take a tour of **Fenway Park**, the country's oldest baseball park and a true icon of the city. Continue your culture crawl with a relaxing afternoon at one of the nearby museums – the **Museum of Fine Arts** (pp110–13) or the **Isabella Stewart Gardner Museum** (p109). Stroll the handsome streets of trendy **South End** and round off the day at one of the city's hottest tables, which you will have to reserve in advance.

Day 2
Morning Explore some of New England's priciest real estate in the historic **Beacon Hill** (pp64–5) neighborhood. Grab a warming beverage and peruse the numerous high-end boutiques and antique shops that line the neighborhood's primary artery, beautiful **Charles Street** (p66).

Evening Head towards the waterfront to enjoy the city's major water-based attraction, the **New England Aquarium** (pp94–5). Join the steady stream of visitors who fill **Quincy Market** (p84) to shop, dine, and watch colorful street performers. Be

Charlestown Navy Yard and the USS *Constitution*

sure to check out neighboring **Faneuil Hall** (p84), one of the city's most historic sights. Later, stroll through the atmospheric **North End** (pp88–9). Stop by **Paul Revere House** (p92) and **Old North Church** (p91), both are particularly photogenic at night.

Day Trips from Boston

The cities and towns that surround Boston hold a treasure of historical and cultural offerings to satisfy any traveler's interests.

- **Arriving** While hiring a rental car is recommended for maximum flexibility, the MBTA covers much of the Greater Boston area so it is possible to do these with public transport.

Charlestown
Situated a short walk from the North End, on the north bank of the Charles River, **Charlestown** (pp122–3) exudes history. Simply follow the well-marked **Freedom Trail** (p58) and you'll arrive at the **Bunker Hill Monument**, site of the infamous Battle of Bunker Hill. Head back towards the water to visit the historic **Charlestown Navy Yard and USS *Constitution***, pride of the post-revolutionary American Navy. Give your feet a rest by hoisting a pint (and some filling pub grub) at one of the nation's oldest watering holes, the **Warren Tavern**. Don't leave town without exploring other historical spaces such as **City Square** and the **John Harvard Mall**.

Cambridge
While often grouped with Boston, **Cambridge** (pp114–21) is a unique city in its own right, renowned for its strong liberal bent and youthful population. To best appreciate the city's place in worldwide academia, begin your visit by exploring the campuses of **Harvard University** and the **Massachusetts Institute of Technology (MIT)**. Harvard's museums alone rival those of many major cities. In the

afternoon, visit important historic sights such as **Christ Church** and **Cambridge Common**, before exploring dining and shopping options in Harvard, Central, Kendall, and Inman squares.

A Week in Eastern Massachusetts

- **Transport** Though parking can be difficult in Eastern Massachusetts, a car is recommended to follow this itinerary.

Day 1: Salem
Infamous as the city that tried and executed witches in the late 1600s, **Salem** *(pp140–43)* today is a vibrant, entrepreneurial city. Explore its unique history at the **Salem Witch Museum** and **Salem Witch Trial Memorial**. Admire one of the region's best art collections with a visit to the **Peabody Essex Museum**, then take a stroll along the pedestrians-only **Essex Street Mall**, stopping to browse colorful costume shops and occult boutiques. Appreciate the city's rich maritime history by visiting the **Salem Maritime National Historic Site**, then enjoy a meal of fresh seafood by the water.

Day 2: Boston
Pick a day from the Boston itinerary on p12.

Day 3: Cape Cod
Take a ferry, plane, bus, or drive to "**The Cape**," *(pp160–63)* as locals call it. Stop at key commercial destination **Hyannis**, which has the fascinating **JFK Museum**. Then drive north, visiting idyllic **Chatham**, where you can marvel at the area's natural beauty and shifting shoreline, and onwards to festive, colorful **Provincetown**.

Day 4: Martha's Vineyard and Nantucket
Take in **Martha's Vineyard's** *(pp156–7)* key attractions, from rustic natural seascapes to the bustling town of **Vineyard Haven** and the old whaling port of **Edgartown**. Take a quick ferry ride to **Nantucket** *(p157)*, then hire a bicycle to explore the charming, grey-shingled neighborhoods that dot the island. If time allows, hop aboard a **whale watch** and try to spot finbacks, minkes, and humpbacks.

Day 5: Plymouth
Step back in time with a visit to one of America's most authentic living-history museums, **Plimoth Plantation** *(pp154–5)*, where costumed staff recreates the settlement c.1627. Be sure to go through the exhibits devoted to Wampanoag (Native American) life in the same era. Head into Plymouth *(p152)* to explore historical relics such as the **Mayflower II** and **Plymouth Rock**. A meal of fresh lobster on

Gothic-style façade of the Salem Witch Museum, Massachusetts

the waterfront provides a perfect end to a historic day.

Day 6: Boston
Pick a day from the Boston itinerary on p12.

Day 7: Concord and Lexington
The opening skirmishes of the American Revolution, in what is now **Minute Man National Historical Park** *(p148)*, forever link these neighboring towns. Explore the historical markers, statues, and battlegrounds found in the park, then visit Concord's literary attractions including the **Old Manse**, home to author Nathaniel Hawthorne, **Emerson House**, where writer Ralph Waldo Emerson lived, and **Walden Pond**, which essayist Henry David Thoreau called home.

The 17th-Century English Village at Plimoth Plantation, Massachusetts

A Week in Northern New England

- **Airports** Arrive at Portland International Jetport or Bangor International Airport, and depart from Burlington International Airport.

- **Transport** While hiring a car will make for an easier journey, various bus and rail services connect major New England cities and towns.

Bass Harbor Head Light, Mount Desert Island, Maine

Day 1: Mount Desert Island

An easy drive from either of Maine's major airports, **Mount Desert Island** condenses the fabled Maine coast and woods into a single magical spot. Explore the intimate fishing villages that dot the southwest corner, and make time to take the seasonal, **27-mile Loop Road** for a taste of the fabled **Acadia National Park** (pp292–3). Spend the night in **Bar Harbor,** the area's busiest port filled with restaurants, shops, and lodging options.

Day 2 and 3: Portland

Though it has burned down four times since its establishment in 1633, **Portland** (pp284–7), Maine's hub remains one of America's most inviting small cities. Take a stroll along **Congress Street** and through the restored **Old Port District**. The working waterfront, where you can grab an inexpensive seafood meal, and nearby beaches all add to the city's charm and atmosphere. Spend the afternoon appreciating one of the country's largest Winslow Homer collections at the **Portland Museum of Art**.

Start day 3 getting to know the city's history at sites such as the **Victoria Mansion**, **Wadsworth-Longfellow House**, and **Neal Dow Memorial**. No visit to Portland is complete without stopping by the **Portland Head Light** or **Portland Observatory** to snap some postcard-worthy photos.

Day 4: New Hampshire's Lakes Region

Sporty types love New Hampshire's largest lake, **Lake Winnipesaukee** (p268). Ringed by mountains, the lake is dotted with 274 islands and numerous sheltered bays and harbors. Hit the water in a canoe, motorboat, or waterskis, or simply jump in for a swim. Visit **Wolfeboro, Meredith,** and **Weirs Beach,** just a few of the charming small towns worth exploring. Those seeking a calming respite or looking to bird-watch should visit **Squam Lake**, best known as the setting for the 1981 film *On Golden Pond*. Finish the day with a visit to historic **Portsmouth** (pp256–7), one of southern New Hampshire's iconic cities.

Day 5: White Mountains

More than 20 summits define the rugged north country of New Hampshire, of which 1,200 sq miles (3,116 sq km) is set aside as the **White Mountain National Forest** (p269). This is the place in northern New England to make the most of the outdoors: there is summer hiking and climbing, superb fall foliage, and winter skiing. Expect to see wonderful scenery and tumbling waterfalls as you drive onwards to **Bretton Woods** (p271) for your overnight stop.

Day 6: Green Mountains

Another day of outdoor activity beckons. **The Green Mountains** (p248) form the backbone of Vermont, running north-south from the Massachusetts border to Quebec. Use one of the charming ski towns of **Killington** (pp244–5) or **Woodstock** (p251) as your base for exploring this fascinating region. It's worth taking the ski gondola up the mountain for the view alone. Options include fishing, hiking, mountain biking, camping, canoeing, skiing, and snowshoeing. State Route 100, which runs between the east and west ranges is among the most striking roads in the country for fall foliage.

Day 6: Burlington

This friendly, colorful **college town** (pp236–9) is situated on New England's largest lake, **Lake Champlain** (p240). Enjoy a narrated cruise on the **Spirit of Ethan Allen III**, the lake's largest cruise ship, to best appreciate the city's setting and history. See what's on at the **University of Vermont** and its **Robert Hull Fleming Museum**. Round off your tour with dinner on scenic **Church Street**, the city's main artery.

Squam Lake, New Hampshire

For practical information on travelling around New England, see pp374–9

Providence Place Mall, Rhode Island

A Week in Southern New England

- **Airports** Arrive at T.F. Green Airport, located just south of Providence, and depart from Hartford's Bradley International Airport or New York's Albany International Airport.

- **Transport** While hiring a car will make for an easier journey, various bus and rail services connect major New England cities and towns.

Day 1: Providence

Providence (pp178–81) is Rhode Island's largest city, chock full of things to keep a traveler busy. Stroll through the **Waterplace Park** and **Riverwalk** before visiting the city's huge, and very popular, **Providence Place Mall** (pp344–5). Uphill from here are the eclectic neighborhood shops and cheap ethnic eateries situated near the **Brown University** campus. From there take in **Benefit Street's "Mile of History,"** which includes more than 100 houses ranging in style from Colonial and Federal to Greek Revival and Victorian. For a peek into the city's impressive history, visit the **John Brown House**, **Governor Stephen Hopkins House**, and the **First Baptist Church in America**.

Day 2 and 3: Newport

The small city of **Newport** (pp186–91) packs an amazing amount of history into a few square miles. To best appreciate the distinct shoreline, take a pleasure cruise from the waterfront. Later, walk some (or all) of the 3.5-mile (5.5-km) **Cliff Walk**, stopping to wonder at some of the nation's most ornate, historic mansions such as the **Breakers**.

On Day 3, visit the **Naval War College Museum** (the site of America's first naval college), the **Redwood Library and Athenaeum** (the country's oldest continuously-operated library), and **Touro Synagogue**, the nation's first synagogue. Sports fans can't leave town without exploring the **International Tennis Hall of Fame**. End the day with a nightcap at the **White Horse Tavern**, which has been pulling pints since 1673.

Day 4: Southeastern Connecticut

In the southeastern corner of the state resides the historic town of **Mystic**, whose **Mystic Seaport** (pp218–19) museum allows you to walk the decks of a ship or watch carpenters replank a vessel. From there, head to the town's popular aquarium. Gain a sense of New England of yesteryear as you pass through the nearby towns of **Stonington**, **New London**, and **Groton**. Visit one of the region's gargantuan casino resorts, **Foxwoods** and **Mohegan Sun** for a lively night to remember.

Day 5: Connecticut Coast and New Haven

Tour the **Yale University** (pp226–9) campus, almost a living museum with its imposing Gothic architecture and historical artifacts. Walk the parks of **New Haven** (pp224–9), and be sure to sample a local pizza. The town is known for its old-school, thin-crust pies (Frank Pepe's is perhaps the most famous). Enjoy a lazy drive along the coast, stopping to visit the charming small towns of **Madison**, **Guilford**, and **Essex** (pp220–21).

Day 6: Hartford and Litchfield Hills

Explore **Hartford's** (pp202–203) wealth of grand buildings and institutions, from the ornate Victorian-Gothic **Connecticut State Capitol** in Bushnell Park to America's first public art museum, the **Wadsworth Atheneum**. The city was also a hotbed of 19th-century publishing and writing; visit **Mark Twain House** (pp204–205) and adjacent **Harriet Beecher Stowe Center** to better appreciate the city's literary history. Tucked into the northwest corner of the state, not far from Hartford, are the undulating **Litchfield Hills** (pp212–13). Enjoy a leisurely drive through some of the area's most bucolic scenery, or step into cold mountain streams to practise fly-fishing. Try to pass through the idyllic 18th- and 19th-century communities of **Bethlehem**, **Norfolk** and **Kent** (p213), which are filled with white churches and tidy town greens.

Day 7: The Berkshires

Seemingly a world apart from Boston, calmer Western Massachusetts contains the famous **Berkshires** (pp170–71). Tour the Colonial-era villages of the hilly region's south including **Great Barrington** or the former mill towns of the north found in **Pittsfield**. Follow music lovers from across the globe to **Lenox**, home of the esteemed summertime institution, **Tanglewood**. Visit the **Massachusetts Museum of Contemporary Art (MASS MoCA)** (p168). Nature lovers can skip the artistic trappings in favor of challenging hikes over mountaintop trails with sweeping views.

Putting New England on the Map

Northern New England shows the region at its most rural. Vermont is famous for its rolling farmland, and New Hampshire for its White Mountains and the spectacular passes between the peaks. Sparsely populated Maine is covered in dense forest and an intricate network of lakes, streams, and rivers, with a rugged coastline. Southern New England has traditionally been the industrial and cultural hub of the region, with Boston its capital. Massachusetts is the historical center of the New England colonies. Tiny Rhode Island contains some of New England's most extravagant mansions, and Connecticut's proximity to New York City has graced many of its towns and cities with a cosmopolitan flavor.

Area Colors
- Vermont
- New Hampshire
- Maine
- Massachussetts
- Connecticut
- Rhode Island
- Boston

Key
- Interstate
- Major road
- Minor road
- Railroad
- International border
- State border

For map symbols *see back flap*

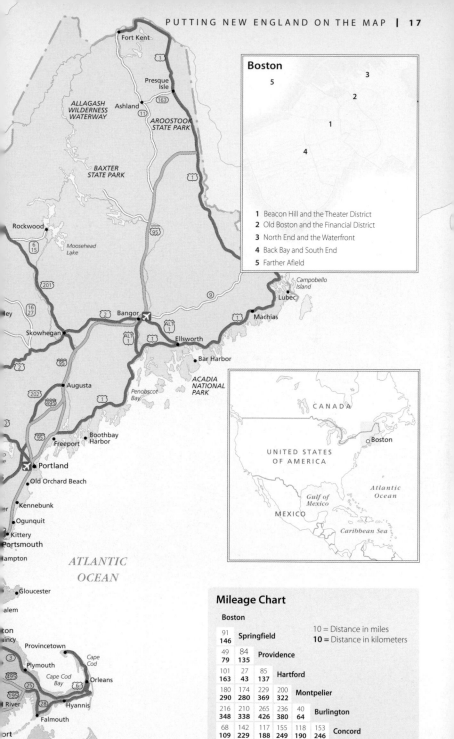

Boston

1 Beacon Hill and the Theater District
2 Old Boston and the Financial District
3 North End and the Waterfront
4 Back Bay and South End
5 Farther Afield

Mileage Chart

Boston

91 **146**	Springfield				10 = Distance in miles				
49 **79**	**84** **135**	Providence			**10** = Distance in kilometers				
101 **163**	**27** **43**	**85** **137**	Hartford						
180 **290**	**174** **280**	**229** **369**	**200** **322**	Montpelier					
216 **348**	**210** **338**	**265** **426**	**236** **380**	**40** **64**	Burlington				
68 **109**	**142** **229**	**117** **188**	**155** **249**	**118** **190**	**153** **246**	Concord			
164 **264**	**254** **409**	**213** **343**	**264** **425**	**197** **317**	**234** **377**	**153** **246**	Augusta		
106 **171**	**189** **304**	**155** **249**	**202** **325**	**171** **275**	**209** **336**	**85** **137**	**59** **95**	Portland	

A PORTRAIT OF NEW ENGLAND

For many people, New England is white-steepled churches, craggy coastlines, and immaculate village greens. However, the region is also home to the opulence of Newport, Rhode Island, the beautiful suburban communities of Connecticut, and the self-assured sophistication of Boston – as well as the picture-postcard villages, covered bridges, timeless landscapes, and back-road gems.

From its beginning, the region has been shaped by both geography and climate. Early explorers charted its coastline, and communities soon sprang up by the sea, where goods and people could be ferried more easily from the Old World to the New. Much of the area's early commerce depended heavily on the ocean, from shipping and whaling to fishing and boat-building. Inland the virgin forests and hilly terrain of areas such as New Hampshire, Vermont, and Maine created communities that survived and thrived on independence. The slogan "Live free or die" on today's New Hampshire license plates is a reminder that the same spirit still lives on.

New England winters are long and harsh, and spring can bring unpredictable weather. As the 19th-century author Harriet Martineau (1802–76) declared, "I believe no one attempts to praise the climate of New England." Combined with the relatively poor growing conditions of the region – glaciers during the last Ice Age scoured away much of New England's precious soil – this has meant that farming has always been a struggle against the capricious forces of nature. To survive in these northeastern states required toughness, ingenuity, and resourcefulness, all traits that became ingrained in the New England psyche. Indeed, the area today is as much a state of mind as it is a physical space.

Few places in America – if any – are richer in historical connections. This is where European civilization first gained a toehold in America. And even long after the American Revolution (1776–83), New England continued to play an important role in the life of the developing nation, supplying many of its political and

Victorian cottage in the Trinity Park district in Oak Bluffs, Massachusetts

◀ Aerial view of a scenic rural village in Stowe, Vermont

Former frontier outpost, Old Fort Western in Augusta, Maine – a view into New England's past

intellectual leaders. That spirit endures. An intellectual confidence, some may call it smugness, persists; some people would say it is with good reason since it was New England that produced the first flowering of American culture. Writers such as Henry David Thoreau (1817–62), Ralph Waldo Emerson (1803–82), Louisa May Alcott (1832–88), and Herman Melville (1819–91) became the first American writers of an international caliber. Even today, New England still figures prominently in the arts and letters, and its famous preparatory schools and the Ivy League universities and other institutions of higher learning continue to draw some of America's best and brightest to the region.

Statue of Samuel de Champlain

Mountains and Seashore

From the heights of the White Mountains – the highest terrain in the northeastern US – to the windswept seashore of Cape

New England-born Louisa May Alcott

Cod, New England offers a stunning range of landscapes. And while industrialization and urbanization have left their stamp, there is plenty of the wild past still in the present. The woods of Maine, for example, look much as they did when American writer and naturalist Henry David Thoreau visited them more than 150 years ago. Vermont's Green Mountains would be instantly recognizable by the explorer Samuel de Champlain (1567–1635) who first saw them almost 400 years ago. But it is not only the countryside that has endured; there are homes scattered throughout New England that preserve an array of early American architectural styles, from Colonial to Greek Revival. Just as the terrain is varied, so, too, is New England's population. The earliest settlers to the region were mostly of English and Scottish stock. Even by the early 19th century New England was still a relatively homogenous society, but this changed dramatically during the mid-1800s as waves of Irish immigrants arrived, driven from their homeland by the potato famines.

This altered the political balance of the area. Whereas the earliest leaders tended to be of British ancestry – men such as

Machine Shed inside the Boott Cotton Mill Museum in Lowell, Massachusetts

President John Adams (1735–1826) and John Hancock (1737–93), signatories of the Declaration of Independence – now Irish-born politicians came to the fore. In 1884 one such man, Hugh O'Brien (1827–95), won the mayoral race in Boston. Meanwhile immigrants from Italy, Portugal, and eastern Europe also arrived, as well as an influx of French-Canadians, who flocked to the mill towns looking for employment. Still, the Irish represented a sizable part of the New England community and their impact on New England society and politics continued to grow, culminating in the election of John F. Kennedy (1917–63) in 1960 as America's first Roman Catholic president. Today some of the fourth-, fifth-, and sixth-generation Irish Americans have ascended to the top of New England's social hierarchy, although there remains a special cachet for people who can trace their ancestry directly to the Pilgrims who first came here aboard the *Mayflower*.

Outdoor Activities

Despite the area's proximity to some of America's most populated areas – a mere 40-mile (64-km) commute separates Stamford, Connecticut, and New York City – it offers a wealth of outdoor activities. There is something here to keep just about any sports enthusiast satisfied. For canoeists and white-water rafters, there are the beautiful Allagash and Connecticut rivers and a captivating collection of lakes. For skiers, resorts such as Killington, Stowe, and Sugarloaf offer some of the best skiing in the eastern US. The region's heavy snowfalls provide a wonderful base for cross-country skiers and snowshoers as well. There's biking on the back roads of New Hampshire and excellent hiking on the Appalachian Trail

White water rafting on the Kennebec River, Maine

Fisherman holding up a large striped bass

and Vermont's Long Trail, considered by many as one of the best hiking trails in the world.

Of course, many popular outdoor activities center around the ocean. There's kayaking among the islands and inlets of the Maine shoreline, wind surfing off Cape Cod, and ample opportunities for sailing, fishing, swimming, and scuba diving up and down the entire New England coast.

The Landscape and Wildlife of New England

Considering its proximity to major cities, rural New England boasts a surprisingly diverse collection of wildlife, including many species of birds, moose, bears, beavers, and, rarely, bobcats. The topography of the region includes rolling hills, dense woodlands, rugged mountains, and a coastline that is jagged and rocky in some areas and sandy and serene in others. Northern Maine has the closest thing to wilderness found in the eastern United States, with hundreds of square miles of trackless land and a vast network of clear streams, rivers, and lakes. New England is also home to the White, Green, and Appalachian mountain ranges.

Bald eagles are found around water, making Maine their favorite New England state.

Coastline

From the crenelated coastline of Maine, which measures almost 3,500 miles (5,630 km) in length, to the sandy beaches of Connecticut, the New England shoreline is richly varied. Here visitors find various sea and shore birds, many attracted by the food provided by the expansive salt marshes that have been created by barrier beaches. A few miles offshore, there is excellent whale-watching.

Mountain Landscape

The western and northern parts of New England are dominated by the Appalachian Mountains, a range that extends from Georgia to Canada. The highest point is 6,288-ft (1,917-m) Mount Washington, also known for drastic weather changes at its summit. Birch and beech trees are plentiful at elevations up to 2,000 ft (610 m). At the higher elevations, pine, spruce, and fir trees are most common.

The great blue heron is the largest of the North American herons. This elegant bird is easily spotted in wetlands and on lakeshores.

White-tailed deer can be found in a range of habitats, from forest edges to open woodland. They are frequently spotted on mountainsides up to 2,000 ft (610 m).

Whales are plentiful off the coast, particularly in the Gulf of Maine, from early spring to mid-October. Finbacks, minke, and right whales are most common, but humpbacks put on the best show, often leaping out of the water.

Coyotes were once all but extinct in the region, but their numbers are on the rise again. They tend to live in forested and mountainous areas, but might be seen in urban areas.

National Wildlife Refuge

With 150 million acres (61 million ha) under its control, the National Wildlife Refuge (NWR) offers protection for some of the country's most ecologically rich areas. The NWR system began in 1903 when President Theodore Roosevelt (1858–1919) established Pelican Island in Florida as a refuge for birds. Thirty-five refuges are located in New England, including 11 in Massachusetts, 6 in Rhode Island, 4 in New Hampshire, 11 in Maine, 1 in Connecticut, and 2 in Vermont. They offer some of the best bird-watching in the region. See www.fws.gov/refuges for more information.

Rachel Carson National Wildlife Refuge, a vast wetland stop for migratory birds

Lakes and Rivers

The rivers and lakes of New England provide fishermen, canoeists, and vacationers in general with a world of outdoor pleasures. The network of waterways is particularly extensive in Maine, which has more lakes than any state in the northeastern United States. Among the rivers, the Connecticut is New England's longest, at more than 400 miles (644 km) in length. It runs from the Canadian border along the Vermont-New Hampshire border and through Massachusetts and Connecticut.

Forests

The logging industry and the switch to agricultural and grazing land – especially for sheep – decimated many of the forests of New England in the 19th and early 20th centuries, but the tide has turned. Vermont, for example, has far more forests today than it did 100 years ago. In the lower elevations, the trees are mostly deciduous, such as ash, maple, and birch, but higher up in the mountains coniferous trees such as balsam fir predominate.

Mallard ducks are a frequent sight throughout New England wetlands. The birds can be seen from April to October, when they migrate to warmer climes.

The pigeon hawk, also known as the merlin, can be found throughout New England, even in urban areas.

Moose are common in Maine, northern Vermont, and New Hampshire. Although they can be spotted in the woods, they are most often seen along the shores of lakes. Drivers should be wary of moose, especially at dawn and dusk.

Chipmunks are seen virtually throughout rural New England, especially in the forests.

Raccoons are commonly seen in wooded areas. They often pay visits to campsites, brazenly foraging for food with dexterous paws.

Fall Foliage

The cool weather in the fall signals more than back-to-school time in New England. It also sounds a clarion call to hundreds of thousands of visitors to head outdoors to gaze in wonder at one of nature's most splendid offerings: the annual changing of leaf colors. Planning foliage tours is an inexact science, however. Generally, leaves start to change earliest in more northern areas and higher up mountainsides. On some mountains in northern New England, for example, the leaves will begin changing color as early as August. In general, the peak period varies from early October in the northern part of the region to late October in the southern section. But this can differ, depending on the weather. Cooler temperatures than normal tend to speed up the leaf-changing timetable and vice versa.

Young boy during fall's pumpkin harvest

Blue sky
The rich palette created by the foliage is made even more dramatic by a backdrop of a deep blue fall sky.

Vermont's Fall Colors

While each of the New England states offers something for "leaf peepers," none can top Vermont. With its rich mix of deciduous trees, the Green Mountain State is anything but just green in late September and October. Inns and hotels tend to be booked up months in advance on the key weekends as the Vermont countryside swells with one of its biggest influxes of out-of-state visitors.

Forest floor
Fallen leaves are more than just beautiful to the eye. They will eventually decay and replenish the humus layer.

Nature's paint box
One of the most remarkable features of the fall foliage season is how it transforms the scenery. Here Quechee Gorge, Vermont's Grand Canyon, has changed its verdant green cloak for one of many colors.

Maple leaf
The maple tree is one of the most common trees in New England. Its leaves change to yellow, red, or orange.

Why Leaves Turn

The changing of leaf colors is not just a capricious act of nature. It is a direct response to the changing realities of the seasons. As daylight hours diminish, the leaves of deciduous trees stop producing the green pigment chlorophyll. With the disappearance of chlorophyll, other pigments that had been hidden behind the chlorophyll's color now burst into view. More pigments are produced by sugars that remain trapped in the leaves. The result is a riotous display that makes this the high point of the year for many visitors. Two of the most spectacular areas for color are Litchfield Hills, Connecticut *(see pp212–13)*, and Penobscot Bay, Maine *(see pp290–91)*. Foliage hotlines give updates and are listed on page 379.

A single crimson leaf aglow on the forest floor

Fall hiking
Hikers should wear bright clothing and stick to well-marked trails and paths in the fall as this is also hunting season in the area.

The Appalachian Trail

The Appalachian Trail is one of the longest footpaths in the world at 2,180 miles (3,508 km). From its southern terminus at Springer Mountain in the state of Georgia to its northernmost point on the summit of Mount Katahdin, Maine, the trail crosses 14 states and two national parks as it winds its way through forests, meadows, and mountains. The trail travels through five of the six New England states, missing only Rhode Island, and reaches its highest point in the northeast on windswept Mount Washington *(see p271)* in New Hampshire. Each year about 400 intrepid souls, called "thru hikers," complete the journey in a single trip. The vast majority of people, however, choose to walk the trail in smaller, more manageable sections. The trail is usually marked by rectangular white blazes painted on trees and rocks, and overnight hikers can take advantage of more than 250 primitive shelters along the route.

Locator Map
▢ New England
--- Appalachian Trail

0 kilometers 50

0 miles 50

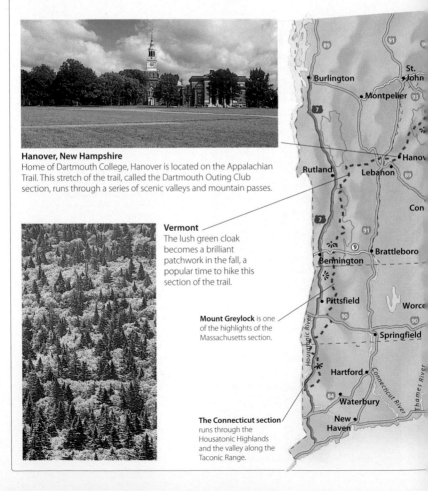

Hanover, New Hampshire
Home of Dartmouth College, Hanover is located on the Appalachian Trail. This stretch of the trail, called the Dartmouth Outing Club section, runs through a series of scenic valleys and mountain passes.

Vermont
The lush green cloak becomes a brilliant patchwork in the fall, a popular time to hike this section of the trail.

Mount Greylock is one of the highlights of the Massachusetts section.

The Connecticut section runs through the Housatonic Highlands and the valley along the Taconic Range.

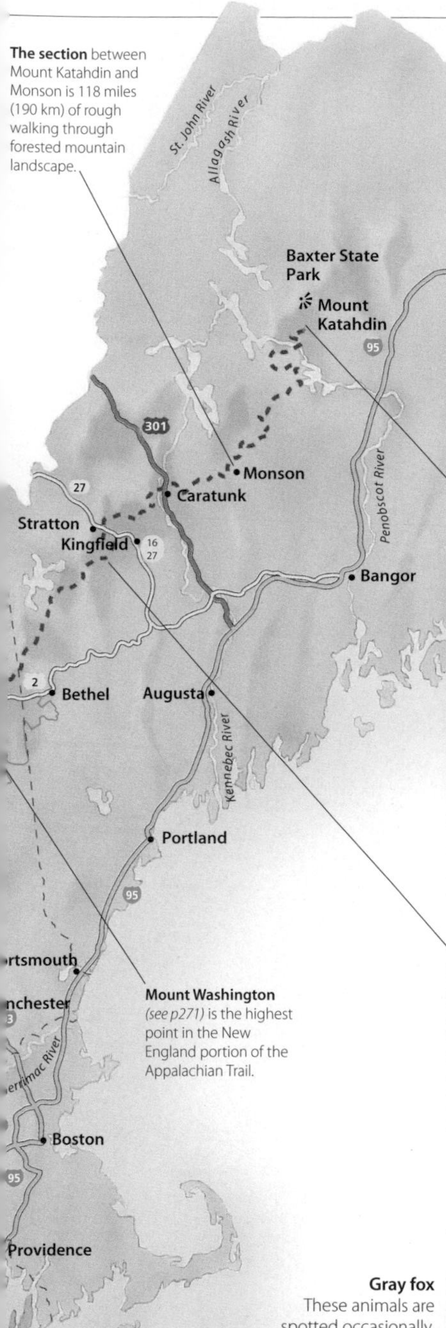
St. John River
Allagash River
Baxter State Park
Mount Katahdin
95
301
Monson
Caratunk
27
Stratton
Kingfield
16
27
Penobscot River
Bangor
2
Bethel
Augusta
Kennebec River
Portland
95
rtsmouth
nchester
errimac River
Boston
95
Providence

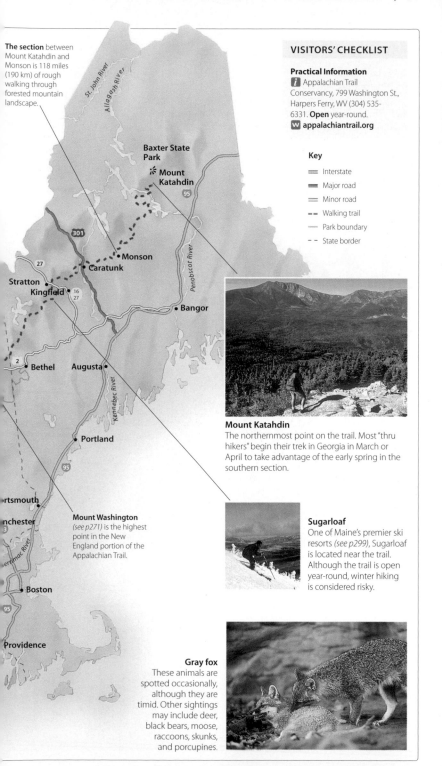

The section between Mount Katahdin and Monson is 118 miles (190 km) of rough walking through forested mountain landscape.

Mount Washington *(see p271)* is the highest point in the New England portion of the Appalachian Trail.

VISITORS' CHECKLIST

Practical Information
Appalachian Trail Conservancy, 799 Washington St., Harpers Ferry, WV (304) 535-6331. **Open** year-round.
appalachiantrail.org

Key

- Interstate
- Major road
- Minor road
- Walking trail
- Park boundary
- State border

Mount Katahdin
The northernmost point on the trail. Most "thru hikers" begin their trek in Georgia in March or April to take advantage of the early spring in the southern section.

Sugarloaf
One of Maine's premier ski resorts *(see p299)*, Sugarloaf is located near the trail. Although the trail is open year-round, winter hiking is considered risky.

Gray fox
These animals are spotted occasionally, although they are timid. Other sightings may include deer, black bears, moose, raccoons, skunks, and porcupines.

Maritime New England

It was the sea that helped open up the region to settlement in the 17th century. The sea also provided New Englanders with a way of life. In the early years, ships worked the fertile waters off Cape Cod for whales, fish, and lobster. Whaling reached its zenith in the 19th century, when hundreds of whaleboats fanned out to the uttermost ends of the Earth. Today the best places to explore the area's rich maritime history are the New Bedford Whaling National Historical Park and the New Bedford Whaling Museum in New Bedford, Massachusetts *(see p125)*, Mystic Seaport *(see pp218–19)*, Connecticut, and the Penobscot Marine Museum in Searsport, Maine *(see p290)*.

Ropes and pulleys were important for hoisting sails and lowering the whaleboats.

Antique whaling harpoons
Harpoons and lances were hand-forged in New Bedford. Harpoons were thrown to attach a line to the whale. When the leviathan tired of pulling boat and men, the lance was used for the kill.

New England's Whalers

Competition in 19th-century whaling was fierce. In 1857 some 330 whalers sailed out of New Bedford, Massachusetts, alone. The Catalpa, portrayed by C.S. Raleigh in his late-1800s painting, is an example of a well-outfitted whaler.

Whaleboats were lowered into the water to hunt and harpoon whales. Whale oil was used for illumination and was a valuable commodity.

Maritime art
Maritime influences still appear throughout New England. This contemporary chest by Harriet Scudder depicts an early whaling scene.

The Ice Trade

The cold winters of northern New England provided the source of a valuable export in the 19th century. In the days before mechanical refrigeration, ice from the region's frozen rivers, lakes, and ponds was cut up into large blocks, packed in sawdust, and shipped as far away as India. To keep the ice from melting, engineers designed ships with special airtight hulls. The ice trade finally collapsed in the late 1800s when mechanical methods for keeping perishables cool began to make ice obsolete for refrigeration in an increasing number of places in the world.

Harvesting ice

Barks were popular whaling vessels in the 19th century because they were maneuverable and could undertake long voyages.

Scrimshaw
New England sailors killed long periods of inactivity on the sea making etchings on whale teeth or jawbones. Ink and tobacco juice added color.

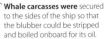

Whale carcasses were secured to the sides of the ship so that the blubber could be stripped and boiled onboard for its oil.

Lighthouses
Nearly 200 lighthouses dot New England's coast, testimony to the area's maritime ties.

Lobster industry
In colonial times, lobster was so common it was used as fertilizer. Today it is considered a delicacy.

New England Architecture

New England architecture encompasses a variety of styles. In the early years of colonization, the influences of England predominated. But after the Revolutionary War (1775–83), the new republic wanted to distance itself from its colonial past. Drawing on French Neo-Classicism, the newest European style of the late 18th century, American architects brought into being a distinctive American version known as Federal. In its efforts to define itself, New England did not reject foreign ideas, however, as evidenced by the Greek Revival style of the early 19th century and the adaptation of English and French Revival styles for the next 100 years.

First Church of Christ in West Hartford, Connecticut

Colonial Style

Colonial style, the style of the period when America was still a British colony, has two aspects: the homes of ordinary people and the more elaborate architecture of public buildings, mansions, and churches. The large wooden houses built in towns and rural areas in New England between 1607 and 1780 constitute one of the area's architectural treasures. Numerous examples survive, and the style has many regional variations. The famous Connecticut "saltbox" houses are an example. They featured distinctive close-cropped eaves and a long back roof that projected over a kitchen lean-to.

Eleazer Arnold House chimney, Providence, Rhode Island

Roof
Shingles became the main roofing material and were frequently used for walls as well.

Chimney
The large chimney provided a vital outlet for smoke.

Jethro Coffin House was built in 1686 and is the oldest surviving structure in Nantucket, Massachusetts. A slot beside the front door allowed inhabitants to see who was standing outside.

Casement window

Windows
Small casement windows were fitted with diamond-shaped panes of glass imported from England.

Door
In keeping with the practical Colonial aesthetics, doors featured a simple, vertical-board design.

Georgian Style

The term Georgian, or Palladian, refers to the mainstream Classical architecture of 18th-century England, which drew on designs of 16th-century Italian architect Andrea Palladio (1508–80). In the colonies and England, these elegant buildings marked the presence of the British ruling class.

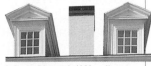

Pedimented dormers, Ladd Gilman House, in Exeter, New Hampshire

Roof
Roofs were less steeply pitched than earlier Colonial-era designs. A delicate balustrade crowns the roof.

Windows
Georgian windows were usually double-hung sash with 6 panes.

Doors
Doors featured a raised-panel design with six or more panels and Classical moldings.

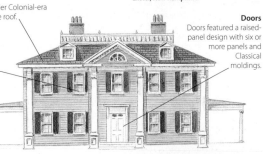

Longfellow House – Washington's Headquarters in Cambridge, Massachusetts, built in 1759. Its facade has Classical columns and a triangular pediment.

Federal Style

American architects viewed the Federal style as a distinctive national statement. Some Federal buildings drew on both Greek and Roman architecture, representing the tenets of democracy and republicanism. Federal style is more restrained than Georgian, with less intricate woodwork.

The Colony House in Newport *(see pp186–91)*, Rhode Island

Roof
Neo-Classical roofs were often flat.

Facade
Neo-Classical facades were less decorated than Georgian. Often stories were separated by bands of stone called string courses.

Fanlights
Fanlights, frequent in Georgian archi-tecture, were also found in Neo-Classical design.

Gardner-Pingree House in Salem, Massachusetts, is known for its graceful proportions.

Greek Revival Style

Popular between 1820 and 1845, this style is a more literal version of Classical architecture than the Federal style. Greek Revival buildings typically borrowed the façades of ancient Greek temples, often sensitively re-creating them in wood.

Samuel Russell House in Middletown, Connecticut, features a white exterior common in Greek Revival structures.

Providence, Rhode Island, church door

Facade
The "temple fronts" of Greek Revival buildings were inspired by the archaeological discoveries in Greece and Turkey in the 18th century.

Columns
These Corinthian columns faithfully follow conventions of ancient Greek architecture.

Colleges and Universities

New England is not only the cradle of American civilization, it is also the birthplace of higher education in the New World. Harvard University *(see pp116–21)* was founded in 1636, only 16 years after the Pilgrims arrived at Plymouth Rock *(see pp152–3)*. Four of the country's eight renowned Ivy League colleges are located in New England: Harvard, Brown *(see p179)*, Dartmouth *(see p267)*, and Yale *(see pp226–9)*. Here higher learning goes hand in hand with tradition and culture. Many of America's most famous art collections and natural history museums are found on campus grounds. As well, many of the top-ranked liberal arts colleges are found here, including Bowdoin and all-women Smith and Wellesley Colleges.

1764 Rhode Island College, later Brown University, is founded in Providence, Rhode Island

1852 The Harvard crew wins inaugural Harvard-Yale Regatta – beginning one of the longest rivalries in US college sports

1778 Phillips Academy is founded by educator Samuel Phillips in Andover, Massachusetts

1781 John Phillips, uncle of Samuel, founds Phillips Exeter Academy in Exeter, New Hampshire

1636 Harvard University is founded in Cambridge, Massachusetts; 12 students enroll in the inaugural year

1701 Puritan clergymen found Collegiate School in Saybrook, Connecticut

1801 Daniel Webster graduates from Dartmouth and goes on to an illustrious career as US statesman and orator

1640	1680	1720	1760	1800	184●
1640	1680	1720	1760	1800	184●

1642 Physics becomes a mandatory subject at Harvard, using text by Aristotle

1777 Brown's University Hall building is used as barracks for Colonial troops during War of Independence

1817 Harvard Law School is established

1832 Yale Art Gallery is founded after US artist John Trumbull donates some 100 pieces of art from his personal collection

1717 Collegiate School is moved to New Haven, Connecticut, and is renamed Yale in 1718 in honor of benefactor Elihu Yale

1844 Yale graduate Samuel Morse sends world's first telegraphic message in Morse code

1853 Franklin Pierce, graduate of Bowdoin College in Brunswick, Maine, is elected 14th president of the United States

1861 Massachusetts Institute of Technology (MIT) is founded

1868 William Dubois is born. Dubois would go on to become the first black person to earn a Ph.D. from Harvard

1919 Philanthropist and Brown University graduate John D. Rockefeller, Jr. donates 8 sq miles (20 sq km) of Maine's Mount Desert Island for use as a preserve. His further gifts would form almost one-third of Acadia National Park *(see pp292–3)*

1925 S.J. Perelman graduates from Brown; goes on to win Academy Award for screenplay of *Around the World in 80 Days* (1956)

1957 Theodor Geisel (Dr. Seuss), Dartmouth alumnus, publishes *The Cat in the Hat*

1992 Yale graduate Bill Clinton is elected 42nd president of the United States

2004 M.I.T. completes Stata Center, designed by Frank Gehry, to house computer science and Artificial Intelligence laboratories

2008 Harvard Law School graduate Barack Obama is elected as the first African-American president of the United States

2010 University of Connecticut women's basketball team sets college record for most consecutive wins by either men's or women's teams

1880	1920	1960	2000	2040

1880	1920	1960	2000	2040

1946 Percy Bridgman becomes first Harvard physicist to receive Nobel Prize in Physics

1969 Women are admitted to Yale's undergraduate program

2000 Yale graduate George W. Bush is elected 43rd president, following in the footsteps of his father George H.W. Bush – Yale graduate and 41st president

1877 Former slave Inman Page becomes first African-American to graduate from Brown

1861 Yale awards country's first Ph.D. degrees

New England Boarding Schools

New England boasts the most prestigious collection of college preparatory, or "prep," schools in the US. The two preeminent institutions are Phillips Academy in Andover, Massachusetts, and Phillips Exeter Academy *(see p260)* in Exeter, New Hampshire. Both are private, coeducational schools and attract the sons and daughters of some of the country's wealthiest and most influential families. Other prominent prep schools include Choate Rosemary Hall in Wallingford, Connecticut, and Groton in Groton, Massachusetts.

Campus of Phillips Exeter Academy

Literary New England

Writing in his seminal work *Democracy in America* (1835), French historian Alexis de Tocqueville (1805–1859) declared, "The inhabitants of the United States have, then, at present, no literature." Less than two decades later that scenario had changed radically. By then, writers such as Ralph Waldo Emerson (1803–82), Henry David Thoreau (1817–62), and Nathaniel Hawthorne (1804–64) were creating works that would take their place among the classics of 19th-century literature – and that was just in one town, Concord *(see pp148–9)*, Massachusetts. Since that first flowering, New England writers have been taking their place among the best in the world.

Author Nathaniel Hawthorne (1804–64)

Ralph Waldo Emerson, speaking to Transcendentalists in Concord

Father of Transcendentalism

Born in Boston, Ralph Waldo Emerson graduated from Harvard University in 1821 and became the pastor of the Second Church (Unitarian) in Boston in 1829. In many ways Emerson turned his back on his formal religious education in the 1830s when he founded the Transcendentalism movement. Among other things, Emerson's writings espoused a system of spiritual independence in which each individual was responsible for his or her own moral judgments. Moving to Concord in 1834, the popular essayist and lecturer soon became known as the "Sage of Concord" for his insightful teachings.

Concord was also the birthplace of Emerson's most famous disciple, Henry David Thoreau. A one-time school teacher, Thoreau worked as a pencil maker before quitting to undertake his lifelong study of nature. Deeply influenced by the Transcendentalist belief that total unity with nature was achievable, Thoreau built a small cabin at Walden Pond *(see p149)* in 1845, living as a recluse for the next two years. In 1854 he published *Walden; or, Life in the Woods*, in which he outlined how people could escape a life of "quiet desperation" by paring

away the extraneous, anxiety-inducing trappings of the industrial age and living in harmony with the natural world.

19th-century Literary Flowering

It was also in Concord that Nathaniel Hawthorne penned *Mosses from an Old Manse* in 1846. Hawthorne later returned to his hometown, Salem *(see pp140–41)*, Massachusetts, where he wrote his best-known work, *The Scarlet Letter* (1850). Moving to Lenox in western Massachusetts, Hawthorne became friends with Herman Melville (1819–91), who wrote his allegorical masterpiece *Moby-Dick* (1851) in neighboring Pittsfield. The book drew its inspiration from the voyage that

Illustration from Herman Melville's *Moby-Dick*

Henry David Thoreau's simple grave in Concord, Massachusetts

Visitor on the porch of the Robert Frost house in New Hampshire

Melville made from New Bedford, Massachusetts, to the South Seas aboard the New England whaler *Acushnet*.

Like Melville, Mark Twain (1835–1910) was not a New Englander by birth. However, it was during his long stay in Hartford *(see pp202–205)*, Connecticut, that he penned the novels that would vault him into worldwide prominence, including *The Adventures of Tom Sawyer* (1876), *The Adventures of Huckleberry Finn* (1885), and *A Connecticut Yankee in King Arthur's Court* (1889).

19th-century Women Authors

Although opportunities for women were limited in 19th-century America, several New England female writers still managed to leave their mark on literature. One of the region's most famous – and mysterious – literary figures was Emily Dickinson (1830–86). Born in Amherst *(see pp166–7)*, Massachusetts, she was educated at the Mount Holyoke Female Seminary *(see p166)* before withdrawing from society in her early 20s. Living the rest of her life in her family's home, Dickinson wrote more than 1,000 poems – the vast majority of which remained unpublished until after her death. Today her finely crafted poems are admired for their complex rhythms and intensely personal lyrics.

Cover of sheet music for Harriet Beecher Stowe's *Uncle Tom's Cabin*

The greatest single indictment of the slavery that would catapult America into civil war came from the pen of Harriet Beecher Stowe (1811–96), who would later become Mark Twain's next door neighbor in Hartford. *Uncle Tom's Cabin; or, Life Among the Lowly* (1852) told the story of a slave family's desperate flight for freedom to a rapt, largely sympathetic audience worldwide. Louisa May Alcott (1832–88) – yet another Concord resident – left a lasting and loving portrait of domestic life in the United States during the Civil War in *Little Women* (1868), a perennial favorite of children.

20th Century

In the 20th century, New England continued to play a defining role in American literature, spawning native writers as diverse as "Beat" chronicler Jack Kerouac *(see p146)* and the "Chekhov of the suburbs," John Cheever (1912–82). The region has also provided a fertile base for transplanted New Englanders. The poet Robert Frost (1874–1963), a native of San Francisco, lived most of his life in Vermont and New Hampshire, and the mountains, meadows, and people of the region figure prominently in his poetry, which won the Pulitzer Prize an unprecedented four times. Poet and novelist John Updike (1932–2009) lived much of his life in Ipswich, Massachusetts, and set both *Couples* (1968) and *The Witches of Eastwick* (1984) in the northeast. Novelist John Irving was born in Exeter, New Hampshire, in 1942. Much of his later fiction is set in New England, including *The World According to Garp* (1978) and *Cider House Rules* (1985). Perhaps the area's best-known living writer is horror master Stephen King (b.1947), a longtime resident of Bangor, Maine. Boston-based mystery writer Dennis Lehane (b. 1966) sets his novels in gritty working-class neighborhoods.

Fright master and longtime Bangor resident Stephen King

NEW ENGLAND THROUGH THE YEAR

New England is really a year-round tourist destination – depending on what it is people are looking to do. Generally, spring is the shortest season. Occurring sometime between April and June, spring in New England can be short-lived but glorious; wildflowers bursting forth in colorful bloom provide a feast for the eyes. Summer is the busiest period for tourism. With the good weather stretching from mid-June into early September, this part of the year is characterized by warm temperatures that have people flocking to lakes and the ocean. Fall is when New England is at its most beautiful, with its lush forests changing from green to a riot of gold, red, and orange. The peak period for fall foliage generally occurs from mid-September to late October. Winter, which usually lasts from December through to mid-April, is often marked by heavy snowfalls – a boon for winter sport enthusiasts.

Cars decorated with flowers in Nantucket's Daffodil Festival

Spring

New England's shortest season is sometimes little more than a three-week interval between winter and summer. As well as being the prime time for maple syrup tapping, spring brings with it a host of festivals.

April

Boston Marathon *(third Monday, April)*, Boston, MA. America's oldest and most prestigious marathon.
Patriot's Day *(third Monday, April)*, Lexington and Concord, MA. Costumed reenactments of the pivotal battles that were waged at the outset of the Revolutionary War.
Daffodil Festival *(late April)*, Nantucket, MA. The town is decked out in millions of yellow daffodils.

May

Lilac Sunday *(early May)*, Boston, MA. The celebration of the Arnold Arboretum historic lilac collection includes tours, performances, and picnics amid the blooms.
Cape Cod Maritime Days *(mid-May)*, Cape Cod, MA. Celebration of seaside life with lectures, boat rides, kayaking, and kite-flying.
Gaspee Days *(mid-May–mid-June)*, Cranston and Warwick, RI. Reenactment of the burning of a British schooner.
Brimfield Antique Show *(May, July, and September)*, Brimfield, MA. Dealers from across the US gather at this show to sell their wares.
Lobster Days *(late May)*, Mystic, CT. A lobsterbake popular with locals and visitors.

Patriot's Day celebration in Lexington, Massachusetts

Delicious lobsters served up during Lobster Days in Mystic, Connecticut

Waterfire *(May–Oct)*, Providence, RI. This dazzling art event features 100 bonfires, which are lit on the city's three rivers.

Early June

Cambridge River Festival *(early June)*, Cambridge, MA. This community festival features food and arts.
Discover Jazz Festival *(early June)*, Burlington, VT. Jazz, blues, and gospel are the highlights of this popular festival.
Circus Smirkus *(early June–mid-August)*. This international youth circus performs around New England.

Summer

New England summers can be hot and humid. This is vacation time for students and families, making the region a very busy place, especially the coastline and beaches.

Average daily hours of sunshine

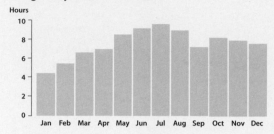

Hours

Sunshine Chart
New England's weather can vary greatly from year to year. Generally, the short spring is cloudy and wet, giving way to better weather in June. July and August are usually the sunniest months. Bright fall days out among the colorful foliage are spectacular.

Late June
Secret Garden Tour *(mid-June)*, Newport, RI. Private gardens open to the public for self-guided walking tour.
International Festival of Art and Ideas *(mid-June–July)*, New Haven, CT. A showcase of performance, visual arts, literature, film, and family events.
Jacob's Pillow Dance Festival *(mid-June–late August)*, Becket, MA. Ballet, jazz, and modern dance feature in the country's oldest dance festival.
Windjammer Days *(late June)*, Boothbay Harbor, ME. Shoreside events complement parade of graceful sailboats.
Stowe Garden Festival *(late June)*, Stowe, VT. Seminars and tours of formal gardens.
Antique Tractor Festival *(late June)*, Farmington, ME. Antique machinery demonstrations, crafts, tractor pulls, and a flea market.
Block Island Race Week *(late June)*, Block Island, RI. The largest sailing event on the coast.
Vermont Quilt Festival *(late June–early July)*, Essex Junction, VT. A quilting celebration.
Williamstown Theater Festival *(late June–August)*, Williamstown, MA. Featuring classical and new theater productions.

July
Independence Day Celebrations *(July 4th)*, throughout New England. Parades, fireworks, and concerts.
Tanglewood Music Festival *(early July–late August)*, Lenox, MA. Boston Symphony and Boston Pops orchestras

One of many festivals celebrating New England's nautical past

give concerts on this grand estate *(see p171)*.
Riverfest *(July)*, Hartford, CT. Fireworks and free concerts along the Connecticut River.
Vermont Cheesemakers Festival *(mid-July)*, Shelburne, VT. More than 40 makers of cheese and other local products offer samples.
American Independence Festival *(mid-July)*, Exeter, NH. Beer festival, fireworks and reenactments.
Newport Regatta *(mid-July)*, Newport, RI. This huge regatta attracts some 300 boats.
Guilford Handcrafts Exposition *(mid-July)*, Guilford, CT. This event features pottery, glass, jewelry, folk art, and quilts.
Lowell Folk Festival *(late July)*, Lowell, MA. Dance troupes, musicians, and ethnic food in historic Downtown Lowell.
Newport Folk Festival *(late July–early August)*, Newport, RI. One of the country's top folk festivals, held at Fort Adams State Park.

August
Maine Lobster Festival *(early August)*, Rockland, ME. Lobster and live entertainment are on the menu at this event.
League of New Hampshire

![July 4th road markings]
July 4th road markings

Craftsmen Annual Fair *(early August)* Newbury, NH. The oldest crafts fair in the US features craft demonstrations, work-shops, performing arts, and 200 booths selling high-quality crafts.
Addison County Fair *(early August)*, New Haven, VT. This is one of the state's largest agricultural fairs.

Newport Jazz Festival *(early August)*, Newport, RI. International jazz stars gather to perform at this festival.
Mystic Outdoor Arts Festival *(mid-August)*, Mystic, CT. This art show attracts 300 artists.
Wild Blueberry Festival *(mid–late August)*, Machias, ME. Foot races, pie-eating contests, and musical comedy celebrate the berry harvest.
Brooklyn Fair *(late August)*, Brooklyn, CT. The country's oldest continuously running agricultural fair has ox pulls and livestock shows.
Champlain Valley Fair *(late August–early September)*, Essex Junction, VT. Horse shows and midway rides are part of this huge fair.
Classic Yacht Regatta *(late August–early September)*, Newport, RI. More than 100 vintage wooden yachts are on parade in this regatta.
Thomas Point Beach Bluegrass Festival *(late August–early September)*, Brunswick, ME. World-class lineup of musicians.

Average monthly precipitation

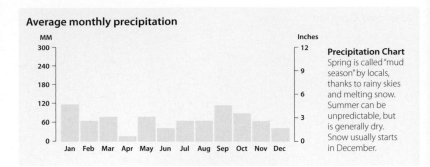

Precipitation Chart
Spring is called "mud season" by locals, thanks to rainy skies and melting snow. Summer can be unpredictable, but is generally dry. Snow usually starts in December.

Autumn

Many people consider the fall to be New England's most beautiful season. Bright, crisp autumn days are made more glorious by the brilliant fall foliage (see pp24–5).

September

Pawtucket Arts Festival (early September), Pawtucket, RI. Music and food for all tastes and colorful dragon boat races are some of the highlights of this festival.
International Seaplane Fly-In (early September), Greenville, ME. Spectators gather on the shores of Moosehead Lake to observe floatplane competitions and sample local food.
Windjammer Festival (early September), Camden, ME. A celebration of Maine's fleet of classic sailing ships.
Vermont State Fair (early September), Rutland, VT. One of the most popular agricultural fairs in the state.
Woodstock Fair (early September), South Woodstock, CT. The state's second-oldest agricultural fair includes crafts, go-cart races, livestock shows, and petting zoos for children.
Norwalk Oyster Festival (early September), East Norwalk, CT. This nationally acclaimed celebration includes fireworks, antique boats, and lots of oyster sampling.
The Big "E" (last two weeks of September), Eastern States Exhibition Ground, West Springfield, MA. One of New England's biggest fairs, with rodeos, rides, and a circus.
Harvest Festivals (late September), throughout New

A Harvest Festival, this one in Keene, New Hampshire

England. Parades, apple picking, and hay rides are just some of the events held around the region to celebrate the fall harvest.
Sugar Hill Antique Show (late September), Sugar Hill, NH. A popular, long-running antique show attracts numerous dealers and their wares.
Fryeburg Fair (late September–early October), Fryeburg, ME. Maine's oldest county fair emphasizes its agricultural roots,

but also offers midway rides and live entertainment.
Northeast Kingdom Fall Foliage Festival (late September–early October), throughout northern Vermont. Different towns hold foliage-related bus tours, hiking parties, and family events.

October

Mount Greylock Ramble (Columbus Day), Adams, MA. The whole community climbs the state's highest mountain.
Woonsocket Autumnfest (early October), Woonsocket, RI. Live music, craft displays, a midway, and a Columbus Day parade are top events.
Haunted Happenings (October), Salem, MA. A month-long festival celebrating the city's witch-related past (see pp140–43) and Halloween.
Wellfleet Oysterfest (mid-October), Wellfleet, MA. Local cuisine, road race, oyster shuck-off, and music.
Keene Pumpkin Festival (late October), Keene, NH. Celebration featuring up to 25,000 lit jack-o'-lanterns.

Brilliant colors, heralding Northeast Kingdom Fall Foliage Festival

Average monthly temperature

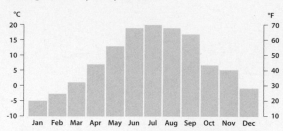

Temperature Chart
New England temperatures vary greatly through the year. In the summer, temperatures of 90° F (32° C) are quite frequent, while the thermometer can dip to 0° F (-18° C) or lower in winter. In general, it is warmer along the coast and in the southern section of New England.

November

Dinner in a Country Village *(Nov–Mar)*, Old Sturbridge Village, Sturbridge, MA. Dinners cooked on open hearths relieve the winter chill.

Holiday Craft Exhibition and Sale *(mid-Nov–Dec 31)*, Brookfield, CT. Craft artists put unique wares up for sale.

Thanksgiving Celebration *(mid–late November)*, Plymouth, MA. Thanksgiving traditions of the past are celebrated in historic homes. Visitors can also enjoy a Thanksgiving dinner at Plimoth Plantation *(see pp154–5)*.

Festival of Light *(late November–early January)*, Hartford, CT. Constitution Plaza is transformed into a spectacular world of more than 200,000 white lights.

Winter

New England winters are often marked by heavy snowfalls, particularly in the mountainous areas farther inland. Temperatures can also plunge drastically overnight and from one day to the next. This, of course, is a boon for people who enjoy winter sports, as New England has some of the most popular ski centers in the eastern US.

December

Christmas at Blithewold *(late November–December)*, Bristol, RI. Traditional Christmas celebrations are celebrated in this beautiful mansion.

Festival of Trees and Traditions *(early December)*, Hartford, CT. Hundreds of beautiful trees and

A traditional Thanksgiving dinner celebration

wreaths are on display at Wadsworth Athenaeum.

Festival of Lights *(early December)*, Wickford Village, RI. This family-oriented festival includes tree- and window-decorating competitions, hayrides, and live music.

Christmas Tree Lighting *(early December)*, Boston, MA. The huge tree in front of the Prudential Tower and Shopping Center is lit up with bright lights.

Candlelight Stroll *(mid-December)*, Portsmouth, NH. The town's historic Strawbery Banke district *(see pp258–9)* is resplendent with antique Christmas decorations.

Boston Tea Party Reenactment *(mid- December)*, Boston, MA. Costumed interpreters bring to life the famous protest that precipitated the Revolutionary War.

New Year's Eve Celebrations *(December 31)*, throughout New England. Family-oriented festivities including fireworks, ice carvings, and performances can be found around the region.

January

Vermont Farm Show *(late January)*, Barre, VT. Vermont's premier winter show includes a variety of agricultural displays and livestock exhibits.

Chinese New Year *(late January–early March)*, Boston, MA. The location for this colorful festival is Boston's Chinatown.

February

National Toboggan Championships *(February)*, Camden, ME. Daredevils of all sizes and ages come to compete in this high-speed, often hilarious, event.

Stowe Derby *(late February)*, Stowe, VT. This is one of the oldest downhill and cross-country skiing races in the country.

March

Boston Flower and Garden Show *(March)*, Boston, MA. Meticulous landscaped gardens and thousands of new blooms announce the end of winter.

St. Patrick's Day Parades *(mid-March)*, Boston and Holyoke, MA. Two of New England's oldest and largest celebrations.

Maple Season *(late March)*, throughout New England. Visitors can see how maple sap is collected and made into syrup.

Musicians in Boston's St. Patrick's Day Parade

THE HISTORY OF NEW ENGLAND

The early history of New England is the history of the United States itself, for it is here that Europeans first gained a toehold in America and where much of the drama of forming a new country was played out. But even after the rest of the country had been populated, New England continued to exert influence on the political, economic, and intellectual life of the country.

No one can say for sure which Europeans first made landfall in New England. Some historians claim that the Vikings, after first reaching Newfoundland around AD 1000, eventually ventured as far south as Massachusetts. Others suggest that Spanish, Portuguese, or Irish explorers were the first Old World visitors. But one thing is sure: none of these peoples actually discovered the area. Native Americans already had called the region home for several thousand years. They were descendants of nomads from central Asia who had journeyed to what is now Alaska via the then-dry Bering Strait between 20,000 and 12,000 years ago. Slowly they migrated east.

The earliest fossil evidence of human activity in the area dates back to 9000 BC. By the time the first European came ashore, the region was populated by about 20,000 Native Americans. Most of them were members of the Algonquin "nation," a loose conglomeration of a dozen or so tribes that occasionally engaged in violent internecine struggles. Their inability to unite would later prove a fatal flaw when confronted by a common foe – white settlers. Unlike their Asian ancestors, the Algonquins, also known as Abenakis ("people of the dawn"), had given up nomadic life. They ate moose, deer, birds, and fish, but grew crops, too – maize, called Indian corn, beans, and pumpkins.

Map of the Northeast, printed in England a month after the Declaration of Independence was signed

◄ *Native American Indians Cooking and Preparing Food* c.1850 by J. Fumagalli

Embarkation and Departure of Columbus from the Port of Palos, undated painting by Ricardo Balaca

The Age of Discovery

The voyage of Christopher Columbus (1451–1506) to the New World in 1492 fired the imagination of maritime nations in Europe. Soon seafarers from England, France, and Spain were setting forth to explore the New World on behalf of their respective kings and queens. In 1497 the Italian explorer John Cabot (c.1425–1499) reached New England from Bristol, England, and claimed the land, along with all the territory north of Florida and east of the Rocky Mountains, for his English patron, Henry VII (1457–1509). By the end of the 16th century, helped largely by the 1588 defeat of the Spanish Armada, England was beginning to achieve mastery of the seas.

In 1606 England's King James I (1566–1625) granted a charter to two ventures to establish settlements in America. The Virginia Company was assigned an area near present-day Virginia; the Plymouth Company was granted rights to a more northern colony. This second group ran into trouble early on. One of its

**King James I
(1566–1625)**

ships strayed off course and was captured by the Spanish near Florida. Another ship made it to New England, but had to turn back to England before winter arrived. In May 1607 two ships left Plymouth, England, with approximately 100 colonists. Three months later they made landfall at the mouth of the Kennebec River, where the settlers constructed Fort St. George. Their first winter proved to be an especially cold and snowy one, and the furs and mineral wealth fell far short of what the colonists expected. After just a year, the so-called Popham Colony was abandoned.

Despite this inauspicious beginning, the Plymouth Company hired surveyor John Smith (1580–1631) to conduct a more extensive evaluation of the territory. In 1614 Smith sailed along the Massachusetts coast, observing the region. His findings, published in *A Description of New England*, not only coined the name of the region, but also painted a glowing picture of this new land and its "greatnesse" of fish and

25,000-12,000 BC Central Asian nomads cross Bering Strait to become first North Americans

7,000-1,000 BC Warming temperatures lead to development of New England's forests

| 25,000 BC | 10,000 BC | AD 1000 | 1500 |

10,000 BC Humans move into New England area after deglaciation

Leif Eriksson in Viking boat

AD 1000 Vikings sail to Newfoundland, Canada, and move south along the coast

timber. Of all the places in the world, concluded Smith, this would be the best to support a new colony.

Colonial New England

While the explorers of the early 17th century probed the shoreline of New England, events were taking place in Europe that would have a far-reaching impact on the settlement of the New World. The Reformation of the 16th century and the birth of the Protestant faith had created an upheaval in religious beliefs – particularly in England, where Henry VIII (1491–1547) had severed ties with Rome and had made sure that parliament declared him head of the Church of England.

Protestant Puritans believed that the Church of England, despite its claim to represent a reformed Christianity, was still rife with Catholic practices and that their faith was being debased in England, especially after James I, who was suspected of having Catholic sympathies, succeeded Elizabeth I in 1603. Puritans were persecuted for their beliefs and found themselves facing a stark choice: stay at home to fight against overwhelming odds or start anew somewhere else.

A small, radical faction of Puritans, known as Separatists, emigrated to Holland. The lifestyle of the Dutch did not live up to the demanding

Puritan governor addresses Colonists in 1621

standards of the Separatists' stern orthodoxy. As a result, they negotiated a deal with the Plymouth Company to finance a "pilgrimage" to America. In September 1620 they set sail. After a grueling 66-day voyage, their ship, the *Mayflower*, landed at what is now Provincetown *(see p160)*, Massachusetts.

It was a short-lived stay. The barren, sandy coast seemed a forbidding place, so the ship sailed on to Plymouth Rock *(see pp152–3)*, where the fatigued Pilgrims disembarked on December 26, 1620. During the winter of 1620–21, half of the Pilgrims succumbed to scurvy and the rigors of a harsh New England winter. But with the arrival of spring, the worst seemed to be behind them. The settlers found an ally among the indigenous people in Squanto (d.1622), a member of the Pawtuxet tribe who had been taken to England in 1605. Squanto had returned to the New World in 1615, and when word reached him that the English had arrived, he soon helped negotiate a 50-year peace treaty between the Pilgrims and the chief of the local Wampanoag tribe. Squanto also taught the newcomers how to live in their adopted home. He showed them how to shoot and trap, and told them which crops to grow. The first harvest was celebrated in the fall of 1621 with a three-day feast of Thanksgiving.

Pilgrims board the *Mayflower* in 1620

1500	1600		1615	1620
1497 John Cabot explores North American coast	**1607** First North American colony founded at Jamestown	**1614** John Smith names territory New England		**1620** Pilgrims land at Plymouth, Massachusetts, aboard the *Mayflower*
1492 Christopher Columbus discovers the New World	**1602** Captain Bartholomew Gosnold lands on Massachusetts coast		**1616** Smallpox epidemic kills large number of New England Indians	*First feast of Thanksgiving*
	John Smith			**1621** Pilgrims celebrate feast of Thanksgiving

The Battle of Bunker Hill

The first major battle of the Revolutionary War took place in Boston on June 17, 1775, and actually was fought on Breed's Hill. The Americans had captured heavy British cannon on Breed's and Bunker hills overlooking Boston Harbor, which gave them a commanding position. Britain's first two attacks on Breed's Hill were repelled by the outnumbered defenders. The Colonial soldiers were running low on ammunition, however, which gave rise to commander Colonel William Prescott's orders, "Don't fire until you can see the whites of their eyes!" Reinforced with 400 fresh troops, British forces made a bayonet charge and seized the hill, forcing the Americans to retreat to nearby Bunker Hill. The British suffered more than 1,000 casualties to approximately 150 for the Americans. The battle reinforced the confidence of the American troops that had first been kindled by their successes at Lexington and Concord.

Bunker Hill Monument, a granite obelisk, honors Colonial casualties.

In the Heat of the Battle

John Trumbull's 1786 painting Battle of Bunker Hill depicts the hand-to-hand combat of the skirmish, fought mainly with bayonets and muskets. Victory came at a price. As one British soldier commented, "It was such a dear victory, another such would have ruined us."

Colonial General Joseph Warren dies in final moments of battle after being shot in the head.

Declaration of Independence Less than a year after the battle, the Second Continental Congress adopted the Declaration of Independence, which outlined the framework for democracy in the United States.

Attack on Breed's Hill
Prior to the infantry assault on the Colonial position, British men-of-war bombarded Breed's Hill with cannonade. Portions of nearby Charlestown caught fire and burned during the bombing.

A British officer
prevents grenadier's coup de grâce.

British Firelocks
Loading a musket involved shaking gunpowder into a pan just above the trigger as well as into the barrel itself. The powder in the barrel was then tamped down with a small rod. This time-consuming process meant that soldiers stood unprotected on the battlefield as they reloaded.

British troops storm Colonial positions with renewed vigor after having suffered massive casualties on first two attempts.

British Major John Pitcairn collapses into his son's arms after being shot in chest, only to die while receiving medical treatment for his wounds.

Colonel William Prescott

Born in Groton, Massachusetts, William Prescott (1726–95) led the Colonial forces during the battle of Bunker Hill. In the initial stages of the fight, British warships bombarded the Americans' fortified position with heavy cannon. The untested Colonial troops were taken aback, especially when a private was decapitated by a cannonball. Sensing his men were disheartened, Prescott, covered in the slain soldier's blood, leapt atop the redoubt wall and paced back and forth in defiance of the bombs bursting around him. His brave gesture galvanized the troops, who went on to make one of the most courageous stands of the Revolutionary War.

Death of Metacomet (King Philip) in 1676

Colonial New England

From this modest beginning, the settlement began slowly to prosper and expand. Within five years the group was self-sufficient. Nine years later the Massachusetts Bay Company was founded, which sent 350 people to Salem *(see pp140–43)*.

A second, much larger group joined the newly appointed governor, John Winthrop (c.1587–1649), and established a settlement at the mouth of the Charles River. They first called their new home Trimountain, but renamed it Boston in honor of the town some of the settlers had left in England.

During the 1630s immigrants started spreading farther afield, creating settlements along the coast of Massachusetts and New Hampshire, and even venturing inland.

However, the colonists' gain proved to be the Natives' loss. Initial cooperation between both groups gave way to competition and outright hostility as land-hungry settlers moved into Indian territory. War first erupted with the Pequot tribe in 1637, which resulted in their near annihilation as a people. The hostility reached its peak at the outset of the King Philip's War (1675–6), when several hundred members of the Narragansett tribe were killed by white settlers near South Kingston, Rhode Island.

Weakening Ties

The sheer distance dividing England and New England and the fact that communication could move no faster than wind-borne ships meant that there was very little contact between Old World and New. The colonists were largely self-governing, and there was no representation from them in the British parliament. Efforts by London to tighten control over the colonies were sporadic and in most cases successfully resisted until the Seven Years' War between Britain and France (1756–1763) assured British domination of North America. Ironically, British success created the conditions that lessened the colonists' dependence on the mother country and also led to their growing estrangement. The colonies, especially New England, would come to feel that they no longer had to rely on British protection against the French in Canada and their Indian allies. Moreover, Britain's efforts after 1763 to derive a revenue from the colonies

England's George III
(1738–1820)

1636 Harvard is founded, becoming America's first college

Harvard booster

1656 Puritans of Massachusetts Bay Colony begin systematic persecution of newly arrived Quakers with imprisonment, banishment, and hanging

1676 King Philip's War ends when Wampanoag chief Metacomet is betrayed and killed

1630   **1660**   **1675**   **1690**

1630 Puritans led by John Winthrop found Boston

1636 Murder of two colonists, supposedly by Pequot Indians, sparks the beginning of Pequot War

Salem gravestone

1692 Salem witch trials begin, leading to the execution of 20 people

to help cover the debt incurred by the war and to contribute to imperial defense met growing resistance. The cry of "No taxation without representation" would become a rallying call to arms for the independence move-ment, with the most vocal protests coming from New England.

The taxation issue came to a head under the reign of King George III (1738–1820), who ascended the throne of Great

Paul Revere's 1770 engraving of the Boston Massacre

Britain in 1760. The Hanoverian king believed that the American colonists should remain under the control of Britain, and enacted a series of heavy taxes on various commodities, such as silk and sugar. In 1765 British parliament passed the Stamp Act, which placed a tax on commercial and legal documents, newspapers, agendas, and even playing cards and dice. The act had a galvanizing effect throughout New England as its incensed inhabitants banded together and refused to use the stamps. They even went so far as to hold stamp-burning ceremonies.

Parliament eventually repealed the act in 1766, but this did not end the issue. In fact, at the same time that the Stamp Act was rescinded, it was replaced by the Declaratory

British stamp for American colony goods

Act, which stated that every part of the British Empire would continue to be taxed however the parliament saw fit. To make sure that the colonists would not flout the law, the British sent two regiments to

Boston to enforce its control. The troops, called Redcoats for their distinctive uniforms, proved decidedly unpopular. A series of small skirmishes between them and local sailors and workers culminated in the Boston Massacre (March 5, 1770), in which the British soldiers opened fire on an unruly crowd, killing five, including a free black man, Crispus Attucks.

Revolutionary Spirit

After the massacre an uneasy truce ensued. A simmering distrust remained between the two sides, and it only needed a suitable provocation to boil over again. That provocation came in the form of yet another proclamation – this one giving the East India Company the right to market tea directly in America, thus bypassing American merchants. When three ships arrived in Boston Harbor in 1773 with a shipment to unload, a group of about 60 men, including local politicians Samuel Adams (1722–1803) and John Hancock (1737–93), disguised themselves with Indian headdresses and then boarded the ships. They dumped 342 tea chests, valued at £18,000, into the harbor. The Boston Tea Party (see p93) was celebrated by the

Protesters during the 1773 Boston Tea Party

(see p93)

704 The *Boston News Letter*, America's first newspaper, is published

1737 John Hancock, an original signatory of the Declaration of Independence, is born

John Hancock's signature

1773 New taxes spur Boston Tea Party

1710	1725	1740	1750	1770

1713 Boatyard in Gloucester, Massachusetts, produces America's first schooner

1770 British soldiers kill five in Boston Massacre

Crowd in Philadelphia celebrating the signing of the Declaration of Independence on July 4, 1776

colonists as a justifiable act of defiance against an oppressive regime. Parliament responded by passing the Intolerable Acts of 1774. These included the closing of the port of Boston by naval blockade until payment was made for the tea that had been destroyed.

On September 5, 1774, 56 representatives from the various American colonies, including New England, met in Philadelphia to establish the First Continental Congress to consider how to deal with grievances against Britain. The first concrete step toward nationhood had been taken.

Minutemen repelling the British, who were trying to march through to Concord

Although the British troops garrisoned in Boston in the mid-1770s represented a formidable force, a large part of New England lay beyond their control. In the countryside, locals stockpiled arms. In 1775 the royal governor of Massachusetts, General Thomas Gage (1721–87), learned about such a cache at Concord (see pp148–9), 20 miles (32 km) west of Boston. He ordered 700 British soldiers to travel there under cover of darkness and destroy the arms.

The Americans were tipped off by dramatic horseback rides from Boston by Paul Revere and William Dawes. By the time the troops arrived at Lexington a few miles to the east of Concord, 77 colonial soldiers had set up a defensive formation, slowing the British advance. The Redcoats pressed onward to Concord, where close to 400 American patriots, called Minutemen for their ability to muster at a moment's notice, repelled the British attack. By the end of that day, April 19, 1775, 70 British had been killed and the casualty toll was 273. American losses were 95.

Boston shipbuilding c.1850

New England also became a world center for the whaling industry, as local ships plied the Seven Seas in search of the leviathans of the deep, which were killed for their oil, baleen, and blubber. The burgeoning shipbuilding industry that had sprung up along the coast also supplied a fleet of fishing boats that trolled the Grand Banks and the waters off Cape Cod, returning with their holds full of cod and halibut.

The days of discussion were now clearly over. Colonial leaders signed the Declaration of Independence on July 4, 1776, and the American Revolution had begun. For the next six years the war would be waged first on New England soil, but then mostly beyond its borders at such key places as the Valley Forge encampment, Pennsylvania, and Yorktown, Virginia. Although the fighting ceased in 1781, the war officially came to an end with the signing of the 1783 Treaty of Paris.

Ultimately it was an invention of the Industrial Revolution that transformed New England into an economic powerhouse. In the late 18th century, the first of Richard Arkwright's (1732–92) cotton spinning machines was imported to North America from England and installed on the Blackstone River at Pawtucket (see pp174–5), Rhode Island. Previously cotton had been processed on individual looms in homes. Arkwright's device permitted cotton spinning to be carried out on factory-sized machines, which increased productivity a thousandfold. Soon mills sprang up, mainly

A New Industrial Power

The fledgling United States of America was rich in natural resources, especially in New England. The region had excellent harbors that gave it access to the West Indies, Europe, and farther afield, where a developing maritime trade (see pp28–9) with the spices, teas, and other riches of the Far East proved increasingly lucrative. Indeed, New England ships became a familiar sight at docks from Nantucket (see p157) to New Guinea and from Portsmouth (see pp256–7) to Port-au-Prince, Haiti.

Antique harpoon

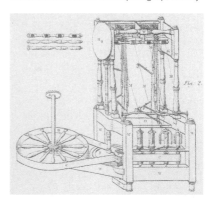

Richard Arkwright's sketch for his revolutionary cotton spinning machine

800 National census results: 5.3 million people

Noah Webster

1805	1810	1815	1820	1825

1806 New Haven's Noah Webster publishes *Compendious Dictionary of the English Language*

1820 Maine gains independence from Massachusetts and becomes 20th state in the Union

in Massachusetts, in towns such as Lowell *(see pp146–7)*, Waltham, and Lawrence. By the mid-19th century, New England held two-thirds of America's cotton mills. The region offered two main advantages: a ready supply of rivers to power the mills' machinery and an increasing flow of cheap labor. Escaping the Potato Famine in the 1840s, numerous Irish immigrants fled to Massachusetts, where the mill towns beckoned with dormitory housing for their employees. Despite their numbers, however, this group faced discrimination. In Boston many such newcomers settled in squalid tenements along the city's waterfront. Eventually the Irish would come to dominate Boston politics, but for much of the 19th century they faced a daily struggle just to survive.

The extent of industrialization was felt in a relatively small area of New England, mostly Massachusetts, Rhode Island, and Connecticut. In the hinterland of Vermont, New Hampshire, and Maine, farming and logging remained the key industries well into the 20th century. These far-flung regions provided some of the manpower for the heartland's factories, as people left the hardscrabble life of subsistence farming for new lives farther south. Northern New England also helped supply the factories with some of their raw materials. The forests of Vermont, for example, were hacked down to make grazing land for sheep, which supplied wool for the textile mills.

Irish peasant contemplating failed crop

Abolitionist New England

New England's role in 19th-century America was not merely one of economic powerhouse. The region also dominated the fields of education, science, politics, and architecture, as well as serving as the cultural heart of the nation, with Boston and its environs producing some of the nation's most influential writers and thinkers. The Massachusetts capital was also the center of a prominent protest against slavery, which was firmly entrenched in the southern states and reviled in much of the North.

William Lloyd Garrison (1805–79) began publishing a newspaper called *The Liberator* in 1831. In Garrison's view, "There is only one theme which should be dwelt upon till our whole country is free from the curse – SLAVERY." His polemics in *The Liberator* drew the wrath of pro-slavery forces. The House of Representatives of the southern state of Georgia offered $5,000 for his arrest. But Garrison continued publishing his newspaper, never missing an issue until it ceased publication at the end of the Civil War (1861–65), when slavery had been expunged from American society. Some residents of New England towns went beyond merely reading and writing about the injustices of slavery. Stirred by Garrison and the so-called abolitionist

Abolitionist William Lloyd Garrison

Colt six-shooters

1830	1845	1860

1835 Connecticut's Samuel Colt invents the six-shooter handgun

1851–2 *Uncle Tom's Cabin* appears in serial form in *The National Era* newspaper

1861 Civil War begins

1831 Abolitionist William Lloyd Garrison publishes first edition of anti-slavery newspaper *The Liberator*

1840 Ireland's first Potato Famine devastates country

1851 Herman Melville publishes *Moby-Dick*, written in the southern Berkshires

1865 Civil War ends, leaving some 620,000 Americans dead

movement, some anti-slavery exponents offered safe houses for what came to be known as the Underground Rail-road. This loosely connected network of escape routes helped slaves fleeing the South make their way to freedom in the North and in Canada, beyond the reach of slave hunters. Towns such as New Bedford (see p125), Massachusetts, Portland (see pp284–7), Maine, and Burlington (see pp236–9), Vermont, served as key "stations" on the slaves' road to freedom. The Underground Railroad was immortalized in Harriet Beecher Stowe's novel Uncle Tom's Cabin; or, Life Among the Lowly (1852).

Declining Power

In the latter part of the 19th century there were signs that the days of New England's industrial preeminence were over. The transcontinental railroad had opened up the West to an army of new immigrants, which flooded in after the Civil War. The New World was a far, far bigger place than it had been when the Pilgrims landed, and the opportunities were boundless. The Great Plains encompassed thousands of square miles of arable land that New England farmers could only dream about. And for those looking for a more temperate climate, many other areas of the US now beckoned.

Meanwhile, the exploitation of natural resources and the development of new technologies were changing the face of industry. The discovery of

Cover of sheet music based on Harriet Beecher Stowe's Uncle Tom's Cabin by artist Louisa Corbauy

petroleum meant that whale oil lost its economic importance, while steam engines offered a way of powering mills that no longer required river waterpower – one of the natural advantages upon which the region had relied.

These problems were compounded by the fact that local labor was organizing to fight for better pay and working conditions, driving some factories to move to the South where labor costs were cheaper. Between 1880 and 1923, the South's share of the cotton-weaving industry rose from 6 percent to almost 50 percent.

The call for unionization even reached into the ranks of the police force, sparking one of America's most bitter labor

Child laborer in cotton spinning plant

1884 Mark Twain publishes The Adventures of Huckleberry Finn, a novel he wrote at his home in Hartford, Connecticut

Modern Red Sox fan

1875

1890

1910

1882 Massachusetts-born poet/philosopher Ralph Waldo Emerson dies

1897 Country's first subway is opened in Boston

1903 Boston Red Sox win first World Series baseball championship

Ralph Waldo Emerson

confrontations. In 1919 Boston's men in blue sought to affiliate themselves with the American Federation of Labor. The city's police commissioner refused the request, and the entire force went on strike. Boston was beset by a wave of crime and riots, prompting the governor to send in the militia. By the time order was restored, at least five people had been killed and dozens had been wounded.

The loss of New England's economic importance was accompanied by a wave of change in the social makeup of the region. What had long been a homogeneous society – largely Protestant and of English or Scottish descent – was transformed by a rapid influx of immigrants. By the turn of the 20th century more than two-thirds of the residents of Massachusetts had at least one parent born outside the country.

The Depression of the 1930s hit the inhabitants of New England particularly hard. Unemployment in some towns topped 40 percent and wages plunged dramatically. World War II provided a temporary boost to the economy as shipyards and munition factories worked

Women making shell casings in a munitions plant during World War II

overtime to provide the military with the tools of their trade. However, with the return of peace, New England struggled to find its way in the new post-war era, and its economy continued to have its difficulties. The glory days, at least economically speaking, seemed to be irretrievable.

New England Rebirth

Even in its worse decline, as factories crumbled and residents headed for greener pastures, New England still possessed advantages that set the stage for recovery. One important factor was its concentration of higher educational institutions *(see pp32–3)*.

Unknown artist's depiction of Harvard University campus c.1857

Calvin Coolidge

1914–1918 World War I

1923 Vermont's Calvin Coolidge is sworn in as country's 30th president by his father

| 1915 | 1925 | 1935 | 1945 | 1955 |

1929 Stock market crash marks beginning of Great Depression

Depression soup kitchen

1939–45 World War II: US enters conflict in 1941

1954 World's first nuclear submarine is built in Groton, Connecticut

Falmouth Heights Beach in Cape Cod

As the Manufacturing Age gave way to the Information Age beginning in the 1960s, knowledge and adaptability became increasingly valuable commodities. With their well-endowed research facilities, venerable institutions such as Harvard University *(see pp116–21)* and the Massachusetts Institute of Technology *(see p115)* attracted a new generation of young entrepreneurs looking to cash in on this newest opportunity. Meanwhile a son of one of Boston's most prominent families was proving that New England's impact on the national political scene was not over yet. John F. Kennedy *(see pp108–109)*, the great-grandson of an Irish potato-famine immigrant, became America's first Catholic president in 1960.

Starting in the mid-1980s, companies producing computer software and biomedical technology set up shop in the Boston suburbs and southern New Hampshire. The meteoric growth of high-tech industries represented a second revolution of sorts – proving far more valuable than the Industrial Revolution of the previous century. Meanwhile certain businesses, such as the insurance trade, weathered the shifts in the economy better than traditional manufacturing ventures, with Hartford *(see pp202–204)*, Connecticut, continuing to serve as the insurance capital of the nation.

One thing that all the economic upheavals did not change was New England's stunning physical beauty: the craggy coastline of Maine, the beaches of Cape Cod *(see pp160–63)*, the picturesque Vermont villages, and the coiled-up mountains of New Hampshire. As America became more prosperous and its workers had more free time in which to spend their mounting disposable income, tourism became an even bigger business than manufacturing had once been. The skiers, fishermen, beachcombers, antique hunters, campers, and others who flocked to the Northeast year-round pumped billions of dollars into the states' economies. By the 1990s tourism ranked alongside manufacturing as one of New England's most profitable industries.

Somehow, it seems fitting. After all, it was the beauty of the area that had helped convince people such as John Smith, close to four centuries ago, that New England had a viable future. And now, that same natural beauty is proving to be both timeless and lucrative, helping to bring about a renaissance in the prosperity of the place where American society had begun so tenuously so many years before.

Vermont's trademark rural landscape

1961 Massachusetts-born John F. Kennedy becomes first Catholic president

1990 Thieves make off with artwork valued at $100 million from Boston's Isabella Stewart Gardner Museum

2005 New England Patriots win the Super Bowl

2004 Red Sox "reverse the curse" and win Baseball World Series

2008 Boston Celtics win their 17th NBA championship

2009 Senator Edward M. Kennedy (D-Mass) dies

| 1960 | 1970 | 1980 | 1990 | 2000 | 2010 | 2020 |

1968 Senator Robert Kennedy is assassinated in Los Angeles

1963 President Kennedy is assassinated in Dallas

1999 John F. Kennedy, Jr. dies in plane crash off Martha's Vineyard

Robert F. Kennedy

2004 Massachusetts legally recognizes gay marriage

2011 Boston Bruins win hockey's Stanley Cup

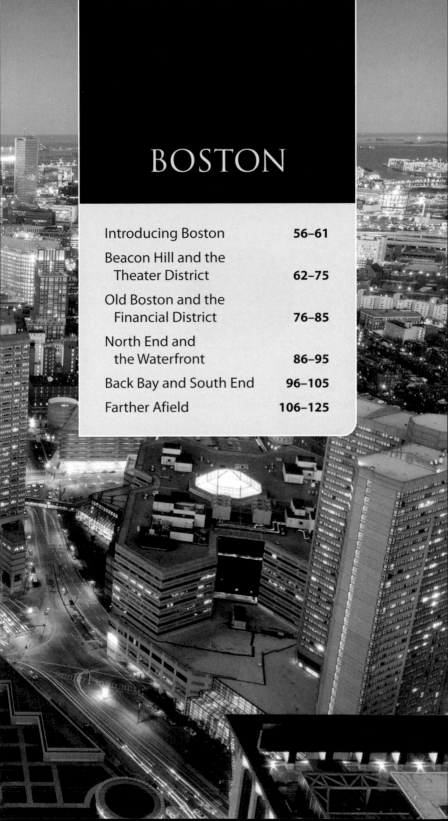

BOSTON

Boston's Best

The city of Boston's Athenian self-image is manifested in dozens of museums, galleries, and archives, paramount of which is the Museum of Fine Arts. The city's importance in America's history has left it with a unique legacy of old buildings, with much fine religious and civic architecture, including Trinity Church and Massachusetts State House. This strong architectural heritage continues to the present day, and includes modern structures such as the John Hancock Tower. Boston's wealth of sights, along with its many parks and gardens, make it a fascinating city to explore.

Boston Common and Public Garden
At the heart of the city, the spacious common, and smaller, more formal Public Garden, provide open space for both sport and relaxation.

Trinity Church
Perhaps Boston's finest building, this Romanesque Revival masterpiece by Henry Hobson Richardson was completed in 1877.

John Hancock Tower
Dominating the Back Bay skyline, with its mirrored façade reflecting the surroundings, the John Hancock Tower is New England's tallest building.

CHARLES ST

BEACON STREET

ARLINGTON ST

BOYLSTON STREET

HUNTINGTON AVE

COLUMBUS AVENUE

WASHINGTON ST

0 kilometers   0.5
0 miles   0.5

Museum of Fine Arts
One of the largest museums in North America, the M.F.A. is famous for its Egyptian, Greek, and Roman art, and French Impressionist paintings.

◀ Brightly-lit city of Boston at night

Old State House
The seat of British colonial government until independence, the building later undertook many different uses. It now houses a museum.

Old North Church
Dating from 1723, this is Boston's oldest surviving church. Due to its role in the Revolution, it is also one of the city's most important historical sites.

New England Aquarium
This aquarium displays a huge array of creatures from the world's oceans. Researchers here are also involved in key international fish and whale conservation programs.

CAUSEWAY

HANOVER ST

COMMERCIAL ST

CONGRESS ST

ATLANTIC AVE

SUMMER ST

Boston Common and Public Garden

Massachusetts State House
Built in the 1790s as the new center of state government, the Charles Bulfinch-designed State House sits imposingly at the top of Beacon Hill.

John F. Kennedy Library and Museum
The nation's 35th president is celebrated here in words and images – video clips of the first president to fully use the media make this a compelling museum.

The Freedom Trail

From Boston Common to Paul Revere House

Boston has more sites directly related to the American Revolution than any other city. The most important of these sites, as well as some relating to other freedoms gained by Bostonians, have been linked together as "The Freedom Trail." This 2.5-mile (4-km) walking route, marked in red on the sidewalks, starts at Boston Common and eventually ends at Bunker Hill in Charlestown. This first section weaves its way through the central city and Old Boston.

Elegant Georgian steeple of Park Street Church

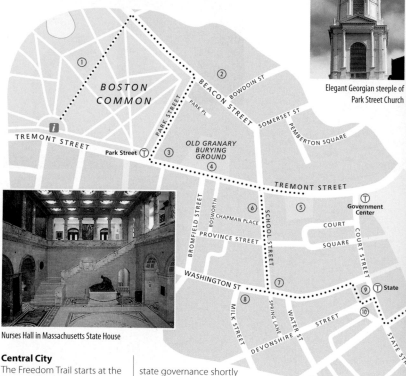

Nurses Hall in Massachusetts State House

Central City

The Freedom Trail starts at the Visitor Information Center on Boston Common ① *(see pp68–9)*. This is where angry colonials rallied against their British masters and where the British forces were encamped during the 1775–76 military occupation. Political speakers still expound from their soapboxes here, and the Common remains a center of activity.

Walking toward the northwest corner of the Common gives a great view of the Massachusetts State House ② *(see pp72–3)* on Beacon Street, designed by Charles Bulfinch as the new center of state governance shortly after the Revolution. Along Park Street, at the end of the Common, you will come to Park Street Church ③ *(see p70)*, built in 1810 and a bulwark of the antislavery movement. The church took the place of an old grain storage facility, which gave its name to the adjacent Granary Burying Ground ④, one of Boston's earliest cemeteries and the final resting place of patriots John Hancock and Paul Revere *(see p124)*. Continuing along Tremont Street you will come to King's Chapel and Burying Ground ⑤ *(see p80)*. The tiny cemetery is Boston's oldest, containing, among others, the grave of city founder John Winthrop. As the name suggests, King's Chapel was the principal Anglican church in Puritan Boston, and more than half of its congregation fled to Nova Scotia at the outbreak of the Revolution. The box pew on the right just inside the front entrance was reserved for condemned prisoners to hear their last sermons before going to the gallows on Boston Common.

Heart of Old Boston

Head back along Tremont Street and turn down School Street, where a hopscotch-like mosaic embedded in the sidewalk commemorates the site of the First Public School ⑥, established in 1635. At the bottom of the street is the Old Corner Bookstore ⑦ (see p81), a landmark more associated with Boston's literary emergence of 1845–65 than with the Revolution.

The Old South Meeting House ⑧, a short way to the south on Washington Street, is a graceful, white-spired brick church, modeled on Sir Christopher Wren's English country churches. As one of the largest meeting halls in Revolutionary Boston, "Old South's" rafters rang with many a fiery speech urging revolt against the British. A few blocks along, the Old State House ⑨ presides over the head of State Street. The colonial government

building, it also served as the first state legislature, and the merchants' exchange in the basement was where Boston's colonial shipping fortunes were made. The square in front of the Old State House is the Boston Massacre Site ⑩, where British soldiers opened fire on a taunting mob in 1770, killing five and providing ideal propaganda for revolutionary agitators.

Follow State Street down to Congress Street and turn left to reach Faneuil Hall ⑪, called the "Cradle of Liberty" for the history of patriotic speeches made in its public meeting hall. Donated to the city by Huguenot merchant Peter Faneuil, the building was Boston's first marketplace.

The red stripe of the Freedom Trail comes in handy when negotiating the way to the North End and the Paul Revere House ⑫ on North Square. Boston's oldest house, it was home to the man known for his famous "midnight ride" (see p124).

Tips for Walkers

Starting point: Boston Common. Maps at Boston Common Visitor Center.
Length: 2.5 miles (4 km).
Getting there: Park Street Station (T Green and Red lines) to start. Free guided tours leave from National Park Visitor Center at Faneuil Hall. Follow red stripe on sidewalk for the full route.
W thefreedomtrail.org

Faneuil Hall, popularly known as "the Cradle of Liberty"

Old State House, the seat of colonial government

Walk

① Boston Common
② Massachusetts State House
③ Park Street Church
④ Granary Burying Ground
⑤ King's Chapel and Burying Ground
⑥ First Public School Site
⑦ Old Corner Bookstore
⑧ Old South Meeting House
⑨ Old State House
⑩ Boston Massacre Site
⑪ Faneuil Hall
⑫ Paul Revere House

0 meters 200
0 yards 200

Key

••• Walk route

For map symbols see back flap

The Freedom Trail

From Old North Church to Bunker Hill Monument

Distances begin to stretch out on the second half of the Freedom Trail as it meanders through the narrow streets of the North End, then continues over the Charles River to Charlestown, where Boston's settlers first landed. The sites here embrace two wars – the War of Independence and the War of 1812.

View from Copp's Hill terrace, at the edge of Copp's Hill Burying Ground

The North End

Following the Freedom Trail through the North End, allow time to try some of the Italian cafés and bakeries along the neighborhood's main thoroughfare, Hanover Street. Cross through the Paul Revere Mall to reach Old North Church ⑬ *(see p91)*, whose spire is instantly visible over the shoulder of the statue of Paul Revere on horseback. Sexton Robert Newman hung two lanterns in the belfry here, signaling the advance of British troops on Lexington and Concord in 1775. The church retains its 18th-century interior, including the traditional box pews.

Gravestone at Copp's Hill Burying Ground

The crest of Copp's Hill lies close by on Hull Street. Some of Boston's earliest gallows stood here, and Bostonians would gather in boats below to watch the hangings of heretics and pirates. Much of the hilltop is covered by Copp's Hill Burying Ground ⑭. This was established in 1660, and the cemetery holds the remains of several generations of the Mather family – Boston's influential 17th- and 18th-century theocrats – as well as the graves of many soldiers of the Revolution.

Boston's first free African American community, "New Guinea," covered the west side of Copp's Hill. A broken column marks the grave of Prince Hall, head of the Black Masons, distinguished veteran of the Revolution, and prominent political leader in the early years of the Republic. The musketball-chipped tombstone of patriot Daniel Malcolm records that he asked to be buried "in a stone grave 10 feet deep" to rest beyond the reach of British gunfire.

Traditional box pews inside Old North Church

Walk

⑬ Old North Church
⑭ Copp's Hill Burying Ground
⑮ Charlestown Navy Yard and the USS *Constitution*
⑯ Bunker Hill Monument

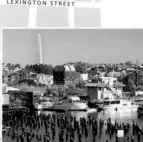

View of Bunker Hill Monument from
Charlestown harborfront

Key

••• Walk route

| 0 meters | | 200 |
| 0 yards | | 200 |

Charlestown

The iron bridge over the Charles River that links the North End in Boston with City Square in Charlestown dates from 1899. Across the bridge, turn right along Constitution Road, following signs to Charlestown Navy Yard ⑮. The National Park Service now operates the Visitor Center at Building 5, with a film and exhibits about the historic role of the Navy Yard and the history of the 18th- through to 20th-century warships that are berthed at its piers. The colonial navy had been no match for the might of Britain's naval forces during the Revolution, and building a more formidable naval force became a priority. This was one of several shipyards that were set up around 1800. Decommissioned in 1974, the yard is now maintained by the National Park Service. Lying at her berth alongside Pier 1, the USS *Constitution* is probably

Lion carving, USS
Constitution

the most famous ship in US history and still remains the flagship of the US Navy. Built at Hartt's shipyard in the North End, she was completed in 1797. In the War of 1812, she earned the nickname "Old Ironsides" for the resilience of her live oak hull against cannon fire. Fully restored for her bicentennial, the *Constitution* occasionally sails under her own power. The granite obelisk that towers above the

Charlestown waterfront is Bunker Hill Monument ⑯, commemorating the battle of June 17, 1775 that ended with a costly victory for British forces against an irregular colonial army, which finally ran out of ammunition. British losses were so heavy, however, that the battle would presage future success for the colonial forces. As a monument to the first large-scale battle of the Revolution, the obelisk, based on those of ancient Egypt, was a prototype for others across the US.

Defensive guns at Charlestown Navy Yard with view of the North End

For map symbols *see back flap*

BEACON HILL AND THE THEATER DISTRICT

By the 1790s, the south slope of Beacon Hill, facing Boston Common, had become the main seat of Boston's wealth and power. The north slope and the land up to the Charles River, known as the West End, was much poorer. Urban renewal has now cleared the slums of the West End, and the gentrification of Beacon Hill has made this one of Boston's most desirable neighborhoods. The area south of Boston Common is more down-to-earth, and home to the city's Theater District.

Sights at a Glance

Historic Streets and Squares

1 Charles Street
2 Louisburg Square
3 Mount Vernon Street
6 Beacon Street
14 Downtown Crossing
16 Chinatown
17 Bay Village

Historic Buildings, Museums, and Theaters

4 Nichols House Museum
5 Hepzibah Swan Houses
8 Park Street Church
10 Boston Athenaeum
11 *Massachusetts State House pp72–3*
12 Museum of African American History
13 Museum of Science
15 Colonial Theatre
18 Shubert Theatre
19 Wang Theatre

Parks and Cemeteries

7 *Boston Common and Public Garden pp62–3*
9 Granary Burying Ground

See also Street Finder maps
1 & 4

0 meters 250
0 yards 250

◀ A typical autumn day in Boston

For map symbols *see back flap*

Street-by-Street: Beacon Hill

From the 1790s to the 1870S, the south slope of Beacon Hill was Boston's most sought-after neighborhood – its wealthy elite decamped only when the more exclusive Back Bay *(see pp96–105)* was built. Many of the district's houses were designed by Charles Bulfinch and his disciples, and the south slope evolved as a textbook example of Federal architecture. Elevation and view were all, and the finest homes are either on Boston Common or perched near the top of the hill. Early developers abided by a gentleman's agreement to set houses back from the street, but the economic depression of 1807–12 resulted in row houses being built right out to the street.

Cobblestone street, once typical of Beacon Hill

❷ Louisburg Square
The crowning glory of the Beacon Hill district, this square was developed in the 1830s. Today, it is still Boston's most desirable address.

Charles Street Meeting House was built in the early 19th century to house a congregation of Baptists.

❶ ★ Charles Street
This elegant street is the main shopping area for Beacon Hill. Lined with upscale grocers and antique stores, it also has some fine restaurants.

Back Bay and South End

Key

— Suggested route

0 meters   50
0 yards   50

For hotels and restaurants in this region see pp310–13 and pp324–9

4 ★ Nichols House Museum
This modest museum offers an insight into the life of Beacon Hill resident Rose Nichols, who lived here from 1885 to 1960.

Locator Map
See Street Finder maps 1 & 4

3 Mount Vernon Street
Described in the 19th century as the "most civilized street in America," this is where the developers of Beacon Hill (the Mount Vernon Proprietors) chose to build their own homes.

Massachusetts State House

Boston Common

5 Hepzibah Swan Houses
Elegant in their simplicity, these three Bulfinch-designed houses were wedding gifts for the daughters of a wealthy Beacon Hill proprietress.

6 Beacon Street
The finest houses on Beacon Hill were invariably built on Beacon Street. Elegant, Federal-style mansions, some with ornate reliefs, overlook the city's most beautiful green space, Boston Common.

Charles Street, lined with shops catering to the residents of Beacon Hill

❶ Charles Street

Map 1 B4. ⓣ Charles/MGH.

This street originally ran along the bank of the Charles River, although subsequent landfill has removed it from the riverbank by several hundred feet. The main shopping and dining area of the Beacon Hill neighborhood, the curving line of Charles Street hugs the base of Beacon Hill, giving it a quaint, village-like air. Many of the houses remain residential on the upper stories, while street level and cellar levels were converted to commercial uses long ago. Though most of Charles Street dates from the 19th century, widening in the 1920s meant that some of the houses on the west side acquired new façades. The Charles Street Meeting House, designed by Asher Benjamin in 1807, was built for a Baptist congregation that practiced immersion in the then-adjacent river. It is now a commercial building. Two groups of striking Greek Revival row houses are situated at the top of Charles Street, between Revere and Cambridge Streets. Charles Street was one of the birthplaces of the antique trade in the US and now has some two dozen antique dealers.

❷ Louisburg Square

Map 1 B4. ⓣ Charles/MGH, Park Street.

Home to millionaire politicians, best-selling authors, and corporate moguls, Louisburg Square is perhaps Boston's most prestigious address. Developed in the 1830s as a shared private preserve on Beacon Hill, the square's tiny patch of greenery surrounded by a high iron fence sends a clear signal of the square's continued exclusivity. On the last private square in the city, the narrow,

Greek Revival bow-fronted town houses sell for a premium over comparable homes elsewhere on Beacon Hill. Even the on-street parking spaces are deeded. The traditions of Christmas Eve carol singing and candlelit windows are said to have begun on Louisburg Square. A statue of Christopher Columbus, presented by a wealthy Greek merchant in 1850, stands at its center.

❸ Mount Vernon Street

Map 1 B4. ⓣ Charles/MGH, Park Street.

In the 1890s the novelist Henry James called Mount Vernon Street "the most civilized street in America," and it still retains that air of urbane culture. Most of the developers of Beacon Hill, who called themselves the Mount Vernon Proprietors, chose to build their private homes along this street. Architect Charles Bulfinch envisioned Beacon Hill as a district of large freestanding mansions on spacious landscaped grounds, but building costs ultimately dictated much denser development. The sole remaining example of Bulfinch's vision is the second Harrison Gray Otis House, built in 1800 at No. 85 Mount Vernon Street. The current Greek Revival row houses next door (Nos. 59–83), graciously set back from the street by 30 ft (9 m), were built to replace the single mansion belonging to Otis's chief development partner, Jonathan Mason. The original mansion was torn down after Mason's death in 1836. The three Bulfinch-designed houses at Nos. 55, 57, and 59 Mount Vernon Street were built by Mason for his daughters. No. 55 was ultimately passed on to the Nichols family in 1885.

Columbus Statue, Louisburg Square

Oliver Wendell Holmes and the Boston Brahmins

In 1860, Oliver Wendell Holmes wrote that Boston's wealthy merchant class of the time constituted a Brahmin caste, a "harmless, inoffensive, untitled aristocracy" with "their houses by Bulfinch, their monopoly on Beacon Street, their ancestral portraits and Chinese porcelains, humanitarianism, Unitarian faith in the march of the mind, Yankee shrewdness, and New England exclusiveness." So keenly did he skewer the social class that the term has persisted. In casual usage today, a Brahmin is someone with an old family name, whose finances derive largely from trust funds, and whose politics blend conservatism with *noblesse oblige* toward those less fortunate. Boston's Brahmins founded most of the hospitals, performing arts bodies, and museums of the greater metropolitan area.

Oliver Wendell Holmes
(1809–94)

Drawing room of the Bulfinch-designed
Nichols House Museum

❹ Nichols House Museum

55 Mount Vernon St. **Map** 1 B4.
Tel (617) 227-6993. Ⓣ Park Street.
Open Apr–Oct: 11am–4pm Tue–Sat;
Nov–Mar: 11am–4pm Thu–Sat.

The Nichols House Museum was designed by Charles Bulfinch in 1804 and offers a rare glimpse into the tradition-bound lifestyle of Beacon Hill. Modernized in 1830 by the addition of a Greek Revival portico, the house is nevertheless a superb example of Bulfinch's domestic architecture. It also offers an insight into the life of a true Beacon Hill character. Rose Standish Nichols moved into the house at 13 when her father purchased it in 1885. She left it as a museum in her 1960 will. A woman ahead of her time, strong-willed and

famously hospitable, Nichols was, among other things, a self-styled landscape designer who traveled extensively around the world to write about gardens.

❺ Hepzibah Swan Houses

13, 15 & 17 Chestnut St. **Map** 1 B4.
Ⓣ Park Street. **Closed** to the public.

The only woman who was ever a member of the Mount Vernon Proprietors, Mrs. Swan had these houses built by Bulfinch as wedding presents for her daughters in 1806, 1807, and 1814. Some of the most elegant and distinguished houses on Chestnut Street, they are backed by Bulfinch-designed stables that face onto Mount Vernon Street. The deeds restrict the height of the stables to 13 ft (4 m) so that her daughters would still have a view over Mount Vernon Street. In 1863–65, No. 13 was home to Dr. Samuel Gridley Howe, abolitionist and educational pioneer who, in 1833, founded the first school for the blind in the US.

❻ Beacon Street

Map 1 B4. Ⓣ Park Street.

Beacon Street is lined with urban mansions facing Boston Common. The 1808 William Hickling Prescott House at No. 55, designed by Asher Benjamin, offers tours of rooms in Federal, Victorian, and Colonial Revival styles on Wednesdays and Saturdays between May and October. The American Meteorological Society in No. 45 was built as Harrison Gray Otis's last and finest house. It had 11 bedrooms and an elliptical room behind the front parlor, where the walls and even the doors are curved.

The elite Somerset Club stands at No. 42-43 Beacon Street. Between the 1920s and the 1940s, Irish Catholic mayor James Michael Curley would lead election night victory marches to the State House, pausing at the Somerset Club to taunt the Boston Brahmins inside.

The Parkman House at No. 33 Beacon Street is now a city-owned meeting center. It was the home of Dr. George Parkman, who was murdered by Harvard professor and fellow socialite Dr. John Webster in 1849. Boston society was torn apart when the presiding judge, a relative of Parkman, sentenced Webster to be hanged.

Elegant Federal-style houses on Beacon Street, overlooking
Boston Common

● Boston Common and Public Garden

Acquired by Boston in 1634 from first settler William Blackstone, the 48-acre (19-ha) Boston Common served for two centuries as common pasture, military drill ground, and gallows site. British troops camped here during the 1775–76 military occupation. As Boston grew in the 19th century, the Boston Common became a center for open-air civic activity and remains so to this day. By contrast, the 24-acre (10-ha) Public Garden is more formal. When the Charles River mudflats were first filled in the 1830s, a succession of landscape plans were plotted for the Public Garden before the city chose the English-style garden scheme of George F. Meacham in 1869. The lagoon was added to the garden two years later.

The Public Garden, a popular green space in the heart of the city

Make Way for Ducklings
Based on the classic children's story by Robert McCloskey, this sculpture is of a duck and her brood of ducklings.

★ George Washington Statue
Cast by Thomas Ball from bronze, with a solid granite base, this is one the finest memorial statues in Boston. It was dedicated in 1869.

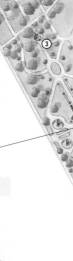

VISITORS' CHECKLIST

Practical Information
Map 1 B4.
Open 24 hrs.
Visitors' Center: 148 Tremont St.;
(617) 426-3115. **Open** 8:30am–
5pm Mon–Fri, 9am–5pm Sat–Sun
(winter: shorter weekend hours).
Swan Boats: Boston Public
Garden. **Tel** (617) 522-1966.
Open Mid-Apr–mid-Sep: 10am–
5pm daily (subject to change).
Ⓦ swanboats.com
Ⓦ bostonusa.com

Transport
Ⓣ Park Street, Boylston Street,
Arlington

Lagoon Bridge
This miniature, ornamental bridge over the Public Garden lagoon was designed by William G. Preston in 1869 in a moment of whimsy. The lagoon it "spans" was constructed in 1861.

★ Shaw Memorial
This relief immortalizes the Civil War's 54th regiment of Massachusetts Infantry, the first free black regiment in the Union Army, and their white colonel Robert Shaw.

KEY

① **The Swan Boats**, originally inspired by Wagner's *Lohengrin*, have been a feature of the Public Garden lake since 1877.

② **Statue of Reverend William Ellery Channing**

③ **The Ether Monument** memorializes the first use of anesthesia in 1846.

④ **Statue of Edward Everett Hale**

⑤ **The Soldiers and Sailors Monument**, erected in 1877, features prominent Bostonians from the time of the Civil War.

⑥ **The Frog Pond** turns into a public outdoor skating rink during winter months.

⑦ **Blackstone Memorial Tablet** recalls the purchase of the common in 1634 and is cited as proof that it belongs to the people.

⑧ **Park Street subway**

⑨ **Brewer Fountain** was purchased at the Paris expo of 1867.

⑩ **Visitors' Center**

⑪ **The Flagstaff**

Parkman Bandstand
This bandstand was built in 1912 to memorialize George F. Parkman, who bequeathed $5 million for the care of Boston Common and other parks in the city.

Central Burying Ground
This graveyard, which dates from 1756, holds the remains of many British and American casualties from the Battle of Bunker Hill (1775). The portraitist Gilbert Stuart is also buried here.

| 0 meters | | 100 |
| 0 yards | | 100 |

Park Street Church at the corner of Tremont and Park Streets

❽ Park Street Church

1 Park St. **Map** 1 C4. **Tel** (617) 523-3383. ⓣ Park Street. **Open** Jul–Aug: 9am–4pm Tue–Fri, 9am–3pm Sat; Sep–Jun: by appointment. ⓣ Jul–Aug: 10:45am, 5:30pm Sun; Sep–Jun: 8:30am, 11am, 4pm, 6pm Sun. ✉ ♿ ⓦ parkstreet.org

Park Street Church's 217-ft (65-m) steeple has punctuated the intersection of Park and Tremont Streets since its dedication in 1810. Designed by English architect Peter Banner, who adapted a design by the earlier English architect Christopher Wren, the church was commissioned by parishioners wanting to establish a Congregational church in the heart of Boston. The church was, and still is, one of the city's most influential pulpits.

Contrary to popular belief, the sermons of Park Street ministers did not earn the intersection the nickname of "Brimstone Corner." Rather, the name came about because during the war of 1812 the US militia, based in Boston, stored its gunpowder in the church basement as safekeeping against bombardment from the British navy.

In 1829, William Lloyd Garrison (1805–79), fervently outspoken firebrand of the movement to abolish slavery, gave his first abolition speech from the Park Street pulpit.

In 1849 a speech entitled *The War System of Nations* was addressed to the American Peace Society by Senator Charles Sumner. Much later, in 1893, the anthem *America the Beautiful* by Katharine Lee Bates debuted at a Sunday service. Today the church continues, as always, to be involved in religious, political, cultural, and humanitarian activities.

❾ Granary Burying Ground

Tremont St. **Map** 1 C4. ⓣ Park Street. **Open** 9am–5pm daily.

Named after the early grain storage facility that once stood on the adjacent site of Park Street Church, the Granary Burying Ground dates from 1660. Buried here were three important signatories to the Declaration of Independence – Samuel Adams, John Hancock, and Robert Treat Paine, along with Paul Revere, Benjamin Franklin's parents, merchant-philanthropist Peter Faneuil, and victims of the Boston Massacre.

The orderly array of gravestones, often featured in films and television shows set in Boston, is the result of modern groundskeeping. Few stones, if any, mark the actual burial site of the person memorialized. In fact, John Hancock may not be here at all. On the night he was buried in 1793, grave robbers cut off the hand with which he had signed his name to the Declaration of Independence, and some believe that the rest of his body was removed during 19th-century construction work.

❿ Boston Athenaeum

10½ Beacon St. **Map** 1 C4. **Tel** (617) 227-0270. ⓣ Park Street. **Open** 8:30am–8pm Mon & Wed, 8:30am–5:30pm Tue, Thu & Fri, 9am–4pm Sat. **Closed** Jun–Aug: Sat. ✉ ⓦ bostonathenaeum.org

Organized in 1807, the collection of the Boston Athenaeum quickly became one of the country's leading private libraries. Sheep farmer Edward Clarke Cabot won the 1846 design competition to house the library, with plans for a gray sandstone building based on Palladio's Palazzo da Porta Festa in Vicenza, a building Cabot knew from a book in the Athenaeum's collection. Included in over half a million volumes are rare manuscripts, maps, and newspapers. Among the

Granary Burying Ground, final resting place for Revolutionary heroes

For hotels and restaurants in this region see pp310–13 and pp324–9

Stone frieze decoration on the Renaissance Revival-style Athenaeum

Athenaeum's major holdings are the personal library that once belonged to George Washington and the theological library supplied by King William III of England to the King's Chapel (see p80). In its early years the Athenaeum was Boston's chief art museum, but when the Museum of Fine Arts was proposed, it graciously donated much of its art, including unfinished portraits of George Washington purchased in 1831 from the widow of the painter Gilbert Stuart.

⓫ Massachusetts State House

See pp72–3.

⓬ Museum of African American History

46 Joy St. **Map** 1 C3. **Tel** (617) 725-0022. Ⓣ Park Street. **Open** 10am–4pm Mon–Sat. **Closed** public hols. 🖼 📷 🅦 afroammuseum.org

Built from town house plans designed by Asher Benjamin, the African Meeting House (the centerpiece of the museum) was dedicated in 1806. The oldest black church building in the United States, it was the political and religious center of Boston's African American society. The interior is plain and simple but rang with the oratory of some of the 19th century's most fiery abolitionists: from Sojourner Truth and Frederick Douglass to William Lloyd Garrison, who

founded the New England Anti-Slavery Society in 1832. The meeting house basement was Boston's first school for African American children until the adjacent Abiel Smith School was built in 1831. When segregated education was barred in 1855, however, the Smith School closed. The meeting house became a Hasidic synagogue in the 1890s, as most of Boston's African American community moved to Roxbury and Dorchester. The synagogue closed in the 1960s, and in 1987 the African Meeting House reopened as the linchpin site on the Black Heritage Trail.

⓭ Museum of Science

Science Park. **Map** 1 B2. **Tel** (617) 723-2500. Ⓣ Science Park. **Open** 9am–5pm Mon–Thu & Sat–Sun, (Jul–early Sep: 9am–7pm), 9am–9pm Fri. **Closed** Thanksgiving, Dec 25. 🖼 🅖 🎧 🅦 mos.org

The Museum of Science straddles the Charles River atop the flood control dam that sits at the mouth of the Charles River. The campus that has developed around it includes a large-format IMAX cinema and planetarium.

With more than 550 interactive exhibits covering natural history, medicine, astronomy, the physical sciences, and computing, the Science Museum is largely oriented to families. The Mugar Omni Theater contains a five-story domed screen with a multidimensional wrap-around sound system, and shows mostly films with a natural science theme. The Charles Hayden Planetarium offers laser shows as well as shows about stars, planets, and other celestial phenomena.

Black Heritage Trail

In the first US census in 1790, Massachusetts was the only state to record no slaves. During the 19th century, Boston's substantial free African American community lived principally on the north slope of Beacon Hill and in the adjacent West End. The Black Heritage Trail links several key sites, ranging from the African Meeting House to several private homes, which are not open to visitors. Among them are the 1797 George Middleton House (Nos. 5–7 Pinckney Street), the oldest standing house built by African Americans on Beacon Hill, and the Lewis and Harriet Hayden House (No. 66 Phillips Street). Escaped slaves, the Haydens made their home a haven for runaways in the "Underground Railroad" of safe houses between the South and Canada. The walking tour also leads through mews and alleys, like Holmes Alley at the end of Smith Court, once used by fugitives to flee professional slave catchers.

Free tours of the Black Heritage Trail are led by National Park Service rangers – (617) 742-5415 – from Memorial Day weekend to Labor Day, 10am, noon, and 2pm Mon–Sat, departing from the Shaw Memorial. Self-guided tour maps are available at the Museum of African American History.

Holmes Alley, once an escape route for slaves on the run

⓫ Massachusetts State House

The cornerstone of the Massachusetts State House was laid on July 4, 1795, by Samuel Adams and Paul Revere. Completed on January 11, 1798, the Charles Bulfinch-designed center of state government served as a model for the US Capitol Building in Washington and as an inspiration for many of the state capitols around the country. Later additions were made, but the original building remains the archetype of American government buildings. Its dome, sheathed in copper and gold, serves as the zero mile marker for Massachusetts, making it, as Oliver Wendell Holmes *(see p67)* remarked, "the hub of the universe."

The State House, from Boston Common

★ House of Representatives
This elegant oval chamber was built for the House of Representatives in 1895. The Sacred Cod, which now hangs over the gallery, came to the State House when it first opened in 1798, and it has since hung over any place where the representatives have met.

KEY

① **The Wings** of the State House, thought by many to sit incongruously with the rest of the structure, were added in 1917.

② **The Great Hall** is the latest addition to the State House. Built in 1990, it is lined with marble and topped by a glass dome, and is used for state functions.

③ **Administrative offices** can be found on the upper floors of the building.

④ **The dome** was sheathed in copper in 1802 to prevent water leakage, and, in 1872, gilded in 23-carat gold.

Main Staircase
Beautiful stained-glass windows decorate the main staircase. They illustrate the varied state seals of Massachusetts from its inception as a colony through to modern statehood.

Hall of Flags

Flags carried into battle by regiments from the state of Massachusetts are housed here. They are displayed beneath a stained-glass skylight depicting seals of the original 13 colonies.

★ Nurses Hall

This marble hall is lined with murals depicting critical events leading up to the American Revolution. The name derives from the statue of an army nurse here, erected to honor all the nurses who took part in the Civil War.

Entrance

Doric Hall

George Washington is among the historical figures represented here. The center doors of the hall are opened only for a state governor at the end of his term or for a visiting head of state.

Senate Chamber

Prior to 1895, this was the meeting chamber of the House of Representatives. Situated directly beneath the State House's magnificent dome, the chamber features a beautiful sunburst ceiling, also designed by Charles Bulfinch.

Brattle Book Shop, a Boston literary landmark

⓮ Downtown Crossing

Washington, Winter & Summer Sts. **Map** 4 F1. Ⓣ Downtown Crossing.

As an antidote to heavy traffic congestion, this shopping-district crossroads, located at the intersection of Washington, Winter, and Summer Streets, was laid out as a pedestrian zone between 1975 and 1978. Downtown's single remaining department store is Macy's, although the area also offers a range of other outlets, including bookstores, camera stores, and a jewelry district. Street vendors and summer lunchtime concerts create a lively scene.

The busy Macy's department store is one of a chain found throughout the US, with the most well-known store in New York. Across Summer Street, the Beaux-Arts building that housed Filene's Department Store remains a local landmark. Currently under redevelopment, it will once again house the original Filene's Basement when work is completed. The "Basement", as Bostonians call it, retains a powerful hold on residents eager for a bargain. Designer clothes at a discount can still be found in the neighborhood at branches of the popular local chains Marshalls and T.J. Maxx.

Another well-known store in the area is Brattle Book Shop, just off Washington Street on West Street. Founded in 1825, this bibliophiles' treasure-house is packed with more than 250,000 used, rare, and out-of-print books, as well as back issues of magazines, maps, prints, postcards, and manuscripts. Outside the store are bins of bargain books priced between $1 and $5.

⓯ Colonial Theatre

106 Boylston St. **Map** 4 E2. **Tel** (617) 426-9366. Ⓣ Boylston. **Open** phone to check. ♿ Ⓦ **citicenter.org**

Clarence H. Blackall designed 14 Boston theaters during his architectural career, among them the Colonial, which is the city's oldest theater in continuous operation under the same name. Although plain outside, the interior is impressively opulent. Designed by H.B. Pennell, the Rococo lobby has chandeliers, gilded trim, and lofty arched ceilings. The auditorium is decorated with figures, frescoes, and friezes. The theater opened on December 20, 1900 with an extravagant performance of the melodrama Ben Hur. Today the theater is best remembered for premiering lavish musical productions, such as Ziegfeld Follies.

Gilt cherub, the Colonial Theatre

⓰ Chinatown

Bounded by Kingston, Kneeland, Washington & Essex Sts. **Map** 4 E2. Ⓣ Chinatown.

This area is the third largest Chinatown in the US after those in San Francisco and New York. Pagoda-topped telephone booths, as well as a three-story gateway guarded by four marble lions, set the neighborhood's Asian tone.

The first 200 Chinese to settle in New England came by ship from San Francisco in 1870, recruited to break a labor strike at a shoe factory.

Another wave of immigration from California in the 1880s was prompted by an economic boom that led to job openings in construction. Boston's Chinese colony was fully established by the turn of the 19th century.

Political turmoil in China immediately following World War II, and more recent arrivals from Vietnam, Laos, Korea, Thailand, and Cambodia, have swelled Chinatown's population. Along with the area's garment and textile industries, restaurants, bakeries, food markets, and dispensers of Chinese medicine are especially numerous along the main thoroughfare of Beach Street, as well as on Tyler, Oxford, and Harrison Streets.

Chinatown Gate (paifang) with a foo lion on each side

⑰ Bay Village

Bounded by Tremont, Arlington
& Charles St South. **Map** 4 D2.
Ⓣ Tufts Medical Center, Boylston.

Originally an expanse of
mud flats, the Bay Village
area was drained in the early
1800s and initially became
habitable with the construction
of a dam in 1825. Many
carpenters, cabinetmakers,
artisans, and house painters
involved in the construction
of Beacon Hill's pricier town
houses built their own modest
but well-crafted residences
here. As a result there are
many similarities between
the two neighborhoods.

Fayette Street was laid out
in 1824 to coincide with the
visit of the Marquis de Lafayette,
the French general who
allied himself with George
Washington. Bay Street, located
just off Fayette Street, features a
single dwelling and is generally
regarded as the city's shortest
street. In 1809, poet and short-
story writer Edgar Allen Poe
was born in a boarding house
on Carver Street, where his
thespian parents were staying
while in Boston on tour with a
traveling theatrical company.

In the 1920s, at the height
of the Prohibition era,
clandestine speakeasies gave
Bay Village its still-prevalent
bohemian ambience. More
recently, the neighborhood has
become a center for Boston's
gay community.

Bay Village's Piedmont
Street is well known for the
W. S. Haynes Company at
No. 12, which has been hand-
crafting flutes and piccolos
since 1888, and has acquired
among musicians a worldwide
reputation for its instruments.

⑱ Shubert Theatre

265 Tremont St. **Map** 4 E2. **Tel** (617)
482-9393. Ⓣ Boylston, Tufts Medical
Center. **Open** phone to check. ♿
Ⓦ citicenter.org

The 1,650-seat Shubert Theatre
rivals the Colonial Theatre for
its long history of staging
major pre-Broadway musical

The vast Grand Lobby of the Wang Theatre

productions. Designed by
the architects Charles Bond
and Thomas James, the
theater features a white Neo-
Classical façade with a pair
of Ionic columns flanking a
monumental, Palladian-style
window over the entrance. The
theater first opened its doors
in 1910, and during its heyday
many stars walked the boards,
including Sarah Bernhardt,
W.C. Fields, Cary Grant, Mae
West, Humphrey Bogart, Ingrid
Bergman, Henry Ford, and Rex
Harrison. Today, dance, theater,
musicals, and opera are
showcased here.

⑲ Wang Theatre

270 Tremont St. **Map** 4 E2.
Tel (617) 482-9393. Ⓣ Boylston,
Tufts Medical Center.
Open phone to check. ♿
Ⓦ citicenter.org

Opened in 1925 as the
Metropolitan Theatre and
later named the Music Hall,
New England's most ornate
variety theater was inspired
by the Paris Opera House,
and was originally intended
to be a movie theater.
Designed by Clarence Blackall,
the theater's auditorium
was once one of the largest
in the world. The theatre
was restored and renamed
as the Wang Center for the
Performing Arts in 1983,
but is now known simply
as the Wang Theatre. The
five-story Grand Lobby
and seven-story auditorium
are designed in Renaissance
Revival style, with gold
chandeliers, stained glass,
ceiling murals, and
jasper pillars.

Today the theater hosts
Broadway road shows, visiting
dance and opera companies,
concerts, motion-picture
revivals, and local productions.
The Wang and Shubert theaters
are now operated by the Citi
Performing Arts Center.

The History of Boston's Theater District

Boston's first theater opened in 1793 on Federal Street. Fifty years
later, with patronage from the city's social elite, Boston had become
a major tryout town and boasted a number of lavish theaters. The
US premiere of Handel's *Messiah* opened in 1839, the US premiere
of Gilbert and Sullivan's *H.M.S. Pinafore* in 1877, and the premiere of
Tchaikovsky's *First Piano Concerto* in 1875. In the late 19th century
theaters came under fire from the censorious Watch and Ward
Society. Later, in the
20th century,
dramas such as
Tennessee Williams'
*A Streetcar Named
Desire* and Eugene
O'Neill's *Long Day's
Journey into Night*
debuted here.
Musicals included
Ziegfeld Follies,
Gershwin's *Porgy
and Bess*, and works
by Rodgers and
Hammerstein.

A Streetcar Named Desire, starring a young Marlon Brando
and Jessica Tandy

OLD BOSTON AND THE FINANCIAL DISTRICT

This is an area of Boston where old and new sit one on top of the other. Some of its sights, situated in the older part of the district closest to Boston Common, predate the American Revolution. Much of what can be seen today, though, was built much more recently. The north of the district is home to Boston's late 20th-century, modernist-style City Hall and Government Center, while to the east is the city's bustling Financial District. This once formed part of Boston's harbor waterfront, a district built on mercantile wealth. Today, the wharves and warehouses have been replaced by skyscrapers belonging to banks, insurance companies, and high-tech industries.

Sights at a Glance

Historic Buildings and Churches

1. Omni Parker House
2. King's Chapel and Burying Ground
3. Old City Hall
4. Old Corner Bookstore
5. Old South Meeting House
6. *Old State House pp82–3*
7. Government Center
8. Faneuil Hall
9. Quincy Market
10. Custom House
11. Post Office Square Park

See also Street Finder maps 1 & 2

0 meters	300
0 yards	300

◄ Quincy Market and the distinctive Custom House tower by night

For map symbols *see back flap*

Street-by-Street: Colonial Boston

An important part of Boston's Freedom Trail *(see pp58–61)* runs through this historic core of the city, the site of which predates American Independence. Naturally, the area is now dominated by 19th- and 20th-century development, but glimpses of a colonial past are prevalent here and there in the Old State House, King's Chapel and its adjacent burying ground, and the Old South Meeting House. Newer buildings of interest include the Omni Parker House, as well as the towering skyscrapers of Boston's financial district, located on the northwest edges of this area.

Irish Famine memorial, Washington Street

Government Center

❷ ★ King's Chapel and Burying Ground
A church has stood here since 1688, although the current building dates from 1749. The adjacent cemetery is the resting place of some of the most important figures in US history.

SCHOOL STREET

❶ Omni Parker House
This hotel *(see p312)* first opened its doors in 1855, then underwent many renovations. Famed for its opulence, the hotel also gained a reputation in the 19th century as a meeting place for Boston intellectuals. The current building was erected in 1927.

❸ Old City Hall
This building served as Boston's City Hall from 1865 to 1969. Today it houses a steak house.

| 0 meters | 50 |
| 0 yards | 50 |

For hotels and restaurants in this region see pp310–13 and pp324–9

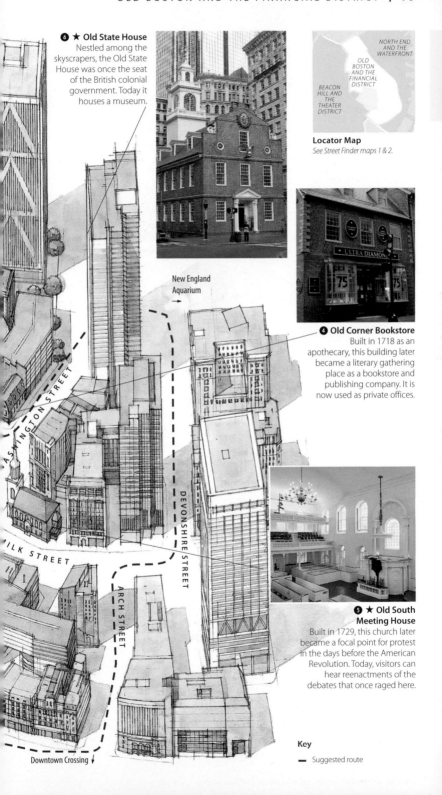

6 ★ Old State House
Nestled among the skyscrapers, the Old State House was once the seat of the British colonial government. Today it houses a museum.

Locator Map
See Street Finder maps 1 & 2.

New England Aquarium →

4 Old Corner Bookstore
Built in 1718 as an apothecary, this building later became a literary gathering place as a bookstore and publishing company. It is now used as private offices.

WASHINGTON STREET

DEVONSHIRE STREET

MILK STREET

ARCH STREET

5 ★ Old South Meeting House
Built in 1729, this church later became a focal point for protest in the days before the American Revolution. Today, visitors can hear reenactments of the debates that once raged here.

Downtown Crossing ↓

Key

— Suggested route

❶ Omni Parker House

60 School St. **Map** 1 C4. **Tel** (617) 227-8600. Ⓣ Park Street, State, Government Center.
Ⓦ omnihotels.com

Harvey D. Parker, raised on a farm in Maine, became so successful as the proprietor of his Boston restaurant that he achieved his ambition of expanding the property into a first-class, grand hotel. His Parker House opened in 1855, with a façade clad in white marble, standing five stories high, and featuring the first passenger elevator ever seen in Boston. It underwent several, rapid transformations during its early years, with additions made to the main structure in the 1860s and a 10-story, French chateau-style annex completed later that century. The building saw many successive transformations, and its latest 14-story incarnation has stood across from King's Chapel on School Street since 1927.

This hotel attained an instant reputation for luxurious accommodations and fine, even lavish, dining, typified by 11-course menus prepared

Simply decorated, pure white interior of King's Chapel on Tremont Street

by a French chef. Among Parker House's many claims to fame are its Boston Cream Pie, which was first created here, and the word "scrod," a uniquely Bostonian term for the day's freshest seafood, still in common usage. Two former Parker House employees later became recognized for quite different careers. Vietnamese revolutionary leader Ho Chi Minh worked in the hotel's kitchens around 1915, while black activist Malcolm X was a busboy in Parker's Restaurant in the 1940s.

Parker House Guests

Boston's reputation as the "Athens of America" was widely acknowledged when members of a distinguished social club began meeting for lengthy dinners and lively intellectual exchanges in 1857. Their get-togethers took place on the last Saturday of every month at Harvey Parker's fancy new hotel. Regular participants included New England's literary elite *(see pp34–5)*: Henry Wadsworth Longfellow, Ralph Waldo Emerson, Nathaniel Hawthorne, and Henry David Thoreau, to name a few. Charles Dickens participated while

John Wilkes Booth, infamous Parker House guest

staying at the Parker House during his American speaking tours, and used his sitting-room mirror to rehearse the public readings he gave at Tremont Temple next door. The mirror now hangs on a mezzanine wall. In 1865, actor John Wilkes Booth, in town to see his brother, a fellow thespian, stayed at the hotel and took target practice at a nearby shooting gallery. Ten days later, at Ford's Theatre in Washington, he pulled a pistol and shot Abraham Lincoln.

❷ King's Chapel and Burying Ground

58 Tremont St. **Map** 1 C4. **Tel** (617) 523-1749. Ⓣ Park Street, State, Government Center. **Open** late May–mid-Sep: 10am–5pm Mon, Thu–Sat, 10–11:15am & 1:30–5pm Tue–Wed, 1:30–5pm Sun; mid-Sep–May: call for hours. ✝ 11am Sun, 12:15pm Wed. Music Recitals: 12:15pm Tue.
Ⓦ kings-chapel.org

British Crown officials were among those who attended Anglican services at the first chapel on this site, which was built in 1688. When New England's governor decided a larger church was needed, the present granite edifice – begun in 1749 – was constructed around the original wooden chapel, which was dismantled and heaved out the windows of its replacement. After the Revolution, the congregation's religious allegiance switched from Anglican to Unitarian. The sanctuary's raised pulpit – dating from 1717 and shaped like a wine glass – is one of the oldest in the US. High ceilings and clear glass windows enhance the sense of spaciousness. The bell inside the King's Chapel is the largest ever cast by Paul Revere *(see p124)*.

Among those interred in the adjacent cemetery, Boston's oldest, are John Winthrop and Elizabeth Pain, the inspiration for adultress Hester Prynne in Nathaniel Hawthorne's moralistic novel *The Scarlet Letter*.

❸ Old City Hall

45 School St. **Map** 2 D4. Ⓣ Park Street, State, Government Center.

This building is a wonderful example of French Second Empire architectural gaudiness and served as Boston's City Hall for over a century from 1865 to 1969. It was eventually superseded by the rakishly imposing new City Hall structure at nearby Government Center (see p84). Now the renovated 19th-century building features a steak house.

Previous occupants of the Old City Hall have included such flamboyant mayors as John "Honey Fitz" Fitzgerald and James Michael Curley. There a re also statues here which memorialize Josiah Quincy, the second mayor of Boston, after whom Quincy Market is named, as well as Benjamin Franklin, who was born on nearby Milk Street in 1706.

19th-century French-style façade of Boston's Old City Hall

❹ Old Corner Bookstore

1 School St. **Map** 2 D4. Ⓣ Park Street, State, Government Center. **Closed** to the public.

A dormered gambrel roof crowns this brick landmark, which opened as Thomas Crease's apothecary shop in 1718 and was reestablished as the Old Corner Bookstore in 1829. Moving in 16 years later, the Ticknor & Fields publishing company became a gathering place for a notable roster of authors: Emerson, Hawthorne, Longfellow, Thoreau, early feminist writer Margaret Fuller, and *Uncle Tom's Cabin* novelist Harriet Beecher Stowe. The firm is often credited with carving out the first distinctively American literature. The earliest editions of the erudite *Atlantic Monthly* periodical were also printed here under editor James Russell Lowell before he handed the reins over to William Dean Howells. Julia Ward Howe's rousing tribute to American Civil War bravado, *The Battle Hymn of the Republic*, first appeared in in the *Atlantic's* February 1862 issue. No publishing activities take place at the Old Corner Bookstore anymore.

Many consider the Old Corner Bookstore the cradle of American literature

❺ Old South Meeting House

310 Washington St. **Map** 2 D4. **Tel** (617) 482-6439. Ⓣ Park Street, State, Government Center. **Open** Apr– Oct: 9:30am–5pm daily; Nov– Mar: 10am–4pm daily. 🅿 ♿ 🔊 📷
W oldsouthmeetinghouse.org

Built in 1729 for Puritan religious services, this edifice, with a tall octagonal steeple, had colonial Boston's biggest capacity for town meetings – a fact capitalized upon by a group of rebellious rabble-rousers calling themselves the Sons of Liberty. Their outbursts against British taxation and other royal annoyances drew increasingly large and vociferous crowds to the pews and upstairs galleries.

During a candlelit protest rally on December 16, 1773, fiery speechmaker Samuel Adams flashed the signal that led to the Boston Tea Party (see p93) down at Griffin's Wharf several hours later. The British retaliated by turning Old South Meeting House into an officers' tavern and stable for General John Burgoyne's 17th Lighthorse Regiment of Dragoons. It was saved from destruction and became a museum in 1877. Displays and a multimedia presentation entitled *If These Walls Could Speak* relive those raucous days as well as more recent occurrences well into the 20th century. The Meeting House offers a series of lectures covering a wide range of New England topics and also holds chamber music concerts and other musical performances. The downstairs shop has a broad selection of merchandise, including books and the ubiquitous tins of "Boston Tea Party" tea.

Directly across Washington Street, sculptor Robert Shure's memorial to the victims of the 1845–49 Irish Potato Famine was added to the small plaza here in 1998.

Old South Meeting House, in stark contrast to the modern city

❻ Old State House

Dwarfed by the towers of the Financial District, this was the seat of British colonial government between 1713 and 1776. The royal lion and unicorn still decorate each corner of the eastern facade. After independence, the Massachusetts legislature took possession of the building, and it has had many uses since, including produce market, merchants' exchange, Masonic lodge, and Boston City Hall. Its wine cellars now function as a downtown subway station. The Old State House houses two floors of Bostonian Society memorabilia and a multimedia show about the Boston Massacre.

Old State House amid the skyscrapers of the Financial District

West Façade
A Latin inscription, relating to the first Massachusetts Bay colony, runs around the outside of this crest. The relief in the center depicts a local Native American.

Keayne Hall
This is named after Robert Keayne who, in 1658, gave £300 to the city so that the Town House, predating the Old State House, could be built. Exhibits in the room depict events from the Revolution.

Entrance

KEY

① **A gold sculpture** of an eagle, symbol of America, can be seen on the west facade.

② **The tower** is a classic example of Colonial style. In 18th-century paintings and engravings it can be seen clearly above the Boston skyline.

③ **The Declaration of Independence** was read from this balcony in 1776. In the 1830s, when the building was City Hall, the balcony was enlarged to two tiers.

★ **Central Staircase**
A fine example of 18th-century workmanship, the central spiral staircase has two beautifully crafted wooden handrails. It is one of the few such staircases still in existence in the US.

For hotels and restaurants in this region see pp310–13 and pp324–9

Site of the Boston Massacre

A circle of cobblestones below the balcony on the eastern façade of the Old State House marks the site of the Boston Massacre. After the Boston Tea Party, this was one of the most inflammatory events leading up to the American Revolution. On March 5, 1770, an angry mob of colonists taunted British guardsmen with insults, rocks, and snowballs. The soldiers opened fire, killing five colonists. A number of articles relating to the Boston Massacre are exhibited inside the Old State House, including a musket found near the site and a coroner's report detailing the incident.

Cobbled circle: site of the Boston Massacre

VISITORS' CHECKLIST

Practical Information
Washington & State Sts.
Map 2 D4.
Tel (617) 720-1713.
W **bostonhistory.org**
Open 9am–5pm daily (reduced hours Jan, extended hours Jul–Aug).
🐾 ♿   🏛

Transport
Ⓣ State.

British Unicorn and Lion
A royal symbol of Britain, the original lion and unicorn were torn down when news of the Declaration of Independence reached Boston in 1776.

★ **East Façade**
This façade has seen many changes. An earlier clock from the 1820s was removed in 1957 and replaced with an 18th-century replica of the sundial that once hung here. The clock has now been reinstated.

Council Chamber
Once the chambers for the royal governors, and from 1780 chambers for the first governor of Massachusetts (John Hancock), this room has seen many key events. Among them were numerous impassioned speeches made by Boston patriots.

City Hall and Government Center, a main city focal point

❼ Government Center

Cambridge, Court, New Sudbury & Congress Sts. **Map** 2 D3. Ⓣ Government Center.

This city center development was built on the site of what was once Scollay Square, demolished as part of the trend for local urban-renewal that began in the early 1960s. This trend had already seen the building of the strikingly Modernist concrete and brick new City Hall, which stands on the eastern side of the square and houses government offices.

Some viewed the development as controversial; others did not lament what was essentially a disreputable cluster of saloons, burlesque theaters, tattoo parlors, and scruffy hotels. The overall master plan for Government Center was inspired by the outdoors vitality and spaciousness of Italian piazzas. Architects I.M. Pei & Partners re-created some of this feeling by surrounding Boston's new City Hall with a vast terraced plaza covering 56 acres (23 ha), paved with 1,800,000 bricks. Its spaciousness makes it an ideal place for events such as skateboard contests, political and sports rallies, food fairs, patriotic military marches, and concerts.

❽ Faneuil Hall

Dock Sq. **Map** 2 D3. Ⓣ Government Center, Haymarket, State. Great Hall: **Open** 9am–5pm daily (closed for events). ♿ 📷 🔊 Ⓦ nps.gov/bost

A gift to Boston from the wealthy merchant Peter Faneuil in 1742, this Georgian, brick landmark has always functioned simultaneously as a public market and town meeting place. Master tinsmith Shem Drowne modeled the building's grasshopper weathervane after the one on top of the Royal Exchange in the City of London, England. Revolutionary gatherings packed the hall, and as early as 1763 Samuel Adams used the hall as a platform to suggest that the American colonies should unite against British oppression and fight to establish their independence; hence the building's nickname "Cradle of Liberty" and the bold posture of the statue of Sam Adams at the front of the building. Toward the end of the 18th century, architect Charles Bulfinch was commissioned to expand the building in order to accommodate larger crowds. The work was completed in 1806, and Faneuil Hall then remained unchanged until 1898, when it was further expanded according to Bulfinch stipulations. In addition to the historic meeting place, this Freedom Trail landmark also

Sam Adams statue, in front of Faneuil Hall

houses the visitor center of the Boston National Historical Park. Opposite the building is the information center for the Boston Harbor Islands.

❾ Quincy Market

Between Chatham & Clinton Sts. **Map** 2 D3. **Tel** (617) 523-1300. Ⓣ Government Center, State. **Open** 10am–9pm Mon–Sat, noon–6pm Sun. ♿ Ⓦ faneuilhallmarketplace.com

This immensely popular shopping and dining complex attracts nearly 18 million people every year. It was developed from the buildings of the old Quincy Market, which was the city's meat, fish, and produce market. These buildings had fallen into disrepair before they underwent a widely acclaimed restoration in the 1970s. The 535-ft (163-m) long Greek Revival-style colonnaded market hall is now filled with a selection of fast food stands and a restaurant-nightclub, located in the spectacular central Rotunda. Completing the ensemble are twin North and South Market buildings – these individual warehouses have also been refurbished to accommodate numerous boutiques, stores, restaurants, and pubs, as well as upstairs business offices.

Gallery of the Greek Revival main dome in Quincy Market's central hall

⓾ Custom House

3 McKinley Square. **Map** 2 E3. **Tel** (617) 310-6300. Ⓣ Aquarium. Museum: **Open** 8am–9pm daily. Tower: **Open** 2pm Sat–Thu. 🅿 🅦 **marriott. com/vacationclub**

Before landfill altered downtown topography, early Boston's Custom House perched at the water's edge. A temple-like Greek Revival structure with fluted Doric columns, the granite building had a skylit dome upon completion in 1847. Since 1915, however, it has supported a 495 ft (150 m) tower with a four-sided clock. For the best part of the 20th century, the Custom House was Boston's only bona fide skyscraper.

The observatory, which is open to the public, offers stunning views of the harbor and the Financial District skyscrapers that tower over it.

The Langham Boston Hotel in Post Office Square Park

Greek Revival Custom House tower, one of Boston's most striking sights

⓫ Post Office Square Park

Franklin, Pearl, High & Congress sts. **Map** 2 D4. Ⓣ State, Aquarium.

Officially named Norman B. Leventhal Park, and occupying land reclaimed when a parking garage was demolished, this beautifully landscaped park is a small island of green amid the soaring skyscrapers of the Financial District. Vines climb a 143-ft (44-m) long trellis along one side of the park, and a fountain made of green glass cascades on the square's Pearl Street side. A focal point for the entire Financial District throughout the year, the Post Office Square Park comes into its own in the summer months, when a small kiosk sells luncheon fare, jazz concerts are often held at midday, and office workers fill the benches and lounge on the well-kept lawns. The green space is blanketed with free Wi-Fi access.

The square is surrounded by several notable buildings, not least the former main post office on Congress Street after which the park is named. The 1929–31 Art Deco masterpiece of geometric and botanical ornamentation that used to be occupied by the post office now houses the John W. McCormack courthouse. The Langham Boston hotel (see p312) is housed in a classic Renaissance Revival showpiece completed in 1922 that once housed the Federal Reserve Bank. Among the original features that have been carefully preserved are the painted dome and murals by N.C. Wyeth. Perhaps the most notable edifice on the square is the "wedding cake"-style 1947 late Art Deco building on the south side of Franklin Street. Originally constructed as the headquarters for the New England Telephone Company, this landmark building also recalls the neighborhood's connection to telephone history. The laboratory of telephone pioneer Alexander Graham Bell was located on nearby Court Street.

Alexander Graham Bell (1847–1922)

A native of Edinburgh, Scotland, and son of a deaf mother, Bell moved to Boston in 1871 to start a career teaching speech to the deaf. Two years later he was appointed as professor of vocal physiology at Boston University. Bell worked in his spare time on an apparatus for transmitting sound by electrical current. History was made on March 17, 1876, when Bell called to his assistant in another room: "Mr. Watson, come here. I want you." The first demonstration of the "telephone" took place in Boston on May 10, 1876, at the Academy of Arts and Sciences. By 1878, he had set up the first public telephone exchange in New Haven, Connecticut.

NORTH END AND THE WATERFRONT

This was Boston's first neighborhood, and one that has been key to the city's fortunes. Fringed by numerous wharves, the area prospered initially through shipping and shipbuilding, with much of America's early trade passing through its warehouses. The more recent importance of finance and high-tech industries, however, has seen the waterfront evolve, its old warehouses transformed into luxury apartment blocks and offices. Away from the waterfront, the narrow streets of the North End have historically been home to European immigrants, drawn by the availability of work. The area today is populated largely by those of Italian descent, whose many cafés, delis, and restaurants make it one of the city's most distinct communities.

Sights at a Glance

Historic Sites and Churches
1 Copp's Hill Burying Ground
3 *Old North Church p91*
4 Paul Revere Mall
5 Paul Revere House

Waterfront Sights
2 Institute of Contemporary Art
6 Waterfront Wharves
7 *New England Aquarium pp94–5*
8 Boston Tea Party Ships and Museum
9 Children's Museum

See also Street Finder map 2

| 0 meters | 450 |
| 0 yards | 450 |

◀ Sailboats on the Charles River with the Boston skyline in the background   **For map symbols** *see back flap*

Street-by-Street: North End

The main arteries of this area are Hanover and Salem Streets. Topped by the Old North Church, Salem Street is indicative of this area's historical connections – indeed the Old North Church is one of Boston's premier Revolutionary sights. In general the area consists of narrow streets and alleys, with four- and five-story tenements, many of which are now expensive condominiums. Hanover Street, like much of the area, has a distinctly Italian feel, while just south of here is North Square, site of the famous Paul Revere House *(see p92)*.

Clough House was built by Ebenezer Clough who helped build the Old North Church. Benjamin Franklin's family home was just next door.

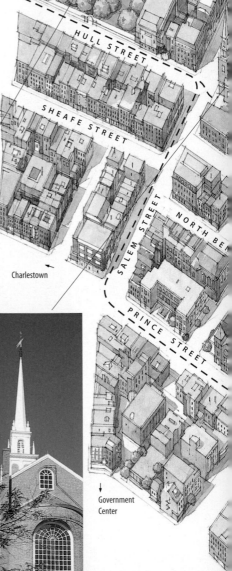

HULL STREET

SHEAFE STREET

SALEM STREET

NORTH BE

PRINCE STREET

Charlestown ←

↓ Government Center

❶ Copp's Hill Burying Ground
During the American Revolution, the British used this low hilltop to fire cannon at American positions across Boston Harbor. Created in 1659, it is the city's second oldest graveyard.

❸ ★ Old North Church
Built in 1723 and famous for the part it played in Paul Revere's midnight ride *(see p124)*, this is Boston's oldest religious building. On festive occasions, the North End still rings with the sound of its bells.

Key

— Suggested route

0 meters   50

0 yards   50

❹ ★ Paul Revere Mall
Linking the Old North Church to Hanover Street, this tree-lined mall dates only from 1933. Its antique feel is enhanced by a statue of Paul Revere, which was modeled in 1885.

Locator Map
See Street Finder map 2

St. Stephen's Church echoes the North End's Italian theme, though only by chance. Long before the first Italians arrived, Charles Bulfinch incorporated Italian Renaissance features and a bell tower into his renovation of an earlier church building.

Hanover Street is the most Italian of all Boston's streets, brought to life by restaurants and cafés, as well as the day-to-day activities of its ethnic community.

➤ The waterfront

❺ ★ Paul Revere House
This is the house where Paul Revere began his midnight ride *(see p120)*. Revere's home from 1770 to 1800, it is now a museum.

STON STREET

EET

CLARK STREET

HANOVER STREET

FLEET STREET

MOON STREET

RDEN COURT

Slate tombstones of Boston's early settlers, Copp's Hill Burying Ground

❶ Copp's Hill Burying Ground

Entrances at Charter & Hull Sts.
Map 2 D2. Ⓣ Government Center, North Station. **Open** 9am–5pm daily.

Existing since 1659, this is Boston's second-oldest cemetery after the one by King's Chapel *(see p80)*. Nicknamed "Corpse Hill," the real name of the hill occupied by the cemetery derives from a local man by the name of William Copp. He owned a farm on its southeastern slope from 1643, and much of the cemetery's land was purchased from him. His children are buried here. Other more famous people interred here include Robert

Quiet, leafy street, typical of the area around Copp's Hill

Newman, the sexton who hung Paul Revere's signal lanterns in the belfry of Old North Church *(see p91)*, and Edmund Hartt, builder of the USS *Constitution (see p123)*. Increase, Cotton, and Samuel Mather, three generations of a family of highly influential colonial period Puritan ministers, are also buried here. Hundreds of Boston's Colonial-era black slaves and freedmen are also buried here, including Prince Hall, a free black man who founded the African Freemasonry Order in Massachusetts.

During the British occupation of Boston, the site was used by British commanders who had an artillery position here. They would later exploit the prominent hilltop location during the Revolution, when they directed cannon fire from here across Boston harbor toward American positions in Charlestown. King George III's troops were said to have used the slate headstones for target practice, and pockmarks from their musket balls are still visible on some of them.

Copp's Hill Terrace, directly across Charter Street, is a prime observation point for

Decorative column, Copp's Hill

views over to Charlestown and Bunker Hill. It is also the site where, in 1919, a 2.3-million-gallon molasses tank exploded, creating a huge, syrupy tidal wave that killed 21 people.

❷ Institute of Contemporary Art

100 Northern Ave. **Map** 2 F5. **Tel** (617) 478-3100. Ⓣ Courthouse. **Open** 10am–5pm Tue, Wed, Sat, Sun (to 9pm Thu, Fri). ♿ 🐾 ⓦ **icaboston.org**

Since 1936, when it introduced Americans to the then-radical work of German Expressionism, the Institute of Contemporary Art has made a point of championing cutting-edge innovation and avant-garde expression. Over the years, the ICA has pushed the envelope of the definition of art, showing creations often outside the usual art-world boundaries, such as an entire exhibition devoted to blowtorches. The ICA was also in the vanguard of showing and interpreting video art when the technology was still in its infancy. For its first 70 years, the ICA was an exhibiting but not a collecting institution, in part on the theory that the definition of "contemporary" changes from minute to minute. That focus changed in 2006 when the ICA moved from its quaint Back Bay building to a dramatic new wood, steel, and glass structure cantilevered above the Harbor Walk on Fan Pier on the South Boston waterfront. The 65,000 sq ft (6,040 sq m) museum is the creation of the design firm Diller Scofidio + Renfro, and includes a 325-seat performing arts theater with clear walls that allow the harbor to serve as a stage backdrop, as well as a media center and art lab for educational programs. The vastly expanded facilities also allow the ICA to focus on collecting 21st-century art.

❸ Old North Church

Christ Episcopal Church is the official name of Boston's oldest surviving religious edifice, which dates from 1723. It was built of brick in the Georgian style similar to that of St. Andrew's-by-the-Wardrobe in Blackfriars, London, designed by Sir Christopher Wren. The church was made famous on April 18, 1775, when sexton Robert Newman, aiding Paul Revere *(see p124)*, hung a pair of signal lanterns in the belfry. These were to warn the patriots in Charlestown of the westward departure of British troops, on their way to engage the revolutionaries.

VISITORS' CHECKLIST

Practical Information
193 Salem St.
Map 2 E2.
Tel (617) 523-6676.
Ⓦ oldnorth.com
Open 9am–5pm daily (extended hours Jun–Oct).
⊕ 9am, 11am. 🅿 🅒 🅜 🅑
(call for tours)

Transport
Ⓣ Haymarket, Aquarium, North Station.

Tower
The tower of the Old North Church contains the first set of church bells in North America cast in 1745.

★ Box Pews
The traditional, high-sided box pews in the church were designed to enclose footwarmers, which were filled with hot coals or bricks during wintry weather.

Chandeliers
The church's distinctive chandeliers were brought from England in January 1724 for the first Christmas season.

Entrance

★ Bust of George Washington
This marble bust of the first US president, modeled on an earlier one by Christian Gullager, was presented to the church in 1815.

❹ Paul Revere Mall

Hanover St. **Map** 2 E2. Ⓣ Haymarket, Aquarium. ♿

This brick-paved plaza gives the crowded neighborhood of the North End a precious stretch of open space between Hanover and Unity Streets. A well-utilized municipal resource, the Mall is always full of local people: children, teenagers, young mothers, and older residents chatting in Italian and playing cards or checkers. Laid out in 1933, and originally called the Prado, its focal point is Cyrus Dallin's equestrian statue of local hero Paul Revere, which was originally modeled in 1885. However, it was not sculpted and placed here until 1940. Bronze bas-relief plaques on the mall's side walls commemorate a number of North End residents who have played an important role in the history of Boston. Benches, a fountain, and twin rows of linden trees complete the space, which has a distinctly European feel.

At the north end of the Mall, across Unity Street, is Old North Church (see p91), one of the city's most important historical sites. To the south is busy Hanover Street, which is lined with numerous Italian cafés and restaurants.

Paul Revere House kitchen, as it was in the 18th century

❺ Paul Revere House

19 North Sq. **Map** 2 E2. **Tel** (617) 523-2338. Ⓣ Haymarket, Aquarium. **Open** mid-Apr–Oct: 9:30am–5:15pm daily; Nov–mid-Apr: 9:30am–4:15pm daily. **Closed** Jan–Mar: Mon. 📷 ♿ 📧 📖 📷 call for hours. 🆆 **paulreverehouse.org**

The city's oldest surviving clapboard frame house is historically significant, for it was here in 1775 that Paul Revere began his legendary horseback ride to warn his compatriots in Lexington of the impending arrival of British troops. This historic event was later immortalized in a boldly patriotic, epic poem by Henry Wadsworth

Longfellow (see p114). It begins "Listen, my children, and you shall hear of the midnight ride of Paul Revere."

Revere, a Huguenot descendent, was by trade a versatile gold- and silversmith, copper engraver, and maker of church bells and cannons. He and his second wife, Rachel, mother of eight of his 16 children, owned the house from 1770 to 1800. Small leaded casement windows, an overhanging upper story, and nail-studded front door all contribute to make it a fine example of 18th-century Early American architecture. In the courtyard along one side of the house is a large bronze bell, cast by Paul Revere for a church in 1804 – Revere made nearly 200 church bells. Three rooms in the house contain period artifacts, including original pieces of family furniture, items made in Revere's workshop, and colonial banknotes. The house, which by the mid-19th century had become a decrepit tenement fronted by stores, was saved from demolition by preservationists' efforts led by one of Revere's great-grandsons.

Next door, the early 18th-century Pierce-Hichborn House is the earliest brick town house remaining in New England.

View toward the Custom House and the Financial District, across Christopher Columbus Park

Rowes Wharf development, typical of Boston's waterfront regeneration

❻ Waterfront Wharves

Atlantic Ave. **Map** 2 E4. Ⓣ Aquarium.

Boston's waterfront is fringed by many wharves, reminders of the city's past as a key trading port. One of the largest of these is Long Wharf, established in 1710 to accom-modate the boom in early maritime commerce. Once extending 2,000 ft (610 m) into Boston Harbor and lined with shops and warehouses, Long Wharf provided mooring for the largest ships of the time. Many sightseeing excursion boats depart from here.

Harbor Walk connects Long Wharf with other adjacent wharves, such as Union, Lewis, and Commercial wharves. Dating from the early 19th century most are now converted to fashionable harborside apartments. Rowes Wharf, to the south of the waterfront, is a particularly fine example of such revitalization.

Built of Bostonian red brick, this modern development features a large archway that links the city to the harbor. It comprises the luxury Boston Harbor Hotel, restaurants, and a marina.

❼ New England Aquarium

See pp94–5.

❽ Boston Tea Party Ships & Museum

306 Congress St. **Map** 2 E5.
Tel (617) 338-1773. Ⓣ South Station.
Open 10am–5pm daily. 🅿
Ⓦ bostonteapartyship.com

Griffin's Wharf, where the Boston Tea Party took place on December 16, 1773, was buried beneath landfill many years ago. Replicas of three British East India Company ships involved in the Tea Party now anchor on the Fort Point Channel, a short distance south of the old Griffin's Wharf site. After boarding the ships and even tossing tea overboard, visitors can enter an interactive museum where exhibits put that historic act of protest into a broader context, explaining how the political tensions between Boston and the British crown led up to the American Revolution.

❾ Children's Museum

300 Congress St. **Map** 2 E5. **Tel** (617) 426-6500. Ⓣ South Station. **Open** 10am–5pm daily (to 9pm Fri). 🅿 ♿
Ⓦ bostonchildrensmuseum.org

Overlooking Fort Point Channel, a pair of rejuvenated 19th-century red-brick wool warehouses contain one of the country's best children's museums. The expansive museum offers a host of interesting exhibits. Youngsters play games, join learning activities, and hoist themselves up a 30-foot (9-m) climbing structure in the New Balance Center addition. The Art Studio provides a hands-on recycling area with materials for projects. Visits to a silk merchant's house transplanted from Kyoto (Boston's sister city) inject a multicultural dimension while careers can be sampled as children work on a mini-construction site.

A towering milk bottle in front of the museum serves as a summer ice-cream stand, and mazes, giant boulders, and performance spaces grace an outdoor park.

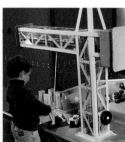

Playing on the mini-construction site at Boston's Children's Museum

❼ New England Aquarium

The waterfront's prime attraction dominates Central Wharf. Designed by a consortium of architects in 1969, the aquarium's core encloses a vast four-story ocean tank, which contains an innumerable array of marine animals. A curving walkway runs around the outside of the tank from top to bottom and provides viewpoints of the interior of the tank from different levels. Also resident at the aquarium are colonies of penguins, playful harbor seals, anacondas, rays, sea turtles, and mesmerizing seadragons. The facility also includes a superb IMAX theatre.

Shark and Ray Touch Tank
The largest shark and ray touch tank on the East Coast is surrounded by shallow edges and viewing windows.

★ Penguin Exhibit
One of the most popular attractions of the aquarium, the penguin pool runs around the base of the giant tank. It contains more than 80 penguins.

★ Whale Watch
A naturalist aboard an Aquarium boat explains marine ecology on 3- to 4-hour educational trips to Stellwagen Bank to see whales and sea birds.

Main entrance

Harbor Seals
An outdoor tank covered by a steel canopy is home to a lively colony of harbor seals.

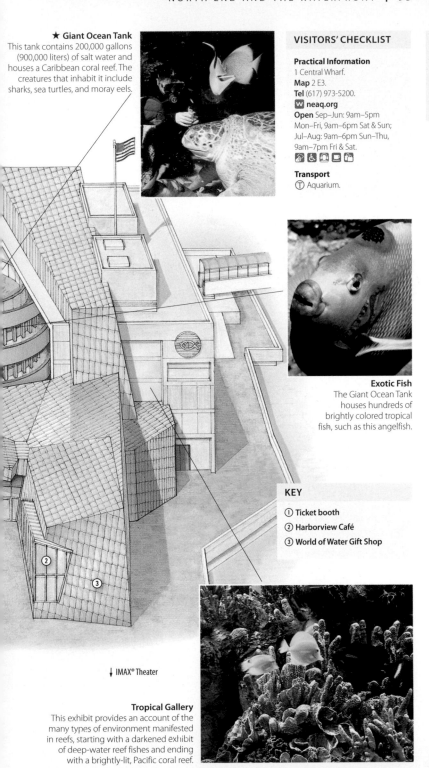

★ Giant Ocean Tank
This tank contains 200,000 gallons (900,000 liters) of salt water and houses a Caribbean coral reef. The creatures that inhabit it include sharks, sea turtles, and moray eels.

VISITORS' CHECKLIST

Practical Information
1 Central Wharf.
Map 2 E3.
Tel (617) 973-5200.
W **neaq.org**
Open Sep–Jun: 9am–5pm Mon–Fri, 9am–6pm Sat & Sun; Jul–Aug: 9am–6pm Sun–Thu, 9am–7pm Fri & Sat.

Transport
T Aquarium.

Exotic Fish
The Giant Ocean Tank houses hundreds of brightly colored tropical fish, such as this angelfish.

KEY

① Ticket booth
② Harborview Café
③ World of Water Gift Shop

↓ IMAX® Theater

Tropical Gallery
This exhibit provides an account of the many types of environment manifested in reefs, starting with a darkened exhibit of deep-water reef fishes and ending with a brightly-lit, Pacific coral reef.

BACK BAY AND SOUTH END

Until the 19th century Boston was situated on a narrow peninsula surrounded by tidal marshes. Projects to fill Back Bay began in the 1850s and were made possible by new inventions such as the steam shovel. The Back Bay was filled by 1880, and developers soon moved in.

Planned along French lines, with elegant boulevards, Back Bay is now one of Boston's most exclusive neighborhoods. The more bohemian South End, laid out on an English model of town houses clustered around squares, is home to many artists and much of Boston's gay community.

Sights at a Glance

Historic Streets and Squares
1 The Esplanade
4 Commonwealth Avenue
5 Newbury Street
7 Copley Square
8 Boylston Street

Historic Buildings, Churches, and Museums
2 Gibson House Museum
3 First Baptist Church
6 Trinity Church pp102–103
9 Boston Public Library

10 John Hancock Tower
11 Berklee Performance Center
12 Boston Center for the Arts

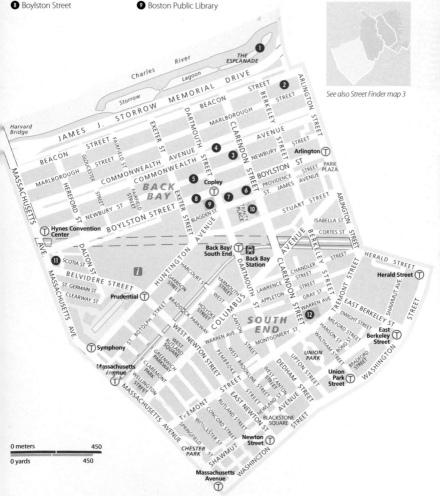

See also Street Finder map 3

0 meters 450
0 yards 450

◀ Interior of the historic Boston Public Library

For

Street-by-Street: Back Bay

This fashionable district unfolds westward from the Public Garden (see pp68–9) in a grid that departs radically from the twisting streets found elsewhere in Boston. Commonwealth Avenue, with its grand 19th-century mansions and parkland, and Newbury and Boylston Streets are its main arteries. Newbury Street is a magnet for all of Boston wanting to indulge in some upscale shopping, whereas the more somber Boylston Street bustles with office workers. Copley Square anchors the entire area and is the site of Henry Hobson Richardson's magnificent Trinity Church (see pp102–103) and the 60-story John Hancock Tower (see p105), which is the tallest building in New England.

Weekly summer and fall farmers' market, Copley Square

❼ Copley Square

This square was a marsh until 1870. It took on its present form only in the late 20th century as buildings around its edges were completed. A farmers' market, concerts, and folk-dancing feature regularly.

COMMONWEALTH AVEN

NEWF

Fenway Park

DARTMOUTH STREET

❽ Boylston Street

The site of the Prudential Tower and Shopping Center and the Hynes Convention Center, Boylston Street is also the location of the fabulous New Old South Church (see p104).

BOYLSTON STREET

❾ ★ Boston Public Library

of the first free ...aries in the ...lding was ... Charles ...murals ...gent.

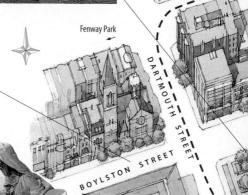

South End

this region see pp310–13 and pp324–9

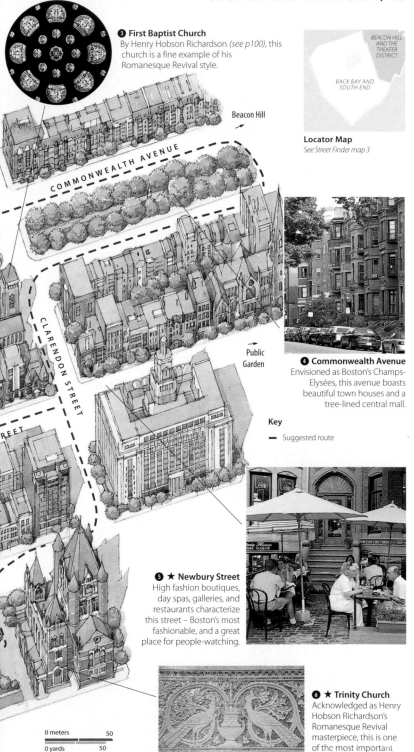

❸ First Baptist Church
By Henry Hobson Richardson *(see p100)*, this church is a fine example of his Romanesque Revival style.

BEACON HILL AND THE THEATER DISTRICT

BACK BAY AND SOUTH END

Locator Map
See Street Finder map 3

Beacon Hill

COMMONWEALTH AVENUE

CLARENDON STREET

REET

Public Garden

❹ Commonwealth Avenue
Envisioned as Boston's Champs-Elysées, this avenue boasts beautiful town houses and a tree-lined central mall.

Key
— Suggested route

❺ ★ Newbury Street
High fashion boutiques, day spas, galleries, and restaurants characterize this street – Boston's most fashionable, and a great place for people-watching.

❻ ★ Trinity Church
Acknowledged as Henry Hobson Richardson's Romanesque Revival masterpiece, this is one of the most important churches in the US.

0 meters   50
0 yards   50

❶ The Esplanade

Map 1 A4. Ⓣ Charles/MGH.
Open 24 hrs daily. ♿

Running along the Boston side of the Charles River, between Longfellow Bridge and Dartmouth Street, are the parkland, lagoons, and islands known collectively as the Esplanade. The park is used extensively for in-line skating, cycling, and strolling. It is also the access point for boating on the river (including gondola rides) and the site of the city's leading outdoor concert space.

In 1929, Arthur Fiedler, then the young conductor of the Boston Pops Orchestra, chose the Esplanade for a summer concert series that became a tradition. The Hatch Memorial Shell was constructed in 1939, and its stage is widely used by musical ensembles and other groups throughout the summer. Fourth of July concerts by the Boston Pops, which are followed by fireworks, can attract upward of 500,000 spectators.

Fountains at the Esplanade, next to the Charles River

❷ Gibson House Museum

137 Beacon St. **Map** 1 A4. **Tel** (617) 267-6338. Ⓣ Arlington. **Open** Tours at 1pm, 2pm & 3pm Wed–Sun. ♿ ✉ 📷 🖥 **thegibsonhouse.org**

Among the first houses built in the Back Bay, the Gibson House preserves its original Victorian decor and furnishings throughout all six stories. The 1860 brownstone and red-brick structure was designed in the popular Italian Renaissance

The original Victorian-style library of the Gibson House Museum

Revival style for the widow Catherine Hammond Gibson, who was one of the few women to own property in this part of the city. Her grandson Charles Hammond Gibson, Jr., a noted eccentric, poet, travel writer, horticulturalist, and bon vivant, arranged for the house to become a museum after his death in 1954. As a prelude to this, Gibson began to rope off the furniture in the 1930s, thus inviting his guests to sit on the stairs to drink martinis made with his own bathtub gin.

One of the most modern houses of its day, the Gibson House boasted such technical advancements as gas lighting, indoor plumbing in the basement, and coal-fired central heating. Visitors can see a full dinner setting in the dining room or admire the whimsical Turkish pet pavilion. It is Gibson's preservation of the 1860s decor (with some modifications in 1888) that makes the museum a true time capsule of Victorian life in Boston.

Detail of Bartholdi's frieze atop the distinctive square tower of the First Baptist Church

❸ First Baptist Church

110 Commonwealth Ave. **Map** 3 C2. **Tel** (617) 267-3148. Ⓣ Arlington. **Open** for Sunday worship. ✝ 11am Sun. ✉ ♿

The Romanesque-style First Baptist Church on the corner of Commonwealth Avenue and Clarendon Street was Henry Hobson Richardson's first major architectural commission and became an instant landmark when it was finished in 1872. Viewed from Commonwealth Avenue, it is one of the most distinctive buildings of the city skyline.

Richardson considered the nearly freestanding bell tower, which he modeled roughly on Italian campaniles, to be the church's most innovative structure. The square tower is topped with a decorative frieze and arches protected by an overhanging roof. The frieze was modeled in Paris by Bartholdi, the sculptor who created the Statue of Liberty, and was carved in place by Italian artisans after the stones were set. The faces in the frieze, which depict the sacraments, are likenesses of prominent Bostonians of that time, among them Henry Wadsworth Longfellow and Ralph Waldo Emerson. The trumpeting angels at the corners of the tower gave the building its nickname, "Church of the Holy Bean Blowers."

Four years after the church was completed, the Unitarian congregation dissolved because it was unable to bear the expense of the building. The church stood vacant until 1881, when the First Baptist congregation from the South End took it over.

❹ Commonwealth Avenue

Map 3 B2. ⓣ Arlington, Copley, Hynes Convention Center.

Back Bay was Boston's first fully planned neighborhood, and architect Arthur Gilman made Commonwealth Avenue, modeled on the elegant boulevards of Paris, the centerpiece of the design. At 200 ft (61 m) wide, with a 10-ft (3-m) setback from the sidewalks to encourage small gardens in front of the buildings, Commonwealth became an arena for America's leading domestic architects in the second half of the 19th century. A walk from the Public Garden to Massachusetts Avenue is like flicking through a catalog of architectural styles. Few of the grand buildings on either side of the avenue are open to the public, but strollers on the central mall of the avenue encounter a number of historic figures in the form of bronze statues. Some have only tangential relationships to the city, like Alexander Hamilton, the first secretary of the US Treasury. The end of the mall features an heroic bronze of Leif Eriksson, erected as a historically unsupported flight of fancy that the Norse explorer landed at Boston. The patrician statue of abolitionist William Garrison is said to capture exactly the man's air of moral superiority. The best-loved memorial depicts sailor and historian Samuel Eliot Morison dangling his feet from a rock.

William Garrison statue on Commonwealth Avenue

❺ Newbury Street

Map 3 C2. ⓣ Arlington, Copley, Hynes Convention Center.

Newbury Street is a Boston synonym for "stylish." The Taj Boston, formerly the Ritz-Carlton Hotel, at Arlington Street sets an elegant tone for the street that continues with a mix of prestigious and often well-hidden art galleries, stylish boutiques, and some of the city's most *au courant* restaurants. Churches provide vestiges of a more decorous era. The Church of the Covenant at No. 67 Newbury contains the world's largest collection of Louis Comfort Tiffany stained-glass windows and an elaborate Tiffany lantern. A chorus and orchestra perform a Bach cantata each Sunday at Emmanuel Church on the corner of Newbury and Berkeley Streets.

Most of Newbury Street was constructed as townhouse residences, but the desirability of these spaces for retail operations has pushed residents to the upper floors, while ground and subsurface levels are devoted to chic boutiques and eateries. Modern-day aspiring celebrities may be spotted at the sidewalk tables of Newbury's "hottest" restaurants, such as Sonsie *(see p325)*.

🏛 **Church of the Covenant**
67 Newbury St. **Tel** (617) 266-7480.
🕐 10:30am Sun. 🅿 ♿ 🔊 📷 🎦 📱
🌐 cotcbos.org

Stylish Newbury Street, with its elegant shops, galleries, and restaurants, the epitome of Boston style

❻ Trinity Church

Routinely voted one of America's finest buildings, this masterpiece by Henry Hobson Richardson dates from 1877. Trinity Church was founded in 1733 near Downtown Crossing, but the congregation moved the church to this site in 1871. The church is a granite and sandstone Romanesque structure standing on wooden piles driven through mud into bedrock, surmounted with granite pyramids. John LaFarge designed the interior, while some of the windows are designed by Edward Burne-Jones and executed by William Morris.

Bas-relief in Chancel
On the wall of the chancel, behind the altar, are a series of gold bas-reliefs. This one shows St. Paul before King Agrippa.

★ North Transept Windows
Designed by Edward Burne-Jones and executed by William Morris, the three stained-glass windows above the choir relate the story of Christmas.

Parish House

KEY

① **The Pulpit** is covered with carved scenes from the life of Christ, as well as portraits of great preachers through the ages.

② **The Bell Tower** was inspired by the Renaissance cathedral at Salamanca, central Spain.

③ **John LaFarge's** lancet windows show Christ in the act of blessing. They were designed at the request of Phillips Brooks – he wanted LaFarge to create an inspirational design for the west nave, which he could look at while preaching.

Chancel
Designed by Charles Maginnis, the present-day chancel was not dedicated until 1938. The seven windows by Clayton & Bell of London show the life of Christ.

David's Charge to Solomon
Located in the baptistry, to the right of the chancel, this beautiful window is also the result of a partnership between Edward Burne-Jones and William Morris. The story shown is one of the few in the church from the Old Testament.

VISITORS' CHECKLIST

Practical Information
Copley Sq.
Map 3 C2. **Tel** (617) 536-0944.
w trinitychurchboston.org
Open 9am–5pm Mon–Sat (to 6pm Tue–Thu), 1–6pm Sun.
🕇 7:45am, 9am, 11:15am, 6pm Sun. Concerts: Sep–mid-June: 12:15pm Fri.

Transport
Ⓣ Copley.

★ **West Portico**
Richardson disliked the original flat façade of Trinity Church, and so modeled the deeply sculpted west portico after St. Trophime in Arles, France. It was added after his death.

Carving of Phillips Brooks and Christ

Phillips Brooks

Born in Boston in 1835 and educated at Harvard, Brooks was a towering charismatic figure. Rector of Trinity Church from 1869, he gained a reputation for powerful sermons. From 1872 Brooks worked closely with Henry Hobson Richardson on the design of the new Trinity Church – at least five sculpted likenesses of him can be seen in and around the building.

Main Entrance

The New Old South Church on the corner of Copley Square

❼ Copley Square

Map 3 C2. Ⓣ Copley.

Named after John Singleton Copley, the great Boston painter born nearby in 1737, Copley Square is a hive of civic activity surrounded by some of Boston's most striking architecture. Summer activities include weekly farmers' markets, concerts, and even folk-dancing.

The inviting green plaza took years to develop; when Copley was born it was just a marshy riverbank, which remained unfilled until 1870. Construction of the John Hancock Tower in 1975 anchored the southeastern side of Copley Square, and the Copley Place development completed the square on the southwestern corner in 1984. Today's Copley Square, a wide open space of trees, grass, and fountains, took shape in the heart of the city in the 1990s, after various plans to utilize this hither- to wasted space were tendered.

A large plaque honoring the Boston Marathon, which ends at the Boston Public Library, was set in the sidewalk in 1996 to coincide with the 100th race. As well as pushcart vendors, the plaza has a booth for discounted theater, music, and dance tickets.

❽ Boylston Street

Map 3 C2. Ⓣ Boylston, Arlington, Copley, Hynes Convention Center.

The corners of Boylston and Berkeley streets represent Boston architecture at its most diverse. The stately French Academic-style structure on the west side was erected for the Museum of Natural History, a forerunner of the Museum of Science (see p71). It has gone on to house upscale shops and restaurants. The east side spouts a Robert A.M. Stern tower and a Philip Johnson office building that resembles a table radio. Boston jeweler Shreve, Crump & Low occupied the Art Deco building at the corner of Arlington Street until relocating nearby to Newbury Street.

Some notable office buildings stand on Boylston Street. The lobby of the New England building at No. 501 features large historical murals and dioramas depicting the process of filling Back Bay. The central tower of the Prudential Tower and Shopping Center dominates the skyline on upper Boylston Street. Adjoining the Prudential is the Hynes Convention Center. It was significantly enlarged in 1988 to accommodate the city's burgeoning business in hosting conventions.

The Italian Gothic-style **New Old South Church**, which is located at the corner of Dartmouth, was built in 1874–5 by the congregation that had met previously at the Old South Meeting House (see p81).

🔼 **New Old South Church**

645 Boylston St. **Tel** (617) 536-1970. **Open** 9am–7pm Mon–Fri, 10am–4pm Sat, 8:30am–4pm Sun. ⏰ 6pm Thu, 9am, 11am Sun. 📶 ♿ 🔲 oldsouth.org

❾ Boston Public Library

Copley Square. **Map** 3 C2. **Tel** (617) 536-5400. Ⓣ Copley. General Library: **Open** 9am–9pm Mon–Thu, 9am–5pm Fri–Sat, 1–5pm Sun. **Closed** public hols; Jun–Sep: Sun. ⏰ 2:30pm Mon, 6pm Tue, 11am Fri–Sat. ♿ 🔲 bpl.org

Founded in 1848, the Boston Public Library was America's first metropolitan library for the public. It quickly outgrew its original building, hence the construction of the Italian *palazzo*-style Copley Square building in 1887–95. Designed by Charles McKim, the building is a marvel of fine wood and marble detail. Bates Hall, on the second floor, is particularly noted for its soaring barrel-vaulted ceiling. Sculptor Daniel Chester French fashioned the library's huge bronze doors, Edward Abbey's murals of the Quest for the Holy Grail line the book request room, and John Singer Sargent's murals of Judaism and Christianity cover a third-floor gallery. The library's collection is housed in the 1971 Boylston Street addition, a modernist structure by architect Philip Johnson.

The vast Bates Hall in the Boston Public Library, noted for its high barrel-vaulted ceiling

⓾ John Hancock Tower

200 Clarendon St. **Map** 3 C2.
Ⓣ Copley. **Closed** to the public.

The tallest building in New England, the 790-ft (240-m) rhomboid that is the John Hancock Tower cuts into Copley Square, with its mirrored facade reflecting the surroundings, including from one angle the original Hancock building, built in 1947, with its red and blue lights that forecast the local weather. The innovative design has created a 60-story office building with 10,344 windows that shares the square with its 19th-century neighbors, the Romanesque Trinity Church and the Italian Renaissance Revival Copley Plaza Hotel, without dwarfing them. It was designed by Henry Cobb of the architect firm of I. M. Pei & Partners and its construction was completed in 1975.

⓫ Berklee Performance Center

136 Massachusetts Ave. **Map** 3 A3.
Tel (617) 266-7455. Ⓣ Hynes/
Convention Center. **Open** call or
consult website for concert details.
Ⓦ berkleebpc.com

The largest independent music college in the world, Berklee College of Music has produced a number of jazz, rock, and pop stars, including producer and arranger Quincy Jones, Dixie Chicks singer Natalie Maines, and jazz-pop pianist/vocalist Diana Krall.

Berklee students as well as faculty frequently use the Berklee Performance Center as a showcase, and often as a venue for making live recordings. The warm acoustics and intimate relationship between the performers and the audience produce what is known among audiophiles as "the Berklee sound."

View over Back Bay and the Charles River from the John Hancock Tower

⓬ Boston Center for the Arts

539 Tremont St. **Map** 4 D3. **Tel** (617)
426-5000. Ⓣ Back Bay/ South End.
Cyclorama: **Open** 9am–5pm Mon–Fri.
Mills Gallery: **Open** noon–5pm Wed
& Sun; noon–9pm Thu–Sat. **Closed**
public hols. 🎭 for performances. ✉
♿ Ⓦ bcaonline.org

The centerpiece of a resurgent South End, the B.C.A. complex includes four stages, an art gallery, and artists' studios as well as the Boston Ballet Building, home to the company's educational programs, rehearsal space, and administrative offices. The Tremont Estates Building at the corner of Tremont Street, an organ factory in the years after the Civil War, now houses artists' studios, rehearsal space, and an art gallery. The largest of the B.C.A. buildings is the circular, domed Cyclorama, which opened in 1884 to exhibit the 50-ft (15-m) by 400-ft (121-m) painting *The Battle of Gettysburg* by the French artist Paul Philippoteaux. The painting was removed in 1889 and is now displayed at Gettysburg National Historic Park. It now serves as performance and exhibition space.

The Stanford Calderwood Pavilion, with a 360-seat and a 200-seat theater, opened in 2004 as the first new theater in Boston in 75 years. **The Mills Gallery** houses exhibitions focusing on emerging contemporary artists, with a strong emphasis on multimedia installations and shows with confrontational, and often provocative, themes.

Richardsonian Romanesque is a popular architectural style in Back Bay

FARTHER AFIELD

Most of Boston's historic sights are concentrated in the central colonial and Victorian city. However, the late 19th and 20th centuries saw Boston expand into the surrounding area. What were the marshlands of the Fenway now house two of Boston's most important art museums, the Museum of Fine Arts and the Isabella Stewart Gardner Museum *(see p109)*. Southeast of the city center, Columbia Point was developed in the mid-20th century and is home to the John F. Kennedy Library and Museum *(see p108)*. West of central Boston, across the

Charles River, lies Cambridge, a city in its own right and sometimes referred to as the "Socialist Democratic Republic of Cambridge," a reference to the politics of its two major colleges, Harvard and the Massachusetts Institute of Technology. Harvard Square *(see p114)* is a lively area of bookstores, cafés, and street entertainers. Charlestown, east of Cambridge, is the site of the Bunker Hill Monument *(see p122)* and the Charlestown Navy Yard, where the US's most famous warship, the USS *Constitution*, is moored.

Sights at a Glance

Towns

❼ Cambridge
❽ Charlestown
⓫ Lexington
⓬ Lincoln
⓭ Quincy

Gardens and Zoos

❶ John F. Kennedy Library and Museum
❷ Fenway Park
❸ Arnold Arboretum

❹ John F. Kennedy National Historic Site
❺ Isabella Stewart Gardner Museum
❻ *Museum of Fine Arts pp110–13*
❾ Wellesley College
❿ Broadmoor Sanctuary
㉒ Museums and Historic Site

Key

▦ Main sightseeing area
▢ Urban area
▬ Highway
▬ Major road
▭ Minor road
— Railroad

0 kilometers 5
0 miles 5

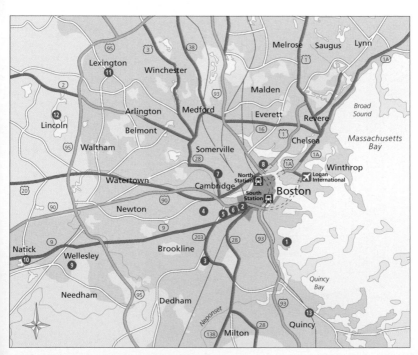

◀ Joseph Warren Statue, Bunker Hill Monument, Charlestown

For map symbols *see back flap*

❶ John F. Kennedy Library and Museum

Columbia Point, Dorchester.
Tel (617) 514-1600. Ⓣ JFK/U Mass.
Open 9am–5pm daily. **Closed** Jan 1,
Thanksgiving, Dec 25. 🐾 ♿ 🎥 🔍
W jfklibrary.org

The soaring white concrete and glass building housing the John F. Kennedy Library stands sentinel on Columbia Point near the mouth of the Boston Harbor. This striking white and black modern building by the architect I. M. Pei is equally dramatic from the interior, with a 50-ft (15-m) wall of glass looking out over the water. Exhibitions extensively chronicle the 1,000 days of the Kennedy presidency with an immediacy uncommon in many other historical museums. Kennedy was among the first politicians to grasp the power of media. The museum takes full advantage of film and video footage to use the president's own words and image to tell his story: his campaign for the Democratic Party nomination, landmark television debates with Republican opponent Richard M. Nixon (who later became infamous for the Watergate Scandal), and his many addresses to the nation.

Spectators enjoying a baseball game at Fenway Park

Several rooms re-create key chambers of the White House during the Kennedy administration, including the Oval Office; gripping film clips capture the anxiety of nuclear brinksmanship during the Cuban missile crisis as well as the inspirational spirit of the space program and the founding of the Peace Corps. Recently expanded exhibits on Robert F. Kennedy's role as Attorney General touch on both his deft handling of race relations and his key advisory role to his brother. The combination of artifacts, displays, and television footage evoke both the euphoria of "Camelot" and the numb horror of the assassination.

❷ Fenway Park

4 Yawkey Way. **Tel** (877) 733-7699.
Ⓣ Kenmore. **Open** through the year,
check website for details on events.
🐾 🎥 daily. **W** redsox.com

Whatever their loyalties, sports fans from all over the world flock to this civic icon, the home of the wildly popular Boston Red Sox. Opened in 1912, this is the oldest Major League baseball park and a shrine to the national pastime.

Tickets to games during the baseball season (April to October) can be hard to come by, but one-hour tours are offered daily throughout the year. Knowledgeable tour guides provide visitors with a behind-the-scenes look at the park's many intricacies, including a stop atop the fabled Green Monster, which stands 37 ft (11 m) above left-field. The venue has also become a popular summertime concert space, hosting big-name acts such as Bruce Springsteen and the Rolling Stones.

❸ Arnold Arboretum

125 Arborway, Jamaica Plain.
Tel (617) 524-1718. Ⓣ Forest Hills.
🚌 39. **Open** sunrise–sunset daily.
Visitors Center: **Open** 9am–4pm
Mon–Fri, 10am–4pm Sat, noon–4pm
Sun. **Closed** public hols. ♿
W arboretum.harvard.edu

Founded by Harvard University in 1872 as a living catalog of all the indigenous and exotic trees and shrubs adaptable to

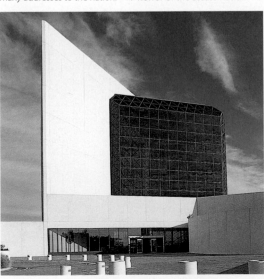
Dramatic, modern structure of the John F. Kennedy Library and Museum

New England's climate, the Arboretum is planted with more than 15,000 labeled specimens. It is the oldest arboretum in the US and a key resource for botanical and horticultural research. The Arboretum also serves as a park where people jog, stroll, read, and paint.

The park's busiest time is on Lilac Sunday in early May when tens of thousands come to revel in the sight and fragrance of the lilac collection, one of the largest in the world. The range of the Arboretum's collections guarantees flowers from late March into November, beginning with cornelian cherry and forsythia. Blooms shift in late May to azalea, magnolia, and wisteria, then to mountain laurel and roses in June. Sweet autumn clematis bursts forth in September, and native witch hazel blooms in October and November. The Arboretum also has fine fall foliage in September and October.

A large scale model of the Arboretum can be seen in the Visitors' Information Center just inside the main gate.

❹ John F. Kennedy National Historic Site

83 Beals St., Brookline. **Tel** (617) 566-7937. Ⓣ Coolidge Corner. **Open** late May–Sep: 9:30am–5pm Wed–Sun. ▨ ⚅ ♿ ⬜ Ⓦ nps.gov/jofi

The first home of the late president's parents, this Brookline house saw the birth of four of nine Kennedy children, including J.F.K. on May 29, 1917. Although the Kennedys moved to a larger house in 1921, the Beals Street residence held special memories for the family, who repurchased the house in 1966 and furnished it with their belongings circa 1917 as a memorial to John F. Kennedy. The guided tour includes a taped interview with J.F.K.'s mother Rose. A walking tour takes in other neighborhood sites relevant to the family's early years.

Central courtyard of the *palazzo*-style Isabella Stewart Gardner Museum

❺ Isabella Stewart Gardner Museum

280 The Fenway. **Tel** (617) 566-1401. Ⓣ MFA. **Open** 11am–5pm Tue–Sun. **Closed** Jan 1, Thanksgiving, Dec 25. ▨ ▨ ♿ Concerts: (call for schedule). Ⓦ **gardnermuseum.org**

The only thing more surprising than a Venetian *palazzo* on The Fenway is the collection of more than 2,500 works of art inside. Advised by scholar Bernard Berenson, the strong-willed Isabella Stewart Gardner turned her wealth to collecting art in the late 19th century, acquiring a notable collection of Old Masters and Italian Renaissance pieces. Titian's *Rape of Europa*, for example, is considered his best painting in a US museum. The eccentric "Mrs. Jack" had an eye for her contemporaries as well. She purchased the first Matisse to enter an American collection and was an ardent patron of James McNeill Whistler and John Singer Sargent. The paintings, sculptures, and tapestries are displayed on three levels around a stunning skylit courtyard. Mrs. Gardner's will stipulates the collection should remain assembled in the manner that she originally intended. Her intentions were thwarted in 1990, when thieves stole 13 priceless works, including a rare Rembrandt seascape. On a more positive note, a wing designed by the Italian architect Renzo Piano opened in 2012 with gallery space and a performance hall for the Gardner's concert series.

The Emerald Necklace

Best known as designer of New York's Central Park, Frederick Law Olmsted based himself in Boston, where he created parks to solve environmental problems and provide a green refuge for inhabitants of the 19th-century industrial city. The Emerald Necklace includes the green spaces of Boston Common and the Public Garden *(see pp68–9)* and Commonwealth Avenue *(see p101)*. To create a ring of parks, Olmsted added the Back Bay Fens (site of beautiful rose gardens and gateway to the Museum of Fine

Jamaica Pond, part of Boston's fine parklands

Arts and the Isabella Stewart Gardner Museum), the rustic Riverway, Jamaica Pond (sailing and picnicking), Arnold Arboretum, and Franklin Park (a golf course, zoo, and cross-country ski trails). The 5-mile (8-km) swath of parkland makes an excellent bicycle tour or ambitious walk.

❻ The Museum of Fine Arts

This is the largest art museum in New England and one of the great encyclopedic art museums in the United States. Its collection includes around 450,000 objects, ranging from Egyptian artifacts to paintings by John Singer Sargent. The MFA's original 1909 Beaux Arts-style building was augmented in 2010 by the 53 galleries of the Art of the Americas Wing, designed by Foster and Partners. In 2011, the museum transformed its west-facing wing, designed in 1981 by I.M. Pei, into the Linde Family Wing for Contemporary Art.

Linde Family Wing

★ Egyptian Mummies
Among the museum's Egyptian and Nubian art is this tomb group of Nes-mut-aat-neru (767–656 BC) of Thebes.

American Silver
The revolutionary Paul Revere *(see p25)* was also a noted silversmith and produced many beautiful objects, such as this ornate teapot.

Fenway Entrance

★ Japanese Temple Room
This room was created in 1909 to provide a space in which to contemplate Buddhist art. The MFA has one of the finest Japanese collections outside Japan.

Calderwood Courtyard

S Co

Huntingdon Entrance

★ Copley Portraits
John Singleton Copley (1738–1815) painted the celebrities of his day, hence this portrait of a dandyish John Hancock *(see p25).*

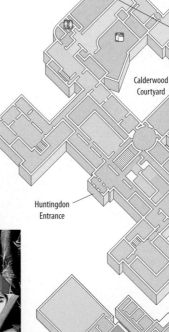

Lower Ground

For hotels and restaurants in this region see pp310–13 and pp324–9

Head of Aphrodite
This rare example of Ancient Greek sculpture dates from about 330–300 BC.

Level 3

Level 2

Level 1

VISITORS' CHECKLIST

Practical Information
Avenue of the Arts, 465 Huntington Ave.
Tel (617) 267-9300.
W mfa.org
Open 10am–4:45pm Sat–Tue, 10am–9:45pm Wed–Fri.
Closed most public hols.
🎫 ♿ 🛍 📷 Lectures, concerts, and films: 🎞 🖥 🎦

Transport
Ⓣ MFA.

Sargent Murals
John Singer Sargent spent the last years of his life creating artwork for the MFA. Originally commissioned to produce three paintings, Sargent instead constructed these elaborate murals, which were unveiled in 1921 and can still be seen today. He went on to create the works of art in the adjacent colonnade until his death in 1925.

Gallery Guide

The Linde Family Wing (west side) displays contemporary art and houses a restaurant and the museum store. European, Classical, Far Eastern, and Egyptian art and artifacts occupy the original MFA building. Arts from North, Central, and South America are displayed over four levels in the Art of the Americas Wing. Works on display are subject to change.

Key

☐ Art of Europe
☐ Contemporary Art
☐ Art of Asia, Oceania, and Africa
■ Art of the Ancient World
■ Art of the Americas
☐ Special/Temporary exhibitions
☐ Non-exhibition space

★ **Impressionist Paintings**
Boston collectors were among the first to appreciate French Impressionism. *Dance at Bougival* (1883) by Renoir is typical of the MFA collection.

Exploring the Museum of Fine Arts

In addition to the major collections noted below, the Museum of Fine Arts has important holdings in the arts of Africa, Oceania, and the ancient Americas. The museum also houses collections of works on paper, contemporary art, and musical instruments. Several galleries are devoted to temporary thematic exhibitions. Other features of the museum include a seminar room, lecture hall, and well-stocked bookstore. The museum also offers several eateries, ranging from an open courtyard café to a fine-dining restaurant.

Boston Harbor by the Luminist painter Fitz Hugh Lane (1804–65)

American Paintings, Decorative Arts, and Sculpture

The M.F.A. displays a wealth of American art that includes more than 1,600 paintings. The earliest works on show are anonymous portraits painted in the late 17th century. The Colonial period is well represented, with more than 60 portraits by John Singleton Copley, perhaps America's most talented 18th-century painter, as well as works by Charles Willson Peale. Other works on display are 19th-century landscapes, including harbor scenes by Fitz Hugh Lane, an early Luminist painter, lush society portraits by John Singer Sargent, and those of other late 19th- century artists who constituted the "Boston School." There are also notable seascapes by Winslow Homer on show, who often painted on the Massachusetts coast,

as well as the muscular figure portraiture of Thomas Eakins. The M.F.A. also houses a sampling of works by 20th-century masters, including Stuart Davis, Jackson Pollock, Georgia O'Keeffe, and Arthur Dove.

The museum's holdings of American silver are superb. As well as works by John Coney, there are two cases containing tea services and other pieces by Paul Revere *(see p92)*. The M.F.A. also traces the development of the Boston style of 18th-century furniture through a definitive collection of desks, high chests,

and tall clocks. The museum's period rooms display decorative arts in their historical context. They include furnishings and the reproduced decor of three circa-1800 rooms from a Peabody mansion designed by Federal-period master architect and wood carver Samuel McIntyre.

European Paintings, Decorative Arts, and Sculpture

This collection of European paintings and sculpture ranges from the 7th to the late 20th century. It showcases numerous masterpieces by English, Dutch, French, Italian, and Spanish artists, including various portraits by the 17th-century Dutch painter Rembrandt. The collection of works from 1550 to 1700 is impressive both for the quality of art and for its size; it includes Francisco de Zurbarán, El Greco, Paolo Veronese, Titian, and Peter Paul Rubens.

Boston's 19th-century collectors enriched the M.F.A. with wonderful French art: the museum features several paintings by Pierre François Millet (the M.F.A. has, in fact, the largest collection of his work in the world), as well as by other well-known 19th-century French artists, such as Edouard Manet, Pierre-Auguste Renoir, and Edgar Degas. Among this collection are the hugely popular *Waterlilies* (1905) by Claude Monet and *Dance at Bougival* (1883) by Renoir. The M.F.A.'s Monet holdings are among the world's largest, and there is also a good collection of paintings by the Dutch artist Vincent van Gogh. Early

Where Do We Come From? What Are We? Where Are We Going? by Paul Gauguin (1848–1903)

Part of the Processional Way of Ancient Babylonia (6th century BC)

20th-century European art is also exhibited.

The Raab Gallery for European Modernism chronicles the major movements of 20th-century art, from Fauvism in the early 1900s through to 1960, with particular emphasis on Expressionist works by Oskar Kokoschka, Ernst Kirchner, Max Beckmann, and Kathe Kollwitz.

The M.F.A. is also renowned for its collections of European decorative arts and sculpture, which are among the most significant in the US. The collections of English silver and porcelain, considered to be some of the world's most comprehensive, are complemented by extensive holdings of 18th-century French decorative arts.

Ancient Egyptian, Nubian, and Near Eastern Art

The M.F.A.'s collection of Egyptian and Nubian materials is unparalleled outside of Africa, and it derives primarily from M.F.A.-Harvard University excavations along the Nile, which began in 1905. One of the highlights is a 1998 installation showing Egyptian Funerary Arts, which uses the M.F.A.'s superb collection of mummies from nearly three millennia to illustrate the technical and art-historical aspects of Egyptian burial practices. Also on display are some exceptional Babylonian, Assyrian, and Sumerian reliefs. Works from ancient Nubia, the cultural region around the Nile stretching roughly between the modern African cities of Aswan and Khartoum, encompass gold and silver artifacts, ceramics, and jewels.

Other highlights from the Egyptian and Nubian collections include two monumental sculptures of Nubian kings from the Great Temple of Amen at Napata (620–586 BC and 600–580 BC). A few of the galleries are set up to re-create Nubian burial chambers, which allows cuneiform wall carvings to be displayed in something akin to an original setting; a superb example is the offering chapel of Sekhem-ankh-Ptah from Sakkara (2450–2350 BC).

Classical Art

The M.F.A. boasts one of America's top collections of Greek ceramics. In particular, the red- and black-figured vases dating from the 6th and 5th centuries BC are exceptional. The Classical galleries of the museum are

Roman fresco, excavated from a Pompeian villa (1st century AD)

intended to thematically highlight the influence of Greek arts on both Etruscan and Roman art. The Etruscan collection has several carved sarcophagi, gold jewelry, bronze mirrors, and colorful terracottas, while the Roman collection features grave markers, portrait busts, and a series of wall panel paintings unearthed in Pompeii on an M.F.A. expedition in 1900–01.

Asian Art

The Asian collection is one of the most extensive that can be found under one roof. A range of works from India, the Near East, and Central Asia is exhibited. Among the highlights are Indian sculpture and changing exhibitions of Islamic miniature paintings and Indian narrative paintings. Elsewhere, works from Korea feature some Buddhist paintings and sculptures, jewelry, and ornaments.

Tang Dynasty Chinese Horse (8th century)

The museum also boasts calligraphy, ceramics, and stone sculptures from China and the largest collection of Japanese prints outside Japan. Extensive holdings and limited display space mean that exhibitions change often, but the M.F.A.'s collections of Japanese and Chinese scroll and screen paintings are, nevertheless, unmatched in the West. The strength of the M.F.A.'s Japanese art collection is largely due to the efforts of enthusiasts such as Ernest Fenollosa and William Bigelow Sturgis. In the 19th century, they encouraged the Japanese to maintain their traditions, and salvaged Buddhist temple art when the Japanese imperial government had withdrawn subsidies from these institutions. This collection is considered to contain some of the finest examples of Asian temple art in the world.

❼ Cambridge

Part of the greater Boston metropolitan area, Cambridge is, nonetheless, a city in its own right and has the mood and feel of such. Principally a college town, it is dominated by Harvard University and other college campuses. It also boasts a number of important historic sights, such as Christ Church and Cambridge Common, which have associations to the American Revolution. Harvard Square is the area's main entertainment and shopping district.

Site of the Washington Elm, on Cambridge Common

🏛 Longfellow House – Washington's Headquarters National Historic Site

105 Brattle St. **Tel** (617) 876-4491.
Open Jun–Oct: 10am–4:30pm Wed–Sun. 🖼 ♿ 📷 💻 **nps.gov/long**

This house on Brattle Street, like many around it, was built by Colonial-era merchants loyal to the British Crown during the Revolution. It was seized by American revolutionaries and served as George Washington's headquarters during the Siege of Boston.

The poet Henry Wadsworth Longfellow boarded here in 1837, was given the house as a wedding present in 1843, and lived here until his death in 1888. He wrote his most famous poems here, including *Tales of a Wayside Inn* and *The Song of Hiawatha*. Longfellow's status as literary dean of Boston meant that Nathaniel Hawthorne and Charles Sumner, among others, were regular visitors.

Street musician, Harvard Square

🏛 Harvard Square

ℹ (617) 491-3434. ♿
💻 **harvardsquare.com**

Even Bostonians think of Harvard Square as a stand-in for Cambridge – the square was the original site of Cambridge from around 1630. Dominating the square is the Harvard Cooperative Society ("the Coop"), a Harvard institution that sells inexpensive clothes, posters, and books.

Harvard's large student population is very much in evidence here, adding color to the character of the square. Many trendy boutiques, inexpensive restaurants, and friendly cafés cater to their needs. Street performers abound, especially on the weekends, and the square has long been a place where pop trends begin. Club Passim, for example, has incubated many successful singer-songwriters since Joan Baez first debuted here in 1959.

🏛 Cambridge Common

Set aside as common pasture and military drill ground in 1631, Cambridge Common has served as a center for religious, social, and political activity ever since. George Washington took command of the Continental Army here on July 3, 1775, beneath the Washington Elm, now marked by a stone. The common served as the army's encampment from 1775 to 1776. In 1997 the first monument in the US to commemorate the victims of the Irish Famine was unveiled on the common.

⛪ Christ Church

Garden St. **Tel** (617) 876-0200.
Open 8am–5pm Mon–Fri & Sun, 8am–3pm Sat. ⛪ 7:45am, 10:15am Sun (Sep–Jun also 5:30pm), 12:10pm Wed. 🖼 ♿ 💻 **cccambridge.org**

With its square bell tower and plain, gray shingled edifice, Christ Church is a restrained example of an Anglican church. Designed in 1761 by Peter Harrison, the architect of Boston's King's Chapel (*see p80*), Christ Church came in for rough treatment as a barracks for Continental Army troops in 1775 – British loyalists had almost all fled Cambridge by this time. The army even melted down the organ pipes to cast musket balls. The church was restored for services on New Year's Eve, 1775, when George Washington and his wife, Martha, were among the worshipers. Anti-Anglican sentiment remained strong in Cambridge, and Christ Church did not have its own rector again until the 19th century.

Simple interior of Christ Church, designed prior to the Revolution in 1761

For hotels and restaurants in this region see pp310–13 and pp324–9

🔲 Radcliffe Institute for Advanced Study

Brattle St. **Tel** (617) 495-8601.
🔲 🔲 radcliffe.edu

Radcliffe College was founded in 1879 as the Collegiate Institution for Women, when 27 women began to study by private arrangement with Harvard professors. By 1943, members of Harvard's faculty no longer taught separate undergraduate courses to the women of Radcliffe, and in 1999 Radcliffe ceased its official existence as an independent college. It is now an institute for advanced study promoting scholarship of women's culture. The first Radcliffe building was the 1806 Federal-style mansion, Fay House, on the northern corner of what became Radcliffe Yard. Schlesinger Library, on the west side of the yard, is considered a significant example of Colonial Revival architecture. The library's most famous

Stained glass, Radcliffe Institute

holdings are an extensive collection of cookbooks and reference works on gastronomy.

🔲 M.I.T.

77 Massachusetts Ave. **Tel** (617) 253-4795. MIT Museum **Open** 10am–5pm daily. 🖼 Hart Nautical Gallery **Open** 10am–5pm daily. List Visual Arts Center **Open** noon–6pm Tue–Sun (to 8pm Thu). 🔲 🔲 🔲 🔲 mit.edu

Chartered in 1861 to teach "exactly and thoroughly the fundamental principles of positive science with application to the industrial arts," the Massachusetts Institute of Technology has evolved into one of the world's leading universities in engineering and the sciences. Several architectural masterpieces dot M.I.T.'s 135-acre (55-ha) campus along the Charles River, including Eero Saarinen's Kresge Auditorium and Kresge Chapel, built in 1955. The Wiesner Building is a major collaboration between architect I. M. Pei and several artists, including Kenneth Noland, whose relief mural dominates the atrium. The building houses the **List Visual Arts Center**, noted for its avant-garde art.

The **Hart Nautical Gallery** in the Rogers Building focuses on marine engineering, with exhibits ranging from models of ships to exhibits of the latest advances in underwater research. The **M.I.T. Museum** blends art and science with exhibits such as Harold Edgerton's groundbreaking stroboscopic flash photographs, and the latest holographic art.

Harvard Square Area

① Cambridge Common
② Christ Church
③ Harvard Square
④ Harvard University Museums
   (see pp118–21)
⑤ Harvard Yard
   (see pp116–17)
⑥ Longfellow House – Washington's Headquarters National Historic Site
⑦ Radcliffe Institute or Advanced Study

Harvard Yard

In 1636 Boston's well-educated Puritan leaders founded a college in Newtowne. Two years later cleric John Harvard died and bequeathed half his estate and all his books to the fledgling college. The colony's leaders bestowed his name on the school and rechristened the surrounding community Cambridge after the English city where they had been educated. The oldest university in the US, Harvard is now one of the world's most prestigious centers of learning. The university has expanded to encompass more than 400 buildings, but Harvard Yard is still at its heart.

Holden Chapel
Built in 1742, the chapel was the scene of revolutionary speeches and was later used as a demonstration hall for human dissections.

★ Old Harvard Yard
This leafy yard dates from the founding of the college in 1636. Freshman dormitories dot the yard, and throughout the year it is a focal point for students.

Harvard University
Information Center ✦

★ John Harvard Statue
This statue celebrates Harvard's most famous benefactor. Almost a place of pilgrimage, graduates and visitors invariably pose for photographs here.

★ Widener Library
This library memorializes Harry Elkins Widener, who died on the *Titanic* in 1912. With more than 3 million volumes, it is the world's largest university library.

★ **Memorial Church**
This church was built in 1931 and copies earlier styles. For example, the steeple is modeled on that of the Old North Church *(see p91)* in Boston's North End.

VISITORS' CHECKLIST

Practical Information
Massachusetts Ave.
Open 24 hrs.
Closed Commencement (date varies, late May–early Jun). &
🎬 🔁 Lectures, concerts and films: Harvard Film Archive:
Tel (617) 495-4700.
Films shown Fri–Mon.
W harvard.edu
Harvard Information Center:
Tel (617) 495-1573.
Harvard Box Office:
Tel (617) 496-2222.

Transport
Ⓣ Harvard.

Sackler and Peabody Museums, and Harvard Museum of Natural History *(see pp120–21)*

Sever Hall
One of the most distinctive of Harvard's Halls, this Romanesque style-building was designed by Henry Hobson Richardson.

KEY

① **University Hall**, designed by Charles Bulfinch, was built in 1816.

② **Massachusetts Hall**, built in 1720, is Harvard's oldest building.

③ **Hollis Hall** was used as barracks by George Washington's troops during the American Revolution.

④ **Memorial Hall**, a Ruskin Gothic building, memorializes Harvard's Union casualties from the Civil War.

⑤ **Fogg Art and Busch-Reisinger Museums** *(see pp118–19)*

⑥ **Tercentenary Theater**

Carpenter Center for Visual Arts
Opened in 1963, the Carpenter Center is the only building in the US designed by the avant-garde Swiss architect Le Corbusier.

| 0 meters | 50 |
| 0 yards | 50 |

Harvard University Museums

Harvard's museums were originally conceived to revolutionize the process of education; students were to be taught by allowing them access to artifacts from around the world. Today, this tradition continues, with the museums housing some of the world's finest university collections: art from Europe and America in the Fogg Art and Busch-Reisinger Museums; archaeological finds in the Peabody Museum; Asian, Islamic and Indian art in the Sackler Museum, and a vast collection of artifacts in the Harvard Museum of Natural History.

Main entrance to the Fogg Art and Busch-Reisinger Museums

Fogg Art and Busch-Reisinger Museums

32 Quincy St. **Tel** (617) 495-9400. **Closed** for renovation; call ahead or check website for details. 🅿 ♿ 🛍
W **harvardartmuseums.org**

Both these museums are currently closed for renovation. The Fogg was created in 1891, when Harvard began to build its own art collection to teach art history more effectively. Both the Fogg and the Busch-Reisinger, which was grafted onto the Fogg in 1991, have select collections of art from Europe and America.

The red-brick Georgian building housing the Fogg was completed in 1927. The collections, which focus on Western art from the late Middle Ages to the present, are organized around a central courtyard modeled on a 16th-century church in Montepulciano, Italy. The ground-floor corridors surrounding the courtyard feature 12th- century capitals from Moutiers St-Jean in Burgundy, France.

Two small galleries near the entrance, and the two-story Warburg Hall, display the Fogg's collections that prefigure the Italian Renaissance. The massive

altarpieces and suspended crucifix in the Warburg are particularly impressive.

The ground floor galleries on the left side of the entrance are devoted to 17th-century Dutch, Flemish, French, and Italian paintings, including four studies for Francesco Trevisiani's *Massacre of the Innocents*, a masterpiece destroyed in Dresden in World War II. Another room details Gian Lorenzo Bernini's use of clay models for his large-scale marbles and bronzes.

The museum's second level features the emergence of landscape as a subject in French 19th-century painting.

Galleries along the front of the building change exhibitions frequently, often focusing on drawings and graphic arts. The highlight of the second level is the Maurice Wertheim collection of Impressionist and Post-Impressionist art, most of it collected in the late 1930s. With a number of important

Light-Space Modulator (1923 – 30) by the Hungarian Moholy-Nagy

paintings by Renoir, Manet, and Degas, the Wertheim gallery is the Fogg's most popular.

Surprises lurk in an adjacent gallery of art made in France 1885-1960, often by expatriate artists. Edvard Munch's 1891 painting of *Rue de Rivoli*, for example, is both bright and impressionistic, in contrast with his collection of bleak Expressionist paintings.

The museum also houses rotating displays from its collection of 19th- and 20th-century African art.

Werner Otto Hall, which contains the Busch-Reisinger Museum, is entered through the second level of the Fogg. The museum's collections focus on Germanic art and

Bernini Model
(1674-75)
Gian Lorenzo Bernini crafted this clay model of a kneeling angel to guide the artisans casting his larger bronze.

First floor

Main entrance

Guide to the Fogg Art and Busch-Reisinger Museums

Western art from the Middle Ages to the present is on the first floor of the Fogg Art Museum. French and American art from the 19th and 20th centuries and 20th-century American art are on the second floor. The Busch-Reisinger focuses on Germanic art.

design from after 1880, with an emphasis on Expressionism. Harvard was a safe haven for many Bauhaus artists, architects, and designers who fled Nazi Germany, and both Walter Gropius and Lyonel Feininger chose the Busch-Reisinger as the depository of their personal papers and drawings.

Periodic exhibitions explore aspects of the work and philosophy of the Bauhaus movement. Although small, the museum owns major paintings and sculptures by 20th-century masters such as Max Beckmann, Lyonel Feininger, Wassily Kandinsky, Paul Klee, Oskar Kokoschka, Emil Nolde, and Franz Marc.

Calderwood Courtyard of the Fogg Art Museum

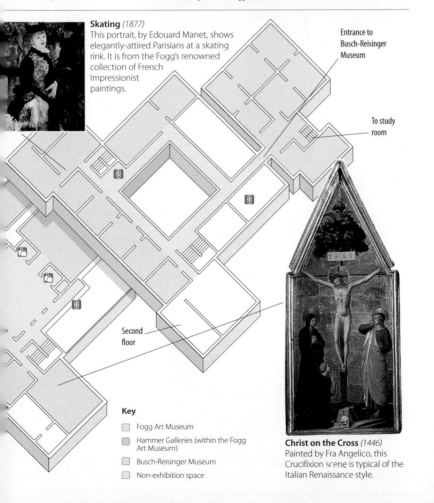

Skating (1877)
This portrait, by Edouard Manet, shows elegantly-attired Parisians at a skating rink. It is from the Fogg's renowned collection of French Impressionist paintings.

Entrance to Busch-Reisinger Museum

To study room

Second floor

Key

- ☐ Fogg Art Museum
- ☐ Hammer Galleries (within the Fogg Art Museum)
- ☐ Busch-Reisinger Museum
- ☐ Non-exhibition space

Christ on the Cross (1446)
Painted by Fra Angelico, this Crucifixion scene is typical of the Italian Renaissance style.

Peabody Museum of Archaeology and Ethnology

11 Divinity Ave. **Tel** (617) 496-1027.
Open 9am–5pm daily. **Closed** Jan 1,
Thanksgiving, Dec 24, 25. 🖼 🖖 🎦
W **peabody.harvard.edu**

The Peabody Museum of
Archaeology and Ethnology
was founded in 1866 as the
first museum in the Americas
devoted solely to
anthropology. The
many collections,
which include
several million artifacts
and more than 500,000
photographic images,
come from all around
the world. Initially, in
the 19th century, the
museum's pioneering
archaeological and
ethnological research
began relatively close
to home with
excavations of Mayan
sites in Central
America. The Peabody
also conducted some
of the first and most
important research
on the precontact
Anasazi people of the
American Southwest
and on the cultural
history of the later
Pueblo tribes of the
same region. Joint
expeditions sponsored
by the Peabody
Museum and the Museum of
Fine Arts *(see pp110–11)* also
uncovered some of the richest
finds of dynastic and predynastic
Egypt. Research continued in all
these areas well into the 20th
century and later broadened to
embrace the cultures of the
islands of the South Pacific.

Native American totem
pole, Peabody Museum

The Hall of the North American
Indian on the ground level
was completely overhauled
so that the artifacts could
be displayed in a way that
puts them in the context
of the time when they
were gathered, when
European and Native
cultures first came into
contact. For example,
the Native American
tribes of the Northern
Plains are interpreted
largely through an
exhibition detailing
the Lewis and Clark
expedition of 1804–
1806; these two
explorers undertook to
find a route, by water,
from East to West
Coast, and on their
way collected
innumerable artifacts.
Other outstanding
exhibits include totem
carvings by Pacific
Northwest tribes and
a wide range of
historic and
contemporary Navajo
weavings. The third
floor is devoted to
Central American
anthropology, with
casts of some of the
ruins uncovered at
Copán in Honduras
and Chichen Itza
in Mexico. The fourth floor
concentrates on Polynesia,
Micronesia, and other islands
of the Pacific, with striking
collections of ceremonial
objects, such as masks.
Small vessels used for fishing
and near-island trading
hang overhead.

Triceratops skull in the Harvard Museum of
Natural History

Harvard Museum of Natural History

26 Oxford St. **Tel** (617) 495-3045.
Open 9am–5pm daily. **Closed** Jan 1,
Thanksgiving, Dec 24, 25. 🖼 🖖 🎦
W **hmnh.harvard.edu**

The Harvard Museum of Natural
History is actually three museums
rolled into one, all displayed on
a single floor of a turn-of-the-
century classroom building. It
includes the collections of the
Mineralogical and Geological
Museum, the Museum of
Comparative Zoology, and
the Botanical Museum. The
straightforward presentation
of labeled objects exudes an
infectious, old-fashioned charm,
yet their initial appearance
belies the fact that these are
some of the most complete
collections of their kind.

The mineralogical galleries
include some of Harvard
University's oldest specimen
collections, the oldest of which
dates from 1783. Virtually every
New England mineral, rock, and
gem type is represented here,
including rough and cut gem-
stones and one of the world's
premier meteorite collections.

The zoological galleries owe
their inception to the great
19th-century biologist Louis
Agassiz and include his personal
arachnid collection. The
collection of taxidermied bird,
mammal, and reptile specimens
is comprehensive, and there is
also a collection of dinosaur
skeletons. Children are most
fascinated by the giant
kronosaurus (a type of prehistoric
sea serpent) and the skeleton
of the first triceratops ever
described in scientific literature.

Frog mask fom Easter Island in the South Pacific, Peabody Museum

There are also fossil exhibits of the earliest invertebrates and reptiles, as well as skeletons of still-living species, including a collection of whale skeletons.

The collections in the botanical galleries include the Ware Collection of Blaschka Glass Models of Plants, popularly known as the "glass flowers." Between 1887 and 1936, father and son artisans Leopold and Rudolph Blaschka created these 3,000 exacting models of 850 plant species. Each species is illustrated with a scientifically accurate lifesize model and magnified parts. While the handblown models were created as teaching aids, they are a unique accomplishment in the glassblowers' art and are as prized for their aesthetic qualities as their scientific utility.

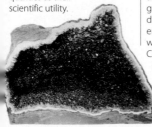

Amethyst specimen in the Harvard Museum of Natural History

Sackler Museum

485 Broadway, Cambridge. **Tel** (617) 495-9400. **Closed** for renovation; call ahead or check website for details. 🅿 ♿ 📷
Ⓦ **harvardartmuseums.org**

Named after a famous philanthropist, physician, and art collector, the Arthur M. Sackler Museum was built to display Harvard's collection of ancient, Asian, Islamic, and late Indian art. Be sure to pick up a gallery map and flyers on the configuration of current exhibitions.

Opened in 1985, the Sackler is housed in a modern building designed by James F. Stirling and his firm of architects based in London, England. The building is itself a bold artistic statement that complements the more traditional Fogg Art Museum that sits directly across from it. Aware that Harvard University had long embarked on a tradition of erecting many unique buildings in the area just north and east of Harvard Yard, Stirling was prompted to introduce the innovatively designed building to the world as "the newest animal in Harvard's architectural zoo." The exterior borrows details and decorative devices from several surrounding buildings, while the starkly modern interior galleries provide optimal display space. The 30-ft (10-m) entrance lobby features a 1997 wall-painting by the late Conceptual artist Sol Lewitt (1928–2007), whose trademark was colorful geometric shapes, which appear to float in space. The original design of the building called for an enclosed walkway over a major street to connect the Sackler to the Fogg, thereby creating a formal gateway to Harvard, but the plan was thwarted by Cambridge neighborhood activists.

Southeast Asian Buddha head, Sackler Museum

The Sackler is best toured by ascending the long staircase to the galleries on the fourth floor and then working back down to the lobby.

Holdings include ancient Greek art with a coin collection from the empire of Alexander the Great, and unusually extensive collections of red and black pottery with decorative friezes. The collections of Chinese art, including many objects which were the gifts of Harvard-affiliated diplomats, are thought to be among the finest of Chinese art in the West. They include Chinese sculpture, Buddhist stone sculpture, and archaic Chinese bronzes, jades, and ceramics. The Southeast Asian collections are particularly interesting for their Buddhist sculptures and figures from Hindu mythology. Also included in the collection are Korean ceramics, Japanese ukiyo-e prints, and former ambassador to India John Kenneth Galbraith's (1908–2006) Indian paintings.

Buddhist sculptures, part of the Sackler's Asian and Indian collections

❽ Charlestown

Situated on the north bank of the Charles River, directly opposite the North End, Charlestown exudes history. The site of the infamous Battle of Bunker Hill, when American troops suffered huge losses in their fight for independence, today the district forms a major part of Boston's Freedom Trail *(see pp58–61)*. As well as sights from the American Revolution, visitors can see USS *Constitution*, pride of the post-revolutionary American Navy, which took part in the 1812 war with Britain. Also of interest is the Charlestown Navy Yard.

Granite obelisk of the Bunker Hill Monument, erected in 1843

🏛 Bunker Hill Monument

Monument Square. **Tel** (617) 242-5641. **Open** 9am–5pm daily (until 6pm Jul & Aug). **Closed** Jan 1, Thanksgiving, Dec 25. **W** **nps.gov/bost**

In the Revolution's first pitched battle between British and colonial troops, which took place on June 17, 1775, the British won a Pyrrhic victory on the battlefield but failed to create an escape route from the Boston peninsula to the mainland. Following the battle, American irregulars were joined by other militia to keep British forces penned up until the Continental Army, under the command of General George Washington, forced their evacuation by sea the following March 17, still celebrated in the Boston area as Evacuation Day.

The citizens of Charlestown began raising funds for the Bunker Hill Monument in 1823, laid the cornerstone in 1825 and dedicated the 221-ft (67-m) granite obelisk in 1843. There is

no elevator, but the 294-step climb to the top is rewarded with spectacular views.

The ground-level museum, completely accessible for the disabled, focuses on the strategies and significance of the Battle of Bunker Hill. High-efficiency lighting fully illuminates the monument at night and reveals the pyramid that caps the obelisk – a design echoed at the tops of the pylons of the nearby Leonard P. Zakim Bunker Hill Bridge. Be aware that during the winter months, the monument may be closed due to ice and snow accumulation on the stairs.

🏛 City Square

When John Winthrop arrived with three shiploads of Puritan refugees in 1630, they settled first in the marshes at the base of Town Hill, now City Square. A small public park now marks the site of Winthrop's Town House, the very first seat of Boston government.

Municipal art in City Square

🏛 John Harvard Mall

Ten families founded Charlestown in 1629, a year before the rest of Boston was settled. They built their homes and a palisaded fort on Town Hill, a spot now marked by John Harvard Mall. Several bronze plaques within the small enclosed park commemorate events in the early history of the Massachusetts Bay Colony *(see p46)*, one plaque proclaiming "this low mound of earth the memorial of a mighty nation." A small monument pays homage to John Harvard, the young cleric who ministered to the Charlestown settlers and who left his name, half his estate, and all his books to the fledgling college at Newtowne when he died in 1638 *(see pp116–17)*.

🏛 Warren Tavern

2 Pleasant St. **Tel** (617) 241-8142. **Open** lunch, dinner daily, brunch Sat–Sun. **W** **warrentavern.com**

Dating from 1780, Warren Tavern was one of the first buildings erected after the British burned Charlestown. It was named after Joseph Warren, president of the Provincial Congress in 1774 and a general in the Massachusetts Army. He enlisted as a private with the Continental Army for the Battle of Bunker Hill, where he was killed. The tavern, once derelict, has been restored to its 18th-century style. By contrast, the food is modern fare.

Old-fashioned clapboard houses on Warren Street

USS *Constitution*, built in 1797, moored in Charlestown Navy Yard

Charlestown Navy Yard

Visitor Center, Building 5. **Tel** (617) 242-5601. **Open** 9am–5pm daily (till 6pm Jul & Aug). **Closed** Jan 1, Thanksgiving, Dec 25. ♿ 📷

w **nps.gov/bost**

Boston's deep harbor and long tides made Charlestown a logical site for one of the US Navy's first shipyards, established in 1800. For 174 years, as the Navy moved from wooden sailing ships to steel giants, Charlestown Navy Yard played a key role in supporting the US Atlantic fleet.

On decommissioning, the facility was transferred to the National Park Service to interpret the art and history of naval shipbuilding. The yard was designed by Alexander Parris, architect of Quincy Market *(see p84)*, and was one of the first examples of industrial architecture in Boston.

Drydock No. 1, built in 1802, was the one of the first docks that could be drained of water – its first occupant was USS *Constitution*. Visitors can also board the World War II destroyer USS *Cassin Young*.

USS Constitution

Charlestown Navy Yard. **Tel** (617) 242-5671. **Open** Apr–Oct: 10am–6pm Tue–Sun; Nov–Mar: 10am–4pm Thu–Sun. Metal detector scan and ID may be required. ♿ 📷 Museum **Open** Apr–Oct: 9am–6pm daily; Nov–Mar: 10am–5pm daily. **Closed** Jan 1, Thanksgiving, Dec 25. 🎫 ♿

w **ussconstitutionmuseum.org**

The oldest commissioned warship afloat, the USS *Constitution* was built in the North End and christened in 1797. She saw immediate action in the Mediterranean protecting American shipping from the Barbary pirates. In the War of 1812, she won fame and her

nickname of "Old Ironsides" when cannonballs bounced off her in a battle with the British ship *Guerriere*. She won 42 battles, lost none, captured 20 vessels, and was never boarded by an enemy. She was nearly scuttled several times. In 1830, Oliver Wendell Holmes penned the poem *Old Ironsides*, which rallied public support to save the ship, while on another occasion, in the 1920s, schoolchildren sent in their pennies and nickels to salvage her. She underwent her most thorough overhaul in time for her 1997 bicentennial, able to carry her own canvas into the wind for the first time in a century. On July 4 each year, she is taken out into the harbor for an annual turnaround that reverses her position at the Navy Yard pier to insure equal weathering on both sides. A small museum documents her history.

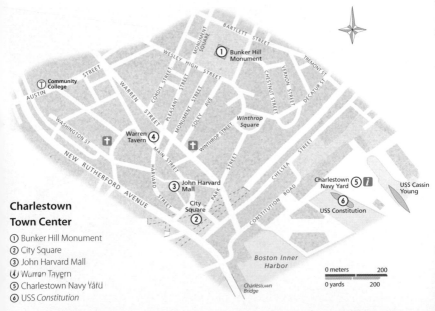

Charlestown Town Center

① Bunker Hill Monument
② City Square
③ John Harvard Mall
④ Warren Tavern
⑤ Charlestown Navy Yard
⑥ USS *Constitution*

❾ Wellesley College

106 Central St., Wellesley. **Tel** (781) 283-1000. Museum: (781) 283-2051. **Open** year-round: call for hours.
W wellesley.edu

Founded in 1875, this top college for women has former First Lady Hillary Rodham Clinton (b.1947), now US Secretary of State, among its graduates. The grounds of the hilly Gothic campus overlooking Lake Waban are a virtual arboretum, with trees tagged for easy identification.

The main attraction is the **Davis Museum and Cultural Center**, with its collection of 5,000 paintings, prints, photos, drawings, and sculptures spanning the ages from classical to contemporary. The dramatic building was the first US project for noted Spanish architect Jose Rafael Moneo (b.1937).

❿ Broadmoor Wildlife Sanctuary

280 Eliot St., S Natick. 🛈 (508) 655-2296. W massaudubon.org
Nature Center: **Open** 9am–5pm Tue–Fri, 10am–5pm Sat, Sun & public hols.
🚪 Trails: **Open** dawn–dusk Tue–Sun. 🐾 ♿

Nine miles (14.5 km) of walking trails go through field, woodland, and wetland habitats at this sanctuary. A boardwalk skirts the bank of Indian Brook before crossing a marsh. The 110-ft (33.5-m) bridge spanning the brook is an ideal lookout from which to photograph beavers, otters, and wood ducks. In winter the sanctuary is popular with snowshoe enthusiasts and cross-country skiers.

US Secretary of State Hillary Rodham Clinton, a former Wellesley College grad

⓫ Lexington

🏠 31,500. 🛈 1875 Massachusetts Ave. (781) 862-2480.
W lexingtonchamber.org

Lexington and neighboring Concord are forever linked in history as the settings for two bloody skirmishes that acted as catalysts for the Revolutionary War *(see p148)*. It was here on April 19, 1775, that armed colonists, called Minute Men, clashed with British troops on their way to Concord in search of rebel weaponry. The *Minute Man* statue stands on the town common, now known as **Lexington Battle Green**. The battle is reenacted each year in mid-April. The local Historical Society maintains three buildings linked to the battle that now display artifacts from that era. **Buckman Tavern** served as both the meeting place for the Minute

Men before the confrontation and as a makeshift hospital for their wounded. Paul Revere alerted the colonists of the advancing British troops and is said to have stopped here following his historic ride *(see box below)*. Revere also stopped at the **Hancock-Clarke House** to warn Samuel Adams (1722–1803) and John Hancock (1737–93), two of the eventual signatories to the Declaration of Independence. **Munroe Tavern** served as headquarters for British forces.

🏛 Historical Society Houses
Hancock-Clarke House: 36 Hancock St.
Buckman Tavern: 1 Bedford St. Munroe Tavern: 1332 Massachusetts Ave.
Tel (781) 862-1703. 🚶

⓬ Lincoln

🛈 (781) 259-2600.
W lincolntown.org

Located just 13 miles (21 km) from Boston at the midway point between Concord and Lexington, Lincoln was once called "Niptown" because it was comprised of parcels of land that were "nipped" from neighboring towns. Today this wealthy rural community is noted for its interesting array of sightseeing attractions.

Buckman Tavern at Lexington, meeting place of the minute men

Paul Revere's Ride

Under the cover of night on April 18, 1775, Boston silversmith Paul Revere (1734–1818) took on a daring mission. Rowing silently past British ships in the harbor, he reached Charlestown, borrowed a horse, and rode to Lexington to spread the alarm: the British were approaching to arrest patriots John Hancock and Samuel Adams in Lexington and seize rebel arms in Concord. Detained by British troops on the way to Concord, he was released just in time to see the first shots fired on Lexington Green. Nearly 100 years later, his heroics were immortalized in the 1860 poem "Paul Revere's Ride" by New Englander Henry Wadsworth Longfellow.

Outdoor sculptures at DeCordova Sculpture Park

The **DeCordova Sculpture Park**, the largest park of its kind in New England, displays some 70 contemporary large-scale American sculptures as part of its changing outdoor exhibition. The estate was bequeathed to the town by wealthy entrepreneur and patron of the arts Julian DeCordova (1850–1945). The on-site museum is famous for its collection of contemporary New England artworks.

Walter Gropius (1883–1969), the director of the original Bauhaus school of design in Germany – and one of the 20th century's most influential architects – fled Adolf Hitler's regime and became a professor at Harvard. In 1937 he designed this modest but unique home by combining traditional New England elements, such as clapboard and fieldstone, with modern flourishes of chrome banisters and acoustical plaster. **Gropius House** stands as a prime example of Bauhaus design.

Art and architecture are also celebrated at the **Codman Estate**, built in 1740 and expanded in the 1790s by merchant John Codman. Home to five generations of the Codman family, the structure was expanded again in 1860, adding 18th-century architectural details to the interior and exterior. The three-story house is set on a 16-acre (6.5-ha) estate and contains wonderful Neo-Classical furnishings.

At **Drumlin Farm**, which is a Massachusetts Audubon Society property, visitors have an opportunity to see a working New England farm in action as well as to enjoy bird-watching and nature walks. The farm has hands-on learning activities for children.

DeCordova Sculpture Park and Museum
51 Sandy Pond Rd. **Tel** (781) 259-8355. Sculpture park: **Open** dawn to dusk daily. Museum: **Open** 10am– 5pm Tue–Sun.
W decordova.org

Gropius House
68 Baker Bridge Rd. **Tel** (781) 259-8098. **Open** Jun–mid-Oct: 11am–4pm Wed–Sun; mid-Oct–May: 11am–4pm Sat & Sun. hourly. first floor only.

Codman Estate
Codman Rd. **Tel** (781) 259-8098. **Open** Jun–mid-Oct: 11am–4pm 2nd & 4th Sat of month. hourly.

Drumlin Farm Nature Center and Wildlife Sanctuary
208 South Great Rd. **Tel** (781) 259-2200. Nature Center: **Open** Mar–Oct: 9am–5pm Tue–Sun; Nov–Feb: 9am–4pm Tue–Sun (trails open same hours).

⑬ Quincy

(617) 471-1000.
W thequincychamber.com

Now a suburb south of Boston, Quincy was once home to four generations of the Adams family, among them the second and sixth presidents of the US. The 12.5-acre (5-ha) **Adams National Historical Park** has 12 buildings, including the John Adams Birthplace, where the second president was born in 1735. His son, John Quincy Adams (1767–1848), was born just steps away at what is now called The John Quincy Adams Birthplace. Other structures include the Old House, home to four generations of the family, and a church, where both presidents and their wives are buried. A trolley provides transportation between sites.

Adams National Historical Park
1250 Hancock St. **Tel** (617) 770-1175. **Open** mid-Apr–mid-Nov: 9am– 5pm daily; Visitor Center open limited hours rest of year. partial.
W nps.gov/adam

Environs

New Bedford, 49 miles (79 km) south, was once a major whaling port. This working-class town lends its name to the **New Bedford Whaling National Historical Park**. The 13-block site commemorates whaling history and heritage. Walking maps and guided tours are available at the visitor center. Among the town's attractions is the excellent **New Bedford Whaling Museum**, which has one of the most comprehensive collections of whaling artifacts in the world, as well as model ships and figureheads. In Fall River, naval veterans at **Battleship Cove** offer year-round tours of a fleet of World War II and Cold War-era warships. In summer, a 1920 vintage wooden carousel operates.

New Bedford Whaling National Historical Park
33 William St. **Tel** (508) 996-4095. **Open** 9am–5pm daily.
W nps.gov/nebe

New Bedford Whaling Museum
18 Johnny Cake Hill. **Tel** (508) 997-0046. **Open** 9am–5pm daily (Jan–Apr: 9am–4pm Mon–Sat, noon–4pm Sun).
W whalingmuseum.org

Battleship Cove
5 Water St., Fall River. **Tel** (508) 678-1100. **Open** 9am–4:30pm daily (later in summer). **W** battleshipcove.org

Model ships on display at the New Bedford Whaling Museum

BOSTON STREET FINDER

The key map below shows the area of Boston covered by the *Street Finder* maps, which can be found on the following pages. Map references, given throughout this guide, for sights, restaurants, hotels, shops, and entertainment venues refer to the grid on the maps. The first figure in the map reference indicates which *Street Finder* map to turn to (1 to 4), and the letter and number that follow refer to the grid reference on that map.

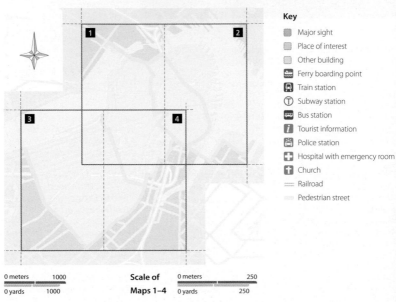

Key

- Major sight
- Place of interest
- Other building
- Ferry boarding point
- Train station
- Subway station
- Bus station
- Tourist information
- Police station
- Hospital with emergency room
- Church
- Railroad
- Pedestrian street

| 0 meters | 1000 |
| 0 yards | 1000 |

Scale of Maps 1–4

| 0 meters | 250 |
| 0 yards | 250 |

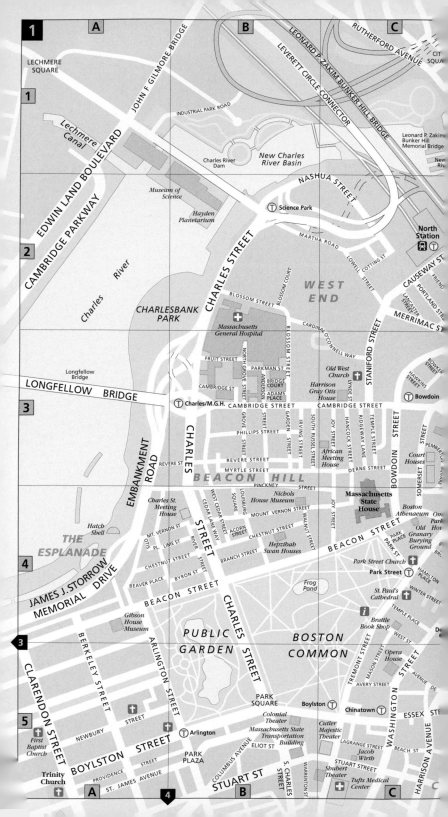

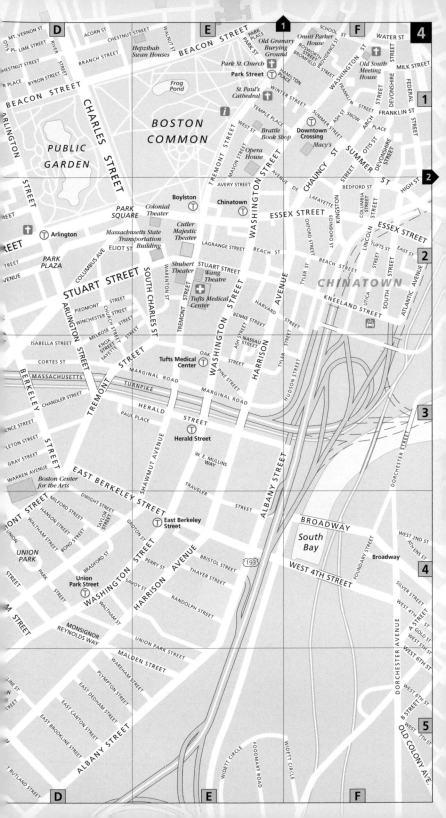

NEW ENGLAND REGION BY REGION

New England at a Glance

Tucked away in the northeasternmost corner of the United States, New England is rich in history and natural beauty. Many of the country's earliest settlements were established within these six states, with the seeds of the Revolutionary War taking root most firmly in Massachusetts. Interspersed along large tracts of rural countryside, heavy forests, and sweeping coastlines, Ivy League universities and college towns bring an influx of modernity to this historically significant region.

Vermont's fall foliage usually peaks in mid-October.

The Towne House in Old Sturbridge Village was built in 1796. Located in Sturbridge, Massachusetts, the village is one of New England's most popular living-history museums *(see p164).*

Mark Twain House in Hartford, Connecticut, is where the famous US author penned many of his most beloved works. The house was commissioned in 1873 for the then hefty sum of $45,000 *(see pp204–205).*

Newport

Lake Champlain

Be

Danville

Montpelier

Middlebury

N
Co

Lincoln

VERMONT
(See pp230–251)

Rutland

White River
Junction

Laconia

NEW HAMPSH
(See pp252–277)

Bellows
Falls

Concord

Bennington

L

MASSACHUS
(See pp136–17)

Lenox

Springfield

South

Norfolk

Provic
RH
ISLA
(See pp

Hartford

CONNECTICUT
(See pp200–229)

Old Lyme

New Haven

0 kilometers   100

0 miles   50

◀ Lush autumn forest surrounding Jordan Pond, Acadia National Park, Maine

Fort Kent

Presque
Isle

Ashland

MAINE
(See pp278–303)

Rockwood

Sugarloaf is one of Maine's
premier ski centers. The mountain
has the most continuous vertical
drop of all New England
ski slopes *(see p362–3)*.

Lubec

angeley

Bangor   Machias

Skowhegan   Ellsworth

Augusta   Bar Harbor

Lobster boats dot the waters near Isle
au Haut at Ferry Landing.

Freeport   Boothbay
            Harbor

Portland

ATLANTIC
OCEAN

**The Chase
House** is
featured in the
Strawbery Banke
restoration
project in
Portsmouth,
New Hampshire
(see pp258–9).

Portsmouth

Gloucester

on

Provincetown

Plymouth

Orleans

iver

Hyannis

Falmouth

The Breakers is one of
Newport, Rhode
Island's most opulent
mansions. Designed
after 16th-century
palaces in Italy, the
70-room masterpiece
was used as the
summer "cottage" for
the wealthy Vanderbilt
family *(see pp190–91)*.

MASSACHUSETTS

Of all the New England states, Massachusetts may have the most diverse mix of natural and man-made attractions. Miles of wide sandy beaches beckon along the eastern seaboard; green mountains and rich culture characterize the Berkshire Hills in the west. America's early architecture has been well protected, from the lanes of Boston to villages dotting coast and countryside.

Many of America's pivotal events have been played out against the backdrop of Massachusetts. In 1620 a group of 102 British Pilgrims sailing to the Virginia Colony were blown off course and forced to land farther north. Their colony at Plymouth *(see pp154–5)* was the first permanent English settlement in North America. More than 100 years later the seeds of the American Revolution took strongest root in Boston, blossoming into the nation of the United States and forever altering the course of world history.

Massachusetts has always been New England's industrial and intellectual hub. The machinery of the American Industrial Revolution chugged to life in the early 19th century in Lowell *(see p146)* and other mill towns. Later the high-tech labs in Cambridge *(see pp114–15)* would help lead the nation into the computer age. In

1944 scientists at Harvard University *(see pp116–17)*, the oldest and most prestigious college in the nation, developed the world's first digital computer. Today the venerable university attracts visitors from around the world wanting to tour its beautiful campus and explore the multitude of treasures in its magnificent museums.

Travelers can also tread the same ground as some of the country's most influential leaders. Quincy *(see p125)* honors the father and son team of John Adams (1735–1826) and John Quincy Adams (1767–1848), the nation's second and sixth presidents. Fashionable Hyannisport on Cape Cod *(see pp158–63)* is home to the Kennedy clan *(see p163)* compound. Of course, the Cape is best known for its expanse of sand dunes and beaches along the Cape Cod National Seashore *(see pp158–9)*.

Part of the stunning sculpture collection at Chesterwood in Stockbridge

◀ Pumpkins laid out in front of an old-style building in Chatham, Massachusetts

Exploring Massachusetts

Massachusetts is a wonderful destination for travelers in that such a diverse array of attractions is squeezed into a relatively small area. Art, music, theater, and dance can be found in abundance in many of the state's larger urban areas and busy college towns. Scenic seascapes, historic villages, and whale-watching junkets await along the coast and Cape Cod *(see pp158–63)*. Understandably, the coastal beaches are popular spots in summer. Venturing inland, visitors will come upon centuries-old towns, verdant forests and meadows, and countless opportunities for antiquing. As is the case with all the New England states, fall is one of the most beautiful times of year to visit.

Blooming wildflowers beside the Deerfield River

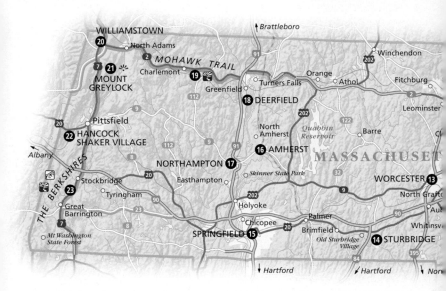

Getting Around

Interstate 93 and Interstate 95 are the two largest and most popular north-south routes leading into Boston. Interstate 495 loops outside Boston, thereby bypassing much of the heavy traffic. Highway 2 and Interstate 90 are the two biggest east-west routes. Boston's Logan International Airport is New England's largest airport. Amtrak has rail links between Boston and New York City and Boston and Portland, Maine with stops in between. Bus lines such as American Eagle, Concord Trailways, Greyhound, and Peter Pan service most of Massachusetts. Passenger and car ferries sail year-round from Cape Cod (leaving from Woods Hole) to Martha's Vineyard and from Hyannis to Nantucket. Advance reservations are essential for cars.

Brant Point, at the entrance to Nantucket Harbor

For hotels and restaurants in this region see pp313–14and pp329–31

Sights at a Glance

The impressive Minute Man Visitor Center
in Lexington

Key

— Highway
— Major road
--- Minor road
— Scenic route
-·- Main railroad
— Minor railroad
— State border
△ Summit

For additional map symbols *see back flap*

❶ Salem

Although it is best known for the infamous witch trials of 1692, which resulted in the execution of 20 innocent people, this coastal town has other, less sensational claims to fame. Founded in 1626 by Roger Conant (1592–1679), Salem grew to become one of New England's busiest 18th- and 19th-century ports, its harbor filled with clipper ships carrying treasures from around the globe. Present-day Salem is a bustling, good-natured town that has the ability to celebrate its rich artistic and architectural heritage, all the while playing up its popular image as the witchcraft capital of America.

An 1842 whaling scene from the Peabody Essex Museum

Exploring Salem
Salem's main attractions are situated in clusters in the harbor and downtown areas. The historic waterfront can be explored on foot, as can the busy area along Essex and Liberty streets (see pp142–3).

Photo opportunities for Salem visitors

🏛 Peabody Essex Museum
East India Sq. **Tel** (978) 745-9500, (866) 745-1876. **Open** 10am–5pm Tue–Sun. ▦ 🎧 ♿ 🖥 🌐 pem.org

The dramatic Moshe Safdie building allows the Peabody Essex soaring galleries to display its collection of more than one million objects, including some of the world's largest holdings of Asian art and artifacts. Among the exhibits are treasures brought back from the Orient, the Pacific, and Africa by Salem's sea captains. Highlights include jewelry, porcelain figures, ritual costumes, scrimshaw, and figureheads.

The museum also displays the only complete Qing-dynasty house outside China.

🏛 Salem Witch Museum
19 1/2 Washington Sq. N. **Tel** (978) 744-1692 or (800) 544-1692. **Open** Jul–Aug: 10am–7pm daily; Sep–Jun: 10am–5pm daily. **Closed** Jan 1, Thanksgiving, Dec 24 & 25. 🎧 ♿ 📷
🌐 salemwitchmuseum.com

Salem's most visited sight commemorates the town's darkest hour. In 1692, 150 people were jailed and 20 executed after being charged with practicing witchcraft. According to some, Nathaniel Hawthorne – who was profoundly disturbed by reports of the events – added a "w" to his last name to distance himself from descendants of Judge Hathorne, the man who

---

Salem City Center

① Peabody Essex Museum
② Salem Witch Museum
③ Salem Witch Trial Memorial
④ Salem Maritime National Historic Site
⑤ Custom House
⑥ House of Seven Gables

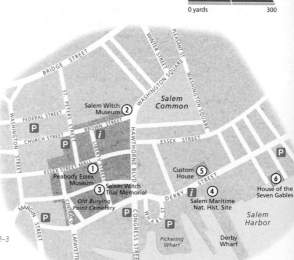

0 meters 300
0 yards 300

WINTER STREET
PLEASANT ST
WASHINGTON SQUARE
BRIDGE STREET
ST PETERS STREET
FEDERAL STREET
WASHINGTON STREET
CHURCH STREET
BROWN STREET
LIBERTY STREET
Salem Witch Museum ②
Salem Common
WASHINGTON SQUARE
HAWTHORNE BLVD
ESSEX STREET
ESSEX STREET MALL
Peabody Essex Museum ①
③ Salem Witch Trial Memorial
Old Burying Point Cemetery
MARGIN STREET
CENTRAL ST
LAFAYETTE ST
CONGRESS STREET
WHARF ST
Custom House ⑤
⑥ House of the Seven Gables
DERBY STREET
④ Salem Maritime Nat. Hist. Site
Salem Harbor
Pickering Wharf
Derby Wharf

Key
▦ Street-by-Street map see pp142–3

Salem Witch Museum, commemorating the infamous 1692 witch trials

presided over the witch trials. Exhibits in the Gothic-style building trace the history of witches and witchcraft and evolving perceptions of witches up to the present day. The town capitalizes on its association with witches each year in October with one of the nation's largest and most colorful celebrations of Halloween.

🏛 Salem Witch Trial Memorial

Charter St. **Open** dawn to dusk.
Located next to the old cemetery, this memorial provides a place for quiet contemplation and public acknowledgment of this tragic event in local history. The memorial was dedicated by Nobel laureate Elie Wiesel in 1992 on the 300th anniversary of the witch trials.

🏛 Salem Maritime National Historic Site

Orientation Center 193 Derby St.
Tel (978) 740-1660. **Open** Apr–Oct:
9am–5pm daily; call for winter hours.
Closed Jan 1, Thanksgiving, & Dec 25.
🅿 📷 🚻 Ⓦ nps.gov/sama

Salem's heyday as a maritime center has been preserved here. At its peak, the town's harbor was serviced by some 50 wharves. Today this waterfront complex maintains three wharves, including the 2,100-ft (640-m) Derby Wharf. The *Friendship*, a reconstruction of an East Indiaman sailing ship built in 1797, is moored here when it is not on tour during the summer.

🏛 Custom House

See Salem Maritime National Historic Site for details.
The federal-style Custom House (1819) was established to collect taxes on imports and now forms part of the Salem Maritime National Historic Site. In the 1840s author Nathaniel Hawthorne (1804–64) worked as a surveyor here. The redbrick structure, described in his novel *The Scarlet Letter* (1850), contains his office and desk.

🏛 House of Seven Gables Historic Site

115 Derby St. **Tel** (978) 744-0991.
Open mid-Jan–Jun, Nov–Dec
10am–5pm daily; Jul–Oct:
10am–7pm daily. **Closed** first 2
weeks Jan, Thanksgiving, Dec 25.
🚻 📷 obligatory. 🚻 partial. 📷
Ⓦ 7gables.org

Fans of author Nathaniel Hawthorne should make a pilgrimage to this 1668 house. The Salem-born writer was so taken with the Colonial-style home that he used it as the setting in his novel *House of Seven Gables* (1851). As well as its famous seven steeply pitched gables, the house also has a secret staircase. The site also contains other early homes, including Hawthorne's birthplace, a gambrel-roofed 18th-century residence moved from Union Street in 1958.

Environs

Just 4 miles (6 km) from town lies the area's most picturesque spot: Marblehead. When President George Washington (1732–99) visited, he said it had "the look of antiquity." This still holds true. Settled in 1629 and perched on a rocky peninsula, this village displays its heritage as a fisherman's enclave and a thriving port. Crisscrossed by hilly, twisting lanes, the historic district is graced with a wonderful mix of merchants' homes, shipbuilders' mansions, and fishermen's cottages. With more than 200 houses built before the Revolutionary War and nearly 800 built during the 1800s, the district is a catalog

Clock Tower at Abbot Hall in Marblehead

of American architecture. Included among the historic buildings is the spired **Abbot Hall**, the seat of local government built in 1876, where *The Spirit of '76* painting (1875) by Archibald Willard (1836–1918) hangs. Built in 1768 for a wealthy business-man, **The 1768 Jeremiah Lee Mansion** has a sweeping entrance hall, mahogany woodwork, and superb wallpaper. A drive along the shoreline reveals the lighthouse at Point O'Neck (1835).

🏛 Abbot Hall

Washington Sq. **Tel** (781) 631- 0000.
Open call for hours. 🚻

🏛 The 1768 Jeremiah Lee Mansion

161 Washington St. **Tel** (781) 631-
1768. **Open** Jun–Oct: 10am–4pm
Thu–Sat. 🚻 📷

Street-by-Street: Historic Salem

Like many New England towns, Salem is enjoying something of a rebirth. Downtown renewal programs have revitalized the city core, particularly around Essex Street. Specialty shops, cobblestone walkways, restaurants, and a pedestrian mall offer visitors an array of diversions, including stores specializing in the occult. Travelers are best served by stopping by the Regional Visitor Center operated by the National Park Service, where they can watch a 27-minute film on the region's history and pick up maps to guide their tour.

Peabody Essex Museum houses the 1765 portrait of Sarah Erving by John S. Copley.

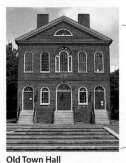

Old Town Hall
The red-brick building is now a popular venue for concerts.

Old Burying Point Cemetery

Salem Witch Village traces the history of witches by looking at their traditions, legends, and – ultimately – their persecution.

DERBY SQUARE

ESSEX STREET

FRONT STREET

LAFAYETTE ST.

CENTRAL STREET

CHARTER STREET

NEW LIBERTY STREET

DERBY STREET

Salem Witch Trials

In 1692 Salem was swept by a wave of hysteria in which 200 citizens were accused of practicing witchcraft. In all, 150 people were jailed and 19 were hung as witches, while another man was crushed to death with stones. No one was safe: two dogs were executed on the gallows for being witches. Not surprisingly, when the governor's wife became a suspect, the trials came to an abrupt and officially sanctioned end.

Early accused: Rebecca Nurse

Key

▨ Pedestrian mall

— Suggested route

0 yards	50
0 meters	50

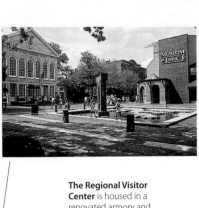

★ **Essex Street Pedestrian Mall**
Renewal programs have turned this cobblestone walkway into a busy mall of shops, cafés, and restaurants.

The Regional Visitor Center is housed in a renovated armory and shows a short film of the region's history.

★ **Gardner-Pingree House**
This 1804 house is elegantly decorated and furnished with period pieces.

Salem Witch Museum

N LIBERTY STREET

ESSEX STREET

BROWN STREET

WASHINGTON SQ. WEST

HAWTHORNE BOULEVARD

R STREET

to waterfront

Statue of Nathaniel Hawthorne
honors the Salem-born author of *The Scarlet Letter* (1850).

Crowninshield Bentley House
Built in 1727, this house typifies the architectural style of mid-18th century dwellings.

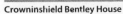

❷ Tour of the North Shore

The scenic tip of the North Shore is a favorite escape for harried Bostonians and vacationers who come for the quaint towns, sandy beaches, and whale-watching excursions that are found here in abundance. Ipswich, founded in 1633, still has more than 40 houses built before 1725. It is also known for its sandy beaches, marshes, dunes and seafood, especially clams. The rocky shores of Cape Ann hold diverse pleasures, including artists' colonies, mansions, and opportunities for swimming and boating.

Fishermen casting into the surf on a North Shore beach

⑧ **Ipswich**
A wealth of 17th century architecture makes this a fine town to explore.

Antiquing
Antique stores can be found throughout the North Shore region, particularly in Essex along Main Street.

① **Manchester-by-the-Sea**
A scenic harbor, luxurious mansions, and a wide beach are town highlights.

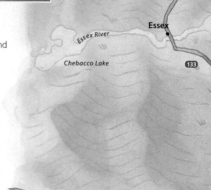

Ipswich River

A1

Castle Neck River

133

Essex

Essex River

Chebacco Lake

133

① 127

2

② **Magnolia**
This Gloucester village is known for magnificent summer homes and the Medieval-style Hammond Castle Museum.

Key

━━ Tour route
── Other road

0 kilometers   3
0 miles   3

③ **Gloucester**
Famous for its *Fisherman's Memorial* statue, this is a lively town with a busy harbor.

The World's First Fried Clam

The town of Essex has a proud culinary distinction: it was here that the clams were first fried. In 1916 Lawrence "Chubby"

Fried clams to go from Woodman's restaurant in Essex

Woodman and his wife were selling raw clams by the road. Following a friend's suggestion, they tried deep-frying a clam. The popularity of the new-dish snack helped Woodman open his own restaurant – still one of the region's most popular today.

Tips for Drivers

Tour length: 31 miles (50 km) with detour to Wingaersheek Beach.
Starting point: Rte 127 in Manchester-by-the-Sea.
Stopping-off points: Seafood abounds in places such as Gloucester, Rockport, Essex, and Newburyport. Lodgings are plentiful, but reservations are advised during the peak period of June to October.

⑦ Wingaersheek Beach
One of the North Shore's most popular beaches, Wingaersheek affords a view of the Annisquam lighthouse.

• Crane Beach

⑥ Rockport
Settled in 1690, the town is home to art galleries and an often photographed structure, the red fishing shed called Motif No.1.

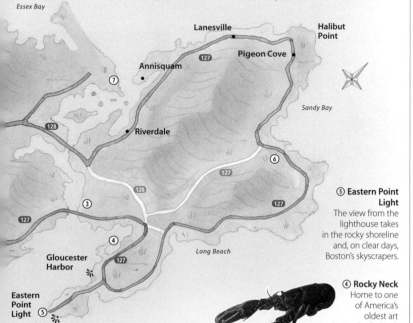

Essex Bay

Lanesville

Halibut Point

Pigeon Cove •

Annisquam

127

⑦

Sandy Bay

• Riverdale

128

⑥

127

⑤ Eastern Point Light
The view from the lighthouse takes in the rocky shoreline and, on clear days, Boston's skyscrapers.

③

128

Long Beach

④

127

127

127

Gloucester Harbor

Eastern Point Light ⑤

④ Rocky Neck
Home to one of America's oldest art colonies, Rocky Neck lays claim to fine seafood restaurants.

Power looms on display in the Boott Cotton Mills Museum

❸ Lowell

🗺 106,000. ✈ 30 miles (48 km) S in Boston. 🚌 ℹ 40 French St., 2nd Floor, (978) 459-6150 or (800) 443-3332. 🌐 merrimackvalley.org

Lowell has the distinction of being the country's first industrial city, paving the way for the American Industrial Revolution. In the early 19th century, Boston merchant Francis Cabot Lowell (1775–1817) opened a cloth mill in nearby Waltham and equipped it with his new power loom. The increase in production was so great that the mill quickly outgrew its quarters and was moved to the town of East Chelmsford (later renamed for Lowell). Set on 400 acres (162 ha) and using power provided by a steep drop in the Merrimack River, the business expanded to include 10 giant mill complexes, which employed more than 10,000 workers.

While the town prospered, it was at the expense of its workers, many of whom were unskilled immigrants exploited by the greedy mill owners. Eventually laborers organized and there were many strikes. The most successful was the 1912 Bread and Roses Strike, which began in neighboring Lawrence and spread to Lowell. While that confrontation helped improve conditions for workers, the relief was temporary. In the 1920s companies began to move south in search of

cheaper labor. The death knell came in 1929. The country was rocked by the Great Depression and the mills closed, leaving Lowell a ghost town.

In 1978 the **Lowell National Historical Park** was established to rehabilitate more than 100 downtown buildings and preserve the town's unique history. The Market Mills Visitor Center on Market Street offers a free introductory video show, walking tour maps, guided walks with rangers, and tickets for summer canal boat tours of the waterways. From March to November, antique trolleys take visitors to the **Boott Cotton Mills Museum**, the centerpiece of the park, where 88 vintage power looms produce a deafening clatter. Interactive exhibits trace the Industrial Revolution and the growth of the labor movement. Also in Lowell, the **American Textile History Museum** traces the evolution of textiles, from Colonial-era weavers to today's high-tech fabrics made from recycled materials.

Lowell has non-industrial attractions as well. The **New England Quilt Museum** displays both antique and contemporary examples of the quilt-maker's art, and sponsors talks and symposia on quilt scholarship and trends in current fiber arts. Painter James McNeill Whistler (1834–1903), most famous for his portrait of his mother, was born in Lowell while

his father was in charge of the railroad works for the city's mills. Whistler's birthplace is now a museum that displays prints of some of his work, but focuses more on 19th- and 20th-century American art.

🏛 **Lowell National Historical Park**
246 Market St. **Tel** (978) 970-5000.
Open Mar–Oct: 9am–5pm daily, Nov–Feb: 9am–4:30pm Mon–Sat, 10am–5pm Sun. 🚌 for canal tours only. 🌐 nps.gov/lowe

🏛 **Boott Cotton Mills Museum**
115 John St. **Tel** (978) 970-5000.
Open late May–Oct: 9:30am–4:30pm daily (call for opening hours off-season). ♿

🏛 **American Textile History Museum**
491 Dutton St. **Tel** (978) 441-0400.
Open 10am–5pm Wed–Sun. **Closed** public hols. 🌐 athm.org

🏛 **New England Quilt Museum**
18 Shattuck St. **Tel** (978) 452-4207.
Open 10am–4pm Tue–Sat, also open noon–4pm Sun May–Dec.
Closed public hols. ♿
🌐 nequiltmuseum.org

🏛 **Whistler House Museum of Art**
243 Worthen St. **Tel** (978) 452-7641.
Open 11am–4pm Wed–Sat.

Bedroom display at the New England Quilt Museum in Lowell

Lowell's Jack Kerouac

Lowell native Jack Kerouac was the leading chronicler of the "beat generation," a term that he coined to describe members of the disaffected Bohemian movement of the 1950s. Although he lived elsewhere for most of his adult life, his remains are buried in the town's Edson Cemetery. Excerpts from Kerouac's most famous novel, *On the Road* (1957), and other of his writings are inscribed on granite pillars in the Kerouac Commemorative Park on Bridge Street.

Jack Kerouac (1922–69)

Part of the Fruitlands Museums' Shaker collection

❹ Sudbury

🏙 18,000. ✈ 24 miles (39 km) E in Boston.

The picturesque town of Sudbury is home to a number of historic sites, including the 1797 First Parish Church and the 1723 Loring Parsonage. Longfellow's Wayside Inn, one of the nation's oldest inns, was built in 1716 and was immortalized in Henry Wadsworth Longfellow's poetry collection entitled *Tales of a Wayside Inn* (1863). In the 1920s the building was purchased by industrialist Henry Ford (1863–1947), who restored it, filled it with antiques, and surrounded it with other relocated structures, such as a rustic gristmill, a schoolhouse, and a general store.

Today, the inn serves both as a mini-museum of Colonial America as well as offering cozy overnight rooms and hearty American fare in its pub-like restaurant.

❺ Nashoba Valley

ℹ 100 Sherman Ave., Devens (978) 772-6976.

Fed by the Nashoba River, Nashoba Valley is an appealing world of meadows and orchards and colonial towns built around village greens. The region is particularly popular in May when the apple trees are in bloom, and again in fall when the apples are ripe for picking and the surrounding hills are ablaze in autumn colors.

The **Fruitlands Museums**, the valley's major attraction, comprises four museums, two outdoor sites, and a restaurant on beautiful hilltop grounds that include nature trails and picnic areas with valley views. Founder Clara Endicott Sears (1863–1960), a philosopher, writer, collector, and early preservationist, built her home here in 1910 and began gathering properties of historical significance. Her first acquisition was Fruitlands, the "New Eden" commune based partly on vegetarianism and self-sufficiency initiated by Bronson Alcott (1799–1888) and fellow Transcendentalists. Alcott was the father of author Louisa May Alcott (1832–88) and was the model for the character of Mr. March in her

Fruitlands Museums' rocking horse

book *Little Women* (1868). The restored farmhouse now serves as a museum and includes memorabilia of Alcott, Ralph Waldo Emerson (1803–82), and other Transcendentalist leaders.

Five years later, Sears acquired a building in nearby Shaker Village. The 1790 structure, the first office building in the village, now houses a collection of traditional Shaker furniture, clothing, and artifacts. The Native American Gallery includes objects from New England and throughout the United States.

Another of the region's attractions is the **Nashoba Valley Winery**, a beautiful 55-acre (22-ha) orchard that produces wines from fruits such as apples, pears, peaches, plums, blueberries, strawberries, and elderberries. More than 100 varieties of apples are grown here. On weekends the winery offers tours.

🏛 **Fruitlands Museums**
102 Prospect Hill Rd, Harvard. **Tel** (978) 456-3924. **Open** mid-Apr–mid-Nov: 11am–4pm Mon–Fri, 11am–5pm Sat–Sun. 🅿 ♿ partial. 🌐 fruitlands.org

🏛 **Nashoba Valley Winery**
100 Wattaquadock Hill Rd, Bolton. **Tel** (978) 779-5521. **Open** year-round: 10am–5pm daily. Winery tours: year-round: 11am–4pm Sat–Sun. 🅿

Henry Wadsworth Longfellow's Wayside Inn, one of the nation's oldest

❻ Concord

The peaceful, prosperous suburban look of modern-day Concord masks an eventful past. This small town was at the heart of two important chapters in US history. The first was marked by a single dramatic event, the Battle of Concord on April 19, 1775, which signaled the beginning of the Revolutionary War. The second spanned several generations, as 19th-century Concord blossomed into the literary heart and soul of the US, with many of the nation's great writers establishing homes here. The influence of both important periods is in full evidence today.

North Bridge in Minute Man National Historical Park

Exploring Concord

At Concord's center lies **Monument Square**. It was also at the center of the battle fought between British troops and Colonists more than 200 years ago. Having seized the gun cache and other supplies of rebel forces, the British soldiers began burning them. Nearby Colonist forces spotted the smoke and, believing the town was being torched, rushed to its defense, precipitating the Revolutionary War.

🏛 Minute Man National Historical Park

North Bridge Visitor Center, 174 Liberty St. **Tel** (978) 369-6993. **Open** mid-Mar–Nov: 9am–5pm daily; Dec–mid-Mar: 11am–3pm daily. **Closed** Jan 1, Thanksgiving, Dec 25. Minute Man Visitor Center, Rte. 2A Lexington. **Tel** (781) 674-1920. **Open** mid-Mar–Oct: 9am–5pm daily; Nov: 9am–4pm daily. **Closed** winter. ♿ 🌐 **nps.gov/mima**

On April 19, 1775, a group of militia, ordinary citizens, and Colonist farmers known as Minute Men confronted British troops who were patrolling the **North Bridge**. The Minute Men fought valiantly, driving three British companies of troops from the bridge and chasing them back to Boston.

This 990-acre (400-ha) park preserves the site and tells the story of the American victory. The Minute Man Visitor Center also features a massive battle mural and a 22-minute multimedia show called "Road to Revolution." The Battle Road Trail traces the five-mile (8-km) path followed by the British as they advanced from Lexington to Concord – the same route they took in their retreat back to Boston.

The park's North Bridge Unit is the place where the first major engagement was fought. This so-called "shot heard 'round the world" set off the war. Across the bridge is the famous **Minute Man statue** by Concord native Daniel Chester French (1850–31). A short trail leads from the bridge to the **North Bridge Visitor Center**. A reenactment of the battle takes place every year in April in Concord and Lexington.

🏛 Concord Museum

Jct of Lexington Rd & Cambridge Tpk. **Tel** (978) 369-9609. **Open** Jan– Mar: 11am–4pm Mon–Sat, 1–4pm Sun; Apr–Dec: 9am– 5pm Mon–Sat, noon– 5pm Sun (Jun–Aug: 9am– 5pm Sun). 🌿 ♿ 🌐 **concordmuseum.org**

Minute Man statue in Concord

The museum's eclectic holdings include decorative arts from the 17th, 18th, and 19th centuries, and the lantern that Paul Revere ordered hung in the steeple of Old North Church to warn of the British advance (*see p124*).

🏛 The Old Manse

269 Monument St. **Tel** (978) 369-3909. **Open** mid-Apr–Oct: 10am–5pm Mon–Sat, noon–5pm Sun. 🌿 📷 🌐 **thetrustees.org**

The parsonage by the North Bridge was built in 1770 by the grandfather of writer Ralph

Along the Battle Road, by John Rush, located in the Minute Man Visitor Center

Concord's Old Manse: home to 19th-century literary giants

Waldo Emerson (1803–82), who lived here briefly. Author Nathaniel Hawthorne (1804–64) and his wife rented the house during the first three years of their marriage (loving inscriptions are scratched into the windows). The house got its name from Hawthorne's *Mosses from an Old Manse* (1846), the collection of short stories he wrote here.

Emerson House
28 Cambridge Tpk. **Tel** (978) 369-2236.
Open mid-Apr–late Oct: 10am–4:30pm Thu–Sat, 1–4:30pm Sun & public hols.
Ralph Waldo Emerson lived in this house from 1835 until his death in 1882, writing essays, organizing lecture tours, and entertaining friends and admirers. Much of Emerson's furniture, writings, books, and family memorabilia is on display.

Walden Pond State Reservation
915 Walden St. **Tel** (978) 369-3254.
Open call for hours.
W mass.gov/dcr/
Essayist Henry David Thoreau (1817–62) lived in relative isolation at Walden Pond from July 1845 to September 1847. During his stay, he compiled the material for his seminal work *Walden; or, Life in t he Woods* (1854). In the book, he called for a return to simplicity in everyday life and respect for nature. Because of Thoreau's deep influence on future generations of environmentalists, Walden

Pond is widely considered to be the birthplace of the conservationist movement.

The pond itself is surrounded by 333 acres (135 ha) of mostly undeveloped woodlands. The area is popular for walking, fishing, and swimming, and today is far from the solitary spot that Thoreau described, even though the reservation limits the number of visitors to no more than 1,000 people at one time.

Fisherman on the tranquil waters of Walden Pond

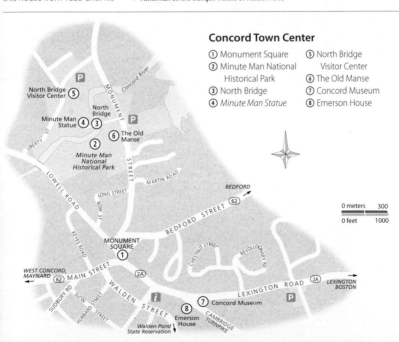

Concord Town Center
① Monument Square
② Minute Man National Historical Park
③ North Bridge
④ *Minute Man Statue*
⑤ North Bridge Visitor Center
⑥ The Old Manse
⑦ Concord Museum
⑧ Emerson House

Mayflower II, replica of the original Pilgrim sailing ship

❼ Plymouth

🏙 52,000. ✈ 40 miles (64 km) NW in Boston. 🚢 to Provincetown (seasonal). ℹ 130 Water St. (508) 747-7533 or (800) USA-1620.
W **visit-plymouth.com**

In 1620, 102 pilgrims aboard the ship *Mayflower* sailed into Plymouth harbor and established what is considered to be the first permanent English settlement in the New World. Today the town bustles with tourists exploring the sites of America's earliest days, including **Plimoth Plantation** (*see pp154–5*), which is 2.5 miles (4 km) from town. The plantation is a living-history museum of the English colonists and Native Americans of the area. Plymouth itself is a popular seaside resort, complete with a 3.5-mile-(6-km-) long beach, harbor cruises, and fishing excursions. In the fall, the surrounding bogs turn ruby red as the annual cranberry harvest gets underway. Plymouth is popular for its "Progress," which takes place most Fridays in August at 6pm and on Thanksgiving Day at 10am. Visitors come to witness the

solemn reenactment of the Pilgrims' slow procession to Burial Hill, where a short service is held.

Most of the historic sights can be accessed on foot by the Pilgrim Path that stretches along the waterfront and downtown areas. A seasonal sightseeing trolley connects sights and features a 40-minute history of the town. Ensconced in a monument at the harbor is the country's most famous boulder, Plymouth Rock, marking the spot where the Pilgrims are said to have first stepped ashore. The *Mayflower II*, a replica of the 17th-century sailing ship that carried the Pilgrims over from England, is moored by Plymouth Rock. At just 106 ft (32 m) in length, the vessel seems far too small to have made a transatlantic voyage, especially considering the horrific weather it encountered. Walking along the cramped deck, visitors will marvel at the Pilgrims' courage. Even after surviving the brutal crossing, many Pilgrims succumbed to illness and

malnutrition during their first winter in Plymouth. Their remains are buried across the street on Coles Hill, which is fronted by a statue of Massasoit, the Wampanoag Indian chief who allied himself with the newcomers and aided the survivors by teaching them the growing and use of native corn. It was with Massasoit and his people that the Pilgrims celebrated their famous first Thanksgiving. Coles Hill offers a panoramic view of the harbor.

Burial Hill at the head of the Town Square was the site of an early fort and the final resting place of many members of the original colony, including Governor William Bradford (1590–1656). Most Fridays in August, citizens dressed in Pilgrim garb walk from Plymouth Rock to the hill to reenact the church service attended by the 51 survivors of the first winter. Perched on a hilltop overlooking town, the 81-ft (25-m) National Monument to the Forefathers is dedicated to the Pilgrims who made the dangerous voyage to the New World. The Pilgrim Mother Fountain was erected in honor of the women who made the original voyage. Twenty-five women set sail from England, but only four of them survived.

Opened in 1824, the **Pilgrim Hall Museum** is one of America's oldest public museums, housing the largest existing collection of Pilgrim-era artifacts, such as the only known portrait of a *Mayflower* passenger, as well as such personal items as bibles, cradles, and the sword of one of the most colorful Pilgrims, Myles Standish (c.1584–1656), a former soldier of fortune who went on to found nearby Duxbury. Exhibitions explore Pilgrim history as well as Native American culture and history, and the interactions between the two groups. To

Statue of Massasoit

Fully functioning water wheel at Jenney Grist Mill

◀ Scenic boardwalk at Duxbury Beach

Pilgrim Hall exhibits furniture, armor, and art

appreciate how quickly the Pilgrims progressed from near castaways to hardy settlers, take in the **Jenney Grist Mill**, a 1970 reconstruction of the 1636 original destroyed by fire in 1847. The restored mill grinds cornmeal with power from a 14-ft (4-m) water wheel.

Plymouth has several historic homes of special interest. Among them is **Spooner House**, constructed in 1749 and continuously occupied by one family until 1954, when James Spooner left his home to the Plymouth Antiquarian Society. Its accumulation of artifacts provides a history of Plymouth life. An American crafts shop can be found in the town's oldest home, c.1640 **Richard Sparrow House**.

The original site of the **Mayflower Society House** was built in 1754 and extensively renovated in 1898. What was the old kitchen is now the office for the General Society of Mayflower Descendants. Its research library has one of the finest genealogical collections in the United States.

Travelers will encounter many of the state's 19 sq miles (49 sq km) of cranberry bogs along the roads of south-eastern Massachusetts inland from Plymouth. Introduced to the English colonists by Native

Americans, the cranberry was first cultivated commercially on Cape Cod in the mid-19th century; about a century later, the center of both growing and processing moved to the Plymouth area. During the autumn harvest season, visitors may see the rectangular bogs flooded as paddle-wheel harvesters thrash the submerged bushes, causing the red berries to separate from the plants and float to the surface, where they are harvested by skimming.

🏛 **Mayflower II**
State Pier. **Tel** (508) 746-1622. **Open** late Mar–Nov: 9am–5pm daily. 🐾

🏛 **Pilgrim Hall Museum**
75 Court St. **Tel** (508) 746-1620. **Open** year round: 9:30am–4:30pm daily. **Closed** Jan. 🐾

🏠 **Jenney Grist Mill**
6 Spring Lane. **Tel** (508) 747-4544. **Open** Apr–Nov: 9:30am–5pm Mon, Tue & Thu–Sat; noon–5pm Sun.

🏠 **Spooner House**
27 North St. **Tel** (508) 746-0012. **Closed** for restoration.

🏠 **Richard Sparrow House**
42 Summer St. **Tel** (508) 747-1240. **Open** Apr–late Dec: 10am–5pm daily; late Dec–Apr: 10am–5pm Thu–Sat. 🐾 ♿ call first. 📷

🏠 **Mayflower Society House**
4 Winslow St. **Tel** (508) 746-3188. **Open** call for hours. 🐾

❽ Duxbury

🏘 15,350. ✈ 34 miles (54 km) N in Boston. 🛈 130 Water St., Plymouth (508) 747-7533.

Duxbury was settled in 1628 by a group of Pilgrims who found that the Plymouth colony was getting too crowded. Two who made the move, John Alden (c.1598–1687) and Myles Standish (c.1584–1656), were on the *Mayflower* crossing. Today the town is best known for its nine-mile- (14-km-) long beach.

The last home of Alden and his wife was the 1653 **Alden House**. The structure has several features of note, including gunstock beams and a ceiling plastered with crushed clam and oyster shells.

King Caesar House, the home of another prominent resident, is one of the town's grandest structures. Ezra Weston II, an 18th-century shipping magnate, had a fortune large enough to earn him the nickname "King Caesar." It also allowed him the luxury of building this stately Federal mansion in 1808. Today the house is furnished with period pieces, French wallpaper, and a small museum celebrating the region's maritime history.

The **Art Complex Museum** has everything from Asian and European art to Shaker furniture and contemporary New England art. A traditional Japanese tea ceremony is held on the last Sunday of the month, June through August.

Shaker piece at Art Complex Museum

🏠 **Alden House**
105 Alden St. **Tel** (781) 934-9092. **Open** Jun–early Sep: noon–4pm Wed–Sat. 🐾 ♿

🏠 **King Caesar House**
120 King Caesar Rd. **Tel** (781) 934-6106. **Open** Jul–Aug: 1–4pm Wed–Sun.

🏛 **Art Complex Museum**
189 Alden St. **Tel** (781) 934-6634. **Open** Mar–mid-Jan: 1–4pm Wed–Sun.

Plimoth Plantation

Plimoth Plantation is a painstakingly accurate re-creation of the Pilgrims' 1627 village, right down to the 17th-century breeds of livestock. Costumed interpreters portray actual original colonists going about their daily tasks of salting fish, gardening, and musket drills. In the parallel Wampanoag Village, descendants of the people who have lived here for 12,000 years speak in modern language about the experiences of the Wampanoag and explore the story of one 17th-century man, Hobbamock, and his family.

Plimoth Plantation
Costumed interpreters mingle with visitors on the village's busy central street.

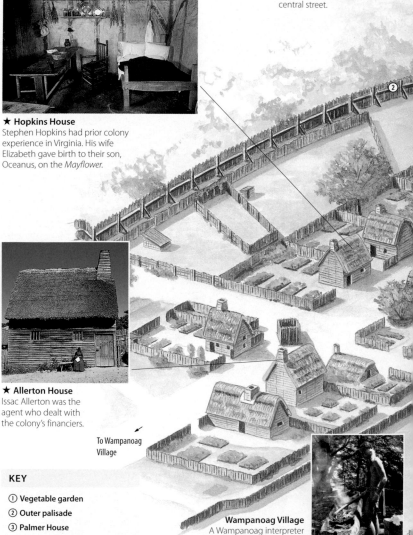

★ Hopkins House
Stephen Hopkins had prior colony experience in Virginia. His wife Elizabeth gave birth to their son, Oceanus, on the *Mayflower*.

★ Allerton House
Issac Allerton was the agent who dealt with the colony's financiers.

To Wampanoag Village

KEY

① Vegetable garden
② Outer palisade
③ Palmer House
④ Dutch Barn

Wampanoag Village
A Wampanoag interpreter explains the creation of a dugout canoe.

Key

- ☐ Illustrated
- ☐ Not illustrated
- 1 Fort/Meetinghouse
- 2 Standish and Alden Houses
- 3 Winslow and Cooke Houses
- 4 Bradford House
- 5 Allerton House
- 6 Cow Shed
- 7 Hopkins House
- 8 Brewster and Browne Houses
- 9 Dutch Barn
- 10 Fuller House
- 11 Forge
- 12 Storehouse

VISITORS' CHECKLIST

Practical Information
Rte 3A. 🛈 137 Warren Ave. (508)
746-1622. **Open** late Mar–Nov:
9:30am–5pm daily. 🚻 ♿ limited
access to certain parts of site;
wheelchairs available upon
request. 📷 🆆 plimoth.org

★ Storehouse
Everyday provisions
were stored here,
along with furs and
other goods to be
shipped to England.

Local Reeds
Used for thatching,
reeds were long-lasting,
easily repaired, and
virtually waterproof.

The Cow Shed
Cows and other
livestock were
housed in what was
often called the
"beasthouse." It
opens into an
enclosed paddock.

0 meters 10
0 yards 10

Martha's Vineyard scene: fishing boat outside fishing shack

❾ Martha's Vineyard

🏘 13,900. ✈ West Tisbury.
🚢 Woods Hole; Hyannis; Falmouth;
New Bedford. ℹ Beach Rd., Vineyard
Haven (508) 693-0085 or (800) 505-
4815. 🌐 mvy.com

The Vineyard, as the locals call it, is the largest of all New England's vacation islands at 108 sq miles (280 sq km). Just a 45-minute boat ride from shore, it is blessed with a mesmerizing mix of scenic beauty and the understated charm of a beach resort. Bicycle trails abound here and opportunities for hiking, surf fishing, and some of the best sailing in the region add to the Vineyard's lure. Each town has its own distinctive mood and architectural style, making for interesting exploring.

Vineyard Haven
Most visitors arrive on Martha's Vineyard aboard ferries that sail into this waterfront town, which was largely destroyed by fire in the 1800s. Vineyard Haven is sheltered between two points of land known as East and West Chop, each with its own landmark lighthouse.

Edgartown
As the center of the island's whaling industry in the early 1800s, Edgartown was once home to wealthy sea captains and merchants. The streets are lined with their homes.

Victorian home with gingerbread ornamentation in Oak Bluffs

The main building of the **Martha's Vineyard Museum** complex is the c.1730 Thomas Cooke House. The beautiful 12-room structure is filled with antique furniture, ship models, scrimshaw, and gear used by whalers.

At the eastern end of the waterfront, visitors can catch the ferry to Chappaquiddick Island, a rural outpost that is popular for its beaches and opportunities for bird-watching, surf fishing, canoeing, and hiking. This quiet enclave was made famous by a fatal accident in 1969, when a car driven by Senator Edward Kennedy (1932–2009) went off the bridge, killing a young woman passenger.

🏛 **Martha's Vineyard Museum**
59 School St. **Tel** (508) 627-4441.
Open 10am–5pm Mon–Sat (mid-Oct–mid-Jun: to 4pm; Jan–mid-Mar: open Sat only). **Closed** public hols. Cooke House: **Closed** mid-Oct–mid-Jun. ♿
🏠 🌐 mvmuseum.org

Oak Bluffs
Tourism began on Martha's Vineyard in 1835 when local Methodists began using the undeveloped area to pitch their tents during their summer revival meetings. The setting proved popular as people came in search of sunshine and salvation. Gradually the tent village gave way to a town of colorful gingerbread cottages, boarding houses, and stores, and was named Cottage City. In 1907 it was renamed Oak Bluffs. The town is home to the **Flying Horses Carousel**, the oldest continuously operating carousel in the country. Today's children delight in riding on it as much as those of the 1870s.

🎠 **Flying Horses Carousel**
Oak Bluffs Ave. **Tel** (508) 693-9481.
Open Apr–mid-Oct: call for hours.
♿ 💻

Western Shoreline
Unlike the Vineyard's busier eastern section, the western shoreline is tranquil and rural. The area, which includes the towns of North and West Tisbury, Menemsha, and

---

Whale-watching

From April to mid-October the waters off Nantucket Island and Cape Cod come to life with the antics of finback, right, minke, and humpback whales. These gentle behemoths bang their massive tails, blow clouds of bubbles, and sometimes fling their entire bodies into the air only to come crashing down in mammoth back or belly flops. Whales are most numerous during July and August, and cruises are offered from many ports, including Provincetown and Barnstable on the Cape, Vineyard Haven on Martha's Vineyard, and the Straight Wharf in the town of Nantucket.

Whale off the coast of Martha's Vineyard

Colored cliffs of Aquinnah on western shore of Martha's Vineyard

Aquinnah (formerly Gay Head but renamed in 1998), is graced by a number of private homes and pristine beaches, many of which are strictly private.

Tiny West Tisbury remains a rural village of picket fences, a white-spired church, and a general store. In Menemsha, a working fishing fleet fills the harbor, and the weathered fishermen's shacks, fish nets, and lobster traps look much as they did a century ago. Windswept Aquinnah at the western edge of the island is famous for its steep multi-hued clay cliffs – a favorite subject of photographers.

⑩ Nantucket Island

🚶 9,000 (year-round). ✈ West Tisbury. 🚢 Hyannis, Harwichport & Oak Bluffs. ℹ Zero Main St. (508) 228-1700. 🖥 nantucketchamber.org

Lying off the southern tip of Cape Cod (see pp160–63), Nantucket Island is a 14-mile-(22-km-) long enclave of tranquility. With only one town to speak of, the island remains an untamed world of kettle ponds, cranberry bogs, and lush stands of wild grapes and blueberries, punctuated by the occasional lighthouse.

In the early 19th century the town of Nantucket was the envy of the whaling industry, with a fleet of about 100 vessels. The town's

Brant Point Light on Nantucket Island

architecture reflects those glory days, with the magnificent mansions of sea captains and merchants – made rich from their whaling profits – lining Main Street. Today the town has the nation's largest concentration of pre-1850s houses.

The **Nantucket Historical Association** (NHA) operates 11 historical buildings in town. One of the most important sites is the Whaling Museum on Broad Street. The expanded museum features a restored 1847 spermaceti candle factory and a rare complete 46-ft (14-meter) skeleton of a sperm whale recovered from Nantucket beach. Historic exhibits include ship models, tools, ship's logs, portraits, and scrimshaw that highlight the era when Nantucket was the world's leading whaling port. The Hawden House, built in 1845, focuses on the lifestyle of the well-off whaling merchants. The Quaker Meeting House is a reminder that from the first meeting in 1701, Quakerism grew to be the religion of Nantucket's elite – a small group still meets here.

Additional sites open for tours are the 1686 Jethro Coffin House, the oldest house on the island, and the 18th-century Old Mill, a wind-powered grain mill still in operating condition. letters, manuscripts, business documents, ships' logs, maps and charts, and

genealogical materials, as well as more than 45,000 photographs.

🏛 Nantucket Historical Association (NHA)

15 Broad St. **Tel** (508) 228-1894. Historic buildings: **Open** call for hours. 📷 🎥 ♿ Whaling Museum only. 🖼 🖥 nha.org

Environs

Just 8 miles (13 km) from the town of Nantucket lies the tiny village of **Siasconset**. The village, which is called "Sconset" by locals, is located on the eastern shore of the island and easily lives up to the description offered by one 18th-century visitor: "Perfectly unconnected with the real world and far removed from its perturbations." Set between cranberry bogs and rose-covered bluffs overlooking the Atlantic Ocean, the village's narrow lanes are lined with miniature cottages that are among the oldest of the island. Many of these fishermen's shanties are constructed out of wood rescued from shipwrecks, accounting for Sconset's old nickname, "Patchwork Village."

Once Sconset was a summer colony for actors, attracting such luminaries of the American stage as Lillian Russell (1861–1922) and Joseph Jefferson (1829–1905), who made the 35-minute ride from the town of Nantucket via an island railroad. Today there are only a few inns remaining. The majority of Sconset's summer visitors own or rent homes, a fact that serves to keep the beaches uncrowded and the village peaceful.

⓫ Cape Cod National Seashore

Stretching more than 40 miles (64 km) from Chatham in the south to Provincetown in the north, Cape Cod National Seashore is one of the Eastern Seaboard's true gems. With the backing of President John Kennedy (1917–63) the seashore was established in 1961 to protect the fragile sand dunes and beaches, salt marshes, glacial cliffs, and woodlands. While the delicate landscape has been under federal protection since then, certain features have been added, including bike trails, hiking paths, and specially designated dune trails for off-road vehicles. Historical structures are interspersed among the seashore's softly beautiful natural features.

Long Point Light

★ Old Harbor Life-Saving Station
This 1897 station houses a museum containing turn-of-the-century rescue equipment and shipwreck paraphernalia. During the summer months, traditional rescue methods are sometimes demonstrated.

★ Province Lands Area
The barren, windswept landscape of the Province Lands Area has long been an inspiration for writers and artists. Here beech forests give way to horseshoe-shaped dunes and white sand beaches.

Key

━━ Major road

═══ Minor road

-- Walking trail

— Park boundary

Overview
Visitors get an overview of the area in the park's visitor centers.

For hotels and restaurants in this region see pp313–14 and pp329–31

VISITORS' CHECKLIST

Practical Information
Rte. 6, Cape Cod. 🛈 Salt
Pond Visitor Center, Rte. 6,
Eastham (508) 255-3421.
Open 9am–4:30pm daily, with
extended summer hours.
🅿 beach and trails.
🔲 nps.gov/caco

★ Atwood Higgins House
This 1730s Colonial-style home typifies the
houses of early settlers to the region.

**★ Atlantic White
Cedar Swamp Trail**
A nature trail, part of
which is a boardwalk
over swamp, leads
through forested
swampland and
stands of scrub oak
and pitch pine to
Marconi Station.

Marconi Beach
This broad and sandy expanse near South Wellfleet is named
after Guglielmo Marconi (1874–1937), who transmitted the
world's first wireless message from this area in 1903.

Wildflowers
These flowers
bloom throughout
the seasons at the
National Seashore.

Head of the
Meadow Beach

Coast Guard Beach

**Highland
Light (Cape
Cod Light)**

Longnook
Beach

Ballston
Beach

N. Parmet Rd.
S. Parmet Rd.

S. Highland Rd.
Longnook Rd.

Collins Rd.

Newcomb
Hollow Beach

Cahoon
Hollow Beach

White Crest
Beach

LeCount
Hollow
Beach

Gross Hill Road

Ocean View Drive

Wellfleet

E. Commercial St.

South Wellfleet

Lieutenant
Island

**Marconi
Station
Site**

Marconi
Beach

Ocean View
Drive

Nauset Light
Beach

Coast
Guard
Beach

Nauset
Marsh

Eastham

Nauset Cable Road

Doane Rd.

Orleans
(Nauset)
Beach

Orleans

Beach Road

Sipson
Island

Pleasant
Bay

Strong
Island

Chatham

| 0 kilometers | 2 |
| 0 miles | 2 |

For map symbols *see back*

⑫ Cape Cod

Millions of visitors arrive each summer to enjoy the bound-less beaches, natural beauty, and quaint colonial villages of Cape Cod. Extending some 70 miles (113 km) into the sea, the Cape is shaped like an upraised arm, bent at the elbow with the Atlantic Ocean and the Cape Cod National Seashore *(see pp158–9)* and ending with the fist at Provincetown. Crowds are heaviest along Route 28, where beaches edge the warmer waters of Nantucket Sound and Buzzard's Bay. Towns along Route 6A, the old Kings Highway, retain their colonial charm, with many of the old homes now serving as antique shops and inns.

Fishermen on their boat in Provincetown harbor

Exploring the Lower Cape

First-time visitors to Cape Cod are almost always confused when they are given directions by locals. This is because residents have divided the Cape into three districts with names that do not make much sense. The Mid- and Upper Cape is actually the southern most portion closest to the mainland, while the Lower Cape is the northernmost section.

The Lower Cape takes in the long elbow of the peninsula that curls northward and forms Cape Cod Bay. The towns of Chatham, Brewster, Orleans, Eastham, Wellfleet, Truro, and Provincetown are all located in this section of Cape Cod.

Pilgrim Monument

The place where the Pilgrims first landed is marked by a bronze plaque on Commercial Street and commemorated by the tallest granite structure in the US, the 252-ft (77-m) **Pilgrim Monument**. On a clear day, the view from the top extends all the way to Boston. Eclectic displays in the adjacent museum include exhibits of Pilgrim history as well as marine and Arctic artifacts.

The **Whydah Pirate Museum** is named for a ship that sank in a storm off Cape Cod after being captured by pirates. It exhibits artifacts such as gold dubloons, weapons, clothing, and West African gold jewelry. The region's rich cultural history is celebrated in the galleries of the **Provincetown Art Association and Museum**, where works by local artists are displayed. One of the town's busiest locales is MacMillan Wharf, the center of nautical activity, including the jumping-off point for whale-watching cruises *(see p156)*.

🏛 **Pilgrim Monument and Provincetown Museum**
High Pole Hill Rd. **Tel** (508) 487-1310. **Open** Apr–Nov: 9am–5pm daily (Jun–mid-Sep: to 7pm). ♿ 🅿

🏛 **Whydah Pirate Museum**
16 MacMillan Wharf. **Tel** (508) 487-8899. **Open** mid-May–Oct: 10am–5pm daily (Jun–Aug: extended hours). ♿ 🅿 📷

🏛 **Provincetown Art Association and Museum**
460 Commercial St. **Tel** (508) 487-1750. **Open** call for hours. ♿ 🅿

Environs
Just 17 miles (27 km) south of Provincetown lies Wellfleet, an early whaling center that possesses one of the Cape's largest concentrations of art

Provincetown

This picturesque town at the northern tip of the Cape has a colorful history. The Pilgrims first landed here in 1620 and stayed for five weeks before pushing on to the mainland. During that time they drew up the Mayflower Compact, a forerunner of the American Constitution. "P-Town," as it is called, later grew into a major 18th-century fishing center. By the beginning of the 20th century, P-Town had become a bustling artists' colony. Today this popular and eccentric town is one of New England's most vibrant destinations and a popular gay resort. However, in the summer months the town's population can swell from 3,500 more than 30,000.

Busy streets of Cape Cod's Provincetown in the summertime

galleries. Farther down the Cape is Eastham, home to the **Old Schoolhouse Museum**, a one-room school built in 1869. Neighboring Orleans is a commercial center with access to the very beautiful Nauset Beach and its much-photographed lighthouse.

🏛 Old Schoolhouse Museum
Nauset Rd, Eastham. **Tel** (508) 255-0788. **Open** call for opening hours.

Chatham

Chatham rests on the very point of the Cape's "elbow," the place where Nantucket Sound meets the Atlantic Ocean. An attractive, upscale community, it offers fine inns, a Main Street filled with attractive shops, and a popular summer playhouse. Housed in an 1887 Victorian train station, the **Railroad Museum** contains models, photos, memorabilia, and vintage trains that can be boarded. Fishing boats unload their catch at the pier every afternoon, and the surrounding waters offer good opportunities for amateur anglers to fish for bluefish and bass.

Chatham is also the best place to plan a trip to the **Monomoy National Wildlife Refuge**. Encompassing two islands, this huge reserve attracts migrating birds and is a nesting habitat for such endangered birds as the piping plover and the roseate tern. Deer are spotted here, as are the numerous gray and harbor seals that bask on the rocks.

🏛 Railroad Museum
Depot Rd. **Tel** (508) 945-5199. **Open** mid-Jun–mid-Sep: 10am–4pm Tue–Sat. ♿

🦅 Monomoy National Wildlife Refuge
Wikis Way, Morris Island. **Tel** (508) 945-0594. Visitor Center: **Open** late May–mid-Sep: 10am–6pm daily. Call for off-season hours and info on boat services. **w** monomoy.fws.gov

Brewster

Named for Elder William Brewster (1567–1644), who was a passenger on the *Mayflower*, Brewster is another town graced with handsome 19th-century houses of wealthy sea captains. It is also home to a particularly lovely church, the 1834 First Parish Brewster Unitarian Universalist Church. Some pews are marked with names of prominent captains.

Children will love the interactive exhibits on display at the **Cape Cod Museum of Natural History**. An observation area looking out on the salt-marsh habitat of birds gives visitors close-up views of the natural world. The 82-acre (33-ha) grounds are laced with three walking trails with boardwalks that cross salt marshes. The museum also offers interesting guided "eco-treks" and cruises to nearby Nauset Marsh and Monomoy Islands.

Naturalists can continue with a more hands-on kind of exploration at any of Brewster's

eight beaches along Cape Cod Bay. These strands taper gradually toward the ocean, and about a mile (1.6 km) of tidal flats is revealed at low tide. The dramatic flats attract a wide variety of visitors, from photographers, to children who like to search for sea life, to clam diggers.

🏛 Cape Cod Museum of Natural History
869 Rte 6A. **Tel** (508) 896-3867. **Open** Jun–Sep: 9:30am–4pm daily. Call for winter opening hours. **Closed** public hols. 🅿 🎫 ♿ **w** ccmnh.org

Red and white Nauset Light on the Lower Cape

Provincetown Artist Colony

Artists, writers, and poets have long been inspired by the sublime natural beauty of Provincetown. The town's first art school opened in 1901 and Hans Hofmann (1880–1966), Jackson Pollock (1912–56), Mark Rothko (1903–70), and Edward Hopper (1882–1967) are among the many prominent artists who have spent time here. Today the town is famous for its art galleries, both large and small. The roster of resident writers includes John Dos Passos (1896–1970), Tennessee Williams (1911–83), Sinclair Lewis (1885–1951), and Eugene O'Neill (1888–1953), whose earliest plays were staged at the Provincetown Playhouse.

Visitor to one of Provincetown's many art galleries

Exploring the Mid- and Upper Cape

Stretching from Bourne and Sandwich in the west to Yarmouth and Harwich in the east, Cape Cod's Mid- and Upper sections offer travelers a broad range of vacation experiences. Be it sunbathing on the tranquil beaches of Nantucket Sound by day or partaking in the fashionable nightlife of Hyannis once the sun has set over Cape Cod Bay, this section of the Cape has a little something for every taste.

Hyannis boatbuilder and his remodeled Russian torpedo boat

Dennis

This gracious village has developed into a vibrant artistic center and is home to the 1927 **Cape Playhouse**, America's oldest professional summer theater, as well as some of the Cape's finest public golf courses. The list of stage luminaries who started their career here is impressive. Playhouse grads include eventual Academy Award-winners Humphrey Bogart, Bette Davis, and Henry Fonda. The Playhouse complex also includes the **Cape Cod Museum of Art**, displaying the works of Cape Cod artists. A short drive to the east, the Scargo Hill Tower is open to the public and offers brilliant views of the surrounding landscape.

🎭 **Cape Playhouse**
820 Rte. 6A. **Tel** (508) 385-3911.
Open call for show times.

🏛 **Cape Cod Museum of Art**
Cape Playhouse grounds. **Tel** (508) 385-4477. **Open** late May–mid-Oct: 10am–5pm Mon–Sat, noon–5pm Sun; call for winter hours. **Closed** public hols; mid-Oct–late May: Mon. ♿ 🎁 ✉ 🌐 ccmoa.org

Hyannis

The Cape's largest village is also a busy shopping center and the transportation hub for regional train, bus, and air service. The harbor is full of yachts and sightseeing boats. Surprisingly, one of Hyannis' most popular forms of transportation does not float. The **Cape Cod Central Railroad** takes travelers for a scenic two-hour round-trip to the Cape Cod canal. Hyannis was one of the Cape's earliest summer resorts, attracting vacationers as far back as the mid-1800s. In 1874 President Ulysses S. Grant (1822–85) vacationed here, followed by President Grover Cleveland (1837–1908) years later. The most famous estate is the Kennedy compound, summer playground of one of America's most famous political dynasties. The heavily screened compound is best seen from the water aboard a sightseeing cruise.

After John Kennedy's assassination in 1963, a simple monument was erected in his honor: a pool and fountain and a circular wall bearing Kennedy's profile. The **John F. Kennedy Hyannis Museum** on the ground floor of the Old Town Hall covers the years he spent vacationing here, beginning in the 1930s, and includes photos, oral histories, and family videos.

🚂 **Cape Cod Central Railroad**
Tel (508) 771-3800 or (888) 797-7245.
Open late May–late Oct: Tue–Sun; call for trip times and departure points.
♿ ♿ 🎁 🌐 capetrain.com

🏛 **John F. Kennedy Hyannis Museum**
397 Main St. **Tel** (508) 790-3077.
Open call for hours. ♿ ♿

Barnstable

This attractive harbor town is the hub of Barnstable County, a widespread region extending to both sides of the Cape. The **Coast Guard Heritage Museum**, located in an 1856 customs house, displays artifacts from the Lighthouse, Livesaving, and Revenue Cutter services. A film

Popular sightseeing mode of transportation: Cape Cod Central Railroad

For hotels and restaurants in this region see pp313–14 and pp329–31

The Kennedy Clan

The center of the Kennedy compound in Hyannis Port is the "cottage" that multi-millionaire Joseph Kennedy (1888–1969) and his wife Rose (1890–1995) bought in 1926. The much-expanded structure was a vacation retreat for the Kennedys and their nine children. John Fitzgerald Kennedy (1917–63), the country's 35th president, and his brothers and sisters continued to summer here long after they had started families of their own. In 1999, JFK's son, John Jr, was flying to the compound for a family wedding when his plane crashed off Martha's Vineyard.

John and Jacqueline Kennedy at their cottage in Hyannis Port

shows lifesaving techniques. The harbor is home to whale-watching cruises, and conservation properties offer fine hiking.

🏛 Coast Guard Heritage Museum
Rte 6A, 3353 Main St. **Tel** (508) 362-8521. **Open** mid-Jun–Oct: 10am–3pm Tue–Sat.

Falmouth
Falmouth, settled by Quakers in 1661, grew into a resort town in the late 19th century. The picturesque village green and historic Main Street reflect a Victorian heritage.

Falmouth's coastline is ideal for boating, windsurfing, and sea kayaking. As well, the town is graced with 12 miles (19 km) of beaches. Old Silver is the most popular beach, but Grand Avenue has the most dramatic views of Vineyard Sound. Nature lovers will find walking and hiking trails, salt marshes, tidal pools, and opportunities for beach-combing and bird-watching. The 3.3-mile (5-km) Shining Sea Bike Path offers vistas of beach, harbor, and woodland on the way to Woods Hole.

Woods Hole
This is home to the world's largest independent marine science research center, the Woods Hole Oceanographic Institution (WHOI).

Visitors to the **WHOI Exhibit Center** can explore two floors of displays and videos explaining coastal ecology and highlighting some of the organization's findings. Exhibits include a replica of the interior of the *Alvin*, one of the pioneer vessels developed for deep-sea exploration.

🏛 WHOI Exhibit Center
15 School St. **Tel** (508) 289-2663. **Open** Apr–Dec: call for hours. 🅿 donation. 📷 Jul–Aug by appt. ♿

Sandwich
The oldest town on the Cape is straight off a postcard: the First Church of Christ overlooks a picturesque pond fed by the brook that powers the waterwheel of a colonial-era gristmill. The church has what is said to be the oldest church bell in the US, dating to 1675. The **Dexter Grist Mill**, built in 1654, has been restored and is grinding again, producing cornmeal that is available at the gift shop.

Antique bottle in Glass Museum

Another industry is celebrated at the **Sandwich Glass Museum**. Between 1825 and 1888, local entrepreneurs invented a way to press glass that was prized for its colors. Nearly 5,000 pieces of Sandwich glass are handsomely displayed here.

The most unique attraction in Sandwich is **Heritage Museums and Gardens**, a 75-acre (30-ha) garden and museum built around the collection of pharmaceutical magnate and inveterate collector Josiah Kirby

Lilly, Jr (1893–1966). The artifacts fill three buildings. The American History Museum, a replica of a revolutionary war fort, includes military miniatures and antique firearms. A collection of 37 antique cars is displayed in a reproduction of a Shaker barn.

The Art Museum contains everything from folk art and a collection of Currier and Ives prints to changing exhibits and a working 1912 carousel – a favorite with visitors. Outside, the grounds are planted with more than 1,000 varieties of trees, shrubs, and flowers, including superb rhododendrons.

🏚 Dexter Grist Mill
Maine & Water Sts. **Tel** (508) 888-4910. **Open** call for hours. 🅿

🏛 Sandwich Glass Museum
129 Main St. **Tel** (508) 888-0251. **Open** Feb–Mar: 9:30am–4pm Wed–Sun; Apr–Dec: 9:30am–5pm daily. 🅿 📷 ♿

🏚 Heritage Museums and Gardens
67 Grove St. **Tel** (508) 888-3300. **Open** May–Oct: 10am–5pm daily; Nov–Mar: call for hours. 🅿 ♿ 🌐 heritagemuseumsand gardens.org

Film star Gary Cooper's 1930 Duesenberg, Heritage Museums and Gardens

Old Sturbridge Village

At the heart of this living history museum are about 40 vintage buildings that have been restored and relocated from all over New England. Laid out like an early 19th-century village, Old Sturbridge is peopled by costumed interpreters who go about their daily activities. A blacksmith works the forge, farmers tend crops, and millers work the gristmill. Inside buildings, visitors will find re-created period settings, early American antiques, and demonstrations of such crafts as spinning and weaving. A gallery, education center, and workshops illuminate 19th-century life.

VISITORS' CHECKLIST

Practical Information
Rte. 20, Sturbridge. **Tel** (508) 347-3362 or (800) 733-1830.
Open mid-Apr–mid-Oct: 9:30am–5pm daily; mid-Oct–mid-Apr: 9:30am–4pm Tue–Sun.
Closed Dec 25. 🅿 🅲 call for times. ♿ some buildings. 🔲 🖥 📷 🆆 osv.org

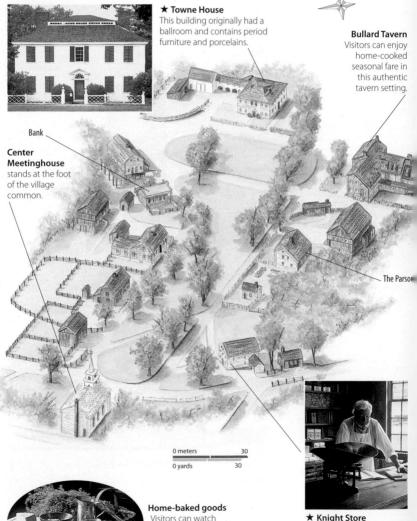

★ Towne House
This building originally had a ballroom and contains period furniture and porcelains.

Bullard Tavern
Visitors can enjoy home-cooked seasonal fare in this authentic tavern setting.

Bank

Center Meetinghouse
stands at the foot of the village common.

The Parson

0 meters 30
0 yards 30

Home-baked goods
Visitors can watch as costumed interpreters go about such daily activities as preparing food.

★ Knight Store
Rural stores provided important links to the outside world by stocking imported goods.

⓭ Worcester

🏔 181,000. ✈ Worcester Airport.
🚌 🚉 ℹ 91 Prescott St (508) 753-2920.

Worcester has always been on the cutting edge. During the American Industrial Revolution, local designers deve- loped the nation's first mechanized carpet weavers and envelope folders. This spirit of invention reached its pinnacle in 1926, when Worcester native Dr. Robert Goddard (1882–1945) launched the world's first liquid-fuel rocket.

Not all of Worcester's forward-thinking has been reserved for the development of new machines, however. Over time this city, which is built on seven hills, became home to 10 colleges and universities plus a center for biological research that in the 1950s developed the first birth-control pill.

Central Massachusetts' premier event space, the **DCU Center**, contains an indoor arena and convention center. Located in the heart of downtown Worcester, the complex is within walking distance of numerous shops, restaurants, and bars. The facility hosts an assortment of events, from big-name concerts and sporting events to family shows and conventions. The arena holds nearly 15,000 spectators and has hosted the likes of Frank Sinatra, Katy Perry, and local icons Aerosmith.

Housed in a handsome late 19th-century stone building, the **Worcester Art Museum** has distinguished itself as an important repository. Its impressive collection contains some 35,000 objects spanning 5,000 years, including a 12th-century chapter house that was rebuilt stone by stone on the premises. The museum's holdings of East and West Asian art and Japanese woodblock prints are balanced wonderfully by a good number of works by such Western masters as Claude Monet (1840–1926), Thomas Gainsborough (1728–88), and Pablo Picasso (1881–1973).

Just 2 miles (3 km) from downtown, the **Ecotarium** promotes a better under-standing of the region's environment and its wildlife. Interactive exhibits invite hands-on learning experiences. The surrounding grounds contain a wildlife center for injured and endangered animals, and New England's only tree canopy walkway (summer only). The 60-acre (24-ha) grounds also hold a planetarium.

DCU Center
50 Foster St. **Tel** (508) 755-6800. **Open** year-round, check website for details on events. W **dcucenter.com**

🏛 Worcester Art Museum
55 Salisbury St. **Tel** (508) 799-4406. **Open** year-round: 11am–5pm Wed-Fri & Sun, 10am–5pm Sat. 🌀 🚻 W **worcesterart.org**

🗺 Ecotarium
222 Harrington Way. **Tel** (508) 929-2700. **Open** year-round: 10am–5pm Tue–Sat, noon–5pm Sun. 🌀 🚻 W **ecotarium.org**

Environs
North Grafton, 10 miles (16 km) southeast, has a long history of clock-making. In the early 19th century brothers Benjamin, Simon, Ephraim, and Aaron Willard were regarded as some of New England's best craftsmen, designing new styles for timepieces. The time-pieces were given such names as Eddystone Lighthouse, Skeleton, and Act of Parliament. Today more than 70 Willard timepieces and elegant tall clocks are on display in the family's original 18th-century homestead.

🏛 Willard House and Clock Museum
11 Willard St., North Grafton. **Tel** (508) 839-3500. **Open** Apr–Dec: 10am–4pm Wed–Sat, 1–4pm Sun; Jan–Mar: Fri–Sun only. 🌀 📷 obligatory. 🚻 partial.

⓮ Sturbridge

Sturbridge's roots are literally in the land. Soon after its founding in 1729, residents planted apple orchards, some of which are still in operation. The town's main attraction is its living-history museum: Old Sturbridge Village *(see p164)*.

The 1748 Parsonage in Old Sturbridge Village

Environs
Located 9 miles (14 km) west, the village of Brimfield blossoms three times each year as America's flea market capital. The Brimfield Antique Show attracts hundreds of dealers, filling every field, sidewalk, and front porch in town. Treasure hunters descend to the village by the thousands to shop for wares ranging from valuable antiques to the truly kitsch.

Scraping recent layers of paint off an antique carousel horse at the Brimfield flea market

⓯ Springfield

🏙 153,000. ✈ 15 miles (24 km) SW in Windsor Locks, CT. 🚌 🚃 ℹ 1441 Main St. (413) 787-1548 or (800) 723-1548. 🌐 **valleyvisitor.com**

Now a center for banking and insurance, Springfield owes much of its early success to guns. The **Springfield Armory** – the first armory in the US – was commissioned by George Washington (1732–99) to manufacture arms for the Colonial forces fighting in the Revolutionary War. Today the historic armory is part of the National Park Service and maintains one of the most extensive and unique firearms collections in the world.

In 1891 Dr. James Naismith (1861–1939), an instructor at the International YMCA Training Center, now Springfield College, invented the game of basketball. **Basketball Hall of Fame** traces the development of the game from its humble beginnings, in which peach baskets were used as nets, to its evolution as one of the world's most popular team sports. Along with its collection of basketball memorabilia, the state-of-the-art museum features interactive displays. Children and adults can play against former stars in virtual reality games or test their own shooting skills.

Court Square on Main Street is the revitalized center of the city, lined with 19th-century churches, civic and commercial buildings, and a 300-ft (91-m) high tower housing carillon bells. Nearby is **The Quadrangle**, a group of

Emblem of the Basketball Hall of Fame in Springfield

five museums of art, science, and history. The G.W.V. Smith Art Museum displays a noted collection of Oriental decorative arts and Japanese armor. Galleries at the Museum of Fine Arts contain European and American paintings, sculpture, and decorative arts. Children love the Springfield Science Museum, with its live animal center, planetarium, and Dinosaur Hall, with a life-sized model of *Tyrannosaurus rex*. The Connecticut Valley Historical Museum concentrates on colonial-era history, while the Wood Museum of Springfield History displays locally made cars and motorcycles.

The Dr. Seuss National Memorial sculpture features the beloved characters of popular children's author and Springfield native Theodor Geisel (1904–91), better known as Dr. Seuss.

🏛 **Springfield Armory National Historic Site**
One Armory Sq. **Tel** (413) 734-8551. **Open** 9am–5pm daily. **Closed** Jan 1, Thanksgiving, Dec 25. 🎦 🕭

🏛 **Basketball Hall of Fame**
1000 W Columbus Ave. **Tel** (413) 781-6500. **Open** 10am–4pm Tue–Fri & Sun, 10am–5pm Sat. **Closed** Thanksgiving, Dec 25, Mon & Tue (Jan–Apr). 🎦 🕭 ♿ 🌐 **hoophall.com**

🏛 **The Quadrangle**
State & Chestnut Sts. **Tel** (413) 263-6800. Five museums: **Open** year-round: call for hours. 🎦 ♿ partial. 🌐 **springfieldmuseums.org**

Environs
Some 11 miles (18 km) north, the hamlet of South Hadley is home to **Mount Holyoke College** (1837), the nation's oldest women's college. Poet Emily Dickinson (1830–86) was one of Mount Holyoke's most famous graduates. The 800-acre (320-ha) campus encompasses two lakes and a series of nature trails. College sites worth a visit include the **Art Museum** and the **Talcott Greenhouse**, which is located in a Victorian-style greenhouse.

Farther north in Hadley, the summit of 954-ft (291-m) Mount Holyoke in **Skinner State Park** offers a panorama of the oxbow

Dinosaur model dwarfing visitor in Springfield's Science Museum

bend in the Connecticut River. The park is well known for massive laurel displays in June and flaming foliage in autumn.

🏛 **Mount Holyoke College Art Museum**
Mount Holyoke College. **Tel** (413) 538-2245. **Open** 11am–5pm Tue–Fri, 1–5pm Sat–Sun. 🕭

🌱 **Talcott Greenhouse**
Mount Holyoke College. **Tel** (413) 538-2116. **Open** year-round: 9am–4pm Mon–Fri, 1–4pm Sat–Sun. 🕭

🥾 **Skinner State Park**
Rte. 47. **Tel** (413) 586-0350. **Open** May–Oct: dawn–dusk. 🥾 on weekends.

⓰ Amherst

🏙 23,000. ✈ 41 miles (66 km) S in Windsor Locks, CT. 🚌 🚃 ℹ 28 Amity St. (413) 253-0700.

This idyllic college town is home to three different institutes of higher learning. The most popular with visitors is Amherst College, with its central green and traditional ivy-covered buildings. Founded in 1821 for underprivileged youths hoping to enter the ministry, the school has grown into one of the most selective small colleges in the US. The college's excellent **Mead Art Museum** includes the Rotherwas Room, an ornately paneled English hall c.1600. Minerals, fossils, and bones star in the **Beneski Museum of Natural History**, also on the college campus. Poet Emily

Dickinson was one of Amherst's most famous citizens. In her early 20s, Dickinson withdrew from society and spent the rest of her life in the family home, where she died in 1886. The second-floor bedroom of the **Emily Dickinson Museum** has been restored to the way it was during the years 1855–86, when the reclusive poet wrote her most important verse. Her work remained unpublished until after her death. Over time critics proclaimed it to be the work of a poetic genius. The **Jones Library** has displays on Dickinson's life and works, as well as collections on poet Robert Frost, who taught at Amherst College in the 1940s.

🏛 **Mead Art Museum**
Amherst College. **Tel** (413) 542-2335. **Open** 9am–5pm Tue–Thu & Sat–Sun, 9am–8pm Fri. **Closed** mid-Dec–late Jan. 🎫 🛗

🏛 **Beneski Museum of Natural History**
Amherst College. **Tel** (413) 542-2165. **Open** year-round: 11am–4pm Tue–Sun.

🏛 **Emily Dickinson Museum**
280 Main St. **Tel** (413) 542-8161. **Open** Mar–mid-Dec: call for hours. 📷 🎫 obligatory.

🏛 **Jones Library**
43 Amity St. **Tel** (413) 256-4090. **Open** 9am–5:30pm Mon–Wed, Fri & Sat, 9am–8:30pm Tue & Thu, 1–5pm Sun. **Closed** Jun–Aug: Sun. Special collections: **Open** year-round: 2–5pm Mon & Sat, 10am–5pm Tue–Fri. 🛗

⓱ Northampton

🏙 30,000. ✈ 36 miles (58 km) S in Windsor Locks, CT. 🚌 ℹ 99 Pleasant St (413) 584-1900.

A lively center for the arts and known for its fine dining, Northampton has a well preserved Victorian-style Main Street lined with craft galleries and shops. The town is also home to the 1871 **Smith College**, the largest privately endowed women's college in the nation. The handsome campus has a notable **Museum of Art** and the **Lyman Plant House and Conservatory**, known for its flower shows and the arboretum

Beautiful bloom at Smith College's Lyman Plant House

and gardens. South of Northampton in Holyoke, visitors can explore the trails in the 3-sq-mile (7-sq-km) **Mount Tom State Reservation**. Nearby is the Norwottuck Rail Trail, a popular walking and biking path that runs along an old railroad bed connecting Northampton to neighboring Amherst.

🏛 **Smith College Museum of Art**
Elm St., Northampton. **Tel** (413) 585-2760. **Open** 10am–4pm Tue–Sat, noon–4pm Sun. 📷

🌿 **Lyman Plant House and Conservatory**
College Lane, Northampton. **Tel** (413) 585-2740. **Open** year-round: 8:30am–4pm daily. **Closed** Thanksgiving, Dec 25–Jan 1.

🌲 **Mount Tom State Reservation**
125 Reservation Rd., Holyoke. **Tel** (413) 534-1186. **Open** year-round: 8am–dusk daily. Visitors' center: **Open** Memorial Day–mid-Oct: Wed–Sun. Call for hours. 🛗 partial.

⓲ Deerfield

🏙 5,300. ✈ 52 miles (84 km) S in Windsor Locks, CT. ℹ 18 Miner St., Greenfield (413) 773-9393.

A one-time frontier outpost that was almost annihilated by Indian raids in the late 17th century, Deerfield survived and its farmers prospered, building gracious clapboard homes along the mile-long (1.6-km) center avenue known simply as "The Street."

Sixty of these remain within **Historic Deerfield** and are carefully preserved. Some of the buildings now serve as museums, exhibiting a broad range of period furniture and decorative arts, including silverware, ceramics, and textiles. The Flynt Center of Early New England Life schedules changing exhibitions on early life in western Massachusetts. Visitors seeking a photo opportunity can drive to the summit of **Mount Sugarloaf State Reservation** in South Deerfield for views of the Connecticut River Valley.

🏛 **Historic Deerfield**
The Street, Old Deerfield. **Tel** (413) 775-7214. **Open** Dec–Mar: call for hours; Apr–Nov: 9:30am–4:30pm daily. **Closed** Thanksgiving, Dec 24, Dec 25. 📷 🌐 historic-deerfield.org

🌲 **Mount Sugarloaf State Reservation**
US 116, South Deerfield. **Tel** (413) 665-2928. **Open** May–Dec: 8am–dusk daily.

White clapboard house and picket fence in historic Deerfield

❶ Tour of the Mohawk Trail

Originally an Indian trade route, this trail was a popular artery for early pioneers. In 1914 the trail, which stretches for 63 miles (100 km) from Orange to North Adams along Route 2, became a paved road. The choicest section of the route, from Greenfield to North Adams, was the first officially designated scenic drive in New England. This twisting road offers magnificent mountain views, particularly in the sharp hairpin curves leading into North Adams, and is one of the most popular fall foliage routes.

② **Charlemont**
The town is dominated by the massive statue *Hail to the Sunrise*.

③ **Hairpin Turn**
This sharp bend in the road offers soaring views of Mount Greylock.

④ **North Adams**
North Adams is near America's only naturally formed marble bridge.

Key

▭ Tour route

— Other road

❷ Williamstown

🏠 8,000. ✈ 47 miles (75 km) W in Albany, NY. 🚌 ℹ Jct Rtes 2 & 7 (413) 458-9077 or (800) 214-3799.

Art lovers make pilgrimages to **The Sterling and Francine Clark Art Institute** to see its private art collection, strong on Old Masters and French Impressionists, including more than 30 Renoirs. The grounds of this hilltop museum also include trails through forest and meadow that are open to hikers and, in winter, snowshoers. The **Williams College Museum of Art** is also notable for a collection that ranges from ancient Assyrian stone reliefs to Andy Warhol's (1927–87) final self-portrait.

The summertime Williamstown Theater Festival, founded in 1954, is known for its high-quality productions, which often feature big-name Broadway and Hollywood stars.

A 19th-century Steinway at The Sterling and Francine Clark Art Institute

🏛 **The Sterling and Francine Clark Art Institute**
225 South St. **Tel** (413) 458-2303.
Open 10am–5pm Tue–Sun (Jul–Aug: daily). 🅿 (Jun–Oct only). 🅖 ♿
🆆 clarkart.edu

🏛 **Williams College Museum of Art**
Main St. **Tel** (413) 597-2429.
Open year-round: 10am–5pm Tue–Sat, 1–5pm Sun. ♿ 🆆 wcma.org

Environs
More art can be found 7 miles (11 km) east in North Adams at the **Massachusetts Museum of Contemporary Art** (MASS MoCA). Seven interconnected buildings, part of a 19th-century factory, with enormous indoor spaces, elevated walkways, and outdoor courtyards display cutting-edge art. The complex is able to house sculptures and paintings that are too large for most conventional museums.

🏛 **Massachusetts Museum of Contemporary Art**
1040 MASS MoCA Way. **Tel** (413) 662-2111. **Open** 11am–5pm Wed–Mon (Jul–Sep: 10am–6pm daily). 🅿 ♿
🏠 🆆 massmoca.org

Degas statue at Clark Institute

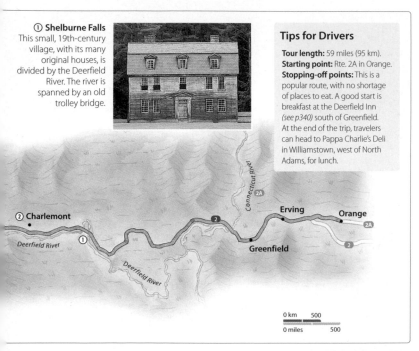

① **Shelburne Falls**
This small, 19th-century village, with its many original houses, is divided by the Deerfield River. The river is spanned by an old trolley bridge.

Tips for Drivers

Tour length: 59 miles (95 km).
Starting point: Rte. 2A in Orange.
Stopping-off points: This is a popular route, with no shortage of places to eat. A good start is breakfast at the Deerfield Inn (see p340) south of Greenfield. At the end of the trip, travelers can head to Pappa Charlie's Deli in Williamstown, west of North Adams, for lunch.

② Charlemont
Deerfield River ①
Deerfield River
Connecticut River
2A
2
Erving
Orange
2A
Greenfield
2

0 km 500
0 miles 500

㉑ Mount Greylock State Reservation

Off Rte. 7, Lanesborough. (Auto road open late-May–Oct). ℹ️ (413) 499-4262. 🆆 mass.gov/dcr/parks

The Appalachian Trail (see pp26–7), the popular 2,000-mile (3,200-km) hiking path running from Georgia to Maine, crosses Mount Greylock's summit. At 3,491 ft (1,064 m), Greylock is the highest peak in Massachusetts and offers panoramic views of five states. The auto road to the summit is open from late May through October. Hiking trails in the 2-sq-mile (5-sq-km) park remain open and are particularly popular during fall foliage season. At the summit visitors can climb Veterans' Memorial Tower for an even more panoramic view.

㉒ Hancock Shaker Village

Rte. 20, outside Pittsfield. **Tel** (413) 443-0188. **Open** mid-Apr–late May: 10am–4pm daily; late May–Oct: 10am–5pm daily. 🆆 hancockshakervillage.org

Founded in 1783, this was the third in a series of 19 Shaker settlements established in the Northeast and Midwest as utopian communities. The Shakers, so-called because they often trembled and shook during moments of worship and prayer, believed in celibacy and equality of the sexes, with men and women living separately but sharing authority and responsibilities. At its peak in the 1830s, there were 300 residents living in the village. Now the community has no resident Shakers.

Summit Veteran's Memorial Tower atop Mount Greylock

Authentic Shaker door latch at Hancock Shaker Village

Twenty of the 100 original buildings have been restored, including the tri-level round stone barn, cleverly designed so that as many as 52 head of cattle could be fed by a single farmhand from a central core. The Brick Dwelling can house up to 100 people, and has a meeting room used for weekday worship and a communal dining room, where traditional Shaker fare is served on select evenings.

Presentations on the Shaker way of life include demonstrations of chair-, broom-, and oval box- making. In the Discovery Room visitors may try on reproduction Shaker clothing and also try their hand at crafts such as weaving. An orientation exhibit and videos in several buildings provide historical background.

For map symbols see back flap

Picturesque Bash Bish Falls in Mount Washington State Forest

❷ The Berkshires

🚗 37 miles (60 km) NE in Albany, NY.
🚆 Pittsfield. ℹ️ 3 Hoosac St., Adams
(413) 743-4500; (800) 237-5747.
🌐 berkshires.org

Visitors have long been attracted to the peaceful wooded hills, green valleys, rippling rivers, and waterfalls of this western corner of Massachusetts. Among the first tourists were writers such as Henry Wadsworth Longfellow (1807–82), Herman Melville (1819–91), and Nathaniel Hawthorne (1804–64). When the three wrote about the natural beauty of the area, the location caught the attention of many of the region's wealthy people, who began to spend their summers here. Now the region is a year-round playground, popular for its culture as well as for the ample opportunities it provides for outdoor recreation.

The area is speckled with small towns and country villages. Great Barrington to the south and Pittsfield to the north are the commercial centers of the region, while Lenox and Stockbridge are cultural meccas. The old cotton and woolen mills in Housatonic are finding new life as art galleries, and Main Street of Sheffield is lined with interesting little antique shops.

Among the most popular walking and hiking trails in the Berkshires are Bartholemew's Cobble in Sheffield and Bash Bish Falls in the **Mount Washington State Forest**. A trail leads to the summit of Monument Mountain and affords beautiful views. Reputedly, it was on a hike up the mountain that Herman Melville first met Nathaniel Hawthorne, forming a friendship that resulted in Melville's dedicating his novel *Moby-Dick* to his fellow author.

🏞 Mount Washington State Forest
Rte 41 S. **Tel** (413) 528-0330. **Open** Memorial Day–Columbus Day. 🏞

Pittsfield
Although primarily a commercial hub, Pittsfield has a growing cultural scene, including the award-winning **Barrington Stage Company**. The town's literary shrine is

Life-sized model of Stegosaurus at Berkshire Museum in Pittsfield

Arrowhead, an 18th-century home in the shadow of Mount Greylock, where Herman Melville lived from 1850 to 1863 and where he wrote his masterpiece *Moby-Dick*. The **Berkshire Museum** has a large collection of items covering the disciplines of history, natural science, and fine art. The museum's aquarium has 20 tanks for local and exotic sea creatures. The galleries are notable for their works by such 19th-century American masters as George Inness (1825–94) and Frederic Church (1826–1900).

🎭 Barrington Stage Company
30 Union St. **Tel** (413) 236-8888.
🌐 barringtonstageco.org

🏠 Arrowhead
780 Holmes Rd. **Tel** (413) 442-1793.
Open late May–mid-Oct: 9:30am–5pm daily; rest of year by appt. 🎫 📷 ♿ first floor only. 🏠 ✉ 🌐 mobydick.org

🏛 Berkshire Museum
39 South St. **Tel** (413) 443-7171. **Open** 10am–5pm Mon–Sat, noon–5pm Sun. **Closed** public hols. 🎫 ♿ 🏠 ✉ 🌐 berkshiremuseum.org

Lenox
In the late 19th century the gracious village of Lenox became known as the "inland Newport" for the lavish summer "cottages" built by prominent families such as the Carnegies and the Vanderbilts. Before the 1929 Great Depression, there were more than 70 grand estates gracing the area. While some of the millionaires have since moved away, many of their lavish homes remain in service as schools, cultural institutions, resorts, and posh inns. One of the more prominent mansions is **The Mount**, built in 1902 by

Gathering hay by oxcart at Hancock Shaker Village

Typical townhouse in the village of Lenox

Pulitzer Prize-winning author Edith Wharton (1862–1937).

Lenox gained new status as a center of culture in 1937 when the 500-acre (202-ha) Tanglewood estate became the summer home of the Boston Symphony Orchestra. Music lovers flock for concerts to the 1,200-seat Seiji Ozawa Hall or the open Music Shed, where many enjoy picnicking and listening to the music on the surrounding lawn. Jazz and popular concerts are interspersed with the classical program. Tanglewood's name is credited to Nathaniel Hawthorne, who lived in a house on the estate at one time and wrote some of his short stories here.

The Mount
2 Plunkett St. **Tel** (413) 551-5111.
Open May–Oct: 10am–5pm daily. 🅿
🎫 ♿ 📷 ♻ 🅆 edithwharton.org

Stockbridge
Stockbridge was founded in 1734 by missionaries seeking to educate and convert the local

Figures of *Andromeda* and *Memory* at Chesterwood

Mohegan Indians. The simple **Mission House** (c.1739) was built by Reverend John Sergeant for his bride. Today the house contains period pieces and Indian artifacts.

The town's quaint main street, dominated by the 1897 Red Lion Inn, has been immortalized in the popular paintings of Norman Rockwell (1894–1978), one of America's most beloved illustrators. The painter lived in Stockbridge for 25 years, and the country's largest collection of Rockwell originals can be seen at the **Norman Rockwell Museum**.

Stockbridge has been home to its share of prominent residents, including sculptor Daniel Chester French (1850–1931), who summered at his **Chesterwood** estate. It was here that French created the working models for his famous *Seated Lincoln* (1922) for the Lincoln Memorial in Washington, DC. The models remain in the studio along with other plaster casts. During the summer months the grounds are used to exhibit sculpture. **Naumkeag Museum**

and Gardens is a graceful 1885 mansion built for Joseph H. Choate, US ambassador to Britain and one of the era's leading attorneys. The 26-room house is appointed with its original furnishings and an art collection that spans three centuries. Of note is the exhibit of Chinese porcelains. The grounds are a work of art also with their formal gardens.

🚏 **Mission House**
19 Main St. **Tel** (413) 298-3239.
Open Memorial Day–Columbus Day; call for tour hours. 📷 ♻

🏛 **Norman Rockwell Museum**
Rte. 183. **Tel** (413) 298-4100. **Open** May–Oct: 10am–5pm daily; Nov–Apr: 10am–4pm Mon–Fri, 10am–5pm Sat–Sun. **Closed** Jan 1, Thanksgiving, Dec 25. 📷 🎫 ♿ 📷 🅆 nrm.org

🚏 **Chesterwood**
4 Williamsville Rd. **Tel** (413) 298-3579.
Open late May–Oct: 10am–5pm daily.
📷 🎫 ♿ partial. ♻
🅆 chesterwood.org

🏛 **Naumkeag Museum and Gardens**
Prospect Hill. **Tel** (413) 298-3239.
Open Memorial Day–Columbus Day: 10am–5pm daily. 📷 ♻

Relaxed setting for the Tanglewood summer concert series

The Arts in the Berkshires

The Berkshires region has one of America's richest summer menus of performing arts. As well as Boston Symphony Orchestra concerts at Tanglewood, Aston Magna presents baroque concerts at several locations. The Berkshire Choral Festival is held in Sheffield, and the Barrington Stage Company performs in Pittsfield. The Jacob's Pillow Dance Festival in Becket, the oldest such event in the nation, presents leading international companies. The Berkshire Theater Festival and the Williamstown Theater Festival are among the oldest and most respected summer theaters in the nation. Shakespeare & Company presents acclaimed productions of the Bard's works, as well as thought-provoking new plays.

RHODE ISLAND

With an area of just over 1,200 sq miles (3,100 sq km), Rhode Island is the smallest of the 50 states. However, its historic towns, unspoiled wilderness areas, and a pristine shoreline dotted with inlets and tranquil harbors make the place a lively and easily explored holiday destination.

For such a small state, "Little Rhody" was founded on big ideals. Driven from the Massachusetts Bay colony in 1636 for his outspoken beliefs on religious freedom, clergyman Roger Williams (1604–83) established a settlement on the banks of Narragansett Bay. He called the town Providence and founded it upon the tenets of freedom of speech and religious tolerance – principles that would be formally introduced in the First Amendment to the US Constitution in 1781. This forward-thinking spirit made Rhode Island the site of America's first synagogue and Baptist church and some of the nation's earliest libraries, public schools, and colleges. In May 1776 Rhode Island followed the lead of New Hampshire and formally declared its independence from British rule.

Although its 400-mile (645-km) shoreline is considered small in comparison to those of neighboring states, Rhode Island has earned its nickname, the Ocean State. In the 17th century, its port towns were primary players in the burgeoning maritime trade with the West Indies. Today some 120 public beaches provide opportunities for swimming, scuba diving, boating, windsurfing, and fishing. Pleasure craft can be seen skimming the waters of Narragansett Bay. Home to the America's Cup yacht races between 1930–85, Newport is well known as one of the world's great yachting centers. But not all of Rhode Island's allure is found on the waterfront. More than 50 percent of the state is covered in woodland. The 28 state parks are ideal for outdoor activities; three allow camping.

Fishing at dusk on beautiful Narragansett Bay

◀ Castle Hill Lighthouse on Narragansett Bay, Newport

Exploring Rhode Island

Not an island at all, the state of Rhode Island does, however, contain dozens of islets and peninsulas along the Atlantic coastline. They dot Narragansett Bay, which takes a huge bite out of the eastern portion of the state. Craggy cliffs, grass-covered bluffs, and golden sand beaches mark the shoreline of the Ocean State, which offers an abundance of opportunities for fishing, swimming, boating, surfing, and other aquatic activities. Inland numerous lakes, reservoirs, and swamps (in South County) maintain the maritime atmosphere. Most activity in Rhode Island centers around its two major cities, Providence *(see pp178–81)* and Newport *(see pp186–91),* but the smaller roads across the western part of the state are perfect for tranquil country drives.

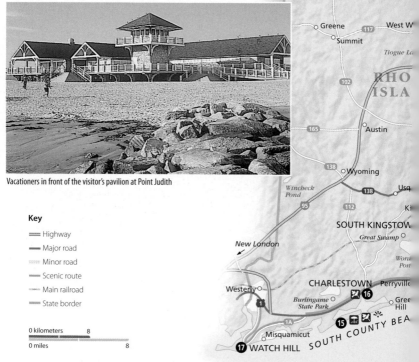

Vacationers in front of the visitor's pavilion at Point Judith

Key

=== Highway

— Major road

===== Minor road

— Scenic route

—•— Main railroad

— State border

```
0 kilometers        8
0 miles             8
```

Sights at a Glance

1. Woonsocket
2. Great Road
3. Pawtucket
4. Bristol
5. *Providence pp178–81*
6. Portsmouth
7. Little Compton
8. Middletown
9. *Newport pp186–91*
10. Jamestown
11. Wickford
12. Saunderstown
13. South Kingstown
14. Narragansett
15. South County Beaches
16. Charlestown
17. Watch Hill

Tour

18. Block Island *pp196–7*

For hotels and restaurants in this region see pp314–15 and pp331–3

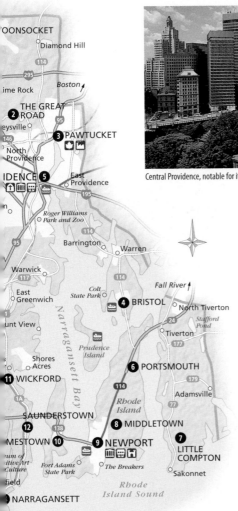

Central Providence, notable for its blend of the historic and modern

Getting Around

Highway 146 follows the Blackstone River Valley south to Providence where it connects with Interstate 95, forming the major north-south artery in the state. For scenery, travelers should stay on Route 1 as it hugs Narragansett Bay and Block Island Sound. An alternative route is 114, which island-hops down the eastern region of the state through Bristol *(see pp176–7)* to Newport.

Amtrak operates rail lines running from Boston through Providence and down as far as Westerly.

Rhode Island Public Transit Authority (RIPTA) provides bus services throughout most of the state, with hourly service between Providence and Newport and a summer service to several South County beaches *(see pp194–5)*.

Year-round ferry services operated by RIPTA are offered from Providence to Newport. Ferries to Block Island also run year-round and depart from Point Judith *(see pp194–5)*.

Yachts by the score in the harbor at Newport

For map symbols *see back flap*

Classroom display at the Museum of Work and Culture, Woonsocket

❶ Woonsocket

🏙 44,000. 🛈 175 Main St., Pawtucket (401) 724-2200 or (800) 454-2882. 🌐 **tourblackstone.com**

A major manufacturing center located on the busy Blackstone River, Woonsocket was transformed from a relatively small village to a booming mill town by the development of the local textile industry in the 19th and early 20th centuries. Although the textile industry declined after World War II, the city remains one of the major manufacturing hubs.

The **Museum of Work and Culture** focuses on the impact of the Industrial Revolution on the region. The day-to-day lives of the factory owners, managers, and immigrant workers are examined and explained with the help of a re-created 1934 union hall, hands-on displays, models, and multimedia exhibits.

🏛 **Museum of Work and Culture**
42 S Main St. **Tel** (401) 769-9675.
Open 9:30am–4pm Tue–Fri, 10am–4pm Sat, 1–4pm Sun. 🐾 🅰

❷ The Great Road

🛈 (401) 724-2200.
🌐 **tourblackstone.com**

An often-overlooked gem, the stretch of Great Road (Route 123) between Saylesville and Lime Rock follows the course of the Moshassuck River for 0.6 mile (1 km) and yields eight historically significant buildings. Four of these buildings are open for limited hours and include the 1680 **Eleazer Arnold House** and the 1704 **Friends Meetinghouse**, New England's oldest Quaker meeting house in continuous use. Constructed in

Eleazer Arnold House near Lincoln on the Great Road

1807 as a toll station and later serving as a hotel, **North Gate**, just off the Great Road, now contains a small museum room decked out with early 18th-century furniture. Farther along the road, **Hannaway Blacksmith Shop** is a one-story, 19th-century structure restored for blacksmith demonstrations and special events.

🏠 **Eleazer Arnold House**
487 Great Rd. **Tel** (401) 728-9696.
Open 11am–4pm Sat & Sun.
🎟 obligatory; call for appt.

🏠 **Friends Meetinghouse**
374 Great Rd. **Tel** (401) 725-2847.
🎟 obligatory; call for appt.

🏠 **North Gate**
Rte. 246. **Tel** (401) 725-2847.
🎟 obligatory; call for appt.

🏠 **Hannaway Blacksmith Shop**
671 Great Rd. **Tel** (401) 333-1100.
🎟 obligatory; call for appt.

❸ Pawtucket

🏙 73,000. 🛈 175 Main St. (401) 724-2200. 🌐 **tourblackstone.com**

This bustling industrial city, built on hills sliced by the Blackstone, Moshassuck, and Ten Mile rivers is generally acknowledged to be the birthplace of America's Industrial Revolution. It was here in 1793 that mechanical engineer Samuel Slater (1768–1835) built the country's first water-powered cotton-spinning mill.

A major historic landmark, the **Slater Mill Living History Museum** includes the restored Slater Mill and the 1810 Wilkinson Mill, complete with an authentic 19th-century machine shop and the only 8-ton (7-tonne) waterwheel in the US. Also on

Pawtucket's Slater Mill Living History Museum, home of the first water-powered cotton-spinning mill in the US

For hotels and restaurants in this region see pp314–15 and pp331–3

McCoy Stadium, playing field of the Pawtucket Red Sox baseball team

the site, the 1758 Sylvanus Brown House is furnished with the machinery and personal effects of Sylvanus Brown, a millwright and pattern-maker.

At the 200-acre (81-ha) **Slater Memorial Park** on the Ten Mile River, there are hiking trails, paddleboats, tennis courts, picnic areas, sunken gardens, and a seasonal 1895 Looff carousel. The park is also home to the city's oldest dwelling, the 1685 **Daggett House**, which contains exhibits of 17th-century furnishings and antiques.

The **Pawtucket Red Sox** baseball team plays games at McCoy Stadium. This minor league team has players who, once they have honed their skills, may move on to play for the Boston Red Sox.

Pawtucket Red Sox logo

🏛 Slater Mill Living History Museum

Roosevelt & Slater Aves. **Tel** (401) 725-8638. **Open** Mar–Apr: 11am–3pm Sat & Sun; May–Oct: 10am–4pm Tue–Sun; Nov–Feb: by appt. 🅿 📷 ♿

🌳 Slater Memorial Park

Newport Ave. **Tel** (401) 728-0500 ext 252. **Open** year-round: 8:30am–dusk daily. ♿

🏛 Daggett House

Slater Park off Rte. 1A. **Tel** (401) 724-5748. 📷 obligatory; call for appt. 🅿

Pawtucket Red Sox

McCoy Stadium, Columbus Ave. **Tel** (401) 724-7300. **Open** Apr–early Sep; call for schedule. 🅿 ♿ **W** pawsox.com

❹ Bristol

🅼 21,650. 🛈 16 Cutler St., Warren (401) 245-0750. **W** eastbaychamberri.org

Bristol blossomed in the late 18th century when its status as a major commercial, fishing, whaling, and shipbuilding center made it the nation's fourth-busiest port. The many elegant Federal and Victorian mansions lining Hope, High, and Thames streets attest to those prosperous days. One such fine home is the 1810 **Linden Place**, where scenes from *The Great Gatsby* (1974) were filmed. The Federal-style mansion was built by General George DeWolf (1772–1844) with money he had made from his sugar plantations in Cuba and the slave trade. Historic walking tours are often available.

The trappings of wealth are also in evidence at **Blithewold Mansion and Gardens**. Built in 1894 for Pennsylvania coal baron Augustus Van Wickle (1856–98), the mansion was rebuilt in 1907. It has many gardens and trees from the Far East. The grounds offer spectacular views of Narragansett Bay *(see p169)*.

Boating has always been popular with the rich and famous, and Bristol's history as the producer of America's greatest yachts is traced at the **Herreshoff Marine Museum/ America's Cup Hall of Fame**. The museum is located on Narragansett Bay, at the site of the legendary Herreshoff Manufacturing Company, which built yachts for eight America's Cup races. Photos, models, and restored ships celebrate the golden age of yachting. The museum also operates a sailing school for adults and children, and hosts classic yacht regattas.

Colt State Park, a 460-acre (186-ha) shoreline park features a 3-mile (5-km) shoreline drive along Narragansett Bay, a bicycle trail, many picnic areas, and playing fields. Also on the park grounds is the **Coggeshall Farm Museum**, a restored 1790s coastal farm with a barn, blacksmith shop, and heirloom breeds of domesticated animals. Cyclists and inline skaters can tour the picturesque East Bay Bike Path, leading some 14.5 miles (23 km) from Bristol to Providence along the coast-hugging route of an old railroad line.

The peaceful rural idyll of Coggeshall Farm Museum

🏛 Linden Place

500 Hope St. **Tel** (401) 253-0390. **Open** May–Columbus Day: 10am–4pm Thu–Sat (Sun: call first). 🅿 📷 ♿

🏛 Blithewold Mansion

101 Ferry Rd. **Tel** (401) 253-2707. Mansion: **Open** mid-Apr–mid-Oct: 10am–4pm Wed–Sun; call for winter hours. **Closed** public hols. Grounds: **Open** 10am–5pm daily. 🅿 ♿

🏛 Herreshoff Marine Museum/ America's Cup Hall of Fame

1 Burnside St. **Tel** (401) 253-5000. **Open** May–Oct: 10am–5pm daily. 🅿 📷 ♿ **W** herreshoff.org

🌳 Colt State Park

Rte. 114. **Tel** (401) 253-7482. **Open** daily. ♿

🏛 Coggeshall Farm Museum

Poppasquash Rd off Rte 114. **Tel** (401) 253-9062. **Open** 10am–4pm Tue–Sun. 🅿 ♿ **W** coggeshallfarm.org

❺ Providence

Sandwiched between Boston and New York on busy I-95, Providence is often overlooked by hurried travelers. This is a pity, since the city is blessed with a rich history well worth exploring. Perched on seven hills, Providence started life as a farming community before taking advantage of its location on the Seekonk River to develop into a flourishing seaport in the 17th century. The city then evolved into a hub of industry in the 19th century, with immigrants from Europe pouring in to work in the burgeoning textile mills.

Interior courtyard at Rhode Island School of Design's Museum of Art

🏛 First Unitarian Church
310 Benefit St. **Tel** (401) 421-7970.
Open daily. ♿ ✝ 10:30am Sun.

🏛 First Baptist Church in America
75 N Main St. **Tel** (401) 454-3418.
Open call for hours. 📷 ♿
✝ 11am Sun (10am in summer).
Founded in 1638 by Roger Williams and built in 1774–5, the First Baptist Church in

Stately buildings along Benefit Street's Mile of History

Exploring Providence
The city is bisected by the Providence River, with the Downtown district (see pp180–81) on the west bank and College Hill to the east. Walking through College Hill, visitors will pass a large number of 18th-century buildings, including the redbrick colonial Market House, built along the waterway in the 1770s and now part of Rhode Island School of Design (RISD).

🏛 Benefit Street's Mile of History
Benefit St. **Tel** (401) 274-1636.
Along Benefit Street's Mile of History there are more than 100 houses ranging in style from Colonial and Federal to Greek Revival and Victorian. This lovely, tree-lined street passes RISD's **Museum of Art**, which houses a small but comprehensive collection of artworks from Ancient Egyptian to contemporary American. Also on Benefit Street is the 1838 Greek Revival **Providence Athenaeum**. This is where author Edgar Allen

Poe (1809–49) courted Sarah Whitman, the woman who was the inspiration for his poem *Annabel Lee* (1849). The library, one of the oldest in America, has a collection dating back to 1753. Other architectural gems include the **First Unitarian Church**, which possesses a 2,500-lb (1,350-kg) bell, the largest ever cast by silversmith and Revolutionary War hero Paul Revere (see p124).

🏛 RISD Museum of Art
224 Benefit St. **Tel** (401) 454-6500. **Open** year-round: 10am–5pm Tue–Sun, 10am–9pm 3rd Thu of month. **Closed** public hols. 📷 ♿ 🅦 risd.edu

🏛 Providence Athenaeum
251 Benefit St. **Tel** (401) 421-6970. **Open** year-round: 9am–5pm Mon–Thu, 9am–5pm Fri–Sat, 1–5pm Sun. **Closed** summer: Sat pm, Sun. 🅦 providenceathenaeum.org

| 0 meters | 250 |
| 0 yards | 250 |

Culinary Archives and Museum ➤

Roger Williams Park and Zoo, Johnson and Wales University
Airport
12 miles (19 km) ✈

America is noted for its Ionic columns, intricately carved wood interior, and large Waterford crystal chandelier.

🏛 Governor Stephen Hopkins House

15 Hopkins St. **Tel** (401) 421-0694. **Open** May–Oct: 1–4pm Fri–Sat. 🎟 📷 obligatory.

The 1707 **Governor Stephen Hopkins House** belonged to one of Rhode Island's two signatories to the Declaration of Independence, and contains fine 18th-century furnishings.

🏛 Brown University

45 Prospect St. **Tel** (401) 863-1000. **Open** call for hours. 🎟 ♿ 📷 🎁 🖥

Founded in 1764, Brown is the seventh-oldest college in the US and one of the prestigious Ivy League schools *(see pp32–3)*. The campus, a rich blend of Gothic and Beaux Arts styles, is a National Historic Landmark. The John Hay Library has an eclectic collection

that includes artifacts and memorabilia relating to President Abraham Lincoln (1809–65), 5,000 toy soldiers and miniatures, and vintage sheet music. Other buildings of note include University Hall, where French and colonial troops were quartered during the American Revolution; Manning Hall, which houses the University Chapel; the John Carter Brown Library, with its fascinating collection of Americana; and the List Art Center, a striking building designed by Philip Johnson (1906–2005) and featuring classical and contemporary art.

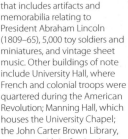

Statue on Brown University campus

🏛 John Brown House

52 Power St. **Tel** (401) 273-7507. **Open** Dec–Mar: 10:30am–3pm Fri–Sat; Apr–Nov: 1:30–3pm Tue–Fri, 10:30am–3pm Sat. **Closed** public hols. 🎟 📷 🎁

This Georgian mansion was built in 1786 for John Brown (1736–1803) and designed by his brother Joseph (1733–85). A successful merchant and shipowner, John played a lead role in the burning of the British customs ship *Gaspee* in a pre-Revolutionary War raid in 1772. The John

Brown House was the most lavish of its era, introducing Providence to many new architectural elements, including the projecting entrance, Doric portico, and the Palladian window above it. There are Neo-Classical pediments over paired doorways, a grand staircase with twisted balusters, ornate plaster ornamented ceilings, and intricate detailing inside arches over windows and mantels.

Sparing no expense, Brown ordered wallpapers from France and furniture from famed cabinetmakers Townsend and Goddard. The 12-room house has been impeccably restored and is a repository for some of the finest furniture and antiques of that period.

The 1786 John Brown House, an excellent example of Georgian architecture

Providence City Center

Downtown Providence

Downtown Providence, to the west of the Providence River, has undergone several renewal phases. In all, $1 billion has been pumped into the rejuvenation project since 1983. Keeping a balance with the old and the new, Providence municipal officials have managed to clean out previously blighted areas by restoring historic buildings, installing more green spaces, and building pedestrian malls and markets. The reclaimed waterfront and developing arts and entertainment district have helped inject new vitality into the city's core. Visitors are best served by exploring on foot so they are free to poke into the numerous shops, cafés, and restaurants.

The Waterfire show, held every summer at Waterplace Park

Exploring Downtown Providence

Providence's rebirth is more than just physical; it is also cultural. The Trinity Repertory Company on Washington Street is home to one of the best theater groups in the country and has performances year-round. Just a block away, the Providence Performing Arts Center, a 1928 movie palace, features Broadway shows, concerts, entertainment for children, and big-screen films, with free lunchtime organ recitals in the spring and fall.

The Trinity Repertory Company, housed in a 1917 historic theater

🔲 Waterplace Park and Riverwalk

Memorial Blvd. **Tel** (401) 751-1177. **Open** dawn–dusk daily.

One of the newest and brightest additions to the downtown area is this 4-acre (1.6-ha) walkway at the junction of the Moshassuck, Providence, and Woonasquatucket rivers. Visitors can stroll the park's cobblestone paths, float under footbridges in rented kayaks,

canoes, or gondolas, or enjoy the free concerts and the Waterfire extravaganza during the summer months.

🏛 The Arcade

65 Weybosset St. **Tel** (401) 598-1199.
🔲🏠🚭🖥

Known as the "Temple of Trade," this 1828 Greek Revival building has the distinction of being the first indoor shopping mall in the US. The massive, three-story stone complex covers an entire block in Providence's old financial district and has been acclaimed as "one of the three finest commercial buildings in 19th-century America" by New York's Metropolitan Museum of Art. Similar columns on the Westminster entrance match the six 22-ft- (6.7-m-) high Ionic granite columns on Weybosset. Inside a skylight extends the entire length of the building, providing light even on rainy days. Restored in 1980, the marketplace is undergoing another restoration and will include micro-loft housing units along with expanded retail offerings.

🏛 Federal Hill

Visitors will know they are in Little Italy once they pass through Federal Hill's impressive arched gateway, decorated with a traditional bronze pine nut. A stripe down the center of the street – in the colors of the Italian flag – confirms that this lively neighborhood in the Federal Hill district is truly Italian in spirit. Bordered by Federal and Broadway streets and Atwells Avenue, the area is marked by

Italian groceries, restaurants, bakeries, import shops, and a pleasant old-world plaza.

🏛 Rhode Island State House

82 Smith St. **Tel** (401) 222-3983.
Open 8:30am–4:30pm Mon–Fri.
Closed public hols. 🚭 self-guided, others by appt. 🔲🏠🖥

Dominating the city landscape, this imposing building was constructed in 1904 by the prominent New York firm McKim, Mead, & White. The white Georgian marble dome is one of the largest self-supported domes in the world. A bronze statue called *Independent Man*, a longtime symbol of Rhode Island's free spirit, tops the magnificent dome. Among the displays in the statehouse are a full-length portrait of President George Washington (1732–99) by Gilbert Stuart (1755–1828), a portrait of Providence resident and Civil War General Ambrose Burnside (1824–81) by Emanuel

Rhode Island State House, with its white marble dome

Roger Williams (1603–1683)

More than an exponent of religious freedom, Roger Williams was also a friend and champion of the area's indigenous inhabitants. He defied the strict restraints of the Massachusetts Bay Colony, believing that all people should be free to worship as they liked without state interference. Banished from Massachusetts for his outspoken views, he established his own colony of Rhode Island and Providence Plantations, obtaining the land from the Narragansett Indians so that "no man should be molested for his conscience sake." It became the country's first experiment in religious liberty.

Leutze (1816–68), and the original state charter of 1663.

🏞 Roger Williams Park and Zoo

1000 Elmwood Ave. **Tel** (401) 785-3510. 🚌 Kennedy Plaza. Park **Open** dawn to dusk daily. Zoo **Open** 9am–4pm daily. **Closed** Dec 25. 🦓 zoo. 🎫 ♿ 📷 🚫
w rogerwilliamsparkzoo.org

In 1871 Betsey Williams, a direct descendant of Roger Williams, donated 102 acres (41 ha) of prime real estate to the city for use as parkland. Since that time, another 320 acres (130 ha) of property have been added to the site. Once farmland, the park now holds gardens and greenhouses, ponds, a lake with paddleboats and rowboats for rent, jogging and cycling paths,

Historic cookbooks from the Culinary Archives and Museum

and a tennis center. Children especially love the carousel and train, the planetarium, and the Museum of Natural History.

Without a doubt, the highlight of the park is the zoo, which has more than 900 animals and 130 species. Dating back to 1872, the zoo is one of the oldest in the nation, but is constantly updated to meet top animal welfare standards. Its Marco Polo Trail, with camels, snow leopards, and Asian black bears, was enhanced with the addition of endangered red pandas, while a raised viewing deck makes it easier to observe the elephants and giraffes in the Fabric of Africa exhibit.

🏛 Culinary Arts Museum at Johnson & Wales University

315 Harborside Blvd. **Tel** (401) 598-2805. **Closed** for renovation; call ahead or check website for details. 📷 🎫 w culinary.org

This one-of-a-kind museum contains half a million items relating to the culinary arts – hardly surprising since Johnson & Wales University is devoted to training chefs. The museum was created in 1979, when Chicago chef Louis Szathmary donated his vast collection of culinary oddities, including a cannibal eating bowl from Fiji and rings worn by bakers that had been excavated at Pompeii. Exhibits include diners that used to be towed from place to place and stoves and ranges.

Roger Williams Park and Zoo, a highlight of downtown Providence

Boats moored at the Sakonnet Wharf near Little Compton

⑥ Portramouth

🏠 16,850. 🛈 23 America's Cup Ave., Newport (401) 845-9123 or (800) 976-5122. 🖥 gonewport.com

Portsmouth figures greatly in Rhode Island history. It was the second settlement in the old colony, founded in 1638 just two years after Providence. The town was also the site of the 1778 Battle of Rhode Island, the only major land battle fought in the state during the American Revolution. Bad weather and fierce British resistance forced the US troops to retreat. With the British in hot pursuit, only the courage of the American rear guard enabled most of the soldiers to escape to the sanctuary of Butts Hill Fort. Today some of the fort's redoubts are still visible from Sprague Street, where plaques recount the battle.

The **Green Animals Topiary Garden** is a more whimsical attraction. Located on a Victorian estate, this lighthearted garden is inhabited by a wild array of topiary creations. In all, some 80 animal shapes – including elephants, camels, giraffes, bears, birds, even a dinosaur – have been trimmed and sculpted from a selection of yew, English boxwood, and California privet. Elsewhere on the grounds, formal flower gardens, a rose arbor, and a museum with an extensive collection of Victorian-era toys delight even the very youngest visitors.

🌳 **Green Animals Topiary Garden** Cory's Lane. **Tel** (401) 847-1000. **Open** May–early Oct: 10am–5pm daily. 🖼

⑦ Little Compton

🏠 3,350. 🛈 23 America's Cup Ave., Newport (401) 845-9123 or (800) 976-5122.

Residents of Little Compton relish their isolated nook at the end of a peninsula that borders Massachusetts with good reason: Little Compton is one of the most charming villages in the entire state, protected from the outside world by the surrounding farmlands and woods.

The white-steepled United Congregational Church stands over Little Compton Commons. Beside the church lies the old Commons Burial Ground, with the gravesite of Elizabeth Padobie (c.1623–1717). The daughter of *Mayflower* Pilgrims Priscilla and John Alden, Padobie was the first white woman born in New England. The 1680 **Wilbor House** was home to eight generations of the Wilbor family. The house is furnished with period pieces and antique household items. Elsewhere on the grounds visitors can explore a one-room schoolhouse and artist's studio. An 1860 barn displays old farm tools, sleighs, a one-horse shay, oxcart, and buggies.

Nearby **Sakonnet Vineyards** is the largest winery in New England. There are free daily wine tastings and guided tours. Beyond the vineyard on Route 77 is Sakonnet Wharf, where the curious can watch fishermen arrive with their catches.

Sakonnet Vineyards in Little Compton

Delightful denizens of the Green Animals Topiary Garden

◀ The Providence skyline at sunset

🏛 Wilbor House
548 W Main Rd. **Tel** (401) 635-4035.
Open call for hours. ♿

🍷 Sakonnet Vineyards
162 W Main Rd. **Tel** (401) 635-8486.
Open late May–mid-Oct: 10am–6pm
daily, mid-Oct–late May: 11am–5pm
daily. 🎥 call for schedule. ♿
🌐 sakonnetwine.com

Environs
Four miles (6 km) northeast is
Adamsville. **Gray's Store** dates
back to 1788 and is the oldest
general store in the country. It
contains the first post office
(1804) in the area and still has its
original soda fountain, candy
and tobacco cases, and ice chest.

Gray's Store, built in 1788, on Main Street
in Adamsville

🏛 Gray's Store
4 Main St. **Tel** (401) 635-4566.
Open 9am–5pm Mon–Sat, noon–
4pm Sun (Nov–Apr: 9am–5pm Thu–
Sat, noon–4pm Sun).

❾ Middletown

🏙 19,950. ℹ 23 America's Cup Ave.,
Newport (401) 845-9123 or (800)
976-5122.

Nestled between Newport (see
pp186–91) and Portsmouth on
Aquidneck Island, Middletown is

Middletown's popular Third Beach

known primarily for its two
popular beaches. **Third Beach** is
located on the Sakonnet River
and is outfitted with a boat
ramp. A steady wind and
relatively calm water make
the beach a favorite among
windsurfers and families with
young children.

Third Beach runs into
the largest and most
beautiful beach on
the island.
Sachuest, or
Second Beach,
is widely
considered one
of the best places
to surf in southern
New England. This
spacious strand is
rippled with sand dunes and
equipped with campgrounds.
Purgatory Chasm, a narrow cleft
in the rock ledges on the east
side of Easton Point, provides a
scenic outlook over both the
beach and 50-ft- (15-m-) high
Hanging Rock.

Second Beach has yet
another advantage; it is

Inhabitant of the
wildlife area

adjacent to the **Norman Bird
Sanctuary**, a 325-acre (132-ha)
wildlife area with 7 miles
(11 km) of walking trails that
are ideal for birding. Some 250
species have been sighted at
this sanctuary, including
herons, egrets, woodcocks,
thrashers, ducks, and swans.
The refuge is home to
numerous four-legged
animals, such as
rabbits and red
foxes. A small
natural history
museum is
also located
on the site, and
during the winter
months the sanctuary
trails are used by
cross-country skiers. Nearby
Tiverton Four Corners is a
charming crossroads village
that combines the bucolic
countryside of riverine
Rhode Island with some of
the commercial sophistication
of Newport. Several galleries
sell clothing, jewelry, weavings,
and pottery made by local
artisans, while cows graze
in the pasture next to the
seasonal ice-cream stand.

🏖 Third Beach
Third Beach Rd. **Tel** (401) 849-2822.
Open Memorial Day–Labor Day:
lifeguards on duty 9am–5pm daily. ♿

🏖 Second Beach
Third Beach Rd. **Tel** (401) 849-2822.
Open Memorial Day–Labor Day:
lifeguards on duty 8am–6pm daily. ♿

🦅 Norman Bird Sanctuary
583 Third Beach Rd. **Tel** (401) 846-
2577. **Open** year-round: 9am–5pm
daily. **Closed** Thanksgiving &
Dec 25. ♿ 🎥

Waterfowl in Middletown's Norman Bird Sanctuary

For hotels and restaurants in this region see pp314–15 and pp

❾ Newport

A center of trade, culture, wealth, and military activity for more than 300 years, Newport is a true sightseeing mecca. Historical firsts abound in this small city. America's first naval college and synagogue are here, as are the oldest library in the country and one of the oldest continuously operating taverns. Any visit to the city should include a tour of the mansions from the Gilded Age of the late 19th century, when the rich and famous flocked here each summer to beat New York's heat. These summer "cottage" retreats of the country's wealthiest families, the Vanderbilts and Astors among them, are some of America's grandest private homes.

Public grass courts at the International Tennis Hall of Fame

Advertisement for carved whalebone, or whale ivory

Exploring Newport

Like Italy, Newport has a distinctly boot-shaped outline. The city's famous mansions are located on the southeastern side, or the heel of the boot. Newport's harborfront is to the west, where the laces would be. The city's most interesting streets, America's Cup Avenue and Thames Street, are here. Pedestrians will find restaurants, shops, and colonial buildings, including the 1726 **Trinity Church**.

🏛 Brick Market Museum and Shop

127 Thames St. **Tel** (401) 841-8770. **Open** 10am–5pm daily. 🅿️ 🈂️
The Brick Market, a commercial hub during the 18th century, is now a museum that provides an excellent introduction to the city's history and architecture. Self-guided tours include an audiovisual exploration of the downtown in a 19th- century omnibus.

✡ Touro Synagogue

85 Touro St. **Tel** (401) 847-4794. **Open** call for times. ✡ Shabbat and all Jewish hols. 🅿️ 🈂️ 🈁 🈂️
America's oldest synagogue, Touro was erected in 1763 by Sephardic Jews who had fled Spain and Portugal in search of religious tolerance. Designed by architect Peter Harrison

(1716–75), it is considered one of the country's finest examples of 18th-century architecture. Services still follow the Sephardic rituals of its founders.

Redwood Library and Athenaeum's stately interior

📖 Redwood Library and Athenaeum

50 Bellevue Ave. **Tel** (401) 847-0292. **Open** 9:30am–5:30pm Mon–Sat (to 8pm Thu). **Closed** public hols. 🈂️ 🈁
🇼 redwoodlibrary.org
Completed in 1750, the Redwood is the oldest continuously operating library in America and is one of the country's earliest examples of temple-form buildings. In addition to rare books and manuscripts, the library's museum collections contain colonial portraits, sculpture, and furniture.

🏛 International Tennis Hall of Fame

194 Bellevue Ave. **Tel** (401) 849-3990. **Open** 9:30am–5pm daily. **Closed** Thanksgiving & Dec 25. 🎾 courts available to public. 🅿️ 🈁
🏠 🇼 tennisfame.com
The hall is housed in the Newport Casino, once a private club for Newport's elite. Founded in 1880, the club installed grass tennis courts to introduce its members to the latest sports rage. The first US National Lawn Tennis Championship, later known as the US Open, was held here in 1881. Today the hall displays everything from antique rackets to the "comeback" outfit worn by Monica Seles (b.1972). The grass courts are the only ones in the US open to the public.

🌿 Cliff Walk

Begins at Memorial Blvd. **Tel** (401) 845-9123. **Open** year-round: dawn–dusk daily. 🈂️
This 3.5-mile (5.5-km) walk along Newport's rugged cliffs offers some of the best views of the Gilded-Age mansions. Local fishermen preserved public access to the trail by going to court when wealthy mansion-owners tried to have it closed. The walk was designated a National Recreation Trail in 1975. The Forty Steps, each step named for someone lost at sea, lead to the ocean.

The breathtaking Cliff Walk, popular with residents as well as visitors

For hotels and restaurants in this region see pp314–15 and pp331–3

🏛 International Yacht Restoration School

449 Thames St. **Tel** (401) 848-5777. **Open** 9am–5pm Mon–Sat (longer summer hours). 🅿 ♿ 🆆 **iyrs.org**

Founded in 1993, this small school provides a fascinating look at yacht restoration. Visitors can observe students from the mezzanine, and tour the waterfront campus to see the famous *Coronet*. Built in 1885, the wooden-hull schooner yacht is one of the oldest and largest of its kind in the world.

Students at work at International Yacht Restoration School

🏯 Fort Adams State Park

Harrison Ave. **Tel** (401) 847-2400. **Open** sunrise–sunset daily. 🅿 Museum of Yachting **Tel** (401) 847-1018. **Open** Jun–Oct: 11am–4:30pm Wed–Mon. 🖼 🚫 🚻

Fort Adams is one of the largest military forts in the US. Completed in 1857 at a cost of $3 million, it was designed to house 2,400 troops. The property surrounding

Fort Adams, centerpiece of Fort Adams State Park

the fort is equipped with facilities for swimming, soccer, rugby, and picnicking. Newport's world-famous music festivals *(see p37)* are held here annually.

The park is also home to the Museum of Yachting, which chronicles Newport's famed yachting history. One of the museum's highlights is its collection of classic luxury boats in its outdoor basin.

🏛 Newport Mansions

Preservation Society of Newport County, 424 Bellevue Ave. **Tel** (401) 847-1000. **Open** Apr–mid-Nov: 10am–5pm daily; winter: call for hours. **Closed** Dec 24 & 25. 🖼 🅿 obligatory. ♿ partial. 🚭

Built between 1748 and 1902, 12 of these summer "cottages," most of them along Bellevue Avenue, are open for guided tours. Modeled on European palaces and decorated with the finest artworks, the mansions were used for only ten weeks of the

VISITORS' CHECKLIST

Practical Information
🗺 24,000. ℹ Newport County Convention & Visitors Bureau, 23 America's Cup Ave (401) 845-9123 or (800) 976-5122. 🎫 Newport Tennis Week (Jul), Newport Jazz Festival (Aug). 🆆 **gonewport.com**

Transport
✈ TF Green Airport, Warwick, 27 miles (43 km) NW. 🚌 Gateway Center, 23 America's Cup Ave. ⛴ Perrotti Park (to Providence)

year. The Breakers *(see pp190–91)* is one of the finest examples.

🏛 Naval War College Museum

686 Cushing Rd. **Tel** (401) 841-4052. **Open** 10am–4:30pm Mon–Fri (Jun–Sep: also noon–4:30pm Sat & Sun). 🅿 ♿

This site preserves the history, art, and science of naval warfare and the heritage of Narragansett Bay. Founded in 1885, the college is the oldest naval institute of higher learning in the world, where education and research is carried out for the U.S. Navy. The museum houses ship models and maritime art. Due to increased security, visitors must call in advance.

Newport City Center

① Trinity Church
② Brick Market Museum and Shop
③ Touro Synagogue
④ Redwood Library and Athenaeum
⑤ International Tennis Hall of Fame

0 meters 300
0 yards 300

Key

■ Street-by-Street map *see pp188–9*

For map symbols *see back flap*

Around Washington Square

Newport's first settlers were religious moderates fleeing persecution at the hands of Puritans in the Massachusetts Bay colony. With its accessible harbor, the town quickly developed into a thriving seaport. However, its location also made it vulnerable. When Rhode Island declared independence from colonial rule in 1776, British forces occupied the city. Before they were driven out in 1780, the occupying army destroyed much of the town. Thanks to preservation efforts, a number of colonial buildings survive. Several of them can be seen on this tour around historic Washington Square, the center of Newport's political and economic life during colonial times.

Architectural detail is typical of the Washington Square district.

White Horse Tavern
Granted its liquor license in 1673, the White Horse claims to be the nation's oldest continuously operating tavern. At one time, state legislators gathered here before sitting at Colony House.

St. Paul's Methodist Church was built in 1805. A simple structure, it reflects the continuation of the Colonial style in the decades after independence.

Bank Newport

Rivera House, currently a bank, was once the home of Abraham Rivera, a prominent member of Newport's Jewish and business communities. Rivera laid the cornerstone of Touro Synagogue.

Statue of Oliver Hazard Perry
Oliver Hazard Perry (1785–1819) defeated British forces in a pivotal naval battle in the War of 1812, securing control of Lake Erie for the US. Perry's former home at No. 29 Touro Street faces the statue.

★ **Brick Market Museum and Shop**
The Brick Market, once the center of commerce, has been renovated to house this museum *(see p186)* that brings to life Newport's economic, social, and sporting past.

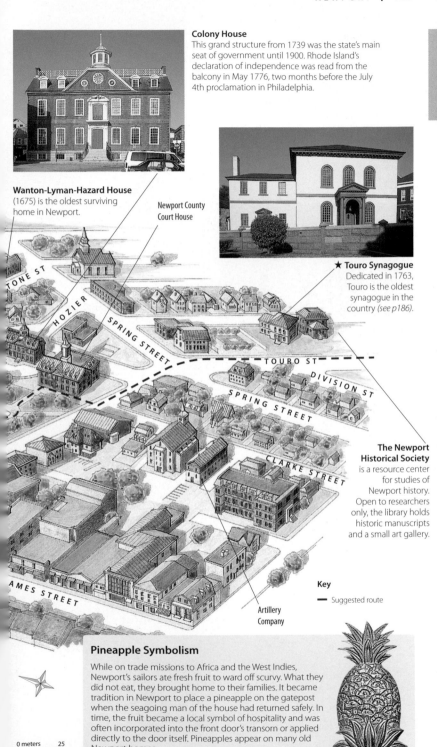

Colony House
This grand structure from 1739 was the state's main seat of government until 1900. Rhode Island's declaration of independence was read from the balcony in May 1776, two months before the July 4th proclamation in Philadelphia.

Wanton-Lyman-Hazard House
(1675) is the oldest surviving home in Newport.

Newport County Court House

★ **Touro Synagogue**
Dedicated in 1763, Touro is the oldest synagogue in the country *(see p186)*.

The Newport Historical Society
is a resource center for studies of Newport history. Open to researchers only, the library holds historic manuscripts and a small art gallery.

Artillery Company

Key
— Suggested route

TONE ST

HOZIER

SPRING STREET

TOURO ST

DIVISION ST

SPRING STREET

CLARKE STREET

AMES STREET

Pineapple Symbolism

While on trade missions to Africa and the West Indies, Newport's sailors ate fresh fruit to ward off scurvy. What they did not eat, they brought home to their families. It became tradition in Newport to place a pineapple on the gatepost when the seagoing man of the house had returned safely. In time, the fruit became a local symbol of hospitality and was often incorporated into the front door's transom or applied directly to the door itself. Pineapples appear on many old Newport homes.

0 meters   25
0 yards   25

The Breakers

The architecture and ostentation of the Gilded Age of the late 1800s reached its pinnacle with the Breakers, the summer home of railroad magnate Cornelius Vanderbilt II (1843–99). Completed in 1895, the four-story, 70-room limestone structure surpassed all other Newport mansions in extravagance. US architect Richard Morris Hunt (1827–95) modeled the building after the 16th-century palaces in Turin and Genoa. Its interior is adorned with marble, alabaster, stained glass, gilt, and crystal.

The Structure
Built in the Italian Renaissance style, the Breakers is alleged to have cost more than $10 million – a huge sum of money in 1895.

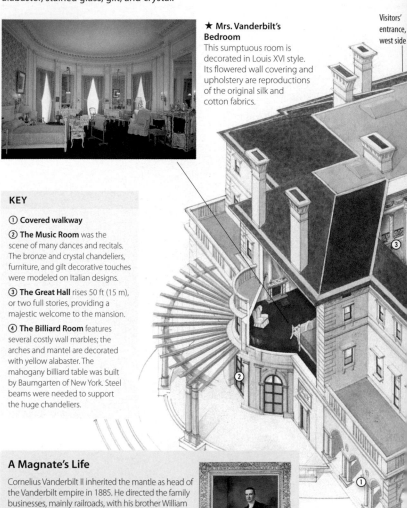

★ **Mrs. Vanderbilt's Bedroom**
This sumptuous room is decorated in Louis XVI style. Its flowered wall covering and upholstery are reproductions of the original silk and cotton fabrics.

Visitors' entrance, west side

KEY

① **Covered walkway**

② **The Music Room** was the scene of many dances and recitals. The bronze and crystal chandeliers, furniture, and gilt decorative touches were modeled on Italian designs.

③ **The Great Hall** rises 50 ft (15 m), or two full stories, providing a majestic welcome to the mansion.

④ **The Billiard Room** features several costly wall marbles; the arches and mantel are decorated with yellow alabaster. The mahogany billiard table was built by Baumgarten of New York. Steel beams were needed to support the huge chandeliers.

A Magnate's Life

Cornelius Vanderbilt II inherited the mantle as head of the Vanderbilt empire in 1885. He directed the family businesses, mainly railroads, with his brother William for 11 years before suffering a paralyzing stroke. He convalesced at the Breakers, but died in 1899 at the age of 56. At the time of his death, the local gossip held that he had more money than the US Mint.

Cornelius Vanderbilt II

★ The Dining Room
The most richly adorned room in the mansion, the two-story, 2,400-sq-ft (220-sq-m) dining room has two huge crystal chandeliers and a stunning arched ceiling.

VISITORS' CHECKLIST

Practical Information
Ochre Point Ave. **Tel** (401) 847-1000. **Open** mid-Nov–Mar: 10am–5pm daily; Apr–mid-Nov: 9am–6pm daily. **Closed** Thanksgiving, Dec 25. 🎫 📷 ♿
ⓦ **newportmansions.org**

Transport
🚌 67.

Upper Loggia
The upper loggia offers a view of the sunrise over the Atlantic Ocean. Its ceiling is painted to look like canopies against a clouded sky.

Sculpted Archways
Ornately carved archways are inspired by Italian Renaissance-style palazzos.

★ The Morning Room
The ceiling of this east-facing room is adorned with paintings of the Four Seasons, the mahogany doors with the Four Elements. All cornices, pilasters, and panels were made in France and shipped to Newport.

Sunbathing on the rocks at Beavertail Lighthouse and State Park

⑩ Jamestown

🏠 5,000. 🛈 23 America's Cup Ave., Newport (401) 845-9123 or (800) 976-5122.

Named for England's King James II (1633–1701), Jamestown is located on Conanicut Island and linked to Newport (see pp186–91) and the mainland by a pair of bridges. During the Revolutionary War, British troops torched much of the town, sparing very few of the houses from that era.

The town is best known for the **Beavertail Lighthouse and State Park**, perched at the southernmost tip of the island. The first lighthouse here was built in 1749 and was subsequently replaced by the present structure in 1856. As with many New England lighthouses, the coastal vistas from Beavertail are beautiful. The winds, currents, and surf can be heavy at times, but on calm days hiking, climbing, and sunbathing on the rocks are favorite pastimes.

Situated on the site of an early fort and artillery battery, **Fort Wetherill State Park** offers great scenic outlooks, picnic tables, and a boat ramp. The park is a popular place for saltwater fishing, boating, and scuba diving. Legend has it that notorious privateer Captain Kidd (1645–1701) stashed some of his plundered loot in the park's Pirate Cave.

🏛 Beavertail Lighthouse and State Park
Beavertail Pt. **Tel** (401) 423-9941. Park: **Open** dawn to dusk daily. Lighthouse: **Open** call for hours. 🎫 ♿

🏛 Fort Wetherill State Park
Fort Wetherill Rd. **Tel** (401) 423-1771. **Open** dawn to dusk daily. 🎫 ♿

⑪ Wickford

🛈 4808 Tower Hill Rd., Wakefield (401) 789-4422 or (800) 548-4662. 🔲 southcountyri.com

Considered a part of North Kingstown (population 26,000), the quaint village of Wickford lies in the northern-most point of Washington County, also known as South County. Wickford's many 18th- and 19th-century houses are a magnet for artists and craftsmen. John Updike (see pp34–5),

author of *Rabbit Run* (1960), had family roots here. The 1745 Updike House on Pleasant Street is just one of some 60 buildings constructed before 1804.

Daytrippers hailing from Providence and Connecticut are apt to jam Wickford's picturesque harbor and shopping streets. At the corner of Brown and Phillips Streets, the Kayak Center of Rhode Island offers extensive paddling tours on Narragansett Bay.

Old Narragansett Church (more commonly called Old St. Paul's) is one of the oldest Episcopal churches in the US, dating back to 1707, with box pews, an organ from 1660, and an upstairs gallery to which plantation slaves were relegated. Artist Gilbert Stuart (1755–1828) was baptized here in a silver baptismal font given to the

Wickford's tranquil harbor

Smith's Castle, just outside of Wickford

church as a gift by England's Queen Anne (1665–1714).

Environs
One mile north of town is **Smith's Castle**, one of America's oldest plantation houses. In 1678 settler Richard Smith built a dwelling on the site. Hardly a castle, the structure served as a garrison for the soldiers who had participated in the 1675 Great Swamp Fight against the Narragansett Indians. The battle resulted in a mass slaughter of Indians, which set off a chain of tragic events culminating in the retaliatory destruction of the garrison and the death of 40 soldiers. Later the structure was rebuilt and acquired by the Updike family in 1692. Subsequent additions and renovations transformed the structure into one of the most handsome plantation houses on the Rhode Island shore. The house contains fine paneling, 17th- and 18th-century furnishings, china, and a chair once owned by Roger Williams *(see pp173, 181)*.

🔲 **Smith's Castle**
55 Richard Smith Dr. **Tel** (401) 294-3521. **Open** call for hours. 🎨 🎴

⑫ Saunderstown

ℹ️ 8045 Post Rd., North Kingstown (401) 295-5566.

Located between Wickford and Narragansett, this town has two main attractions. The gambrel-roofed **Gilbert Stuart Birthplace** was built in 1751 along the Mattatuxet River. Stuart (1755–1828), whose portraits of US presidents were

to bring him lasting fame, was born here. His best-known portrait, that of George Washington, graces the US one-dollar bill.

On the first floor of the house, Stuart's father built a large kitchen and snuff mill, the first in America, powered by a wooden waterwheel. The upstairs living quarters are furnished with authentic period pieces.

Also in town is the 18th-century **Silas Casey Farm**. Still in operation, the farm has been occupied by the same family since 1702. The 360-acre (146-ha) property is ringed by almost 30 miles (48 km) of stone walls. Organic vegetables are grown on the farm and sold at a farmers' market on Saturday mornings.

Plaque at Stuart Birthplace

🔲 **Gilbert Stuart Birthplace**
815 Gilbert Stuart Rd. **Tel** (401) 294-3001. **Open** May–mid-Oct: 11am–4pm Thu–Sat & Mon, noon–4pm Sun. **Closed** mid-Oct–Apr. 🎨 🎴

🔲 **Silas Casey Farm**
2325 Boston Neck Rd. **Tel** (401) 295-1030. **Open** Jun–mid-Oct: 9am–2pm Sat. **Closed** mid-Oct–May. 🎨 🎴 ♿

⑬ South Kingstown

🏔️ 26,700. ℹ️ 230 Old Tower Hill Rd., Wakefield, **Tel** (401) 783-2801.

South Kingstown is a 55-sq-mile (142-sq-km) town that encompasses 15 villages,

including Kingstown, Green Hill, Wakefield, and Snug Harbor. The town is home to the **Museum of Primitive Art and Culture**. Located in an 1856 post office, the museum displays weapons, tools, and implements of aboriginal cultures around the world, including a range of artifacts from prehistoric New England.

After visiting the museum, travelers can enjoy some of the region's outdoor charms. Sightseers, particularly those with cameras, will want to make the trek to the top of the observation post at Hannah Robinson Rock and Tower, where they are greeted with expansive views of the Atlantic Ocean and the Rhode Island seashore.

The South County Bike Path is a 5.6-mile (9-km) paved trail, starting at the Kingstown train station, which takes cyclists through Great Swamp, the scene of the 1675 slaughter of 2,000 Narragansett Indians at the hands of soldiers and settlers – one of the bloodiest battles ever fought in New England. The swamp is now a pristine 5-sq-mile (13-sq-km) wildlife refuge called the **Great Swamp Management Area** and is home to creatures such as coyotes, mink, wild turkeys, and ring-necked pheasants. Nature trails lead visitors through dense woodland, past a dike to a boardwalk into a marsh. Birders should pack binoculars and visit the refuge during the spring songbird migration. Avoid hunting season.

🏛️ **Museum of Primitive Art and Culture**
1058 Kingstown Rd. **Tel** (401) 783-5711. **Open** 10am–2pm Wed. 🎨

🦌 **Great Swamp Management Area**
Liberty Lane off Great Neck Rd. **Tel** (401) 789-3094. **Open** dawn to dusk daily.

Whale-watching off Point Judith, a popular summer activity

⓮ Narragansett

🏙 18,000. ✈ TF Green Airport.
ℹ 36 Ocean Rd. (401) 783-7121.

In the late 19th century this town's waterfront area gained national fame as a fashionable resort, complete with a large casino. In 1900 a devastating fire razed the 1884 casino and many of the lavish hotels. All that remains of the ornate 1884

casino are **The Towers**, two stone towers linked by a Romanesque Revival-style arch.

Today rolling dice have given way to rolling waves, as the town beach offers some of the best surfing on the East Coast. Nearby the **South County Museum** depicts early Rhode Island life with displays of children's toys, farm tools, weapons, a cobbler's shop, a general store, and a working print shop.

🏛 The Towers
35 Ocean Rd. **Tel** (401) 782-2597.
Open call for tours & events schedule or visit the website.
🌐 thetowersri.com

🏛 South County Museum
Strathmore St. off Rte 1. **Tel** (401) 783-5400. **Open** May, Jun, Sep: 10am–4pm Fri–Sat; Jul & Aug: 10am–4pm Wed–Sat. 🅿

Environs
Located at the south end of the Narragansett peninsula, **Point Judith** and **Galilee** are departure points for numerous whale-watching cruises, sightseeing boat tours, ferries to Block Island (see pp196–7), and

charters for deep-sea fishing. Toward the end of World War II, a German U-boat was sunk just 2 miles (3 km) off the Point Judith Lighthouse. Today the lighthouse affords beautiful views of the ocean. Galilee is famous for its Blessing of the Fleet festival in late July. The Galilee Salt Marsh is popular for birding.

⓰ Charlestown

🏙 6,000. ✈ 🚌 ℹ 4945 Old Post Rd. (401) 364-3878.

This small town stretches along 4 miles (6.4 km) of lovely beaches, encompassing the largest saltwater marsh in the state and several parks. It is also a convenient base for nature lovers. The 3-sq-mile (8-sq-km) **Burlingame State Park** on Watchaug Pond is equipped with campgrounds, nature trails, swimming and picnic areas, trails for road and mountain bikes, as well as fishing and boating. Birders will enjoy the Audubon Society's **Kimball Wildlife Sanctuary**, located on the south side of the park. The

---

⓯ South County Beaches

Driving along Highway 1 between Narragansett and Watch Hill, travelers will pass some 100 miles (161 km) of pristine white sand beaches. These thin strands of sand are all that separate Block Island Sound from a series of tidal salt ponds, some of which have been designated national wildlife refuges. The ponds are big lures for bird-watchers hoping to study the egrets, sandpipers, and herons that swim and wade in the salty marshes. Many of the beaches are free to the public, except for parking fees.

Key
▬ Major road
═ Other road

⑤ **Misquamicut State Beach**
The state's largest beach has gentle surf and a nearby old-time amusement park with rides for children.

To Westerly

Westerly State Airport

Haversham
Quonochont Pond
Quonochontaug
Weekapaug

Winnapaug Pond

Watch Hill Road

Atlantic Avenue

Watch Hill

sanctuary is a habitat for many kinds of waterfowl and migrating birds, and has a network of easy footpaths.

More outdoor enjoyment can be found at the 172-acre (70-ha) **Ninigret Park**. Tracks lead cyclists and bladers through the grounds, which are graced with a spring-fed swimming pond, tennis courts, and baseball fields. During the winter months, the trails are used by cross-country skiers. Every clear Friday night, the park leaves the gates open to allow visitors to participate in stargazing

activities at the **Frosty Drew Observatory**, which is open year-round. (The facility is unheated, so dress accordingly.)

⊠ Frosty Drew Observatory
61 Park Lane, Ninigret Park.
Tel (401) 364-9508. **Open** year-round: Fri (weather allowing).
w frostydrew.org &

⊠ Burlingame State Park
Rte. 1A. **Tel** (401) 322-8910.
Open Apr–early Sep: dawn–dusk daily. 🦌 for camping facilities.

⊠ Kimball Wildlife Sanctuary
Prosser Trail. **Tel** (401) 949-5454.
Open dawn–dusk daily.

⊠ Ninigret Park
Rte. 1A. **Tel** (401) 364-1222.
Open dawn–dusk daily. 🦌 &

⑰ Watch Hill

ℹ 1 Chamber Way, Westerly (401) 596-7761.

A village within the town of Westerly, Watch Hill has been an upscale beach haven for the rich and famous since the 19th century. Strolls along Bay Street yield beautiful views of the gingerbread-trimmed Victorian houses on rocky hills above the beach. Visitors to Watch Hill can enjoy the relaxed atmosphere, with a little window shopping or sunbathing at the beach. The 1867 **Flying Horse Carousel** on the beach is a favorite of children. The vantage point of the Watch Hill Lighthouse offers views of neighboring Connecticut's Fishers Island.

▦ Flying Horse Carousel
Bay St. **Tel** (401) 348-6007. **Open** mid-Jun–Labor Day: 11am–9pm daily (from 10am Sat–Sun); late May–mid-Jun & Labor Day–mid-Oct: weekends only. 🦌 ▢ ⬛

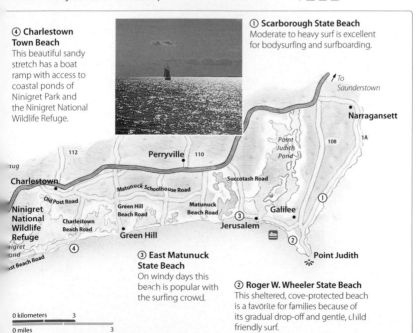

Nature trails through the Kimball Wildlife Sanctuary

④ Charlestown Town Beach
This beautiful sandy stretch has a boat ramp with access to coastal ponds of Ninigret Park and the Ninigret National Wildlife Refuge.

① Scarborough State Beach
Moderate to heavy surf is excellent for bodysurfing and surfboarding.

↗ *To Saunderstown*

Narragansett

Point Judith Pond

108   1A

112   **Perryville** 110

aug

Charlestown

Old Post Road

Matunuck Schoolhouse Road

Succotash Road

Ninigret National Wildlife Refuge

Green Hill Beach Road

Charlestown Beach Road

Green Hill

Matunuck Beach Road

③

Jerusalem

Galilee

①

②

Point Judith

igret ond
st Beach Road

④

③ East Matunuck State Beach
On windy days this beach is popular with the surfing crowd.

② Roger W. Wheeler State Beach
This sheltered, cove-protected beach is a favorite for families because of its gradual drop-off and gentle, child friendly surf.

0 kilometers   3
0 miles   3

For map symbols see back flap

⑱ Tour of Block Island

Lying 13 miles (21 km) off the coast, the haven of Block Island has long been a favorite getaway spot for New Englanders. With 25 percent of its wild landscape under protection, Block Island is a wonderful destination for outdoor enthusiasts who enjoy such activities as swimming, fishing, sailing, bird-watching, kayaking, canoeing, and horseback riding. Some 30 miles (48 km) of natural trails entice hikers and cyclists alike to experience the island's natural beauty firsthand.

Colorful lobster buoys ashore on Block Island

④ Great Salt Pond

Completely protected from the ocean, Great Salt Pond has three marinas and is an excellent spot for kayaking and fishing. New Harbor is Block Island's prime marina and boating center.

③ Rodman's Hollow

Nature trails lead hikers through the glacial depression of Rodman's Hollow Natural Area. The wildlife refuge is home to hawks and white-tailed deer. One path takes visitors to the beach at Black Rock Point at the southern extremity of the island.

Dead Man's Cove

Cormorant Point

Grace Cove Road

Champlin Road

Beacon Hill

West Side Road

Beacon Hill Road

Center Road

Cooneymus Swamp

Dickens Road

Cooneymus Road

③

Black Rock Road

Black Rock Point

Key

▬ Tour route

═ Other road

0 meters   500
0 yards   500

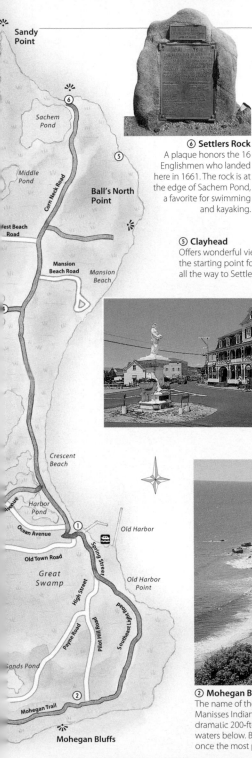

Sandy Point

Sachem Pond

Middle Pond

West Beach Road

Corn Neck Road

Ball's North Point

Mansion Beach Road

Mansion Beach

⑥ Settlers Rock
A plaque honors the 16 Englishmen who landed here in 1661. The rock is at the edge of Sachem Pond, a favorite for swimming and kayaking.

Tips for Drivers

Tour length: 18 miles (29 km).
Getting there: Regularly scheduled flights from Westerly, RI, and chartered flights from other mainland airports. Year-round ferry service from Point Judith, RI. Ferries carry cars by advance reservations only, (401) 783-7996.
Stopping-off point: Old Harbor, the island's only village, has inns and several quaint restaurants overlooking the ocean (see pp314 and 331).

⑤ Clayhead
Offers wonderful views of the Atlantic Ocean and is the starting point for a popular nature trail that goes all the way to Settlers Rock.

① Old Harbor
This village is the main hub of activity on the island. Victorian houses, hotels, and shops line the streets, and anglers can charter boats to fish for striped bass, bluefish, flounder, and cod.

Crescent Beach

Harbor Pond

Ocean Avenue

Old Town Road

Great Swamp

High Street

Payne Road

Pilot Hill Road

Southeast Light Road

Spring Street

Old Harbor

Old Harbor Point

Sands Pond

Mohegan Trail

②

Mohegan Bluffs

② Mohegan Bluffs
The name of the bluffs goes back to 1590, when local Manisses Indians tossed 50 Mohegan invaders off these dramatic 200-ft- (61-m-) high red clay cliffs into the waters below. Built in 1875, the Southeast Light was once the most powerful in New England.

CONNECTICUT

Connecticut is quintessential New England. Its quiet charm is evident everywhere, in scenic villages replete with white steepled churches, immaculate village greens, covered bridges, and old-fashioned clapboard houses ringed by stone walls. Even the state's most bustling cosmopolitan centers contain enclaves of picturesque serenity that invite visitors to poke about at their leisure.

The third-smallest state in the US, Connecticut is brimming with history. One of the country's original 13 colonies, Connecticut has always been a trendsetter, beginning with its adoption in 1639 of the Fundamental Orders of Connecticut – the New World's first constitution. It was on Connecticut soil that the nation's first public library, law school, and amusement park were built. Scholars and soldiers can thank the fertile minds of state residents for giving them the first dictionary and pistol, gourmands for the hamburger and corkscrew, and children for the three-ring circus, lollipop, and Frisbee.

Water has played an important role in shaping the state. The Housatonic, Naugatuck, Connecticut, and Thames rivers have been feeding the interior woodlands for thousands of years and acted as the main transportation arteries for early inhabitants. Fueled by waterpower, mill towns sprang up along the rivers, eventually giving way to larger commercial centers. Today these waterways are the arenas of canoeists looking for their next adventure. Houseboats and tour boats offer road-weary passengers unique views of the picturesque towns that hug the banks.

Autumn's annual explosion of color makes it the favorite time of year for visitors to meander along Connecticut's byways, hike the Berkshires, wander the Appalachian Trail *(see pp26–7)*, and indulge in the seasonal bounty of country inns. In addition, the state calendar bulges with eclectic events. Old-fashioned county fairs are held concurrently with cutting-edge performing arts showcases and regattas. When people have had their fill of ballooning and antiquing, they can sample the wares in one of the state's late-summer oyster festivals.

Mystic Seaport's calm harbor

◀ Tower of the Center Church in downtown Hartford

Exploring Connecticut

Compact enough to cross in a few hours, Connecticut has treasures that entice travelers to stay for days. The magnificent shoreline, stretching 105 miles (170 km) from Greenwich near the New York State line northeast to Rhode Island, is scalloped by coves, inlets, and harbors, and dotted with state parks, beaches, and marinas. The coast is punctuated by historically significant houses, culminating in Mystic Seaport *(pp218–19)*, a recreated 18th- and 19th-century seafaring village. The area also attracted America's Impressionist artists. Their works are shown in the state's many museums *(pp206–207)*. Inland hills and valleys are dotted with tiny postcard- perfect villages.

Hartford's Bushnell Park

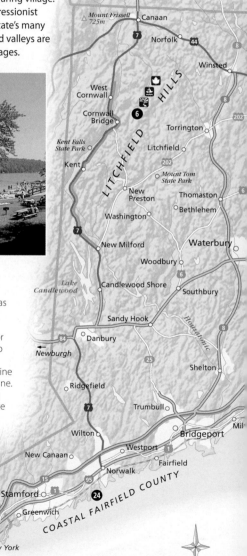

Beach at Mount Tom State Park

Getting Around

Hugging the coast, Interstate 95 serves as the primary east-west link. Interstate 84 follows a similar route from Danbury through Hartford and beyond. The major north-south artery is Interstate 91. Metro North runs trains from New York City to New Haven. Amtrak's New York-Boston line makes stops along Connecticut's shoreline. Several major bus companies, including Peter Pan and Greyhound, offer interstate services. Seasonal ferries operate New London-Block Island, Rhode Island, and year-round services run New London-Orient Point, New York, as well as Bridgeport–Port Jefferson.

0 kilometers 10
0 miles 10

Sights at a Glance

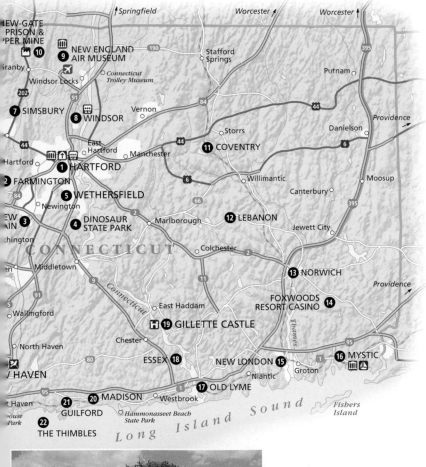

Boat tours cruising the 365 picturesque islands of The Thimbles

Key

— Highway
— Major road
··· Minor road
— Scenic route
-·- Main railroad
-··- Minor railroad
— State border
△ Summit

For additional map symbols *see back flap*

❶ Hartford

Serving first as an ancient Saukiog Indian settlement and later as a Dutch trading post, Connecticut's capital was founded in 1636 by the Reverend Thomas Hooker (1586–1647) and a group of 100 Englishmen from the Massachusetts Bay Colony. By the late 19th century, Hartford was basking in its Golden Age, thanks to both an economic boom in the insurance industry and a cultural flowering typified by resident authors Mark Twain *(see pp204–205)* and Harriet Beecher Stowe *(see pp34–5)*. An ambitious revitalization program has helped breathe new life into the downtown core.

The imposing façade of the Wadsworth Atheneum

Exploring Hartford

Approaching the city by car, travelers are greeted by sunlight gleaming off the gold-leaf dome of the hilltop **State Capitol**. Many of Hartford's most popular attractions are easily accessed on foot from the Capitol building, which has an information office for tourists.

🚇 Old State House

800 Main St. **Tel** (860) 522-6766. **Open** year-round: 10am–5pm Mon–Fri. **Closed** public hols, Tue in summer. 🎨 ♿ 📷 🎤 🅦 ctosh.org

The 1796 State House, designed by Charles Bulfinch (1763–1844), is the country's oldest Capitol building. Its graceful center hall, grand staircase, and ornate cupola make the Old State House one of the nation's finest examples of Federal architecture. An interactive audio tour highlights points of interest such as the Great Senate Room and the courtroom where the slave ship *Amistad* trial of 1839 was held. Outdoors there is a seasonal farmers' market.

🏛 Center Church and Ancient Burying Ground

675 Main St. Church **Tel** (860) 249-5631. **Open** by appt. 📷 by appt. Burying Ground **Tel** (860) 280-4145. **Open** 10am–4pm daily.

Five stained-glass windows designed by US artist Louis Comfort Tiffany (1848–1933) grace the 1807 Center Church (First Church of Christ in Hartford). The church's Ancient Burying Ground contains some 415 headstones dating back to 1648, including that of Hartford's founding father Thomas Hooker. Across Main Street is the 527-ft- (160-m-) high Travelers Tower office building, the tallest man-made observation post in the state.

Alexander Calder's *Stegosaurus*

🏛 Wadsworth Atheneum

600 Main St. **Tel** (860) 278-2670. **Open** 11am–5pm Wed–Sun (from 10am Sat & Sun; to 8pm first Thu of month). **Closed** pub hols. 🎤 (reduced fee 5–8pm first Thu of month). 🎨 ♿ 🖥 📷 🅦 wadsworthatheneum.org

Established in 1842, this museum has the distinction of being the oldest continuously operating public art museum in the country. Its extensive collection has 45,000 pieces and spans five centuries. It is particularly strong in Renaissance, Baroque, and Impressionist works, as well as in European decorative arts. The museum is noted for its extensive collection of American paintings, including works by Thomas Cole (1801–48) and Frederic Church (1826–1900). Outside in the Burr Mall is the monumental red steel sculpture called *Stegosaurus* (1973) by Connecticut resident Alexander Calder (1898–1976).

🌳 Bushnell Park

Trinity and Elm Sts. **Tel** (860) 232-6710. **Open** year-round. 🎨 May–Sep. ♿ Carousel **Open** May–mid-Oct: 11am–5pm Tue–Sun. 🎤

Shaded by 100 tree varieties, the 40-acre (16-ha) park is the lush creation of noted landscape architect and Hartford native Frederick Law Olmsted (1822–1903). Children adore the park's 1914 Bushnell Carousel, with its 48 hand-carved horses, ornate "lovers' chariots," and refurbished Wurlitzer band organ. The 115-ft- (35-m-) tall Soldiers and Sailors Memorial Arch honors those who saw duty in the American Civil War (1861–65).

East Senate Chambers of Hartford's Old State House

State Capitol

210 Capitol Ave.
Tel (860) 240-0222.
Open 9am–5pm Mon–Fri,
tours every hour 9:15am–
1:15pm Mon–Fri (also
2:15pm Jul & Aug).

The State Capitol
was designed by
Richard Upjohn
(1828–1903) in
the high Victorian-
Gothic style. It is
constructed primarily
of marble and granite
and has a golden
dome. Highlights of the
grand interior are the oak
woodwork and the ornate
oak charter chair.

The Bushnell

166 Capitol Ave. Box office **Tel** (860)
987-5900. call (860) 987-6033 for
tour schedule. **W bushnell.org**
This leading performing
arts venue features Broadway-
style extravaganzas as well as
more modest productions.
Highlights of the free tours
include the historic theater,
a state-of-the-art modern
stage, and a 14-ft (4.27-m)
chandelier by Seattle glass
artist Dale Chihuly.

Soldiers and Sailors
Memorial

Harriet Beecher Stowe Center

77 Forest St. **Tel** (860) 522-
9258. **Open** year-round:
9:30am–4:30pm Wed–Sat (&
Tue Jun–Oct), noon–4:30pm
Sun. **Closed** public hols.
obligatory. first floor.
**harriet
beecherstowe.org**

Located next to the
Mark Twain House
(see pp204–205), this
home is adorned
with gingerbread
ornamentation typical
of late 19th-century Victorian
design. Harriet Beecher Stowe's
fame as the author of the anti-
slavery novel *Uncle Tom's Cabin*
(1852) overshadowed her skill
as an interior decorator,
demonstrated by the
elegance of her

1871 home. The Stowes lived
here until Harriet's death in 1896.

Elizabeth Park Rose Gardens

Prospect Ave. **Tel** (860) 231-9443.
Gardens **Open** dawn to dusk daily.
Each year in this 90-acre (28-ha)
park more than 900 varieties
of roses bloom on around
15,000 bushes. The park has
delightful herb, perennial,
and rock gardens.

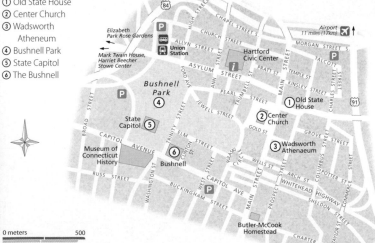

The Connecticut State Capitol, overlooking Bushnell Park

Hartford City Center

① Old State House
② Center Church
③ Wadsworth Atheneum
④ Bushnell Park
⑤ State Capitol
⑥ The Bushnell

Mark Twain House and Museum

Mark Twain (1835–1910) – a former Mississippi riverboat pilot, humorist, and author – lived here from 1874 to 1891 and penned six novels. Based on a floor plan sketched out by Twain's wife, Olivia, the 19-room home is a masterpiece of the Picturesque-Gothic style. The home's expansive upper balconies, peaked gables, towering turrets, and painted brick combine the sense of high style and playfulness personified by its owners. The adjoining museum has extensive exhibits on Twain and his times, including a film by award-winning New England documentary filmmaker Ken Burns.

North face of Mark Twain House, showing peaked gable and turret

★ Billiard Room
Twain worked on some of his best-known works, including *The Adventures of Tom Sawyer* (1876), in the tranquility of the Billiard Room.

★ Library
The ornate fireplace mantel, carved in Scotland in the 1850s, was purchased by the Clemenses in 1873.

KEY

① **Turret-style bay windows**

② **The Conservatory** has a statue of Venus, similar to works by Karl Gerhardt (1853–1940). Twain helped finance Gerhardt's studies in Europe.

③ **The decorative treatment** of the railings is indicative of the "Stick" style of the 1870s.

For hotels and restaurants in this region see pp315–316 and pp333–5

★ **Master Bedroom**
Twain rhapsodized about the Master Bedroom, claiming it possessed "the most comfortable bedstead that ever was [and one that brings] peace to the sleepers."

VISITORS' CHECKLIST

Practical Information
351 Farmington Ave. **Tel** (860) 247-0998. **Open** 9:30am–5:30pm Mon–Sat, noon–5:30pm Sun. **Closed** Tue (Jan–Mar only), Jan 1, Easter Sunday, Thanksgiving, Dec 24 & 25. 🅿 📷 obligatory, last tour 4:30pm. ♿ first floor only. 🆆 **marktwainhouse.org**.

Transport
🚌 all buses marked E Farmington Ave.

Entrance
The massive wooden door leads into the Entrance Hall, famous for its silver stenciling applied by Louis C. Tiffany's firm in 1881.

Mark Twain

Raised in the frontier town of Hannibal, Missouri, on the banks of the Mississippi River, young Samuel Langhorne Clemens (better known as Mark Twain) was exposed to a strange cast of characters. Steamboat captains, gamblers, circus performers, actors, and minstrel showmen were just some of the people who passed through the town. As an adult, Twain worked as a typesetter, printer, miner, journalist, soldier, lecturer, editor, and even steamboat captain before finally trying his hand at writing full-time in 1870.

Graceful exterior of the Hill-Stead Museum in Farmington

🏛 Hill-Stead Museum
35 Mountain Rd. **Tel** (860) 677-4787.
Open 10am–4pm Tue–Sun.
Closed public hols. 🅿
📷 obligatory. ♿ partial.
W hillstead.org

🏠 Stanley-Whitman House
37 High St. **Tel** (860) 677-9222.
Open May–Oct: noon–4pm Wed–
Sun; Nov–Apr: call for hours.
🅿 📷 ♿ partial.

❷ Farmington

🏠 21,050. ℹ One Constitution Plaza,
2nd Floor, Hartford (860) 787-9640.

Perched on the banks of the surging Farmington River, this quiet enclave has long been the starting point for canoeists, fishermen, and bird-watchers. The skies above the Farmington River Valley are also a busy place, popular with hang gliders and hot-air balloonists taking in the spectacular vistas from on high. Several companies offer champagne flights over the scenic valley, while others offer candlelit tours of the town's historic homes.

The interior of the **Hill-Stead Museum** has remained unchanged since the 1946 death of its original owner Theodate Pope Riddle (1867–1946). Pope, one of the country's first female architects, designed the Colonial–Revival mansion, which was completed in 1901. Her will stipulated that upon her death nothing in the house could be changed, altered, or moved. The result is a fascinating home frozen in the Edwardian period. On display is the Pope family's fine collection of French and American Impressionist paintings, including works by Edgar Degas (1834–1917), Édouard Manet (1832–83), Mary Cassatt (1845–1926), and James Whistler (1834–1903). The museum also contains splendid examples of American and European furniture and decorative arts. Particularly noteworthy on the grounds of the 150-acre (61-ha) estate is the sunken garden. The **Stanley-Whitman House** is a well-preserved example of the

framed overhang style of early 18th-century architecture of New England. The house, furnished with Colonial pieces, is often used as a venue for craft demonstrations and exhibits. Elsewhere in Farmington, admirers of old cemeteries will find many markers of interest in the Ancient Burying Ground, with gravestones dating back to 1661. In the Riverside Cemetery, one tombstone marks the grave of Foone, an African slave who drowned in the town's canal after being freed in the *Amistad* trial (see p202).

Environs
Twenty miles (32 km) south of Farmington lies the blue-collar town of Waterbury. The town is proud of its ethnic roots, as

Arts of the West by Thomas Hart Benton at the New Britain Museum of American Art

Impressionist Art Trail

Between 1885 and 1930 Connecticut was a magnet for many American artists. Childe Hassam (1859–1935), J. Alden Weir (1852–1919), Willard Metcalf (1858–1925), and others depicted marshes, seascapes, harbors, and farms in a style called American Impressionism. Their works are in nine museums on a self-guided trail that winds from Greenwich to New London.

Sights at a Glance

① Bruce Museum, Greenwich
② Bush-Holley Historic Site, Cos Cob
③ Weir Farm, Ridgefield and Wilton
④ Yale University Art Gallery, New Haven
⑤ New Britain Museum of American Art, New Britain
⑥ Hill-Stead Museum, Farmington
⑦ Wadsworth Atheneum, Hartford
⑧ Florence Griswold Museum, Old Lyme
⑨ Lyman Allyn Art Museum, New London

evidenced by its 240-ft- (73-m-) tall Clock Tower, modeled on the city hall in Siena, Italy. A hands-on exhibit at the **Mattatuck Museum** relates the state's industrial history, including Waterbury's role as the "Brass City" during the 19th and early 20th century.

Ⅲ Mattatuck Museum
144 W Main St., Waterbury. **Tel** (203) 753-0381. **Open** year-round: 10am–5pm Tue–Sat, noon–5pm Sun. **Closed** public hols. 🖼️ 🚻 🔊 ♿ ☐
W mattatuckmuseum.org

❸ New Britain

🏙️ 73,000. ℹ️ One Constitution Plaza, 2nd Floor, Hartford (860) 787-9640.

New Britain is midway between Boston and New York. Travelers to either city should stop to visit the **New Britain Museum of American Art**, whose distinguished collection spans art from the Colonial era to the present. Almost every major US artist is represented here, including Georgia O'Keeffe (1887–1986), Andrew Wyeth (b.1917), Alexander Calder

(1898–1976), and Isamu Noguchi (1904–88). The American Impressionist collection is also important. One gallery is dedicated to the seminal "Arts of Life in America" mural series by Thomas Hart Benton.

Ⅲ New Britain Museum of American Art
56 Lexington St., New Britain. **Tel** (860) 229-0257. **Open** 11am–5pm Tue–Wed & Fri; 11am–8pm Thu; 10am–5pm Sat; noon–5pm Sun.
🖼️ **W** nbmaa.org

❹ Dinosaur State Park

400 West St., Rocky Hill. **Tel** (860) 529-8423. Park: **Open** 9am–4:30pm daily. Exhibit center: **Open** 9am–4:30pm Tue–Sun. **Closed** public hols. 🖼️
W dinosaurstatepark.org

During the lower Jurassic period some 200 million years ago, the dinosaurs that roamed this region literally left their mark on the land. Today some 500 prehistoric tracks are preserved beneath this park's huge geodesic dome. Also on

One of 500 ancient tracks at Dinosaur State Park

display is a life-size model of an 8-ft (2-m) *Dilophosaurus*, the creature that most likely left the prints. Two large dioramas tell the story of the Connecticut Valley during the Triassic and Jurassic periods. Highlights of this exhibit are a model *Coelophysis* and a cast of a skeleton unearthed in New Mexico. A thrill for children and amateur paleontologists is the chance to make plaster casts of the tracks from May through October. (Call ahead to find out what to bring.) The park also has 2.5 miles (4 km) of hiking trails through a variety of habitats.

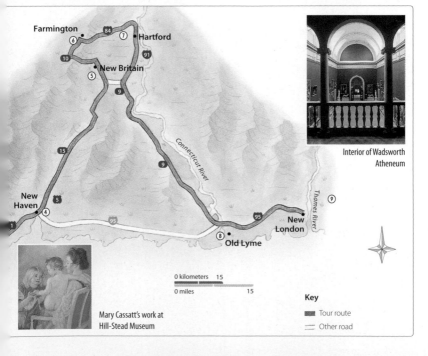

Interior of Wadsworth Atheneum

Mary Cassatt's work at Hill-Stead Museum

Key

▬ Tour route
⌁ Other road

0 kilometers 15
0 miles 15

⑤ Street-by-Street: Wethersfield

Now an affluent Hartford suburb, Wethersfield began as the state's first settlement in 1634. In 1640 its citizens held an illegal public election – America's first act of defiance against British rule. The town also hosted the 1781 Revolutionary War conference between George Washington (1732–99) and his French allies, during which they finalized strategies for the decisive American victory in Yorktown. Preserved within a 12-block area, Old Wethersfield stands as a primer of American architecture, with numerous houses from the 18th to 20th centuries. The centerpiece is the Webb-Deane-Stevens Museum, a trio of dwellings depicting the differing lifestyles of three 18th-century Americans: a wealthy merchant, a diplomat, and a leather tanner.

A Connecticut River-style entrance built in 1767

133 Main Street
This 1787 house was the home of Reverend Joseph Emerson, who ran the Female Seminary at the Old Academy at 150 Main.

Church and Main
The house atop the street sign marks the area of one of Connecticut's first suburban subdivisions.

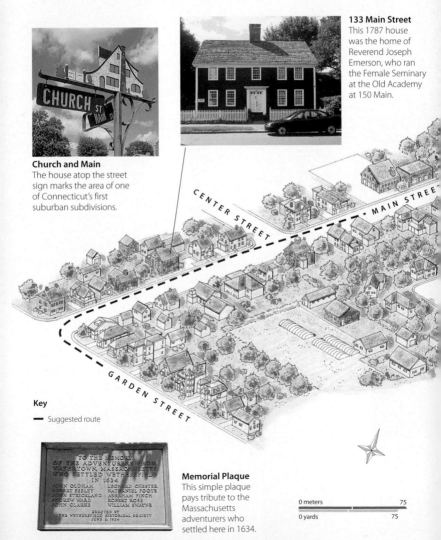

Key

— Suggested route

Memorial Plaque
This simple plaque pays tribute to the Massachusetts adventurers who settled here in 1634.

| 0 meters | 75 |
| 0 yards | 75 |

◀ Gothic façade of the Harkness Tower at Yale University, New Haven

★ **First Church of Christ**
One of only three Colonial meeting houses left in the state, the 1761 church included presidents George Washington (1732–99) and John Adams (1735–1826) among its worshipers.

VISITORS' CHECKLIST

Practical Information
🗺 26,000. ℹ Connecticut Heritage River Valley, (860) 721-2939 or (860) 787-9640.
w centerofct.com and
w historicwethersfield.org

Transport
✈ Bradley International Airport, 17 miles (27 km) N in Windsor Locks. 🚌 from Hartford.

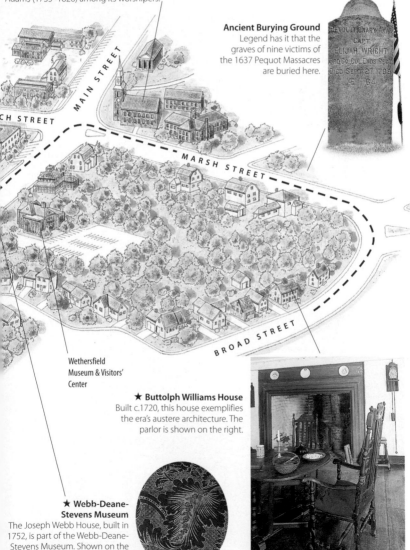

Ancient Burying Ground
Legend has it that the graves of nine victims of the 1637 Pequot Massacres are buried here.

MAIN STREET

CH STREET

MARSH STREET

BROAD STREET

Wethersfield Museum & Visitors' Center

★ **Buttolph Williams House**
Built c.1720, this house exemplifies the era's austere architecture. The parlor is shown on the right.

★ **Webb-Deane-Stevens Museum**
The Joseph Webb House, built in 1752, is part of the Webb-Deane-Stevens Museum. Shown on the right is wallpaper from one of the upstairs bed chambers.

For hotels and restaurants in this region see pp315–16 and pp333–5

❻ Litchfield Hills

Nestled in the folds and foothills of the Berkshire Hills and Taconic Mountains in the northwesternmost section of Connecticut, the Litchfield Hills region covers some 1,000 sq miles (2,590 sq km), or one-quarter of the state. Many people consider this to be the most scenic part of Connecticut. Anchored by the Housatonic River, the bucolic landscape of woods, valleys, lakes, and wildlife offers unparalleled opportunities for canoeing, kayaking, white-water rafting, tubing, fly-fishing, and hiking. In autumn, traffic along the winding roads can slow as the brilliant fall foliage entrances sightseers. A steady influx of the wealthy into the area has resulted in the gentrification of Litchfield's 26 towns and villages, with boutiques and bistros popping up beside traditional craft shops and historic homes and gardens.

Fishing at Mount Tom State Park outside Litchfield

Bristol

🏠 62,000. ℹ️ Litchfield (860) 567-4506.

Bristol's past as a premier clock manufacturing center is celebrated at the American Clock and Watch Museum on Maple Street. Housed in an 1801 mansion, this vast collection includes 5,000 clocks and watches.

Bristol is also home to the Lake Compounce Theme Park, the nation's oldest amusement park. Complete with one of the fastest and longest wooden roller coasters on the East Coast, a white-water raft ride, and a 185-ft- (56-m-) drop tower, the park on Lake Avenue has been entertaining families since 1846. More family fun can be found on Riverside Avenue in the form of the Carousel Museum of New England. Its collection of antique carousel pieces is one of the finest in the world.

Woodbury

🏠 9,400. ℹ️ Litchfield (860) 567-4506.

With many shops and dealers, this is a popular haunt for antique lovers. Antique furnishings from the late 18th century can also be found at the Glebe House on Hollow Road. This minister's farmhouse is surrounded by the Gertrude Jekyll Garden, the noted English landscaper's only garden on US soil. The town is also blessed with five churches from various eras that have been wonderfully preserved.

New Preston

ℹ️ Litchfield (860) 567-4506.

New Preston offers access to 95-acre (38-ha) Lake Waramaug State Park. The lake is especially beautiful in the autumn, when the glorious colors are reflected on its mirrorlike surface. Visitors can rent canoes for peaceful paddles around the shoreline, and some 80 campsites cater to enthusiasts who want to linger and enjoy the great outdoors. The Hopkins Vineyard, perched above the lake, offers wine tastings along with tours of its facilities.

Litchfield

🏠 8,850. ℹ️ Northwest Connecticut (860) 567-4506. 🌐 litchfield hills.com

Picturesque Litchfield has many noteworthy historic buildings, such as South Street's 1784 Tapping Reeve House and Law School, the country's first law school.

Just on the outskirts of town on Route 202, Mount Tom State Park has trails leading to the 1,325-ft (404- m) summit. The lake is ideal for scuba diving, swimming, boating, and fishing.

Elegant Bellamy-Ferriday House and Garden in Bethlehem

Bethlehem
🏠 3,700. 🛈 Litchfield.

One of the town's highlights is the Bellamy-Ferriday House and Garden, the 18th-century home of Reverend Joseph Bellamy (1719–90), founder of the first theological seminary in America. Located on Main Street, this 13-room house (open May–Oct) displays Ferriday family delftware, furniture, and Oriental art.

West Cornwall
🛈 Litchfield.

Tiny West Cornwall is best known for its covered bridge. The 1841 bridge, which spans the Housatonic River, is only one of two such spans in the state open to car traffic.

Norfolk
🏠 2,000. 🛈 Litchfield.

Founded in 1758, this small village is located in the northwest corner of the state. Its village green is known for two key reasons: a monument that was designed by architect Stanford White (1853–1906) and US sculptor Augustus Saint-Gaudens *(see pp266–7)*; and the Music Shed. The latter is an auditorium on the Ellen Batell Stoeckel Estate that hosts the highly acclaimed annual Norfolk Chamber Music Festival.

Re-created Algonkian village at the Institute for American Indian Studies

Washington
🏠 3,950. 🛈 Litchfield.

At the Institute for American Indian Studies, situated on Curtis Road, those with a bent for history can examine a pre-contact Algonkian village, artifacts from 10,000 years ago, and exhibits of northwest Connecticut's Woodland Indians. The grounds contain a re-created archaeological dig.

Kent
🏠 2,900. 🛈 Litchfield.

Art lovers should go out of their way to visit this small community. It is well known for having the highest concentration of galleries in the region, including the interesting Heron American Craft Gallery and the Kent Art Association Gallery.

North of town travelers indulge in outdoor fun at Kent Falls State Park. A short hike into the 295-acre (119-ha) park will reward visitors with stunning views of what many people consider the most impressive waterfall in Connecticut. Picnic facilities overlook the idyllic scene.

Scenic road through Litchfield Hills

Litchfield Hills

The beautiful scenery of Litchfield County attracts many kinds of sightseers. Its scenic roads are perfect for cycling and driving tours. Adventurous travelers can tour the region on hot-air balloon excursions available in Litchfield.

Key

━━ Major road

═══ Minor road

Picturesque bridge over the Connecticut River outside the town of Windsor

❼ Simsbury

🏠 22,000. 🅸 Hartford (860) 787-9640

Originally a quiet colonial farming community, Simsbury grew into something of a boomtown in the early 18th century with the discovery of copper in the region. The wheels of US industry started turn- ing here with the opening of the nation's first steel mill in 1728.

Three centuries of local history are squeezed into the **Phelps Tavern Museum**. The museum is located in the home of sea Captain Elisha Phelps. Period rooms and galleries have been used to create an authentic inn from 1786 to 1849, an era when such wayside inns were central to New England's social life. The tavern museum is part of a 2-acre (1-ha) complex that includes a museum store and award-winning period gardens.

🏛 **Phelps Tavern Museum**
800 Hopmeadow St. **Tel** (860) 658-2500. **Open** year-round: noon–4pm Thu–Sat. **Closed** public hols. 🗗 🖰

❽ Windsor

🏠 27,800. 🅸 Hartford (860) 787-9640.

Windsor was settled in the early 1630s by Pilgrims from Plymouth (see pp152–63), making it the oldest permanent English settlement in the state – a claim disputed by the residents of nearby Wethersfield (see pp210–11). A drive along Palisado Avenue passes several historic houses.

The 1758 **John & Sarah Strong House** is an old surviving frame structure named after the newlyweds who built it and lived in it for four years before heading west to settle. It has an excellent collection of furnishings reflecting the history of Windsor. Next door is the **Dr. Hezekiah Chaffee House**, a three-story brick Georgian-Colonial built in the mid-18th century. The home is appointed with period furniture and features changing exhibits. Visitors may also tour the adjoining Palisado Green. Here nervous settlers built a walled stockade during the 1637 war with the Pequot Indians. Further down the road stands the 1780 Georgian home of the state's first senator, Oliver Ellsworth (1745–1807). Today the **Oliver Ellsworth Homestead** contains interior design details from the era, including the original wallpaper.

🏛 **John & Sarah Strong House**
96 Palisado Ave. **Tel** (860) 688-3813. **Open** year-round: 10am–4pm Tue–Sat. **Closed** public hols. 🗗 includes admission to Dr. Hezekiah Chaffee House. 🖰

🏛 **Dr. Hezekiah Chaffee House**
108 Palisado Ave. **Tel** (860) 688-3813. **Open** year-round: 10am–4pm Tue–Sat. **Closed** public hols. 🗗 includes admission to John & Sarah Strong House. 🖰

🏛 **Oliver Ellsworth Homestead**
778 Palisado Ave. **Tel** (860) 688-8717. **Open** mid-May–mid-Oct: noon–4pm Wed, Thu & Sat. 🗗

Environs
Fifteen miles (24 km) north of Windsor, the **Connecticut Trolley Museum** takes visitors on a nostalgic journey. A round-trip through the grounds on an antique trolley highlights permanent displays of classic trolley cars dating from 1894 to 1949. The Connecticut Fire Museum and a Bus Museum are also part of the complex.

🏛 **Connecticut Trolley Museum**
58 North Rd., East Windsor. **Tel** (860) 627-6540. **Open** Apr–mid-Jun: 10am–4:30pm Sat, noon–4pm Sun; mid-Jun–Labor Day: 10am–3:30pm Mon, Wed–Fri, 10am–5pm Sat, noon–4:30pm Sun; off season call for hours. 🗗 access to both museums. 🖲 ceraonline.org

Sea captain's home, Phelps Tavern Museum

For hotels and restaurants in this region see pp315–16 and pp333–5

❾ New England Air Museum

Bradley International Airport, Windsor Locks. **Tel** (860) 623-3305. **Open** 10am–5pm daily. **Closed** Jan 1, Thanksgiving, & Dec 25. 🅿 🅒 ♿ 🏠 W neam.org

Aviation fans can indulge their flights of fancy at the largest aviation museum in the Northeast. The impressive collection of 80 aircraft spans the complete history of aviation beginning with pre-Wright Brothers flying machines right up to present-day jets and rescue helicopters. Located near Bradley International Airport, the museum is housed in and around two cavernous hangars. Highlights include a Bunce-Curtiss Pusher, a vintage 1909 Blériot and a Sikorsky VS-44 Flying Boat, the last of the four-engined flying boats.

To experience the thrill of flying, visitors can strap themselves into a simulator of the Grumman Tracer.

One of the planes on display at the New England Air Museum

Old New-Gate Prison and Copper Mine insignia

❿ Old New-Gate Prison and Copper Mine

ℹ 115 Newgate Rd., East Granby. **Tel** (860) 653-3563. **Open** call for hours. 🅿 🅒 ♿ 🏠

When financial woes forced the sale of this less than prosperous 18th-century copper mine, its new proprietors found a novel but grim use for the dark hole in the ground. In 1773 the local government transformed the nation's first chartered copper mine into the state's first colonial prison. Over the course of its infamous career, the jail held everyone from horse thieves to captured British soldiers. New-Gate represented a particularly brutal form of punishment, with prisoners living and sleeping in damp, sunless tunnels. Mercifully, the prison was abandoned in 1827, although tours of its lower chamber still inspire shivers.

⓫ Coventry

🗺 11,350. ℹ Hartford (860) 787-9640.

Coventry is the birthplace of Nathan Hale (1755–76), one of the inspirational heroes of the American Revolution (1775–83). Just minutes before he was to be hanged by the British for being a spy, the 21-year-old Coventry schoolteacher uttered his now famous last words, "I only regret that I have but one life to lose for my country."

The **Nathan Hale Homestead** is an anomaly in that its namesake never actually lived in the house. The existing structure, located on the site where Hale was born, was built by Hale's brothers and father in 1776, the same year he was executed.

Some of Hale's belongings are on display, including his Bible, army trunk and boyhood "fowling piece." Nearby, Strong-Porter House was built by Hale's great uncle in 1730.

Between June and October, the Nathan Hale Homestead is the site of the popular **Coventry Regional Farmers' Market**, with organic and heirloom produce for sale. Held on Sundays, this lively market also features live entertainment, food demonstrations, petting animals, and handmade goods from local artisans.

🏠 **Nathan Hale Homestead**
2299 South St. **Tel** (860) 742-6917. **Open** Jun–Aug: noon–4pm Wed–Sat, 11am–4pm Sun; Sep & Oct: noon–4pm Fri & Sat, 11am–4pm Sun. 🅿 🅒 ♿ partial.

🎪 **Coventry Regional Farmers' Market**
Open Jun–Oct: 11am–2pm Sun. W coventryfarmersmarket.com

The 1730 Strong-Porter House in Coventry

⓬ Lebanon

🏙 6,500. 🚆 Hartford. 🚌 🚉 New London. 🛈 Mystic (860) 536-8822 or (800) 863-6569.

This Eastern Connecticut community is steeped in American Revolution history. It was here on the 160-acre (65-ha) common that French hussars trained before joining their American allies in Yorktown for the climactic battle of the conflict. Lebanon native and artist John Trumbull (1756–1843), whose paintings can be seen in Hartford's Wadsworth Atheneum (see p202) and New Haven's Yale University Art Gallery, put down his paintbrush long enough to design the town's 1807 Congregational Church.

Also overlooking the green is the **Governor Jonathan Trumbull's House**. Father to John and governor of the colony and the state of Connecticut from 1769 to 1784, Trumbull was the only governor of the 13 colonies to remain in office before, during and after the Revolutionary War. Behind the house is the **Doctor William Beaumont Homestead**, birthplace of one of the world's pioneers of gastric medicine.

🏛 **Governor Jonathan Trumbull's House**
169 W Town St. **Tel** (860) 429-7194. **Open** mid-May–mid-Oct: 1–6pm Fri, 10am–5pm Sat, 11am–5pm Sun. 🅿

🏛 **Doctor William Beaumont Homestead**
169 W Town St. **Tel** (860) 642-6579. **Open** mid-May–mid-Oct: noon–4pm Sat. 🅿

Environs
Twelve miles (19 km) to the east, Canterbury is home to the

Prudence Crandall Museum. Crandall (1803–90) raised the ire of citizens when, in 1832, she admitted a young black student to her private school for girls. Undaunted by threats of boycotts, Crandall kept the school open and attracted students, many of whom were black, from other states. Public outcry was such that the local government pushed through a law forbidding private schools to admit black children from out of state. Crandall was subsequently jailed and brought to trial. It was only after an angry mob attacked the school in 1834 that the heroic Quaker woman reluctantly closed its doors forever. Today the museum commemorates Crandall's struggle and traces local black history.

🏛 **Prudence Crandall Museum**
Canterbury Green. **Tel** (860) 546-7800. **Open** call for hours. **Closed** mid-Dec–Mar. 🅿

⓭ Norwich

🏙 35,000. 🛈 Mystic (860) 536-8822 or (800) 863-6569.

Norwich has the dubious distinction of being the birthplace of Benedict Arnold (1741–1801), forever synonymous with traitor for betraying Colonial forces during the American Revolution. In contrast, the Colonial Cemetery contains graves of soldiers, both American and French, who died fighting for the American cause during the war.

A two-story colonial structure consisting of a pair of annexed saltboxes, the **Christopher Leffingwell House**, is named

after a financier of the Colonial side in the American Revolution. During the war, Leffingwell's house and tavern were used for secret meetings. The interior, full of late 17th- and 18th- century furniture, has never been remodeled, making it of special interest.

🏛 **Christopher Leffingwell House**
348 Washington St. **Tel** (860) 889-9440. **Open** Apr–Oct: noon–4pm Sat. **Closed** public hols. 🅿 🎥

Environs
Located 5 miles (8 km) south of Norwich is the **Shantok Village of Uncas**, final resting place of Native American leader Uncas (d.1683). Inspiration for James Fenimore Cooper's novel *Last of the Mohicans* (1826), Uncas provided early colonists with the plot of land for the original Norwich settlement and sided with them during the Pequot War of the 1630s. An obelisk memorializing Uncas was erected here in 1840.

🏛 **Shantok Village of Uncas**
Rte 32 S of Norwich. **Open** dawn to dusk daily. 🎥

A Leffingwell sculpture

⓮ Foxwoods Resort Casino

Rte 2. **Tel** (800) 369-9963. Casino: **Open** 24 hrs daily. ♿ 🏨 🍴 🖥 🎭 🚼 🛍

First of the Native American-operated casinos in New England, this gaming facility has hundreds of games tables, more than 6,300 slot machines, and high-stakes bingo and poker. In addition, the 4,000-seat MGM Grand Theater attracts international stars.

Also on casino grounds is the **Mashantucket Pequot Museum**, a state-of-the-art research and exhibition center of Native American history. Multimedia displays and touch-screen computers provide a detailed study of the natural history of the area and its earliest inhabitants. Walking

The War Office in Lebanon, once Jonathan Trumbull's store

For hotels and restaurants in this region see pp315–16 and pp333–5

Life-size Native American figures at the Mashantucket Pequot Museum

through a replica Pequot Village c.1500, visitors come upon life-size figures depicting local Native American life.

🏛 Mashantucket Pequot Museum

110 Pequot Trail. **Tel** (860) 396-6800 or (800) 411-9671. **Open** 10am–4pm Wed–Sat. **Closed** Jan 1, Thanksgiving Eve, Thanksgiving, Dec 24 & 25. 🅿 🖼 ♿ 🎦 ⊘ 🆆 **pequotmuseum.org**

⓯ New London

🏙 26,000. 🚌 🛈 Mystic (860) 536-8822 or (800) 863-6569.

British forces led by traitor Benedict Arnold razed New London during the American Revolution. Rebounding from the attack, the town enjoyed newfound prosperity with the whaling industry during the 19th century. The four colonnaded Greek Revival mansions along Whale Oil Row attest to the affluence of that era.

Remarkably, many homes survived Arnold's torching, including the **Joshua Hempsted House**. Built in 1678, the dwelling is insulated with seaweed and represents one of the few 17th-century homes left in the state. Connecticut College houses the **Lyman Allyn Art Museum**, particularly known for

its 19th-century American paintings. Also on campus, the 1-sq-mile (3-sq-km) college Arboretum encompasses a variety of ecosystems, native trees and shrubs, trails, and ponds. At the edge of town is **Monte Cristo Cottage**, boyhood home of Nobel Prize-winning playwright Eugene O'Neill (1888–1953). The two-story cottage, which served as the setting for his Pulitzer Prize-winning play *Long Day's Journey into Night* (1957), is now a research library, with some of O'Neill's belongings on display.

🏠 Joshua Hempsted House

Jct of Hempstead, Jay, & Truman Sts. **Tel** (860) 443-7949. **Open** mid-May–mid-Oct: 1–4pm Sat & Sun (Jul–Aug: also Thu & Fri). 🅿 🖼 obligatory.

🏛 Lyman Allyn Art Museum

625 Williams St. **Tel** (860) 443-2545. **Open** year-round: 10am–5pm Tue–Sat, 1–5pm Sun. **Closed** public hols. 🅿 🖼 by appt. ♿

🏠 Monte Cristo Cottage

325 Pequot Ave. **Tel** (860) 443-5378 ext 227. **Open** late May–early Sep: noon–4pm Thu–Sat, 1–3pm Sun. 🅿

Environs

Directly across the river Thames from New London is the town of Groton. The USS *Nautilus*, the world's first nuclear-powered submarine is berthed at the

Submarine Force Museum on the Naval Submarine Base. **Fort Griswold Battlefield State Park** is where British troops under Benedict Arnold killed surrendered American soldiers in 1781. A 134-ft (41-m) obelisk memorial and a battle diorama mark the event.

🏛 Submarine Force Museum

Crystal Lake Rd. **Tel** (860) 694-3174. **Open** May–Oct: 9am–5pm Wed–Mon; Nov–Apr: 9am–4pm Wed–Mon. **Closed** first week Nov, public hols. ♿

🏞 Fort Griswold Battlefield State Park

Monument & Park Aves. **Tel** (860) 449-6877. Museum: **Open** late May–Labor Day: 9am–5pm Wed–Sun. Park: **Open** year-round: 8am–sunset daily.

Sea lion sculpture on the rocks at Mystic Aquarium

⓰ Mystic

🏙 2,600. 🛈 27 Coogan Blvd. (860) 536-8822 or (800) 863-6569.

When shipbuilding waned, Mystic turned to tourism. Today Mystic Seaport *(see pp218–19)* and **Mystic Aquarium** make the town bustle. Seals and sea lions cavort in the outdoor Seal Island; indoors is a colony of African black-footed penguins and 3,500 sea creatures. They have one of the largest outdoor beluga tanks in the U.S. and there are daily shows in a 14,000-seat theater.

🏛 Mystic Aquarium

55 Coogan Blvd. **Tel** (860) 572-5955. **Open** Apr–Oct: 9am–5pm daily; Nov & Mar: 9am–4pm daily; Dec–Feb: 10am–4pm daily. **Closed** Jan 1, Thanksgiving, Dec 25. 🅿 ♿ ⊘ 🆆 **mysticaquarium.org**

World's first nuclear-powered sub, USS *Nautilus*, berthed at Groton

Mystic Seaport

What began as a modest collection of nautical odds and ends housed in an old mill in 1929 has grown into the world's largest maritime museum. The 19-acre (7-ha) working replica of a 19th-century port is a complex of more than 40 buildings open to the public, including a bank, chapel, tavern, rope-making shops, and one-room schoolhouse from the 19th century. Despite its fascinating exhibits of ship models and authentic scrimshaw, Mystic Seaport's main attraction remains its preservation shipyard and its fleet of antique ships, including the *Charles W. Morgan*, the last remaining vessel in the nation's fleet of 19th-century whalers.

Seagoing Connection
Almost every building sports a nautical motif.

Whaleboat Exhibit
A fully equipped whaleboat contains all the gear carried in such vessels in the late 19th century. It is housed in a shed on Chubb's Wharf.

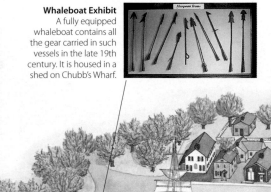

KEY

① **Middle Wharf**

② **Burrows House** is an early 19th century home of a shopkeeper and his milliner wife that re-creates coastal domestic life.

③ **Village Green Bandstand** is sometimes used as a concert venue, especially for July 4th celebrations.

④ **The *L.A. Dunton***, a 1921 schooner, is one of the last existing examples of the once-popular New England round-bow fishing vessels.

⑤ **The *Joseph Conrad*** was built in Denmark in 1882 and is one of the museum's three largest ships. It serves as a training vessel.

Shipcarver's Shop
Independent craftsmen carved figureheads and other decorations, such as this American eagle, for shipbuilders.

★ **The Charles W. Morgan**
The last wooden whaling ship in the world was built in 1841. During restoration of the *Charles W. Morgan* visitors can still board the vessel and walk the deck.

Thomas Oyster House
Initially used as a culling shop to sort oysters by size, the 1874 building was later used to shuck oysters before shipping them on ice.

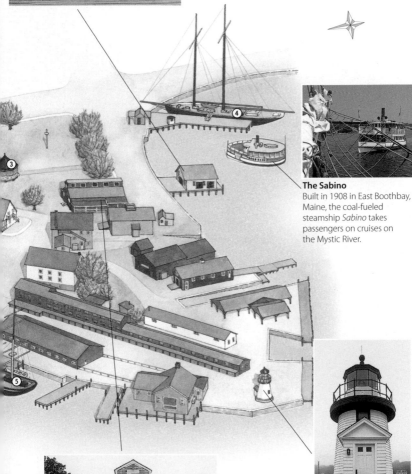

The Sabino
Built in 1908 in East Boothbay, Maine, the coal-fueled steamship *Sabino* takes passengers on cruises on the Mystic River.

Lighthouse
This copy of the 1901 Brant Point Lighthouse on Nantucket, houses a multimedia exhibit on lighthouse history (open Apr–Oct).

★ **Mystic River Scale Model**
Inside is a 50-ft- (17-m-) long model giving a bird's-eye view of Mystic circa 1870. It has over 250 detailed buildings.

The Harpist by Alphonse Jongers at the Florence Griswold Museum

ⓘ Old Lyme

🏠 6,800. 🛈 27 Coogan Blvd., Mystic (860) 536-8822 or (800) 863-6569.

Once a shipbuilding center, Old Lyme is home to numerous 18th- and 19th- century houses. Originally built for merchants and sea captains, many became residences of the artists who established a colony here in the early 1900s.

The **Florence Griswold Museum** is intimately linked to the arts. The mansion became the home of Captain Robert Griswold and his daughter Florence. An art patron, Florence began letting rooms in the 1890s to New York artists looking for a summer by the sea. She hosted Henry Ward Ranger (1858–1916), Childe Hassam (1859–1935), and Clark Voorhees (1871–1933), spawning the Old Lyme Art Colony.

This stop on the American Impressionist Art Trail *(see pp206–207)* features more than 900 works by artists who at one time lived in the house or nearby. Many of Griswold's guests painted on the wall panels of the dining room as thanks for her generosity. There is also a modern gallery which houses changing exhibitions. It is a work of art in itself, with a rippling aluminum canopy entrance, curvilinear walls and skylights to provide soft illumination.

🏛 **Florence Griswold Museum**
96 Lyme St., Old Lyme. **Tel** (860) 434-5542. **Open** year-round: 10am–5pm Tue–Sat, 1–5pm Sun. 🅿 📷 ♿

⓲ Essex

🏠 2,500. 🛈 One Constitution Plaza, 2nd Floor, Hartford (860) 787-9640 or (800) 793-4480.

In surveys naming America's top small towns, Essex is often found at the head of the list. Sited on the Connecticut River, the village is surrounded by a series of sheltered coves and has a bustling marina and tree-lined, virtually crime-free streets.

The **Connecticut River Museum**, a restored 1878 warehouse, is perched on a dock overlooking the water. Its collection and exhibits of maritime art and artifacts tell the story of this once-prominent shipbuilding town, where the *Oliver Cromwell* – the first warship built for the American Revolution (1775–83) – was constructed. The museum's conversation piece is a replica of the world's first submersible craft, the *Turtle*, a squat, single-seat vehicle built in 1775. Transportation is also the focus at the **Essex Steam Train & Riverboat Ride**, where guests take an authentic, coal-belching steam engine for a 12-mile (19-km) scenic tour. At the midpoint, passengers can take a 90-minute cruise down the river aboard a riverboat.

🏛 **Connecticut River Museum**
67 Main St. **Tel** (860) 767-8269. **Open** 10am–5pm Tue–Sun (daily late May–early Sep). **Closed** Jan 1, Labor Day, Thanksgiving, Dec 24 & 25. 🅿 📷 ♿

🚂 **Essex Steam Train & Riverboat Ride**
Exit 3 off Rte. 9. **Tel** (860) 767-0103 or (800) 377-3987. **Open** May–Dec: call for ride times. 🅿 📷 ✎
🌐 essexsteamtrain.com

Environs
Five miles (8 km) north of Essex is Chester, home to **The Norma Terris Theatre**, which presents new musicals. Across the Connecticut River the town of East Haddam offers spectacular views of river traffic from the **Goodspeed Opera House**. This late-Victorian "wedding cake" gem is the setting for new musicals and revivals, which are staged from April to December.

🎭 **The Norma Terris Theatre**
N Main St. / Rte. 82, Chester. **Tel** (860) 873-8668. **Open** call for show times. 🅿 ♿

🎭 **Goodspeed Opera House**
Rte. 82, East Haddam. **Tel** (860) 873-8668. **Open** call for show times. 🅿 ♿

Replica of the first submersible at Connecticut River Museum

⓳ Gillette Castle

See pp222–3.

⓴ Madison

🏠 16,000. 🛈 One Constitution Plaza, 2nd Floor, Hartford (860) 787-9640 or (800) 793-4480.

Madison is a resort town full of antique stores and boutiques, including a specialty store that stocks British kippers, bangers, and pork pies. Several historic homes are open for viewing, including the 1685 **Deacon John Grave House**. The structure has served as tavern, armory, courthouse, and infirmary, but has always belonged to the Graves. One of the oldest artifacts on display is the family's bookkeeping ledger, with entries from 1678 to 1895.

Madison is also home to **Hammonasset Beach State Park**, the largest shoreline park in the state. Poking into Long Island Sound, the peninsula has a 2-mile- (3-km-) long beach that attracts swimmers, sailors, scuba divers, and sunbathers. The park has walking trails, picnic areas, and a 550-site campground.

 Deacon John Grave House
581 Boston Post Rd. **Tel** (203) 245-4798. **Open** mid-Jun–early Sep: call for hours.

Hammonasset Beach State Park
I-95, exit 62. Park: **Tel** (203) 245-2785. Campground reservations: **Tel** (877) 668-2267. Park: **Open** 8am–dusk daily.

The boardwalk at Hammonasset Beach State Park in Madison

㉑ Guilford

 20,000. One Constitution Plaza, 2nd Floor, Hartford (860) 787-9640 or (800) 793-4480. **w** ctvisit.com

In 1639 Reverend Henry Whitfield (1597–1657) led a group of Puritans from Surrey, England, to a wild parcel of land near the West River. There they established the town of Guilford. A year later, fearing an attack by local Mennuncatuk Indians, the colonists built a three-story stronghold out of local granite. The Tudor Gothic-style fort, the oldest stone dwelling of its type in New England, now serves as the **Henry Whitfield State Historical Museum**. The austere interior has a 33-ft-(10-m-) long great hall and 17th-century furnishings.

Guilford is graced by dozens of historic 18th-century homes. Both the **Hyland House**, a classic early saltbox *(see p30)*, and the 1774 **Thomas Griswold House** are open to view. **Dudley Farm**, a 19th-century working farm and living history museum,

demonstrates the agricultural techniques of the era. In mid-July craftsmen gather on the scenic Guilford Green to celebrate the arts at the annual Guilford Handcraft Exposition *(see p37)*.

Henry Whitfield State Historical Museum
248 Old Whitfield St. **Tel** (203) 453-2457. **Open** May–mid-Dec: 10am–4:30pm Wed–Sun; mid-Dec–Jan: by appt only.

Hyland House
84 Boston St. **Tel** (203) 453-9477. **Open** Jun–Labor Day: noon–4:30pm Tue–Fri & Sun, 11am–4:30pm Sat. **Closed** Columbus Day. obligatory.

Thomas Griswold House
171 Boston St. **Tel** (203) 453-3176. **Open** call for hours.

Dudley Farm
2351 Durham Rd. **Tel** (203) 457-0770. **Open** May–Oct: 10am–1pm Thu–Sat, 1–4pm Sun.

㉒ The Thimbles

from Stony Creek Dock (203) 488-8905. (203) 777-8550.

From Stony Creek, travelers can cruise to the Thimble islands aboard one of several tour boats that operate in the area. Many of the 365 islands are little more than large boulders visible only at low tide. Some of the privately owned islands sport small communities. One colorful legend about this clutch of islands centers on circus midget General Tom Thumb (1838–83) courting a woman on Cut-In-Two Island. Another has the privateer Captain Kidd (1645–1701) hiding plundered treasure on Money Island while being pursued by the British fleet. Today cruisers watch seals or take in glorious fall colors.

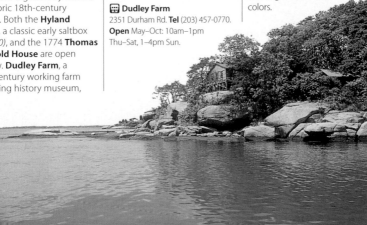

The Thimbles, home to seals, whales, and colorful legends

⑲ Gillette Castle

Ostentatious and bizarre, Gillette Castle is the antithesis of New England architectural grace. However, visitors to the 24-room granite mansion always leave with a smile. Actor William Gillette (1853–1937) based the design of his 1919 dream home on medieval castles, complete with battlements and turrets. The castle is rife with such oddities as Gillette's homemade trick locks, furniture set on wheels and tracks, a cavernous 1,500-sq-ft (139-sq-m) living room, and a series of mirrors starting in his bedroom that permitted him to see who was arriving downstairs in case he wished to be "indisposed" or make a grand entrance.

Park and goldfish pond, a pleasing vista

The View
The castle has a view of the Connecticut River and its traffic. Gillette lived on a houseboat for five years while the castle was constructed.

Castle Grounds
Following Gillette's death, the castle and its 117 acres (47 ha) became a state park. His railroad with its two locomotives used to carry guests on a three-mile (5-km) tour through the property. Now visitors walk the trails.

KEY

① At the **Main Entrance**, the huge oak door through which visitors must pass is equipped with an elaborate homemade lock.

② **The Study** is where Gillette spent much of his time. The chair at his desk is on a set of small tracks so it can be easily moved back and forth.

③ **Servants' quarters**

④ **The Library** holds the self-educated Gillette's book collection that ranges far and wide.

⑤ **Mezzanine**

⑥ **Outdoor terrace**

William Gillette

An eccentric playwright and actor, Gillette caught the acting bug early, leaving college at age 20 to tread the boards. His most famous role, repeated many times in repertory, was Sherlock Holmes. He was reputed to have made $3 million playing the fictional sleuth. Gillette spent $1 million to build his folly. His will stipulated that it should never fall into the hands of "any blithering saphead."

Castle Exterior
Constructed on a steel framework, the castle is built of fieldstone bought from local farmers and lifted up the hill on an aerial tram designed by Gillette.

★ **The Great Hall**
Exposed stone walls are five feet (1.5 m) thick in some places, and heavy oak covers steel beams. Gillette had a generator installed to provide power, but the castle is still dark and baronial.

❷ New Haven

The land on which Connecticut's second most populous city stands was purchased from the Quinnipiac Indians in 1638 for a few knives, coats, and hatchets. The city's location on the coast where the West, Mill, and Quinnipiac rivers flow into Long Island Sound has helped make it one of the state's major manufacturing centers. Over the centuries, items ranging from clocks and corsets to musical instruments, carriages, and Revolutionary War cannonballs have been made here. In 1716 Yale University *(see pp226–7)* moved from Saybrook to New Haven, establishing the city as a center for education, technology, and research. Today New Haven also offers opportunities for attending theater, opera, dance performances, and concerts.

Amistad Memorial

Tiffany stained-glass window at First Church of Christ

Exploring Downtown New Haven

The 16-acre (6-ha) New Haven Green is the central section of the original nine symmetrical town squares the Puritans laid out in New Haven, the first planned city in America. The Green has been the focal point of local life ever since, serving as the setting for many of New Haven's activities and festivals. Three churches, all built between 1812 and 1815, sit on the Green on Temple Street. United Church on the Green (often called North Church for its northern location) is in the style of London's St. Martin-in-the-Fields. Graced by a beautiful Tiffany stained-glass window, the First Church of Christ (Center Church) is considered an architectural masterpiece of the American Georgian style. The crypt beneath the church holds the remains of some of the city's original colonists. Among the notables buried here are Benedict Arnold's first wife, Margaret, and James Pierpont (1659–1714), one of the founders of Yale University. Trinity Church on the Green was one of the first Gothic-style churches in America.

Looming on the corner of Court and Church streets is the monumental Greek Revival post office, now the Federal District Court, designed in 1913 by James Gamble Rogers (1867–1947), architect of many of Yale University's Gothic Revival buildings. City Hall faces the Green on Church Street and epitomizes high Victorian style, with its polychrome limestone-and-sandstone façade. In front of City Hall, the 14-ft- (4-m-) tall bronze Amistad Memorial, which honors Senghe Pieh (also known as Joseph Cinque), leader of the *Amistad* revolt *(see p202)*, is on the exact site of the jail where the mutinous slaves were held.

In late April the Green becomes the stage for Powder House Day, a reenactment of one of Benedict Arnold's few celebrated moments. At the start of the American Revolution, Arnold, then a captain in the militia, seized control of a municipal arsenal and led his troops to Boston to help bolster the sagging Colonial forces.

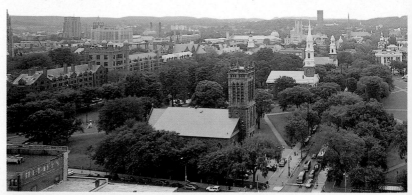
Church spires around New Haven Green

🏛 New Haven Museum and Historical Society

114 Whitney Ave. **Tel** (203) 562-4183. **Open** 10am–5pm Tue–Fri, noon–5pm Sat. **Closed** public hols. 🅿 📷

This handsome Colonial Revival house traces the city's cultural and industrial growth from 1638 to the present. Exhibits include such items as Eli Whitney's cotton gin, the sign that hung over Benedict Arnold's George Street shop, a fine collection of colonial pewter and china, and permanent galleries on the *Amistad* and the city's maritime history.

🏛 Grove Street Cemetery

227 Grove St, gate at N end of High St. **Tel** (203) 787-1443. **Open** year-round: 8am–3:30pm daily. 📷 ♿

Established in 1797 and covering 18 acres (7 ha), this was the first cemetery in the US to be divided into family plots. Walking through its 1848 Egyptian Revival gate, visitors will find a veritable who's who of New Haven. Eli Whitney (1765–1825), Noah Webster (1758–1843), Charles Goodyear (1800–1860), and Samuel F.B. Morse (1791–1872) are just some of the distinguished citizens buried in this cemetery.

The colorful 1916 carousel at Lighthouse Point Park

New Haven Parks

Among New Haven's many attractive parks, the 84-acre (34-ha) **Lighthouse Point Park** on Long Island Sound is a standout. The park has nature trails, a picnic grove, a splash pad, swimming facilities, a 1916 Coney Island-style carousel, and an 1847 lighthouse. **East Rock Park** offers a spectacular view of Long Island Sound, New Haven, and the harbor and is crisscrossed by 10 miles (16 km) of nature trails. The 123-acre (50-ha) **Edgewood Park** has a duck pond, nature trail, in-line skating rink, and playground. Black Rock Fort, from the Revolutionary War period, and Fort Nathan Hale, vintage Civil War era, offer splendid views of New Haven Harbor.

🏞 Lighthouse Point Park

2 Lighthouse Rd. **Tel** (203) 946-8790. Park: **Open** year-round: dawn–dusk daily. Beach: **Open** Memorial Day–Labor Day: dawn–dusk daily. 🅿 ♿

🏞 East Rock Park

E Rock Park. **Tel** (203) 946-6086. **Open** year-round: 8am–dusk daily.

🏞 Edgewood Park

Edgewood Ave. **Tel** (203) 946-8028. **Open** year-round: dawn–dusk daily. ♿

🏛 Eli Whitney Museum

915 Whitney Ave., Hamden. **Tel** (203) 777-1833. **Open** noon–5pm Wed–Fri & Sun, 10am–3pm Sat. **Closed** public hols. 🅿 ♿ 🌐 eliwhitney.org

On the northern outskirts of New Haven in the suburb of Hamden is the Eli Whitney Museum. One of the nation's earliest inventors, Whitney (1765–1825) was best known for developing the cotton gin, thereby automating the labor-intensive task of separating cotton from its seeds. Another of his inventions, a musket with interchangeable parts, revolutionized manufacturing. The museum contains examples of Whitney's achievements but the primary emphasis is on hands-on children's learning activities which emphasize creativity and inventiveness.

🏞 Connecticut Audubon Coastal Center

1 Milford Point Rd., Milford. **Tel** (203) 878-7440. Center **Open** year-round: 10am–4pm Tue–Sat, noon–4pm Sun. **Closed** gate closed at dusk. 🅿 📷 ♿ 🌐 ctaudubon.org

Just 15 miles (16 km) southwest of New Haven, travelers come upon the Connecticut Audubon Coastal Center, one of the state's best birding sites. This 8.4-acre (3-ha) bird and wildlife sanctuary and nature center is situated on Long Island Sound at the mouth of the Housatonic River. Visitors can take nature walks along the beach and around the salt marsh and climb a 70-ft (21-m) tower overlooking Long Island Sound.

Eli Whitney Museum in Hamden, just north of New Haven

🏛 Shore Line Trolley Museum

17 River St., East Haven. **Tel** (203) 467-6927. **Open** May–Dec: call for hours. 🅿 ♿ partial. 📷 🌐 bera.org

Five miles (8 km) to the east of New Haven in East Haven is the Shore Line Trolley Museum. The oldest rapid-transit car and first electric freight locomotive are among 100 vintage trolleys from 1878 onward on display. The museum also offers a 3-mile (5-km) trolley ride through salt marshes and woods on the oldest suburban trolley line in the country.

The 1840 lighthouse at Lighthouse Point Park

Yale University

Founded in 1701, this Ivy League school is one of the most prestigious institutions of higher learning in the world. The list of Yale's distinguished alumni includes Noah Webster (1758–1843), who compiled the nation's first dictionary, Samuel Morse (1791–1872), inventor of Morse code, and five US presidents, including George W. Bush (b.1946). While its law and medical schools attract much of the attention, Yale's other graduate programs (ranging from divinity to drama) are no less demanding. In some ways avant-garde, in others staunchly traditional, Yale admitted its first female Ph.D. student before the turn of the 20th century, but didn't become fully co-educational until 1969.

Wrexham Tower, Branford College, on the Yale campus

Exploring Yale Campus

Yale's campus comprises much of New Haven's downtown core, with the main section located on the western flank of the New Haven Green. Campus buildings reflect the architectural eclecticism that runs through the university. **Connecticut Hall** is Yale's oldest building and the only one left of a row of Georgian buildings on the **Old Campus**, Yale's original quadrangle. Nathan Hale *(see p215)* and US President William Howard Taft (1857–1930) had rooms here when they were students. After World War I,

Yale's oldest building, Connecticut Hall, constructed in 1717

James Gamble Rogers (1867–1947) designed the **Memorial Quadrangle**, a beautiful Gothic complex that is now the heart of the campus. Another Rogers design, **Harkness Tower**, completed in 1921, was modeled on St. Botolph's Tower in Boston, England, and has a facade covered with sculptures celebrating Yale's history and traditions. Each day at noon and again at 6pm the beautiful sounds of the bell tower's carillon can be heard throughout New Haven. On the Memorial Gate near the tower, the school's motto is inscribed: "For God, for country, and for Yale."

Post-World War II architects have left their mark on campus, too. The **Yale School of Art and Architecture** is as controversial today as when it was built in the 1960s. From the outside this 36-level building seems to stand only seven stories tall. The collection of buildings that makes up Ezra Stiles and Morse

VISITORS' CHECKLIST

Practical Information
Across from New Haven Green.
🚇 149 Elm St. (203) 432-2300.
Call individual sites for hours. 🗓
♿ 🎭 International Festival of Arts and Ideas (Jun). 🌐 **yale.edu**

Colleges at Broadway and Tower is by architect Eero Saarinen (1910–61), who based the design on an Italian mountain village. Philip Johnson's Kline Biology Tower, Yale's skyscraper, was completed in 1965.

🏛 Yale Center for British Art

1080 Chapel St. **Tel** (203) 432-2800. **Open** year-round: 10am–5pm Tue–Sat, noon–5pm Sun. **Closed** public hols. 🗓 ♿ 🎭 🌐 yale.edu/ycba

In 1966 Philanthropist Paul Mellon (1907–99) donated his collection of British art to the university. This was no small gift, considering it consisted of more than 50,000 paintings, prints, drawings, watercolors, and rare books and documents. Needing the right space to display its artistic windfall, the university hired American architect Louis Kahn (1901–74) to design an elegant new center. Thus was born this important collection

Library Court in the Yale Center for British Art

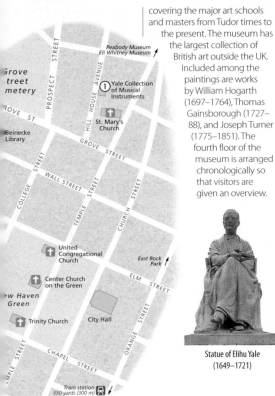

Yale University Campus

① Yale Collection of Musical Instruments
② Beinecke Library
③ Sterling Memorial Library
④ Memorial Quadrangle
⑤ Harkness Tower
⑥ Old Campus
⑦ Connecticut Hall
⑧ Yale Center for British Art
⑨ Yale University Art Gallery
⑩ Yale School of Art and Architecture

Statue of Elihu Yale
(1649–1721)

0 meters 200
0 yards 200

covering the major art schools and masters from Tudor times to the present. The museum has the largest collection of British art outside the UK. Included among the paintings are works by William Hogarth (1697–1764), Thomas Gainsborough (1727–88), and Joseph Turner (1775–1851). The fourth floor of the museum is arranged chronologically so that visitors are given an overview.

🏛 Sterling Memorial Library

128 Wall St. **Tel** (203) 432-2798.
Closed to the public.

This striking library boasts stained-glass windows and Gothic arches and is the largest on the Yale University campus. It contains some 4 million items, including rare Babylonian tablets.

Gothic entrance to the Sterling Memorial Library

🏛 Beinecke Rare Book and Manuscript Libraries

121 Wall St. **Tel** (203) 432-2977.
Open year-round: 9am–7pm Mon–Thu, 9am–5pm Fri, noon–5pm Sat.
Closed Sat in Aug & public hols.

American architect Gordon Bunshaft (1909–90) built the walls of this library out of translucent marble. This unique design helps filter the sunlight, which could harm the library's illuminated medieval manuscripts and 7,000 books. The library owns a host of rare books and manuscripts, but its prized possession is one of the world's few remaining Gutenberg Bibles.

🏛 Yale University Art Gallery
1111 Chapel St. **Tel** (203) 432-0600.
Open 10am–5pm Tue–Sat (Sep–Jun:
until 8pm Thu), 1–6pm Sun.
Closed public hols. 🎫 ♿ 📷
🆆 artgallery.yale.edu

This major collection of Asian,
African, European, American, and
pre-Columbian art comprises
more than 100,000 objects and
reflects the generosity and taste
of Yale alumni and benefactors.
While the museum was founded
in 1832, its main building was
completed in 1953 and is
considered architect Louis Kahn's
first masterpiece. After a series of
alterations, Yale chose to restore
the signature window walls,
refurbish the geometric ceilings,
and reinstate Kahn's open plan
to the galleries.
   The gallery's vast collection
highlights art as far back as
ancient Egypt. It is famous for its

Entrance to the Peabody Museum of
Natural History

American paintings, furniture,
and decorative arts. Among its
prized American pieces is John
Trumbull's *The Battle of Bunker
Hill* (1786). It also includes works
by artists such as Picasso, Van
Gogh, Monet, and Pollock.

🏛 Peabody Museum of Natural History
170 Whitney Ave. **Tel** (203) 432-5050.
Open year-round: 10am–5pm Mon–
Sat, noon–5pm Sun. **Closed** public
hols. 🍴 🎫 ♿ 📷 🆆 yale.edu/
peabody

Visitors entering the museum
are dwarfed by the imposing
skeleton of a 67-ft- (20-m-)
high *Brontosaurus* – an
apt introduction to this
outstanding museum, famous
for its collection of dinosaurs.
Children migrate to the
Great Hall of Dinosaurs, where
they can mingle with the
mastodon and socialize with
the *Stegosaurus*. Included
among the many fossils
and realistic dioramas is a
75-million-year-old turtle.
Archelon, at 10 ft (3 m), ranks
as the largest turtle that ever
roamed the planet.

㉔ Tour of Coastal Fairfield County

Travelers following Interstate 95 are bound to strike it
rich along the "Gold Coast," so nicknamed because
of the luxurious estates, marinas, and mansions
concentrated between Greenwich and Southport.
This, the southernmost corner of the state, has attractions
sure to meet everyone's taste. The shoreline is dusted
with numerous beaches offering a variety of summer
recreation opportunities. Nature preserves, arboretums,
planetariums, and the state's only zoo will appeal to
naturalists of all ages. People of a more artistic bent
can visit the area's numerous small galleries or visit
some of its larger, well-established museums.

New Canaan Historical Society building

**Stamford's First
Presbyterian Church** has
the largest mechanical-
action organ in the state.

⑥ Greenwich
Blessed with a
stunning coastline,
this town is home
to the Bush-Holley
Historic Site, the
state's first Impres-
sionist art colony.

⑤ Stamford
This major urban
area has a lively
downtown and the
First Presbyterian
Church, which is
shaped like a fish.

*Putnam
Lake*

Horseneck Brook

Mianus River

⑤
Stamford

🛈 ●⑥Greenwich

The Peabody's third floor has a slightly more contemporary feel, with displays ranging near and far – from daily life in Ancient Egypt to modern biodiversity in Connecticut. Elsewhere, visitors can admire exhibits on Native American or Pacific Island cultures, or examine minerals, meteorites, and exhibits on the solar system.

🏛 Yale Collection of Musical Instruments

15 Hillhouse Ave. **Tel** (203) 432-0822. **Open** Sep–Jun: 1–4pm Tue–Fri, 1–5pm Sun. **Closed** Jul–Aug. 🅿 📷 by appt. ♿ partial. 🌐 yale.edu/musicalinstruments

A must-stop for the musically inclined, this stunning collection of instruments, considered among the top ten of its kind, has 800 objects, including historic woodwind and stringed instruments. The collection was started by New Haven piano manufacturer Morris Steinert (1831–1912). Steinert's love of music (he also founded the New Haven Symphony) saw him travel to Europe to collect and restore antique instruments, especially claviers and harpsichords, forerunners to his beloved piano. Some of the collection's violins and harpsichords date back centuries. The museum holds a series of concerts from September to April. Many of the concerts are performed using the historic instruments.

Angelic detail on Yale's graceful High Street Bridge

Key

▰▰ Tour route

— Other road

④ New Canaan
The drive into town, which is set in a bucolic landscape of woods, streams, and rolling fields, is spectacular in fall.

① Bridgeport
Circus impresario P.T. Barnum was once mayor of this city, home to such attractions as the Beardsley Zoo, the Barnum Museum, and the Discovery Museum.

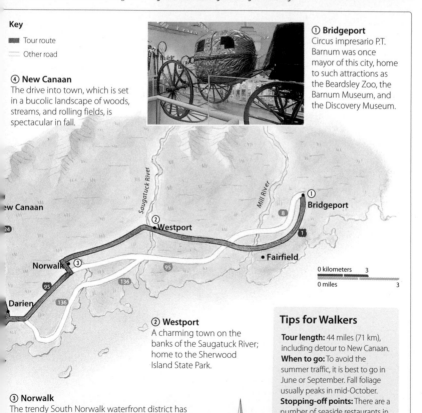

② Westport
A charming town on the banks of the Saugatuck River; home to the Sherwood Island State Park.

③ Norwalk
The trendy South Norwalk waterfront district has historic buildings, restaurants, shops, and cafés, as well as the Maritime Aquarium at Norwalk.

Tips for Walkers

Tour length: 44 miles (71 km), including detour to New Canaan. **When to go:** To avoid the summer traffic, it is best to go in June or September. Fall foliage usually peaks in mid-October. **Stopping-off points:** There are a number of seaside restaurants in Greenwich and Norwalk.

VERMONT

Vermont was given its name by explorer Samuel de Champlain in 1609. The word means "Green Mountain" in French, and must have seemed most suitable when he gazed upon the fertile landscape. Almost 400 years later, Vermont is still very much an enclave of unspoiled wilderness, with thick forests blanketing the rolling hills and the valley lowlands.

In all there are just about 600,000 people living in Vermont, one of the most rural states in the Union. The countryside is replete with manicured farms where the state's trademark black and white Holstein cattle graze against a backdrop of natural beauty. The pastoral landscape, dotted with pristine villages and covered bridges, evokes the idealized images found in paintings by longtime resident Norman Rockwell *(see p245)*. An anti-billboard law ensures that the countryside is not blighted by obtrusive advertisements.

Vermonters may be small in number, but they are nationalistic and often have led the country's conscience on social and political issues. The Stars and Stripes are a familiar sight in Vermont; the American flag, "Old Glory" as is it known, decorates many a front porch.

It is hardly surprising that people from around the world are attracted to this green corner of the US. Each season brings new opportunities to enjoy nature. When the countryside is covered in a blanket of snow, picturesque towns are transformed into bustling ski centers. Outdoor enthusiasts have long known that Vermont possesses some of the best boating, hiking, camping, and fishing in the country. Vermont is also a magnet for painters, writers, musicians, and poets who enrich the cultural life of the state. Regional theaters, museums, and art galleries are prominent attractions. But Vermont is at its scenic best in the fall, when thousands of "leaf peepers" come to see the natural phenomenon of leaves changing color *(see pp24–5)*. What makes the season so special here is the variety of colors that the trees manifest, from the palest mustard to flaming scarlet.

Grazing Holstein cows, a favorite breed in Vermont, in a typical state setting

Beautiful view of the sunset over Lake Champlain

Exploring Vermont

Unlike New England's coastal states, with attractions most often found along the water's edge, Vermont's highlights are sprinkled liberally throughout the state. The northeastern region boasts mountains, forests, and the fjordlike Lake Willoughby *(see pp234–5)*. Snaking down the western border, Lake Champlain and its islands *(see p240)* provide the backdrop for the collegial spirit of Burlington *(see pp236–9)* and the one-of-a-kind Shelburne Museum *(see pp242–3)*. Pre-Revolutionary War villages grace the south and provide good base camps for hikers looking to trek the Appalachian Trail *(see pp26–7)* or enjoy the splendor of the Green Mountain National Forest *(see p248)*.

Burlington's waterfront, well used by sailors and boaters

Key

═══ Highway
▬▬ Major road
▭▭▭ Minor road
── Scenic route
▬▬▬ Main railroad
─── Minor railroad
▬▬▬ International border
▬▬ State border
△ Summit

0 kilometers 25
0 miles 25

Sights at a Glance

1 St. Johnsbury
2 Lake Willoughby
3 Bread and Puppet Museum
4 Stowe
5 *Burlington pp236–9*
6 Lake Champlain
7 *Shelburne Museum pp242–3*
8 Ben & Jerry's Ice Cream Factory
9 Montpelier
10 Mad River Valley
11 Middlebury

12 Killington
13 Manchester
14 Green Mountain National Forest
15 Bennington
16 Wilmington
17 Brattleboro
18 Grafton
19 Woodstock

For hotels and restaurants in this region see pp316–17 and pp335–6

Montreal
Isle La Motte
North Hero
Grand Isle
Grand Isle **6**
BURLINGTON 5
South Burlin
SHELBURNE MUSEUM 7
Vergennes
Bristol
MIDDLEBURY 11
Mt Moosalamoo 790m
Brandon
Fair Haven
Rut
Poultney
Wallin
MANCHESTER
Arlington
15
BENNINGTON
Pittsfield

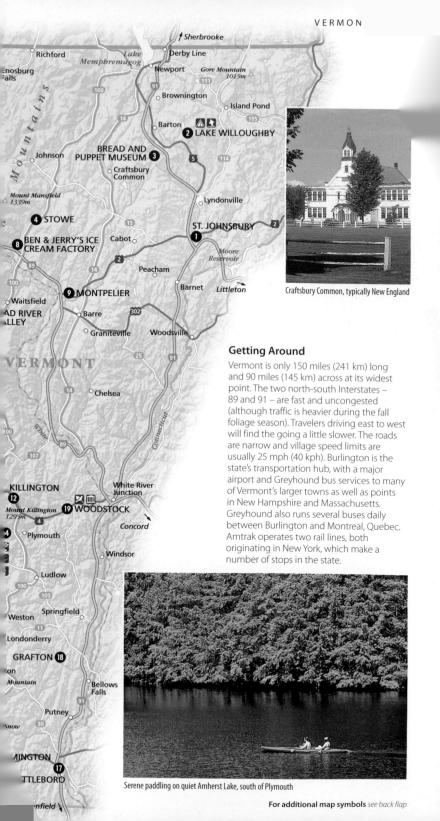

Sherbrooke
Richford
Lake Memphremagog
Derby Line
Enosburg Falls
Newport
Gore Mountain 1015m
Brownington
Island Pond
Mountains
Barton
2 LAKE WILLOUGHBY
Johnson
BREAD AND PUPPET MUSEUM **3**
Craftsbury Common
Mount Mansfield 1339m
Lyndonville
4 STOWE
ST. JOHNSBURY
1
Cabot
8 BEN & JERRY'S ICE CREAM FACTORY
Moore Reservoir
Peacham
Waitsfield
Barnet
Littleton
AD RIVER LLEY
9 MONTPELIER
Barre
Graniteville
Woodsville
VERMONT

Craftsbury Common, typically New England

Chelsea

White River Junction

KILLINGTON
12
Mount Killington 1293m
19 WOODSTOCK
Concord
Plymouth
Windsor

Ludlow
Springfield
Weston
Londonderry
GRAFTON **18**
Bellows Falls
Putney
Snow
MINGTON
17
TTLEBORO
nfield

Getting Around

Vermont is only 150 miles (241 km) long and 90 miles (145 km) across at its widest point. The two north-south Interstates – 89 and 91 – are fast and uncongested (although traffic is heavier during the fall foliage season). Travelers driving east to west will find the going a little slower. The roads are narrow and village speed limits are usually 25 mph (40 kph). Burlington is the state's transportation hub, with a major airport and Greyhound bus services to many of Vermont's larger towns as well as points in New Hampshire and Massachusetts. Greyhound also runs several buses daily between Burlington and Montreal, Quebec. Amtrak operates two rail lines, both originating in New York, which make a number of stops in the state.

Serene paddling on quiet Amherst Lake, south of Plymouth

For additional map symbols *see back flap*

Johnsbury

. ✈ 77 miles (125 km) W in
gton. 🚌 ℹ 51 Depot Sq. (802)
3678 or (800) 639-6379.
nekchamber.com

his small industrial town, which is the unofficial capital of Vermont's northeast region – also called the "Northeast Kingdom" – sits on a promontory at the convergence of the Moose, Sleeper, and Passumpsic rivers. The town is named for Saint Jean de Crèvencour, who was a friend of Revolutionary War hero Ethan Allen. It was the Frenchman who suggested that "bury" be added to the name because there were too many towns called St. John.

It was here in 1830 that mechanic Thaddeus Fairbanks (1796–1886) invented the platform scale, an easier and more accurate method of weighing than the balances of the time. The Fairbanks scale, as it came to be known, put St. Johnsbury on the map and boosted the growth of other pioneer industries, notably the manufacturing of maple products.

The Fairbanks family collected art and antiques, which now are housed in the **Fairbanks Museum and Planetarium** – one of the area's finest natural history museums. This Romanesque-style brick Victorian building, now on the National Historic Register, contains over 150,000 artifacts, including 4,500 stuffed birds and animals, and tools, dolls, and toys. Also on Main Street is the **St. Johnsbury Athenaeum**

Art on walnut wall panels at St. Johnsbury Athenaeum Art Gallery

Tranquil waters of Lake Willoughby

Art Gallery, a Victorian gem with gleaming woodwork, paneled walls, and circular staircase. The gallery highlights the landscapes of the Hudson River School of painting. Popular in the 19th century, the movement was the first native school of American art, and focuses on the beauty of the natural world. Albert Bierstadt (1830–1902), whose massive canvas *Domes of Yosemite* (1867) hangs here, was one of its leaders.

🏛 Fairbanks Museum and Planetarium

1302 Main St. **Tel** (802) 748-2372. Museum: **Open** 9am–5pm Tue–Sat, 1–5pm Sun (& Apr–Oct: 9am–5pm Mon). Planetarium: **Open** call for show times. 🎫 ♿ 📷
Ⓦ **fairbanksmuseum.org**

🏛 St. Johnsbury Athenaeum Art Gallery

1171 Main St. **Tel** (802) 748-8291. **Open** 10am–5:30pm Mon–Fri, 9:30am–5pm (3pm in summer) Sat. 🎫 ♿ 📷 Ⓦ **stjathenaeum.org**

Environs

Nineteen miles (30 km) to the west is Cabot, where one of the state's best-known agricultural products – cheddar cheese – is made. The **Cabot Creamery**, a farmers' cooperative, was started in 1919 and now produces a mind-boggling 100 million lbs (45.5 million kg) of cheese a year. The creamery offers tours and free tastings.

🧀 Cabot Creamery

Main St., Cabot, Rte. 215. **Tel** (802) 563-3393 or (800) 837-4261. **Open** Jun–Oct: 9am–5pm daily; Nov–Dec & Feb–May: 9am–4pm Mon–Sat; Jan: 10am–4pm Mon–Sat. **Closed** Jan 1, Thanksgiving. 🏠 ♿
Ⓦ **cabotcheese.com**

❷ Lake Willoughby

Rte. 5A ne ar Barton. **Tel** (802) 748-6687.

Travelers heading east from Barton climb a crest on the road only to be met with the breathtaking view of this beautiful body of water. The narrow glacial lake, which plunges 300 ft (90 m) in certain areas, is flanked by two soaring cliffs: Mount Pisgah at 2,750 ft (840 m) and Mount Hor at 2,650 ft (810 m). Jutting straight out of the water, the mountains give the lake the appearance of a rugged Norwegian fjord or a resort in Switzerland, garnering it the nickname the "Lucerne of America."

With trails leading around both promontories, this is a haven for hikers and swimmers looking for a secluded spot. There are wonderful picnic and camping areas along the beaches at either end of the 5-mile (8-km) lake. Several resorts and bed and breakfast establishments ring the shores. The lake itself offers plenty of recreational opportunities – fishing, boating, scuba diving – and there are three nearby golf courses.

Environs

Because of its isolated location 11 miles (18 km) northwest of Lake Willoughby, Brownington has retained the look of an 18th-century village, with few modern touches. The **Old Stone House** museum documents the history of the region. Twenty-two miles (35 km) to the north of the lake lies Derby Line – really two communities in one. The northern half, which is in Que Canada, is called Rock Islan

The border between Canada and the US runs through the middle of the **Haskell Free Library and Opera House**, a stately granite and brick building constructed in 1904.

Part of the audience sits in the US, but the stage is in Canada. The building's wealthy benefactor, Mrs. Martha Stewart Haskell (1831–1906), wanted both communities to enjoy her gift.

Old Stone House

109 Old Stone House Rd. **Tel** (802) 754-2022. **Open** call for hours. obligatory.

Haskell Free Library and Opera House

93 Caswell Ave. **Tel** (802) 873-3022. Library: **Open** 10am–5pm Tue–Wed & Fri, 10am–6pm Thu, 10am–2pm Sat. Opera House: **Open** May–Oct: call for hours. **Closed** Sun & Mon.

❸ Bread and Puppet Museum

Exit 25 Rte. 122 near Glover. **Tel** (802) 525-3031 or (802) 525-1271. **Open** Jun–Oct: call for hours and show times. **W** breadandpuppet.org

An extraordinary place down a quiet rural road, this museum is a century-old, two-story building, which once served as a barn to shelter dairy cattle. The cattle have gone, but every

...election of fanciful creatures at the ...d and Puppet Museum

inch of space is taken up by paintings, masks, and other theatrical knick-knacks, most notably puppets of all shapes and sizes, dressed in outlandish costumes in every style. The props belong to the internationally famous Bread and Puppet Theater company, founded in 1962. Guided tours of the museum are the best way to glimpse the history behind the artistry. The troupe members live communally on the surrounding farm. Their productions are notable for the masterful use of giant puppets.

Typical Vermont church in Craftsbury Common

Environs

Small and graceful Craftsbury Common, just 14 miles (22 km) southwest, is pure Americana. Gnarled old trees, planted in 1799 to commemorate the death of George Washington (1732–99), the first president of the US, line the main street. The village green is flanked by handsome clapboard homes with black shutters, and is anchored at one corner by a typical New England church with a white wooden steeple. In winter the area is popular with cross-country skiers.

The Austrian-style Trapp Family Lodge

❹ Stowe

3,500. ✈ 40 miles (64 km) W in Burlington. 51 Main St. (802) 253-7321 or (877) 467-8693.
W gostowe.com

It is hardly surprising that the Von Trapp family, whose daring escape from Austria during World War II was the inspiration behind the 1965 movie *The Sound of Music*, chose Stowe as their new home. The pretty village is ringed by mountains, which reminded them of the Alpine region they had left behind. Their Trapp Family Lodge *(see p317)* is part of the 4.2-sq-mile (10.9-sq-km) estate. The giant wooden chalet is one of the area's most popular hotels.

The village has been a major ski and outdoor activity center since the 1930s. In winter it draws hordes of skiers looking to enjoy the region's best slopes *(see pp362–3)*. Mountain Road begins in the village and is lined with chalets, motels, restaurants, and pubs; it leads to the area's highest peak, 4,393-ft (1,339-m) Mount Mansfield. Many local spas and resorts offer gourmet meals, and massages and other health treatments.

In summer there are still opportunities to enjoy the outdoors. Visitors can hike, rock-climb, fish, and canoe, or walk, cycle, or inline skate along the paved, meandering 5.5 mile (8.5 km) Stowe Recreational Path. It winds from Stowe's village church across the West Branch River, then through woodlands.

Burlington

Burlington is one of Vermont's most popular tourist destinations. It is a lively university town with almost half of its population of just under 40,000 made up of students or people associated with the University of Vermont (UVM) and the city's four colleges. One of the oldest universities in the country, UVM was founded in 1791, the same year that Vermont officially joined the United States. Burlington's strategic location on the eastern shore of Lake Champlain *(see p240)* helped it prosper in pioneer times, and today it is Vermont's center of commerce and industry. The town is also rich in grand old mansions, historic landmarks, interesting shops, and restaurants, and has an attractive waterfront. The famed American Revolution patriot Ethan Allen (1738–89), omnipresent throughout the state, has his final resting place here in Greenmount Cemetery.

The restored Flynn Center for the Performing Arts, close to City Hall Place

Exploring Burlington

The center of Burlington is compact and easy to explore on foot. Battery Street, near the waterfront, is the oldest, most historic part of the city and a jumping-off point for ferries to New York State and sightseeing trips around Lake Champlain. More than 200 handsome buildings in the downtown core have been renovated, and visitors will find many architectural landmarks, including the First Unitarian Church *(see pp238–9)*.

Battery Park, at the north end of Battery Street where it meets Pearl Street, was the site of a battle between US soldiers and the British Royal Navy. Burlington saw several skirmishes during the War of 1812, and scuba divers have found military artifacts at the bottom of the lake. Five shipwrecks, three lying close to Burlington, can be explored by divers who register with the Waterfront Diving Center on Battery Street.

These days Battery Park is a much more peaceful place. Lake Champlain is at its widest point here, and visitors who stroll through the park are rewarded with lovely views of Burlington Bay and the backdrop

of the Adirondack Mountains on the other side of the lake. Entertainment is presented in the park on selected evenings in summer.

Burlington's cultural life comes to the fore during its annual jazz festival in June. Venues for this popular concert series include City Hall Place, Waterfront Park, the Church Street Marketplace *(see pp238–9)*, and the Flynn Center for the Performing Arts. A former vaudeville theater and movie palace, the Flynn has had its Art Deco interior carefully restored, and now stages a variety of cultural events throughout the year. Vermont is well known for

Statue in Battery Park

Key

🖼 Street-by-Steet map *see pp238–9*

0 meters 250
0 yards 250

Lake steamer with a full complement of sightseers

its many artists working in craft media. The Frog Hollow Vermont State Craft Center, located on Church Street, serves as a sales gallery for work by artist members and as a source of information on classes in craft media across the state.

🚢 Spirit of Ethan Allen III

Burlington Boat House, College Street. **Tel** (802) 862-8300. **Open** 10am–6:30pm daytime and sunset dinner cruises (reservations necessary). 🎫 🅿️ ♿ 🖼
🆆 **soea.com**

Tall-stack steamers used to ply the waters of Lake Champlain. Today visitors can board a three-decker cruise ship, *Spirit of Ethan Allen III*, which holds 363 passengers. During the 90-minute trip, the captain narrates entertaining tales of the Revolutionary War.

🏛 Robert Hull Fleming Museum

61 Colchester Ave. **Tel** (802) 656-0750. **Open** May–mid-Sep: noon–4pm Tue–Fri, 1–5pm Sat & Sun; mid-Sep–Apr: 9am–4pm Tue–Sat (to 8pm Wed), 1–5pm Sun. **Closed** mid-Dec–mid-Mar, public hols. 🎫 ♿ 🖼

The museum is located on the campus of the **University of Vermont**, up on a hillside overlooking the city. Built in 1931, the elegant Colonial Revival building houses a huge collection of artifacts – more than 19,000 items – ranging from ancient Mesopotamia to modern times. Some of the items on display include European and American paintings and sculptures, as well as Native Indian crafts and glassware.

Statue of Penelope in the Fleming Museum

🏠 Shelburne Farms

1611 Harbor Rd. **Tel** (802) 985-8686. Dairy **Open** mid-May–mid-Oct: 9:30am–3:30pm daily. Farm Store **Open** year-round: 10am–5pm daily. 🎫 🅿️ ♿ partial.
🆆 **shelburnefarms.org**

Seven miles (11 km) south of town are Shelburne Museum *(see pp238–9)* and Shelburne Farms, a historic 2.2-sq-mile (5.7-sq-km) estate. The parklike grounds of the latter include rolling pastures, woodlands, and a working farm. Tours are given of the dairy. There is a children's farmyard.

Burlington Town Center

① First Unitarian Church
② Church Street Marketplace
③ City Hall Place
④ Flynn Center for the Performing Arts
⑤ Battery Park
⑥ Waterfront Park
⑦ *Spirit of Ethan Allen III*
⑧ Robert Hull Fleming Museum
⑨ University of Vermont

Part of the stately University of Vermont campus

For map symbols *see back flap*

eet-by-Street: Historic District

four-block section known as the Church Street Marketplace ocated at the center of the city's historic district. The eighborhood has been converted into a pedestrian mall complete with trendy boutiques, patio restaurants, specialty stores, factory outlets, craft shops, and, naturally, a Ben & Jerry's *(see p240)*. The marketplace, thronged with shoppers and sightseers at the best of times, is at its most vibrant in the summer months, with numerous street performers and musicians adding color and action. The district also has its share of historical attractions, including the 1816 First Unitarian Church.

Richardson Building
This 1895 chateau-style building was a 19th- centur department store.

The Masonic Temple
is Church Street's tallest structure.

★ First Unitarian Church
Standing at the head of Church Street, the First Unitarian Church was built in 1816 and stands as the oldest house of worship in Burlington.

The Burlington Montgomery Ward Building, built in 1929, is on the National Register of Historic Places. Its graceful lines and colorful facade typify pre-Depression architecture.

Central-Union Blocks
This was the first major development on upper Church Street. It now houses restaurant and pubs.

Pedestrian Mall
This section of the mall – particularly lively on weekends – is popular among students and tourists for its many shops and terraces. Cafés, pubs, and restaurants are housed in Queen Anne-style buildings from the late 1800s.

Merchants Bank was built in 1895 by Burlington architect Sydney Greene.

★ City Hall
This 1928 building marks the southern boundary of the marketplace and is made of local brick, marble, and granite.

Key

▢ Pedestrian mall

— Suggested route

0 meters — 25
0 yards — 25

Abraham Block was once considered the most striking commercial block in the state.

City Hall Park
The park is a popular outdoor concert venue. It features a poured concrete fountain and two granite monuments. One honors those who died in the Civil War; the other, soldiers who died in World War II.

Sailing and boating, popular on beautiful Lake Champlain

❻ Lake Champlain

Vermont-New York border from Whitehall to Alburg. ✈ Burlington. 🚌 ℹ️ 60 Main St., Burlington (802) 863-3489 or (877) 686-5253.
Ⓦ vermont.org

Said to be the home of "Champ," a water serpent that could be a distant cousin of Scotland's Loch Ness Monster, Lake Champlain was named for French explorer Samuel de Champlain (1567–1635). He discovered and explored much of the surrounding region. Some 120 miles (190 km) long and 12 miles (19 km) wide, the lake has its western shore in New York State, while the eastern sector is in Vermont. Seasonal hour-long ferry rides run regularly between Burlington and Port Kent, New York.

Sometimes called the sixth Great Lake because of its size, Champlain has 500 miles (800 km) of shoreline and about 70 islands. At the lake's northern end, the Alburg Peninsula and a group of thin islands (North Hero, Isle La Motte, and Grand Isle) give glimpses of the region's colorful past.

At Ste. Anne's Shrine on Isle La Motte is a statue of Champlain. Grand Isle is home to America's oldest log cabin (1783). The villages of North and South Hero were named in honor of brothers Ethan and Ira Allen. Their volunteers, the Green Mountain Boys, helped secure Vermont's status as a separate state.

Some of Lake Champlain's treasures are underwater, preserved in a marine park where scuba divers can explore shipwrecks resting on sandbars and at the bottom of the lake.

The **Lake Champlain Maritime Museum** at Basin Harbor gives an overview of the region's marine history. On display are ship models, old divers' suits, and photographs of Lake Champlain steamers, the most famous of which was the SS *Ticonderoga*, built in 1906. Visitors can board a full-scale replica of a 1776 gunboat.

🏛 **Lake Champlain Maritime Museum**
4472 Basin Harbor Rd., Vergennes. **Tel** (802) 475-2022. **Open** late May–Oct: 10am–5pm daily. 🅿️ ♿
Ⓦ lcmm.org

❼ Shelburne Museum

See pp242–3.

Gold dome of the Vermont State House in Montpelier

❽ Ben & Jerry's Ice Cream Factory

Rte. 100, Waterbury. **Tel** (802) 882-1240 or (866) BJTOURS. **Open** tours: Jul–mid-Aug: 9am–9pm daily; mid-Aug–Oct: 9am–7pm daily; Nov–Jun: 10am–6pm daily. 🅿️ ♿ 🚻 📷
Ⓦ benjerry.com

Although Ben Cohen and Jerry Greenfield hail from Long Island, New York, they have done more than any other "flatlanders" to put Vermont's dairy industry on the map. In 1977 these childhood friends paid $5 for a correspondence course on making ice cream and parlayed their knowledge into a hugely successful franchise.

Ben & Jerry's bus, gaily decorated with dairy cows

Ben and Jerry use the richest cream and milk from local farms to produce their ice cream and frozen yogurt. The Ben & Jerry trademark is the black and white Holstein cow, embellishing everything in the gift shop.

Tours of the factory start every 15 to 30 minutes and run for half an hour. Visitors learn all there is to know about making ice cream. They are given a bird's-eye view of the factory floor, and at the end of the tour a chance to sample the products and sometimes test new flavors.

❾ Montpelier

🏙 8,400. ✈ 40 miles (64 km) NW in Burlington. 🚌 🚉 ℹ️ (877) 887-4968.
Ⓦ central-vt.com

Montpelier is the smallest state capital in the US, but its diminutive stature is advantageous. The city is impeccably clean, friendly, and easily seen on foot. Despite its size, Montpelier has a grand, imposing building to house its state politicians and legislators. The **Vermont State House**, which dates back to 1859, replaced an earlier building that was destroyed by fire. It is now a formidable Greek Revival structure, complete with a gil cupola and giant fluted pillars of granite that were hewn from one of the quarries at neighboring Barre.

The **Vermont History Museum**, run by the local historical society, is housed in a replica of a 19th-century hotel. The museum has an additional center in Barre.

Vermont State House

115 State St. **Tel** (802) 828-2228. **Open** year-round: 8am–4pm Mon–Fri. Jul–mid-Oct: 10am–3:30pm Mon–Fri, 11am–2:30pm Sat. **Closed** public hols.

Vermont History Museum

109 State St. **Tel** (802) 828-2291. **Open** 10am–4pm Tue–Sat.

Environs

Seven miles (11 km) to the south, Barre (pronounced "berry") is the self-proclaimed granite capital of the world. In the 19th century, Italian and Scottish stonemasons came here to work the pale, white and blue-gray rock.

The region is still a hive of granite-related activity, with several large plants producing stone for tombstones (many have ended up in Barre's Hope Cemetery on Merchant Street), statues, and monuments. In nearby Graniteville, the **Rock of Ages Quarry** is the biggest such operation. Visitors can watch – from the safety of an observation deck – as the stone is being hewn from the huge 475-ft (134-m) pit. On

weekdays visitors can also take a self-guided tour to see artisans at work.

Rock of Ages Quarry

773 Main St., Graniteville. **Tel** (802) 476-3119. **Open** late May–mid-Sep: 9:15am–3:35pm Mon–Sat; mid-Sep–mid-Oct: 9:15am–3:35pm daily. **Closed** Jul 4. **rockofages.com**

❿ Mad River Valley

Central VT along Rte. 100. ℹ️ Rte. 100, Waitsfield (802) 496-3409 or (800) 828-4748. 🏠 Waitsfield, mid-May–Columbus Day: 9:30am–1pm Sat. **madrivervalley.com**

Located in central Vermont, Mad River Valley is most famous for outdoor activities that include hiking, cycling, hunting, and especially skiing.

One popular stop is the Mad River Glen ski area (see p362), which attracts die-hard traditionalists who enjoy their sport the old-fashioned way – without fancy high-speed gondolas (though there are four chairlifts) and snowmaking equipment. With only a couple of dozen trails, Mad River Glen caters to the country's most skilled skiers – in fact, its motto is "Ski it if you can."

Sugarbush, on the other hand, has more than 100 trails and a vertical drop of 2,650 ft (800 m). It is the polar opposite of Mad River Glen. This trendy resort, which caters to beginners and intermediate skiers as well as

Moss Glenn Falls near Warren in Mad River Valley

those who are more advanced, has the most modern snowmaking facilities and lifts. It was very popular with the 1960s "jet set," but now a more "retro" crowd who own time-share condos frequents the slopes. A state-of-the-art express "people mover" connects what used to be two separate ski areas: Lincoln Peak and Mount Ellen.

Activities in and around Waitsfield, the small, fashion-able, and wealthy community that is the center of this tourist region, include hiking, hunting, and – of all things – polo. The local landmark is a round barn, which is one of only a dozen remaining in the state. It is a venue for cultural functions and art exhibits. It sits next to an elegant inn and restaurant that has been converted from an 1806 farmhouse.

Bucolic scenery outside of Waitsfield, a popular summer destination

urne Museum

just an eclectic repository, the Shelburne
celebrates three centuries of American
ty, creativity, and diversity. Here folk art,
tools, duck decoys, and circus memorabilia
displayed on the same grounds as scrimshaw,
d paintings by such US artists as Winslow Homer
1836–1910) and Grandma Moses (1860–1961).
Established in 1947 by collector Electra Webb (1888–
1960), the museum's 39 exhibition buildings and their
contents constitute one of the nation's finest museums.

★ **Circus Building**
The horseshoe-shaped building
houses a 500-ft- (152-m-) long
miniature circus parade. The west
entrance foyer features this 3,500-
piece miniature circus.

Museum Store
Handicrafts by New
England artisans are
sold here.

Round Barn Gallery
All three floors of this 1901 barn feature changing
exhibits. The visitor center is located on the top floor.

Key

☐ Illustrated

☐ Not illustrated

1 Museum Store and
   Entrance
2 Round Barn Gallery
3 Circus Building and
   Carousel
4 Railroad Station
5 Beach Gallery

6 Beach Lodge
7 *Ticonderoga*
8 Electra Havemeyer Webb
   Memorial Building
9 Lighthouse
10 Webb Gallery
11 Covered Bridge
12 Meeting House
13 Horseshoe Barny

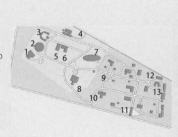

V

★ **Railroad Station**
The station was built in 1890 in Shelburne, Vermont, and relocated here. It houses a variety of railroad memorabilia, including telegraphy systems, vintage railroad maps, a restored stationmaster's office, and men's and women's waiting rooms.

VISITORS'

Practical Informa
Rte. 7, 7 miles (11 kr
Burlington. **Tel** (802) 9⟨
Open mid-May–late Oc⟨
10am–5pm Mon–Sat, noo⟨
Sun. **Closed** late Oct–mid-N⟨
🅿♿🚻📷🎫 flash
photography restricted in
some buildings.
W shelburnemuseum.org

1871 Lake Champlain Lighthouse
Built to warn ships off reefs in the lake, the building now houses art exhibits and tells of the lives led by light-house keepers.

KEY

① **Vintage 1920s carousel**

② **Beach Lodge**, built to resemble an Adirondack hunting lodge, contains a variety of big-game trophies.

③ **Locomotive 220**, a 1915 10-wheel steam locomotive, hauled freight and passenger trains. Engine 220 could pull 12.5 tons (11 tonnes) of dead weight.

★ **Ticonderoga**
A National Historic Landmark, the *Ticonderoga* was still in operation when Webb bought it in 1951. Today the former Lake Champlain steamship is open for visitors to explore.

...ury

...iles (58 km) N in
93 Court St. (802)
00) 733-8376.
...mont.com

...bury, founded in 1761,
archetypal New England
...n. It has not one, but two
...age greens, or "commons,"
...all-spired churches, a
prestigious college, and a
collection of Colonial-era
homes. In all Middlebury
lays claim to more than 300
buildings that were constructed
during the 18th and early 19th
centuries. Chief among them
are the Congregational Church,
the Battell and Beckwith
commercial blocks, and the
Middlebury Inn, a classic brick
Georgian-style hostelry with
shuttered windows that
dates back to 1827.

The town sits on
Otter Creek, which at
one time
powered the
machinery for a
thriving wool and
grain industry.
But the town gets
its name from the
days of stage
coaches when
Middlebury
served as the
transit point on
Vermont's main north-south
and east-west routes. Morgan
horses, one of the first US native
breeds, were often seen on this
route. Today visitors can tour
the **University of Vermont
Morgan Horse Farm**, which is
dedicated to the preservation
and improvement of this
versatile and historic breed.
Between 60 and 80 stallions,
mares, and foals are cared for by
agricultural science students.
History buffs will enjoy the
**Henry Sheldon Museum of
Vermont History**, an 1829
house that documents the early
19th century through its
collection of furniture, textiles
and clothing, and portraits.

Folk art and folk ways
meet the 21st century at the
Vermont Folklife Center where
multimedia exhibits using
computers and iPods help bring

Peaceful campus of Middlebury College

Morgan Horse Farm

rural culture to life. The center's
Heritage Shop features quilts,
decoys, baskets, and other
objects made by contemporary
folk artists. The 500-acre
(200-ha) campus
of **Middlebury
College** is a
delightful place
to explore,
with graceful
architecture, an
art gallery, and
green spaces.
The college's
Bread Loaf
campus in
nearby Ripton is
nestled in the
Green Mountain
National Forest
(see p248) near
the scenic Robert Frost
Interpretive Trail. Named for the
famous American poet who
spent summers here from 1938
to 1962, the path is flanked with
quotations from Frost's poems
set on plaques.

🐴 University of Vermont Morgan Horse Farm
Rte. 23 NW of Middlebury in
Weybridge. **Tel** (802) 388-2011. **Open**
May–Oct: 9am–4pm daily.

🏛 Henry Sheldon Museum of Vermont History
1 Park St. **Tel** (802) 388-2117. **Open**
10am–5pm Tue–Sat, 1–5pm Sun (call
for winter hours). **Closed** Feb.

🏛 Vermont Folklife Center
88 Main St. **Tel** (802) 388-4964.
Open 10am–5pm Tue–Sat.

🏫 Middlebury College
College St. **Tel** (802) 443-5000.
Open year-round: Mon–Fri.

⑫ Killington

🏔 1,000. ✈ 5 miles (8 km) W in
Rutland. ℹ Rte 4, West Killington
(802) 422-3333 or (800) 621-6867.

Sporty types who like outdoor
adventure and a lively social life
head for this year-round resort.
Killington has a highly
developed tourism
infrastructure, with hundreds
of condominiums, vacation
homes, ski lodges and B&Bs,
golf courses, hiking and bike
trails, and an adventure center
with water slides and a
climbing wall. It operates the
largest ski center *(see p362)*
in the eastern United States,
with 200 runs for alpine skiing
and snowboarding spread
across seven peaks including
nearby Pico Mountain.
Killington itself is the second-
highest peak in Vermont at
4,240 ft (1,295 m). Two of the
best cross-country ski centers
in the eastern US – Mountain

One of the numerous trails at Killington,
Vermont

Top Inn and Mountain Meadows Ski Touring – are also situated in the Killington area.

The ski season here usually lasts eight months, longer than anywhere else in Vermont, and one of the gondolas that ferry skiers to the peaks runs during the summer and fall as well. It is worth taking a ride to the top for the spectacular views. On a clear day, visitors can glimpse parts of five states and distant Canada. Killington also keeps busy throughout the summer with arts and crafts shows, barbecues, and music festivals.

⓭ Manchester

🗺 3,860. 🚘 33 miles (53 km) N in Rutland. 🚌 ℹ️ Suite 1, 5046 Main St. (802) 362-2100 or (800) 362-4144. 🌐 **manchestervermont.net**

Manchester is actually made up of three separate communities: Manchester Depot and Manchester Center, the outlet centers of New England, and Manchester Village. The sum of these parts is a picturesque destination surrounded by mountains, typical of scenic southern Vermont. There are two major ski areas: Stratton, a large complex with more than 90 trails and a hillside ski village with shops and restaurants; and Bromley, a busy, family-oriented ski area.

Manchester has been a popular vacation resort since the 19th century, when wealthy urbanites used to head to the mountains to escape the summer heat. The town's marble sidewalks fringed by old shade trees, the restored Equinox Resort *(see p316–17)*, and several stately homes evoke that era. Today's tourists take pleasure in following the Equinox Skyline Drive, a toll road, with its panoramic view of the countryside from the crest of Mount Equinox. Many visitors spend their time hunting for brand-name bargains in the designer outlets and factory stores.

One of Manchester's largest and most elegant houses is **Hildene**, a 24-room Georgian Revival manor house built by Robert Lincoln (1843–1926), a lawyer, diplomat, and the son of President Abraham Lincoln (1809–65). Among the mansion's most notable features are its 1,000-pipe Aeolian organ and Lincoln family memorabilia. The grounds are graced with an impeccable formal garden. In winter, 8 miles (14 km) of trails are open to cross-country skiers.

Also housed in a stately Georgian mansion, the **Southern Vermont Arts Center** rotates its permanent collection of 700 paintings and photographs. The hilly 400 acres (160 ha) also contain a striking sculpture garden and a short nature trail. Elsewhere, the **American Museum of Fly**

Antique kitchenware on display at elegant Hildene

Fishing claims to house the largest collection of fly-fishing paraphernalia in the world. The collection includes hundreds of rods, reels, and flies used by famous people such as singer Bing Crosby, literary giant Ernest Hemingway, and former US president Jimmy Carter.

Manchester is also the site where Charles Orvis established his fly rod shop in 1856; the finest of the company's rods are still built there. The extensive retail operation of the **Orvis Flagship Store** carries the full line of Orvis rods, reels, flies, clothing, and fly-tying equipment and supplies. The store also operates free introductory and intermediate fly-fishing classes on select dates throughout the summer.

🏛 **Hildene**
Rte. 7A. **Tel** (802) 362-1788. **Open** year-round: 9:30am–4:30pm daily. **Closed** Easter, Thanksgiving, Dec 25–27. 🔳 🔳 🌐 hildene.org

🏛 **Southern Vermont Arts Center**
West Rd. **Tel** (802) 362-1405. **Open** May–Dec: 10am–5pm Tue–Sat, noon–5pm Sun. 🔳 🔳 🔳

🏛 **American Museum of Fly Fishing**
4104 Main St. **Tel** (802) 362-3300. **Open** Jan–May: 10am–4pm Tue–Sat; Jun–Dec: 10am–4pm Tue–Sun. 🔳 🔳 🌐 amff.com

🏠 **Orvis Flagship Store**
4180 Main St. **Tel** (802) 362-3750. **Open** 10am–6pm Mon–Fri, 9am–6pm Sat, 10am–5pm Sun. 🌐 orvis.com

Norman Rockwell in Vermont

Painter and illustrator Norman Rockwell, famous for idealized depictions of small-town America, lived in Arlington at the height of his career, from 1939 to 1954. His paintings were so detailed they looked almost like photographs, and the magazine covers that he designed for publications such as *Saturday Evening Post*, the *Ladies' Home Journal*, and *Look*, have become collectors' items. Admirers of his work should be sure to visit the Norman Rockwell Museum in Stockbridge, Massachusetts *(see pp170–71)*.

Norman Rockwell surveys his work surrounded by friends and his son c.1944

⓮ Green Mountain National Forest

Forest Supervisor, Green Mountain National Forest, 231 N Main St., Rutland. **Tel** (802) 747-6700. Hapgood Campground: **Tel** (877) 444-6777 for reservations (all other campgrounds on first-come, first-served basis). **Open** year-round. to campgrounds. **recreation.gov**

This huge spine of greenery and mountains runs for 350,000 acres (142,850 ha) – almost the entire length of the state – along two-thirds of the Green Mountain range. The mountains, many more than 4,000 ft (1,200 m) high, have some of the best ski centers in the eastern United States, including Sugarbush *(see p241)* and Mount Snow *(see p250)*. A large network of snowmobile and cross-country ski trails are also maintained throughout the winter months.

The National Forest is divided into northern and southern sectors, and encompasses six wilderness areas; sections of the forest have remained entirely undeveloped – no roads, no electricity, and even paths may be poorly marked or non-existent. While hard-core backcountry hikers and campers may enjoy this challenge, the majority of travelers will prefer to roam the less primitive areas of the forest. Picnic sites and campgrounds are found throughout, along with more than 500 miles (805 km) of hiking paths, including the challenging Long and Appalachian trails *(see pp26–7)*.

Woodward Reservoir in the Green Mountain National Forest

Many lakes, rivers, and, reservoirs offer excellent boating and fishing opportunities. On land, bike paths (both mountain and road) are numerous and specially designated paths are open to horseback riders. Regardless of their mode of transportation, visitors are encouraged to stay on the paths in order to preserve the delicate ecosystem. Markers indicate designated lookout points and covered bridges. The town of Stratton in the southern portion of the Green Mountain range offers recreational activities such as golf, horseback riding, sailing, and fly-fishing, as well as alpine and cross-country skiing. The Stratton Arts Festival is held in the fall. Nearby Bromley Mountain Ski Center has been a popular family resort since the 1930s.

⓯ Bennington

16,800. Rte. 7 (802) 447-3311 or (800) 229-0252. Wed & Fri. **bennington.com**

Although it is tucked away in the southwest corner of the Green Mountain National Forest bordering Massachusetts and New York State, Bennington is no backwoods community. The

Dense woodlands of the Green Mountain National Forest

◀ Picturesque countryside during autumn in Vermont

third-largest city in the state, Bennington is an important manufacturing center and home to Bennington College, the faculty of which once included cutting-edge engineer Buckminster Fuller (1895–1983).

Three covered bridges (just off Route 67) herald the approach to town. These 19th-century wooden structures, built with roofs to protect them against the harsh Vermont winter, were nicknamed "kissing bridges" because in the days of horses and buggies they provided a discreet shelter for courting couples to embrace.

Bennington was established in 1749 and a few decades later Ethan Allen arrived on the scene to lead the Green Mountain Boys, a citizen's militia originally created to protect Vermont from the expansionist advances of neighboring New York. Allen would later make his name as a patriot during the Revolutionary War by leading his men into battle and scoring several decisive victories against British forces.

The revolutionary era comes alive during a walking tour of the **Old Bennington Historic District** just west of the downtown core, where a typical New England village green is ringed by pillared Greek Revival structures and Federal-style brick buildings. The 1806 **First Congregational Church**, with its vaulted plaster and wood ceilings, is a striking and much-photographed local landmark. Next to it is the Old Burying Ground, resting place of five Vermont governors and the

The pulpit of Bennington's First Congregational Church

beloved poet Robert Frost *(see pp34–5)*.

Looming over the Historic District is the 306-ft- (93-m-) high **Bennington Battle Monument**, a massive stone obelisk that, when it was built in 1891, was the tallest war monument in the world. It commemorates a 1777 battle in nearby Willoomsac Heights, when the colonial forces defeated the British army and their allies, leading to the surrender of their commander, General John Burgoyne (1722–92). An elevator takes visitors to an observation area that affords panoramic views of Vermont and the neighboring states of New York and Massachusetts. The turbulent times of the Revolutionary and Civil wars are also recalled at the **Bennington Museum and Grandma Moses Gallery**. The museum houses several dozen paintings by famed folk artist Anna Mary "Grandma" Moses (1860–1961), who lived in the Bennington area. A farmer's wife with no formal training in art, Moses started painting landscapes as a hobby when she

The 1891 Bennington Battle Monument

was in her mid-70s. She was "discovered" by the critics in 1940, when a collection of her art was shown at a private exhibition in the Museum of Modern Art in New York City. At that time the 79-year-old primitive artist was being hailed as an important new talent. By the time she died in 1961 at the age of 101, Grandma Moses had produced some 1,600 works of art, including a series of tiny country scenes painted on mushrooms. The collection in Bennington includes her only known self-portrait.

The Museum's comprehensive collection of Americana also includes uniforms, furniture, and examples of pottery from Bennington's ceramics industry, which reached its peak in the mid-19th century. The display of American glassware includes examples of the decorative Art Nouveau style that was popularized by Louis Comfort Tiffany (1848–1933).

Portrait of Governor Paul Brigham

🏛 **Old Bennington Historic District**
Tel (802) 447-3311 or (800) 229-0252.

⛪ **First Congregational Church**
Monument Ave. **Tel** (802) 447-1223. 🕐 11am Sun (also 9:30am Jul–Aug). 📷

🏛 **Bennington Battle Monument**
15 Monument Circle. **Tel** (802) 447-0550. **Open** mid-Apr–late Oct: 9am–5pm daily. 📷 ♿

🏛 **Bennington Museum and Grandma Moses Gallery**
75 Main St. **Tel** (802) 447-1571.
Open 10am–5pm Thu–Tue.
Closed Jan, Thanksgiving, Dec 25. 📷
♿ 📷 🌐 benningtonmuseum.org

For hotels and restaurants in this region see pp316–17 and pp335–6

⑯ Wilmington

🏔 1,950. ✈ 8 miles (13 km) NW in West Dover. ℹ 21 W Main St. (802) 464-8092 or (877) 887-6884.

Wilmington is the largest village in the Mount Snow Valley, with several dozen restaurants and stores catering to the tourists who come to enjoy outdoor sports at the nearby mountain. Like so many of Vermont's small towns, its Main Street is lined with restored 18th- and 19th-century buildings, many listed on the National Register of Historic Places.

Standing 3,600 ft (1,100m) tall, **Mount Snow** is named after the original owner of the land, farmer Reuben Snow, although most visitors believe the name refers to the abundance of white stuff that during winter is the resort's *raison d'être*.

In the late 1990s, more than $35 million was spent on upgrading the ski center, which now has 102 trails, many of them wooded, spread over 610 acres (247 ha). Mount Snow was one of the first ski resorts in the US to provide facilities for snowboarders, with dedicated learning areas for beginners and facilities for advanced surfers. The center also opened the first mountain-bike school in the country. Outdoor summer attractions include 45 miles (72 km) of challenging bike trails (some are also ski runs), hiking routes, an inline skate and skateboard park, and a climbing wall. The 18-hole **Mount Snow Golf Club** provides a more sedate diversion.

⛷ Mount Snow
Rte. 100. **Tel** (802) 464-3333 or (800) 245-7669. **Open** year-round. 🅿 ♿
ⓦ **mountsnow.com**

⛳ Mount Snow Golf Club
Rte. 100. **Tel** (802) 464-4254; call for tee times. **Open** 7am–dusk Mon–Fri, 6am–dusk Sat–Sun & public hols. 🅿

⑰ Brattleboro

🏔 12,500. ✈ 20 miles (32 km) NE in Keene, NH. 🚌 🚉 ℹ 180 Main St (802) 254-4565 or (877) 254-4565. 📅 May–Oct: Wed & Sat.
ⓦ **brattleborochamber.org**

Perched on the banks of the Connecticut River on the New Hampshire border, Brattleboro is the first major town that northbound travelers encounter as they enter the state. Fort Dummer was established here in 1724, making it the state's first European settlement. For that reason, Brattleboro has adopted the slogan "Where Vermont Begins."

A bustling center of commerce and industry, the town is also a hub of tourism. As is the case with so many other Vermont towns, there is a historic district with many Colonial-era buildings of architectural interest. In the 1840s, after the Vermont Valley Railroad was laid to provide a vital link to the outside world, natural springs were discovered in the area and Brattleboro took on a new personality as a spa town where people came for "cures" and health treatments. The former railroad station is now home to the **Brattleboro Museum and Art Center**, which offers rotating exhibitions by artists of regional and international stature. The Brattleboro Music Center, on Walnut Street, stages a broad range of programs, including a chamber music series. The town's **Estey Organ Museum** is housed in the former factory building

Estey organs were manufactured in Brattleboro for more than 100 years

where the famous reed, pipe, and electronic organs were manufactured, prior to being shipped around the world.

🏛 Brattleboro Museum and Art Center
10 Vernon St. **Tel** (802) 257-0124. **Open** Apr–mid-Feb: 11am–5pm Wed–Mon. 🅿 ♿
ⓦ **brattleboromuseum.org**

🏛 Estey Organ Museum
108 Birge St. **Tel** (802) 246-8366. **Open** by appointment only. 🅿
ⓦ **esteyorganmuseum.org**

⑱ Grafton

🏔 600. ✈ 47 miles (76 km) N in Rutland. ℹ (877) 887-2378.

A thriving industrial center in the early 19th century, Grafton suffered a steady decline until by the 1960s it was almost a ghost town. But in 1963 Dean Mathey (1890–1972), a wealthy investment banker, established a foundation with the mandate to restore historic structures and revitalize commercial life. Today the village is an architectural treasure trove of 19th- century buildings.

Two tourist attractions are also thriving commercial enterprises: the **Grafton Village Cheese Company**, with its hearty cheddars, and the Old Tavern at Grafton *(see p316)*, a hostelry since 1801. Over the years, the inn has hosted author Rudyard Kipling (1865–1936), and President Theodore Roosevelt (1858–1919).

Verdant farmlands around the town of Wilmington

For hotels and restaurants in this region see pp316–17 and pp335–6

🏠 Grafton Village Cheese Company
533 Townshend Rd. **Tel** (800) 472-3866. **Open** year-round: 10am–6pm daily. 🍴 ♿

Environs
Eighteen miles (29 km) to the north lies the hamlet of Plymouth Notch. The tiny community was the birthplace of Calvin Coolidge (1872–1933), the 30th president of the US. The **Calvin Coolidge State Historic Site** encompasses an 1850s general store and post office once run by Coolidge's father, a cheese factory, a schoolhouse, and the Coolidge family home.

In Weston, 21 miles (34 km) west of Plymouth Notch, visitors will find the **Vermont Country Store**. The store is famous for its enormous and eclectic array of merchandise, selected by its owners, the Orton family. Not only are these items highly original – be they badger-hair shaving brushes or handblown glasses that sea captains once used to forecast the weather – they are also always of the highest quality.

🏛 Calvin Coolidge State Historic Site
Rte 100A. **Tel** (802) 672-3773. **Open** late May–mid-Oct: 9:30am–5pm daily. 🏞 ♿ 🚻

One of the many beautiful homes in the village of Woodstock

🏠 Vermont Country Store
Rte 100, Weston. **Tel** (802) 824-3184. **Open** year-round: 9am–5:30pm daily.

⑲ Woodstock
🏠 1,000. ✈ 31 miles (50 km) W in Rutland. 🚌 ℹ Mechanic St. (802) 457-3555 or (888) 496-6378.
🌐 **woodstockvt.com**

Even in Vermont, a state where historic, picturesque villages are common, Woodstock stands out. Founded in 1761, the town is an enclave of renovated brick and clapboard Georgian houses. The restoration of the town came about as a result of the generosity of philanthropists such as the Rockefeller family and railroad magnate Frederick Billings (1823–90). An early proponent of reforestation, Billings personally financed the planting of 10,000 trees.

Billings Farm & Museum is still a working entity. The 1890 farmhouse has been restored and there are seasonal events such as plowing competitions in the spring and apple-cider pressing in the fall. The museum also traces Vermont's agricultural past with old photographs and exhibits of harvesting implements, butter churns, and ice cutters.

The **VINS Nature Center** is a reserve where injured birds of prey are cared for until they can be returned to the wild. As well as operating conservation programs and summer day camps for children, the naturalists here give frequent presentations about the owls, falcons, and eagles that have come under their care.

🏛 Billings Farm & Museum
River Rd. **Tel** (802) 457-2355. **Open** May–Oct: 10am–5pm daily; call for winter hours. 🏞 ♿ 🚻
🌐 **billingsfarm.org**

🦅 VINS Nature Center
Rte 4, Quechee. **Tel** (802) 359-5000. **Open** mid-Apr–Oct: 10am–5pm daily; Nov–Apr: call for hours. 🏞 🍴 ♿
🌐 **vinsweb.org**

Environs
Six miles (10 km) east of town is the stunning Quechee Gorge. The best view of the chasm is on Route 4, which crosses the gorge via a steel bridge. A short hiking trail leads from the parking lot on the east side down to the Ottauquechee River below.

The Rise of Calvin Coolidge
Calvin Coolidge was born in tiny Plymouth to parents who ran a general store. His humble upbringing endowed him with traits that would carry him to the presidency in the 1920s: honesty, frugality, and industry. Known as "Silent Cal," because he wasted little time on small talk, Coolidge guided the US to a period of economic prosperity before the onset of the Great Depression of 1929.

Boyhood home of Calvin Coolidge

NEW HAMPSHIRE

New Hampshirites are known for their fiercely independent nature, born of necessity in the early 1600s when European settlers established outposts in this mountainous and heavily forested region. This natural beauty is still in evidence, in the soaring peaks of the White Mountains, the pristine water of Lake Winnipesaukee, and the small, but scenic coastline.

There can be no better expression of New Hampshire's individualistic spirit than the state motto, "Live Free or Die," which is stamped on every state license plate. Six months before the July 4, 1776 signing of the Declaration of Independence, New Hampshire became the very first state to formally declare its separation from Great Britain. Ever cautious of centralized government, modern New Hampshirites proudly point out that they pay no personal state income tax, nor is sales tax levied on most consumer goods in the state – a boon for tourists looking for bargains.

The landscape that helped forge the determined mindset of early settlers has changed little in the ensuing centuries. It is estimated that more than 90 percent of the state is undeveloped, with dense forest covering more than three-quarters of its land. The northern part of the state is wild country, its woodlands bisected by the mighty Connecticut River and rippled by the tall peaks of the White Mountains *(see p269)*. Campers, climbers, and canoeists reign here. The hundreds of lakes and ponds that quilt central New Hampshire attract vacationers year-round looking to boat, fish, cross-country ski, and snowmobile. In the southwest, sightseers drive across rolling farmland that is punctuated by scenic villages and covered bridges. Even the industrial heartland of the Merrimack Valley is predominantly rural. A mere 15-minute drive from the downtown cores of the state's major commercial centers of Concord *(see pp262–3)* and Manchester *(see p262)* will transport travelers to the tranquility of dairy farms or quiet country roads.

Early October view of the Presidential Range in the White Mountains

◀ Visitors at Rocky Gorge Falls along the Kancamagus Highway, New Hampshire

Exploring New Hampshire

New Hampshire's compact borders make it ideal for sightseeing. Some attractions can be enjoyed on foot, as with the spectacular boardwalked chasm of Franconia Notch *(see pp276–7)*, or by car, as with a breathtaking fall-foliage tour along the Kancamagus Highway *(see p274)*. The remains of colonial battlements, the Shaker villages at Enfield *(see p266)* and Canterbury *(see pp264–5)*, and the historic homes of poets, politicians, and presidents are sprinkled throughout the state. Called the Granite State for its extensive granite formations and quarries, New Hampshire's rough edges are softened somewhat in its many fine museums. The Currier Museum of Art *(see p262)* is one such establishment, giving visitors the chance to view work by some of the world's great masters.

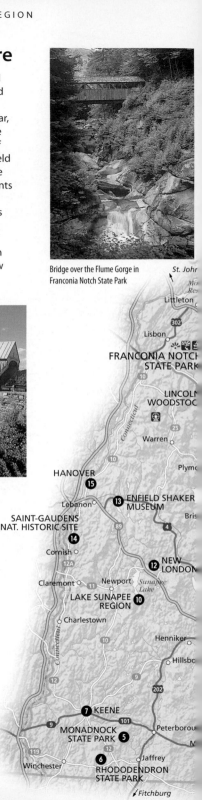

Bridge over the Flume Gorge in Franconia Notch State Park

Lengthy Cornish-Windsor Bridge outside Cornish

Getting Around

Interstates 93 and 89 are the largest and most popular north-south routes in the state, with numerous smaller roads branching off to more remote areas. Drivers should be aware of two New Hampshire realities: heavier traffic during peak fall-foliage season, especially on the weekends; and moose crossings. While moose sightings are thrilling, collisions with the huge animals can be extremely dangerous. Travelers should drive with caution at all times. The Amtrak "Northeaster" service stops in Exeter, Durham, and Dover. Travelers may also take Amtrak to White River Junction, Vermont, or to Boston and link up with a bus line from there. Commercial bus lines servicing the area include C&J Trailways, Concord Coach Lines, and Greyhound bus lines *(see p375)*. The state's largest airport is found in the south in Manchester *(see p374)*, although Maine's Portland International Airport is a good jumping-off point for northeastern New Hampshire.

For hotels and restaurants in this region see pp317–18 and pp336–8

Sights at a Glance

1. Portsmouth
2. Exeter
3. Hampton
4. America's Stonehenge
5. Monadnock State Park
6. Rhododendron State Park
7. Keene
8. Manchester
9. Concord
10. Lake Sunapee Region
11. *Canterbury Shaker Village pp264–5*
12. New London
13. Enfield Shaker Museum
14. Saint-Gaudens National Historic Site
15. Hanover
16. White Mountains/White Mountain National Forest
17. North Conway
18. Jackson
19. Pinkham Notch
20. Bretton Woods
21. Kancamagus Highway
22. Lincoln-Woodstock
23. Crawford Notch State Park
24. *Franconia Notch State Park pp276–7*

Tour

16. Lake Winnipesaukee *p268*

Key

▬▬ Highway
▬ Major road
▭▭▭ Minor road
▬ Scenic route
▰▰▰ Main railroad
— Minor railroad
▬ International border
▬ State border
△ Summit

Panorama of Saco River Valley from North Conway

0 kilometers   30
0 miles   30

For additional map symbols *see back flap*

❶ Portsmouth

When settlers established a colony here in 1623, they called it Strawbery Banke *(see pp258–9)* in honor of the berries blanketing the banks of the Piscataqua River. In 1653 the name was changed to Portsmouth, a reflection of the town's reputation as a hub of maritime commerce. First a fishing port, the town enjoyed prosperity in the 18th century as a link in the trade route between Great Britain and the West Indies. During the years leading up to the American Revolution, the town was a hotbed of revolutionary fervor and the place where colonial naval hero John Paul Jones (1747–92) built his warship, the *Ranger*.

Favorite with tourists: Portsmouth's Market Street

Exploring Portsmouth

Girded by the Piscataqua River and the North and South Mill ponds, compact Portsmouth is easily explored on foot. The town's past permeates the downtown core, especially along busy Market Street. Historic buildings, some constructed in the 19th century by wealthy sea captains, have been restored and turned into museums, boutiques, and restaurants. The city also has a number of brew pubs and microbreweries that produce local ales. More than 70 historic sites, including houses and gardens, can be found along the Portsmouth Harbor Trail, a walking tour of the Historic District.

Beautiful exterior of Moffatt-Ladd House in Portsmouth

🏛 Governor John Langdon House

143 Pleasant St. **Tel** (603)-436-3205. **Open** Jun–mid-Oct: 11am–4pm Fri–Sun. **Closed** Labor Day. 🅿 🎦 ♿

The son of a farmer of modest means, John Langdon (1741–1819) became one of Portsmouth's most prominent citizens. Langdon enjoyed great prosperity as a ship captain, merchant, and shipbuilder before becoming the governor of New Hampshire and a US senator. In 1784 he built this imposing Georgian mansion. The house is known for its ornate Rococo embellishments. The grounds feature a grape arbor and a large rose garden.

🏛 Moffatt-Ladd House

154 Market St. **Tel** (603) 436-8221. **Open** mid-Jun–mid-Oct: 11am–5pm Mon–Sat, 1–5pm Sun. 🅿 🎦 ♿

One of Portsmouth's first three-story homes, this elegant 1763 mansion was built for wealthy maritime trader and sea captain John Moffatt. The house's boxy design was a precursor to the Federal style of architecture that would later become popular

throughout the country. The house, located on the Portsmouth Harbor Trail, is graced by a grand entrance hall, a series of family portraits, and period furnishings.

🏛 Wentworth-Gardner House

50 Mechanic St. **Tel** (603) 436-4406. **Open** mid-Jun–mid-Oct: noon–4pm Wed–Sun. **Closed** public hols. 🅿 ♿

Also located on the Portsmouth Harbor Trail, this 1760 house is considered to be one of the best examples of Georgian architecture in the country. The house's beautiful exterior has rows of multi-paned windows, symmetrical chimneys, and a pillared entrance. The interior has 11 fireplaces, hand-painted wallpaper, and graceful carvings that took artisans a year to complete.

John Paul Jones

Born in Scotland, John Paul Jones (1747–92) went to sea as a cabin boy when he was only 12 years old. He worked his way up to being the first mate on a slave ship, then later the commander of a merchant vessel in Tobago. A hard taskmaster, Jones escaped to America before he was to go on trial for the deaths of several sailors he had punished. Regarded as an outlaw by the British, Jones went on to become an illustrious naval commander for the US. During the American Revolution, Jones led a series of daring raids up and down the British coast for which he was awarded a gold medal by Congress.

USS *Albacore*

Albacore Park, 600 Market St. **Tel** (603) 436-3680. **Open** mid-May–mid-Oct: 9:30am–5pm daily; mid-Oct–mid-Jan & mid-Feb–mid-May: 9:30am–4pm Thu–Mon. 🅿 🆆 **ussalbacore.org**

This sleek submarine was the fastest underwater vessel of its type when it was launched from the Portsmouth Naval Shipyard in 1953. It gives visitors access to the cramped quarters of submariners and an idea of what life was like for the 55 crew members. Exhibits in the visitor center trace the vessel's history.

🚌 Water Country

Rte 1 S of Portsmouth. **Tel** (603) 427-1111. **Open** Jun–Labor Day: call for hours. 🅿 🚻 🆆 **watercountry.com**

Thrilling water rides, a huge wave pool, a pirate ship, and a man-made lagoon await visitors to New England's largest water park. Smaller children can enjoy the slides and fountains in designated areas, while the more adventurous thrill-seekers can careen down looping water slides.

VISITORS' CHECKLIST

Practical Information
🗺 26,000. ℹ 500 Market St. or Market Sq. (603) 436-1118. 🖃 mid-May–Oct: 8:30am–1pm. 🎪 Market Square Day (Jun), Prescott Park Arts Festival (Jul–Aug daily). 🆆 **portsmouthchamber.org**

Transport
🚌 10 Ladd St. ✈ 36 Airline Ave.

🏛 Children's Museum of New Hampshire

6 Washington St., Dover (12 miles/ 20 km N of Portsmouth). **Tel** (603) 742-2002. **Open** 10am–5pm Tue–Sat (& Mon in summer), noon–5pm Sun. 🅿 🅰 🆆 **childrens-museum.org**

This facility features a riverside playground as well as interactive exhibits where kids can command a submarine, don lab coats to excavate dinosaur fossils, play musical instruments from around the world, and explore visual and textural patterns. There is also a human-scale kaleidoscope.

Popular destination on summer days: Water Country

0 meters 100
0 yards 100

Portsmouth City Center

① Gov. John Langdon House
② Moffatt-Ladd House
③ Wentworth-Gardner House

Key

🟦 Street-by-Street map *see pp258–9*

For map symbols *see back flap*

Street-by-Street: Strawbery Banke

This outdoor museum near the waterfront is located on
the very spot on which Portsmouth was founded. Tracing
the history of the town, this 10-acre (4-ha) site contains 40
historic buildings that depict life from 1695 to 1955. Those
houses open to the public are furnished in period style and
contain interesting collections of decorative arts, ceramics,
and assorted artifacts. Many of the buildings are set amid
gardens cultivated according to their eras, from early pioneer
herb gardens to formal Victorian flower beds.

Pitt Tavern
This Revolutionary War-
era inn was frequented
by George Washington.

Aldrich House and Garden
The garden of the restored Colonial
Revival home of poet Thomas Bailey
Aldrich (1836–1907) blooms with
flowers celebrated in
his verse.

COURT STREET

ATKINSON STREET

JEFFERSON STREET

COURT STREET

WHIDDEN PLACE

WASHINGTON STREET

Key

— Suggested route

0 meters   50

0 yards   50

★ Chase House
Built c.1762, this
elegant home is
furnished with
sumptuous pieces
from several
periods.

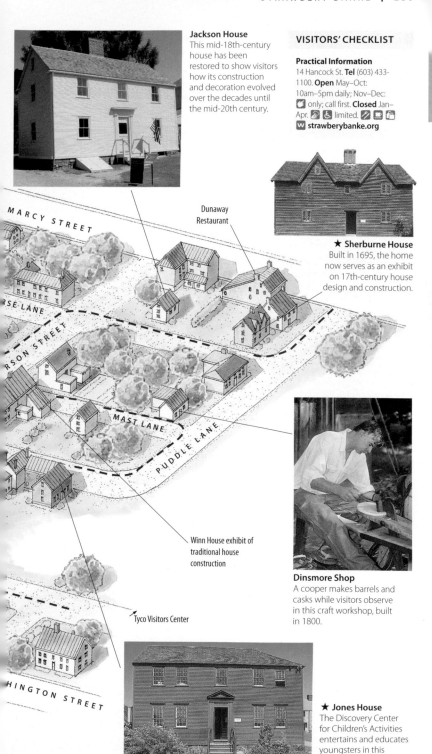

Jackson House
This mid-18th-century house has been restored to show visitors how its construction and decoration evolved over the decades until the mid-20th century.

Dunaway Restaurant

★ **Sherburne House**
Built in 1695, the home now serves as an exhibit on 17th-century house design and construction.

MARCY STREET

RSE LANE

RSON STREET

MAST LANE

PUDDLE LANE

Winn House exhibit of traditional house construction

Dinsmore Shop
A cooper makes barrels and casks while visitors observe in this craft workshop, built in 1800.

Tyco Visitors Center

HINGTON STREET

★ **Jones House**
The Discovery Center for Children's Activities entertains and educates youngsters in this c.1790 structure.

❷ Exeter

🏙 14,500. ✈ 15 miles (24 km) E in Portsmouth. ℹ 24 Front St (603) 772-2411. 🔲 exeterarea.org

The quiet little town of Exeter southwest of Portsmouth was much less tranquil during the century and a half leading up to the American Revolution (1775–83). The community sprang up around the falls linking the freshwater Exeter River and the salty Squamscott River. It was founded in 1638 by the Reverend John Wheelwright (1592–1679), an outspoken cleric who was thrown out of the Massachusetts colony for his radical views.

During the turbulent years leading up to American Independence, outraged townspeople openly defied the British government. They drove off officials who had been dispatched to cut down trees for the British Navy, burned their leaders in effigy, and finally declared independence from Britain, setting a precedent for the rest of the colonies.

Dominating the center of town, Phillips Exeter Academy stands as one of the country's most prestigious preparatory schools. The complex of more than 100 ivy-clad brick buildings fronted by manicured lawns was founded in 1781.

Other points of interest include the **Gilman Garrison House**, a late 17th-century fortified log building, and the **American Independence Museum**, which displays an original copy of the Declaration of Independence in mid-July, and also owns two drafts of the US Constitution.

🏛 **Gilman Garrison House**
12 Water St. **Tel** (603) 436-3205. **Open** call for opening hours. 🅿 🎥 obligatory. ♿

🏛 **American Independence Museum**
1 Governors Lane. **Tel** (603) 772-2622. **Open** late May–Oct: 10am–4pm Wed–Sat. 🅿 🎥 obligatory. 🖼 ✉

Exterior of the American Independence Museum in Exeter

❸ Hampton

🏙 15,000. ✈ 12 miles (19 km) N in Portsmouth. ℹ 1 Lafayette Rd. (603) 926-8718. 🔲 hamptonchamber.com

One of New Hampshire's oldest towns, Hampton is situated at the geographic center of the many state parks and public beaches that line Highway 1A, the coast road. Public recreation areas stretch from Seabrook Beach, a sandy shore dotted with dunes, to the rugged shoreline of **Odiorne Point State Park** in Rye to the north. The park has biking trails, tidal pools, and a boardwalk spanning a salt-water marsh. The park's Science Center also runs interpretive nature programs that are especially appealing to young visitors. Ten miles (6 km) to the south of the factory outlet shopping mecca of North Hampton, travelers will come upon the popular **Hampton Beach**. This miniature version of Atlantic City (without the gambling) comes complete with a venue that hosts big-name entertainers and an old-fashioned boardwalk lined with video arcades, ice cream shops, and stalls selling T-shirts and tacky souvenirs. Open year-round, Hampton Beach is busiest during hot summer months, when vacationers come to enjoy the miles of clean, golden beaches, including a separate area designated for surfers. Swimmers and jet skiers test the waters, para-sailers soar overhead, and deep-sea fishing and whale-watching charter boats are available from Hampton Harbor. Hampton Beach is not the place for people looking for quiet, but it is geared toward family fun, with game arcades, water slides, magic shows, and a series of free concerts and fireworks.

🏞 **Odiorne Point State Park**
Rte. 1A, Rye Beach. **Tel** (603) 436-7406. 🎥 Science Center: **Tel** (603) 436-8043. **Open** 10am–5pm daily (Nov–Mar: only Sat–Mon). **Closed** Jan 1, Thanksgiving, & Dec 25. 🅿 ♿ Park: **Open** year-round: 8am–dusk. 🅿

🏖 **Hampton Beach**
Tel (603) 926-8717. 🔲 hamptonbeach.org

Away from the casino and busy boardwalk, the blue skies and tranquil surf of Hampton Beach

❹ America's Stonehenge

Haverhill Rd., N. Salem. **Tel** (603) 893-8300. **Open** 9am–5pm daily. **Closed** Thanksgiving, Dec 25. 🖼 **W** stonehengeusa.com

Although not nearly as imposing as its British namesake, this is an intriguing place nonetheless. Believed to be one of the oldest man-made complexes this side of the Atlantic, the 30-acre (12-ha) grounds of America's Stonehenge are scattered with standing stones, walls, and stone chambers. Archaeologists, historians, and astronomers have argued for decades about the origins of the site, with credit going to everyone from ancient Greeks to wayward aliens. Today one of the most popular theories has Native American tribes constructing this megalithic complex as a giant calendar to measure the movements of the sun and the moon. Excavations have turned up a wealth of ancient remains, including stone pottery, tools, and petroglyphs that have been carbon-dated to between 3,000 and 4,000 years old. One of the more gruesome parts of the site is the 5-ton (4.5-tonne) Sacrificial Table, carved with grooves that researchers believe may have been troughs for collecting the blood of victims. Special events are held at the site during the spring and fall equinox and at the winter and summer solstice.

Mount Monadnock, popular with climbers and hikers

❺ Monadnock State Park

Off Rte. 124, W of Jaffrey. **Tel** (603) 532-8862. Campground reservations: (877) 647-2757. **Open** year-round. 🖼 🏕 **W** nhstateparks.org

Standing some 3,165 ft (965 m) high, Mount Monadnock has two claims to fame. It is said to be one of the world's most climbed mountains (it is not unusual to find several hundred hikers milling around its peak) and it has spawned a geological term. A "monad-nock" is an isolated hill or mountain of resistant rock rising above a plain that has been created by glacial activity.

The mountain's popularity has a lot to do with its campsites, scenic picnic areas, and numerous hiking trails. Within the 8-sq-mile (20-sq-km) park, there are 40 miles (64 km) of trails, many of which lead to the summit. The climb to the peak of the metamorphic schist pinnacle takes more than three hours, but on clear days intrepid hikers are rewarded with gorgeous views of all six New England states.

Markers along the trails have been erected in memory of such men of letters as Ralph Waldo Emerson (1803–82) and Henry David Thoreau (1817–62), both of whom climbed to the peak. The visitor's center gives an overview of the hiking trails and information about the local flora and fauna.

The campsites are open year-round and in the winter months the trails are popular with cross-country skiers.

❻ Rhododendron State Park

Off Rte. 119, W of Fitzwilliam. **Tel** (603) 532-8862. **Open** year-round: dawn–dusk daily. 🖼 ♿ partial.

New England's largest grove of wild rhododendrons bursts into a celebration of pink and white in June through mid-July. The 4.2-sq-mile (10.9-sq-km) park has more than 16 acres (6 ha) of giant rhododendron bushes. Walking through the rhododendrons, some of which grow to more than 20 ft (6 m) high, is a feast for the senses in summer, but there are floral highlights in other seasons as well. In the spring the woodland park is carpeted with trilliums. By May the apple trees are heavy with blossoms. During summer, visitors will find flowering mountain laurel and wildflowers such as jack-in-the-pulpit and delicate pink lady slippers. The park is equipped with picnic areas and hiking trails that offer spectacular views of Mount Monadnock and the surrounding peaks.

ancient ruins of America's Stonehenge

ene

50. ✈ 58 miles (93 km) W of
...ester. 🚌 𝒊 48 Central Sq.
352-1303.

...ene is the largest town in
...outhern New Hampshire's
Monadnock region. The nation's
first glass-blowing factory was
founded in nearby Temple in
1780, and soon after Keene
became one of the region's
hotbeds of arts and crafts. By
the 19th century the town was
famous for the production of
high-quality glass and pottery
and for its thriving wool mill.
The **Horatio Colony Museum** is
the former home of a descendant of the mill-owning family.
Its period furnishings give a
good idea of upper-class life in
the mid-19th century. Today the
focus of Keene's thriving cultural
life is Keene State College,
located on what is reputed to
be the widest Main Street in the
world. The college has several
theaters and art studios where
events are staged throughout
the year.

🏛 **Horatio Colony Museum**
199 Main St. **Tel** (603) 352-0460.
Open May–mid-Oct: 11am–4pm
Wed–Sun. 📷 obligatory.

Environs
Half a dozen covered bridges (see
p267) lie within a 10-mile (16-km)
radius of Keene, giving the region
the nickname "Currier and Ives
country." Road markers direct
drivers to each span. These "kissing
bridges," where young couples
would steal secret embraces as
they rode their buggy through
them, have long been favorite
subjects of photographers.

West Swanzey or Thompson Covered Bridge near Keene

❽ Manchester

🏔 105,250. ✈ 1 Airport Rd. 🚌
𝒊 54 Hanover St (603) 666-6600.
🎪 (603) 622-7531.

In 1805 a modest mill was built
on the east bank of the
Merrimack River. Fueled by
waterpower, the Amoskeag Mill
continued to expand until by
the beginning of the 20th
century it claimed the title as
the largest textile mill in the
world. At its peak, the
operation employed some
17,000 people and its complex
of brick buildings stretched for
more than 1 mile (1.5 km).
Today the structures that
once held workers and heavy
machinery are used for
restaurants, college classrooms,
and even residential housing.

This former industrial center
is now known for the **Currier
Museum of Art**, New
Hampshire's premier art
museum. In order to display
more of its impressive collection
of fine and decorative arts, the
museum has undergone an
ambitious renovation program
that added a massive 33,000 sq ft

(3,066 square meters) of space.
The entire second floor is
dedicated to 18th- and
19th-century American artists,
including the Impressionists
and members of the Hudson
River School. The museum's
holdings of modern paintings
and sculptures include works
by Pablo Picasso (1881–1973)
and Henri Matisse (1869–1954).
A gallery features regional
artists, while a café occupies
the sky-lit Winter Garden.

The museum's largest piece is
the nearby Zimmerman House,
designed in 1950 by pioneering
American architect Frank Lloyd
Wright (1867–1959) as an
exemplar of his Usonian homes.
Shuttles take visitors from the
museum to the house, and
guided tours (by advance
reservation April through
December) of its interior
highlight textiles and furniture
designed by Wright.

🏛 **Currier Museum of Art**
150 Ash St. **Tel** (603) 669-6144.
Open 11am–5pm Wed–Mon (from
10am Sat). 🏠 Zimmerman House:
Open Apr–Dec (call for tour hours).
🏠 📷 ♿ 🏠 🖥 📷 🅦 **currier.org**

❾ Concord

🏔 37,500. ✈ 25 miles (49 km) N of
Manchester. 🚌 𝒊 40 Commercial St.
(603) 224-2508.

New Hampshire's capital is a
quiet little town, but thanks to
its prominent political position,
it has been associated with a
number of important historica
figures. Mary Baker Eddy (18⁻
1910), founder of the Christ

The granite and marble façade of the State House, in Concord

Concord Coaches

In 1827 Concord-based wheelwright Lewis Downing and coach builder J. Stephens Abbot built the first Concord Coach, designed to withstand the unforgiving trails of the undeveloped West. The 1-ton (1-tonne) stagecoaches were, in their own way, as revolutionary as the Internet is today because they helped facilitate communications across the vast emerging hinterland. Wells Fargo, the famous transportation company, relied heavily on the coaches during the California Gold Rush (1848–55) to carry mail and passengers on parts of the route between New York City and San Francisco.

Science Church, spent much of her life here. The **Pierce Manse** was the one-time home of Franklin Pierce (1804–69), the 14th president of the US.

The 1819 **State House**, built from New Hampshire granite and Vermont marble, is one of the oldest in America. Inside the building are several hundred paintings of the state's better known residents and political figures.

In its heyday, the Eagle Hotel on Main Street, which is now used as an office building, hosted the likes of presidents Andrew Jackson and Benjamin Harrison, as well as aviator Charles Lindbergh, and former first lady Eleanor Roosevelt.

Concord schoolteacher Christa McAuliffe (1948–86) unfortunately gained her fame through tragedy. On January 28, 1986, McAuliffe boarded the *Challenger* space shuttle as the first civilian to be launched into space by NASA. Seventy-three seconds after the lift-off, with her husband and children watching from the ground, the shuttle exploded into a fireball and crashed, killing McAuliffe and her six fellow astronauts.

McAuliffe's memory lives on at **The McAuliffe-Shepard Discovery Center**, which also honors New Hampshire native and astronaut Alan Shepard, who was the first American to be launched into space. The futuristic center is capped by a giant glass pyramid. In addition to exhibits and planetarium shows, visitors can see a scale model of a space shuttle and a replica of the Mercury-Redstone rocket from Shepard's flight on May 5, 1961. Special astronomy programs are offered on Friday evenings.

🏠 Pierce Manse
14 Horseshoe Pond Lane. **Tel** (603) 225-4555. **Open** mid-Jun–early Sep: 11am–3pm Tue–Sat. 🚻 ✅ 🏠

🏠 State House
107 N Main St. **Tel** (603) 271-2154. Visitor center: **Open** year-round: 8am–4pm Mon–Fri. ♿ 🏠

🏛 The McAuliffe-Shepard Discovery Center
2 Institute Dr. **Tel** (603) 271-7827. **Open** 10am–5pm Mon–Thu, 10am–9pm Fri, 10am–5pm Sat & Sun. Call for show times. 🚻 ♿ 🏠 **Closed** week after Labor Day.
W starhop.com

⑩ Lake Sunapee Region

ℹ️ 143 Main St., New London (603) 526-6575 or (877) 526-6575.

This scenic region, dominated by 2,743-ft- (835-m-) high Mount Sunapee and the 10-mile- (16-km-) long lake at its feet, is a major drawing card for outdoor enthusiasts, particularly boaters and skiers. Many locals have vacation and weekend homes here, and an increasing number of retirees are also moving to the region, attracted not only by the scenery but also by the activity-oriented lifestyle.

Lake Sunapee (its name is said to be derived from the Penacook Indian words for "wild goose water") has been attracting visitors for well over a century. In the mid-19th century, trains and steamships used to transport tourists to hotels that rimmed the lake. The steamships have long since gone, but vacationers can rent canoes, picnic on the beach, or take a narrated trip on a sightseeing boat. **Mount Sunapee State Park**'s namesake peak attracts hikers and climbers during the summer months and skiers during the winter. The Mount Sunapee resort in the park is the largest ski area between Boston and the White Mountains.

🏞 Mount Sunapee State Park
Rte. 103. **Tel** (603) 763-5561. **Open** Jun–Labor Day. 🚻 ♿ Mount Sunapee Resort: **Tel** (603) 763-4020.

…ightseeing boat on Lake Sunapee

erbury Shaker Village

ded in 1792, this village was occupied for 200 aking it one of the longest-lasting communities of gious group in the country. Shakers also lived in by Enfield *(see p266)*. Their belief in strict separation the rest of the world and in celibacy eventually led to eir demise. The last member of this colony died in 1992, and now 25 of the original buildings are part of the village. Millponds, nature trails, and traditional gardens punctuate the 690-acre (280-ha) site. Skilled artisans re-create Shaker crafts, herbal products, and cooking.

Canterbury Shaker Village
The village is dominated by the central Dwelling House (below).

Shaker Brooms
The common flat broom was invented in 1798 by Shaker Brother Theodore Bates. Shakers believed that cleanliness mirrored spiritual purity.

★ **Dining Room**
This area once held as many as 60 Shakers per sitting.

KEY

① **Brethren's retiring room**

② **The belfry** is a distinctive shape and contains a bell made by Revere and Sons.

③ **Dormer rooms** were used for summer sleeping.

Key

☐ Illustrated building

1 Trustees' Office
2 The Infirmary
3 Meeting House
4 Dwelling House
5 Sisters' Shop
6 Carriage House
7 Creamery
8 Carpenter Shop
9 Fire House/Power House
10 Laundry
11 Shaker Box Lunch and Farm Stand
12 School House
13 Syrup Shop
14 Shaker Table
15 Visitor Center

VISITORS' CHECKLI

Practical Information
288 Shaker Rd., Canterbury.
Tel (603) 783-9511; Greenwood'.
Restaurant (603) 783-4238.
Open mid-May–Oct: 10am–5pm
daily; Nov & Dec: some weekends.
🏛 📷 🍴 🎁 🛍 **W** shakers.org

Popular Stop
Historic buildings, a restaurant, and a gift shop make Canterbury a favorite tourist destination.

Welcome to
CANTERBURY
Shaker Village
CREAMERY RESTAURANT
SHAKER GIFT SHOP
OPEN DAILY 10AM - 5PM

★ **Old Library and Archives**
The library contains 1,500 Shaker books and documents, and is open by appointment only.

★ **Sisters' Retiring Room**
Men and women had separate sleeping quarters. Each one is equipped with traditional Shaker furniture.

New London

28 miles (45 km) NW in
...on. Main St. (603) 526-
... or (877) 526-6575.
sunapeevacations.com

New London's perch atop a crest gives it an enviable view of the surrounding forests during the fall foliage season. The bucolic setting also serves as a wonderful backdrop for the town's rich collection of colonial and early 19th-century buildings. Of these, the architectural centerpiece is **Colby-Sawyer College**, an undergraduate liberal arts school founded in 1837. The college organizes numerous cultural programs, including plays, lectures, films, concerts, and art exhibitions. More cultural fun can be had farther down the street at the **New London Barn Playhouse**. Housed in a refurbished 1820s barn, the theater stages popular plays and musicals during the summer months.

Colby-Sawyer College in New London

Colby-Sawyer College
Main St. **Tel** (603) 526-2010.
Open year-round: 9am–5pm Mon–
Fri.

New London Barn Playhouse
84 Main St. **Tel** (603) 526-4631 or (603) 526-6710. **Open** mid-Jun–Sep: call for hours.

⑬ Enfield Shaker Museum

Rte. 4A, Enfield. **Tel** (603) 632-4346.
Open 10am–5pm Mon–Sat, noon–
5pm Sun (winter: closes 4pm).
shakermuseum.org

Facing religious persecution in Britain in the mid-18th century, several groups of Shakers, a sect that broke away from the Quakers, fled to North America under the spiritual guidance of Mother Ann Lee (1736–84). The Shaker village at Enfield was founded in 1793, one of 18 such communities in the US.

Between the founding of Enfield and the 1920s, the Shakers constructed more than 200 buildings, of which 13 remain. And while they farmed more than 4.6 sq miles (12 sq km)

of land, property was under the ownership of the community, not individuals. Members were celibate and they were strict pacifists, devoting their "hands to work and hearts to God." At one time the Enfield Shakers numbered over 300, but, as in similar communities, their numbers gradually dwindled. In 1923 the last 10 members moved to the Canterbury Shaker Village (see pp264–5) north of Concord. The last Canterbury Shaker died in 1992 at the age of 96.

The exhibits at the museum illustrate how the Shakers lived and worked. Visitors will come across fine examples of Shaker ingenuity, including one of their many inventions: sulfur matches. The buildings are filled with the simple but practical wooden furniture for which the Shakers, who were consummate craftspeople, were famous. The 160-year-old Great Stone Dwelling, the

largest such structure ever built by these industrious people, is a model of stately workmanship.

⑭ Saint-Gaudens National Historic Site

Rte. 12A N of Cornish-Windsor Bridge.
Tel (603) 675-2175. Buildings:
Open late May–Oct: 9am–4:30pm daily. Grounds: **Open** year-round.
nps.gov/saga

This national historic site celebrates the life of Augustus Saint-Gaudens (1848–1907), the preeminent US sculptor of his time. When he began to summer here in 1885, it marked the beginning of the town's evolution into an art colony. Artists, writers, and musicians alike were attracted to the town by the talent of Saint-Gaudens, whose family had emigrated to the US from Ireland when he was just a baby. Something of a world traveler, Saint-Gaudens became an apprentice cameo cutter in New York and later studied at the École des Beaux-Arts in Paris. He also won several commissions in Rome. By the time that he returned to New York, his reputation as a brilliant sculptor had been well established. His work, usually of heroic subject matter, can be found throughout the

Saint-Gaudens' angel

Great Stone Dwelling in the Enfield Shaker Museum

country. New England is home to many Saint-Gaudens masterpieces, including Boston's Shaw Memorial (1897).

Eventually Saint-Gaudens grew tired of the big-city pace, buying an old tavern near the Connecticut River and turning it into a home and studio.

Model for Boston's Shaw Memorial

Many of his greatest works were created here, including the famous statue of Abraham Lincoln (1809–65) in Lincoln Park, Chicago. Today this historic 1805 structure is filled with the sculptor's furniture and samples of his small, detailed sketches for large bronzes. A number of his sculptures are scattered around the 150-acre (61-ha) property, which is laid out with formal gardens and pleasing walking trails flanked by tall pines and hemlocks.

Environs

Just 2 miles (3 km) south of the Saint-Gaudens site, visitors will come upon the Cornish-Windsor Bridge. Spanning the Connecticut River between New Hampshire and Vermont, the structure is the longest

covered bridge in New England at 460 ft (140 m). Three other covered bridges can be found in the vicinity of Cornish.

⑮ Hanover

🏠 9,200. ✈ 6 miles (10 km) SE in Lebanon. 🚌 ℹ️ 216 Nugget Arcade Building (603) 643-3115.
🌐 **hanoverchamber.org**

Hanover, with a traditional village green ringed by historic brick buildings, is the archetypal New England college town. Situated in the upper valley region of the Connecticut River, it is a pleasant stop for visitors following the Appalachian Trail, which goes right through the center of town. Hanover is the home of **Dartmouth College**,

the northernmost of the country's Ivy League scho[...] The college was originally known as Moor's Indian Cha[...] School, and was founded in 1769 to educate and convert Abenaki Natives. Today some 4,500 students participate in programs that include one of the oldest medical schools in America, the Thayer School of Civil Engineering (1867), and the Amos Tuck School of Business Administration (1900). The school's famous graduates include statesman Daniel Webster (1782–1852) and former vice president Nelson Rockefeller (1908–79).

The college has a number of noteworthy sights. The **Baker/Berry Memorial Library** is decorated by a series of thought-provoking murals tracing the history of the Americas painted by Mexican artist José Clemente Orozco (1883–1949) in the early 1930s. The **Hood Museum of Art** has a diverse collection that includes Native American and African art, early American and European paintings, and works by such noted modern artists as Pablo Picasso (1881–1973).

🏛️ **Dartmouth College**
Tel (603) 646-1110. 📷 ♿

🏛️ **Baker/Berry Memorial Library**
Dartmouth College. **Tel** (603) 646-2560. **Open** year-round: call for hours. ♿

🏛️ **Hood Museum of Art**
Dartmouth College. **Tel** (603) 646-2808. **Open** year-round: 10am–5pm Tue & Thu–Sat, 10am–9pm Wed, noon–5pm Sun. 📷 ♿ ✉️ 🏠
🌐 **hoodmuseum.dartmouth.edu**

Gallery in Dartmouth's Hood Museum of Art in Hanover

Covered Bridges

American bridge builders began covering their wooden spans in the early 19th century to protect the truss work and planking from the harsh weather. Originally the bridges were built by locals, meaning that each one had design elements specific to its region. Covered bridges built in farming communities were wide enough and tall enough to accommodate a wagon loaded with hay. Bridges leading into town had the added luxury of pedestrian walkways. The bridges, though, were more than just river crossings. Fishermen cast their lines beneath the spans, children used them as platforms from which to dive into the water below, birds nested among the rafters, and social dances were sometimes held beneath their roofs.

One of New Hampshire's covered bridges outside Cornish

Tour of Lake Winnipesaukee

This stunning lake has a shoreline that meanders for 240 miles (386 km), making it the biggest stretch of waterfront in New Hampshire. Ringed by mountains, Winnipesaukee is scattered with 274 islands. Around its shores are sheltered bays and harbors, with half a dozen resort towns where visitors can enjoy activities ranging from canoeing to shopping for crafts and antiques.

Tips for Drivers

Tour length: 70 miles (113 km).
Starting point: Alton, at junction of Hwys 11 & 28.
Stopping-off points: Popular Weirs Beach eateries include Donna Jean's Diner and Patio Garden Restaurant. In Center Sandwich, Corner House Inn oozes historic Yankee style. Wolfeboro has many places to eat, including Wolfetrap Grill, Bailey's Bubble, and West Lake Asian Cuisine.

④ **Squam Lake**
This pristine body of water was where the movie *On Golden Pond* (1981) was filmed. The lake is ideal for boating and fishing.

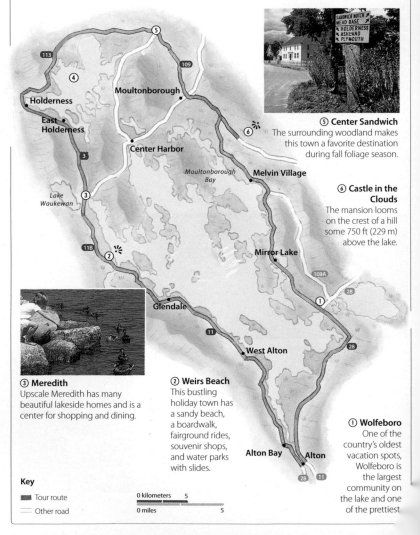

⑤ **Center Sandwich**
The surrounding woodland makes this town a favorite destination during fall foliage season.

⑥ **Castle in the Clouds**
The mansion looms on the crest of a hill some 750 ft (229 m) above the lake.

③ **Meredith**
Upscale Meredith has many beautiful lakeside homes and is a center for shopping and dining.

② **Weirs Beach**
This bustling holiday town has a sandy beach, a boardwalk, fairground rides, souvenir shops, and water parks with slides.

① **Wolfeboro**
One of the country's oldest vacation spots, Wolfeboro is the largest community on the lake and one of the prettiest

Key

▬▬ Tour route
‑‑‑ Other road

0 kilometers   5
0 miles   5

For map symbols *see back flap*

⑰ White Mountains/ White Mountain National Forest

ℹ️ Headquarters: 71 White Mountain Drive, Campton (603) 536-6100. 🔲 🌲 🔲 fs.fed.us/r9/ forests/white_mountain Camping: reservations: **Tel** (877) 444-6777. 🔲 **recreation.gov**

New Hampshire's heavily forested northland is an outdoor paradise, encompassing a national forest, several state parks, more than 1,200 miles (1,900 km) of hiking trails, several dozen lakes, ponds and rivers, and 23 campgrounds. The White Mountain National Forest, a small portion of which lies in neighboring Maine, sprawls over 1,203 sq miles (3,116 sq km).

The most beautiful wilderness area in the state, the National Forest is home to an abundance of wildlife, including a large population of moose. These giant members of the deer family are very shy, but they can be seen from the road at dawn or dusk, lumbering back and forth from their feeding grounds or standing in a swampy pond.

This region offers all manner of outdoor activities – from bird-watching and skiing to rock climbing and kayaking – but even less sporty travelers will revel in the spectacular scenery visible from their car. More than 20 summits soar to over 4,000 ft (1,200 m). Driving through the White Mountains,

Brightly colored engine of the Conway Scenic Railroad

Saco RANGER STATION · WHITE MOUNTAIN *National Forest*

Ranger station marker

visitors encounter one scenic vista after another: valleys flanked by forests of pine, waterfalls tumbling over rocky outcrops, and trout rivers hissing alongside the meandering roads.

In 1998 a stretch of road, the 100-mile- (161-km-) long White Mountains Trail, was designated as a National Scenic and Cultural Byway. The trail loops across the Mount Washington Valley, through Crawford Notch (see p275), North Conway, and Franconia Notch (see pp276–7).

Brilliant fall foliage colors, interspersed with evergreens, transform the rugged countryside into a living palette. The leaves of different trees manifest a rich variety of shades – flaming red maples, golden birch, and maroon northern red oaks. Driving during the fall can be a beautiful but slow-moving experience since thousands of "leaf peepers" are on the roads.

Accommodations can also be difficult to find unless booked well in advance.

⑱ North Conway

🔲 2,500. ✈️ 70 miles (112 km) SE in Portland, ME. ℹ️ 2617 Main St (603) 356-3171 or (800) 367-3364.

The gateway to the sublime beauty of the White Mountains, North Conway is, surprisingly, also a bustling shopping center. This mountain village now has more than 200 factory outlets and specialty shops lining its Main Street. Prices are low in the first place, even for designer names such as Calvin Klein, Ralph Lauren, and Tommy Hilfiger, but because there is no sales tax in New Hampshire, all purchases become even better bargains.

Locals are quick to point out that there are many other attractions in and around North Conway, including canoe trips on the Saco River and a ride into the mountains in an old-fashioned train aboard the **Conway Scenic Railroad**. At the **Story Land** theme park children can ride on an antique German carousel, a pirate ship, or Cinderella's coach.

🚂 Conway Scenic Railroad
Rte. 16 in North Conway. **Tel** (603) 356-5251 or (800) 232-5251. **Open** call for schedule. 🔲 🔲 🔲 🔲 **conwayscenic.com**

🎠 Story Land
Rte. 16 in Glen. **Tel** (603) 383-4186. **Open** Jul–Aug: 9am–6pm daily; late May–Jun & Labor Day–Columbus Day: 10am–5pm Sat–Sun. 🔲 🔲

Breathtaking view from Cathedral Ledge just outside North Conway

For hotels and restaurants in this region see pp317–18 and pp336–8

Red and white covered bridge leading into Jackson

⑲ Jackson

🏔 750. ✈ 77 miles (125 km) SE in Portland, ME. **ℹ** Rte. 16B (603) 383-9356 or (800) 866-3334.

This mountain village is tucked away on a back road off Route 16B, but drivers will not miss it because the entrance is marked by its distinctive red and white covered bridge. The picturesque 200-year-old community is, along with the nearby villages of Intervale, Bartlett, and Glen, the main center for accommodation in the Mount Washington area.

Jackson was at one time a favorite getaway spot for big-city Easterners, but the hard times of the Great Depression of the 1930s saw the town slip into disrepair. Developers rediscovered this quiet corner of New Hampshire in the 1980s and began restoring several of the town's best hotels.

Jackson is a popular base camp for winter sports enthusiasts because the region is blessed with more than 110 downhill ski runs and a network of more than 200 miles (320 km) of cross-country trails. The main ski centers are Black Mountain, the Wildcat Ski Area, and the Attitash Mountain Resort (see p363). With 273 acres (113 ha) of skiable terrain served by 12 lifts, Attitash is the state's biggest ski center.

Summer sports abound here as well. The region's numerous peaks and valleys make this prime hiking and mountain-biking country, and a restored 18-hole course gives golfers the chance to play a round against one of the most scenic backdrops in New England. After having worked up a sweat, bikers and hikers can cool off under the waterfalls of the Wildcat River in Jackson Village.

⑳ Pinkham Notch

ℹ Rte. 16 N of North Conway (603) 466-2721. **Open** 6:30am–10pm daily.

Named after Joseph Pinkham, who according to local lore explored the area in 1790 with a sled drawn by pigs, this rocky ravine runs between Gorham and Jackson. The lofty Presidential Range girds the western flank of Pinkham Notch, while the 4,415-ft (1,346-m) Wildcat Mountain looms to the east.

Backcountry adventurers love this part of the state because of its great variety of activities. Skiing at the Wildcat Ski Area is among the best in the state, and its high elevation makes for a long season, running from November to April. In the summer, visitors can ride to the summit aboard the aerial gondola. Picnic areas at the top offer great views of Mount Washington and the Presidential Range.

Hiking trails lace Pinkham Notch, including a section of the fabled Appalachian Trail (see pp26–7). These well-maintained paths range from less demanding nature walks suitable for whole families to lung-testing climbs best attacked by serious hikers. Along the way, visitors are led past some of the region's most captivating sights, including waterfalls, rivers, scenic overlooks, and pristine ponds tucked away in thick woodland.

Sublime beauty of the Presidential Range from Pinkham Notch

Striking exterior of the Mount Washington Hotel and Resort

Lucky travelers may spot raccoons, beaver, deer, and even the occasional moose.

㉑ Bretton Woods

🏨 550. ✈ 96 miles (155 km) SE in Portland, ME. ℹ (603) 745-8720 or (800) 346-3687. 📷
W visitwhitemountains.com

This tiny enclave situated on a glacial plain at the base of the Presidential Range has an unusual claim to fame: it hosted the United Nations Monetary and Financial Conference in 1944. The meetings established the International Monetary Fund and laid the groundwork for the World Bank, a response to the need for currency stability after the economic upheavals of World War II. The delegates also set the gold standard at $35 an ounce and chose the American dollar as the international standard for monetary exchange.

The setting for this vital meeting was the **Mount Washington Hotel and Resort** *(see p317)*. It is easy to imagine the reaction of delegates when they first caught sight of this grand Spanish Renaissance-style hotel from a sweeping curve in the road. Opened in 1902, the hotel's sparkling white exterior and crimson roof stand out in stark contrast to Mount Washington, looming 6,288 ft (1,917 m) skyward behind the edifice. The hotel has entertained a host of distinguished guests, including

British Prime Minister Sir Winston Churchill (1874–1965), inventor Thomas Edison (1847–1931), baseball star Babe Ruth (1895–1948), and three presidents.

Apart from its sublime setting, what makes the hotel so impressive is its sheer size. Designated a National Historic Landmark, the 200-room structure was built by 250 skilled craftsmen from Italy. Today the hotel is surrounded by more than 27 sq miles (70 sq km) of parkland, and its facilities include a 27-hole golf course laid out by the famous Scottish designer Donald Ross (1872–1948). Nearby Bretton Woods ski area *(see p363)* offers alpine skiing along with 62 miles (100 km) of cross-country trails.

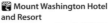

Sir Winston Churchill, a Mount Washington visitor

🍴 Mount Washington Hotel and Resort
Rte. 302, Bretton Woods. **Tel** (603) 278-1000 or (800) 314-1752. ♿ 📷
W mtwashington.com

Environs
The Mount Washington Valley, in which Bretton Woods is located, is dominated by the 6,288-ft (1,917-m) peak of

Mount Washington, the highe[st] in the northeastern United States. Other imposing peaks belonging to the Presidential Range – Adams, Jefferson, Madison, Monroe, and Eisenhower – surround Mount Washington, which has the dubious distinction of having the worst weather of any mountain in the world. Unpredictable snowstorms are not unusual, even during the summer months; the highest wind ever recorded on Earth was clocked here in April 1934: 230 mph (370 kph). During the last century, the mountain has claimed the lives of almost 100 people caught unaware by Mount Washington's temperamental climate. On clear days, however, when the mountain is in a good mood, nothing compares to the panoramic view from the top. Brave souls hike to the summit by one of the many trails, drive their own cars up the winding Mount Washington Auto Road, or puff their way slowly to the top in the deservedly famous **Mount Washington Cog Railroad**. Billed as "America's oldest tourist attraction," the railroad started operating in 1869.

The train, powered by steam locomotives, chugs its way up the cog track to the top of the mountain belching steam. The 3.5-mile (5.6-km) route to the top is one of the steepest tracks in the world, climbing at a heart-stopping 37 percent grade at some points. At the top, passengers can visit the Sherman Adams Summit Building, with the Summit Museum, and Mount Washington Observatory, which records weather conditions and conducts research.

🍴 Mount Washington Cog Railroad
Off Rte. 302, Marshfield Base Station. **Tel** (603) 278-5404 or (800) 922-8825. **Open** Apr–Dec: call for hours and train schedule. 🅿 ♿ 📷 🚻
W thecog.com

Mount Washington Cog Railroad

Perfect spot on Chocorua Lake for the view of Mount Chocorua

❷ Kancamagus Highway

Rte. 112 between Lincoln & Conway.
ℹ️ Saco District Ranger Station, 33 Kancamagus Hwy. (603) 447-5448.

Touted by many as the most scenic fall-foliage road in New England, this stretch of highway runs through the White Mountain National Forest (see p269) between Lincoln and Conway. The road covers about 34 miles (55 km) of Route 112 and offers exceptional vistas from the Pemi Overlook as it climbs 3,000 ft (914 m) through the

Sabbaday Falls, a highlight of the Kancamagus Highway

Kancamagus Pass. Descending into the Saco Valley, the well-traveled road joins up with the Swift River, following the aptly named waterway into Conway. The highway provides fishermen with easy access to the river, home to brook and rainbow trout.

Campgrounds and picnic areas along the entire length of highway give travelers ample opportunity to relax and eat lunch on the banks of cool mountain streams. Maintained by the US Forest Service, the campgrounds are equipped with toilets and one has shower facilities; most are operated on a first-come, first-served basis. Well-marked trails also allow drivers to stretch their legs in the midst of some of the most beautiful scenery in the state. One of the most popular trails is the short loop that leads travelers to the oft-photographed Sabbaday Falls. Closer to Conway, road signs guide drivers to several scenic areas that afford views of cascades, rapids, and rivers.

The area is home to a wide variety of wildlife, including resident birds such as woodpeckers and chickadees, as well as migratory songbirds who breed here in the summer. Larger inhabitants include deer, moose, and the occasional black bear.

Clark's Trading Post in North Woodstock

❷ Lincoln-Woodstock

🏠 1,300. ✈️ 66 miles (106 km) SW in Lebanon. ℹ️ Rte. 112 & Connector Rd., Lincoln (603) 745-6621 or (800) 227-4191. 🌐 **lincolnwoodstock.com**

Not including its convenient location near the White Mountains (see p269), the region's main attraction is **Clark's Trading Post**, a strange combination of circus acts, amusement park rides, and museums. Children especially love the trained bears and the over-the-top performers. A session at Clark's "blaster boat" marina, in which participants try to ram each other's boat, is where the younger set can blow off the steam that may have built up on a leaf-peeping drive.

Environs
Tiny Lincoln is located just 3 miles (5 km) northwest of North Woodstock. The town's location

at the western end of the Kancamagus Highway and at the southern entrance to Franconia Notch State Park *(see pp276–7)* have turned it into a base camp for both backwoods adventurers and stick-to-the-road sightseers. Nearby **Loon Mountain** is one of the state's premier ski resorts. However, in the summer it offers a number of activities, from guided nature walks and tours of caves to horseback riding, mountain biking, and a gondola ride to the summit.

Challenging climbing wall at Loon Mountain outside of Lincoln

Clark's Trading Post
Rte. 3, Lincoln. **Tel** (603) 745-8913. **Open** late May–mid-Oct: call for hours & show times.

Loon Mountain
E of I-93, near Lincoln. **Tel** (603) 745-8111 or (800) 229-5666. **W** loonmtn.com

View from the Willey House in Crawford Notch State Park

❷ Crawford Notch State Park

Rte. 302 between Twin Mountains & Bartlett. **i** (603) 374-2272 or (877) 647-2757. Camping: **Tel** (877) 647-2757 for reservations. **Open** mid-May–mid-Oct (campground until mid-Dec).

This narrow pass, which squeezes through the sheer rock walls of Webster and Willey mountains, gained notoriety in 1826. One night a severe rain sent tons of mud and stone careening into the valley below, heading straight for the home of innkeeper Samuel Willey and his family. Alerted by the sounds of the avalanche, the family fled outdoors, where all seven were killed beneath falling debris. Ironically the lethal avalanche bypassed the house, leaving it unscathed. Several writers, including New Englander Nathaniel Hawthorne *(see p34),* have immortalized the tragedy in literature. The house still stands today and is now in service as a visitors center.

Once the notch was threatened by overlogging. However, the establishment of the state park in 1911 has ensured protection of this rugged wilderness. Today white-water boaters come here to test their mettle on the powerful Saco River, which carves its way through the valley. Fishermen ply the park's more tranquil ponds and streams in search of sport and a tasty dinner of trout or salmon.

People who prefer to keep their feet dry can still enjoy the water on a short hiking trail leading to the Arethusa Falls. Towering more than 200 ft (61 m) in the air, this magnificent cascade is New Hampshire's tallest waterfall. Elsewhere drivers will get wonderful views of the Silver Cascades and Flume Cascades waterfalls without leaving the comfort of their car.

Robert Frost and New Hampshire

The natural beauty of New Hampshire was an inspiration to one of America's best-loved poets: Robert Frost (1874–1963). Born in San Francisco, California, the four-time winner of the Pulitzer Prize moved to Massachusetts with his family when he was 11. After working as a teacher, a reporter, and a mill hand, Frost moved to England in 1912. Upon his return to the US in 1915, Frost settled in the Franconia Notch area *(see pp276–7).* The majestic setting inspired him to pen many of his greatest works, including his famous poem *Stopping by Woods on a Snowy Evening* (1923).

Robert Frost farm in Derry, New Hampshire

㉕ Franconia Notch State Park

This spectacular mountain pass carved between the Kinsman and Franconia ranges is graced with some of the state's most spectacular natural wonders. Foremost among them was the Old Man of the Mountain, a rocky outcropping on the side of a cliff that resembled a man's profile, until the nose and forehead came crashing down in 2003. Other attractions compensate for the loss including a boardwalk and stairways which lead visitors through the Flume Gorge, a narrow, granite chasm slashed in two by the Flume Brook, while an aerial tramway carries passengers to the summit of Cannon Mountain in eight minutes. Also within the park is Boise Rock, a picnic area by a mountain spring that offers views of the Cannon Cliffs and Echo Lake.

Glacial Boulder
This glacial boulder is one of the sights on the Flume Trail.

Key

▬▬▬ Interstate

▬▬▬ Major road

▬▬▬ Minor road

– – Walking trail

– – Aerial tramway

···· Bus shuttle

★ The Basin
The waterfall at the Basin empties into a large granite pothole.

Kinsman Pond Trail

Cascad

Basin-Cascade Trail

Indian Head Trail

Mount Pemigewasset Trail

Cascade Brook Trail

The Basin

Pemi Trail

Recreational.T

To Concord

93

To Plymouth

3

P

The Pool

The Flume

Flume Slide Trail

Liberty Spring Trail

★ Flume Gorge
The granite walls of this narrow gorge tower more than 90 ft (27 m) above visitors walking along the boardwalk. A two-mile (3-km) self-guided trail leads hikers past points of interest.

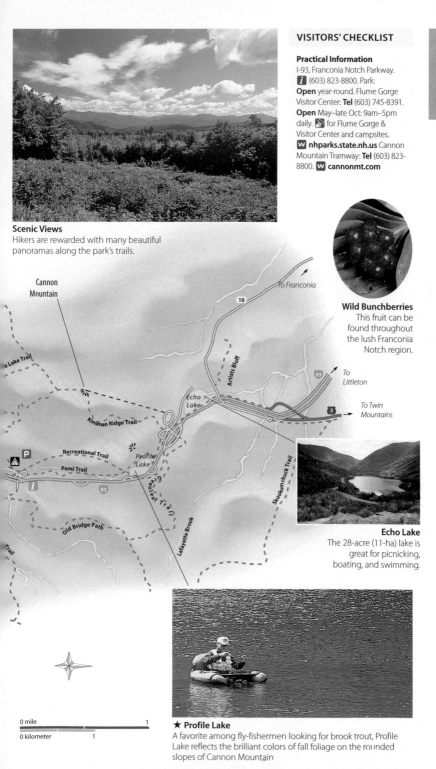

Scenic Views
Hikers are rewarded with many beautiful panoramas along the park's trails.

VISITORS' CHECKLIST

Practical Information
I-93, Franconia Notch Parkway.
📋 (603) 823-8800. Park:
Open year-round. Flume Gorge
Visitor Center: **Tel** (603) 745-8391.
Open May–late Oct: 9am–5pm
daily. 🎫 for Flume Gorge &
Visitor Center and campsites.
Ⓦ **nhparks.state.nh.us** Cannon
Mountain Tramway: **Tel** (603) 823-
8800. Ⓦ **cannonmt.com**

Wild Bunchberries
This fruit can be found throughout the lush Franconia Notch region.

Cannon Mountain

To Franconia

To Littleton

To Twin Mountains

e Lake Trail

Kinsman Ridge Trail

Artists Bluff

Echo Lake

Recreational Trail

Pemi Trail

Profile Lake

Skookumchuck Trail

Boat Leat Trail

Old Bridge Path

Lafayette Brook

Echo Lake
The 28-acre (11-ha) lake is great for picnicking, boating, and swimming.

0 mile   1

0 kilometer   1

★ Profile Lake
A favorite among fly-fishermen looking for brook trout, Profile Lake reflects the brilliant colors of fall foliage on the rounded slopes of Cannon Mountain.

For map symbols *see back flap*

MAINE

Maine truly is the great outdoors. More than 5,500 miles (8,850 km) of inlets, bays, and harbors make up its spectacular coastline. Inland deep forests and jutting mountain peaks complement 32,000 miles (51,500 km) of rivers and 6,000 glacial lakes. However, for all its wild mystique, Maine also includes quaint villages, appealing cities, and discount shopping meccas.

Maine has a long and rich history. While some historians maintain that the Vikings probed the rocky coast as early as the 11th century, European settlement began in earnest 500 years later, beginning with the Popham Beach colony of 1607. Although this original colony was short-lived, it spawned a succession of similar settlements at Monhegan (1622), Saco (1623), and Georgeana (1624). The last – renamed York *(see p282)* in 1652 – became the English America's first chartered city in 1642.

While Maine has always been one of the more sparsely populated states in the Union, it has been at the center of numerous territorial disputes, beginning with its abrupt seizure by Massachusetts in 1652 (an unhappy forced marriage, which ended in 1820 when Maine was granted statehood). Between 1675 and 1748 a series of four bloody wars was fought between British colonials and their French counterparts in Quebec. At the outset of the Revolutionary War (1775–83), Portland *(see pp284–7)* was bombarded and burned by the British as an example to other colonies harboring similar anti-Loyalist sentiments.

Traveling through Maine it is easy to see what all the fuss was about. The state's trove of unspoiled wilderness is interspersed with wonderfully preserved relics of its past. Beautiful Colonial homes can be found throughout the state. The importance of seafaring in the region's history is evident in the lighthouses *(see p283)*, maritime museums, and the sea captains' mansions found up and down the coast. And although tourism is now Maine's number one industry, the state has remained remarkably undeveloped, retaining much of the natural splendor that first attracted settlers so many centuries ago.

Hot summer shoreline along Old Orchard Beach

◀ The rocky Maine coastline as seen from the town of Ogunquit

Exploring Maine

Maine's most popular attractions are found dotted along its coast, beginning in the southeast with the beach playgrounds of Ogunquit *(see pp282–3)*, Old Orchard *(see p283)*, and the resort towns of the Kennebunks *(see p283)*. The scenery gets more dramatic as travelers move north through Boothbay Harbor *(see p289)*, Pemaquid Point *(see p289)*, and Muscongus Bay. The tiny villages are perfect starting points for sailing and kayaking excursions. Yachts and windjammers ply the waters of the Penobscot Bay region *(see pp290–91)*, while Acadia National Park *(see pp292–3)* stands as Maine's coastal jewel. Farther north, the rising sun first strikes the US at Cobscook Bay. World-class hiking, boating, and mountain-biking opportunities are found inland among the state's many mountains, lakes, and rivers.

Key

━━━ Highway
━━ Major road
┄┄┄ Minor road
━━ Scenic route
– – Track
•━•━ Main railway
━━ Minor railway
▬▬ International border
▬▬ State border
△ Summit

Stone fortifications at Fort William Henry on Pemaquid Point

Getting Around

Interstate 95 is the only major artery in the state. As a result, the smaller scenic routes along the coastline are often congested with summer traffic. Many coastal towns can be reached from Boston by Greyhound bus line. Amtrak runs a service from Boston to Portland with stops en route. Maine State Ferry Service has numerous routes to and from various seashore destinations. Both Portland and Bangor have international airports. The scarcity of public roads in northern Maine means that occasionally logging roads are used, which are operated much like toll roads and are best tackled with four-wheel drive vehicles.

For hotels and restaurants in this region see pp318–19 and pp338–9

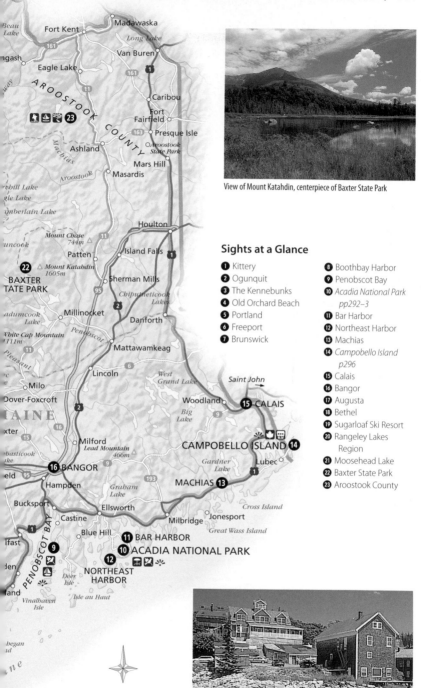

View of Mount Katahdin, centerpiece of Baxter State Park

Sights at a Glance

1. Kittery
2. Ogunquit
3. The Kennebunks
4. Old Orchard Beach
5. Portland
6. Freeport
7. Brunswick
8. Boothbay Harbor
9. Penobscot Bay
10. *Acadia National Park pp292–3*
11. Bar Harbor
12. Northeast Harbor
13. Machias
14. *Campobello Island p296*
15. Calais
16. Bangor
17. Augusta
18. Bethel
19. Sugarloaf Ski Resort
20. Rangeley Lakes Region
21. Moosehead Lake
22. Baxter State Park
23. Aroostook County

0 kilometers 30

0 miles 30

Picturesque Stonington village on Deer Isle

For additional map symbols *see back flap*

1 Kittery

9,500. 49 miles (78 km) NE in Portland. I-95 and US Rte. 1, (207) 439-1319. **mainetourism.com**

The southern coast of Maine begins at the Piscataqua River and Kittery, a town with a split personality. Founded in 1647, Kittery boasts the oldest church in the state, the 1730 **First Congregational Church**. Many fine old mansions line the streets, including the John Bray House, one of the oldest dwellings in Maine. **Fort McClary**, now a state historic site, has fortifications dating to the early 1800s and a hexagonal blockhouse, and the **Kittery Historical and Naval Museum** is filled with ship models and exhibits explaining maritime history. Despite its wealth of historical attractions, Kittery is best known for a more contemporary lure – the more than 100 factory outlet stores promising bargains along Route 1, where shoppers can buy name brands at a discount.

First Congregational Church
23 Pepperrell Rd. **Tel** (207) 439-0650. 8am & 10am Sun.

Fort McClary State Historic Site
Rte. 103 E of Kittery. **Tel** (207) 384-5160. **Open** late May–Sep: 9am–dusk daily.

Kittery Historical and Naval Museum
Rogers Rd. **Tel** (207) 439-3080. **Open** Jun–mid-Oct: 10am–4pm Tue–Sat; call for winter hours. partial.

Hexagonal Fort McClary block-house in Kittery

Environs

Four miles (6 km) from Kittery, visitors will come upon York Village. Settled in the 1630s, the village later grew into an important trading center, its wharves and warehouses filled with treasures from the lucrative West Indies trade. A collection of nine historic buildings maintained by the Old York Historical Society, **Old York** traces town history over three centuries. A repository for historical items, Old York has a superb collection of regional decorative arts housed in more than 30 period rooms and galleries. Tours begin at Jefferds' Tavern, a colonial hostelry, and include two historic homes, a 1745 one-room schoolhouse, and the John Hancock Warehouse, named after its owner, an original signatory of the Declaration of Independence. Down the street, the 1719 Old Gaol (jail) stands as one of the country's oldest public buildings. Dark, foreboding dungeons tell of harsh conditions faced by the felons who served their sentences within the jail's 3-ft- (1-m-) thick walls.

Old York
Lindsay Rd. **Tel** (207) 363-4974. **Open** Jun–mid-Oct: 9:30am–4pm Mon–Sat. last tour at 4pm. indoors. **oldyork.org**

2 Ogunquit

900. 36 miles (58 km) NE in Portland. 36 Main St (207) 646-2939. **ogunquit.org**

It is easy to see why the Abenaki Indians called this enclave Ogunquit, or "Beautiful Place by the Sea." Maine beaches do not come any better. From mid-May to Columbus Day, trolleys shuttle visitors to this powdery three-mile (5-km) stretch of sand and dunes that curves around a backdrop of rugged cliffs. Atop the cliffs is the 1.25-mile (2-km) Marginal Way, a footpath that offers walkers dramatic vistas of the ocean. Perkins Cove, home of the only pedestrian drawbridge in the US, is a quaint jumble of fishermen's shacks now transformed into art galleries, shops, restaurants, and docks with fishing and cruise boats.

Lobster trap buoys

This picturesque outpost attracted an artist's colony as early as 1890, establishing it as a haven for the arts. The handsome **Ogunquit Museum of American Art** was built in 1952 by the

Scenic ocean vista at Marginal Way in Ogunquit

For hotels and restaurants in this region see pp318–19 and pp338–9

eccentric but wealthy Henry Strater, who served as its director for more than 30 years. Constructed of wood and local stone, the museum has wide windows to allow views of the rocky cove and meadows. A 3-acre (1-ha) sculpture garden and lawns also make the most of the breathtaking setting. The permanent collection includes art by many notable American painters.

🏛 **Ogunquit Museum of American Art**

543 Shore Rd. **Tel** (207) 646-4909. **Open** May–Oct: 10am–5pm daily. **Closed** Labor Day. 📷
🌐 ogunquitmuseum.org

❸ The Kennebunks

✈ 30 miles (48 km) NE in Portland. ℹ 17 Western Ave., Kennebunk (207) 967-0857.
🌐 visitthekennebunks.com

First a thriving port and busy shipbuilding center, then a summer retreat for the wealthy, the Kennebunks are made up of two villages, Kennebunkport and Kennebunk.

The profusion of fine Federal and Greek Revival structures in Kennebunkport's historic village is evidence of the fortunes made in shipbuilding and trading from 1810 to the 1870s. With its 100-ft- (30-m-) tall white steeple and belfry, the 1824 South Congregational Church is a favorite subject for photographers. History of a different sort can be found at the **Seashore Trolley Museum**, where some 200 antique streetcars are housed, including one vehicle from New Orleans named "Desire." Visitors can embark on a tour of the countryside aboard one of the restored trolleys.

The scenic drive along Route 9 offers views of surf along rocky Cape Arundel. At Cape Porpoise hungry travelers can sample lobster pulled fresh from the Atlantic. Kennebunk is

Kennebunkport signpost

famous for its beaches, most notably Kennebunk Beach, which is actually three connected strands. One of the town's most romantic historic homes is the 1826 Wedding Cake House. According to the local lore, George Bourne was unexpectedly called to sea before his marriage. Although a very hastily arranged wedding took place, there was no time to bake the traditional wedding cake. Instead, the shipbuilder vowed to his bride that upon his return he would remodel their home to look like a wedding cake. Today the Gothic spires, ornate latticework, and ginger-bread trim offer proof that Bourne was a man of his word. Housed in four restored 19th- century buildings, **The Brick Store Museum** offers glimpses into the past with displays of decorative arts. It also offers architectural walking tours of the town's historic area (May–October).

Maine's Lighthouses

For centuries mariners have been guided to safety by Maine's picturesque lighthouses. The coast is dotted with 63 such beacons, some accessible from the mainland and others perched on offshore islands. Portland Head Light was commissioned by the country's first president, George Washington (1732–99), and built in 1791, making it the oldest lighthouse in the state. It, like several other beacons, is open to the public and houses a small museum focusing on local marine and military history.

Nubble Lighthouse near Old York

🏛 **Seashore Trolley Museum**
195 Log Cabin Rd., Kennebunkport. **Tel** (207) 967-2712. **Open** late May–mid-Oct: 10am–5pm daily; early May & late Oct: 10am–5pm Sat–Sun. 📷 ♿ 🌐 trolleymuseum.org

🏛 **The Brick Store Museum**
117 Main St., Kennebunk. **Tel** (207) 985- 4802. **Open** year-round: 10am–4:30pm Tue–Fri, 10am–1pm Sat. **Closed** pub hols. 📷
🌐 brickstoremuseum.org

❹ Old Orchard Beach

🏘 9,000. ✈ 13 miles (21 km) NE in Portland. 🚌 ℹ 11 First St. (207) 934-2500 or (800) 365-9386.

One of Maine's oldest seashore resorts, Old Orchard Beach's 7 miles (11 km) of sandy shoreline and low surf make it a favorite spot for swimming. Kids love the pier lined with game booths, food stands, a roller coaster, a 60-ft (18-m) water slide, and a 36-hole miniature golf course with waterfalls. A floating marina caters to water sports.

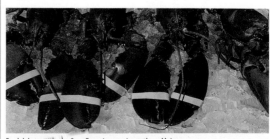

Fresh lobster from the Cape Porpoise area in southern Maine

❺ Portland

Poet and Portland native Henry Wadsworth Longfellow (1807–82) described Maine's largest city as "the beautiful town that is seated by the sea." Longfellow was inspired by Portland's fortunate location on the crest of a peninsula with expansive views of Casco Bay and the Calendar Islands on three sides. Once a prosperous port and an early state capital, Portland has been devastated by no less than four major fires, resulting in a preponderance of sturdy stone Victorian buildings that line many of its streets today.

Distinctive building in Portland's downtown arts district

Exploring Portland

A thriving arts community and a downtown with interesting shopping and dining are all part of a stroll along Congress Street and through the restored Old Port Exchange area (see pp286–7). The West End has fine homes and a splendid Western Promenade overlooking the water. The working waterfront and nearby beaches all add to the city's charm and atmosphere.

🏛 Neal Dow Memorial

714 Congress St. **Tel** (207) 773-7773.
Open 11am–4pm Mon–Fri.
Neal Dow (1804–97), one of Portland's prominent citizens, built this Federal-style mansion in 1829. Twice serving as the city's mayor, Dow was an abolitionist and prohibitionist who also championed the causes of women's rights and prison reform. The Dow family's furnishings, paintings, china, and silver are displayed. The home is also the headquarters of The Maine Women's Christian Temperance Union.

🏛 Victoria Mansion

109 Danforth St. **Tel** (207) 772-4841.
Open May–Oct: 10am–4pm Mon–Sat, 1–5pm Sun; late Nov & Dec: 11am–4:30pm daily. **Closed** Jan–Apr, Jul 4, Nov & Dec 25. 🎟 📷 every half hour. 📷

This sumptuous brownstone villa was completed in 1860 to serve as the summer home of Ruggles hotelier Sylvester Morse (c.1816–93). The interior has extraordinary interior detail, such as painted trompe l'oeil walls and ceilings, wood paneling, marble mantels, and a flying staircase.

🏛 Portland Museum of Art

7 Congress Sq. **Tel** (207) 775-6148.
Open year-round: 10am–5pm Tue, Wed, Thu, Sat, Sun, 10am–9pm Fri; late May–mid-Oct: 10am–5pm Mon. 🎟
♿ 🖥 portlandmuseum.org
Portland's premier fine art collection fills three distinctive buildings, spanning Federal, Beaux-Arts,

and post- modern design. One gallery showcases paintings and extensive graphic art by the Portland area's most famous artist, Winslow Homer (1836–1910). Other highlights include works by Andrew Wyeth (1917–2009), Paul Gauguin (1848–1903), and Pablo Picasso (1881–1973). Also on display are glass, ceramics, and furniture.

Victoria Mansion, with its lavishly decorated interior

Portland City Center

① Neal Dow Memorial
② Victoria Mansion
③ Portland Museum of Art
④ Children's Museum & Theatre of Maine
⑤ Wadsworth-Longfellow House

Coastal fishing on the outskirts of Portland

🏛 Children's Museum & Theatre of Maine

142 Free St. **Tel** (207) 828-1234.
Open year-round: 10am–5pm Tue–Sat, noon–5pm Sun; May–Sep: 10am–5pm Mon. **Closed** public hols. 🅿 📷

This historic brick building houses three floors of interactive exhibits, including a tidepool touch tank, a replica space shuttle, and a camera obscura. Young actors occasionally perform shows in the Children's Theatre.

⌂ Wadsworth-Longfellow House

489 Congress St. **Tel** (207) 879-0427.
Open May–Oct: 10am–5pm daily (from noon Sun). 🅿 📷 ♿ first floor. 📷

Poet Henry Wadsworth Longfellow grew up in this 1785 house, which contains family mementos, portraits, and furnishings.

⌂ George Tate House

1270 Westbrook St. **Tel** (207) 774-6177.
Open Jun–mid-Oct: 10am–4pm Wed–Sat, 1–4pm 1st Sun of month. **Closed** Oct–May, Jul 4, & Labor Day. 🅿

In 1755 George Tate, an agent of the British Royal Navy, constructed an elegant gambrel-roofed home with rich wood paneling, patterned floors, a dogleg staircase, and eight fireplaces. Now a National Historic Landmark, the house has fine period furnishings. Tours of the garden are on the first Wednesday of the month.

🏛 Maine Narrow Gauge Railroad Co. & Museum

58 Fore St. **Tel** (207) 828-0814.
Open 10am–4pm Mon–Fri (daily during train season). ♿ Train ride: **Open** mid-May–Oct on the hour; call for other times. 🅿

Scenic trips along a 3-mile (5-km) stretch of the waterfront are the highlight of this museum dedicated to the railroad that served much of Maine from the 1870s to the 1940s. Exhibits include vintage locomotives.

⌂ Portland Observatory

138 Congress St. **Tel** (207) 774-5561.
Open late May–mid-Oct: 10am–5pm daily. **Closed** Jul 4. 🅿 📷 ♿ 📷

Constructed in 1807, this octagonal landmark is the last surviving 19th-century signal tower on the Atlantic. The 102-step climb to the upper deck is worth the effort.

🏛 Museum at Portland Head Light at Fort Williams Park

1000 Shore Rd. **Tel** (207) 799-2661.
Open late May–mid-Oct: 10am–4pm daily; mid-Apr–May & mid-Oct–Dec: 10am–4pm Sat & Sun. 🅿 ♿

First illuminated in 1791 by order of President George Washington (1732–99), the lighthouse has been the subject of poetry, postage stamps, and photographs. The keeper's house is now a museum with exhibits on the history of the world's beacons. The large surrounding park, just 4 miles (6.5 km) from downtown, has a beach and picnic areas.

Portland Observatory atop Munjoy Hill

On the map (left column):

FRANKLIN ARTERIAL

Maine Narrow Gauge Railroad Co. & Museum

Convention, Visitors Bureau & Information Center ℹ

Maine State Pier

United States Customs House

Mariner's Church

Portland Pier

0 meters 400
0 yards 400

Key

▪ Street-by-Street map *see pp286–7*

Street-by-Street: Old Port

This once-decaying neighborhood near the harbor has
been restored and is now the city's liveliest area, filled
with shops, art galleries, restaurants, and bars. The Old
Port's narrow streets are lined with classic examples
of Victorian-era commercial architecture, including
venerable structures that once served as warehouses
and ships' chandleries. From the docks, ships take
passengers out for deep-sea fishing excursions and
harbor tours. Cruises include mail-boat rides and
excursions to the Calendar Islands, where visitors can
enjoy everything from cycling to sea kayaking.

Lively District
The Old Port has numerous pubs and
outdoor terraces.

Centennial Block
has a facade made
of Maine granite.

Charles Q. Clapp Block
This distinctive building was
designed by self-taught
architect Charles Quincy
Clapp in 1866.

First National Bank is a
typical example of Queen
Anne commercial style.
Its sandstone and brick
exterior features a corner
tower and tall chimneys.

Mary L. Deering Block,
built for the prominent
Deering family, is a mix
of Italian and Colonial
Revival styles.

Dolphins Statue
The statue
is situated in the
small cobblestone
area in the middle
of the Old
Port district.

Seaman's Club
Built after the devastating fire of
1866, the building is known for its
striking Gothic windows.

For hotels and restaurants in this region see pp318–19 and pp338–9

★ **United States Custom House**
Built following the Civil War (1861–5), this regal building contains gilded ceilings, marble staircases, and chandeliers.

Antique shops can be found throughout the Old Port district.

State of Maine Armory was designed to resemble a fortress and once was home to several units of the reserve militia known as the National Guard.

0 meters 50
0 yards 50

Key

— Suggested route

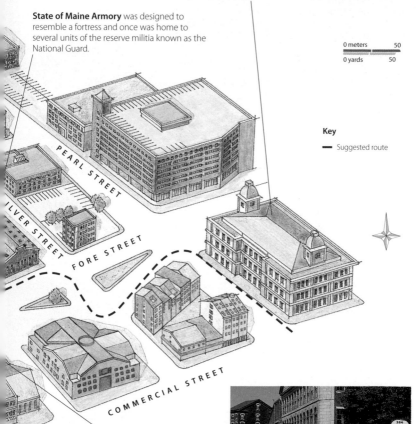

★ **Mariner's Church**
Built in 1828, the building is an eclectic mix of Greek Revival and Federal styles, and is now used to house a variety of shops and businesses.

❻ Freeport

🏘 7,000. ✈ 17 miles (31 km) SW in Portland. ℹ 23 Depot St. (207) 865-1212 or (800) 865-1994.
🌐 **freeportusa.com**

Although Freeport dates back to 1789, shoppers would argue that it did not arrive on the scene until 1917, when the first L.L. Bean clothing store opened its doors. Today this retail giant is open 24 hours a day, 365 days a year, and, with more than 3.5 million customers annually, L.L. Bean is easily Maine's biggest man-made attraction. Since the 1980s more than 150 other brand-name outlets have opened here.

Travelers who make it past the shops will discover a working harbor in South Freeport, where seal-watching tours and sailing cruises depart. The shoreline includes **Wolfe's Neck Woods State Park**, 233 acres (94 ha) of tranquility wrapped along Casco Bay.

Freeport's most unusual sight is the **Desert of Maine**. Originally a late-1700s farm, the area was severely over-tilled and over-logged. The topsoil eventually disappeared altogether, giving way to glacial sand deposits and creating a 40-acre (16-ha) desert of sand dunes. Visitors can walk the nature trails with a guide who narrates the history of the area, or ride on an open cart. The farm museum is housed in a 1783 barn.

L.L. Bean and Outlet Shopping

Leon Leonwood Bean (1872–1967) likely would be amazed if he could see the result of his dislike for cold, wet feet. The hunting shoe he developed in 1912 with leather uppers on rubber overshoe bottoms began a company that now claims more than a billion dollars in sales worldwide and carries anything needed for outdoor excursions. Bean's showroom has grown into a mammoth flagship store that includes a 785-sq-ft (73-sq-m-) pond stocked with trout.

Bust of L.L. Bean

🏞 **Wolfe's Neck Woods State Park**
Wolfe's Neck Rd. **Tel** (207) 865-4465.
Open Apr–Oct: 9am–dusk daily. 🏞
🚻 ♿

🏜 **Desert of Maine**
95 Desert Rd. **Tel** (207) 865-6962.
Open May–mid-Oct: tours 9am–4:30pm daily. 🏞 ♿
🌐 **desertofmaine.com**

❼ Brunswick

🏘 21,000. ✈ 33 miles (53 km) SW in Portland. 🚌 ℹ 2 Main St., Topsham (207) 725-8797.

Brunswick is best known as the home of Bowdoin College and as the land entry for the scenic panoramas of the town of Harpswell – a peninsula and three islands jutting out into Casco Bay.

Founded in 1794, the college claims a number of distinguished alumni, including explorers Robert Peary (1856–1920) and Donald MacMillan (1874–1970). The **Peary-MacMillan Arctic Museum**

Peary-MacMillan Arctic Museum on Bowdoin College campus

honors the two, who in 1909 became the first to reach the North Pole. Exhibits trace the history of polar exploration and display the journals of both men.

The **Pejepscot Historical Society** offers displays of Brunswick history in its three museums and offers tours of both Skolfield-Whittier House, a 17-room Italianate mansion built in 1858 by a shipyard

Seemingly endless acres of sand in Desert of Maine, Freeport

owner, and the Joshua L.
Chamberlain House, a Civil
War museum.

🏛 Peary-MacMillan Arctic Museum
Hubbard Hall, Bowdoin College.
Tel (207) 725-3416. **Open** year-round:
10am–5pm Tue–Sat; 2–5pm Sun.
Closed public hols. ♿

🏛 Pejepscot Historical Society
159 Park Row. **Tel** (207) 729-6606.
Open Jun–Oct: call for opening hours
and tour times. 📷

Environs
Nine miles (14 km) east lies
Bath, long a shipbuilding center.
Its stately homes were built with
the profits from this lucrative
industry. In 1608 colonists
constructed the *Virginia*, the first
British boat produced in the
New World. Since then, some
4,000 ships have been built
here. The **Maine Maritime
Museum** operates one of the
country's few surviving wooden
shipbuilding yards. The modern
Maritime History Building annex
is a repository of nautical models,
paintings, and memorabilia.

Nautical art from the Maine Maritime
Museum in Bath

🏛 Maine Maritime Museum
243 Washington St. **Tel** (207) 443-
1316. **Open** 9:30am–5pm daily.
Closed Jan 1, Thanksgiving, & Dec 25.
📷 🎥 call for times. ♿ partial. 📷

❽ Boothbay Harbor

🏘 2,500. ✈ 38 miles (61 km) N in
Augusta. 🛈 192 Townsend Ave. (207)
633-2353 or (800) 266-8422.
🌐 boothbayharbor.com

The boating capital of the mid-
coast, Boothbay Harbor bustles
with the influx of summer tourists.
Dozens of boating excursions cast
off from the dock. Visitors might
choose to take an hour's sail along
the coast aboard a majestic
windjammer, a 41-mile (66-km)

Boothbay Harbor's busy boardwalk area

cruise up the Kennebec River, or
the popular day trip to the artists'
retreat on Monhegan Island *(see
p291)*. Sightseers can participate
in a wide range of activities,
including puffin and whale-
watching expeditions. The
harbor is at its best in late June,
when majestic tall
ships parade in
under full sail
for the annual
Windjammer
Days festival.

Boothbay WHALE WATCH

Boothbay Harbor whale
watch sign

The town itself is
chock-a-block with shops
and galleries. **Maine State
Aquarium**, a haven for parents
of restless children on rainy
days, is equipped with a
large touch tank filled with
sea creatures, which can
be touched.

🐟 Maine State Aquarium
194 McKown Point Rd., West
Boothbay Harbor. **Tel** (207) 633-9559.
Open late May–early Sep: 10am–5pm
daily. 📷 🎥 ♿

Environs
A scenic 30-mile (48-km) drive
up the coast brings travelers
to Pemaquid Point, complete
with shelves of granite cliffs
that jut from the sea. Rising
dramatically above a bluff and
offering panoramic views of
the coastline, the 1827
Pemaquid Point Light houses
the **Fisherman's Museum** in
the old lightkeeper's home.
The **Pemaquid Art Gallery** is
on the grounds and shows the
work of local artists. There is a
bonus for history buffs at the
8-acre (3-ha) **Colonial Pemaquid
State Historic Site**, which
includes a 1695 graveyard and

a replica of **Fort William Henry**.
English colonists fought French
invaders at this spot in several
forts that date from the early
17th century onward. A small
museum contains a diorama of
the original 1620s settlement
and displays a collection of
tools, pottery
shards, and
household
items that
reflect the rustic lives
of the early settlers.

🏛 Pemaquid Point Light
Rte. 130. **Tel** (207) 677-2492.
Open mid-May–mid-Oct: 10:30am–
5pm daily. 📷 ♿ Fisherman's
Museum: **Tel** (207) 677-2494.
Open May–Oct: call for hours. ♿
Pemaquid Art Gallery: **Tel** (207) 677-
2752. **Open** Jun–Oct: call for hours.

🏛 Colonial Pemaquid State Historic Site/Fort William Henry
Off Rte 130. **Tel** (207) 677-2423.
Open late May–early Sep: dawn
to dusk. 📷

Pemaquid Point Light and the
Fisherman's Museum

❾ Penobscot Bay

Penobscot Bay is picture-book Maine, with high hills seemingly rolling straight into the ocean, wave- pounded cliffs, sheltered harbors bobbing with fishing boats, and lobster traps piled high on the docks. Windjammer sailboats, ferries, and numerous cruise ships carry passengers to offshore islands, setting sail from ports such as Rockland, Camden, and Lincolnville, popular stops on the bay's western shore. The former shipbuilding centers of Searsport and Bucksport lie beyond. The more remote eastern shore leads to serene, perfectly preserved villages such as Castine and Blue Hill.

Sailboats moored in the safe confines of Camden Harbor

Secluded cliff-top view of Penobscot Bay

Exploring Penobscot Bay

To sail across Penobscot Bay covers a mere 35 miles (56 km) from its southernmost outpost of Port Clyde to its northern tip at Stonington. However, typical of Maine's ribboned coast, the same voyage takes almost 100 miles (160 km) by car. Either mode of transportation will offer stunning views of one of Maine's coastal highlights.

Rockland

ℹ️ 1 Park Drive (207) 596-0376 or (800) 562-2529.

Long a fishing town and commercial center, Rockland is now evolving into a tourist destination. These days lobster boats share the harbors with excursion boats, state ferries, and the schooners of Maine's windjammer fleet. However, the Lobster Festival, on the first full weekend of August, remains the town's biggest event.

On land the Farnsworth Art Museum and Wyeth Center showcases artists inspired by the Maine landscape, including Rockwell Kent (1882–1971), Edward Hopper (1882–1967),

and N.C. (1882–1945), Andrew (1917–2009), and Jamie (b.1946) Wyeth. The Maine Lighthouse Museum has a superb collection of lenses and other artifacts as well as a lighthouse-themed gift shop. Two miles (3.2 km) south of Rockland on Route 73, the Owls Head Transportation Museum houses aircraft, cars, bicycles, and carriages, and occasionally hosts air shows.

Camden

ℹ️ Commercial St, Public Landing (207) 236-4404 or (800) 223-5459.
🌐 visitcamden.com

The compact village is ideal for exploring on foot. Shady streets are lined with elegant homes and spired churches, and a host of shops border the waterfront. Among the fine inns on High Street is the Whitehall, with a room dedicated to Pulitzer Prize-winning poet Edna St. Vincent Millay (1892–1950), who went to school in Camden.

From mid-May to mid-October a short road at Camden Hills State Park on Route 1 is open to the top of 796-ft (242-m) Mount Battie. Standing on this point overlooking

Penobscot Bay, Millay was inspired to write her first volume of poetry.

Searsport

ℹ️ Main & Steamboat (207) 548-6510.

Searsport was once a major shipbuilding port. Now a handful of restored sea captains' homes on Church Street house the collection of the Penobscot Marine Museum (open late May to late October). An extensive collection of maritime art, ship models, navigational instruments and imported goods and displays of shipbuilding tools help tell the story of those glory days.

Considered to be the antiques capital of Maine, the town is chock-a-block with shops and has large flea markets on weekends in the summer.

Bucksport

ℹ️ 52 Main St (207) 469-6818. 📷

Bucksport looks across the Penobscot River to the 125-acre (51-ha) Fort Knox State Park that surrounds a pentagonal Civil War-era fortress. From May

Vintage aircraft at Owls Head Transportation Museum

Penobscot Bay and its Islands

Penobscot Bay is famous for its islands. Although some are no more than a pile of bald granite boulders, others are lush paradises that cover thousands of acres and are prime territory for birders, hikers, and sea kayakers. While some of these retreats are inhabited, most are completely wild, home only to harbor seals and seabirds such as puffins and great cormorants.

Key

━━ Major road

═══ Minor road

0 kilometers 20

0 miles 10

---

through October, visitors can explore barracks, storehouses, and underground passages. The park also features the Penobscot Narrows Bridge Observatory, which provides 360-degree views from 420 ft (128 m) above the river.

Castine

🛈 Emerson Hall, Court St (207) 326-4502.

Founded in the early 17th century and coveted for its strategic location overlooking the bay, Castine has flown the flags of France, Britain, Holland, and the US.

Relics of Castine's turbulent past can still be seen at Fort George on Wadsworth Cove Road, the highest point in town. Fort George was built by the British in 1779 and witnessed the American Navy's worst defeat during the Revolutionary War, a battle in which more than 40 colonial ships were either captured or destroyed. The fort is always open. Across from Fort George on Battle Avenue is the Maine Maritime Academy.

On Perkins Street, the two-story Wilson Museum has a collection that includes everything from Balinese masks and pre-Inca pottery to minerals and farm tools. It is closed during the fall and winter months.

Blue Hill

🛈 Blue Hill Town Hall (207) 374-3242.

Surrounded by fields of blueberries and with many of its white clapboard buildings listed on the National Historic Register, Blue Hill is a living postcard. Visitors will get a great view if they climb up Blue Hill Mountain.

Deer Isle

🛈 Rte 15 at Eggemoggin Rd (207) 348-6124.

Deer Isle, reached from the mainland via a graceful suspension bridge, is actually a series of small islands linked by causeways. Island highlights include the towns of Deer Isle and Stonington, and the famous Haystack Mountain School of Crafts.

Isle au Haut

🛈 Rte 15 at Eggemoggin Rd (207) 348-6124.

A mail boat from Stonington covers the 8 miles (13 km) to Isle au Haut. Almost half the island,

White-tailed deer, a common sight throughout the Penobscot Bay area

some 4 sq miles (11 sq km), belongs to Acadia National Park *(see pp292–3)* and offers 20 miles (32 km) of hiking.

Monhegan Island

🛈 (207) 596-0376 or (800) LOBCLAW.

This unspoiled enclave has no cars and no commotion. Only a half mile (0.8 km) wide and 1.7 miles (2.7 km) long, this island is smaller than New York City's Central Park, and is a favored retreat for birders and hikers who enjoy rough trails along rocky cliffs and through deep forest. Painter Jamie Wyeth is one of the prominent current members of a summer artists' colony. Cruise companies operate round-trip excursions from Port Clyde, Boothbay Harbor, and New Harbor.

North Haven Island

🛈 (207) 867-4433.

Eight miles (13 km) long and 3 miles (5 km) wide, North Haven is a refined summer colony and home to 350 hardy year-round residents. Much of the island remains open fields and meadows filled with wildflowers.

Vinalhaven

🛈 (207) 863-4826.

Tiny Vinalhaven is a perfect place for a swim or a hike. Inland moors and green spaces are balanced by a granite shoreline and a harbor bustling with lobster boats.

⑩ Acadia National Park

Located primarily on Mount Desert Island, the 35,000-acre (14,164-ha) Acadia National Park, a wild, unspoiled paradise, is heavily visited in summer. Wave-beaten shores and inland forests await travelers. The park's main attraction is the seasonal Loop Road, a 27-mile (43-km) drive that climbs and dips with the pink granite mountains of the east coast of the island before swinging inland past Jordan Pond, Bubble Pond, and Eagle Lake. Visitors who want a closer, more intimate look at the flora and fauna can do so on foot, bike, or horseback.

Vintage Carriage Roads
Forty-five miles (72 km) of old broken-stone carriage roads can be used for hiking and cycling.

Acadia's Wildlife
The park is home to numerous animals including woodchucks, white-tailed deer, red foxes, and the occasional black bear.

★ **Bass Harbor Head**
Craggy Bass Harbor Head exemplifies Maine's rock-bound shoreline. The 1858 Bass Harbor Head lighthouse affords magnificent views of the ocean.

Thompson Island

Indian Point   **Town Hill**

Somesville

Round Pond

Echo Lake

Pretty Marsh

Long Pond

Echo Lake Beach

Seal Cove Pond

Seal Cove

Seal Cove Road

Mount Desert Oceanarium

Bass Harbor Marsh

Key

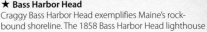

— Major road
— Minor road
— Scenic route
— Park boundary

0 kilometers   2
0 yards   2

Bass Harbor Head

VISITORS' CHECKLIST

Practical Information

ℹ️ Hulls Cove Visitor Center, off Rte. 3 in Hulls Cove. **Tel** (207) 288-3338. **Open** May–Oct: 8am–4:30pm daily (Jul–Aug: to 6pm). 🅿️ 🚻 ♿

🌐 nps.gov/acad

Transport

🚌 Bangor-Bar Harbor.

★ Cadillac Mountain

The 1,527-ft- (465-m-) tall Cadillac Mountain is the highest point on the Atlantic Coast. Hiking trails and an auto road lead to spectacular panoramas at the summit.

Jordan Pond

Many visitors stop at beautiful Jordan Pond, where a restaurant serves lunch, tea, and dinner from late May to late October.

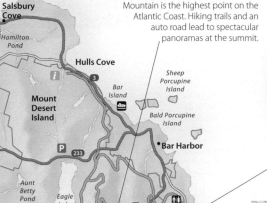

★ Sand Beach

Sand Beach is one of only two lifeguarded beaches in the park, but the ocean water, which rarely exceeds 55° F (15° C), discourages many swimmers.

★ Thunder Hole

The ocean's relentless pounding on the island's cliffs has created the natural phenomenon known as the Thunder Hole. When the tide rises during heavy winds, air trapped in this crevice is compressed and expelled with a resounding boom.

For map symbols *see back flap*

Rolling hills near Eagle Lake on the outskirts of Bar Harbor

⓫ Bar Harbor

🚌 5,000. ✈ 11 miles (17 km) NW in Trenton. 🚌 Island Explorer (free). 🛈 1201 Bar Harbor Rd., Trenton, (800) 345-4617 or 1 West St, Bar Harbor (mid-May–mid-Oct only). 🌐 **barharbormaine.com**

With a commanding location on Frenchman Bay, Bar Harbor is Mount Desert Island's lively tourist center. Artists Thomas Cole (1801–48) and Frederic Church (1862–1900) discovered the area's beauty in the 1840s and their brilliant work attracted the wealthy. In the 19th century, the town was a haven for the Astors and the Vanderbilts, among other rich American families.

Today Bar Harbor is a thriving waterside resort that attracts 5 million visitors a year. From here people can explore Acadia National Park *(see pp292–3)* or the mid-Maine coastline.

🏛 Bar Harbor Historical Society Museum

33 Ledgelawn Ave. **Tel** (207) 288-0000. **Open** Jun–Oct: 1–4pm Mon–Sat.

In 1947 a fire destroyed 26.5 sq miles (69 sq km) of wilderness

Chartered cruise boat in Bar Harbor

For hotels and restaurants in this region see pp318–19 and pp338–9

and a third of Bar Harbor's lavish summer homes, all but ending the village's reign as a high-society enclave. A display of early photographs shows the grand old days and the devastating effects of the fire. Happily for visitors, several of the remaining summer showplaces have been turned into gracious inns.

🎭 Criterion Theater

35 Cottage St. **Tel** (207) 288-3441. 🅿 A perennial favorite, this is an Art Deco gem that is listed on the National Register of Historic Places. The theater offers films, live music, and theater performances.

🏛 Abbe Museum

26 Mount Desert St. **Tel** (207) 288-3519. **Open** late May–Nov: 10am–5pm daily; call for winter hours. **Closed** Jan. 🅿 ♿

This museum celebrates Maine's Native American heritage with exhibits, hands-on programs and workshops taught by Native artists. There is a seasonal branch next to the Wild Gardens of Acadia, which has some 300 species of local plants.

⊠ Mount Desert Oceanarium & Lobster Hatchery

Rte 3. **Tel** (207) 288-5005. **Open** late May–mid-Oct: 9am–5pm Mon–Sat. 🅿 🅿 ♿ 🏠

Mount Desert Oceanarium, 8.5 miles (14 km) northwest of town, is where to see harbor seals, explore a salt marsh on Thomas Bay Marsh Walk, or visit the Maine Lobster Museum and separate lobster hatchery, where the hatching and raising process is explained. Children can enjoy the touch tank.

⊠ Acadia Zoo/Kisma Preserve

Rte 3 in Trenton. **Tel** (207) 667-3244. **Open** May–late Dec: 9:30am–dusk daily. 🅿 ♿

A popular family attraction, this zoo/preserve is located in Trenton across the bridge from Mount Desert Island, where pastures, streams, and woods shelter some 45 species of animals, including reindeer, wolves, monkeys, and moose. A barn has been converted into a rainforest habitat for monkeys, birds, reptiles, and other denizens of the Amazon.

⓬ Northeast Harbor

✈ 12 miles (19 km) N in Trenton. 🛈 18 Harbor Dr. (207) 276-5040. 🌐 **mountdesertchamber.org**

Northeast Harbor is the center of Mount Desert Island's social scene. The village has a handful of upscale shops, a few dining places, many handsome but rambling summer mansions and a scenic harbor where boats set sail for nearby Cranberry Islands.

🔅 Asticou Terrace and Thuya Lodge and Gardens

Rte 3 S of Rte 198 jct. **Tel** (207) 276-3727. **Open** May–Oct: dawn to dusk. 🦽 for gardens. **ⓦ gardenpreserve.org**

The Harbor can best be admired from the stunning Asticou Terraces. A granite path snakes along the hillside, yielding ever-wider vistas as it ascends, with benches and a gazebo placed at strategic viewpoints. At the top of the hill are Thuya Lodge, with collections of paintings and books, and Thuya Gardens, with flowerbeds and a reflecting pool that descends to the harbor's edge.

Environs

Somes Sound, a finger-shaped natural fjord that juts 5 miles (8 km) into Mount Desert Island, separates Northeast Harbor from quiet Southwest Harbor, famed for its yacht-builders Hinckley and Morris. The village is also home to the **Wendell Gilley Museum of Bird Carving**. The village artisan was a pioneer in the art of decorative bird carving, and the museum preserves about 100 of more than 10,000 birds he carved. It's a good introduction to local species. Museum workshops range from introductory classes to projects focused on specific birds. A drive or bike ride beyond Southwest Harbor leads to unspoiled villages, including Bass Harbor, where tourists are few and visitors can explore the 1858 Bass Harbor Head Light.

🏛️ Wendell Gilley Museum of Bird Carving

Main St. **Tel** (207) 244-7555. **Open** Jun–Oct: 10am–4pm Tue–Sun (to 5pm Jul & Aug); May & Nov–Dec: 10am–4pm Fri–Sun.

⓭ Machias

🅰 2,900. ✈ 91 miles (146 km) W in Bangor. ℹ 12 East Main St. (207) 255-4402.

Situated at the mouth of the river of the same name, Machias retains many of the handsome homes that sprang up during its days as a prosperous 19th-century lumber center. The town's name comes from the Micmac Indians and means "bad little falls," a reference to the waterfall that cascades in the center of town. There is a good view of the falls from the footbridge in Bad Little Falls Park.

Machias proclaims itself as the wild blueberry capital of Maine. It also lays claim to the region's oldest building, the 1770 **Burnham Tavern**, now a museum with period furnishings, paintings, and historic photographs. It was here that plans were made for the first naval battle of the Revolutionary War in 1775 *(see pp47–8).* Following that meeting, local men sailed out into Machias Bay on the small sloop *Unity* and captured the British man-of-war HMS *Margaretta*. Models of the two ships can be seen at

Whimsical sculpture in Asticou Gardens

The Lobster Industry

Harbors filled with lobstering boats and piers piled high with traps are familiar sights in the state that is America's undisputed lobster capital. Maine harvests over 50 million lbs (23 million kg) of this tasty crustacean each year. No visit is complete without a trip to a lobster pound, where patrons pick a live lobster from the tank, wait for it to be steamed, and savor the sweet meat at a picnic table overlooking the water.

Lobster fishermen

the **Gates House**, a restored 1807 Federal-style home in nearby Machiasport.

The town is set on the Machias River, a demanding canoeing route. **Roque Bluffs State Park** to the southwest of town offers swimming in a 60-acre (24-ha) freshwater pond and a 1-mile- (1.6-km-) long sweep of beach. The park has a launching ramp for sea kayaks, which are popular in Machias Bay. Birders go to nearby Jonesport for boat trips to Machias Seal Island, home to puffins, Arctic terns, and razorbill auks.

🏛️ Burnham Tavern

Main St. **Tel** (707) 255 6930. **Open** mid-Jun–Sep: 9:30am–4pm Mon–Sat. 🦽 🔲

🏠 Gates House

Rte. 92, Machiasport. **Tel** (207) 255-8461. **Open** Jul–Aug: 12:30– 4:30pm Tue–Fri. 🦽

🔅 Roque Bluffs State Park

Roque Bluffs Rd., Roque Bluffs. **Tel** (207) 255-3475. **Open** mid-May–mid-Oct: 9am–dusk. 🦽 ♿

Footbridge in Bad Little Falls Park in Machias

⓮ Campobello Island

In 1964 2,800 acres (1,133 ha) of Campobello Island were designated as a memorial to President Franklin Delano Roosevelt (1882–1945). The main settlement of Welshpool was where the future president spent most of his summers, until 1921 when he contracted polio. Undaunted, Roosevelt went on to lead the US through the Great Depression and World War II. The highlight of the park – which actually lies in Canada – is Roosevelt Cottage, a 34-room summer home that displays Roosevelt's personal mementos. A passport is required for border crossing.

VISITORS' CHECKLIST

Practical Information
ℹ️ Rte. 774. **Tel** (506) 752-2922.
Cottage: **Open** late May–mid-
Oct: 9am–5pm daily. Grounds:
Open year-round. 🅿️ ♿
Ⓦ fdr.net

Key
▬ Major road
═ Minor road
▭ Scenic route
— Park boundary
-- Walking trail

★ **Roosevelt Cottage**
Built in 1897, the sprawling wood-frame structure is one of a cluster of cottages that once belonged to wealthy families.

Mulholland Point has an 1885 lighthouse and a waterfront picnic site that offers good views of the FDR Memorial Bridge and Lubec.

Lower Duck Pond Bog is a prime habitat for such birds as killdeer, American black duck, and great blue heron.

Liberty Point
A pair of observation decks perched on the rugged cliffs afford far-ranging views of the coastline and the ocean.

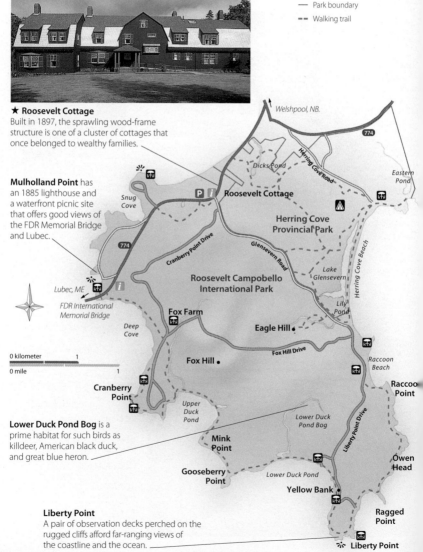

Welshpool, NB.

Dicks Pond

Herring Cove Road

Eastern Pond

774

Snug Cove

Roosevelt Cottage

Lubec, ME

774

Cranberry Point Drive

Herring Cove Provincial Park

Glensevern Road

Lake Glensevern

Herring Cove Beach

FDR International Memorial Bridge

Roosevelt Campobello International Park

Lily Pond

Deep Cove

Fox Farm

Eagle Hill •

Fox Hill Drive

Raccoon Beach

0 kilometer   1
0 mile   1

Fox Hill •

Cranberry Point

Upper Duck Pond

Mink Point

Lower Duck Pond Bog

Liberty Point Drive

Raccoon Point

Owen Head

Gooseberry Point

Lower Duck Pond

Yellow Bank •

Ragged Point

Liberty Point

Privately-owned Hamilton's Folly mansion in Calais

⓯ Calais

🏘 4,000. ✈ 229 miles (424 km) W in Bangor. 🛈 39 Union St. (207) 454-2211.

Perched on the west bank of the St. Croix River opposite St. Stephen, New Brunswick, Calais is Maine's busiest border crossing to Canada. The two countries share jurisdiction over nearby St. Croix Island, where in 1604 explorers Samuel de Champlain (1567–1635) and the Sieur de Monts (c.1560–1630) established the first white settlement in North America north of Florida. The island is accessible only by boat, a difficult trip due to strong currents and tides that can run as high as 28 ft (8.5 m).

Ripe blueberries in Calais

Calais was devastated by a gigantic fire in 1870. One of the few buildings that survived the conflagration is Hamilton's Folly mansion at No. 78 South Street. The Victorian house was so dubbed by locals because of its ostentatious design – a tribute to excess that bankrupted its owner.

Outdoor activities abound here. The St. Croix River is a challenging waterway for canoeists and a prime spot for salmon fishing. Three miles (5 km) southwest of Calais is the Baring Unit of the **Moosehorn National Wildlife Refuge**, 26.5 sq miles (69 sq km) of wilderness that beckons hikers, bird-watchers, and naturalists. Man-made eagle nesting platforms have been erected along Route 1 north of town. Visitors should watch

for the 400-sq-ft (120-sq-m) observation deck on this road for the best views. Also, there are a number of commercial farms that allow visitors to pick their own blueberries.

🦌 Moosehorn National Wildlife Refuge

Charlotte Rd. S of Calais. **Tel** (207) 454-7161. Park: **Open** year-round: sunrise–sunset daily. Office: **Open** year-round: 8am–4:30pm Mon–Fri. ♿

⓰ Bangor

🏘 33,200. ✈ 287 Godfrey Blvd. 🚌 🛈 519 Main St. (207) 947-0307.

The world's leading lumber port in the 1850s, Bangor remains the commercial center of northern Maine. The town's Penobscot River harbor was once loaded with ships carrying pine logs from nearby sawmills. This past is saluted with a 31-ft (9.5-m), 3,200-lbs (1,450-kg) statue of the mythical lumberjack Paul Bunyan on Main Street. Industrial might aside, Maine's second-largest city also draws visitors because of its ideal location as a base camp for treks to Acadia National Park *(see pp292–3)* and the forestlands that stretch to the north.

The city has a number of noteworthy residences from both the past and the present. The stately homes spared by a 1911 fire still line the West Market Square Historic District and the Broadway area. Maine-born horror author Stephen King lives in a mansion at No. 47 West Broadway, complete with a wrought-iron fence festooned with iron bats and cobwebs. The Greek Revival 1836 Thomas Hill House is headquarters for the **Bangor Museum and Center for History**, and offers historic walking tours.

One of Bangor's most pleasant green spaces is the **Mount Hope Cemetery**. Established in 1834, the cemetery is beautifully landscaped with ponds, bridges, and paved paths that attract strollers and inline skaters. This spirit of movement is also celebrated at the **Cole Land Transportation Museum**. The museum's collection contains more than 200 vehicles dating from the 19th century, ranging from fire engines and horse-drawn logging sleds to antique baby carriages.

🏛 Bangor Museum and Center for History

159 Union St. **Tel** (207) 942-5766. **Open** Jun–Sep: 10am–3pm Tue–Fri. 📷 📹 🌐 bangormuseum.org

🪦 Mount Hope Cemetery

State St. **Open** 7:30am–dusk Mon–Fri. 📹 ♿

🏛 Cole Land Transportation Museum

405 Perry Rd. **Tel** (207) 990-3600. **Open** May–early Nov: 9am–5pm daily. 📷

Bangor's West Market Historic District

⑰ Augusta

🏙 20,000. ✈ 75 Airport Rd. 🚌
ℹ 21 University Dr (207) 623-4559.

Maine's state capital is a relatively quiet city of 20,000. The 1832 Maine State House, the centerpiece of the government complex on the Kennebec River, was built of granite quarried from neighboring Hallowell. Major expansions have left only the center block from the original design by Boston architect Charles Bulfinch (1763–1844). Exhibits include political portraits and battle flags. Across the street, the Blaine House has been serving as the governor's mansion since 1919. The 28-room Colonial-style home was built in 1832 for a local sea captain.

The **Maine State Museum** has exhibits spanning "12,000 years of Maine history." One highlight is the "Made in Maine" exhibit, which re-creates a water-powered woodworking mill. The **Old Fort Western** is a restoration of one of New England's oldest surviving wooden forts, dating from 1754. The fort was built on the site where the Plymouth Pilgrims *(see pp154–5)* had established their trading post the previous century.

🏛 Maine State House
State & Capitol Sts. **Tel** (207) 287-1400.
Open year-round: 8am–5pm Mon–Fri.
🎫 ♿

Costumed interpreter at Old Fort Western in Augusta

Imposing facade of the Maine State House in Augusta

🏛 Blaine House
192 State St. **Tel** (207) 287-2121.
Open year-round: 2–4pm Tue–Thu & by appt. 🎫 call to arrange. ♿

🏛 Maine State Museum
State Capitol Complex, State St.
Tel (207) 287-2301. **Open** year-round: 9am–5pm Mon–Fri, 10am–4pm Sat.
Closed public hols. 🎫 🎫 ♿
🌐 **maine.gov/museum/**

🏛 Old Fort Western
16 Cony St. **Tel** (207) 626-2385.
Open late May–mid-Oct: call for hours. 🎫 ♿
🌐 **oldfortwestern.org**

Lifeguard's chair on the shore of tranquil Sebago Lake

Environs
Heading southwest from Augusta, travelers will get a rare look at the last active Shaker community in the US. Established in the 18th century, the Sabbathday Lake Shaker Community is home to a handful of residents who still adhere to their traditional beliefs of simplicity, celibacy, and communal harmony. Tours of the 18-building village include a stop at the **Shaker Village Museum** to see the beautiful furniture and ingenious inventions that became Shaker trademarks.

Nestled at the feet of Maine's western mountain ranges, Poland Springs is famous for its water. Farther west is Sebago Lake, a favorite among fishermen for its delicious salmon.

🏛 Sabbathday Shaker Village Museum
707 Shaker Rd., New Gloucester.
Tel (207) 926-4597. **Open** late May–mid-Oct: 10am–4:30pm Mon–Sat.
🎫 🎫 ♿ 🌐 **shaker.lib.me.us**

⑱ Bethel

🏙 2,500. ✈ 70 miles (113 km) S in Portland. ℹ 8 Station Place (207) 824-2282 or (800) 442-5826.
🌐 **bethelmaine.com**

A picturesque historic district, a major New England ski resort, and proximity to the White Mountains give Bethel year-round appeal. First settled in 1796, the town grew into a farming and lumbering center, and with the coming of the railroad in 1851 quickly became a popular resort. The line-up of classic clapboard mansions on the town green includes the Federal-style **Moses Mason House** (c.1813), which has period pieces and Rufus Porter murals on two floors.

Scenic drives are found in all directions, taking in tiny, unspoiled colonial hamlets such as Waterford to the south and beautiful mountain terrain to the north. **Sunday River Ski Resort** *(see p362)*, 6 miles (10 km) north of town in Newry, has 8 mountains and more than 100 ski trails. Evans Notch, a natural pass through the White Mountain peaks, offers many memorable views, including the Roost, a suspension bridge high above the Wild River and a favorite with photographers. **Grafton Notch State Park** has even more spectacular scenery along its drives, hiking trails and picnic areas. The park's special spots include waterfalls bearing such fanciful names as Screw Auger and Mother Walker, and beautiful panoramic views from Table Rock and the top of Old Speck Mountain.

⊞ Moses Mason House
10–14 Broad St. **Tel** (207) 824-2908. **Open** Jul–Aug: 1–4pm Tue–Sun, or by appointment year-round. 🎨 ✅ ♿
W bethelhistorical.org

⛷ Sunday River Ski Resort
Off Rte. 2 in Newry. **Tel** (207) 824-3000 or (800) 543-2SKI. **Open** 9am–4pm Mon–Fri, 8am–4pm Sat–Sun. 🎨

⛺ Grafton Notch State Park
Rte. 26 NW of Newry. **Tel** (207) 824-2912. **Open** mid-May–mid-Oct. 🎨

⓳ Sugarloaf

ℹ (207) 237-2000 or (800) 843-5623.

Maine's highest ski mountain, Sugarloaf is the centerpiece of this touristic village packed with hotels, restaurants, and hundreds of condominiums. Downhill skiers have been flocking to the **Sugarloaf** ski center *(see p362)* for years, attracted by the more than 100 trails and a vertical drop of 2,800 ft (870 m). The center also offers cross-country skiing, snowshoeing, and ice skating.

In summer, the emphasis shifts to the resort's 18-hole golf course, boating on the lakes and rivers, and hiking in the surrounding Carrabassett Valley. The resort is also famous for a network of more than 50 miles (80 km) of mountain-biking trails through terrain ranging from flat trails to challenging circuits full of steep climbs and descents.

Screw Auger Falls in Grafton Notch State Park

⛷ Sugarloaf
Carrabassett Valley. **Tel** (207) 237-2000 or (800) 843-5623. **Open** 8:30am–3:50pm daily. 🎨 ✅ ♿ in lodge. 🔋

⓴ Rangeley Lakes Region

ℹ 6 Park Rd. (207) 864-5364 or (800) 685-2537. **W** rangeleymaine.com

Set against a backdrop of mountains, this rustic area encompasses a series of pristine lakes that have long been a magnet for any kind of outdoor enthusiast. In summer fishermen ply the waterways for trout and salmon, while canoeists frequently spot a moose or two lumbering along the shoreline. The area is now popular with mountain

Moose crossing sign

bikers, but the beauty of the place has never been a secret. Hikers have been enjoying the vistas from the summit of **Bald Mountain** and tramping the section of the Appalachian Trail running along **Saddleback Mountain** for decades.

Elsewhere, the popular **Rangeley Lake State Park** provides vacationers with facilities for swimming, fishing, birding, boating, and camping, and 1.2 miles (2 km) of lakefront. Toward the southeast, **Mount Blue State Park** is home to Lake Webb, a favorite haunt of fishermen because of its plentiful population of black bass, trout, and salmon. The park is dominated by the towering 3,187-ft (971-m) Mount Blue.

⛰ Bald Mountain
Tel (207) 864-7311.

⛰ Saddleback Mountain
Tel (207) 864-5671. **Open** 9am–4pm Mon–Fri; daily during the ski season.

⛺ Rangeley Lake State Park
South Shore Dr., Rangeley. **Tel** (207) 864-3858. **Open** mid- May–Oct: 9am–dusk. 🎨

⛺ Mount Blue State Park
West Rd., Weld. **Tel** (207) 585-2347. **Open** daylight hours. Camping; **Tel** (207) 624-9950. 🎨 ✅ ♿

Snowboarding on Sugarloaf, Maine's second-highest mountain at 4,237 ft (1,290 m)

The dramatic 1,800-ft- (550-m-) high cliffs of Mount Kineo on Moosehead Lake

㉑ Moosehead Lake

ℹ️ Rte. 15, Greenville (207) 695-2702 or (888) 876-2778.
🌐 **mooseheadlake.org**

Forty miles (64 km) long and blessed with 320 miles (515 km) of mountain-rimmed shoreline, Moosehead Lake is one of the largest bodies of freshwater within any state in the Northeast. A popular destination for hunters, fishermen, hikers, and canoeists since the 1880s, the region is attracting a whole new breed of outdoor enthusiasts: mountain bikers, skiers, and snowmobilers.

Greenville, the region's largest town, is the starting point for excursions into the deep boreal forests known as the Great North Woods, including seaplane services that fly visitors to remote fishing camps in the most extensive wilderness region of New England. Greenville is also the chief base for moose-watching expeditions, which can take the form of aerial reconnaissance, exploration of boggy sites via timber roads, or trips aboard canoes or inflatable boats to observe moose as they feed in shallow waters.

The **Moosehead Marine Museum** tells of the history of the steamboat in Greenville, beginning in 1836 when the town was a logging center. One of the museum's prized possessions is the *Katahdin*, a restored 1914 steamboat and the last of a fleet of 50 such boats that plied the lake during the peak lumbering years. The *Katahdin* offers lake cruises and excursions to Mount Kineo, the sheer cliff face of which is the most prominent landmark on the lake. Local Native Americans considered the mountain sacred. The tiny settlement of Rockwood, the closest town to Mount Kineo, provides views of the mountain from rustic lakeside lodgings.

🏛 **Moosehead Marine Museum**

12 Lily Bay Rd., Greenville. **Tel** (207) 695-2716. Museum: **Open** late Jun–mid-Oct: 10am–4pm Mon–Sat. Cruises: **Open** Tue–Sat: call for times. ♿ 🌐 **katahdincruises.com**

㉒ Baxter State Park

ℹ️ 64 Balsam Dr, Millinocket (207) 723-5140. Office: **Open** 8am–4pm Mon–Fri; late May–mid-Oct: 8am–4pm daily. Park: **Open** mid-May–mid-Oct & Dec–Mar. 🌐 **baxter statepark authority.com**

This park was named for Governor Percival Proctor Baxter (1876– 1969). Baxter was instrumental in the effort to preserve this magnificent land, purchasing more than 200,000 acres (81,000 ha) and donating it to the state over 30-odd years with the stipulation that it was never to be developed. The park encompasses 46 mountain peaks, 18 of them over 3,000 ft (900 m), including Katahdin, Maine's tallest.

The park's 200 miles (320 km) of hiking trails are unsurpassed, and range from demanding climbs to easy family walks. Henry David Thoreau *(see p34)* tried the trek in 1846, but never made it to the 5,267-ft (1,605-m) summit of Katahdin. However, thousands of hikers are successful each year, and the trails are crowded with climbers in summer and fall. Some hardy souls can be seen completing the last steps of the famous Appalachian Trail *(see pp26–7)*, which runs from Springer Mountain, Georgia, to its terminus atop Katahdin.

Deer, bear, raccoons, and other wildlife are abundant in this park, and ponds such as Grassy, Sandy Stream, and Russell are favorite watering spots for Maine's official state animal: the moose.

Majestic Mount Katahdin, a popular hiking destination

◀ Lake Millinocket in Baxter State Park, Maine

Autumn colors in Aroostook State Park

㉘ Aroostook County

i 11 W. Presque Isle Rd., Caribou (207) 498-8736 or (888) 216-2463. **W** visitaroostook.com

Maine's largest and most northern county, Aroostook covers an area greater than the combined size of Connecticut and Rhode Island. The region is best known for agriculture, with some 1 million acres (405,000 ha) producing nearly 2 billion lbs (907 million kg) of potatoes each year, plus lush crops of clover, oats, barley, and broccoli. In summer endless acres of potato fields are covered with blossoms, a vision in pink and white. Another 4 million acres (1,620,000 ha) of land is forested, mostly owned by paper companies that process the lumber in 50 local pulp and paper mills.

In summer, hikers trek the trails in **Aroostook State Park**, fly-fishermen plumb the streams for salmon and trout, and canoeists and kayakers paddle the Allagash River. When the heavy winter snows come, snowmobilers arrive in large numbers to explore the entire 1,600 miles (2,500 km) of the Interstate Trail System.

Aroostook County begins in the south in Houlton, a quiet town with a Market Square Historic District of 28 19th-century buildings. A French dialect can be heard in the northern St. John Valley, the legacy of Acadians who settled here in 1785. The **Acadian Village** consists of 16 original and reconstructed buildings from the early days. In New Sweden, a cluster of historic buildings, including a log house and a one-room school, recalls a Swedish colony that settled not far from Caribou in the late 19th century.

📷 Aroostook State Park
87 State Park Rd., S of Presque Isle. **Tel** (207) 768-8341. **Open** year-round: for camping; mid-May–mid-Oct: daylight hours; accessible for cross-country skiing and snow-mobiling in winter. 🚗 📷 🍴 ♿

🏚 Acadian Village
Rte. 1, Van Buren. **Tel** (207) 868-5042. **Open** mid-Jun–mid-Sep: noon–5pm daily. 🚗

Finely crafted tools of the trade for fly fisherman

Environs
Starting at Lake Chamberlain and extending north for more than 90 miles (145 km), the **Allagash Wilderness Waterway** is one of New England's most stunning natural areas. The waterway and its many lakes and streams have been protected since 1966. The Allagash has also been

designated a National Wild and Scenic Rivers System.

The state owns the land flanking the waterway for 500 ft (150 m) on each side, assuring a protected habitat for dozens of animals and more than 120 bird species. Anglers will find numerous brook trout and whitefish.

A trek up or down the Allagash system is the ultimate canoe trip in the state, and one that generally takes between five and ten days. Especially beautiful spots are Allagash Lake, a tranquil side trip where no motors are allowed, and Allagash Falls, a dramatic 40-ft (12-m) drop that necessitates carrying the canoe (called "portaging") for about a third of a mile (0.5 km). The canoeing season runs from late May to early October.

🦫 Allagash Wilderness Waterways
i Maine Bureau of Parks and Lands. 106, Hogan Rd. Bangor (207) 941 4014 **Open** year round 🚗

Frog in the protected habitat of the Allagash Wilderness Waterway

Maine's Great Rafting Rivers

Maine is famous for three whitewater rivers, the Kennebec, the Dead, and the west branch of the Penobscot. The first two rivers meet near the town called The Forks, southwest of Moosehead Lake, where more than a dozen rafting companies offer equipment and guided trips (see p357). The Millinocket area services paddlers bound for the Penobscot, famed among rafters for its challenging drop through a vertical walled canyon below the Ripogenus Dam.

Kennebec River rafters in the challenging whitewater

For hotels and restaurants in this region see pp318–19 and pp338–9

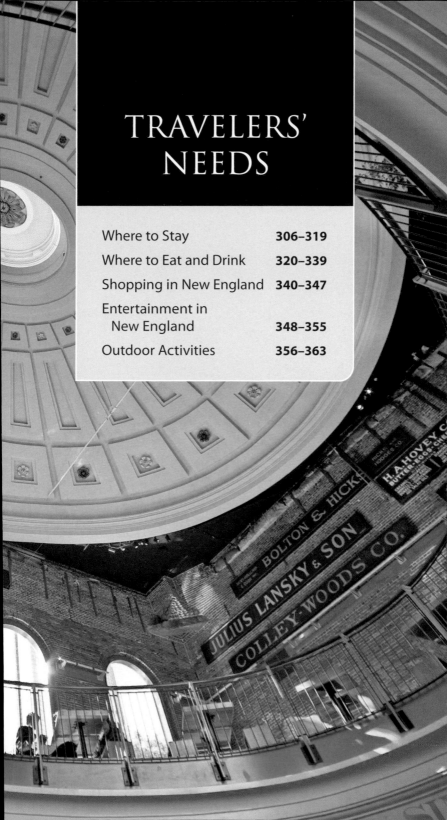

TRAVELERS' NEEDS

WHERE TO STAY

The incredibly varied accommodations of the New England states are tailored to suit virtually all tastes and budgets. If you are looking to commune with nature and save a few dollars at the same time, you can take your pick of campsites *(see p356–9)* sprinkled liberally throughout the six states. Rustic country inns and bed and breakfasts (B&Bs) are plentiful, offering travelers quaint facilities and a more personal touch. Hotels and motels are also popular choices, conveniently located in or around busy tourist destinations and on major roads throughout the region. From the most posh hotel in Boston to a historic Vermont B&B or a rugged back-country camping experience in Maine, New England has suitable accommodations for everyone. During the summer vacation season, lodgings can sometimes be hard to come by, so it is always best to book in advance. This is also true during the busy fall-foliage season.

Foxwoods Resort Casino near Mystic, Connecticut *(see p315)*

Hotels

New England has no shortage of hotel chains. The majority of the large chains, such as Holiday Inn, Hilton, Hyatt, Marriott, and Holiday Inn, offer standard amenities that include such things as a bar, dining room, and exercise facilities. Although one hotel room is generally indistinguishable from the next, they are all impeccably clean and come equipped with a television, room service, and a private bathroom – comforts not always found in B&Bs. Luxury hotels, usually found in city centers, can be very lavish. Lush decor, fine dining, and valet services are the earmarks of such establishments. The area's large casinos and resorts are also known for their lavishness.

Most hotels will hold your reservation only until 6pm, especially during the tourist season. It is always best to notify the reservation clerk should you be arriving late.

Motels

If you are on a budget, motels offer you the best and most flexible value for your money. Often found on the outskirts of cities and towns, motels also dot the New England roads most frequented by travelers. While you will not find the same amenities as in the big hotels, motels will offer you convenience and comfort at significantly lower prices. A standard motel room is equipped with a private bathroom, color TV, and heat and air conditioning. The more modern places usually have two double beds, making it easier to accommodate the whole family in a single room.

Bed and Breakfasts and Inns

American B&Bs can differ greatly from their European counterparts. Very often they are not the cozy one- or two-room guest lodgings located in the owner's personal residence like those you would come across in Europe. Increasingly, New England B&Bs are professionally operated businesses in which guests live in separate accommodations from the owner or caretaker. This style of B&B tends to be larger in size and have more rooms than its more traditional counterpart. The loss of intimacy usually comes with the added bonus of private bathrooms and added services. Of course, traditionalists can still find small, cozy B&Bs throughout New England. Regardless of size, all B&Bs offer distinctive lodgings and breakfast, which may vary in size and style from one establishment to another. Like B&Bs, inns come in all shapes and sizes, from the very rustic to the large resort-style lodging. Not only do inns serve breakfast and dinner, the larger ones can come with such "extras" as swimming pools, gardens, and taverns. Depending on their location, many are affiliated with local tennis or golf clubs.

Rose Farm Inn *(see p314)*, in a quiet country setting on Rhode Island's Block Island

Omni Mount Washington Hotel in Bretton Woods, New Hampshire *(see p317)*

Because some B&Bs and inns are historic homes appointed with beautiful antique furniture, they usually prohibit smoking and often do not allow children. The **New England Inns and Resorts Association**, or one of its state branches, is a good lodging resource.

Prices and Reservations

Rates and availability can fluctuate from season to season. Prices are generally highest during peak tourist periods (July–August and mid-September–late October) and in the cities, coastal areas, and other prime vacation destinations. The reverse is true with ski resorts, when winter months are the most expensive. Booking your accommodations well in advance is always

the safest way to avoid complications. This is especially true if youare looking forward to staying at a B&B or inn in which rooms are limited.

Many hotels in urban areas such as Boston cater to business travelers and may offer reduced rates from Friday to Sunday. Conversely, many of the rural lodgings, popular with the weekend crowd, slash their prices substantially during the week.

Always inquire about package deals offered by motels and hotels. Discounted meals and free passes to local attractions are sometimes thrown in as added incentives for you to stay with them. Some inns and B&Bs also work in conjunction with each other to promote inn-to-inn tours for cyclists and cross-country skiers, offering special rates for accommodations along

Beautiful room at the Red Lion Inn in Stockbridge, Massachusetts *(see p314)*

the tour route. To avoid unpleasant surprises, it is always prudent to ask about any restrictions, including those on children, pets, and smoking.

How to Make Reservations

Most hotels have toll-free reservation numbers, and some offer discounts on Internet bookings. Room rates are usually quoted for two people sharing a room, including tax (and breakfast, if it is offered); all B&Bs, of course, provide a morning meal. For longer stays, it is customary to prepay one night in advance.

Hidden Extras

You should be aware that the prices quoted for many accommodations do not include taxes, which can increase the bill significantly – even in the haven of New Hampshire, which has no sales

Sleek interiors at XV Beacon, Boston, Massachusetts *(see p313)*

tax, but does have lodging and restaurant taxes. Hotels in large urban areas often charge for their parking facilities, sometimes substantially. In Boston, for example, parking costs could amount to $35–$45 per day. Also be aware of added service fees which can sometimes be as high as 15 percent.

Business Travelers

As access to high-speed wireless Internet rapidly becomes a common amenity, even in modest motels and many B&Bs, the modern business traveler can stay connected to the office and the world at large. Internet access is often free at small properties but pricey at major chain hotels. Some modern urban hotels offer multi-line phones, in-room fax machines, and private voice mail.

Disabled Travelers

Although federal law requires that all businesses provide access and facilities for the disabled, the practical reality is that this is not always the case. The vast majority of large private and chain hotels are modern enough to be equipped with the necessary facilities, including visual notification of the fire alarm, incoming phone calls, and the doorbell. Many also have some suites designated specifically for the disabled. However, many of New England's older buildings and B&Bs have narrow hallways that can obstruct wheelchairs and have no ramps. As always, it is best to check in advance.

Where to Stay in Boston

The centrally-located Back Bay has the greatest concentration of hotels, convenient for tourists as well as for business travelers. In the gentrifying South End, an increasing number of restored Victorian town-houses have been converted into B&Bs. Accommodations in the downtown Financial District near the waterfront cater to

Bedroom at the Inn on Covered Bridge Green *(see p316)* in Arlington, Vermont

business people during the week, but often offer good value to vacationers on the weekends. Across the Charles River, Cambridge has a large number of hotels, particularly around Harvard Square and among the Kendall Square office towers. In more suburban Brookline along the Green Line Trolley routes west of the Back Bay, several guesthouses as well as more upscale B&Bs offer additional alternatives. One plus for travelers: Boston hotels now house many of the city's top restaurants, including Clio in the Eliot Hotel, Mooo at Fifteen Beacon, Bond at the Langham Hotel, and L'Espalier at the Mandarin Oriental.

Boston hotels are particularly busy in May and June for college graduations, July and August for summer vacations, and September and October for the fall-foliage season. Throughout the course of a year, many Boston hotels, including the hotels around the Boston Convention and Exhibition Center and in Cambridge's Kendall

Square, cater to business travelers. This means that the rates are often lowest on weekends.

The city does have a good selection of smaller hotels and B&Bs, often offering more personal service and charm than the big convention hotels. If you are looking for a classic B&B – a room or two in the owner's home – you should contact one of the B&B booking agencies, such as the **Bed & Breakfast Agency of Boston**, **Host Homes of Boston**, or the **Bed and Breakfast Associates Bay Colony, Ltd**. A popular trend is the "boutique" hotel, a small, elegantly appointed accommodation with solicitous service. Be warned: these luxury boutiques are among the most expensive lodging options.

Hostels

Hostels have long been a way for people – especially students – to slash their traveling budget. However, unlike the more extensive European model, New England's hostel network is somewhat underdeveloped. The good news is that some of the region's prime locations (including Boston and Cape Cod) do have hostels. A list of member hostels and their locations is available from **Hostelling International – American Youth Hostels**

Boston's Seaport Hotel *(see p312)*, busy during the summer

(HI/AYH). **HI/AYH Eastern New England Council** provides information on hostels in New Hampshire, Maine, and Massachusetts. Located in the heart of the Theater District, the modern HI-Boston Hostel offers a variety of rooms, including some very affordable six-bed dormitories and several private rooms with en-suite bathroom. Guests enjoy free Wi-Fi and daily continental breakfast.

Recommended Hotels

The lodging options featured in this guide have been selected across a wide price range for

The stylish Hotel Pemaquid *(see p319)* in New Harbor, Maine

Luxurious room at the Taj Boston hotel, Massachusetts *(see p310)*

their excellent facilities, good location, and value. From rustic, family-owned inns and relaxing beachfront resorts to stylishly modern boutique hotels, these hotels run the gamut across all price levels and environments. For the finest in service and amenities, consider a stay in one of New England's award-winning luxury hotels. For a more intimate experience, the region contains numerous acclaimed inns and B&Bs, and some of the nation's most historic lodging options. Key urban areas host plenty of full-service business hotels ideal for the working traveler, and those

who don't mind sacrificing a bit of comfort and location can find wallet-friendly motels on the edge of town.

Hotels are listed by area, and within these areas by price. For the best of the best, look out for hotels featured as "DK Choice". These establishments have been highlighted in recognition of an exceptional feature – a stunning location, notable history, inviting atmosphere. The majority of these are exceptionally popular among local residents and visitors, so be sure to inquire regarding reservations or you may be left on the outside looking in.

DIRECTORY

Bed and Breakfast and Inn Agencies

Bed & Breakfast Agency of Boston
Tel (800) 248-9262 or (617) 720-3540; (0800) 89-5128 from UK.
Ⓦ boston-bnbagency.com

Bed and Breakfast Associates Bay Colony, Ltd.
PO Box 57166, Babson Park Branch, Boston, MA 02457-0166.
Tel (888) 486-6018 or (617) 720-0522.
Ⓦ bnbboston.com

Host Homes of Boston
PO Box 117, Waban Branch, Boston, MA 02468-0001. **Tel** (800) 600-1308 or (617) 244-1308.
Ⓦ hosthomesofboston.com

New England Inns and Resorts Association

PO Box 1089, North Hampton, NH 03862-1089.
Tel (603) 964-6689.
Ⓦ newenglandinnsandresorts.com

Hostels and Budget Accommodations

Best Western International
Tel (800) 528-1234.
Ⓦ bestwestern.com

Boston International Youth Hostel
12 Hemenway St, Boston, MA 02115.
Tel (617) 536-9455.
Ⓦ bostonhostel.org

Days Inn
Tel (800) 329-7466.
Ⓦ daysinn.com

Fairfield Inn
Tel (800) 228-2800.
Ⓦ marriott.com/fairfield-inn/travel.mi

Hostelling International
8401 Colesville Rd, Suite 600, Silver Spring, MD, 20910.
Tel (301) 495-1240. (membership information).
Tel (800) 909-4776. (reservation service).
Ⓦ hiusa.or

Hostelling International Eastern New England Council
218 Holland St, Somerville MA 02144.
Tel (617) 718-7990.
Ⓦ hinewengland.org

Cape Cod Chamber of Commerce
5 Patti Page Way, Centerville, MA 02632.
Tel (508) 362-3225.
Ⓦ capecodchamber.org

North of Boston Convention and Visitors Bureau
10 State St, Suite 309, Newburyport, MA 01950.
Tel (978) 225-1559.
Ⓦ northofboston.org

Where to Stay

Boston

Back Bay and South End

**Best Western
Roundhouse Suites** $
Business
891 Massachusetts Ave.
Tel *(617) 989-1000*
W bestwestern.com
Modern, spacious suites in a
former railroad roundhouse.

Midtown Hotel $
Motel   **Map** 3 B4
220 Huntington Ave., 02115
Tel *(617) 262-1000*
W midtownhotel.com
60s-style motor inn with secure
parking and connecting rooms.

82 Chandler Bed & Breakfast $$
Inn/B&B   **Map** 4 D3
82 Chandler St., 02116
Tel *(617) 482-0408*
W 82chandler.com
Five Victorian-style rooms with
private baths and air conditioning.

Chandler Inn $$
Business   **Map** 4 D3
26 Chandler St., 02116
Tel *(617) 482-3450*
W chandlerinn.com
This 55-room hotel is good for
business travelers. Rooms have
TVs and phones with voicemail.

Charlesmark $$
Boutique   **Map** 3 C2
655 Boylston St., 02116
Tel *(617) 247-1212*
W charlesmarkhotel.com
Stylish hotel. Rooms have custom-
made furniture and state-of-the-
art amenities. Breakfast included.

Clarendon Square Inn $$
Inn/B&B   **Map** 3 C4
198 West Brookline St., 02118
Tel *(617) 536-2229*
W clarendonsquare.com
South End brick townhouse inn
with large modern suites.

Colonnade Hotel $$
Luxury   **Map** 3 B3
120 Huntington Ave., 02116
Tel *(617) 424-7000*
W colonnadehotel.com
Some of the largest, most comfort-
-able rooms in Back Bay, and the
city's only outdoor rooftop pool.

**Commonwealth Court
Guest House** $$
Inn/B&B   **Map** 3 A2
284 Commonwealth Ave., 02116
Tel *(617) 424-1230*
W commonwealthcourt.com

Rent rooms by the week or month.
Each has a kitchenette, cable TV,
and maid service twice a week.

Gryphon House $$
Inn/B&B
9 Bay State Rd., 02215
Tel *(617) 375-9003*
W gryphonhouseboston.com
Huge, elegant rooms with
fireplaces in a 1895 brownstone.

Hotel 140 $$
Business   **Map** 3 C3
140 Clarendon St., 02116
Tel *(617) 585-5600*
W hotel140.com
The country's first YMCA refur-
bished as a modern hotel with
all the basic amenities.

Hotel Commonwealth $$
Luxury
500 Commonwealth Ave., 02215
Tel *(617) 933-5000*
W hotelcommonwealth.com
Features high-tech essentials
coupled with the elegant
ambience of 19th-century France.

Newbury Guest House $$
Inn/B&B   **Map** 3 B2
261 Newbury St., 02116
Tel *(617) 670-6000*
W newburyguesthouse.com
Great location amid the city's most
famous shopping street. Rooms
feature eclectic furnishings.

Eliot Hotel $$$
Luxury   **Map** 3 A2
370 Commonwealth Ave., 02215
Tel *(617) 267-1607*
W eliothotel.com
Graceful 19th-century landmark
hotel with smart, spacious suites.

Fairmont Copley Plaza $$$
Luxury   **Map** 3 C2
138 St James Ave., 02116
Tel *(617) 267-5300*
W fairmont.com
New York Plaza's sister hotel
features opulent public areas and
exceptionally grand suites.

Lenox Hotel $$$
Luxury
710 Boylston St., 02116
Tel *(617) 536-5300*
W lenoxhotel.com
Family-run Edwardian landmark
with intimate rooms; splendid
corner suites.

Mandarin Oriental $$$
Luxury   **Map** 3 B2
776 Boylston St., 2199
Tel *(617) 535-8888*
W mandarinoriental.com
Large rooms and state-of-the-
art electronics. Offers a full-
service spa and high-profile
dining options.

DK Choice

Taj Boston $$$
Luxury   **Map** 4 D2
15 Arlington St., 02116
Tel *(617) 536-5700*
W tajhotels.com/boston
First opened in 1927 as the
original Ritz-Carlton, this is
one of New England's most
inviting hotels. Most of the
city's major attractions are
within walking distance.
This grand dame epitomizes
opulence, decorum, and "old
Boston" style. The lobby bar
is legendary.

Beacon Hill and the
Theater District

Boston Park Plaza $$
Historic   **Map** 4 D2
50 Park Plaza, 02116
Tel *(617) 426-2000*
W bostonparkplaza.com

Elegant interiors at the Taj Boston hotel, Boston

Vintage elegance at this 1927 landmark. Features eight excellent on-site restaurants.

Courtyard Boston Downtown Hotel $$
Business   Map 3 E2
275 Tremont St., 02116
Tel *(617) 426-1400*
W mariott.com
Glittery, dramatic, with first-rate amenities and conference rooms; a lingering 1920s allure.

John Jeffries House $$
Inn/B&B   Map 1 B3
14 David G. Mugar Way, 02114
Tel *(617) 367-1866*
W johnjeffrieshouse.com
Period artwork, Neo-Federal style public areas, and cheerful rooms, most with kitchenettes.

W Hotel $$
Luxury   Map 1 B5
100 Stuart St., 02116
Tel *(617) 261-8700*
W starwoodhotels.com
Trendy chain hotel with a celebrity chef restaurant and lobby bar.

Beacon Hill Hotel $$$
Luxury   Map 1 B4
25 Charles St., 02114
Tel *(617) 723-7575*
W beaconhillhotel.com
Euro-chic rooms. The on-site bistro is a culinary destination.

Four Seasons $$$
Luxury   Map 4 E2
200 Boylston St., 02116
Tel *(617) 338-4400*
W fourseasons.com
Luxurious yet low-key, frequented by rock stars and dignitaries.

Liberty Hotel $$$
Luxury   Map 1 B3
215 Charles St., 02114
Tel *(617) 224-4000*
W libertyhotel.com
This hotel is an outstanding redesign of the iconic, former Charles Street Jail. Excellent facilities and amenities.

Ritz-Carlton Boston Common $$$
Luxury   Map 4 E2
10 Avery St., 02111
Tel *(617) 574-7100*
W ritzcarlton.com
Height of contemporary elegance overlooking the Boston Common.

Wyndham Boston Beacon Hill $$$
Business   Map 1 B3
5 Blossom St., 02114
Tel *(617) 742-7630*
W wyndham.com
In the heart of Massachusetts General Hospital campus. Good

Entrance to Irving House B&B , Cambridge, Massachusetts

shopping and dining options close by.

Brighton

Days Hotel $$
Business
1234 Soldiers Field Rd., Brighton, 02135
Tel *(617) 254-1234*
W dayshotelboston.com
On the Charles River and a short ride from Harvard Square. Comfortable, good service.

Brookline

Beech Tree Inn $$
Inn/B&B
83 Longwood Ave., Brookline, 02446
Tel *(617) 277-1620*
W thebeechtreeinn.com
Victorian-style B&B features rooms with private baths and a common parlor. Close to eateries,

Bertram Inn $$
Inn/B&B
92 Sewall Ave., Brookline, 02446
Tel *(617) 566-2234*
W bertraminn.com
Private home with elegant rooms in a residential area .

Holiday Inn Boston-Brookline $$
Business
1200 Beacon St., Brookline, 02446
Tel *(617) 277-1200*
W holidayinn.com
One of the few large-scale hotels in the area. Convenient for Fenway Park and Kenmore Square.

Inn at Longwood Medical Center $$
Business
342 Longwood Ave., Brookline, 02115
Tel *(617) 731-4700*
W innatlongwood.com
Best Western affiliate; comfortable rooms, en-suite bathrooms.

Cambridge

A Friendly Inn at Harvard $
Inn/B&B
1673 Cambridge St., Cambridge, 02138
Tel *(617) 547-7851*
W afinow.com
Queen Anne-style house with 17 large rooms. Friendly service.

Courtyard Boston Cambridge $$
Business
777 Memorial Dr., Cambridge, 02139
Tel *(617) 492-7777*
W mariott.com
Fabulous views of the Charles, large desks, and an indoor pool are highlights of this riverfront hotel.

Harvard Square Hotel $$
Business
110 Mt Auburn St., Cambridge, 02138
Tel *(617) 864-5200*
W harvardsquarehotel.com
In the heart of the city's cultural core, this former motor inn has modern rooms. Friendly service.

Holiday Inn Express $$
Business
250 Monsignor O'Brien Hwy., Cambridge, 02141
Tel *(617) 577-7600*
W hiecambridge.com
Dependable roadside lodging with good work areas. Limited free parking.

Hotel Marlowe $$
Luxury
25 Edwin H. Land Blvd., Cambridge, 02141
Tel *(617) 868-8000*
W hotelmarlowe.com
An elegant hotel with trendy rooms. Hosts evening wine receptions. Pet friendly.

Hotel Veritas $$
Boutique
1 Remington St., Cambridge, 02138
Tel *(617) 520-5000*
W thehotelveritas.com
Stylish hotel near the campus. Has intimate rooms and a lovely cocktail lounge.

Hyatt Regency Cambridge $$
Business
575 Memorial Dr., Cambridge, 02139
Tel *(617) 492-1234*
W cambridge.hyatt.com
River-facing rooms have great sunset views. Good public spaces, 24-hour business centre.

Irving House $$
Inn/B&B
24 Irving St., Cambridge, 02138
Tel *(617) 547-4600*
W irvinghouse.com
An older rooming house; quiet environs and handy location.

For more information on types of hotels *see p309*

Modern rooms at the Royal Sonesta, Cambridge, Massachusetts

Isaac Harding House $$
Inn/B&B
288 Harvard St., Cambridge, 02139
Tel *(617) 876-2888*
W harding-house.com
An 1860s Victorian home with
comfortable, spacious rooms –
some share baths.

Le Meridien Cambridge $$
Business
20 Sidney St., Cambridge, 02139
Tel *(617) 577-0200*
W lemeridiencambridge.com
Contemporary hotel, ideal for
exploring Central Square's many
acclaimed restaurants.

Mary Prentiss Inn $$
Inn/B&B
6 Prentiss St., Cambridge, 02140
Tel *(617) 661-2929*
W maryprentissinn.com
Greek Revival house with
traditional "historic B&B"-style
decor. Some rooms have
fireplaces and whirlpool tubs.

Royal Sonesta $$
Business
*5 Cambridge Pkwy., Cambridge,
02142*
Tel *(617) 806-4200*
W sonesta.com
Modern hotel with a great art
collection and striking riverside
location. Good meeting spaces.

The Kendall Hotel $$
Historic
350 Main St., Cambridge, 02142
Tel *(617) 577-1300*
W kendallhotel.com
Century-old firehouse now an
antique-filled boutique hotel.

Sheraton Commander $$$
Business
16 Garden St., Cambridge, 02138
Tel *(617) 547-4800*
W sheratoncommander.com
Modern hotel close to the
Harvard campus. Rooms are
elegant and well-equipped.
Pet friendly.

The Charles Hotel $$$
Luxury
1 Bennett St., Cambridge, 02138
Tel *(617) 864-1200*
W charleshotel.com
Chic hotel with a personal touch;
also has a jazz club, and a leading
Boston restaurant.

Charlestown

Constitution Inn $$
Inn/B&B **Map** 2 D1
*150 3rd Ave., Charlestown Navy Yard,
Charlestown, 02129*
Tel *(617) 241-8400*
W constitutioninn.org
Caters to military personnel, but
welcomes all.

East Boston

Hyatt Harborside $$
Business
101 Harborside Dr., 02128
Tel *(617) 568-1234*
W harborside.hyatt.com
A large glass wall makes the most
of the view. Spacious rooms.

North End and the Waterfront

Harborside Inn $$
Boutique **Map** 2 D3
185 State St., 02109
Tel *(888) 723-7565*
W harborsideinnboston.com
Modern, spaces redesigned from
an 1858 spice warehouse.

Marriott Long Wharf $$
Business **Map** 2 E3
296 State St., 02109
Tel *(617) 227-0800*
W marriottlongwharf.com
Spacious rooms with great harbor
views. Close to major attractions.

Seaport Hotel $$
Business **Map** 2 5F
1 Seaport Lane, 02210
Tel *(617) 385-4000*
W seaportboston.com

Comfortable rooms offer large
workspaces and flatscreen TVs.
There is a 24-hour business
center and a heated indoor pool.

Boston Harbor Hotel $$$
Luxury **Map** 2 E4
70 Rowes Wharf, 02110
Tel *(617) 439-7000*
W bhh.com
Renowned for its winter wine
festival and summer entertain-
ment series. The rooms are plush
and there's an on-site spa.

The Langham Boston $$$
Luxury **Map** 2 D4
250 Franklin St., 02110
Tel *(617) 451-1900*
W langhamhotels.com
In the Art Nouveau former
Federal Reserve Bank building.
Second Empire furnishings.

Old Boston and the Financial District

Ames Hotel $$
Luxury **Map** 2 D3
1 Court St., 02108
Tel *(617) 979-8100*
W ameshotel.com
In the historic Ames building;
modern style, old world
architecture. Great location.

Hilton Boston Downtown $$
Business **Map** 2 E4
89 Broad St., 02110
Tel *(617) 556-0006*
W hilton.com
Art Deco-style hotel popular with
business execs. The sedate library
is great for one-on-one meetings.

Nine Zero $$
Boutique **Map** 1 C4
90 Tremont St., 02108
Tel *(617) 772-5800*
W ninezerohotel.com
Contemporary luxury hotel offers
in-room spa services and hosted
evening wine hour.

Omni Parker House $$
Historic **Map** 2 D4
60 School St., 02108
Tel *(617) 227-8600*
W omniparkerhouse.com
Opulent downtown landmark
and America's oldest hotel in
operation has elegant rooms
and suites.

Millennium Bostonian $$$
Luxury **Map** 2 D3
26 North St., 02109
Tel *(617) 523-3600*
W millenniumhotels.com
Rooms run the gamut from tiny
to palatial in this elegant oasis,
close to Faneuil Hall Marketplace.

XV Beacon $$$
Luxury Map 1 C4
15 Beacon St., 02108
Tel *(617) 670-1500*
W xvbeacon.com
Chic boutique hotel with design-conscious decor. All rooms feature high-tech extras.

Somerville

La Quinta Inn and Suites $
Business
23 Cummings St., Somerville, 02145
Tel *(617) 625-5300*
W lq.com
Spacious rooms and suites with simple decor. Complimentary shuttle service and breakfast.

Massachusetts

AMHERST: Allen House Inn $$
Inn/B&B
599 Main St., 01002
Tel *(413) 253-5000*
W allenhouse.com
Victorian B&B that celebrates the English and American Arts & Crafts Movement.

CHARLEMONT: Warfield House Inn $
Inn/B&B
200 Warfield Rd., 01339
Tel *(413) 339-6600*
W warfieldhouseinn.com
Mountain-top inn with sweeping views. Each room includes a hot tub and wood-burning fireplace.

CHATHAM: Chatham Wayside Inn $$$
Luxury
512 Main St., 02633
Tel *(508) 945-550*
W waysideinn.com
Rooms in both the original stagecoach inn and a modern wing. Some offer whirlpool spa jets and private patios.

Exterior of the XV Beacon, Boston, Massachusetts

DK Choice

CONCORD: Colonial Inn $$
Historic
48 Monument Sq., 01742
Tel *(978) 369-9200*
W concordscolonialinn.com
One of the state's top choices for historic lodging, located just steps from key sights such as the Old North Bridge. For the full historical effect, ask for one of the 15 rooms in the original inn. Colonial Revival features add to the atmospheric charm in both rooms and the tavern.

CONCORD: North Bridge Inn $$
Historic
21 Monument St., 01742
Tel *(978) 371-0014*
W northbridgeinn.com
A renovated 1885 home with each of the six suites named after a local 19th-century author.

EDGARTOWN: Winnetu Oceanside Resort $$$
Luxury
31 Dunes Rd., 02539
Tel *(508) 310-1733*
W winnetu.com
Bright rooms, suites, and cottages. Plenty of kid-friendly activities.

FALMOUTH: Palmer House Inn $$
Inn/B&B
81 Palmer Ave., 02540
Tel *(508) 548-1230*
W palmerhouseinn.com
Queen Anne-style inn and adjacent guest house. Stained-glass windows, antiques, and lace all provide the historic touch.

GLOUCESTER: Ocean View Inn and Resort $$
Historic
171 Atlantic Rd., 01930
Tel *(978) 283-6200*
W oceanviewinnandresort.com
Edwardian-style summer mansions and contemporary motel rooms, many of which feature stunning ocean views.

GREAT BARRINGTON: Monument Mountain Motel $
Motel
247 Stockbridge Rd., 02130
Tel *(413) 528-3272*
W monumentmountainmotel.com
Ideally located for outdoor activities and summer arts. Has connecting family units.

IPSWICH: Inn at Castle Hill $$
Inn/B&B
280 Argilla Rd., 01938
Tel *(978) 412-2555*
W theinnatcastlehill.com

Tranquil inn within a preserve noted for its birdlife. Nearby beach features sand dunes and hiking trails.

LENOX: Canyon Ranch $$$
Luxury
165 Kemble St., 01240
Tel *(413) 637-4100*
W canyonranch.com
Luxurious resort spa. All-inclusive packages present an innovative approach to health and wellness.

NANTUCKET: Century House $$$
Luxury
10 Cliff Rd., 02554
Tel *(508) 228-0530*
W centuryhouse.com
The island's oldest family-run inn, a short walk from the town center. Graceful 19th-century ambience.

NEW MARLBOROUGH: Old Inn on the Green $$
Historic
134 New Marlborough Branch Rd., 01230
Tel *(413) 229-7924*
W oldinn.com
Historic inn, dating back to 1760, located on the village green. Spacious rooms feature antiques, quilts, and folk art.

NORTH ADAMS: Porches Inn $$
Inn/B&B
231 River St., 01247
Tel *(413) 664-0400*
W porches.com
Early 20th-century millworkers' houses, now a trendy inn next to Museum of Contemporary Art.

PLYMOUTH: John Carver Inn $$
Inn/B&B
25 Summer St., 02360
Tel *(508) 746-7100*
W ohncarverinn.com
Colonial Revival-style inn. Pilgrim-themed indoor pool features an 80-foot water slide.

PROVINCETOWN: Seaglass Inn & Spa $$$
Luxury
105 Bradford St. Ext., 02657
Tel *(508) 487-1286*
W seaglassinnandspa.com
Quiet, private accommodation with luxuriant gardens, a large heated pool, and several decks.

SALEM: Hawthorne Hotel $$
Inn/B&B
18 Washigton Square West, 01970
Tel *(978) 744-4080*
W hawthornehotel.com
Federal-style hotel famous for its Halloween costume ball. Book in advance during fall foliage and Halloween.

For more information on types of hotels *see p309*

SANDWICH: Sandy Neck Motel $
Motel
669 Route 6A, 02537
Tel *(508) 362-3992*
W sandyneck.com
Close to Sandy Neck Beach. Well-maintained grounds feature communal barbeque stations.

SOUTH WELLFLEET: Wellfleet Motel & Lodge $
Motel
170 Route 6, 02663
Tel *(508) 349-3535*
W wellfleetmotel.com
A variety of rooms and suites; popular with visitors to Cape Cod Rail Trail and Audubon Sanctuary.

SPRINGFIELD: La Quinta Inn & Suites Springfield $
Business
100 Congress St., 01104
Tel *(413) 781-0900*
W lq.com
Pocket-friendly option near some major attractions. Continental breakfast included.

STOCKBRIDGE: Red Lion Inn $$$
Luxury
30 Main St., 01262
Tel *(413) 298-5545*
W redlioninn.com
Famous Victorian-style inn dating to the 1700s and more modern guest houses.

STURBRIDGE: Comfort Inn $
Business
215 Charlton Rd., 01566
Tel *(508) 347-3306*
W sturbridgecomfortinn.com
Modern accommodation with both indoor and outdoor pools and well-maintained grounds.

WEST DENNIS: GuestLodge $
Inn/B&B
221 Main St., 02670
Tel *(508) 394-8472*
W guestlodge.net
A wide selection of rooms close to Cape Cod attractions.

WILLIAMSTOWN: The Williams Inn $$
Inn/B&B
1090 Main St., 01267
Tel *(413) 458-9371*
W williamsinn.com
Three-story inn close to the town center. Blends traditional and contemporary style.

WORCESTER: Quality Inn $
Business
50 Oriol Dr., 01605
Tel *(508) 852-2800*
W qualityinn.com
Suites with fully-equipped kitchens; located near most of the city's main attractions.

Key to Price Guide *see p310*

Rhode Island

BLOCK ISLAND: 1661 Inn and Hotel Manisses $$
Inn/B&B
5 Spring St., 02807
Tel *(401) 466-2421*
W blockislandresorts.com
The 21-room inn is open year-round, while the Victorian-style hotel closes mid-Oct to Mar. Some rooms lack TVs and share baths.

BLOCK ISLAND: Rose Farm Inn $$
Inn/B&B
1005 High St., 02807
Tel *(401) 466-2034*
W rosefarminn.com
Peaceful, natural setting with plenty of wildlife. No TVs or ACs. Open mid-Apr to mid-Oct.

BRISTOL: Bristol Harbor Inn $$
Inn/B&B
259 Thames St., 02809
Tel *(401) 254-1444*
W bristolharborinn.com
French Provincial-style rooms in a former distillery and warehouse.

CHARLESTOWN: General Stanton Inn $
Historic
4115 Old Post Rd., 02813
Tel *401-364-8888*
W generalstantoninn.com
Atmospheric low ceilings and huge fireplaces; partially dates back to 1667

MIDDLETOWN: Newport Beach Hotel and Suites $$
Luxury
1 Wave Ave., 02840
Tel *(401) 846-0310*
W newportbeachhotelandsuites.com
Well-appointed rooms, great facilities, excellent location.

NEWPORT: Hyatt Regency Newport $$
Luxury
1 Goat Island, 02840
Tel *(401) 851-1234*
W newport.hyatt.com

Rooms feature deluxe amenities and water views. Guests enjoy outdoor activities on the broad lawns and gardens.

NEWPORT: Castle Hill Inn and Resort $$$
Luxury
590 Ocean Dr., 02840
Tel *(401) 8493800*
W castlehillinn.com
A stunning waterfront locale, scenic private cottages, and fine dining options.

NEWPORT: The Chanler at Cliff Walk $$$
Luxury
117 Memorial Blvd., 02840
Tel *(401) 847-1300*
W thechanler.com
European-style boutique hotel offers excellent ocean views and individually-appointed rooms.

NEWPORT: Vanderbilt Grace Hotel $$$
Luxury
41 Mary St., 02840
Tel *(401) 846-6200*
W vanderbiltgrace.com
Formerly the famous Vanderbilt Hall mansion. Has indoor and outdoor pools and a charming terrace garden.

NORTH KINGSTOWN: Hamilton Village Inn $
Inn/B&B
642 Boston Neck Rd., 02852
Tel *(401) 295-0700*
W hamiltonvillageinn.com
This year-round inn is good for exploring the greater Newport area. Simple rooms.

PROVIDENCE: Courtyard Providence Downtown $$
Business
32 Exchange Terrace, 02903
Tel *(401) 272-1191*
W marriott.com
Low-rise hotel in the heart of down-town, connected by a walkway to shopping and convention centers.

Rich interiors at the Red Lion Inn, Stockbridge, Massachusetts

DK Choice
PROVIDENCE: Hotel Providence $$
Luxury
311 Westminster St., 02903
Tel *(401) 861-8000*
W *hotelprovidence.com*
Leading boutique hotel, blends modern design sensibilities with an appreciation of classic formality. Full European flair and New England charm, with a handy location in the heart of the city's thriving arts and theater district.

WARWICK: La Quinta Airport $
Inn/B&B
36 Jefferson Blvd., 02888
Tel *(401) 941-6600*
W *lq.com*
Pets are welcome too; close to the T.F. Green Airport.

WESTERLY: Sand Dollar Inn $
Inn/B&B
171 Post Rd., 02891
Tel *(401) 322-2000*
W *sandmotel.info*
Set two miles from the beach. Also offers a fully-equipped cottage and a private apartment.

WOONSOCKET: Pillsbury House B&B $
Inn/B&B
341 Prospect St., 02895
Tel *(401) 766-7983*
W *pillsburyhouse.com*
1875 home full of Victorian style; an excellent base for exploring the Blackstone Valley.

Connecticut
BRIDGEPORT: Holiday Inn $
Business
1070 Main St., 06604
Tel *(203) 334-1234*
W *holidayinn.com*
Convenient location with inexpensive covered parking.

COVENTRY: Daniel Rust House $$
Historic
2011 Main St., 06238
Tel *(860) 742-0032*
W *thedanielrusthouse.com*
An inn since 1800; atmospheric dining room and tavern feature an open hearth fireplace.

ESSEX: The Griswold Inn $$
Historic
36 Main St., 06426
Tel *(860) 767-1776*
W *griswoldinn.com*
Charming inn, dating back to 1776, is filled with original Currier & Ives prints and paintings.

GREENWICH: The Cos Cob Inn $
Inn/B&B
50 River Rd., 06830
Tel *(203) 661-5845*
W *coscobinn.com*
Federal-style inn whose walls are covered with American impressionist paintngs.

GREENWICH: The Delamar $$
Luxury
500 Steamboat Rd., 06830
Tel *(203) 661-9800*
W *delamargreenwich.com*
Old-world charm combined with bespoke services and modern technology. Elegant.

GROTON: Best Western Olympic Inn $
Motel
360 Route 12, 06340
Tel *(860) 445-8000*
W *bestwestern.com*
Basic, with large suites and weekend shuttle service to Mohegan Sun casino.

HARTFORD: Hilton Hartford $$
Business
315 Trumbull St., 06103
Tel *(860) 728-5151*
W *hilton.com*
A short walk from key attractions. Guests enjoy a fitness center and indoor pool.

KENT: Fife 'N Drum $$
Inn/B&B
53 North Main St., 06757
Tel *(860) 927-3509*
W *fifendrum.com*
A historic inn and adjacent house, a short stroll from upscale boutiques and galleries.

LAKEVILLE: Wake Robin Inn $$
Inn/B&B
106 Sharon Rd., 06039
Tel *(860) 435-2000*
W *wakerobininn.com*
Extensive property: the inn has 23 rooms, and there's a motel. Also has a lovely walking trail.

LEDYARD: Stonecroft Country Inn $$
Inn/B&B
515 Pumpkin Hill Rd., 06339
Tel *(860) 572-0771*
W *stonecroft.com*
Elegant country retreat that's a listed historic Georgian colonial farmhouse. Most rooms have fireplaces.

MADISON: Madison Beach Hotel $$$
Luxury
93 West Wharf Rd., 06443
Tel *(203) 245-1404*
W *madisonbeachhotel.com*
Contemporary resort in a

The atmospheric Daniel Rust House, Coventry, Connecticut

beachfront Victorian building. All rooms have balconies.

MASHANTUCKET: Foxwoods Resort Casino $$
Luxury
350 Trolley Line Blvd., 06338
Tel *(860) 312-3000*
W *foxwoods.com*
One of the world's largest casino resorts with six casinos, over 25 restaurants, four hotels, and endless shopping options.

MONTVILLE: Mohegan Sun $$
Luxury
1 Mohegan Sun Blvd., 06382
Tel *(888) 226-7711*
W *mohegansun.com*
All-purpose entertainment destination with casinos, famous performers, gourmet dining, shopping, and many amenities.

MYSTIC: Hyatt Place $$
Business
224 Greenmanville Ave., 06355
Tel *(860) 536-9997*
W *mystic.place.hyatt.com*
Close to Mystic Seaport. There's a 24-hour fitness center, guest kitchen, and business facilities.

MYSTIC: Whaler's Inn $$
Inn/B&B
20 East Main St., 06355
Tel *(860) 536-1506*
W *whalersinnmystic.com*
Friendly inn, close to shops. Requires minimum two-night stay on weekends and holidays except in winter.

NEW HAVEN: Omni New Haven $$
Luxury
155 Temple St., 06510
Tel *(203) 772-6664*
W *omnihotels.com*
Large hotel near Yale University, museums, and other attractions. Elegant interiors.

For more information on types of hotels *see p309*

DK Choice
NEW HAVEN: Study at Yale $$
Luxury
1157 Chapel St., 06511
Tel *(203) 503-3900*
W studyhotels.com
A sleek hotel across from Yale School of Art. Rooms have large flatscreen TVs, leather reading chairs, seersucker robes, and iPod docking stations. A farm-to-table restaurant completes the modern atmosphere.

NORWALK: Four Points by Sheraton $
Motel
426 Main Ave., 06851
Tel *(203) 849-9828*
W fourpointsnorwalk.com
Three-story highway stop; close to the attractions of South Norwalk and chic dining options.

OLD LYME: Bee & Thistle Inn $$
Inn/B&B
100 Lyme St., 06371
Tel *(860) 434-1667*
W beeandthistleinn.com
Charming inn features carved staircases, canopy and four-poster beds, and Oriental carpets.

OLD SAYBROOK: Saybrook Point Inn $$$
Luxury
2 Bridge St., 06475
Tel *(860) 395-2000*
W saybrook.com
An intimate spa hotel. Offers private balconies, whirlpool tubs, and working fireplaces.

SIMSBURY: Iron Horse Inn $
Inn/B&B
969 Hopmeadow St., 06070
Tel *(860) 658-2216*
W ironhorseinnofsimsbury.com
Former stagecoach inn. Rooms have refrigerators and micro-waves. There's an outdoor pool.

SOUTHPORT: The Delamar $$
Boutique
275 Old Post Rd., 06890
Tel *(203) 259-2800*
W delamarsouthport.com
Upscale luxury hotel features custom furnishings, marble floors, and museum-quality art.

STONINGTON: The Inn at Stonington $$
Inn/B&B
60 Water St., 06378
Tel *(860) 535-2000*
W theinnatstonington.com
Traditional clapboard-style inn. Most rooms have a fireplace and luxury bath.

WOODBURY: Curtis House Inn $
Historic
506 Main St., 06798
Tel *(203) 263-2101*
W curtishouseinn.com
Connecticut's oldest inn, dating back to 1735, has an old-time, quirky style. Breakfast included.

WOODSTOCK: Inn at Woodstock Hill $$
Inn/B&B
94 Plaine Hill Rd., 06281
Tel *(860) 928-0528*
W woodstockhill.com
Typical traditional New England architectural features. Popular for weddings and Sunday brunch.

Vermont

ARLINGTON: Inn on Covered Bridge Green $$
Historic
3587 River Rd., 05250
Tel *(802) 375-9489*
W coveredbridgegreen.com
Fully-equipped cottages at this 1792 farmhouse and former home of illustrator Norman Rockwell near Battenkill River.

BRATTLEBORO: Latchis Hotel $
Business
50 Main St., 05301
Tel *(802) 254-6300*
W latchis.com
Art Deco hotel with a movie theater. Modest rooms with refrigerators and coffeemakers.

BURLINGTON: Sheraton Burlington Hotel $$
Business
870 Williston Rd., 05403
Tel *(802) 865-6600*
W sheratonburlington.com
The state's largest hotel, next to the University of Vermont campus, close to downtown, Lake Champlain, and the airport.

Exterior of the Bee & Thistle Inn, Old Lyme, Connecticut

BURLINGTON: Willard Street Inn $$
Inn/B&B
349 South Willard St., 05401
Tel *(800) 577-8712*
W willardstreetinn.com
Charming 19th-century mansion filled with antiques and repro-duction Victorian furniture

CHITTENDEN: Mountain Top Inn $$
Inn/B&B
195 Mountain Top Rd., 05737
Tel *(802) 483-2311*
W mountaintopinn.com
Rooms, chalets, and pet-friendly cabins. Rates cover breakfast and many sporting activities.

EAST MIDDLEBURY: Waybury Inn $
Inn/B&B
457 East Main St., 05740
Tel *(802) 388-4015*
W wayburyinn.com
Robert Frost's favorite. Updated rooms include private baths.

ESSEX: The Essex $$$
Luxury
70 Essex Way, 05452
Tel *(802) 878-1100*
W vtculinaryresort.com
Short drive from famous skiing spots. Some rooms offer fireplaces, whirlpool tubs, and kitchenettes.

GRAFTON: The Old Tavern at Grafton $$
Historic
92 Main St., 05146
Tel *(802) 843-2231*
W graftoninnvermont.com
Tranquil former stagecoach stop. No TVs or phones in the rooms.

KILLINGTON: Mountain Meadows Lodge $$
Inn/B&B
285 Thundering Brook Rd., 05751
Tel *(802) 775-1010*
W mountainmeadowslodge.com
On a glacial lake within the Appalachian Trail; the perfect base for outdoor enthusiasts.

KILLINGTON: The Inn at Long Trail $$
Inn/B&B
709 Route 4, 05751
Tel *(800) 325-2540*
W innatlongtrail.com
Rustic lodge legendary among hikers and skiers of the Appalachian and Long Trails.

MANCHESTER: The Equinox Resort $$$
Historic
3567 Main St., 05254
Tel *(802) 362-4700*
W equinoxresort.com

Woodstocker Inn, Woodstock, Vermont

Stunning public spaces and large rooms at this 18th-century resort. Most activities are extra.

MIDDLEBURY: Swift House Inn $$
Inn/B&B
25 Stewart Lane, 05753
Tel (802) 388-9925
W swifthouseinn.com
Rooms scattered between a Federal-era main, modernized carriage, and a gatehouse on a hill.

MONTPELIER: The Inn at Montpelier $$
Inn/B&B
147 Main St., 05602
Tel (802) 223-2727
W innatmontpelier.com
Stately Federal-era inn with a large veranda and wood-burning fireplaces.

NORTH HERO: North Hero House Inn $$
Inn/B&B
3643 Route 2, 05474
Tel (802) 372-4732
W northherohouse.com
On the Lake Champlain islands; rooms are spread across four buildings. Open May–Nov.

RICHMOND: The Richmond Victorian Inn $
Inn/B&B
191 East Main St., 05477
Tel (802) 434-4410
W richmondvictorianinn.com
Modest inn. No air conditioning. Children over six welcome.

SHELBURNE: Inn at Shelburne Farms $$
Inn/B&B
1611 Harbor Rd., 05482
Tel (802) 985-8498
W shelburnefarms.org/staydine
A late 19th-century mansion, centerpiece of a historic farm that makes cheese and offers property tours.

STOWE: Alpenrose Motel $$
Inn/B&B
2619 Mountain Rd., 05672
Tel (802) 253-7277
W gostowe.com/saa/alpenrose
Modest, caters primarily to winter sports enthusiasts. Some units are pet-friendly.

DK Choice

STOWE: Trapp Family Lodge $$
Inn/B&B
700 Trapp Hill Rd., 05672
Tel (802) 253-8512
W trappfamily.com
This is the world-famous resort of the family that inspired *The Sound of Music*. Set within massive grounds, the 96-room property features a large Austrian-style main lodge and 100 cozy guest chalets. Guests enjoy nightly live entertainment, a range of recreational activities (sleigh rides, cross-country skiing, maple sugaring), and exquisite cuisine that pairs nicely with beer from the on-site brewery.

STOWE: Stowe Mountain Lodge $$$
Luxury
7412 Mountain Rd., 05672
Tel (802) 253-3560
W stowemountainlodge.com
All-seasons resort, a good base for nature lovers. Custom-designed rooms feature warm tones and comfy furnishings.

WOODSTOCK: The Woodstocker Inn $$
Inn/B&B
61 River St., 05091
Tel (802) 457-3896
W woodstockervt.com
"Green" B&B that prides itself on using organic and energy-efficient products.

New Hampshire

ALTON BAY: Bay Side Inn $$
Inn/B&B
86 Route 11D, 03810
Tel (603) 875-5005
W bayside-inn.com
Family-operated inn on Lake Winnipesaukee with a lakeside sundeck. Open May–Oct.

BETHLEHEM: Adair Country Inn $$
Inn/B&B
80 Guider Lane, 03754
Tel (603) 444-2600
W adairinn.com
A tranquil hideaway, built as a country retreat in 1927.

DK Choice

BRETTON WOODS: Omni Mount Washington Hotel $$$
Luxury
310 Mt Washington Hotel Rd., 03585
Tel (603) 278-1000
W brettonwoods.com
Since 1902, this elegant hotel has offered high-quality service in a beautiful natural setting. A favorite New England retreat of dignitaries from far and wide, the hotel is a prime example of Spanish Renaissance architecture. Besides numerous public areas and dining facilities, guests enjoy a signature spa, thrilling year-round canopy tour and Donald Ross-designed golf course.

BRIDGEWATER: Inn on Newfound Lake $$
Inn/B&B
1030 Mayhew Turnpike, 03222
Tel (603) 744-9111
W newfoundlake.com
Classic country stagecoach inn since 1840. The welcoming restaurant and lively lounge attract patrons from miles away.

CONCORD: The Centennial Inn $$
Inn/B&B
96 Pleasant St., 03301
Tel (603) 227-9000
W thecentennialhotel.com
In a restored 1892 Victorian brick mansion, antique decor and suites in the turrets.

EXETER: The Exeter Inn $$
Inn/B&B
90 Front St., 03833
Tel (603) 772-5901
W theexeterinn.com
Georgian-style inn; elegant rooms filled with antiques and reproduction furniture.

For more information on types of hotels *see p309*

Old-fashioned decor at the Franconia Inn, New Hampshire

FRANCONIA: The Franconia Inn $
Inn/B&B
1300 Easton Rd., 03580
Tel *(603) 823-5542*
W franconiainn.com
Striking views and year-round
activities such as rock climbing,
hiking, snowshoeing, and skiing.

**HAMPTON: Ashworth by
the Sea** $$
Inn/B&B
295 Ocean Blvd., 03842
Tel *(800) 345-6736*
W ashworthhotel.com
Elegant beachfront hotel, open
all year. Most of the spacious
rooms have ocean views.

HANOVER: Chieftain Motor Inn $
Motel
84 Lyme Rd., 03755
Tel *(603) 643-2550*
W chieftaininn.com
Two-story motel with complimen-
tary canoe rentals and a heated
pool. Family rooms sleep up to six.

HANOVER: Hanover Inn $$
Inn/B&B
2 South Main St., 03755
Tel *(603) 643-4300*
W hanoverinn.com
Colonial-style inn, popular with
scholars and dignitaries.

KEENE: Carriage Barn B&B $
Inn/B&B
358 Main St., 03431
Tel *(603) 357-3812*
W carriagebarn.com
Cheerfully decorated rooms with
local country antiques.

KEENE: Lane Hotel $$
Historic
30 Main St., 03441
Tel *(603) 357-7070*
W thelanehotel.com
Carved out of an upscale
department store and done up
with reproduction furnishings.

MANCHESTER: Econo Lodge $
Inn/B&B
75 W. Hancock St., 03102
Tel *(603) 624-0111*
W econolodge.com

Basic, comfortable rooms. Pet-
friendly, breakfast included.

**MANCHESTER: Hilton Garden
Inn Manchester Downtown** $$
Business
101 S. Commercial St., 03101
Tel *(603) 669-2222*
W hgi-manchester.com
A short walk from the main
attractions and Verizon Wireless
arena. Modern amenities.

**NEW CASTLE: Wentworth by
the Sea** $$$
Luxury
588 Wentworth Rd., 03854
Tel *(603) 422-7322*
W wentworth.com
Meticulously-restored, historic
grand hotel popular at the
mouth of Portsmouth harbor.

**NORTH SUTTON: Follansbee
Inn** $$
Inn/B&B
2 Keyser St., 03260
Tel *(603) 927-4221*
W follansbeeinn.com
Lakeside location. Free use of kay-
aks, boats, and other equipment.

**PORTSMOUTH: Sheraton
Harborside Portsmouth** $$
Business
250 Market St., 03801
Tel *(603) 431-2300*
W sheratonportsmouth.com
Modern hotel, in the heart of
Plymouth, offers redwood sauna,
fitness room, and a large pool.

**WEIRS BEACH: Lake
Winnipesaukee Motel** $
Motel
350 Daniel Webster Hwy., 02347
Tel *(603) 366-5502*
W lakewinnipesaukeemotel.com
Open May–Oct and in Feb for ice-
fishing and snowmobiling. Private,
two-bedroom house available.

**WHITFIELD: Mountain View
Grand Resort & Spa** $$
Historic
101 Mountain View Rd., 03598
Tel *(603) 837-2100*
W mountainviewgrand.com

Dating back to 1865, it is ideally
situated for hikers and alpine
skiiers. Stunning views of the
Presidential and Kilkenny ranges.

**WOLFEBORO: The
Wolfeboro Inn** $$
Inn/B&B
90 North Main St., 03894
Tel *(603) 569-3016*
W wolfeboroinn.com
Offers its own private beach on a
small lake. Rooms feature country
squire-style appoinments.

Maine

BANGOR: Fairfield Inn $
Business
300 Odlin Rd., 04401
Tel *(207) 990-0001*
W marriott.com
Offers amenities such as indoor
pool, hot tub, and fitness room.

**BAR HARBOR: Atlantic Eyrie
Lodge** $$
Inn/B&B
6 Norman Rd., 04609
Tel *(207) 288-9786*
W atlanticeyrielodge.com
Good base for exploring Bar
Harbor. Some rooms have full
kitchens; all have ocean views.

**BAR HARBOR: Mira Monte
Inn** $$
Inn/B&B
69 Mount Desert St., 04609
Tel *(207) 288-4263*
W miramonte.com
Welcoming, family-owned B&B
constructed in 1864.
Open May–Oct.

**BELFAST: Colonial Gables
Oceanfront Village** $
Inn/B&B
7 Eagle Ave., 04915
Tel *(207) 338-4000*
W colonialgables.com
Offers both cottages and rooms.
Many units have cooking facilities.

**BETHEL: Bethel Inn and
Country Club** $$
Luxury
21 Broad St., 04217
Tel *(207) 824-2175*
W bethelinn.com
Popular resort with four colonial-
style buildings, golf course and
tennins courts.

**CAMDEN: Camden Maine
Stay Inn** $$
Historic
22 High St., 04843
Tel *(207) 236-9636*
W camdenmainestay.com
Grand, 1801 house, barn, and

carriage house complex furnished in an eclectic style.

CAPE ELIZABETH: Inn by the Sea $$$
Luxury
40 Bowery Beach Rd., 04107
Tel *(207) 799-3134*
W innbythesea.com
A certified "Green Lodging" destination. Rooms feature local artwork and luxurious touches.

CARIBOU: Caribou Inn and Convention Center $
Business
19 Main St., 04736
Tel *(207) 498-3733*
W caribouinn.com
Catering to snowmobilers; busiest during Jan and Feb. Pet-friendly.

CARRABASSETT VALLEY: Sugarloaf Mountain Resort $
Inn/B&B
5092 Sugarloaf Rd., 04947
Tel *(207) 237-2000*
W sugarloaf.com
A popular ski resort; choose a casual slope-side inn, full-service hotel, or condo unit.

FREEPORT: Harraseeket Inn $$
Inn/B&B
162 Main St., 04032
Tel *(207) 865-9377*
W harraseeketinn.com
High-end retreat offers fireplaces, Jacuzzis, and an indoor pool.

FRYEBURG: Oxford House Inn $$
Inn/B&B
548 Main St., 04037
Tel *(207) 935-3442*
W oxfordhouseinn.com
Charming 1913 residence with four beautifully decorated rooms.

GREENVILLE: Kineo View Motor Lodge $
Motel
50 Overlook Dr., 04441
Tel *(207) 695-4470*
W kineoview.com
Modest family-run three-story motel. Spectacular views,

GREENVILLE: Greenville Inn $$
Inn/B&B
40 Norris St., 04441
Tel *(207) 695-2206*
W greenvilleinn.com
Beautifully appointed Victorian inn has rooms and cottages.

KENNEBUNKPORT: Captain Jefferd's Inn $$
Historic
5 Pearl St., 04046
Tel *(800) 839-6844*
W captainjefferdsinn.com
Sea captain's mansion, built in

1804, retains its antique charm and has beautiful gardens.

KENNEBUNKPORT: The Colony Hotel $$
Inn/B&B
140 Ocean Ave., 04046
Tel *(207) 967-3331*
W thecolonyhotel.com
Overlooking the ocean; with a heated saltwater pool and private surf beach. Open mid-May–late Oct.

DK Choice

KENNEBUNKPORT: The White Barn Grace $$
Historic
37 Beach Ave., 04043
Tel *(207) 967-2321*
W gracehotels.com
Dating back to 1820, this property offers a variety of handsome lodging options. Rooms, suites, and cottages are all filled with fresh flowers and fruit, plus a range of modern amenities. The natural stone-heated swimming pool and full-service spa provide relaxation. Local, seasonal cuisine is served in the acclaimed restaurant.

MONHEGAN ISLAND: The Island Inn $$
Inn/B&B
Monhegan Harbor, 04852
Tel *(207) 596-0371*
W islandinnmonhegan.com
1816 Inn with no heating but lots of fireplaces and duvets. Open late May–early Oct.

NEW HARBOR: Hotel Pemaquid $
Historic
3098 Bristol Rd., 04554
Tel *(207) 677-2312*
W hotelpemaquid.com
Former farmhouse near the coast that first welcomed guests in 1888. Open mid-May–mid-Oct.

NEWCASTLE: Newcastle Inn $$
Inn/B&B
60 River Rd., 03907
Tel *(207) 563-5685*
W newcastleinn.com
Perfect for exploring the peninsulas of mid-coast Maine. Select from the main inn, a cottage, and a former carriage house.

OGUNQUIT: The Cliff House Resort & Spa $$
Historic
591 Shore Rd., 03907
Tel *(207) 361-1000*
W cliffhousemaine.com
Iconic oceanside resort built in 1872. Open Apr–mid-Dec.

PORTLAND: The Inn at St. John $
Inn/B&B
939 Congress St., 04102
Tel *(800) 636-9127*
W innatstjohn.com
Venerable inn built in 1897 to accommodate rail passengers.

PORTLAND: Portland Regency Hotel $$
Business
20 Milk St., 04101
Tel *(207) 774-4200*
W theregency.com
Former Armory in the heart of the Old Port. Rooms feature Colonial-style furnishings.

PORTLAND: Residence Inn Portland Downtown/ Waterfront $$
Business
145 Fore St., 04101
Tel *(207) 761-1660*
W marriott.com
Modern all-suite hotel that is a good base for leisure travelers.

RANGELEY: Rangeley Inn $
Inn/B&B
2443 Main St., 04970
Tel *(207) 864-3341*
W therangeleyinn.com
Includes a main inn, motor lodge, and two lakeside cabins. Popular for skiing in winter. Open Jun–Mar.

ROCKLAND: Limerock Inn $$
Inn/B&B
96 Limerock St., 04841
Tel *(207) 594-2257*
W limerockinn.com
Queen Anne-style mansion with landscaped gardens; a stroll away from Farnsworth Museum.

TENANTS HARBOR: East Wind Inn $$
Inn/B&B
21 Mechanic St., 04860
Tel *(207) 372-6366*
W eastwindinn.com
Spread across three buildings and furnished with a mix of country furniture and local antiques.

The White Barn Grace, Kennebunkport, Maine

For more information on types of hotels *see p309*

WHERE TO EAT AND DRINK

To many outsiders, New England has long been synonymous with simple, hearty, somewhat boring fare. While it is true that a traditional meal of the past often consisted of cod or boiled beef and cabbage served with potatoes, the contemporary regional menu is substantially more varied and tempting. Local cheeses, fruits, and vegetables from rural areas complement the exquisite seafood, often caught fresh the same day, which is found up and down the coast. In addition, the New England dining experience includes a host of ethnic flavors, thanks to a steady stream of immigrants into the large urban areas. Boston (Massachusetts), Portland (Maine), and Providence (Rhode Island) are the region's top dining destinations. Boston's restaurant scene is particularly vibrant; the city's top restaurants serve a medley of styles, such as French and Italian, often using other Mediterranean and Asian accents. Boston was once called "Bean Town" because of the popularity of its baked beans; now it has quality Indian, Southeast Asian, Latin American, and Caribbean restaurants.

Opening Hours

Most restaurants serve breakfast from 6 or 7am until 11am or noon. Some serve breakfast all day. The choice is varied, with some spots offering little more than a bagel and a coffee and others whipping up portions of eggs, bacon, and sausages hefty enough to keep you going almost all day. Lunch can run anytime from 11:30am until 2:30pm, and is equally varied. In downtown areas; businesspeople can be seen gulping down a sandwich at the counter of a local deli or sitting down to enjoy a sumptuous restaurant meal. In many places, the lunch menu is the same as it is for dinner, with smaller portions and significantly lower prices. Some restaurants close for a few hours between lunch and dinner, while smaller family-run places may stay open throughout the afternoon, making them a good bet for eating at more unusual times.

Traditionally, New Englanders tend to serve up large dinners.

Radio Room at the Good News Café *(see p335)* in Woodbury, Connecticut

You can usually sit down between 5:30 and 10:30pm. Some Boston restaurants, notably those in Chinatown and Kenmore Square, stay open late, supported mostly by the ravenous crowds heading home from the dance clubs and bars. As a general rule, urban areas will have a much higher percentage of dinner-only establishments, while finding a casual eating spot open after 3pm in the countryside can be challenging. State and local laws vary on the hours during which alcohol may be served, but in most parts of New England bars begin to close at midnight, with a few staying open until 1am or 2 am in the urban areas. Food service, even at bars, usually finishes by 10pm or 11pm. On Sundays, alcohol sales are generally prohibited before noon, although some Boston establishments, notably in the South End, are allowed to serve cocktails with their amazing Sunday brunches. Hotels are also exempt from the alcohol prohibition and often serve champagne cocktails with their Sunday brunches. It is not uncommon for restaurants to close on Mondays, as well as during quiet afternoon periods. As always, you should check in advance.

Reservations

Finer restaurants often require a reservation, though in most cases (especially weeknights) these can be made at short notice. In rural areas and small cities, reservations are only an issue during peak season – July and August on the coast and the Berkshires, September and October in the mountains, and December, January and February in ski country.

Paying and Tipping

Waiters are generally paid fairly low wages and they earn the bulk of their income through tips. This means that all restaurants with table service expect some sort of gratuity at the end of the

Elegant dining room at Rialto, Cambridge *(see p327)*

Casual outdoor seating at Local 188, Maine *(see p339)*

meal. Each state charges a different meal tax, but it is standard practice to leave between 15–20 percent of the bill as the tip. If the service is good or bad, adjust the tip rate accordingly.

Alcohol and Smoking

The legal drinking age is 21, so underage travelers should be aware that they will be denied access to most bars and will not be allowed to order wine with dinner in restaurants. Most places are strict about this and often require you to show photographic ID before you are served. Passports are generally the best form of identification, since many people are unfamiliar with driver's licenses from abroad. The legal age to purchase cigarettes is 18; identification may be required. Smoking is banned in almost all restaurants and bars throughout New England.

Dress Codes

New England is a relaxed place where people dress on the casual side when they are dining out. This is especially true along the coast, where the casual beach atmosphere carries over into restaurants. There, shorts and T-shirts are commonplace. However, some establishments do have strict dress codes. Formal evening wear is uncommon, but in some of the finest restaurants it will not appear out of place.

Children

Children are welcome in most mid-range restaurants, although restaurants in urban business areas are often less accustomed to them. Avoid restaurants that feature a large bar and young crowds, as they are less likely to permit under 21s on the premises.

Entrance to L'Espalier in Boston, Massachusetts *(see p325)*

Disabilities

Federal and state legislation has made most restaurants in New England at least partially accessible by wheelchair and many more are accessible to people with other disabilities. Historic structures are sometimes exempted from the accessibility requirements. Entrances are generally ramped, doors may be fitted with an automatic opener, and restrooms usually include the appropriate stalls and sinks.

Recommended Restaurants

The restaurants featured in this guide have been selected across a wide price range for their value, good food, atmosphere, and location. From authentic, no-frills seafood shacks to pricey temples of gastronomy, these restaurants run the gamut across all price levels and cuisine types. Bordering the chilly waters of the Atlantic Ocean, New England is renowned for its seafood offerings. Large cities such as Boston, Providence, and New Haven all have large Italian communities with a preponderance of acclaimed Italian and pizza eateries on offer. Many of the region's most acclaimed restaurants serve French and New American fare. Ethnic restaurants also abound, serving tasty Chinese, Thai, and Indian fare to budget-minded diners.

Restaurants are listed by area, and within these areas by price. Since venues often host private events or close unexpectedly due to any number or issues, it's always wise to consult a restaurant's homepage or call before visiting. For the best of the best, look out for restaurants featuring the "DK Choice" symbol. These establishments have been highlighted in recognition of an exceptional feature – a celebrity chef, exquisite food, an inviting atmosphere. The majority of these are popular among local residents and visitors, so be sure to inquire regarding reservations or you may be facing a lengthy wait for a table.

New England's Maple Syrup

During the spring thaw in late March and early April, New England farmers hammer spigots into the trunks of their sugar maple trees in order to collect the trees' clear, slightly sweet sap in buckets. Traditionally sap is then poured into vats back at the "sugarhouse" and boiled for hours. When most of the excess water has been evaporated, an amber-colored syrup is left – a highly concentrated, thoroughly delicious product that is distinctly New England. The finest quality syrup goes best on pancakes and waffles and over ice cream.

The Flavors of New England

The geography and history of New England have produced some fine and highly distinctive culinary traditions. The long coastline accounts for the region's abundance of superb seafood, while the ethnic make-up of the area has led to some gastronomic highlights. Native Americans enjoyed staples such as corn, maple syrup, and cranberries. Early settlers brought dishes from England and Ireland, including hearty stews (known as boiled dinners) and puddings that remain popular to this day. Thanks to several Italian communities, New England boasts some of the best and most authentic pizza in America, and recipes from Portuguese fishermen pepper many menus.

New England apples

Typical lobster dish served at a beachfront restaurant

Gifts from the Sea

Seafood is at the heart of New England cuisine. The cold waters along the coast yield a bounty of delicious fish such as scrod (young cod), haddock, and swordfish. Maine lobster is a coveted delicacy. Tanks of live lobsters are shipped to restaurants all around America, but nowhere are they as succulent and sweet as they are in their home state. Lobster is at its best when eaten at one of the informal outdoor lobster pounds that are found all along the shoreline. Here, diners can choose their own freshly caught specimen from a tank and then sit back and enjoy the view, while it is being steamed or boiled. Lobster is usually served with melted butter in which to dip the meat, and cups of clear steaming seafood broth.

The Mighty Clam

No food is more ubiquitous in the region than clams. They are served in so many different ways: steamed, stuffed, baked, minced in fish cakes, or in the famous New England clam chowder. Fried clams, a dish said to have been invented in Essex, Massachusetts, are found on almost every seafood menu. The large hard-shelled quahog clam – a delicacy from Rhode Island – is used to make stuffed

Corn on the cob — Baked potato — Steamed clams — Melted butter — Boiled lobs
A typical New England clambake dinner

Local Dishes and Specialties

Like most Americans, New Englanders tend to have a light lunch and their main meal in the evening. Some New England dining experiences are too good to miss. Breakfasts are hearty, perhaps because of the cold winters, and at least one should include wild blueberry pancakes or muffins, and another an omelette made with tangy Vermont cheddar. Other musts are a lunch of lobster roll (chunks of sweet lobster meat in a mayonnaise-based dressing, stuffed into a toasted bun), New England clam chowder, and one of the region's famous

Maple Syrup   clambake dinners. A visit to Boston is hardly complete without sampling the superb local scrod and the rich classic cream pie, both found on menus all over the city along with Vermont's favorite ice cream, Ben and Jerry's.

Blueberry pancakes Wild blueberries are stirred into batter to make a stack of these thick pancakes.

Colorful display of pumpkins at a local farmers' market

Dairy Delights

Vermont is home to over 1,500 dairy farms, where herds of well-fed cows produce the milk that goes into some of New England's famous dairy produce. This includes a selection of rich ice creams and the highly acclaimed Vermont cheddar cheese. Some of the best and most widely available cheeses are produced by the Cabot Creamery Cooperative, which is owned directly by a group of dairy farmers. The Vermont Cheese Council offers a map showing 39 dairies that make a variety of cheeses. Some welcome visitors.

clams known as "stuffies". There is also a distinctive Rhode Island-style chowder which is made with a clear broth, unlike the more usual chowder which is enriched with either milk or cream.

Sweet Offerings

Sugar maples, which bring a dazzling display of color to the hillsides in fall, yield yet more riches in late winter, when the trees can be tapped and their sap boiled down to produce maple syrup. This is served on pancakes and made into sweets (candy) and sauces. New England also produces vast acres of wild blueberries, apples, and pumpkins that lend themselves to a variety of delectable desserts. Well into the 19th century, molasses from the Caribbean was used as a sweetener, and is still added to many traditional sweet dishes, such as Indian pudding, a delicious slow-baked confection of spiced cornmeal, molasses, eggs, and milk.

Freshly picked wild blueberries, from the bumper summer harvest

WHAT TO DRINK

Poland Spring water This bottled water from Maine is the local favorite.

Frappé A New England-style milkshake made with ice cream and chocolate syrup.

Sakonnet Wines From Rhode Island, these are among the finest wines in the region.

Samuel Adams and Harpoon beers New England's best known brands are brewed in Boston.

Micro-brewery beers Some of the best are made by Thomas Hooker in Hartford, Connecticut; Smuttynose in Portsmouth, New Hampshire; and Magic Hat in Burlington, Vermont.

Baked scrod Fillets of young cod (scrod) are rolled in breadcrumbs and baked, then served with tartare sauce.

New England clam chowder Fresh clams, either left whole or chopped, and chunks of potato fill this creamy soup.

Boston cream pie Layers of sponge cake, sandwiched with egg custard, are topped with chocolate icing.

Where to Eat and Drink

Boston

Back Bay and the South End

B.Good $
American　　　　　Map 3 B2
272 Newbury St., 02116
Tel *(617) 236-0440*
Inexpensive option for a snack or light meal, specializes in healthy fast food. The leafy patio is a top choice for *al fresco* eats.

El Pelon Taquería $
Mexican
92 Peterborough St., 02215
Tel *(617) 262-9090*
A favorite grab-and-go spot for those heading to or from Fenway Park. Try the fish tacos and the *El Guapo* burrito.

Flour Bakery + Café $
American　　　　　Map 3 C5
1595 Washington St., 02118
Tel *(617) 267-4300*
A popular neighborhood meeting spot. Area residents and medical staff stop by for gourmet sandwiches, coffee, and freshly baked goods.

Mike's City Diner $
American　　　　　Map 3 C5
1714 Washington St., 02118
Tel *(617) 267-9393*
There's often a line outside for this classic, breakfast- and lunch-only diner. Filling, greasy classics take up most of the menu.

Trident Booksellers & Café $
American　　　　　Map 3 A3
338 Newbury St., 02115
Tel *(617) 267-8688*
The in-store café and bar serves light and casual meals ranging from breakfast eggs to lunch wraps, as well as dinner dishes such as lasagna.

Audubon Circle Restaurant Bar $$
New American
838 Beacon St., 02215
Tel *(617) 421-1910*
Trendy sandwiches and burgers prove popular with Red Sox fans heading to or from Fenway Park. The patio is a local favorite.

Joe's American Bar & Grill $$
American　　　　　Map 3 B2
181 Newbury St., 02116
Tel *(617) 536-4200*
Endless menu of classic favorites, from giant salads to prime burgers. The staff are kid-friendly.

Parish Café $$
American　　　　　Map 3 B2
361 Boylston St., 02116
Tel *(617) 247-4777*
Renowned for its creative sandwiches designed by Boston's top chefs. During warm weather, the sidewalk patio offers terrific views of the street scene.

Aquitaine $$$
French　　　　　Map 4 D4
569 Tremont St., 02118
Tel *(617) 424-8577*
A Parisian-style bistro popular for its snazzy wine bar and French market cooking. Black truffle vinaigrette makes Aquitaine's steak-frites Boston's best.

Brasserie Jo $$$
French　　　　　Map 3 B3
120 Huntington Ave., 02116
Tel *(617) 425-3240*
Airy hotel-restaurant captures the savoir faire of 1940s Paris. Hearty French classics such as steak *roquefort* and *coq au vin* pair nicely with the inviting wine list.

Bravo $$$
New American
465 Huntington Ave., 02116
Tel *(617) 369-3474*
The Museum of Fine Arts' dining destination focuses on light and healthy dishes like crisp salads and pastas tossed with vegetables.

Clio $$$
New American　　　Map 3 A2
370A Commonwealth Ave., 02215
Tel *(617) 536-7200*　　**Closed** *Sun*
Local culinary titan Ken Oringer presides over the grand Eliot Hotel's claim to culinary fame. Luxurious entrées complement the richly appointed dining room.

The sophisticated and popular Clio, at the Eliot Hotel, Boston

---

Price Guide
Prices are based on a three-course meal per person, with a half-bottle of house wine, including tax and service.
$　　　　　under $35
$$　　　　$35 to $60
$$$　　　over $60

Davio's $$$
Italian　　　　　Map 4 D2
75 Arlington St., 02116
Tel *(617) 357-4810*
Choose from a versatile menu of steaks, veal chops, and handmade pastas. Also has a children's menu.

Deuxave $$$
New American　　　Map 3 A2
371 Commonwealth Ave., 02116
Tel *(617) 517-5915*
Highbrow cocktails and modern American fare with local, seasonal ingredients, served in chic surroundings.

Douzo $$$
Japanese　　　　　Map 3 C3
131 Dartmouth St., 02116
Tel *(617) 859-8886*
One of the city's popular spots for sushi and intricate Japanese dishes. Specialties include Phoenix Rolls, Red Spider, and Spicy Tuna Crispy Rice.

Gaslight Brasserie $$$
French　　　　　Map 4 E4
560 Harrison Ave., 02118
Tel *(617) 422-0224*
Stylish bistro that specializes in the casual cuisine of the French provinces. Free parking is an added bonus.

Grill 23 & Bar $$$
Steakhouse　　　　Map 4 D2
161 Berkeley St., 02117
Tel *(617) 542-2255*
Big-ticket steakhouse harks back to the days of exclusive, Prohibition-era supper clubs. Prime-aged beef with an inventive spin is served in a sumptuously classic interior.

Hamersley's Bistro $$$
New American　　　Map 4 D4
553 Tremont St., 02116
Tel *(617) 423-2700*
Iconic neighborhood bistro, featuring the best of local produce. Lively bar scene and outdoor patio. The chicken may just be the city's most famous.

Island Creek Oyster Bar $$$
Seafood
500 Commonwealth Ave., 02215
Tel *(617) 532-5300*
Far more than an oyster bar, this

Elegant interiors at the famed L'Espalier, Boston

large hotel-restaurant provides a plethora of creative, seasonal fare in casual surroundings.

Jae's Café $$$
Asian   Map 3 B4
520 Columbus Ave., 02118
Tel *(617) 421-9405*
Light, fresh dishes drawn from Korea, Japan, China, and Southeast Asia served in relaxed environs.

DK Choice

L'Espalier $$$
French   Map 3 B2
774 Boylston St., 02199
Tel *(617) 262-3023*
Staffed by impeccable waiters and brilliant cooks, this romantic destination restaurant serves some of New England's most acclaimed contemporary French cuisine. Chef-owner Frank McClelland's vegetarian entrées featuring produce from his own farm are every bit as sophisticated as those with meat. Inventive desserts, unrivaled cheese dishes, and a to-die-for wine list complete the gourmet scene.

Masa $$$
New American   Map 4 D3
439 Tremont St., 02116
Tel *(617) 338-8884*
Refined New American dishes with southwestern accents, complemented by margaritas, colorful decor, and good wines.

Orinoco $$$
Latin American   Map 3 C5
477 Shawmut Ave., 02118
Tel *(617) 369-7075*   **Closed** *Mon*
Cheerful dining room serves inviting, exotic Latin American and Venezuelan fare. The diverse cocktail list features something for every taste.

Petit Robert Bistro $$$
French   Map 3 A2
468 Commonwealth Ave., 02215
Tel *(617) 375-0699*
Simple, clean French bistro fare in the heart of Kenmore Square. The sunken sidewalk patio features a replica Eiffel Tower.

Sonsie $$$
Italian   Map 3 A3
327 Newbury St., 02115
Tel *(617) 351-2500*
Enjoy pizzas, pastas, and well-made cocktails. The Wine Room offers over 200 wines.

Stephanie's on Newbury $$$
American   Map 3 B2
190 Newbury St., 02116
Tel *(617) 236-0990*
The menu has everything from salads and burgers to pasta dishes and well-made martinis.

Summer Shack $$$
Seafood   Map 3 A3
50 Dalton St., 02115
Tel *(617) 867-9955*
One of New England's legendary chefs delivers straightforward preparations of fresh seafood in casual, fun environs. The bar is a welcoming spot for solo diners.

Tapéo $$$
Spanish   Map 3 B2
266 Newbury St., 02116
Tel *(617) 267-4799*
A neighborhood stalwart, popular for its intensely flavorful tapas and extensive Spanish wine list. In summer, the large patio is filled with groups enjoying pitchers of sangria.

The Elephant Walk $$$
Asian-French
900 Beacon St., 02215
Tel *(617) 247-1500*
A vivid, sophisticated menu alternates between authentic

Cambodian and French dishes. There is an extensive wine list.

Toro $$$
Spanish   Map 3 C5
1704 Washington St., 02118
Tel *(617) 536-4300*
It's a battle to secure a table at the city's most popular spot for upscale tapas and Latin fare. The menu is filled with trendy, imported items and hard-to-find-elsewhere dishes.

Tremont 647 $$$
New American   Map 3 C4
647 Tremont St., 02118
Tel *(617) 266-4600*
The chef's barbeque has won national competitions, his menu is also filled with eclectic, New American eats. The sidewalk patio and "pajama brunch" are neighborhood favorites.

Turner Fisheries $$$
Seafood   Map 3 C2
10 Huntington Ave., 02116
Tel *(617) 424-7425*   **Closed** *Sun, Mon*
The Westin Copley Place's largest restaurant places an emphasis on large portions of fresh seafood, much of it local. Opt for either the airy outer room with windows onto Copley Square or the cozier lounge near the bar.

Beacon Hill and the Theater District

Anna's Taqueria $
Mexican   Map 1 B3
242 Cambridge St., 02114
Tel *(617) 227-8822*
This popular cafeteria-style burrito chain serves as a dependable spot for no-frills Mexican bites. A favorite of neighborhood students and the medical community.

For more information on types of restaurants *see p321*

Fresh crabs on display at the New Jumbo Seafood Restaurant, Boston

Jacob Wirth $$
German-American **Map** 1 B5
31 Stuart St., 02116
Tel *(617) 338-8586*
A true Boston landmark: an old fashioned beer hall serving since 1868. Live piano music featured on Friday nights.

King & I $$
Thai **Map** 1 B3
145 Charles St., 02114
Tel *(617) 227-3320*
Savory, well-priced Thai staples in a small, casual interior; the take-out is popular.

New Jumbo Seafood Restaurant $$
Chinese **Map** 4 F3
5 Hudson St., 02111
Tel *(617) 542-2823*
A bustling Chinatown eatery that replicates the complex seafood cuisine of China's Guandong province, featuring imported ingredients such as dried shrimp and jellyfish.

Panificio Bistro & Bakery $$
Italian **Map** 1 B3
144 Charles St., 02114
Tel *(617) 227-4340*
This popular bakery specializes in rustic Italian breads, pastries, and well-made coffee drinks; also serves light meals all day long in the homey dining room.

Penang $$
Asian **Map** 1 C5
685 Washington St., 02111
Tel *(617) 451-6373* **Closed** *Fri, Sat*
Largely a Malaysian menu, ranging from inexpensive noodle staples and spicy curry dishes to more contemporary concoctions.

Shabu-Zen $$
Asian **Map** 4 F2
16 Tyler St., 02111
Tel *(617) 292-8828*
One of Chinatown's busiest restaurants; a casual social spot for enjoying traditional hot pot fare.

75 Chestnut $$$
American **Map** 1 B4
75 Chestnut St., 02108
Tel *(617) 227-2175*
Converted townhouse that offers one of Beacon Hill's most welcoming dining experiences. The upscale bistro fare can be enjoyed while watching sports in the casual bar area.

Artu $$$
Italian **Map** 1 B2
89 Charles St., 02114
Tel *(617) 227-9023* **Closed** *Mon, Wed*
Tuscan specialties such as seasoned chicken and roasted veggies come straight off the exposed, sizzling grill to the table. Casual subterranean environs.

Beacon Hill Bistro $$$
French-American **Map** 1 B4
25 Charles St., 02114
Tel *(617) 723-7575*
Authentic bistro setting in which to enjoy a New American spin on

Entrance to the award-winning Beacon Hill Bistro , Boston

French bistro cuisine. The tiny bar is perfect for sampling from the well-chosen wine list.

Bristol Lounge $$$
New American **Map** 4 D2
200 Boylston St., 02116
Tel *(617) 351-2037*
The Four Seasons' all-purpose restaurant is one of the city's best spots for afternoon tea, upscale dining with kids, or a romantic rendezvous.

Figs $$$
Italian **Map** 1 B4
42 Charles St., 02114
Tel *(617) 742-3447*
A popular spot where local celeb-chef Todd English delivers special thin-crust pizzas with gourmet toppings. Also serves hand-made pastas, salads, and home-made desserts.

Lala Rokh $$$
Middle Eastern **Map** 1 B4
97 Mount Vernon St., 02108
Tel *(617) 720-5511*
Authentic Persian cuisine served in romantic surroundings. Citrus-based glazes and relishes give meats a lovely piquant flavor.

No. 9 Park $$$
New American **Map** 1 C4
9 Park St., 02108
Tel *(617) 742-9991*
Hob-nob with Beacon Hill high flyers in this bold bistro over-looking Boston Common. Inventive gourmet fare pairs nicely with the imaginative wine list.

Scampo $$$
Italian **Map** 1 B3
215 Charles St., 02114
Tel *(617) 536-2100*
Celebrity chef Lydia Shire wows customers with upscale Italian-accented fare in the trendy Liberty Hotel.

Teatro $$$
Italian **Map** 4 E2
177 Tremont St., 02111
Tel *(617) 778-6841* **Closed** *Mon*
A glamourous scene prevails at this flashy *trattoria*, serving Italian classics such as hand-made pastas, grilled thin-crust pizzas, and fresh seafood. There's also a great wine list.

Toscano Restaurant $$$
Italian **Map** 1 B4
47 Charles St., 02114
Tel *(617) 723-4090*
Situated in the heart of scenic Charles Street in relaxed environs. Serves a straightforward menu of Italian favorites prepared with aplomb.

Troquet $$$
New American   **Map** 1 B5
140 Boylston St., 02116
Tel *(617) 695-9463* **Closed** *Sun, Mon*
A stylish restaurant where wines
get top billing, with suggested
small plates of New American
bistro fare paired with the
owner's diverse wine selections.

Brookline

Zaftigs Delicatessen $$
American
335 Harvard St., Brookline, 02446
Tel *(617) 975-0075*
Great Jewish-style deli with a
ton of menu options, from filling
breakfast fare to towering
sandwiches and hearty soups.

Cambridge

Russel House Tavern $$
New American
14 JFK St., Cambridge, 02138
Tel *(617) 500-3055*
Modern takes on American
classics and regional favorites.
Diners choose between the
bustling bar area, casual dining
room, and popular patio space.

Catalyst $$$
New American
*300 Technology Sq., Cambridge,
02139*
Tel *(617) 576-3000*
Trendy restaurant serving
locally-inspired fare. Offers
craft beers and a good selection
of wines. Multiple seating
options, including a patio and
a lively bar.

Craigie on Main $$$
New American
853 Main St., 02138
Tel *(617) 497-5511* **Closed** *Mon*
French-inspired dishes prepared
with locally-sourced organic
ingredients. The menu changes
daily, based on the ingredients of
the day. The bar area-only burger
is legendary.

East Coast Grill $$$
American
1271 Cambridge St., Cambridge, 02139
Tel *(617) 491-6568*
This Pacific Rim-influenced Inman
Square fish house also serves up
some of the area's best barbeque
fare. "Hell Nights" attract lovers of
exceptionally spicy fare.

EVOO $$$
New American
350 3rd St., Cambridge, 02142
Tel *(617) 661-3866*
Eclectic cuisine, mirroring the
high-tech Kendall Square
surroundings. The chef packs

his menu with all the fine local
produce he can get his hands on.

Henrietta's Table $$$
American
1 Bennett St., Cambridge, 02138
Tel *(617) 661-5005*
Serving generous portions of
classic American fare, the Charles
Hotel's inviting bistro amply
rewards hearty appetites. House-
infused liquors can be enjoyed
at the small, social bar area.

Hungry Mother $$$
New American
*233 Cardinal Medeiros Ave.,
Cambridge, 02141*
Tel *(617) 499-0090* **Closed** *Mon*
One of the area's most in-
demand restaurants, this
unassuming little eatery serves
upscale interpretations of
American southern fare.

Oleana $$$
Eclectic
134 Hampshire St., Cambridge, 02139
Tel *(617) 661-0505*
Award-winning chef Ana Sorton's
mastery of exotic spices is evident
in the intriguing, multi-ethnic
cuisine. Diners choose between
the casually elegant dining room
and lovely back patio.

Restaurant Dante $$$
Italian
*40 Edwin H Land Blvd., Cambridge,
02142*
Tel *(617) 497-4200*
The chef's Italian heritage shines
through in the appetizing family
recipes and home-made pastas
at this riverside Cambridge hotel-
restaurant. Beautiful outdoor
patio with scenic views.

Rialto $$$
New American
1 Bennett St., Cambridge, 02138
Tel *(617) 661-5050*
One of New England's best-

Intimate seating at EVOO, Cambridge,
Massachusetts

known female chefs, Jody
Adams, takes a luscious
approach to hotel dining, with
an emphasis on fresh, local
ingredients. The comfortable
and soothing dining room is
ideal for special occasions.

Salts $$$
New American
798 Main St., Cambridge, 02139
Tel *(617) 876-8444* **Closed** *Sun, Mon*
This gracious hideaway near
MIT serves contemporary
American fare with fresh
ingredients and a selection
of handcrafted wines. The
40 seats fill up quickly, so
reserve ahead.

West Bridge $$$
New American
1 Kendall Sq., Cambridge, 02141
Tel *(617) 945-0221*
One of the area's most adventur-
ous culinary restaurants. Serves
French-inspired food with a New
England perspective in a modern
and comfortable environment.

The bar area at West Bridge in Cambridge, Massachusetts

For more information on types of restaurants *see p321*

The historic Warren Tavern, Charlestown, Massachusetts

Charlestown

Warren Tavern $
American
2 Pleasant St., Charlestown, 02129
Tel *(617) 241-8142*
This is one of the most historic pubs in America, dating back to 1780. Choose from a lenghty beer list and varied menu of familiar comfort fare.

North End and the Waterfront

James Hook & Co. $
Seafood **Map** 2 E5
15 Northern Ave., 02110
Tel *(617) 423-5501*
Seafood market located right on Fort Point Channel. Enjoy the freshly cooked lobster, clams, crab, and fish to-go.

Pizzeria Regina $
Italian **Map** 2 D2
11 1/2 Thacher St., 02113
Tel *(617) 227-0765*
The city's best known pizza spot hasn't changed much over the decades. Expect affordable wine and amazing brick-oven pies.

Barking Crab $$
Seafood **Map** 2 E5
88 Sleeper St., 02210
Tel *(617) 426-2722*
This colorful fish shack is most congenial in the summer, when diners can sit outdoors at picnic tables.

No Name Restaurant $$
Seafood
15 Fish Pier St. W., 02210
Tel *(617) 423-2705*
Fish Pier's only restaurant serves fresh seafood, simply fried or broiled, in bare-bones environs. Popular with families and tour groups.

Bricco $$$
Italian **Map** 2 D3
241 Hanover St., 02113
Tel *(617) 248-6800*
A lively, stylish *trattoría*, very popular for socializing over Abruzzo-style pastas or rabbit casserole. Window tables provide colorful North End views.

Daily Catch $$$
Italian **Map** 2 D3
323 Hanover St., 02113
Tel *(617) 523-8567*
Closet-sized eatery caters to fans of classic Italian seafood dishes, heavy on the garlic. Many items are served in a sizzling pan.

Legal Sea Foods $$$
Seafood
255 State St., 02109
Tel *(617) 742-5300*
Legendary local chain where diners can always count on getting immaculately fresh fish in a fine-dining setting. The clam chowder is unrivaled; raw clams and oysters, impeccable.

Maurizio's $$$
Italian **Map** 2 E2
364 Hanover St., 02113
Tel *(617) 367-1123*
A buzzy spot where the chef draws on his Sardinian heritage to create dishes that often include brilliant preparations of fish.

Meritage $$$
New American **Map** 2 E4
70 Rowes Wharf, 02110
Tel *(617) 439-3995* **Closed** Sun, Mon
Wine lovers truly appreciate this hotel-restaurant known for its varied, modern American menu in which all items feature suggested wine pairings.

Pomodoro $$$
Italian **Map** 2 D2
319 Hanover St., 02113
Tel *(617) 367-4348*
The eponymous red sauce here is arguably the tastiest in the North

End. Roasted vegetables and veal dishes are excellent, and portions are large.

Prezza $$$
Italian **Map** 2 E2
24 Fleet St., 02113
Tel *(617) 227-1577*
One of the longest wine lists in town guarantees just the right glass to accompany hearty Tuscan fare as well as sinfully rich desserts.

Taranta $$$
Italian **Map** 2 D3
210 Hanover St., 02113
Tel *(617) 720-0052*
An artistic, environmentally-conscious blend of Sardinian and Catalan cuisine spells intriciate recipes and intense flavors.

Trade $$$
New American **Map** 2 E5
540 Atlantic Ave., 02210
Tel *(617) 451-1234*
Downtown workers fill this airy, after-work hot spot for Mediterranean-inspired bites, craft beers, and designer cocktails. Huge windows look out onto the Kennedy Greenway.

Old Boston and the Financial District

Les Zygomates $$$
French **Map** 4 F2
129 South St., 02111
Tel *(617) 542-5108* **Closed** Sun
Reasonably priced French bistro fare. The whimsically designed bar area comes alive with young professionals; live jazz performances often held here.

Nebo $$$
Italian **Map** 2 E5
520 Atlantic Ave., 02210
Tel *(617) 723-6326* **Closed** Sun
Enjoy upscale pizzas and pastas in a clean, welcoming space facing the Rose Kennedy Greenway.

Diners at the popular fish shack – Barking Crab, Boston

Bright decor at Redbones, Somerville, Massachusetts

Notable for its gluten-free menu of delectable Old World delights.

O Ya $$$
Japanese   Map 2 D5
9 East St., 02111
Tel *(617) 654-9900* **Closed** *Sun, Mon*
One of the city's most acclaimed restaurants, serving exceptionally pricey modern Japanese fare. It's hard to find, as it's tucked away near South Station.

Somerville

Diva $$
Indian
246 Elm St., Somerville, 02144
Tel *(617) 629-4963*
Sleekly appointed Indian bistro, part of a local chain, serves carefully prepared Indian classics and designer cocktails.

Redbones $$
Barbeque
55 Chester St., Somerville, 02144
Tel *(617) 628-2200*
A down-and-dirty kitchen slings some of the best barbeque in the area. The raucous atmosphere mirrors the young, upbeat crowd. Free valet service for those arriving on bicycles.

Dalí $$$
Spanish
415 Washington St., Somerville, 02143
Tel *(617) 661-3254*
The area's most beloved spot for authentic tapas is hidden away on the Cambridge-Somerville border. Exceptionally romantic vibe makes it a favorite of celebratory couples.

Wellesley

CK Shanghai $$
Chinese
15 Washington St., Wellesley, 02481
Tel *(781) 237-7500*
Many Boston chefs flock to the suburbs to taste the clever use of New England ingredients in Shanghai cuisine. Dim sum served on Sundays.

Massachusetts

AMHERST: Amherst Chinese Food $
Chinese
62 Main St., 01002
Tel *(413) 253-7835*
Spicy, flavorful Cantonese and Szechuan specialties (stir-fries, steamed dishes, vegetarian soups), made using organic produce from a nearby farm.

AMHERST: Judie's $
Eclectic
51 N. Pleasant St., 01002
Tel *(413) 253-3491*
Eclectic food (giant popovers, vegetarian risotto cakes) and afternoon tea served in a sunny greenhouse.

BREWSTER: Chillingsworth $$$
French
2449 Main St., 02631
Tel *(508) 896-3640*
Since 1976, this restaurant has set the fine dining bar for Cape Cod with elegant French fare and top-notch service. More casual fare is served in the bistro and bar areas.

DEERFIELD: Champney's $$$
American
81 Old Main St., 01342
Tel *(413) 774-5587*
Dating back to 1884, this historic inn's restaurant brings a varied approach to seasonally-driven dishes. A friendly gathering place for locals.

DENNIS: Scargo Café $$
American
799 Main St., 02638
Tel *(508) 385-8200*
Located across the Cape Playhouse, ideal for a pre-show bite. Diners enjoy creative, contemporary American fare and welcoming service.

ESSEX: Woodman's of Essex $$
Seafood
121 Main St., 01929
Tel *(978) 768-6057*
Old-time year-round favorite for world-famous fried clams, huge steamed lobsters, clam cakes, and other seafood treats. Casual, no-frills environment.

LENOX: Bistro Zinc $$$
French
56 Church St., 01240
Tel *(413) 637-8800*
Popular upscale bistro, features a long zinc bar and the atmosphere of a Provencal country *boîte*. Menu is a mix of contemporary dishes and familiar French favorites.

MARTHA'S VINEYARD: Net Result $
Seafood
79 Beach Rd., 02554
Tel *(508) 693-6071* **Closed** *Mon–Wed; Dec–May*
Fish market-cum-café churns out inexpensive fish dishes and sushi, as well as steamed lobster. Operated by the island's largest seafood distributor.

MARTHA'S VINEYARD: Brant Point Grill $$$
American
50 Easton St., 02554
Tel *(508) 325-1320* **Closed** *Oct–May*
Set on the harbor with unbeatable views; hosts many notable visitors. An island favorite for its high-end wine list, fresh seafood, and artfully prepared dishes.

MARTHA'S VINEYARD: Sweet Life Café $$$
New American
63 Circuit Ave., 02557
Tel *(508) 696-0200* **Closed** *Fall/Winter*
A Victorian house with three dining rooms and a garden terrace in which to enjoy upscale New American cooking.

NANTUCKET: Ventuno $$$
Italian
21 Federal St., 02554
Tel *(508) 228-4242* **Closed** *Nov–May*
Northern Italian fare with panache. The daily seafood catch is a feature, as are vegetables locally farmed on the island and the Cape.

NATICK: Casey's Diner $
American
36 South Ave., 01760
Tel *(508) 655-3761*
Tiny old-time diner, famous for its steamed hot dogs, salty locals, and amusing memorabilia.

For more information on types of restaurants *see p321*

Romantic ambience at Old Inn on the Green, Massachusetts

NEW MARLBOROUGH: Old Inn on the Green $$$
American
134 Hartsville New Marlborough Rd., 02130
Tel *(413) 229-7924* **Closed** *Mon–Tue*
Four candlelit dining rooms are the stage for imaginative presentations of local produce and ingredients. Popular fixed-price menu is a culinary bargain.

NORTH ADAMS: Gramercy Bistro $$$
New American
87 Marshall St., 01247
Tel *(413) 663-5300* **Closed** *Tue*
Contemporary cuisine with French and Italian touches. Conveniently located across the street from the Massachusetts Museum of Contemporary Art.

NORTHAMPTON: Northampton Brewery $
American
11 Brewster Ct., 01060
Tel *(413) 584-9903*
One of New England's oldest brewpubs serves up straightforward, beer-friendly appetizers and dishes. Plenty of TVs for watching sports with rowdy local fans.

NORTHAMPTON: Eastside Grill $$
American
19 Strong Ave., 01060
Tel *(413) 586-3347*
Rich, spicy specialities of the American South, served with aplomb by a friendly staff. The nondescript exterior belies the lively scene inside.

PLYMOUTH: East Bay Grille $$
American
173 Water St., 02360
Tel *(508) 746-9751*

Traditional American fare served on scenic Plymouth Harbor. Strong emphasis on seafood. Relaxed environment, with waterfront views from an in-demand patio.

PLYMOUTH: Lobster Hut $$
Seafood
25 Town Wharf, 02360
Tel *(508) 746-2270*
Local institution on the waterfront, steps from the *Mayflower II*. Classic fish shack menu served to a steady stream of tourists and hungry locals. Self-service.

ROCKPORT: Lobster Pool $$
Seafood
329 Granite St., 01966
Tel *(978) 546-7808* **Closed** *Oct–Apr*
This is a typical fish shack, known for its fair prices and spectacular sunset views. Lobster served in various forms, plus fresh local seafood and home-made pies.

SALEM: Finz Seafood & Grill $$$
Seafood
76 Wharf St., 01970
Tel *(978) 744-8485*
Cheerful waterfront restaurant serves fresh seafood and New American fare. A lively bar scene picks up when musical performances are hosted in the lounge.

SANDWICH: Marshland Restaurant $
American
109 Route 6A, 02537
Tel *(508) 888-9824*
Classic Yankee cooking executed with special care. Locals covet the recipe for stuffed *quahogs* (hard-shelled clams). Attached take-out bakery.

SANDWICH: Belfry Inne & Bistro $$$
Eclectic
8 Jarves St., 02563
Tel *(508) 888-8550* **Closed** *Jan*
A menu of "world's greatest hits," served in an atmospheric, de-sanctified church. Impeccably executed dishes run the gamut from Thai noodles to lobster truffle risotto.

SAUGUS: Kowloon Restaurant $
Chinese
948 Broadway, 01906
Tel *(781) 233-0077*
Old-time Chinese-American favorites such as sizzling *pupu* platters and sweet-and-sour-chicken served at this giant eatery perched majestically atop a hill.

SPRINGFIELD: Student Prince $$
German
8 Fort St., 01103
Tel *(413) 734-7475*
A local institution, one of the region's few German eateries. Home-made sausages and a beer stein collection complete the authentic experience.

STURBRIDGE: Publick House $$$
American
277 Main St., 01566
Tel *(508) 347-3313*
This welcoming roadside inn has fed weary travelers since 1771 and continues to serve old-school, warming fare. Fittingly close to Old Sturbridge Village.

SUDBURY: Longfellow's Wayside Inn $$$
American
72 Wayside Inn Rd., 01776
Tel *(978) 443-1776*
Colonial-era stagecoach inn offering a number of seating

options – from a Tap Room to the famous Old Bar Room – in which to enjoy retro-minded fare (lobster pie, prime rib, baked scrod).

SWAMPSCOTT: Red Rock Bistro $$$
American
141 Humphrey St., 01907
Tel *(781) 595-1414*
Casual, contemporary fare served in a scenic waterfront spot. Laid out to ensure that most diners enjoy breathtaking views. Take-out window proves popular in summer.

DK Choice

WALTHAM: La Campania $$$
Italian
504 Main St., 02452
Tel *(781) 894-4280*
One of the most acclaimed eateries in Eastern Massachusetts. It serves upscale Italian fare in a welcoming farmhouse setting. Authentic Neapolitan dishes from a wood-burning brick oven and home-made pasta made with fresh ingredients impress the fussiest of area gourmands. The antique dining room is filled with rural Italian bric-a-brac. Impressive wine list contains lots of big Italian reds.

WELLESLEY: Blue Ginger $$$
Asian
583 Washington St., 02482
Tel *(781) 283-5790*
TV superchef Ming Tsai lures foodies to quiet Wellesley to sample his upscale Pan-Asian fare. Extensive wine list pairs nicely with the eclectic menu.

WELLFLEET: Catch of the Day Seafood Grill $$
Seafood
975 Route 6, 02667
Tel *(508) 349-9090* **Closed** *mid-Oct–late May*
The town's famous oysters are on offer at this casual seafood eatery and market. Simply select your fish from the market and specify how you'd like it prepared, or enjoy a hearty fisherman's stew.

WILLIAMSTOWN: Gala Steakhouse and Bistro $$$
New American
222 Adams Rd., 01267
Tel *(413) 458-9590*
Upscale dining room in the Orchards Hotel. One of western Massachusetts's most romantic dining spots, serving fine steaks and modern bistro fare.

The Tap Room at Longfellow's Wayside Inn, Massachusetts

Rhode Island

BLOCK ISLAND: Eli's $$
Italian
456 Chapel St., 02807
Tel *(401) 466-5230* **Closed** *Winter*
Friendly eatery serves up imaginative pastas with flare. With only 50 seats, the casual dining room can get packed; arrive early or expect to wait.

BLOCK ISLAND: Atlantic Inn $$$
American
359 High St., 02807
Tel *(401) 466-5883*
A formal favorite among urbane locals for its spectacular ocean views and sophisticated modern fare. Veranda tables are prized for the sunset dining ambience.

BLOCK ISLAND: Manisses Dining Room $$$
American
5 Spring St., 02807
Tel *(401) 466-2836* **Closed** *Nov–Apr*
The classy Hotel Manisses' formal *boîte*, an attractive place in which to sample freshly-caught local seafood, home-made pastas, and elaborate desserts.

BRISTOL: Lobster Pot $$
Seafood
199 Hope St., 02809
Tel *(401) 253-9100*
Extremely fresh basic as well as sophisticated preparations served across three dining rooms and a patio with stunning harbor views.

CHARLESTOWN: Wilcox Tavern $$$
American
5153 Old Post Rd., 02813
Tel *(401) 322-1829* **Closed** *Mon–Wed; Winter*
Colonial-style tavern dates back to about 1730, serving classic hearty fare (prime rib, baked stuffed flounder). Fittingly located on one of New England's oldest roads.

GALILEE: George's of Galilee $$
Seafood
250 Sand Hill Cove Rd., 02882
Tel *(401) 783-2306*
Bustling waterfront landmark in one of the region's leading fishing ports. Diners come from all over the state for seafood platters, clam cakes, and chowders.

HARRISVILLE: Wright's Farm Restaurant $
American
84 Inman Rd., 02830
Tel *(401) 769-2856*
All-you-can-eat chicken dinners are the drawing card at this legendary restaurant, hosting more than 1,000 diners weekly.

MIDDLETOWN: Atlantic Beach Club $$
American
55 Purgatory Rd., 02842
Tel *(401) 847-2750*
Choose between casual daytime patio dining and a more formal dining room. Local seafood is prepared in any number of ways, and the varied menu has something for everyone.

Veranda tables at the Atlantic Inn, Rhode Island

For more information on types of restaurants *see p321*

NARRAGANSETT: Coast Guard House $$
American
40 Ocean Rd., 02882
Tel *(401) 789-0700*
Renovated 1888 Coast Guard station provides views of the beach. Straightforward seafood offerings and large portions of familiar American fare. Popular Sunday brunch service.

NEWPORT: Crazy Dough's Pizza $
Italian
446 Thames St., 02840
Tel *(401) 619-3343* **Closed** *Mon*
Top choice for pocket-friendly eats in a sea of pricey tourist haunts. Award-winning pizzas and calzones, made using fresh ingredients.

NEWPORT: Brick Alley Pub $$
American
140 Thames St., 02840
Tel *(401) 849-6334*
One of Newport's most popular restaurants, always packed with families enjoying selections from a far-ranging casual menu. Many menu items come with an unlimited soup and salad buffet.

NEWPORT: Restaurant Bouchard $$
French
505 Thames St., 02840
Tel *(401) 846-0123* **Closed** *Tue*
French-trained chef Albert Bouchard wows the fussiest of gourmands with his elegant interpretations of French classics. Attentive service and classy environs make it a top choice for special occasions.

NEWPORT: Salvation Café $$
Eclectic
140 Broadway, 02840
Tel *(401) 847-2620*
A laid-back staff mirrors the colorful atmosphere featuring vivid local art. The diverse menu

incorporates everything from Thai fare to roasted local seafood.

NEWPORT: Scales & Shells $$$
Seafood
527 Thames St., 02840
Tel *(401) 846-3474*
Welcoming eatery sports a raw bar to go along with its lengthy menu of seafood and pasta offerings. Many patrons stick to cold beer in these casual environs.

NEWPORT: The Black Pearl $$$
New American
Bannister's Wharf, 02840
Tel *(401) 846-5264* **Closed** *Jan–Feb*
A rundown sail loft on Bannister's Wharf, transformed into one of the city's most charming dining spots. Diners enjoy a varied menu featuring seafood caught in nearby waters.

NEWPORT: The Mooring $$$
American
Sayers Wharf, 02840
Tel *(401) 846-2260*
Located on the historic Downtown Waterfront, offering panoramic views of Narragansett Bay. Varied menu contains numerous seafood and steak offerings. Lively bar area.

NEWPORT: White Horse Tavern $$$
American
26 Marlborough St., 02840
Tel *(401) 849-3600*
One of the oldest taverns in America, serving upscale American fare in candlelit environs. Low-beamed ceilings, hearth fires, and colonial bric-a-brac complete the experience.

PROVIDENCE: Caserta Pizzeria $
Pizza
121 Spruce St., 02903
Tel *(401) 621-3618*
This old-time pizzeria churns out

inexpensive pies in spartan environs. Families pop in for a quick pie or for take-out.

PROVIDENCE: East Side Pockets $
Middle Eastern
278 Thayer St., 02906
Tel *(401) 453-1100*
Family-owned eatery serving inexpensive wraps and platters. A favorite of bargain-seekers and vegetarians.

PROVIDENCE: Olneyville N.Y. System Restaurant $
American
20 Plainfield St., 02903
Tel *(401) 621-9500*
Nondescript eatery has won national attention for its old-style hot dogs, a true state delicacy. Try the coffee-flavored milk.

PROVIDENCE: Rick's Roadhouse $
Barbeque
370 Richmond St., 02903
Tel *(401) 272-7675*
A wide selection of beers, bourbons, and whiskies pair well with smoky barbeque fare. The wood-fired grill provides an inviting aroma to the casual environs.

PROVIDENCE: Venda Ravioli $
Italian
265 Atwells Ave., 02903
Tel *(401) 421-9105*
An Italian gourmet shop with a huge selection. It also serves bountiful Italian meals from late breakfast through early supper at tables at the back of the store.

PROVIDENCE: Don Jose Tequilas $$
Mexican
351 Atwells Ave., 02903
Tel *(401) 454-8951*
This casual eatery provides a

Entrance to the Brick Alley Pub, Rhode Island

Bar area at Al Forno, Rhode Island

lively break from the city's Little Italy neighborhood. Traditional Mexican dishes and fresh margaritas are especially popular.

PROVIDENCE: Farmstead Inc. $$
New American
186 Wayland Ave., 02906
Tel *(401) 274-7177* **Closed** *Mon*
Popular farm-to-table restaurant, it reflects the nuances and spirit of the season and features a strong selection of domestic and imported artisan cheeses.

DK Choice

PROVIDENCE: Al Forno $$$
Italian
577 S. Main St., 02903
Tel *(401) 273-9760* **Closed** *Sun, Mon*
Diners come from far and wide to sample nationally-renowned, upscale Italian fare. Wood-fire grilled meats, thin-crust pizzas, and bubbling baked pasta dishes all jockey for attention. An extensive wine list features something for everyone. Seasonal, local ingredients are dotted through-out the menu. The kitchen's talents have spawned numerous cookbooks.

PROVIDENCE: Capital Grille $$$
Steakhouse
1 Union Station, 02903
Tel *(401) 521-5600*
Pricey cuts of premium-aged beef and big-ticket classics are served with panache.

PROVIDENCE: Capriccio $$$
Italian
2 Pine St., 02903
Tel *(401) 421-1320*
Grand style continental cuisine continues to hold forth in a grotto-like, candlelit dining room. Modern

Northern Italian dishes pair nicely with the well-chosen wine list.

PROVIDENCE: New Rivers $$$
New American
7 Steeple St., 02903
Tel *(401) 751-0350* **Closed** *Sun*
A pair of 1870s storefronts on College Hill, housing a 40-seat dining room and an intimate bar, offer a bistro menu packed with plenty of culinary surprises.

PROVIDENCE: Siena $$$
Italian
238 Atwells Ave., 02903
Tel *(401) 521-3311*
Northern Italian fare in the heart of Federal Hill. Wood-grilled pizzas and home-made pastas are popular. Free valet parking.

Connecticut

DARIEN: Coromandel $$
Indian
25 Old Kings Hwy., 06820
Tel *(203) 662-1213*
One of the state's most lauded Indian restaurants, serving South Indian specialties. Goan and northern dishes also available.

FARMINGTON: Apricots $$$
New American
1593 Farmington Ave., 06032
Tel *(860) 673-5405*
This airy, two-story barn overlooking a scenic river has a wine list that matches the creative cuisine. The pub downstairs is a popular after-work haunt.

GREENWICH: Burgers, Shakes & Fries $
American
302 Delavan Ave., 06830
Tel *(203) 531-7433* **Closed** *Sun*
Serves gourmet burgers, fresh side orders, and creamy milk-shakes in a casual atmosphere.

GREENWICH: Penang Grill $$
Asian
55 Lewis St., 06830
Tel *(203) 861-1988* **Closed** *Sun*
Stylish yet casual eatery churns out Chinese-Malaysian fare with speedy service. Certain dishes are exceptionally fiery; spice levels can be adjusted on request.

GUILFORD: Whitfield's on Guilford Green $$
American
25 Whitfield St., 06437
Tel *(203) 458-1300*
A contemporary café located in a late-18th-century home filled with bright artwork. The varied menu includes hearty steaks and home-made pasta dishes, as well as smaller plates for sharing.

HARTFORD: Black-Eyed Sally's $$
Barbeque
350 Asylum St., 06103
Tel *(860) 278-7427* **Closed** *Sun*
A Downtown eatery churning out Southern-style barbeque and Cajun fare, with live music on the side. Expect a crowd when there's an event at the nearby arena.

HARTFORD: Max Downtown $$$
New American
185 Asylum St., 06103
Tel *(860) 522-2530*
Contemporary fare served in stylish environs at this flagship of a local chain with locations in the city and suburbs. A favorite of the after-work crowd.

HARTFORD: Peppercorn's Grill $$$
Italian
357 Main St., 06103
Tel *(860) 547-1714* **Closed** *Sun*
This handsome two-level eatery serves Northern Italian dishes including home-made pastas. Meat and fish arrive hot off the fiery wood-grill.

KENT: Fife 'n Drum $$
Eclectic
53 N. Main St., 06757
Tel *(860) 927-3509* **Closed** *Tue*
Live piano music often accompanies the fine French, Italian, and American meals here. A lengthy wine list complements the cuisine.

LEDYARD: Paragon $$$
New American
Grant Pequot Tower, Foxwoods, Route 2, 06339
Tel *(860) 312-5130* **Closed** *Mon–Wed*
Elegant continental cuisine with views of the countryside. Seasonal menus spotlight gourmet ingre-dients such as fresh oysters, Maine lobsters, and dry-aged steaks.

For more information on types of restaurants *see p321*

Outdoor tables at Abbott's Lobster in the Rough, Connecticut

LITCHFIELD: West Street Grill $$$
New American
43 West St., 06759
Tel *(860) 567-3885*
Comfortably casual setting for enjoying New American fare. Inexpensive, straightforward lunch offerings stand in contrast to the pricier, more creative dinner menu.

MANCHESTER: Cavey's $$$
French-Italian
45 E. Center St., 06040
Tel *(860) 643-2751*
Two rooms serving two cuisines: Northern Italian in the casual upstairs; gourmet modern French in the formal downstairs, where jackets are suggested for men.

MONTVILLE: Bobby Flay's Bar Americain $$$
New American
1 Mohegan Sun Blvd., 06382
Tel *(860) 862-8000*
The popular TV chef here treats diners to his interpretations of classic French bistro fare and top-notch seafood.

MYSTIC: Mystic Pizza $
Pizza
56 W. Main St., 06355
Tel *(860) 536-3700*
Famous from its role in the Julia Roberts movie of the same name, this no-frills institution remains popular for its tasty pies. Lots of TVs and a well-stocked bar.

MYSTIC: Flood Tide Restaurant $$
American
3 Williams Ave., 06355
Tel *(860) 536-8140*   **Closed** *Tue*
Serves local seafood and familiar American fare. Casual environs and a children's menu make this a particularly family-friendly spot.

NEW BRITAIN: Fatherland $
Polish
450 S. Main St., 06051
Tel *(860) 224-3345*
Home-style Polish cooking in a welcoming space. Popular with homesick members of the state's largest Polish expat community.

NEW HAVEN: Frank Pepe's Pizzeria $
Pizza
157 Wooster St., 06511
Tel *(203) 865-5762*
Opened in 1925, this no-frills spot for thin-crust pizza attracts foodies from all over for what some consider to be the world's best white clam pizza.

DK Choice

NEW HAVEN: Louis' Lunch $
American
263 Crown St., 06511
Tel *(203) 562-5507*   **Closed** *Sun, Mon*
While some may question it, most people agree that the humble hamburger can trace its origins back to this famed lunch counter, which first served a ground beef patty on a bun back when it opened in 1895. Today, it remains mostly unchanged, with an old-time environment that matches its small menu and low prices. Steamed in vintage vertical broilers, each burger provides a true taste of history.

NEW HAVEN: Bentara $$
Malaysian
76 Orange St., 06510
Tel *(203) 562-2511*
Authentic Malaysian dishes served in spacious, high-ceilinged dining rooms decorated with Asian artifacts. Most dishes blend sweet, pungent, spicy, and salty notes.

NEW HAVEN: Union League Café $$$
French
1032 Chapel St., 06510
Tel *(203) 562-4299*   **Closed** *Sun*
An acclaimed restaurant in a historic setting, it serves traditional French dishes with a contemporary twist, using local and organic produce and artisanal cheeses.

NEW HAVEN: Zinc $$$
New American
964 Chapel St., 06510
Tel *(203) 624-0507*   **Closed** *Sun*
Stunning minimalist decor suits the vibrant, Asian-tinged modern cuisine made with local, organic ingredients. Situated directly on New Haven Green.

NOANK: Abbott's Lobster in the Rough $
Seafood
117 Pearl St., 06340
Tel *(860) 536-7719* **Closed** *Nov–May*
Fresh local seafood served at plain picnic-style tables facing the harbor on Mystic River. Patrons are allowed to bring their own beer and wine.

OLD SAYBROOK: Fresh Salt $$$
New American
Saybrook Point Inn, 2 Bridge St., 06475
Tel *(860) 388-1111*
This upscale eatery puts a European spin on local produce and fresh seafood. The stellar raw bar is a prime spot for enjoying oysters on the half shell.

PLAINVILLE: Confetti $$
Italian
393 Farmington Ave., 06062
Tel *(860) 793-8809*
An oasis of hearty Italian fare in an inviting setting. The kitchen focuses on seafood, with ingredients like fresh calamari offered in multiple preparations.

SIMSBURY: Metro Bis $$$
New American
928 Hopmeadow St., 06070
Tel *(860) 651-1908*   **Closed** *Sun*
Lively American bistro sporting Asian and Mediterranean touches on its varied menu. The intriguing wine list specializes in New World varieties.

SOUTH NORWALK: SoNo Seaport Seafood $$
Seafood
100 Water St., 06854
Tel *(203) 854-9483*
A casual dining spot serving fresh seafood, fried or grilled, with a view of working fisher-men right outside. Take-out

is available at the adjacent fish market.

STONINGTON: Noah's $$$
Seafood
113 Water St., 06378
Tel *(860) 535-3925* **Closed** *Mon*
A local fixture for affordable local seafood, Mediterranean dishes, and home-made desserts, since 1979. The casual environs include one of the area's liveliest bar scenes.

VERNON: Rein's Deli $
American
435 Hartford Tnpk., 06066
Tel *(860) 875-1344*
A popular, affordable stop along the NYC-Boston corridor. This NYC-style, family-owned deli has been satisfying motorists' sandwich cravings for decades.

WEST HARTFORD: Plan B Burger Bar $$
American
138 Park Rd., 06119
Tel *(860) 231-1199*
Lively haunt wildly popular for its fine steaks and gourmet burgers. A wide selection of craft beers and boutique bourbons complete the experience.

WOODBURY: Good News Café $$$
American
694 Main St. S., 06798
Tel *(203) 266-4663* **Closed** *Tue*
Fresh organic ingredients from local farmers is the focus of this award-winning restaurant's creative menu. "To Go" menu is available for diners in a hurry.

Vermont

BURLINGTON: American Flatbread Burlington Hearth $
Pizza
115 St. Paul St., 05401
Tel *(802) 861-2999*
Gourmet wood-fired pizzas made with local, organic ingredients keep the crowds coming at this eco-friendly eatery. Craft beers and organic salads also served.

BURLINGTON: Penny Cluse Café $
American
169 Cherry St., 05401
Tel *(802) 651-8834*
Penny Cluse Café is a friendly spot that serves breakfast and lunch daily. The varied menu runs from gingerbread pancakes to fish tacos. Especially popular for weekend brunch.

BURLINGTON: India House Restaurant $$
Indian
207 Colchester Ave., 05401
Tel *(802) 862-7800*
A casual spot specializing in traditional North Indian food. One of the city's best options for vegetarians.

BURLINGTON: The Vermont Pub & Brewery $$
American
44 College St., 05401
Tel *(802) 865-0500*
Vermont's oldest craft brewery serves hearty American fare alongside freshly brewed beers. Lengthy menu features lots of fun plates perfect for sharing.

BURLINGTON: Leunig's Bistro $$$
Eclectic
115 Church St., 05401
Tel *(802) 863-3759*
Located in a 1920s building. Its award-winning grill and bistro serves a varied menu of French classics and Mediterranean-tinged American dishes.

BURLINGTON: Trattoria Delia $$$
Italian
152 St. Paul St., 05401
Tel *(802) 864-5253*
This family-run restaurant emphasizes an Old World ambience and serves regional Italian specialties. Stone walls, exposed beams, and a fireplace add to the atmosphere.

GRAFTON: Grafton Inn $$$
Eclectic
92 Main St., 05146
Tel *(800) 843-1801*
Housed in an 1801 inn, the menu incorporates numerous modern global touches. Ingredients include herbs from the inn's garden, and local meat and dairy products.

KILLINGTON: The Foundry at Summit Pond $$
American
Summit Pond & Killington Rd., 05751
Tel *(802) 422-5335*
Bistro-style fare served in an atmospheric building that was designed to look like an old mill. The lounge often features live entertainment.

LOWER WATERFORD: The Rabbit Hill Inn $$$
New American
48 Lower Waterford Rd., 05848
Tel *(802) 748-5168* **Closed** *Wed (except during peak foliage season)*
This tranquil and romantic 1795 country inn is the stage for one of the state's most acclaimed restaurants. New American fare served à la carte or via a seasonal tasting menu.

MANCHESTER CENTER: Little Rooster Café $
American
Rt. 7A and Hillvale Dr., 05255
Tel *(802) 362-3496*
A popular stop near outlet shopping for filling breakfasts and lunches. Belgian waffles and over-stuffed sandwiches are crowd favorites.

Exterior of the Grafton Inn, Vermont

For more information on types of restaurants *see p321*

MIDDLEBURY: American Flatbread $
Pizza
137 Maple St., 05753
Tel *(802) 388-3300* **Closed** *Sun, Mon*
A local institution, this popular pizzeria utilizes local, organic produce. It is a great spot for sampling award-winning, local craft beers.

MONTPELIER: La Brioche $
American
89 Main St., 05602
Tel *(802) 229-0443* **Closed** *Sun*
Pastry chefs of tomorrow train at this bakery-café operated by the New England Culinary Institute. Menu includes fresh soups, salads, and sandwiches.

MONTPELIER: NECI on Main $$
New American
118 Main St., 05602
Tel *(802) 223-3188* **Closed** *Mon*
Students of the New England Culinary Institute staff this energetic spot located just down the street from the school. The menu is dotted with French touches, with an emphasis on fresh, local ingredients.

DK Choice

QUECHEE: Simon Pearce Restaurant $$$
New American
1760 Quechee Main St., 05059
Tel *(802) 295-1470*
Located in a restored mill overlooking the Ottauquechee River, Simon Pearce enjoys a scenic location. After checking out the namesake glass-blowing studio, where the glassware and pottery used by the restaurant are produced, guests fill the romantic dining room to enjoy fresh, modern American cuisine and an award-winning wine list.

Simple, classy interiors of NECI on Main, Vermont

SHELBURNE: Restaurant at the Inn at Shelburne Farms $$$
New American
1611 Harbor Rd., 05482
Tel *(802) 985-8498*
Creative regional cuisine in a historic mansion overlooking Lake Champlain. Many ingredients on the contemporary, ever-changing menu come from the estate's garden and dairy.

STOWE: Pie in the Sky $
Italian
492 Mountain Rd., 05672
Tel *(802) 253-5100*
Before or after hitting the slopes, skiers fuel up with pizzas, baked pastas, and giant calzones here. The weekday all-you-can-eat option is a good bargain.

STRATTON: Verde $$$
New American
19 Village Lodge Rd., 05360
Tel *(802) 297-9200*
Contemporary, upscale bistro fare featuring locally-grown ingredients is the culinary star of this mountain resort. Look out for the grass-fed Vermont beef on the menu.

WATERBURY: Hen of the Wood $$$
New American
92 Stowe St., 05676
Tel *(802) 244-7300* **Closed** *Sun, Mon*
This restaurant's straightforward preparations showcase the wealth of premium ingredients found nearby in the lush Green Mountains and Champlain Valley.

WESTON: Inn at Weston $$$
New American
630 Main St., 05161
Tel *(802) 824-6789*
The ever-changing menu in this place is always interesting. Members of the Vermont Fresh network supply top-notch, seasonal meat and dairy produce.

WOODSTOCK: Bentley's Restaurant $$
American
3 Elm St., 05091
Tel *(802) 457-3232*
A friendly hang-out hosting trivia contests and live music to go along with its varied menu of hearty American fare. Deep, comfortable couches add to the warm atmosphere.

New Hampshire

BEDFORD: Bedford Village Inn $$$
New American
2 Olde Bedford Way, 03110
Tel *(603) 472-2001*
This luxury inn's restaurant serves upscale regional cuisine in eight unique dining rooms. Oenophiles will delight in the lengthy wine list.

CANTERBURY: Greenwoods $$
American
288 Shaker Rd., 03224
Tel *603-783-9511* **Closed** *Nov–mid-May*
Visitors to the Shaker Village's restaurant enjoy hearty, Shaker-inspired cuisine in a reconstructed blacksmith shop.

CENTER SANDWICH: Corner House Inn $$$
American
22 Main St., 03227
Tel *(603) 284-6219* **Closed** *Tue*
Local residents have been dining on classic American fare at this country inn for more than a century. Diners have four cozy dining rooms to choose from.

CONCORD: The Common Man $$
American
25 Water St., 03301
Tel *(603) 228-3463*
American comfort food served in

Scenic location of the Simon Pearce Restaurant, Vermont

relaxed environs. Choose between the spacious downstairs dining room or the inviting upstairs pub.

DURHAM: Three Chimneys Inn $$$
American
17 Newmarket Rd., 03824
Tel *(603) 868-7800*
Enjoy fine American cuisine served in a beautiful 1649 mansion. A full menu is served in the elegant dining room as well as the historic pub on the lower level.

EXETER: Epoch Restaurant and Bar $$$
New American
2 Pine St., 03833
Tel *(603) 778-3762*
Creative, upscale fare served in an elegant atmosphere. Dining room can become crowded with conference guests; reservations are essential during peak times.

HAMPTON: Bonta $$$
New American
287 Exeter Rd., 03842
Tel *(603) 929-7972* **Closed** *Sun, Mon*
Handsome eatery serving New American fare with Mediterranean touches, plus fine steaks and chops. Polished mahogany bar often hosts live music.

HANOVER: Lou's $
American
30 S. Main St., 03755
Tel *(603) 643-3321*
A go-to spot for hearty comfort fare. Over four generations of Dartmouth College students have filled their bellies with traditional breakfast and lunches.

HANOVER: Pine $$$
New American
2 S. Main St., 03755
Tel *(603) 643-4300*
Gourmet breakfast, lunch, and dinner options in a boutique hotel. Stunning views of the Dartmouth College campus, especially from the *al fresco* terrace.

KEENE: Elm City Brewing Company $$
American
22 West St., 03431
Tel *(603) 355-3335*
Handcrafted draft beers and hearty pub fare in a renovated 19th-century woolen mill. Being a college town hangout, expect a boisterous atmosphere.

KEENE: Luca's Mediterranean Café $$
International
10 Central Sq., 03431
Tel *(603) 358-3335*

Red Arrow Diner, New Hamphire

Mediterranean-inspired dishes served in casual environs. French, Italian, and Spanish classics with occasional forays into north African, Greek, and Turkish fare.

LITTLETON: Miller's Café & Bakery $
American
16 Mill St., 03561
Tel *(603) 444-2146* **Closed** *Mon*
A lunch-only café housed in a former mill building with great views of the Ammonoosuc River. The friendly staff mirrors the congenial surroundings.

MANCHESTER: Red Arrow Diner $
American
61 Lowell St., 03101
Tel *(603) 626-1118*
Dating back to 1922, this historic diner serves classic American fare 24 hours a day. Friendly service.

MANCHESTER: Café Momo $$
Nepali
1065 Hanover St., 03104
Tel *(603) 623-3733* **Closed** *Mon*
Authentic Nepali cuisine served in a colorful environment. Namesake momos (traditional dumplings) and spicy curries prove popular.

DK Choice

MEREDITH: Hart's Turkey Farm Restaurant $$
American
233 Daniel Webster Hwy., 03253
Tel *(603) 279-6212*
The country-style turkey dinner is a staple of New England dining. This restaurant specializes in serving up Thanksgiving on a plate every day, and also offers turkey pot pie, turkey livers, and even turkey tempura. A huge selection of non-turkey dishes is also available, such as prime rib and a full line of seafood.

NASHUA: MT's Local Kitchen & Wine Bar $$
New American
212 Main St., 03060
Tel *(603) 595-9334*
This eatery delivers fanciful modern bistro fare in style. Exposed brick walls, white linen tablecloths, and a chic jazz bar all lend to the sophisticated vibe.

NEW CASTLE: Wentworth Dining Room $$$
New American
588 Wentworth Rd., 03854
Tel *(603) 422-7322*
Scenic harbor views and a fireplace add to the romantic atmosphere. Upscale regional cuisine with an emphasis on fresh local ingredients.

NEW LONDON: The Coach House $$$
New American
353 Main St., 03257
Tel *(603) 526-2791* **Closed** *Sun, Mon*
Tourists and locals alike enjoy casual elegance and fine local ingredients served in a charming New England atmosphere. The wine list is impressive.

NEWMARKET: Rocky's Famous Burgers $
American
171 Main St., 03257
Tel *(603) 292-3393*
Popular eatery; serves a variety of half-pound burgers (beef, bison, chicken, veggie) with a sense of humor; free fries if you pin a photo of your pet dog on the wall.

NORTH CONWAY: Moat Mountain Smoke House and Brewing Co. $
Barbeque
3378 White Mtn. Hwy., 03860
Tel *(603) 356-6381*
Friendly, casual brewpub pairs its popular handcrafted ales with a variety of slow-cooked barbequed meats (pulled pork, ribs, brisket).

For more information on types of restaurants *see p321*

Portsmouth Gas Light Co., New Hampshire

PORTSMOUTH: Portsmouth Gas Light Co. $$
American
64 Market St., 03801
Tel *(603) 430-8582*
All under one roof: Italian and American fare in the dining room, casual pizza downstairs, and a bar-nightclub on the third floor.

PORTSMOUTH: The Oar House $$$
New American
55 Ceres St., 03801
Tel *(603) 436-4025*
Upscale fare served in a restored 1803 warehouse. Decor reflects the city's maritime heritage.

WALPOLE: L.A. Burdick Restaurant $$
New American
47 Main St., 03608
Tel *(800) 229-2419* **Closed** *Sun*
As part of an ever-growing chocolate empire, this restaurant serves a bistro menu only in the afternoon, leading up to world-class desserts.

WEST LEBANON: Three Tomatoes Trattoria $$
Italian
1 Court St., 03766
Tel *(603) 448-1711*
A popular spot right across from the Lebanon Green. Thin-crust pizzas from a wood-fire oven are favored by college students.

Maine

BANGOR: Thistles Restaurant $$$
Mediterranean
175 Exchange St., 04401
Tel *(207) 945-5480* **Closed** *Sun, Mon*
Features fresh local seafood with a Spanish accent. Live music makes it one of the most avant-garde spots in town.

BAR HARBOR: Lompoc Café and Brewpub $$
Eclectic
36 Rodick St., 04609
Tel *(207) 288-9392* **Closed** *Sun*
Intimate café and bar with a heated outdoor dining room and a *bocce* garden. Enjoy house-made microbrews along with an interesting eclectic menu.

BAR HARBOR: West Street Café $$$
Seafood
76 West St., 04609
Tel *(207) 288-5242* **Closed** *Dec–May*
Welcoming eatery near the down-town waterfront, popular for its array of fresh seafood, steak, pasta dishes, and home-made pies.

BATH: Mae's Café & Bakery $
American
160 Centre St., 04530
Tel *(207) 442-8577*
Top-notch bakery-café serves dependable breakfast, brunch, and lunch in an old house.

BELFAST: Chase's Daily $$
Vegetarian
96 Main St., 04915
Tel *(207) 338-0555* **Closed** *Mon*
Combination bakery-restaurant-market serves up creative vege-tarian and vegan fare featuring organic veggies. Small but well-chosen wine and beer selection.

BETHEL: Bethel Inn and Country Club $$$
New American
21 Broad St., 04217
Tel *(207) 824-2175* **Closed** *Sun–Thu*
New England gourmet cuisine, dished up in lovely, candlelit surroundings. Glassed-in veranda allows for scenic views. Live piano music often featured.

BOOTHBAY HARBOR: Brown's Wharf Restaurant $$
Seafood
121 Atlantic Ave., 04538
Tel *(207) 633-5440* **Closed** *Sun, Mon; Oct–May*
Casual spot in the middle of the harbor, serving fresh seafood to a friendly mix of locals and tourists.

GREENVILLE: The Greenville Inn $$$
New American
40 Norris St., 04441
Tel *(207) 695-2206*
Gourmet restaurant, housed in an 1895 mansion in remote northern Maine. Large round dining room and smaller Victorian room have sweeping views.

KENNEBUNKPORT: The Clam Shack $
Seafood
2 Western St., 04046
Tel *(207) 967-2560* **Closed** *Oct–Apr*
Take-out stand provides a typical seaside experience of fried and steamed seafood. Fresh-cut onion rings are a popular accompaniment.

KENNEBUNKPORT: Stripers at Breakwater Inn & Spa $$$
New American
127 Ocean Ave., 04046
Tel *(207) 967-5333* **Closed** *Sep–Apr*
Upscale yet casual spot. A prime place for enjoying lobster with sunset views of the river and ocean. Raw bar lounge and breezy patio also available.

KITTERY: Warren's Lobster House $$
Seafood
11 Water St., 03904
Tel *(207) 439-1630*
Vintage 350-seat seafood house perched above the old Route 1 bridge. House specialty is twin steamed lobsters.

LINCOLNVILLE BEACH: Lobster Pound $
Seafood
2521 Lincolnville Hwy., 04849
Tel *(207) 789-5550*
Serves classic seafood dishes such as stews, chowders, and boiled lobsters as well as steaks and burgers. Nice views from the enclosed patio.

OGUNQUIT: Barnacle Billy's $
Seafood
70 Perkins Cove Rd., 03907
Tel *(207) 646-5575* **Closed** *Nov–Mar*
Classic, bare-bones Maine lobster house with basic seafood menu in casual, seaside surroundings.

PORTLAND: Duckfat $
New American
43 Middle St., 04101
Tel *(207) 774-8080*
This cozy eatery attracts crowds thanks to its signature namesake treat: duck-fat fried potatoes. An assortment of casual small plates and craft beers are also offered. Diminutive sidewalk patio.

PORTLAND: El Rayo Taqueria $
Mexican
101 York St., 04101
Tel *(207) 780-8320*
This converted gas station houses a popular spot for fresh, fiery Mexican fare.

PORTLAND: Local 188 $$
New American
685 Congress St., 04102
Tel *(207) 761-7909*

Diners at the bustling Local 188 in Portland's Arts District, Maine

Located in Portland's Arts District, this colorful café feeds the senses of both foodies and artists. Local singles love the buzzing lounge area featuring views of the open kitchen.

PORTLAND: Fore Street $$$
New American
288 Fore St., 04101
Tel *(207) 775-2717*
Upscale American fare, featuring fresh ingredients from Maine's community of farmers, fishermen, foragers, and cheesemakers. High vaulted ceilings and a brick hearth add to the warm environs.

PORTLAND: Hugo's $$$
New American
88 Middle St., 04101
Tel *(207) 774-8538* **Closed** *Sun, Mon*
This nationally-renowned restaurant specializes in inventive modern fare, served in *prix-fixe* and tasting menus. The bar offers a less expensive, à la carte menu.

DK Choice

ROCKLAND: Primo Restaurant $$$
New American
2 S. Main St., 04841
Tel *(207) 596-0770* **Closed** *Mon–Wed, Nov–Apr*
Nationally acclaimed restaurant known for its innovative market cuisine, provides a complete farm-to-table experience. Dishes are prepared with locally-sourced seafood and fresh vegetables. Choose between formal dining areas or a more casual bar area in which a less expensive menu is offered.

SOUTH FREEPORT: Harraseeket Lunch & Lobster $
Seafood
36 Main St., 04078
Tel *(207) 865-3535* **Closed** *Oct–Apr*
Time-honored lobster pound serves up fried and steamed seafood right on the water's edge. Head to the back counter for steamed lobsters to-go.

TENANTS HARBOR: Cod End Cookhouse $
Seafood
Commercial St., 04860
Tel *(207) 372-8981* **Closed** *early-Sep–mid-Jun*
Simple Maine comfort fare in the only restaurant in town: a no-frills eatery that serves as the *de facto* town meeting spot.

WALDOBORO: Moody's Diner $
American
1885 Atlantic Hwy., 04572
Tel *(207) 832-7785*
A Maine institution, where locals, vacationing families, and long-haul trick drivers mix. Old-school diner menu includes an array of comfort fare, from blueberry pancakes to chicken pot pie.

WALDOBORO: Morse's Sauerkraut & European Deli $
German
3856 Washington Rd., 04572
Tel *(207) 832-5569* **Closed** *Wed*
Authentic German café and market, selling hard-to-find, imported specialties and award-winning, home-made sauerkraut and pickles.

WELLS: Billy's Chowderhouse $
Seafood
216 Mile Rd., 04090
Tel *(207) 646-7558* **Closed** *Jan*
Located behind the Wells barrier beach, this casual spot is ideal for whiling away an afternoon drinking beer and snacking on wine-steamed mussels.

Elegant interiors at the nationally-acclaimed Primo, Maine

For more information on types of restaurants *see p321*

SHOPPING IN NEW ENGLAND

New England offers a wide and ever-growing variety of high-quality stores and merchandise. For gifts with regional flavor, maple syrup and maple sugar candy, especially plentiful in the northern states of Vermont, New Hampshire, and Maine, fit the bill. Many coastal souvenir shops carry beautiful replicas of whalebone scrimshaw carvings. Regional arts and crafts can be found everywhere. Some of

New England's best-known shopping is in factory outlet stores in Freeport and Kittery, Maine and North Conway, New Hampshire, where brand-name goods are sold at a discount. The region's best and most varied shopping is found in Boston. Long known as an excellent center for antiques, books, and quality clothing, the shopping options have evolved to become vibrant and eclectic.

Large glass atrium of the busy Shops at Prudential Center in Boston

store, a huge food court, and a multitude of smaller specialty stores. The city's most upscale shopping destination, **Heritage on the Garden** looks out over Boston's Public Garden, and features the boutiques of top European designers, fine jewelers, and stores selling other luxury goods.

Outside the center of town, across the Charles River, **Cambridgeside Galleria** has over 120 stores and a pond-side food court. For last-minute purchases, **Boston Store** at Logan Airport Terminal C has stores, restaurants, banking, and Internet access.

Sales

There are two major sale seasons in New England. In July, summer clothes go on sale to make room for fall fashions, and in January, winter clothing and merchandise is cleared after the holidays. Most stores also have a sale section or clearance rack throughout the year.

Payment and Taxes

Major credit cards and traveler's checks with identification are accepted at most stores. Sales tax in the New England states ranges from 5 to 7 percent. In some states, clothing items may be exempt. New Hampshire is unique in that it has no sales tax.

Opening Hours

Most stores open at 10am and close at 6pm from Monday to Saturday, and from noon to 5 or 6pm on Sunday. Many stores

stay open later on Thursday nights, and major department stores often stay open until 9pm during the week. Weekday mornings are the best times to shop. Saturdays, lunch hours and evenings can be very busy.

Shopping Malls in Boston

Shopping malls – clusters of stores, restaurants, and food courts all within one complex – have become top destinations for shopping, offering variety, dining, and entertainment. With long winters and a fair share of bad weather, New Englanders flock to malls to shop, eat, and, in the case of teenagers, simply hang out.

Copley Place, with its elegant restaurants and more than 75 stores over two levels, is based around a dazzling 60-ft (18-m) atrium and waterfall. Across a pedestrian overpass, **Shops at Prudential Center** encompasses Saks Fifth Avenue department

Department Stores in Boston

Boston's major department stores offer a large and varied selection of clothing, accessories, cosmetics, housewares, and gifts. Some also have restaurants and beauty salons, and provide a variety of personal services. For those wanting to shop at several

An elegant display of contemporary fashion at Barneys New York

stores, **Concierge of Boston** provides a shopping service in metropolitan Boston. At Downtown Crossing *(see p74)*, a bustling shopping district between Boston Common and the Financial District, generations of Bostonians once shopped at Filene's and Filene's Basement, both now closed. Sitting at the heart of this area is **Macy's**, the legendary New York emporium, offering an impressive array of fashions, cosmetics, housewares, and furnishings.

On the bustling waterfront, **Louis Boston** consists of carefully curated departments that run the gamut from eyewear and accessories to home goods. The men's collection has won national acclaim, and the staff is renowned for its customer relations.

Heading uptown, through Boston Common and Public Garden to Boylston Street, you can spot the Prudential Tower, centerpiece of a once nondescript but fully revitalized complex of stores, offices, and restaurants. It includes the venerable **Saks Fifth Avenue**, which caters to its upscale clientele with renowned service, a luxurious ambience, and strikingly stylish displays. For the ultimate high fashion, high profile shopping experience,

stop by **Neiman Marcus** (NM) in Copley Place, which specializes in haute couture, precious jewelry, furs, and gifts. The store is well known for its Christmas catalog, with gift suggestions that have included authentic Egyptian mummies, vintage airplanes, a pair of $2-million diamonds, and robots to help out around the house. Contrasting Manhattan chic against NM's Texas cheekiness is **Barneys New York**, a large-scale outlet of the premier New York retail trendsetter.

Sign for Brattle Book Shop

Not only can shoppers sample exotic perfumes inside "smelling columns," they can rely on the in-store concierge to book their theater tickets and make dinner reservations. Next door is **Lord & Taylor**, well known for its classic American designer labels, juniors' and children's departments, and menswear. The store also carries a range of crystal, china, and gifts.

Specialty Districts in Boston

From the fashionable boutiques to the many stores selling cosmopolitan home furnishings or ethnic treasures, to the varied

Boutiques of trendy Newbury Street

art and crafts galleries, Boston has evolved to cater to every shopping need. Charles Street has been one of the nation's leading centers of fine antiques for generations, while Newbury Street is known for couture and art galleries. A younger and more trendy gallery scene has emerged in the SoWa (south of Washington Street) section of the South End.

Home decor stores also tend to cluster in the South End, especially along the 1300 block of Washington Street. Shoppers seeking contemporary designer furniture find a treasure trove on the 1000 block of Massachusetts Avenue in Cambridge. Despite the inroads made by online book dealers, Harvard Square retains one of the greatest concentrations of bookstores in the United States. See Specialty Dealers *(pp342–3)*.

DIRECTORY

Shopping Malls

Boston Store
Terminal C Logan International Airport, East Boston.
W massport.com

Cambridgeside Galleria
100 Cambridgeside Pl., Cambridge.
Tel (617) 621-8666.

Copley Place
100 Huntington Ave.
Map 3 C3.
Tel (617) 262-6600.
W simon.com

Heritage on the Garden
300 Boylston St. **Map** 4 D2. **Tel** (617) 426-9500.

Shops at Prudential Center
800 Boylston St.
Map 3 B3. **Tel** (800) 746-7778.
W prudentialcenter.com

Department Stores

Barneys New York
5 Copley Place, 100 Huntington Ave. **Map** 3 C3. **Tel** (617) 385-3300.

Concierge of Boston
165 Newbury St.
Map 3 C2.
Tel (617) 266-6611.
W concierge.org

Lord & Taylor
760 Boylston St.
Map 3 B3.
Tel (617) 262-6000.

Louis Boston
60 Northern Ave.
Map 2 F5.
Tel (617) 262-6100.
W louisboston.com

Macy's
450 Washington St.
Map 4 F1.
Tel (617) 357-3000.

Neiman Marcus
5 Copley Place, 100 Huntington Ave.
Map 3 C3.
Tel (617) 536-3660.

Saks Fifth Avenue
Prudential Tower and Shopping Center.
Map 3 B3.
Tel (617) 262-8500.

Boston Fashion and Antiques

Bostonians have always preferred their traditions reinvigorated with an edge, making both clothing and decorative arts distinct from other parts of the country. While the top national names in apparel are well represented, so are virtual unknowns with fresh ideas. The city is also a major international center for fine arts in craft media as well as home to the region's top purveyors of antiques – some of which were made right here in Boston.

Men's Fashion

Gentlemen seeking the quintessential New England look should head to **Brooks Brothers** on Newbury Street, longtime purveyors of traditional, high-quality menswear. America's foremost fashion house, **Polo/Ralph Lauren** offers top-quality and high-priced sporting and formal attire, while **Jos. A. Bank Clothiers** sells private label merchandise as well as major brands at discounted prices. Professors and students alike patronize the venerable **Andover Shop** and **J. Press** in Cambridge for top-quality Ivy-League essentials.

Women's Fashion

No woman need leave Boston empty-handed, whether her taste is for the haute couture of **Chanel** or the earthy ethnic clothing at **Nomad**. Newbury Street's high-fashion boutiques include **Kate Spade**, **Betsy Jenney**, and **Max Mara**. Local retailer **Life is Good** offers affordable casual clothes with optimistic mottoes. On Boylston Street, **Ann Taylor** is the first choice for modern career clothes, while **Talbots**, a Boston institution, features enduring classics.

Other Cambridge shops include **A Taste of Culture**, which sells beautiful woolens from Peru; **Settebello**, with its elegant European apparel and accessories; and **Clothware**, which emphasizes natural fiber clothing by local designers.

Discount and Vintage Clothes

First among discount chains is **Marshall's**, promising "brand names for less" and offering bargains on clothing, shoes, and accessories. Trendsetters head to **H&M**, the popular Swedish retailer, for the latest fashions for adults and kids.

Vintage aficionados love the vast collections at **Bobby from Boston**, a longtime costume source for Hollywood and top fashion designers. **Keezer's** has provided generations of Harvard students with used tuxedos and tweed sports jackets. **Second Time Around**, with locations in both Boston and Cambridge, offers a select array of top-quality, gently worn contemporary women's clothing.

Shoes and Accessories

Many Boston stores specialize in accessories. **Helen's Leather** is known for jackets, briefcases, purses, and shoes, as well as Western boots. At Downtown Crossing, **Foot Paths** carries a range of shoes from major manufacturers. Stylish Spanish shoes and bags are the specialty at **Stuart Weitzman** at Copley Place, while the adventurous will find more unusual shoes at **Berk's** and **The Tannery** in Cambridge.

For sports gear, **Niketown** shows video re-runs of sports events while shoppers peruse the latest designs in clothing and footwear. Visitors don't mind going out of the way for huge discounts on athletic and street shoes and apparel at the **New Balance Factory Outlet** store.

Antiques

There are several multi-dealer antiques emporiums in town. **The Boston Antique Company** searches local estates for tableware, art, jewelry, and vintage corkscrews. In Cambridge, **Cambridge Antique Market** encompasses more than 100 dealers, offering antiques, collectibles, furniture, jewelry and more.

Charles Street, Boston's antiques mecca, also features specialty shops for those with specific tastes. Collectors of fine Asian antiques should not miss **Alberts-Langdon, Inc.** and **Judith Dowling Asian Art**, for everything from screens and scrolls to lacquer-ware, ceramics, and paintings.

Antique jewelry is a specialty at **Marika's Antiques Shop**, along with paintings, porcelain, glass, and silver. **Twentieth Century Ltd.** excels in glittery costume jewelry from top designers.

Danish Country carries Scandinavian furniture, while **JMW Gallery**, near South Station, specializes in 19th- and early 20th-century American objects associated with the Arts and Crafts Movement.

Fine Crafts

Collectors with a more contemporary bent will find several distinguished galleries with a wide variety of American crafts. **Mobilia** in Cambridge has a national reputation for its jewelry, ceramics, and other objects. The **Society of Arts and Crafts**, established in 1897, has a shop and gallery, with exhibits from the 350 artists it represents. The **Cambridge Artists' Cooperative**, owned and run by over 250 artists, offers an eclectic collection ranging from hand-painted silk jackets to ornaments and jewelry. **Mudflat Gallery** is a showcase for the work of almost 50 ceramic artists.

Specialty Dealers

There are shops specializing in everything from posters to rare books, early maps to tribal rugs. Top-brand and vintage watches are a specialty at **European Watch Co.**, while the **Bromfield Pen Shop** has been the purveyor of new, antique, and limited edition pens since 1948. For vintage posters from the 19th and 20th centuries, try **International Poster Gallery** on Newbury Street. **Brattle Book Shop** has a huge selection of used, out-of-print and rare books, magazines and vintage photographs. **Eugene Galleries** features antiquarian maps, prints, and etchings, as well as a comprehensive selection of books. Harvard Square is one of the best places in the United States for bookstores. Specialists abound, including the legendary **Grolier Poetry Book Shop**, and the comic book and graphic novel specialist **Million Year Picnic**. The **Harvard Coop Bookstore** has a nearly encyclopedic selection of new books, while **Harvard Bookstore** offers used and remaindered books in addition to a wide range of carefully chosen new titles.

DIRECTORY

Men's Fashion

Andover Shop
22 Holyoke St.,
Cambridge.
Tel (617) 876-4900.

Brooks Brothers
46 Newbury St.
Map 4 D2.
Tel (617) 267-2600.

J. Press
82 Mount Auburn St.,
Cambridge.
Tel (617) \547-9886.

Jos. A. Bank Clothiers
399 Boylston St.
Map 4 D2.
Tel (617) 536-5050.

Polo/Ralph Lauren
93/95 Newbury St. **Map** 3
C2. **Tel** (617) 424-1124.

Women's Fashion

A Taste of Culture
1160 Massachusetts Ave.,
Cambridge.
Tel (617) 868-0389.

Ann Taylor
800 Boylston St. **Map** 3
B3. **Tel** (617) 421-9097.

Betsy Jenney
114 Newbury St. **Map** 3
C2. **Tel** (617) 536-2610.

Chanel
5 Newbury St. **Map** 4 D2.
Tel (617) 859-0055.

Clothware
1773 Massachusetts
Ave., Cambridge.
Tel (617) 661-6441.

Kate Spade
117 Newbury St. **Map** 3
C2. **Tel** (617) 262-2632.

Life is Good
285 Newbury St. **Map** 3
B2. **Tel** (617) 262-5068.

Max Mara
69 Newbury St. **Map** 3 C2.
Tel (617) 267-9775.

Nomad
1741 Massachusetts Ave.,
Cambridge.
Tel (617) 497-6677.

Settebello
52 Brattle St., Cambridge.
Tel (617) 864-2440.

Talbots
500 Boylston St. **Map** 3 C2.
Tel (617) 262-2981.

Discount and Vintage Clothes

Bobby from Boston
19 Thayer St. **Map** 4 E4.
Tel (617) 423-9299.

H&M
350 Washington St. **Map**
4 F1. **Tel** (617) 482-7081.
100 Newbury St. **Map** 3
C2. **Tel** (617) 859-3192.

Keezer's
140 River St., Cambridge.
Tel (617) 547-2455.

Marshall's
500 Boylston St. **Map** 3
C2. **Tel** (617) 262-6066.

Second Time Around
176 Newbury St. **Map** 3
B2. **Tel** (617) 247-3504. 8
Eliot St., Cambridge.
Tel (617) 491-7185.

Shoes and Accessories

Berk's
50 John F. Kennedy St.,
Cambridge.
Tel (617) 492-9511.

Foot Paths
489 Washington St. **Map**
4 F1. **Tel** (617) 338-6008.

Helen's Leather
110 Charles St. **Map** 1 B3.
Tel (617) 742-2077.

New Balance Factory Outlet
40 Life St., Brighton.
Tel (617) 779-7429.

Niketown
200 Newbury St. **Map** 3
B2. **Tel** (617) 267-3400.

Stuart Weitzman
Copley Place. **Map** 3 C3.
Tel (617) 266-8699.

The Tannery
39 Brattle St., Cambridge.
Tel (617) 491-1811.

Antiques

Alberts-Langdon, Inc.
135 Charles St. **Map** 1 B3.
Tel (617) 523-5954.

The Boston Antique Company
119 Charles St. **Map** 1 B3.
Tel (617) 227-9810.

Cambridge Antique Market
201 Msgr. O'Brien Hwy,
Cambridge.
Tel (617) 868-9655.

Danish Country
138 Charles St. **Map** 1 B3.
Tel (617) 227-1804.

JMW Gallery
144 Lincoln St. **Map** 4 F2.
Tel (617) 338-9097.

Judith Dowling Asian Art
133 Charles St. **Map** 1 B3.
Tel (617) 523-5211.

Marika's Antiques Shop
130 Charles St. **Map** 1 B3.
Tel (617) 523-4520.

Twentieth Century Ltd.
73 Charles St. **Map** 1 B4.
Tel (617) 742-1031.

Fine Crafts

Cambridge Artists' Cooperative
59a Church St.,
Cambridge.
Tel (617) 868-4434.

Mobilia
358 Huron Ave.,
Cambridge.
Tel (617) 876-2109.

Mudflat Gallery
36 White St., Cambridge.
Tel (617) 491-7976.

Society of Arts and Crafts
175 Newbury St.
Map 3 B2.
Tel (617) 266-1810.

Specialty Dealers

Brattle Book Shop
9 West St. **Map** 1 C4.
Tel (617) 542-0210.

Bromfield Pen Shop
5 Bromfield St. **Map** 1 C4.
Tel (617) 482-9053.

Eugene Galleries
76 Charles St. **Map** 1 B4.
Tel (617) 227-3062.

European Watch Co.
232 Newbury St.
Map 3 B2.
Tel (617) 262-9798.

Grolier Poetry Book Shop
6 Plympton St.,
Cambridge.
Tel (617) 547-4648.

Harvard Bookstore
1256 Massachusetts Ave.,
Cambridge.
Tel (617) 661-1515.

Harvard Coop Bookstore
1400 Massachusetts Ave.,
Cambridge.
Tel (617) 499-2000.

International Poster Gallery
205 Newbury St.
Map 3 B2.
Tel (617) 375-0076.

Million Year Picnic
99 Mt. Auburn St.,
Cambridge.
Tel (617) 492-6763.

Shopping in New England

Although New England does not immediately conjure up images of unrestrained shopping, in reality there are bargains to be had on a huge variety of consumer goods as well as regional specialties. With a few notable exceptions including Boston *(see pp340–3)*, the greatest concentration of stores generally occurs outside the downtown area, usually along the highways at the outskirts of town. Some of New England's best-known shopping experiences occur at the factory outlet stores in Freeport and Kittery in Maine, and North Conway in New Hampshire, where brand-name clothing and other goods are offered at discount prices.

Shopping Malls

With free parking and a wide range of stores gathered under one roof, malls are popular throughout the region. Here you can find fashions for the whole family, home furnishings, electronic goods, books, toys, music, beauty products, jewelry, sporting goods, food courts, and virtually anything else you could need.

Large department stores are increasingly serving as anchor stores to mall complexes. These "magnet" stores include upscale retailers such as Seattle-based Nordstrom, Lord & Taylor, and branches of Manhattan retail giant Macy's. For widest appeal, these pricey emporiums often share mall space with popular discount chains such as J.C. Penney, Kohl's, big-box electronics retailer Best Buy, and Sears.

The **Natick Mall**, New England's largest shopping complex, is located 15 miles (24 km) from Boston. In addition to 250 stores, the sprawling complex includes condominiums, multiple dining options, and plenty of parking space. The **Arcade** in Providence, Rhode Island, is considered the first indoor marketplace in America. **Providence Place**, a 13-acre (5.3-ha) shopping complex in the heart of the city, has over 170 stores. Highlights include one of New England's two Nordstrom department stores, an IMAX theater and Dave & Buster's, a combination restaurant and amusement arcade.

Downtown Hartford, Connecticut, has been overshadowed by nearby malls. Only 7 miles (11.2 km) southwest, **Westfarms Mall** boasts 160

shops, including the first Nordstrom in New England as well as Lord & Taylor for those with deep pockets. Twelve miles (19 km) east of Hartford, **The Shoppes at Buckland Hills**, one of the state's biggest and most successful malls, caters to families by offering a play area for children and a carousel in the large food court. The success of the mall has attracted many other retailers to the surrounding area. In an ironic nod to the past, **Evergreen Walk** is a recreation of a typical main street, lined with house-wares shops such as Country Curtains and Williams Sonoma; fashion retailers such as The Gap, J. Jill, and Talbots; and restaurants and ice cream shops. For a different kind of experience, **Olde Mistick Village** in Mystic, Connecticut, is designed to resemble a colonial village, with more than 60 shops and restaurants set among duck ponds and gardens. Along with clothing and household items, merchandise ranges from scrimshaw carvings to Christmas ornaments, from Irish imports to folk art.

In New Hampshire, options include the **Mall of New Hampshire** in Manchester with about 125 specialty stores as well as J.C. Penney, Sears, and Macy's anchor shops and the somewhat smaller **Steeplegate Mall** in Concord with about 75 shops. New Hampshire is the only state in New England that does not have a sales tax, making savings on shopping purchases even greater. The **Maine Mall**, only 6 miles (10 km) south of Portland, has not reduced the lively boutique

shopping scene at the Old Port. Nonetheless, it attracts a large crowd to its 140 stores, anchored by Macy's, Best Buy, and The Sports Authority, the country's largest full-line sporting goods dealer. The mall also boasts about 20 eateries.

In bucolic Vermont, the largest mall is **University Mall** in South Burlington, with about 70 shops, including toy and clothing stores for children, anchor stores Sears and J.C. Penney, and a food court.

Travelers looking for a unique shopping environment should visit **Thornes Marketplace** in Northampton, Massachusetts. A Victorian-era department store building was converted into a five-story mall with retailers offering something for every-one: upscale home accessories and clothing, trendy merchan dise for college students, ethnic imports, crafts items, and organic foods.

Discount and Outlet Shopping

Dedicated bargain hunters will want to pay a visit to some of New England's famed outlet centers, where many top designers and major brand manufacturers offer late-season and over-stocked clothing and goods at big discounts. Generally sold at 20 to 30 percent less than retail prices, some items can be found reduced by as much as 75 percent. In addition to clothing, outlets are good places to find bargains on kitchen goods, linens, china, glassware, leather goods, luggage and sporting goods.

In Wrentham, Massachusetts, 33 miles (53 km) southwest of Boston, are the **Wrentham Village Premium Outlets**. The stores here sell designer clothing, housewares, and accessories from many leading manufacturers. Serving the upscale Long Island Sound community, the **Tanger Factory Outlet Center** in Westbrook, Connecticut, emphasizes fashion and style in its mix of about 65 shops. **Kittery** *(see p282)*, Maine, is an even larger outlet destination, with about 120 shops lining a 1-mile (1.6-km) stretch of busy Route 1. Merchants offer everything from footwear and designer clothes to sports equipment, perfume, books, china, glass, and gifts. There are also numerous restaurants. Many shoppers prefer **Freeport**, farther up the coast, about a 20-minute drive north of Portland. Outlets, individual shops, and eateries mingle along the streets of the historic village, making it easy to park the car and stroll from Jones New York to Talbots or to check out leather goods and luggage at Dooney & Bourke or Hartmann Factory Store.

The **Manchester Designer Outlets** in Manchester, Vermont, focus on some of the top names in the fashion world, such as Michael Kors, Escada, Giorgio Armani, and BCBG Max Azria, in addition to Jones New York, Polo/Ralph Lauren and Tse for soft, luxurious cashmere. Other designers to look out for include Kenneth Cole and Kate Spade New York.

Settlers' Green Outlets in North Conway, New Hampshire, was one of the first major outlet centers in the region. The 3-mile (5-km) stretch along Route 16 is lined with factory outlets selling fashion, furniture, and outdoor gear.

Outdoors Outfitters

With mountains to climb, streams to fish, woods to hike, and lakes and oceans to paddle, New England has an abundance of outdoors outfitters who offer everything from custom flyrods to specialized rock-climbing gear. They also sell "outdoors chic" casual clothing for those more interested in looking the part than breaking a sweat. The regional leader in outdoor sporting equipment (especially hunting and fishing gear) is **L.L. Bean**, which has its flagship store in Freeport, Maine. The hunting and fishing section is open daily around the clock. The 23,000 sq ft (2137 sq m) flagship store of **Orvis** in Manchester, Vermont (*see p245*), sits on the company's extensive campus, where visitors can tour the adjacent signature flyrod factory or practice flycasting in company trout ponds. **REI Boston** has outdoor gear for all seasons, including equipment for rent, and it operates outdoor classes for all levels. **Eastern Mountain Sports** focuses on climbing, trekking, mountain biking, and kayaking. Its flagship store is located in Peterborough, New Hampshire. Outdoor stores at the North Conway Factory Outlets include Eddie Bauer, Norm Thompson, and Chuck Roast who sell warm and durable winter outerwear.

DIRECTORY

Shopping Malls

The Arcade
65 Weybosset St.,
Providence, RI.
Tel (401) 454-4568.
W arcadeprovince.com

Evergreen Walk
501 Evergreen Way
South Windsor, CT.
Tel (860) 432-3398.
W thepromenadeshops
atevergreenwalk.com

Maine Mall
364 Maine Mall Rd.,
South, Portland, ME.
Tel (207) 774-0303.
W mainemall.com

Mall of New Hampshire
1500 S. Willow St.,
Manchester, NH. **Tel** (603)
669-0433. W simon.com

Natick Mall
1245 Worcester St., Natick,
MA. **Tel** (508) 655-4345.
W natickmall.com

Olde Mistick Village
I-95, exit 90, CT.
Tel (860) 536-4941.
W oldemistickvillage.
com

Providence Place
1 Providence Pl.,
Providence, RI.
Tel (401) 270-1000.

The Shoppes at Buckland Hills
194 Buckland Hills Dr.,
Manchester, CT.
Tel (860) 644-1450.
W theshoppesat
bucklandhills.com

Steeplegate Mall
270 Loudon Rd.,
Concord, NH.
Tel (603) 224-1523.
W steeplegatemall.com

Thornes Marketplace
150 Main St.,
Northampton, MA.
W thornesmarket
place.com

University Mall
Dorset St. at Williston Rd.,
South Burlington, VT.
Tel (800) 863-1066.
W umallvt.com

Westfarms Mall
500 Westfarms Mall
Rd., Farmington, CT.
Tel (860) 561-3024.
W shopwestfarms.com

Discount and Outlet Shopping

Freeport Merchants Association
Freeport, ME.
Tel (800) 865-1994.
W freeportusa.com

Kittery Outlets
Kittery, ME.
Tel (888) 548-8379.
W thekitteryoutlets.com

Manchester Designer Outlets
Manchester, VT.
Tel (802) 362-3736.
W manchesterdesigner
outlets.com

Settlers' Green Outlets
North Conway, NH.
Tel (888) 667-9636.

Tanger Factory Outlet Center
314 Flat Rock Pl.,
Westbrook, CT.
Tel (860) 399-8656.
W tangeroutlet.com

Wrentham Village Premium Outlets
Wrentham, MA.
Tel (508) 384-0600.
W premiumoutlets.com

Outdoor Outfitters

Eastern Mountain Sports
1 Vose Farm Rd.,
Peterborough, NH.
Tel (603) 924-7231.
W ems.com

L.L. Bean
95 Main St., Freeport, ME.
Tel (800) 441-5713.
W llbean.com

Orvis Headquarters
4180 Main St.,
Manchester, VT.
Tel (802) 362-3750.
W orvis.com

REI Boston
401 Park Dr., Boston, MA.
Tel (617) 236-0746.
W rei.com

Antiques, Crafts, Books, and Country Stores in New England

While the highway-side shopping centers are the focus of mercantile New England, the goods closely associated with the region are more likely to be found in shops along the byways or in the villages. Visitors looking for gifts with a regional flavor might consider maple syrup, found widely in Vermont and New Hampshire. Coastal shops often have excellent reproductions of scrimshaw whalebone carvings. The nostalgia-oriented country stores often sell the most typical goods of the region, from freshly ground cornmeal to carved wooden toys.

Antiques and Flea Markets

Perhaps the region's most famous antiquing event is the thrice-yearly Brimfield Antique Show *(see p165)* in Brimfield, Massachusetts. On Cape Cod, scenic Route 6 is peppered with antique shops, especially the charming towns of Dennis and Brewster. Up to 300 dealers fill the parking lot of the **Wellfleet Drive-In Theater** for the flea market on weekends from May through mid-October. The towns of the southern Berkshires are also known for antiquing. **Great Barrington Antiques Center** and **The Emporium Antique Center** cover a broad range of Americana. In Sheffield, **Painted Porch Country Antiques** displays rustic antiques from France, England, and Canada in decorator settings.

Shops continue as Route 7 crosses the border to Vermont. This state's largest antiques emporia is **Vermont Antique Mall** at Quechee Gorge Village, with more than 450 booths.

Connecticut's Litchfield Hills is another antiques hotbed. The town of Woodbury has dozens of high-quality shops, including **Country Loft Antiques**, which sells many wine implements. The **New Woodbury Antiques and Flea Market** operates on Saturdays all year selling a wide range of new and collectible merchandise. The former mill town of Putnam has reinvented itself as an antiques center. Chief among the shops is **Antiques Marketplace**.

In Rhode Island, go to Spring Street and lower Thames Street in Newport for a variety of shops with select, upmarket merchandise. One of the state's largest flea markets is held on weekends from April through October at Charlestown's **General Stanton Inn**. Up to 200 dealers offer a wide range of antiques and collectibles.

In Maine, Route 1 between Kittery and Scarborough is lined with antiques shops and one of the largest is **Arundel Antiques** with more than 200 dealers. The seafaring town of Searsport has a mix of multi-dealer shops and weekend flea markets. In season, **Hobby Horse Flea Market** features indoor and outdoor stalls. For nautical antiques, quilts and old tools, visit **Pumpkin Patch Antiques Center**.

New Hampshire's antiquing areas include Route 4 between Concord and Durham, Route 101A in Milford, and Route 119 in Fitzwilliam. The highly regarded **Northeast Auctions** conducts five major auctions a year in Manchester and Portsmouth, as well as smaller estate sales. The **Londonderry Flea Market** operates on weekends from mid-April through October.

Crafts Galleries

New Hampshire has the region's best-established program to support local craftspeople. The **League of New Hampshire Craftsmen** was founded in 1932 and its annual fair in early August is one of the most important in the region. The League also operates seven crafts galleries throughout the state.

The **Frog Hollow Vermont State Craft Center** began modestly in 1971 by offering pottery classes for children. Now it offers a wide array of programs and operates a gallery that displays traditional and contemporary work by about 250 Vermont artisans.

In Connecticut, the **Brookfield Craft Center** was founded in 1954. It offers classes, and showcases the work of American craftspeople through its exhibitions and gallery.

Fifteen Maine potters have formed a collective to market their work through the **Maine Potters Market** in Portland. The functional and decorative pieces represent a wide range of styles and colors. Nearby **Abacus American Craft Gallery** displays the work of American artists, including many from New England.

The Berkshire hills of Massachusetts are home to many crafts artists, including ceramist Thomas Hoadley. His work and that of other local and national artists is displayed in the **Hoadley Gallery**.

Book Dealers

Specialists in antiquarian and used books abound in New England, but few stores have the variety of out-of-print volumes – especially of cookbooks and culinary titles – as **New England Mobile Book Fair**. For sheer volume of used books, check out **Old Number Six Book Depot** in Henniker, New Hampshire, or **Big Chicken Barn Books** in Ellsworth, Maine. Illustrated books and Vermontiana are specialties of **Monroe Street Books** in Middlebury, Vermont, while **Harbor Books** in Old Saybrook, Connecticut, has a broad range of new and used nautical books. **Tyson's Old & Rare Books** in East Providence, Rhode Island, specializes in American history, nautical themes, and Native American literature.

Country Stores

New England's country stores offer an old-fashioned atmosphere and specialize in local foods: honey, maple syrup, cheese, mustards, and jams. At **Brown & Hopkins Country Store** in Chepachet, Rhode Island, well-worn pine planks line the floors and a glass case of penny candy sits by the door. The **Williamsburg General Store** in Williamsburg, Massachusetts, is located in an 1870 building and offers delicious baked goods as well as kitchen tools, herbs, spices, mustards, jellies, and syrups. In Vermont, the **Weston Village Store** has a pressed tin ceiling and scuffed wooden floors. Sturdy pottery, weathervanes and wooden bowls supplement the wide selection of cheese and fudge. The **Vermont Country Store** sells outdoor clothing, quirky but useful gadgets, and local foodstuffs. In Sugar Hill, New Hampshire, **Harman's Cheese & Country Store** is known for its aged white cheddar. **The Old Country Store and Museum** in Moultonborough also offers cheddar cheese, along with cast iron cookware.

DIRECTORY

Antiques and Flea Markets

Antiques Marketplace
109 Main St., Putnam, CT.
Tel (860) 928-0442.
W putnamantiques.com

Arundel Antiques
Route 1, Arundel, ME.
Tel (207) 985-7965.

Country Loft Antiques
557 Main St. S., Woodbury,
CT. Tel (203) 266-4500.
W countryloftantiques.com

The Emporium Antique Center
319 Main St., Great
Barrington, MA. Tel (413)
528-1660. W emporium
antiquecenter.com

General Stanton Inn Flea Market
4115 Old Post Rd.,
Charlestown, RI. Tel (800)
364-8011. W general
stantoninn.com

Great Barrington Antiques Center
964 S. Main St., Great
Barrington, MA. Tel (413)
644-8848. W great
barringtonantiques
center.com

Hobby Horse Flea Market
383 Main St., Searsport,
ME. Tel (207) 548-2981.
W hobbyhorseflea
market.com

Londonderry Flea Market
RR 102 Londonderry, NH.
Tel (603) 883-4196.
W londonderryflea
market.com

New Woodbury Antiques and Flea Market
44 Sherman Hill Rd.,
Woodbury, CT.
Tel (203) 263-6217.
W thenewwoodbury
fleamarket.com

Northeast Auctions
W northeastauctions.
com

Painted Porch Country Antiques
102 S. Main St., Sheffield,
MA. Tel (413) 229-2700.
W paintedporch.com

Pumpkin Patch Antiques Center
15 W. Main St., Searsport,
ME. Tel (207) 548-6047.

Vermont Antique Mall
Route 4, Quechee, VT.
Tel (802) 281-4147.
W vermontantique
mall.com

Wellfleet Drive-In Theater Flea Market
Route 6, Wellfleet, MA.
Tel (508) 349-0541.
W wellfleetcinemas.com

Crafts Galleries

Abacus American Craft Gallery
44 Exchange St., Portland, ME.
Tel (207) 772-4880.
W abacusgallery.com

Brookfield Craft Center
286 Whisconier Rd.,
Brookfield, CT.
Tel (203) 775-4526.
W brookfield craft.org

Frog Hollow Vermont State Craft Center
85 Church St., Burlington,
VT. Tel (802) 863-6458.
W froghollow.org

Hoadley Gallery
21 Church St., Lenox, MA.
Tel (413) 637-2814.
W hoadleygallery.com

League of New Hampshire Craftsmen
32 Main St., Center
Sandwich, NH. Tel (603)
284-6831 (May–Oct only).
W nhcrafts.org 36 N.
Main St., Concord, NH.
Tel (603) 228-8171. 13
Lebanon St., Hanover, NH.
Tel (603) 643-5050. 81
Main St., Littleton, NH.
Tel (603) 444-1099. 279
Daniel Webster Hwy.,
Meredith, NH. Tel (603)
279-7920. 98 Main St.,
Nashua, NH. Tel (603)
595-8233. 2526 White
Mountains Hwy./Route
16. North Conway, NH.
Tel (603) 356-2441. 15 N.
Main St., Wolfeboro, NH.
Tel (603) 569-3309.

Maine Potters Market
376 Fore St., Portland, ME.
Tel (207) 774-1633.
W mainepotters
market.com

Book Dealers

Big Chicken Barn Books
1768 Bucksport Rd.,
Ellsworth, ME.
Tel (207) 667-7308.

Harbor Books
146 Main St., Old
Saybrook, CT.
Tel (860) 388-6850.

Monroe Street Books
70 Monroe St. (Route 7
N.), Middlebury, VT.
Tel (802) 398-2200.

New England Mobile Book Fair
82–84 Needham St.,
Newton Highlands, MA.
Tel (617) 964-7440.

Old Number Six Book Depot
166 Depot Hill Rd.
Henniker, NH.
Tel (603) 428-3334.

Tyson's Old & Rare Books
178 Taunton Ave., East
Providence, RI.
Tel (401) 431-2111.

Country Stores

Brown & Hopkins Country Store
1179 Putnam Pike,
Chepachet, RI.
Tel (401) 568-4830.

Harman's Cheese & Country Store
1400 Route 117, Sugar
Hill, NH.
Tel (603) 823-8000.

The Old Country Store and Museum
1011 Whittier Hwy.,
Moultonborough, NH.
Tel (603) 476-5750.

Vermont Country Store
Route 100, Weston, VT.
Tel (802) 824-3184.

Weston Village Store
Route 100, Weston, VT.
Tel (802) 824-5477.

Williamsburg General Store
12 Main St., Williamsburg,
MA. Tel (413) 268-3036.

ENTERTAINMENT IN BOSTON

From avant-garde performance art to serious drama, and from popular dance music to live classical performances, Boston offers an outstanding array of entertainment options, with something to appeal to every taste: the Theater District offers many excellent plays and musicals; the Wang Theatre hosts many touring productions; and Symphony Hall is home of the renowned Boston Symphony Orchestra. Boston is also well acquainted with jazz, folk, and blues as well as being a center for more contemporary music, played in big city nightclubs. In summer, entertainment often heads outdoors, with many open-air plays and concerts, such as the famous Boston Pops at the Hatch Shell.

Practical Information

The best sources for information on current films, concerts, theater, dance, and exhibitions include the arts and entertainment sections of the *Boston Globe*, *Boston Herald*, and *Improper Bostonian*. Even more up-to-date listings can be found on the Internet at the following sites: www.bostonmagazine.com; www.boston.com; and www.bostonusa.com.

Boston entertainment listings magazines

Boston. For advance tickets these are **Ticketmaster** and **Live Nation**. Tickets can be purchased from both of these agencies over the telephone, in person, or online.

Half-price tickets to the majority of non-commercial arts events as well as to some commercial productions are available from 10am on the day of the performance at **BosTix** booths. Purchases must be made in person and only cash is accepted. BosTix also sells discount tickets in advance. Special Boston entertainment discount vouchers, available from hotel lobbies and tourist offices, may also offer savings on some shows.

Booking Tickets

Tickets to popular musicals, theatrical productions, and touring shows often sell out far in advance, although theaters sometimes have a few returns or restricted-view tickets available. You can either get tickets in person at theater box offices, or use one of the ticket agencies in

Districts and Venues

Musicals, plays, comedies, and dance are generally performed at venues in the Theater District,

Tchaikovsky's *Nutcracker*, danced by the Boston Ballet *(see p350)*

although larger non-commercial theater companies are distributed throughout the region, many being associated with colleges and universities.

The area around the intersection of Massachusetts and Huntington Avenues hosts a concentration of outstanding concert venues, including Symphony Hall, Berklee Performance Center at Berklee College of Music, and Jordan Hall at the New England Conservatory of Music.

Many nightclub and dance venues are on Lansdowne and nearby streets by Fenway Park and around Boylston Place in the Theater District. The busiest areas for bars and small clubs offering live jazz and rock music are Central and Harvard Squares in Cambridge, Davis Square in Somerville, and Allston. The principal gay scene in Boston is found in the South End, with many of the older bars and clubs in neighboring Bay Village.

Boston's Symphony Orchestra performing at Symphony Hall *(see p350)*

Open-air and Free Entertainment

The best free outdoor summer entertainment in Boston is found at the Hatch Shell *(see p100)*. The Boston Pops *(see p350)* performs here frequently during the week around July 4, and all through July and August jazz, pop, rock, and classical music is played. On Friday evenings from late June to the week before Labor Day, the Hatch Shell also shows free big-screen family films.

Music is also performed in the summer months at the **Blue Hills Bank Pavilion** on the waterfront, which holds live jazz, pop, and country music concerts. City Hall Plaza and Copley Plaza have free concerts at lunchtimes and in the evenings, and the **Museum of Fine Arts** *(see pp110–13)* operates a summer musical concert series in its courtyard. Most of the annual

Free open-air music concert outside Boston City Hall *(see p84)*

concerts and recitals of the **New England Conservatory of Music** *(see p350)* are free, although some require advance booking.

Other free open-air entertainment includes productions of Shakespeare on the Boston Common in July and August, sponsored by **Commonwealth Shakespeare**, and concerts by artists from the Berklee College of Music at the **Institute of Contemporary Art**.

An area that has more unusual open-air entertainment is Harvard Square, famous for its nightly and weekend scene of street performers. Many recording artists paid their dues here, and other hopefuls still flock to the square in

Entrance to the Shubert Theatre *(see p75)*

the vain hope of being discovered – or at least of earning the cost of dinner.

Details of all free entertainment happening in the city are listed in the arts and entertainment sections of the *Boston Globe*, *Boston Herald*, and *Improper Bostonian*.

Disabled Access

Many entertainment venues in Boston are wheelchair-accessible. **Very Special Arts Massachusetts** offers a full Boston arts access guide. Some places, such as **Jordan Hall**, the **Cutler Majestic Theatre**, and the **Wheelock Family Theatre**, have listening aids for the hearing impaired, while the latter also has signed and described performances.

DIRECTORY

Booking Tickets

BosTix
Faneuil Hall Marketplace.
Map 2 D3. Copley Sq.
Map 3 C2.
Tel (617) 262-8632.
w bostix.org

Live Nation
1 Hamilton Pl.
Map 1 C4. Various outlets.
Tel (800) 745-3000.
w livenation.com

Ticketmaster
Various outlets.
Tel (866) 448-7849.
w ticketmaster.com

Open-air/Free Entertainment

Blue Hills Bank Pavilion
290 Northern Ave., South Boston. **Map** 2 F5.
Tel (617) 728-1600.
w livenation.com

Commonwealth Shakespeare
Parkman Bandstand, Boston Common. **Map** 1 C4. **Tel** (617) 426-0863.
w commshakes.org

Institute of Contemporary Art
100 Northern Ave.
Map 2 E5.
Tel (617) 478-3100.
w icaboston.org

Museum of Fine Arts
465 Huntington Ave.
Tel (617) 267-9300.
w mfa.org

New England Conservatory of Music
290 Huntington Ave.
Tel (617) 585-1260.
w necmusic.edu

Disabled Access

Cutler Majestic Theatre
219 Tremont St.
Map 4 E2.
Tel (617) 824-8000.
w cutlermajestic.org

Jordan Hall
30 Gainsborough St.
Tel (617) 585-1260.
w necmusic.edu

Very Special Arts Massachusetts
89 South St. **Map** 4 F2.
Tel (617) 350-7713; TTY
(617) 350-6536.
w vsamass.org

Wheelock Family Theatre
200 Riverway, Brookline.
Tel (617) 879-2300. TTY
(617) 879-2150.
w wheelockfamily theatre.org

The Arts in Boston

Although some theaters are closed on Mondays, there is rarely a night in Boston without performing arts. For classical music lovers, the season revolves around the Boston Symphony Orchestra, with many Brahmins *(see p67)* occupying their grandparents' seats at Symphony Hall. Bostonians are also avid theatergoers, opting for touring musical productions in historic theaters as well as ambitious contemporary drama at repertory theaters. (Occasionally shows preview in Boston before debuting on Broadway.) The prestigious Boston Ballet performs at the Opera House and other smaller venues. With huge student and expat populations, the city also enjoys a healthy cinema scene, with annual film festivals and a number of art-house theaters.

Classical Music and Opera

Two cherished Boston institutions, the **Boston Symphony Orchestra** and its popular-music equivalent, the Boston Pops, have a long history of being led by some of America's finest conductors. The BSO performs a full schedule of concerts at Symphony Hall from October through April. The Boston Pops takes over for May and June, performing at the Charles River Esplanade *(see p100)* for Fourth of July festivities that are the highlight of the summer season.

The students and faculty of the **New England Conservatory of Music** present more than 450 free classical and jazz performances each year, many in Jordan Hall *(see p349)*. **Boston Lyric Opera** has assumed the task of reestablishing opera in Boston, through small-cast and light opera at venues around the city.

Boston's oldest musical organization is the **Handel & Haydn Society** (H&H), founded in 1815. As the first American producer of such landmark works as Handel's *Messiah* (performed annually since 1818), Bach's *B-Minor Mass* and *St. Matthew Passion*, and Verdi's *Requiem*, H&H is one of the country's musical treasures. Since 1986, the society has focused on performing and recording Baroque and Classical works using the period instruments for which the

composers wrote. H&H gives regular performances in Boston at Symphony Hall, Jordan Hall, and other venues.

Classical music is ubiquitous in Boston. **Emmanuel Music**, for example, performs the entire Bach cantata cycle at regular services at Emmanuel Church on Newbury Street. The Isabella Stewart Gardner Museum *(see p109)* hosts a series of chamber music concerts, continuing a 19th-century tradition of professional "music room" chamber concerts in the homes of the social elite.

The **Celebrity Series of Boston** brings world-famous orchestras, soloists, and dance companies to Boston, often to perform at Jordan Hall and Symphony Hall.

Theater

Though much diminished from its heyday in the 1920s, when more than 40 theaters were in operation throughout Boston, today the city's Theater District *(see pp62–75)* still contains a collection of some of the most architecturally eminent, and commercially productive, early theaters in the United States. Furthermore, during the 1990s, many of the theaters that are currently in use underwent major programs of restoration to bring them back to their original grandeur, and visitors today are bound to be impressed as they catch a glimpse of these theaters' past glory.

The main, commercially run theaters of Boston – the **Colonial**, **Wilbur**, and Shubert *(see p75)* theaters, and the **Opera House** and the Wang Theatre *(see p75)* – often present Broadway productions that have already premiered in New York and are touring the country. They also present Broadway "tryouts" and local productions.

In stark contrast to some of the mainstream shows on offer in Boston, the most avant-garde contemporary theater in the city is performed at the **American Repertory Theater** (ART), an independent, non-commercial company associated with Harvard University *(see pp116–17)*. ART often premieres new plays, particularly on its second stage, but is best known for its often radical interpretations of traditional and modern classics. By further contrast, the **Huntington Theatre**, allied with Boston University, is widely praised for its traditional direction and interpretation. For example, the Huntington was the co-developer of Pulitzer Prize-winning plays detailing 20th-century African American life, by the late August Wilson, an important chronicler of American race relations.

Several smaller companies, including **Lyric Stage**, devote their energies to showcasing local actors and directors and often premiere the work of Boston-area playwrights. Many of the most adventurous companies perform on one of the four stages at the **Boston Center for the Arts**.

Dance

The city's largest and most popular resident dance company, the **Boston Ballet** performs an ambitious season of classics and new choreography between October and May at the opulent Opera House and other venues. The annual performances of the *Nutcracker* during the Christmas season are a Boston tradition. The somewhat more modest **José Mateo Ballet Theatre** has developed a strong and impressive body of repertory choreography. The company performs in the neo-Gothic Old Cambridge Baptist Church, which is situated near Harvard Square. Modern dance in Boston is represented by many small companies, collectives, and independent choreographers, who often perform in the **Dance Complex** and **Green Street Studios** in Cambridge. Boston also hosts many other visiting dance companies, who often put on performances at the **Cutler Majestic Theatre**.

Cinema

Situated in Harvard Square (see p114) close to Harvard Yard, the **Brattle Theater**, one of the very last repertory movie houses in the Greater Boston area, primarily shows classic films on a big screen. For example, the Brattle was instrumental in reviving movie-goers' interest in the Humphrey Bogart, black-and-white classic *Casablanca*. Something of a Harvard institution, the Brattle has long served as a popular "first date" destination.

Serious students of classic and international cinema patronize the screening programs of the **Harvard Film Archive**, for its range of foreign, art, and historical films. The **Kendall Square Cinema** multiplex is the city's chief venue for non-English language films, art films and documentaries. Multiplex theaters showing mainstream, first-run Hollywood movies are found throughout the Boston area. Some of the most popular are **AMC Loews Boston Common 19**, located at Boston Common, and the **Regal Fenway 13** in the suburb of Brookline.

Tickets for every kind of movie in Boston are often discounted for first shows of the day.

DIRECTORY

Classical Music and Opera

Boston Lyric Opera
various venues.
Tel (617) 542-6772.
W blo.org

Boston Symphony Orchestra
Symphony Hall, 301 Massachusetts Ave.
Map 3 A4.
Tel (617) 266-1200, (617) 266-1492.
W bso.org

Celebrity Series of Boston
various venues.
Tel (617) 482-6661.
W celebrityseries.org

Emmanuel Music
Emmanuel Church, 15 Newbury St.
Map 4 D2.
Tel (617) 536-3356.
W emmanuelmusic.org

Handel & Haydn Society
various venues.
Tel (617) 266-3605.
W handelandhaydn.org

New England Conservatory of Music
Jordan Hall, 30 Gainsborough St.
Map 3 A4.
Tel (617) 585-1260.
W necmusic.edu

Theater

American Repertory Theater
Loeb Drama Center, 64 Brattle St., Cambridge.
Tel (617) 547-8300.
W amrep.org

Boston Center for the Arts
539 Tremont St.
Map 4 D3.
Tel (617) 933-8600.
W bcaonline.org

Colonial Theater
106 Boylston St.
Map 4 E2.
Tel (617) 426-9366.
W bostoncolonialtheatre.com

Huntington Theatre
264 Huntington Ave.
Map 3 B4.
Tel (617) 266-0800.
W huntingtontheatre.org

Lyric Stage
140 Clarendon St.
Map 3 C3.
Tel (617) 585-5678.
W lyricstage.com

Opera House
539 Washington St.
Map 4 E1.
Tel (617) 259-3400.
W bostonoperahouse.com

Wilbur Theatre
246 Tremont St.
Map 4 E2.
Tel (617) 931-2000.
W ticketmaster.com

Dance

Boston Ballet
various venues.
Tel (617) 695-6955.
W bostonballet.org

Cutler Majestic Theatre
219 Tremont St.
Map 4 E2.
Tel (617) 824-8000.
W cutlermajestic.org

Dance Complex
536 Massachusetts Ave., Cambridge.
Tel (617) 547-9363.
W dancecomplex.org

Green Street Studios
185 Green St., Cambridge.
Tel (617) 864-3191.
W greenstreetstudios.org

José Mateo Ballet Theatre
400 Harvard St., Cambridge.
Tel (617) 354-7467.
W balletheatre.org

Cinema

AMC Loews Boston Common
Boston Common.
Map 4 E2.
Tel (617) 423-5801.
W amctheatres.com

Brattle Theater
40 Brattle St., Cambridge.
Tel (617) 876-6837.
W brattlefilm.org

Harvard Film Archive
24 Quincy St., Cambridge.
Tel (617) 495-4700.
W hcl.harvard.edu/hfa

Kendall Square Cinema
1 Kendall Square, Cambridge.
Tel (617) 499-1996.
W landmarktheatres.com

Regal Fenway 13
201 Brookline Ave.
Tel (617) 424-6266.

Music Venues in Boston

Boston's mix of young professionals and tens of thousands of college students produces a lively nightlife scene, focused on live music, clubs, and bars. Since the 1920s, Boston has been especially hospitable to jazz, and it still has an interesting jazz scene, with the world-renowned Berklee College of Music playing an important part. Cambridge is an epicenter of folk and acoustic music revivals and alt-rock, while Lansdowne Street (behind Fenway Park) is the main district for rock clubs. Virtually every neighborhood has a selection of friendly bars, many with live music. The city's audiences, considered to be among the country's most eager and receptive, make Boston a must-stop destination for national touring acts.

Rock Music

The **House of Blues** chain of clubs specializing in indoor rock and blues concerts began in Harvard Square in 1992. In 2009, a giant House of Blues opened in the Fenway district. Heavily booked throughout the year with both established and up-and-coming rock and pop acts – many from New England – the venue also offers an extremely popular Sunday brunch that features Southern-style food accompanied by live gospel music. In keeping with this theme, a box of mud from the Mississippi Delta is buried beneath the main stage.

Royale, one of Boston's most popular clubs, offers the occasional big-time concert with international performers including Robyn and Ziggy Marley, but it makes its name by hosting some of the city's most raucous club nights, with world-famous DJs and hordes of scantily clad clubbers.

Located on the edge of Boston University's campus, the **Paradise Rock Club** has long been a local institution (the likes of U2, Coldplay, and the Police have all graced the stage). The front lounge offers a relaxed spot for an inexpensive pre-show meal and sometimes hosts smaller acts.

In a city that's chock full of historical sites, the **Orpheum Theatre** stands out as the oldest concert venue. The original home of the New England Conservatory of Music *(see pp350–51)* dates back to 1852

and serves as Boston's premier venue for acts that are too big for the clubs but can't quite fill an arena. While the sightlines are above-average, the venue loses major points for having a no food or beverage policy in the stands (concert-goers are forced to enjoy their overpriced beers in the stuffy lobby).

Arena-level acts head to the 18,000-seat **TD Garden**, home of the Boston Bruins (NHL) and Celtics (NBA), or Boston University's **Agannis Arena**, which is roughly half the size of the Garden. Come summertime, those same acts head outdoors to play the massive **Comcast Center for the Performing Arts** – located 30 miles (48 km) southwest of Boston – and smaller **Blue Hills Bank Pavilion** *(see p349)*, which enjoys scenic skyline views from its South Boston waterfront home.

At the other end of the size spectrum are places like the **Green Dragon Tavern** near Quincy Market, known for its Irish and cover bands; **Midway Café**, in Jamaica Plain, for live local blues and rock; and the **Brighton Music Hall**, a diminutive venue that hosts an assortment of local and national acts.

The Middle East, Cambridge's premier all-purpose club, offers three distinct stages in which to enjoy everything from local folk collectives and belly dancing to national rock acts. The eponymous restaurant provides a relaxed spot for a pre- or post-show drink or snack.

For anyone who's always wanted to be close enough to taste a rock star's sweat, **TT the Bear's** is the place. This diminutive club, located just behind the Middle East, puts fans right in the middle of the action, with nothing separating those at the front from the low stage.

Also located in Cambridge are the **Lizard Lounge** and **All-Asia Café**, tiny clubs that host wildly eclectic schedules, and **Plough & Stars** and **Toad**, both of which are popular with local singer-songwriters.

Away from the city center, up- and-coming Somerville is home to **P.A.'s Lounge** and **Sally O'Brien's**, a pair of dive bars that are good for cheap drinks and local rock acts.

Jazz and Blues

As one would expect from one of the nation's most respected music schools, **Berklee Performance Center** houses the best acoustics and sight-lines in Boston. The auditorium hosts everything from jazz legends and big band revues to contemporary acts. The only drawback is that no food or drink is allowed in the seats.

On a nondescript stretch of Massachusetts Avenue resides **Wally's Cafe**, one of the city's hidden gems. This atmospheric jazz club hosts live music 365 days a year, with bebop, swing and Afro-Cuban Latin jazz. Now and then professionals pop up, but most lineups comprise students and amateurs. On weekends, there's usually a line.

The majority of national jazz touring acts stick to one of three clubs: **Regattabar** (in Harvard Square's swish Charles Hotel), **Ryles Jazz Club** (in Cambridge's Inman Square) and **Scullers Jazz Club** (in the Doubletree Hotel, on the Brighton-Cambridge border).

Those looking to avoid paying steep cover charges stick to lower-key spots like Central Square's **Cantab Lounge**, Allston's **Wonder Bar** and **Les Zygomates**, a stylish French bistro in Boston's gentrifying Leather District that hosts free live jazz most nights.

Folk and World Music

Since 1958, Harvard Square has been home to **Club Passim**, one of the country's seminal folk clubs. The small venue held the Northeast's first hootenanny, and has seen everyone from Bob Dylan to Joan Baez play here. **Johnny D's Uptown Restaurant & Music Club** in Somerville's

Davis Square is one of the area's most diverse music clubs, where you might stumble upon a hillbilly jam or Latin funk artist. There's a live jazz brunch and blues jam on Sunday's. The **Somerville Theatre** is a stuffy venue that's popular with world music acts, while just down the street is **The Burren**, an Irish pub

that hosts lively sessions and Celtic acts. The Museum of Fine Arts' **Remis Auditorium** has wonderful acoustics for world music gigs. International acts ranging from Afro-pop to ska play at large venues across Boston in a concert series presented by promoters **World Music**.

DIRECTORY

Rock Music

Agganis Arena
925 Commonwealth Ave., Boston.
Tel (617) 358-7000.
W **agganisarena.com**

All-Asia Cafe
334 Massachusetts Ave., Cambridge.
Tel (617) 497-1544.
W **allasiabar.com**

Blue Hills Bank Pavilion
290 Northern Ave.
Tel (617) 728-1600.
W **livenation.com**

Brighton Music Hall
158 Brighton Ave., Allston, MA.
Tel (617) 779-0140.
W **crossroadspresents. com**

Comcast Center for the Performing Arts
885 S Main St., Mansfield, MA. **Tel** (508) 339-2331.
W **livenation.com**

Green Dragon Tavern
11 Marshall St.
Tel (617) 367-0055.
W **somerspubs.com**

House of Blues
13–15 Lansdowne St.
Tel (888) 693-2583.
W **houseofblues.com**

Lizard Lounge
1667 Massachusetts Ave., Cambridge, MA.
Tel (617) 547-0759.
W **lizardloungeclub. com**

The Middle East
472/480 Massachusetts Ave., Cambridge.
Tel (617) 864-3278.
W **mideastclub.com**

Midway Café
3496 Washington St., Jamaica Plain.
Tel (617) 524-9038.
W **midwaycafe.com**

Orpheum Theatre
1 Hamilton Place.
Map 1C4.
Tel (617) 482-0106.

P.A.'s Lounge
345 Somerville Ave., Somerville.
Tel (617) 776-1557.
W **paslounge.com**

Paradise Rock Club
969 Commonwealth Ave.
Tel (617) 562-8800.
W **thedise.com**

Plough & Stars
912 Massachusetts Ave., Cambridge.
Tel (617) 576-0032.
W **ploughandstars.com**

Royale
279 Tremont St.
Tel (617) 338-7699.
W **royaleboston.com**

Sally O'Brien's
335 Somerville Ave., Somerville, MA.
Tel (617) 666-3589.
W **sallyobriensbar.com**

TD Garden
1 Causeway St.
Map 1C2.
Tel (617) 624-1000.
W **tdgarden.com**

Toad
1912 Massachusetts Ave., Cambridge.
Tel (617) 497-4950.
W **toadcambridge.com**

TT The Bear's
10 Brookline St. (Central Square), Cambridge.
Tel 617-492-BEAR (2327).
W **ttthebears.com**

Jazz and Blues

Berklee Performance Center
Berklee College of Music, 136 Massachusetts Ave.
Map 3 A3.
Tel (617) 266-7455.
W **berkleebpc.com**

Cantab Lounge
738 Massachusetts Ave., Cambridge.
Tel (617) 354-2685.
W **cantab-lounge.com**

Les Zygomates
129 South St.
Tel (617) 542-5108.
W **winebar.com**

Regattabar
Charles Hotel, 1 Bennett St., Cambridge.
Tel (617) 395-7757.
W **regattabarjazz.com**

Ryles Jazz Club
212 Hampshire St., Cambridge.
Tel (617) 876-9330.
W **rylesjazz.com**

Scullers Jazz Club
Doubletree Guest Suites, 400 Soldiers Field Rd., Brighton.
Tel (617) 562-4111.
W **scullersjazz.com**

Wally's Cafe
427 Massachusetts Ave.
Tel (617) 424-1408.
W **wallyscafe.com**

Wonder Bar
186 Harvard Ave., Allston, MA.
Tel (617) 351-2665.
W **wonderbarboston. com**

Folk and World Music

The Burren
247 Elm St., Somerville, MA.
Tel (617) 776-6896.
W **burren.com**

Club Passim
47 Palmer St., Cambridge.
Tel (617) 492-7679.
W **clubpassim.org**

Johnny D's Uptown Restaurant & Music Club
17 Holland St., Somerville.
Tel (617) 776-2004.
W **johnnyds.com**

Remis Auditorium, Museum of Fine Arts
465 Huntington Ave.
Tel (617) 267-9300.
W **mfa.org**

Somerville Theatre
55 Davis Square, Somerville, MA.
Tel (617) 625-5700.
W **somervilletheatre online.com**

World Music
various venues.
Tel (617) 876-4275.
W **worldmusic.org**

Pubs, Clubs, and Sports Bars

While large-scale events and concerts abound, the regular nightlife of Boston revolves primarily around drinking establishments. The legal drinking age here is 21, and you may be asked to show proof of identification *(see p367)* if you appear to be under 35. Not all bars and clubs are clearly marked, but they can usually be identified by their address and the cluster of smokers puffing away near the entrance in all weather. (Smoking is not permitted in clubs and bars in New England.) Ironically, the window for nightlife is short, as most venues don't liven up until 10pm, and Boston's drinking laws shut off alcohol service at 1 or 2am, depending on the neighborhood.

Sports Bars

Bostonians love sports, and while most bars have at least one game on the television over the bar, hard-core fans want more, and the city's dozens of sports bars oblige with multiple channel offerings. The **Cask 'N' Flagon**, adjacent to Fenway Park (to the west of Back Bay), is perfect for celebrating victory or softening the pain of defeat, while **Jillian's Boston** is just up the street, drawing a mixed-gender crowd for billiards and sports-watching. At **Kings**, big-screen sports televisions vie with bowling lanes, while **Jerry Remy's Sports Bar** has giant, wall-to-wall televisions. The area near North Station is filled with bars catering to Boston Celtics and Boston Bruins fans. One of the most notable is **The Fours**, where the sandwiches are named for sports legends and the memorabilia extends beyond basketball and hockey to boxing and baseball. One of the friendliest neighborhood sports bars of South Boston is the **Boston Beer Garden**, where locals refer to the city's hockey team as the "Broonz."

Pubs & Brewpubs

With the largest per capita population of Irish descendants in the US, it's not surprising that Boston has many Irish pubs, which offer a convivial setting for good hearty food, pints of Guinness and live music. Among these are **Kinsale**, near Government Center, where the entire bar was transported brick by brick from Ireland; the **Phoenix Landing Bar and Restaurant**, a mock Irish pub in Cambridge's Central Square lined with mahogany and screening English football on cable TV on weekend nights; **The Burren**, which has some of the finest musicians in the city; and the smaller **Druid**, where as the evening wears on, crowds of young professionals give way to recent Irish immigrants. **The Independent** in Somerville's Union Square is a good place to catch Irish bands, as well as unplugged rock. Darts and stout are the main draws at **The Field**, which is reputed to serve more Guinness on draft than any other bar in the US. The **Plough and Stars** ranks as one of the city's most seriously literary bars. It also features English League football on weekends.

Boston was in the forefront of the national brewpub craze in the 1980s, but of that first wave of artisanal brewers, only **John Harvard's Brew House** in Harvard Square and **Cambridge Brewing Company** in Kendall Square continue to flourish. Successful newcomer **Boston Beer Works** has a built-in clientele by virtue of its location next to Fenway Park and Boston University. No serious drinker or student of Boston history should miss **Doyle's Café**, famous for its continuing role in Boston political campaigns and a flagship bar for nearby Boston Beer Co., which debuts its seasonal Sam Adams brews here.

Gay Clubs & Bars

Boston's gay scene comes into sharpest focus in the South End and Bay Village, but bars and clubs are found throughout the city that hold gay nights. These events are often a staple of otherwise straight nightclubs. **Club Café Bar & Lounge** runs separate front and back dance rooms with different themes every night. Girls take over the club for women's T-dance on Sunday nights. A suave cabaret scene can be found in the venue's **Napoleon Room**. The perpetually packed **Fritz Lounge** is a stalwart South End bar. Boston's longest-running gay club, **Jacques**, features raucous drag shows and cabarets, as well as occasional karaoke sessions that lure wild crowds. The leather and denim set are drawn to the sociable, mellow Ladder District bar, **The Alley**, and to Boston's largest gay cruise bar, **Ramrod** in the Fenway. The weekly *Bay Windows* newspaper provides more information, as do other listings.

Nightclubs

Boston has a club for almost every type of dance music. Little happens until at least 11pm. The **Emerald Lounge**, is a swanky hotel venue that attracts crowds with its trendy environs and lively DJ nights. The **Grand Canal** near North Station spins techno and house music for a youthful clientele. Located in the rear of a stylish restaurant, the **Gypsy Bar** has a Latin night as well as house and techno music. Chandeliers and full-length mirrors add drama at cavernous **The Estate** on Piano Row. **Precinct** in Somerville's Union Square has lively music every night, ranging from Irish rockers to local singer-songwriters to good-times, old-fashioned rock-and-roll. More middle-of-the-road is the **Royale** in the Theater District, with classy touches like doormen instead of bouncers, marble walls, and a vast dance floor.

Comedy Clubs

Many clubs and bars program occasional evenings of standup comedy, and several specialize in it. **Nick's Comedy Stop**, on the other hand, tends to focus on homegrown talent, grooming performers who often go on to the "big time." Located in Cambridge's nightlife-busy Central Square, **Improv Boston** mixes audience-participation cabaret, skit comedy, revues, the occasional hootenanny, and even serious theater. The very name of **Improv Asylum** explains it all: lunatic comedy based on audience suggestions. Local comedian Dick Doherty hosts the shenanigans (including open mic nights) at **Dick's Beantown Comedy Vault**. Somewhat edgier laughs from newcomers and television comedy writers can be had at **The Comedy Studio**. National comedy acts and stand-up performances by TV stars are held at the **Wilbur Theatre**.

DIRECTORY

Sports Bars

Boston Beer Garden
732 East Broadway, South Boston.
Tel (617) 269-0990.
W bostonbeergarden. com

Cask 'N' Flagon
62 Brookline Ave.
Tel (617) 536-4840.
W casknflagon.com

The Fours
166 Canal St.
Map 1 C2.
Tel (617) 720-4455.
W thefours.com

Jerry Remy's Sports Bar
1265 Boylston St.
Tel (617) 236-7369.
W jerryremys.com

Jillian's Boston
145 Ipswich St.
Tel (617) 437-0300.
W jilliansboston.com

Kings
50 Dalton St. **Map** 3 A3.
Tel (617) 266-2695.
W kingsbowlamerica. com

Pubs & Brewpubs

Boston Beer Works
61 Brookline Ave.
Tel (617) 536-2337.
W beerworks.net

The Burren
247 Elm St., Somerville.
Tel (617) 776-6896.
W burren.com

Cambridge Brewing Company
1 Kendall Sq., Building 100.
Tel (617) 494-1994.
W cambrew.com

Doyle's Café
3484 Washington St., Jamaica Plain.
Tel (617) 524-2345.
W doylescafeboston. com

Druid
1357 Cambridge St., Cambridge.
Tel (617) 497-0965.
W druidpub.com

The Field
20 Prospect St. (Central Sq.), Cambridge.
Tel (617) 354-7345.
W thefieldpub.com

The Independent
75 Union Sq., Somerville.
Tel (617) 440-6022.
W theindo.com

John Harvard's Brew House
33 Dunster St., Cambridge.
Tel (617) 868-3585.
W johnharvards.com

Kinsale Irish Pub & Restaurant
2 Center Plaza.
Map 1 C3.
Tel (617) 742-5577.
W classicirish.com

Phoenix Landing Bar and Restaurant
512 Massachusetts Ave., Cambridge.
Tel (617) 576-6260.
W phoenixlanding bar.com

Plough and Stars
912 Massachusetts Ave., Cambridge.
Tel (617) 576-0032.
W ploughandstars.com

Gay Clubs & Bars

The Alley
14 Pi Alley. **Map** 4 F4.
Tel (617) 263-1449.

Club Café Bar & Lounge
209 Columbus Ave.
Map 4 D3.
Tel (617) 536-0966.

Fritz Lounge
26 Chandler St.
Map 4 D3.
Tel (617) 482-4428.

Jacques
79 Broadway.
Map 4 F4.
Tel (617) 426-8902.

Napoleon Room
209 Columbus Ave.
Map 4 D3.
Tel (617) 536-0966.

Ramrod
1254 Boylston St.
Tel (617) 266-2986.

Nightclubs

Emerald Lounge
200 Stuart St.
Map 2 B5.
Tel (617) 457-2626.
W emeraldultralounge. com

The Estate
1 Boylston Pl.
Map 4 E2.
Tel (617) 251-7000.

Grand Canal
57 Canal St.
Map 2 D2.
Tel (617) 523-1112.

Gypsy Bar
116 Boylston St.
Tel (617) 482-7799.

Precinct
70 Union Sq., Somerville.
Tel (617) 623-9211.
W precinctbar.com

Royale
279 Tremont St.
Map 4 E2.
Tel (617) 338-7699.

Comedy Clubs

The Comedy Studio
Hong Kong Restaurant, 3rd Floor, 1236 Massachusetts Ave., Cambridge.
Tel (617) 661-6507.
W thecomedystudio. com

Dick's Beantown Comedy Vault
124 Boylston St.
Map 1 B5.
Tel (800) 401-2221.
W dickdoherty.com

Improv Asylum
216 Hanover St.
Map 2 D3.
Tel (617) 263-6887.
W improvasylum.com

Improv Boston
40 Prospect St., Cambridge.
Tel (617) 576-1253.

Nick's Comedy Stop
100 Warrenton St.
Tel (617) 438-1068.
W nickscomedy stop.com

Wilbur Theatre
246 Tremont St.
Map 4 E2.
Tel (617) 931-2000.
W ticketmaster.com

OUTDOOR ACTIVITIES

Squeezed within New England's relatively compact borders there is a wealth of outdoor activities. Mountain ranges, forests, rivers, and miles of coastline have been preserved as natural playgrounds for outdoor enthusiasts ranging from people just looking for a quiet afternoon in the sun to serious backcountry trekkers. While the majority of unspoiled, rugged wilderness is found in the northern states of New Hampshire, Vermont, and Maine, there are still plenty of outdoor adventures to be had in the much more densely populated south. Visitors will find plenty to do on sea and land throughout Massachusetts, Rhode Island, and Connecticut.

Visitors camping on the coast of Maine

Camping

Always a popular activity in New England, camping can also save you money on accommodations – depending on how much you are willing to rough it. While there are designated primitive camping areas in the backcountry of selected national forests, the more established campgrounds make up the majority of sites. Standard campgrounds, usually found in state and national forests, are equipped with facilities such as toilets, garbage disposal, and often facilities for hot showers. The tent sites at such places are usually spaced well apart and cost between $12 and $20 a night. For the hardcore camper, primitive campsites found in national forests offer only the bare minimum: rudimentary cooking areas, pit toilets, and cold running water. These sites are perfect for the frugal outdoor enthusiast, usually costing around $10 a night.

On the opposite end of the spectrum, private campgrounds are models of luxury. Most cater to large recreational vehicles (RVs) and motor homes, with running water and electrical hookups. Hot showers and sewage hookups are often provided as well. Many upscale campgrounds have a host of recreational facilities that range from swimming to miniature golf courses. These sites are somewhat more expensive, costing $20 to $40 dollars or so a night.

Government-run campgrounds usually follow the summer season from the end of May through to early October. For the most part, private campgrounds have a much longer season, with some staying open year-round. Regardless of the type of camping that will be done, it is always a good idea to reserve a campsite early, especially during the busy summer months. Contact the **National Park Service** or the **National Recreation Reservation Service** for campground information and reservations. As a safety measure, always remember to notify someone of your itinerary and your approximate time of arrival at your destination should you decide to camp or hike by yourself.

Hiking

Hiking trails crisscross almost all of New England, with the two most popular being the New England section of the Appalachian Trail *(see pp26–7)* and Vermont's 265-mile (426-km) Long Trail. Both trails can be quite challenging in spots, with extremely steep mountain climbs to stunning vistas. Maine's Baxter State Park *(see p302)* and New Hampshire's White Mountain National Forest *(see p269)* are both well known for their extensive networks of demanding trails.

Not all nature walks need be difficult, however. Acadia National Park *(see pp292–3)* in Maine has an excellent system of easier hiking trails that lead past some of the most breathtaking coastal scenery. The **Rails-to-Trails Conservancy**

Boston's Swan Boats offering gentle cruises *(see pp68–9)*

provides information and maps on 1,359 trails along abandoned railroad tracks that have been converted into convenient and accessible paths for cyclists and pedestrians alike. These paths stretch across a vast portion of New England. Companies such as **New England Hiking Holidays** organize excursions that last between two and five days, so that you can choose an itinerary to suit your fitness and experience level.

Easy biking amid New England wildflowers

Hiking at Center Sandwich, New Hampshire

Biking

In addition to the more formal bike paths, the region possesses hundreds of miles of quiet back roads that are a cyclist's paradise. The pastoral scenery is beautiful, but the distances between towns are rarely so great that you will feel isolated. Cape Cod *(see pp158–63)* is famous for its wonderful bike paths, as is Nantucket *(see p157)* with its network of easy trails leading to pristine beaches. Many people believe that the best way to see Martha's Vineyard *(see pp156–7)*, Block Island *(see pp196–7)*, and the Litchfield Hills *(see pp212–13)* is by bike. Various outfitters such as **VBT** offer organized bike tours for some of New England's most scenic regions, supplying everything from bicycles and protective gear to maps and accommodations.

Mountain bikers also have plenty to choose from. Some ski areas let bikers use their lifts and slopes in the summer, and many of the region's forests are open to biking. Acadia National Park, Mount Desert Island *(see pp292–3)*, and the White *(see p269)* and Green *(see p248)* mountains all have excellent facilities. To avoid damaging the surrounding environment, mountain bikers should stick to the marked trails. Cyclists should wear helmets and other protective gear.

DIRECTORY

Canoeing and Rafting

Maine Island Trail Association
58 Fore St., Portland, ME 04101. **Tel** (207) 761-8225.
W mita.org

Raft Maine
PO Box 78, West Farms, ME 04985.
Tel (800) 723-8633.
W raftmaine.com

Hiking and Biking

Appalachian Trail Conservancy
799 Washington St., PO Box 807, Harpers Ferry, WV 25425-0807.
Tel (304) 535-6331.
W appalachiantrail.org

Green Mountain Club
4711 Waterbury-Stowe Rd., Waterbury Center, VT 05677.
Tel (802) 244-7037.
W greenmountainclub. org

New England Hiking Holidays
PO Box 1648, North Conway, NH 03860.
Tel (603) 356-9696 or (800) 869-0949.
W nehikingholidays. com

Rails-to-Trails Conservancy
2121 Ward Ct NW, Washington, DC 20037.
Tel (202) 331-9696.
W railtrails.org

VBT
614 Monkton Rd., Bristol, VT 05443.
Tel (802) 453-4811 or (800) 245-3868.
W vbt.com

Technical or Rock Climbing

Acadia Mountain Guides Climbing School
92 Main St., Orono, ME 04473 or 228 Main St., Bar Harbor, ME 04609 (summer only).
Tel (888) 232-9559 or (207) 288-8 186.
W acadiamountain guides.com

New England Climbing
W neclimbs.com

Rhinoceros Mountain Guides
55 Mountain View Rd., Campton, NH 03223.
Tel (603) 726-3030.
W rhinoguides.com

Fishing

If you like to fish, you will love New England. Deep-sea fishing is best at Point Judith in Rhode Island, where you can rent boats through the **Rhode Island Party and Charterboat Association**. Farther up the coast at Cape Cod, surfcasters test the waters for striped bass and bluefish, which are most plentiful between July and October. Brook trout, walleye, and bass are plentiful in the inland streams and lakes, especially in Maine. Contact the **Maine Sporting Camp Association** for information regarding the state's top fishing camps and lodges. Fly-fishermen seeking to hone their skills can do so in one of the highly regarded programs run by **Orvis** in Manchester, Vermont. Fresh-water fishing licenses are mandatory throughout New England and can be obtained at fishing supply stores.

Turbulent rapids in one of New England's mountain rivers

Canoeing, Kayaking, and White-Water Rafting

Maine is the premier destination for paddlers, beginning with sea kayakers who flock here each summer to ply the waters along the 3,500-mile (5,630-km) coast. One of the state's most popular excursions is the 350-mile (563-km) Maine Island Trail, which goes from Portland to Machias. Maine's latticework of rivers is ideal for canoeing, with its most famous trek being down the challenging Allagash Wilderness Waterway *(see p303)*. New Hampshire's Androscoggin River is another demanding waterway best tested by experienced paddlers. Canoeists

Whale-watching on a regional cruise ship

looking for a more leisurely ride can skim across the calm waters of northern New England's lakes and ponds.

White-water rafting is the paddler's roller-coaster ride and, once again, Maine is the region's best theme park. The state's three major rivers, the Penobscot, Kennebec, and Dead, offer gut-wrenching tests of rafters' skills. **Raft Maine** will put you in touch with the proper outfitter. New Hampshire's Saco River is another favorite among the white-water set.

Boating

New England's reputation as one of the world's great cruising areas is well deserved. The thousands of miles of shoreline are dotted with hundreds of anchorages. Penobscot Bay, Maine, and Newport, Rhode Island, are both considered sailing meccas. For those who want something a little calmer than the Atlantic Ocean, New England has countless lakes, large and small, including popular cruising destinations such as Sebago Lake, Lake Champlain, and Lake Winnipesaukee.

Boat rentals are available at many seaside and lakeside resorts in New England. A few outlets will rent a large sailboat for a day or night. These so-called "bareboat charters" are only for experienced sailors, particularly in Maine, where water and weather conditions can be treacherous. **Hinckley Yacht Charters** in Southwest

Harbor, Maine, is one of the area's larger companies, with 25 sail and power crafts available. This company will also provide fully crewed yacht charters. Top-notch windsurfing sites and windsurfing equipment rentals are also available at many locations up and down the New England coast.

Cruises

Whale-watching cruises have become one of the region's most popular activities, with more and more coastal towns trying to cash in. Not quite an exact science, a successful whale-watching trip relies both on the experience of the ship's captain and on the guidance offered by high-tech sounding gear to find these majestic mammals. Many companies will offer a rain check if no whales are sighted.

Plan whale-watching trips carefully. Choose a calm day. Choppy water causes most people to become seasick. If you fear you will get sick, buy some ginger capsules at a health food store and take the recommended dose just before boarding.

Sightseeing and nature cruises are also available throughout New England. For a different view of the city, **Boston Harbor Cruises** offers sunset tours throughout the summer. River cruises are available on several New England waterways, including both the Charles and the

Group rafting run on the Cold River at Charlemont, Massachusetts

Boats at pier in Edgartown Harbor, Martha's Vineyard

Connecticut rivers in Massachusetts and Connecticut's Mystic River.

Windjammer cruises are also popular in Massachusetts, Rhode Island, and Maine.

Bird-Watching

With its diverse habitats, ranging from mountains to coastal marshes and sand flats to conifer and mixed hardwood forests, New England offers some of the most interesting birding in the U.S.

Massachusetts, home to the first Audubon Society in America, is famous for several areas, most notably the northeast coast at Newburyport, Cape Cod, and around the Berkshires. At Machias Seal Island, Maine, birders have a good opportunity to sight nesting colonies of Atlantic puffins. Special boat excursions to the island are offered by local charters.

National parks along with national wildlife refuges and protection areas are often the best places to bird since they are protected and unspoiled. **The US Fish and Wildlife Service** can provide information on the location of refuges and the birding opportunities at each. Every state's **Audubon**

Society will provide information on birding in the state as well as on Audubon field trips to various hotspots.

Golf

New England has more than its share of outstanding golf courses – in all price ranges and at all levels of difficulty. Dedicated golf vacationers have a choice between some stunning coastal and mountain resorts. Of the former, Samoset Resort, located in Rockport, Maine, stands out above all the rest.

With ocean views on 14 holes, Samoset has been called the most visually appealing course in New England. Two other terrific coastal links, the Seaside course at New Seabury and the Ocean Edge Resort and Golf Club, are located on Cape Cod.

For a full-fledged mountain golf holiday, consider the Equinox resort in Manchester, Vermont. It features a championship 1927 Walter J. Travis design surrounded by the Green Mountains. Some famous ski

destinations offer great golf as well. In western Maine, Sugarloaf Golf Club presents a memorable Robert Trent Jones, Jr. layout that *Golf Digest* has ranked among the top ten for both memorability and aesthetics. Mount Snow is ranked as one of Vermont's top five courses. Both courses also offer summer golf schools, as does Quechee in Vermont. Other worthwhile mountain courses include The Balsams in northeastern New Hampshire and Cranwell Resort and Golf Club in the Berkshires.

The signature of New England: a beautiful, well-kept golf course

Technical or Rock Climbing

With New England's Green Mountains and White Mountains, it's little surprise that this part of the country offers some great climbing.

In Maine the vast majority of cliff climbing falls along its rugged south coast, with high-quality routes in a setting that is truly stunning. Acadia National Park is the most popular destination. Alpine climbers will also find a worthy test in Maine. Mount Katahdin, the state's highest peak, has some of the longest routes in New England.

New England's best climbing, however, is found in New Hampshire, where Cannon Cliff, Cathedral Ledge, and Whitehorse Ledge make up a triumvirate of diverse, challenging peaks. New Hampshire also offers bouldering and sport climbing at several sites, the best of which is Rumney in the center part of the state.

Connecticut and Rhode Island are not especially famed for their climbing, but both offer several quite good bouldering sites, most notably at Lincoln Woods, Rhode Island.

Climbing in Massachusetts is varied, with the central area of the state offering longer scenic routes and Boston providing some of the country's best urban cragging.

Vermont has few developed sites, though the treacherous sport of ice climbing is practiced at Smuggler's Notch and Lake Willoughby.

Hunting

With its wide range of game spread across its diverse woodlands, New England offers something for every hunter. Among the big game are white tail deer, bear and moose, while small game includes rabbit, hare, and squirrel. For those interested in bird hunting,

Climber in bold ascent of New Hampshire's White Mountains

turkey, duck, goose, pheasant, quail and grouse can be found. The hunting seasons are concentrated in the late summer and fall, with limited exceptions. Hunters in all six states require licenses. In most cases, the fees are significantly higher for out-of-state hunters. Guns must be kept unloaded during transport in all states, and in some of them, a secure transport case is mandatory. There are also regulations that govern transport of game out-of-state. For specific information on regulations in each state,

Ruffed grouse

contact the government department responsible for wildlife management in that state.

Hang Gliding and Paragliding

Good hang gliding and paragliding sites abound in New England. That's no surprise, considering the large number of accessible places throughout the Green Mountains and the White Mountains. The best place to start is Morningside Flight Park in Charlestown, New Hampshire. It is the only full-time flight school and flying center in New England, and it has a 450-ft (137-m) summit launch site on the premises. Not far away in Vermont, Mount Ascutney is known as the premier cross-country hang gliding site in New England, with flights having reached the Atlantic coast.

Southern New England is not without its advantages, however. Two of the best sand cliff launches are located in Cape Cod, Massachusetts, and Block Island, Rhode Island. Training is essential before attempting these sports. It is important to check local regulations before making any flight. You will find that many sites require memberships or have strict guidelines about landing areas. At state sites in Vermont, gliders must sign a waiver before making any flight. Contact the state association or a local club before making any jump.

Daring way to view the Berkshires at North Adams, Massachusetts

DIRECTORY

Bird-Watching

Audubon Society of New Hampshire
84 Silk Farm Rd., Concord, NH 03301.
Tel (603) 224-9909.
W nhaudubon.org

Audubon Society of Rhode Island
12 Sanderson Rd., Smithfield, RI 02917-2600.
Tel (401) 949-5454.
W asri.org

Audubon Vermont
255 Sherman Hollow Rd., Huntington, VT 05462.
Tel (802) 434-3068.
W vtaudubon.org

Connecticut Audubon Society
2325 Burr St., Fairfield, CT 06430.
Tel (203) 259-6305 or (800) 996-8747.
W ctaudubon.org

Maine Audubon Society
20 Gilsland Farm Rd., Falmouth, ME 04105.
Tel (207) 781-2330.
W maineaudubon.org

Massachusetts Audubon Society
208 S Great Rd., Lincoln, MA 01773.
Tel (781) 259-9500 or (800) 283-8266.
W massaudubon.org

United States Fish and Wildlife Service
Regional Office, 300 Westgate Center Dr., Hadley, MA 01035-9589.
Tel (413) 253-8200.
W fws.gov/northeast

Boating

Hinckley Yacht Charters
Great Harbor Marina, PO Box 950, Southwest Harbor, ME 04679.
Tel (800) HYC-SAIL or (207) 244-5008.
W hinckleycharters. com

Camping

Connecticut Campground Owners Association
193 Main St., East Hartford, CT 06108.
Tel (860) 521-4704.
W campconn.com

Department of Environmental Protection

79 Elm St., Hartford, CT 06106.
Tel (860) 424-3000.
W dep.state.ct.us/rec/

Maine Campground Owners Association
10 Falcon Rd., Suite 1, Lewiston, ME 04240.
Tel (207) 782-5874.
W campmaine.com

Maine Department of Conservation
18 Elkins Lane, Augusta, ME 04333.
Tel (207) 287-3821.
W state.me.us/doc/ parks

Massachusetts Department of Conservation and Recreation
251 Causeway St., Suite 600, Boston, MA 02114.
Tel (617) 626-1250.
W mass.gov/dcr

National Park Service Northeast Region
Custom House, 200 Chestnut St., Philadelphia, PA 19106.
Tel (800) 365-2267 or (215) 597-7013.
W nps.gov/nero

National Recreation Reservation Service
Tel (518) 885-3639 or (877) 444-6777.
W recreation.gov

New Hampshire Campground Owners Association
PO Box 1074, Epsom, NH 03234.
Tel (800) 822-6764.
W ucampnh.com

New Hampshire Division of Parks and Recreation
PO Box 1856, Concord, NH 03302.
Tel (603) 271-3556.
W nhparks.state.nh.us

Rhode Island Department of Parks and Recreation
2321 Hartford Ave., Johnston, RI 02919-1719.
Tel (401) 222-2632.
W riparks.com

Vermont Department of Forests, Parks and Recreation
103 S Main St., Waterbury, VT 05671.
Tel (802) 241-3655.
W vtstateparks.com

Cruises

Bar Harbor Whale Watch Company
1 West St., Bar Harbor, ME 04609.
Tel (207) 288-2386 or (800) WHALES-4.
W whalesrus.com

Boston Harbor Cruises
One Long Wharf, Boston, MA 02110.
Tel (617) 227-4320 or (877) 733-9425.
W bostonharborcruises. com

Fishing and Hunting

Maine Sporting Camp Association
HC 76, Box 620, Greenville, ME 04441.
W mainesportingcamps. com

Orvis
Rte. 7A, Manchester, VT 05254.
Tel (802) 362-3750 or (888) 235-9763.
W orvis.com

Rhode Island Party and Charterboat Association

PO Box 3198, Narragansett, RI 02882.
Tel (401) 737-5812.
W rifishing.com

Hang Gliding and Paragliding

Morningside Flight Park
357 Morningside Lane, Charlestown, NH 03603.
Tel (603) 542-4416.
W flymorningside. kittyhawk.com

Vermont Hang Gliding Association
W vhga.aero

Winter Activities

Far from lamenting the end of the stunning fall foliage season, New Englanders instead begin readying themselves for winter activities. Skis and snowboards are pulled out and dusted off, snowmobiles are tuned up, and skates are sharpened in anticipation of cold weather and the slate of outdoor fun it brings. In New England top-notch ski hills and cross-country ski and snowmobiling trails are never far away. This is especially true in the region's northernmost reaches, where the annual blanket of snow is thickest and, for outdoor enthusiasts, most inviting.

Sleigh ride through Hancock Shaker Village in Pittsfield, Massachusetts

Skiing

People have been downhill skiing on New England's rounded peaks for more than a century. While the region does not have the elevation of the Rockies, it does offer many large hills, some with a vertical rise of more than 2,000 ft (610 m). The best skiing and snowboarding is concentrated in the three northern states. Vermont has the most high-quality peaks,

with **Killington** offering the most trails at 191. But it is **Stowe** that can claim the title of New England's ski capital. A world-famous resort set in the quaint village of the same name, Stowe has the state's highest peak and offers excellent trails for skiers of all levels. For the experienced skier, **Mad River Glen** near Waitsfield provides a stern test in one of the most pristine settings in the world. It also forbids snowboarding.

The White Mountains in New Hampshire have a plethora of good ski hills; downhill, alpine, and cross-country trails are arguably the best in the Northeast. In Maine, **Sugarloaf** and **Sunday River** are considered to be the best hills in the state.

Downhill ski trails in New England are accurately rated following a standard code: Easier = green circle; More Difficult = blue square; Most Difficult = black diamond; and Expert = double diamond. Rental equipment is available at all resorts, as are skiing and snowboarding lessons for all levels. Where price is concerned, in general, the larger, more famous resorts charge more for lift tickets. If you have time, look for off-site sellers. They typically offer reduced prices. Also ask about package deals and senior or child discounts.

Cross-country ski trails are also plentiful in New England. Towns such as Craftsbury Common, Vermont, and **Jackson, New Hampshire** have miles of groomed trails. State parks also often provide good trails. These are good areas for other winter activities such as sliding and snowshoeing. **Catamount Trail**, set aside for skiers and snowshoers, runs 300 miles (482 km) down the length of Vermont. Many renowned downhill resorts also offer cross-country trails. The trails at the **Trapp Family Lodge Ski Center** in Stowe are considered among the best in New England.

Low in the turn at Vermont's majestic Stowe resort

Snowmobiling

Snowmobiling is extremely popular all across New England, but Maine is truly the mecca for this activity. The state is interconnected by 12,500 miles (20,000 km) of trails and has more than 85,000 registered snow-mobiles using them. Resorts such as **Northern Outdoors** in The Forks and the **New England Outdoor Center** in Millinocket will rent snow-mobiles and accommodations, and supply guides for excursions. Most agencies require that renters have a valid driver's license.

Skating

In winter, New England has plenty of frozen lakes and rivers for skating. Always check with local authorities to be sure the ice is safe.

Winter also brings droves of bundled-up skaters to the Boston Common Frog Pond in Boston. Rentals are available in the warm-up shed or alternatively at the **Beacon Hall Skate Shop**. The **Department of Conservation and Recreation** runs numerous indoor rinks in Boston, Cambridge, and the surrounding communities.

Freestyle skiing, common at New England ski resorts

DIRECTORY

Skiing

Attitash Mountain Resort
PO Box 508, Rte. 302, Bartlett, NH 03812.
Tel (800) 223-7669 or (603) 374-2368.
W attitash.com

Bretton Woods Mount Washington Resort
Rte. 302, Bretton Woods, NH 03575.
Tel (800) 314-1752 or (603) 278-1000.
W brettonwoods.com

Catamount Trail Association
1 Main St., Suite 350, Burlington, VT 05401.
Tel 802-864-5794.
W catamounttrail.org

Jackson Ski Touring Foundation
PO Box 216, 153 Main St., Jackson, NH 03846.
Tel (800) 927-6697 or (603) 383-9355.
W acksonxc.org

Killington
4763 Killington Rd., Rutland, VT 05751.
Tel (800) 621-MTNS or (802) 422-6200.
W killington.com

Mad River Glen
Rte. 17, Fayston, VT 05673.
Tel (802) 496-3551.
W madriverglen.com

Ski Maine Association
Box 7566, Portland, ME 04112.
Tel (207) 773-7669.
W skimaine.com

Ski New Hampshire
PO Box 528, North Woodstock, NH 03262.
Tel (603) 745-9396 or (800) 887-5464.
W skinh.com

Ski Vermont
26 State St., PO Box 368, Montpelier, VT 05601.
Tel (802) 223-2439.
W skivermont.com

Stowe Mountain Resort
5781 Mountain Rd., Stowe, VT 05672.
Tel (800) 253-4754 or (802) 253-3000.
W stowe.com

Sugarloaf
5092 Access Rd., Carrabassett Valley, ME 04947.
Tel (800) THE-LOAF or (207) 237-2000.
W sugarloaf.com

Sunday River Ski Resort
Sunday River access road, Newry, ME 04261.
Tel (800) 543-2SKI or (207) 824-3000.
W sundayriver.com

Trapp Family Lodge Ski Center
700 Trapp Hill Rd., Stowe, VT 05672.
Tel (800) 826-7000 or (802) 253-8511.
W trappfamily.com

Snowmobiling

Maine Snowmobile Association
PO Box 80, Augusta, ME 04332.
Tel (207) 622-6983.
W mesnow.com

New England Outdoor Center
PO Box 669, Millinocket, ME 04462.
Tel (800) 634-7238.
W neoc.com

New Hampshire Snowmobile Association
614 Laconia Rd., Tilton, NH 03276.
Tel (603) 273-0220.
W nhsa.com

Northern Outdoors
PO Box 100, 1771 Route 201, The Forks, ME 04985.
Tel (800) 765-7238.
W northernoutdoors.com

Snowmobile Association of Massachusetts
PO Box 386, Conway, MA 01341.
Tel (413) 369-8092.
W sledmass.com

Skating

Beacon Hill Skate Shop
135 South Charles St., Boston, MA 02116.
Tel (617) 482-7400.

Department of Conservation and Recreation
251 Causeway St., Boston, MA 02114.
Tel (617) 626-1250.
W mass.gov/dcr

SURVIVAL GUIDE

PRACTICAL INFORMATION

New England offers a wide variety of recreational activities within a relatively small area. Vacationers can hike the White Mountains of New Hampshire in the morning, swim at Maine's Ogunquit Beach in the afternoon, and take in the Boston Symphony Orchestra at night. Tourism is a major part of the local economy, with numerous agencies and facilities geared toward ensuring that visitors have an enjoyable stay. Accommodations and restaurants *(see pp306–39)* come in all price ranges, allowing you to sleep and eat in comfort even on a limited budget. For people without cars, transportation is readily available in Boston and throughout the six states *(see pp376–9)*. The following pages offer some practical advice for people traveling around New England, from general guidelines on personal security and health *(see pp370–71)* to some basic financial and media information *(see pp372–3)*.

When to Go

New England is a four-season vacation destination, but it is particularly popular in the summer and fall. Generally speaking, the peak tourist period is from mid-June, when schools let out, through October. During this time, accommodations and restaurant reservations can be hard to come by, especially in the busy resort towns along the coast.

There is another rush during fall-foliage season *(see pp24–5)*, which lasts from sometime in mid-September to late October. During this month-long stretch, the hotels and B&Bs farther inland near the woods are booked solid.

The length of the ski season depends entirely on the weather. It is not unheard of for New England winters to run from late November right through March, during which time New Hampshire and Vermont, which possess

Enough signs to keep visitors busy in Center Sandwich, New Hampshire

the bulk of New England's ski centers *(see pp362–3)*, are busiest.

If you are planning a backwoods vacation, it is prudent to avoid wooded areas in April and May, when the ground can be extremely muddy and swarms of hungry black flies fill the air. Don't be fooled by their small size; they have a nasty bite.

Visas and Passports

All travelers to New England and the US, including Canadians, should have a machine-readable biometric passport that is valid for six months longer than their intended period of stay. Holders of a valid EU, Australian, or New Zealand passport in possession of a return ticket do not need visas if staying 90 days or less in the US. However, visitors must apply for entry in advance via the Electronic System for Travel

Authorization, or ESTA (https://esta.cbp.dhs.gov). Applications must be made at least 72 hours before travel. Sometimes foreign visitors must prove they carry sufficient funds. Ask your travel agent, check with the US Department of State (travel.state.gov), or contact the US embassy in your home country for current requirements.

Customs Information

Visitors over the age of 21 are allowed to enter the US with two pints (1 liter) of alcohol; 200 cigarettes, 50 cigars, or 4 lb (2 kg) of smoking tobacco; and gifts worth up to $100. Prohibited items include meat products, dairy products aged less than 90 days, and all fresh fruit. Travelers entering the country with more than $10,000 in cash or traveler's checks must declare the money to customs officials upon entry.

Snowboarding, popular with the young, daring, and fit

◀ Clay cliffs lining Lucy Vincent Beach on Martha's Vineyard, Massachusetts

Acadia National Park Visitor Center, Maine

Tourist Information

The state tourism offices are great sources of information, and they can provide road maps, brochures, and listings of accommodations, events, and attractions free of charge. Some offices also hand out discount vouchers for lodgings and restaurants. Many towns have a visitors' bureau that dispenses local information. State Welcome Centers found along motorways also provide information for tourists.

Admission Prices

While many of New England's attractions are free to visit, some have an admission charge. Check in advance for admission infor-mation, and ask about special discounts for groups, children and seniors. Some museums offer an evening slot when admission is free or by voluntary donation.

Opening Hours

Most stores open from 9 or 10am–6pm Monday to Saturday, although they often stay open until 9 or 10pm on Thursday and Friday. Stores are now open on Sunday too.

Most New England banks are open from 9am–4 or 5pm Monday to Friday. Many banks are also open on Saturday mornings from 9am–noon or 1pm.

The larger museums are usually open from 10am–5pm Tuesday to Sunday, but always check in advance. Smaller museums may have seasonal hours and even be closed during the winter.

Many gas stations and convenience stores stay open 24 hours a day. Offices are generally open from 9am–5pm Monday to Friday and do not close for lunch.

Etiquette and Smoking

The legal drinking age throughout New England is 21. Most young people will be asked to produce a photo ID as proof of age in order to buy alcohol or enter a bar; your passport is usually your best bet. Drinking in public spaces is against the law, and the penalties for driving under the influence of alcohol are severe, including the loss of your driver's license.

Cigarettes can be sold only to people aged 18 or over. It is against the law to smoke in public buildings, such as hospitals, and on public conveyances, including subways and buses. A few restaurants permit smoking in designated outdoor sections, though most are completely smoke-free.

Accessibility to Public Conveniences

Tourist information booths and welcome centers are equipped with toilets, and rest areas are usually found upon entering states on major highways.

There are several automatic coin-operated toilets around Boston. Public libraries and government buildings also provide a handy stop for those in need of a restroom during business hours, and most coffee shops and bars require only a small purchase in order to use their facilities.

Taxes and Tipping

Listed prices rarely include applicable taxes or expected gratuities. All New England states, with the exception of New Hampshire, levy their own sales tax. All states charge taxes on hotel rooms and restaurant meals, and some cities have extra taxes, too. Many accommodations tack on additional surcharges to bills, such as housekeeping and parking fees; these can increase the total by up to 15 percent. To avoid unpleasant surprises at the end of a stay, inquire about any extra charges before checking in.

A gratuity is given for most services. Travelers should give waiters 15–20 percent of the bill, bartenders $1–$2 per drink, barbers 10–15 percent of the bill, and taxi drivers between 10 and 20 percent of the fare. Porters usually get $1 per piece of luggage, and hotel maids at least $1 per night.

A tip of 15–20 percent of the bill is expected by waiters

Taxes in New England

State	Lodging	Meal	Sales
Connecticut	12%	6.35%	6.35%
Maine	7%	7%	5%
Massachusetts	12.5–15%	6.25–7%	6.25%
New Hampshire	9%	9%	–
Rhode Island	13%	8%	7%
Vermont	9%	9%	6%

Youngsters enjoying water-based activities at a lakeside wharf

Travelers with Special Needs

While US federal law requires that businesses are accessible to the disabled, some historic buildings may have limited facilities for wheelchair users. Most hotels and restaurants are equipped for people with special needs, and an increasing number of small inns are refitting their rooms. Many outdoor recreation areas, including all national parks, also provide restrooms and facilities for the disabled, including tour buses and wheelchair-friendly trails.

Disabled travelers visiting New England are advised to call venues in advance or to contact organizations such as the **Society for Accessible Travel and Hospitality** or **Mobility International** for help. Both groups provide information and comprehensive guides on disabled access throughout the region.

Traveling with Children

New England is a fairly child-friendly place. Many museums, zoos, and aquariums offer hands-on and interactive exhibits that encourage younger participants. The multitude of state parks, forests, and public beaches give children lots of space to burn excess energy.

Many establishments and services cater to families by having children's menus and reduced admission rates. Most hotels and motels make cots or rollaway beds available (sometimes for a nominal fee) so that children can stay in the same room as their parents. The same is generally not true for inns and bed and breakfasts (B&Bs), some of which will not take children under a certain age.

Senior Travelers

Senior travelers are eligible for myriad discounts, ranging from car rentals and lodgings to entry to museums and national parks. Depending on the place, the minimum qualifying age for seniors can be as low as 50. A valid form of ID is required. For more information, visitors to New England should contact

Senior travelers getting around in Lenox, Massachusetts

the **American Association of Retired Persons (AARP)** or **Elderhostel**, also known as Road Scholar. This Boston-based international senior-travel organization offers educational tours in New England and throughout the US, for those over 50.

Gay and Lesbian Travelers

New England has a number of vibrant gay communities, including Provincetown *(see pp160–61)*, on the far end of Cape Cod; Ogunquit *(see pp282–3)*, Maine; Northampton *(see p167)*, Massachusetts; and Boston's South End *(see pp97–105)*. In addition, New England is considered one of the US's main strongholds in support of gay marriage, which is currently legal in all New England states except Maine and Rhode Island.

Bay Windows, New England's largest gay and lesbian newspaper, includes arts and cultural listings for all six states.

International Student Identity Card (ISIC)

Traveling on a Budget

Students from abroad should buy an **International Student Identity Card (ISIC)** from the ISIC website before traveling to New England. Numerous discounts are available to cardholders at such places as hostels, museums, and theaters. This is especially true in Boston. The **Student Advantage Card** offers a similar deal, but this is available only to American university students.

Budget-minded travelers should look out for lunch menus which are commonly less expensive at restaurants than dinner menus. Some establishments also offer unlimited lunch buffets. To save money on accommodation, check www.priceline.com or www. hotwire.com where many hotels offer up to 50% off their normal rates.

What to Take

Given the region's notoriously inconsistent weather – "if you don't care for the weather, wait a few minutes and it's likely to change" is a common adage – it's wise to pack for an array of conditions. Layers are recommended, as is rain gear.

All of New England's main cities are easily manageable on foot, so comfortable footwear is a must. Foreign travelers visiting remote parts of the region may have a difficult time finding electrical converters to purchase, so they should therefore come prepared.

Electricity

Electricity flows at the standard US 110–120 volts AC (alternating current). Foreign-made electrical appliances may require a US-style plug adapter and a voltage converter.

Responsible Tourism

Long considered one of America's most environmentally conscious regions, New England continues to gain national acclaim for its forward-thinking initiatives and policies. Examples include state zoning laws requiring LEED (Leadership in Energy and Environmental Design) certification for certain developments and a requirement that all Boston taxicabs go hybrid by 2015. Organizations like **Boston Green Tourism** help guide out-of-towners toward the area's numerous eco-certified hotels, restaurants, and shops. The "green movement" has spread throughout New England's economic landscape. Visitors find it easier and easier to be environmentally aware while touring the area, as recycling bins are quite common and community farmers' markets selling local produce and artisan foodstuffs can be found in every corner of every state.

DIRECTORY

Tourist Information

Connecticut Commission on Culture and Tourism
One Constitution Plaza, Hartford, CT 06103.
Tel (860) 256-2800 or (888) 288-4748.
🆆 ctvisit.com

Greater Boston Convention and Visitors Bureau
2 Copley Place, Suite 105, Boston, MA 02116.
Tel (888) 733-2678 or (617) 536-4100.
Map 3 C3.
🆆 bostonusa.com

Maine Office of Tourism
59 State House Station, Augusta, ME 04333-0059.
Tel (207) 287-5711 or (888) 624-6345.
🆆 visitmaine.com

Massachusetts Office of Travel & Tourism
10 Park Plaza, Suite 4510, Boston, MA 02116.
Tel (617) 973-8500 or (800) 227-6277.
Map 1 B5.
🆆 massvacation.com

New Hampshire Division of Travel & Tourism Development
172 Pembroke Rd., PO Box 1856, Concord, NH 03302.
Tel (603) 271-2665 or (800) 386-4664.
🆆 visitnh.gov

Rhode Island Tourism Division
315 Iron Horse Way, Suite 101, Providence, RI 02908.
Tel (800) 250-7384.
🆆 visitrhodeisland.com

Vermont Department of Tourism and Marketing
National Life Building, 6th Floor, Drawer 20, Montpelier, VT 05260.
Tel (800) VERMONT.
🆆 vermontvacation. com

Travelers with Special Needs

Mobility International
🆆 miusa.org

Society for Accessible Travel and Hospitality
347 Fifth Ave., Suite 605, New York City, NY 10016.
Tel (212) 447-7284.
🆆 sath.org

Senior Travelers

American Association of Retired Persons (AARP)
601 E. St. NW, Washington, DC 20049.
Tel (888) 687-2277.
🆆 aarp.org

Elderhostel (Road Scholar)
11 Ave. de Lafayette, Boston, MA 02111.
Tel (800) 454-5768.
Map 4 F2.
🆆 roadscholar.org

Gay and Lesbian Travelers

Bay Windows
Tel (617) 464-7280.
🆆 baywindows.com

Traveling on a Budget

International Student Identity Card (ISIC)
🆆 isic.org

Student Advantage Card
280 Summer St., Boston, MA 02210.
Tel (617) 912-2011 or (800) 333-2920.
Map 2 E5.
🆆 studentadvantage. com

Responsible Tourism

Boston Green Tourism
🆆 bostongreentourism. org

Useful Websites

City of Boston
🆆 cityofboston.gov

Boston Globe Online
🆆 boston.com

Visit New England. com
🆆 visitnewengland. com

Yankee Magazine
🆆 yankeemagazine. com

Personal Security and Health

New England's comparatively low crime rate makes it a safe vacation destination. Even the region's largest metropolitan area, Boston, is considered quite safe. Nonetheless, it is a good idea for travelers to exercise a few simple precautions to ensure that they remain out of harm's way. This same rule of thumb applies to the wilderness areas. Despite being almost free of crime, these areas possess a number of natural hazards that can be minimized with a little effort.

Motorized police patrol on Surfside Beach, Nantucket, Massachusetts

Police

Three agencies share law enforcement duties: city police, sheriffs (who patrol county areas), and the state Highway Patrol, which deals with traffic accidents and offenses outside city boundaries. Law enforcement officials are friendly and often helpful when not otherwise engaged in official duties. Their uniforms are dark blue.

What to be Aware of

As with all large urban centers, New England's major cities – Boston, Burlington, Worcester, Springfield, New Haven, Hartford, Providence, and Portland – have pockets of crime. Generally speaking, the main tourist areas are safe as most of the problems occur in neighborhoods not usually frequented by visitors. It is best to avoid wandering into areas that are off the beaten track. The number of street people, or panhandlers, in cities is on the rise, but these people are almost always harmless.

Pickpockets are sometimes at work in the busy centers and will target anyone who looks like a tourist. Your best defense is common sense. Avoid wearing expensive jewelry and carry cameras and camcorders securely. Carry only small amounts of cash, and opt instead for credit cards and traveler's checks. Money belts or pouches worn under your clothing provide maximum security against pickpockets, especially in crowded areas such as buses and malls. While theft in hotels is not common, it is prudent to store valuables in the safe when you are out.

Always lock your car when leaving it unoccupied. Valuables left in the open in unattended cars are easy targets for smash-and-grab thieves, so store them in the trunk. In major urban areas, avoid walking through parks and strange neighborhoods at night. Always use automatic teller machines (ATMs) on busy, well-lit streets.

Before you leave home, make a photocopy of all important documents, such as your passport and visa or ESTA application number, and take it with you, keeping it separate from the originals. Also make a note of the numbers of your traveler's checks and credit cards, in case they are stolen.

In an Emergency

For emergency medical, fire, or police services, call 911. The call is free from public phones. Emergency phone boxes are located along major highways and connect instantly to the emergency services. The **Travelers' Aid Society** may provide assistance or referrals to stranded travelers.

Lost and Stolen Property

Although the chances of retrieving lost or stolen property are very slim, you should report all missing items to the police and get a copy of the police report for your insurance claim. A stolen passport should be reported to your embassy or consulate. Most credit card companies have toll-free numbers to report a lost or stolen card, as do **American Express** and **Thomas Cook** for lost traveler's checks, which can often be replaced within a few hours. In the event of loss or theft, it is useful to have a record of your valuables' serial numbers and receipts as proof of possession. If you have lost something, try retracing your steps and think of the taxi companies and bus or train routes you were using when the item went missing. Most taxi and transport companies run a Lost and Found service, which can be reached via the general access phone number (see p377).

A crowded Boston street, where pickpockets can operate

Fire engine

Ambulance

Police car

Hospitals and Pharmacies

New England has a number of acclaimed hospitals and research facilities, such as **Massachusetts General Hospital**, should you need medical treatment. If you need a prescription dispensed, there are pharmacies (drug stores) in every city in the region, some staying open 24 hours, such as **CVS Pharmacy**. Ask your hotel for the nearest one. Those with known medical issues visiting small towns and remote areas should take precautions and locate the nearest medical facility in advance. If you need to see a dentist, some clinics offer emergency care, including **Tufts Emergency Dental Clinic**.

Outdoor Safety

A wide variety of outdoor recreational activities are on offer in New England, some of which entail certain risks. Helmets and other protective items are essential, and often mandatory, for such activities as white-water rafting and mountain biking, as are life jackets for all types of boating. Hikers should always stay on marked trails; those who are hiking or camping alone should notify someone of their destination and estimated time of arrival. Campers should never feed animals and are advised to suspend food from a tree branch to avoid visits from bears. If you see a bear, don't look it in the eyes. Back away slowly and do not run. Extinguish campfires carefully using water. Mountain hikers and rock climbers should always be prepared for sudden changes in the weather, while ocean swimmers are advised to use beaches with lifeguards and ask about undertows.

Wear a hat and apply sun block in the summer. Hikers should wear bright-colored clothes and avoid forests and fields during hunting season (May and the fall). To avoid any risk of catching Lyme disease from ticks, cover up well when walking through woods and fields.

Hiking trail marker

Travel and Health Insurance

As the US does not have a national health program, emergency medical and dental care, though excellent, can be very expensive. Medical travel insurance is highly recommended in order to defer some of the costs of an unscheduled stop in a US hospital. Even with medical coverage, you may have to pay for services when you receive them, then claim reimbursement from your insurance company later. Ensure the policy you choose covers trip cancellation, baggage and document loss, emergency medical care, and accidental death. You may need extra cover for certain activities.

DIRECTORY

In an Emergency

All emergencies (police, fire, medical)
Tel 911 (toll-free, or dial 0 for the operator.)

Travelers' Aid Society
727 Atlantic Ave., Boston, MA 02111.
Tel (617) 542-7286. Map 4 F2.
w travelersaid.org
(For other New England branches, look in the Yellow Pages or dial 411 for directory assistance).

Lost or Stolen Property

American Express
Tel (800) 528-4800 (cards).
Tel (800) 221-7282 (checks).

Diners Club
Tel (800) 234-6377.

Discover
Tel (800) DISCOVER.

MasterCard
Tel (800) 826-2181.

Thomas Cook
Tel (888) 713-3424 (cash, passport, or checks).

Visa
Tel (800) 336-8472.

Hospitals and Pharmacies

Area Hospitals
Tel 411 for directory assistance.

Beth Israel Deaconess Medical Center
330 Brookline Ave., Boston, MA 02215.
Tel (617) 667-7000.
w bidmc.org

CVS Pharmacy (open 24 hours)
587 Boylston St., Boston, MA 02116.
Tel (617) 437-8414.
Map 3 C4.
w cvs.com

Massachusetts General Hospital
55 Fruit St., Boston, MA 02114.
Tel (617) 726-2000.
Map 1 B3.
w massgeneral.org/

Tufts Emergency Dental Clinic
1 Kneeland St., Boston, MA 02111.
Tel (617) 636-6828. **Map** 4 E2.

Banks and Local Currency

Outside of Boston, not many banks exchange foreign currency, so visitors from abroad should use credit or automatic teller machine (cash machine) cards. Never carry all your money and credit cards with you at the same time, and keep in mind that most banks and foreign currency exchanges are closed on Sundays.

Banks and Foreign Exchange Bureaus

Most New England banks are open 9am–5pm Monday to Friday. Many are also open 9am–noon or 1pm on Saturdays. Most banks are closed on Sundays, and all are closed on public holidays. Foreign exchange bureaus tend to be open 9am–5pm weekdays.

Traveler's checks can usually be cashed at banks with a recognized photo ID, such as a passport. The main branches of national banks in large urban areas will exchange foreign currency for a small fee, but outside the major cities, not many facilities offer this service. Among the best-known agencies for changing currency are American Express Travel Agency and Travelex Currency Services.

Always ask about hidden charges or commissions before making a transaction. For the best rates, avoid exchanging your money at airports or train and bus stations. In general, you will get the best rates at big city banks or private exchange bureaus in larger centers.

ATMs

Automatic teller machines (ATMs) are available throughout New England, even in tiny villages. Look for them in the foyers or by the entrances of banks. ATMs are also found in airports, train stations, shopping malls, supermarkets, large gas stations, and along the streets of major cities. Widely found bank-card networks include Cirrus, Plus, NYCE, and Interlink. The machines will also dispense money to credit cards such as VISA and MasterCard.

Before leaving home, ask your bank if your card can be used in the US.

Credit Cards

The most commonly accepted credit cards in New England are MasterCard, VISA, and American Express, with Diners Club and the Discover Card sometimes accepted as well. Credit and debit cards can be used at most restaurants, retail stores, hotels, and gas stations, as well as to reserve tickets over the phone and to book a rental car. The biggest benefit of credit cards is that they offer you much more security than carrying around large sums of cash, and they can be very useful to have in emergency situations (see p371).

Banknotes and Coins

The US currency is the dollar. There are 100 cents to a dollar. Banknotes come in denominations of $1, $5, $10, $20, $50, and $100, while coins come in 1-, 5-, 10-, 25-, and 50-cent pieces. Gold-tone $1 coins are also in circulation, though not very popular; you will receive them mainly as change from vending machines. Each coin has a popular name: 25-cent pieces are called quarters; 10-cent pieces, dimes; 5-cent pieces, nickels; and 1-cent pieces, pennies.

1-dollar bill ($1)

5-dollar bill ($5)

10-dollar bill ($10)

20-dollar bill ($20)

50-dollar bill ($50)

100-dollar bill ($100)

25-cent coin (a quarter)

10-cent coin (a dime)

5-cent coin (a nickel)

1-cent coin (a penny)

Communications and Media

Many cities and towns in New England offer free wireless Internet access in public places, and a copy of a daily local newspaper (some of which are free) is never far away. For updates on the news, traffic, and weather, consult the numerous specialized websites that residents count on in their day-to-day lives.

International and Local Telephone Calls

Local phone calls are fairly inexpensive, but long-distance calls incur additional charges. Check rates by dialing 0 and asking the operator, but do not get the operator to put the call through, since this costs extra. The cheapest way to make long-distance calls is with a disposable calling card. These can be purchased for as little as $5 at convenience stores and train station kiosks.

Cell Phones

If you wish to bring your own cell phone, ask your provider if they offer an international plan that covers the US. However, it may be easier and cheaper to buy a disposable phone in the US. Pre-paid cell phones can be bought from around $25 throughout New England. Replacement chargers and adapters can be found in any electronics store.

Public Telephones

Public phones can usually be found in train stations and shopping centers. All pay phones accept coins, and many also take phone and credit cards. Local calls cost 50¢–$1 for three minutes; long-distance rates vary and include both a fixed call charge and a per-minute charge. All numbers with an 800, 866, 877, or 888 prefix are free of charge, as are calls from a pay phone to directory assistance (411 for local, 00 for international) and the emergency services (911). Operator assistance (0 for local, 01 for international) has a charge. Making a call from a hotel room can carry a hefty surcharge, and it is usually cheaper to use the pay phone in the lobby.

Internet and Email

Internet-enabled cell phones have led to the decline of the cybercafé, though **FedEx**, of which there are numerous locations throughout New England, have computers with Internet access available for rental. Terminals with online access can also be found in the **Boston Public Library** and in many hotels, though you may have to pay. Some colleges and universities allow visitors to use their Internet terminals for free. From coffee shops to public parks, wireless Internet hot spots dot the region.

Postal Services

Post offices are open 9am–5pm weekdays, with some branches offering a Saturday service. All are closed on Sundays and federal holidays. Letters and small parcels (less than 13 oz) with the correct postage can be placed in any blue mailbox. Domestic mail takes one to five days for delivery, faster if you use Priority Mail or Express Mail's next-day delivery. Use airmail when sending mail overseas. Couriers like **FedEx**, **UPS**, and **DHL** provide a faster service but also cost more.

Boston post office, Charles Street

DIRECTORY

Internet and Email

Boston Public Library
700 Boylston St., Boston, MA 02116. **Map** 3 C2.
Tel (617) 536-5400.

FedEx
187 Dartmouth St., Boston, MA 02116. **Map** 3 C2. **Tel** (617) 262-6188. W local.fedex.com

Postal Services

Boston Main Post Office (extended hours)
25 Dorchester Ave., Boston, MA 02210.
Tel (617) 654-5302.

Cambridge Main Post Office (extended hours)
770 Massachusetts Ave., Cambridge, MA 02139. **Map** 3 C5.
Tel (617) 575-8700.

DHL
420 E St., Boston, MA 02127.
Tel (800) 225 5345.

FedEx Office Print & Ship Center
125 Tremont St., Boston, MA 02116. **Map** 4 E1.
Tel (617) 423-0234.

UPS Customer Center
647 Summer St., Boston, MA 02127. **Tel** (800) 742-5877.

Newspapers and Magazines

The Boston Globe is the most widely read newspaper in New England. The *Boston Herald* is a popular tabloid-style daily. National publications like the *New York Times*, *Wall Street Journal*, and *USA Today* are also easily available.

Television and Radio

Hotels usually have access to the main networks (CBS, NBC, Fox, ABC), as well as some cable channels such as ESPN (for sports) and CNN (news). Public station PBS has classic films and documentaries.

Radio stations on FM frequencies tend to stick to a particular type of music (rock, jazz, Top 40, and so on). AM stations are usually geared toward talk-radio shows.

TRAVEL INFORMATION

The most common ways to get to New England are by plane or by car. However, trains and buses also provide decent access to many areas, particularly the southern states in the region. Boston's Logan International Airport handles international and domestic flights, and some of the longest journeys within the region can be accomplished by a quick flight on a regional carrier. Boston is also the hub for rail and bus services coming in from all over the US and parts of Canada. Amtrak is the only rail option, but the presence of several bus carriers competing with one another has led to greatly reduced fares, with direct Boston to New York services for as little as $1.

The international check-in area at Boston Logan International Airport

Arriving by Air

Boston's Logan International Airport (BOS) is the region's busiest, although some domestic and international carriers use Manchester Boston Regional Airport (MHT), in New Hampshire, which serves Vermont and Maine; T.F. Green Airport (PVD) in Warwick, Rhode Island, which serves Providence; and Bradley International Airport (BDL) in Windsor Locks, Connecticut, which serves Hartford. A few major commercial airlines also fly into Bangor (BGR) and Portland (PWM), Maine; and Burlington (BTV), Vermont. Other gateways to New England include Montreal, Quebec, and, of course, New York City's three major airports.

Tickets and Fares

Planning your vacation early will allow you to shop around for the best fares. Even with the small fees they may charge, travel agents are often your best bet in your search for savings. Alternatively, **Expedia** is a good online source of inexpensive tickets, while **Kayak** gives you instant access to the best published prices on the web. Flights are busiest between June and October, as well as around the major holidays (Easter, Labor Day, Thanksgiving, Christmas). Book well in advance if you wish to fly during these times. In general, you will get the lowest fares if you travel at non-peak times – prices usually drop substantially after Labor Day, for instance.

Internal Flights

Small domestic airlines cover specific geographical regions, and also offer a few national flights. With fewer flights than the major carriers, they often have much lower fares. Some regional commuter airlines shuttle passengers around with small, single-prop planes flying to various destinations including islands off the coast. **Cape Air** flies smaller routes throughout New England and is especially useful for those visiting Cape Cod. **Nantucket**

Passenger jet in flight

Airport	Information	Distance from City
Logan International Airport (Boston, MA)	(800) 235-6426	3 miles (4.8 km) from Downtown Boston W massport.com/logan
Manchester Boston Regional Airport (Manchester, NH)	(603) 624-6556	6 miles (9.5 km) from Downtown Manchester W flymanchester.com
T.F. Green Airport (Warwick, RI)	(401) 737-8222	10 miles (16 km) from Downtown Providence W pvdairport.com
Bradley International Airport (Windsor Locks, CT)	(860) 292-2000	12 miles (19 km) from Downtown Hartford W bradleyairport.com

Airlines fly between Hyannis (Cape Cod) and Nantucket.

On Arrival

International travelers will be given a customs and immigration form to complete during their flight and to hand in to customs officials at the airport. At the immigration area there are two lines – one for US citizens and another for non-US citizens. If you are entering the country via New York's busy JFK, be warned that the immigration lines there are often long and the process can be time-consuming.

Arriving by Train

Amtrak is the major railroad in the US. One of its busiest routes serves southern and central New England up to Boston. Amtrak's high-speed Acela regional train links New York to Boston, cutting about 45 minutes off the regional service's regular travel time of four hours. While Acela is available at a premium price, it is still cheaper than most airfares and has the added benefit of taking you from downtown to downtown without the added expense of taxis or shuttle buses.

A rail service also runs between Boston and Portland, Maine; in the summer, there is a stop at Maine's popular Old Orchard Beach.

Arriving by Car

Beginning in Florida, I-95 (known as Route 128 in the Boston area) is one of the most popular drives for travelers from the South. This major highway sticks close to the coast as it passes through

A modern Greyhound bus

Connecticut and Providence, Rhode Island, en route to the outskirts of Boston. Circumventing the city, the highway continues up through New Hampshire and Maine before crossing the border into Canada. Truck traffic on I-95 can be heavy, especially when the route approaches Boston.

From the north, the two major gateways into New England are I-89 and I-91. The latter crosses from Canada into Vermont at Derby Line, then follows a relatively straight line south along the Vermont/New Hampshire border, through Massachusetts and Connecticut all the way down to New Haven. I-89 starts in Vermont's northwesternmost corner, then cuts diagonally from Burlington to Concord, New Hampshire, where it links up with I-93 into Boston.

The major western points of entry into New England are I-84 and I-90 (toll road) from New York state.

Arriving by Bus

You can get just about anywhere in New England by bus, so long as you are not in a hurry. Many of the bus companies serve particular sections of the region. **Concord Coach Lines** has routes in Maine and New Hampshire, while **Peter**

Pan has stops in Connecticut and western Massachusetts. Other parts of Massachusetts, such as Cape Cod and the South Shore, are served by **Plymouth & Brockton**. **Greyhound Lines** is a nationwide carrier with stops throughout New England. Greyhound works in conjunction with Peter Pan lines.

Most major bus lines offer discounted rates for students and seniors (with proper ID), and offer unlimited travel during a set period.

DIRECTORY

Tickets and Fares

Expedia
W expedia.com

Kayak
W kayak.com

Internal Flights

Cape Air
Tel 886-227-3247.
W flycapeair.com

Nantucket Airlines
Tel 800-635-8787.
W nantucketairlines.com

Arriving by Train

Amtrak
Tel (800) 872-7245.
W amtrak.com

Arriving by Bus

Concord Coach Lines
Tel (617) 426-8080.
W concordcoachlines.com

Greyhound Lines
Tel (617) 526-1800.
W greyhound.com

Peter Pan
Tel (800) 343-9999.
W peterpanbus.com

Plymouth & Brockton
Tel (508) 746-0378.
W p-b.com

Train station in North Conway, New Hampshire

Getting Around Boston

The public transportation network in Boston and Cambridge is very good. In fact, it is considerably easier to get around by public transit than by driving, with the added benefit of not having to find a parking space. All the major attractions in the city are easily accessible by subway, bus, or taxi. The central sections of the city are also extremely easy to navigate on foot.

One of Boston's MBTA buses

Green Travel

Most places in the Boston area can be easily reached by public transit. The city's public transportation network, the MBTA (Massachusetts Bay Transportation Authority), is committed to providing alternatives to the car and works with the Environmental Protection Agency on projects such as locomotive-engine pollution control devices. The MBTA is also replacing its diesel-powered buses with natural gas-powered vehicles.

Boston's tourism moniker of "America's Walking City" hints at how easy it is to see the city on foot. Most attractions require nothing more than sensible shoes, while the Esplanade Trail along the Charles River and the Minuteman Bikeway offer ample opportunities for bikers, joggers, and walkers.

Websites such as https://. hopstop.com offer public transport and walking directions to almost anywhere.

Finding Your Way in Boston

Much of Boston is laid out organically, rather than in the sort of strict grid found in most American cities. When trying to orient yourself, it helps if you think of Boston as enclaves, or neighborhoods around a few central squares. In general, uphill from Boston Common is Beacon Hill, downhill is Downtown, while Back Bay begins west of Arlington Street. The North End sticks out from the north side of Boston, while the Waterfront is literally that – where Boston meets the sea.

MBTA Subway and Trolley Buses

Run by the **MBTA**, Boston's combined subway and trolley network is known as the "T". The T operates 5am–12:45am daily (from 6am on Sundays). Weekday service is every 3–15 minutes, less frequent at weekends. There are five lines: Red, from south of the city to Cambridge; Green, from the Museum of Science westward into the suburbs; Blue, from near the Government Center to Logan Airport and on to Revere; Orange, linking the northern suburbs to southwest Boston; and Silver, a surface bus that runs from Roxbury to Logan Airport via South Station. Maps of the system are available at Downtown Crossing MBTA station.

Admission to subway stations is via turnstiles into which you insert a paper "Charlie" ticket ($2.50) or plastic "Charlie" card ($2). These can be bought from MBTA vending machines. Day or week Link passes for unlimited travel can be purchased at Downtown Crossing, South Station, Back Bay, Government Center, and North Station subway stops.

MBTA Buses

The MBTA bus system expands the transit network to cover more than 1,000 miles (1,600 km). Buses are often crowded, though, and schedules can be hard to get. Two useful sightseeing routes are Haymarket–Charlestown (from near Quincy Market to Bunker Hill) and Harvard–Dudley (from Harvard Square via Massachusetts Avenue through Back Bay and the South End to Dudley Square in Roxbury). Cash, a paper "Charlie" ticket ($2), or a plastic "Charlie" card ($1.50) is required for the fare.

Taxis

Finding a taxi in Boston and Cambridge is easy, except when it rains. Taxis can be found at stands in tourist areas or hailed on the street. Taxis may pick up fares only in the city for which they are licensed – Boston taxis only in Boston, Cambridge taxis only in Cambridge. If you need to be somewhere on time, it is wise to call a taxi company and arrange a pickup time and place in advance.

Rates are calculated by both mileage and time of day, beginning with a $2.60 pickup fee when the meter starts running. Taxis in Boston and Cambridge tend to be more expensive than in other US

Boston taxis waiting for fares at one of the city's many taxi stands

cities. Taxis to and from Logan Airport are required to charge an airport fee ($2.75); taxis coming into the city from the airport also charge for the harbor tunnel toll ($5.25). Other surcharges may apply late at night. A full schedule of fares should be posted inside the vehicle.

The driver's photograph and permit as well as the taxi's permit number will be displayed inside all legitimate taxicabs.

Walking in Boston

Boston is a great walking city: it is compact, and virtually all streets are flanked by sidewalks. It is nonetheless essential to wear comfortable walking shoes with adequate cushioning and good support. Boston is mainly a city of neighborhoods, so it is usually best to use public transportation to reach a particular area, and then walk around to soak up the atmosphere. Walking also allows you to see parts of the city that are impractical to explore by car because the streets are too narrow – for example, Beacon Hill, parts of the North End, and Harvard Square.

Traveling by Boat

With more than 6,000 miles (9,656 km) of coastline, New England offers numerous public boats and ferries for both leisure and transport purposes. Some attractions, like the Boston Harbor Islands, are reachable only by boat, with ferries by **Boston's Best Cruises** departing from Long Wharf. Visitors can make longer journeys to Salem or to Provincetown on Cape Cod, which is served by the **Baystate Cruises**. From Cape Cod there is the option of going further by ferry to Nantucket and Martha's Vineyard.

DIRECTORY

Subway, Trolley Buses, and Buses

MBTA
Tel (617) 222-3200 (route and schedule information).
W mbta.com

Taxis

Boston Cab Dispatch, Inc
Tel (617) 262-2227 (Boston).

Boston Town Taxi
Tel (617) 536-5000 (Boston).

Checker Cab of Cambridge
Tel (617) 497-9000 (Cambridge).

Yellow Cab
Tel (617) 547-3000 (Cambridge).

Traveling by boat

Baystate Cruises
Tel 877-783-3779.

Boston's Best Cruises
Tel (617) 770-0040.

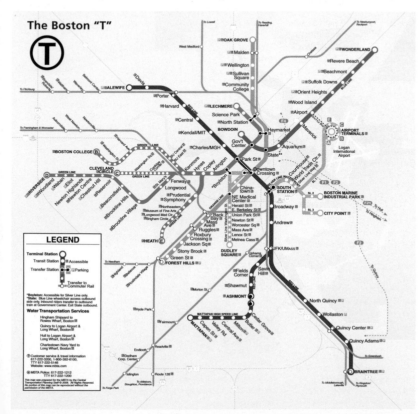

Driving in New England

While flying is the fastest and most efficient way to get to New England, driving is by far the best way to explore the region. In fact, much of this area's charm is found along scenic jaunts down the coast and driving tours during fall-foliage season. It is important to remember that large parts of the region are essentially wild, so you should always be prepared for any eventuality, such as a breakdown. This is doubly true in the winter, when sudden blizzards and whiteouts caused by blowing snow can leave motorists stranded. Boston's public transit system makes it easy to be without a car (*see pp376–7*), but once outside the city you will need a vehicle to do your best exploring.

Country roads beckoning drivers to leave the crowds behind

A rented convertible, perfect for exploring in good weather

Car Rental

The major car rental chains have outlets in most of New England's largest cities and airports. These national chains include **Avis**, **Budget**, **Enterprise**, **Hertz**, **National**, **Rent-A-Wreck**, and **Thrifty**. While their rates are somewhat higher than those offered by smaller local companies, they usually provide an extremely efficient service.

In order to rent a car, you must be 21 and possess a valid driver's license. People under the age of 25 will usually have to pay an additional fee. A major credit card is normally required as well, unless you are prepared to put down a hefty cash deposit. Credit cards sometimes provide coverage against damage or theft of the vehicle, but it is wise to check what the terms are with your credit card company prior to traveling. Make sure that your car rental agreement includes Collision Damage Waiver (CDW) – also known as Loss Damage Waiver (LDW) – or else you will be liable for any damage to the car, even if it was not your fault. This supplemental insurance can cost between $10 and $20 extra a day.

Sightseeing by car, stopping where and when you want

Speed Limits

It is important to pay attention to road signs, since speed limits can vary from one place to the next depending on your proximity to a town or city. In general, the maximum speed on an interstate highway ranges from 55 to 65 mph (88–105 km/h). On smaller highways, it can range between 30 and 55 mph (50–88 km/h). Cities and towns set their speed limits between 20 and 35 mph (32–56 km/h), and drastically lower around hospitals and schools.

Police pick strategic points along highways – often right after a sign requesting drivers to lower their speed – to set up their radar equipment in order to catch those who are going too fast. Do not try to pay tickets or fines directly to the police officer who pulled you over; this can be interpreted as attempted bribery and can land you deeper in hot water.

Driving Tours

There are a number of books on the market listing the best driving tours of the region. Some magazines, such as **Yankee**, which can be purchased at most newsstands, might include a complete itinerary of recommended routes, historic stops, and the best places to eat and stay. Tours vary from a single day to an entire week and take in everything from dramatic coastal scenery and tiny fishing villages to mountainous terrain and country towns. Of course, the favorite season for drivers is the fall, when the rural roads are flanked by the brilliant colors of leaves *(see pp24–5)*.

State tourism offices *(see p369)* can give you the contact details of organizations that arrange foliage tours. Each state also has a **Foliage Hotline** number that gives frequently updated foliage reports. Remember, though, that traffic on New England's roads peaks during the fall.

Parking

New England is one of the most densely populated regions in America, and space is at a premium. As a result parking spaces can be hard to find in some destinations. Larger cities tend to provide a variety of parking options, from cheaper municipal lots and highly contested metered spaces to pricier private lots and valet services. First-time visitors to the region's cities should allow extra time when driving to more popular destinations. Also be aware of marked towing zones.

Gasoline

Except when driving through remote areas, motorists will rarely have trouble locating a gas station. However, many locations close at night, with 24-hour stations hard to come by, even in the larger cities. Prices fluctuate wildly; in general, gas stations in smaller, remote towns charge more than those in more densely populated areas. Without fail, motorists can save money by pumping their own gas rather than opting for full service.

DIRECTORY

Car Rentals

Avis
Tel (800) 831-2847.
W avis.com

Budget
Tel (800) 527-7000.
W budget.com

Enterprise
Tel (800) 736-8222.
W enterprise.com

Hertz
Tel (800) 654-3131.
W hertz.com

National
Tel (800) 227-7368.
W nationalcar.com

Rent-A-Wreck
Tel (800) 944-7501.
W rentawreck.com

Thrifty
Tel (800) 847-4389.
W thrifty.com

Driving Tours

Yankee
W yankeemagazine.com

Foliage Hotlines

Connecticut
Tel (888) 288-4748.

Maine
Tel (800) 777-0317.

Massachusetts
Tel (800) 227-6277.

New Hampshire
Tel (800) 258-3608.

Rhode Island
Tel (800) 556-2484.

Vermont
Tel (800) 837-6668.

Safety Tips

The steps listed below will help to ensure a safe road trip. The National Highway Traffic Safety Administration website (www.nhtsa.gov) has more information on road safety.

- Passengers should wear their seat belts at all times. Infants and young children should be secured in a car seat in the back seat. Follow child-seat instruction manuals precisely. A rear-facing child seat should NEVER be placed in the front seat of a vehicle equipped with an air bag.

- Check your oil, radiator reservoir, brake fluids, and your fan belt before setting off on a long drive. Also check your tires for tread wear and the correct air pressure, and see that your spare tire is roadworthy.

- In winter, be sure you have extra gloves, boots, and warm clothes. If you get stuck in an out-of-the-way place, stay in your car. Keep the motor running for warmth, but open your window slightly to guard against carbon monoxide buildup. Make sure your exhaust pipe is clear of snow.

- Check road conditions on the radio, especially in winter. Heavy snowfalls can leave many areas impassable. Individual state transportation departments often have hotlines dispensing up-to-date information.

- Be wary of large animals on the road. Hitting a moose poses more of a threat to you than it does to the animal.

Sign on a Vermont highway warning drivers to watch for moose

General Index

'I squashed into the doorway and p[...] [...]ard. It bumped against Mack's leg a[...] [...]nd stumbled out the other s[...] [...] stayed revolving round the d[...] [...]. I felt as if I wanted to go on s[...] [...]pinning. Maybe if I twirled really f[...] [...]p there would be this humming sound an[...] [...]erything would be a blur and I'd shoot out somewhere else entirely, a warm bright world where everyone liked me and laughed at my jokes.
I stepped into the grubby foyer of the Royal Hotel instead . . .'

Life in the Royal Hotel – a run down bed and breakfast hotel for homeless families – is no joke for ten-year-old Elsa and her family. But when things go dangerously wrong, Elsa suddenly has the chance to be a real star!

'An unsentimental and truthful book that is even better for a strong sense of mischief' *Independent on Sunday*

'Jacqueline Wilson has a rare talent for confronting a serious subject head on and managing to make it amusing . . . A highly entertaining read' *Good Book Guide*

Shortlisted for the 1995 Carnegie Medal

The Bed and Breakfast Star

Jacqueline Wilson
Illustrated by Nick Sharratt

CORGI YEARLING BOOKS

For Frances Stokes
(Froggy to her friends)

THE BED AND BREAKFAST STAR
A CORGI YEARLING BOOK : 0 440 86540 9

First published in Great Britain by Doubleday,
a division of Transworld Publishers

PRINTING HISTORY
Doubleday edition published 1994
Corgi Yearling edition published 1995

Text copyright © 1994 by Jacqueline Wilson
Illustrations copyright © 1994 by Nick Sharratt

The right of Jacqueline Wilson to be identified as the author of
this work has been asserted in accordance with the Copyright,
Designs and Patents Act 1988

Set in Century Schoolbook by
Chippendale Type Ltd, Otley, West Yorkshire

Corgi Yearling Books are published by Random House Children's Books,
61–63 Uxbridge Road, London W5 5SA,
a division of The Random House Group Ltd,
in Australia by Random House Australia (Pty) Ltd,
20 Alfred Street, Milsons Point, Sydney, NSW 2061, Austrlia,
in New Zealand by Random House New Zealand Ltd,
18 Poland Road, Glenfield, Auckland 10, New Zealand
and in South Africa by Random House (Pty) Ltd,
Endulini 5a Jubilee Road, Parktown 2193, South Africa

Printed and bound in Great Britain by
Cox & Wyman Ltd, Reading, Berkshire.

Do you know what everyone calls me now? *Bed and Breakfast*. That's what all the kids yell after me in the playground. Even the teachers do it. Well, they don't say it to my face. But I've heard them. 'Oh yes, that Elsa. She's one of the bed-and-breakfast children.' Honestly. It sounds like I've got a duvet for a dress, cornflake curls, two fried-egg eyes and a streaky-bacon smile.

I don't look a bit like that. Well, I hope I don't! I'm Elsa.

Do you like my name? I hope you do like it or Elsa'll get upset. Do you get the joke? I made it up myself. I'm always cracking jokes. People don't often laugh though.

I bet you don't know anyone else called Elsa. There was just this lion called Elsa, ages ago. There was a book written about her, and they made a film. They sometimes show it on the television so maybe you've seen it. My mum called me after Elsa the lion. I was a very tiny baby, smaller than all the others in the hospital, but I was born with lots of hair. Really. Most babies are almost bald but I had this long tufty hair and Mum used to brush it so that it stood out all round my head like a lion's mane. I didn't just look like a lion. I sounded like one too. I might have had very tiny little lungs but I had the loudest voice. I bawled day and night and wore all the nurses out, let alone my mum. She says she should have left me yelling in my hospital cot and slipped off out of it without me. She was joking. Mum's jokes aren't always funny though – not like mine.

That was my very first BED.

It's not very comfy-looking, is it? No wonder I bawled.

Here's my second BED.

I used to pretend I was a real lion in a cage. I didn't half roar.

We've still got my old duck cot. We've lost lots of our other things but we've always carted that around with us. I used to turn it into a play-house

or a car

and once it was even my castle.

But then my sister Pippa was born and I lost a house and a car and a castle and she gained a bed. I gave it a good spring-clean for her and tried to make it as pretty as possible, but I don't think she really appreciated it.

Pippa did a lot more sleeping and a lot less yelling than me. She's not a baby now. She's nearly five. Half my age. Half my size though. She's not a little titch like me. She'll catch me up soon if I don't watch out.

I've also got a brother, Hank. Hank the Hunk. He had the duck cot too.

He only fitted it for five minutes. I'm tiny and Pippa is tall but Hank is enormous. He's

not just long, he's very wide too. He's still not much more than a baby but if you pick him up you practically need a crane and if you put him on your lap you get severely squashed. If you stand in his way when he comes crawling by, then you're likely to get steam-rollered.

Pippa and Hank aren't my proper sister and brother. They're halves. That sounds silly, doesn't it. As if they should look like this.

We've all got the same mum. Our mum. But I've got a different dad.

My dad never really lived with Mum and me. He did come and see me sometimes, when I was little. He took me to the zoo to see the real lions. I can remember it vividly though Mum says I was only about two then. I liked seeing those lions. My dad held me up to see them. They roared at me, and I roared back. I think I maybe went on roaring a bit too long and loud. My dad didn't come back after that.

Mum said we didn't care. We were better off without him. Just Mum and me. That was fine. But then Mum met Mack. Mack the Smack. That's not a joke. He really does smack. Especially me.

You're not supposed to smack children. In lots of countries smacking is against the law and if you hit a child you get sent to prison. I wish I lived in one of those countries. Mack smacks a lot. He doesn't smack Pippa properly, he just gives her little taps. And he doesn't smack Hank because even Mack doesn't hit babies. But he doesn't half whack me. Well, he doesn't *always* smack. But he lifts his hand as if he's going to. Or he hisses out of the side of his mouth: 'Are you asking for a good smacking, Elsa?'

What sort of question is that, eh? As if I'd prance up to him and say, 'Hey, Uncle Mack, can I have a socking great smack, please?'

Mum sometimes sticks up for me. But sometimes she says I'm asking for it too. She says I give Mack a lot of cheek. I don't. I just try out a few jokes on him, that's all. And he doesn't ever get them. Because he's thick. Thick thick thick as a brick.

I don't know why my mum had to marry him. And guess who got to be the bridesmaid at their wedding! Mum wanted me to wear a proper long frilly bridesmaid's frock but it looked ever so silly on me. My hair still sticks out all over the place like a lion's mane and my legs are so skinny my socks always wrinkle and somehow they always get dirty marks all over them and my shoes go all scuffed at the

toes right from when they're new. The brides-
maids' frocks in the shop were all pale pink
and pale blue and pale peach and pale lilac.
Mum sighed and said I'd get my frock filthy
before she'd had time to get up and down the
aisle.

So we forgot about the frock and Mum
dressed me up in this little black velvet jacket
and tartan kilt because Mack is Scottish. I even
had a sprig of lucky Scottish heather pinned to
my jacket. I felt like I needed a bit of luck.

Mack moved in with Mum and me after the
wedding. After I grew out of the duck cot I used
to share the big bed with Mum and that was
fun because there was always someone to chat
to and cuddle.

That was my third BED.

But then Mack got to share the big bed with Mum and I had a little campbed in the living-room. BED number four. And I kept falling out of it every time I turned over at first. But I didn't mind that campbed. I played camping.

But it was really too cramped to play camp. We only had a little flat and Mack took up so much *space*.

There certainly wasn't going to be room for a new baby too. (That was Pippa. She wasn't born then. She was just a pipsqueak in Mum's tummy.) Mum had our name down for a bigger council flat but the waiting list was so long it looked like we'd be waiting for ever.

Then one of Mack's mates up in Scotland offered him a new job up there so he went back up to Scotland and we had to go too. We stayed with Mack's mum. I was scared. I thought she might be like Mack.

But she wasn't big, she was little. She didn't smack, but she wasn't half strict all the same. I wasn't allowed to do anything in her house. I couldn't even play properly. She wouldn't let me get all my toys out at once. She said I had to play with them one at a time.

So I started playing with some of her stuff. She had some lovely things – ornaments and photo albums and musical boxes. I didn't break anything at all but she still went spare.

'You're no allowed to go raking through my things! Away and watch the television like a good wee bairn.'

That's all you were supposed to do in her house. Watch the telly. We watched it all the time.

My Scottish sort-of Gran wasn't so bad though. She did pass the sweets round while we were watching her telly. She called them sweeties.

'Are you wanting a sweetie, hen?' she'd say to me.

And I'd go cluck-cluck-cluck and flap my arms and she'd laugh and say I could be awful comic when I wanted. On Sundays we had special sweeties, a home-made fudge she called tablet. Oh, that tablet. Yum yum YUM.

16

I could eat tablet all day long. I didn't eat much else at my sort-of Gran's. She said I was a poor wee bairn who needed fattening up but she kept giving me plates of mince and tatties. I don't like mince because it looks as if someone has already chewed it, and I don't like mashed potatoes because I'm always scared there's going to be a lump. So I didn't eat much and she got cross with me and Mum got cross with me and Mack got cross with me.

The worst bit about living there was the bed. BED number five. Only it wasn't my bed, it was my sort-of Gran's. I had to share it with her. There wasn't room in her bedroom for my campbed, you see, and she said she wasn't having it cluttering up her lounge. She liked it when I stopped cluttering up the place too. She was always wanting to whisk me away to bed early. I was generally still awake when she came in. I used to peep when she took her corset off.

She wasn't so little when those corsets were off. She took up a lot of the bed once she was in it. Sometimes I'd end up clutching the edge, hanging on for dear life. And another thing. She snored.

We were meant to be looking for our own place in Scotland but we never found one. Then my sister Pippa got born and Mack fell out with his pal and lost his job. Mum got ever so worried. She didn't get on very well with my sort-of Gran and it got worse after Pippa was born.

So we moved back down South and said we were homeless. Mum got even more worried. She thought we'd be put in a bed-and-breakfast hotel. She said she'd never live it down. (Little did she know. You don't have to live it down. You can live it *up*.)

But we didn't get put in a bed-and-breakfast hotel then. We were offered this flat on a big estate. It was a bit grotty but Mack said he'd fix it up so it would look like a palace. So we moved in. It was a pretty weirdo palace, if you ask me. There was green mould on the walls and creepy-crawlies in the kitchen. Mack tried slapping a bit of paint about but it didn't make much difference. Mum got ever so depressed and Mack got cross. Pippa kept getting coughs and colds and snuffling, because of the damp.

I was OK though. My campbed collapsed once and for all, so I got to have a new bed.

BED number six. It had springs and it made the most wonderful trampoline.

I had a lot of fun in those flats.
I didn't want to leave.

But Mack got this new
job and started to make a
lot of money and he said
he'd buy Mum her
own proper house and
Mum was over
the moon.

Yippee!

I thought it was great once we'd moved into the new house. I liked that house ever so much. It wasn't damp, it was warm and cosy and when Pippa and I got up we could run about in our pyjamas without getting a bit cold. Pippa stopped being a boring old baby and started to play properly. She shared my new bed now but I didn't really mind that much because she liked my stories and she actually laughed at my jokes. We kept getting

the giggles late at night when we were supposed to be asleep, but Mum didn't often get cross and Mack didn't even smack any more. Hank the Hunk got born and he was happy too.

But we didn't live happily ever after.

Mack's job finished. He got another for a bit but it didn't pay nearly so well. And then he lost that one. And he couldn't get another. Mum worked in a supermarket while Mack looked after Pippa and Hank. (*I* can look after myself.)

But Mum's money wouldn't pay all the bills. It wouldn't pay for the lovely new house. So some people came and took nearly all our things away. We had to leave our new house. I cried. So did Pippa and Hank. Mum cried too. Mack didn't cry, but he looked as if he might.

We thought we'd have to go back to the mouldy flat. But they'd put another family in there. There wasn't any room for us.

So guess where we ended up. In a bed-and-breakfast hotel.

Bed and Breakfast

We went to stay at the Royal Hotel. The Royal sounds very grand, doesn't it? And when we were down one end of the street and got our first glimpse of the Royal right at the other end, I thought it looked very grand too. I started to get excited. I'd never stayed in a great big posh hotel before. Maybe we'd all

have our own rooms with satellite telly and people would make our beds and serve us our breakfasts from silver trays. As if we were Royalty staying in the Royal.

But the Royal started to look a bit shabby the nearer we got. We saw it needed painting. We saw one of the windows was broken and patched with cardboard. We saw the big gilt lettering had gone all wobbly and some of it was missing. We were going to be staying in the oyal H t l.

'O Yal Htl,' I said. It sounded funny. 'O Yal Htl,' I repeated. I thought of a song we sang at school about an old man river who just went rolling along. 'O Yal Htl,' I sang to the same tune.

'Will you just shut it, Elsa?' said Mack the Smack.

'I can't shut, I'm not a door,' I said. 'Hey, when is a door not a door? When it's ajar!'

No-one laughed. Mum looked as if she was about to cry. She was staring up at the Royal, shaking her head.

'No,' she said. 'No, no, no.' She started off quietly enough, but her voice got louder and louder. *'No, no, no!'*

'Come on, it's maybe not that bad,' said Mack, putting his arm round her.

Mum was carrying Hank. He got a bit squashed and started squawking. Pippa's mouth went wobbly and she tried to clutch at Mum too.

'I don't like this place, Mum,' she said. 'We don't have to go and live here, do we?'

'No, we don't, kids. We're not living in a dump like this,' said Mum. She kicked the litter in the driveway. An old Chinese take-away leaked orange liquid all over her suede shoes.

'For heaven's sake,' Mum wept. 'Look at all this muck. There'll be rats. And if it's like this outside, what's it going to be like inside? Cockroaches. Fleas. I'm not taking my kids into a lousy dump like this.'

'So where *are* you going to take them?' said Mack. 'Come on, answer me. Where?'

Hank cried harder. Pippa sniffed and stuck her thumb in her mouth. I fiddled with my hair. Mum pressed her lips tight together, as if she was rubbing in her lipstick. Only she wasn't wearing any make-up at all. Her face was as white as ice-cream. When I tried to take her hand, her fingers were as cold as ice too.

She shook her head. She didn't know how to answer Mack. She didn't have any other place to take us.

'I'm sorry,' said Mack. 'I've failed you, haven't I?' He suddenly didn't seem so big any more. It was as if he was shrinking inside his clothes.

'Oh don't be daft,' said Mum wearily. She joggled Hank and wiped Pippa's nose and tried to pat my hair into place. We all wriggled and protested. 'It's not your fault, Mack.'

'Well, whose fault is it then?' Mack mumbled. 'I've let you down. I can't get work, I can't even provide a proper home for you and the kids.'

'It's not your fault. It's not anybody's fault.

It's just . . . circumstances,' said Mum.

I saw a horrible snooty old gent, Sir Come-Stances, pointing his fat finger in our direction, while all his servants snatched our house and our furniture and our television and our toys. I was so busy thinking about him that I hardly noticed Mum marching off into the entrance of the Royal, Hank on one hip, Pippa hanging on her arm. Mack shuffled after her, carrying all our stuff. He turned round when he got to the revolving door.

'Elsa!' he called irritably. 'Don't just stand there looking gormless. Come on!'

'What's a gorm, Mack? And how come I've lost mine?'

'*Elsa!* Are you asking for a good smacking?'

I decided it was time to scuttle after him. I squashed into the doorway and pushed hard. It bumped against Mack's leg and he yelled and stumbled out the other side, cursing. I stayed revolving round the door by myself. I felt as if I wanted to go on spinning and spinning. Maybe if I twirled really fast like a top then there would be this humming sound and everything would blur and I'd shoot out into somewhere else entirely, a warm bright world where everyone liked me and laughed at my jokes.

I stepped into the grubby foyer of the Royal Hotel instead. There was a dark carpet on the

27

floor, red with lots of stains. The thick wall-paper was red too, with a crusty pattern like dried blood. The ceiling was studded with pale polystyrene tiles but several were missing. I wondered if anyone went away wearing one as a hat without noticing.

There was a big counter with a bell. We could see through a glass door behind the counter into an office. A woman was sitting in there, scoffing sweets out of a paper-bag and reading a big fat book. She didn't seem to notice us, even though Hank was crying and Mack was creating a commotion hauling all our cases and plastic bags around the revolving doors and into the hallway.

Mum touched the bell on the counter. It gave a brisk trill. The woman popped another pear-drop in her mouth and turned a page of her Jackie Collins. Mum cleared her throat loudly and pinged on the bell. I had a go too. And Pippa. The woman turned her back on us with one swivel of her chair.

'Oi! You in there!' Mack bellowed, thumping his big fist on the counter.

The woman put down her book with a sigh, marking her place with a sweet wrapper. She stretched out her arm and opened the glass door a fraction.

'There's no need to take that tone. Manners don't cost a penny,' she said in a pained voice.

'Well, we did ring the bell,' said Mum. 'You must have heard it.'

'Yes, but it's nothing to do with me. I'm only switchboard. That bell's for management.'

'But there doesn't seem to *be* any management,' said Mum. 'This is ridiculous.'

'If you want to make a complaint you must put it in writing and give it to the Manager.'

'Where is this Manager then?' asked Mack.

'I've no idea. I told you, it's nothing to do with me. I'm only switchboard.' She closed her glass door and stuck her nose back in her book.

'I don't believe this,' said Mum. 'It's a total nightmare.'

I shut my eyes tight, hoping like mad that it really was a nightmare. I badly wanted to be back in bouncy bed number six in the lovely new house. I put my hands over my ears to blot out Hank's bawling and tried hard to dream myself back into that bed. I felt I was very nearly there . . . but then Mack's big hand shook my shoulder.

'What are you playing at, Elsa? Stop screwing up your face like that, you look like you're having a fit or something,' said Mack.

I glared and shook my shoulder free. I shuffled away from him, scuffing my trainers on the worn carpet. I saw a door at the end of the hallway. It had a nameplate.

I pushed the door open and peeped round. There was a little man in a brown suit sitting at a desk. A big lady in a fluffy pink jumper was sitting at the desk too. She was perched on the man's lap and they were *kissing*. When they saw me the lady leapt up, going pink in the face to match her jumper. The little man seemed to be catching his breath. No wonder. The lady was *very* big, especially in certain places.

'Excuse me,' I said politely. After all, I'd just been told that manners don't cost a penny.

'Come on now, out of here,' said the big lady, shooing at me as if I was a stray cat. 'And don't hang around the reception area either. I'm sick and tired of you kids turning this hotel into a play-park. You go up to your room, do you hear me?'

'That's right. Go to your room, little girly,' said the man in the brown suit, trying to brush all the bitty pink hairs away.

'But I haven't *got* a room,' I said. 'We've only just come here and we don't know where to go.'

'Well, why didn't you *say?*' said the fluffy pink lady, and she flounced out of the room, beckoning me with one of her long pink finger-nails.

Hank was still howling out in the hall. Pippa was whispering and Mum was muttering and Mack was pacing the carpet like a caged animal, looking as if he was ready to bite someone.

'*So* sorry to have kept you waiting,' said the big lady, and she nipped round the corner of the counter and smiled a big pink lipsticky smile. 'On behalf of the management, I'd like to welcome you to the Royal Hotel. I hope your stay with us will be a pleasant one.'

'Well, we're hardly here on holiday,' said Mum, wrestling with Hank. She sat him down on the counter to give her arms a rest. Hank perked up a little. He spotted what looked like a very very big pink bunny rabbit and started crawling rapidly towards it, drooling joyfully.

'Please try to keep your children under control!' said the big lady, swatting nervously at the advancing baby. 'I'll have to process all your particulars.'

This took for ever. Hank howled mournfully, deprived of his cuddle with the giant pink bunny. Mum sighed. Mack tutted and strutted, working himself up into a temper. Pippa started hopping about and holding herself. There was going to be a puddle on the carpet if we didn't watch out.

'Mum, Pippa's needing the toilet,' I hissed.

'Shut *up*, Elsa,' said Pippa, squirming.

Mum cast an experienced eye at Pippa.

'You'd better take her, Elsa,' she said.

The big lady paused whilst sorting through our particulars and pointed the way down the hall and round the corner. I took Pippa's arm and hurried her along. We passed the Manager's office. His door was ajar. Like my joke.

We had a quick peek at him. He was still sitting at his desk. He'd kicked his shoes off and put his feet up. One of his socks had a hole.

His toe stuck through and looked so silly that Pippa and I got the giggles. The Manager heard and looked cross and we scooted quickly down the corridor. We had to dash, anyway, because it was getting a bit dodgy for Pippa to be laughing in her current circumstances.

Things got dodgier still because we seemed to take a wrong turning and blundered around unable to find the toilets. We came across a gang of boys as we rounded a corner. They were busy writing something on the wall with black felt-tip pen.

'Don't ask them, they'll laugh at us,' said Pippa urgently.

They laughed at us anyway, making rude comments about us as we rushed past. You know the sort of things boys shout out.

'They are *rude*,' said Pippa.

They were ruder than Pippa realized. She can't read yet. *I* read what they were writing on the wall.

We hurried on, turned another corner, and suddenly I saw one of those funny little lady outlines stuck up on the door.

I don't know why they design the lady in that weird sticky-out frock. And she hasn't got any arms, poor thing, so she'd have a job using the loo herself, especially when it came to pulling the chain.

I was still busy contemplating this little lady while Pippa charged inside. I heard the door bang shut.

'Did you make it in time, Pippa?' I called.

'Shut *up*,' Pippa called back.

It sounded as if her teeth were gritted. I stepped inside to find out why. There was someone else in the Ladies. A girl about my own age was sitting on the windowsill with her feet propped on the edge of the washbasin. She was reading a book. Well, she had her eyes on the page, but you could tell we were disturbing her a bit.

'Hello,' I said.

She nodded at me, looking a bit nervous.

'I'm Elsa. And that's my sister Pippa sitting in the toilet.'

'Don't keep *telling* everyone!' Pippa shouted from inside.

'Sisters!' I said, raising my eyebrows.

'Brothers are worse,' said the girl. 'I've got three.'

'I've got one too. He's only a baby but he's still awful. I have to look after him sometimes.'

'I have to look after my brothers all of the time. Only I get fed up because they keep pestering me. So sometimes I slip in here for a bit of peace.'

'Good idea. So what's your name, then?'

'Naomi.'

'Hi, Naomi. I'm Elsa.'

'Yes, you said.'

'How long have you been here then?'

'Sitting in the basin?'

'No! In this place. The hotel.'

'About six months.'

'You haven't! Gosh.'

I was too busy thinking to carry on chatting. I'd thought we'd stay in the hotel a week or two at the most. As if we really were on holiday. I hadn't realized we might be stuck here for months and months.

Pippa pulled the chain and came out of the toilet. Naomi swung her skinny legs out of the way so that Pippa could wash her hands. There weren't any towels so I let Pippa wipe her hands on my T-shirt. Naomi settled her feet back again.

I looked at her. I looked at the tap.

'I could give your feet a little paddle,' I said.

'Don't,' said Naomi.

I thought about it.

'No, OK.'

I smiled at her. She smiled back. Things were looking up. I'd only just got here and yet I'd already made a friend.

I took Pippa's damp hand and we set off back down the corridor.

'I like that girl,' said Pippa.

'That's my friend. Naomi.'

'She can be my friend too. I like her hair. All the little plaits. Will you do my hair like that, Elsa?'

'It looks a bit too fiddly. Come on, quick.' We were going past the boys again. They said some more rude things. Really awful things.

'You think you're so clever, but you can't even spell,' I said, snatching the felt-tip. I crossed out the worst word and wrote it correctly.

That showed them. Pippa and I skipped on down the corridor and eventually found our way back to the foyer.

'There you are! I was beginning to think you'd got lost,' said Mum.

The big lady was handing over a key to Mack.

'One room for all five of us?' said Mack.

'It's a family room, with full facilities.'

Mack stared at the number tag.

'Room six-oh-eight?'

'That's right.'

'That doesn't mean we're up on the sixth floor, does it?'

'You got it.'

'But we've got little kids. You can't shove us right up at the top, it's stupid.'

'It's the only room available at the moment. Sorry,' said the big lady, fluffing up her jumper.

'There is a lift?' said Mum.

'Oh yes, there's a lift,' said the big lady. 'Only the kids have been messing around and it's not working at the moment. We're getting it fixed tomorrow. Meanwhile, the stairs are over there.'

It took us a long while and several journeys to get us and all our stuff up those stairs.

But at long last we were all crowded into room 608. Our new home.

I thought a family room would have room for a family. Something like this:

Only room 608 wasn't quite how I'd imagined. It was a bit cramped to say the least. And by the time we'd squeezed inside with all our stuff, we couldn't even breathe without bumping into each other.

'Home sweet home,' said Mum, and she burst into tears.

'Don't start on the waterworks,' said Mack. 'Come on, hen, it's not as bad as all that.'

'It's worse,' said Mum, trying to swallow her sobs. It sounded as if she was clucking. Like a hen. Mack calls her that when he's trying to be

42

nice. And he sometimes calls Pippa 'Ma Wee Chook', which is probably Scottish for chick. Hank is too big and barging about to be a chick. He's more like a turkey. I don't get called anything. I am not part of Mack's personal farmyard.

I stepped over all our stuff and climbed across a bed or two and made it to the window. It was probably a good thing it had bars, especially with Hank starting to pull himself up. He'd be able to climb soon and he's got so little sense he'd make for the window first thing. But I didn't like the bars all the same. It felt as if we were all in a cage.

It wasn't just us and our family. We could hear the people in room 607 having an argument. And the people in room 609 had their television on so loudly it made our room buzz with the conversation. The people underneath us in room 508 were playing heavy-metal music and the floor bumped up and down with the beat. At least the sixth floor was the top floor, so there was no-one up above us making a racket.

'It's bedlam,' said Mum.

Bedlam is some old prison place where they put mad people, but it made me think of beds. I flopped down on to one of the single beds. It gave a creak and a groan. I didn't bounce a bit on this bed. I just juddered to a halt. Bed number seven was a disappointment.

I tried the other single bed, just in case that was better. It was worse. The mattress sagged right down through the bedsprings. I set them all jangling as I jumped on.

'Elsa! Will you quit that!' Mack yelled.

'I was just trying out my bed, that's all. Sussing out where we're all going to sleep.' I decided to crack a bed joke to cheer us all up. 'Hey, where do baby apes sleep?'

'Give it a rest, Elsa, eh?' Mum sniffed.

'No, listen, it's good this one, really. Where do baby apes sleep? Can't you guess? Baby apes sleep in apricots.' I waited. They didn't even titter. '*Apricots*,' I said clearly, in case they hadn't got it first time round.

'Sh! Keep your voice down. Everyone can hear what you're saying,' said Mum.

'Then why isn't everybody laughing?' I said. 'Look, don't you get it? Baby apes . . . '

'That's *enough*!' Mack thundered. 'Button that lip.'

Honestly!

44

Then I had to unbutton, because I'd just thought of something.

'What about Hank? There isn't a bed for him,' I said.

We all looked round the room, as if a bed might suddenly appear out of nowhere.

'This will be Hank's little bedroom in here,' said Pippa, opening a cupboard door that stuck right out into the room, taking up even more of the space. It wasn't another bedroom. It was the shower and the loo and the washbasin, all cramped in together.

'We're going to be able to save time, you know. I reckon you could sit on the loo and clean your teeth and stick your feet in the shower all at the same time,' I said. 'Let's have a try, eh?'

'Look, come out of there, Elsa, and stop mucking about,' said Mum. 'This is ridiculous. Where *is* Hank going to sleep?'

'I'll go downstairs and tell them we're needing another bed,' said Mack.

'Yes, but where are we going to put it?' said Mum. 'There's no room to move as it is.'

'Maybe we'll have to take it in turns to move,' I said. 'You and Mack could stand in the shower while Pippa and Hank and I play for a bit, and then you could yell "All change" and we'll cram into the shower and you two could walk round and round the beds for a bit of exercise.'

I thought it an extremely sensible idea but they didn't think so.

'You'll be the one standing in the shower if you don't watch it,' said Mack. 'And the cold water will be on too.' He laughed. That's *his* idea of a joke.

He went all the way downstairs to tackle the big lady about another bed. Mum sat on the edge of the double bed, staring into space. Her eyes were watery again. She didn't notice when Hank got into her handbag and started licking her lipstick as if it was an ice lolly. I grabbed him and hauled him into the tiny shower space to mop him up a bit. The hot water tap in the basin was only lukewarm. I tried the shower to see if that had any hot. I couldn't work out how to switch it on. Pippa squeezed in too to give me a hand. I suddenly found the right knob to turn. I turned it a bit too far actually.

Mack's joke came true. It wasn't very funny. But at least we all got clean. Our clothes had a quick wash too. I dried us as best I could. I thought Mum might get mad but she didn't say a word. She just went on staring, as if she was looking right through the wall into room 607. They were still having their argument. It was getting louder. They were starting to use a lot of rude words.

'Um!' said Pippa, giggling.

Mack came storming back and he was mumbling a lot of rude words too. The hotel management didn't supply beds for children under two.

'Hank will have to go back in his cot,' he said, and he started piecing the bits of the old duck cot together again.

'But it's falling to bits now. And Hank's so big and bouncy. He kept thumping and jumping last time he was in it. He'll smash it up in seconds,' I said.

'And that's not Hank's cot any more. It's my Baby Pillow's bed,' said Pippa indignantly.

'Baby Pillow will have to sleep with you, my wee chook,' said Mack.

'But he won't like that. Baby Pillow will cry and kick me,' said Pippa.

'Well, you'll just have to cry and kick him back,' said Mack, reaching out and giving her a little poke in the tummy. He noticed her T-shirt was a little damp.

'Here, how come you're soaking wet?' said Mack, frowning.

I held my breath. If Pippa told on me I wouldn't half be for it. Yes, for it. And five it and six it too.

But Pippa was a pal. She just mumbled something about splashing herself, so Mack grunted and got on with erecting the duck cot for Hank. I gratefully helped Pippa find Baby Pillow and all his things from one of the black plastic rubbish bags we'd carted from our old house.

My sister Pippa is crackers. Mack was always buying her dolls when he was in work and we were rich. All the different Barbies, My Little Ponies, those big special dolls that walk and talk and wet, but Pippa's only ever wanted Baby Pillow. Baby Pillow got born when Mum had Hank. Pippa started carting this old

48

pillow round with her, talking to it and rocking it as if it were a baby. He's rather a backward baby if he's as old as Hank, because he hasn't started crawling yet. If I'm feeling in a very good mood I help Pippa feed Baby Pillow with one of Hank's old bottles and we change his old nappy and bundle him up into an old nightie and then we tuck him up in the duck cot and tell him to go to sleep. I generally make him cry quite a bit first and Pippa has to keep rocking him and telling him stories.

'We won't be able to play our game if Hank's got to go in the duck cot,' Pippa grumbled.

But when Mack had got the cot standing in the last available spot of space and we tried stuffing Hank into his old baby bed, Hank himself decided this just wasn't on. He howled indignantly and started rocking the bars and cocking his leg up, trying to escape.

'He'll have that over in no time,' said Mack. 'So what are we going to do, eh?'

He looked over at Mum. She was still staring into space. She was acting as if she couldn't hear Mack or even Hank's bawling.

'Mum?' said Pippa, and she clutched Baby Pillow anxiously.

'Hey, Mum,' I said, and I went and shook her shoulder. She wasn't crying any more. This was worse. She didn't even take any notice of me.

'Here,' said Mack, grabbing Hank, hauling him out of the cot and dumping him into Mum's lap.

For a moment Mum kept her arms limply by her side, her face still blank. Hank howled harder, hurt that he was getting ignored. He raised his arms, wanting a hug. He stretched higher, lost his balance, and nearly toppled right off Mum's lap and on to the floor. But just in time Mum's hands grabbed him and pulled him close against her chest.

'Don't cry. I've got you,' said Mum, sighing. She blinked, back in herself again.

'Where's the wee boy going to sleep, then?' Mack asked again.

Mum shrugged.

'He'll have to sleep with one of his sisters, won't he,' she said.

'Not me!' I said quickly.

'Not me either,' said Pippa. 'He wets right out of his nappies.'

Hank went on crying.

'He's hungry,' said Mum. 'We could all do with a drink and a bite to eat. I'm going to go and find this communal kitchen. Here Hank, go to Daddy. And you girls, you get all our stuff unpacked from those bags, right?'

Yes, everything was all right again. Mum rolled up her sleeves and got the cardboard box with our kettle and our pots and pans and some tins of food and went off to find the kitchen. Mack romped on the bed with Hank, and he stopped crying and started chuckling. Pippa said Baby Pillow was still crying though, and she insisted she had to tuck him up in the duck cot and put him to sleep.

So I got lumbered doing most of the unpacking. There were two bags full of Pippa's clothes and Hank's baby stuff. There was an old suitcase stuffed with Mum and Mack's clothes and Mum's hairdryer and her make-up and her precious china crinoline lady. And there was my carrier bag. I don't have that many clothes because I always get them mucked up anyway. I've got T-shirts and shorts for the summer, and jumpers and jeans for the winter, and some knickers and socks and stuff. I've got a

51

Minnie Mouse hairbrush though it doesn't ever get all the tangles out of my mane of hair. I've got a green marble that I used to pretend was magic. I've got my box of felt-tip pens. Most of the colours have run out and Pippa mucked up some of the points when she was little, but I don't feel like throwing them away yet. Sometimes I colour a ghost picture, pretending the colours in my head. Then there are my joke books. They are a bit torn and tatty

because I thumb through them so often.

I hoped Mum would be ever so pleased with me getting all our stuff sorted out and the room all neat and tidy but she came back so flaming mad she hardly noticed.

'This is ridiculous,' she said, dumping the cardboard box so violently that all the pots and pans played a tune. 'I had to queue up for ages just to get into this crummy little kitchen, and then when some of these other women were finished and I got my chance, I realized that it was all a waste of time anyway. You should see the state of that stove! It's filthy. I'd have to scrub at it for a week before I'd set my saucepans on it. Even the floor's so slimy with grease I nearly slipped and fell. What are we going to do, Mack?'

'You're asking Big Mack, right?' said Mack, throwing Hank up in the air so he shrieked with delight. 'Big Mack says let's go and eat Big Macs at McDonald's.'

Pippa and I shrieked with delight too. Mum didn't look so thrilled.

'And what are we going to live on for the rest of the week, eh?' she said. 'We can't eat out all the time, Mack.'

'Come on now, hen, give it a rest. You just now said we can't eat in. So we'll eat out today. Tomorrow will just have to take care of itself.'

'The sun will come out tooomorrow . . .' I sang. I maybe don't have a very sweet voice but it is strong.

'Elsa! Keep your voice down!' Mum hissed.

Mack pulled a silly face and covered up his ears, pretending to be deafened.

We sang the Tomorrow song at school. It comes from a musical about a little orphan girl called Annie. Occasionally I think I'd rather like to be Little Orphan Elsa.

Still, I cheered up considerably because McDonald's is one of my all-time favourite places. Mum changed Hank and we all got ready to go out. It was odd using the little loo in the bedroom. Pippa didn't like it with everybody listening so I trekked down the corridor with her to find a proper ladies' toilet. If Mum saw it she'd get flaming mad again. Pippa got even more upset, hopping about agitatedly, so I ended up trailing her down six flights of stairs and down the corridor to the toilet where we met Naomi. I hoped she might still be there, but she'd gone. The boys weren't hanging around any more either. The rude words were still on the wall though.

We'd worked up quite an appetite by the time we'd trudged up the stairs to put on our jumpers and then down all over again with Mum and Mack and Hank. It was a long long walk into the town to find the McDonald's too. Pippa started to lag behind and Mum kept twisting her ankle in her high heels. I started to get a bit tired too, and my toes rubbed up against the edge of my trainers because they're getting too small for me. Mum moaned about being stuck in a dump of a hotel at the back of beyond and said she couldn't walk another step. Mack stopped at a phone box and said he'd call a cab then, and Mum said he was crazy and it was no wonder we'd all ended up in bed and breakfast.

It was starting to sound like a very big row. I was getting scared that we'd maybe end up with no tea at all. But then we got to a bus stop and a bus came along and we all climbed on and we were in the town in no time. At McDonald's.

Mack had his Big Mac. Mum had chicken nuggets. I chose a cheeseburger and Pippa did too because she always copies me. Hank nibbled his own French fries and experienced his very first strawberry milkshake.

It was great. We didn't have a big row. We didn't even have a little one. We sat in the warm, feeling full, and Mack pulled Pippa on

to his lap and Mum put her arm round me, and Hank nodded off in his buggy still clutching a handful of chips.

We looked like an ordinary happy family having a meal out. But we didn't go back to an ordinary happy family house. We had to go back to the Bed-and-Breakfast hotel.

The people in 607 were still arguing. The people in 609 still had their television blaring. The people in 508 were still into heavy-metal music. And it was even more of a squash in room 608.

We all went to bed because there wasn't much else to do. Mum and Mack in the double bed. Pippa and Hank either end of one single bed. Me in the other. Baby Pillow the comfiest of the lot in the duck cot.

Hank wasn't the only one who wet in the night. Pippa did too, so she had to creep in with me. She went back to sleep straightaway, but I didn't. I wriggled around uncomfortably, Pippa's hair tickling my nose and her elbow digging into my chest. I stared up into the dark while Mack snored and Hank snuffled and I wished I could rise out of my crowded bed, right through the roof and up into the starry sky.

Sugar Sandwiches for Breakfast

We've always had different breakfasts. Mum's never really bothered. She just likes a cup of coffee and a ciggie. She says she can't fancy food early in the morning. She cooks for Mack though. He likes great greasy bacon sandwiches and a cup of strong tea with four sugars. I'd like four sugars in my tea but Mum won't let me. It's not fair. She does sometimes let me have a sugar sandwich for my breakfast though, if she's in a very good mood. I say *she* needs to eat a sugar sandwich to sweeten herself up.

Pippa likes sugar sandwiches too, because she always copies me. Hank has a runny boiled egg that certainly runs all over him. His face is

bright yellow by the time he's finished his breakfast, and he always insists on clutching his buttered toast soldiers until he's squeezed them into a soggy pulp. Sometimes I can see why Mum can't face food herself. Mopping up my baby brother would put anyone off their breakfast.

Mum certainly didn't look like she wanted any breakfast our first morning at the Royal. She'd obviously tossed and turned a lot in the night because her hair was all sticking up at the back. Her eyes looked red and sore. I'd heard her crying in the night.

'How about you taking the kids down to breakfast, Mack?' she said pleadingly. 'I don't think I could face it today. I'm feeling ever so queasy.'

'Aw, come on, hen. I can't cope with all three of them on my own. I'm not Mary Piddly Poppins.'

'You don't have to cope with me,' I said indignantly.

'I sometimes wish to God I didn't,' Mack growled.

He's always like that with me. Ready to bite my head off. He's the one who's like a lion, not me.

I wish I could figure out some way of taming him.

'I'll feed Hank for you, Mum, and see that Pippa has a proper breakfast,' I promised kindly.

'Your mum's going to have a proper breakfast herself,' said Mack. 'That's what she needs to make her feel better. A good cooked breakfast. And if we're getting it as part of this lousy bed-and-breakfast deal then we ought to make sure we all eat every last mouthful.'

'All right, I'm coming,' said Mum, slapping a

bit of make-up on her pale face and fiddling with her hair. She took out her mirror from her handbag and winced. 'I look a right sight,' she wailed.

'You look fine to me,' said Mack, giving her powdered cheek a kiss. 'And you'll look even better once you've got a fried egg and a few rashers of bacon inside you.'

'Don't, Mack! You're going to make me throw up,' said Mum.

I'd throw up if Mack started slobbering at me like that.

We trailed down all the stairs to the ground floor, where this breakfast room was supposed to be. Mack started sniffing, his hairy nostrils all aquiver.

'Can't smell any bacon sizzling,' he said.

We soon found out why. There wasn't any bacon for breakfast. There wasn't very much of anything. Just pots of tea and bowls of corn-flakes and slices of bread, very white and very square, like the ceiling tiles in reception. You just went and served yourself and sat at one of the tables.

'No bacon?' said Mack, and he stormed off to the reception desk.

'Hank needs his egg,' said Mum, and she marched off after Mack, Hank balanced on her hip.

Pippa and I sighed and shrugged our shoulders. We straggled off after them.

The big lady was behind the desk. She was wearing a fluffy blue jumper this time. I hoped she'd painted her fingernails blue to match, but she hadn't. Still, Mack was certainly turning the air blue, shouting and swearing because there weren't any cooked breakfasts.

'It's your duty to provide a proper breakfast. They said so down at the Social. I'm going to report you,' Mack thundered.

'We don't have any duty whatsoever, sir. If you don't care to stay at the Royal Hotel then why don't you leave?' said the big lady.

'You know very well we can't leave, because we haven't got anywhere else to go. And it's a disgrace. My kids need a good breakfast – my baby boy needs his protein or he'll get ill,' said Mum.

She spoke as if Hank was on the point of starving right this minute, although she was sagging sideways trying to support her strapping great son. He was reaching longingly for this new blue bunny.

The big lady stepped backwards, away from his sticky clasp.

'We're providing extra milk for all the children at the moment. We normally do provide a full cooked breakfast but unfortunately we are temporarily between breakfast chefs, so in these circumstances we can only offer a continental breakfast. Take it – or leave it.'

We decided to take it.

'Continental breakfast!' said Mum, as we sat at a table in the corner. 'That's coffee in one of them cafetière thingys and croissants, not this sort of rubbish.' She flapped one of the limp slices of bread in the air. 'There's no goodness in this!'

There were little packets of butter and pots of marmalade. And sugar lumps. Lots of sugar lumps.

I got busy crushing and sprinkling. I made myself a splendid sugar sandwich. Pippa tried to make herself one too, but she wasn't much good at crushing the lumps. She tried bashing them hard on the table to make them shatter.

'Pippa! Give over, for goodness sake. Whatever are you doing?' said Mum, spooning cornflakes into Hank.

'It's Elsa's fault. Pippa's just copying her,' said Mack. 'Here, give me that sugar bowl and stop messing around. You'll rot your teeth and just have empty gums by the time you're twelve.'

I covered my teeth with my lips and made little gulpy noises to see what it would be like. I tried sucking at my sandwich to see if I'd still be able to eat without teeth. I swallowed before the lump in my mouth got soft enough, and choked.

'Elsa! Look, do you have to show us all up?' Mum hissed.

'Stop it!' said Mack. 'Otherwise you'll get a good smacking, see?'

I saw. I was trying like anything to stop choking. I got up, coughing and spluttering, and went over to the service hatch to get myself some more milk. There was a big black lady with a baby serving herself. I wondered if she might be Naomi's mum and asked her between coughs.

She said she wasn't, but helpfully banged me on the back. I took a long drink of milk and peered all round the room, hoping to spot Naomi. There were old people and young people and lots of little kids, black people and white people and brown people and yellow people, quiet people and noisy people and absolutely bawling babies. But I couldn't spot Naomi anywhere. Maybe she had her breakfast sitting in the washbasin in the Ladies.

I did spot one of the boys who'd been writing rude words all over the wall. He saw me looking at him and crossed his eyes and stuck out his tongue. I did likewise.

'Elsa!' Mum came and yanked me back to our table. 'Don't you dare make faces like that.'

I pulled another face, because I was getting fed up with everyone picking on me when it wasn't my fault. Then I saw a lovely lady with lots of little plaits come into the breakfast room. She had two little boys with her, and she was carrying a toddler. And there was a girl following on behind, her head in a book.

'NAOMI!' I yelled excitedly, jumping up.

Mack was taking a large gulp of tea at that precise second. Somehow or other the tea sprayed all down his front. He didn't look too happy. I decided to dash over to Naomi pretty sharpish.

'Hi, Naomi. I've been looking out for you. Is this your mum? Are these your brothers?'

I said hello to them all and they smiled and said hello back.

'Is that your dad over there? That man shouting at you,' said Naomi.

'No fear,' I said. 'What are you reading then, eh?'

I had a quick peer. The cover said *Little Women* and there was a picture of four girls in old-fashioned frocks.

'*Little Women*?' I said, thinking it a rather naff title.

'It's a lovely book, one of the classics,' said Naomi's mum proudly. 'My Naomi's always reading it.'

'Boring,' I mumbled, peering at the pages.

'*The Cursed Werewolf seized the young maiden and ripped her to pieces with his huge yellow teeth. . .*'

'There's a werewolf in *Little Women?*' I said, astonished.

'Sh!' said Naomi, giving me a nudge. She turned her back so that her mum couldn't see and quickly lifted the dustjacket off *Little Women*. She had a different book entirely underneath. *The Cursed Werewolf Runs Wild.*

'Ah,' I said. I decided I liked Naomi even more.

I sat down at their table, even though Mack was bellowing fit to bust for me to come back at once OR ELSE. Naomi's little brothers looked utterly angelic above the table, all big eyes

and smiley mouths, but they were conducting a violent kicking match out of sight. One of the kicks landed right on my kneecap. I gave a little scream and both boys looked anxiously at their mum. I didn't tell tales, but I seized hold of several skinny legs and tickled unmercifully. They squirmed and doubled up.

'Boys!' said Naomi's mum. 'Stop messing about.'

She was trying to feed the baby but he kept fidgeting and turning his head away, not wanting his soggy old cornflakes.

'Come on, Nathan,' said Naomi's mum.

Nathan shut his mouth tight and let cornflake mush dribble down his chin.

'How about feeding him like an aeroplane?' I suggested. 'My baby brother Hank likes it when I do that. Here, I'll show you.'

I took the spoon, filled it with flakes, and then let my arm zoom through the air above Nathan's head.

'Here's a loaded jumbo jet coming in to land,' I said and made very loud aeroplane noises.

Nathan opened his mouth in astonishment and I shoved the spoon in quick.

'Unloading bay in operation,' I said, and I unhooked the empty spoon from his gums.

'Come on then, Nathan, gobble gobble, while I go looking for the next aeroplane. Hey, how about a Concorde this time?'

Nathan chewed obediently while I reloaded the spoon and held it at the right Concorde angle. I revved up my sound system.

Unfortunately, my dear non-relative Uncle Mack was revving up his own sound system. After one last bellow he came charging like a bull across the breakfast room.

I landed Concorde, unloaded the new cargo of cornflakes inside Nathan, and tried turning the spoon into a bomber plane with mega-quick, whizz-bang missiles.

Mack certainly exploded. But not in the way I wanted.

'How dare you make this ridiculous noise and bother these poor people,' he roared, yanking me up from the table.

'Oh no, she's been no bother at all,' said Naomi's mum quickly. 'So Elsa's your daughter, is she?'

'No!' I said.

'No!' Mack said.

It was about the only thing we ever agreed on.

'Elsa is my stepdaughter,' said Mack. He said the word 'step' as if it was some disgusting swear word. 'I've done my best to bring her up as if she was my own, but she gets right out of hand sometimes.'

I wished I was out of his hand at that precise moment. He was holding me by the shoulders, his fingers digging in hard.

'Well, she's been a very good girl with us, helping me keep my family in order,' said Naomi's mum.

'Yes, she got my baby brother Nathan to eat up all his cornflakes,' said Naomi.

'It's a pity she can't help out with her own brother and sister then,' said Mack. 'Come on, Elsa, your mum needs you.'

He gave a jerk and a pull. I had to go with him or else get my arm torn off. I looked back at Naomi.

'The Cursed Werewolf!' I mouthed, nodding at Mack.

Naomi nodded, grinning at me sympathetically.

I needed sympathy. Mack was in a foul mood.

'What do you think you're doing, rushing

around yelling your head off?' he yelled, rushing around.

I could sense it wasn't quite the right time to point out that I was only following my step-daddy's example. He got me sat back at our table and started giving me this right old lecture about learning to do as I was told. Pippa started fidgeting and shifting about on her chair as if she were the one getting the lecture, not me.

'I'm needing to go to the toilet,' she announced.

'Well, off you go then,' said Mack.

'I can't find it by myself,' said Pippa.

'I'll take her,' I said, jumping at the chance.

I clutched Pippa's hand and escaped the Werewolf's copious curses. Some of the boys were back down the corridor, writing more rude words on the walls. An old lady with a hoover rounded a corner and saw what they were up to.

'Here, you clean that off, you little var-mints,' she yelled, aiming her vacuum at them.

They laughed and said the words to her.

'Dirty beasts,' said the hoover lady.

She saw us gawping.

'Cover your ears up, girls. And you'd better close your eyes too. These little whatsits are

desecrating this hotel. Blooming desecrating
it, that's what they are.' She banged up
against the boys with the vacuum, running the
suction nozzle up and down the nearest's shell
suit.

'Get off, will you! My mum's only just bought
me this,' he yelled indignantly.

'I'm just trying to clean you up, laddie. Get
some of the dirt off you. Now clear off, the lot of
you, or I'll fetch the Manager.'

They straggled away while she held her
vacuum aloft in victory. Pippa and I giggled.
Mrs Hoover followed us into the Ladies so she
could have a quick smoke.

'Dear oh dear, this place will be the death of me,' she said, lighting up. She tucked her ciggies and matches back in her pocket and flexed her legs in her baggy old trousers. 'It used to be a really classy establishment back in the old days. A really nice business hotel. You could get fantastic tips and everyone spoke to you ever so pleasant. Now you just get a mouthful of abuse. They're all scum that stay here now. Absolute scum.'

She said this very fiercely and then blinked a bit at me.

'No offence meant, dearie. You seem very nice little girls, you and your sister.'

'Are we just a bit scummy round the edges then?' I said.

'You what? Oh, give over!' She drew on her cigarette, chuckling.

'What's scum?' said Pippa, emerging from the toilet and going to wash her hands.

'That's scum,' I said, wiping my finger round the edge of the grey basin.

'Now dear, don't shame me. I used to keep this place so clean you could eat your dinner out of one of them basins. But now I just lose heart. And the management's so mean, they keep cutting down the staff. How can I keep all this place spick and span, eh, especially with my legs.' She patted at her trousers and shook her head. Then she had another glance at the basin. 'Look, that's a footprint, isn't it? Dear goodness, would you credit it? They're actually putting their feet in the basins now.'

'I wonder who on earth that could be,' I said, winking at Pippa.

'I know!' said Pippa, not understanding my meaningful wink.

'No you don't,' I said quickly. 'Here, we could help you do a bit of the cleaning if you like, Pippa and me. I'm good at vacuuming. It's fun.'

I wasn't in any hurry to get back to the breakfast room and Mack. I wanted him to cool down a bit first. So Mrs Hoover sat stiffly on the stairs and did a bit of dusting and Pippa pottered about with a dustpan and brush while I switched on the vacuum and sucked up all the dust on the shabby carpet.

I kept imagining Mack was standing right in front of me. I'd charge at him and knock him flying and then get out a really giant suction nozzle. I wouldn't just snag his shell suit, *oh* no. I'd hoover him right out of existence.

74

I was galloping along the corridor, laughing fit to bust, when the real Mack suddenly came round the corner. He didn't look very cool at all. He looked as if he might very well be at boiling point.

'What the heck are you playing at, Elsa?'

'I'm not playing, I'm helping do the housework.'

'Switch it off! And don't answer me back like that,' Mack said. 'We thought you'd both got lost. You've been gone nearly half an hour. Didn't you realize you'd be worrying your mum? Elsa!'

'I thought you didn't want me to answer you,' I said.

Mack took a step nearer to me, breathing fire.

'Don't be cross with the kiddie, she's been ever such a help,' said Mrs Hoover. 'She's got this carpet up a treat, I'm telling you. And the little one's been sweeping the stairs, haven't you, pet?'

'Yes, well, I'll thank you to mind your own business,' said Mack, snatching Pippa up into his arms. 'You come with Daddy, chook. We've been worried sick, wondering what had happened to you.

75

Mum's been right up to our room and back, thinking you'd gone up there.'

Mack stomped round the corner, still clutching Pippa, and tripped right over the gang of giggling boys writing more dirty words on the wall.

'Get out of my way, you kids,' Mack thundered.

Pippa peered at the words from her new vantage point. She stared at the worst word of all. She remembered. She said it loudly and clearly.

'What did you say, Pippa?' said Mack, so taken aback he nearly dropped her.

So she said it again. Unmistakably.

'I'm reading, Dad,' she said proudly.

The boys absolutely cracked up at this, sniggering and spluttering.

'I'll wipe the smile off your silly faces!' Mack shouted, practically frothing at the mouth. 'How dare you write mucky words on the wall so that my little girl learns dirt like that?'

They stopped sniggering and started scattering, seeing that Mack meant business. Mack caught hold of one of them, the boy I'd made the face at. He was pulling faces again now, trying to wriggle free.

'It wasn't me that wrote that word, honest!' he yelled. 'It was her.'

He pointed to me. All his pals stopped and pointed to me too.

'Yes, it was that girl.'

'Yes, that one with all the hair.'

'Yeah, that little girl with the loud voice.'

It looked like I was in BIG TROUBLE.

I was.

I tried to explain but Mack wouldn't listen.

He hit. And I hurt.

Sweets for Treats

Mack stayed in a horrible mood all that day. All that *week*. And Mum wasn't much better. She didn't get mad at me and shout. She didn't say very much at all. She did a lot of that sitting on the bed and staring into space. Sometimes Mack could snap her out of it. Sometimes he couldn't.

I hated to see Mum all sad and sulky like that. I tried telling her jokes to cheer her up a bit.

'Hey Mum, what's ten metres tall and green and sits in the corner?'

'Oh Elsa, please. Just leave me be.'

'The Incredible Sulk!'

I fell about. But Mum didn't even smile.

'OK, try this one. Why did the biscuit cry?'

'What biscuit? What are you on about?'

'Any biscuit.'

'Can I have a biscuit, Mum?' said Pippa.

'Look, just listen to the *joke*. Why did the biscuit cry, eh? Because his mother was a wafer so long.'

I paused. Nobody reacted.

'Don't you get it?'

'Just give it a rest, Elsa, please,' Mum said, and she lay back on her bed and buried her head under the pillow.

I stared at Mum worriedly. I so badly wanted her to cheer up.

'Mum? Mum.' I went over to her and shook her arm.

'Leave her be,' said Mack.

I took no notice.

'Mum, what happened to the lady who slept with her head under the pillow?'

Mum groaned.

'When she woke up she found the fairies had taken all her teeth out!'

Mum didn't twitch.

'Elsa, I'm telling you. Leave her alone,' Mack growled.

I tried just one more.

'Are you going to sleep, Mum? Listen, what happened to the lady who dreamed she was eating a huge great marshmallow?'

'Can I have a marshmallow?' said Pippa.

'When she woke up her pillow had disappeared!'

Mum didn't move. But Mack did.

'I'm warning you, Elsa. Just one more of your stupid jokes and you're for it!'

'Dad, can I have some biscuits or some sweets or something? I'm hungry,' Pippa whined.

'OK, OK.' Mack fumbled in his pocket for change. 'Take her down to that shop on the corner, Elsa. Here.'

'What do Eskimos use for money? Ice lolly!'

'I thought I told you. NO MORE JOKES!'

'OK, OK.' I grabbed Pippa and scooted out the room.

'Why are adults boring?' I asked her, as we went down the stairs. 'Because they're groan-ups.'

I roared with laughter. I'm not altogether sure Pippa understood, but she laughed too to keep me company. The big bunny lady in reception put her pointy finger to her lips and went 'Sh! Sh!' at us.

'She sounds like a train,' I said to Pippa. 'Hey, what do you call a train full of toffee?'

'Oh, toffee! Are you buying toffee? I like toffee too.'

'No, Pippa, you're not concentrating. What do you call a train full of toffee? A chew-chew train.'

Pippa blinked up at me blankly. I laughed. She laughed too, but she was just copying me like she always does. I wished she was old enough to appreciate my jokes. I longed to try them all out on Naomi, but she was at school.

That was one of the advantages of going to live at the O Yal Htl. I couldn't go to my old school because it was miles and miles away. No-one had said anything about going to any other school. I certainly wasn't going to bring the subject up.

I took hold of Pippa's hand and we went out of the hotel and down the road to where there was this one shop selling sweets and ciggies and papers and videos – all the things you need.

Some of the boys from the hotel were mucking around at the video stands, whizzing them round too fast and acting out bits from the films. One of them lunged at me with his hands all pointy, pretending to be Freddie from Elm Street.

81

'Ooooh, I'm so fwightened,' I said, sighing heavily. 'What are you lot doing here, anyway? Are you bunking off from school?'

They shuffled a bit so I was obviously right.

'Don't you tell on us or you'll get it, see,' said another, trying to act dead tough.

'Don't worry. *I* don't tell tales,' I said, looking witheringly at the funny-face boy who had told on me.

He shuffled a bit more, his face going red.

'Yeah, well, I didn't think your dad would get mad at you like that,' he said quickly.

'He's not my dad. He's just my mum's bloke, that's all.'

'Did he hit you? We heard you yelling.'

'You'd yell if he was laying into you.'

'Here. Have this,' said the funny-face boy, and he handed me his big black magic-marker pen, the one I'd used to correct his spelling to write the truly worst word ever.

'Hey, are you giving this to me?' I said.

'Yeah, if you want.'

'You bet I want! My own black felt-tip's run out. Hey, what goes black and white, black and white, black and white?'

'Hmm?' he said, looking blank.

But one of his mates spoilt it.

'A nun rolling down a hill,' he said, grinning. 'That's an *old* joke.'

'OK, OK, what's black and white and goes ha-ha?'

I paused. This time I'd got them.

'The nun that pushed her!'

Funny-face suddenly snorted with laughter. The others all sniggered too. Laughing at my joke! I'd have happily stood there cracking jokes all day but the man behind the counter started to get narked so the boys sloped off while Pippa and I chose our sweets. It took a long time, especially as Pippa kept chopping and changing. Once or twice she changed her mind *after* she'd had a little experimental lick of a liquorice bootlace or a red jelly spider, but the man behind the counter couldn't see down far enough to spot her.

We ended up with:

We ate them on the way back to the hotel.
We weren't in any hurry to get back. Mack had
been so grouchy recently he'd even got mad at
Pippa.

I meant to save a chocolate bar for Naomi,
and a toffee chew or two for her brothers, but I
seemed to get ever so hungry somehow, and by
the time Naomi got back from school there
were just a few dolly mixtures left (and they
were a bit dusty and sticky because Pippa had
been 'feeding' them to Baby Pillow half the
afternoon).

'Never mind, I'll give them a little wash
under the tap,' said Naomi, going into the
Ladies.

She and I scrunched up together on the
windowsill, feet propped on the basin, and we
read the worst bits of her Cursed Werewolf
book and got the giggles. My Pippa and her
Nicky and Neil and Nathan kept on plaguing
us so we filled the other basins with water and
hauled them up so they could have a little

paddle. They were only meant to dangle their feet. They dangled quite a bit more.

I was scared I'd get into trouble with Mum and Mack for getting Pippa soaked, but luckily Mum didn't notice and Mack had gone out for a takeaway and taken Hank with him. Hank loves to go anywhere with Mack. He's a really weird baby. He thinks his dad is great.

I think Mack is great too. A great big hairy warthog.

Pippa and Nicky and Neil and Nathan weren't the only ones who got soaked when they went paddling in the basins. The floor in the Ladies turned into a sort of sea too. Naomi and I tried to mop it up a bit but we only had loo paper to do it with so we weren't very successful.

Mrs Hoover had to mop it up properly and she wasn't very pleased. I felt bad about it so the next day Pippa and I helped her with her hoovering. I'd got lumbered with Hank as well, but I tried hard to get him to flick a duster. He seemed determined to use it as a cuddle blanket but Mrs Hoover didn't mind.

'Oh, what a little sweetie! Bless him!' she cooed.

'Have you got some sweeties?' Pippa asked hopefully.

'You're just like my little granddaughter, pet. Always on at her Nan for sweeties. Here you are, then.' Mrs Hoover gave us both a fruit drop. Hank had to make do with chewing his duster, because he might swallow the fruit drop whole and choke.

'Yum yum, I've got an orange. I nearly like them best. I like the red bestest of all,' said Pippa hopefully.

I tutted at her but Mrs Hoover tittered.

'You're a greedy little madam,' she said, handing over a raspberry drop too.

'What do you say, Pippa, eh?' I said.

'Thank you ever so much Mrs Hoover.'

'You what?' said Mrs Hoover, because Mrs Hoover wasn't her real name at all, it was just our name for her. Her real name was Mrs Macpherson but I didn't like calling her that because it reminded me too much of my Mack Person. My least favourite person of all time.

He'd given me another smack because Pippa and I were playing hunt the magic marble in our room and I'd hidden it under the rug covering the torn part of the carpet. How was I to know that Mack would burst back from the betting shop and stomp across the rug and skid on the marble and go flying?

I couldn't help laughing. He really did look hilarious. Especially when he landed bonk on his bum.

'I'll teach you not to laugh at me!' he said, scrabbling up.

He did his best.

But I've had the last laugh. I sloped off into the Ladies all by myself and had a little fun with my new black magic-marker pen.

Mega-Feast for Lunch

I soon got into a Royal Hotel routine. I always woke up early. I'd scrunch up in bed with my torch and my joke books and wise up on a few more wisecracks. I'd tell the jokes over and over until I had them off by heart. I'd often roll around laughing myself.

Sometimes I shook the bed so much Pippa woke up wondering if she was in the middle of an earthquake. If I caused earthquakes Pippa was liable to cause her own natural disasters. Floods.

Mum kept getting mad at her and saying she was much too big to be wetting the bed and she didn't let Pippa have anything to drink at teatime but it still didn't make much difference. Pippa cried because she was so thirsty and she *still* wet the bed more often than not.

So another of my little routines was to sneak all Pippa's wet bedclothes down to the laundry room before Mum and Mack woke up. There were only two washing machines and one dryer. You usually couldn't get near them. But early in the morning everyone was either fast asleep or getting the kids ready for school so there was a good chance I could wash the sheets out for my leaky little sister.

The only other people around were some of the Asian ladies in their pretty clothes. They looked like people out of fairy tales instead of ordinary mums in boring old T-shirts and leggings. They sounded as if they were saying strange and secret things too as they

whispered together in their own language. Some of their children could speak good English even though they'd only been over here a few months, but the mums didn't bother. They generally just stuck in a little clump together.

I felt a bit shy of them at first and I think they felt shy with me too. But after a few encounters in the laundry room we started to nod to each other. One time they'd run out of washing powder so I gave them a few sprinkles of ours. The next day they gave me half a packet back *and* a special pink sweet. It was the sweetest sweet I'd ever eaten in my life. It was so sweet it started to get sickly, and when I got back to room 608 I passed it on to Pippa. She enjoyed it hugely for a while but it finally got the better of her too. We rubbed a little on Hank's dummy and it kept him quiet half the morning.

Keeping Hank quiet was a task and a half at the hotel. He'd always been a happy sort of baby, even if he did act like a bit of a thug at times, bashing about with his fat fists and kicking hard with his bootees. But he'd never really whined and whimpered that much. Now he didn't seem to do much else. It was probably because he was so cooped up. He was just getting to the stage when he wanted to crawl around all over the place and explore. But he couldn't really crawl in room 608. It was much too little and crowded.

It was dangerous too. If you took your eye off him for two seconds he'd be doing this

or this

or this.

There was only one way to keep him out of mischief.

He didn't like it one little bit. He wanted to be up and about.

Mum and Mack didn't want to be up and about at all. They just wanted to sleep in. Most days they even stopped bothering to go down to breakfast. So Pippa and Hank and I had our breakfast and then we helped Mrs Hoover and then we played about in the corridor. We set Hank down at one end and charged up to the other end and had a very quick game before he caught up with us.

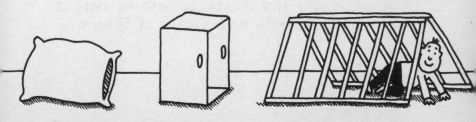

Hank got so good at crawling he could probably win a gold medal at the Baby Olympics. If we wanted any peace at all we had to change his crawling track into an obstacle race.

Sometimes we collected several babies and had a proper race. The other brothers and sisters placed bets. That was good. Pippa and I coined it in, because Hank always won.

We got a bit noisy and sometimes Mack would come staggering out into the corridor and tell us all to pipe down. He'd yell if he was in a bad mood but he didn't frighten anyone now. The kids just muttered amongst themselves about pimply bums and brain transplants and cracked up laughing. All the girls had read the jokes in the Ladies toilet downstairs. Even some of the boys had dashed in and out for a dare.

Mack and Mum often didn't get up properly until lunchtime. Lunch was my favourite meal of the day because I could nip along to the shop on the corner and choose it. I had to make sure I bought a packet of ciggies for Mum and the *Sun* for Mack, and maybe something boring like a carton of milk or a packet of biscuits –

but then I could buy crisps and Coke and chocolates and sweets and anything else I fancied with the money left over. Pippa and I always had a Mega-Feast.

SAMPLE WEEK'S MENU OF THE MEGA-FEAST

Monday: Apple juice, Mini Cheddars, Toffee Crisp, Woppa, Spearmint chew

Tuesday: Strawberry Ribena, Californian corn chips, Cadbury's Flake, Buster bar

Wednesday: Lucozade, Chicken Tikka Hula Hoops, Bounty, Flying Saucers

Thursday: Dr Pepper drink, Chipsticks, Galaxy, Sherbert Fountain

Friday: Coke, Salt-and-vinegar crisps, Crunchie, Fizz cola-bottle sweets

Saturday: Strawberry Break Time Milk, Pork scratchings, Picnic, Dolly-beads

Sunday: Lilt, Skips (chilli flavour), Fruit-and-nut chocolate, Giant Bootlace

This is all times two, because Pippa always copied me. Hank generally wanted a lick here and a munch there after he'd had his bottle and his baby tins, but there was still heaps left for us.

We sometimes went out in the afternoons. Once we went to the park.

I liked it best of all when Mack went down the betting shop and took Hank along too and Mum and Pippa and me went to the shops. Not the shop on the corner. Not the Kwik-Save or the off-licence or the chip shop down the road. The real shops in the town. Especially the

Flowerfields Shopping Centre. It's this great glass shopping mall with real flowers blossoming in big bouquets all round the entrance, and painted flowers spiralling over the door of each individual shop, and there are lovely ladies wandering round in long dresses who hand you a flower for free.

Mum and Pippa and I could spend hours and hours and hours wandering round the Flowerfields Shopping Centre.

Of course we couldn't ever buy the books or the tapes or the toys or the outfits. But we could go back the next day and the next and read and listen and play and try them on all over again. And then when we had to trail all the way back to the Oyal Htl and we were all tired and we didn't even have the money for the bus, we could still smell our flowers and pretend they were big bouquets.

I made up this story to myself that I was a famous comedienne and I'd just done this amazingly funny routine on stage and everyone had laughed and laughed and then they'd clapped and clapped and begged for an encore and showered me with roses . . .

'Hey, Mum, Pippa, what do you get if you cross a rose with a python?'

'Oh Elsa, please, give it a rest.'

'I don't know what you get – but don't try to smell it!' I laughed. Then I tried again.

'What did one rose say to the other rose?'

'Hello, Rose,' said Pippa. She laughed. 'Hey, I said the joke!'

'Don't you start too,' Mum groaned.

'That's not a joke, Pippa. It's not funny. No, *listen*. What did one rose say to the other rose? It said . . . Hi, Bud. See? *That's* funny.'

'No it's not,' said Mum.

I ignored her.

'All right then. What did the bee say to the flower?'

'Hi, flower?' said Pippa. 'Is that right? Have I said the joke now?'

'No! Pippa, you can't just say any old thing. It's got to be a joke. Now, what did the bee say to the flower? It said, Hello honey.'

'And I'm going to say Goodbye Sweetie if you dare come out with one more of your daft jokes,' said Mum, but she didn't really mean it. She was just joking herself.

Mum could still be a lot of fun, especially going round Flowerfields – but when we got back to room 608 she wilted like the flowers.

We spent the evenings indoors. So did everyone else around us. The people in room 607 had more arguments. The people in room 609 still had their telly blaring. The people underneath in room 508 still played their heavy-metal music. You could feel our room vibrating with the noise.

100

We tried going downstairs to the television lounge. Well, that was a laugh. There wasn't anywhere to lounge, like a sofa or a comfy armchair. There were just these old vinyl straight-back chairs, the same sort as in the breakfast room, but even older, so you had to play musical chairs finding the ones without the wobbly legs. There wasn't much of a television either. It was supposed to be colour but the switch wouldn't stay stable, so people's faces were gloomy grey for a bit and then suddenly blushed bright scarlet for no reason. There was something wrong with the sound too. It was all blurry and every time anyone talked there was a buzzing sound.

'I'm starting to feel that way myself,' said Mum, putting her hands over her ears.

'Don't throw another moody on me, for goodness sake,' said Mack. 'I can't stick this. I'm going out.'

Mum hunched up even smaller in her chair after he'd gone. I went over to her and tried putting my arm round her. She didn't seem to notice.

'Good riddance to bad rubbish,' I said fiercely.

We both knew where he'd gone. Down the pub. He'd drink all our money and then try to scrounge from some mates. And then he'd come staggering back and be all stupid and snore all night and in the morning he'd have such a sore head he'd snap at the least thing.

I got ten out of ten for an accurate prediction. But by the afternoon he was acting sorry. He'd won a bet down at the betting shop so he took Mum out in the evening while I babysat and then on Sunday morning he got up ever so early. I heard him go out before anyone else was awake. I couldn't help hoping he was maybe doing a runner. But he came back at ten o'clock, staggering again, but this time it was because he was carrying a television.

'I got it for a fiver at a car-boot sale,' he said triumphantly. 'There! Now we don't have to sit in that stupid lounge. We can watch our own telly. Great, eh?'

It wasn't a colour television, just a little old black-and-white portable set. It took ages to retune it when you changed channels, and of course you couldn't get Sky. But it *was* our own television. We could put the sound up so loud you could hardly hear the arguments in 607 and if we tuned into the same programme as the people in 609 it was like we were listening in stereo.

Mum didn't get so droopy now she had the television to watch. She switched on as soon as she woke up and it was still on long after I settled down to sleep. I liked to listen to it as I snuggled under the covers. But sometimes I put my head right down under my duvet and put my hands hard over my ears so that they made their own odd roaring noise and then I switched on this tiny private little television inside my own head. It was much better than the real thing because I could make up all my own programmes.

I was the lady on breakfast television interviewing people in my bedroom

and I was in all the soaps

and I won all the quizzes

and *Gladiators*

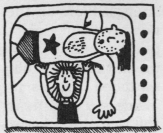

and I was in *Blue Peter*

and I was in
lots of films

and best of all I had my very own comedy show
and it was a huge success.

One Slurpy Square of Yorkie Bar

Just when I'd got into this happy little routine at the Royal, Mum went and mucked it all up. She stopped drooping. She started dashing about. She said we weren't going to be stuck in this crummy bed-and-breakfast dump a day longer. She went to the housing department and the social services and the DSS. She armed herself with Hank and Pippa and me, and whenever we were stuck too long in a queue she sent Pippa and me off sniping into enemy territory in quest of a toilet and she primed her Hank hand grenade and set him off howling.

Mum went into battle day after day, but it
didn't make any difference to where we lived.
We had to stay put because there wasn't anywhere else for us to go. But someone down the
Social told Mum about this drop-in centre
where the kids could play and you got cheap
food, so Mum thought she'd give it a go.

I didn't like the sound of it.

It wasn't that bad actually, just this big
room, half of it for the mums and half a crèche
for the kids. It was a bit of a crush in the crèche
and there was just this one woman going
crackers trying to keep all the kids chirpy.

We soon got them sorted out.

But then someone from the Council came and said the centre had to be closed because there wasn't any more money to fund it. Mum started moaning and creating, saying this drop-in centre was practically saving her life because we were stuck in a bed-and-breakfast hotel and it was no place for little kids. The Council Someone got a bit stammery because Mum can get ever so fierce when she feels like it, and he promised to put Hank's name down on the day nursery waiting list.

'Oh, very funny,' said Mum. 'He'll be twenty-one before he gets a blooming place.'

'This little girly here will be old enough for proper school soon,' he said, timidly patting Pippa.

Then he turned to me.

Oh-oh. I should have seen it coming and scarpered.

'Why isn't this girl in school, hmm? Now, I *can* help you here. We'll get her registered at the local school straightaway and she can start on Monday morning.'

Thanks a lot.

It had been the one ultra big bonus of life at the Oyal Htl. NO SCHOOL.

I knew Naomi and Funny-Face and most of the other kids at the hotel had to go. I'd hoped I'd not got noticed. I don't like school. Well, my first school was OK. There was a smiley teacher and we could play with pink dough and we all got to sing these soppy old nursery rhymes. I could sing loudest and longest.

But then we moved up to Scotland and I had to go to a new school and it was all different and I got teased because of the way I talk. Then we moved back down South and lived in the flats and that school was the sort where even the little kids get their heads held down the toilet. That was a pretty grim way of getting your hair washed. I didn't go a bundle on that school. But then the next one, my last school, wasn't so bad. That was when we were living in the lovely house and we were almost an ordinary family and even Mack didn't smack. Well, not so much.

It was a bit depressing though. They gave me all these tests and stuff and I couldn't do a lot of it. They thought I was thick. *I* thought I was thick. I had to go to these extra classes to help me with my reading and my writing and my sums. The other kids laughed at me.

I like it when people laugh at my jokes. But I can't stand it when they laugh at *me*.

But I had this really great remedial teacher, Mr Jamieson, only everyone called him Jamie, even us kids. He was very gentle and he didn't yell at you when you couldn't do something. He worked with me and whenever I learnt the least little thing he smiled and stuck his thumb up and said I was doing really fine. So I

felt fine and I learnt a lot more and then Jamie got me to do some other tests and it turned out I wasn't thick at all. I was INTELLIGENT.

Jamie asked me about all the other schools and he said that it was no wonder I hadn't been able to learn much, because I'd had so many changes. But now I could get stuck in and swoop through all the stuff I didn't know and Jamie said I'd soon end up top of the class, not bottom. So there.

But then Mack lost his job and we lost our house and we ended up in the Oyal Htl, miles and miles and miles away from my old school.

Still, if I had to go to school, that was the one I wanted to go to. So that I could still see Jamie.

'Of course you can't go, Elsa. You'd have to get two buses. And then walk miles. We can't afford the fares. And you'd wear out your trainers in weeks. No, you're to go to this Mayberry School where the other kids go.'

Only they didn't all go, of course. Naomi went. The Asian kids went. One or two others. But Funny-Face and nearly all the boys bunked off every day.

I decided that's what I'd do. I might know I was intelligent, but this school might give me the wrong sort of tests. I could easily end up being thought thick all over again. There was no guarantee at all I'd find another Jamie.

I started hanging around more with Funny-Face and the others. I had to work hard to get them to like me. I had to tell them lots and lots of jokes. They soon got sick of my usual repertoire. Get that fancy word. I'm *not* thick. I know lots and lots of things, though they're not usually the sort of things they like you to know in school. All comedians have to have a repertoire – it's all the jokes in their act. So to impress Funny-Face and his Famous Five followers I had to tell a few rude jokes. Naughty jokes. Blue jokes. Dirty jokes. You know the sort.

The trouble was that Pippa still hung round me most of the time, and she heard some of the jokes too. I told her and told her and told her that she mustn't repeat them, but one time she forgot. She told Mack.

And then guess what. SMACK.

'It wasn't my fault this time,' said Funny-Face afterwards.

'It was my fault,' said Pippa, and she burst into tears.

'You didn't mean to,' I said, giving her a cuddle. 'Here, don't cry, you soppy little thing. It's me he smacked, not you.'

'You don't hardly ever cry,' said Pippa.

'She's tough,' said Funny-Face, and he sounded admiring.

'Yeah, that's me. Tough as old boots,' I said, swaggering.

So on the Monday I was due to start school I set off with Naomi, but the minute we got down the road I veered off with Funny-Face and the Famous Five.

'Hey, Elsa. Why don't you come with me?' Naomi said, looking disappointed. 'I thought we were friends. Why do you want to go off with all the boys?'

'We are friends, Naomi. Course we are. I just don't want to go to this dopey old school, that's all. I'll see you after, same as usual, and we'll play in the toilets and have fun.'

'But it isn't a dopey school, really. And I hoped we'd get to be in the same class. I even swopped desks with this other girl so there'd be a place for you to sit beside me.'

'Oh Naomi,' I said, fidgeting. She was starting to make me feel bad. But I really didn't want to go to school. I didn't even want to be in Naomi's class and sit beside her. Naomi looked like she was really brainy, being a bookworm and all that. I knew I was intelligent, Jamie said so, but I hadn't quite caught up with all the things I'd missed, and maybe it would still look as if I was thick. I didn't want Naomi knowing.

So I went off with Funny-Face and the others. I bunked off with them all day long. It was OK for a while. We couldn't hang about the hotel or risk going round the town because someone would spot us and twig we were bunking off school, but we went to this camp place they'd made on a demolition site. It

wasn't much of a camp, just some corrugated iron shoved together with a blue tarpaulin for a roof. It was pretty crowded when we were all crammed in there knee-to-knee, and there was nothing to sit on, just cold rubbly ground.

'Well, you could make it a bit comfier, couldn't you?' said Funny-Face.

'Yeah, you fix it up for us, Elsa,' said one of his henchboys.

'Why me?' I said indignantly.

'You're a girl, aren't you?'

I snorted. I wasn't going along with that sort of sexist rubbish. They seemed to think they were Peter Pan and the Lost Boys and I was wet little Wendy.

'Catch me doing all your donkey work,' I said. 'Hey, what do you get if you cross a zebra and a donkey? A zeedonk. And what do you get if you cross a pig and a zebra? Striped

114

sausages.' I kept firing jokes at them as the resident entertainer, and so they stopped expecting me to be the chief cook and bottle-washer into the bargain.

They started bullying the littlest boy, a runny-nosed kid not much older than Pippa, getting him to run round the site finding sacks and stuff for us to sit on. He tripped over a brick and cut both his knees and got more runny-nosed than ever, so I mopped him up and told him a few more jokes to make him laugh. It was heavy going. His name was Simon and he certainly seemed a bit simple. But he was a game little kid and so I stuck up for him when the boys were bossing him around and when we were all squatting on our makeshift cushions and Funny-Face started passing round a crumpled packet of fags, I wouldn't let Simon sample a smoke.

'You don't want to mess around with ciggies, my lad, they'll stunt your growth,' I said firmly, and I gave him a toffee chew instead.

I spurned Funny-Face's fags too. I can't stick the smell and they make me go dizzy and I've seen my mum cough-cough-coughing every morning. But even though Simon and I didn't participate in the smoking session it still got so fuggy in the camp my head started reeling. It came as a relief when the blue tarpaulin suddenly got ripped right off and we were exposed by this other dopey gang of boys also bunking off from school. They threw a whole pile of dust and dirt all over us as we sat there gasping, and then ran away screeching with laughter.

So then, of course, Funny-Face and the Famous Five started breathing fire instead of inhaling it, and they went rampaging across the demolition site to wreak their revenge. I rampaged a bit too, but it all seemed a bit ridiculous to me. There was a pathetic sort of war with both gangs throwing stones rather wildly. Simon got over-excited and wouldn't keep down out of range, so he got hit on the head.

It was only a little bump and graze but it frightened him and he started yelling. The boys just stood about jeering at him, though they looked a bit shamefaced. So I rushed over to him going 'Mee-Maa Mee-Maa Mee-Maa' like an ambulance, and then I made a big production of examining him and pretending his whole head had been knocked off and he needed a major operation. Simon was so simple he believed me at first and started crying harder, but when he twigged it was all a joke he started to enjoy being the centre of attention as a major casualty of war.

The war seemed to have petered out anyway, and the rival gang wandered off down the chip shop because it was nearly lunchtime.

That proved to be a major drawback to bunking off. None of us lot had any lunch. We didn't have any spare cash either. As DSS kids we were entitled to a free school lunch but they just issued you with a ticket, not actual dosh you could spend. So as we weren't at school we were stuck. I began to wish I hadn't been so generous with my toffee chew.

One of the boys found half a Yorkie bar he'd forgotten about right at the bottom of his bomber-jacket pocket. The wrapping paper had disintegrated and the chocolate was liberally sprinkled with little fluffy bits and after he'd passed it round for everyone to nibble it was all slurpy with boy-lick too – but it was food, after all, so I ate a square.

I was still starving all afternoon and getting ever so bored with bunking off. I had to keep an eye on the time so as I knew when to go back to the Oyal Htl as if I'd just been let out of afternoon school. When you keep on looking at the time it doesn't half go s-l-o-w-l-y. Half a century seemed to plod past but it was only half an hour.

But e-v-e-n-t-u-a-l-l-y it was time to be making tracks. And then I found out I'd been wasting my time after all. Mum had decided to trot down to the school with Hank and Pippa to see how I'd got on for my first day. Only I wasn't there, obviously, so she went into the school to find me and of course the teacher said I hadn't ever arrived.

Mum was MAAAAAAAAD.

And then Mack got in on the act and you can guess what he did.

So I stormed off in a huff all by myself.

I sat there and it hurt where Mack had hit me and my tummy rumbled and I felt seriously fed up. But I didn't cry.

And then I heard footsteps. The clacky-stomp of high heels. It was Mum come to find me. I thought at first she might still be mad, but she sat right down beside me, even though she nearly split her leggings, and she put her arms round me. I did cry a bit then.

'I'm sorry, sausage,' she said, nuzzling into my wild lion's mane. 'I know he's too hard on you sometimes.

But it's just that you won't
do as you're told. And you've
got to go to school, Elsa.'

'It's not fair. I don't want
to go to that rotten old
school where I don't know
anyone.'

'You know that nice Naomi. She's your
friend! Oh, come on now, Elsa, you're never
shy. You!' Mum laughed and tweaked my nose.

'The others all bunk off. The boys.'

'I don't care about them. I care about you.
My girl. Now listen. You don't want to go to
school. *I* don't want you to go to school. I'd
much sooner have you round the hotel keeping
the kids quiet for me. I've missed you something chronic today.'

'Really?' I said, cheering up considerably.

'Yes, but *listen*. You've *got* to go to school
because it's the law, see, and if you don't go
they can say I'm not looking after you properly. You know the Social are always on to us
as it is. We don't want to give them any excuse
whatsoever to whip you into Care.'

She'd got me there. So I had to go the next
morning. I set off with all the other kids – and
then when we got to the end of the road,
Funny-Face and the Famous Five all called to
me.

'Come on then, Elsa.'

'Come with us, eh?'

'Come to the camp.'

Little Simon even came and held my hand and asked if I'd come and play ambulances with him. His face fell a mile when I had to say no. So I gave him a packet of Polos and showed him how to poke his pointy little tongue through the hole. That cheered him up no end.

'Elsa! Why aren't you coming?' said Funny-Face. 'You chicken or something?'

'Hey, why did the one-eyed chicken cross the road? To get to the Bird's Eye shop.'

'That is a fowl joke,' said Funny-Face.

We both cracked up.

'Come on. You can be good fun . . . for a girl,' said Funny-Face.

'You can be quite perceptive . . . for a boy,' I said, and I waved to him and walked off with Naomi.

'Is he your boyfriend then?' she said.

'Look, *I'm* the one that's meant to make the jokes,' I said. 'Him!'

'He fancies you all the same,' said Naomi. 'You and him will be slinking off to room one hundred and ten soon.'

120

'Naomi!' I nudged her and she nudged me back and we both fell about giggling.

The Manager and the bunny lady can't let Room 110 because the damp's got so bad all the wallpaper's peeled off and the Health Inspector's been round. But someone nicked a spare key and some of the big kids pair off, boy and girl, and sneak into the empty room together. They don't seem to mind the damp.

But catch me going anywhere with Funny-Face. Least of all Room 110.

Naomi and I had a laugh about it, like I said, but as I got nearer and nearer the school there suddenly didn't seem anything to laugh at.

'Cheer up, Elsa. It's OK, really it is. Look, tell me a school joke.'

I swallowed. My mouth had suddenly gone dry. For once I didn't really feel in a jokey mood. Still, a comedienne has to be funny no matter what she feels like.

'OK, so there's this geography teacher, right, and he's asking all the kids where all these mountains are, and he says to the little thick one, "Where are the Andes?" and the little thick one blinks a bit and then pipes up, "At the end of my armies." '

My own andies were cold and clenched tight. I felt like the little thick one all right.

Pizza and Porky-Pies

I was right to feel edgy. I didn't like this new school at all.

I didn't get to sit next to Naomi in her class. I was put in the special class, which was a bit humiliating for a start. They said it was just for a little while, to see how things worked out. Hmm. Fine if they did work out. But what if they didn't? Where do you go if you're too thick even for the special class? Do they march you right back to the Infants?

I didn't like my teacher in this strange class I got stuck in.

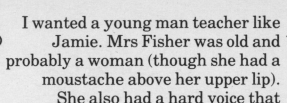 I wanted a young man teacher like Jamie. Mrs Fisher was old and probably a woman (though she had a moustache above her upper lip).

She also had a hard voice that could rip right through you, though when I first got shoved in her class she stretched her thin lips in a smile and said in ever such sugary, sweetie tones that she was pleased to meet me, and oh what a pretty name Elsa is, and here was my notebook and have this nice sharp pencil, dearie, and why don't you sit at the front where I can see you and write me a little story about yourself.

She was trying to kid on she was really interested in me, but she couldn't fool me. When she took us all out in the playground to have P.E., she got talking to one of the other teachers. The other teacher saw me barging around doing batty things with a bean bag and asked Mrs Fisher who I was. Mrs Fisher didn't even tell her my name. She just said: 'Oh, that's just one of the bed-and-breakfast children.'

I'm not even a she. I'm a That. Some sort of boring blob who doesn't have a name, who doesn't even have a sex.

Elsa the Blob. Hey, I quite like that idea. I could be a great big giant monster Blob and

squelch around obliterating people. Mack is still first on my list but Mrs Fisher comes a close second.

I wrote her a little story about myself all right. I wrote that my real name is Elsarina and I'm a child star – actress, singer and comedienne – and I've been in lots of adverts on the telly and done panto and heaps of musicals, and I was actually currently starring in a travelling repertory performance of *Annie* – me playing Annie, of course. And I wrote that my mum and the rest of my family are all in showbiz too, part of the company, and *that's* why we're currently living in a hotel, because we travel around putting on our shows.

I tried to make it sound dead convincing. But when she read it she just gave me one of those smug old smiles.

'This is certainly some story, dear,' she said. 'Rather a *fairy* story, I'm afraid.'

The other kids tittered, though they didn't know what she was on about. She handed me my story back with all my spelling and punctuation mistakes underlined. There seemed to be more red ink on the page than pencil.

But I was not deterred. If I was meant to be thick then some of the kids in the class were as dense as drains, and gurgled into the bargain. So I tried out my Elsarina story on them, and they were all dead impressed, even the big tough guys. I gave them a few quick samples of my comic routine out in the playground and some of them laughed and then I treated them to a rendition of 'The Sun Will Come Out Tomorrow'. I forget what a powerful voice I've got. One or two of them ran for cover, but those that stayed seriously seemed to appreciate my performance.

School didn't seem quite so bad at this stage. I had my little group of fans who happily drank in everything I told them. I got a bit carried away and started elaborating about my mum being this really beautiful actress and yet she could belt out a song and dance up

125

a storm in this really classy cabaret
act . . . and every so often I seemed to
step outside myself and hear my own
voice and I could see I was tempting
fate telling all these lies. Well, they
weren't completely lies. Mum *did* use
to be beautiful before she met up with
Mack and had some more kids so that
she lost her lovely figure and gained a
few worry lines. She could *still* look
beautiful if only she'd bother to slap on
some make-up and do her hair properly. She really did use to sing and
dance too. She'd sing along to all the
records on the radio in a happy husky
voice and she'd dance away, wiggling
her hips and waggling her fingers. So
Mum *could* sing and dance and if
only she'd had the right breaks then
I'm sure she really could be a star . . .

All the same, I shut up at lunchtime when I
met Naomi. It was great to have my own
special friend to wander round the playground
with. School dinners weren't so bad either.
They weren't a patch on my Mega-Feast at
home with Pippa, but you were allowed to
choose what you wanted, so I had a big plateful
of pizza and chips, and I set all our lunch table
laughing with a whole load of pizza jokes that

aren't fit for publication. Even my silly old chip joke went down well salted.

'Hey, you lot, what are hot, greasy and romantic? Chips that pass in the night!'

The afternoon wasn't so great because we had to divide up into groups to do all this dumb weighing and measuring. I could do that easy-peasy but I didn't have much clue when it came to how you write it all down. I didn't want to admit this so I made a lot of it up, and then of course Mrs Fisher came nosing around and when she saw all my calculations she sighed and scored a line right through them, so it was obvious to everyone I'd got it all wrong. She sat down with me and tried to explain how to do it. I felt stupid in front of all the others and so I couldn't take it in. She had to go through the whole gubbins again, speaking e-v-e-r s-o s-l-o-w-l-y because she obviously thought she had a right moron on her hands. The other kids started to snigger by this stage, so when Mrs Fisher at last left us in peace I had to work hard to regain their respect. I started on about my stage clothes and my mum's stage clothes and my little sister Pip-pa's stage clothes, and once I'd started on Pippa I couldn't stop, and soon I'd turned her into this adorable little child star with chubby cheeks and a head of curls and though she

hadn't started school yet she could sing and dance like a real little trooper.

I was certainly going a bit over the top here, because even Mack and Mum admit that Pippa is plain. Well, the poor kid can't help it, being lumbered with Mack as a dad. She hasn't got chubby cheeks, she hasn't got curls (Mum did have a go with her curling tongs once when Pippa was going to a party but her hair ended up looking like it had exploded). She isn't even little – she's nearly as big as me though she's half my age – and as for singing and dancing, well, Pippa can't ever remember the words to any song, let alone the tune, and the only sort of dancing she can do is slam-dancing, though she doesn't *mean* to barge straight into you.

But I built her up into such a little Baby Wonder that the kids in my class were drooling, and they all wanted to see the show with me and this mega-brilliant little brat and our glamorous movie-star mummy.

'Sorry, folks, we've been sold out for weeks because the show's so popular,' I said breezily, though my heart was beating fit to bust.

That shut them up for a few seconds, but then I started to wonder about going-home time. Mum had caught me out yesterday by trailing round to the school. What if she did it again today? What if she'd just pulled on her oldest old T-shirt and leggings and hadn't bothered to do her hair? All the children would see her for themselves. And even if I could somehow manage to convince them that she was just practising for a forthcoming searingly realistic drama on the telly about a careworn young mother ground down by the system, they'd see Pippa too.

It might help matters if my whole family were present and correct. I could tell them that Mack was all set for a remake of King Kong. He didn't even need to bother with a costume.

I shot out of school the moment the bell
went. It was a huge great relief to see that
Mum wasn't there, though I couldn't help
feeling a weeny bit miffed all the same,
because she *said* she'd come. She wasn't back
at the hotel either. None of them were. I
couldn't get into room 608 because I didn't
have a key, so I had to mooch about the
corridors for ages. Naomi came along but she
was a bit narked with me because I hadn't
waited for her after school, and she couldn't
play with me now anyway because she had to
help her mum with her brothers. Then Funny-
Face sloped into view, scuffing his trainers and
spitting. He was even more narked with me
because my mum had stirred things up yesterday and the school had done a check on their
registers and sent the truant officer round and
now Funny-Face and the Famous Five had to
turn up at school tomorrow or *else*.

'Or else you'll all get into trouble and Elsa'll
get into trouble for getting you lot into trouble,'
I said, pulling a funny face at Funny-Face.

130

He didn't pull one back. He called me a lot of rude names, even the infamous one he wrote on the wall that I had to correct.

I swept away loftily and pretended I didn't care. But I felt a bit friendless by now. And I was starting to get dead worried that I might be familyless too.

Why had they all pushed off without telling me where they were going? What if they'd finally got fed up with me and packed up and scarpered? I knew Mack didn't want me. He'd go like a shot and he'd take Pippa and Hank because they were his kids and he cared about them. But Mum wouldn't walk out on me, would she? Although only this morning, when the drains all went wrong and someone else's dirty water came bubbling up in our basin, she burst into tears and said she couldn't stick this rotten dump a day longer. So maybe . . . maybe she had gone too.

The ceiling suddenly seemed a long long way off. I felt I was getting smaller and smaller until I wasn't much more than a squeak. I hunched up on the floor with my head on my knees and held on tight in case I disappeared altogether.

'Elsa? What on earth are you doing? What's up, eh?' said Mum, coming down the corridor.

Yes, it was Mum, and I was so very pleased to see her even though she sounded cross. And I was very pleased to see Pippa even though she was all sniffly with her nose running. And I was very pleased to see Hank even though he was howling his head off and needing his nappy changed. And I was . . . No. I wasn't very pleased to see Mack. I wouldn't ever go *that* far.

'Where have you *been*? I've been back from school ages and ages!'

'Yeah, well, I'm sorry, love, but it's not our fault. We had a right ding-dong with that useless Manager this morning because we're all going to end up getting typhoid or cholera stuck in this poxy dump, and the tight-fisted pig won't even send for a plumber to fix things, would you believe! Anyway, he said we could clear off if we didn't like it here, and so I said we were doing our best to do just that, but we didn't have any place to go, so *then* we went down the Housing Office, all of us, and would you believe they kept us waiting *all* day. They weren't even going to see us at all because we didn't have some stupid appointment, but we sat it out and I knew you'd be waiting, pet, but I couldn't do anything, could I?'

'So what happened, Mum? Are we getting a house?'

'Are we heck,' said Mum. 'They just mumbled on about priority families and exceptional circumstances and said even if this dump was affecting our health we'd have to get some really bad complaint and it would all have to be written up in medical reports and even then, if we were all at death's door, they couldn't blooming well guarantee us a house or even a mouldy old flat like we used to have.'

'So I asked what *would* guarantee us a house – did one of you kids have to snuff it altogether, is that it?' Mack said. 'It's getting dangerously close too. Look at little Pippa, all sniffles. She can't get rid of that cold, and as for the baby, well, I don't like the sound of his chest at all.'

Mack sighed over Hank, who was still exercising his magnificent lungs. They certainly sounded in full working order.

'Yeah, Mack started to get really stroppy. Well, I did too, especially when they said they couldn't even guarantee us a proper set of rooms here like we're entitled to, instead of us having to squash up like sardines. They said there was nothing further they could do at this moment in time, and threatened to set the police on to us unless we left the office.'

Mum sighed theatrically, the back of her hand to her forehead. She mightn't be a proper actress but it certainly sounded as if she'd been giving a good performance down at the Housing Office. She threatened to go back again tomorrow, wondering if she could get us rehoused by sheer persistence.

'Yes, good thinking, Mum,' I said, encouraging her so she wouldn't come to collect me from school and crack my credibility.

Only I needn't have bothered. Someone else started telling the wrong sort of tales the very next day. Someone with a funny face. And a great big mouth.

Funny-Face got shoved in the special class too. Right next to me, at the front, under the Fisher's pop eyes. This reminded me of 101 Popeye the Sailorman jokes – *you* know – and I swopped some of them with Funny-Face and we both got terrible snorty giggles, and Mrs Fisher's eyes popped so much they almost rolled down her cheeks, and her mouth went so tight her lips disappeared.

'I'm glad you two are finding school so amusing,' she said, dead sarcastic. 'Perhaps you'd like to share your little jokes with me, hmm?'

Perhaps not. If she heard some of the wilder Popeye jokes she'd go off pop herself.

So Funny-Face and I were getting on famously until playtime. And then one of the kids in the class asked if Funny-Face performed too.

'You what?' said Funny-Face.

'Are you a child star like Elsarina and Pipette?' They elaborated on the famous fictional talents of me and my family, and Funny-Face

fell about, thinking this was just another joke,
a wind-up on my part.

'You lot aren't half loopy,' said Funny-Face.
'How come you've fallen for all this rubbish?
Elsa isn't a famous star! She's just a bed-and-
breakfast kid, like me. And cripes, you should
see her mum and her dopey little sister —
stars!'

That was enough. Funny-Face saw stars
then. Because I punched him right in the nose.

All the children started shouting 'Fight!
Fight! Fight!' I was all set to have a proper
fight even though I'm generally gentle, and
Funny-Face was bewildered but wanted a fight
too because I'd made his nose bleed. But as
soon as we'd squared up to each other Mrs
Fisher came flying forth and she seized Funny-
Face in one hand and me in the other. She shook
us both very vigorously indeed, practically

clonking our heads together, and told us we were very rough, naughty children and we had to learn not to be violent in school.

Then, as she stalked off, she said just one word. Well, she muttered it, but I heard. And Funny-Face did too. She said, *'Typical.'* She meant we were typical bed-and-breakfast kids indulging in typical disruptive behaviour. And I suddenly felt sick, as if I needed my bed and might well throw up my breakfast.

Funny-Face didn't look too clever either. He wiped the smear of blood from his nose and pulled a hideous face at Mrs Fisher's back, crossing his eyes and waggling his tongue.

I giggled feebly.

'Why did the teacher have crossed eyes, eh? Because she couldn't control her pupils.'

It was one of my least funny jokes but Funny-Face guffawed politely.

'Well, she's not going to control us, is she, Elsa?'

'You bet she's not.' His nose was still bleeding. I felt up my sleeve for a crumpled tissue. 'Here,' I said, dabbing at him.

'Leave off! You're acting like my mum,' said Funny-Face.

'Sorry I socked you one,' I said.

'Yeah, well, if that old trout hadn't come along I'd have flattened you, see. Just as well for you. Though you can hit quite hard – for a girl.'

'If you start that I'll hit you even harder,' I said, but I gave his nose another careful wipe. 'We're still mates, aren't we?'

'Course we are. Though why did you have to attack me like that, eh?'

'Because of what you said about my mum and my sister.'

'But you were the one telling porky-pies, not me! Why did you spin all those stupid stories about them? I mean, it's daft. As if you lot could ever be in showbiz.'

'We could, you know,' I said fiercely. 'Well, maybe not my mum. Or Pippa. But *I'm* going to be some day. I'll be famous, just you wait and see. I'll be a comedienne – that's a lady who tells jokes – and I'll have my own show and I'll get to be on the telly, you'll see, maybe sooner than you think.'

It was sooner than I thought, too. Because when Funny-Face and I went home from school that day there was a camera crew filming in the foyer of the Royal Hotel!

Television and no Tea

'What on earth's going on?' said Funny-Face. 'Hey, is this for telly? Are we going to be on the telly?'

He pulled a grotesque funny face for the camera, waving both his arms.

I sighed scornfully. I wasn't going to behave like some idiotic amateur. I eyed up all the people and spotted the man in the tightest jeans and the leather jacket. That one just had to be the director. I walked right up to him, smiling.

'Hello, I'm Elsa, I live here and I'm going to be a comedienne when I grow up. In fact, I've got my whole comedy act worked out right now. Would you like to listen?'

The director blinked rapidly behind his trendy glasses, but he seemed interested.

'You live here, do you, Elsa? Great, well, we're doing a programme called *Children in Crisis*, OK? Shall we do a little interview with you and your friend, eh? You can tell us all about how awful it is to have to stay in a bed-and-breakfast hotel, right?'

'Wrong, wrong, wrong!' said the bunny lady receptionist, rushing out from behind her desk. Even the telephonist lady had chucked her Jackie Collins and was peering out from behind her glass door, all agog.

141

'Go and get the Manager, quick,' the bunny lady commanded, shooing the telephonist lady up the corridor. 'Now listen to me, you television people. You're trespassing. Get out of this hotel right this minute or I'll call the police and have you evicted.'

'I can tell any joke you like. We'll have a police joke, OK? What did the policeman say to the three-headed man? Hello hello hello. Where does the policeman live? Nine nine nine Let's be Avenue. What's the police dog's telephone number? Canine canine canine.'

'Very funny, dear,' said the director, though he didn't laugh. 'Now, once we get the camera rolling I want you to say a bit about the crowded room you live in and how damp it is and maybe there are nasty bugs in the bath, yeah?'

'How dare you! This is a scrupulously clean establishment, there are no bugs here, no infestations of any kind!' the bunny lady screeched, so cross that the fluff on her jumper quivered.

'Bugs, OK, I'll tell you an insect joke, right? You've got this fly and this flea, yes, and when they fly past each other what time is it? Fly past flea.' I laughed to show that this was the punchline.

'Mmm, well. Simmer down now, sweetie, we

want you looking really sad for the camera. And you, sonnie, do you think you could stop pulling those faces for five seconds?'

'OK, I can look sad, it's all part of a comedienne's repertoire. Look, is this sad enough?'

'Well, you needn't go to extremes. Cheer up just a bit.'

'Hey, I've thought of another insect joke. There were these two little flies running like mad over a cornflake packet – and do you know why? Because it said, "Tear along dotted line".'

I laughed, but that made me cheer up a bit too much. And then the Manager came charging up and started shouting and swearing at the television people and they tried to film him and he put his hand over the camera and I started to get the feeling I might have lost my big chance to make it on to the television.

'Phone the police this minute!' the Manager commanded.

'I know some more police jokes,' I said, but no-one was listening.

'Who put you up to this? Who invited you in, eh? Has one of the residents been complaining? Which one? You tell me. If they don't like it here they can get out,' the Manager shouted, making wild gestures. He nearly clipped me on the head and I ducked. 'It was your mum and dad, wasn't it, little girl!'

'That man's not my dad.'

'The big Scottish bloke, he was throwing his weight around and moaning about his basin.'

'What animal do you find in a toilet? A wash-hand bison,' I said, but I seemed to have lost my audience.

The police arrived and there was a big argy-bargy which ended in the camera crew having to squeeze all their stuff back round the revolving door, while the Manager continued to rant and rave to me, saying it was all my family's fault and we'd better start packing our bags right this minute.

I began to feel very much like a Child in Crisis. I whizzed out after the camera crew, desperate for one last chance to get on the telly.

'Hey, don't go, don't pack up!' I yelled, as I saw them heaving their gear into a van. 'Look, couldn't we do an interview in front of the hotel, eh? I'll be ever so sad – I could even try to cry if you like. Look, I can make my face crumple up – or I tell you what, I'll go and get my little sister and brother from our room, they're great at crying—'

'Sorry, sweetie, but I think this is a waste of time,' said the director. 'I don't need this sort of hassle. And besides, you're a great little sport but you're not the sort of kid I'm looking for. I need someone . . . ' He waved his hand in the air, unable to express exactly what he wanted. Then he stopped and stood still.

'Someone like that little kid there!' he said, snapping his fingers.

I looked for this favoured little kid. And do you know who it was? Naomi, mooching along the road, trailing a brother in either hand, looking all fed up and forlorn because I'd rushed off with Funny-Face instead of waiting for her.

'Hey, sweetie, over here!' The director waved at her frantically. 'Where did you spring from, hmm? You don't live in the bed-and-breakfast hotel by any chance?'

Naomi nodded nervously, clutching her little brothers tight.

'Great!' He threw back his head and addressed the clouds. 'A gift!'

'We don't want any gifts. We don't take stuff from strangers,' said Naomi, and she started trying to hustle her brothers away. She hustled a little too abruptly, and Neil tripped and started crying.

'Hey, shut up, little squirt,' said Funny-Face. 'You're going to be on the telly. Can I still be on it too, mister?'

'And me?' I said urgently.

'Well, you can maybe sort of wander in the background,' said the director. 'But no clowning. No funny faces. And absolutely *no* jokes.'

I didn't actually feel like cracking any jokes right that minute. Naomi was going to be the star of the show. Not me, even though I'd been perfecting my routine and practising on everyone all this time. Naomi, who couldn't crack a joke to save her life, little meek and mousey Naomi!

OK, I thought. Maybe just *one* joke to try to cheer myself up. So I whispered all to myself,

'What do you get if you cross an elephant with a mouse? Socking great holes in the skirting board!' I couldn't help laughing. You can't really do that quietly. The director glared in my direction. 'Dear goodness, you dippy kids! I don't want merriment, I don't want laughter, I don't want JOKES.'

'OK, OK, no jokes,' I said, and I pinched my lips together with my fingers so he could see I was serious. Only it was such a pity. The mouse and elephant joke had triggered off a whole herd of elephant jokes inside my head, and they were trumpeting tremendously.

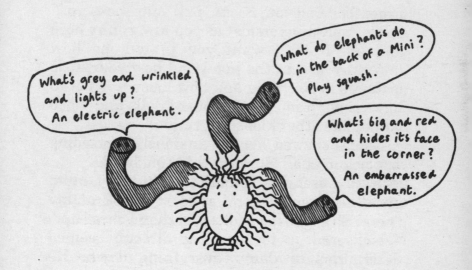

What's grey and wrinkled and lights up? An electric elephant.

What do elephants do in the back of a Mini? Play squash.

What's big and red and hides its face in the corner? An embarrassed elephant.

'Well *I* can't tell jokes,' said Naomi truthfully. 'I can't dance or sing or anything. So you'd really better pick Elsa.'

'Oh Naomi,' I said, immensely touched. 'You can't do all the showy things, but you're ever so brainy. You could get to be on one of the quiz shows, eh?'

'Never mind quiz shows. This little girl's perfect for *Children in Crisis*. Now just stand here, sweetie – little brothers too, that's it, and I'll ask you a few questions while the camera rolls, right?'

'No, wait! Neil, come and get your nose wiped and stop that silly sniffling,' Naomi said urgently. 'And you, Nicky, pull your socks up.'

'No, we want you just as you are, runny nose and all! Now, I want you to tell me how miserable it is in the hotel and how your little brothers keep crying and how lousy it is not to have enough money for lots of dolls and video games like other kids. OK, action!'

Naomi chewed her lip anxiously, not going into action at all. She was thinking hard.

'It *is* miserable sometimes. But my mum gives me a cuddle or I read my book or my friend Elsa tells me a joke and then I cheer up.'

I cheered up too, but the director seemed determined to damp everything down. He practically told Naomi what she had to say.

148

The first time she had a go she came out all weird and wooden, and she kept looking up at the director anxiously and hissing, 'Is that right? Have I remembered it?'

'No, sweetie, don't keep saying that. Just act natural, for pity's sake,' said the director, practically tearing his hair.

The bunny lady receptionist came clopping out into the street in her high heels, wagging her pointed nails at the television crew.

'Now look! You're harassing our tenants. We'll call the police again. The Manager's on the phone right this minute. And as for you kids, I'm warning you. We don't have to house you, you know. If you've got any complaints then you can push off somewhere else.'

She clip-clopped back into the hotel. Naomi stared after her worriedly, her eyes filling with tears.

'Does she mean that? She wouldn't really throw us out, would she?' Naomi whispered. 'We haven't got anywhere else to go. And it's so unfair, because we've put up with ever such a lot – we've even had those horrible bugs, cockroaches, squiggling all over the floor. One even got in the toe of our baby Nathan's bootee, and yet the Manager wouldn't even send for the pest-control people. He said it was our fault because we were dirty! And my mum cried when he said that because we're as clean as we can be – we bath every day even when there isn't any hot water, and my mum keeps the room spotless, and that's not easy with the four of us kids. I don't know what we're going to do, because we've been waiting six months and we still can't get a flat and if we get turned out the hotel then us kids will have to go into Care and we've got to stay with our mum.'

'We want our mum,' said Nicky.

'Mum! Mum!' wailed Neil.

'Perfect!' said the director. The cameras had been rolling for all of Naomi's outburst. 'Absolutely great, sweetie. Lovely emotive stuff. Right folks, I think we can hit the road now.'

'But what about us?' said Naomi, wiping her eyes. 'Are we going to get thrown out?'

'Mmm? Oh, I shouldn't think so,' he said vaguely.

He'd turned his back on us. He didn't know. He didn't even care. He just wanted to make a good television programme.

I put my arm round Naomi.
'We'll be OK,' I said, giving her a hug. 'Don't take any notice of him. He's just been using us. Still, it looks like you really will be on the telly after all, Naomi.'

Naomi didn't seem very thrilled about the idea. She still worried and worried that her family might get thrown out.

'Look, they've threatened us too. That Manager thinks it's all my mum and Mack's fault. We'll all be thrown out together. We'll have to set up a little camp. It's OK, Naomi. Don't get in such a state.'

I tried to cheer her up, but it wasn't easy.

'I wish you hadn't got us all involved with those telly people,' Naomi said, sighing.

That's what Mum and Mack were saying too in room 608. Only they were saying it a lot more angrily. I could hear them yelling from right down the corridor.

'Oh-oh,' I said.

'It's all your fault, you stupid Scottish git!' Mum was screaming. 'You shouldn't have phoned them. Now that Manager will make our lives a misery.'

'It's a flaming misery as it is. It couldn't be worse. I was simply trying to help, so stop giving me all this hassle, woman.'

I slunk into the room. Pippa was crouched in the duck cot, clutching Baby Pillow. Hank was grizzling in bed, needing his nappy changed. I mopped them up and crept off with them. I don't think Mum and Mack even noticed.

It was getting near teatime and there were lots of cooking smells coming from the kitchen. Mum still said it was a filthy hole and we couldn't cook in there or we'd go down with a terrible disease. I was starting to get so starving hungry I was willing to risk the terrible disease, but we didn't have anything to cook.

Naomi's mum was stirring a very interesting bean stew that smelt ever so rich and tasty. She had baby Nathan on her hip, and he was smacking his lips in happy anticipation.

152

Naomi told her mum all about the television people and the Manager's threats, but Naomi's mum didn't get mad at all. She just went on stirring her stew.

'We'll be fine, little old lady,' she said to Naomi. 'You're such a worry-guts. Here, tea's just about ready. Have you got the plates set out in our room?'

She saw Pippa and Hank and me looking at her hungrily.

'Do you kids want to come and join us for tea?' she said cheerily.

We wanted to extremely badly, but there didn't look that much of a stew and it seemed a bit mean to eat their food so I said we'd be having our own tea in a minute.

But when I did a quick sortie back to room 608 the row was getting louder and fiercer and I knew there was no point disturbing them. So Pippa and Hank and I hung around the kitchen some more. Simple Simon's mum came along and she cooked a whole load of chips in the greasy old chip-pan – so many that they almost came bubbling over the top. They smelt so good and she had such a lot that I decided we'd have a few if we got offered. Only we didn't.

Simon's mum is very fierce.

'What are you kids staring at?' she said

sharply. 'Clear off out of it. Go and get your own tea.'

But that was easier said than done. The row was still roaring. So we sat outside the room, our tummys rumbling. Mack came storming out eventually. He tripped right over me actually. I felt like calling him a Great Scottish Git too, but I sensed it wasn't quite the moment. I knew where he was going. Down the pub. And he wouldn't be back for ages.

At least that meant we could get in our room. But Mum didn't seem up to considering something ordinary like tea. She was in bed crying and when I tried to talk to her she pulled the covers up over her head. She went on crying for a bit and then she went to sleep.

I felt really funny for about five minutes. Not funny ha-ha. Funny peculiar and horrible. It hadn't been a good day. I wasn't going to be on television. I didn't have any tea. I felt like getting into my own bed and pulling the covers up and having a good cry.

But Pippa and Hank were looking up at me and I couldn't let them down. I switched on the telly and said they could stay up as long as they liked because Mum was asleep and Mack was out. And I hunted round the room for food and found some stale sliced bread and a pot of raspberry jam.

154

'We're going to have a really special tea, you'll see,' I said, scrabbling through Mum's handbag for her nail scissors. I got snipping and scraping and made us ultra-special jam sandwiches.

I made a clown jam sandwich for Hank.

I made a teddy jam sandwich for Pippa and Baby Pillow.

And I made a great red movie-star-lip jam sandwich for me,

and the jammy lips kissed me for being such a good girl.

I woke up early and read my joke books in bed . . .

Why are tall people lazier than short people? Because they're longer in bed, ha ha!

. . . and then Pippa woke up for a cuddle and Hank woke up for a bottle and soon it was time to get up.

Mum didn't wake up. Mack didn't wake up either. He was snoring like a warthog with catarrh.

So I had to speak up to make myself heard. Mum stirred at last.

'Will you stop that shouting, Elsa!'

'I'm *not* shouting,' I said, wounded. 'I'm simply speaking up a little because that Scottish git is snoring fit to bust.'

Mum stirred more vigorously.

'Don't you dare call Mack names like that, you cheeky little whatsit!'

'But that's what *you* called him just last night.'

We started to have a little argument. I might have got a bit heated. Suddenly the warthog stopped snoring. It reared up in the bed, a horrible sight.

'If you don't stop that shouting and screaming right this minute, Elsa, I'll give you such a smacking you'll never dare say another word.'

He glared at me with his bleary eyes and then slowly subsided back under the covers. Hank gave a worried hiccup. Pippa started sucking her fingers. I blinked hard at the bulk in the bed. I opened my mouth, but Pippa shook her head and clutched me with her dribbly little hands. I gave her a hug to show her it was OK. I wasn't going to speak. Mack might be an idle lout but he doesn't make idle threats. He always follows them through.

I waggled my tongue very impressively at

the bed instead. Mum still had her eyes open
but she didn't tell me off. When I went to take
Pippa and Hank downstairs for breakfast she
sat up in bed and held her arms out to me.

'I'm sorry, love,' she whispered. 'I didn't
mean to get you into trouble. You're a good girl
really, I know you are. I don't know what I'd do
without you.'

I cheered up a bit then, but when we went
down to breakfast the bunny lady said loudly
to the switchboard lady: 'Oh-oh, there's one of
the little trouble-makers.' She pointed at me

with a lilac fingernail to match a new purple
fluffy jumper. 'The Manager wants to see your
dad in his office,' she announced.

'He's not my dad,' I said and walked straight past, Hank on my hip, Pippa hanging on my hand.

'Mack is my dad,' Pippa whispered. 'Is he going to get into trouble, Elsa?'

'I don't know,' I said uncomfortably. Maybe we were all in trouble. Maybe we really were going to get chucked out.

We went to sit with Naomi and her family at breakfast. They were looking dead gloomy too. Naomi's mum didn't smile at me the way she usually did.

'I'll tell you a really good joke about cornflakes,' I said.

'No jokes, Elsa,' she said, sighing.

'OK, I'll tell you this cornflake joke tomorrow. It's a cereal,' I said. I roared with laughter. It wasn't *that* funny, but I wanted to lighten the atmosphere.

Naomi's mum stayed resolutely gloomy. Naomi chewed her lip anxiously. Even Nicky and Neil couldn't crack a smile.

'What's up, eh?' I said, starting to feed baby Nathan, playing the aeroplane game.

He at least seemed happy enough to play, but Naomi's mum caught hold of my arm and took away my spoon.

'No, leave him be. Leave all my family be. Haven't you done enough?'

'Oh, Mum,' said Naomi. 'It isn't Elsa's fault.'

'She was the one who talked you into that television interview,' said Naomi's mum. 'And now the Manager says we'll have to go.'

'Well, he says we've got to go too. But he doesn't mean it. He just wants to scare us,' I said. I tried to sound reassuring but I was getting scared too. 'Look, I'll go and see the Manager. I'll tell him it was all down to me if you like. Then at least you'll be OK.'

So after we'd had breakfast I lumped Hank along to the Manager's office, Pippa trailing behind us. I didn't have a hand free to knock so we just went barging straight into his office. The Manager wasn't on his own. He wasn't having a little cuddle with the bunny lady. He was with Mrs Hoover, and he didn't look at all cuddly. He was telling Mrs Hoover off, wagging his finger at her.

'What's the matter?' I said. 'Why is he being nasty to you, Mrs Hoover?'

'You! Out of my office this instant,' said the Manager. 'It's your mum and dad I want to see, not you lot.'

'I keep telling you, I haven't *got* a dad. That Scottish bloke is nothing to do with me,' I insisted.

'Oh yes! Thank you for reminding me. Yes, my receptionist informs me that there's more disgusting graffiti about a Scots person inside the ladies' downstairs cloakroom,' said the Manager, still wag-wag-wagging that finger at poor Mrs Hoover.

'She didn't do that! I know for a fact that Mrs Hoover didn't write all that stuff on the walls,' I said quickly, my heart thumping. Everyone seemed to be getting into trouble because of me and it was awful. I decided to make a clean breast of things. (What a weird expression. I haven't got a breast yet for a start. And it wasn't even clean because the basin in room 608 was getting so gungy I hadn't felt very much like washing recently.)

'All the Mack jokes – they're mine,' I said.

The Manager and Mrs Hoover both blinked at me.

'You wrote all that revolting rubbish?' said the Manager.

'I thought some of the jokes were quite funny,' I mumbled.

'You children! Vandals! Hooligans!' said the Manager.

'It was just me. Not Pippa. She can't write yet – and even if she could, she quite likes her dad. It's just me that can't stick him. But you can stop telling Mrs Hoover off because, like I said, it was me.'

'Oh Elsa,' said Mrs Hoover. 'He knows I didn't write it, silly. He's cross because I can't clean it all off. Only I keep telling him, that felt-tip just won't budge even though I scrub and scrub.'

'I never see you scrubbing. The hotel is a disgrace. No wonder we have television crews traipsing in here making trouble. If I'm reported to the authorities it will be all your fault.'

'If you get reported to the authorities it'll be because you run a lousy hotel,' said Mrs Hoover. 'How can I possibly hope to keep a huge place like this anywhere near up to standard? Why don't you employ more staff?'

'I'll be employing one less member of staff if you don't watch your tongue,' said the Manager.

'All right then. That suits me. You can stick your stupid job,' said Mrs Hoover, whipping off her overall and throwing it right in his face.

Then she turned on her heel and flounced straight out of his office. I decided it wasn't quite the right time to plead Naomi's case to the Manager. I ran after Mrs Hoover instead.

'Oh gosh, have you really lost your job now? And it's my fault because I did all the scribbling on the walls,' I wailed. 'Oh Mrs Hoover, I'm so sorry!'

'Mrs Whoosit?' said Mrs Hoover. 'Here, is that what you kids call me? Well, don't you fret yourself, pet. I've had it up to here hoovering for that dreadful man. I'll get another cleaning job, they're not that hard to come by even nowadays.'

But I couldn't be absolutely sure she was telling the truth. I wished I was as little as Pippa so she could pick me up and give me a big hug to reassure me. I felt little inside. And stupid. And sad. And sorry.

I was extra loud and noisy and bouncy and bossy at school to try to make myself feel big again. It didn't work. I kept telling jokes to Funny-Face and he kept laughing, but Mrs Fisher was frowning and she made us stay in at playtime and write out I MUST LEARN TO BEHAVE PROPERLY IN THE CLASSROOM fifty times.

Funny-Face is not very good at writing. His words wobble up over the line and slide down below it. His spelling's a bit wobbly too. He missed out one of the 's's in classroom. Mrs Fisher pointed this out huffily. I was scared she might make him do it all over again, so I tried to lighten things a little.

'Why can't you remember there are two 's's in class?' she said crossly. 'I've told you enough times.'

'Which 's' did he leave out this time, Mrs Fisher?' I said.

It was a joke. A bit of a feeble one, but a joke all the same. Only Mrs Fisher just thought I was being cheeky.

Do you know what happened? We had to stay in at lunchtime too. Funny-Face had to write out CLASSROOM another fifty times, and I had to write out a fresh fifty: I MUST LEARN NOT TO BE CHEEKY IN THE CLASSROOM.

'That's silly, anyway,' I muttered. 'That sounds like I can be cheeky in the hall and cheeky in the corridors and cheeky in the toilets and cheeky all over the place. And I wasn't blooming cheeky to start with. I was just joking.'

'You and your
@!+!@ jokes!'
said Funny-Face,
laboriously drawing 's's.

'Hey, don't be like that. Listen, this boy was kept in at lunchtime just like us and his teacher said he had to write out this sentence of not less than fifty words, right? So do you know what he wrote?'

'No, and I don't care,' said Funny-Face. 'Here, I've got all these poxy 's's in the right place, haven't I?'

'Yes. Though hang on, you've started to miss out your 'o's now. There are two in classroom. Like us two in this classroom. But listen to the punchline bit of my joke. This boy wrote, "I went to call my cat in for the night so I stood at the door and called: 'Here, kitty, kitty, kitty, kitty, kitty . . . ' " '

'Shut *up*, Elsa.'

'No, I haven't done enough kittys – there are supposed to be fifty. And you've missed out another 'o' there – *and* there.'

'You'll be going O in a minute, when I punch you right in the nose,' Funny-Face growled.

'What do you give a pig with a sore nose? Oinkment,' I said, snorting like a little pig myself because I think that's one of my funnier jokes.

Funny-Face didn't think it funny at all.

'Why don't you shut your cakehole?' he said, and he sounded so menacing I did what he said.

I wished he hadn't used that expression. We still hadn't been allowed to have our dinners and I kept thinking very wistfully of cake. When horrible old Mrs Fisher eventually let us go, we had to squeeze in right at the end of second-sitting dinners, when all the goodies had long since gone. Not one chip left. We had to make do with a salad, and no-one ever chooses bunny food from choice. I know some excellent bunny jokes but I decided it might be better to keep them in their burrow in my head. Funny-Face still didn't look ready for mirth as he chomped his way morosely through his lettuce.

We had a new teacher in the hall in the afternoon to take us for singing. It was a relief to be free of the Fishy-Eye and I was all set to sing my cares away. I didn't know many of the songs but I've always been good at improvising. So I threw back my head and let rip. But the teacher stopped playing the piano. Her face was all screwed up as if she had a terrible headache.

'Who is making that . . . noise?' she asked.

We stared at her. What did she mean? We were all making a noise. We were singing.

Only she didn't seem to appreciate that. She made us start again, this time without the piano. I decided not to let this faze me. I sang out joyfully. The teacher shuddered.

'You!' she said, pointing.

I peered round. No, it wasn't anyone else. She was pointing at me.

'Yes, you. The little bed-and-breakfast girl.'

The other children around me sniggered. I

felt my face start to burn, like the Royal Hotel's toast.

'Could you try not to sing so loudly, please?' said the teacher.

'Why?' I said, astonished.

'Because you're singing rather flat, dear. And completely out of tune. In fact, it might be better if you didn't sing at all, even softly. How about just nodding your head in time to the music?'

The other kids collapsed, nudging each other and tittering.

'Some stage star, eh! She can't even sing in tune,' they hissed.

I had to spend the whole singing lesson with my mouth shut, nid-nodding away like Little Noddy. I didn't feel much like making a noise after that. I hardly said anything on the way home from school. Funny-Face kept having a go at me, but I didn't respond.

'What's up, Elsa?' said Naomi, putting her arm round me. 'Here, I'm sorry my mum got mad at you. It wasn't really fair for her to pick on you.'

'Oh, I don't know. That's what everyone does. Pick on me,' I said gloomily.

'Hey, don't be like that. You're always so cheerful. I can't bear it when you're all sad. Tell us a joke, go on.'

But for the first time in my life I didn't even feel like telling jokes. Mum gave me a big hug when I went up to room 608. She sent Mack out for a special Kentucky chicken tea.

'To make up for last night, lovie,' said Mum. 'Sorry about that. And Mack's sorry he got snappy too. He's feeling better now.'

Mack might be feeling better, Mum might be feeling better. I didn't feel better at all.

I normally love Kentucky chicken take-aways. I like to sit cross-legged on the floor with Pippa and kid on we're American pioneers like in *Little House on the Prairie*, and we're eating a chicken our Pa has raised and there are prowling bears outside who can smell it cooking but we're safe inside our little log cabin.

'Play our game,' Pippa commanded, but somehow I couldn't make it work.

I usually finish off the game by pretending Hank is a baby bear cub and we all feed him bits of chicken (Hank loves this game too) and then we have a jolly sing-song. But now I didn't feel I ever wanted to sing again.

I didn't want to say anything.

I didn't want to tell jokes.

I didn't want to be me.

'Do try and cheer up, Elsa,' said Mum. 'Come on, you're going to have to go to bed if you sulk around the room like this.'

'I don't care,' I said.

So I went to bed really early, before Pippa — even before Hank. Of course it was difficult to get to sleep when the light was on and the telly was loud and there were two and a half people and a baby still racketing round the room, but I put my head way down under the covers and curled up in a little ball with my hands over my ears.

When I woke up I couldn't hear anything even when I took my hands away. I stuck my head out the covers. I could hardly see anything either in the dark. It seemed like the middle of the night.

And yet . . . someone was cooking supper somewhere. I could smell chips. People sometimes stayed up really late and made midnight snacks. I licked my lips. I hadn't eaten all my Kentucky chicken because I'd felt so fed up. I could do with a little snack now myself.

I wondered who was cooking in the kitchen. I'd got to know most of our sixth floor by now. Most of them were quite matey with me. I wondered if they'd consider sharing a chip or two.

I eased myself out of bed. Pippa mumbled

something in her sleep, but didn't wake up. I picked my way across the crowded floor, tripping over Pippa's My Little Pony and stepping straight into a Kentucky chicken carton, but eventually reached the door. I opened it very slowly so that it wouldn't make any noise and crept outside into the corridor. Then I stood still, puzzled. There was a much stronger smell now. And there was a strange flickering light coming from right down the end, in the kitchen. And smoke. You don't get smoke without . . . FIRE!

We Nearly Have Our Chips!

For just one second I stood still, staring. And then I threw back my head and gave a great lion roar.

'FIRE!' I shouted. 'FIRE FIRE FIRE!'

I banged on room 612, I banged on room 611, I banged on room 610, I banged on room 609, charging wildly back down the corridor and bellowing all the while.

'FIRE FIRE FIRE FIRE FIRE FIRE FIRE FIRE FIRE!'

I shouted so long and so loud it felt as if there was a fire in my own head, red and roaring. And then I got to room 608 and I went hurtling inside, screaming and shouting as I snapped on the light.

'FIRE!' I flew to Mum and shook her shoulder hard. Mack propped himself up on one elbow, his eyes bleary. 'Shut that racket!' he mumbled.

'I can't! There's a fire along in the kitchen. Oh, quick, quick, Mum, wake up! Pippa, get up, come on, out of bed.'

Mum sat up, shaking her head, still half-asleep. It was Mack who suddenly shot straight out, grabbing Hank from one bed, Pippa from the other.

'It's OK, Elsa. I'll get them out. You wake the others along the corridor,' he said, busy and brisk.

'Oh good lord, what are we going to do?' Mum said, stumbling out of bed, frantic. 'Quick kids, get dressed as soon as you can – I'll do Hank.'

'No, no, there's no time. We've just got to get out,' said Mack. 'No clothes, no toys, no messing about – OUT!'

'Baby Pillow!' Pippa yelled, struggling, but Mack held her tight.

'I've got him,' I said, snatching Baby Pillow from Pippa's bed.

Then I went charging down the corridor, calling, 'FIRE FIRE FIRE!' all over again.

The smoke was stronger now, and I could hear this awful crackling sound down the corridor. One of the men went running towards the kitchen in his pyjamas, but when he got near he slowed down and then backed away.

'Get everyone out!' he shouted. 'The whole kitchen's ablaze. Keep yelling, little kid. Wake them all up, loud as you can.'

I took a huge breath and roared the dreadful warning over and over again. Some people came running out straight away. Others shouted back, and someone started screaming that we were all going to be burnt alive.

'No-one will be burnt alive if you all just stop panicking,' Mack shouted, charging down the corridor, Pippa under one arm, Hank under the other, Mum stumbling along in her nightie behind them. Mack was only wearing his vest and pants and any other time in the world I'd have rolled around laughing, he looked such a sight.

But we all looked sights. People came blundering out of their bedrooms in nighties and pyjamas and T-shirts and underwear. Some were clutching handbags, some had carrier bags, several had shoved their possessions in blankets and were dragging them along the corridor.

'Leave all your bits and bobs behind. Let's just get out down the stairs. Carry the kids. Come on, get cracking!' Mack yelled. He banged his fist against the fire alarm at the end of the corridor and it started ringing.

'You nip down to the fifth floor and get that alarm going too, Elsa!' Mack yelled. 'And keep calling "Fire!" to get that dozy lot woken up properly. Go on, pal, you're doing great.'

176

I shot off down the stairs and searched for the fifth-floor fire alarm – but it had already been broken weeks ago by some of the boys and no-one had ever got round to mending it. But I wasn't broken. I was in full working order.

'FIRE!' I roared. 'Get up, get out! Come on, wake up! FIRE FIRE FIRE!'

I ran the length of the corridor and back, banging on every door, screeching until my throat was sore. Then I rushed back down the stairs, pushing past sleepy people stumbling in their nightclothes, desperate to find Mum and Pippa and Hank and Mack, wanting to make sure they were safe.

'Elsa! Elsa, where are you? Come here, baby!'

It was Mum, forcing her way back up the stairs, shouting and screaming.

'Oh Elsa!' she cried, and she swooped on me, clutching me as if she could never let me go. 'I thought you were with us – and then I looked back and you weren't there and I had to come back to get you even though Mack kept telling me you were fine and you were just waking everyone up . . . Oh Elsa, lovie, you're safe!'

'Of course I'm safe, Mum,' I said, hugging her fiercely. 'But I've got to get cracking down on the fourth floor now. No-one else has got such a good voice as me. Listen. FIRE!'

I nearly knocked Mum over with the force of my voice.

'Goodness! Yes, well, I don't see how anyone can sleep through that. But it's OK, they've got the other fire alarms going now and some of the men are seeing that everyone's getting out. They've rung for the fire engines. So come on now, darling – hang on tight to my hand,' said Mum.

We made our way down the stairs, clinging to each other. There was no smoke down on the lower floors but people were still panicking, surging out and running like mad, pushing and shoving. One little kid fell down but his mum pulled him up again and one of the men popped him up on his shoulders out of harm's way. The stairs seemed to go on for ever, as if we were going down and down right into the middle of the earth, but at last the lino changed to the cord carpeting of the first floor and then even though our feet kept trying to run downwards, we were on the level of the ground floor.

The Manager was there in a posh camel dressing gown, wringing his hands.

'Which one of you crazies set my hotel on fire?' he screamed. 'I'll have the law on you!'

'And we'll have the law on you too, because your fire alarms aren't working properly and we could all have got roasted to a cinder if it wasn't for my kid,' Mack thundered. He was still clutching Pippa in one arm, Hank in another. He turned to me – and for one mad moment I thought he was going to try to pick me up too. 'Yeah, this little kid here! She raised the alarm. She got us all up and out of it. Our Elsa.'

I'm not Mack's Elsa and I never will be – but I didn't really mind him showing off about me all the same.

'That Elsa!'

'Yes, little Elsa – she yelled "Fire!" fit to bust.'

'She was the one who woke us up – that little kid with the loud voice.'

They were all talking about me as we surged outside the hotel on to the pavement. Lots of people came and patted me on the back and said I'd done a grand job, and one man saw I was shivering out in the cold street and wrapped his jumper right round me to keep me warm. Someone had dragged out a whole pile of blankets and the old ladies and little kids got first pick. There weren't enough to go round.

'Come on, Jimmy, you can be a gent too,' said Mack, seizing hold of the Manager and 'helping' him out of his cosy camel dressing gown. He draped it round a shivery Asian granny who nodded and smiled. The Manager was shaking his head and frowning ferociously. He looked even sillier than Mack now, dressed in a pair of silky boxer shorts and nothing else. The bunny receptionist looked a bit bedraggled too without her angora jumper and with her fluffy hair in curlers. Switchboard looked startling in red satin pyjamas – a bit like a large raspberry jelly. Now that everyone was safe out in the street this fire was almost starting to be fun.

Then we heard a distant clanging and a big cheer went up. The fire engines were coming! We all crowded out of their way, and firemen in yellow helmets went rushing into the hotel with all their firefighting equipment. Lots of the kids wanted to go rushing in after them to watch. Funny-Face had to be frogmarched away by his mum, and Simple Simon and Nicky and Neil started their own fire-engine imitations, barging around bumping into people. Even baby Hank cottoned on and started shrieking like a siren.

Several ambulances arrived although no-one had actually been hurt, and the police came too. And guess who else? A television crew. Not the *Children in Crisis* people. These were from one of the news stations. And there were reporters too, running around with notebooks, and photographers flashing away with their cameras although all the people in their underwear started shrieking. Everyone asked how the fire started and who discovered it and someone said 'Elsa' and then someone else echoed them and soon almost everyone was saying 'Elsa Elsa Elsa'.

Me!

People were prodding me, pushing me forwards towards the cameras and the microphones and the notebooks. It was my Moment of Glory.

And do you know what? I can hardly bear to admit it. I came over all shy. I just wanted to duck my head and hide behind my mum.

'Come on now, lovie. Tell us all about it. You were the one who raised the alarm, weren't you? Come on, sweetheart, no need to be shy. It sounds as if you've been very brave,' they said. 'Tell us in your own words exactly what happened.'

I opened my mouth. But no words came out. It was as if I'd used up all my famous voice yelling 'Fire!' so many times.

So someone else started speaking for me. The wrong someone. The someone who really doesn't have anything to do with me. We're not even related. Though now he was acting as if he was my dad and I was his daughter.

'The poor wee girl's still a bit gob-smacked –
and no wonder! My, but she did a grand job
raising the alarm,' Mack boasted, strutting all
around. He was careful to hold in his tummy

all the time the cameras were pointing his
way. He couldn't flex his arm muscles properly
because he was still carrying Pippa and Hank,
but he kept carefully arranging his legs as if
he was posing for Mister Universe. He didn't
half look a berk. He sounded a right berk too,
prattling on and on about his wee Elsa. If I'd
had any voice left at all I'd have contradicted
him furiously.

Then little Pippa piped up.

'Yes, my sister Elsa's ever so big and brave. She rescued my baby!'

'She rescued the baby?' said the reporters, looking at Hank.

'Yep, she went and got him out of his cot. I was crying and crying because I thought he'd get all burnt up and Dad and Mum wouldn't let me go back for him—'

'They wouldn't go back for the *baby*?' said the reporters, their eyes swivelling from Hank to Mum and Mack.

'Not *our* baby. It's just Pippa's pillow. She calls it her baby,' said Mum quickly. Then she realized the cameras were aiming at her, and she clutched her nightie with one hand and did her best to tidy her hair with the other. 'Don't worry, we made sure we had our baby Hank safe and sound. But certainly if it hadn't been for our Elsa then we could still be in our beds right this minute –

charred to cinders,' said Mum dramatically.

'Yes, Elsa banged on our door and woke us all up. We'd be dead if it wasn't for her. She rescued all of us,' said Naomi's mum.

'Me and all *my* babies,' she said, showing them off to the camera.

'Elsa's my best friend,' said Naomi, nodding her head so that her plaits jiggled.

'Elsa's *my* best friend too and she rescued us and all,' said Funny-Face, and then he pulled the funniest face he could manage, all cross-eyes and drooly mouth until his mum gave him a poke.

My mum was giving me a poke too.

'Come on then, pet. Haven't you got anything to say for yourself? All these nice gentlemen want you to say a few words about the fire. Come on, lovie, this is your big chance,' Mum hissed.

I knew it. I swallowed. I wet my lips. I took a deep breath.

'Fire,' I mumbled. It was as if my voice could still only say one thing. I concentrated fiercely, trying to gain control. Fire crackled through my thoughts. My brain suddenly glowed.

'Do you know what happened to the plastic surgeon who got too close to the fire?' I said, in almost my own voice.

185

'What plastic surgeon? There was a medical man in there? Did he get out OK?' the reporters clamoured.

'He melted!' I said, and fell about laughing.

They blinked at me, missing a beat.

I decided to forge right ahead like a true professional.

'What were the two Spanish firemen called?'

'We haven't got any Spaniards in our team,' said one of the firemen, wiping the sweat from his brow and replacing his helmet.

'OK, but what would they be called? Hosé and Hose B! Do you get it?'

He didn't look very sure. Mum gave me a violent nudge.

'Elsa, stop telling those silly *jokes*!'

But once I got started I couldn't ever seem to stop.

'Why did the fireman wear red trousers?' I paused for a fraction. Everyone was still staring at me oddly. 'His blue ones were at the cleaners!'

'Pack it in, Elsa,' Mack hissed, looking like he wasn't so sure he wanted me to be his wee Elsa after all.

'It's the shock,' said Mum firmly. 'She's just having a funny five minutes.'

'Only she's not being flipping funny,' said Mack.

'Yep, I think we'd better cut the jokes,' said the television man gently.

'I'll try harder,' I said desperately. 'I'll try a new set of jokes, OK? Or I could put on a silly voice . . . ?'

'Why not use your own voice, Elsa? And why do you have to try so hard? Just be yourself. Act natural,' said the television man, chucking me under the chin. 'Let's start again, hmm? Tell us in your own words exactly what happened.'

'But if I just say any old thing, without any jokes, then I'm not funny,' I wailed.

'Who says you've got to be funny?'

'Well, I want to be a comedienne and get to be famous.'

'You don't have to be funny to be famous. And we don't really want people chortling when this goes out on the news. We want to touch the heart. We've got a super story here. You're a great little kid, Elsa. You'll come over really well on television if you just *relax*.'

'It's kind of difficult to act relaxed when you're standing on the pavement in your T-shirt and knickers and a whole bunch of strangers are asking you questions,' I said, sighing.

I wasn't trying to be funny. But the weirdest thing happened. Everyone chuckled appreciatively.

'So what happened, Elsa? You woke up in the middle of the night and . . . ?'

And so I started to tell them exactly what happened. I said I thought the smell was someone cooking chips and I started to get peckish and slipped out of bed to go and beg a few chips for myself. (They laughed again.) Then I told about tripping over Pippa's My Little Pony. (More laughter – and I still hadn't told a single joke!) Then I went on about the fire and dashing up and down the corridor banging on the doors and yelling. (I waited for them to laugh again, but this time they listened spellbound.) The television man asked what I'd yelled and I said 'Fire' and he said that wasn't very loud and *I* said well, I did it a lot louder. And he said show us. So I did. I threw back my head and roared.

'F-I-I-I-I-I-I-I-I-I-I-I-I-I-I-I-I-I-R-E!!!'

That nearly blew them all backwards. Most people had their hands over their ears. Some shook their heads, dazed. Then someone laughed. They all joined in. Someone else cheered. Someone else did too. Lots of cheers. For me. FOR ME!

It really was my Moment of Fame. I hadn't blown it after all.

My interview went out on the television. I thought I sounded sort of stupid, but everyone else said it went splendidly. (Well, Mum moaned because her hair was a sight and she didn't have any make-up on, and Mack fussed because they'd cut out most of his bits and he was only shown from the waist up so no-one could see his great hairy legs.) But they didn't cut *any* of my bits.

I might not have made it into the *Children in Crisis* documentary. But guess what. My news interview was repeated later in the year in a special compilation programme called *Children of Courage*. And I got to do another interview with a nice blonde lady with big teeth, and Mum spent some of Mack's betting money on a beautiful new outfit from the Flowerfields Shopping Centre for my special telly appearance. Mum made me try on lots of frilly frocks but they all looked *awful*.

So she gave up and let me choose instead. I wanted black jeans (so they wouldn't show the dirt). Mum bought me a black top too, and tied her red scarf round my neck, and then guess what we found at a car-boot sale? Red cowboy boots! They were a bit big but we stuffed the toes with paper and I looked absolutely great.

The blonde lady with the big teeth loved my outfit too. She said I looked just like a cowboy. I was a bit nervous so without thinking I got launched into a cowboy joke routine.

'Who wears a cowboy hat and spurs and lives under the sea? Billy the Squid!'

She laughed! It wasn't *that* funny, one of my oldest jokes actually, but she laughed and laughed and laughed. She said she loved jokes, the older and cornier the better, and she said I could maybe come on her special show one day and do my own comedy routine !!!!!

We couldn't go back to bed in room 608 when the firemen put the fire out at last. It wasn't all burnt to bits. It was only the kitchen that had cooked itself into little black crumbs. But the whole corridor was thick with smoke and sloshy with water and all the rooms looked as if someone had run amok with giant paint-brushes and vats of black paint. All our stuff was covered in this black treacle, and there was a sharp smell that scratched at your nostrils.

'Sorry, folks. You'll have to stay in temporary accommodation for a few weeks,' said the Chief Fireman, shaking his head.

He looked surprised when all the residents of the Royal gave a hearty cheer. The Manager was prancing about in his silk boxer shorts, pointing out that only a few of the rooms were seriously fire damaged, and that the first few floors were barely affected. There was a lot of rushing around consulting, and eventually it was decided that only the people living on the top two floors need be evacuated.

Us sixth-floor and fifth-floor people hugged and danced and shouted. All the other residents booed and argued and complained. Naomi and I had a big hug because she's on the fifth floor so she could come too. Then Funny-Face came and clapped hands with me because though he's on the fourth floor their room is right below the burnt kitchen and water had swirled right down through the room underneath and was dripping through to them, so they couldn't stay either.

We were all ferried off in police cars and coaches to this church hall, where several big bossy ladies with cardigans over their nighties handed out blankets and pillows and sleeping bags. They gave us paper cups of hot soup too – which we needed, because the church hall was freezing. The floor was slippery lino and fun to skid across in your socks, but not exactly cosy or comfy when we settled down to go to sleep. I didn't exactly rate bed number eight – and it soon got crowded because Pippa unzipped my sleeping bag and stuck herself in too. She kept

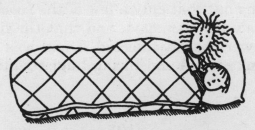

having nightmares and twitching and I had to keep waking her up and dragging her off to the toilet because I was all too aware of what would happen if I didn't.

There was only one toilet and there were queues for it all night long. It was worse in the morning. There was only the one small wash-basin too, and most people didn't have their toothbrushes or flannels or towels anyway.

'I don't know why we were flipping cheering last night,' said Mum, trying to wipe round Hank's sticky face with a damp hankie. 'Compared with this draughty old dump the Royal is practically a palace.'

'We can't stay here,' said Mack, sitting up and scratching. 'I'm going right down that Housing Department first thing.'

'Oh yeah?' said Mum, looking at him. 'You're walking down the road in your underpants, right? Don't forget you haven't even got any trousers any more. And look at me! This is all I've got – the old nightie that I'm wearing. All my clothes, all my make-up, my crinoline-lady ornament . . . all gone! Even if they're not ruined by that smoke then someone will be bound to nick them before I can get back to claim them.' She started to cry so I went and put my arms round her.

'Don't cry, Mum,' I said, hugging her tight.

'You've still got us.'

Mum snuffled a bit but then hugged me back.

'Yes, that's right, Elsa. I've still got my family. My Mack. My baby. My little girl. And my special big girl.'

The special big girl went a bit snuffly herself then. I was glad that Funny-Face in the next row of sleeping bags was still fast asleep or he might have jeered. He looked oddly little, snuggled up under the blanket. And he sucked his thumb and all!

More big bossy ladies breezed into the hall and started heating up a big urn of tea. They had lots of packets of biscuits too. I helped hand them round to everyone. We could have seconds and even thirds. A Bourbon, a short-bread finger and a chocolate Hob Nob make quite a good breakfast.

Then the ladies started dragging in great black plastic sacks crammed with clothes.

'Come and help yourselves! There should be enough for a new outfit for everyone.'

'Oh, big deal,' Mum grumbled. 'It's just tatty old junk left over from jumbles. I'm not wearing anyone's old Crimplene cast-offs.'

She watched Funny-Face's mum trying to squeeze herself into a tight black skirt.

'She's wasting her time. She'll never get that

over her big bum,' Mum mumbled, and when Funny-Face's mum had to give up the attempt, Mum darted out and snatched the skirt herself.

'There! I thought so! That's a Betty Barclay skirt. I've seen them on sale in Flowerfields. Hey, look, does it fit?' Mum pulled it up over her narrow hips and stood preening. 'I wonder if there's a jacket to go with it, eh?'

Mum started skimming her way through the plastic sacks and came up with all sorts of goodies – even a pair of patent high heels her exact size. She had more trouble finding stuff for Mack, considering the only size he takes is *out*-size. She found a jumper that could just about go round him, but the biggest trousers could barely do up and the legs ended way above his ankles. Hank was a bit of a problem too – there were heaps of baby clothes, but he's such a *big* baby that the average one-year-old's sleeping suit came unpopped every time he breathed out and bent him up double into the bargain. Pippa was fine, fitting all the little frocks a treat, but I looked such a fool in the only one my size that Mum threw it back in the pile. (Naomi tried it on instead and looked gorgeous, but then she always does.) Funny-Face was delving in a sack of boys' clothes so I had a sift through too and found some jeans

and a jumper and a really great baseball
bomber jacket with a picture of a lion on the
back!

'Well, we're all kitted out like a dog's dinner,
but we've still got no place to go,' said Mack.

But he was wrong.

Oh, you'll never guess where we ended up!

Someone from the Social and the man from
the Housing Office came round to the church
hall to tell us. We were all going to be temporarily accommodated in another hotel. Not a
special bed-and-breakfast DHS dumping
ground. A *real* hotel. The Star Hotel. With
stars after its name.

When we stepped through those starry glass doors it was like finding fairyland. There were soft sofas all over the reception area, and thick red carpet and flowers in great vases, and a huge chandelier sparkled from the ceiling. All us lot from the Oyal Htl crowded into the reception area, and Mum and Mack and Naomi's mum and Funny-Face's mum and dad and all the other grown-ups sprawled on the sofas while we all ran round and round the red carpet and up and down the wide staircase and rang all the bells on the lifts.

The Star Manager came out of his office to meet us. He didn't look terribly thrilled to see us, but he shook us all by the hand, even the littlest stickiest kid, and welcomed us to the Star Hotel. Then there was a lot of hoo-ha and argy-bargy about rooms, with the Manager and his chief receptionist going into a huddle. This receptionist was dark instead of blonde, and fierce instead of fluffy, but she also had long pointy fingernails and she started to tap them very impatiently indeed. But at last it was all sorted out and she handed all of us little cards instead of keys.

We were in suite 13. It might be an unlucky number for some people, but it was lucky lucky lucky for us.

Note I said suite, not room. As we shot up one floor in the lift and padded along the thickly carpeted corridor, Pippa licked her lips hopefully, thinking we were going to be given a sweety sweet. Even I didn't twig what suite really meant.

Suite 13 wasn't just one room. It was a set of

three rooms, just like a little flat. Only there was nothing little about suite 13. It was really big – and *beautiful.* The main room was blue, with deeper blue velvet curtains and a dark blue coverlet on the huge bed. There was a painting on the wall of a boy in a blue velvet suit and a blue glass vase on the bedside table filled with little blue pretendy rosebuds. There was a dressing table with swivel mirrors so you could see the back of your head, and a blue leather folder containing notepaper and envelopes, and a blue felt-tip pen patterned with stars. There was a big television too – a colour one – and it even had Sky!

There was a bathroom leading off this main room. It was blue too, with a blue bath, blue

basin, even a blue loo. They all shone like the sea they were so sparkly clean. Laid out on the gleaming tiled shelf were little blue bottles of shampoo and bath gel and tiny cakes of forget-me-not soap. Mum sniffed them rapturously, her eyes shining.

Mack kicked his shoes off and lay on the big bed, Hank sitting astride his tummy. The bed was so big that even Mack could fit right inside it, and his feet wouldn't stick out at the end. I thought we might *all* have to fit inside it, because it was the only bed in the room.

Then I saw another door and opened it. There was another bedroom, with three single beds, three little beside tables, and three little wooden chairs with carved hearts and painted roses. It was just like the three bears fairy

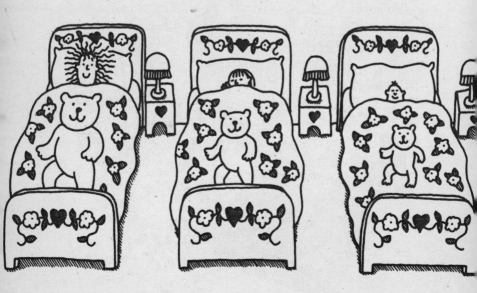

story – and there were bears on the duvets too, and a painting of Goldilocks up on the wall. The carpet and wallpaper were pale blue but the ceiling was a deep navy, with stars scattered all over it. That night when I slept in my wonderful, soft, splendid bed number nine I could still see the stars, even with the light switched off. They glowed luminously in the dark, my own magic midnight stars. I didn't want to sleep, just in case this was all a wonderful dream and when I woke up I'd be back in the grotty old Oyal Htl.

But it wasn't a dream at all. I woke up early and lay luxuriating in my bed and then I crept into Mum and Mack's room. They were all cuddled up together, looking friendly even though they were fast asleep. I sat down at the dressing table and practised a few funny faces and then I took a piece of paper and the felt-tip pen and wrote letters to all my friends.

*** Star Hotel ***

Dear Jamie,
I hope you haven't forgot me, I'm Elsa, and I don't like my new school much but I do like my new home. It's ever such a posh hotel and if it's nearer your school maybe I can come back which would be GREAT.

Love from Elsa

P.S. I'm the girl they said was thick but you said I was INTELLIGENT.

★★★ Star Hotel ★★★

Dear Mrs Hoover, Sorry
Mrs Macpherson,
    Hey, this hotel is
HEAPS better than the Royal.
Why don't you come and work
here? I bet you'd like it and
I'd give you a hand. The walls
have all got fancy paper so
no-one ever scribbles on them.
            Love From Elsa

★★★ Star Hotel ★★★

Dear Naomi,
    Isn't it super here. My
bedroom's got stars on the
ceiling, has yours? I hope we
don't have to go back to the
Royal for ages and ages.
See you at breakfast.
        Love from your friend Elsa
            ✗ ✗ ✗

★★★ Star Hotel ★★★

Dear Funny-Face,
    There are lots of bushes
and trees and stuff at the
end of the Star Hotel garden
so maybe we could make
a camp ???
            See you.
                Elsa

★★★ Star Hotel ★★★

Dear Pippa,
    I will read you this letter
seeing as you can't read
yet yourself. It is from me,
Elsa, and it's just to say
HELLO and we'll play lots
today.
        Love from your big sister
                Elsa

✗✗✗✗✗✗✗✗✗✗✗✗

★★★ *Star Hotel* ★★★

Dear Hank,
    Hello Big Baby

Love from your big
sister Elsa

XXX

★★★ *Star Hotel* ★★★

Dear Mum,
    It's so lovely here I don't
think you'll ever be sad
or cross ever again, eh?
    Lots and lots of love
        from Elsa

XXXXXXXXXXXX

★★★ *Star Hotel* ★★★

Dear Mack,
    Och Aye the Noo.
That's all the Scotch
    I know.

            From Elsa

★★★ *Star Hotel* ★★★

Dear Elsa,
    I am having a lovely time
here. I have been writing
lots and lots of letters. I even
wrote one to the warthog !!!
    But I am too happy to hate
anyone and there are stars
on my ceiling and I have
stars in my eyes because it
is so super here at the Star
Hotel.   Love and XXX
        from Elsa

There! I used up all the notepaper and gave myself a big appetite for breakfast.

Ooooh the breakfast! You have it in a lovely room with a dark pink swirly carpet and pink fuzzy paper on the walls and rose-pink cloths on the tables. You sit at a table and spread a rose-pink napkin on your lap and a waitress in a black frock and a white apron comes and asks what you want to drink. Then you go and help yourself to whatever you want to eat from the breakfast bar. You can have whatever you want. Lots and lots and lots of it.

Even Mum had more breakfast than usual. She had freshly squeezed orange juice and black coffee and toast and butter and marmalade.

Mack had tea and a bowl of porridge because he's Scottish and then he had a big plate of

bacon and egg and mushroom and fried potatoes and more bacon because that's his
favourite, and he tucked the extra bacon into
toast to make a bacon butty.

Pippa didn't copy me! She chose all by herself. Apple juice and Cocoa Pops and milk and
a soft white roll and butter and honey.

Hank had hot milk and a little bowl of
porridge like his dad and a runny egg and tiny
toast soldiers. He loved this breakfast and
wanted to wave his arms about to show his
appreciation and he dropped a few crumbs
(more than a few, actually) on the carpet, but
no-one seemed to mind and the waitress tickled him under the chin and said he was a
chubby little cherub!

Mum and Mack and Pippa and Hank all
knew exactly what they wanted for breakfast.
I was the one who simply couldn't decide
because it all looked so delicious. So guess

what. I had almost all of it.

I had milky tea and cranberry juice and cornflakes sprinkled with rainbow sugar and then muesli with extra sultanas and apple

rings and then scrambled egg on toast with tomato sauce and then sausages stuck in a long roll to make a hot dog and then a big jammy Danish pastry and I ate it all up, every little bit. It was the best breakfast ever.

What with the cranberry juice and the cherry jam in the pastry I ended up looking like Dracula. And that reminded me of a Dracula breakfast joke and that got me started.

I told jokes to Mum and Mack and Pippa and Hank and I shouted them to Naomi and Funny-Face across the tables and I tried them out on our waitress too because she seemed friendly and she said I was a proper caution. Do you want to hear a small sample?

What does Dracula like for breakfast?
Readyneck.

What do ghosts like for breakfast?
Dreaded wheat.

What do cannibals like for breakfast?
Buttered host.

What do Frenchmen eat for breakfast?
Huit heures bix.

How would a cannibal describe a man in a hammock?
Breakfast in bed.

What happens when a baby eats Rice Krispies?
It goes snap, crackle and poop.

I *must* stop rabbiting on like this. Well. Just one more.

What do you get if you pour boiling water down a rabbit hole?

Hot cross bunnies!

I'm not hot. I feel super-cool.
I'm not cross. I'm happy happy happy.
I'm not a bunny. I'm Elsa and I roar like a lion.

Hey, what do you get if you cross a lion with a parrot?
I don't know, but if he says 'Pretty Polly' you'd better

SMILE

THE
HUNT

A DEVIL'S ISLE NOVEL

CHLOE NEILL

First published in Great Britain in 2017
by Gollancz
an imprint of the Orion Publishing Group Ltd
Carmelite House, 50 Victoria Embankment
London EC4Y 0DZ

An Hachette UK Company

1 3 5 7 9 10 8 6 4 2

A CIP catalogue record for this book is
available from the British Library.

ISBN 978 1 473 21538 2

Printed and bound in Great Britain by Clays Ltd, St Ives plc

www.gollancz.co.uk
www.chloeneill.com

I was born for a storm, and a calm does not suit me

– Andrew Jackson

CHAPTER ONE

Early January
New Orleans

It had once been a lovely kitchen, with pale wood and granite, a
pretty view of a courtyard garden, and an enormous refrigerator
still dotted with photographs of what looked like a big, happy family. Father, mother, daughter, sons, and an enormous black dog, big
enough for the kids to ride on.

But they were long gone now, cleared out like nearly everyone
else in New Orleans when Paranormals flooded into our world, leaving most of our city and much of the South in ruins.

I was searching through what they'd left behind, looking for a
diamond in the rough.

"There is a house in New Orleans . . ."

I winced at the throaty croak that echoed from the other end of
the kitchen. "Like a frog being strangled," I muttered.

"They call the Rising Sun!"

I leaned around the cabinet door. "Moses!"

Inside the pantry, something thudded, rolled. "What? I'm working here."

"The singing."

A head, small and pale, with glossy black horns and irritable green eyes, peered around the pantry door. "What about it?"

"It's not great."

He snorted, doubt written across his face. "Says you."

"Yeah, says me."

Moses walked out of the pantry, three feet of Paranormal attitude. And, for the five weeks we'd been sneaking around New Orleans, my best friend.

"Someone might hear you," I reminded him.

He grumbled a curse, walked through the shadowed kitchen in my direction. He held up a bloated silver can, its seams bursting from age, heat, and rot. By the size, I guessed it was tuna fish. Very gnarly tuna fish.

"Jackpot," Moses said.

"You aren't going to eat that," I said. "It's spoiled."

"Don't be persnickety." He sniffed at the metal, closed his eyes in obvious pleasure. "More flavor this way." He held it out. "You want a sniff?"

My stomach flipped in revolt. "I do not. It would probably kill me."

He waved off the concern. "I've done this tons of times. Maybe I just have a stronger constitution than you, Claire."

"Hmm," I said noncommittally. Better to avoid going too far down that rabbit hole.

Moses was supposed to be locked up in Devil's Isle, the prison for Paras and anyone else touched by magic. Some Paras had wanted our world for their own; others, like Moses, had been forced to fight via magical conscription. Unfortunately, the Paranormal Combatant Command, the federal agency in charge of Paras, didn't much care about that detail.

I was a Sensitive, a human affected by magic that had seeped in from the Beyond. That magic gave me telekinesis, but at a cost: Too much magic would destroy my mind and body. Keeping that balance was a trick I was trying to master.

I'd kept my power secret until a cult called Reveillon—people who believed magic in any form, including the city's remaining Paranormals, should be eradicated—had attacked Devil's Isle. I'd had to use my magic to bring down Reveillon's founder. The PCC now considered me its enemy—and didn't get the irony.

There were signs the PCC might eventually come to its senses, acknowledge that magic wasn't all bad and not all Paranormals had been our enemies on purpose. It had even authorized temporary leave for a select few Paranormals who'd fought in the Battle of Devil's Isle.

Sensitives like me hadn't gotten the same consideration. We weren't Paras, and we weren't humans. We were different. Paras couldn't become wraiths—the pale, skeletal monsters into which Sensitives transformed if we failed to control our magic, to balance all that heady power. If we weren't careful, the magic would corrupt us, turn us into twisted creatures obsessed with absorbing more and more power.

So despite my efforts in the battle, there'd be no pass for me. I was too unpredictable, too dangerous, too untrustworthy.

Moses, having already snuck out of Devil's Isle and having skipped out again during the battle, didn't need a pass. He was already on the lam.

We'd tried playing the game, helping Containment, the PCC unit in charge of Devil's Isle, track down Reveillon and fighting on their side. And except for the few token passes, nothing had changed.

So we'd been sneaking around New Orleans, working to avoid Containment. And since they were treating us like criminals, we figured we'd might as well act like criminals. We'd decided our job was to challenge the PCC and its refusal to acknowledge the truth about magic, about Paranormals, about Sensitives.

Along with the other members of our crew, which we called Delta, we'd been covering Reveillon's antimagic billboards with our own messages, using contacts outside the war Zone to rally the rest of the world to our side and gathering supplies for the Devil's Isle clinic.

The facility—and the wraiths secured there—weren't on Containment's priority list. Reveillon's attacks had put a big crimp in the PCC's supply chain, so even if the clinic had been on that list, consumables were getting harder to come by. We were in this house to gather up what we could for delivery to Lizzie, who ran the clinic.

Moses walked toward the kitchen island with his slightly sideways gait, then slung a mesh bag of equally swollen cans onto the granite countertop and added his newest find to it. "You find anything?"

It took me a moment to reorient. I closed the cabinet, held up a carton of sea salt and a tin of tea bags. "Salt's half full, and the tea bags still smell mostly like tea." No small feat, given they'd been stewing in heat and humidity. "Still," I said, "you'd think there'd be more here."

"It's a nice house," he said, glancing around the room. "It would have been one of the first ones sacked after the war—or during the battle."

"Yeah," I said.

Reveillon had ransacked Devil's Isle—and every neighborhood the members had blown through along the way. They'd been like a hurricane scouring their way across New Orleans. Not the first storm the Big Easy had faced down. But over time, hell and high water took their toll.

Reveillon's members had hurt the city and those who lived here—

and some, including Liam Quinn, didn't live here anymore. The bounty hunter I'd fallen for had been hit by magic, and he'd left New Orleans to fight his resulting demons.

I hadn't heard from him since.

I knew Liam was with his grandmother Eleanor in what Malachi called the "southern reach," the bayous and marshes of southern Louisiana, where small communities of Paras worked to stay out of Containment's crosshairs—and out of Devil's Isle.

Malachi, another of my Paranormal friends, had told us that much when he'd returned from reuniting Liam and Eleanor.

But that was all I knew about Liam's location or the effects of the magical hit he'd taken. It was a point of pride that I hadn't asked Malachi for any more details, for updates as one week after another passed. I'd tried to force thoughts of Liam to the back of my mind, giving him the time and space he apparently needed. In the meantime, I'd focused on Delta, on our new work for New Orleans, on controlling my magic. Because even though I knew why he'd gone, it still hurt to be left behind.

I put my hands on my hips and sighed as I looked at our meager harvest. "Oh, well. You add it to the bottled water, the aspirin, the radio. That's something."

"It's something," he said. "You know they don't take things for granted."

They hadn't. If anything, they'd been too grateful, and that didn't make me feel any better about Containment or our situation.

"Oh, found one more thing," Moses said, pulling something from the bib of his denim overalls. He'd found the overalls during a previous scavenger hunt. They were way too big for him—the pants rolled up at the bottom—but he loved that front pocket.

He moved toward me, offered his hand. In his small, meaty palm sat a silver robot with a square body perched on blocky feet. Probably three inches long, with a canister-shaped head topped by a tiny antenna. A metal windup key emerged from its back.

"It was wedged behind a drawer," Moses said.

"It's old," I said, taking it gingerly and looking—as my father had taught me—for a manufacturer's mark or date, but I didn't find anything. "Probably from the fifties or sixties." That was much older than the fancy cabinets and countertops in there. "Must have missed it when they renovated the house. Let's fire it up." Carefully, I cranked the key, listened to the gears catch and lock, then set the toy on the countertop.

The gears buzzed like hornets as it moved forward, its feet rotating in sequence, the little antenna bobbing. We watched silently as it marched to the end of the countertop. Moses caught it before it reached the end, turned it around, and sent it back in my direction.

"Huh," he said, monitoring its progress with surprising affection in his eyes. "I like that."

"Yeah," I said, "so do I."

We wound it again and let the toy repeat its parade across the granite.

"Shame they missed it when they left," he said.

"What did they miss?"

We both turned sharply, found a man behind us.

Malachi was tall, over six feet, with the broad shoulders of a soldier. He looked like an angel: tousled blond curls that reached his shoulders, a square jaw, luminous ivory wings that folded and magically disappeared while we watched, and eyes of shimmering gold. That gold was a signature of some Paranormals—and it was the color I'd seen in Liam's eyes after he'd been hit and before he'd run.

Malachi had been a general in the Consularis army—the caste of Paras who'd ruled the Beyond before the war, the same Paras who'd been magically conscripted to fight us by their enemies, the Court of Dawn.

We hadn't heard the usual *thush* of wings that signaled Malachi had alighted—and apparently walked right through the front door. He wore jeans, boots, and a faded Loyola T-shirt.

Malachi smiled at Moses, then let his gaze linger on me. My heart met that look, delivered by a man beautiful enough to be carved in marble and preserved for eternity, with an answering thump. It was an instinctive response, triggered by the sheer power of his gaze.

Paras had very different conceptions of romance and attraction. We were just friends—even if we'd become better friends over the last few weeks—but that didn't make his power any less potent.

"They missed our new toy," I said, answering his question. I wound it again and set it to work.

"Ah," he said, then picked it up to study it. "An automaton."

"Or humans' sixty-year-old idea of one. How'd you find us?"

"We followed the sound of mating cats," Malachi said, sliding a sly smile to Moses.

Moses lifted his middle finger. "I got your mating cats right here."

I guess the gesture translated. Good to know. "We?" I asked.

"Someone wanted to talk." He glanced back as footsteps echoed on the hardwood floors at the other end of the shotgun house.

A man stepped into the doorway, his figure only a shadow in the harsh sunlight behind him.

For a moment, I was lost in memory, back at Royal Mercantile, my store in the French Quarter. Or it had been, before I'd been forced to abandon it. In my mind, I was in an antique bed on a rough-hewn floor, a slip of a breeze coming through the windows and a man sleeping next to me. Dark hair. Blue eyes. Body lean and honed like a weapon.

The man I'd fought beside.

The man who'd left.

Then he took a step forward. Memory faded, putting another man in the doorway. Similar to the one who'd left, but not the same.

"Gavin," Moses said.

This wasn't Liam, but his brother. But it was still surprising that he was standing here with Malachi. I hadn't seen him since the battle.

"Claire. Mos."

"What are you doing here?" I asked.

Gavin didn't waste any time. "Jack Broussard is dead."

Broussard was a Containment agent, and a generally despicable human.

"No loss there," Moses said.

"Maybe not," Gavin replied. "But they're saying Liam killed him."

CHAPTER TWO

"Liam's not in New Orleans," Malachi said simply. "He couldn't have done it."

"There's supposedly physical evidence he did," Gavin said. "And Liam and Broussard had a bad history. That seems to be enough."

Liam was a bounty hunter, or had been, and Broussard had been his handler before their relationship had soured. Because Liam understood Paranormals weren't all our enemies, Broussard believed Liam was a traitor to humankind. That was the kind of attitude Delta was fighting against.

"Tell us what happened," Moses said, crossing his arms.

"Broussard didn't show up for a shift at the Cabildo," Gavin said. Containment headquartered in the historic building on Jackson Square. "Containment sent someone to take a look, and they found him in his house. It was bloody. His throat had been slit." He paused, seemed to collect himself. "The knife was one of Liam's—a hunting knife I gave him. Had an engraved blade. And 'For Gracie' was scrawled on the wall—in Broussard's blood."

The silence was heavy, mixed with eddies of horror and fury.

Gracie was Gavin and Liam's late sister, a young woman killed by wraiths. Her death had haunted them, and that was one of the obstacles that had stood between me and Liam.

Moses narrowed his eyes. "Someone's setting your brother up."

"That's how it reads to me."

"Bastards," Moses spat. "Scum-sucking bastards for using your sister like that."

"Yeah," Gavin said, running a hand through his hair. "I can't argue with that."

"Why set Liam up?" I asked. "Containment doesn't have anything against him—or didn't. Do they know he has magic?"

"Not that I'm aware of," Gavin said.

"Maybe Containment didn't arrange the frame-up," Malachi said. "Maybe the killer did. He or she could have a vendetta against Liam, or may not care who's blamed, as long as it's directed away from him or her."

"Yeah," Gavin said with a heavy sigh. He looked tired, I realized, his skin a little paler than usual, his eyes shadowed with fatigue. "I lean toward that. Containment's issued a bounty for him."

"Gunnar wouldn't do that." Gunnar Landreau was second-in-command at Containment, and one of my best friends.

"He wouldn't have a choice," Gavin said. "An agent's been murdered, and the evidence points to Liam. Gunnar's hands are tied. Containment's already been looking for him. Now that the bounty's issued, the search is going to get more intense. Containment is also looking for Eleanor."

"For leverage," I said, sickness settling in my belly.

"Probably," Gavin said. "I hear they've been through her place in Devil's Isle, tore up what wasn't already torn up after the battle. I haven't been to Liam's, but I imagine it didn't fare any better."

"How do you know all this?" Moses asked. "You talk to Gunnar?"

He shook his head. "I just got back into town, had a drink with a source at the Cabildo. That's where I got the details."

"You're here to warn us," I said. "Because now they'll want us for another reason—to find Liam."

Gavin nodded. "Containment's been looking for you, but they haven't been looking very hard. They know you helped in the battle; Gunnar knows you helped. But with this, they'll double their efforts to take you in."

Moses snorted. "They can try."

"We'll be careful," I said. "What are you going to do about Liam?"

"We're going to warn him," Gavin said. "Me and Malachi. That's the other thing we wanted to tell you. We'll be gone for at least a couple of days, more likely three."

"You know where Liam is?" Moses asked. "I mean, specifically?"

The bayous and marshes of southern Louisiana covered thousands of square miles. They were also isolated and difficult to get through.

"We know where they were," Malachi said. "Erida checks in when she can." Erida was a goddess of war and one of Malachi's people. She'd accompanied Eleanor into the bayous. But to make it harder for Containment to find them, Erida, Eleanor, and the other Paras moved frequently. "I received a message three days ago. By the time we get to that location, she'll have moved again."

"It's a place to start," Gavin said with a nod. "That's all we need."

"They could follow you back to him," I said. "That might be their plan—to send you running to him, to Eleanor. And if they find him, they might find the others."

I didn't know how many Paras lived in the bayou, but I knew their existence needed to remain a secret. Given the smile on Gavin's face, he wasn't very concerned about that.

"They might think we'll lead them to Liam and the others. But I've walked through PCC recon camps without being spotted. If I don't want to be seen, I won't be seen. And I'm fairly confident Malachi has the same skills."

"I do," Malachi confirmed. "It's not without risk. But we can't not warn them of what might be coming. Of the storm they may be facing. And we can't wait until Erida checks in again."

I had a sudden image of Liam on his knees in front of the cypress house, hands linked behind his head, gun at his back. Whether from fear or premonition, a cold sweat snaked up my spine. Because Liam Quinn was still mine.

"I'm going with you."

"No," Gavin said automatically. "It's too dangerous."

I gave him my best stare. "You want me to remind you what we faced down five weeks ago? What I faced down?"

"I don't mean physical danger; I know you can hold your own, not that I'm eager to throw you into a fight." He moved toward me. "Like I said, Containment wants you even more now. Parading you around isn't the best idea."

"I wouldn't be parading," I said flatly. "And they'll expect me to be in New Orleans. Near the store, near my friends. They won't be looking out there."

"Claire might help Liam," Malachi said. "Could be good for him."

"And he'll string me up if anything happens to her," Gavin said, flashing him a look. "You want to take that punishment for me?"

"If Liam wanted to keep an eye on me," I said, "he could have stayed in New Orleans."

Gavin opened his mouth, closed it again. "I can't really argue with that."

Moses snorted. "That's a damn lie. You'd argue with a signpost just for the fun of it."

"That's the Irish in me," Gavin admitted.

"That's the mule in you," Moses corrected. "Anyway, I think it's a good idea." He narrowed his eyes at me. "Gets her off my back for a little while."

I just rolled my eyes. I'd missed one day of visiting him since the battle—during a gnarly tropical storm—and he'd hounded me for a week.

Gavin tapped his fingers on the countertop as he considered. *Tap-tap-tap. Tap-tap-tap.* "Give us a minute?" he said, glancing up at Moses and Malachi.

Not one to take orders from Gavin, Malachi looked at me. When I nodded, he gestured to Moses, and they walked into the next room, leaving us alone.

"I don't want you to get hurt," Gavin said, then held up a hand when I started to argue. "I don't mean by Containment."

He softened his tone. "He hasn't been gone very long, not really. And if he's trying to come to terms with his magic, he may not be ready for company." He paused, and my stomach clenched at what I knew was coming next. "He may not be ready for you."

That was the other side of the coin. The possibility that time had changed his mind, or his heart, had been gnawing at me. And the teeth grew sharper each day that passed without a message.

But it was a risk I had to take. I'd given him time and space to cope. Now it was time to act. To flip the coin.

Gavin must have seen the hurt in my eyes. "Liam wouldn't feel good about running away. About bailing on you, on New Orleans, on me, on the life he was finally beginning to build here. But that doesn't mean he's ready to come back."

I nodded. "I know."

"And you still want to go?"

I turned to lean back against the counter, crossed my arms. "I don't like that he left. I know why he did it, but I don't like it. And I don't feel good about being left behind, probably any more than you do."

Gavin didn't answer with words, but there was no mistaking the quick flinch. Liam had hurt both of us. He might have had his reasons, but the pain was still there, the wounds still fresh.

"But he's in danger," I continued. "Eleanor's in danger. I'm not going to sit on my ass in New Orleans while you guys do the hard work." I looked over at him. "If it was me out there, he'd look for me. Even if he thought my feelings had changed."

He looked like he wanted to argue, but realized there wasn't anything to argue about.

"And Containment?"

"You suddenly a coward?" I asked with a grin.

He puffed out his chest. "I'm not afraid of Containment. Or anything else. But still." He made a vague gesture in the direction of my hair. "Your hair . . . It's noticeable."

Rolling my eyes, I pulled my long red hair into a bun and unsnapped the Saints cap I'd fastened to the back of my jeans. Then I stuffed my hair into it, adjusted the fit.

"Boom," I said, and flicked the cap's bill. "Instant disguise. I won't get caught."

"You willing to stake your life on that?"

I lifted my brows. "I've been staking my life on it since I learned I had magic. And since the battle. You think I've spent that time underground?"

"Not according to what Malachi's told me." He glanced over at me. "I saw the billboard on Magazine. 'Free the Consularis. Seek the truth.' And a pretty little triangle in the bottom corner. The Greek symbol for delta."

"It's amazing what you can do with seven-year-old house paint."

"It was one of Reveillon's?"

"It was. Now it's one of ours."

Gavin shook his head, but there was pride in his eyes. "He ever tell you you're stubborn?"

"Connolly," I said, grinning and reminding him of my last name. "I'm also Irish. And you know I can handle myself."

To prove my point, I raised a hand, gathered up the tendrils of power that lingered in the air, and used them to lift the robot off the counter and into my hand. When it was in my grip, I scratched a bit of grime from its body.

"You're getting better," Gavin said. "Smoother."

I had gotten better, both at controlling it and expelling the leftover magic to keep it from wrecking me.

"I've been practicing." Robot still safe in my palm, I looked up at him. "We go, we talk to them, we come back. An easy two days," I said, repeating his promise. "Three at the most."

"Rude, using my words against me."

"Handy, giving me words to use."

Gavin leaned on the countertop, muttered something in the Cajun French he and Liam used when their emotions ran high. But my arrow had found its mark. "Fine. We meet at Moses's place at dawn." His expression changed. "In the meantime, Malachi said you have a place to stay. A place that's safe."

"He's right." The fewer the people who knew about the former Apollo gas station my father had rehabbed, the building where I now lived, the safer it would remain. It had to stay safe because it was the last bastion of a trove of magical objects my father had saved from destruction. So I wouldn't give Gavin any more details.

Gavin nodded. "I figure you, like Liam, had reasons for the choices you made."

I narrowed my gaze. "Now who's using words against whom?"

———————

Gavin left. "We'll talk," Malachi said, and then he was gone, too.

"Was he telling you or me?" I asked Moses.

"Could be either," Moses said. "But I'm pretty sure he meant you."

Moses and I packed up the things we'd found, then closed up the house again. We walked in silence through the alley that bisected the block.

"Did you know Broussard well?" I asked as we moved through shadows made by the high afternoon sun. It wasn't exactly discreet to walk through the city in broad daylight, but there were so few people in the neighborhood—and the sound of anyone was so easily heard in the silence of the city—that we usually risked it.

"Not well," he said, pausing to kick at a shining spot of metal in the gravel. "Knew enough to stay away from him. Saw the world as good or bad. You were either on his side or on the wrong side." Apparently not impressed by whatever he'd found on the ground, he started walking again.

"Yeah. Liam said something similar. You know anyone who'd want him dead? Maybe any Paras in Devil's Isle?"

Moses snorted. "Who didn't want him dead? But hated him enough to take him out? No." He stopped and leaned down, pulled a random bit of wire from a patch of scraggly grass, regarded it with a nod, stuffed it into his bag. Moses had never met an electronic component he didn't like; he'd had a store of discarded radios, computers, televisions, and every other available gadget in Devil's Isle before it had been destroyed.

As a woman estranged from her store, I could sympathize.

"Humans," he said when we were moving again, "think they're the only things we think about. Seven years we've been in Devil's

Isle. We've got lives and worries, probably the same kind of crap humans worry about."

Malachi had warned me once not to make assumptions about Paras. He'd been right then, just as Moses was right now.

"So who does that leave? Did he have enemies?"

"You mean other than Liam? They want to frame him for this, they couldn't have picked a better fall guy."

"Yeah. No love lost there." I glanced at him. "Maybe you could poll your Para friends? Find out what they know?"

"How would I do that? They're in Devil's Isle, and I'm out here in the wasteland." But he took a big huff of fresh air and held it in for a moment, as if savoring the sensation.

"I know you and Solomon communicate," I said. Solomon was the Paranormal kingpin of Devil's Isle. He was also Moses's cousin.

"That would be illegal. And risky."

I stopped, gave him a dry look. It took a minute, but eventually he withered a little, hunched his shoulders.

"I'll find out what I can."

"Good man. And I guess I'm going into the bayou."

"It's a good decision."

I looked back at him. "I thought you were opposed to it."

"The danger, yeah." He lifted a shoulder. "But not the idea. It's Liam, and you're Claire. I may not be people, but I got a sense of how they work."

"He may not want to see me."

Moses rolled his eyes.

"He left," I pointed out.

"You know why he left." His voice was low, quiet, and a little bit sad. "He'll want to see you. He'll *need* to see you."

I hoped so. Because I didn't really have a backup plan.

"Look," he said, "let's just put it out there. He left, and even if he has his reasons, it's real damn hard not to take that personally. But you haven't been whining and moping. You got your shit together, and you hung out with me." He pointed a stubby finger at me. "Now you go find that boy, and you call his ass out."

I thought of Gavin's warning. "What if he won't talk to me?" The words spilled out and with them the fear.

"Well, fuck that," Moses said, and started walking again. "He'll talk to you, if only because he's gotta face this Broussard situation. He may have his issues, but he's not a coward." He looked at me speculatively, onyx horns glinting in the sunlight. "I figure he gets a good look at you, he probably remembers how good he had it."

That made me feel better. "And what are you going to do while I'm gone?"

"Try and get my damn comp up and running. Managed to find a working power supply, but I still can't get the OS to boot."

We reached the end of the alley, prepared to turn right down the sidewalk, and stopped short. Across the street, a man in fatigues sat inside a Containment-branded jeep. Another man walked toward him, opened the front passenger door, and climbed inside. RECOVERY was printed in large letters on the side.

Moses and I were the types they wanted to recover: Paras and Sensitives who weren't in Devil's Isle, where we belonged.

"Shit," Moses said, stepping back into the shadows. "We wait here or run?"

There was no way to tell if they were here for us—if they'd followed us across the neighborhood—or if there were others on the hit list today. "Wait," I said. And watch. Figure out what they did, and which way we'd need to run.

The sounds came first, high-pitched and spitting with anger.

"A wraith?" Moses said.

But as two agents dragged the man out, I realized we weren't that lucky.

The man they'd found wasn't a wraith or a Sensitive. He was a Para, short and slender, with elfish features, pointed ears. His name was Pike. He was a friend of Liam's who'd helped protect Eleanor when she'd lived in Devil's Isle.

"I didn't know he made it out," Moses said, voice tight with concern.

"Me, either." I hadn't seen Pike during the battle or in the brief time after that I'd been in the Quarter, and I hadn't been back inside Devil's Isle since. If he'd been on the streets the entire time, I hadn't seen him there, either.

I didn't know Pike well. If Liam trusted him, Pike was smart enough to be careful. But Containment had ways of finding people. I glanced up and around, looking for the magic monitor, found it hanging on a light pole across the street. The light blinked green. The power was on in this sector of the city, and Pike had done something magical, which tripped the alarm.

I started forward, but Moses's fingers tightened on my arm. I tried to shake him loose, but he held firm. He may have been small, but he had plenty of strength.

"Let go," I said. "I have to help him."

"You can't just run out there. We're outnumbered."

"I can use magic." I could clear a path for Pike, get the agents out of his way, and put him somewhere safe—as long as I could do it quickly. I could use only so much magic without having to manage its side effects.

"Okay," Moses whispered, "let's assume you get out there and kick some ass with your magic, and they *don't* take you into Devil's Isle. Gavin already told you they've moved you up the most wanted list. You do this, you definitely can't risk going into the bayou."

And wasn't that a shitty choice? I felt angry, guilty, helpless. "We can't just let them take him."

"He'll go back inside," Moses said. His voice was quiet. "There are worse places for him to be."

"Even if freedom's the other option?"

"There's a time and place," he said. "And out here on the street, in broad daylight in front of operational magic monitors ain't either of those."

Pike hadn't stopped struggling, so the agents forced a jacket on him—a special restraint usually used to control wraiths—and moved him into the back of the vehicle.

A moment later, they climbed inside and were gone. When the neighborhood was quiet again, the birds began to chirp.

"We'll talk to Lizzie," Moses said. "Make sure she's got an eye on him."

Right now that didn't feel like much consolation.

It had been a gas station—a corner business with atomic-era architecture and a couple of garage bays. It was now a bunker and a secret archive of banned magical objects. And my home sweet home.

Inside, there were long wooden tables and shelves along the walls, each holding priceless and completely illegal weapons, books, masks, and other items. My father had hidden them here to keep them away from Containment bonfires.

For now, I was outside and above the magic. I lay on a blanket on the roof, where the low walls gave me cover from Containment patrols.

Tomorrow would be the first night I'd spent out of New Orleans in years. My father had refused to evacuate, even when the city was bombarded. We'd lived together in a house until he died, and then I moved into Royal Mercantile. After the Battle of Devil's Isle, I'd walked to the gas station and spent the first of many nights here. It had become my home, my new piece of New Orleans.

Tonight I watched the sun sink in the west, sending streaks of brilliant orange and purple across the sky. The sight was beautiful enough that I could nearly pretend the world was whole again. But nearly wasn't enough. Nothing—and no one—in the Zone was whole anymore.

The gas station sat on what had been a busy road. But in the weeks I'd been here, I'd seen fewer than a dozen people nearby. An older couple lived up the street in a double camelback. A man lived two blocks up in the kingdom he'd made of a former Piggly Wiggly. Everyone else had been moving: passersby, nomads, Containment officers.

"I understand I missed some excitement."

I jumped at the sound of Malachi's voice, sat up to find him standing behind me, his body a dark silhouette against the brilliant sky. "You have got to stop doing that."

His wings retracted, changing his shape from Paranormal to human. "You have got to listen harder."

I shouldn't have been surprised; Malachi had a habit of visiting me at night. Darkness reduced the chance he'd be seen, and I think he enjoyed the company and the quiet. I hadn't let him inside the building—too many secrets there—but I'd given him the address. I knew I could trust him to keep the location secret, and I didn't have to worry about his evading Containment if they somehow found out about it.

"Containment agents found Pike," I said. "They took him in."

He walked toward me, sat down on the edge of the blanket. His body was big and warm, and he smelled faintly like woodsmoke. "Moses told me."

I stared hard at the horizon, guilt punching through my chest. "I should have helped him."

"There's a time and a place."

"That's what Moses said."

"He was right. We have to pick our battles. They aren't all winnable."

I glanced at him. His face was inscrutable, his golden eyes shimmering in the fading light as he scanned the horizon, as if keeping watch for marauders. "Is that a lesson you learned here, or in the Beyond?"

"Here," he said thoughtfully. "In the Beyond, we were in power and took much for granted." He glanced at me. "I've told you it was an orderly society. Rigidly so. If it hadn't been so rigid—if we'd been able to evolve, to change—perhaps we'd have been able to prevent the war."

"Maybe," I said. "Or maybe the Court would have been dissatisfied with everything you offered to do. Sometimes the ones who cry loudest for war don't really want change. They just want the fight and the power."

He nodded. "Humans and Paras are very similar in that respect."

I sat up, crossed my legs. "You didn't object to Gavin's request—to leaving New Orleans and traveling into the wilderness. Is that a winnable battle?"

"I don't know. But I've been in that particular wilderness before. There's a lot to recommend it."

"I don't like snakes."

Malachi smiled, ran a hand through his tousled curls. "Then the bayou may not be the best place for you."

"What is?" I asked. I didn't really fit in anywhere right now. "What's the real story about Broussard?"

"I don't know anything beyond what Gavin said. But whatever it is, Liam seems to be the key."

"The key to what?"

"I don't know. Something important enough to kill a Containment agent for. Or something important enough to frame Liam for. Or both."

I looked up at the stars that had begun to pierce the settling darkness. "Life is never simple."

"Death is simpler." He smiled a little. "But too simple for most."

"At least everybody gets a turn."

He lay back, looked up at the stars. "That's one thing we certainly all have in common."

CHAPTER THREE

I sat on the floor. It was just dawn, and sunlight would have filtered through the windows if they hadn't been painted over to shield the magical goods inside from prying eyes. I still wore pajamas—a V-neck T-shirt and shorts. I hadn't yet begun to pack for the trip.

I'd committed to going. And I was going. But in the meantime, I was having seriously cold feet.

I knew why Liam had left. Understood well the fear and doubts he'd have had about gaining magic. I'd had doubts, too, and I hadn't had a sister who'd been killed by wraiths, by magic gone bad. Having gained magic, he would have to deal with those complicated feelings.

And it was probably worse for him, because he didn't clearly fit on the human-Sensitive-Paranormal scale. Unlike me, he and Eleanor hadn't just absorbed magic; they'd gotten it through strikes by magical weapons.

But five weeks still felt like a long time. A long time with no messages, no checking in, no making sure that I was all right. Maybe it was selfish of me, maybe not. But the silence hurt. Maybe, like Gavin had warned me, Liam's feelings had changed.

If they had, what was I going to say to him? How was I going to face that down?

I shook my head. At least I'd find out one way or the other, I reminded myself, and ignored the hollowness in my chest. I wouldn't have to wait, and I wouldn't have to wonder. Plus, I'd get out of New Orleans for a little while. I'd spend time with Malachi and Gavin, who were usually entertaining, and I'd see parts of Louisiana I hadn't seen before. If we found them, I'd see Eleanor again.

We hadn't even left yet, and I was lining up the consolation prizes.

"Way to be brave, Connolly." I muttered it to myself, but climbed to my feet, then took the small back staircase to the basement.

I walked to the far wall, grabbed one of the hanging backpacks that was already half full of emergency supplies my father had decided we'd needed, and began adding to it.

Today, I was going into the bayou. I'd see Liam. And the shape of my future would become clear.

The sky was gray with clouds and humidity, and even the breeze was heavy and wet and carried the scents of earth and water. The scents of New Orleans.

The temperature would continue to climb and the humidity probably wouldn't diminish, but we'd also be facing bugs of every variety, and God only knew what other crawling and flying horrors rural Louisiana would have to offer, so I opted for long cargo pants and a short-sleeved shirt, and folded a thin waterproof jacket into my pack in case of deluge.

In Louisiana, there was always a chance of deluge.

My travel mates stood together in the alley behind Moses's house— one human and two Paranormals. Moses, in a shirt of screaming red that made him look more like an impish devil than made me comfortable, Gavin in lived-in jeans and a technical shirt, and Malachi in a V-neck and jeans. Gavin had the strap of an army surplus pack in one hand, a double-barreled shotgun in the other.

He looked at me, smiled. There was so much Quinn in that smile. "Looks like we're all here. Would y'all like the good news first or the bad news?"

"I'd prefer there not be any bad news," I said, adjusting my pack. "Is that an option?"

"No," Gavin said. "I talked to Gunnar this morning. He doesn't think Liam's guilty, but the theory's got legs within Containment. There are folks who think Liam had too much leeway dealing with Paras and got special treatment because of his family."

Eleanor was an Arsenault, an old and wealthy Creole family connected to very powerful people outside the Zone—the people we'd been contacting in our efforts to bring to light the truth about magic.

"They sound like allies of Broussard," I said.

"Yeah. They have no trouble believing this is Liam's doing. And they've increased the amount of the bounty."

"It's only been a day," I said, concern for Liam tightening my gut. "They never increase that quickly." I'd done a little bounty hunting with Liam; it had been good cover for keeping an eye on Containment. Increases in bounties were rare, and happened only when time had passed without a lead on the particular prey.

"And what's the good news?" Malachi asked.

"It's not raining. Yet."

We just looked at him.

Shameless, Gavin lifted a shoulder. "As leader of this particular mission, I figured you needed the stick and the carrot. Except I didn't have any carrots. So I went with the weather."

Moses shook his head, lips pursed. "You this good on all your missions?"

"There's a reason I usually work alone," Gavin said, shouldering the pack.

"Where, exactly, are we going?" I asked. There was no one else around, but I dropped my voice anyway. This wasn't the time to attract attention.

"Houma," Malachi said. "Vicinity of Erida's last location."

Houma was about an hour's drive from New Orleans.

"There," he continued, "we'll meet some friends, see if we can get a sense of where she went."

"Friends?" I asked.

"Paranormals with passes."

I lifted my eyebrows. "I was actually beginning to think that was a myth. Since Moses didn't get one, I mean. Or you."

"I won't request freedom I already own," Malachi said. "And Containment isn't in a position to give us passes from Devil's Isle, since we're already out."

I couldn't really argue with that.

Gavin gestured to the beat-up jeep at the curb. "The wheels will take us to Houma. Then we'll leave the vehicle, travel on foot."

"If we get to the Gulf, we've gone too far?" I asked.

"Something like that." Gavin looked me over, took in the pants, shirt, shoes, and gave a nod of approval. "What's in the bag?"

"Water, poncho, knife, atomic bug spray." I might not have been out of New Orleans in a while, but I'd been in it long enough. I had a pretty good idea how to survive in the wet and the heat.

"Good," Gavin said with a smile.

"I'll meet you at Houma," Malachi said.

"Wait," I said, sliding him a narrowed glance. "What do you mean you'll 'meet' us? You aren't going with us?"

He smiled. "I mean I don't need a ride." He unfolded his wings, and twelve feet of ivory stretched out behind him, feathers gleaming in the sun.

"You're going to fly the whole way?"

"Boy, will his arms be tired!" Moses said, waving a fake cigar.

Gavin's eyes narrowed at me. "I hear you let him have a joke book."

"He found it in an abandoned house, which made it fair game. I couldn't exactly stop him from taking it."

He shook his head. "Let's hit the road. Every mile toward Houma is another mile away from jokes that start with 'Two Paranormals walked into a bar.'"

"I need a minute," Moses said to me, then moved a few feet away.

"I believe you're being beckoned," Malachi said.

"Evidently," I said, and joined Moses. "You rang?"

"I want you to remember something," he said, pointing a stubby finger up at me. "You've worked hard for the last few weeks, done some good around here. Whatever happens, no one can take that away from you."

I lifted my brows, surprised at the emotion in his eyes. "You under the impression I'm gonna have a breakdown in the bayou?"

"I'm just saying, whatever he says or does"—he paused, seemed to look for the right words—"there's more to the world than dames."

I looked at him for a minute, appreciating the thought but confused by the message. And then I figured it out. "You didn't just take the joke books. You took the detective novels, too, didn't you?"

"They're good," he said with an embarrassed shrug that I found almost absurdly endearing. "I like this Sam Spade character. Straight shooter. Anyway." He cleared his throat. "You be careful out there."

"I'll be fine," I told him. "But I don't like leaving you here alone."

"You think I can't take care of myself?" He pointed a thumb at his chest, which was puffed out a little. "I'm the one who's been taking care of you—not the other way around." But there was something soft and sweet in his eyes.

"You're right. You'll tell Lizzie why I'm gone?"

"That you're taking a relaxing spa weekend? Sure thing."

"Hilarious, as always." I hugged him. "Be careful."

"No need to get emotional," he said, but his arms were steel bands around me. "You're only gonna be gone a few days."

Assuming we found him and managed to make it back alive.

"We'll be fine," I said, trying to assure both of us.

"Damn right you will. Now get in that jeep, start your hunt, and claim your bounty."

The clouds had burned off by the time we reached the edge of New Orleans, and the sun beat down on Highway 90 like a drum, sending up shimmering waves of heat. It was much too early to be this warm, but magic hadn't just affected electricity; it had made our weather less predictable.

We stayed on the highway as long as we could, then veered off to Old Spanish Trail when Gavin caught sight of a Containment convoy—jeeps and trucks heading into New Orleans with goods and sundries to be distributed to stores around the city.

Royal Mercantile would probably be getting some of the freight. Bottled water, soap, maybe a few sticks of butter packed in dry ice for the trip. But that was Tadji's responsibility now. She was my beautiful and brilliant best friend, the woman I'd given the choice to run the store or let it sit until I came home again.

She'd decided to enter the exciting world of postwar retail and was doing a damn fine job of it, based on what I'd seen the couple of times I'd managed to sneak into the Quarter. She'd apparently gathered up every volunteer left in the neighborhood to fix glass broken in the battle, to reorganize overturned furniture and scattered stock. From what I could tell, business was booming. Tadji might have been trained as a linguist, but she was really, really good at merchandising. Even in the mostly deserted Quarter, people had milled around, looking at the goods and making purchases.

I wondered if the convoy had skipped this road to keep from destroying the vehicles and the cargo. I had to grab the jeep's handle as we bounced over pitted asphalt.

"Are you hitting the potholes on purpose?"

"Man's gotta have a hobby," Gavin said.

The narrow highway ran between railroad tracks on one side and the remains of stores, small houses, and mobile homes on the other. Rural parts of the state hadn't been hit by Para attacks as hard as the urban areas, but there were even fewer services out here, and a lot of people hadn't stayed after the war. Plenty of solitude, if that's what you preferred, but the living was hard.

We passed a store on stilts, a bait shop with "fresh" painted in rough black letters along one exterior wall. The windows were boarded up, and a rusting car sat on blocks in front. Once again, my mind tripped back to my store, to the Quarter.

I pulled out my water bottle, took a drink, trying to focus on something else.

"Tadji's handling Royal Mercantile," Gavin said.

I guess his mind had taken the same turn.

"Yeah," I said, screwing the lid back on the bottle.

"Have you talked to her?"

I shook my head. "I check in on the store every once in a while. But I don't want to put her in danger. The less she knows about me, the better." As far as I was concerned, plausible deniability was my friend's best option. "Have you talked to her?"

He shook his head. "I haven't been around." The vehicle shuddered, and he slammed a hand on the dashboard, which seemed to settle the issue. "I left after the battle."

My eyebrows lifted. Yesterday, he said he'd just gotten back into town, but I didn't know he'd been gone the entire time. I'd assumed he'd been here but was doing his own thing—or he'd been avoiding me. That he'd been out of town made me feel a little better, and more curious.

"Where were you?"

"Reconnaissance contract," Gavin said.

"For Containment?"

"For Containment. They were surprised by Reveillon. They don't want to be surprised again."

"Do they think there are more Reveillon members out there?"

Gavin made a sarcastic sound. "Nobody doubts there are more Reveillon members out there. Or at least sympathizers. Plenty of people hate magic, blame magic for what the Zone's become. Containment's looking for organizing, collective action. Any sign that people are clustering again, planning violence, posing a threat."

"Find anything?"

"Lot of talk, no action to speak of." He gave me a sideways glance. "Did you think I was in New Orleans and just avoiding you?"

He'd nailed it, which made my cheeks burn. "Kind of, yeah."

He shook his head, looked back at the road. "We're family, Claire. Granted, kind of a weird, dysfunctional family, but family all the same."

"Yay," I said, and spun an imaginary noisemaker. But family was family. And it wasn't so bad to have this one.

Before we hit Houma, the rain started up, the kind of heavy and steady downpour that set in for the day.

Twenty minutes later, Gavin pulled the car off the highway and onto a long gravel drive.

At the end of it, stately as a queen, sat a plantation house. White, with two stories, both lined with porches, fluted columns, and floor-to-ceiling windows. The front yard featured a boxwood hedge in a pretty pattern, and the drive was marked by enormous oak trees whose branches bent in graceful arcs toward the ground, with Spanish moss draped like scarves across the boughs.

There weren't many plantation houses left in Louisiana. There'd once been dozens along the Mississippi River outside New Orleans. The Civil War had knocked down some of them. Time and history had knocked down others. The war with Paras had done a number on the rest, especially after Paras targeted the petroleum facilities that shared the prime real estate along the river.

This house had survived, and it looked like it had been well cared for. It wasn't the only thing that had gotten attention. Row after row of skinny green stalks filled the fields around the structure. It was sugarcane, acres and acres of it stretching across the delta to the horizon. A dozen Paras—or so I guessed, given the rainbow hues of their skin tones—were pulling weeds among the stalks.

Gavin moved slowly down the drive and came to a stop in the shade of an oak tree. A wooden sign swinging in the rain read VACH-ERIE PLANTATION.

"What are we doing here?" I asked, after we'd climbed out of the car.

"One, leaving the car, so grab your pack."

I did as he suggested, shouldering it on. "And two?"

He met my gaze over the hood of the car. "Malachi's friends work here. The Paranormals with passes."

"Correct," Malachi said.

This time I'd caught the soft flutter of wings.

"Back up," I said. "Paranormals who have passes out of Devil's Isle are working in sugarcane fields?"

Malachi looked at me, his golden eyes keen. "What did you think they'd be doing outside Devil's Isle?"

"I'd assumed they were out there"—I made a vague gesture—"enjoying freedom." Not pulling weeds at a plantation house.

"They are entitled to employment," Malachi said. "And feeding the Zone is a big industry."

"I'm not arguing they don't have the right to work. But, I mean—working in sugarcane fields? Does that make anyone else uncomfortable?"

"You mean the overtones of indentured servitude?" Gavin asked.

"Yeah, let's start there." And jump right into slavery. "How is this freedom?"

"Because they're paid," Malachi said, and there was tension in his voice now. "Because they can be productive after seven years of feeling like victims. Because they can sleep outside Devil's Isle for the first time in years. And because it was the only option given."

So passes weren't really the magnanimous gesture that Containment made them out to be.

"I'm sorry," I said. "That's pretty conniving on Containment's part. And it's not really comfortable, given, well, U.S. history."

Malachi nodded. "Paras have their own history and uncomfortable parallels. The landowners are allies, and the Paras want their wages and their freedom. They know this is their best route to that—at least for now."

At least, he meant, until Containment proved it wasn't willing to go further. Containment had acted in good faith by giving the passes, so the Paras would act in good faith, too. For now.

"Come on," Malachi said.

Gavin and I followed him toward the house, then around it to several barns and outbuildings. The grass was short, the areas between buildings dotted with enormous copper kettles probably used for preparing cane syrup.

"They sleep in the main house," Malachi said. "While they're getting ready for the harvest, they'll repair the barn and the house, work on the subsidiary crops. When the cane's ready, they'll trim it, cut it, process it."

The detail made me smile. "You a farmer now?"

He looked down at me, a curl falling over one eye. "I take an interest in my friends' interests."

"Does that mean we're friends?"

"Close enough."

"Is it safe for you to be here?" I asked him.

"The humans here know me as a friend of the Paras." He smiled a little. "They believe I'm connected with a charitable organization, and I haven't bothered to correct them."

"Is it safe for Claire to be here?" Gavin lifted his gaze to the magic monitors that dotted the grounds.

"The monitors are inoperable," Malachi said. "Although Containment isn't aware of it."

A whistle split the air, high-pitched enough to break all wineglasses in a five-mile radius. I put my hands over my ears a little too late.

"Damn," Gavin said, wincing. "Please destroy that whistle immediately."

"Not a whistle," Malachi said. "A skill."

A man emerged from behind one of the outbuildings, his skin pale, his hair long and white and straight. He was on the short side, his body lean and compact beneath bright orange scrubs. The color,

I guessed, was for visibility, should he or any of the other Paras attempt to escape.

"And the line between freedom and imprisonment gets thinner still," I murmured.

"Uncomfortable," Gavin quietly agreed.

"Djosa," Malachi said. "This is Gavin and Claire, human and Sensitive."

We nodded to one another.

"What brings you here, General?" Djosa asked, his voice deep, his diction precise.

Malachi had been a general in the Consularis military.

"We're looking for Erida and two travelers with her," he said. "Neither of them Sensitives. Both changed by power from others. One without sight. One with golden eyes."

His brows lifted. "You don't know where your subordinate is hiding?"

"We know where she *was*. We do not know where she *is*."

Djosa gave us a suspicious look. "I imagine that's for her security and yours."

"It is," Malachi agreed. "But circumstances require that we find her."

"Because?"

"Because the humans are being hunted," Malachi replied. "And we bring a warning."

"Or you lead soldiers right to them."

"We're being careful," Malachi said, impatience growing in his voice. "We acknowledge the risk, but there's no helping it. They must be told."

"We don't know anything about where they are or might be." He looked back at the fields. "And we need to get back to work."

"Do you like the work?" I asked him.

"Would you?"

"Probably not," I admitted.

He seemed to appreciate the honest answer. "This isn't forever," he said determinedly. "It's for now, and it's freedom. Maybe not the freedom we want forever, but the freedom we can get now."

He held up his hands, his skin marbled with dirt and stained green from weeds. "Do you know how long it's been since I've had earth beneath my fingers? Since I've felt her heart beating? Felt her stirring beneath me?"

Given the lust in his voice, he might as well have been talking about a woman. That created some uncomfortable mental imagery.

"Too long," Djosa answered, saving me from filling the silence. "This is a chance for us. It may not be the best chance, but it's the one we've been given. And when you've been in our skin for seven years, you take freedom as it comes."

Good enough for me. It was his life, not mine, and we all had to find our path.

Screaming pulled our attention away from Djosa. A woman who looked to be human—slender, with tan skin, straight dark hair, and dark eyes full of concern—ran out of the barn.

"Djosa!" she screamed, waving him toward her. "Help!"

Djosa didn't waste any time, but took off at a sprint toward her. We let Malachi take the lead, then followed him.

The barn was enormous, a tall wooden rectangle with a sharply pitched tin roof. The double doors stood open. We were about to follow Djosa inside when three men emerged from the door and jumped into our path.

They had tan skin, hooded eyes, hair dark as ravens, and a cascade of dark feathers that appeared to run from the crest of their heads to the bottom of their feet. "Appeared to," because they were wearing the same bright orange scrubs as Djosa.

The trio split apart and moved around us, the shifting light illuminating purple and black tones in their gleaming feathers.

The feathers along their spines lifted like the hackles of an angry dog, and the men made low, snipping noises as they circled, raising hands that revealed gleaming talons nestled among finer feathers.

They prepared for attack, so I did, too. I reached out a hand, felt for the magic in the air, just in case I needed it.

"These are the Tengu," Malachi said, spreading his hands out as if to shield me and Gavin from an attack—or to keep us from drawing first. "They don't know us. Give them a moment to settle."

They didn't seem interested in settling. Ominous magic colored the air, staining it black. I could feel the magic circling around us now, spinning like a hurricane and bending the cane around us, as we stood in the eye of the storm. The Tengu screamed, the sound sharp as fingernails on a blackboard.

"I don't think they're settling," Gavin murmured, blading his body for a counterattack.

"Kahsut."

The simple word, spoken by Malachi, apparently in a language from the Beyond, echoed around us. It was more than a word; it was a bone-deep order, full of power.

I wasn't sure if the Tengu recognized the word or understood the demand, but they stopped moving and lowered their arms. Then each of them knelt in front of Malachi and gave another whistling cry.

"Are they your . . . subjects?" Gavin quietly asked, clearly groping for the right word.

"Not precisely," Malachi said, then repeated the word. The Tengu rose and shifted away from us, giving us room to walk.

Subjects or not, he got results.

The path now cleared, we walked into the barn. A dirt floor, with hay in piles and rusting implements leaning against the walls. A piece of bright green farm machinery was parked near the opposite end, streaked by shafts of sunlight.

In the middle of the space, a woman lay on the floor, her skin and hair the same pale shades as Djosa's, her legs folded like she'd simply fallen in place. Even from a dozen feet away, it was clear to see her skin was sallow, her body shaking with chills, or fever, or both. There were red dots on her arms, and her breath wheezed in and out.

Djosa knelt at her left side and took her hand in his.

"Anh," Malachi said to the woman who'd yelled for us and who now stood behind Djosa, looking worriedly at the woman on the floor. "What's happened?"

"She was ill," Anh said. I hadn't realized how petite she was— barely over five feet, and delicately boned. "But she refused to stop working. She'd had chills, collapsed suddenly. Now she's burning up, and her breathing is shallow. Her heart is beating so fast."

I could have imagined it was just a difference in biology, except for everyone's obvious concern. "What's her name?" I asked.

"Cinda," Djosa said, without looking up. "Her name is Cinda."

One of the Tengu moved closer, began chattering at Malachi in what I assumed was the same language Malachi had used to calm them.

"They believe she was exposed to something out here," Malachi translated, then paused while the Tengu spoke again. "Something she wasn't exposed to in Devil's Isle."

Another pause, and Malachi's brows lifted as he listened. "Containment warned them this might happen, gave them immunity boosters before they left Devil's Isle . . . to strengthen them against the enemies here."

"The enemies?" I asked as more people came into the barn, humans and Paras who smelled of earth and sweat, who'd probably left their work to investigate.

"Wildlife," Gavin said. "Animals and bugs, humans from outside Devil's Isle. New vectors."

"Freedom made her ill," I quietly said.

"Yeah." There was regret in Gavin's voice.

"We need to get her to a hospital," Malachi said. "I assume the closest one's in New Orleans?"

Djosa shook his head. "They won't treat her. They'll send her back to Devil's Isle. Our passes last one week," he explained. "We sleep here, in the big house, because they don't want to transport us back and forth every day. That's too much trouble if the power goes out. And if Containment decides she's hurt," he continued, anger rising in his words, "they won't let her out again."

Anger burned in my chest, but it was useless against the tide of Containment's power.

"We can't just leave her like this," Anh said. "That can't be the only option."

"Are you sure she'd trade her freedom for her life?" Malachi asked Djosa, his voice calm and composed even in the midst of panic.

"Yes," Djosa said, his gaze clear. "She would. But this is just an illness. She'll get rest, and she'll be fine. She'd want to take the chance."

"Then we treat her," Malachi said, and looked at Anh. "Prepare a bed inside the house, away from the others. Only she will sleep there. You have ice?"

Anh nodded.

"Get ice, a fan if you have a generator. You need to get her temperature down. She'll need liquids, salt. Go," he said. Anh dashed off.

I wished I'd brought the salt I'd found yesterday; it hadn't even occurred to me that it might be useful.

"I cannot heal her," Malachi said, crouching beside Djosa. "But I can perhaps soothe her. That may help."

"Do it," Djosa said, wiping his brow. The barn was in the shade, but there was no breeze in it, and the air was stifling.

"Maybe we should move people back," I said, since we had no other way to help. Gavin nodded, turned to the crowd.

"All right, everyone," he said, "let's give them some room to help her."

The Paras and humans, united by hard work and concern for their colleague, shuffled around and backed up as Malachi pushed the damp hair from Cinda's face. He closed his eyes, his lashes crescents against his golden skin, and placed his hands, palm down, above her heart.

She whimpered, and he smiled down at her with warm and confident kindness. Exactly the kind of expression you'd expect to see on an angel. If you hadn't seen them fight in the war.

"There's no need to be afraid," Malachi said. "Consularis are strong. Djosa is strong, and you've inherited your strength from him."

So Djosa was Cinda's father, I guessed.

"Illness is part of life," Malachi said, "just as pain is part of healing. It is a natural reaction. I cannot interrupt that process, but I can make you more comfortable while your body heals."

Malachi didn't touch Cinda, but moved his hands above her body, back and forth, as if manipulating air—or maybe energy.

I'd felt Malachi's magic before, when we'd snuck Moses out of Devil's Isle and when he'd begun to train me to better use my magic. We'd managed a few more lessons in the last few weeks, and I'd sensed it then, too.

Here in this hot and dusty barn, as his magic unfurled around us,

I realized that those had been mere glimpses of the breadth of it. Like looking into a greenhouse and seeing shapes and petals through a filter of fogged glass.

This was like standing in a field of brilliant crimson poppies.

Malachi was a master of control, and he often seemed distant because of it. But his magic was wild the way wolves were, untamed like the staggering peak of a snowy and rugged mountain. And it was strong—the strongest magic I'd ever felt from a Paranormal. It was like the torrent of a raging river. This was real magic, not the pale frost that I could access.

After a few minutes of steady movement, Cinda appeared to relax, and her breathing calmed again. Malachi slowly lifted his hands, then stepped away as Anh rushed back in.

"We're ready," she said.

At Malachi's nod, Djosa picked Cinda up, limp in his arms, and carried her out of the barn.

We waited for a moment in the humming silence, while the other workers went back to their tasks.

Malachi led me and Gavin outside, then pointed toward a stand of trees about a hundred yards away. "The trail begins there, and it's blazed. Follow it to the woods."

"You want us to leave?" I asked.

"I want to be sure she's comfortable, and she doesn't need an audience for that. We also don't want to wear out our welcome, as we've yet to get information about Liam and the others.

"Get started," he continued. "The trail forks a quarter mile into the woods. Go left when you reach the fork. You'll find a creek about twenty yards down. The water's potable, and there's shade. You can fill your bottles and wait there. I'll meet you when I'm done."

"All right," Gavin said, glanced at me, and I nodded.

"Be careful," Malachi said, then turned and strode toward the house.

"Are you okay?" Gavin asked when we were alone. "Your pupils are still dilated."

My cheeks warmed. "He's got powerful magic."

"I bet," Gavin murmured. "Let's get moving."

CHAPTER FOUR

The trail was hard dirt that skimmed between a sugarcane field on one side and a treelined creek bed on the other. The woods were in front of us, a dark wall battling back oppressive sunshine. The temperature dropped ten degrees the second we stepped into shade, but the trees and foliage quickly formed a canopy over the path, closing in the humidity.

"It's like trying to breathe through a wet blanket," I said, wiping my brow.

"Yeah," Gavin said, pausing to inspect a tree along the trail—and the small symbols carved into it.

"Para trailblazing?" I asked.

"Yeah. I don't know the meaning, but at least we know we've hit the trail."

We walked until trees surrounded us on all sides and we could no longer see the fields open behind us.

"Creek's nearby," Gavin said as the sound of moving water grew louder.

A few seconds later, the trail spit us out to a short bluff over the narrow creek, which flowed invitingly between tree-covered banks. "Steps" had been worn into the sharp drop to the water, held in place by roots that popped up through the dirt.

"And here we are," he said. We took off our backpacks, pulled out our bottles, and headed down the bank. Gavin went first, sliding a little in the slick mud, and turned back to offer me a hand when he hit the bottom.

"You want help?"

"Not going to say no to that offer," I said, taking his strong fingers and easing my way toward the water. I ran-skipped the final few feet, then grabbed a tree limb to keep from pitching into the creek.

"Momentum's a bitch," Gavin said with a grin, uncapping his bottle.

"Yeah." But the view was nearly worth it. The water wasn't deep—only a foot or so—but it was crystal clear, moving quickly over a rocky bottom. A tree limb dipped nearly to the surface on the opposite bank, and Spanish moss hung like lace above the ribbon of water as it flowed past.

Except for the gurgle of water over rock, the world was completely silent. If anything else moved in the woods, the sound was muffled by the stream. That was a reason to take a minute to relax—and a reminder that we needed to be aware.

"It's beautiful here."

"Yeah," Gavin said, taking a drink from the bottle he'd already filled. "There's a reason I don't spend much time in the city. Out here, it's easy to pretend the war never happened. That everything's peaceful again and you're alone in paradise."

I looked at him. "You like going solo."

"I'm used to it," he said, but didn't elaborate. A tender spot, I guessed.

I dipped my bottle into the stream until it was full again, took a long drink. The water was sweet and cold, probably untouched by humans since the war.

That was one of the few benefits of the battles that had racked

Louisiana. Most humans and industry were long gone, and nature had reclaimed the land in their absence. A few years ago, pesticides probably would have made the creek water undrinkable. The world had, in some ways, healed itself.

I screwed on the bottle cap again, then splashed water on my face and dried it with the bottom of my T-shirt.

Back on the bluff, which was easier to get up than climb down, I looked it over for enemies—snakes, spiders, ants—and took a seat.

"I'm going to take a moment," Gavin said, gesturing into the woods. "A private moment."

"I don't need the details," I said, holding up a hand. "Do what you need to do. I'll be right here."

"Stay put," he said with a warning glance. "We don't know who or what's roaming around these woods looking for Liam or you."

"Not a problem," I said, patting the log. "Me and Mr. Tree will hang out right here."

With a nod, he wandered back down the trail.

He'd been gone less than a minute when I heard his footsteps behind me. "Found the little boys' room already?" I asked.

It took me a moment to realize they weren't Gavin's footsteps.

And that was a moment too late.

The hand that clapped over my mouth was thick and callused and smelled of dirt and gasoline.

"Keep ya mouth shut, and you'll be fine." His voice was over my head and to my right. He was tall, and the spread of heat radiating at my back indicated he was wide as well. His other hand was clamped on my shoulder.

"You got her?" The second man stepped out from behind a tree. Average height, average weight, average looks, dark hair, pale skin.

He wore a T-shirt, jeans, and boots. No uniform, which meant he wasn't a Containment agent. Or he wasn't on duty as one, anyway.

"I got her," the man behind me said.

My heart was pounding so fiercely it might have broken through my chest. But panic wouldn't help me, so I made myself stay calm and hoped they might let their guard down.

"Let me go," I said, when he moved his hand away from my mouth. But he kept his meaty hold on my shoulder.

"Oh, we can't do that." The second man's voice had a rough edge, as if he'd dragged each word over a serrated blade. "You appear to be Claire Connolly, and I know plenty of Containment agents who'd like to question you. And what's more, my research says you know one Liam Quinn. He's right at the top of my list, and I understand he's been seen in these parts."

"We aren't gonna hurt you," the man behind me said. "Just take you into New Orleans."

Not a trip I wanted to take today, and certainly not with these two. But before I could object, Gavin stepped onto the trail, his eyes wide, an apple halfway to his mouth. If he was alarmed to see me in my current position, he hid it well.

"Well, hello there," he said, crunching into the apple, as he looked from man to man and then to me. "I am not sure what I've come across here, but I don't want any trouble."

"True enough, friend," the second man said. "This is Containment business, so just be on your way."

"Containment business?" Gavin looked excited. "That's actually really great. I don't suppose you gentlemen have any matches to trade? Mine got soaked, and I've been looking for someone on the trail for two hours."

"Your name?" the second one asked.

"You can call me Lafitte," Gavin said, naming the most famous pirate in the history of New Orleans. "I'm not aiming to make friends." He held up his hands. "You don't have what I need, I'll be on my way."

The man behind me let me go, giving me a look at his face. He was older, easily a hard-earned sixty, with long, frizzy gray hair and a mustache of the same color that fell well below his chin. He wore jeans and a T-shirt with a leather vest covered in patches.

He reached into his pocket, pulled out an old Altoids tin. And from that, he extracted three thick matches.

"Thank God," Gavin said, relief clear on his face. "I've got MREs, an extra knife, some wire and rope I found up the way. Any of that interest you?"

"All of it," the younger man said, "if you want the matches."

Gavin's gaze narrowed, jaw working as he considered. "Price isn't worth it for me. Two MREs, wire, and rope."

"You aren't exactly in a bargaining spot."

Gavin's brows lifted. "I'm not?"

"You don't seem to know who we are."

"I can't say that I do."

"Hunters," said the older man. "And lots of people want to talk to her."

Gavin looked at me doubtfully. "About what? She doesn't look like much of a threat."

"She did something that pissed off Containment," the older man said. "The details ain't no business of mine."

"I guess I can't argue with that." Gavin took another bite of the apple. "Bounties make for good work? I haven't gone that route yet, prefer staying outside New Orleans—which is Gomorrah if you ask me—but I'm always looking for viable employment."

"It's viable," the younger one said, "if you're skilled."

"Sure," Gavin said, eagerness in his nod. "Of course."

"Biggest bounty is for Liam Quinn," the older one said, excitement coloring his words. "Biggest bounty Containment's issued in three years."

There was a hard knot in my stomach. Gavin's eyes shifted quickly to mine, a warning in his gaze that told me to keep my mouth shut.

"Jimmy," the younger one said, "zip it."

Jimmy pursed his lips. "Sorry, Crowley."

Crowley was the older one. He nodded, looked at Gavin again. "We've got business now. If you want the trade, let's get on with it."

"Sure thing." Gavin took a final bite of the apple and tossed the rest into the woods. Then he wiped his hand on his pants, pulled his backpack off his shoulder, and set it on the ground. "Shit," he said, wincing as he yanked at the zipper. "Damn thing's stuck again."

"Let's go," Crowley said, after Gavin had wrestled with it for another solid minute.

Gavin looked up, held out the bag. "You want to give it a go?"

Crowley stepped forward, and Gavin took his chance. He used the bag like a baseball bat, slamming it toward Crowley. But Crowley dodged at the last moment, so the bag only smacked his shoulder.

"Son of a bitch!" Crowley yelled. He took a knife from the leather holster on his belt and sliced down, aiming for Gavin's chest. Gavin, who still held the bag in one hand, spun it again, this time knocking the knife away so it disappeared into the foliage. Crowley growled and charged, pushing them both to the ground.

His hand still around my arm, Jimmy yanked me back down the trail toward Vacherie. I tried to pull away, but he outweighed me by more than a hundred pounds and didn't mind dragging me.

"We have to make a damn living, too," he muttered, his uneven fingernails digging into the skin on my arm.

"Everybody does," I said neutrally, my gaze darting around the narrow trail, looking for something I could use.

Since he wasn't sure why Containment wanted to talk to me, I didn't think it was a good idea to call up magic and clarify that for him. So unless Gavin got to me first, I'd have to deal with Jimmy on my own.

And when I saw what I needed, I made my move.

"Ow!" I cried. I leaned down, touched my ankle gingerly, then hopped a bit for good measure. "I stepped on something wrong. I think I might have sprained it, maybe?" I let my voice do a simpering little whine.

"Freaking women in the woods," Jimmy muttered. He dragged me over to a chopped-off cypress stump and pushed me down onto it. "What the hell's wrong with you?"

When he leaned over to look at my foot, I brought my knee up hard against his chin.

Kneecap slammed into jaw and sent pain ricocheting up my leg. Jimmy howled and stumbled backward, his momentum stopped by a tree on the other side of the trail.

"Son of a bitch!" he said, his words muffled by the hand he'd slapped over his mouth.

While I scrambled to my feet and snagged a thick branch that lay beside the stump, he pulled his fingers away, and his eyes went hot with anger at the sight of the blood on them.

He roared and jumped up again. I waited until he was close, then dodged to the side, lifted the branch, and brought it down across his back. He stumbled forward, hit the cypress stump, then rolled over it to the ground. He was up in a second, clothes striped with mud and moss and plenty of piss and vinegar in his glare.

I raised the branch again, but he was on me before I could swing. He grabbed it and tried to pull it away, but I put my weight into it, and his mud-slicked fingers lost their purchase. He cursed and I stumbled and hit the ground. The branch skittered off.

Jimmy wiped blood from his face. "You couldn't just go quietly?" He stalked forward, and I scrambled backward, trying to give myself enough space to get to my feet. "You get into trouble with Containment, that's your fault. Man has a right to make a living out here, damn it."

Since Liam and Gavin were hunters, too, I didn't object to the principle. But I objected to being anyone's prisoner. "I don't have anything to say to Containment."

"That's not what Containment says."

I finally managed to get to my feet, sweat snaking down my back from the heat, the humidity, and the fight. My heart was still pounding, my adrenaline high. "I guess that makes us enemies. Why don't we both just walk away?"

"I don't think so." Jimmy reached out and swiped at me, but I managed to avoid him. Problem was, the path was narrow, bounded by swampy woods on both sides. Jumping into that mess wasn't going to help me get away from him. "Why don't you be a good little girl and come with me?"

"Because I'm not a good little girl." I kneed him in the balls. And when he hit the ground, moaning and scrunched up with pain, I grabbed the branch from the ground and knocked him in the back of the head.

"Freaking women in the woods," I said, chest heaving. Then I tossed the branch away.

There was clapping behind me. I looked back, found Gavin leaning against a tree and applauding me congenially.

"Thanks for the help," I muttered, wiping my hands on my pants.

"Didn't need my help," he said. "You can handle yourself on your own."

"Thanks," I said dryly. "You get your guy?"

"He's out."

I cocked my head toward the man on the trail. "I guess we'll need to do something with him."

"You wanna kill him?" he asked.

Once upon a time, that question would have horrified me a lot more than it did now.

Still. "No, I don't want to kill him. I'd really like to get out of this trip without anybody dying," I said. The fight did confirm this trip had been a good idea, though; Liam and Eleanor needed warning. And they needed it fast.

"Lafitte?" I asked.

"Beau Q. Lafitte," Gavin drawled. "One of the identities I use on ops."

"And nobody guessed 'Lafitte' was borrowed from 'Jean Lafitte'?"

"It's Louisiana," he said with a grin. "Anyone who recognizes it wants to hear the backstory."

"Which is?"

"He's Beau's grandfather, a dozen generations back. And in between, you've got your wenches, privateers, the illegitimate son of a U.S. senator."

"That's a lot of fake backstory."

"I spend a lot of time alone," Gavin said. "I made a chart."

This time, I heard the flutter, saw the silhouette of wings against the sky as Malachi maneuvered through the trees and touched down on the trail with impressive grace.

He looked at Jimmy. "Bounty hunter?"

"Yep," I said, then gestured down the trail. "There's another one that way."

"They're going to wake up soon," Gavin said.

"They won't trail us to the others." Malachi's statement was as much warning as promise.

Gavin smiled. "I've got an idea about that. You know Montagne Désespérée?"

Malachi didn't smile, but there was definitely amusement in his eyes. "I do."

"What's that mean? 'Desperate Mountain'?" I translated.

"'Hopeless Mountain,'" Gavin corrected. "Right off Bayou Black. And it's not a place you want to be stranded. Which is unfortunate for them."

Montagne Désespérée couldn't have even impersonated a mountain, except by the standards of flat southern Louisiana. It was a hump of land about twenty yards across, like a man's balding dome topped with scrubby vegetation and ringed by cypress knees and dark water. And it would be the temporary home of Jimmy and Crowley, whom Malachi and Gavin had hefted down the trail.

"This isn't an accidental hill," Malachi said, looking it over.

"No," Gavin said. "Built by Native Americans five or six thousand years ago. It used to be higher. But again, the water's rising."

"How do we get over there?" I asked, glancing dubiously at the swamp that lapped at our feet, water bugs skimming like ice-skaters across its surface.

"In a skiff," Gavin said. "I just have to remember where to find it." He picked up a stick and began poking into the leaves, fronds, and moss that littered the ground and probably held more than a few spiders and snakes.

I stayed well back from the search. And sure enough, after a couple of minutes, Gavin hit something wooden and hollow, then used the branch to push debris off a gnarly-looking boat upside down in the dirt, well hidden from passersby. But not, apparently, from people in the know.

"How did you know that would be there?" I asked.

"Because it's not my first time on Hopeless Mountain," Gavin grumbled, and I knew I'd need to weasel the entire story out of him later.

"Let's flip her," he said, and we took positions along the boat, pushed it up and over, and found the oars wedged beneath the seats. We carried it to the water and set the nose firmly in the muck at the edge so it wouldn't float away. Gavin watched for a minute, hands on his hips, waiting to be sure the bottom didn't leak and fill with water.

"Who left you here?" Malachi asked.

"That's a story that doesn't need telling. Suffice it to say I woke up on the mountain one morning with a helluva headache and no skiff."

"You swam for it?"

"After I gathered up the nerve. Place is teeming with gators. But I made it out again. Point is, if you're on the correct side of the bayou," Gavin said, "the skiff's here for the borrowing. If not, you take your chances with the water.

"Boat's fine," he pronounced, then glanced over at the hunters, now on the ground and still unconscious. Then he looked at me. "Three in the boat at a time. You want to help or watch?"

"Land is fine by me."

We moved Crowley first. Gavin and Malachi paddled the short distance to the hill while I watched Jimmy. Then they unloaded Crowley, made the return trip, and repeated the process.

"What do you think?" Gavin asked me, arms crossed as he looked over their work. He and Malachi had placed the two men beside each other against a tree, arms slung over each other's shoulders like buddies sleeping off a bender.

"I think they're going to be pissed when they wake up." I slapped a bug on my elbow, hoping for at least a couple of reasons that I wasn't going to be in the vicinity when that happened. "How long will they be here?"

"Probably less than twenty-four hours," Gavin said. "If they don't want to wade back to shore, shrimpers will find them."

"I'm surprised there are shimpers this far out," I said.

He shrugged. "Life was already hard in this area, so the war wasn't much of a change. Anyway, these two *couillons* will only have to wait out the mosquitoes." Right on cue, he slapped a bug on his neck.

Malachi and I helped Gavin turn the boat upside down and cover it again. Then Gavin picked up his backpack, slung it over one shoulder. "Let's get moving. Just in case they had friends."

Malachi's conversation with the Paras had kept him out of the bounty hunters' sight. Since he'd come back with a snack, we could forgive his missing the fight.

"Sweet rice cakes," he said, offering a waxed paper package containing two small round snacks in pretty pastel colors. "It's one of Anh's family recipes."

Gavin grabbed one and took a bite. "Nice."

I took the other one, nibbled on the edge. It was sweet and soft, and textured on the inside like a honeycomb.

"I believe her parents were from Vietnam," Malachi said. "They were here before the war and stayed when it was over."

"They give you any information?" Gavin asked, stuffing the rest of the cake into his mouth and licking sugar from his fingers.

"Djosa says he saw Erida," Malachi said. "But not Liam or Eleanor, and they don't know where Erida was going."

"Is he telling the truth?" Gavin asked.

Malachi nodded. "He might evade, but I don't think he'd lie about the details. But he did have one suggestion—that we visit the Bayou Black Marina and speak with a woman named Cherie."

"Hey," Gavin said, brightening up, "I know her. She's actually a friend of mine."

When we both looked at him, he hunched his shoulders. "What? I have friends."

Malachi's brows lifted. "Seriously?"

Gavin looked at Malachi, then me.

"He's been working on sarcasm," I explained. "I think he's getting pretty good at it."

"You let Moses have a joke book, and you're teaching Malachi about sarcasm. Of all the things you could illuminate about the human experience, you opted for those?"

"Man's gotta have a hobby," I said with a grin. "Didn't you say that once?"

Gavin grumbled and led the way down the trail again.

It was the ugliest building I'd ever seen, and it sat like a sentinel at the edge of Bayou Black.

Maybe less a building than a three-year-old's imitation of a building—flotsam and jetsam assembled into a rough cube perched on top of wooden piles to keep it out of the water.

But letting the water take it might have been a small mercy. The walls were shards of other buildings—red shiplap and weathered cypress and aluminum siding—and the windows were oddly sized and mismatched, probably salvaged from the same buildings. It was ringed by a rickety dock that connected land and sea and hosted a single skinny gas pump.

"That is . . . interesting," Malachi finally said from our spot on the shoreline.

"It's ugly as sin," Gavin said. "And the proprietor's a pain in the ass. But she knows her stuff."

"And there will be shade," I said, wishing we'd decided to hunt down the Arsenault clan on a cloudy day.

"Let's go," Gavin said, and we strode across the bouncing dock to the door.

The inside didn't look any better than the exterior. Mismatched tables and mismatched chairs atop a sheet of linoleum that curled around the edges. There was a bar on the far end made of an old shop counter with a glass front, the case now filled with faded buoys and tangles of fishing nets.

Only one chair was occupied—by a man whose tan skin had the texture of sandpaper. He was roughly bear shaped, wore a T-shirt, jeans, and rubber boots, and worked on a bowl of food with grim determination. He looked up when we entered, apparently found nothing worth commenting on, and returned to his lunch.

There may not have been much to look at, but there was plenty to feel. An air conditioner roared in a small window on the other end of the room, and the bar was at least twenty degrees cooler than the air outside. The striking difference made my head spin, and I didn't mind a bit.

"Close the goddamn door." The voice came from behind the bar. The woman—tall, broad-shouldered, and dark-skinned—stepped around it. Her hair was short and dark, her eyes narrowed with irritation. "You think electricity comes in with the tide?"

"I think if you've got AC in here," Gavin said, walking to the bar as Malachi closed the door, "electricity isn't a problem."

"It's always a damn problem." She looked him over. "What's not a problem is that sweet, sweet face. You are a beautiful example of a man."

Gavin's eyes narrowed. "It's good to see you, too, Cherie. Can we steal a few minutes of your time?"

She looked over at us, took in me and Malachi. "Six ears is three times the price."

"I can pay," Gavin assured her. He pulled bills from his pocket and put the wad on the counter. She slipped the packet into a pocket of snug, worn jeans in a practiced move that said this was clearly not her first bribe.

"Your friends?" she asked, looking us over.

"Call them Tom and Jerry."

She looked dubious, but gestured at a table. "Take a seat," she said. She opened a cooler behind the bar, and condensation rose into the air like steam. She pulled out an unlabeled bottle of what I guessed was homebrew, popped the top, walked back to our table.

I guess the payment didn't include beverages.

Cherie pulled out a chair and practically fell into it. The movement shook the entire structure, and I had to swallow the urge to grip the edges of the table for support. At least if the building crumbled beneath us, we would hit the water.

"Helluva morning," she said, and took a long pull from the bottle. "PCC patrol rolled through here a few hours ago."

My heart tripped at the possibility they'd already narrowed down Liam's location—and made it farther and faster than us.

"PCC patrol?" Gavin asked. "Looking for someone?"

"Don't know. They drove past on the levee road, didn't stop." Gaze narrowed, she looked at Gavin. "You here because of Containment?"

Gavin slid a questioning gaze to the loner at the table.

"Don't worry about him," she said. "That's Lon. Shrimper. Lives in his trawler half mile up the water. He doesn't hold with Containment."

"In that case, I'm here because of my brother."

She chewed on that for a good fifteen seconds. "Word is, your *frère's* wanted for the murder of a Containment agent."

"Incorrect," Gavin said. "He wasn't in New Orleans when it happened."

"Heard that, too."

"That's why we're here. We need to find him. You know where he is?"

She shook her head, twirled her bottle on the table. "I haven't seen him, don't know anyone who has. Could be I could speculate. For the right price."

Gavin's patience was obviously wearing thin. "I already paid you."

"For the time," she said, and took a drink. "Not for the answers."

For a long moment, she and Gavin just looked at each other, poker players gauging each other's hands. "What do you want?"

"Booze. We can't get shit but skunky beer up here." Still, she took another pull on the bottle. "Skunky beer's better than nothing, but it don't help business much."

She didn't seem to get the irony of "better than nothing," given that she was demanding more from us. But there was no point in complaining. Not when we needed information, and not when I could do something about it.

"Done," I said. Getting goods into Containment was my particular skill, after all. And even if I wasn't at the helm of Royal Mercantile, I still had contacts.

Gavin kicked me under the table, but I ignored it.

Cherie narrowed her eyes at me. "You answered fast. Maybe I didn't ask for enough."

"You didn't let me finish." I leaned forward. "Done—if you give us the right information."

She watched me for a moment, calculating. "What kind of booze?"

"Depends on what they're bringing in that week. But if it's on the truck, I can get it."

She wet her lips thirstily. "I might know where you can find a friend of his. Word is, there's a woman living in a cabin near Dulac, only been there a few days. Word is, she doesn't see in this world, but she sees in others."

That was Eleanor, almost certainly. But I kept my expression neutral and didn't let her see the victory in my eyes.

"That's an unusual condition," Gavin said carefully.

"It is," she agreed. "The kind of thing that would interest Containment. Or maybe already has."

"The PCC patrol?" Gavin asked.

"Don't know, but that certainly seems possible." Our time apparently up—or because she didn't like the Containment talk—Cherie rose and pushed back her chair with a squeak of metal. "Word about bounties spreads fast around here. Take a break if you need it, but don't stay too long." She grabbed her bottle by the neck and headed back to the bar.

"Thank you, Cherie."

She held up the bottle as she walked away, her back to us. "Get me some decent brew, we'll call it even."

"We're going to end up owing a lot of people on this trip," Gavin muttered when we'd stepped outside again. "Let's get out of here. Being out in the open is making me twitchy."

"Also," Malachi said, "you may need new friends."

CHAPTER FIVE

We made good time toward Dulac, but even still, it was slow going. The farther south we moved, the thicker the mosquitoes and the deeper the humidity. We found more water, but I was sweating it out as quickly as I was taking it in.

We walked for two hours, until woods gave way to grasslands and fields, land with a road and a few houses on stilts became occasional slips of earth between bayou or marsh. And that water was rising. From the middle of one road, we could see the remains of three aboveground tombs slipping into the advancing water.

"It was a full cemetery," Gavin said. "But land in southern Louisiana is sinking. The Mississippi's controlled to keep it from flooding, but flooding is what deposits the silt that puts land in the bayou. Without the silt, the Gulf gets closer; the water gets higher. The tombs are slipping into the bayou, like most everything else around here."

"And there's no one to pull them out again," I quietly said.

Gavin nodded.

The thought of my loved ones' remains sliding alone into the water was disturbing and incredibly sad—and it made me eager to find high ground.

"What's the plan for tonight?" I asked.

"Depends on Dulac," Gavin said, breaking a granola bar in half and offering a piece to me. I took it. "And whether we find anyone there."

"They won't be in the city proper," Malachi said. "It would be too easy to track them—as we've done. There's a cabin in the area we've used before. But if they aren't there, we may still be looking when night falls." He looked at me. "Either way, we'll find a place to sleep."

"Away from the water," I said as a chunk of mortar from one of the tombs splashed into the bayou. "High and dry."

"No argument," Gavin said.

We crossed the road and moved into a drier area of knee-high grass that had probably grown unfettered since the war began.

"Let's take a break," Gavin said, pointing at a hand-operated water pump in the shade of a weathered barn with old gas and oil signs nailed to its sides.

We stepped into the shade, took off our packs.

"I'm going to check out the barn," Gavin said. "See if there's any sign of them, or anything worth grabbing."

We hadn't passed any evidence of people in a few miles; even the stilt houses had looked empty. So there likely wasn't much to find. On the upside, odds were also low that we'd be taking someone else's property.

Gavin disappeared around the corner . . . and then his body flew backward toward us, bowed in the middle like he'd taken a kick to the gut. He hit the ground with an audible *"Ooof."*

And before we could move toward him, Erida stepped out of the barn's shadow, a satisfied smile on her face.

I moved to Gavin, went to my knees beside him, patted his cheeks. "Hey, you all right?"

"No," he said, eyes still closed, wincing as he rubbed a hand over his abdomen. "She still standing there?"

"Yep."

"She look at all bothered by my jab?"

Erida was tall, with dark curly hair that spilled over an army-green tank top, buff leggings, and knee-high boots. Her skin was tan, her features lush, and her eyes narrowed. This wasn't the first time she and Gavin had come to blows—and it wasn't the first time she'd won.

"No," I said quietly. "But I'm sure she's suffering on the inside."

In truth, she looked perfectly unruffled.

But while Erida didn't look flustered by Gavin, she looked pretty unthrilled to see me. I'd seen that look on her face before, a kind of flat disdain, the first time I'd met her in the New Orleans church we'd used as a meeting site before the battle.

"Ow," Gavin said, pushing himself to his feet. "Was that really necessary?"

"I owed you from the last time," she said, putting a hand on her hip. Her voice was faintly accented, and plenty arrogant. Not surprising for a goddess of war.

Swearing under his breath and gripping his ribs with one hand, Gavin walked back to her. "Let's call a truce for now."

She just lifted her gaze to Malachi, the question in her eyes.

"Peace is faster," he said with a nod. "We're looking for Eleanor and Liam."

"What's happened?"

"It's involved," Gavin said.

Erida's thick, dark brows lifted. Then she shifted her gaze to the woods. "He's at a fishing cabin up the road. Checking traps. He'll be back soon."

Liam was nearby.

We'd met Djosa, Anh, Cinda, the Tengu, then Cherie. We'd moved from Houma to Vacherie, from Bayou Black to Dulac. One person at a time, one place at a time, we'd been getting closer to him. And now we were nearly there.

For weeks, I'd wondered what it would feel like to stand right here, to be on the verge of seeing him again. Every muscle in my body seemed to tense in anticipation, in hope, in fear. So many emotions, all of them pummeling me.

"Eleanor?" Gavin asked. "She all right?"

"She is. She's at the main house." Erida looked surprised by the question, but then her face went all business. "You weren't followed?" she asked her boss.

"No." Malachi's response was flat.

"Very well, then," she said, and turned on her heel. "Follow me."

The field where the barn sat gave way to another border of trees. And that border gave way to the bayou.

Cypress trees, dark water, and Spanish moss covered the land on both sides of the path Erida led us down. The sounds of wind blowing through grass gave way to the croaks of bullfrogs and insects, to the whoops of enormous birds, and when we reached a patch of open water, the swoop of a pelican.

The house sat near the shore, wooden and unpainted, the planks probably made of cypress—wood that would last in the heat and humidity. It was a small, two-story box with a peaked roof and deep front porch, and it stood on ten-foot stilts that kept the water out of the living room.

Eleanor Arsenault sat on one of two white wooden rocking chairs that flanked the front door. She was a lovely woman. Slender, with medium skin, cropped gray hair, and a regal face. She wore a simple dress and white sneakers, and a delicate knitted wrap around her shoulders even in the heat and humidity. There was more color in her cheeks than I remembered; maybe being out here had healed her in some important way.

"I've brought guests," Erida said as we approached the house.

"Well, I believe that's Claire," Eleanor said with a smile, leaning forward, eyes bright. The magical attack had taken her sight but left her with the ability to see magic, the unique shades and tints that colored power from the Beyond.

"And Malachi," she added, her eyes going bright with pleasure. She didn't need to see Gavin to be glad of his arrival. "And my grandson. You've come a long way."

Gavin climbed the steps, took her hand, and pressed a kiss to her cheek. "You look well, Eleanor."

"I feel well, although I'm surprised to see you." She glanced in my direction. "Claire, your color is beautiful. Deep and rich—more than the last time I saw you." Her voice softened. "It's been a while, hasn't it?"

"It has. It's good to see you again, Eleanor. I'm glad you're safe."

"I am." But her smile faded. "I have to wonder what brings you here—and away from New Orleans."

"Let's talk inside," Malachi said to Erida. "Give them a few moments."

When they crossed the creaking porch planks and disappeared into the house, Gavin gave Eleanor the details, told her about the murder, the accusations, the bounty.

Her hand, small and elegant, flew to her chest. "But Liam hasn't even been there. Someone is blaming him for something he didn't do . . . on purpose."

"That would be my guess," Gavin said.

"They're looking for him," she went on, "and if they're looking for him, they're probably looking for me." Eleanor didn't bother with tears; she just narrowed her gaze, screwed her features into what I guessed was DNA-deep Creole stubbornness. "I don't hold with false accusations. I assume you're here to warn us?"

"We are," Gavin said. "Erida said he's checking traps?"

She nodded. "He's at the cabin."

"How far?" Gavin asked.

"Not far at all," Eleanor said, and the words sent another flurry of nerves through my belly.

She looked toward Gavin. "There's firewood in the shed behind the house. Would you be a dear and grab a few cords for later? The smoke helps with the mosquitoes."

His expression said he knew he was being dismissed, but he didn't argue. "Sure thing," he said, flicking a glance my way.

If she was dismissing Gavin, I assumed she had words for me. I wasn't sure how I felt about that.

"Come," Eleanor said, patting the arm of the second rocking chair. "Have a seat."

I did so, the chair creaking beneath me, and let my gaze shift to the bayou in front of us, the sway of moss in the light breeze.

"How are you, Claire?"

"I'm managing. How are you?"

She closed her eyes, lifted her face to the sunlight that filtered through the trees. "I'm good. It's peaceful here. Not easy living, but peaceful."

Silence fell, broken only by the sounds of birds and insects. I looked over the water, watched the sun begin to dip into the bayou, watched the light go golden. An egret flew past, long and white and elegant as a dancer, and unfolded its legs to drop onto a cypress stump.

"He missed you."

The words were a lance, and they found their mark.

"I'm not sure if he's able to tell you that yet, but don't doubt that he missed you. I'm sure you know he had reasons to leave—good ones. But it never feels good to be left behind." Eleanor looked toward me. "Or, I think, to come looking for the one who left you."

"Not easy," I agreed. "Kind of terrifying." I paused, gathering my words like carefully picked flowers. "I've missed him. Worried about him. And sometimes I've been angry at him.

"Malachi and Gavin didn't want me to come," I said after a moment. "I'm still not sure if my coming was a good idea or not, if I'm interrupting him or breaking some unspoken request for space and time. But I needed to come. It's time to face the music, for both of us."

Eleanor smiled as she rocked. "I had a sense you'd be good for him. I'm glad to know I was right."

I appreciated the sentiment, but that she thought I was good for him didn't mean he felt the same way.

"His magic?" I asked, but she shook her head.

"That's for him to tell."

"It has a color?" I wasn't entirely sure what that would tell me—the color of his magic. But it was one characteristic that she would know, and that I thought she might confess.

"It doesn't have *a* color," she said after a moment. "It has *all* the colors."

I didn't know what she meant, so I waited in silence for her to elaborate. And when she didn't, I realized she wasn't going to say anything else. I'd have to wait—just as I'd been waiting—to see what magic had done to him.

"I won't tell you what to do," Eleanor said. "You have your own feelings, your own reasons, and you're entitled to them. I'm sure the last month hasn't been easy for you. It hasn't been easy for him, either. Even though he believes he did the right thing, he also knows it was the wrong thing for both of you.

"What have you been doing for the last few weeks?" she asked, and it took me a moment to catch up with the conversation shift.

"Spending time with Moses. Trying to do what we can for Paranormals. And to change Containment's mind."

She smiled cannily. "Good. It's good to have a companion in Moses. And it's good to give those in power a little pinch every once in a while. It reminds them who they work for."

She reached out, patted my hand. "Thank you for listening to me, Claire. Liam and Gavin are my boys, and I love them more than good sense should allow. And I want them to be happy. I imagine you could use a little of that, too."

"There's happiness out there," I said, thinking of bloated cans and tiny robots. "Sometimes it's easier to find than others."

Gavin rounded the corner, arms full of wedges of wood, sweat on his brow. I hopped up and opened the door so he could carry the load inside, where a stone fireplace with a deep hearth dominated a small sitting room. A single hallway led to the rest of the house, probably to the kitchen, bedroom, and bathroom.

"Damn," Gavin said, when he'd added the wood to the pile on the hearth and wiped his hands on his pants. "Hard to believe a fire's necessary when it's this hot out."

"Anything that keeps the bugs away," I said.

"I guess."

Erida and Malachi came in with Eleanor. "Time to get Liam?" Malachi asked.

"Yeah," Gavin said, using the hem of his shirt to wipe his forehead. "Let me get a drink."

"Cold water in the fridge," Erida said. He nodded and headed in that direction.

"What will we find?" Gavin asked over his shoulder.

"He's angry," Eleanor said. "Getting used to his new reality."

"Picked a helluva way to do it," Gavin muttered. He came back with a Mason jar of water and continued, "Middle of the bayou, PCC roaming around. But that's my *frère*. God forbid he should do anything the easy way." He drank the entire container of water, then looked at Erida. "Cabin's down the road, you said?"

She nodded. "Walk until the road ends, then take the trail to the right. Maybe half a mile down from there."

Gavin nodded. "Claire and I will go." He looked at me. "Unless you prefer to stay here."

He was giving me an out, and I knew it. Giving me an opportunity to pretend I was just along for the ride—or giving himself an opportunity to prepare Liam for the fact that I was here.

For a moment, I considered it. I considered playing the coward, sitting in the rocking chair and letting the world spin around me, letting fate fall where it would. But I didn't like the idea of being cowardly. Not when I'd come this far.

And selfish or not, I didn't want to give Liam the chance to adjust, to prepare, to school his face if regret was going to show there. I wanted to know his heart. So I'd see him, and he could see me. And we'd both see.

"I'm going," I said. I saw the approval in his eyes.

We walked outside, and Eleanor gave me a fierce nod.

"I'd say we're all on your side," Gavin murmured with a laugh as we walked back to the road.

While I appreciated the sentiment, I needed only one person on my side right now. And the time had come to face that particular fire.

"Not a road," Gavin said as he and I squelched toward the trail. "Just muck between trees."

Since my shoes were covered in it, I couldn't argue.

We picked our way through and across the muck, then down the narrow trail that led to even lower ground. By that point we were sloshing between cypress knees.

The bayou was beautiful—the water, the trees, the haunting stillness. There was something undeniably wild and vital here. But that also made it seem undeniably ominous. I was convinced that every tendril of Spanish moss brushing my shoulder was a cottonmouth with an attitude. Two snapping turtles eyed us warily from a log that poked up through the murky water, and I heard splashing in the distance that I was pretty certain was an alligator on the hunt.

"If a gator is man-eating," I wondered, pushing away a tangle of moss, "does it eat woman as well?" I was making jokes because I was nervous, because my body was jittering like a live wire. And not just because of the wild things in the woods.

"A timely question," Gavin said. "If one charges at me, I'll push you in front."

"That's very thoughtful."

We reached the end of the trail, where dirt gave way to clumps of grass and scrubby palms that nearly hid the cabin a few yards away. It was a smaller version of the main house, with unpainted planks, a roof of tin, and a small porch in front.

"I'll see if he's inside," Gavin said.

"I'll wait," I said. But only because the cabin was tiny and looked empty to boot. Not because my heart was beating so hard I could hear it in my ears.

I could see a strip of glassy water through the trees, so I headed toward it, passed a pile of ancient and rotting buoys and traps, reached a short, weathered dock.

And there he was.

Liam Quinn stood at the end of the dock in jeans and dark green rubber boots, his short-sleeved shirt soaked through with sweat.

He looked completely different, and exactly the same. The same leanly muscled body, the same black hair, the same strong, square chin, and the wide mouth that tended to curl up at one corner when he was pleased. Broad shoulders, long legs, strong hands. But his cheekbones, already honed, seemed sharper, and every muscle was more distinct, as if the generous sculptor who'd created him had come back to refine his work.

Muscles bunched, moved as he added bait to a mesh crawfish trap, then dropped it into the water. He pulled up a second trap from the bayou, emptied the wriggling contents into a bucket on his left, baited it with leftovers from a bucket on his right, and dropped it back into the water. Another trap, and then another, and another. They'd feast on crawfish tonight.

Liam looked natural here, completely at home surrounded by woods and water. I wondered if he'd learned this skill—smoothed the rough edges of the movements—at his family's cabin near Bayou Teche. There was something so practiced in the movement, so hypnotic in the dance of it, that I forgot myself. I just watched him, *admired* him, while pent-up emotions rushed back to the surface.

A crack as loud as a gunshot split the air—and jolted me out of my reverie.

His head shot up, like a wolf scenting danger, eyes widening as he stared at the tree limb—more than a foot in diameter and nearly ten feet long—falling toward him from a tree that stretched above the bayou.

Instinct had him throwing up his arms, but that wouldn't save him. And I wouldn't let him be hurt on my watch.

Moving just as quickly, I grabbed a fistful of magic, wrapped the invisible filaments around the branch, and brought it to a jerking stop eighteen inches above his head.

Still staring, he dropped his arms, and his gaze. And for the first time in weeks, we looked at each other.

The world went quiet, its revolution slowing, as his eyes locked onto mine like a weapon on a target. The vivid blue was still ribboned through his eyes, but they were shot through now with streaks of gold, a residual effect of the magic that had struck him.

Liam Quinn had always been beautiful. Now there was something devastating about him.

I half concentrated on the magic, spent the rest of it to search his face, his feelings. I saw utter surprise, as if I was the last person he'd expected to find standing on the dock behind him.

Something else lurked there, too. Something darker that I didn't understand.

"Claire."

The word was full of emotion, but he didn't take even a single step toward me. Instead, his body was rigid, like he was holding himself back.

I didn't trust myself to pick apart why that might have been. And I didn't say anything, afraid that voicing his name would give away too much about my own feelings and the fact that seeing him here, today, only solidified them.

Foliage crackled, and Gavin stepped onto the dock. He glanced at me, at Liam, and at the branch hovering above Liam's head.

"You threatening to kill him, or stopping that thing from doing it?"

"Stopping it," Liam quietly said.

Gavin nodded. "Then there's no point in overdoing it." He touched the hand I still held outstretched, the hand that still gripped the tangled reins of magic.

I flicked my fingers and sent the branch soaring into the water, where it landed with a splash, bobbed once, then twice, and moved on downstream.

Liam looked as surprised by the quick release as he had by my being there in the first place. Good. I liked the idea that I'd awed him.

"I guess we found you," Gavin said.

That statement broke the spell, had Liam pulling back into himself. The surprise on his face disappeared, and his other expressions shuttered.

"I guess you did." His tone was as flat as his gaze. "Why are you here?"

"Because you've become suddenly popular," Gavin said, glancing around. "Let's get out of the heat, sit down. We need to talk."

We waited while Liam finished rebaiting the traps and grabbed the bucket of crawfish. Then we walked back to the cabin.

I wouldn't have thought my heart could beat faster than it had when I'd looked into his eyes for the first time. But now it raced with a different kind of nerves and challenged the hollowness that made my chest ache.

We'd seen each other, and there'd been no hug, no embrace, not even a look of excitement or gratitude or relief. There'd been nothing. That flatness sent a chill down my spine and a frisson of worry through my belly. Had his feelings changed? Had that been the obvious and simple reason I hadn't heard from him?

Maybe this had been a mistake.

"Go on in," Liam said, flicking a glance my way as he dealt with the crawfish at a small table on the porch.

"You all right?" Gavin whispered as we walked through the screen door. The question added embarrassment to my churning emotions.

"I'm not sure."

Like the main house, the fishing cabin had walls and a floor made from planks of wood, with what looked like old newspapers stuffed into the gaps. There was a wooden bench topped by a pelt of dark, shiny fur and a kitchenette with a gas camping stove and a sink. A small wooden table sat in the opposite corner, its top a slice of cypress with wavy edges. Two wooden chairs were tucked beneath. Through the open doorway, we could see the foot of a small brass bed covered by a handmade quilt.

"This is like Grandfather's place," Gavin said when Liam came in behind us.

"Yeah." Liam gestured to the chairs. When we took seats, he walked to the sink, turned on a water spigot that probably was hooked up to a rainwater cistern. He washed his hands and dried them on a tea towel. Then he opened a plastic cooler on the small counter, pulled out three bottles of water, passed two of them to us.

He didn't make eye contact when he handed me the bottle, was careful to avoid touching me. Gavin must have noticed it, too, because his brows lifted in surprise.

Liam walked to the fur-covered bench and sat down. His body seemed bigger in this small room, as if his strength strained against the walls.

"What's the problem?" he asked. He glanced at me, seemed to satisfy himself that I was in one piece, then looked at Gavin. "Eleanor?"

"She's fine. With Erida at the main house. It's about Broussard."

Liam's brows lifted. He hadn't been expecting to hear that. "What about him?"

"We've come too far to beat around the bush," Gavin said, "so I'll get to the point. He's dead, and you're the prime suspect."

For a moment, Liam just stared at him. "What?"

"Broussard was murdered, killed in his house. They think you did it, because 'For Gracie' was scrawled on the wall above the body."

There was no hiding the emotion in Liam's gaze now, no suppressing the rage that boiled there. "Someone is using our sister's death to frame me for murdering a Containment agent." His voice was low, dangerous. A panther, angry and pacing.

"That's part one," Gavin said. "Your knife was used to slit his throat."

Brow furrowed, Liam felt for the small utility knife holstered on his belt. "What knife?"

"Well, not that one, obviously. The blade mounted to the antler handle. The one I gave you—what was it, two years ago? Three? The one I found in Mobile."

The confusion in Liam's eyes faded to what I thought was speculation. "I haven't seen that knife in months. I don't even own it anymore."

"You gave away my knife?"

"You gave the knife to me. It was mine to keep or give away."

Gavin rolled his eyes, made a frustrated sound. "Who'd you give it to?"

"Not to anyone who'd kill Broussard."

"All evidence to the contrary," Gavin sniped. "I want a name."

"I'm not giving you one."

"Stubborn bastard," Gavin murmured. "Who has the knife?"

Liam shook his head, which sent Gavin on a tear of Cajun French.

"This isn't helping," I said sharply, cutting through the cursing.

They both looked at me, then dragged hands across their jaws. I wondered if the move had been buried in their DNA.

"I don't know who has it," Liam said. "That's the truth. I could find out. But that needs to be . . . careful."

There was humming silence for a moment. "All right," Gavin said. "Sleep on it. Then you owe me names. There's a bounty on your head, and I'm not giving you up that easy."

Liam finished off his water, began to strip the label from the bottle. He did that when he was agitated. "Is someone eager to get me back to New Orleans, or just to pass the blame?"

"Hard to say." Gavin finished his water as well and recapped the bottle. "Could be either. Both."

"If Containment wants to close the book on the murder," Liam continued, "they say Broussard's dead, Liam Quinn did it, so no need to look further?"

"That's my guess, and Gunnar's. There are people in Containment who believe it. You've got a few enemies. Maybe not as many as Broussard, but enough to make trouble."

Liam pushed the wadded label into his pocket and began to flip the bottle idly in his hand. After a moment, he looked up. "Who'd Broussard piss off?"

"We don't know," Gavin said. "We don't know of any specific enemies, or at least not any new ones. Plenty of people didn't like him. We don't know anyone who hated him enough to kill him."

"Who'd I piss off?" Liam wondered. "I mean, why me particularly?"

"Maybe someone," Gavin said. "Maybe no one. Could be as simple as opportunity: someone knows you had a beef with Broussard, thinks you're a convenient target."

"Only if they don't think too closely about the fact that I didn't have the opportunity to kill him."

"Your innocence doesn't seem to matter," Gavin said.

"Have you talked to Gunnar?" Liam looked at me. It was the first question he'd asked me directly.

"Not since the battle."

"He hasn't come by Royal Mercantile?"

"Couldn't say. Tadji's running the store now. I haven't been there since the battle."

Whatever he was feeling, his face gave nothing away. "I see."

"Containment's offered passes for some of the Paras," Gavin said. "But they haven't changed their position regarding Sensitives. Claire used magic during the battle. Ergo . . ."

"Ergo," Liam quietly agreed. He shifted his gaze away, his expression still unreadable. And again, I wavered between feeling hurt, worrying about him, and being flat-out confused.

"Speaking of, you need to be careful out here. We talked to Cherie; she said a PCC patrol had been by the marina. And we met two hunters on the way in. They wanted to execute the bounty on you, take Claire in for the field goal."

Liam looked at me. "You're all right?"

"I'm fine. It was a minor incident, all things considered."

Emotion flared gold in his eyes. "An attack on you isn't minor. I don't want you getting hurt on my account." He said nothing else. He didn't reach out, didn't try to comfort or soothe. But if his feelings for me had disappeared, or faded away, why the emotion?

When Gavin cleared his throat, Liam shifted his gaze toward him. "I assume you didn't let them follow you here?"

Gavin gave him a look of brotherly irritation. "It's not my first day on the job. We left them at Montagne Désespérée."

For the first time, a corner of Liam's mouth lifted. Even after many nights and miles apart, and regardless of his feelings, that wicked smile had a powerful effect. "Not a bad idea."

Gavin grunted. "Easy for you to say." He looked at me, pointed at Liam. "He's the bastard who left me there."

I risked a glance at Liam. "And why did you do that?"

"He needed a time-out." He watched me for a moment, and I met his gaze beat for heavy beat. "Your magic is better."

"I've been practicing. How is yours?"

To his credit, he didn't look away. "Fine."

"The magic was enough to make you leave," I said, "but not enough for you to talk about?"

"It's not that simple." Liam rose, obviously restless, and put the bottle in a bucket. Then he came back and looked down at us, his gaze settling on me again. "You're here to warn me?"

If the question was a test, I didn't know the right answer. It was Gavin who spoke.

"Yes," he said. "They've also mentioned looking for Eleanor. If they're willing to plant evidence and send out hunters, they're willing to do worse. We want to be sure you're both safe."

Liam acknowledged that with a nod. "Then thank you for warning me."

Gavin nodded, and Liam headed for the door. "It's getting dark. Let's get back to the house."

By the time we made it, darkness had fallen.

"You'll stay here tonight," Eleanor said. "We'll have a fire."

Since I was bone-deep tired—physically and emotionally—that sounded good to me.

The Quinn boys prepared the bonfire, logs and branches in a brick fire pit, and arranged camp chairs around it.

Eleanor and I took neighboring chairs, watching forks of flame lift and crackle. Beyond the fire's reach, the world was dark, but the bayou was loud with frogs, insects, and the calls of animals.

Liam came out and took a seat on Eleanor's other side, the chair angled just enough for his gaze to fall on me.

And fall it did. Intense and searching. But he still hadn't given voice to anything he was feeling, whatever that might have been.

"Dinner," Malachi said, and I shifted my gaze from the fire to the enamel mug he offered. The metal was hot, and the steam that wafted up smelled of meat and onion and the bright green flavor I recognized as filé.

He sat down beside me, his broad shoulders and muscular body almost comically large in the slender chair.

"Nothing for you?" I asked. He'd brought only the one cup.

He shook his head and crossed his arms, watching Liam warily beneath half-closed lids. I'd assumed Malachi and Liam had discussed Liam's magic, but maybe I'd been wrong. Maybe Gavin and I weren't the only ones who hadn't seen it, who didn't know what kind of power he was carrying. Or how it had affected him.

"I'm fine," he said.

"Spoon," Gavin said behind him, pulling two from his pocket, offering one to me. "I'm not entirely sure what variety of gumbo this is."

"Probably crawfish," I said. "Or didn't you recognize the traps?"

"I don't trap," Gavin said, fanning a mouthful of still-steaming gumbo. "Hot," he confirmed, and swallowed with a wince.

I pulled out a spoonful, but let it cool before I took a stingy bite. It was thick enough to stand the spoon straight up, dark as coffee, and absolutely delicious.

"Not a bad way to spend an evening," Gavin said, casting a glance at Liam. He leaned forward as if studying the fire, hands clasped in front of him.

"The fire is good," I said. "The bayou is . . . intimidating."

Gavin smiled. "Didn't spend much time out of the city, did you?"

"I camped at City Park once for a field trip. But otherwise, no." Even the gas station, which was supposed to be an emergency bunker, was loaded with tech, including the air conditioner, dehumidifier, and solar generator that had kept my father's collection safe.

A steady beat began to fill the air, and it took me a moment to realize what I was hearing.

"Is that—is that the Go-Go's?" Eighties pop didn't find its way into the Zone very often.

"It is," Erida said, pulling a chair to the fire. Like Malachi, she didn't carry a bowl. But she did have a beer, which raised my opinion of her. Or at least made her seem a little more human. "Our esteemed general has a great love of eighties music."

I looked at Malachi, tried to imagine him—tall and broad-shouldered, a young god's cap of wavy curls—dancing to Bananarama or Michael Jackson, or wailing away on an air guitar to Journey. The image didn't work.

"Please provide details," I said.

Malachi smiled. "It's . . . hopeful." He lifted a shoulder and seemed faintly embarrassed by the entire discussion. "And very different from the music of the Beyond."

He'd said the Beyond was orderly and regimented. "So what did you have?" I smiled at him. "Baroque classical music? Maybe lyres? Golden harps?"

"Consularis Paranormals do not care for instruments," Erida said.

"Don't do instruments?" Gavin asked, pulling a shrimp from its tail with his teeth and tossing the tail into the darkness over his shoulder.

"Instruments are unnecessary when the voice is prepared," Malachi said, his gaze on Erida. "That's the tradition in our society."

"So, like a cappella?" I asked.

"Yes," Erida said. "Although with complexities not recognized in the human form."

"Dozens of voices in careful and precise layers," Malachi said. "Well-ordered, as are most things in the Beyond. Intricately constructed, each song prepared and performed for a very particular circumstance."

No wonder he liked eighties music. It wasn't "intricately constructed," and it was certainly more emotional and spontaneous than the music he was describing.

"Give us a taste," Gavin said.

"Please," Eleanor added. "I'd really enjoy it."

Malachi looked at Erida, who nodded.

I couldn't have said when the song began, only that it slowly surrounded us. No words, just the gentle rise and fall of their voices, which danced together, then swirled apart into higher and lower notes, then dipped back together again. The melody was complex, even with only two voices performing the parts, and it lifted goose bumps along my arms.

By the time they stopped, my head was swimming. Residual magic, I guessed.

"Damn," Gavin said, running a hand over his head. "Powerful stuff."

"What was it about?" I asked.

"It's a tale of battle and bravery," Erida said. "And the honor of loss."

"There's nothing honorable in loss," Liam said.

"In your world, that may be true," Erida said. "Our world was different."

Their world sounded cold and constrained. That didn't justify the Court's attempt to bring their revolution to our door, but I could understand how they'd have felt straitjacketed.

"We've now told you about one of our rituals," Malachi said, glancing at me. "Tell us one of yours."

"One of ours? You've lived among humans for years."

"I've lived *near* humans for years," he said, "but outside their communities, and in a place mostly denuded by war."

I hadn't thought of it that way, of how much he'd have missed by living in the Zone instead of outside it. Not to mention the fact that nearly all humans would have considered him an enemy if they'd known what he truly was.

"Okay," I said, and let my mind wander to the place where I kept my memories of life before the war. "Kids had slumber parties, where you'd go sleep at someone else's house for fun."

Malachi blinked. "Why would it be fun to sleep in someone else's home?"

"Because there would be food," Gavin said. He'd finished his gumbo and stretched out, ankles crossed, and hands linked across his flat abdomen. "And music. Booze, if you were old enough." He grinned. "Girls, if the parents were out of town."

"So it was a mating ritual?" Malachi asked.

"No," Gavin said with a laugh. "The kids at slumber parties weren't usually old enough for that. And if they were, there wasn't much slumbering."

"We had football games," I said. "A game involving a ball and a march down a field. You'd have liked it," I said to Malachi. "It's regimented and orderly, like two armies facing each other across a battle line. That's how a lot of people in Louisiana spent their weekends."

"Marching down a field or facing off across a battle line?"

I knew he was teasing me. "Watching football on television. And drinking beer."

"That doesn't sound very rigorous," Erida said. I didn't think she was teasing.

"Don't tell the members of my fantasy league that," Gavin said. At Erida's raised brow, he shook his head. "Never mind."

"So humans," Malachi began, "for entertainment, slept in a stranger's house and watched strangers engage in battle?"

"It's a little more complex than that," Gavin said, and lifted his gaze to his silent brother. "And what about you, Liam? What rituals do you remember that you'd like to enlighten our friends about?"

"Do plumbing and electricity count?"

"They do," Eleanor said with a smile. "Very much so. I love a good ceiling fan in the summertime."

I glanced at Liam, expecting to see at least a half-smile on his face, but his body had gone rigid. I looked up, watched silent warning flash across Erida's and Malachi's faces, and followed the direction of their gazes.

Deep in the trees, where cypress knees emerged from shadowed water, hovered a pale green light. It was the color of spring leaves, and it floated like a cloud a few feet above the ground. But there was no bulb or fork of flame. Just a fog that grew nearer, transforming dark and silhouetted branches into threatening claws.

"*Feu follet*," Gavin whispered. "Will-o'-the-wisp."

The hair lifted on the back of my neck. But Liam and Malachi rose. Erida and Gavin moved closer to Eleanor.

Instinct told me to snatch a torch from the fire, run back to the house, and lock myself inside. But I wasn't going to run—and certainly not in front of this crowd—so I slowly stood, locked my knees tight, and moved behind Liam and Malachi.

Without taking his gaze off the light, Gavin reached out, took Eleanor's hand, whispered something to her. She nodded, glanced casually in the direction of the light . . . and smiled.

"Friends," she said quietly, taking another sip from her teacup, as smoothly as a woman at high tea. I trusted her instinct and relaxed a little, but kept my gaze on the light.

It drew closer, the single cloud separating into a dozen smaller pinpoints.

Malachi chuckled. "Not will-o'-the-wisps," he said.

"No," Erida agreed. "Just run-of-the-mill Peskies."

Peskies were tiny Paras with dragonfly wings, curvy bodies, and not a scrap of clothing. They were about twice the size of hummingbirds and four times as nasty.

They didn't like being called "run-of-the-mill." They let out shrieks sharp as an ice pick and began to dive-bomb us. One buzzed around my face, her wings moving so quickly they were a haze behind her. Then she gave me an ugly stare and flipped me off.

The gesture *definitely* translated.

"Right back at you, honey," I said, and got a double eagle in response.

"Don't antagonize the Peskies," Liam said, his gaze still on the trees.

"She flipped me off first," I grumbled, and swatted her away when she tried to blitz me again. That triggered a stream of foreign cursing. But I didn't need to understand the words to get the gist.

They stepped out of the woods in sequence, led by a tall man with a barrel chest and thin legs in jeans, a T-shirt, and rubber boots. He carried a bucket in one hand, a shotgun in the other. Although a gun in the hand of a stranger should have made me wary, the three kids—all with their father's skinny legs—appeared behind him, all smiles.

All four of them had tan skin, high cheekbones, and dark hair that came to sharp widow's peaks.

"Good evening," said the man in front. "Looks like a good fire."

"Roy," Liam said, walking to him and offering a hand, which Roy pumped heartily. *"Comment ça va?"*

"Comme ci, comme ça." He shrugged. *"C'est la vie."*

"Looks like you've got a Peskie infestation," Liam said.

Roy grinned. "Found 'em in one of my muskrat traps. Released 'em, for all the good it did. They been following me 'round since."

"They like you," Malachi said. "They're grateful for the rescue. And they're enjoying the crawfish."

"Who doesn't?" Roy said. "You speak their language?"

"Enough of it."

"Roy Gravois," Liam said, "Malachi, a general in the Consularis army. My brother, Gavin Quinn. Claire Connolly. And you know Erida and Eleanor."

Roy nodded at us in turn, his gaze stopping when he got to me. "Nice to put a face to a name."

I nodded, and couldn't help but wonder which of them had mentioned me. "Nice to meet you."

"Roy lives up bayou," Liam said. "Takes the crawfish before they get down to me."

"Problem is, you don't bait your traps worth a damn." Roy looked back, held out a hand to those who'd come with him. "My family: Adelaide, Claude, and Iris." He pointed to each of the kids in turn.

"All members of the United Houma Nation," Liam said.

"Born and bred," Roy agreed with a nod.

"Roy," Eleanor said, "would you like some gumbo? We made too much."

Roy smiled at Eleanor. "I'm good. Just came by to return these tools." He offered Liam the bucket. "Appreciate the loan."

Liam took them. "You fix the generator?"

"Did. I tell you what I was doin' with it?"

Liam shook his head.

"Took the windshield wiper motor outta the old Plymouth on the Fortner place. Hooked it up to a pole, then plugged it into the generator, made my own little spit. Roasted the rest of the wild boar last night."

"Cajun ingenuity," Liam said with a grin. "The boar good?"

"*Mais ya*," Roy said, kissing the tips of his fingers.

The conversation carried on like that for a few more minutes— food, trapping, life in the bayou.

Like on the dock, he seemed comfortable here. Maybe that was something positive that had come out of whatever had happened to him during the battle; he'd been able to come home, at least in some way.

I wondered if it also meant he should stay here. Live here. Which made my heart ache painfully.

"Listen," Liam said, "while you're here, you should know—there's possibly trouble on the horizon."

"What kinda trouble?"

When Liam glanced at the kids warily, Roy nodded.

"It's all right if they hear. If there's trouble, I want them prepared. They can handle it."

Liam nodded. "Containment agent in New Orleans was killed a couple days ago. I'm the prime suspect."

Roy's brows lifted. "Interesting you killed a man in the city while you were out on the water with me."

"Isn't it, though?"

"They issue a bounty?"

"They did."

The initial curiosity in Roy's face faded, and his gaze narrowed. "They wrong accidentally, or on purpose?"

"We have the same question. Given I wasn't even in the parish at the time, we think it's on purpose. But we aren't sure why he was killed, and we aren't sure why they settled on me, other than because Broussard and I didn't much get along."

Roy made a snorting sound. "If we killed everyone we didn't get along with, the world would be a much smaller place."

Liam smiled.

"Have you seen anyone looking around?" Gavin asked, rising from his spot at Eleanor's side and stepping forward.

"Haven't seen an agent or hunter this far south in years. Present company excluded." Roy grinned. "They know better than to come into the southern reach without a guide. End up lost and stranded on a good day, gator meat on a bad."

"Be on the lookout," Liam advised.

"For storms, for gators, for hunters, and for agents," Roy said. "We'll stay careful." He looked down at Claude. "Right?"

When Claude nodded, Roy ruffled his hair, pulled him close. "Should get home, get the little ones to bed and check on Cosette and the baby." He looked back at Liam. "What you gonna do about those charges?"

"Not sure yet."

Roy nodded thoughtfully. "You need a character witness, you call me. You need someone to talk about your expertise on the water, you'll have to call somebody else."

With another jaunty wink, Roy and his family disappeared into the trees again, Peskies lighting their way.

We took turns adding branches to the fire, stoking it to keep the flames dancing in the humidity and occasionally slapping at the mosquitoes that hadn't been deterred by the rising smoke.

I grew more comfortable as the night went on. Not that I was getting used to the bayou, but I was getting used to the sounds—the frogs, rustles, splashes that signaled things moving in the dark. And I was getting used to Liam sitting near me, to the gravity of his body only a few feet from mine.

Somewhere around midnight, Gavin stretched, yawned. "We should call it a night. We've got an early day tomorrow."

"I'll sleep at the cabin," Liam said, rising.

Gavin nodded. "I'll join you."

"Claire can sleep in the house with us," Eleanor said.

I looked at Malachi. "And where will you go?"

"I prefer to be outside."

Yes, we'd spent more time together in the last few weeks, and I'd gotten to know more of his thoughts and moods. But he was still a mystery to me in so many ways. "Where will you sleep outside?"

"Wherever seems best," Malachi said. "I'll see you all in the morning." And he walked into the darkness, disappearing beyond the edge of firelight.

"Let's get you settled," Erida said, rising. I did the same, and followed her into the house without another backward glance. Liam hadn't made a move to talk to me, at least not yet. And while I was pretty sure we'd need to have some kind of talk, I wasn't emotionally or physically equipped to do it tonight.

The steps creaked beneath us, and the porch and floorboards did the same. Erida pulled a rolled-up green sleeping bag from a high shelf, then pointed to a small, empty room off the kitchen. "You can sleep in there. There's a cot in the back room. It's folded up, but you can get it, bring it in if you don't want to sleep on the floor."

She said it like a dare, as if she expected me to refuse and demand a feather bed and silk sheets.

"Either way is fine," I said.

"You may not think that after you see the cot. But the spiders are probably gone."

I tried not to think about the possibility of dozens of legs crawling on me in my sleep. "The floor is fine. I've slept on worse." I held out a hand, and she offered me the sleeping bag.

"I knew your father."

That jerked me out of my arachnoid nightmare. I looked over at her. "What?"

"There were many of us in New Orleans. Hidden there, at least until we fled. We were, at first, convinced humans would come to understand the difference between Court and Consularis, and release from prison those who hadn't chosen to fight. They did not."

The words were spoken like a judgment, a declaration of guilt. There'd be no acquittal for humans from Erida.

"How did you know him?" I asked.

"He helped us. When he became aware of his power, like other humans in his position—he became more sympathetic. He was a good man. He—"

She stopped herself, went silent and still for a solid fifteen seconds. So still she might have been a statue of some ancient human goddess. And since she seemed to be grappling for words, I waited her out.

"He was kind," she said at last. "He was good and he was kind. He helped those of us stuck in New Orleans when he could, gave us supplies. He gave us trust and friendship."

But when she said "friendship," there was something beyond friendship in her eyes. Longing, if I had to put money on it.

I'd seen my father with women, a date or two here and there with the divorced mother of a middle school friend, the woman who baked croissants at the European bakery on Magazine. But I hadn't seen him with Erida. Hadn't seen Erida before the moment she'd walked into Delta's church.

"Friendship," I quietly said.

She looked at me, met my gaze, and didn't say a word. Much like Malachi, she held her cards close to the chest.

"Did you see his magic?" I asked.

She gave me a questioning look.

"I didn't know he was a Sensitive," I said. "I didn't know anything about his magic, about what he'd done to help until . . ." Until Broussard had spilled the beans. And now Broussard and my father were both dead. "He loved me, but he didn't tell me as much as he should have."

"He was a bringer of light," she said quietly.

I nodded. "That's what I heard."

"He didn't know about you, either?"

I shook my head.

"I see," she said, but her voice said she didn't really see but maybe was trying to reconcile the man she'd known with the one I'd just described.

She wasn't the only one.

"I also knew your mother." Her gaze stayed on mine, but her expression had gone very cool.

I tried to maintain control of my own expression, to keep the fear that flooded my veins from overwhelming me, from showing on my face.

My father had told me my mother had died when I was a child, many years before the war, before Paranormals had even entered our world. I didn't remember her; it should have been impossible for Erida to know her.

But the war had expanded what was possible. Stretched and contorted it. I'd seen a woman with red hair, a woman who looked like me, trying to force open the Veil at Talisheek. The same woman whose photograph had rested in a trunk in the gas station's basement.

I had good friends, but I didn't have a family, and I longed for that connection, for something that had been gone a long time from my life. But I was afraid of what I might learn. Because if there was some connection between me and that woman, it meant my father had lied to me my entire life.

And it meant the woman who'd tried to open the Veil, who'd nearly destroyed us, was my mother. So the questions I might have asked— *Is she alive? Is she our enemy?*—stayed strangled and unspoken.

I wasn't ready to accept either possibility, so I shook my head. "My mother died a long time ago."

Erida watched me carefully for a moment. "I see," she finally said. "Then perhaps I was mistaken."

The ice turned to heat that burned in my chest, tightened my throat. I nodded at her. "Sure."

"Well," she said after a long silence, "you'll have an early morning. You should get some sleep."

And then she was gone, leaving me with more questions than answers.

CHAPTER SEVEN

Chicory coffee was scenting the small house when I woke. Gavin offered me a spatterware cup that matched the one in his hand, while I blinked myself awake in the sleeping bag.

I sat up groggily and took the mug, the enamel still hot. The first sip was so sweet it made my teeth ache.

"Eleanor apparently didn't get quite enough sugar in Devil's Isle," Gavin said with a grin. The shoulders of his T-shirt were dark with moisture from his still-damp hair.

"And apparently she's making up for lost time." I gestured to his shirt. "You take a swim this morning?"

"Me and the gators," he said with a wink. "Water's great if you want a turn."

It took less than a second of consideration to decline the offer. "There isn't enough money in the world to get me to take a bath with a gator."

He grinned. "You step into the bayou, you might find just that, cher. Get that coffee in you and get dressed. There's omelet in the kitchen, with crawfish pulled out of the traps this morning. We're leaving in twenty."

I didn't have an appetite, but I gave myself time for a few heartening sips of coffee. Then I poured water into a basin in the small bathroom and cleaned up as well as I could. I'd slept in my clothes in case we needed to make a quick getaway, so I changed what I needed to, brushed my teeth, and twined my hair into a braid that would keep it out of my face for the journey home. Then I shoved everything else back into my bag and zipped it up.

I went outside, dropped the bag on the porch, and headed for the dock again. This time, it was empty, so I walked a few feet out over the water.

A low fog covered the bayou, thick as a cloud. It was speared by sunlight, which reflected off the fog and cast an eerie light across everything. Everything was still, like I'd walked into a photograph of a bayou frozen in time.

An arrow of white split the stillness—an egret flying from one bank to the other. It disappeared among the trees, and bullfrogs began to croak in the vacuum of sound.

It was beautiful here. Desolate and empty in some ways, teeming with life in others. This was a world that had existed before humans and had managed to survive them.

Today, we would walk away from the bayou, and from the people who lived there. I wasn't ready to face the loss that would mean again—either walking away from Liam or watching him let me walk away. But I had to prepare myself, emotionally and physically. And I had to be ready for the journey and whatever we might face. With hunters on the prowl, there was a good chance I'd need magic before we got back to New Orleans. I had to be ready for that, too.

Sensitives absorbed magic daily, which would rot us from the inside out. Once a Sensitive became a wraith, there was no way back. Simply using magic didn't help, as Sensitives' bodies just tried to absorb more, to fill the vacuum that using the magic created. The only way to get rid of it was to consciously let it go, send it back into the universe.

It had been a few days since I'd done that, and that was dangerous. It felt like a living thing within me, something that wriggled and burned and ached to turn me inside out. Something that wanted more.

So I had to take steps.

As I walked back to the bank, I saw a short stool on the porch. Like the table in the cabin, the top had been cut from a slice of cypress. I grabbed it, found a quiet spot with a view of water and cypress, and took a seat.

I hadn't brought the box I usually used to store the excess magic. I hadn't wanted the weight of it in my backpack, and I hadn't wanted it to accidentally open along the way and spill the magic back into the world, where it would keep creating the same problem. I needed an alternate holder. I found one in the cleanly cut cypress stump a few feet away. Probably the same tree sacrificed for the table and stool.

"Apologies in advance," I said, then closed my eyes, let my mind drop down to the spot where I imagined the magic sank and gathered and filled. Its shimmering filaments hummed with power, as if anticipating more. The magic always wanted more. That I knew that now—that we were so connected I could sense its desires—was disconcerting. But it's where I was. Removing it was the only control I had, so that was what I would do.

I gathered up as many of the threads as I could metaphorically hold and pulled them up and away from their hidden center. I struggled against them for a moment, against their tentacular grip on my body, but demanded that they move, and they did. Movement, after all, was my particular gift. And curse.

I directed them away from my body, let them pour into the wood until I felt lighter, until the pulse of power was softer, a hum instead of a drumbeat.

Then I blew out a breath and opened one eye to take a squinting look at the stump.

I hadn't blown it up. I hadn't set it on fire, and it wasn't glowing with otherworldly radiation. It just sat there, as stumps tended to do, and went about its stump business.

"Success," I muttered, giving myself a mental high five. Then I stood up, stretched muscles that felt loose and relaxed, and glanced at the slow-moving water.

Like a lithe and nimble god, Liam rose from the bayou, body wet and slick and naked down to his now-damp cargo pants. Water dripped from his torso, sleeking down the curves of his hips.

It took a moment for me to grasp that he was real, and not some mirage conjured by my traitorous imagination. Eyes closed, he ran his hands through his hair, tightening every lean cord of muscle.

And then his eyes opened, and his gaze met mine . . . and we stared at each other until the air seemed to sizzle with electricity, with heat.

This time, he didn't seem surprised to see me.

"Sorry," I said, turning on my heel before the image of his body seared further into my brain. "I was just taking a look before we left. At the bayou," I added quickly.

"It's fine," Liam said, but the tightness in his voice said exactly the opposite. He pulled down a towel hanging from a nearby branch, slung it around his neck. "I'm glad you're here."

I turned around slowly, looking for a sign of what he might be feeling. Was he glad I was here because he'd wanted to see me? Or because he appreciated the warning?

But once again, his face gave nothing away. And that left me asking, once again, what he was trying to hide. Or hide from.

"Are you all right?" I asked him.

"I'm fine."

But there was a tightness in his voice, something behind the words, something he clearly wasn't ready to talk about. A conflict I didn't understand.

"Really?" I asked. "You don't seem okay."

Gold flashed in his eyes. "What do I seem, Claire?"

"I don't know. You tell me. Or show me," I murmured, and took a step closer. For the first time I was near enough to feel the magic that spun around him.

Instinctively, I lifted a hand to touch the threads of it, to let them brush through my fingers—and Liam took a step back, putting space between us.

"You don't want to do that."

Before I could ask what he meant, Gavin stepped into the clearing.

"Sorry to interrupt, but we need to get going. We're getting a later start than I'd intended."

My chest went tight, stuffed with words that needed to be said before there were miles and miles between us again. Before I lost him again.

Liam shook his head, kept his eyes on me but spoke to Gavin. "I'm going with you."

"Oh, no, you aren't, brother mine." Gavin took a step closer, a fight brewing in his eyes. "I didn't haul my ass down here into the bayou so you could turn yourself over to Containment. I came down here to keep you out of trouble. You and Eleanor both."

"I'm the one accused of murder," Liam said, sliding his gaze to his brother. "You think I'm going to stay here, cower here, while someone frames me? Convicts me in absentia?"

"You seemed okay with coming down here after the battle."

"That was different," Liam said, each word carefully bitten off. "There were reasons—" He shook his head. "I can't get into that right now. If someone's willing to frame me, they're willing to do worse. If I don't go back, if I don't challenge this, who else will stop it?"

"We will," Gavin said. "That's why we're here, after all. You go back, you endanger everyone."

"I stay here, I endanger everyone. Including Eleanor, Erida, Roy and his family. Plenty of hunters aren't concerned about who they hurt to get their quarry. If I'm here, they might use him—or the kids—to find me. If I'm gone, he can be honest, tell them where I've gone, maybe even get a little money out of it."

"And they'll tail you back to New Orleans," Gavin said. "Where Containment is waiting to haul you in. If something happens to you because I made the call to come down here, I won't be able to live with that."

Liam took a step toward Gavin. I'd seen them come to blows before, and I wasn't sure if we were headed there now. "Someone murdered Broussard in my name. I can't live with *that*."

Gavin didn't answer. The sounds of the bayou crept into the waiting silence.

"I go with you," Liam said, "and you're there to help me, or I go back by myself. Which do you prefer?"

Gavin cursed, then turned and stalked back to the house, fury in every step. I followed him, and Liam followed me, close enough that I could feel the punch of heat from his body.

Malachi and Erida waited on the porch.

Liam gave his hair a scrub with the towel, then tossed it over a railing, took a T-shirt from a waiting duffel bag, and pulled it over his head.

"Going somewhere?" Malachi asked.

"With you," he said.

Malachi looked at Gavin, who glared back. "Stubborn ass is going back whether we like it or not. He might as well go with us."

I guess that decided that. And I decided I'd probably better not think too hard about what it meant for me. I was going to have to either wait Liam out or decide he wasn't worth it. And I wasn't ready to make that decision.

Erida shifted slightly, drawing our attention to her. "I can stay with Eleanor, but I think we'd need to move again. Perhaps make it look like the house has been deserted for a while."

"I think that's a good idea," Gavin said. "At least until this Broussard situation is done."

Erida nodded.

"And now that you've made a plan, do I get to speak in my own defense?"

We looked back. Eleanor had stepped onto the porch. Gavin moved forward to help her, but Erida held out a hand, shook her head.

Eleanor moved slowly to the rocking chair, using her hands as guides, then sat carefully down. "I'm content to stay out here," she said. "The bayou is growing on me. But Liam should go back to New Orleans. His home is there, not here. This is his birthplace. And I'm not saying he shouldn't come visit every once in a while." She shifted her gaze, settled it near Liam. "I've loved spending this time with you. But it's time for you to go home. As if you haven't been planning that all along."

Her gaze slid toward me, and I felt my body jerk, but refused to give in to the temptation to play with those words, to let them roll around in my mind, so full of possibility. He'd been planning to come back? When? How?

And, most important, why?

"Plans go awry," Liam said, and that snipped off the growing stem of hope. "I don't want to leave you alone."

- Eleanor smiled like a cat who's done a fine job of pinning the canary. "My boy, I lived on this earth for decades before you were a glint in your father's Irish eyes. You have business to attend to. It's time you attend to it."

She rocked once, wood creaking against wood. "Now, be on your way, and get that business done."

And like the bayou's Creole queen, Eleanor looked over the trees and water and waited for her bidding to be done.

Liam having no counterargument to his formidable grandmother—and who could?—we helped Erida prepare some of Eleanor's belongings, including the book in which she'd cataloged the colors of the magic she'd seen over the years. Malachi found Roy, who steered a boat up to the dock. It was big and pale green, a former trawler with the net spars removed.

We helped Eleanor into the boat, and then they were gone, ready to move even farther downriver, farther toward the flat saltwater marshes and the Gulf of Mexico.

When the sound of the motor had drifted away, Gavin put a hand on Liam's shoulder. "To everything there is a season."

The hand dropped away when Liam growled.

"You may not have had enough coffee," Gavin muttered. "But it's too late now. Let's hit the road."

We walked in single file: Gavin, me, Liam, and when he wasn't doing above-the-ground scouting, Malachi. I could feel the weight of Liam's gaze on my back, like his stare was a tangible thing. His silence was nearly as oppressive as the heat and humidity, but we were focused on making progress.

It didn't help that I didn't know what to say to him and he wasn't ready to say anything to me. Every sticky mile made me more irritated about that.

"Anybody need a break?" Gavin asked. The trail veered away from the levee to our left, which held back the Mississippi, and toward the railroad tracks on our right.

Gavin walked to a short line of trees, pulled off an orange, sniffed. "Ripe," he said. He plucked a few more, began passing them out. Even Malachi took one, and we climbed up the levee to eat them. The path up was steep, but the top was rounded. Below us, the river frothed brown as it rushed south.

"I always thought it looked like café au lait," Gavin said, throwing off his pack and taking a seat.

"Which is how you ended up a hundred yards downriver one fateful Saturday afternoon."

Gavin grinned at Liam. "Got me out of Sunday school, which was fine by me."

I put down my backpack, sat on it, and began peeling my orange. Only then did I realize we hadn't passed an orange tree on the way to Dulac. We were taking a different route back.

"We bypassed the marina," I said.

Gavin chewed, nodded. "Didn't want to push our luck."

"You don't trust Cherie?" I asked.

Liam made a sound of doubt and began to peel the orange rind in a single long spiral, just like he'd peeled the label from his bottle the day before.

"Cherie's out for herself," Gavin said. "And no one else. I can't fault her for it in this day and age. But you have to stay wary."

"She's probably already sent people our way," Liam said.

"She might have," Gavin said. "But we needed information. That's the risk we took."

If she was going to tell Containment about us, I wasn't going to hurry in getting booze sent her way.

"So where are we going?" Liam asked. "This isn't a straight path to New Orleans."

"Jeep's at Houma," Gavin said. "Vacherie Plantation."

Malachi nodded. "I want to check on Cinda."

"Who's Cinda?" Liam asked.

"One of mine," Malachi said, biting into a segment of fruit. "She was ill when we passed through the first time. I'd like to see how she's doing."

"And maybe Anh has some more of those rice cakes."

Malachi gave Gavin a dour look.

"But obviously check on Cinda first," Gavin amended. "Because the care of our Paranormal friends is more important than my stomach." He glanced speculatively at Liam. "That work for your agenda, frère?"

"Fine by me."

"You given any thought to where you'll be staying in the city? Can't get you back into your town house in Devil's Isle."

"I'll borrow a house." He would sleep in an abandoned home, he meant. "That's safest for everyone. And I want to see Broussard's house—the scene."

"Wait until we talk to Gunnar," Gavin said. "Maybe he can make arrangements for me, and I can get you in."

"I can't make any promises." The orange denuded, Liam pulled off a segment and took a bite, then gazed over the water.

"You won't do us or Eleanor any good if you get caught," Malachi said.

Liam looked at him. "I'm a pretty good judge of what I should and shouldn't be doing."

Malachi slid his gaze to me. "I'm not sure that's accurate."

Gavin snorted, then covered it with a fairly unconvincing cough. "I want your opinion, I'll ask for it."

"Not opinion," Malachi said. "Fact."

Liam's gaze went hot. "You have something you want to say to me?"

"No." Malachi's expression was utterly bland. "Should I?"

Liam tossed away the rest of his orange and stood up, gold blazing in his eyes.

"Ladies," Gavin said, "this isn't helping. Malachi, please quit antagonizing him. You're too old to be acting like idiots. Well, I presume." He looked at Malachi. "I'm not actually sure how old you are."

"I think we need to discuss some things," Liam said, his eyes still narrowed on Malachi's. "Feel free to take a walk."

"I'm available for a conversation," Malachi said.

I rolled my eyes, then rose and pulled on my backpack. "Let's walk," I told Gavin. "We've got miles to go before we get to Vacherie."

"The voice of reason," Gavin said, following me down the levee. I glanced back once, saw Malachi and Liam—light and dark—facing each other like warriors preparing for battle.

"He's not helping anything," I said.

"He's not trying to help. He's trying to be a pain in Liam's ass, and it's working."

"And what good does he think that's going to do?"

Gavin looked at me. "You cannot be that naive. He's trying to get Liam to pull out the stick that's wedged thoroughly up his ass and talk to you. He's obviously still in love with you, Claire."

I snorted. "Whatever. He's barely had two words to say to me."

"Stick, ass," Gavin reminded me with a smile. "He's as stubborn as they come, and I'd know, seeing as how we've got the same genetics. My guess is the magic's eating at him. Maybe also guilt about

Gracie, anger at being stuck out here while you're in New Orleans alone. If you can't see that on his face, you aren't looking. Or maybe that's the problem—you aren't looking. He stares at you like you're the first water he's seen in months. I know you've at least seen those looks he's been giving Malachi."

"There's nothing between me and Malachi. We're just friends, and Malachi's antagonizing him."

"Yeah, but you can't antagonize someone who doesn't give a shit. Trust me—he cares. He'll just have to work his way around to figuring that out, or telling you about it."

And how long was I supposed to wait?

It was twenty minutes before Malachi and Liam caught up to us again, and after noon by the time we reached Vacherie. We'd grabbed a few oranges for the road, but were still hungry.

"Rice cakes," Gavin said again. "Just to confirm, that's item number two on the agenda. Checking on Cinda being item number one."

"You're so magnanimous," Liam said. The first words he'd spoken in miles.

"Diplomacy is my particular art," Gavin said. Which nobody really believed.

We reached the edge of the woods and saw the house perched like a crown amid the fields. And from somewhere on the plantation, the sound of wailing and weeping carried toward us on the breeze.

"*No,*" Malachi said, pushing in front of us, his body bowed and tense. "No, no, no." He ran forward and his wings unfolded with a sharp *snap*, then propelled him into the air.

Cinda was my first thought. She'd taken a turn for the worse.

I ran down the trail and toward the plantation, ignoring Gavin's calls behind me. I flew out of the knee-high sugarcane and emerged in front of the barn to stand beside Malachi.

I saw the Tengu first, standing in a semicircle, hands linked, feathers lifted. Paranormals followed, crying and keening, then two men with a linen-covered board on their shoulders, a body laid carefully upon it.

He wore white, and his hands were crossed over his chest, his hair falling white around the shoulders of the men who carried him. It wasn't Cinda; it was Djosa.

"*No,*" Malachi said again, an exhalation and a cry. Then he stepped in line with the rest of the mourners as they walked.

"Oh, shit," Gavin murmured as he and Liam joined me.

More Paranormals joined the procession, and we watched silently as Djosa was borne from the barn to a grass path between cane fields.

I glanced at Gavin, unsure of the etiquette.

"It's all right to follow," he said. "But let's keep our distance."

The Tengu began to sing, a keening cry of sadness and loss as the group moved through the fields beneath the glaring sun. The Paras carrying Djosa must have been parched, but none seemed to complain. Given what little I knew about the Consularis, I guessed they saw the task as a privilege, a way to honor their fallen friend.

The sown fields gave way to tangled and gnarly woods, where nature was winning its battle against the forces of human agriculture. Humidity closed in around us again, and even the smells changed, became damper and greener.

We wound through the woods to a small clearing where I could just make out broken stones that littered the ground. This was a cemetery, a very old one that had probably been used by the plantation since its inception. There were no elaborate aboveground tombs here, and barely any markers. Just a small plot of land where the deceased could be laid to rest beneath live oaks and moss.

But they weren't going to put Djosa in the ground. They'd built a small platform of two-by-fours and plywood, and carefully placed the board that held his body atop it. The Tengu moved closer, picked at his hair and clothes to resettle them. To arrange them.

A Para I hadn't seen before stepped forward, began to speak to the crowd in their particular language. And it was a crowd, I belatedly realized, that didn't include Cinda. I wondered if she'd been too ill to attend her father's funeral.

Gavin pulled off his cap. I did the same thing, so my braid fell across my shoulders.

Drawn by the movement, the Tengu looked in our direction, caught sight of us.

They went crazy again—feathers raised like an animal's hackles, voices that had been singing now screaming. With fear or fury, I wasn't sure, but they didn't want us there. Didn't want us watching. The other Paras turned, shot nasty looks in our direction, made it clear they didn't welcome either the interruption or our presence.

Without argument, we left them alone with their grief.

CHAPTER EIGHT

We were sweating by the time we took seats beside the jeep and beneath the oak tree in front of the main house. We waited nearly an hour for Malachi to walk around the hill. In the meantime, I stayed quiet, while Gavin and Liam talked through Containment's personnel roll, trying to pick out the person who might have had some vendetta against Liam.

"It was an illness," Malachi confirmed when he joined us. "Djosa had been feeling weak, tired. Felt worse before we arrived yesterday, but didn't want to seem weak in front of me." He looked away, shook his head as he gazed at the plantation house.

I wasn't sure how to comfort him, so I went for the obvious thing, which still felt pointless. "We're sorry for your loss."

Malachi nodded. But there was something hard in his eyes—something that said he wouldn't be forgetting about Djosa's death anytime soon.

Southerners—whether in New Orleans or out of it—loved to talk about lessons. What you learned even from bad experiences. What they were supposed to teach you. How they were part of a bigger plan. But I was having trouble seeing how this man's death could have been part of anyone's plan.

Gavin pushed himself up from the ground, wiped his hands on his jeans. "He shouldn't have gotten sick at all."

"No," Malachi agreed. "He shouldn't have."

"At the risk of sounding incredibly callous," Gavin said, "we should get moving. Presuming it's contagious, you don't need any further exposure. We don't want you getting sick, and we don't want to take anything home with us, spread it further."

"I'll go my own way," Malachi said, then glanced at me. "Would you like a ride into New Orleans?" He extended his wings, the ivory feathers reflecting back the sunlight that dappled through the tree limbs.

Although the thought of getting a bird's-eye view of New Orleans was interesting, the thought of flying all the way back in the arms of a rogue Paranormal was not.

"Rain check," I said.

"We'll see you there," Gavin said. "We should probably meet tonight, discuss the plan of attack, so to speak." He slid his brother a glance. "Since this is no longer just a warning mission, but an investigatory one."

Liam nodded. "We need to find out what we can about Broussard's death. The why, the how, the when. That will lead us to the culprit."

"I'll speak with Moses," Malachi said, and gave Liam the address. "We'll meet there, unless it's not safe." He nodded at me.

"I know the system," I assured him. A string of Mardi Gras beads—yellow, with enormous plastic monkeys holding enormous plastic bananas—hanging on the front door meant the coast was clear. If the beads were gone, it wasn't safe, and we were supposed to keep on walking.

"Then it's a date," Malachi said, and took to the sky.

I held a hand over my eyes, watched his body rise, wings smooth and powerful against the thick air, until he became a thin sliver of white against the brilliant sky and then disappeared.

When I looked back again, Gavin was clapping Liam on the back, then walking toward the jeep, singing as he strolled, *"Do you know what it means to miss New Orleans . . ."*

At least he was better at it than Moses.

Liam wasn't any more communicative in the jeep than he had been during the walk.

"If we play I Spy or the alphabet game," Gavin said, catching his gaze in the rearview, "will you contribute to the discussion?"

"Doubtful."

"Grouchy ass," Gavin muttered.

He went back to singing and tapping his fingers on the steering wheel—until he suddenly went quiet.

"Forget the words?" I murmured, my eyes closed as I tried to take a catnap in the passenger seat.

"No," he said, and there was no humor in his voice. "Look. Road-block."

My eyes flashed open, and I blinked in the brilliant sunlight, caught a glimpse of four vehicles, two on each side of the divided highway. On the side heading into New Orleans, the vehicles were parked nose to nose, just enough space between them to allow one car to pass at a time.

Gavin swung the jeep onto a gravel road, sending a spray of dirt and gravel into the air.

"I'm sure they won't notice that and think it's suspicious," Liam muttered.

"Defensive maneuvers," Gavin said.

"Why is there a roadblock around New Orleans?" I asked. Had something happened in the two days we'd been gone? "Was there another attack on Devil's Isle?"

"Doubtful," Gavin said. "Someone would have gotten word to Malachi."

"Is this because of Broussard?" Liam asked.

"It couldn't possibly be," Gavin said, tapping the top of the gearshift. "Shutting down access to New Orleans to find a suspect in one murder? Not to diminish what happened to Broussard, but that's not procedure. That's overkill."

"The entire thing is overkill," Liam said. "The murder, the literal writing on the wall, the frame job. Maybe this is bigger than Broussard."

"Maybe," Gavin said, but he didn't seem convinced. He glanced back, looked at his brother. "What's the plan?"

"I can swim in," Liam said.

"Swim in?" I asked, meeting his gaze in the rearview mirror. "You're going to swim into New Orleans?"

"Just to the river," Liam said. "Containment doesn't patrol the canals. You stay low along the wall, and you can move in and out of the city pretty easily."

"You want to meet down the road?" Gavin asked.

Liam shook his head. "I'll take the ferry when I get to the river. Meet you at Moses's place."

"That's a long trip," I said.

Liam's gaze on me was intense. "It's safer for all of us if we split up."

"And speaking of safety," Gavin said, looking at me, "the roadblock wouldn't be for you, but that doesn't mean they won't take you in if they can. Can you swim?"

"I can swim, but I'm not strong enough to go through miles of canals." And that didn't take into account the gators, snakes, rats, and nutria, among other things. "So no."

"Then you pretend to be someone else," Gavin said, turning in his seat to glance at me. "Grab that cap, please."

"I'll do you one better," I said, and rummaged through the backpack at my feet to find the wig I'd thrown in. It was cut into a short, dark bob, not unlike Darby's. She was a former employee of PCC Research and a member of Delta.

I pulled off the cap, twisted up my braid, then leaned over and stuffed the wig on. It took a little adjusting in the mirror to get it straight and to tuck up the stray ends, but I didn't look like an obvious redhead anymore. I pulled the cap down over it, then turned to Gavin, lifted an eyebrow.

"Not bad." His appraising look turned to an appreciative one. "Not bad at all." He wiggled his eyebrows suggestively.

"Focus," Liam said, elbowing the back of Gavin's seat.

"A man can focus on multiple things at once."

"*Focus.*" This time I said it. I checked the car's side mirrors again, since I was expecting a Containment vehicle to come storming down the gravel road any minute.

"Be careful," Gavin said.

Liam nodded. "I know how to stay below the radar."

"Then let's do this," Gavin said, starting the car again.

Liam climbed out, shut the door, and glanced through my open window. "Be careful," he said, and gave me a long look before walking away.

"Is he brave, or stupid?" I asked.

"Both, obviously." Gavin's face changed, became serious, as he pulled the car around to head back to the highway.

"I'm with Containment," Gavin reminded me, "or close enough. Hunter on my way into the city for a meeting. And you are?"

"Your girlfriend, along for the ride. Name's . . . Mignon."

"Excellent choice," he said. "I've always wanted to date a Mignon."

I sat back, crossed my arms, and tried to ignore the butterflies in my belly. I'd been purposely avoiding not just Containment but nearly everyone and everything from my previous life that Containment could have used to get to me. Now we were running toward the trouble, and there was no turning back.

Gavin waved out the window as we came to a stop. Two agents in dark fatigues, guns strapped to their waists, approached us.

"Sir," said the one on Gavin's side. "Ma'am." He was big and beefy, with pale skin, shorn hair, a square jaw, and a puggish nose.

"Agent," Gavin said. "I'm no sir, and she's no ma'am." He yanked away an ID clipped to his visor, offered it to the agent. "I'm Special Ops."

The agent looked at the badge, then up at Gavin again. "Reason for visiting New Orleans?"

"I live there, as my badge says." He checked his watch. "And in particular, I've got a meeting with Gunnar Landreau in half an hour."

"And your business outside New Orleans?" the agent asked.

"Not at liberty to disclose to anyone without sigma clearance. Containment can confirm."

The agent lifted his eyes to me. "And you?"

"Field trip," I said, sounding as bored as possible. "Although this ain't exactly what I had in mind."

The agent gave the badge another careful study, then looked at me and did the same. "Step out of the car, please."

"Sure," Gavin said. "But can I ask why?"

"You're on the list."

Shit, I thought.

"What list is that?"

"You may have information about persons of interest."

"I'm sure I do, having sigma status. But as I noted, I'm not authorized to give out that information."

"We're looking for Liam Quinn. Your brother."

Gavin's jaw went tight in a pretty good imitation of someone very, very angry at Liam.

"*Merde*," he muttered, really pushing the Cajun accent. "The hell has he done this time?"

"Killed a Containment agent, name of Broussard."

Gavin visibly jerked, then pulled his sunglasses off very, very slowly. "Say what?"

"Killed Broussard in his own home. Bounty's been issued. He's a wanted man, and Containment wants him inside sooner rather than later."

"I guess so—you've got a roadblock. But I ain't seen that *couillon* in weeks. We had what you might call a bit of a falling-out after the battle."

He gestured to the roadblock. "Containment thinks he's outside NOLA?"

That was a good strategy lesson: Containment knocks down your door, take the opportunity to get what information you can.

"Don't know. Just following orders."

"Of course you are." He swore, shook his head. "He thinks I'm going to save his ass again, he is very mistaken. *Tête dur.*" Gavin wet his lips, looked at the agent conspiratorially. "How much is the bounty?"

The agent threw out a number that would have kept Royal Mercantile in the green for months. Containment was serious about getting Liam.

Gavin whistled. "I didn't ask this question, but just so I'm sure—family members get the bounty, should they come across him?"

"I believe so." He stepped away for a moment, had a conversation with the other agent, spoke into his communicator. Gavin, who looked completely cool from the neck up, squeezed my hand.

The agents came back.

Let us go, I murmured. *Just let us go.*

"Sir, please step out of the car," the agent said again. "We need to take a look inside."

Gavin nodded. "Of course, Agent. I'm being an asshole, and you're just doing your job. I'm coming out," he said, then opened the door, climbed outside. "But if I'm late for my meeting," he added with a grin, "could you write me a note?"

I exited under the watch of the other agent.

"Hands on the hood, please." We were both steered to face opposite sides of the hood, and we put our palms on the car. After baking in the sun, the hood was hot enough to fry an egg. But at least it kept my hands from visibly shaking.

Gavin winked at me, which helped a little. But I knew some of that was bravado he didn't feel. If someone was willing to frame Liam and put Containment on his trail, it wasn't hard to believe they'd bring in his brother, too.

They opened the doors, began sorting through the Jeep's contents. Gavin's backpack, my backpack. I did a quick mental inventory of what I'd thrown in there and if there was anything damaging.

"Well," said one of the agents.

I froze, swallowed down a hard ball of fear, and glanced around the vehicle.

The agent, whose cheeks were flushed pink, held up by two fingers the raunchiest bit of black lingerie I'd ever seen. Cheap black lace with bows and cords, and strategic cutouts that seemed to defeat the point of wearing lingerie in the first place.

I glared at Gavin.

He managed to scrounge up a blush, coughed delicately. "So, I may not have cleaned out that bag very well after its last use."

Since I was playing a role, I figured I might as well go for the gold. "You asshole!" I lunged at him across the hood of the car, managed to get in a couple of slaps on his arms before the agent dragged me out of range, pulled back my arms. "What the hell is that? Why the hell is there lingerie—*lingerie*—in your bag?"

He held up his hands, all innocent. "Mignon, baby, it's nothing. I swear."

"You *asshole*! Was it Lucinda's? You promised me you wouldn't see her again! You *promised!*"

He looked at the agent who held my arms. "Could you please give us a minute here?"

"Ma'am," the agent said, "you going to control yourself?"

I curled my lip at Gavin. "You mean like how he controls himself? Can't keep his fly zipped. Can't keep his damn hands to himself."

"*Ma'am.*"

"Yes," I said. "Yes, *fine*. I can control myself."

He let me go, and I adjusted my shirt, then brushed a hand over the wig to smooth it.

When I turned back to Gavin, glaring at him over the hood, the agent stepped carefully away and joined the other agent at the back of the jeep.

"You're violent," Gavin murmured.

"You're a pervert."

"It's not *my* underwear."

"Yeah, that was my point. Do I want to know why you have it?"

"You do not," he said matter-of-factly. "Lucinda?"

"Mean girl from sixth grade. Hated her." I couldn't let it go. "Were you hoping you'd find a little company on this trip?"

"I mean, I'm not saying I can't appreciate a good time when I find it, but no. I really did forget it was in there."

Probably best not to dig too deeply into the rest of it.

Five awkward minutes later, the agent came back and avoided all eye contact with me.

"You're free to go," he said. "We appreciate your cooperation, and we're sorry for the, um, domestic issues."

"Not your fault he's an asshole," I said, giving Gavin one last leer.

The agent nodded awkwardly, looked back at Gavin. "If you see your brother, call Containment. He needs to be stopped before he hurts someone else."

"I couldn't agree more," Gavin said, and we climbed into the car again. "We appreciate your service."

We pulled away, both of us still checking the mirrors, waiting to be followed. But the cars stayed parked where they were.

"That was easy," I said.

"Too easy," Gavin said, his gaze still flicking between the road and the rearview mirror. "And . . . there it is."

I checked the side mirror. About a quarter mile behind us, a silver sedan pulled onto the highway.

"Who is it?"

"A Containment tail would be my guess. They probably assume I'm lying about Liam—or they hope I am—and figure I'll either lead them directly to him or I'll take them to a drop-off spot, and they can lie in wait."

"You don't actually have one of those, do you? A drop-off spot?"

He smiled. "Not one, no. More like"—he paused, lips moving silently—"eleven, at last count. Twelve? No. Eleven."

"Why?"

"It's a big city. You never know where you're going to wake up."

I snorted. "That sounds like a personal problem."

Gavin grinned. "Personal, but never a problem. A tail, though, would be a problem. And confirms that Containment is very serious about finding Liam. What the hell did he do to get so much interest?"

"Wrong place, wrong time?"

"I don't know. I really don't."

We watched the sedan draw closer.

"How, exactly, do they plan to tail you? It's pretty obvious they're back there."

"Multiple cars," he said. "They'll do a handoff a mile or two up the road. Watch," he said. And sure enough, the sedan drew closer, then pulled into the other lane and passed us, as if totally oblivious to our car.

"This car will pull off the road ahead. Another car will pull in behind me, follow me until they hopscotch again, and so on. It's a good trick."

"And you've got a plan to deal with it?"

"Of course I've got a plan. Which, unfortunately, is going to mean ditching this jeep. Which is a bummer, because I really like it. Found it in the Garden District behind an old bookstore. Full bottle of Jack Daniel's." He smiled, patted the dash lovingly. "She's been good since the beginning. Alas. I'll leave the keys in it for the next person who might need it. And maybe I'll come across a Range Rover." He glanced at me. "You buckled up?"

"I am," I said, and pulled the seat belt to check the tension, just in case.

"Then sit back and enjoy the ride."

With a grin on his face, he gunned it.

Between the two of them, I'd figured Gavin for the risk-taker, Liam for the planner. If Gavin's driving was any sign, I'd been exactly right.

Gavin knew how to handle a tail. He played oblivious, weaving through Carrollton—up and down side streets, occasionally stopping to chat up some random person he spotted on the street and forcing the cars tailing him to stop and hide. I kept the wig in place while we drove. There was no point in riling them up with the thought of more quarry.

After half an hour of cruising through the city, and no loss of interest by the agents watching us, Gavin waited until the next handoff, then took a chance and pulled the jeep into an alley, driving through it until he found an empty garage. He backed in and turned off the engine while I jumped out and closed the garage door.

The trick worked. They drove right past us. We waited and listened for them to circle back, and when the coast was clear, we pulled out and headed toward Mid-City.

I'd already given Gavin my drop-off location, an alley a few blocks from the gas station that wasn't close enough to clue him in to my secret lair. I wanted a shower and food before I headed to Moses's place for round two.

"I don't suppose you'll let me drop you off right in front, so I'll know where you are, can keep an eye on you?"

"I will not." I climbed out of the car, grabbed my backpack. "Thanks for the ride. If you tail me, I'll be pissed."

"You're entitled to your privacy," Gavin said. He paused for a moment, seemed to debate saying what he said next. "Look, Claire. You and Liam are none of my business."

"But you're going to power through it?"

"I think you should consider something."

One arm atop the jeep, I sighed, looked back in. "What?"

"You're cocooning."

"I'm—what?"

"Cocooning." He stuck his thumbs beneath his arms and pretended to flap wings. "Like a butterfly."

I just kept looking at him.

"Jesus, you're both being purposefully obtuse. You're hunkering down in this secret lair of yours so you won't hurt anybody. Gunnar or Tadji or the store."

"I don't have a secret lair." But I totally did. And even if I did, wasn't that the right thing to do?

"Don't you think Liam was doing exactly the same thing?"

"Maybe," I said. "But he's back now. Whose side are you on?"

"He's my older brother, and you're my friend. So I'm on my side, naturally. I'll see you at Moses's."

I closed the door. "If I don't show up in a couple of hours, you can come back here and start your search."

"Fair enough," he said. "And Liam?"

I shouldered the backpack on. "That wasn't a question."

"I've gotten him back to New Orleans. The rest is up to you. So get to it."

In a war zone, a long shower was a miracle. That was especially true after a day of moving bayou residents, wandering trails, witnessing a Paranormal funeral, and getting stopped by a Containment roadblock.

I was tired, my legs ached, and I was starving. I wouldn't have minded spending the night in the station, futzing with one of the projects I'd started to keep myself busy. The backup dehumidifier that didn't want to turn over, or the few Paranormal artifacts that needed repair. But that wasn't in the cards. Containment was on the hunt, and we were on the clock.

I capped off my shower by eating a can of peaches with a fork. It had been sunny when I'd arrived at the gas station, was pouring by the time I left. I pulled up my Windbreaker hood and started my second hike of the day.

By the time I arrived at Moses's house, dusk had nearly fallen. An enormous white Range Rover was parked outside, and since I didn't know anyone who drove one, I figured Gavin had made quick work of finding a new car.

There were still plenty of vehicles in the city, but not many luxury cars or SUVs that hadn't been stripped or trashed, or turned into rusting hulks after seven years of sitting. And yet, he'd somehow managed to find one in a matter of hours—presumably one that ran. I hoped that kind of luck was contagious.

The beads were on the door, so I took the steps to Moses's Creole cottage, but paused for a moment on the porch to prepare myself for round two with Liam. Whatever that might involve.

I found Gavin and Malachi in the small front room of the house. It had what rental sites would have called "Authentic New Orleans Charm." Brick walls, old hardwood floors, floor-to-ceiling windows.

Along with narrow rooms, old plumbing, and the constant risk of flood.

Before his place in the Quarter had been torched, Moses had amassed a huge collection of electronics. He was making a pretty good dent in filling up this room around his workstation—a padded stool and metal desk. There was a couch for visitors, but unless he'd gotten into a decorating mood while we'd been gone, the race car bed in the back room was the only other piece of furniture in the house.

Because he was small of stature, it fit Moses perfectly.

"You bring me anything?" he asked from his stool, swiveling to look me over.

"Did I bring you anything?" I asked, closing the door.

Moses gestured to Gavin and Malachi. "These two take a field trip, leave me to guard the entire city, don't even bring me a souvenir."

Knowing an opportunity when I had one, I unzipped my backpack, pulled out two of the oranges we'd nabbed near the levee. "I guess they aren't as nice as I am."

"I knew you'd come through," he said, hopping down from the stool, taking the oranges and putting them proudly on one corner of the desk.

Gavin leaned toward me. "You didn't get those for him."

"No comment."

"Now that we're all assembled," Moses said, "shall we get to business?"

"We're actually still missing one," Gavin said, just as we heard a perfectly timed knock at the door. He opened it and let Liam inside.

Liam had cleaned up and changed into a snug DEFEND NEW ORLEANS T-shirt that highlighted every nook and cranny of strong muscle and taut skin.

He gave Malachi and Gavin quick looks. Gave me a longer one as a lock of dark hair fell over his face. He brushed it back, then looked at Moses, who'd hopped onto his stool again and was giving Liam a wary gaze. "Well, well. Look what the damn cat drug in."

"Mos," Liam said with a nod.

Moses lifted his brows. "That's all you got to say?"

"It's good to see you," Liam said. "It's just been a long day."

"Long five weeks, more like," Moses muttered, sending me a look I dutifully ignored. "Where the hell you been?"

"Where it's wet," Liam said.

"Eleanor?"

"She's good."

They stared at each other for a moment, and smiled, and that was that. Weeks evaporating like fog over the bayou.

"Well," Moses said, "I'm glad to see your ugly face again. How was the trip home?"

"Malachi lost a friend," Gavin said.

"A friend?" Moses asked, and Malachi told him about our visit to Vacherie and the death of the Paranormal.

"Damn," Moses said. "Can't stay in Devil's Isle, can't leave it, either."

"Roadblock on the way back into the city," Gavin said. "Nearly got pinched. They wanted Liam, wouldn't give us details. We also met a couple of bounty hunters on the way down there. They said Containment had a bounty for Liam, wanted to talk to Claire."

"Talk, my ass," Moses said. "They want to haul you away." He pointed a finger at me. "I didn't go to all this trouble for you to get rounded right up."

I couldn't help grinning. "What trouble, exactly, did you go to? And be specific."

He just snorted, glanced at Liam. "Looks like they didn't waste any time coming after you, either."

"Evidently not."

"And since that's why we're all here," I said, "you find out anything about Broussard while we were gone?"

"Lizzie doesn't know a damn thing," Moses said. "Plenty of people have plenty of things to say about him, none of it friendly, but none of it specific. Usual complaints, far as I can tell."

"He was an asshole," Liam said. "Pretentious. Narrow-minded. But that's not unusual among humans, much less agents. I will give credit, say he usually thought he was doing the right thing. He and I just disagreed about what was right."

Including, I thought, *whether I'd been harboring magic-wielding fugitives.*

"But that's not our only source of information. While you've been frolicking through the meadows, I've also been working on this gorgeous girl." Moses waved a hand at the electronics on the desk.

It was shaped vaguely like an elephant, but I was pretty sure that was just a coincidence. Large gray body on a platform with four feet, power cords serving as the trunk and tail. A couple of monitors were squeezed in beside cases full of dangling wires and what I thought were speakers and fans.

"Does it work?" Liam asked.

"Does now that I found a power supply a couple houses down. In the damn garage, if you can believe that. People hid all their good shit before they left."

"How dare they?" I asked with mock outrage. Moses ignored the question and the tone.

"Since we're all here and this machine is up and running, I think it's time to see what we can do with it."

"What are you going to try?" I asked, moving closer.

"Try? I'm not going to *try* anything. I'm going to *do*. In particular, I'm going to worm my way into Containment-Net and see what we can see about Mr. Broussard."

"Should I mention that's illegal?" I asked. It wasn't the first time he'd hacked his way in; he'd done it the very night we'd met in order to erase evidence that I'd used magic. In other words, he'd saved my ass.

"Of course you shouldn't." He typed furiously, one screen replacing another as he worked through Containment's systems. "Figured we'd check Broussard's files, take a look at what he's been working on."

"In case what he was working on got him killed," I concluded.

"That's it," Moses muttered as he typed. "Added some new security, think I can't make my way through it? Assholes. Gunnar's the only good one in that entire group. Not counting you two," he said, glancing back at the Quinn boys.

"Technically," Gavin said, "I'm an independent contractor and Liam's"—he glanced speculatively at his brother—"in his post–independent contractor stage."

Liam grunted his agreement.

"All right," Moses said. "Recent docs." He clicked on a folder with Broussard's name on it, revealing another set of folders.

"Put his docs in reverse chronological order," Liam suggested. "Let's see what he was viewing before he died."

"On that." Moses moved from folder to folder, pounded keys, then repeated the process. "Here we go," he said after a moment, when the screen filled with bright green text.

If that text was supposed to mean something, I didn't get it. It was a mishmash of letters and numbers and symbols, like someone had simply rolled a hand across a keyboard.

"Is it encrypted?" Gavin asked, moving forward with a frown and peering at the screen.

"Don't think so," Moses said as he continued to type. He did something that made the text shrink, then rotate, then expand, then shrink again. "Huh," he said. "Not encrypted. Just not the entire file. It's a stub."

"A stub?" I asked.

"What's left of a file after someone tries to delete it." He looked back at us. "Deleting a file doesn't really destroy it, at least not completely, and sometimes not at all. There's almost always at least something left—the stub."

He swiveled back to the screen. "This looks like someone tried to do a pretty thorough delete, dumped a lot of the bytes, but not all of them. This is what's left." He typed, then hit the ENTER key with gusto.

One of the tower's panels flew off, followed by a fountain of orange sparks and flame. The panel hit the brick wall and bounced to the floor, and the machine began to whistle.

"Shit!" Moses said, swatting at it with his hand.

The brothers moved faster than I did. While Gavin grabbed a towel from a nearby stack and covered the flames to block access to oxygen, Liam yanked the power cord—overstuffed with plugs— from the wall.

Without power, the screens went dark, and the hum of electronics went suddenly silent. Gavin futzed with the towel and the case until he was satisfied the fire was out.

The room smelled like burning plastic, and a haze of smoke gathered near the ceiling.

"Huh," Moses said after a moment, brushing smoke away from his face and leaning around to get a look at the case.

"Do try not to burn the house down," Gavin said. "Tends to make Containment pay attention."

"You think that bus you've parked outside won't?" Liam asked.

"It's New Orleans," Gavin said matter-of-factly. "Anything goes in the Big Easy."

Moses hopped off the stool, gave the case a thump with his fist. When nothing happened, he peered inside it, began fiddling with parts.

He yelped in pain, and we all jumped forward to help. But he pulled his hand out, perfectly fine, and wiggled his fingers. "Humans," he said affectionately, and shook his head. "So gullible."

"This is the problem," he said, then extracted a black box—probably four by four by three inches—with a very melted corner. "Power supply. Hoped it would last a little longer. If you wanna get back into the file, I need another one." He looked at me and Liam speculatively, which put me instantly on my guard. "I need a favor."

"What?" I asked.

"This," he said. He tossed the box at Liam. "House down the road's got a pretty good stockpile of parts, and I think I saw another one of these in there. It's a Boomer 3600. Number will be written on the side."

"Which house?"

He gestured vaguely to the left. "The one with the shutters."

"Mos," I said with remarkable patience, "it's New Orleans. They all have shutters." When he opened his mouth, I held up a finger. "And don't say the one with the balcony."

He grinned. "Got me there. It's the butter one."

"The butter one," Liam repeated.

"I think he means yellow."

I asked Moses, with brows lifted.

"That's it, Sherlock. Two houses down, in the garage."

"Be more specific," I said.

"There's a house, with a garage, and there's a pile of damn computer parts in said garage. It's just like that box Liam is currently holding, and it will be inside a case that looks like mine." He gestured over his shoulder with his thumb at the stack of ten or fifteen empty computer cases, which didn't help narrow things much.

"You'll know it when you see it." He turned back to the pile of tools beside his keyboard, pulled out a screwdriver, tossed it at me. "*Go*," he said emphatically.

The order given and screwdriver in hand, we headed for the door.

It was pretty obvious he was setting us up, putting us together so we'd have to talk to each other. I didn't disagree that the conversation needed to be had, but it had been a long day, and I didn't feel much like being manipulated. If Liam wanted to talk, he could damn well open his mouth.

After checking that the coast was clear, we walked down the block. It was quiet out compared to the bayou. Maybe the city's wildlife was also waiting to hear what we'd have to say to each other.

But we didn't say anything. We just walked, and I worked really hard to pretend being out here with Liam was no big deal. To pretend I couldn't sense him beside me, strong and cruelly handsome.

"This one," I said, coming to a stop. Even in the dark, the color was clearly buttery. There wasn't an attached garage, so we walked down the driveway—two strips of gravel nearly covered now by grass—to a courtyard behind. The entrance to the garage was on the other side of the courtyard, a narrow box just big enough for one car. It had a pull-down door with a row of glass panels across the top and painted white handles along the bottom.

We each took a handle, lifted, then turned on the skinny flashlights we'd borrowed from a stash in Moses's living room.

"Damn," I said, staring at the volume of junk stuffed inside the narrow space. There were boxes, crates, electronics, and bundles piled to the ceiling.

"Stockpiler? Or hoarder?" Liam asked.

"Who knows?" I said, glancing around. "Doesn't look like it's been disturbed much, except for that." I pointed the flashlight at the narrow path that wound through the piles. "Probably Moses's trail."

Liam nodded, and I stepped into the path, followed it around a pile of busted bikes and television sets.

"I bet he picked this house because of this garage," Liam said, shifting things behind me.

"Probably. Electronics without corrosion are hard to come by."

The trail spiraled into the center of the garage, where the junk shifted to electronics. Cases, wires, connectors, screens. There were a lot of cases that looked like Moses's, so I started to pick through those.

He must have heard me moving around. "You got something?"

"Maybe." I shone the light into the cases, one after the other, until I saw a dusty box similar to the one Moses had had, with 3600 in red letters across the side.

"Found it," I said, and set about unscrewing it from the case. After a moment of work, it popped free into my hand. I didn't see any corrosion, but it was hard to tell with just a flashlight.

Prize won. I put away the screwdriver and began to weave my way back to the garage door. I stopped when I came to an old metal sign. SNOBALL was written across the rectangular piece of metal in pink three-dimensional block letters, each topped with a mound of snow. Flavors—strawberry, rainbow, praline—had been punched across the bottom.

Snoballs were the New Orleans version of shaved ice, a summertime tradition that hadn't survived the war. I hadn't seen a sign like this before, and I loved the memory it triggered.

My first instinct was to grab it for the shop, either to hang in the store or sell to someone looking for tangible reminders of the city's history.

But I didn't have a store to hang it in.

"Are you okay?"

"Just feeling nostalgic." I held up the power supply. "Got what we needed."

Liam nodded. We walked back to the garage door, and both reached for the same handle. Our fingers brushed, and the shock of hunger that arced through me left me nearly breathless.

Proximity shouldn't have made me suddenly ravenous, weak with want and need. I shouldn't have wanted to grab fistfuls of his hair, meld my mouth with his. I shouldn't have wanted to fall into his arms, to feel safe—and understood. But I did.

And I wasn't the only one affected; Liam's groan was a low, deep rumble. Then he stepped away, putting space between us, and ran a hand through his hair.

"What's going on?" I even sounded breathless. "Tell me what happened to you—what happened at the battle."

He shook his head. "You wouldn't understand."

I didn't think he meant to hurt me. But that didn't matter much.

"What wouldn't I understand, Liam? Magic? What it's like to run from it?"

"This is different."

"How?"

Liam shook his head, the war he was waging clear on his face.

"I don't know who you are right now," I said. "And I don't know what you want from me."

"I want nothing. And everything." He took a step closer, heat pumping from his body, muscles clenched like a man preparing for battle. "I haven't stopped wanting you. But it's inside me like an organism, a living thing full of fuel and anger. You think I'm going to bring that to your door?"

"I don't need protecting."

"Don't you?" He grabbed my hand, pressed it against his chest. His heart pounded like a war drum. "Feel that, Claire. That's because you're here. Because I see you, and I want to claim you like a goddamn wolf."

I stared at him while heat pulsed between our joined hands, and goose bumps rose along my arms. And it was long seconds before I had the composure to pull my hand away. I fisted my fingers against my chest, like that would cool the burn and diminish the power of his touch.

"Tell me about your magic."

My question had been a whisper, but it still seemed to echo through the garage.

I watched him shut down, shutter his expressions. But there was something he couldn't hide, a flash of something in his eyes. Not just anger, and not just stubbornness. There was *fear*. I recognized a man facing down his demons, because I'd faced down demons of my own. I was still facing them down.

"If you won't tell me what you're going through, I can't help you. And I can't fight your monsters on my own."

When he stayed silent, although it made my chest ache to do it, I walked out and left him behind.

The air had already been heavy with humidity, with heat. Now it was heavy with things left unspoken, things that weighed on both of us.

When we reentered Moses's house, everyone turned to look at us. To gauge what had happened—and what might happen next.

"Power supply," I said, walking to Moses and handing him the box. "You need anything else, you can find it yourself."

His gaze narrowed, but he turned it on Liam. "I'm so glad the trip was productive."

"Install the damn thing," Liam said.

Moses muttered something under his breath, then hopped off the stool and began to tinker with parts in the case. Plastic, now charred and black, went flying, as he made room for the new piece. He hooked it up, plugged in the system, and looked back at the screen.

But there was only silence. No whirring motors, no bright letters.

"Hmm," Moses said.

"Maybe it was corroded," Gavin said.

"Might have a trick," Moses muttered, then reared back and whopped the case with the side of his fist.

The entire tower shuddered, let out a belch of grinding plastic, and then whirred to life.

"And away we go," he said, and we all moved closer to watch the screen. Liam slipped in beside me, putting his body between me and Malachi.

That was fine. He could do whatever he wanted.

And so could I.

It took Moses a few minutes to get back into Containment-Net, and Gavin cast wary glances at the tower the entire time, waiting for another round of sparks. But the system held together, and Moses made it back to the stub of the file Broussard had reviewed.

"Here we go," he muttered. "File was called . . . Icarus."

"Isn't that a myth?" Gavin asked. "The guy who flew too close to the sun and his wings melted?"

"Yeah," I said, "that's the myth."

"That mean anything to anybody in this context?" Gavin asked. "Regarding Containment or New Orleans or Paranormals?"

When we shook our heads, Gavin looked at Malachi. "The theory is that a lot of our myths come from the Beyond. That we anticipated your existence, or were visited before."

"I know the theory," Malachi said. "And I know the myth. But there's no comparable story in the Beyond. We don't need wings made of wax."

"Fair enough," Gavin said, and glanced at Moses.

"I don't know anything from my corner of the world, either," Moses said, turned back to the screen, pressed a couple more keys. "Presuming Containment's telling the truth about when he died— and who knows if it is—Broussard opened this file less than an hour before he kicked."

"Coincidence?" Gavin asked.

"Maybe," Liam said quietly. "But it's the only lead we've got."

"Did Broussard create the file?" I asked.

It apparently took a moment for him to check. "He did not. The stub doesn't show who created it, only that it wasn't Broussard. It's some kind of binary security feature. 'Yes' if the creator looked at it, 'No' if a stranger to the file's looking at it." Moses traced a finger across the screen, following a line of letters. "I can tell you he sent this file to someone. Can't tell who, but based on the metadata, he looked at it, transmitted it. And that's the last task he performed."

"Can we see the stub again?" Liam asked. "Or what was left of it?"

"You got it," Moses said, then clicked keys emphatically. There was a music to his typing, like he was building songs with the percussion of stubby fingers on keys. "Here we go," he said, and swiveled back so we could see the screen.

"No flames," Gavin said, stepping forward. "That's a good start."

"Har-dee-har-har," Moses said as he frowned at the screen.

"I can't make heads or tails out of it," Gavin said.

The numbers and letters didn't mean anything to me. But the longer I stared at it, the more I thought I could make out a shape.

"It looks like part of a model," I said.

"A model of what?" Gavin asked.

"A molecule, maybe?" I frowned at it, trying to remember something of Mrs. Beauchamp's chemistry class. "We had to make one for our eighth grade science fair with painted foam balls and straws."

When they all gave me blank looks, I waved it off, then pointed at two clusters of letters. "Here and here," I said, "like these are foam balls, and see how they're kind of linked together by these things?" I pointed at the lines, now crooked, that I thought were supposed to connect them. "But instead of balls and straws, there are numbers and letters."

"A molecule," Gavin said. "So this is something scientific." He glanced around the room. "I don't think any of us are scientifically inclined, other than Balls-and-Straws over here, but anybody got any ideas?"

"None," Liam said.

"Science in the Beyond is differently constructed and imagined," Malachi said. "But even so, this doesn't look familiar. We need to talk to Darby."

This would be right up her scientifically minded alley.

"I think I can clean it up," Moses said, fingers busy at the keys again. "Let me do that, and I'll get you a hard copy. She can work her scientific magic on it."

Malachi nodded. "All right."

"It's also probably time to go see Gunnar," Gavin said. "Tell him what we know, and find out what he knows." He glanced at me. "I assume you want to go?"

"Of course. It would be good to see him." The thought of it made me simultaneously excited and nervous. I was pretty sure we had the kind of friendship that could make it through an absence, but this was the first time we'd been apart for so long.

"I'm going to dig around here a little more," Moses said. "Maybe I can find something else."

"Like what?" I asked.

"Identity of the person who created the file, when, maybe a note about related docs. I'll see what else he worked on, in case this is a blind. Lots of information to look through. Whoever among your ilk invented metadata gets a thumbs-up from me."

"We'll be sure to tell him or her," Gavin said, then gestured to the door. "Saddle up."

Once upon a time, St. Charles Avenue had been an ode to architecture, a boulevard marked by one mansion after another, and the lead-in to a neighborhood of gentility and Southern wealth.

The Landreaus had owned one of those houses, the so-called Palm Tree House, which was as yellow as the cottage near Moses's, had long porches, fancy columns, and dozens of palm trees. The family had refused to give up on or abandon New Orleans. Instead, they'd repaired the damage war had done to the house and lived there still—Gunnar, his parents, and his siblings. It was a testament to their love of New Orleans—and their absolute stubbornness.

It also occurred to me that every one of my friends was stubborn. Probably in part because it was the stubborn people who'd stayed.

Gavin parked on the otherwise empty street, and we took the cobblestone sidewalk to the front door. The house was dark but for the front room, which glowed with light.

He gave the brass door knocker a questioning look, then rapped it lightly.

Seconds later, the door was yanked open. And the man standing there—tall and handsome, with dark, rakish hair that fell over his forehead and teasing, intelligent brown eyes—opened his arms.

I ran past Gavin and into Gunnar's arms.

"It's been too long," Gunnar said. He was tall enough to rest his head atop mine, and his arms were banded around me like I might fly away if he didn't hold tight enough.

"Yeah, it has." I reached up to knuckle away the only tear I'd let fall. "It's good to see you."

He brushed back my hair, pressed a kiss to my forehead. "It's good to see you, too." He looked up, offered nods to Gavin and Malachi, then glared at Liam.

"Well. Look who's here." If anything, Gunnar's embrace tightened. "Let me guess—you pissed off everyone outside New Orleans, too, so you've come home again?"

"Landreau," Gavin said, cutting off the argument. "We need to talk. Can we come in?"

"Just telling it like it is," Gunnar said. He looked down at me, concern in his eyes. "But do come in. I actually have something for you," he said, then released me to push open the door.

She sat on the couch, one leg tucked under the other, a binder in her lap. Her dark hair was curled now into tight ringlets that brushed her shoulders.

"What's going—," Tadji began, then looked up. Her brown eyes went wide with surprise. Then she made a half-scream sound before jumping up, dumping the binder on the floor, and running toward me, the flowy tank she'd paired with leggings and boots shimmering in the air like wings as she moved.

She yanked me into the house, then wrapped me in a fierce hug that almost broke the few ribs Gunnar hadn't managed to crack. She squealed as we swayed back and forth—at least until she let me go and slapped me on the arm. Hard.

"Ow!" I exclaimed, rubbing it. "What was that for?"

"For showing yourself," she said, her eyes brimming with tears. "You're not supposed to be running around the Garden District."

But she pulled me into a hug again. "And I have missed the crap out of you."

Then she pulled back again, slapped my other arm. "Why are you here?"

"Stop the cycle of violence," Gunnar said, extending a hand between us. "Claire, Tadji's glad to see you and concerned about seeing you." He smiled at her. "That cover it?"

"It does." But her eyes were narrow. "For now."

"Good," he said. "There's water in the refrigerator, and the bar's open," he said, as the others filed inside. But no one moved for booze. Not when there was work to be done first.

He closed the door, then turned back to me, ran his hands up and down my arms. "And how are you?" he asked quietly.

"It's been a long couple of days."

Gunnar's gaze found Liam. "I take it that's how long he's been in the universe again."

I nodded, really glad to be back among my allies. "Pretty much."

"He say anything about what happened? Why he left? Maybe groveling for mercy for leaving you behind?"

"Not yet."

Gunnar nodded, looked at Liam. "Never fear, Claire-belle. If the way he looks at you is any indication, it's on its way."

"Where are your parents?" I asked, thinking the house seemed unusually quiet. "Your brother and sister?"

"They left after the battle," he said. "Couldn't stay in the Zone any longer." He glanced back at the room, the fancy Southern décor, like he might be imagining them there, cooking or talking or laughing.

"I'm sorry," I said, and squeezed his hand.

He nodded. "I'm managing. I assume you want to talk about Broussard?" he asked as we moved to stand with the others.

"Among other things," Gavin said. "Let's sit down."

Gunnar didn't look thrilled about taking orders in his own home. But when Gavin took a seat on a yellow gingham sofa, Gunnar went to the windows and began lowering the shades.

"All right," he said, when he'd secured our privacy. "Let's talk."

We joined Gavin on the couches in the living room. Or everyone but Liam did. He stood by the window, apart from the rest of us.

Gavin did the talking, telling Gunnar the parts of the story he hadn't yet heard—from our trip to the bayou, to the bounty hunters, to the roadblock.

Gunnar didn't speak until he looked at me. "You walked into the bayou?"

"Yes."

"With gators and snakes?"

"Yep."

"Should I be pissed you hiked around southern Louisiana even though the Containment heat's been turned up? Or should I be proud you walked among gators and snakes?"

"Technically," Gavin said, before I could answer, "we drove for part of it."

Gunnar slid his gaze to Gavin. "This was your idea?"

"All due respect, since she was a trouper, Claire's really not the focus of this particular story," Gavin said. "We're more concerned about Broussard and this very obvious frame job. And Icarus."

"What's Icarus?"

Gunnar's expression was blank, and he looked genuinely confused. Which was probably what Gavin had been testing.

"The last file Broussard reviewed before he was killed. Assuming Containment's telling the truth about his time of death."

"I'm not going to ask how you know what files Broussard was looking at. But I don't know what Icarus is, and I don't have any more details about the murder than I did the last time we talked." Gunnar looked at Liam. "I'm not involved in the investigation."

"You're second-in-command of Devil's Isle," I said. "How are you not involved?"

"Because you've been shut out," Malachi guessed, and Gunnar nodded.

"He was killed outside Devil's Isle, so his murder is technically outside our jurisdiction. Any normal day, that wouldn't matter. But it seems to matter now, and to people at a higher pay grade than mine. Investigators have been assigned. I don't have access to files, reports, or anything else. I'm shut out completely."

"This the Commandant's doing?" Gavin asked.

"Above his pay grade, too. I don't know who's pulling the strings, but it's someone in the PCC, someone who ranks high enough to shut out the Commandant." He looked at Liam. "Being that I'm the curious sort, I talked to one of those investigators, asked what he believes set you off—why you attacked Broussard when Gracie has been gone for nearly a year. He didn't have a satisfactory answer; he's just assuming you did it."

"That's a shitty investigation," Gavin said.

"It is. I realize Containment isn't perfect. But it's usually minimally competent. That's not what this is."

"It's bigger," I said.

"Yeah. Let's go back to Icarus. What is it?"

"We don't know," Gavin said. "Found a stub of a file that someone tried very diligently to erase."

"And someone else, probably a Para with electronic skills, managed to dig out?" Gunnar asked.

"No comment," Gavin said with a thin smile.

"And did this individual get anything of substance in that stub?"

"It looks like something scientific," Gavin said, glancing at me. "But we don't have enough information to figure out how or what it is."

"You going to talk to Darby?"

"That's the plan."

Gunnar nodded. "That he looked at the file last could be just coincidence."

"Could be," Gavin said. "But it's the lead we've got, so we're following it through."

"Who else knew Liam and Broussard didn't like each other?" I asked. "Does that narrow it down?"

"It doesn't," Gunnar said, and looked over at Liam. "I assume you don't disagree?"

"No," Liam said. "He didn't like me or trust me, and he wasn't shy about sharing that with others."

Gunnar furrowed his brow and nodded. "I can look into this Icarus deal quietly. Assuming it's not personal nonsense he happened to store on our network, it could be a PCC project. If it is, it's not one I'm privy to."

"Is that unusual?" Liam asked.

"Not necessarily. We oversee operations in Devil's Isle, Containment operations in the New Orleans quadrant. That's a small slice of the PCC's pie. But Broussard was one of our people. I'd know about anything he was working on."

"And what was he working on?" Liam asked.

"Nothing unusual," Gunnar said, meeting his gaze. "We're more than a month past the battle and still processing the intel on Reveillon, working through the individuals we arrested. He's been in on that. But Reveillon's old news, according to Gavin's report."

Gavin nodded. "Sporadic discussion in the Zone. No action I could find."

"Like I said, I'll look into it. And I'll let you know what I find."

"There's more," I said, and looked at Malachi. "There are Paranormals at Vacherie. One's sick, and one was sick but passed away. Both were friends of Malachi's."

"Man, I'm sorry," Gunnar said.

Malachi nodded.

"What kind of illness?"

I described what we'd seen. "Does that ring any bells for you? Sound familiar? It's unusual, and we want to make sure it's not spreading."

"I'm not aware of anything," Gunnar said. "Lizzie would know better than me, since she's at the clinic, but she'd have reported something unusual, and she didn't. She did tell me she appreciated your package."

That was something, anyway. "The Paras are being treated at the farm, because they think if they come into the clinic, they won't be able to leave again."

"That's a possibility," Gunnar agreed after a moment. "Based on the phrasing of the regulation."

I nodded. "If you've got any extra medics, maybe you could send someone out to look at them?"

"I'll see what I can do."

"Appreciate it," Malachi said, and Gunnar gave him a nod.

"Go back for a minute," Liam said. "What package did you give Lizzie?" He'd introduced me to her; she'd been his friend first.

"Goods for the clinic," Gavin said. "Delta's been busy in the last few weeks."

"Gunnar arranged the logistics," I explained. "Moses and I scavenge. Lizzie gets whatever we can find for the clinic, and we don't get nabbed for dropping it off."

"How do you do that?" Liam asked.

"Delivery entrance," Gunnar said.

"Devil's Isle doesn't have a delivery entrance."

"It does now," Gunnar said with a smile. "The battle did some damage to the walls. We took the opportunity to do some upgrades."

"They're going to build a gym," Malachi said. "For the residents."

"A gym?" Gavin asked.

"Recreation facility," Gunnar said, "for the kids who've been born in Devil's Isle."

"Innocent kids," I said, and he nodded.

"Yeah. Kids who need an outlet."

"How'd you get the taxpayers to foot the bill for that?" Liam asked.

Gunnar's smile widened. "They didn't. It will be built thanks to a very large donation from the Arsenault Foundation."

Liam's brows lifted in surprise. I guess Eleanor hadn't told him about that, assuming she'd known. The decision could have been made by her friends in Washington.

"There've been a lot of changes while I've been gone."

His words seemed to change the temperature of the room, putting a chill in the air.

"Then maybe you shouldn't have left," Gunnar said. "You ready to talk about that? Because several of us have questions."

"*Many* questions," Tadji said. "And also some declarative sentences."

Liam looked at me, the heat in his eyes sizzling enough to scorch. "I did what I had to do."

"Which was?" Tadji prompted.

There was silence for a long time. And then he looked at me. "What was necessary."

The pain in his eyes was clear enough, and the room went quiet. And so the mystery of Liam's missing weeks still hung in the air.

"Have you been eating?"

I looked at Gunnar, and it took a moment for my brain to catch up with the abrupt shift. "What?"

His gaze narrowed. "You've lost weight you didn't need to lose. I'm making you a grilled cheese sandwich."

"I don't need a grilled cheese sandwich." Never mind that my weight was none of Gunnar's business. But that didn't stop him from playing big brother.

"Tough. I don't need you out there on your own, forgetting to eat."

"I don't forget to eat." I just didn't care that much about it these days. Which, when you put it that way, made it sound like he was right. My jeans had felt a little looser.

Not taking my word for it, Gunnar rose to go into the kitchen.

"I guess we're having grilled cheese," Tadji said, then stood and took my hand. "Come on, Claire. Let's get you fed."

I could feed myself. And did, when I needed food. But the grilled cheese still hit the spot. So did the second one that I accepted after everyone else was satisfied. Gunnar felt better for having done it, and the bread and cheese laid a nice foundation for the alcohol.

We were having an impromptu reunion, after all. And now that the business was done, we decided to make the most of it.

Gunnar played tender at the built-in bar on the other side of the room. "What's everyone drinking?"

He was answered by a chorus of requests.

"Excellent," he said. "You get Sazeracs or you get nothing."

"Claire makes a fantastic Sazerac," Tadji said.

"Oh, I know," Gunnar said with a grin as he added bitters to highball glasses. "Who do you think taught her how to do it?"

"I assumed she taught you," Tadji said with a wink.

"The memory is somewhat hazy," Gunnar said.

She grabbed the first two glasses he'd filled, then gestured toward the door.

"Claire and I are going to take a walk. You gentlemen do what you will."

"Poker?" Gavin asked.

"You cheat," Liam said.

"You just don't like losing." He glanced at Malachi speculatively. "You ever played poker?"

"I have not."

Gavin's grin said all we needed to know about how that was going to go.

Tadji said to me, "Let's go into the orangery."

"You just like saying 'orangery.'"

"True. But mostly I like being in houses that have them."

In that case she'd come to the right place.

The Landreau house was enormous—a late 1920s mansion with a lot of style.

The orangery was pretty much as described: an octagonal peninsula off the back of the house. Five orange trees in terra-cotta pots were blossoming in front of the windows, perfuming the air with floral and citrus scents.

The floor was covered in marble tile, and the ceiling was a cage of glass and steel. If you needed a break from sniffing orange blossoms, there were wicker couches and chairs with deep cushions, and small stone-and-metal tables with matching chairs.

We took seats on the couches. Tadji was already barefoot, and she tucked her feet beneath her as she sat.

"Now that we can talk," she said, turning to face me, "what the hell is the story with Liam?"

"I don't exactly know," I finally said, and told her about our conversation in the garage.

"What do you think happened?"

"No idea. I assume it has something to do with his magic, and that it's not good. But that's based on the look in his eyes. He won't talk about it, and I'm not going to fall at his feet just because he's here."

"Nor should you." She thought for a minute, swirling the liquid in her glass, and nodded. "Ball's in his court until he fesses up."

"Agreed." I took a drink.

It was potent, but layered with flavors. Complex, just like New Orleans. Gunnar did make a pretty good Sazerac.

"I heard about Burke," I said. "Have you heard from him?"

Tadji and Burke, a former Delta member, had been progressing their relationship very slowly—at her request. But he'd been reassigned after the battle, shipped back to DC and PCC headquarters.

"He's doing all right, as far as I can tell."

"And how are you?"

She was quiet for a moment. "Do you believe that absence makes the heart grow fonder?"

"Evidence says yes."

"Well," she said, "then let's just leave it at that."

She was clearly eager to change the subject, so I shifted it back to my first love. "The store looks good."

She looked at me, eyes wide with surprise. And then they narrowed with obvious anger. "What do you mean, 'The store looks good'?"

"Which part are you unhappy about?"

"First of all, the store looks phenomenal," she said, counting off on her fingers. "Second of all, you shouldn't know that. You shouldn't know anything about the store, because you're supposed to be staying away from it."

Perversely, the irritation in her voice made me feel better. If she was angry that I *had* seen her at the store, that meant she wasn't angry that I *hadn't*. She didn't feel burdened by taking it over, or at least not enough to be angry at me over it. That lifted some of the psychic weight I'd been carrying around.

"I just wanted to check on things. How's the dissertation?" I asked, trying to change the subject for my own benefit this time.

"Two more chapters done."

I stared at her. "While running the store on your own? How are you doing that?"

Tadji grinned, pushed hair behind her ear. "Honey, I'm not doing it on my own. I've hired people. There's money in the budget to do that now."

Touché, I thought, with only a little shame that I hadn't been able to get the store to that kind of profitability.

"And, it turns out, I really like being busy. It makes me more productive to have a tight schedule. It's harder to make excuses when you know you have less time. So I made myself a schedule, and I work in the back office while Ezell—he's one of my probationary hires—watches the store."

"There isn't a back office."

She just looked at me, the same way Liam had looked at Gunnar when Gunnar told him about the delivery entry to Devil's Isle.

"Damn, you're good."

"I know," she said with a cheeky grin.

"How do things feel in the Quarter?" I'd missed seeing my regular customers, getting a feel for Containment by watching soldiers moving in and out of the neighborhood. Being in isolation was, well, isolating.

"There's a weird mood," she said, setting her drink on the coffee table.

"How so?"

She frowned, crossed her arms. "Before the battle, we'd gotten comfortable. Maybe not entirely comfortable with Devil's Isle, but we'd gotten used to the way things were."

I nodded. We'd learned to survive during the war. When it was over, it had taken time for us to accept that we were safe, that a battalion of Valkyries wasn't heading for the city, golden weapons at the ready. But we'd made new lives, begun to accept our new world.

"Since the battle," she continued, "it's like we're waiting for the other shoe to drop. For another battle to begin. People look over their shoulders a lot more, wondering if there are more Reveillon members out there.

"But at the same time," she said, "there's a new kind of camaraderie because we fought together. Citizens and soldiers and Paras. We hold coffee klatch on Thursday nights. Someone brings coffee, someone brings a snack, I bring the room and the electricity. And we talk. We're honest. That's a pretty big change."

"It's good," I agreed. "It's very good." I thought of Broussard and the apparent frame job. If anyone knew the word on the streets of New Orleans, it was the woman who ran Royal Mercantile.

And I felt a little pang that I wasn't that woman right now.

"What are you hearing about Containment?"

She glanced back at the doorway, checking that we had privacy. "Nothing about Icarus. If that's part of this. I haven't heard the word since my last myth and mythology class."

"If you hear anything specific, let me know."

"I will." She crossed her legs. "What have you been doing since the battle? Other than delivering goods to the clinic and occasionally spying on my store?"

That was pretty much it. Like everyone else in the Zone, I'd been surviving. There wasn't much to say beyond that. But I told her what there was to tell.

"And how is Moses?" she asked with a grin.

"Grouchy."

"So about the same."

"Pretty much."

She paused. "What are you going to do about Liam?"

"I don't know. I guess just see where it goes."

She patted my leg. "You look exhausted, and you've had a helluva day. You'll get some sleep, let it simmer, and have a clearer outlook."

I hoped she was right. Because right now things were pretty damn murky.

CHAPTER ELEVEN

I was hoping for a ride back to the gas station. It was more than four miles from Gunnar's house, and I'd done plenty of miles today. Besides, the Sazerac was doing its job. My legs felt all warm and soft. By the time we got back to the living room—a good two-minute walk from the orangery—I was ready for bed.

But we found the living room empty.

"Maybe the poker went bad, so they decided to go with a duel?"

"Possible," I said, "but I don't think Gunnar would allow that."

Voices lifted from the doorway on the other side of the room, so we walked that way. And stared.

At the very formal dining table, in a room with walls papered in large flowers, sat four attractive men, shirts discarded, locked in combat. They faced each other in pairs, right hands locked together.

They were arm wrestling.

"Did I drink straight absinthe?" Tadji asked, cocking her head at the scene.

"If so, we both did."

"Not that I'm complaining," Tadji said, her gaze full of appreciation.

Gunnar glanced up at us, sweat popping out on his brow, biceps bulging as he and Gavin struggled for control. "Gun. Show," he muttered through teeth clenched in concentration.

"And are we fighting for money," Tadji asked, "or just to caress our egos?"

"For glory," Gavin said, but didn't take his gaze off his opponent.

Malachi and Liam didn't talk at all. They just stared at each other, knuckles white with effort as they battled.

"Go blow in his ear," Tadji whispered. "Distract him."

"Which one of them?"

"That's my girl," she said with a grin. "Gentlemen, it's getting late. So if you'll wrap up . . . whatever this is, someone needs to give my girl here a ride back to her sanctuary."

There were manly grunts, guttural screams, and finally fists pounded the table.

Gunnar beat Gavin.

Liam beat Malachi.

More power to them.

Gavin rubbed his wrist. "Haven't had a workout like that in a while."

"Y'all have the brains of a fourteen-year-old boy," Tadji said. "Collectively."

"Probably." He glanced at Liam. "Big brother managed a good win."

Without comment, Liam stood and put his T-shirt back on. And didn't bother to avert his gaze. He watched me as I watched him, and there shouldn't have been so much power in a look, in the simple act of a beautiful man pulling a shirt on.

"Oh, you are hosed," Gunnar muttered, sliding behind me to grab his own shirt. "Not that I can fault your taste."

"Physically, no," I said. "But emotionally?"

"Maybe he'll have convincing things to say."

Maybe. But he had to be willing to talk. And he wasn't there yet. I didn't know what could happen between us—but I knew it could only start with honesty.

"You can sleep here," Gunnar said to me. "Plenty of bedrooms."

The idea was inviting—spending the night in a cozy bed in this castle of a house, knowing that I wouldn't be alone. But my being here would put him in danger, and that wasn't worth the risk.

"Thanks, but no, thanks. I'll head home."

"When will I see you again?" Tadji asked, concern pinching her features.

"I don't know." I'd tried to reassure myself that solitude wouldn't last forever. But so far, Containment was still Containment. "Hopefully sooner rather than later."

"If I find out anything on my end," Gunnar said, "I'll let you know. I'm going to have to look into it very discreetly. So it may not be tomorrow. But I'll let you know as soon as I have information."

"We can meet at Moses's house in the morning," I suggested. "Maybe he's found something else about the stub."

Gunnar nodded. "Fine by me."

"While we're making arrangements," Liam said, "I want to see Broussard's place."

Gunnar was quiet for a moment. "That will take time to arrange. The building's sealed, and I don't have authority to let you in."

"How long?"

"A few days, maybe. I'll have to call in a favor."

That didn't calm Liam's obvious impatience. "I'm accused of killing him. I have the right to see the scene, to see what I'm accused of."

"You don't, actually," Gunnar said. He was as calm as Liam was agitated. "You're a suspect in a particularly gruesome murder, and you are absolutely not allowed to contaminate the scene."

"Or risk adding your DNA to the evidentiary mix," I said. "You'd implicate yourself."

"Claire has a point." Gunnar held up his hands. "I'll work as quickly as I can. But you'll only make things worse for yourself if you go without my okay."

"I'm not making any promises."

"Stubborn ass," Gunnar muttered.

"It's genetic," Gavin said, then looked at me. "Since we're wrapping up here, you want a ride back?"

Thank God. "You can take me to the alley. That's as far as you can go."

"If I had a nickel . . . ," Gavin said.

"I'll go, walk you the rest of the way," Malachi said.

"You know where she lives?"

Gavin's question was pouty; Liam's gaze was downright hostile.

"He's already public enemy number one," I said. "Not much harm in his knowing. And there's no need to add anyone else to the list."

After the dark ride back to Mid-City, Gavin turned into the alley.

"Thank you for the ride," I said as Malachi and I climbed out.

"Sure thing," Gavin said. "I'll see you tomorrow?"

"Yep."

Liam looked at me through his open window, a challenge in his eyes. "Be careful," he quietly said.

The tone of his voice, the possessiveness in it, lifted goose bumps on my arms even while it irritated me. "I'm always careful."

"Claire."

I looked back at him, watched gold flare in his eyes. "I told you what I need, Liam."

His jaw clenched, but after a moment the stubbornness in his expression faded, shifted into clear regret. *"Claire,"* he said again, this time an entreaty.

I shook my head. "I get all of you. Or you get none."

He looked away. That I knew we were both hurting was the only reason I wasn't more angry with him.

"Humans, sometimes, are just the worst," I said, when the Range Rover's lights disappeared around the corner. It didn't help that I was tired and feeling helpless. And already missing Tadji, and feeling a little hopeless about that.

"No argument there," Malachi said.

We walked quietly to the gas station. We stopped across the street, where Malachi would wait and watch for me to get safely inside.

Maybe it was time to make a gesture. To take a chance on doing something big. Something right.

"Come on," I said, motioning toward the building. "I want to show you something."

He looked surprised but intrigued. "All right," he said.

We waited to ensure that the coast was clear, and then I headed for the door. "With me," I said.

"You want me to come in?"

"It's only fair," I said, and unlocked it.

We walked inside. I closed and locked the door behind us, then flipped on the overhead lights.

Malachi stared at the room, walked slowly to the first table, looked down at the objects there. *"Claire,"* he said.

"My father saved them from Containment fires," I said.

He walked to the middle table, long and narrow and hewn of thick, dark planks, and picked up a golden bow, ran the tip of his finger down the sinewy string.

"You've kept this secret." He put it down again, then looked back at me, considered. "To ensure that Containment doesn't find out about it."

I nodded. "And that no one gets hurt because they try to find out."

Malachi nodded, looked back at the table. "I don't know how I feel about that."

"Welcome to my world. They'd destroy the weapons if they could. Containment, I mean."

"Or use them for their own purposes." He walked around the table, surveyed the objects on the next one. "I can hardly take it all in."

"I said the same thing the first time."

Malachi frowned at some objects, smiled at others. "There are Consularis and Court objects here."

"Are there? I'd wondered. I don't know anything about how my father gathered these things, but I figured he'd take whatever he could get. I started to catalog it, but I don't know the proper names of everything, and I felt a little stupid writing down human ones."

Malachi was looking at what appeared to be a square tambourine— a rigid form hung with tiny cymbals and bells. "Do you know what this is?"

"Tambourine?"

He smiled. "Something like that. It's called an *Ilgitska*. It's used in a sexual ceremony."

"A sexual ceremony?" I asked, giving it a second look.

"We liked our ceremonies," he said with a smile, probably because of the flush in my cheeks. He picked it up, slapped it against the palm of his hand.

The sound was complex, from the delicate and pretty *ping* of bells to the deep, hollow tones of small brass spheres. I could admit there was something sensual about it, as if each tone had been carefully modulated to stoke desire.

What a weird day this had been. And what a weird night it had become.

"Sound has power," he said with a smile, setting the instrument on the table again. "Your father has done a great service, saving these things."

I nodded. "Thank you. I'd like to think so. I only learned about this a little before the battle. He didn't tell me when he was building the collection, and I didn't know until after he was gone. That hurts. But I know why he kept me from it."

"To keep you safe," Malachi said.

"Yeah. One of the many things he kept from me." I took a deep breath, readied myself, and turned to him. "I need to ask you about Erida."

"You can ask, although I may not be able to answer. What do you want to know?"

I still paused before saying it. "Erida and my father."

He didn't answer immediately. "Was that the question?"

"It was an opener," I said lamely. "They were friends?"

He looked at me for what felt like a really long time. "They were friends," he said finally. "And more."

That confirmed it. "They were lovers," I said. "I thought that might have been the case, after what she told me last night. But I didn't know he was seeing anyone. I never saw her, and he never said anything."

Malachi nodded. "They were very discreet, I understand. By necessity. If they had been found out, she would have been incarcerated, and he would have been punished for harboring a Paranormal."

"Did you know my mother?"

"I did not know her. I've apparently seen her."

"What do you mean?"

"I did not know she was your mother at the time I saw her. Erida told me later."

I told him what I'd believed to be true.

"I'm sorry your father didn't tell you the truth."

"So am I." Because that's what we'd come to. That my father had been lying to me. "Erida said she knew her, but I didn't know her—or anything about her."

"She was a lovely woman, although I understand she was cold."

I nodded. "Come with me." We walked through the kitchenette, then through the narrow door that led to the basement.

The room had probably once been storage for the gas station, and a way to access cars on the first floor via hatches that opened beneath them. It now held rows of metal shelves with water and canned goods, as well as the small cot where I slept.

It also held the trunk that contained only one item—the photograph of the woman with red hair.

Liam and I had taken the photograph away the night we'd discovered this place; I'd taken it back after the battle, put it back in the place where I'd found it.

I lifted the trunk lid and pulled out the picture. I offered it to Malachi, without looking at the image. I'd looked at it too many times already.

"I found the photograph here," I said. "There's no writing on it. I assumed my father had left it, but I didn't know why. She looks like me. And after talking to Erida . . ."

Malachi nodded. "I understand this is your mother. She does look like you." His voice was gentle now.

I looked up at him. "You could both be wrong. This could be a misunderstanding or a coincidence." But that sounded stupid and naive even to me. And I was the one who'd believed a lie for more than twenty years. Who'd been lied to for more than twenty years.

"I understand your father told everyone she was gone. He told Erida the truth only after she found a photograph of her."

My stomach clenched again. "This photograph?" Is that why it had been in the trunk? Had he locked it away so she wouldn't have to see it?

"I don't know. I'm sorry."

I nodded. "Has Erida been here?"

"I knew nothing about this place. If Erida had known, I believe she'd have told me." He looked around. "Or perhaps it would be more accurate to say that I believe she would have told me if she'd known what it held. I don't know how much your father told her."

I nodded, made myself look down at the picture. "This woman was at Talisheek."

His brows lifted. "Was she?"

"Not on our side. She was with the group that had tried to reopen the Veil. Does she work for Containment?"

"I don't know. I don't know anything about her. I don't believe your father spoke about her, and I don't believe Erida asked many questions. But Erida may know more than I do, more that she hasn't told me. You should talk to her."

When I didn't speak, he looked back at me. "It's not her fault your father lied to you."

I knew that, too. But that didn't make it easier.

"You're right." I put the photograph away and closed the lid of the trunk, wishing I could compartmentalize my feelings as easily.

I didn't sleep. Not really.

My brain was spinning with new truths and old lies. Liam and his unknown demons. My mother, my father and his lies.

I tried to flip back through the catalog of memories, of every time I'd asked about my mother, and everything he'd told me in response. I tried to remember his expressions. Had he looked like he was lying?

And that wasn't even the biggest question. The hardest question. If she was alive, where had she been for the last twenty-two years? Why had she left my father, and why had she left me? Why had she willingly let me go? Did she wonder what I looked like, if I'd survived the war, who I'd grown up to be?

Given the life I'd seen my father lead, I still believed he was a good man, a decent man. Nothing Erida or Malachi had told me changed that. But he hadn't been an honest man. Not about this place, not about magic, not about who he'd been, not about Erida, not about my mother.

Layers of lies, stacked one atop the other. And I was left to unravel them all.

CHAPTER TWELVE

It was already scorching by the time I got to Moses's place. It didn't help my mood when I learned it was missing one magically enhanced human.

"Liam was supposed to stay here," I said to Moses. "He shouldn't be wandering around New Orleans alone."

"He left a note," Moses said, offering up the small sheet of paper pulled from a notebook, the edges still frayed.

"'Went to take a look,'" I read aloud, then looked at Moses. "A look at what?"

"He's here because Broussard's dead. My guess? Broussard's house."

My eyes narrowed. "He should have stayed in the damn bayou. Should have stayed there where Eleanor could keep an eye on him. And he certainly should have stayed here with you until someone could watch his back. Gunnar told him not to go over there."

"If you were in his position, would you do anything different?"

I growled, then glanced around. "Malachi?"

"Sent a pigeon." In the Zone, they were one of the most reliable ways to pass messages. "Said he was going back to Vacherie to check in on the Paras."

I nodded. That meant I was closer to Broussard's place than Malachi was, so it was up to me to find Liam. At least I'd get a look at the scene of the crime.

"You better get moving," Moses said. "I'll stay here in case he comes back."

"You get anything else out of that Icarus file?"

"I'm still looking. Quit rushing my genius."

Everyone was grouchy today. "Stay here, lay low, and keep geniusing."

He grinned toothily. "I got canned foods and a working comp. I don't need to go anywhere else."

Whatever kept him safe.

Broussard made a good living, if his place was any indication. There wasn't a lot of money in the Zone, but he'd managed to get into a gorgeous house in the Garden District just a stone's throw from St. Charles and not far from Gunnar's.

Broussard's house sat behind a fenced front yard full of palm trees and hedges, and a long driveway that would have made plenty of New Orleanians jealous, before or after the war.

The house was an ivory box with symmetrical windows and blue shutters. Double stairs curved up to a red front door. And yellow police tape marked it as a crime scene.

I stood beneath an oak tree on the neighboring property, watching for any sign of Liam. If he was in there, he was being quiet about it.

"At least he hasn't lost his damn mind completely," I murmured. I crept along the hedge that divided the properties, looking for a way in. I found a floor-to-ceiling window already pushed open. Probably how he'd have gotten inside.

I darted across the yard and slipped through the window, which opened into a dining room. Pine floors, plastered walls with crown molding, an enormous inlaid table with curving chairs, an antique rug. The ceilings were high, as were the doorways.

I moved into the hallway, the walls lined with paintings in gilded frames. This was the kind of house my father would have loved to live in, if he'd been able to keep an antique for more than a few days, instead of putting it in the store for sale.

Across from the dining room was a formal living room with the same windows and molding, a brick fireplace that stretched to the ceiling, and a hearth of shiny tiles in shades of green.

The floor above me creaked. I took the double staircase to the second floor.

Liam stood on the landing, staring at the wall.

I was prepared to lay into him—for leaving Moses's house alone, for walking into a crime scene—and then I saw what he was staring at.

FOR GRACIE was painted on the wall in what looked like blood, and there was a stain the same color on the floor in front of it.

Liam's body was rigid, his eyes blazing with anger, as if he might be able to burn the letters off the wall by strength of will alone.

"Liam."

His body jerked, but he didn't turn around. He hadn't heard me come in, which proved he shouldn't have been here alone. He might not have heard hunters, either.

"Are you all right?"

"Would you be?"

"No," I said. "No, if I saw the name of someone I loved spread across the wall, an excuse for someone else's murder, I'd be absolutely furious. But still. You shouldn't have come without Gunnar's okay. Without him clearing a path."

He turned, looked at me for the first time, and I gasped before I could help myself. His eyes glowed golden, fury and grief battling on his face.

"I couldn't wait anymore. They're using me, my family, to hurt people. I want to know why."

I nodded. I couldn't argue with that. And since we were already here, we'd might as well investigate.

"All right," I said. "What do we know?"

He looked back at me, the question clear in his eyes.

"I came here to find you, and I did," I said. "I'm not going to leave you here alone with Containment roaming around."

I didn't mean that as an insult, as a snipe because he'd done exactly that to me after the battle—he'd left me in New Orleans, with Containment roaming around. But it sounded that way, and silence fell again, thick and uncomfortable.

Big-girl panties, I told myself, and walked closer to the wall. "Is it blood?"

I could feel his gaze on mine for a minute, evaluating. And then he shifted his attention back to the wall. "Yes. Don't know if it's Broussard's, but you can smell that it's blood."

I could, now that I'd gotten closer. I looked over at him. "The name and the knife are the only facts that tie the murder to you. You ready to talk about the knife?"

"No."

I sighed. "Then let's bypass the evidence against you for the moment. Let's see if there's something here that tells us about the actual killer. Maybe we'll find something out of place, something that suggests why Broussard was targeted."

His expression didn't change much, but he nodded.

"All right, then. The writing." The letters were written in big, wide streaks, not unlike the way business names and slogans might have been painted onto store windows once upon a time.

"The letters weren't written with just a fingertip."

Liam looked at me. "What?"

I held a finger in front of the wall. "The line's too wide." I fisted my hand, held it against the wall. "And that movement's just awkward."

"Maybe they used something they found here."

We looked around. There was nothing on the landing, no pots of faux flowers or knickknacks that could have been adapted to the task.

"Maybe they came prepared," I said. "To kill Broussard, and to blame someone else for his murder. To blame you for it. So they brought a paintbrush or something. And maybe they were sloppy about it. See any fingerprints?"

Liam stepped closer, peered at the wall. I did the same thing. But if there were fingerprints, I couldn't tell from a look at a dark second-floor landing.

"Can't tell," he said.

"Me, either."

I stepped back, looked at the stain on the floor.

"His throat was slit. Effective, and I guess kind of intimate, because you have to be up close. But it's also not very heat of the moment. You don't accidentally slit someone's throat. That's not something you build up to in a fight. That's something you come here to do."

"And why?" Liam asked. "Money? Love? Punishment?"

"Not money," I said. "There are plenty of nice antiques down there, and none of them were taken."

"You do know antiques."

"I do. Granted, it's hard to get rid of antiques in New Orleans right now. But if the perp's willing to kill for money, why not grab a couple of things on the way out?"

"You're right. I don't see anything obviously missing."

"As for love, you know anything about him being in a relationship?"

Liam shook his head. "No, but I don't think I would have."

"And we don't know anything about punishment. Maybe Icarus matters, maybe it doesn't. We don't know yet."

"That's pretty much it." His gaze locked onto his sister's name again, and I decided it was time to get him away from this spot.

"Let's look around," I said.

The hallway split left and right. "I'll go right."

"Then I'll go left."

We parted in the middle of the landing. The hallway on the left had several open doors. Bathroom, which looked pretty standard. What I supposed was a guest room, since it held a perfectly made bed, a nightstand, and a bureau. I checked a couple of drawers, found nothing. And nothing in the closet, either.

A long linen closet filled the other side of the hallway. I pushed open one sliding door. Most of the cubbies and hanging bars were empty, except for one tower of shelves that held folded sheets and pillowcases. I gave them a quick pat-down, but didn't find anything interesting.

The hallway ended in a doorway, the door half-closed. I listened, ensured that nothing was moving on the other side, then pushed it open.

And found Broussard's office.

"Here we go," I murmured, stepping inside.

The room was big, an enormous curving desk nestled in an octagonal bay window. Hardwood floors, a heavy credenza with bookshelves on the other side of the room. A couple of potted plants, a nice rug in the middle of the room.

The books were old, with leather spines, and they weren't about any particular subject. Probably ordered them by the yard to fill up the space.

I moved around the desk. Old-fashioned leather blotter. Pen cup. Memo pad. All of it monogrammed with an equally old-fashioned "B." But there was no pad of paper, and there was no computer. I pulled out my penlight, shone it on the desktop, and found a perfectly clean square where a computer had once been.

"Crafty," I murmured, then sat down in the desk chair—also large and leather. Being careful not to leave fingerprints, I used the hem of my shirt to pull open the left and right drawers, found the usual desk-drawer stuff. Paper clips. Scissors. Stapler. The middle drawer was a keyboard tray. The keyboard was still there, the cord dangling loose at the back.

I looked through the rest of the room, didn't find anything interesting. If Broussard kept secret or controversial information here, it wasn't in his office. Or at least not anymore.

"His computer's gone," I told Liam when we met on the landing again. "You can actually see the edges where the dust had gathered."

"So they took his comp and didn't bother to clean up after themselves."

"That would be my guess. You notice anything else missing?"

"No—although I've never been in here before, so it's hard to say. But there's nothing obvious. No blank space on the wall where a picture was removed, no wall safe with the door hanging open."

"Would have been super handy to find one of those, maybe with a little scrap of paper with the bad guy's name on it."

Liam grinned. "Handy, but unlikely." His expression darkened when his gaze fell on the wall again. "Nothing of value taken, and nothing obvious missing but his computer. He was killed expediently and the perp seemed to be prepared. That confirms our theory—that Broussard found something he wasn't supposed to, and someone didn't want him looking at it."

"Icarus, maybe."

"Maybe. The computer would be a help. Maybe we'll get lucky and find that they've hooked it up to Containment-Net and Moses can somehow backtrack into it."

That would be lucky, and stupid of the perp. But if this was a Containment matter, it was certainly possible.

"You clean up after yourself?" Liam asked. "No fingerprints?"

I shook my head. "I'm good."

"Then we should get out of here," he said. "Containment could come back anytime."

Unfortunately, we'd already overstayed our welcome.

They roared through the front door. Three of them—two men and a woman, all three dressed in black fatigues and combat boots, hair clipped short in military fashion, Containment patches on their arms.

All three pointed guns at us.

"Hands in the air," said the man in front.

"No problem," Liam said, lifting his hands as we walked down the final flight of stairs into the wide hallway. "I'm glad you're here. We've got some information for you."

I managed not to blink, figured he had a plan, and tried to look relieved.

The agents looked momentarily confused, but they were well enough trained that they stayed in position, weapons still pointed. "What information?"

"We saw someone running out of here with a box. Not sure what was in it." Hands still in the air, he pointed at me with a finger. "We saw the tape around the house, figured we better see what was happening. They ran out past us, knocked her down." He bobbed his head toward the open window. "Headed downriver, I think."

The Quinn boys were definitely crafty. And disturbingly good liars.

"You're Liam Quinn," said the female agent. She glanced at me, my hair. "And you're Claire Connolly. We've seen your pictures."

Liam frowned. "I'm not sure what you—did you see the man running? With the box? He looked like a looter, honestly. Ran back down St. Charles?"

The agents had their doubts, but the earnestness in his voice was convincing, even to me. Like synchronized birds in flight, they simultaneously looked out the window.

Liam took the opportunity. He ran forward, taking down the agent in front, then sending the other two off balance. They hit the floor like bowling pins.

"Go!" Liam shouted to me, and began to grapple with the man on the ground.

I didn't have a weapon, not that getting into a gunfight with Containment was a good idea. But I also wasn't about to run and leave him alone with three agents and the same number of weapons. I wasn't that much of a hypocrite.

The two of us would still be outnumbered. But at least the odds would be better.

The female agent was closest, so I went to her first, used the same trick Liam had, and tried to haul her to the floor.

Already off balance, we landed in the dining room doorway together. I smashed my elbow, felt the vibration in the nerve in my teeth. The fingers on my right hand went numb, so I grabbed at the gun with my left, tried to wrangle it out of her grasp.

"Stop!" she yelled, and tried to kick me, but I kept my grip, and my focus, on her hand. I slammed it against the floor, once, twice, a third time.

The gun bounced loose.

I was up in a moment, grabbed it, was about to aim it in Liam's general direction, when a bus hit me from behind.

I'd forgotten about the third agent. And that wasn't smart.

He was at least two hundred pounds of bulk and muscle. I hit the floor on my stomach, his weight added to that, with enough force to push the air out of my lungs and send the gun skittering across the room. He moved to his knees and pulled my wrists behind me.

"I told you to put your goddamn hands in the goddamn air!" he said, nearly yanking my shoulder out of joint.

I didn't want to use magic. Not like this, not in front of Containment agents who already believed we were monsters.

But the woman was on her feet, going for her gun. Liam was still tangled up with the second agent, fists and sweat flying as they grappled. If they took us in after this, we'd be in trouble. Not only a Sensitive and a murder suspect, but fugitives who'd resisted arrest and injured officers in the process.

I didn't have a choice, and that just made me angrier.

I tried to gauge my best options, then gathered up filaments of magic that waited at the ready to be twined and used. To be manipulated against humans.

Alone in the air, the evanescent strands weren't powerful enough to trigger a magic monitor. But gathered together, as I was doing now, they were. An alarm began to wail outside, and the monitor issued an audio warning. *"Containment has been alerted. Containment has been alerted. Containment has been alerted."*

No shit, I thought, and reached out mentally toward the room across the hall, threw the magic at the ornate poker beside the brick-and-tile fireplace in the living room, and zipped it toward me so fast the air sang from the movement.

"Watch out!" The agent scrambled off me. "She's using magic!"

I reached out with the poker and knocked the gun from his hand. It skittered across the hardwood and beneath a sofa. Out of easy reach.

"Good enough," I murmured, and gripped the poker like a baseball bat. "Who's next?"

The air exploded, pain searing across my biceps like God's own fire. I looked back and saw the female agent literally holding the smoking gun.

"You *shot* me."

She'd calmed down, concentration and heat back in her eyes. "You're Claire Connolly, a Sensitive. You're outside Devil's Isle in direct violation of the Magic Act. You will put the weapon down and surrender yourself into the custody of Containment."

"Containment has been alerted. Containment has been alerted."

I ignored the irritating drone of the alarm, the violent throb of pain in my arm, and stared back at her. The flame of my anger was hot enough to scorch anything in its path.

"I'm Claire Connolly, a Sensitive. I helped warn you about Reveillon, and I fought in the Battle of Devil's Isle." I pointed a finger at my chest. "*I* took him down. And you want to arrest me."

She wet her lips nervously. "I'm ordered to take you in. You have magic."

"Not by choice."

"I'm ordered—"

"I don't give a crap about your orders. One of us is going back to the Cabildo today, but it won't be me."

When I felt the other agent moving behind me, I decided we'd had enough talk.

There was more magic in the air, and it waited to be used. Yearned to be used. I knitted it together, wrapped the tendrils around her gun, and yanked it out of her hand. Whatever I felt about Containment, given how much trouble we were already in, I wasn't going to pull a gun on her, so I stuffed it into my jeans.

I saw the shifting of her eyes, but didn't realize until it was too late that she was passing a message to her partner.

He hit me first, grabbing my legs and sending me to the floor. She piled on top, ripping her gun out of my jeans with a scrape against my skin. And then her weight was gone, and he grabbed my arms again and put a knee in my back, mashing my face and chest into the hard floor. I couldn't see, could hardly breathe, couldn't even think about magic.

That's when the world went hot.

It was a kiss by lightning, an embrace by pure electricity. Power subsumed me, coated me, and very nearly drowned me. Had I been stunned? Shot not by a gun but by one of the electric stunners some Containment agents carried?

It took a moment to realize this wasn't human power.

It was magic. Pure and barely controlled.

It was Liam.

I shifted my gaze to look, could just barely see him across the room, standing over the unconscious body of the other agent. The agent on my back couldn't see him; he was too focused on wrangling the handcuffs I could hear jangling behind me. It was better that he hadn't looked, that he was completely oblivious to the golden gleam in Liam's eyes, the fury on his face.

His magic burned like fire, with a rawness that I hadn't felt from Malachi's magic. But I still wasn't sure what it could do. What he could do with it.

He taught me quickly enough.

He condensed his power, his magic, and wrapped it around mine. The same way I braided filaments of magic to manipulate them, he braided the forks of our magic together, and then he used it. He lassoed the agent on my back with the magic and lifted him into the air.

Gasping, I turned over and watched the agent floating upward, his eyes wide with shock.

Liam was controlling my magic. Directing it and making it stronger by adding his own to the mix, like he'd turned up the volume on my own telekinesis.

And then Liam, or I, or the two of us together, tossed the agent across the room like a discarded toy. He flew into the opposite wall, knocking down a gilt-framed portrait on the way, then hitting the floor, eyes closed.

But the envelope taped to the wall—an envelope that had been hidden behind the painting—remained.

It would have to wait.

The female agent aimed the gun again, fired twice in quick succession.

My arm was up and moving before I could register the sound, and certainly before I could grab magic out of the air. I held out a hand, slowed the bullets to a crawl, and then a stop. And then I brushed them away. They clinked to the ground.

"I didn't ask for this," I told her. "Go back to the Cabildo and tell them that."

Tears wobbling in her eyes, she climbed to her feet and ran for the door.

Liam released his magic.

As if that had been holding me aloft, too, I fell to my knees, breathed heavily as silence fell over the room, sunlight glittering through the dust we'd raised during the fight.

I looked down at my fingers, half expecting to see power pouring out like white-blue plasma and my skin charred from the heat. But they were fine. I'd been filled with magic, but my body seemed to be holding. At least for now.

"You're all right?"

I nodded, didn't look at him. "I'm fine."

"Your arm?"

Right. Adrenaline had muted the pain, but it came back now with a vengeance. I winced, rotated my arm and took a look. There was blood, but not a lot.

"Just skimmed me." I looked up. He was sweating from the effort, his knuckles bruised, the hem on his T-shirt nearly ripped off, and there was a cut across his cheekbone. "Are you okay?"

He nodded. He still hadn't come closer, so I figured I needed to be the one who said it.

"You can manipulate the magic of others."

He winced at "manipulate," but there was no helping it, since that was exactly what he'd done. "Yeah."

"Handy." And potentially dangerous, especially in the wrong hands. I didn't think his were the wrong hands, though.

"I didn't hurt you?"

I shook my head, which made it throb with pain. "Just a little worn-out. I'll be fine. Packs a powerful punch."

"Yeah." He ran a hand through his hair. "I've been working on that. Not perfected yet."

He looked at the empty bit of wall space—and the manila envelope taped there.

Then he walked to me, offered a hand. He seemed surprised when I didn't hesitate, when I put my hand in his, let him pull me to my feet.

We approached the wall and Liam pulled the envelope away, was about to run a finger under the sealed tab when a new siren cut through the quiet. Containment had arrived. Again.

"That's our cue to exit," Liam said. He slid the envelope into his shirt, then tucked in the hem to keep it safe. He quickly rehung the painting, then looked at me. "You ready?"

I nodded.

This time, we ran together.

CHAPTER THIRTEEN

We aimed for Moses's house, but stopped about halfway there, just in case we'd been followed or Containment was watching. We didn't want to lead them right to him.

We found a courtyard garden nearly overgrown by mandevilla and jasmine, and all the more hidden because of it. It was cool here, the air perfumed with flowers and brick laid in intricate patterns underfoot. I sat on the ground, my back against the only wall not yet covered with a tangle of green.

He stood near the far wall, looking out at the street through a window made of carefully arranged bricks. He was smart enough to give me room, to give me space. Just like I'd given him once upon a time.

"Welcome to the outcast club," I quietly said, breaking the ice that had gathered between us despite the heat.

"So far, it's a shitty club."

"It doesn't get better." I thought of the Paranormals at Vacherie, the suspicion in their eyes. "Humans are suspicious of you; Paras are suspicious of you. But you do have that cool eye thing going."

He glanced at me, gold still shining in his eyes.

"But harder to hide your magic," I said.

He looked back at me. "Do you see now?"

There was something grave in his voice. Something sad, and something angry.

"Do I see what?"

"Your magic is neutral. Mine is furious."

His hands were fisted on his hips, his lean body still stiff.

"During the battle, he hit me with a blast of magic." He turned back, fingers against his chest like a cage. "I could feel it, sinking in. Affecting me. Changing me. It wasn't just magic, Claire. It was Ezekiel's magic."

Ezekiel had been the leader of Reveillon, a Sensitive who'd suppressed his own magic and been destroyed by it.

I just looked at him, confused. "I don't know what you mean."

"When she was hit, Eleanor lost her vision, but gained her sight. The Para that hit her was a seer, and the weapon carried residual power."

I hadn't known that—hadn't even known it was possible that humans who gained power directly from Paras were affected by it that way.

Did the magic make the Paranormal, or did the Paranormal color the magic?

"And you think Ezekiel's magic had some of him in it?"

He turned back to me, gold churning in his eyes like a tempest. "I know that it did. It took a few seconds before I could move again, before I could do anything other than lie there, the magic like needles in my skin."

"I remember. I went to get Lizzie. You were gone when I got back."

He nodded. "I got to my feet, and it ravaged me, Claire. I had no power over it." His gaze softened, like he was staring at a memory. "A Reveillon member was beside me, on his knees. He'd been hit by something—there was a knot on his head, and he was staring at the ground, totally dazed. And none of that mattered. Because I wanted to kill him. Before I knew it, my hands were wrapped around his neck, and I could feel Ezekiel's fire in my skin, beneath my hands."

Liam stared down at his hands. He extended his fingers, then clenched them into fists, as if he could feel those flames and that power again.

"It was a battle," I said. My voice sounded quiet, far away. "He was trying to kill you. All of us. There's no shame in wanting him dead, or in killing him. That's just war."

"Not sitting there on the ground, only half aware of what was happening. But to the magic that didn't matter." He looked back at me.

Something clenched in my stomach at the look in his eyes. It was feral.

No, I realized. It was *Paranormal*. I knew only some of the basics of Paranormal biology, but I'd seen that primal hunger before—in the eyes of Paras who'd wanted to kill me and everyone else during the war.

"I was so angry. So full of hate I could hardly see through it. It was a haze across my vision." His eyes focused again, and he looked at me. "I held his life, quite literally, in my hands."

"You could use Ezekiel's magic." And it had been a sight—the hot fire that had burst from Ezekiel's mouth. He could literally scream fire.

Liam nodded.

"And still, even though the Reveillon member tried to kill you, you didn't kill him."

"I could have. I could have so easily done it. I could feel his pulse beneath my hands, and see that look of disgust in his eyes. Even dazed, he could see what I was. What I'd become. And when he realized what I could do, that disgust turned to fear. He pissed himself, sitting there, waiting to die."

He went quiet, the memory all but poisoning the air around us.

"You *chose* not to kill him," I insisted.

"No, I *managed* not to kill him." Liam walked toward me, held his thumb and forefinger a millimeter apart. "That's the difference between life and death, Claire."

He paused, seemed to collect himself. "You're worth too much to risk. So I removed myself from the situation. And I removed myself from New Orleans."

I stared at him. "You could have told me."

"How could I tell you that? That I could have taken that man's life as easily as snapping my fingers? That I could have that kind of anger—and that kind of power—inside me? When I'm channeling Ezekiel?"

"Ezekiel was a sociopath."

"And I'm not?"

"No. He'd have done what he wanted and damn the consequences. You just tried to save my life, and yours. You could have killed those agents, but you didn't."

"You could feel the anger?"

I paused, decided there was no point in lying to him, and nodded.

We didn't know if someone had created the Veil or if it had grown organically between our world and the Beyond. If someone created it, maybe this was why. Maybe magic was too much for us—too much temptation, too much power, too much risk. Maybe we couldn't be trusted with it any more than Paranormals could. If magic wasn't the problem, who was good enough, strong enough, to wield it?

Liam looked away, his features fierce, waging his own battle. "I couldn't bring that to your door."

"You think I wouldn't understand?" I stood up, faced him. "That magic is wonderful and terrible? That it makes you feel invincible—and totally vulnerable? Because I do." I put a hand on my chest. "I do,

Liam. I know it better than anyone else. Because, like you, I wasn't born with it. I wasn't used to it. It just *was* one day. And everything changed.

"But even if you had to leave to deal with it to ensure you had control, that was weeks ago, Liam. You couldn't send a message? You couldn't take five minutes to let us know where you were, how you were?"

He turned away, walked back to the gap in the bricks. "It took a long time to get myself ready," he said. "To understand who I was. I had to know who I was before I put you at risk again. Erida helped me—helped me figure out what I could and couldn't do. Helped me try to become myself again." He took a step closer, and I didn't move back. "You think I walked away from you, but I didn't. I took myself away so I could keep you safe, so I could learn control."

I looked up into his eyes, saw the doubts that still flickered there. "And can you learn to live with what you are?"

His jaw worked, chewing over words he couldn't bring himself to say. "I don't know. I care more about whether you can."

"I have magic. I'm an enemy of the state. I've killed. And a bounty hunter once dragged me into Devil's Isle because he figured there was more to life than my becoming a prisoner to my magic."

Liam considered that for a moment. "I don't recall dragging you."

He said it lightly, almost sarcastically. And it loosened some tight knot of tension between us.

"It was mostly emotional," I said, and watched him for a moment. Watched the battle rage in his eyes. And figured that taking this danger away from me was exactly the kind of thing Liam Quinn would do.

"All right," I said.

His brows lifted. "All right what?"

"All right, I accept your story."

"That's good, because it's true." He swallowed, looked to be gathering up his own courage. "And the rest of it?"

Us, he meant.

"I guess I want you to tell me when you're ready."

I walked toward him. Saw the heat flare in his eyes, hotter with each step I took. Then I held out a hand. "Envelope."

His eyes narrowed. "You're cruel, Connolly."

I arched an eyebrow.

"Fine." He took the envelope from his shirt, offered it.

"Thank you."

I removed the sheet of paper, found an invoice addressed to Javier Caval from a place called Henderson Scientific, which was based in Seattle.

"An order for pipettes, a refractometer, polymerase, and other things I don't understand." I passed it to Liam. "This make any sense to you?"

"It doesn't," he said, looking it over. "I mean, not beyond the fact that it's scientific equipment. Lab stuff."

The invoice's memo line said the goods should be routed to Laura Blackwell, president of ADZ Logistics, and listed another address.

"Javier Caval," Liam said. "That name sounds familiar."

"From New Orleans? Containment?"

"I'm not sure. But add him to the list of people we know are involved."

"What about Laura Blackwell?" I asked, and Liam shook his head.

"Don't know her," Liam said.

"So we think Broussard found this invoice. Saved it and hid it, because he thought it was a link in whatever chain he was trying to build. The person who killed him didn't find it."

"They didn't find the paper," Liam agreed. "But that doesn't mean

Broussard didn't go off half-cocked about whatever he'd found. That was his style."

"So what do we do?"

He pointed to Caval's address. "This place is closer. So we check it out."

I stared at him. "We just left two Containment agents unconscious. We need to get out of here."

"One person is already dead in my name," he said quietly. "Did you want to stop looking when you found the gas station?"

I'd been ready to aim a snarky retort in his direction. But I couldn't argue with that. He was right. I'd pushed ahead, and he'd been there with me.

"If they catch you, they won't bother asking questions. Someone wants you to be the fall guy. I know you want to stop this. To fix it. But you can't take chances like that."

"Everyone with magic takes chances. Just by existing here."

I looked at him for a long moment. "All right," I said, rising. "We follow this through. But maybe work on controlling your magic."

A corner of his mouth lifted. "I'll do my best."

All a girl could ask for.

We stood on the neutral ground across the street, looking at the house. It was a newer house by New Orleans standards, probably built after World War II, with white clapboard, a single dormer window beneath a high pitched roof. The deep porch was held up by square columns that narrowed as they rose to the roof. The steps in front were concrete, and no wood or paint had been wasted on decoration—or cleaning up the char marks that still stained the front and sides of the house. The front yard was dirt except for a few scraggly patches of grass.

"I've been here before," Liam said. "This is a Containment safe house."

"A safe house? For who?"

"Humans who talk when they shouldn't, Paras who help when they shouldn't, the occasional controversial visitor. Because despite all the talk, Containment is politically pragmatic."

"But they'll still bitch about Paranormals, paint them with the same brush?"

"That just makes them human," Liam said, the grimness in his voice matching the anger in mine.

"This is another connection to Containment. To whatever's happening here."

"Yeah," Liam said, "I noticed that, too."

"How did you know it was a safe house?"

"Had to park a bounty here three or four years ago. Yale graduate who decided he was going to tell the truth about Devil's Isle conditions."

"You picked him up."

"And parked him here until the PCC could get him out of the Zone again. I think he was a well-meaning kid, but he figured throwing some money around New Orleans would get him special access, special treatment." Liam smiled, crossed his arms. "He was incorrect."

That stirred a memory. "Was this in the summer? And the guy wore this dark Capitol Hill Windbreaker every day?"

Liam looked surprised. "That was him. He come into the store?"

"He did, actually. Came in to get MREs, tried to talk up some of the customers and agents about the prison." I frowned, remembering. "How'd you know what he meant to do?"

Liam's smile went sly. "Because I'm good at my job."

"And as humble as your brother."

We were getting into a rhythm, having the kind of conversation we'd have had before he left. I'd missed that in the same way I'd missed talking with Gunnar and Tadji—I could be myself around all three of them, with no pretensions. Just comfortable in my own skin.

Before we got too far afield, I looked back at the house. "Not much to look at."

"That's the point of a safe house," Liam said with a smile. "Nothing to look at means the house doesn't raise anyone's suspicions. If you were driving past, you wouldn't bother to look twice at this place. That's good op sec."

"Op sec?"

"Operational security," he said.

"What are we likely to find in there?"

"I'm not sure." He cast a gimlet eye on the porch. "But the front door's ajar. That doesn't bode well for anyone using this place as a refuge."

He looked around and, gauging that the coast was clear, climbed the concrete steps.

We stood quietly for a moment, waiting for movement or sound. And then Liam pushed the door open.

The odor that emerged didn't leave many questions about the fate of whoever was inside.

I put my arm over my face, but there was no masking the scent—sweet and rotten and so horrifically strong. And I was suddenly seventeen again, standing in the house across the street from ours. There'd been a barrage of fighting the night before, and I'd wanted to check on the woman who lived there.

Mrs. McClarty was a widow. Her husband died in the first attack on the city; her son had enlisted and had been killed in the Battle of Baton Rouge. She had two daughters, who she'd sent from the Zone to live with relatives before the border had been closed. Because she was alone, we kept an eye on her.

"Mrs. McClarty?" I'd called, and when she didn't answer after a couple of knocks—and when I couldn't see anything through the lace curtain on the front window—I turned the knob and pushed open the door.

It moved with a squeak and let out the thick scent of death. I should have walked away, but I couldn't. I was too young, too curious.

She sat at the kitchen table, her head on the linen tablecloth, arms at her sides. Her eyes were open and blankly staring. A half-drunk mug of coffee, coral lipstick staining the rim, sat in front of her.

She hadn't been killed in the battle the night before; her house hadn't been shelled. She'd been killed by life even while war raged around her.

To my mind back then, that was inspiring and sad. She'd survived the worst of the war, which was a kind of miracle. But she wouldn't have known at that time, and her survival hadn't been worth much in the end, because she still wound up like the rest of us would.

When I'd walked back into our house, my father had stood in the living room with a peanut butter sandwich and an apple on a plate. "Lunch?" he'd asked.

He must have seen the look on my face, because he'd dropped them both and run toward me. When I told him what I'd seen, he wrapped his arms around me.

They'd carried her out a few hours later. Her daughters didn't come back, and no one else took care of the house, so it began to die just like she had. The roof caved in, and the house fell in on itself. And as far as I was aware, that was the end of the McClartys' presence in New Orleans.

I couldn't look at the house then, or think of it now, without experiencing that horribly ripe smell all over again.

"Claire."

I blinked. Liam's hand was on my arm, steadying me. "I'm all right. I'm okay."

"Flashback?"

I nodded. "The smell."

He nodded. "Yeah. I think we're probably too late to question anyone, but I want to take a look. You can stay here if you need to."

I shook my head. "I'll go."

I just wouldn't breathe in while I did.

It was a simple house with slightly shabby furnishings. A worn couch, comfy recliner, scratched dining room table. It was comfortable, and looked lived in and loved. Very different from the showiness of Broussard's house.

A man lay on his back on the floor of the rear bedroom. His body was swollen with death and heat, and the fluids he'd lost in death stained the floor beneath him. Blood and worse, from the gunshot wound in the middle of his forehead. And he wore Containment fatigues.

"Murdered," Liam said.

He moved closer, crouched nearby.

"His hands," he said, and I glanced down. His palms, fingers bore streaky remnants of what I guessed was blood, but it hadn't come from his body. There was no blood anywhere else on him, and the blood on the floor hadn't been disturbed.

Where else might a man have gotten blood under his fingernails?

"He killed Broussard," I said quietly. "Or put Gracie's name on the wall."

"Seems to be a distinct possibility," Liam said.

I held my breath as I walked closer, careful not to step in anything and disturb evidence, or leave a mark that anyone could trace back to me. J. CAVAL was embroidered in gold thread on his pocket flap.

"We found Caval," I said, through the sleeve I was holding over my mouth.

Another wave of odor hit me, and I could feel my gorge rising. "Outside," I said, and didn't wait for him to follow. I dashed to the door, made it to the front porch, and lost what little I'd eaten that morning.

He gave me a moment, then came out, offered his handkerchief in silence.

"Sorry," I said, wiping my mouth and wishing for a tankard of ice water. "Got to me."

"Take your time." He put a hand at my back. We stood there for a few minutes, and I rested my forehead on the porch banister while he rubbed my back in slow, soothing circles.

"It's not the smell per se. Not exactly. It just . . . reminds me."

Liam nodded. "The war?"

I nodded. "Neighbor. I found her."

He gave me another moment to settle.

"Broussard found the invoice," I theorized when I was in control again. "He approached Caval about it. Caval killed Broussard. And someone killed Caval."

"That's what it looks like to me."

"Someone is keeping this from Gunnar, maybe from the Commandant." I wanted to talk to him again. To tell him what we'd seen. But we'd taken a big enough risk going to his house last night. We couldn't go back today.

"Let's get back to Moses's," Liam said. "We'll think it through, regroup, and come up with a plan."

We needed one.

Given the battle we'd already fought, we were extra cautious on the way to Moses's house. We backtracked twice, stopped two additional times to make sure we weren't leading anyone to him. When the coast seemed clear enough, we walked inside.

We walked in together, and we weren't sniping at each other. But there was probably no mistaking the grim expressions on our faces.

"What now?" Moses asked. He was across the room, standing on a chair stacked on a table and picking through a box of parts I was pretty sure hadn't been there this morning.

"Did you bring more stuff in here?"

His gaze narrowed. "My damn house, my damn rules." He pulled out a half-naked Barbie doll. "Could be something for you in here?"

The question was asked with such naked affection I couldn't help but smile. "I am full up on half-naked dolls, but thank you for the very kind offer."

There was a flush across his cheeks when he threw her back in the box. "Suit yourself."

"I don't know what I'd do without you, Mos."

"You'd hear a lot less swearing," Liam said.

"There is that."

"There is what?" Gavin asked, walking into the room with a glass of iced tea in one hand and what I thought was a fried chicken leg in the other.

"Where you'd get that?" Liam asked with narrowed eyes.

"Your scientist lady brought it."

"Darby," she corrected, following Gavin into the room, with her own drumstick and what looked like disappearing patience. "Friend at the lab made it, and we had extra. I wasn't sure if Moses was eating." Hand on her hip, she glared at him.

She was curvy, with pale skin and dark hair in a sleek bob around her face. She favored retro clothes that my dad would have loved, and that made her curves look that much more lush. Today, she'd paired pink ankle-length pants with a pale green short-sleeved shirt that had a Peter Pan collar and tiny pearl buttons on the placket. She wore dark glasses with cat-eye frames and a rolled red bandanna held her hair back.

"I eat!" Moses protested. "Had two cans of potted meat today!"

"More like *rotted* meat," Gavin muttered. "Am I right?"

Moses pointed at him. "That's your word. Your *human* word. It was fine." He sniffed the air. "That stuff, that chicken, smells too fresh."

Darby rolled her eyes, smiled at me. "Hey, Claire. How was the bayou?"

"Wet."

She grinned, looked at Liam. "And welcome back to you. How's Eleanor?"

"Good, thanks. Erida's with her."

"She's still fierce, I assume."

"You asking about Erida or Eleanor?"

Darby smiled. "Either or both."

"Malachi not here?" I asked, glancing around. "We have information."

"Not back yet," Gavin said, pulling off breading and meat with his teeth.

My stomach grumbled, and I obeyed the demand. "Hold that

thought," I said, and headed toward the food. The morning hadn't been appetizing, but the hunger and travel had left me ravenous.

Moses's little kitchen was surprisingly tidy for a man who liked spoiled food. True to Darby's retro style, the chicken was tucked into a red-and-white-checked towel inside a small basket, and the tea was in a Tupperware pitcher the color of avocados.

I poured myself a glass and went back into the living room the same way Gavin and Darby had, with chicken and sweet tea.

Moses had found what he was looking for—a black box with wires that dangled like tentacles—and made his way toward his stool.

"So what's the story?" he asked, short fingers linked together like creatively arranged sausages.

"Well," I said, jumping in before Liam could talk, "I find this one at Broussard's house, standing in front of the murder scene. Long story short, he didn't do it."

"Well, no shit on that one," Moses said.

"No shit on that one," I agreed. "Among other reasons, we may have found the guy who did do it, after we fought with some Containment agents. He's dead."

"The agents?" Darby asked, eyes wide.

"The man we think was Broussard's killer," Liam said. "Small-caliber GSW to the head, and what we're guessing is Broussard's blood still on his hands."

"Busy morning," Gavin said, glancing between us, probably trying to guess if we were still fighting.

When I gave him a look, he just smiled sheepishly. He was a Quinn, just as nosy and stubborn as his brother, and he wasn't about to apologize for it.

"How does it go together?" Moses asked. "Lay out the story for me."

Liam walked to one of the tall windows, leaned against the wall so he could look outside and stay alert, and crossed his arms. "Broussard finds something he isn't supposed to. Something related to this Icarus project."

"The file," Darby said, and Liam nodded.

"He's killed in his home, and not much time elapses between his looking at the file and his TOD," he said. "His computer's missing, and we find an envelope taped behind a picture." Liam nodded at me, and I pulled out the invoice I'd folded and put in my pocket, offered it to Gavin.

Gavin put down his tea, looked over the document. "Invoice for scientific equipment." He passed it to Darby. "Thoughts?"

"Basic lab equipment," she said. "ADZ Logistics. I don't know that company, but I know that name. Laura Blackwell. I'm pretty sure she worked at PCC Research when I did."

"We haven't looked for ADZ yet," Liam said. "The name at the bottom, Caval, is the man we found dead. Broussard had hidden the envelope. Hard to say how long he'd known about Icarus, but he'd apparently managed to put some of its pieces together."

"He thought he'd found a smoking gun," Gavin said. "Something he wanted to keep safe."

"And nearby," I said. "But either word got out that he'd put two and two together, or he confronted the wrong people. Caval decides, or he's instructed, to take Broussard out. He does, leaves a note blaming Broussard's death on Liam. Caval goes to the safe house, is killed before he can even wash his hands."

"He was in a hurry," Gavin said.

Liam nodded. "And he was killed in a different style. Knife for Broussard, gunshot for Caval."

"It's cleaner," I said. "Faster, more expedient."

"Professional," Liam agreed with a nod.

"This is top-of-the-line stuff," Gavin said. "Big enough to merit a Containment safe house and two hits."

"More evidence this is connected to Containment," Liam said. "It's getting uglier."

"Oh, yeah," Darby said. "It is. But very interesting scientifically."

"Discuss," Liam said, when we all looked at her.

"You've got the floor," Gavin said.

"So I've been looking at your file. It's not a molecule. It's actually much more complicated than that." She paused for dramatic effect. "It's a complete biological synthesis."

We were apparently too ignorant to understand the import of that assessment, because you could have heard crickets in the following silence.

"Okay," Liam said. "I'll be the first one to admit I have no idea what she's talking about. What does that mean?"

"It means the file wasn't just illustrating the structure of a molecule," Darby said. "They were *building* something."

"Elaborate," Gavin said.

"Well, without getting into the hairy details, some labs focus on creating new structures—new proteins, new bacteria, new viruses. I can't give you much detail from the stub. There's just not much there, but it looks like a protocol for synthesizing something."

"You can't tell what?" Gavin asked.

She shook her head. "There's not enough left of the file, and what's there is pretty garbled."

"What would you use it for?" I asked with a frown. "The thing you've biologically synthesized."

"Anything. Replacement tissue, research, curiosity, to test drugs. Whatever."

"So the last thing Broussard looks at before he dies is some kind of biological research file."

"Does the invoice look like the kind of stuff they'd need for that?"

Darby nodded. "Creating new tissue is an incredibly complicated process. It needs lots of time, lots of money, lots of very smart people. And plenty of equipment."

"So . . . what?" Gavin asked, swallowing chicken. "Maybe they're trying to figure out how to give humans Paranormal skills? Grow wings or something?"

"Eh, we're several years past the war. I can't imagine they're like, 'Oh, let's suddenly start testing Paranormal tissue to see what makes it tick.' That's not a new research question."

"If someone didn't want Broussard knowing about this, maybe it's too expensive?" I suggested. "Or it's not going well?"

"Or it's generally top secret," Liam said. "But this is merely speculation until we get more information."

Information came in the form of an opening door. Malachi walked in, wearing jeans and a T-shirt that belied his true nature.

That something had happened was clear on his face. He looked absolutely grim, like a man worn thin by exhaustion and grief.

"What's wrong?" Darby asked, moving toward him.

He looked at me. "Cinda's dead."

CHAPTER FOURTEEN

"**C**inda's dead," Malachi said again. "Along with another. Two more are sick."

"'I'm sorry' seems like a totally insufficient thing to say," Darby said. "But that's all I've got."

"The words are insufficient," Malachi agreed. "I gave mine to Anh and the others, and they felt insufficient, too."

"The same illness?" I asked.

He nodded. "The illness seems the same—starts as fatigue. Then chills, fever. Rapid heartbeat, rapid breathing. Confusion. Red dots across the skin."

"Hmm," Darby said. "I'm not a diagnostician, but that doesn't sound like your run-of-the-mill infection."

Malachi nodded. "We presume it's contagious, since they live, work, and eat together. And we aren't aware of any other vector."

Darby frowned. "Strangers on the property? New food or water source? Environmental changes?"

"Other than leaving Devil's Isle, no. Anh has lived on the property for five years. She hasn't been ill with anything like this, and she wasn't aware of anything on the property that would cause an exposure problem."

"Did Gunnar get a Containment unit out there?"

Malachi nodded. "Volunteer. The Zone equivalent of Doctors Without Borders. But without hospitalization, there are limits to what they can do in the field." He pulled from his pocket two small vials of crimson liquid, offered them to Darby.

"Blood test?" she asked. She swirled one of the vials, held it up to the light.

"Please."

"Your wish is my command," she said, giving a jaunty head bob. At our blank stares, she asked, "*I Dream of Jeannie*?" Then she waved her hand. "Never mind."

It seemed science wasn't the only thing we didn't know much about.

"How else can I help you?" Darby asked, frowning as she looked up at Malachi. "I'm a lab person, not the doctor you need, but maybe I can find someone to help with diagnosis?"

Malachi shook his head. "I need to talk to Lizzie, but I can't get close to Devil's Isle." He looked at me.

"Yes," I said. "Of course. I'll go tonight, after dark."

"Today of all days," Liam said in a tight voice. "After what happened earlier today, you're going to try to sneak into Devil's Isle? You were in a shoot-out with Containment."

Put like that, it didn't sound very smart. But what choice did we have?

"Delta is as Delta does," I said. "And we've got our delivery procedure, remember? I can handle myself."

That was a lesson I'd been learning. That I could handle myself. I liked learning that.

"I'll go with you."

The concern that furrowed his brow was clear.

"No, you won't. I'll be quieter, faster, less noticeable on my own. This isn't my first rodeo."

"Liam," Gavin said quietly, "this is the package Gunnar talked about. She's been doing this for five weeks."

She's been doing this since you've been gone, he meant. Which was the absolute truth. But it wasn't a truth that Liam wanted to face, given the pained look on his face.

"I hate to bring this up during this non-tender moment," Gavin said, "but there's an illness spreading among Paranormals at the same time Containment's running some kind of secret project involving a biological thingamajig."

"Synthesis," Darby offered.

"That," Gavin said. "Coincidence?"

"There's a biological synthesis?" Malachi asked, and we gave him the brief rundown about our visit to Broussard and Caval, and Darby's preliminary findings.

"I don't think 'science' is a strong enough link between the illness and Icarus," Liam concluded. "There's no evidence the Paras are sick because of anything Containment's done, and we don't know Containment is working on anything that could make anyone ill. They could be trying to create a new product for skin grafts or something." He glanced at Darby. "Right?"

"You got it."

Liam looked at Moses. "You get anything from that file?"

"Oh, are we remembering I'm in the room now?" His voice was the perfect mix of egotistical and long-suffering. That was pretty much Moses to a T.

"Please proceed," Liam said.

He turned to his computer, began typing. "Did more digging on the Icarus file. As we know, Broussard accessed it not long before he died. But that wasn't the first time he'd looked at it. He'd opened it fourteen times over the last two weeks."

"Fourteen times for the same file?" Liam asked with a frown. "That's a lot of views for a file he didn't create."

"Obsessed," Gavin said. "Which squares with what we know about him. He was obsessed with Liam, too."

"He fixated," Liam agreed.

"And there's this." Moses punched a key, had paper spitting out from an old-fashioned dot matrix printer on a shelf beneath his keyboard. He reached down, ripped off the paper, handed it to Liam. "Once again, the idiots who tried to delete the file didn't think about the metadata. Can't get everything out of the file, but I can tell you the address where it was created."

"I want to tear off the perforations," Gavin said, but Liam swatted his hand away.

"Well, what do you know?" He passed the paper to Gavin, glanced at me. "Same address as ADZ Logistics on the Henderson invoice."

"And there's a link in the chain," Gavin said, ripping off the paper's edges with a satisfying *zip*. "Somewhere in Gentilly, looks like."

Gentilly was a neighborhood on the lake side of Devil's Isle.

"We need to surveil the building," Liam said.

Gavin nodded. "Tomorrow morning. It will be getting dark soon, and the building's going to empty out. They won't work at night; the power goes out too often."

"And after what happened today," I said, "if this building matters to Containment, they're going to put extra staff outside it."

Gavin nodded at me. "She's right. We can get out at dawn, get spots, and be in position when the doors open. We'll see who comes and goes, and that will tell us what's happening in there."

"All right," Liam said. "We'll meet in the morning, go take a look."

"Someone needs to get a message to Gunnar tonight," I said. "Tell him about Caval. Killer or not, he needs to be found. His body dealt with."

"And the DNA tested," Darby said. "If that's Broussard's blood on his hands, it will pretty much exonerate Liam from the murder. And then we can just deal with Icarus, and whatever Containment's trying to hide."

"I'll do that," Gavin said, and gave his brother a look. "If only we knew how the goddamn knife got there."

"I'm working on it," Liam said.

"Work harder, please, so we can exonerate your ass."

"You know what we need?" Darby asked. "We need a break." She walked to Moses, looked over the piles. "You got a DVD player in this mess? Or a VCR?"

"Yeah. Why? You gonna put one back together?"

"No, I want to watch it. I've got a stack of movies in the UV."

"You've got a utility vehicle?" Gavin hoofed it to the window, glanced outside. "Darby, that's a golf cart. With an old Coke cooler welded onto the back." He mostly sounded confused.

"Friend of mine at the lab did that," she said with a grin. "We're calling it Rogue Lab."

"Good name," Liam said with a smile. "And very creative welding job."

The cooler was red, probably from the fifties, and had rounded corners and pretty white script. It also had a lot of rust, which made me feel better about the fact that someone had bolted it to a golf cart.

"Keeps the rain off," she said. "And Containment doesn't even look twice. Chick in glasses on a golf cart apparently doesn't inspire a lot of concern. Anyway, there's movies in the box." She looked around at the group. "See if Moses can get a player up and running. It'll be getting dark soon, anyway."

The chatting and plotting began. What would they watch, what would they eat, who got the limited couch real estate in Moses's living room.

They were all eager for company, for normalcy. I understood the urge, and usually I would have been up for it. But not tonight. It was still early, but I was wiped out, emotionally and physically. Murders, battles, and confessions from Liam had left me completely drained— not to mention the hangover from Liam's unexpected magic. That was going to need some time of its own.

I had a lot to think about, and I needed time and space and quiet to do it.

I could feel his gaze on me, the hope in it. But he was going to have to let that simmer a bit. God knew he'd made me do some simmering.

"Rain check," I said. "I'm going to see Lizzie, remember?"

Moses looked back at me, his brow furrowed with disappointment. "Damn it. It's family movie night."

I smiled, but shook my head. "Things to do, people to see."

Moses wrinkled his nose, like I'd mentioned taking out the garbage. "Spoilsport."

"I am," I agreed. I looked at Gavin, Liam. "We surveil at dawn?"

"Fine by me," Gavin said.

"Same," Liam said.

"Why don't I drive you back?" Darby said to me, gesturing toward the window and the UV that sat at the curb. "I could zip you wherever you need to be."

"Actually," Liam said, glancing at me, "I've got some business to attend to, and I think you might be interested in it. You game?"

The spark in his eyes piqued my interest. "Depends. What's the business?"

"We need to see a girl about a knife."

We escaped from the house after Moses gave Liam his own portion of crap about skipping family movie night, then stood on the curb, looking at Darby's UV.

We'd carried the VCR tapes inside; in exchange she'd given us the key. But we hadn't yet climbed in.

"It would be a walk."

"How long?"

He considered. "About a mile."

I did the math, thinking about the three miles I'd need to walk round-trip tonight to get to Devil's Isle, the walking I'd already done today. "I can't ride in this thing. Let's walk."

"Agreed." Liam got the key back to Darby, and then we started walking.

"Where are we going, exactly?"

"To see Blythe."

Blythe was a bounty hunter, a striking woman with dark, choppy hair and sharp cheekbones, generous lips, and plenty of silver tattoos. Very gorgeous and, if I had to take a guess, very impulsive.

She was also Liam's ex-girlfriend.

"You gave her the knife."

"Yeah." Liam ran a hand through his hair, looked a little sheepish. I figured that was the correct response. "All due respect to my brother, I hated that knife. Handle was awkward, blade wasn't balanced, and you couldn't hide it worth a damn."

"So you gave it to your then-girlfriend?"

"Technically, I think she stole it."

"Of course she did." I didn't know much about Blythe, but that seemed to fit. "And why am I along for this particular ride?"

He kept his eyes on the road ahead of us. "You wanted me to trust you, to trust myself. This seems as good a first step as any."

In a city of gorgeous, empty houses, from the historic to the glamorous, Blythe lived in a third-floor apartment in the middle of an otherwise abandoned complex. There was no architecture to speak of, the swimming pool was empty but for a rusting Chevy Suburban, and the courtyard was overrun with weeds.

"Why here?" I asked.

"Anonymity," Liam said. "She's in the middle of the complex, on the top floor. Gives her visibility, but keeps her from standing out."

In any other place and time, I might have said she was paranoid. But not in the Zone. Not in New Orleans.

We took the stairs to the third floor and the outdoor hallway populated with front doors. Liam stopped in front of one—number 313—that didn't look any different from the others. Double anonymity.

He knocked on the door. There was a thump, then shuffling, the jangling of a lock.

The woman who opened the door had tousled hair and wore a tank top over a hot pink bra and mid-calf silver leggings. Her feet were bare, her eyes lined with kohl. A silver snake covered her right biceps, and a silver dragon wound around her left.

"Well, I declare," she said, in an exaggerated accent that was more 'Bama than bayou. "Look who's here. Liam Quinn, the prodigal son returned." She slid her gaze to me. "And little Saint Claire, who I understand isn't so saintly anymore."

I smiled. "Would you like to see an example of my work?"

She smiled back. "Not unless you want to see how my cuffs work. I'm still on the job."

Liam ignored the bait. "Can we come in, Blythe?"

"Why?"

"Broussard. We need information."

She looked at him for a moment. "Were you followed?"

"Are you under the impression I forgot how to do my job?"

"Just checking," she said. "A girl's gotta be careful these days." She waved us in and gave the hallway a second look before closing and relocking the door.

The entry opened into a narrow hallway that led to a small living room. There was a small kitchen on the other side of the entry, and a hallway that ran to the left, which I assumed led to a bed and bath.

The architecture was Generic Apartment. On the basis of what I knew about her so far, the décor seemed to be completely Blythe: Southern, rock 'n' roll, postwar, and a little bit trashy.

There was a motorcycle in the living room, squeezed in beside a worn love seat and a bergère chair covered in rose velvet. The walls bore enormous paintings of fancy men and women at a garden party, all completely naked from the waist down. Ironically, Blythe's clothes— shirts, undergarments, dresses, and pants—were scattered across everything in the room.

"Sorry about the mess," she said, and walked around the bike to perch on the love seat's rolled arm. "Until very recently, I was entertaining company." She winked bawdily, and I wasn't sure how much of the persona was an act and how much was just her vibrant personality. "You want a drink?"

"We're good," Liam said.

"You kill Broussard?"

"I did not."

"I didn't figure you for that. Wasn't really your style. What information you want?"

"I need to know what happened to my knife."

Her face went completely blank. "What knife?"

"Antler handle. The one my brother gave me. Curiously, it was missing one morning after you visited."

"That must mean it was a good visit." She pushed off the love seat, walked into the kitchen. She emptied out a glass, poured a finger of rye whiskey into it, and gulped it.

"Damn," she said with a wince. "Not nearly late enough for rye."

"The knife," Liam prompted.

She held up her hands. "I'm not saying I took it. But if I did, I don't have it anymore. Had a sweetheart, gave it away." She put the glass down, looked at Liam. "It wasn't a very good blade."

"I'm aware."

"Who were you dating?" I asked.

"A very delicious agent named Lorenzo." She patted the kitchen countertop. "We had some very good times."

"Don't need the play-by-play," Liam said. "Last name?"

"Caval. Lorenzo Caval."

Bingo.

"I don't suppose he has a brother named Javier?" I asked.

"Matter of fact, that's Lorenzo's younger brother." She frowned. "Why do you ask?"

"Javier's dead."

Liam's voice was plenty serious, but Blythe didn't get it. "Quit fucking around."

When Liam stayed quiet, her smile fell away, and so did some of the cockiness, the faux accent. "You're serious."

"We are," Liam said. "Found him dead in a Containment safe house. By the look of things, he took out Broussard, and someone took him out."

"Jesus," Blythe said, and turned around, leaned back against the cabinet, crossed her arms. "I knew they were involved in something, but not something that would get them killed."

"What kind of something?" Liam asked.

"No idea," she said, and shook her head when Liam gave her a dangerous stare.

Blythe groaned, turned back to the counter, and poured another finger of whiskey into the glass. "I don't know. My job is to stay on Containment's good side. Not the other way around. I take legit bounties, and I don't get in anyone's way."

"They had something going with Containment," I said.

"They're agents. Of course they had something going with Containment." Blythe knocked back the whiskey like it was bad medicine, slammed the glass down hard enough to make it ring. Then she sighed. "Like I said, I don't have details. They were both impulsive. Lorenzo more so than Javier. Lorenzo figured he was some kind of Special Ops badass." She looked back at us, eyes narrowed. "Was he?"

"It's possible they were involved in a Containment research project. We don't have all the details, either."

"I know Lorenzo doesn't like Paras," she said. "Their mom was a single parent, and she was killed in the war. Lorenzo idolized her, from what I could tell. Took her death hard."

"You know how or when he got involved with the project?"

Blythe shook her head. "That was before my time. But I had the sense it had been a while, that he was pretty enmeshed in whatever it was. He was what I'd call a 'soldier's soldier.' Liked fighting, liked battle, liked having enemies. And then there was the money."

"Money?" Liam asked. "From Containment?"

"Don't know where it came from. Just that he had plenty of it. I do remember him and Javier fighting about it one night. We were hanging, having some drinks, and Javier said something about the money, how good it was." She frowned, crossed her arms, concentrated on the floor as she replayed the memory. "Lorenzo freaked out, started saying how it wasn't about the money but the principle. Started throwing shit around. Not my kind of scene."

"Violent?"

"I'd say Lorenzo liked violence, if that's a different thing."

Liam nodded, considered.

"Did you talk about Broussard to Lorenzo?" I asked, and her gaze shot to mine. There was an expression of amused puzzlement on her face, like she was trying to figure out the joke.

She shrugged. "Probably. We're colleagues, after all."

She didn't get the meaning behind my question. But Liam did. "Someone wrote 'For Gracie' on the wall above Broussard's body and planted the knife to make me look guilty. Which means he understood I had a beef with Broussard and what I cared about."

Blythe's gaze dropped, moved nervously around the room. "Damn it," she murmured. "I don't know. Probably?" She looked up at Liam pleadingly. "Maybe I blew off steam. I don't know. People talk."

I took that as a yes, and watched Liam's face harden into stern lines.

"Have you seen him lately?"

She shook her head. "It's been five or six months." She shrugged. "I lost interest, ghosted him. He was a very serious guy, and I am not a very serious girl."

"Address?"

Blythe rolled her eyes toward the ceiling, then relented. "He's in the barracks in the Quarter."

"The former Marriott?" Liam asked.

She nodded.

"All right," Liam said. "Thank you for the information, Blythe. We appreciate it."

"I don't want it coming back on me."

"It won't," Liam said. "We're breaking it all down."

"She's got issues," I said. Thunder rumbled ominously above us as we headed back toward Moses's house. "Partying hard-ass layered over someone who's more broken than she wants to admit."

Liam glanced down at me. "How'd you get that in a twenty-minute conversation?"

I shrugged. "A lot of agents came into Royal Mercantile. They all dealt with the pressure, with the stress, differently. Some were quiet. Some, like her, were loud. But most had the same gooey centers."

"The Caval brothers do not have gooey centers."

I held up a hand for a high five. "That's an award-winning segue."

Liam slapped my palm. "It was good. But serious. Both Caval brothers were involved in this. And getting paid for it."

"Javier Caval is dead. Lorenzo Caval had your knife." I grimaced. "Javier Caval kills Broussard, Lorenzo Caval kills Javier? That's pretty dark."

"Yeah, if that's how it went down, it is dark. But Lorenzo apparently wasn't above knocking his brother around because of his imagined moral high ground."

"The war created lots of monsters."

"Yeah," Liam said. "And sometimes it just gave monsters an excuse."

"We can't go to the barracks."

"Finally, a place in New Orleans you won't go."

"There are lots of places in New Orleans I won't go. But, yeah, I'm not stupid. We pass this information along to Gunnar, and we let him handle it."

"That's very wise, Saint Claire."

"Don't push it, Quinn."

CHAPTER FIFTEEN

I t was pouring by the time I got back to the gas station. I grabbed something to eat and balanced out my magic, getting myself ready for my trip to Devil's Isle.

Since I was already going, I searched through my cabinets, looking for something I could take to Lizzie. My father had stocked the gas station pretty well. But I'd been here for several weeks, and the stuff Moses and I found usually went right to the clinic, so I'd been working through my own stash. And I couldn't rely on my garden plot; a tended garden was another sign of activity. I couldn't risk putting a garden close enough to the gas station to actually make it feasible.

I still had plenty of MREs and the stuff I couldn't stand eating any more often than I had to—including the potted meat Moses loved, even though mine wasn't spoiled. But I figured I could spare another can of crushed tomatoes; it was too hot in New Orleans to make red gravy or soup. I didn't plan to make pumpkin pie, so the canned pumpkin could go, too. A couple of rolls of gauze, a bottle of alcohol, and one of peroxide.

It wasn't a lot, but it was something.

When the moon rose over a sodden New Orleans, I pulled a

jacket over a tank and jeans, stuffed the goods into my messenger bag, and locked up the gas station.

It was a solid three miles downtown, but I loved walking in the dark, even if I was a little more tired today than I might have been. The darkness made me feel invisible, which made me feel powerful. I could slip around houses, through alleys. As long as I was careful, I could see without being seen.

I varied my routes toward Devil's Isle—Bienville, Lafitte, Esplanade, Orleans. Names that were part of the history of the city, even if their streets were mostly empty now. Always a few houses with lights on or candles burning. But most were dark, standing silent and still, as if waiting for the moment when their families would come home again. NOLA was a city that preferred the dark. Shadows softened the rough edges, and moonlight made her sing.

Tonight, I'd taken Canal, planning to hop over to St. Louis Avenue. If I followed that straight down toward the river, I'd pass St. Louis Cemetery No. 2. Like most native New Orleanians, I had a love for the city's older cemeteries, for the tall, narrow tombs, the history, the strange dance of voodoo and Catholicism.

I nearly screamed when a cat jumped in front of me, sleek and black, with eyes that shifted between green and gold in the moonlight.

He sat down on the sidewalk, stared up at me inquisitively.

Maybe I should get a cat. Maybe having someone to come home to at the end of the day would do me good. My father had actually stored tins of cat food in the gas station, maybe expecting he'd eventually take a cat there.

I'd have said having a cat would be a lot less emotionally risky than having a boy, except that I'd had a cat before. Her name was Majestic, and she'd deigned to let me own her until the war began. She ran off after the first Valkyrie attack on New Orleans and never came home again.

The cat that stared up at me now didn't have a collar or tags, so I ventured the question.

"You want to come home with me, live in a gas station?"

Those clearly hadn't been the magic words. With what looked like an imperious sniff, the cat lifted its tail and jogged into the silent street, then disappeared into the dark.

I guess he preferred freedom, hard as it was, to being a captive.

I adjusted my bag, started walking again. And made it nearly a block before I heard the footsteps behind me.

My heart began to race. But this wasn't my first night in the city. If it was Containment, it wasn't even my first Containment fight of the *day*.

But I needed to know either way. I stopped, pretended to tie my shoe, and the footsteps fell silent, too. I stared walking again, and the footsteps picked up again. One block, then another, then another.

He or she was about forty feet behind me. And either the person wasn't very good at tailing people or wasn't worried about being caught.

Unfortunately, the magic monitors in this part of town were armed and ready; the closer you got to Devil's Isle, the better they were maintained. That meant it was tree-branch time again. Or the New Orleans equivalent.

I reached a four-way stop marked by palm trees and Creole cottages. I turned the corner, which put me out of my tracker's direct line of sight, then darted around the next cottage into the narrow space between the houses.

I searched the ground, looking for something I could use, grabbed a wrought-iron bar that had probably been part of a window guard, given the turned metal near the top and bottom.

The footsteps drew closer. I judged my timing, and then jumped out, leading with the bar.

And stared up into Liam's eyes.

"Do you have a death wish?" My voice was as fierce as I could make a whisper. The houses around us were dark, but that didn't mean no one was listening.

"Not especially," he said, his gaze on the iron bar. He used a fingertip to push it away. "Nice weapon."

"It's what I could find. What the hell are you doing out here? We decided I was going alone."

"You decided. I made no commitment either way. You shouldn't be roaming around by yourself."

"I can take care of myself."

"I know," he said. "You absolutely can. But maybe you've got someone who'd like to help you take care."

I stared at him, at a loss for words. "How am I supposed to respond to that?"

"Positively."

If I ignored the insinuation, I could admit it would be good to have another set of hands in case of trouble, and I had a pretty good sense that the trip to Devil's Isle would do him good.

I sighed and tossed the bar away. "I assume if I tell you to go home, you're going to skulk around behind me anyway?"

"Pretty much."

"You've got to go where I tell you. No sneaking inside to get to your town house."

Something hard passed across his eyes. "I know I can't go back there."

"Fine," I said, and started walking. "Do you have any idea how loud you are? I'm half surprised Containment didn't hear you coming, send out a patrol."

"I think you've been around Moses too long."

I lifted my brows and he just smiled. "You introduced us."

"Yeah, so part of that blame falls on me."

"Part of it?"

"No more than ninety, ninety-five percent."

It had been designed to keep Paranormals in, to segregate them from the humans in and outside the Zone, to keep us safe from their magical machinations. But it had also been designed to intimidate, and the concrete wall that surrounded the former Marigny, the current Devil's Isle, was plenty imposing for that.

It was more than grim. Concrete and steel and barbed wire, with an electrified grid on top to keep fliers inside and at bay. The sections of the wall repaired after the battle were a little lighter than the old ones, but the grid still glowed eerily green, reflecting the color back on the wet asphalt. If you listened closely enough, you could hear the buzz of electricity and sizzling dust motes.

"We're going to the Quarter side," I told Liam, and steered him to the upriver side of the triangle, instead of the newly rebuilt front gate that rested in its river-facing point.

We walked toward the river, waited across the street beneath the shade of an oak tree, its branches arcing over us like guarding fingers.

Reveillon's explosives had taken out large segments of the wall. Containment had taken the opportunity to finagle the architecture, building a concrete divot into the wall big enough to accommodate a loading dock.

A bright yellow truck was currently pulled up to the dock, its nose facing the street as agents moved boxes out of the back and piled them along the concrete platform. Floodlights illuminated the dock, showing the streak of red paint across the truck's front panel, and CONTAINMENT written in block letters in reverse across the windshield so the car in front of the truck could read the text in the rearview.

"Well," Liam said when we reached the dock, "that's imposing." He let his gaze rise to the enormous steel gate that kept the loading dock secure when it wasn't in use.

"Welcome to the shiny new delivery entrance," I said. "Crazy it took domestic terrorism to get them to add one."

"Before, they were focused on literal containment," Liam said. "They wanted Paras behind a wall, away from everyone else. That was the primary concern. Probably wouldn't have imagined the prison would still be here seven years later."

"Poor planning on their part," I said.

"Intentionally poor planning," he said, and we watched agents begin to load items into the back of the truck they'd just emptied.

"Taking things out of Devil's Isle?" he wondered, as a man loaded a neon orange box into the truck, the paint so bright it nearly glowed in the dark.

"Apparently so," I said. "Let's get moving."

Liam followed me fifty feet farther down the wall. Then I drew to a stop and pointed at the small metal door in the wall, set atop three concrete steps.

"The door opens into a corridor, and that corridor leads to a small room in one of the clinic's back annexes," I explained. "The door's opened, and Lizzie gets notified. She's the only one with access to it."

"So she could walk out of Devil's Isle if she wanted."

"She could. Could have done it during the battle, too. But she won't. That's not who she is."

"She stays inside, agrees to continue caring for the patients, and they don't put cameras on the door so you can make deliveries," Liam said. "That's a good system."

"It's a compromise system, but it's better than nothing." It reminded me why Moses and I skulked around in dusty, moldy houses full of sadness and unfulfilled hopes. Because at the other end of this corridor were Paras with wounds that still hadn't healed, Sensitives who'd become wraiths. People we'd never be able to save.

"Let's give it a minute," I said. Just because there weren't cameras near the door didn't mean there weren't human patrols keeping an eye on us.

"Lower-level agents aren't supposed to know about this," I murmured, stepping back into the shadows as a couple of agents zoomed by in a jeep. "Just Gunnar and a few of the higher-ups, and even then it's 'don't ask, don't tell.' I don't get caught, and they don't come looking."

"I don't like it," Liam whispered. "I understand it, but I don't like it."

"There's a lot not to like in the Zone," I said, pulling the chain from under my shirt. "But we stay here anyway." I waited until the jeep rounded the sharp edge of the prison, then touched his arm.

"Let's go," I said, and we bolted across the street and up the stairs. It didn't escape my notice that he put his back to me, guarding me with his body while I futzed with the lock. But I wasn't going to argue about it.

I unlocked the door and pushed it open.

As always, I half expected to see a Containment agent waiting, and I could feel Liam tense behind me, probably from the same thought. But the corridor, while dimly lit and not really welcoming, was empty.

"It could take her a few minutes," I said quietly, stepping inside.

"Should I close the door?"

"You want to be inside Devil's Isle behind a locked door?"

"No," he said. And that from a man who'd lived in Devil's Isle. He pushed it closed just enough to keep agents outside from getting suspicious, but not enough to engage the lock.

"What now?" he asked.

I leaned back against the bare concrete wall. "Now we wait."

The minutes ticked by. Five, then ten, then fifteen. The longest I'd ever waited to make a drop was seven minutes. We could have left—dropped off the package and left Lizzie to find it—but we needed to talk to her.

Still. Fifteen minutes felt like a long time. I was nearly convinced some rogue agent had intercepted Lizzie when the door opened at the other end of the hall. Liam and I jumped to careful attention.

Lizzie stepped inside, closed it behind her. She wore pale blue scrubs, the visible skin showing forks of fire that danced like moving tattoos. But that was no ink; it was actual fire, an impressive and dangerous part of who she was.

She nodded at me, cast a suspicious look at Liam. I'd proven myself to her, at least as far as she was willing to trust me. But Liam had been AWOL for a long time, and if her expression was any indication, she wasn't thrilled about the fact that he had been gone.

She walked forward, her feet silent in thick rubber clogs. "Sorry for the delay. Minor crisis, but it's fixed now." She glanced at Liam. "I heard you were back."

"I am."

"Containment's all abuzz about you." She glanced at me. "And you, too. Hear you put on a pretty impressive show earlier today."

"We were checking out Broussard's house. They found us."

"And you made your escape." She cocked her head at the bruise on Liam's cheekbone. "That hurt?"

"Doesn't feel great."

"I bet not."

"You heard anything new inside about Broussard?" I asked. "About why he was killed, or who killed him?"

She shook her head. "Plenty of speculation about whether it was or wasn't Liam. Plenty of complaints about Broussard. But it's all been talk. Some have said it was a Reveillon member who didn't get snatched, maybe someone in Containment jealous of Broussard's position, but nothing specific. No names."

I nodded. "You've heard about the Paras at Vacherie?"

Lizzie nodded. "Word got to me. Haven't seen anything like that here. Just the usual complaints."

"Any idea what's happening?"

"Based on what little I know, sounds like an infection of some kind. A serious one, maybe something that affects blood or bone. A systemic infection they're having trouble beating."

"Would that normally be fatal?" I asked.

"It certainly could be without the right care. Among other things, fevers are dangerous, and they can cause big problems. But the red flag for me was the petechiae."

"Say that again," Liam said.

"Petechiae," Lizzie repeated. "The red marks. They're caused by internal bleeding that seeps through the skin. Can indicate sepsis—when an infection has spread through the body, and the immune response makes the situation worse."

"So you think it's an infection?"

"From here," Lizzie said. "But I'm miles away, haven't seen a patient, and I'm working based on communications from laypeople and the one nomedic who's been to Vacherie."

"Nomedic?" I asked.

"Nomad medic," Lizzie said with a smile. "The volunteer docs who travel through the Zone. Lifesavers, but very unique individuals."

Learned something new every day.

"My staff's on alert about the symptoms. If we see anything like that, we'll let you know." Her features softened. "Tell Malachi I'm sorry."

"I will."

Lizzie's gaze shifted to Liam, and she looked at him for a long, quiet time. "You leave because of the magic?"

"Yeah," he said after a moment. "Yeah, I did."

She nodded, watched him again. "I can see it."

That made me jerk. I'd thought she'd been staring him down because she was angry and hurt, and trying to figure out exactly how much anger and hurt were there.

"Like Eleanor?" I asked.

"Not quite. I can't usually do it," she said, frowning at me. "I can't see any of yours. But there's an aura around Liam. A haze."

"It was Ezekiel's magic."

"And he was a Sensitive."

Liam nodded.

Lizzie moved forward, eyes narrowed as she looked him over. "Sensitive plus human shouldn't equal Sensitive, should it? Unless there's something in that DNA of yours. Eleanor was hit by a weapon, after all. Not the usual way of obtaining power."

"I'd give it back if I could."

"I can see that. I can see that you're fighting it."

He looked surprised by that. "I'm not fighting it. I think it's fighting me."

This time she grinned. "Magic in a human body. Of course it's fighting."

"Because Ezekiel was evil."

"He wasn't evil." She pulled a stethoscope from the pocket of her shirt, wrapped it around her neck. "He was dying. Death by magic."

The fate of all Sensitives who didn't learn to control the magic. And an important distinction that Liam needed to hear.

"That wasn't the magic's fault," she said. "Or his. I'm not condoning what he did. He was a sad and narrow-minded fool. But if he'd been given the right tools?" She lifted a shoulder. "Might have been a different story."

She took another step closer to Liam. "You have the tools. You have knowledge and people. As long as you stay out of here, you'll be fine."

I think she'd given me the same speech.

"I'm trying my best," Liam said.

"Good. That's all any of us can do." Lizzie looked at me speculatively. "And speaking of trying our best, what did you bring me?"

I opened my bag, offered up the goodies. She packed them into the wrinkled plastic grocery bag she pulled from a pocket.

"This will be great," she said, holding up the square bottle of peroxide. "Surprisingly effective on cold-iron wounds." Paranormals didn't heal well from attacks by cold-iron weapons; that's why they'd been so effective and changed the tide during the war. "Stupid I didn't try it earlier, but it's a human treatment, not a Para one. Doesn't even exist in the Beyond."

There was a scratch at the clinic door that had Liam and me whipping around, readying ourselves for a fight. A Containment agent, or a wraith that had escaped his room?

"Don't fret over that," Lizzie said. "Just a visitor." She put the bottle in the bag with the other gear, then walked back to the door. "Someone wants to see you."

Lizzie opened the door, then stepped out of the way. "Come on in," she said.

There, sitting expectantly at the door, was Foster Arsenault, Eleanor's golden Lab and a very good friend of Liam's.

Liam murmured something low, something in Cajun, and went to one knee. Foster bolted toward him, tail wagging like a tornado.

"Oh, buddy," Liam said, burying his face in the dog's neck. "I'm so sorry."

I had to look up at the fluorescent lights in the ceiling, breathing through pursed lips, trying to force the tears back. When Foster made a whooping whine that sounded like a complaint, I laughed, let the tears fall anyway, and wiped them away.

"I think he's mad at you," Lizzie said with a grin.

"He should be," Liam said, scratching Foster's chin so his back leg thwacked rhythmically against the floor. "I left him, too."

"You did," she agreed. "Gavin took him to Pike, and Pike brought him to me right after the battle. He wanted a chance on the outside, was worried how Foster would handle it. I told him I'd find a family for him while you were gone, let him hang out in the clinic for a couple of days. I hoped it might do the patients good."

"Did it?"

"It did," she said, stroking Foster's head. Tongue lolling, he sprawled on the floor and basked in the attention. "And now I can't seem to get rid of him. The Paras enjoy him. And he seems to calm the wraiths."

That snapped my head up. "He does?"

She nodded. "Animal therapy isn't a cure, but it helps. I'm not sure why, but I don't really care. Anything that makes their lives easier and doesn't hurt anyone else is fine by me." She looked up at me. "Better a dog than permanent sedation."

I nodded. That was an easy choice to make.

"How's Pike doing?" Liam asked, stroking Foster's flank. "Claire told me he got snatched."

She grinned. "Pike? He's great. Living in your house."

Liam opened his mouth, wisely closed it again. "I probably owe him that."

"Damn right you do." Lizzie sighed, then looked down at Foster. "You ready to get back to work?"

He made a rolling bark that sounded like a song, got to his feet, and headed for the door.

"If only all our staff was so efficient," she said with a smile. Then she looked at Liam. "It's good to see you. But you made a hell of a mistake, leaving."

She let her gaze flick to me, then back to him. "Maybe you've got a chance to fix that. If I were you, I'd be groveling."

That was a note I was happy to leave on.

It had been a market, a meeting spot, a place to discuss and protest. And it had been a place for the rebellion of joy, where dance and music and camaraderie battled back, at least for a little while, against the difficulties of life.

Congo Square was a park on the lake side of the Quarter, just off Rampart and St. Peter. It had once been a field at the edge of the city, then a park lined with bricks and trees, and then, for a little while during the war, the place where doctors set up tents to help those injured in battle. The tents were gone, and rain had washed away the blood that had stained the brick during the war. Even now, the bricks still had scars from the fighting, great gouges where Paranormals' weapons had pierced and shattered them.

That didn't stop the hardy people who'd stayed from taking back the park. Because Congo Square was for New Orleans, for the survivors.

Even though the world was dark, there were three dozen people in the park. A woman sold yaka mein from a pot in the back of her truck, and a man fried beignets in an enormous kettle nearby. In one corner, a beautiful woman with dark skin, a tignon wrapped around her head, listened while the woman in front of her, her tiny frame and wrinkled skin putting her easily in her eighties or nineties, blotted her eyes with a tissue. The woman, a priestess or conjurer, pulled something from a hidden pocket in her skirt, pressed it into the older woman's hand, and sent her on her way. A gris-gris maybe, a powerful voodoo charm that was banned, like every other form of magic.

But these were all sideshows for the main attraction—the music and dance. In the middle of the park, a circle of men and women stood with drums of every shape and size. Some were handheld, not much bigger than tambourines. Others were more than a foot long and hung from wide straps around the neck or shoulders. Some were too big to hold, their glossy vessels in chrome stands that seemed too beautiful to have survived the war.

But they had survived and now built—one drum at a time—a song that was just as layered and complex as the city itself.

Rat tat. Rat tat tat. Rat tat. Rat tat tat.

Foom. Bum bum. Foom. Bum bum.

Chik chik chik. Chik chik chik. Chik chik chik. Chik chik chik.

In front of the drummers, women danced. They wore white blouses and circle skirts in a patchwork of colors, bells on their ankles adding another layer to the song as they spun, stamped their feet, swung their arms.

The drums beat through me, like my heart had adopted their rhythm. For a little while, it was like the war hadn't come to New Orleans at all. Like tourists might be lined up at Café Du Monde and outside the voodoo shops, like Bourbon Street would be a giant boozy party.

"It's why we stay," Liam quietly said. "And it's why we fight."

I couldn't argue with that.

It was nearly midnight by the time we reached the gas station. We stopped across the street, taking precautions.

"Thanks for letting me tag along. It was good to see Foster."

"It was good for you to see him."

He nodded, and we stood in silence that was almost companionable but for the tension in the air.

Neither of us was ready to walk away. Neither of us was ready to move closer.

"I should get inside, try to get some sleep."

He nodded, and his body tensed. He'd wanted to reach out, I realized. Wanted to touch me, but was working to hold himself back. We were holding ourselves back from each other, still looking for that place of comfort and trust. But I didn't think we'd find it tonight. Not out here in the darkness.

"Good night, Liam."

"Good night, Claire."

And we went our separate ways.

CHAPTER SIXTEEN

I got up before dawn, snuck out of the station before the sun was up, and hopped on the scraggly bike I'd found in an alley behind the station and fixed up. The bike had been my consolation prize; I'd found a motorized Simplex in a warehouse off Canal Street, but didn't have the parts to get it running again.

We had picked a house as a neutral meeting spot for our Icarus building surveillance. It was halfway between mine and Moses's, although only Malachi and Liam knew enough about the gas station to understand that geometry.

Since Malachi had stayed behind today—figuring someone needed to stay with Moses, just in case—I met Liam and Gavin there, at the low cottage overgrown with palm trees, a years-old For Sale sign still hanging by one corner in the front yard.

"No one's going to buy this place now," Gavin said quietly as I climbed into the Range Rover he'd parked at the curb.

"No," I agreed.

Even in the milky predawn light, it was obvious the house was in bad shape. The roof had caved into the middle of what had probably been the living room, and plants had grown in the void, a few stalks and branches already reaching up and out toward the sky, searching for sunlight.

If that wasn't a metaphor for those of us who'd stayed, I don't know what was.

The humidity was oppressive even though the sun hadn't yet risen. Since we were possibly heading to a Containment building, I tucked my hair under a cap, the damp tendrils that escaped blowing in the breeze from the SUV's rolled-down windows.

Liam seemed more relaxed as we drove toward ADZ, but his eyes still held that spark of intensity, of interest, of possessiveness.

"How's your arm?" he asked.

"Sore and bruised, but okay. Thanks." I'd have a scar, but I figured that just added to the mystique.

Gavin glanced at me in the rearview. "What's wrong with your arm?"

"She got shot yesterday."

Gavin's eyes went wide, and the vehicle wobbled as he jerked the wheel. "You got shot? By Containment?"

"It just grazed me. I mean, it didn't feel good, but I've done worse to myself in the store." My dad had done a pretty good job of teaching me how to repair things instead of throwing them out and buying something new. Learning to use saws and hammers brought plenty of cuts and bruises with it.

Since I wasn't ready to walk down memory lane with my dad, I put the thoughts aside.

Gavin whistled. "Figures you didn't tell your guardians. They wouldn't have let you out of the house."

I snorted. "They'd have tried not to." I thought I could probably get around Malachi and Moses, although Malachi would have a pretty easy time finding me. He could surveil from the sky.

"You talk to Gunnar?" Liam asked.

"Not directly," Gavin said. "Passed along a message about Caval, signed it with an alias he'll recognize."

"Beau Q. Lafitte?" I guessed.

"*Mais*, you aren't still using that name?" Liam asked.

"Damn right I am. It's got years of life left in it. Unlike this eyesore of a building," he said, driving slowly past the address on the invoice.

He was right; it wasn't much to look at. Low and squat, made of white-painted brick with long horizontal windows. Probably built in the 1970s, with lots of orange and avocado on the inside. There was no landscaping to speak of, just a long strip of low grass behind a strip of parking spaces. The sign in front, equally squat and unimaginative, read ADZ LOGISTICS in plain black letters. If this was some kind of Containment outfit, maybe they wanted to be unassuming.

"Doesn't exactly look like a hub for innovation or research," Gavin murmured.

"No, it doesn't," I said. "But if you're involved in the murder of a Containment agent, you probably try to keep your work on the down low."

"Probably so," Gavin agreed.

"We've got more information about Caval," Liam said, and told him what we'd learned from Blythe.

"Blythe gave your knife away?" Gavin whistled. "That's cold-blooded."

He drove to the next stop sign, then headed across the neutral ground to the southbound lanes of Elysian. He pulled into the parking lot of an abandoned insurance agency and positioned the car so we could see the building.

ADZ's parking lot was empty, and the building was dark. Hard to tell if anyone actually used the place now. We'd have to wait to learn that truth.

And wait we did.

Dawn began to color the sky after twenty minutes of sitting in the car, twenty minutes of listening to Gavin eat a granola bar louder than I'd have thought possible of a human.

"Like a damn chipmunk," Liam said.

"Boy's gotta have energy. Never know what you're going to get into."

"The bottom of that wrapper, it appears."

"You're hilarious, brother. I missed your wry sense of humor and wit."

Liam punched Gavin, and it jostled him and sent granola crumbs into the air like flakes of delicious snow.

Gavin muttered something in Cajun French that didn't sound flattering. But I just sat in the backseat and smiled, my gaze on the road. For the little while that we'd been a group of friends—that short period between my being attacked by a wraith and the battle—I'd gotten used to their sniping. It was good to hear them irritate each other again.

But when a car turned onto the road—the first we'd seen since parking—we went quiet. We all hunched down a little and watched a white Mercedes pull into the lot.

"Damn," Gavin said. "Nice wheels."

"No kidding," Liam muttered.

A woman in a suit stepped out of the car, closed the door behind her.

A woman with long red hair. The woman from the photograph.

"Merde," Liam murmured. But I didn't even think to respond. Before I knew what was happening, I was out of the vehicle.

"Claire!" Liam's whisper through the open window was fierce and demanding, but I didn't process it. The sound was only a buzz in my ears. I was striding across the street, the neutral ground, the other lanes.

This was my mother. And she'd parked at the Icarus building.

I started running, and the cap flew off my head. I hadn't bothered to consider what I might say when I caught up to her. It didn't seem to matter. I just wanted answers. Or acknowledgment. Or both.

She was a beautiful woman. Tall and slender, with red hair, green eyes, and pale skin. She wore a suit of burnt orange, a cream-colored camisole beneath the jacket, heels in the same shade.

She was nearly to the front door when I stepped in front of her. She didn't flinch, just studied me until awareness dawned in her eyes.

"You're my mother."

She looked at me with clinical detail. "You're Claire Connolly?"

My throat suddenly tight with emotion, I could manage only a nod.

"Then yes. My name is Laura Blackwell. I'm your biological mother." She said it matter-of-factly, like she was confirming the humidity level.

My thoughts spun so quickly it literally made me dizzy. Laura Blackwell, the president of ADZ Logistics, the woman identified on the lab invoice, was my *mother*.

When I continued to stare at her, she rolled her eyes and motioned to the building. "I'm a busy woman, Claire, so while I assume you have questions, I need to get back to work." She looked at me expectantly.

"You left us."

"If by 'us' you mean yourself and your father, yes. I did."

A full five seconds of silence followed that with no elaboration. "Why?" I asked.

"I wasn't cut out to be a spouse or mother. Your father's interests diverged from mine, and I realized I didn't have the instinct for motherhood. You were a well-behaved child, but I simply wasn't interested in you, intellectually or emotionally. Your father wanted a child, and I could admit to some curiosity about the biological processes. I considered it a kind of experiment. I hypothesized that the maternal feeling would grow, but it didn't."

She looked at me expectantly, as if she'd provided an entirely reasonable explanation and was confident that I would buy it immediately.

She sounded like a scientist, a woman who—not unlike Broussard—saw the world in very clear terms. In black and white with no shades of gray, even while she was talking about emotions and abandonment.

"So that was it? You decided being a mother wasn't for you, so you walked away?"

"You're being emotional."

"I'm human."

"Then try harder. As my child, you should have ample intelligence at your disposal." She sighed. "As you didn't appear to know my name, I assume your father upheld his end of the bargain."

My blood ran cold. "What bargain?"

"He wouldn't discuss me, and I wouldn't interfere with his raising you, ask for alimony, complicate the divorce, or cause any of those other irritations. Not that I would have interfered—I had no interest in it. But giving you a 'normal childhood' seemed his only concern."

Because he'd had integrity, and knew how to love, I thought. And had somehow managed to negotiate a life for me even while his heart was probably breaking.

"Did you love him?"

"I was fond of him, of course, but that's hardly the point. There's no logic in tying yourself to someone else if you aren't happy. I wasn't happy, so I moved on."

With a slender manicured finger, she pushed back her sleeve, checked the time on a delicate gold watch, then looked at me again.

"I've given you all the time I have. It will have to be enough. I hope you know that I don't regret having had a child."

She said it like she was making an offering, like her lack of regret was a gift. As consolation prizes go, it wasn't much.

The anger rose so quickly I had to clench my fingers to keep from striking her, from slapping that smile off her face. How dared she talk about regret? She'd broken my father's heart, walked out on him, walked out on me without another look. She might not have felt regret, but she also apparently hadn't felt any sense of honor, any sense of obligation to follow through on the commitment she'd made by having a child in the first place. She'd just, apparently, moved on to better things.

It wasn't the first or last time a parent had walked out on a child. But it had never occurred to me that someone could be so cold about it. She was a blank canvas, and seemed baffled, or maybe exasperated, that I didn't see it her way.

For a moment, I felt like I was floating outside my body, watching myself try to sort through my roiling emotions. I knew, as I seemed to watch myself watching her, as I stared down at mother and daughter, that it would take time to process the emotions. To accept who she was, and be grateful that my father had shielded me.

That unleashed another torrent of emotions—but this time on his behalf. She had no idea what he'd gone through as a single parent, to keep me safe and alive and fed, especially after the war started, when the money dried up and he had to get what he could from selling MREs and bottled water.

"How could you just walk away, like you had no responsibilities?"

"I did have responsibilities. Important ones. I made good on those."

"Like Icarus? Is that one of your responsibilities?"

Her body went rigid, her face very controlled. And there was something else in her eyes—something I didn't know her well enough to assess. But it was a lot darker than the bafflement it had replaced.

"I have nothing more to say to you. And since you seem like a relatively intelligent person, perhaps you've gotten lucky and have more of my brain than your father's." She plastered a smile on her face, a bitterly cold smile. "Icarus is none of your business. It is mine, and I protect what's mine very, very carefully. You can walk away right now, or I can call a Containment agent and have you taken out."

She looked at me expectantly.

"I'll just be going," I said, and it took every ounce of control I had to say that civilly.

She nodded. "I assume I won't be seeing any more of you. I don't need the distraction."

Five-to-one odds said she'd be calling Containment whether I walked away or not. So I planned to head in the opposite direction of Gavin and Liam, to keep attention away from them.

But the plan didn't matter.

They came around the corner, three Containment agents with comm devices in hand, stunners on their belts. They'd gotten ahead of me. She'd signaled them somehow while we were still in the parking lot. While we were talking, while she was meeting her grown daughter for the first time, she'd called them.

Betrayal was a knife in my heart, but she was unapologetic. If anything, she looked irritated by my response. She held up her palm, showed me the small device she held. A panic button of some sort.

"You're disrupting my work," she said flatly. "I don't have time for this. And if you've run afoul of Containment, that's not my problem. You're your own responsibility.

"George!" she called out to one of them without taking her eyes off me. "We have an intruder."

"You called Containment on me?" I could barely force the words out.

"You're interrupting my work." Again, that irritation.

"Hands in the air," one of the agents said, and for the second time in as many days, I lifted my hands. But this time, I kept my gaze on my mother.

"I'm glad you left us."

Her jerk was so small, so minor, that most people probably wouldn't have noticed it. But I did.

"I don't have time for this. I have work to do." She looked at one of the agents, tall and slender with dark skin and deeply brown eyes. "You've got it, Chenille?"

"Ma'am," Chenille responded. Her gaze kept flicking back and forth between us, obviously noticing the resemblance. But it didn't change the grim determination in her expression.

"We aren't done," I called out as she opened the door.

She glanced back at me, one perfect red eyebrow lifted dubiously. "Aren't we? It certainly appears to me that you're done, Ms. Connolly." With that, she slipped inside, leaving me alone with the agents.

My mother turned me in to Containment.

I closed my eyes, thinking this was it—my last moment of freedom. I'd be taken into Devil's Isle to waste away until the magic took me. Destroyed me.

I willed Gavin and Liam to leave, to stay in the vehicle and drive away. To get themselves to safety. Maybe they'd be able to come up with a plan to get me, too, or maybe not. At least I wouldn't have to worry about them.

But then things got more complicated.

A truck zoomed down the street and pulled up to the curb. Big and green and jacked up on enormous tires, with angry guitars blasting through the windows. There were two men in the cab, two men in the back. And two of them looked very familiar—Crowley and

Jimmy, the hunters who'd attacked us outside Vacherie. They'd come back to New Orleans. Had they guessed we'd show up here? Did they know about her, or about ADZ?

They jumped out, the man from the front passenger seat holding up a piece of paper and pointing at me.

"I've got a duly authorized bounty on that woman," Crowley said, in that unusual gravelly voice of his. "On Claire Connolly!"

Every system in my body seemed to freeze at the word "bounty."

Before, I'd been just a person of interest, a human with an outstanding warrant. Creating a reward for my capture would bump me right up on the hunters' priority lists. It wasn't much of a surprise that they'd done it, not after what had happened at Broussard's house. But it still sent a wave of sickness through my stomach. It was one thing to live quietly, to stay out of Containment's sight. It was entirely another to know that hunters had been actively searching me out.

Apparently refusing to abandon me, Liam and Gavin ran across the street. Gavin waved a piece of paper in the air like a competing bounty. Probably registration on the vehicle. But I doubted that would stop the Quinn boys. And neither would the fact that there was definitely a bounty on Liam, and probably one on Gavin now, too.

"Hey!" Gavin called out. "Hey! Over here! She's ours!"

Everyone looked back, their expressions surprised or confused or concerned as they moved forward. Gavin held up the paper one last time, then shoved it into his pocket. "We've got dibs on Claire Connolly. Agent Jackson offered us the bounty personally."

Crowley stepped forward. "You know that's not how it works," he said, then slid a look to Liam. "We got here first, so we get the bounty."

"How the hell'd you get off Montagne Désespérée?" Gavin asked.

"Shrimper," Jimmy said, just as Gavin had predicted.

Crowley's and Liam's eyes narrowed as they looked each other over. "You attacked them?" Liam asked.

"I tried to bring your friends here in for questioning." Crowley's jaw was tight with anger. "I'm guessing this is your brother."

"You'd be right," Gavin said. "Bummer you didn't figure that out when you had your chance."

Crowley's gaze didn't leave Liam. "Seems like I've got a pretty good chance now. If you aren't careful, the both of you, we'll take the couple other bounties available to us for the Quinn brothers. I'm not going to do that now due to professional courtesy. Unless you get in my way."

Liam's features were hard, his eyes shifting blue and golden. And that hadn't escaped the other bounty hunter's notice. "You're going to want to back off and walk away."

Crowley's stare stayed steady. This was just business for him—a lot of money and probably a little pride. "Why should I?"

"Because she's mine."

Crowley's brows lifted. "So that's how it goes, is it? And what if I don't walk away? You going to kill me, too?" Several heads in the group turned to stare at Liam. "Or maybe we should just cut to the chase and execute all our bounties right now."

"Everyone step back," Chenille said. "We've got the prisoner, and we're taking her in."

"Can't step back," Crowley said. "You don't even have a wagon here. Rules are, we locate a target at the same time as Containment, the one with wheels wins the prize. We got transpo, we get the bounty."

"We've got a superior claim," Gavin said again, shaking his head.

"Bullshit," Crowley said, slid his glance to Chenille. "How about a trade? I'll take Connolly, and you can take the brothers Quinn."

Chenille's lips curled in the way of villains everywhere. "They're wanted, too?"

"They are," Crowley said. "Might even go without argument, if they think they'll make it to the prison same time as Ms. Connolly here."

"You'll take us in over your dead body." Liam's voice was fierce.

"Or yours," Crowley said. He pulled a toothpick from his pocket, slipped it between his teeth, chewed. "Makes the transport easier."

For a moment, there was nothing but tense silence, everyone gauging the others, watching to see who'd strike first. With the sun beating down, I wouldn't have been surprised to see tumbleweeds drifting by.

We played chicken . . . until Crowley made the first move.

He jumped forward, grabbed my arm, dragged me across the parking lot, and shoved me behind him, his meaty hand still around my arm. He was bigger than me, stronger than me, and I wasn't going to dislodge his fingers by sheer force. I'd have to get creative.

His other men took that as their signal to move. They jumped out of the truck, and two of them began engaging the Containment officers. The third, either brave or stupid, headed for Liam and Gavin.

"I like these odds," Gavin said, swinging when the man lunged for him. The man was big, but spry enough to dodge the shot. He ducked, then grabbed Gavin by the waist and tried to throw him down.

He was bigger than Gavin, heavy and bulky compared to Gavin's lean ranginess, but Gavin managed to stay on his feet as they moved backward, hit a light pole.

Liam strode forward, chin down and a bullish expression on his face. He grabbed the man by his shoulders, ripped him away from Gavin, and tossed him bodily a few feet away.

"That's my baby brother, asshole."

"Oh, now you come to my rescue?" Gavin asked, using one hand to push himself up, the other to support the spot on his back where he'd been mashed into the steel post.

"Better late than never," Liam said, adjusting his stance while the man rose again and made another lunge.

"You need better moves," Liam said, neatly dodging to the side and avoiding the blitz. But the man skidded to a stop on the concrete, came back again, tried to jump on Liam's back.

"Son of a—," Liam yelled, his body bowed under the weight of the man.

Instinctively, I yanked my arm away from Crowley, but barely made a dent. "Not yet, little lady," he said, and began dragging me toward the truck.

No way was I going in the back of that truck.

What the hell? I figured. They already knew I was a Sensitive. Seeing me do magic now was just icing on the cake.

I reached out for power, felt a few delicate tendrils in the air. By some freak of geography, there weren't many out there, so I was going to need to make this count. Best way to threaten a bully? With his own weapon.

I wrapped magic around the butt of his gun, yanked it out of his holster, then popped it into my hand.

"You're going to want to get your hand off me."

He instinctively felt for his holster, and I saw the jolt when he realized it was empty. Slowly, he looked at me.

"Well," he said with a leering grin, "looks like the bounty was telling the truth." He raked his gaze over me, making me feel grimy. "But maybe I'll have some use for you."

I whipped the knife from his other holster, and when it was

seated in my hand, I pointed it toward his balls. "Say that to me again, Crowley. I dare you."

"Put the gun down!"

We looked back. Two of the agents and two of Crowley's men were rolling on the ground. Liam was helping Gavin stand. Chenille had a gun and swung it from person to person, unsure which of us was the best target.

It was time for us to take our leave. I had a pretty good idea how to make that happen.

I put the knife in my pocket, raised the gun at Crowley. "Turn around and face her."

Crowley muttered under his breath, but turned around.

I glanced at Liam, gave him a nod, then used the rest of the magic I'd gathered to push Crowley toward Chenille. He hit her like a bull, sending both of them to the ground.

We took our chance, running back across the street toward the SUV. Along the way, I snatched up my ball cap, rolled and stuffed it into my back pocket.

Liam was in the lead. "Keys!" he shouted at Gavin, who threw the keys over Liam's head and into his waiting hands. Liam yanked open the door and we jumped inside. Then his keys were in the ignition and we were zooming down the street.

We were a quarter mile down the road when their engine roared behind us. The bounty hunters were giving chase. Booms echoed through the air, and we ducked as metal pinged against the vehicle's exterior.

"Son of a bitch! This is my brand-new car!"

"It's neither new nor your car," Liam pointed out, speeding up along the straightaway.

"Plan?" I asked.

"Not getting taken to Devil's Isle"—Liam winced as the car caught a pothole—"and not leading them to Moses."

"I like both of those plans," Gavin said, grabbing the chicken stick as the vehicle bounced.

"Need enough of a lead," Liam murmured, his eyes shifting between the road and the rearview, "and then we're golden."

He gunned it, putting a half mile between us and the truck.

"Now we need a switch," Liam said, and jerked the car into a hard right turn onto a side street that slung us all against the left side of the car.

"Damn it," Gavin muttered. "I liked this car."

"They've seen it."

"I get that, but it doesn't mean I have to like it. Alley coming up on your left, two hundred feet."

Another tight turn, and Liam slid the Range Rover into the alley with scant inches on each side, then floored it over pockmarked asphalt and gravel.

"There!" Gavin yelled. "There's a truck in the garage twenty feet back. On your right."

Liam threw the car into a stomach-hurling reverse, and we lurched forward as he drilled backward through the narrow lane, then screeched to a stop.

He parked the Range Rover kitty-corner so it blocked the alley behind us. We climbed out of the SUV and walked past a dilapidated house and into the garage Gavin had spotted.

Weeds grew through the garage's dirt floor. But the truck was . . . interesting. It was a Ford, probably from the forties, relatively small and plenty curvy, the original paint long ago rusted into mottled red.

Liam's gaze narrowed. "This isn't a truck. It's a paperweight."

"Probably runs better than yours," Gavin said. "Just need to find out if it moves."

I walked toward the cab, running my fingers over the bed. The body felt solid, and the tires were new. And there was something I liked about the narrow bed, huge curving wheel wells, and chrome details.

There was a thin layer of dust on the door handle. The truck hadn't been driven in a while, so at least we weren't poking around in someone's everyday car. That didn't give me much comfort about the mechanics, but I liked the look of it. It was love at rusty first sight.

"I want it."

They both looked back at me.

"This thing?" Gavin asked.

"This thing. I like it, and I want it. Keep an eye out," I said, then opened the driver's-side door. I checked beneath the floor mats, behind the visors, but didn't find a set of keys. Fortunately, the car was old enough to work a trick I'd learned from my father, who'd been afraid I'd find myself stuck in New Orleans without a way home.

I grabbed my hat, pulled it on and stuffed my hair beneath it. "Pocketknife?" I asked, holding out a hand to Liam. He watched me curiously while Gavin stood at the edge of the garage, keeping an eye on the street.

Liam pulled a multi-tool from his pocket, handed it over.

"Thanks," I said, and slid onto the front seat.

Either the leather was in really good shape, or it had been part of the apparent restoration. Half the work was done for me on the hot-wiring, too. The panel that covered the wires beneath the steering wheel was gone, the wires new and labeled with tape. That was a very good sign. Even if the body was rough, someone had taken the time to replace the wires. That meant there was a pretty good chance the mechanics were good, too.

"Thank you," I murmured, carefully stripped a bit of insulation from the ignition wires, twisted them together, and connected the bundle to the battery.

The engine roared to life, echoing like thunder in the narrow garage.

I stuffed the bundle back into the cavity, then sat up and revved the engine. "Squeeze in, and let's get the hell out of here."

Gavin climbed in, slid over on the leather bench seat. "Damn, Claire. You are a badass."

"I can fix things," I said simply, but I noted the pride and interest in Liam's eyes.

I patted the dashboard. "I'm going to call her Scarlet."

"She's not exactly subtle," Liam said, but there was no disapproval in his voice. Just caution. "You'll have to be careful."

"Oh, I will." Because she was mine now.

I put Scarlet in reverse, stretched an arm on the back of the bench seat, and brought her into the light again.

learned, when we were bumping back toward Mid-City, that while I liked Scarlet's curves, I did not like her suspension.

"Well," Gavin said, "that was an interesting trip."

"What was that paper you were waving around?"

"Vehicle registration," Gavin said with a grin.

Nailed it.

"You want to tell us what happened out there?" Gavin asked the question, but I could feel Liam's gaze on me.

I forced words out, even though my chest had gone tight with emotion. "That's Laura Blackwell. The woman whose name was on the ADZ Logistics invoice. The president of the company."

The car was silent for a moment, and I assumed they were debating whether to ask me to elaborate. I saved them the trouble.

"She's my mother," I said, looking out the window to watch the buildings pass.

"Your mother?" Liam said quietly. "She wasn't dead."

"No. My father lied to me." And I was still working my brain around that one. "She apparently left my father, and didn't want to revisit that part of her life. I guess he wanted to close that chapter."

"I'm sorry, Claire."

I nodded. "She didn't tell me anything about Icarus. She said she'd 'protect what was hers.'"

"And yet she called Containment on her own daughter," Gavin said, then whistled low. "What a stone-cold bitch."

"Can't argue with that. And I guess Containment has issued a bounty on me now."

"And me," Gavin said happily, adjusting in his seat and squeezing his shoulders between me and Liam on the bench. Maybe people had been smaller when this car was built. Or it hadn't been meant for the tall, broad-shouldered Quinn boys. "About damn time. I was beginning to feel left out. Now we're the Three Wanted Amigos."

"Oh, good," Liam murmured.

"Here's my question," Gavin said. "How'd Crowley manage to get there at just the right time? That's a pretty damn big coincidence."

"No way that was coincidence," I said. "Either they'd been watching the building, thinking we might show up if we connected it to Icarus, which seems really unlikely, or someone inside called Crowley when they saw me."

"Containment guards were patrolling," Gavin said. "More evidence this is a Containment problem."

I didn't like the implications. But the connections to Containment were undeniable.

"The more we learn about this," Liam said, "the deeper into Containment it goes."

Gavin nodded. "And the more they try to rein us in."

"We're running out of time."

Liam meant me and him and Gavin—and everyone else on the run. And he meant New Orleans. And he meant Paranormals. Everyone still touched by a war that had never really ended. Only the tactics had changed.

"Yeah," I said. "Something is brewing again. And someone doesn't want us to know what it is."

Without a better option, we went back to Moses's place. Our being there was enough to put him at risk, but there wasn't any help for it.

We walked inside, found Moses at the computer table with an open can of beans, the lid ragged-edged and sticking up from the can.

"Lunch?" he asked with a smile, but it faded when he looked at us. "What the shit happened? You get into a scuffle again?"

"Containment showed up at the building, as did Crowley's bastards." Liam pulled a handkerchief from his pocket, then came over and pressed it to my temple.

"Glass, I think," he said quietly, his brow pinched in concentration as he dabbed carefully at my forehead. I hadn't felt a cut there—at least not separate from the million other little injuries—but the pressure stung a little.

I winced, hissed air through my teeth.

Liam went still. "You all right?"

I nodded. "I'm fine. Thanks."

He lifted my hand, held it to the handkerchief. "Keep pressure on it."

"Sure."

Moses was looking at me when Liam walked away, and he raised his brows comically a few times. The narrow-eyed stare I gave him put a little pink in his cheeks.

Malachi walked into the room, looked us over, then frowned at the sight. "What happened?"

"Long story short," Gavin said, "Claire just outed herself to her mother, who works at ADZ, there's a bounty on all of us now, and

Crowley and Containment got into a gunfight over the bounties." He held up a finger. "And I had to get rid of the Rover, and Claire knows how to hot-wire a car."

Malachi looked at me, a mix of pity and anger in his eyes. "That was a dangerous thing to do, to confront her. But necessary, I suppose."

I just nodded, feeling miserable by the reminder.

"No point beating her up for trying to talk to family," Moses said. He cocked his head to the side. "She was at ADZ, eh?"

I nodded. "Going into the building. She called Containment on us."

"No wonder your father got rid of her. Good riddance, I say."

But my father hadn't gotten rid of her. She'd gotten rid of him, and me, soon enough that I didn't have a single clear memory of her face.

Tears—of sadness, of frustration, of pent-up emotion—stung my eyes, and I looked away, blinked them back.

"I need to get some air," I said, and headed outside before anyone could stop me.

I walked down the street in broad daylight, angry and hurt enough in that moment that I'd have dared Containment to take me. And I'd have thrown everything I had at them. Every last ounce of magic.

I was so tired of pretending.

A few doors down, past Moses's butter house, was a cottage with a swing bolted to the roof of the front porch. Plastic beads, which would probably never degrade, still hung from the gingerbread at the house's corners.

I tested the steel chain, the slats of wood. And when it held, I sat down, pushed off with my feet. The swing rocked back and forth, then back again. I closed my eyes and let myself grieve, let sadness cover me like the dark water near Montagne Désespérée.

I heard him walking toward me, his footsteps on the sidewalk.

Liam walked purposefully. Not slowly, but intentionally. He took his time.

The porch creaked when he stepped onto it. I kept my eyes closed, let him look me over.

"I'd ask if you were all right, but that seems like a stupid question."

"I don't know what I am." I rubbed my hands against my eyes, my damp cheeks.

Silence, then: "Can I sit?"

I opened my eyes, scooted over to one side of the swing, wrapped a hand around one of the chains. The swing shivered when he sat, but it held.

"I'm disappointed," I said. "Does that make sense?"

He pushed the swing back. "It does."

"I feel stupid saying that. Disappointed about my mother. I thought she was gone, that I'd never have a chance to so much as see her. And now I've had that chance, and she's not what I wanted. Not even close."

"She never was," Liam quietly said.

"I know. That's what hurts the most."

"It's okay to grieve."

"I guess." I rested my head on the back of the swing, looked up at the porch's ceiling. Someone had painted a mural there—a second line marching down the street behind a bride and groom, all bold colors and slashes of paint. There was water damage in some spots, flaking paint in others. But it was still a beautiful representation of what had been.

"Before the war," I heard myself saying, "when other kids went shopping with their mothers, or their moms dropped them off at school, or whatever, I wondered what that was like. My dad tried hard to keep me from feeling different. But I did. I did feel different, but I didn't grieve, because I hadn't exactly lost anything."

"It was already gone," Liam said.

I nodded. "Yeah. And now, I got it back, but that's almost worse. I've learned that my father lied to me—probably to protect me. That my mother was cold and didn't care anything about me. That she was still in town and apparently working for Containment, although I'm not certain if he knew that. And that's on top of learning he was a Sensitive, collected magical objects, and was dating Erida. And he didn't tell me about any of it."

"You've had a hard few weeks."

My sigh was half exhaustion, half laugh. "Yeah. Something like that."

Silence fell again, the only sound the creak of the swing as Liam pushed it back and forth, back and forth.

"Magic killed Gracie," Liam said. "Now I'm magic. I've had to deal with that, to accept it."

"You're just wrong."

He shook his head. "You don't get it, Claire. Your magic is different."

"Magic is magic. It isn't good or bad any more than that tree"—I pointed to a magnolia overtaking the postage stamp of a front yard—"is good or bad. It's entirely what we make of it."

The swing was perpendicular to the run of the porch, so we faced the side of the house next door, a cottage not unlike this one. He kept his gaze on that house, with its blue paint and rotting wood.

"You didn't inherit evil from Ezekiel," I quietly said. "That's not the way it works. And magic didn't kill Gracie. *Ignorance* did. Ignorance and fear that kept the wraiths who killed her from getting help when they'd needed it. Wraiths didn't cast a spell on her, and no spell was cast on them. They were victims of human ignorance just like she was, because we refused to let them control their magic. They were victims of the war, just like Gracie."

I nudged him with a shoulder. "Once upon a time, you introduced me to Moses so I'd understand that not all Paras were bad. I'd say that operates for humans, too."

"It's impolite to throw my words back at me."

"Yeah, it is."

We rocked in silence for a few more minutes. And when Liam put his hand over mine, I didn't pull away.

By the time we made it back to Moses's house, Darby had joined them, her utility vehicle parked in the narrow space between his house and the one next door.

Her ensemble—a red top and circle skirt with white polka dots—was a big contrast to her grim expression.

"We were waiting for you to get back," Malachi said kindly, then nodded at Darby.

She didn't waste any time. "They were definitely synthesizing something."

"Who was?" Gavin asked, obviously confused. I couldn't blame him.

"Whoever created the Icarus file. I was right about it being the plan, for lack of a better word, for the synthesis—the creation—of something biological."

Malachi's brows lifted. "What kind of something?"

"A virus."

"Oh, shit," Gavin said.

No details necessary to think a government department creating a virus was a bad thing. A very, very bad thing.

"What kind of virus?" Liam asked.

"Call it what you will," she said. "It's a completely *new* virus. A virus that was created in the lab from scratch. Thus, the term 'synthesized.' It's got elements of other viruses. Protein structures borrowed here, phage structures borrowed there, but the makeup, the totality, is completely new." She lifted her gaze to Malachi, and she looked absolutely bleak. "And the research isn't just theoretical."

The air seemed to leave the room completely.

"Vacherie," Malachi said.

She nodded. "I tested the vials." She pulled a folder from a vintage leather satchel on top of one of Moses's stacks, then took out a sheet of paper that showed two graphs.

She came toward us, pointed to the graph. "That's from the stub file—the bit we found on Containment-Net." Then she pointed to the graph on the right. "That's the test of the Vacherie Paranormals' blood."

The lines on the graphs were almost exactly the same.

"*Merde,*" Liam said as Gavin crossed himself.

"Icarus involves a virus," Malachi said. "A virus that sickens and kills Paranormals."

But not just Icarus, I thought as sickness overwhelmed me and the edges of my vision went dark. I reached out for the wall with a hand, let myself slide to the floor so I wouldn't keel over.

"Claire!" Darby said, and I heard her voice move closer. "What's wrong? Are you all right? Are you sick?"

"Tell her," I said, staring at the floor. "I can't—Just tell her."

"Claire's father told her that her mother was dead," Liam quietly said. "Turns out, she's not. She's the president of ADZ Logistics. She's part of Icarus."

Even Darby went pale. "Oh my God." She held up a hand. "Wait, just wait. Let's not panic. Just because she runs ADZ doesn't mean she was involved in this."

"She's involved. She's Laura Blackwell."

"What does she look like?"

I gave her the description.

"PCC Research," Darby said. "I remember seeing a woman like that at PCC Research, or before I left, anyway. She was very beautiful. A striking woman. She wasn't in my division, and we were very segmented, so I didn't know her. I just saw her around."

"What division?" Liam asked.

Darby's milk-white skin went somehow more pale. "Biologics."

My mother was alive.

My mother was a scientist.

My mother was a *murderer.*

"I need a really good Cajun swear," I said miserably.

"Start with *'fils de putain,'*" Gavin said. "Means 'son of a bitch.'"

I repeated it back to him, and only slightly mangled it.

"Not bad," he said. "We need to work on the accent, but that's not bad."

Liam slid to the floor beside me. He didn't touch me, probably could sense I wasn't ready for that. But the fact that he'd literally moved down to my level just to be supportive nearly wrecked me.

"How does the virus work?" Malachi asked. "How did it kill them?"

Darby stood up, looked at Malachi. "Given the symptoms you've described, I'm thinking it acts like a bacterial infection, triggers the crazy immune response—the septicemia or septic shock."

"How could Containment have infected them?" I asked, looking at Malachi. "You said they got boosters before they left Devil's Isle, right? Shouldn't that have protected them from illnesses, even this one?"

"Wait," Darby said, throwing out a hand. "What do you mean, 'boosters'?"

"Immunity-boosting injections," Malachi said, "given to the few Paranormals who got passes just before they left Devil's Isle."

"Maybe they weren't immunity boosters," Liam said darkly, then looked at Malachi. "Did all the Paras at Vacherie receive the injections?"

Malachi was quiet for a moment, but his expression seemed frozen with rage. "All but one. He was late to the clinic check-in and missed it."

"Is he sick?" Darby asked.

Malachi shook his head. "Not him. But all the others received the injections. And they're either sick or dead."

"It's a small sample," Darby said. "Too small to be certain, but awfully coincidental if the one guy who didn't get the injection also didn't get sick. Is anyone in Devil's Isle sick?"

"Not according to Lizzie," Liam said.

"If you want to hurt Paras, why inject only the ones who are leaving Devil's Isle?" Gavin asked. "You could do more damage administering injections to those staying behind."

"Because Devil's Isle is in the middle of New Orleans," Liam said. "It's surrounded by humans. And Containment doesn't want them sick."

"Where the Paras are in isolated areas," Malachi said, "there are only a few humans around."

"So maybe they're still testing it," Gavin said, "or very carefully deploying it."

Liam nodded. "You deploy first to Paras heading outside New Orleans until you confirm it's not contagious, that it won't spread to humans."

"Gunnar wouldn't have let this happen." They were the first words I'd said in a while, and they were twisting my stomach into knots. I looked pleadingly at Malachi. "He wouldn't have."

"She's right," Liam said. "Gunnar's a stand-up guy. He's part of Containment, but chain of command isn't as important to him as integrity. He wouldn't have authorized the intentional infection of

Paras, and certainly not their murder. And if he hadn't authorized it, but someone wanted to do it anyway, he'd have spread the word."

"Which means he probably didn't know about it," Gavin said. "So either Containment's not in it, or they're in it up to their eyeballs, but only a very few people have access."

"Containment's in it," Liam said. "The file was on their network. Containment guards were outside the building where Blackwell was working. The Caval brothers are involved, as is a Containment safe house."

"I'm stuck on the efficiency thing," Gavin said. "Why would any-one in Containment, or affiliated with Containment, do this? You want to take out Paranormals, take them out in Devil's Isle. Hell, they could have let Reveillon have the run of the place. Why even bother fighting back?"

"Because Reveillon killed Containment agents," Malachi said. "They wouldn't have just destroyed Devil's Isle and the Paras in it. They'd have completely seized power. That's different."

"Maybe," I said, "but if you destroy Paranormals, you destroy the reason for Containment's existence. No Paranormals, no federal money, no Devil's Isle."

Liam looked at Malachi. "Do you know how many received the injections?"

Malachi shook his head. "Not precisely. We understand there are approximately forty Paras with passes right now."

"Forty counts of murder," Moses said, his voice low and stained dark with anger.

"Forty-two if you count Broussard and Caval," Liam said. "Brous-sard found out about Icarus, about Caval."

"They killed Broussard because he found out too much," I said to Liam. "And they pinned his death on you because it made sense and bought them some time. Steered the investigation away from what Broussard had been looking into."

"Yeah," Liam said, "that sounds about right."

"We need to talk to Containment," Darby said. "Stop the vaccinations immediately."

"And how do we help those who have already been infected?" I asked.

"What about an antiviral?" Gavin asked, looking to Darby. "They've been developed for some viruses, haven't they?"

"Antivirals take luck and money—and, most important, time," Darby said. "We don't have any of those resources right now. And that plan assumes this particular virus would be susceptible to an antiviral. Not all viruses are."

"Maybe we'll get lucky," Gavin said. "You've got brains and a lab. It's worth looking into."

"I won't refuse to help," Darby said, "but you can't rely on that. You're going to have to do this the old-fashioned way—you're going to have to go to the source."

"We have to tell Gunnar the whole story," I said. "We have to warn him."

"Forty targets," Liam quietly said. "God willing we can save some of them."

Darby would pass the message to Gunnar, this time on the way back to her lab. We decided to meet in our old haunt, an old church in the Freret neighborhood. Gunnar hadn't been there before, but it was time to bring him into that particular circle, and we hadn't met at the church in weeks anyway. Gavin stayed with Moses. Malachi could come separately, as he always did.

I asked Moses for a small favor before we left, and he provided it without comment. Then we drove Scarlet to the church, simple and beautiful and largely abandoned.

Two short steps led to double doors in front. The walls were planks of white wood, the paint peeling, the words on the sign out front long since worn away, except for APOSTLES. Maybe that was the only word that mattered.

We parked around the corner and took the standard wait-and-watch approach before climbing out and walking to the front steps. The doors were unlocked but heavy. Liam pushed one open, and we slipped inside.

The church had a small foyer and a larger sanctuary, wooden from floor to vaulted ceiling. The quiet, the dark, the sameness of it made me feel a little better about everything. When it felt like everything was changing, the few places that had stayed the same were comforts.

I walked to the lectern at the front and put my palms flat on its surface, the wood smooth where other people had done the same thing throughout the church's history. I slid my hands to each side the way a preacher might have while looking over his congregation, pondering their burdens and sins, trying to figure out how best to reach them. A hundred years of wisdom and power worn like a stain into the wood. Maybe some of it would seep into my fingers; we needed all the help we could get.

"What an absolute horror show."

"It's not your fault," Liam said.

"She's my mother. My blood."

"And instead of making the kinds of decisions she makes, you're doing what you can to fix the world, not tear it down."

We heard a flutter of wings overhead, a soft *coo*. A mourning dove, its feathers a pale and shimmering gray, landed on one of the exposed wooden beams that held up the church's roof.

"I've always thought the sound of doves was creepy," Liam said as he looked up and studied the bird.

"Agreed. And very sad."

Without warning, the heavy oak doors began to rattle and shake, like they were being assaulted from the outside.

"Shit," Liam said, and pulled a gun from his pocket. It was smaller than the .44 he kept in his truck. Black and sleek, it looked like a Containment service weapon, for those who preferred guns over stunners.

I came around the lectern, stood beside him, body braced for a fight. "Containment shouldn't know where we are. Gunnar wouldn't tell."

The doors flew open, bodies silhouetted against the brilliant sunlight outside.

"*Whoa*," Gunnar said, his features clearing as he stepped into the room, keeping his body in front of the doorway to protect the rest of them from any violence we might accidentally do. "It's just us."

"Sorry," Liam said, putting the gun away. Malachi and Erida stepped inside behind Gunnar.

"Door got stuck," Gunnar said. "We figured we'd beaten you here, or we would have just knocked."

"They're coming for you," Malachi said.

"What do you mean?" Liam asked.

"Containment," Gunnar said. "They've increased the bounties on all of you."

"Because of what happened earlier?"

"Which was what?" Gunnar asked. "We were told to meet here, but didn't get details."

"What are you doing here?" Liam asked Erida, ignoring Gunnar's question. His tone was as sharp as his gaze. "You're supposed to be with Eleanor."

"I don't take orders from you," she said, tossing her dark hair over her shoulder. She wore leggings, knee-high boots, and a short-sleeved top, and looked ready for either military action or a polo competition. "And I wouldn't have come if Eleanor was not safe. She's with Roy, and she's safe. I'd stake my life on it."

"You have," Liam growled.

"Why do we need help?" Gunnar asked. "What's going on?"

"You found Caval?" Liam asked.

Gunnar's eyes went hard. "I did. Received a message from what was possibly the worst alias I've ever come across that Broussard's killer was an agent named Caval and telling me where to find him. Forensics found him, is testing the DNA." He looked at Liam. "I assume you found him like that?"

"We did. How we got there is involved, and we'll get to that. How long will the testing take?"

"Should have the results later today, tomorrow at the latest. If it's Broussard's blood, that will help put you in the clear. Would help more if we could explain the murder weapon."

"Let me lay it out for you," Liam said. "We believe the Paras who've been dying have been infected with a virus—the same virus found in the Icarus file Broussard located on Containment-Net. We think Containment, or an outfit connected to Containment and run by a scientist named Laura Blackwell, synthesized the virus. We think Containment administered it to Paras with passes via an 'immunity booster.' It's the reason the Paras at Vacherie got ill and the reason they're dead now. It's the reason Broussard is dead."

Gunnar just stared at him, and I saw the instant rejection in his eyes. The dismissal of the possibility that his organization was responsible for something like that. "You've got it wrong. There is no way in hell Containment would administer a virus to Paras or anyone else."

"We've got it right," Malachi said. "Blood samples verify." He offered Gunnar the papers Darby had printed.

"Three dead?" Gunnar frowned, ran a hand through his wavy hair as he looked down at the papers.

"So far," Liam said, "of the forty who received injections. They're all potential victims."

"There's no illness inside Devil's Isle," Gunnar said. "I'd know."

"The only Paras who received the injections, as far as we're aware, have passes," Liam said. "None have returned yet."

"I don't know anyone named Laura Blackwell," Gunnar said. "If she's part of this, whoever she is, she's not on our payroll."

"If she's not being paid by Containment, she's being paid by the PCC," Liam said. "Containment's in this, neck-deep." He glanced at me, hesitant to take that next step.

I might as well pony up. "And she's my mother."

Gunnar blinked, then stared. "She's your— But your mother is dead."

"No, she's very much alive and working at a place on Elysian called ADZ Logistics. She's my mother, was married to my father, left shortly after I was born because she wasn't interested in being a parent."

"Oh, Claire," Gunnar said. "I'm sorry. And what a dick move."

"No argument," I managed.

"The Icarus file that Broussard found was created at ADZ," Liam explained. "We went to surveil, and she was the first one to drive into the lot. Claire confronted her, and she called Containment on us."

"Darby discovered the file was a plan for the synthesis of a biologic," Malachi said. "Paras with passes have been getting ill, and she matched the virus that sickened them to that synthesis and the so-called immunity boosters."

"You have hard evidence the injections contain the virus?"

Malachi's gaze was hot. "We have her test results. Would you like to sample the injection and see?"

"I'm not doubting you. I wish I could doubt you. I want you to be wrong."

"But?" Liam asked.

"But I couldn't find anything about Icarus, so I asked an ally in the department. He laughed it off, said I had too much going on to worry about a pet project from someone in DC."

"Interesting," Liam said.

"Isn't it?" Gunnar looked at me, sympathy in his eyes. "I'd tell you that you shouldn't have confronted your mother. Except I'd have done exactly the same thing in your situation. Not that that does a lot of good."

I nodded. "Yeah. Not my wisest move. But it had to be done."

"I'm really sorry."

"So am I."

Gunnar looked at Liam. "And Broussard? Caval?"

Liam nodded. "Broussard was killed by Javier Caval. He and his brother, Lorenzo, were involved in a Containment project—some sort of black ops program that paid very, very well. And because fate is a twisted bitch, a mutual friend gave Lorenzo my knife—the one used to kill Broussard."

I took up the story. "We think it's possible he might have killed Javier; apparently they had a falling-out over the project. Lorenzo lives in the barracks on Canal, and that's all we've got on him."

"I knew the Caval brothers," Gunnar said. "Not well, but I knew of them. Some minor demerits for causing trouble, starting fights."

"Impulsive?" I asked, and Gunnar nodded.

"I'm not aware they're involved in anything unusual. But then again, I probably wouldn't be. That's for their division commanders. I need to get someone to the barracks," he said, almost to himself. "Pick Lorenzo up, see what he knows."

He considered that for a moment, then looked at Malachi. "I presume you're in communication with the Paras at Vacherie?"

He nodded. "The nomedic, as he's referred to, is still there, treating as he can."

"Good," Gunnar said, then ran a hand through his hair. "As soon as I leave here, I'll make arrangements for medics at the other facilities." He looked at Malachi. "And I'll make sure this isn't held against them for leave purposes. They worked too fucking hard for what little freedom they were granted."

"I agree, and I appreciate it."

Gunnar paced to one end of the church and back, his brows furrowed as he looked at the floor, worked through his mental steps. "I have to talk to the Commandant," he said when he reached us again. "About stopping the injections, about stopping the project, which is against so many laws and international treaties it would take me an hour to explain it."

"Not to mention fundamentally wrong." Malachi's voice was a low rumble of anger.

Malachi wasn't the only one pissed. "I'm not saying it's not wrong," Gunnar said. "I'm saying it's illegal. Inside my organization, that matters."

"When it suits you."

Gunnar took a step toward him. "We stood between the armies that came from your world to destroy ours. Are we perfect? No. Have we been doing the best we can to keep peace in this world? To salvage what we could? Yes."

"I will not stand over more dead bodies."

"Hey," I said, and stepped between them. "Both of you, back off. This situation royally sucks, and it can suck for multiple reasons at the same time. It's not a damn competition."

They stared at each other for another long minute before moving apart again.

"If strings are being pulled in DC, it's going to be tricky."

"He can't just sit on this," I said. "He can't not do anything."

"I didn't say he wouldn't act," Gunnar said. "But there's a chain of command. It's the military, and it's part of the game. If we want him to bypass that system, we're going to have to make a pretty damn convincing case. Well, *I* will. Because that's my job."

"Mentioning Eleanor's name might help get things moving in DC," Liam said, glancing at Gunnar. "She's connected enough, and she'd be on board. Use that however you need to."

"Appreciate it," Gunnar said, with an expression that backed up the words. "We're going to need all the help we can get."

CHAPTER EIGHTEEN

We waited at the church, biding our time, to learn what, if anything, the Commandant would or could do to stop the nightmare.

We sat on the floor where pews had once been. Malachi, Erida, Liam, me. Liam had pulled bottles of water from the priest hole under the floor, passed them around. We waited quietly, talking through what we knew of the project and what we didn't yet know.

I heard the rumbling first, the sound of a thundering engine a few blocks away. Then garbled words filled the air.

"What is that?" Erida asked. We rose and moved into the foyer, peered through the stained glass to look outside.

It was a Containment vehicle, a heavy-duty truck with its bed covered by canvas. A troop carrier, probably. A man stood in the back of the truck, megaphone in hand.

"Attention! Containment has issued bounties for Liam Quinn, Claire Connolly, Gavin Quinn. If you have information regarding these individuals, please communicate with a Containment agent or your block captain. Attention, Containment has issued . . ."

The truck rumbled on, its passengers oblivious to the fact that it had just driven past two of the three fugitives they wanted most of all.

"Someone is running scared," Malachi said, glancing back at us. "They aren't insulated enough—or the project isn't far enough along— that they believe they're immune from setbacks. They're afraid you'll stop them."

"Good," I said. "Because we will."

We just had to stay free long enough to do it.

What he didn't say, of course, was that that concern might also cause Laura Blackwell and Lorenzo Caval to go crazy. To hurt more people.

It took three hours for the door to shake and be pushed open again. Gunnar came in, and once again, he wasn't alone.

A woman stepped in behind him. A beautiful woman. Pale skin and long, dark hair pulled into a high knot. Her eyes were a glassy blue that edged toward green, her nose thin and straight, her lips lush. She was tall and lean, wore jeans and a Tulane T-shirt with the kind of self-assurance that told me she could wear a uniform or a cock-tail dress with the same confidence.

"This is Rachel Lewis. She's a colleague, and she's trustworthy," Gunnar said, the word spoken like a kind of promise. Which was good, because everyone looked at her with obvious suspicion.

Probably sensing that, she met each of our eyes in turn, checking, appraising, and promising she wasn't an enemy. And then her gaze— liquid and intense—fell on Malachi, and she went absolutely still.

I glanced at him, found the same intensity on his face, except that it was marked with temper. Usually cool, calm, and collected, Mala-chi now looked ruffled, on alert, by the slender woman who stood in front of him.

"Captain," he said, biting off the word like it had left a bitter taste in his mouth.

"General," she said. If her emotions were roiling like Malachi's seemed to be, she was doing a much better job of hiding it. And wasn't that interesting? Had we finally met someone who challenged his remarkable control?

"You're acquainted?" Gunnar asked.

"During the war," she said, without taking her eyes off Malachi. I could understand that, too. He was a very intense eyeful. "There was a unit of human and Para soldiers who assisted with the closing of the Veil."

"Black ops," Gunnar put in, and she nodded.

"But we haven't seen each other since." Even with her pretty Southern accent, her words were clipped.

"No," Malachi said, and there was nothing pleasant in his tone now. "We haven't."

"Well," Gunnar muttered, "let's sidestep whatever this is and get down to business. The Commandant is very concerned about what we've found. Rachel is the Commandant's operations director, and she's on loan to us for the time being."

"I take it the Commandant believes us?" Liam asked.

"There's no documentation that confirms Icarus is a project of Containment in New Orleans."

"No *official* documentation," Liam said, and Gunnar nodded.

"Exactly. But Containment resources are clearly being used," Gunnar said. "You've found ample evidence of that."

"How do you reconcile that financially?" I asked.

"The orders came down from on high," Gunnar said. "Long story short, Icarus began as a joint project of the Senate's Armed Services Committee and the FBI. It was initiated after the Veil was identified, before the war. A countermeasure in case something came through."

"Preventive genocide?" Malachi asked.

"I'd definitely call it a biological weapon," Gunnar said. "Beyond that, we're assuming facts they didn't know. There was only the unknown, a lot of fear, and a desire to protect the public, for better or worse.

"The plans didn't get very far," he continued. "There were vague ideas about synthesizing something with biological stopping power, but since they didn't know anything about what was living in the Beyond—or specifically about Paranormal anatomy—they didn't move past the idea stage. When the war started, the project was put on hold, and the materiel, money, and personnel shifted to conventional weapons."

"Like cold iron," I said.

"Like cold iron," Gunnar agreed. "Laura Blackwell was on the synthesis team, but she lost her job when funding was cut off. And that was the end of Icarus. Or it was supposed to be."

"And then what?" Liam asked.

"The war kept going. Tens of thousands dead, property destroyed. The more reasonable politicians realized that developing a virus to infect an entire world was pretty fucking unethical. But not everyone was reasonable."

"Fear makes people . . . well, people," Liam said.

"It does," Gunnar agreed, his face hard.

The plan was obviously unethical, but it was understandable in wartime, when humans had been concerned for their very existence. I'd seen the army that still waited on the other side of the Veil. Those soldiers weren't overly concerned about our genocide; it was their primary motivation.

On the other hand, biological agents weren't choosy. They would kill soldiers and civilians both, the guilty and the innocent. However horrible war was, it wasn't supposed to be that bad.

"The unreasonable politicians?" I prompted.

"They restarted Icarus. Created ADZ Logistics as a shell company and funneled money through the PCC directly to that entity."

"And Laura Blackwell was back in the lab," I said.

Gunnar nodded ruefully. "That's what it looks like."

"What's next?" Malachi asked.

"A lot of work on a lot of levels," Gunnar said. "Big picture—the Commandant is communicating with several members of the Senate's Oversight Committee, requesting a review of Icarus.

"As for Broussard," he continued, looking at Liam, "the blood on Caval's hands was verified as Broussard's, and the writing on the wall at Broussard's house included one of Caval's fingerprints."

"Lorenzo?" I asked.

Gunnar shook his head. "AWOL. Cleaned out his bunk. No obvious link to Icarus left behind. His sheets, pillow were still there, and they will be tested. But it doesn't matter for now. There's ample evidence Liam is innocent, and the Commandant has demanded the charges be dropped immediately. He can't rescind the bounty because of the magic Liam used at Broussard's house, because there were witnesses, and the Magic Act is still in place. But the murder charges are off the table."

I reached out, squeezed Liam's hand. "Good," I said. "That's something, anyway."

Gunnar nodded. "One step at a time." He glanced at Rachel, gave her the go-ahead to continue.

"We're working on warrants right now," she said. "As soon as the lawyers do their jobs, we'll go to ADZ Logistics, where a group of Containment agents and a team from the CDC will inspect the premises and seize any remaining biologicals."

"You need warrants to inspect a Containment site?" Liam asked.

"No," Rachel said. "But it's not technically a Containment site. It's privately owned, as far as all official records show."

"It's off the books," Liam said.

"It is," Rachel acknowledged with a nod.

"As we discussed earlier," Gunnar said, "we've sent additional physicians to work sites. Leave has been temporarily halted until we're sure it's safe."

"So you'll punish Paranormals?" Malachi accused.

"We'll keep them inside Devil's Isle," Rachel said. "For better or worse, it is the most secure and safest facility we can provide for them at this time. There are also no instances of illness inside Devil's Isle, which Lizzie has confirmed. You're welcome to confirm that with her directly, if you can."

There was a challenge in her voice. Captain Lewis was good.

"If this is being directed at the higher levels," Liam said, "the Commandant will take heat."

"He is aware of that," she said. "But as long as Devil's Isle remains under his command, he'll act accordingly."

"We'll help however we can," I said.

Rachel gave Malachi a quick glance before looking at her watch. "I'd like to get back so we can go over the op."

"Sure," Gunnar said. "Sure." He looked around the church. "You all good for tonight?"

"We're fine," Liam said. "We'll meet back here in the morning?"

"Let's make it Moses's house," I said. "He gets testy when he's not included."

"Can't argue with that," Liam said. "Dawn, then."

Arrangements were made, and Gunnar and Rachel left.

"I need to make some contacts," Malachi said. "I'll see you in the morning."

"I've also got something I need to take care of," Liam said, then glanced at me. "You can get back okay?"

I nodded.

"Then I'll see you."

The promise, however vague, was enough to have a blush rising in my cheeks. He'd spoken those words to me, for me, and my body eagerly responded.

Since we were preparing to face the music all the way around, I approached Erida, the only one who hadn't yet arranged her getaway.

"Can I talk to you before you leave?"

If the request made her suspicious, she didn't show it. But then, her poker face was nearly as good as Malachi's. "All right."

"Maybe outside?"

Her brows lifted, but she nodded, followed me through the back of the church and outside again. The sun was setting, the sky streaked with orange and purple.

I walked a few feet away, giving myself time to prepare, then turned back to her. "I know you and my father were lovers. Is that why you hate me?"

Her body jerked at the question. It didn't bother me that I'd shocked her.

"I don't hate you, Claire. I don't even really know you."

Given what I'd seen lately, I didn't think knowing someone was a requirement for hating them. So I stayed quiet.

"If you mean," she went on, her voice softer, "do I hate you because you are your mother's daughter . . ." She paused, seemed to gather her thoughts. "I didn't know your mother well. I only knew what he told me, that she had broken your father's heart."

"He told me she was dead."

"You mentioned that," she said. If she'd judged my father for the lie, it didn't show in her face.

"And now I know she isn't. You'd know that now, too."

She inclined her head. "Malachi told me."

"I thought my father and I had this nice simple life. Antiques and MREs. That my mother had died, but we survived together." I looked at her. "But that's not true. She was still alive. He had magic, and he had you." I paused. "Why didn't he tell me?"

As if to give herself time, Erida went over to the wisteria that climbed over the church's back wall, ran her finger across a cluster of lavender flowers. Then she turned back. "I don't know. I thought he had, and that you simply didn't want to be near a woman you saw as a poor replacement for your mother."

"He told you that?"

"No," she said, with a soft smile. "I thought perhaps he sought to soothe my feelings. I imagine he wanted to keep you safe in the way he knew how—by keeping you away from magic and keeping magic away from you."

The same protective instinct that had driven Liam into the bayou.

"He loved you, Claire, and he wanted to build a wall around you to keep you safe. So he compartmentalized his life."

"You shielded Royal Mercantile from the magic monitors." It was a guess, but I was pretty sure I was right.

She nodded. "He was concerned he might use his magic without thinking, trigger the alarms, and bring Containment. He didn't want you left alone if he got dragged into Devil's Isle."

But I ended up in Devil's Isle anyway. Not dragged, but there because I'd used my magic, triggered Containment, and had to ask Moses to erase the evidence.

"He had such plans for you and the store, for life when things got back to normal. He was working on a second location for the store— an old Apollo gas station in Carrolton."

So he'd told her about the gas station, or at least part of it. "You don't know if he finished it?" I tried to keep my voice neutral, but it was hard.

Grief was clear in her eyes. "I don't know. I shielded it while he was restoring it, but I had to leave New Orleans. Fighting in Shreveport was getting heavier, and I was needed. I was gone for two months . . . and he was gone by the time I got back."

"I'm sorry."

"I know you lost him. But I lost him, too."

I nodded.

"I haven't been to the building since he died. It's been so long, I'm not even sure I could find it again."

We'd both lost my father. Maybe it was time to find something new.

"I know where it is," I said. "He finished it. Maybe I can show it to you sometime."

She looked at me for a long time, a dozen emotions swirling across her face. "I'd like that," she finally said, the deal between us done, and maybe something forged.

I drove Scarlet back to the gas station, parked her in a narrow slot in the alley behind it, covered her with a couple of tarps I found in a nearby garage. They'd keep her safe for now, or at least make her appear uninteresting to casual observers.

It was ironic that I couldn't park my newly adopted car in the gas station I lived in, but none of the garage doors were operable. They'd all been closed and sealed to keep the temperature and humidity consistent. So until I came up with a better plan, it was the alley for her.

I came around the block, waited halfheartedly for a bit to ensure that all was clear, and then stared.

The Snoball sign I'd found in Moses's butter house—and walked away from—was propped beside the gas station door. The grime had been cleared away so the metal gleamed, the letters brilliant and enticing.

I walked toward it, knelt, and ran a finger down the raised ridges of each letter. Memories of another time, as if swollen by the history they contained.

The air changed, shifted, raising the hair at the back of my neck. Slowly, I rose to my feet and glanced behind me.

Liam stood fifteen feet away, hands at his sides, longing laid bare on his face. His eyes shimmered—blue, then gold, then blue, his brows drawn together with an intensity that reminded me of a warrior, of a wolf. Of a man on a mission.

Lust rose so hot, so bright, it might have been a forming star.

"You looked like you wanted that. Back at the house near Moses's, I mean."

I nodded, and felt like gossamer glass, fragile and ready to break. It took two tries to get out "Thank you. It will look good in there."

Liam nodded.

"I'm sorry," he said, and I could see the truth of it in his eyes. "I'm so sorry I left you alone."

I ran to him, and he welcomed me with strong arms.

"I'm sorry," he said into my hair. "I'm so sorry. I thought I was doing the right thing."

In his arms, I broke, shattered into a million pieces. "You left us."

"I know. And I'm so sorry."

"I didn't know my mother. She left. The war came, and my friends left. My teachers left. My father died. He left." I looked at him, let him see the truth in my eyes. And when he realized it, regret settled into his face. "The battle came, and you left. You left when we needed each other most."

"I thought I was saving us, shielding you. Instead, I put myself far away from the one person who makes me stronger. Because we're stronger together." He tipped my chin up. "I love you, Claire. Maybe it's too soon for that; maybe it's too late. I don't even care if you say it back. I love you. And I will never leave you again."

I lifted my head, searched for his mouth. He met my lips softly, careful but hopeful. His fingers slid into my hair as he moved closer, melding the long line of his body with mine.

I felt my body warming, loosening, relaxing for the first time in weeks, melting in the heat of his arms.

The rain fell suddenly, the sky letting go just as we had, and soaked us to the bone immediately.

He pulled back, pushed wet hair from my face. "We should probably get inside. If you're okay with that."

"I demand it," I said with an answering grin.

Before I could argue, and probably because he knew I would, he picked me up, carried me to the door.

I unlocked it and flipped on the lights, but Liam switched them off again.

"Don't need lights," he murmured, shutting the door and leaving us in darkness. The room was pitch-black, and there was a moment of exquisite anticipation before he found my mouth again and steered me backward until my hips hit the lip of a table.

He hoisted me onto it, pulled me hard against his body while rain pelted the roof like a corps of drummers. His mouth pummeled mine, assaulted and possessed it. He kissed me like a man long denied, like a man returning from war.

And maybe that wasn't far from the truth.

I dug my fingers into his hair and wrapped my legs around his waist, nearly moaned from the feel of him, hard and ready, at my core.

Our kisses became brutal, full of heat and anger and promise. I pulled back, yanked at the hem of his shirt, slid my hands against the bunched muscles of his abdomen. His body was strong, lean muscle honed from hard and honest work.

He pulled the T-shirt over his head and I let my hands roam against skin still damp from the downpour, every inch of skin and muscle taut.

"Your body . . . is a wonderland," I said, when I couldn't think of any other way to finish that sentence.

Liam snorted, pulled my shirt over my head, found my breasts with his hands. I arched forward into his fingers as fire erupted under my skin, fire that only he could control.

Then even that bit of lace was gone, and we were down to rain-sodden jeans. I caught my lip between my teeth, smiled at him as I reached for the snap of his jeans.

"Are you sure—?"

I cut off his question with a kiss. "I need you," I murmured against his lips. "I've needed you for a long time. I just didn't know it until we met. And then I told myself I didn't. And then you came back."

"And I'm not leaving again."

"You may have mentioned that."

Then the rest of his clothes were heaped on the floor, and he was hot and heavy in my hand, his arms braced on the table as he dropped his forehead to mine, struggled to breathe. He reached back, pushed artifacts carefully but decisively away, and pressed me into the table-top. Then his hand was at my core, inciting.

"Now," I said, and his hands were at my jeans, and then I was bared to him, too.

He was already hard, his body primed and ready. "Now," he agreed. He thrust, locked our bodies together. He paused, his body shaking with desire, arms corded as he sought to gain control.

"Claire," he muttered, his breath heavy at my temple.

"Don't stop now," I said, and wrapped my arms around his neck as he climbed onto the table above me, his gorgeous face above mine, one hand behind my head to cushion it, as his hips worked.

"Never," he said, and pressed his mouth to mine, found my center again, and sent us both over the edge.

CHAPTER NINETEEN

I woke with a mission. It was stupid, and it was dangerous, but there was a fire in my belly, enough curiosity to kill a very fat cat, and enough anger to get me up and moving before the sun rose.

And before Liam climbed out of my bed, where he still lay, one hand thrown over his head, the other on his abdomen.

I ate half an energy bar that was somewhere between hardtack and cardboard, chasing it down with a bottle of water.

I hid my hair beneath a cap, pulled on a tank top, capri leggings, and tennis shoes. I'd stay cool in the humidity that already fogged across the city, and in case I was noticed, I'd look like a jogger. At least at first glance. And if nobody questioned whether there were many joggers in postwar New Orleans.

She didn't live far away, according to the information Moses had waiting on a note on his front porch, tucked between the screen door and the main door. That had been the favor I'd asked of him yesterday.

We needed to find out where Laura Blackwell might strike, where she might try to deploy her particular weapon. Maybe, if I watched her, I'd find some clue. I wasn't sure what that might be—a giant photograph of a spot where the Veil crossed, a printed set of Google directions accidentally discarded in her yard? I'd know it when I saw it; the point was the looking.

But that's not why I was doing it. That was just the collateral benefit.

I wanted to know who this woman was. And maybe, in the tiniest hidden recess of my heart, in the Corner of Lost Causes, I wanted to be proven wrong.

She lived near Tulane in the Audubon neighborhood, one of the fancier areas of New Orleans. It was too far to walk, but I didn't want to chance getting caught and having to dump Scarlet. So I left her at home, safe and covered, and rode my bike downtown.

I came within a block of her address, stopped, and stared.

Where there'd once been a grid of streets with small cottages, camelbacks, and shotguns, a tall brick wall towered. The bricks were clean and ran in perfectly aligned rows down the wall, which bowed prettily until it curved around away from me. I got off the bike, locked it to a tree, and walked toward the gate.

There was a pretty cottage-style gatehouse in the middle of the divided avenue that led inside. The cottage house was dark, and the gate was open. I wasn't sure if I'd happened to visit when there wasn't a guard, or if the gatehouse was just for show, because there weren't enough people left in New Orleans to cause concern.

I made my decision and crept closer.

I stayed close to the wall, walked inside.

The houses were brick with tile roofs. All of them new, all of them immaculate. The roads were no longer grids, but sweeping avenues that curved around landscaped lawns and sidewalks marked by trees and wrought-iron benches.

They'd torn down the houses that had been here before and constructed an entirely new neighborhood. One that was gated and walled from the need around it. It was Devil's Isle in reverse—the renovation of a neighborhood with a wall to keep unmentionables out.

The sun was beginning to color the sky as I followed the main road around. The houses weren't just new; they were enormous. Two stories, lots of dormers, two- or three-car garages, huge windows with pretty mullions.

This was a beautiful neighborhood. Before the war, it would have fit well in a suburb for the wealthy who commuted into the city for work every day. But to be here? Now? The only big business in New Orleans was Devil's Isle, and Devil's Isle was run by the PCC—Containment, specifically. Maybe the PCC had set up the neighborhood for the Containment bigwigs. Maybe the Commandant lived here, in one of these set-back houses with the cobblestone sidewalks and hanging ferns.

A street sign atop a fluted black pole—gas lamp mounted on top—told me I'd reached the place I wanted: Hidden Ridge Circle.

I wrapped my fingers around the pole, the painted metal cool beneath my hand, and tried to catch my breath. I hadn't been running, but being close to her again made my lungs feel like they'd been belted, tightly wrapped and very constricted.

I could walk away now. She'd almost certainly call Containment again if she saw me, and it would be hard to hide among these sweeping lawns, especially when my only way out was the narrow gap in the wall.

But I had to look. My feet were already carrying me forward, bearing me to the end of the dead-end circle where my mother lived.

It was a story and a half high, with a small brick porch. The windows were bare, the house lit even in the early hours of the morning.

I adjusted my cap, rolled my shoulders, and began walking like I belonged there.

And then I was there, standing in front of the house.

In front of my mother's house.

There wasn't a single item of decoration outside except for the number on the house. No chairs on the porch, no flowers in urns by the door, no extraneous plants in the landscape. Just the solid brick house in a corner of a gated neighborhood of fraternally similar houses.

I bent down to tie my shoe, glanced to the side to look in the front window. It was probably supposed to be a dining room, but the room was empty except for the wrought-iron chandelier that hung low in the middle of the ceiling, waiting for a table to be slid into place beneath it.

I could see the edges of a kitchen beyond, but nothing else.

I stood up, stretched, took a look at the yard. It sloped gently to the back, a hill created where there hadn't been one before; this part of New Orleans had been as flat as the rest of it. If I wanted another look inside, I'd have to get closer.

I walked around to the back of the house, where a live oak's branches skimmed over the lawn. Since the tree was dozens of years older than the houses, they must have managed to build around it.

There was a wooden deck at the back. Light blazed through windows above it. I crept beneath the wooden slats across a bed of mulch, then around to the stairs—the only way I'd be able to get high enough to see. I took a testing step, putting my weight on one tread to ensure it was quiet, before moving to the next.

The window came into view halfway up the stairs. I peeked inside, was immediately faced by disappointment when I didn't see her in the eat-in kitchen. I took the opportunity to study it.

There were no knickknacks, no art, no kitsch in the kitchen. No canisters or napkin holders or towels or bottles. Just empty granite countertops and tall cherry cabinets. The kitchen table was the same shade, but there were no place mats, no centerpiece. A family room flanked the kitchen on the other side. I could see a couch, a coffee table, and nothing else. No pictures, no television.

The emptiness had to be something she'd chosen; if she could get the house, she could get the stuff to put in it.

She walked in. Tall and slender, long red hair falling over her shoulders. She was a lovely woman; in other circumstances, I might have said that I'd have been happy to look like her when I grew up. Now? Not so much.

She wore a belted robe of pale turquoise that draped silkily to the floor. She opened an enormous glass-doored refrigerator, pulled out a plate of food, and moved it to the table. Leftovers for breakfast, or something she'd already prepared?

She sat down at the kitchen table, where she'd already placed a napkin, fork, and small cup of orange juice. A laptop was closed in front of her, and a manila folder lay to her right. Her feet, which were bare, were flat on the floor as she put the napkin in her lap, opened the folder, and began to eat.

And that was it. She read and ate methodically. She certainly didn't look sad or deprived. She just looked . . . focused.

This wasn't the kind of life I'd said I wanted. And yet it was exactly the kind of life I had. Except that I lived alone by circumstance. Not by design.

My mother. Living alone in her mansion, in a neighborhood of mansions, in a city still broken and stained by war. A woman who'd married and borne a child and then left. A woman who'd created a killer no one could see coming.

Feeling suddenly ill, I crept down the stairs, waited at the bottom with a hand on the railing until my breathing slowed to normal levels.

Whoever she was, I was still me. I was still Claire. And that was fine. That was enough.

I'd just keep saying that until it felt true.

I walked toward the front yard, stopped when I saw a truck newly parked in the driveway.

It was the same yellow truck we'd seen in the loading dock at Devil's Isle, with the same streak of red paint across the front panel. A man climbed out of the back with a clipboard. He strode quickly to the front door, rang the bell, waited for Laura to open it.

She did so without smile or "hello," without even meeting his gaze. She reached for the clipboard, signed, and looked at him expectantly.

The driver opened the back of the truck—and pulled out what looked like the same neon orange box loaded at the Devil's Isle dock. It was no less bright today, and in the morning light I could see dark numbers stenciled along one side.

My mother opened the door for him, let him take the crate into her house. Then she closed the door in his face.

He gave the door a dour look before jogging back to the truck and speeding away.

So what did my mother have from Devil's Isle, and why? What could Devil's Isle have to offer her?

"You looking for something?"

I turned quickly, found the neighbor on his front porch, small dog tucked under his arm like a football. My heart stopped, then thudded hard twice before starting up again.

I didn't know how much he'd seen. So I decided to pretend there'd been nothing to see at all. I offered a nervous laugh, and didn't have to fake the nerves.

"Shin splint," I said, pointing to my lower leg. "Just trying to walk it off. I was hoping the break would help me loosen it up. Running on concrete just *kills* me." I gestured to the truck with a smile.

"And then I got a little nosy. Not often you see a delivery truck like that around here!"

"Sure," he said, and didn't sound at all convinced.

"Anyway, I better get going. Have a good one!"

I jogged out of the neighborhood, found my bike, and raced home.

I walked into the gas station, expecting darkness and silence and safety.

Expecting him to be gone.

I hadn't expected much of Liam Quinn. Wasn't that always my mistake? My prejudice?

He wore jeans and a T-shirt, his feet bare. He stood in front of one of the tables, palms braced on the tabletop as he stared down at an open book.

There was something so right about his standing there, about his bare feet and intense expression. Like he was a warrior poet, a scholarly knight.

He looked up when I walked in, his body instantly on alert. And he didn't relax much when he realized it was me. He didn't ask me where I'd been. Could probably see I was flustered. Might have been able to see the grief in my eyes. But he didn't ask about it. Not yet.

For my part, I had absolutely no idea what to say or do.

He filled in the blank. "It's your place. But I'm staying until you kick me out. And if you try to kick me out, I might not go."

I closed and locked the door. "All right."

"How do you feel about that?"

"I have no idea."

He watched me for a moment. "Fair enough."

Hope was like an ember in my belly. Small and hot and greedy. But that wasn't thinking. It wasn't even feeling. It was anticipation, and anticipation wouldn't get me through this moment. Whatever this moment was. So I ignored it, focused on what was.

I walked toward him, and it took a couple of tries to get words out. "What are you reading?"

"I'm not entirely sure." He showed me the cover. It was a big book with leather binding, the paper inside thin enough to see through. The pages were covered in minuscule calligraphy in a language that didn't look even remotely familiar.

"A spellbook?" I asked.

"Do Paras need spellbooks?"

"I have no idea. That would be a good question for Malachi."

Liam nodded, closed the book. "For all we know, could be recipes. Or a romance novel."

"Love in the Beyond?"

"Something like that. I assume it happens."

"Did you see the tension between Malachi and Rachel? That was pretty interesting."

"I'd rather not think about Malachi at the moment."

His body brushed against mine, and lust bolted through me, leaving me nearly breathless. If this was going to be our relationship, if I was going to get weak in the knees every time our paths crossed, I was in trouble.

His lips were on my ear, growling and nipping, sending shivers down my body. "I can't stop thinking about you."

He was doing a pretty damn good job of making me think about him, too. "We have problems to deal with."

"Like?"

"A biomedical conspiracy?"

"Oh. That." He turned our bodies, pinning me back against the table, his thigh between mine. And then his lips crushed against mine, his body hot and hard and ready, his mouth eager.

"I want you again," he murmured. "I have a lot of making up to do. And if we can't have pleasure, if we can't live, what are we fighting for?"

I couldn't find a single reason to argue with him.

"You want to tell me where you were this morning?" he asked, when we were walking to Moses's house.

"You won't like it."

His jaw tightened. "Try me," he said after a minute, in a tone that confirmed to me he wouldn't like it.

"I went to see my mother."

I'd been right. His jaw twitched, and every other muscle in his body tensed as well.

"At her house," I added.

"How did you—? Moses," he said, answering his own question. "You got her address from Moses."

"He did me a favor."

"That was . . . reckless," he finally said.

"You did know that about me." He'd called me that plenty of times. While he didn't like worrying, I was pretty sure he was turned off by cowardice and turned on by whatever category of bravery "reckless" fell into.

"I'd hoped it had worn off."

"You hoped, in the time I've been living alone in a gas station full of illegal magical objects, while being hunted by Containment and hanging out with illegal magical people, that I'd become less reckless?"

He was silent for a moment. "Good point. And what did you find?" His voice had softened with something that sounded like pity, and made me want to curl up in an uncomfortable ball.

"I found her. Sitting at a table, eating her breakfast. She was alone in an enormous house—not even a picture on the wall—everything just so. Just the way she liked it."

He reached out, took my hand, squeezed it.

"There's no room for me in her life. Maybe never was. Maybe not my father, either."

"That matches what she told you at the building."

"I know. Maybe I thought she was lying. Or maybe I just wanted to see for myself. Who she is, why she's done what she's done. Maybe I thought that if I saw her, I'd understand better. She's my *mother*. If that's the extent of her life, it's sad, at least to me. But I don't know if that's the extent of it. I don't know any more about her than she does about me."

"Do you want to know more?"

"I don't know. I didn't expect to walk into a fairy tale. But I didn't expect to pity her, either. I didn't go just for my own benefit," I said, changing the subject. "I wondered if I'd see anything that was useful. And I might have found something."

"Reckless," he said again as we reached Moses's house. "And what did you find?"

I nearly answered, but caught a whiff of something in the air. Something delicious.

I glanced back at the road. Darby's utility vehicle was parked at the curb. "Breakfast," I said. "I found breakfast."

Technically, it was second breakfast. But I'd earned it with the morning's exercise. And it looked to be worth it.

Darby stood in the middle of the room in a pale green dress with a nipped-in waist, her dark hair gleaming. And she held a silver tray of chocolate chip cookies. Real chocolate chip cookies. Not freeze-dried. Not dairy- and gluten-free. Not rehydrated.

Cookies.

"How do you do this in a war zone?" I asked her, gesturing to the ensemble.

"Practice and denial," she said with a grin. "And we're working on a little something in the lab that keeps the power on."

"If there's going to be food every time I come over here," Gavin said, a cookie in each hand, "I'm coming over here more often." He looked us over. "Coincidence, you two arriving at the same time."

Liam didn't take the bait, but stared his brother down.

"About damn time," Gavin muttered, taking another bite. "But don't mind me."

Liam took two cookies, handed me one. "Thank you, Darby."

"You're welcome."

She offered the tray to Moses, but his lip curled. "Gross."

Malachi took one, tried a careful nibble. His eyes lit up like a kid's on Christmas. No words, just another careful bite. And then another. I wasn't sure he cared much for human food; Darby's cookies might have changed his mind. And for good reason—they were delicious.

"Damn," Liam said, taking a bite. "These are amazing."

"You'd be surprised what lab equipment can do."

Liam swallowed hard.

"I'm kidding. *Kidding.*" She put the tray on a pile of electronics. "What's the latest?"

"Gunnar not here yet?"

"He isn't," Gavin said as he and Malachi both reached for another cookie.

"Don't ruin your dinner," Liam told him, which advice Gavin completely ignored.

"I think I saw something this morning," I said, and told them about my visit to see Laura Blackwell. I'd decided to call her that. It was the best way I could think of to cope with it.

"On my way out, a truck pulled up." I looked at Liam. "Remember that big yellow truck we saw at the loading dock? The one with the paint on the front panel?"

"I don't remember the paint, but yeah."

"Same truck pulled into her driveway. And the driver gave her something he'd loaded out on Devil's Isle."

"What was it?" Gavin asked. He'd stopped eating his cookie.

"I don't know. Didn't see what it was. Only the box. Blinding neon orange." I estimated the dimensions with hand gestures. "Had stenciled numbers on one side."

Darby bobbled on her heels, took a stumbling step backward before "Oh, shit," she said. "Oh, shit."

Gavin caught her by the elbow, steadied her again. "What's wrong?"

"The numbers stenciled on the sides—were they 'three-oh-five'?"

A wave of sickness roiled my stomach. "Yes. Why?"

Gavin led her to the couch. "Sit down. Take a breath." He looked back at Moses. "Bottled water?"

"Kitchen," Moses said. "I'll get it." He hopped down, disappeared into the kitchen, and we all looked back at Darby.

"Darby," Malachi prompted, "what's in the box?"

"I can't be sure, but . . ." She trailed off, rubbing a finger over her lips as she stared into the middle distance, preparing herself for something.

"In the early years, like Gunnar was saying, the PCC was trying to learn about the Veil. Where it came from, what it was made of, what it could do. When I joined PCC Research, we were young and curious and stupidly excited to have discovered this thing. One of our tasks was figuring out a way to look through it. Some kind of device that could let us see what was happening on the other side."

"A periscope," Liam suggested.

"A porthole through the portal," Darby said with a rueful smile. "That's what we called it, and thought we were pretty clever."

Moses came back, offered her the bottle of water. Darby took it with a smile of thanks, but didn't twist the lid.

"We futzed around for a little while, played with optics and lenses, tried to stick them through the Veil. At first, we couldn't manage it because the Veil's not a tangible thing. It's energy—a passageway made of energy. A doorway from our world to theirs. Then we got this idea."

She took a moment to gather herself, while the rest of us waited, completely silent. "We decided we could use harmonics to disrupt the energy in a tiny portion of the Veil and make a little window." She mimed pushing curtains aside. "We created this awkward little machine—the decharger—and got it to work once."

"What did you see?" I asked, thinking of the battalions of warriors I'd seen.

Darby smiled. "Nothing but rolling hills. Which is one of the reasons we were so damn surprised when the war actually started. Hindsight."

Several of us grunted in agreement.

"Anyway, the Veil was breached right after that, so it wasn't necessary anymore. And then I was fired, and that was the end of my work on the decharger."

"The decharger was in the orange box," I said.

She nodded. "Yeah, but I haven't heard anything about it in a really long time."

"Someone heard about it," I said. "Laura, maybe because she was at the PCC before."

"Claire and Liam first saw it being moved out of Devil's Isle," Gavin said. "Why would a PCC Research implement be stored there?"

"There were buildings in the Marigny used for Containment

storage before it became the prison," Darby said. "It was probably in one of those. But what would she want it for?"

"If it was working," Malachi asked, "could it be used to slip something into the Beyond? Through the window?"

"Like what?" Darby asked, but then her expression fell, and the room went absolutely silent.

"Like a virus," Liam said.

"You use the decharger to open the Veil," I said, "and you use the virus you've already created and, what, just toss it in?" I looked at Darby.

"Aerosol," she said, misery clear in every line of her face. "She'd need an aerosolized version of the virus for actual deployment through the Veil."

Gavin reached out to squeeze Darby's shoulder supportively. She put her hand over his, tried for a weak smile.

"How much product would she need to pull this off?" he asked. "Does she have enough to do real damage?"

"The size of a virus is measured in nanometers," Darby said. "Tiny. You can fit a lot of them into a small space. In 1979, a missing filter at an anthrax plant in the Soviet Union killed a hundred people in a few hours. That was an *accidental* release."

"Presumably she wouldn't have wanted the decharger unless she had something to deploy," Gavin said.

"So she's got a virus, and she's got a way to sneak it into the Beyond," I summarized. "But we don't know how much she's got, or how many Paras she could kill."

"Say that Cajun swear again," Moses requested.

"Fils de putain." This time, the Quinn boys said it together.

"No," Darby said, and walked across the room, kicked at the wall with a heel, then looked back at us. "The PCC wouldn't do this. We aren't at war. There'd be no reason for it."

"Maybe they don't know."

She looked back at me. "What do you mean?"

"Gunnar said the PCC is funding the research," I said. "That doesn't mean they want to deploy it this way, for genocide."

"That would mean it's Blackwell's doing." Liam's voice was somber, and he reached out, squeezed my hand, offered the same kind of support Gavin had given Darby a moment ago. A reminder that I wasn't alone. That we were in this together.

"Or hers and Lorenzo Caval's," I said. "I obviously don't know Blackwell very well. But after our conversation yesterday and what I saw this morning, I'd say she's really focused on her science, her work. Single-minded." I rubbed my neck, trying to relieve the tension that had gathered there. "Maybe I'm projecting, but she seems unbalanced. Not because she left us for work, but because she seems to wear blinders about everything else." I told them what I'd seen of the house, of her manner.

"It was just a snapshot, what I saw. But there was something really, I guess, *absent* about it."

"She has a mission."

I looked at Liam and said, "Yeah, but not based on some moral code. I don't think she cares about Paras or humans, for that matter. She has a *task*, and she's not going to stop until she gets it done."

"And you add in Lorenzo Caval," Liam said, "who hates Paras because of his mother's death."

"Yeah. Now add those together—single-minded scientific focus and Paranormal bloodlust."

"And you get murder," Moses said.

"Yeah." I paused. "She was at Talisheek, when Nix tried to open the Veil."

"I thought about that," Liam said.

"Maybe she wanted to sneak in a sample," Darby said. "Was hoping for an early test of the aerosolized virus."

I nodded in agreement.

"If she does this," Darby said—"infects the Beyond, and kills all those people—it's my fault."

"It's not," Malachi said. "Claire's right—the context does matter. This device wasn't created for murder. It was created for curiosity—for the basic human instinct to learn. She's warping that, corrupting it."

"We have to do something," Darby said. "We have to tell someone, or—"

There was a knock at Moses's door.

Gavin checked the peephole. "Gunnar," he said, and opened the door.

This time, Gunnar was alone. He wore fatigues, his service weapon belted at his waist. And he didn't look injured, which meant he hadn't been hurt during the raid on the ADZ building.

That was a little more weight off my chest.

"What did you find?" Darby asked, jumping to her feet.

"Not a damn thing. ADZ was cleared out completely. A couple of desks, a couple of refrigeration units that couldn't be hauled away quickly or easily. That was it."

There was a lot of swearing, including a few more attempts at Cajun.

"How'd they move so fast?" Liam asked.

"Could be your visit yesterday scared them off," Gunnar said. "Could be Lorenzo Caval has contacts in Containment, and we've got a leak. Probably heard about the warrant, or about the op, and made his move."

"Rachel?" Malachi asked.

Gunnar barely managed to hide a smile. "She's fine. I'll tell her you asked."

Malachi didn't look thrilled about that, but he didn't object.

Gunnar's gaze fell on the plate of cookies. "Chocolate chip?"

"Yeah," Darby said. But the excitement had gone out of her voice. "Help yourself."

"Thanks. I'm starving."

"Broussard set all this in motion," Gunnar said. "Found the file, figured out at least some of the rest of it. They probably figured they were nearing the beginning of the end."

"And speaking of endings," Moses said, "we think Blackwell's written a really shitty one."

"Brace yourself," Gavin recommended, and Gunnar stuffed the rest of the cookie into his mouth.

"Go," he murmured over it.

"PCC Research built a window into the Veil once upon a time," I said. "Pretty good chance that's now in Blackwell's hands, and she's going to try to deploy the virus there."

Gunnar choked, coughed, and wasn't helped by Gavin's slap on the back.

"And how do we know that?" Gunnar wheezed, and we walked him through the details.

"The decharger was just delivered today," Darby said. "If it was in a storage facility in the Marigny, it hasn't been maintained. It's going to need work. Maybe substantial work."

If nothing else, Laura Blackwell seemed to be a planner. I glanced at Gunnar. "What did Caval do for Containment?"

"Electrical engineer. Worked on the generators."

Of course he was, and of course he did.

"Damn it," Darby muttered. "Damn it all right to hell."

"If she's going to deploy it through the Veil, she's going to have to get to the Veil."

But the Veil, which ran like a fault line along the ninetieth line of longitude, was thousands of miles long.

"We need to identify her target location," Liam said. "Talisheek?"

That was where the Veil had opened the first time, and where defense contractors had nearly opened it again last year.

"It's guarded now," Gunnar said.

"She's a scientist," I said. "She'll want to put the virus through in the most, I guess, efficacious place. The place with the highest chance of success." I looked at Malachi, my stomach sinking with a horrible realization. "In the Beyond, does the Veil pass through any large cities? Population hubs?"

A shadow passed over his eyes when he figured out what I was suggesting. "You think she'll equate success and Paranormal deaths."

"I think they both might." And I wished I could apologize for her, wished that might have meant something. I wished there was a connection between Laura Blackwell and me other than a slim biological thread—something I could use to keep her from doing this horrible, horrible thing.

"In the Beyond, the Veil runs primarily through rural areas," Malachi said. "We were aware of it before you were, and we avoided it when building our cities."

That was something, but it didn't help us narrow down the strike zone. Even if we divided the Veil into sections and tried to assign people to search them all, there was a good chance we wouldn't find her in time.

Maybe there was a building she'd want to be near, a battlefield that was meaningful to her. Or maybe she'd pick the spot that required the least effort—the one easiest to get to.

"We don't have enough information," I said.

"Puzzle it out the best you can," Gunnar said, grabbing another cookie and heading for the door. "I'm going back to the Cabildo. I'll get back to you—or send Rachel—as soon as I can. I need more warrants."

He looked back and narrowed his gaze at me. "And don't do anything rash while I'm gone."

He closed the door heavily behind him, sending a cloud of dust into the air.

"I think he meant me," I said, and there were general murmurs of agreement.

"Of course he meant you, Red," Moses said with a grin. "You're the only one needs supervising."

"I don't need supervising."

But even Liam's look was doubting.

Since they were so certain I was going to do something reckless, I figured I might as well oblige.

"He's battling bureaucracy and people with power," I said, looking at all of them. "She could be making a move right now."

Moses rolled his eyes. "She's setting you up, in case you can't tell. Preparing to drop the hammer."

"You want to go to her house," Liam said, and I nodded.

"She's probably not there," I said. "But evidence might be. And if I can be the one who stops her, I'm damn well going to try."

CHAPTER TWENTY

"I guess we can be grateful you were reckless the last time," Liam said as we bumped toward my mother's house and her pretty walled neighborhood. Gavin, Liam, and I were squeezed into Scarlet's front seat. "Else we wouldn't know about the box or the decharger."

"You should always be grateful I'm reckless. It's one of my better qualities."

I gunned it, the rebuilt V-8 under the hood roaring like thunder, then patted Scarlet's dash. "That's my girl. My sweet, sweet girl."

"She ever touch you like that?" Gavin asked Liam with a grin.

"No comment."

"You're both hilarious," I said. "Maybe we could talk about what we're going to do when we confront my apparently evil mother."

They both went quiet.

"That wasn't sarcasm," I said. "I'm serious. She's evil, and though I'm still processing the emotions of learning that my mother is the scientist version of Maleficent, I'm very eager to take her down."

"Well," Gavin said when we reached the neighborhood. "She's spared no expense for herself."

"Being morally disgusting evidently pays well," I said, pulling

Scarlet to a stop a couple of streets away in front of a house that was obviously empty—windows open, floors and walls bare.

"I think you're right," Liam said, "and there's a good chance she's not here. But just in case." Liam pulled his .44 from his waistband, then looked at me. "You armed?"

"No. But I'll be fine."

We climbed out of the car, tried to walk as nonchalantly as possible down the quiet suburban street. We strode up to the front door just as casually, found the house dark.

I knocked, waited for a response. And when nothing happened, I tried the door.

"Locked," I said.

"Can you use magic?" Liam asked.

"No. Magic monitors are armed," I said, gesturing over my shoulder at the pole-mounted monitors along the curb.

"Not worth the risk," Gavin said, then pulled the gun from its holster. "Stand back."

"That's not exactly low-key," Liam said.

"Yeah, neither is this bitch, and neither is her plan." Gavin aimed, and we scuttled to the other side of the porch.

Two pops, and the door swung open.

"And I call you reckless," Liam muttered.

"Yeah," I said. "And I'm not the one with a gun."

The house was empty.

I took the second floor, walking slowly through each room, taking in the tall ceilings and attractive paint colors, the crown moldings. And the complete absence of décor. The master bedroom held a bed, dresser, nightstand. The nightstand held a single lamp and an old-fashioned wind-up alarm clock. Prevented her from being late, I guessed, when the power went out.

The nightstand's drawers were empty, the dresser's full of neatly folded clothes in tidy piles. Even the socks were paired and fitted into an organizer that looked a little like an egg crate. I didn't see any evidence that she'd packed a bag, but how would I know?

The bathroom held the usual necessities. The makeup and bath products were high-end brands, must have been shipped into the Zone, but there was nothing extraneous. Nothing that didn't have a specific purpose. And here, like downstairs, we saw no art, no flowers, no cocktail tables or objects. There were four smaller bedrooms on this floor; all were empty except for a yoga mat in the room closest to the master.

I went downstairs again, found Liam in the kitchen.

"Coffeepot's still warm," he said, checking the glass carafe with a fingertip. "She hasn't been gone long."

Gavin came in through another door, the orange box in his arms. "Empty," he said. "But here. Confirms she's in possession of PCC property and her likely intent."

"Getting it through the Veil," Liam said, and Gavin nodded.

"You find anything?" he asked.

"Nothing useful," I replied.

"She gets nervous, decides to abandon this place," Liam said, hands on his hips as he looked around. "Goes into the wind. Or she decides she's ready, and she's off to deploy. Doesn't care if we know where she lives, because she's on task, focused."

"I don't think she'd run," I said. "She doesn't seem to care what people think, and she's got some kind of federal benefactor, maybe thinks she's untouchable."

Liam nodded. "Agreed."

I glanced back, realized the laptop was still sitting on the table.

"Computer," I said. I pulled out the chair, sat down in the same spot where my mother had sat with her coffee and orange juice, and turned the machine on.

It wasn't even password-protected. The computer's desktop blinked on, showing a photograph of Jackson Square after dusk.

"She left her computer behind?" Gavin asked, moving closer. He and Liam stood behind the chair, looked over my shoulder.

"She was in a hurry," I said. And that made me worry even more.

The computer's desktop was immaculate. No random files, no temporarily stored documents or gifs. Just a neat line of links to the hard drive and important folders.

I spent ten minutes opening documents and folders, searching the hard drive for anything that might give us a clue about her location. Plenty of scientific documents that I didn't understand, but I figured Darby would be interested in them.

I skipped those, opened up the Internet browser, then pulled up her search history. And my heart stuttered.

The last phrase she'd searched had been "sola fluids."

"What's a sola?"

"A what?" Liam asked, moving closer.

"Sola. It's what she searched for last. 'Sola fluids.'"

"Not 'sola,'" Gavin said, walking toward us. "So La. As in 'Southern Louisiana.'" He peered over my shoulder. "SoLa Fluids. It's a petroleum processor on the river. One of the few still operating in the Zone."

"Where is it?" I asked.

"Near Belle Chasse."

"The Veil runs through Belle Chasse," Liam said. "There was a skirmish there during the war. A few Court Paras tried to go back through."

"I remember." Their effort hadn't worked, but the fight had been the topic of conversation in the Quarter for weeks.

"Belle Chasse," I murmured, thinking it over. The Veil ran through it, it was close to New Orleans, and it was probably a place she'd heard about before. She wouldn't want to leave this to chance. And there was nothing else on the computer that looked like she was trying to nail down the geographic part of the search.

"I think that's the best we're going to do from here," I said. "Let's find Gunnar."

Gavin was already striding to the door. "Moral of this story?" he said. "Murderers should always clear their browser history."

I grabbed the computer and followed them out.

There were days when it was nice to be free of the burden of cell phones. There were no three a.m. e-mails, no social media stress, no worries about Internet arguments with strangers.

And no way to easily arrange for the arrest and capture of a homicidal maniac.

We dropped Gavin off near Moses's house so he could find a vehicle, then drove directly to the Cabildo, Containment's HQ. We waited outside while Gunnar talked to the Commandant about what we'd found and where we thought she might strike.

The guards outside the building gave us the stink eye. But whatever Gunnar had said to them on his way in had them staying in position, weapons still holstered.

Fifteen minutes later, he came out. And he didn't look happy.

"Senator Jute McLellan," he said, climbing into the truck and slamming the door. The truck vibrated from the ferocity of his anger. "Go back to Moses's."

"Which is who?" Liam asked when I put the truck in gear and drove away from the Cabildo before the agents could change their mind.

"The head of the subcommittee that's been sneaking funds to

ADZ. War disrupts the economy, and Senator McLellan doesn't care for that. So he and his friends decided Icarus was a wise investment."

"No more Paranormals, no more war?" I asked.

"Pretty much." He smiled slyly. "Capital police are now on their way to have a very long talk with Senator McLellan."

"Good," Liam said. "Assuming they can make it stick."

"No evidence to date that he's involved in the research, just the funding, so his lawyers will probably have a field day. But the money was appropriated, and that's got his mark all over it. He'll have plenty to answer for."

"And closer to home?" Liam asked.

"Commandant has scrambled jets out of Pensacola," Gunnar said. "And there are a few troop carriers on the ground with some fancy ordnance that the army's been working on. But we might still beat them to the spot."

"And in the meantime," I guessed, "we do what we can."

"We do what we can," Gunnar said. "So drive fast."

Refusing to give up after the loss of his briefly beloved Range Rover, Gavin pulled up to Moses's house in an enormous red Humvee.

"Only in a war zone, where gas is hard to get, would my brother drive something like that."

"I'm in a war zone," Gavin said through the open window. "I'm driving a vehicle that's ready for war."

Admittedly a better argument.

The rest of us stood outside Moses's house, preparing to stop my mother. Moses watched us from the top step of his front porch.

"She'll be there," he said, pointing generally southeast and toward the ninetieth line of longitude. "Or somewhere along here. We go in teams, secure the virus, take her down. In whatever order necessary."

He glanced at me, concern in his eyes.

"I'm fine," I said. "Really. She's not my mother. Not in any way that counts."

It was the first time I'd said it, and it was absolutely true. We had a biological connection. Shared genetic material. My origin story was connected to her, but that was the only thing between us. She hadn't been my mother in any way that mattered then, and she wasn't now. She wasn't confused, or lost, or whatever fairy tale I might have told myself growing up. She was just a woman.

Saying it aloud lifted the rest of the weight from my chest.

Liam reached out, squeezed my hand, and didn't let go.

"Claire, Liam, Darby, and I approach her directly," Gunnar said. "We aren't entirely sure where she'll be positioned, but I'd like two teams—Rachel and Malachi, and Erida and Gavin—to approach from the other directions. We're at six o'clock, you're at two and ten."

The split made sense—one Paranormal and one human on each of those teams—but no one looked happy about their particular team. Which was probably fine by Gunnar.

"Darby, tell us what we're looking for."

"The decharger's pretty small," she said, and held out her hands to form a small square. "Maybe four by four. It's a black disk, about two and a half or three inches thick. You'd press it flat against the Veil," she said, mimicking the move. "It's powered by the Veil itself."

"And the virus? The aerosolizer?"

"She could be bringing the virus in any kind of container. It depends on how it needs to be stored and how much she was able to process. Probably a canister. Something that would fit into a generator, or gun. And the mechanism has to be small enough to fit into the window created by the decharger."

"Disk, canister, generator, gun," Gunnar said. "Generally, keep an eye out for metal and plastic."

"Pretty much," Darby said with a nod.

"We'll take the virus and the decharger, and give them to Darby. She'll secure and transport."

Darby held up an old, dirty Igloo cooler, patted the side. "High-security transport, right here."

"Claire, Liam, and I will ride in the truck. Gavin will take Darby, Rachel, Erida. Malachi will fly in. Any questions?"

We all shook our heads.

"Then let's hit the road."

Ten minutes later, Gunnar was practically jumping in the front seat of the truck. "Can this thing go any faster?"

"I'm driving eighty on a postwar highway," I said. "Unless you want me to flip the truck"—we all grimaced as I hit a bump and we went momentarily airborne before thudding down again—"then no, we aren't going any faster."

Like the road to Houma, the road to Belle Chasse was mostly empty. Empty businesses and houses, then a stretch of green on both sides of a pitted highway. And somewhere ahead of us, a woman and a weapon of mass destruction.

We slowed as we neared the target area, the white towers and spires of the Apollo refinery looming in the distance like a twisted Oz.

Gunnar and Liam peered through the windows as I drove, looking for a vehicle, a sign, a woman with red hair.

But I saw her first.

"There," I said, and slowed the truck, pointed to the field on the river side of the road.

She stood on the levee half a mile up the road, the wind whipping her hair like Medusa's snakes. Scientist that she was, she'd traded in the sharp suit for cargo pants and a trim tank.

There was something small and black in her hands. There was a plastic box also at her feet, and a canister hanging from a strap around her neck. Aerosolizer and virus, I guessed.

She was staring in front of her, as if trying to locate the Veil, figure out what she was looking at, how exactly to accomplish her work. That meant we weren't too late. There was no sign of Lorenzo Caval, but there wasn't time to wait for him.

We had to move.

The Hummer slowed behind us, then pulled up alongside. A shadow passed over, wings momentarily blocking out the sun, and then Malachi landed on the road in front of us, ivory wings casting sharp shadows on the asphalt.

Hair tousled from the flight, he looked like an avenging angel. And today, that probably wasn't far from the truth.

"He is just . . . gorgeous," Gunnar said, his voice a little gravelly.

That broke the tension in the car by a long shot. "I thought we had to focus on the mission?" I said.

"He's part of the mission," Gunnar said. "A very admirable part."

As Malachi retracted his wings, Rachel and I rolled down our respective windows. But her gaze didn't move from him as he strode toward us.

"You got her?" I asked.

"On the levee," Gavin said, leaning forward.

"Caval?" Malachi asked.

"No sign of him," Liam said. "Could be Blackwell decided he's disposable."

"Or maybe he's completely AWOL," I said. "Got smart, relatively speaking, and decided it was better to bail before she did this thing."

Gunnar didn't look convinced by either option. "A man willing to kill his own brother out of a completely warped sense of priorities isn't worried about being caught. He's worried about the mission. We go as planned," he decided, "but stay alert."

"We'll keep going," Gavin said, "come up from behind."

"I'll circle around, come over from the river side," Malachi said.

Gunnar nodded. "We aren't going to wait for you to get into position. We go now, secure the virus before she attempts to deploy it."

"I'm sorry," I said to no one in particular as we climbed out of the car. "I'm sorry for whatever she's about to do."

"You didn't make her choices for her."

I looked up at Malachi, saw understanding in his eyes, and nodded.

"You're right," I said, looking back at my mother again. "But I'm going to be the one who stops her."

"I want to talk to her first," I said as we walked across the field—which was at least a couple of acres wide. Laura had descended from the levee and was walking in small circles, probably trying to nail down exactly where she needed to aim.

She'd been near the Veil at Talisheek, but didn't have magic, so she wouldn't be able to sense it or see it. She'd have to rely on longitude to find it, and even then it waved back and forth across the line of longitude.

But I could sense it fine. It was difficult to grasp the sheer size of the Veil. It wasn't a curtain drawn between us. It was a split in our world, extending up and side to side infinitely. It shimmered high enough to reach the atmosphere, far enough that it disappeared across the horizon. It was big and it was powerful, and it was holding back the river of magic and Paranormals on the other side.

In preparation for her work, Laura had pulled out the decharger. She held it in one hand while inserting the virus cartridge into a device shaped a little like a fire extinguisher.

"Laura."

She froze, turned back, aiming her biological weapon. I didn't think it would do anything to me—no humans had gotten sick yet—but I still lifted my hands.

I was getting sick of doing that lately. Of feeling like a criminal.

Her lip curled angrily. "I don't have time for you. I have work to do."

I could see them moving in my peripheral vision. "Your work is over. You're surrounded, and we'll be taking the decharger, the virus, and the weapon."

"I'm not turning anything over. I have work to do. A job to finish." She turned around to face the Veil, lifted the decharger.

"And did I mention Containment troops are en route? You turn them over to us now, and this will go a lot easier for you."

"Goddamn it." I heard Gunnar's voice behind me. "Ms. Blackwell, I don't want to shoot you, but I will. If it's between you and the Veil, I'll take you out."

She didn't move for a moment, then glanced back over her shoulder. "Why are you being irrational? This is science. The culmination of years of research."

"And you'd destroy a civilization that was millennia in the making."

She turned back, gasped as Malachi landed in front of her, wings extended and golden fury in his eyes.

She took a stumbling step backward, and Gavin was there to grab her. He pinned her arms while Malachi strode forward, not bothering to hide his wings, and wrenched the decharger away from her.

"You are a disgrace to humans, and to your daughter."

"Darby!" Gunnar called, and she ran forward, holding the cooler open, held it out while Liam removed the canister from the gun, laid it carefully inside the box.

"Got it," Darby said, and slid the cover back into place. "Virus container contained."

"That's my work," my mother said vehemently, struggling in Gavin's grip. "That's a lifetime of work."

"Suffice it to say," Liam said, "you should have focused on something a little less nasty."

"And speaking of focus," Gunnar said as he cuffed her, "where's Caval?"

"I don't know what you're talking about."

"You do," Gunnar said. "And it was pretty stupid of you not to let him help you today. The two of you together could have actually accomplished your genocide. But you didn't. We beat you." He pointed at Malachi. "A Para beat you." Then me. "And the daughter you abandoned beat you. But you'll have plenty of time to think about how they beat you when you're in prison."

The words that spewed from her mouth were overwhelmed by the noise that filled the air: sirens roaring toward us as Containment cruisers and armored vehicles raced toward the levee.

"And here comes the cavalry," Gunnar yelled over the din. He pulled a comm unit from his belt. "Prisoner and package are contained," he said.

All of the vehicles visibly slowed—all but one, which steamed toward us, undeterred by Gunnar's order. And then it lifted its muzzle and pointed the weapon directly at us.

"Caval," I murmured, and watched, hypnotized, as a streaking star shot from the muzzle and flew toward us.

"Incoming!" Gunnar screamed, pushed me and Liam to the ground, then grabbed Laura Blackwell and pulled her down, too.

They hit the ground together, the shot flying barely inches over their heads. And it didn't stop. The round kept on going, heading for the thing directly behind them, the enormous, invisible target.

While we watched in horror, the round hit it square on, and the usually invisible Veil shimmered and rippled like pebble-strewn water, shuddered like video from a broken camera.

"Holy shit," Gunnar said, while we all held our breath.

The scar was small at first, so little it was nearly invisible, a bit of dust that had ghosted across my vision and would be cleared away when I blinked.

I looked back, watched Containment agents wrench open the vehicle's door and drag a man from it. A man who looked a lot like Javier Caval.

We'd found Lorenzo.

But the hole expanded, and the char around the edge became clearer, like a cigarette burn in fabric. And it was growing larger, the circle expanding exponentially with each millisecond that passed.

"Malachi!" I screamed, and heard the *thwack* of wings on the wind behind me.

"No," he said, and the horror in his voice nearly buckled my knees. "No!"

It took me too long to realize that if I could move objects, maybe I could move the separate sides of the Veil, stitch them back together with magic. After all, the edges of the tear wrought by Paranormals had been locked together by Sensitives. Why wouldn't we be able to lock them together now?

I reached out for the power. The air was swimming with magic, but not the familiar kind. It was magic from the Beyond, from the same place the rest of our world's magic derived. But this magic was real, original. It hadn't been filtered through the Veil, through the atmosphere and objects of this world. It was pure, different from anything I'd felt before. And maybe because it hadn't been filtered through the human world, it hurt.

I began to spin the filaments of magic around me, pain erupting across my arms like pins and needles in a limb that had fallen asleep.

And all the while, the gap in the Veil grew ever larger.

"No," I said through clenched teeth, gathering every shred of strength I had, every ounce of energy in reserve. I looped magic around one side of the Veil's breach and then the other, used magic to try to force them together.

Sweat broke out on my arms, the pain like fire across them as I desperately tried to bring one side toward the other, to stretch what remained.

I wiped sweat from my brow and tried again. But it didn't work. I could move the Veil only when there was Veil to move. It was disintegrating faster than I could hold it together.

"Claire."

"No," I said to Liam, then shook off his hand. "No. I'm going to do this. I'm going to fix this. Help me, Liam. You have to help me."

"Claire, baby, I would. But you can't fix this."

I didn't want him to be right. But he was.

No matter how hard I tried, how hard I pulled, there was nothing left of the Veil to stitch together. Not enough magic to patch the hole that Containment had created.

The gap was big enough now to see through. Instead of seeing more of Louisiana, we could see glimpses of the Beyond—and the crimson uniforms of those who waited for us on the other side.

Laura Blackwell hadn't infected the Beyond.

She'd helped destroy the Veil.

CHAPTER TWENTY-ONE

The charring edges of the Veil disappeared into the distance. If anything remained of the barrier, it was too far away to matter now.

The Beyond now filled our vision, obscuring what we might have seen of Louisiana.

They were mounted on white destriers, a dozen that I could see. Paranormals all of them, and all in battle gear. Golden armor with long crimson robes beneath, golden helmets topped by crimson combs or feathers, and gleaming golden weapons in their hands. The horses were enormous white stallions with thick legs, long curling manes, and wide and flaring nostrils.

I didn't see the female commander who'd waited in the Beyond the last time the Veil had nearly been opened, the woman who'd looked into my eyes with murder in hers. But that didn't ease my fears. They were different shapes, sizes, skin tones. But they all looked ready to fight.

Some of the Paras had wings like Malachi's. Others had streaks of crimson down their foreheads, noses, and chins, and the same crimson along the tips of their fingers. They were called Seelies, members of the Court of Dawn, the faction that had broken through the Veil and led the war against us.

"The Court of Dawn!" Malachi screamed. "Be ready!"

We had a few humans and Paras, a few Containment vehicles, and a couple dozen soldiers—only enough people to threaten a scientist into backing down.

They had two dozen mounted soldiers with armor that resisted human weapons, or had before Containment had tweaked the ordnance. God only knew what would happen now.

"General!" Rachel ran toward Malachi. "Would you like the field?"

He stared at her for a moment. Then his expression shifted, went hard, and he looked back at his meager troops. Paranormals had a long way to go toward parity, but that Containment was giving Malachi control of the human troops was a pretty big deal, or so it seemed to me.

"Create an arc," he said, and began pointing to locations. "Soldiers in front, armored vehicles at each end, pointed into the Beyond. You take that end," he told her, pointing to his right. "I'll take the other. They'll try to flank us; it's what they're trained to do. Don't let them, Captain."

That single word—his saying her title—contained enough heat to scorch. And the look in her eyes said she knew it. I had a sense that a kiss between Malachi and Rachel would have plenty of heat.

The promise of that, the reminder of love and connection, made me feel incrementally better. I looked back at the Beyond. Or as good as one could feel when staring down a group of people who wanted us dead and our world to boot.

"What about us?" Erida asked.

"Take as many as you can, and don't stop short of killing them. They won't stop short of killing you." The loathing in Malachi's eyes looked ancient, built from years of anger and mistrust.

A horn trumpeted from their world, long and low and wavering, and lifted the hair on the back of my neck. A flashback threatened, but I shook it off. Not here, not now.

The woman at the front of the line of horses screamed, and they let loose.

The Battle of Belle Chasse had begun.

"We'll stand together," Liam said, gripping my hand as we took positions in the front line. My hand was damp, my heart beating like a timpani as the soldiers galloped toward us.

Liam's eyes were completely gold now, as dense and shimmering as Malachi's. But there was no mistaking the human fury in his eyes, or the look of hatred he directed at those who would destroy us.

"Stay with me," he said. "We stay together, work together, we'll be fine."

But then the army crossed into our world, and all hell broke loose.

As if guessing our plan, one of the Seelies, her white hair streaming beneath her gilded helmet, charged us.

"Claire!" Liam called out as I moved first, darting to the side when she arrowed her stallion between us with an evil grin.

She was close enough that my hair rustled as she passed, close enough that I could smell the clove scent of her skin, the warm odor of horse, her well-oiled armor.

She circled around and came again, whipped the bow from her back with one hand and the arrow from her horse-mounted quiver with the other, and fired.

I smiled, gathered magic, made my best guess about velocity . . . and grabbed the arrow in midflight.

It shivered in the air two feet from my face. Holding it steady, I turned, pivoted it with a fingertip, and looked up at her. "You want to walk back into the Beyond?"

She screamed and charged.

I propelled the arrow toward her, and she barely dodged it, the metal tip grazing her shoulder. She screamed again, launched another arrow, fired.

Her movements were so fast I didn't have time to prepare, to grab that arrow. I hit the ground on my stomach, heard the arrow whiz over my head, and then her stallion was nearly on me.

I screamed as I was hauled to my feet and looked up into golden eyes.

But this time, it wasn't an enemy.

Liam crushed his mouth to mine. "Together," he said.

My head was spinning, but I nodded. "We'll try it again." I had only a moment before the next round. "Behind you!" I yelled, and pulled him to the side, inches from where a golden lance slid into the ground.

I'd seen one of those before, knew they were heavy. But with the two of us together . . .

"I have an idea. But it's a little dirty."

"They'll kill us if they can," he said. "Dirty's fine."

I glanced back. The soldier who'd thrown the lance—a man this time, a Seelie with dark skin and beard with the same crimson stripe—galloped toward us.

"A Seelie walked into a bar," I said, and Liam nodded.

"Right there with you," he said, and took my hand.

There was plenty of magic in the air, especially now that it was funneling through the open Veil, but it was weird and wild, and that much harder to wield. It took precious seconds to pry the enormous lance from the ground, to get it horizontal. And we had only seconds to move.

"On three," Liam said. "One, two, *three!*"

We raised the lance to the Para's chest height.

The horse galloped toward us, passed cleanly beneath the bar. But the rider hit the bar, then hit the ground, and didn't get up. We let the lance fall; it was heavy enough, dense enough, that it didn't even bounce.

The earth shook, and we looked to see smoke rising from a mortar round fired on the other side of the battlefield where soldiers, horses, and Paranormals had fallen.

Fuck war, I thought, and let myself look away. I had to if I was going to get through this.

Behind us came a banshee scream. A female Seelie, golden sword lifted over her head, ran toward us, her gaze aimed at me, maybe because I was smaller and she believed I was weaker, the easier target.

But Liam had decided no one would get to me. No one would get past him.

His eyes glowing gold, he put a hand on the ground like a sprinter on the block, then pushed off. They ran toward each other. Liam leaped, propelling his body an inhuman ten feet into the air—maybe borrowing her magic for the trip—arms back and ready to strike.

They met with a blaze of fire and power that sent a shock wave of magic through the air; then they hit the ground with enough force to put a dent in the earth and send dirt flying.

The Seelie swung the sword. Liam blocked it.

I watched for a moment to intervene, for a chance to lend him a hand, to grab the sword or the woman, but they were a blur of action as he fed off her magic and matched her strike for strike.

I was so focused I heard it before I realized what it was—the buzz in the air, the sound of speed and danger. And even when I looked up, all I could see was the gleaming edge of the golden arrow headed straight toward me.

"No!"

Erida leapt toward me, pushed me toward the ground.

I heard the arrow land with a horrible punch of flesh, and Erida jerked above my body.

"Oh, no," I murmured, maneuvered out from under her and tried to roll her over—or as much as I could, given the arrow piercing the middle of her chest. "Oh, Jesus, Erida. Why did you do that?"

She smiled a little. "That's not very gracious of you."

"I'm grateful and pissed off . . ." I trailed off, looked her over, tried to figure out some way to help her, to move the arrow.

But there was only acceptance in her eyes. She reached out, squeezed my hand. "I did it for your father. Because I loved him best of all. And you were his child. He was gone before I wanted him to go. But this is a gift I can give him, even now."

Bon dieu, I thought, borrowing one of Liam's favorite phrases as tears streamed down my face.

She shivered, blood at the corner of her mouth.

And I knew what I could give her. "The gas station," I said. "Remember what you told me about it?"

Jaw clenched, she nodded.

"He finished, Erida. But it's not just a gas station. It's a museum. All those magical artifacts Containment tried to burn, tried to get rid of, he saved. Books, weapons, objects. Hundreds of them."

She squeezed my hand, tried to smile against the pain. "He saved them."

"He did." I wasn't exactly sure why, but I could make a good guess. "And there's a bunker in it, too. Food, beds, a kitchen." I swallowed back tears, tried to dig out the strength to do this. "It wasn't just going to be a store. I think he saved the objects for you, and I think he meant for the three of us to live together. To be a family. Me and you and him."

Tears slipped from her eyes, gratitude clear in them. "Thank you, Claire. Thank you for that."

"Thank you for making him happy, Erida. Even if it wasn't for nearly long enough."

She squeezed my hand again, then closed her eyes tightly against an obvious burst of pain. There was a sudden intake of breath, and then her eyes opened and she went still, even as the battle waged behind us.

Liam shielded me, watched me, and waited. I brushed the hair from her face, then linked her hands atop her chest and climbed to my feet. I would grieve for Erida, for what she'd meant to my father. But I couldn't do it now.

There was fighting to be done.

There was more blood. More death. The Paras, for their part, were fierce warriors. But though Containment's new mortar rounds were still being tested, they were ferocious. They cut through armor just as they'd cut through the Veil. Unfortunately, only half a dozen rounds had been manufactured thus far. And they'd all been depleted today.

When smoke spread like fog across the field, the scents of gunpowder and blood in the air, the world fell quiet.

Malachi emerged through the smoke that swirled around his boots. His wings were folded but still visible. The top arc on his left wing was ripped, his blood brilliantly crimson against the ivory feathers.

"Is this it?" Liam asked.

"This was probably a sentinel unit assigned to watch the Veil for breaches," Malachi said.

Liam surveyed the devastation. "They're only the first wave."

"The first part of the first wave," Malachi corrected. "A guard unit. They'd have passed along a signal, a warning, the moment the Veil began to open." He wiped sweat and smoke from his face. "A battalion will be next, whichever is closest. And when they come, they'll come with weapons and death. We need to prepare."

He walked toward Gunnar, who was talking to a few of the troops.

Liam reached out, squeezed my hand. "I'm going to go speak to them."

"Go ahead." I watched him walk away—temporarily, this time—and then turned back to Laura and Caval. They were on their knees twenty feet away.

There was a bruise across Laura's cheekbone, a smear of blood from a cut on her collarbone. But unlike many of the others, they were alive. They were the reason for it all.

I strode toward them, stared down at them. "How could you be so selfish?"

She pushed her hair from her eyes. "I did what I was asked to do."

"You were fired. Icarus was killed. But you decided to keep going. To keep developing a weapon."

Her eyes were clear, and utterly free of guilt. Free of conscience, if that was possible. "I had a job to do, a mission. I wasn't going to just stop because someone got scared. Because someone wanted to ignore reality. You think Paranormals are our friends? Look around you."

She would never change her mind. She was at least forty, and wasn't able to see the world outside her myopic vision. And it didn't matter. I didn't matter to her, and she didn't have to matter to me. I wasn't her responsibility, and she wasn't mine.

I looked at Caval. "You destroyed the Veil."

His smile was wide and totally without doubt. "We beat them before. We'll beat them again."

"You won't be beating anyone," I said. "You'll both be in prison. Locked away for the rest of your lives. Away from your money, away from your lab. You'll have plenty of time to think about all your achievements."

"We have friends."

"Not anymore," I said. "The jig is up, and your friends are as much underwater as you are."

Liam and Gunnar walked back with half a dozen Containment agents.

One of the agents, an MP badge on her fatigues, stepped forward. "Laura Blackwell and Lorenzo Caval. You're under arrest for murder, several counts, terroristic acts, and other charges that will be made known to you."

They were pulled to their feet, and two of the agents took the prisoners toward one of the vehicles for transportation.

But the other agents stayed behind. And they looked at me and Liam with grim expressions. They'd seen us do magic. Big magic. Powerful magic. Liam had been cleared of murder, but we'd still violated the law.

We were still criminals.

One of the agents stepped forward. Gunnar tried to move in front of us, to protect us, but I held out a hand, shook my head.

"Claire Connolly and Liam Quinn, I'm sorry, but you're under arrest for multiple violations of the Magic Act. We're going to need to take you in."

"No," I said. "I don't believe you will." Because I was absolutely done.

The agent's eyebrows lifted.

"We won't be putting our hands in the air. We won't be going with you and we won't be going into Devil's Isle." I took Liam's hand, smiled at him. "Little help?"

"Always."

I reached for the magic, gasped at the sheer volume of it. It was flowing from the Beyond now, filaments filling the air like millions of fireflies. So much magic I could feel it floating between my fingers.

"Damn," Liam said, swallowing hard. "There's a lot of it."

And there'd be more than this eventually. More magic in our world, more humanity—if that was a thing—in theirs. Because the Veil had been ripped open, and there was no turning back.

The agent put a hand on his weapon.

"Nor will you be pointing those at us," I said, and lifted my hand.

Liam's magic joined mine, braided around it, and together we lifted every weapon in the group into the air, let them float twenty feet above their heads.

Some of the agents jumped, scrambling to keep their guns. Others just stared at us, openmouthed and afraid—or openmouthed and completely awed.

"In a few hours," I said, "maybe sooner, battalions of Paranormal troops are going to storm through that gap and into our world. They've been waiting for an opportunity to go to war, and Lorenzo Caval just gave them one."

"Call the Commandant," Liam told them. "Tell him to get ready for war."

I squeezed his hand, my partner and my friend. "And tell him we're ready to fight."

Photo by Dana Damewood Photography

Chloe Neill, *New York Times* bestselling author of the Chicagoland Vampires Novels (*Blade Bound, Midnight Marked, Dark Debt*), the Dark Elite novels (*Charmfall, Hexbound, Firespell*), and the Devil's Isle Novels (*The Veil, The Sight*), was born and raised in the South but now makes her home in the Midwest—just close enough to Cadogan House, St. Sophia's, and Devil's Isle to keep an eye on things. When not transcribing Merit's, Lily's, and Claire's adventures, she bakes, works, and scours the Internet for good recipes and great graphic design. Chloe also maintains her sanity by spending time with her boys—her favorite landscape photographer (her husband), and their dogs, Baxter and Scout. (Both she and the photographer understand the dogs are in charge.)

chloeneill.com
facebook.com/authorchloeneill
twitter.com/chloeneill